PRAISE FOR *NEW YORK TIMES*
BESTSELLING AUTHOR GARTH NIX:

SABRIEL

"Rich, complex, involving, hard to put down, this is excellent high fantasy."—*Publishers Weekly* (starred review)

"*Sabriel* is a winner."—Philip Pullman, author of *The Golden Compass*

"Nix has created an ingenious, icy world in the throes of chaos. The action charges along at a gallop, imbued with an encompassing sense of looming disaster. A page-turner for sure."—ALA *Booklist* (starred review)

LIRAEL

"What makes *Lirael* a delight is the magic that Nix brings to his story and to his characters. It is filled with twists and turns, playful inventiveness and dark magic, and is sure to satisfy his many readers."—*Locus*

"Readers who like their fantasy intense in action, magisterial in scope, and apocalyptic in consequences will revel in every word."—*Kirkus Reviews* (starred review)

ABHORSEN

"Thought-provoking fantasy."—*Publishers Weekly* (starred review)

"Terror, courage, bitterness, love, desperation, and sacrifice all swirl together in an apocalyptic climax. Breathtaking, bittersweet, and utterly unforgettable."—*Kirkus Reviews* (starred review)

GARTH NIX

THE ABHORSEN CHRONICLES

SABRIEL

LIRAEL

ABHORSEN

Nicholas Sayre and
the Creature in the Case

An Imprint of HarperCollinsPublishers

Eos is an imprint of HarperCollins Publishers.

The Abhorsen Chronicles
Copyright © 2009 by Garth Nix
Sabriel: Copyright © 1995 by Garth Nix.
Lirael: Copyright © 2001 by Garth Nix.
Abhorsen: Copyright © 2003 by Garth Nix.
"Nicholas Sayre and the Creature in the Case":
Copyright © 2005 by Garth Nix.

Library of Congress Catalog Card Number: 2008925692
ISBN 978-0-06-144182-0 (pbk.)

Typography by Henrietta Stern
❖
First Edition

09 10 11 12 13 CG/RRDC 10 9 8 7 6 5 4 3 2

CONTENTS

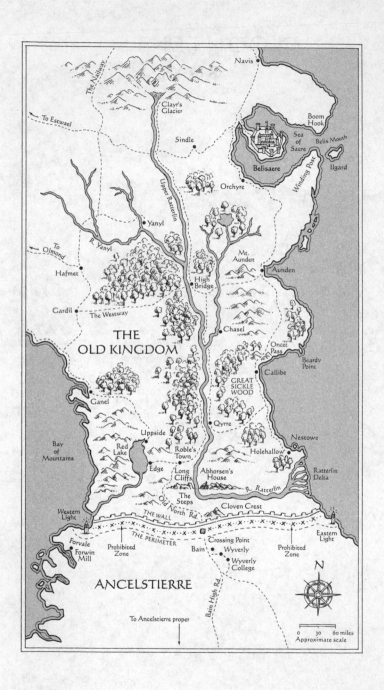

The Neilwey

To Estwael

Navis

Clayr's Glacier

Sindle

Boom Hook

Sea of Saere

Belis Mouth

Belisaere

Ilgard

Upper Ratterlin

Orchyre

Winding Post

Yanyl

To Olmond

R. Yanyl

Hafmet

Mt. Aunden

Aunden

High Bridge

Gardil

The Westway

THE
OLD KINGDOM

Chasel

Oncet Pass

Beardy Point

Callibe

GREAT SICKLE WOOD

Ganel

Qyrre

Bay of Mountains

Uppside

Red Lake

Roble's Town

Holehallow

Nestowe

Ratterlin Delta

Edge

Long Cliffs

Abhorsen's House

R. Ratterlin

The Steps

Old North Rd.

Cloven Crest

Western Light

THE WALL

THE PERIMETER

Eastern Light

Forvale
Forwin Mill

Prohibited Zone

Bain

Crossing Point

Wyverly

Wyverly College

Prohibited Zone

ANCELSTIERRE

Bain High Rd.

N

To Ancelstierre proper

0   30   60 miles
Approximate scale

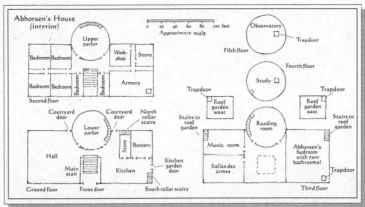

Abhorsen's House (interior)

0 20 40 60 80 100 feet
Approximate scale

Second floor

Bedroom | Bedroom | Workshop | Store
Bedroom | Bedroom | Bedroom | Bedroom | Armory

Upper parlor

Ground floor

Hall | Lower parlor | Courtyard door | Courtyard door | North cellar stairs | Store | Buttery
Main stair | Front door | Kitchen | Kitchen garden door | South cellar stairs

Fifth floor

Observatory □ — Trapdoor

Fourth floor

Study □

Third floor

Trapdoor — Roof garden west
Roof garden east — Trapdoor

Stairs to roof garden | Reading room | Stairs to roof garden

Music room | Abhorsen's bedroom with two bathrooms!
Salles des armes | Trapdoor

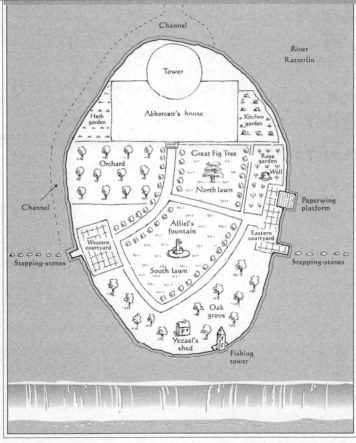

Channel

River Ratterlin

Tower

Channel

Abhorsen's house

Herb garden | Kitchen garden

Orchard | Great Fig Tree | Rose garden | Well

North lawn | Paperwing platform

Alliel's fountain | Eastern courtyard

Western courtyard

Stepping-stones | Stepping-stones

South lawn

Oak grove

Yezael's shed

Fishing tower

SABRIEL

To my family and friends

CONTENTS

Prologue

It was little more than three miles from the Wall into the Old Kingdom, but that was enough. Noonday sunshine could be seen on the other side of the Wall in Ancelstierre, and not a cloud in sight. Here, there was a clouded sunset, and a steady rain had just begun to fall, coming faster than the tents could be raised.

The midwife shrugged her cloak higher up against her neck and bent over the woman again, raindrops spilling from her nose onto the upturned face below. The midwife's breath blew out in a cloud of white, but there was no answering billow of air from her patient.

The midwife sighed and slowly straightened up, that single movement telling the watchers everything they needed to know. The woman who had staggered into their forest camp was dead, only holding on to life long enough to pass it on to the baby at her side. But even as the midwife picked up the pathetically small form beside the dead woman, it shuddered within its wrappings, and was still.

"The child, too?" asked one of the watchers, a man who wore the mark of the Charter fresh-drawn in wood ash upon his brow. "Then there shall be no need for baptism."

His hand went up to brush the mark from his forehead, then suddenly stopped, as a pale white hand gripped his and forced it down in a single, swift motion.

"Peace!" said a calm voice. "I wish you no harm."

The white hand released its grip and the speaker stepped into the ring of firelight. The others watched him without welcome, and the hands that had half sketched Charter marks, or gone to bowstrings and hilts, did not relax.

The man strode towards the bodies and looked upon them. Then he turned to face the watchers, pushing his hood back to reveal the face of someone who had taken paths far from sunlight, for his skin was a deathly white.

"I am called Abhorsen," he said, and his words sent ripples through the people about him, as if he had cast a large and weighty stone into a pool of stagnant water. "And there will be a baptism tonight."

The Charter Mage looked down on the bundle in the midwife's hands, and said: "The child is dead, Abhorsen. We are travelers, our life lived under the sky, and it is often harsh. We know death, lord."

"Not as I do," replied Abhorsen, smiling so his paper-white face crinkled at the corners and drew back from his equally white teeth. "And I say the child is not yet dead."

The man tried to meet Abhorsen's gaze, but faltered and looked away at his fellows. None moved, or made any sign, till a woman said, "So. It is easily done. Sign the child, Arrenil. We will make a new camp at Leovi's Ford. Join us when you are finished here."

The Charter Mage inclined his head in assent, and the others drifted away to pack up their half-made camp, slow with the reluctance of having to move, but filled with a greater reluctance to remain near Abhorsen, for his name was one of secrets, and unspoken fears.

When the midwife went to lay the child down and leave, Abhorsen spoke: "Wait. You will be needed."

The midwife looked down on the baby, and saw that it was a girl child and, save for its stillness, could be merely sleeping. She had heard of Abhorsen, and if the girl could live . . . warily she picked up the child again and held her out to the Charter Mage.

"If the Charter does not—" began the man, but Abhorsen held up a pallid hand and interrupted.

"Let us see what the Charter wills."

The man looked at the child again and sighed. Then he took a small bottle from his pouch and held it aloft, crying out a chant that was the beginning of a Charter; one that listed all things that lived or grew, or once lived, or would live again, and the bonds that held them all together. As he spoke, a light came to the bottle, pulsing with the rhythm of the chant. Then the chanter was silent. He touched the bottle to the earth, then to the sign of wood ash on his forehead, and then upended it over the child.

A great flash lit the surrounding woods as the glowing liquid splashed over the child's head, and the priest cried: "By the Charter that binds all things, we name thee—"

Normally, the parents of the child would then speak the name. Here, only Abhorsen spoke, and he said:

"Sabriel."

As he uttered the word, the wood ash disappeared from the priest's forehead, and slowly formed on the child's. The Charter had accepted the baptism.

"But . . . but she is dead!" exclaimed the Charter Mage, gingerly touching his forehead to make sure the ash was truly gone.

He got no answer, for the midwife was staring across the fire at Abhorsen, and Abhorsen was staring at—nothing. His eyes reflected the dancing flames, but did not see them.

Slowly, a chill mist began to rise from his body, spreading towards the man and midwife, who scuttled to the other side of the fire—wanting to get away, but now too afraid to run.

He could hear the child crying, which was good. If she had gone beyond the first gateway he could not bring her back without more stringent preparations, and a subsequent dilution of her spirit.

The current was strong, but he knew this branch of the river and waded past pools and eddies that hoped to drag him under. Already, he could feel the waters leaching his spirit, but his will was strong, so they *took only the color, not the substance.*

He paused to listen, and hearing the crying diminish, hastened forward. Perhaps she was already at the gateway, and about to pass.

The First Gate was a veil of mist, with a single dark opening, where the river poured into the silence beyond. Abhorsen hurried towards it, and then stopped. The baby had not yet passed through, but only because something had caught her and picked her up. Standing there, looming up out of the black waters, was a shadow darker than the gate.

It was several feet higher than Abhorsen, and there were pale marshlights burning where you would expect to see eyes, and the fetid stench of carrion rolled off it—a warm stench that relieved the chill of the river.

Abhorsen advanced on the thing slowly, watching the child it held loosely in the crook of a shadowed arm. The baby was asleep, but restless, and it squirmed towards the creature, seeking a mother's breast, but it only held her away from itself, as if the child were hot, or caustic.

Slowly, Abhorsen drew a small, silver handbell from the bandolier of bells across his chest, and cocked his wrist to ring it. But the shadowthing held the baby up and spoke in a dry, slithery voice, like a snake on gravel.

"Spirit of your spirit, Abhorsen. You can't spell me while I hold her. And perhaps I shall take her beyond the gate, as her mother has already gone."

Abhorsen frowned, in recognition, and replaced the bell. "You have a new shape, Kerrigor. And you are now this side of the First Gate. Who was foolish enough to assist you so far?"

Kerrigor smiled widely, and Abhorsen caught a glimpse of fires burning deep inside his mouth.

"One of the usual calling," he croaked. "But unskilled. He didn't realize it would be in the nature of an exchange. Alas, his life was not sufficient for me to pass the last portal. But now, you have come to help me."

"I, who chained you beyond the Seventh Gate?"

"Yes," whispered Kerrigor. "The irony does not, I think, escape you. But if you want the child . . ."

He made as if to throw the baby into the stream and, with that jerk, woke her. Immediately, she began to cry and her little fists reached out to gather up the shadow-stuff of Kerrigor like the folds of a robe. He cried out, tried to detach her, but the tiny hands held tightly and he was forced to overuse his strength, and threw her from him. She landed, squalling, and was instantly caught up in the flow of the river, but Abhorsen lunged forward, snatching her from both the river and Kerrigor's grasping hands.

Stepping back, he drew the silver bell one-handed, and swung it so it sounded twice. The sound was curiously muffled, but true, and the clear chime hung in the air, fresh and cutting, alive. Kerrigor flinched at the sound, and fell backwards to the darkness that was the gate.

"Some fool will soon bring me back, and then . . ." he cried out, as the river took him under. The waters swirled and gurgled and then resumed their steady flow.

Abhorsen stared at the gate for a time, then sighed and, placing the bell back in his belt, looked at the baby held in his arm. She stared back at him, dark eyes matching his own. Already, the color had been drained from her skin. Nervously, Abhorsen laid a hand across the brand on her forehead and felt the glow of her spirit within. The Charter mark had kept her life contained when the river should have drained it. It was her life-spirit that had so burned Kerrigor.

She smiled up at him and gurgled a little, and Abhorsen felt a smile tilting the corner of his own mouth. Still smiling, he turned, and began the long wade back up the river, to the gate that would return them both to their living flesh.

The baby wailed a scant second before Abhorsen opened his eyes, so that the midwife was already halfway around the dying fire, ready to pick her up. Frost crackled on the ground and icicles hung from Abhorsen's nose. He wiped them off with a sleeve and leaned over the child, much as any *anxious father does after a birth.*

"How is the babe?" he asked, and the midwife stared at him wonderingly, for the dead child was now loudly alive and as deathly white as he.

"As you hear, lord," she answered. "She is very well. It is perhaps a little cold for her——"

He gestured at the fire and spoke a word, and it roared into life, the frost melting at once, the raindrops sizzling into steam.

"That will do till morning," said Abhorsen. "Then I shall take her to my house. I shall have need of a nurse. Will you come?"

The midwife hesitated, and looked to the Charter Mage, who still lingered on the far side of the fire. He refused to meet her glance and she looked down once more at the little girl bawling in her arms.

"You are . . . you are . . ." whispered the midwife.

"A necromancer?" said Abhorsen. "Only of a sort. I loved the woman who lies here. She would have lived if she had loved another, but she did not. Sabriel is our child. Can you not see the kinship?"

The midwife looked at him as he leant forward and took Sabriel from her, rocking her on his chest. The baby quietened and, in a few seconds, was asleep.

"Yes," said the midwife. "I shall come with you, and look after Sabriel. But you must find a wet-nurse . . ."

"And I daresay much else besides," mused Abhorsen. "But my house is not a place for——"

The Charter Mage cleared his throat, and moved around the fire.

"If you seek a man who knows a little of the Charter," he said hesitantly, "I should wish to serve, for I have seen its work in you, lord, though I am loath to leave my fellow wanderers."

"Perhaps you will not have to," replied Abhorsen, smiling at a sudden thought. "I wonder if your leader will object to two new members joining her band. For my work means I must travel, and there is no part of the Kingdom that has not felt the imprint of my feet."

"Your work?" asked the man, shivering a little, though it was no longer cold.

"Yes," said Abhorsen. "I am a necromancer, but not of the common kind. Where others of the art raise the dead, I lay them back to rest. And those that will not rest, I bind—or try to. I am Abhorsen . . ."

He looked at the baby again, and added, almost with a note of surprise, "Father of Sabriel."

Chapter One

THE RABBIT HAD been run over minutes before. Its pink eyes were glazed and blood stained its clean white fur. Unnaturally clean fur, for it had just escaped from a bath. It still smelt faintly of lavender water.

A tall, curiously pale young woman stood over the rabbit. Her night-black hair, fashionably bobbed, was hanging slightly over her face. She wore no makeup or jewelry, save for an enamelled school badge pinned to her regulation navy blazer. That, coupled with her long skirt, stockings and sensible shoes, identified her as a schoolgirl. A nameplate under the badge read "Sabriel" and the Roman "VI" and gilt crown proclaimed her to be both a member of the Sixth Form and a prefect.

The rabbit was, unquestionably, dead. Sabriel looked up from it and back along the bricked drive that left the road and curved up to an imposing pair of wrought-iron gates. A sign above the gate, in gilt letters of mock Gothic, announced that they were the gates to Wyverley College. Smaller letters added that the school was "Established in 1652 for Young Ladies of Quality."

A small figure was busy climbing over the gate, nimbly avoiding the spikes that were supposed to stop such activities. She dropped the last few feet and started running, her pigtails flying, shoes clacking on the bricks. Her head was down to gain momentum, but as cruising speed was established, she looked up, saw Sabriel and the dead rabbit, and screamed.

"Bunny!"

Sabriel flinched as the girl screamed, hesitated for a moment, then bent down by the rabbit's side and reached out with one pale hand to touch it between its long ears. Her eyes closed and her face set as if she had suddenly turned to stone. A faint whistling sound came from her slightly parted lips, like the wind heard from far away. Frost formed on her fingertips and rimed the asphalt beneath her feet and knees.

The other girl, running, saw her suddenly tip forward over the rabbit, and topple towards the road, but at the last minute her hand came out and she caught herself. A second later, she had regained her balance and was using both hands to restrain the rabbit—a rabbit now inexplicably lively again, its eyes bright and shiny, as eager to be off as when it escaped from its bath.

"Bunny!" shrieked the younger girl again, as Sabriel stood up, holding the rabbit by the scruff of its neck. "Oh, thank you, Sabriel! When I heard the car skidding I thought . . ."

She faltered as Sabriel handed the rabbit over and blood stained her expectant hands.

"He'll be fine, Jacinth," Sabriel replied wearily. "A scratch. It's already closed up."

Jacinth examined Bunny carefully, then looked up at Sabriel, the beginnings of a wriggling fear showing at the back of her eyes.

"There isn't anything under the blood," stammered Jacinth. "What did you . . ."

"I didn't," snapped Sabriel. "But perhaps you can tell me what you are doing out of bounds?"

"Chasing Bunny," replied Jacinth, her eyes clearing as life reverted to a more normal situation. "You see . . ."

"No excuses," recited Sabriel. "Remember what Mrs.

Umbrade said at Assembly on Monday."

"It's not an excuse," insisted Jacinth. "It's a reason."

"You can explain it to Mrs. Umbrade then."

"Oh, Sabriel! You wouldn't! You know I was only chasing Bunny. I'd never have come out—"

Sabriel held up her hands in mock defeat, and gestured back to the gates.

"If you're back inside within three minutes, I won't have seen you. And open the gate this time. They won't be locked till I go back inside."

Jacinth smiled, her whole face beaming, whirled around and sped back up the drive, Bunny clutched against her neck. Sabriel watched till she had gone through the gate, then let the tremors take her till she was bent over, shaking with cold. A moment of weakness and she had broken the promise she had made both to herself and her father. It was only a rabbit and Jacinth did love it so much—but what would that lead to? It was no great step from bringing back a rabbit to bringing back a person.

Worse, it had been so easy. She had caught the spirit right at the wellspring of the river, and had returned it with barely a gesture of power, patching the body with simple Charter symbols as they stepped from death to life. She hadn't even needed bells, or the other apparatus of a necromancer. Only a whistle and her will.

Death and what came after death was no great mystery to Sabriel. She just wished it was.

It was Sabriel's last term at Wyverley—the last three weeks, in fact. She had graduated already, coming first in English, equal first in Music, third in Mathematics, seventh in Science, second in Fighting Arts and fourth in Etiquette. She had also been a runaway first in Magic, but that wasn't printed on the certificate.

Magic only worked in those regions of Ancelstierre close to the Wall which marked the border with the Old Kingdom. Farther away, it was considered to be quite beyond the pale, if it existed at all, and persons of repute did not mention it. Wyverley College was only forty miles from the Wall, had a good all-round reputation, and taught Magic to those students who could obtain special permission from their parents.

Sabriel's father had chosen it for that reason when he had emerged from the Old Kingdom with a five-year-old girl in tow to seek a boarding school. He had paid in advance for that first year, in Old Kingdom silver deniers that stood up to surreptitious touches with cold iron. Thereafter, he had come to visit his daughter twice a year, at Midsummer and Midwinter, staying for several days on each occasion and always bringing more silver.

Understandably, the Headmistress was very fond of Sabriel. Particularly since she never seemed troubled by her father's rare visitations, as most other girls would be. Once Mrs. Umbrade had asked Sabriel if she minded, and had been troubled by the answer that Sabriel saw her father far more often than when he was actually there. Mrs. Umbrade didn't teach Magic, and didn't want to know any more about it other than the pleasant fact that some parents would pay considerable sums to have their daughters schooled in the basics of sorcery and enchantment.

Mrs. Umbrade certainly didn't want to know how Sabriel saw her father. Sabriel, on the other hand, always looked forward to his unofficial visits and watched the moon, tracing its movements from the leather-bound almanac which listed the phases of the moon in both Kingdoms and gave valuable insights into the seasons, tides and other ephemerae that were never the same at any one time on both sides of the Wall. Abhorsen's sending of himself always appeared at the dark of the moon.

On these nights, Sabriel would lock herself into her study (a privilege of the Sixth Form—previously she'd had to sneak into the library), put the kettle on the fire, drink tea and read a book until the characteristic wind rose up, extinguished the fire, put out the electric light and rattled the shutters—all necessary preparations, it seemed, for her father's phosphorescent sending to appear in the spare armchair.

Sabriel was particularly looking forward to her father's visit that November. It would be his last, because college was about to end and she wanted to discuss her future. Mrs. Umbrade wanted her to go to university, but that meant moving farther away from the Old Kingdom. Her magic would wane and parental visitations would be limited to actual physical appearances, and those might well become even less frequent. On the other hand, going to university would mean staying with some of the friends she'd had virtually all her life, girls she'd started school with at the age of five. There would also be a much greater world of social interaction, particularly with young men, of which commodity there was a distinct shortage around Wyverley College.

And the disadvantage of losing her magic could possibly be offset by a lessening of her affinity for death and the dead . . .

Sabriel was thinking of this as she waited, book in hand, half-drunk cup of tea balanced precariously on the arm of her chair. It was almost midnight and Abhorsen hadn't appeared. Sabriel had checked the almanac twice and had even opened the shutters to peer out through the glass at the sky. It was definitely the dark of the moon, but there was no sign of him. It was the first time in her life that he hadn't appeared and she felt suddenly uneasy.

Sabriel rarely thought about what life was really like in the Old Kingdom, but now old stories came to mind and dim memories of when she'd lived there with the Travelers. Abhorsen was a powerful sorcerer, but even then . . .

"Sabriel! Sabriel!"

A high-pitched voice interrupted her thought, quickly followed by a hasty knock and a rattle of the doorknob. Sabriel sighed, pushed herself out of her chair, caught the teacup and unlocked the door. ·

A young girl stood on the other side, twisting her nightcap from side to side in trembling hands, her face white with fear.

"Olwyn!" exclaimed Sabriel. "What is it? Is Sussen sick again?"

"No," sobbed the girl. "I heard noises behind the tower door, and I thought it was Rebece and Ila having a midnight feast without me, so I looked . . ."

"What!" exclaimed Sabriel, alarmed. No one opened outside doors in the middle of the night, not this close to the Old Kingdom.

"I'm sorry," cried Olwyn. "I didn't mean to. I don't know why I did. It wasn't Rebece and Ila—it was a black shape and it tried to get in. I slammed the door . . ."

Sabriel threw the teacup aside and pushed past Olwyn. She was already halfway down the corridor before she heard the porcelain smash behind her, and Olwyn's horrified gasp at such cavalier treatment of good china. She ignored it and broke into a run, slapping on the light switches as she ran towards the open door of the west dormitory. As she reached it, screams broke out inside, rapidly crescendoing to an hysterical chorus. There were forty girls in the dormitory—most of the First Form, all under the age of eleven. Sabriel took a deep breath, and stepped into the doorway, fingers crooked in a spell-casting stance. Even before she looked, she felt the presence of death.

The dormitory was very long, and narrow, with a low roof

and small windows. Beds and dressers lined each side. At the far end, a door led to the West Tower steps. It was supposed to be locked inside and out, but locks rarely prevailed against the powers of the Old Kingdom.

The door was open. An intensely dark shape stood there, as if someone had cut a man-shaped figure out of the night, carefully choosing a piece devoid of stars. It had no features at all, but the head quested from side to side, as if whatever senses it did possess worked in a narrow range. Curiously, it carried an absolutely mundane sack in one four-fingered hand, the rough-woven cloth in stark contrast to its own surreal flesh.

Sabriel's hands moved in a complicated gesture, drawing the symbols of the Charter that intimated sleep, quiet and rest. With a flourish, she indicated both sides of the dormitory and drew one of the master symbols, drawing all together. Instantly, every girl in the room stopped screaming and slowly subsided back onto her bed.

The creature's head stopped moving and Sabriel knew its attention was now centered on her. Slowly it moved, lifting one clumsy leg and swinging it forward, resting for a moment, then swinging the other a little past the first. A lumbering, rolling motion, that made an eerie, shuffling noise on the thin carpet. As it passed each bed, the electric lights above them flared once and went out.

Sabriel let her hands fall to her side and focused her eyes on the center of the creature's torso, feeling the stuff of which it was made. She had come without any of her instruments or tools, but that led to only a moment's hesitation before she let herself slip over the border into Death, her eyes still on the intruder.

The river flowed around her legs, cold as always. The light, grey and without warmth, still stretched to an entirely flat horizon. In the distance, she could hear the roar of the First Gate.

She could see the creature's true shape clearly now, not wrapped in the aura of death which it carried to the living world. It was an Old Kingdom denizen, vaguely humanoid, but more like an ape than a man and obviously only semi-intelligent. But there was more to it than that, and Sabriel felt the clutch of fear as she saw the black thread that came from the creature's back and ran into the river. Somewhere, beyond the First Gate, or even farther, that umbilical rested in the hands of an Adept. As long as the thread existed the creature would be totally under the control of its master, who could use its senses and spirit as it saw fit.

Something tugged at Sabriel's physical body, and she reluctantly twitched her senses back to the living world, a slight feeling of nausea rising in her as a wave of warmth rushed over her death-chilled body.

"What is it?" said a calm voice, close to Sabriel's ear. An old voice, tinged with the power of Charter Magic—Miss Greenwood, the Magistrix of the school.

"It's a Dead servant—a spirit form," replied Sabriel, her attention back on the creature. It was halfway down the dorm, still single-mindedly rolling one leg after the other. "Without free will. Something sent it back to the living world. It's controlled from beyond the First Gate."

"Why is it here?" asked the Magistrix. Her voice sounded calm, but Sabriel felt the Charter symbols gathering in her voice, forming on her tongue—symbols that would unleash lightning and flame, the destructive powers of the earth.

"It's not obviously malign, nor has it attempted any actual harm . . ." replied Sabriel slowly, her mind working over the possibilities. She was used to explaining purely necromantic aspects of magic to Miss Greenwood. The Magistrix had taught her Charter Magic, but necromancy was definitely not on the syllabus. Sabriel had learned more than she wanted to know about necromancy from her father . . . and the Dead themselves. "Don't do anything for a moment. I will attempt to speak with it."

The cold washed over her again, biting into her, as the river gushed around her legs, eager to pull her over and carry her away. Sabriel exerted her will, and the cold became simply a sensation, without danger, the current merely a pleasing vibration about the feet.

The creature was close now, as it was in the living world. Sabriel held out both her hands, and clapped, the sharp sound echoing for longer than it would anywhere else. Before the echo died, Sabriel whistled several notes, and they echoed too, sweet sounds within the harshness of the handclap.

The thing flinched at the sound and stepped back, putting both hands to its ears. As it did so, it dropped the sack. Sabriel started in surprise. She hadn't noticed the sack before, possibly because she hadn't expected it to be there. Very few inanimate things existed in both realms, the living and the dead.

She was even more surprised as the creature suddenly bent forward and plunged into the water, hands searching for the sack. It found it almost at once, but not without losing its footing. As the sack surfaced, the current forced the creature under. Sabriel breathed a sigh of relief as she saw it slide away, then gasped as its head broke the surface and it cried out: "Sabriel! My messenger! Take the sack!" The voice was Abhorsen's.

Sabriel ran forward and an arm pushed out towards her, the neck of the sack clutched in its fingers. She reached out, missed, then tried again. The sack was secure in her grasp, as the current took the creature completely under. Sabriel looked after it, hearing the roar of the First Gate suddenly increase as it always did when someone passed its falls. She turned and started to slog back against the current to a point where she could easily return to life. The sack in her hand was heavy and there was a leaden feeling in her stomach. If the messenger was truly Abhorsen's, then he himself was unable to return to the realm of the living.

And that meant he was either dead, or trapped by something that should have passed beyond the final gate.

Once again, a wave of nausea overcame her and Sabriel fell to her knees, shaking. She could feel the Magistrix's hand on her shoulder, but her attention was fastened on the sack she held in her hand. She didn't need to look to know that the creature was gone. Its manifestation into the living world had ceased as its spirit had gone past the First Gate. Only a pile of grave mold would remain, to be swept aside in the morning.

"What did you do?" asked the Magistrix, as Sabriel brushed her hands through her hair, ice crystals falling from her hands onto the sack that lay in front of her knees.

"It had a message for me," replied Sabriel. "So I took it."

She opened the sack, and reached inside. A sword hilt met her grasp, so she drew it out, still scabbarded, and put it to one side. She didn't need to draw it to see the Charter symbols etched along its blade—the dull emerald in the pommel and the worn bronze-plated cross-guard were as familiar to her as the school's uninspired cutlery. It was Abhorsen's sword.

The leather bandolier she drew out next was an old brown belt, a hand's-breadth wide, which always smelled faintly of beeswax. Seven tubular leather pouches hung from it, starting with one the size of a small pill bottle; growing larger, till the seventh was almost the size of a jar. The bandolier was designed to be worn across the chest, with the pouches hanging down. Sabriel opened the smallest and pulled out a tiny silver bell, with a dark, deeply polished mahogany handle. She held it gently, but the clapper still swung slightly, and the bell made a high, sweet note that somehow lingered in the mind, even after the sound was gone.

"Father's instruments," whispered Sabriel. "The tools of a necromancer."

"But there are Charter marks engraved on the bell . . . and the handle!" interjected the Magistrix, who was looking down with fascination. "Necromancy is Free Magic, not governed by the Charter . . ."

"Father's was different," replied Sabriel distantly, still staring at the bell she held in her hand, thinking of her father's brown, lined hands holding the bells. "Binding, not raising. He was a faithful servant of the Charter."

"You're going to be leaving us, aren't you?" the Magistrix said suddenly, as Sabriel replaced the bell and stood up, sword in one hand, bandolier in the other. "I just saw it, in the reflection of the bell. You were crossing the Wall . . ."

"Yes. Into the Old Kingdom," said Sabriel, with sudden realization. "Something has happened to Father . . . but I'll find him . . . so I swear by the Charter I bear."

She touched the Charter mark on her forehead, which glowed briefly, and then faded so that it might never have been. The Magistrix nodded and touched a hand to her own forehead, where a glowing mark suddenly obscured all the patterns of time. As it faded, rustling noises and faint whimpers began to sound along both sides of the dormitory.

"I'll shut the door and explain to the girls," the Magistrix said firmly. "You'd better go and . . . prepare for tomorrow."

Sabriel nodded and left, trying to fix her mind on the practicalities of the journey, rather than on what could have happened to her father. She would take a cab as early as possible into Bain, the nearest town, and then a bus to the Ancelstierre perimeter that faced the Wall. With luck, she would be there by early afternoon . . .

Behind these plans, her thoughts kept jumping back to
Abhorsen. What could have happened to trap him in Death?
And what could she really hope to do about it, even if she did
get to the Old Kingdom?

Chapter Two

THE PERIMETER IN Ancelstierre ran from coast to coast, parallel to the Wall and perhaps half a mile from it. Concertina wire lay like worms impaled on rusting steel pickets; forward defenses for an interlocking network of trenches and concrete pillboxes. Many of these strong points were designed to control the ground behind them as well as in front, and almost as much barbed wire stretched behind the trenches, guarding the rear.

In fact, the Perimeter was much more successful at keeping people from Ancelstierre out of the Old Kingdom, than it was at preventing things from the Old Kingdom going the other way. Anything powerful enough to cross the Wall usually retained enough magic to assume the shape of a soldier; or to become invisible and simply go where it willed, regardless of barbed wire, bullets, hand grenades and mortar bombs—which often didn't work at all, particularly when the wind was blowing from the North, out of the Old Kingdom.

Due to the unreliability of technology, the Ancelstierran soldiers of the Perimeter garrison wore mail over their khaki battledress, had nasal and neck bars on their helmets and carried extremely old-fashioned sword-bayonets in well-worn scabbards. Shields, or more correctly, "bucklers, small, Perimeter garrison only," were carried on their backs, the factory khaki long since submerged under brightly painted regimental or personal signs.

Camouflage was not considered an issue at this particular posting.

Sabriel watched a platoon of young soldiers march past the bus, while she waited for the tourists ahead of her to stampede out the front door, and wondered what they thought of their strange duties. Most would have to be conscripts from far to the south, where no magic crept over the Wall and widened the cracks in what they thought of as reality. Here, she could feel magic potential brewing, lurking in the atmosphere like charged air before a thunderstorm.

The Wall itself looked normal enough, past the wasteland of wire and trenches. Just like any other medieval remnant. It was stone and old, about forty feet high and crenellated. Nothing remarkable, until the realization set in that it was in a perfect state of preservation. And for those with the sight, the very stones crawled with Charter marks—marks in constant motion, twisting and turning, sliding and rearranging themselves under a skin of stone.

The final confirmation of strangeness lay beyond the Wall. It was clear and cool on the Ancelstierre side, and the sun was shining—but Sabriel could see snow falling steadily behind the Wall, and snow-heavy clouds clustered right up to the Wall, where they suddenly stopped, as if some mighty weather-knife had simply sheared through the sky.

Sabriel watched the snow fall, and gave thanks for her Almanac. Printed by letterpress, the type had left ridges in the thick, linen-rich paper, making the many handwritten annotations waver precariously between the lines. One spidery remark, written in a hand she knew wasn't her father's, gave the weather to be expected under the respective calendars for each country. Ancelstierre had "Autumn. Likely to be cool." The Old Kingdom had "Winter. Bound to be snowing. Skis or snowshoes."

The last tourist left, eager to reach the observation platform.

Although the Army and the Government discouraged tourists, and there was no accommodation for them within twenty miles of the Wall, one busload a day was allowed to come and view the Wall from a tower located well behind the lines of the Perimeter. Even this concession was often cancelled, for when the wind blew from the north, the bus would inexplicably break down a few miles short of the tower, and the tourists would have to help push it back towards Bain—only to see it start again just as mysteriously as it stopped.

The authorities also made some slight allowance for the few people authorized to travel from Ancelstierre to the Old Kingdom, as Sabriel saw after she had successfully negotiated the bus's steps with her backpack, cross-country skis, stocks and sword, all threatening to go in different directions. A large sign next to the bus stop proclaimed:

PERIMETER COMMAND
NORTHERN ARMY GROUP

Unauthorized egress from the Perimeter Zone is strictly forbidden.

Anyone attempting to cross the Perimeter Zone will be shot without warning.

Authorized travelers must report to the Perimeter Command H.Q.

REMEMBER—NO WARNING WILL BE MADE

Sabriel read the note with interest, and felt a quickening sense of excitement start within her. Her memories of the Old

Kingdom were dim, from the perspective of a child, but she felt a sense of mystery and wonder kindle with the force of the Charter Magic she felt around her—a sense of something so much more alive than the bitumened parade ground, and the scarlet warning sign. And much more freedom than Wyverley College.

But that feeling of wonder and excitement came laced with a dread that she couldn't shake, a dread made up of fear for what might be happening to her father . . . what might have already happened . . .

The arrow on the sign indicating where authorized travelers should go seemed to point in the direction of a bitumen parade ground, lined with white-painted rocks, and a number of unprepossessing wooden buildings. Other than that, there were simply the beginnings of the communication trenches that sank into the ground and then zigzagged their way to the double line of trenches, blockhouses and fortifications that confronted the Wall.

Sabriel studied them for a while, and saw the flash of color as several soldiers hopped out of one trench and went forward to the wire. They seemed to be carrying spears rather than rifles and she wondered why the Perimeter was built for modern war, but manned by people expecting something rather more medieval. Then she remembered a conversation with her father and his comment that the Perimeter had been designed far away in the South, where they refused to admit that this perimeter was different from any other contested border. Up until a century or so ago, there had also been a wall on the Ancelstierre side. A lowish wall, made of rammed earth and peat, but a successful one.

Recalling that conversation, her eyes made out a low rise of scarred earth in the middle of the desolation of wire, and she realized that was where the southern wall had been. Peering at it, she also realized that what she had taken to be loose pickets between lines of concertina wire were something different—tall constructs more like the trunks of small trees stripped of every branch. They seemed familiar to her, but she couldn't place what they were.

Sabriel was still staring at them, thinking, when a loud and not very pleasant voice erupted a little way behind her right ear.

"What do you think you're doing, Miss? You can't loiter about here. On the bus, or up to the Tower!"

Sabriel winced and turned as quickly as she could, skis sliding one way and stocks the other, framing her head in a St. Andrew's Cross. The voice belonged to a large but fairly young soldier, whose bristling mustaches were more evidence of martial ambition than proof of them. He had two gilded bands on his sleeve, but didn't wear the mail hauberk and helmet Sabriel had seen on the other soldiers. He smelled of shaving cream and talc, and was so clean, polished and full of himself that Sabriel immediately catalogued him as some sort of natural bureaucrat currently disguised as a soldier.

"I am a citizen of the Old Kingdom," she replied quietly, staring back into his red flushed face and piggy eyes in the manner which Miss Prionte had taught her girls to instruct lesser domestic servants in Etiquette IV. "I am returning there."

"Papers!" demanded the soldier, after a moment's hesitation at the words "Old Kingdom."

Sabriel gave a frosty smile (also part of Miss Prionte's curriculum) and made a ritual movement with the tips of her fingers—the symbol of disclosing, of things hidden becoming seen, of unfolding. As her fingers sketched, she formed the symbol in her mind, linking it with the papers she carried in the inner pocket of her leather tunic. Finger-sketched and mind-drawn symbol merged, and the papers were in her hand. An

Ancelstierre passport, as well as the much rarer document the Ancelstierre Perimeter Command issued to people who had traffic in both countries: a hand-bound document printed by letterpress on handmade paper, with an artist's sketch instead of a photograph and prints from thumbs and toes in a purple ink.

The soldier blinked, but said nothing. Perhaps, thought Sabriel, as he took the proffered documents, the man thought it was a parlor trick. Or perhaps he just didn't notice. Maybe Charter Magic was common here, so close to the Wall.

The man looked through her documents carefully, but without real interest. Sabriel now felt certain that he was no one important from the way he pawed through her special passport. He'd obviously never seen one before. Mischievously, she started to weave the Charter mark for a snatch, or catch, to flick the papers out of his hands and back into her pocket before his piggy eyes worked out what was going on.

But, in the first second of motion, she felt the flare of other Charter Magic to either side and behind her—and heard the clattering of hobnails on the bitumen. Her head snapped back from the papers, and she felt her hair whisk across her forehead as she looked from side to side. Soldiers were pouring out of the huts and out of the trenches, sword-bayonets in their hands and rifles at the shoulder. Several of them wore badges that she realized marked them as Charter Mages. Their fingers were weaving warding symbols, and barriers that would lock Sabriel into her footsteps, tie her to her shadow. Crude magic, but strongly cast.

Instinctively, Sabriel's mind and hands flashed into the sequence of symbols that would wipe clean these bonds, but her skis shifted and fell into the crook of her elbow, and she winced at the blow.

At the same time, a soldier ran ahead of the others, sunlight glinting on the silver stars on his helmet.

"Stop!" he shouted. "Corporal, step back from her!"

The corporal, deaf to the hum of Charter Magic, blind to the flare of half-wrought signs, looked up from her papers and gaped for a second, fear erasing his features. He dropped the passports, and stumbled back.

In his face, Sabriel suddenly realized what it meant to use magic on the Perimeter, and she held herself absolutely still, blanking out the partly made signs in her mind. Her skis slipped farther down her arm, the bindings catching for a moment before tearing loose and clattering onto the ground. Soldiers rushed forward and, in seconds, formed a ring around her, swords angled towards her throat. She saw streaks of silver, plated onto the blades, and crudely written Charter symbols, and understood. These weapons were made to kill things that were already dead—inferior versions of the sword she wore at her own side.

The man who'd shouted—an officer, Sabriel realized—bent down and picked up her passports. He studied them for a moment, then looked up at Sabriel. His eyes were pale blue and held a mixture of harshness and compassion that Sabriel found familiar, though she couldn't place it—till she remembered her father's eyes. Abhorsen's eyes were so dark brown they seemed black, but they held a similar feeling.

The officer closed the passport, tucked it in his belt and tilted his helmet back with two fingers, revealing a Charter mark still glowing with some residual charm of warding. Cautiously, Sabriel lifted her hand, and then, as he didn't dissuade her, reached out with two fingers to touch the mark. As she did so, he reached forward and touched her own—Sabriel felt the familiar swirl of energy, and the feeling of falling into some endless galaxy of stars. But the stars here were Charter symbols, linked in some great dance that had no beginning or end, but contained and described the world in its movement. Sabriel knew only a small fraction of the symbols, but she knew what they danced, and she felt the purity of the Charter wash over her.

"An unsullied Charter mark," the officer pronounced loudly, as their fingers fell back to their sides. "She is no creature or sending."

The soldiers fell back, sheathing swords and clicking on safety catches. Only the red-faced corporal didn't move, his eyes still staring at Sabriel, as if he was unsure what he was looking at.

"Show's over, Corporal," said the officer, his voice and eyes now harsh. "Get back to the pay office. You'll see stranger happenings than this in your time here—stay clear of them and you might stay alive!

"So," he said, taking the documents from his belt and handing them back to Sabriel. "You are the daughter of Abhorsen. I am Colonel Horyse, the commander of a small part of the garrison here—a unit the Army likes to call the Northern Perimeter Reconaissance Unit and everyone else calls the Crossing Point Scouts—a somewhat motley collection of Ancelstierrans who've managed to gain a Charter mark and some small knowledge of magic."

"Pleased to meet you, sir," popped out of Sabriel's school-trained mouth, before she could stifle it. A schoolgirl's answer, she knew, and felt a blush rise in her pale cheeks.

"Likewise," said the Colonel, bending down. "May I take your skis?"

"If you would be so kind," said Sabriel, falling back on formality.

The Colonel picked them up with ease, carefully retied the stocks to the skis, refastened the bindings that had come undone and tucked the lot under one muscular arm.

"I take it you intend to cross into the Old Kingdom?" asked

Horyse, as he found the balancing point of his load and pointed at the scarlet sign on the far side of the parade ground. "We'll have to check in with Perimeter HQ—there are a few formalities, but it shouldn't take long. Is someone . . . Abhorsen, coming to meet you?"

His voice faltered a little as he mentioned Abhorsen, a strange stutter in so confident a man. Sabriel glanced at him and saw that his eyes flickered from the sword at her waist to the bell-bandolier she wore across her chest. Obviously he recognized Abhorsen's sword and also the significance of the bells. Very few people ever met a necromancer, but anyone who did remembered the bells.

"Did . . . do you know my father?" she asked. "He used to visit me, twice a year. I guess he would have come through here."

"Yes, I saw him then," replied Horyse, as they started walking around the edge of the parade ground. "But I first met him more than twenty years ago, when I was posted here as a subaltern. It was a strange time—a very bad time, for me and everyone on the Perimeter."

He paused in mid-stride, boots crashing, and his eyes once again looked at the bells, and the whiteness of Sabriel's skin, stark against the black of her hair, black as the bitumen under the feet.

"You're a necromancer," he said bluntly. "So you'll probably understand. This crossing point has seen too many battles, too many dead. Before those idiots down South took things under central command, the crossing point was moved every ten years, up to the next gate on the Wall. But forty years ago some . . . bureaucrat . . . decreed that there would be no movement. It was a waste of public money. This was, and is to be, the only crossing point. Never mind the fact that, over time, there would be such a concentration of death, mixed with Free Magic leaking over the Wall, that everything would . . ."

"Not stay dead," interrupted Sabriel quietly.

"Yes. When I arrived, the trouble was just beginning. Corpses wouldn't stay buried—our people or Old Kingdom creatures. Soldiers killed the day before would turn up on parade. Creatures prevented from crossing would rise up and do more damage than they did when they were alive."

"What did you do?" asked Sabriel. She knew a great deal about binding and enforcing true death, but not on such a scale. There were no Dead creatures nearby now, for she always instinctively felt the interface between life and death around her, and it was no different here than it had been forty miles away at Wyverley College.

"Our Charter Mages tried to deal with the problem, but there were no specific Charter symbols to . . . make them dead . . . only to destroy their physical shape. Sometimes that was enough and sometimes it wasn't. We had to rotate troops back to Bain or even farther just for them to recover from what HQ liked to think of as bouts of mass hysteria or madness.

"I wasn't a Charter Mage then, but I was going with patrols into the Old Kingdom, beginning to learn. On one patrol, we met a man sitting by a Charter Stone, on top of a hill that overlooked both the Wall and the Perimeter.

"As he was obviously interested in the Perimeter, the officer in charge of the patrol thought we should question him and kill him if he turned out to bear a corrupted Charter, or was some Free Magic thing in the shape of a man. But we didn't, of course. It was Abhorsen, and he was coming to us, because he'd heard about the Dead.

"We escorted him in and he met with the General commanding the garrison. I don't know what they agreed, but I imagine it was for Abhorsen to bind the Dead and, in return, he was to be granted citizenship of Ancelstierre and freedom to cross the Wall. He certainly had the two passports after that. In any case, he spent the next few months carving the wind flutes you can see among the wire . . ."

"Ah!" exclaimed Sabriel. "I wondered what they were. Wind flutes. That explains a lot."

"I'm glad you understand," said the Colonel. "I still don't. For one thing, they make no sound no matter how hard the wind blows through them. They have Charter symbols on them I had never seen before he carved them, and have never seen again anywhere else. But when he started placing them . . . one a night . . . the Dead just gradually disappeared, and no new ones rose."

They reached the far end of the parade ground, where another scarlet sign stood next to a communication trench, proclaiming: "Perimeter Garrison HQ. Call and Wait for Sentry."

A telephone handset and a bell-chain proclaimed the usual dichotomy of the Perimeter. Colonel Horyse picked up the handset, wound the handle, listened for a moment, then replaced it. Frowning, he pulled the bell-chain three times in quick succession.

"Anyway," he continued, as they waited for the sentry. "Whatever it was, it worked. So we are deeply indebted to Abhorsen, and that makes his daughter an honored guest."

"I may be less honored and more reviled as a messenger of ill omen," said Sabriel quietly. She hesitated, for it was hard to talk about Abhorsen without tears coming to her eyes, then continued quickly, to get it over and done with. "The reason I am going into the Old Kingdom is to . . . to look for my father. Something has happened to him."

"I had hoped there was another reason for you to carry his sword," said Horyse. He moved the skis into the crook of his left arm, freeing his right, to return the salute of the two sentries who were running at the double up the communication trench, hobnails clacking on the wooden slats.

"There is worse, I think," added Sabriel, taking a deep breath to stop her voice from breaking into sobs. "He is trapped in Death . . . or . . . or he may even be dead. And his bindings will be broken."

"The wind flutes?" asked Horyse, grounding the end of the skis, his salute dying out halfway to his head. "All the Dead here?"

"The flutes play a song only heard in Death," replied Sabriel, "continuing a binding laid down by Abhorsen. But the bound are tied to him, and the flutes will have no power if . . . they will have no power if Abhorsen is now among the Dead. They will bind no more."

Chapter Three

"I AM NOT ONE to blame a messenger for her tidings," said Horyse, as he handed a cup of tea over to Sabriel, who was sitting on what looked like the only comfortable chair in the dugout which was the Colonel's headquarters, "but you bring the worst news I have heard for many years."

"At least I am a living messenger . . . and a friendly one," Sabriel said quietly. She hadn't really thought beyond her own concern for her father. Now, she was beginning to expand her knowledge of him, to understand that he was more than just her father, that he was many different things to different people. Her simple image of him—relaxing in the armchair of her study at Wyverley College, chatting about her schoolwork, Ancelstierre technology, Charter Magic and necromancy—was a limited view, like a painting that only captured one dimension of the man.

"How long do we have until Abhorsen's bindings are broken?" asked Horyse, breaking into Sabriel's remembrance of her father. The image she had of her father reaching for a teacup in her study disappeared, banished by real tea slopping over in her enamel mug and burning her fingers.

"Oh! Excuse me. I wasn't thinking . . . how long till what?"

"The binding of the dead," the Colonel reiterated, patiently. "How long till the bindings fail, and the dead are free?"

Sabriel thought back to her father's lessons, and the ancient grimoire she'd spent every holiday slowly memorizing. *The Book of the Dead* it was called and parts of it still made her shudder. It looked innocuous enough, bound in green leather, with tarnished silver clasps. But if you looked closely, both leather and silver were etched with Charter marks. Marks of binding and blinding, closing and imprisonment. Only a trained necromancer could open that book . . . and only an uncorrupted Charter Mage could close it. Her father had brought it with him on his visits, and always took it away again at the end.

"It depends," she said slowly, forcing herself to consider the question objectively, without letting emotion interfere. She tried to recall the pages that showed the carving of the wind flutes, the chapters on music and the nature of sound in the binding of the dead. "If Father . . . if Abhorsen is . . . truly dead, the wind flutes will simply fall apart under the light of the next full moon. If he is trapped before the Ninth Gate, the binding will continue until the full moon after he passes beyond, or a particularly strong spirit breaks the weakened bonds."

"So the moon will tell, in time," said Horyse. "We have fourteen days till it is full."

"It is possible I could bind the dead anew," Sabriel said cautiously. "I mean, I haven't done it on this sort of scale. But I know how. The only thing is, if Father isn't . . . isn't beyond the Ninth Gate, then I need to help him as soon as I can. And before I can do that, I must get to his house and gather a few things . . . check some references."

"How far is this house beyond the Wall?" asked Horyse, a calculating look on his face.

"I don't know," replied Sabriel.

"What?"

"I don't know. I haven't been there since I was about four. I think it's supposed to be a secret. Father had many enemies, not just among the dead. Petty necromancers, Free Magic sorcerers, witches—"

"You don't seem disturbed by your lack of directions," interrupted the Colonel dryly. For the first time, a hint of doubt, even fatherly condescension, had crept into his voice, as if Sabriel's youth undermined the respect due to her as both a Charter Mage and necromancer.

"Father taught me how to call a guide who will give me directions," replied Sabriel coolly. "And I know it's less than four days' travel away."

That silenced Horyse, at least for the moment. He nodded and, standing cautiously, so his head didn't hit the exposed beams of the dugout, he walked over to a steel filing cabinet that was rusting from the dark brown mud that oozed between the pale planks of the revetment. Opening the cabinet with a practiced heave of considerable force, he found a mimeographed map and rolled it out on the table.

"We've never been able to get our hands on a genuine Old Kingdom map. Your father had one, but he was the only person who could see anything on it—it just looked like a square of calfskin to me. A small magic, he said, but since he couldn't teach it, perhaps not so small . . . Anyway, this map is a copy of the latest version of our patrol map, so it only goes out about ten miles from the crossing point. The garrison standing orders strictly forbid us to go farther. Patrols tend not to come back beyond that distance. Maybe they desert, or maybe . . ."

His tone of voice suggested that even nastier things happened to the patrols, but Sabriel didn't question him. A small portion of the Old Kingdom lay spread out on the table and, once again, excitement stirred up within her.

"We generally go out along the Old North Road," said Horyse, tracing it with one hand, the sword calluses on his fingers rasping across the map, like the soft sandpapering of a master craftsman. "Then the patrols sweep back, either south-east or south-west, till they hit the Wall. Then they follow that back to the gate."

"What does this symbol mean?" asked Sabriel, pointing to a blacked-in square atop one of the farther hills.

"That's a Charter Stone," replied the Colonel. "Or part of one now. It was riven in two, as if struck by lightning, a month or so ago. The patrols have started to call it Cloven Crest, and they avoid it if possible. Its true name is Barhedrin Hill and the stone once carried the Charter for a village of the same name. Before my time, anyway. If the village still exists it must be farther north, beyond the reach of our patrols. We've never had any reports of inhabitants from it coming south to Cloven Crest. The fact is, we have few reports of people, fullstop. The Garrison Log used to show considerable interaction with Old Kingdom people—farmers, merchants, travelers and so on—but encounters have become rarer over the last hundred years, and very rare in the last twenty. The patrols would be lucky to see even two or three people a year now. Real people that is, not creatures or Free Magic constructs, or the Dead. We see far too many of those."

"I don't understand," muttered Sabriel. "Father often used to talk of villages and towns . . . even cities, in the Old Kingdom. I remember some of them from my childhood . . . well, I sort of remember . . . I think."

"Farther into the Old Kingdom, certainly," replied the Colonel. "The records mention quite a few names of towns and cities. We know that the people up there call the area around the Wall 'the Borderlands.' And they don't say it with any fondness."

Sabriel didn't answer, bending her head lower over the map, thinking about the journey that lay ahead of her. Cloven Crest might be a good waypoint. It was no more than eight miles away, so she should be able to ski there before nightfall if she left fairly soon, and if it wasn't snowing too hard across the Wall. A broken Charter Stone did not bode well, but there would be some magic there and the path into Death would be easier to tread. Charter Stones were often erected where Free Magic flowed and crossroads of the Free Magic currents were often natural door-ways into the realm of death. Sabriel felt a shiver inch up her spine at the thought of what might use such a doorway and the tremor passed through to her fingers on the map.

She looked up suddenly, and saw Colonel Horyse looking at her long, pale hands, the heavy paper of the map still shuddering at her touch. With an effort of will, she stilled the movement.

"I have a daughter almost your age," he said quietly. "Back in Corvere, with my wife. I would not let her cross into the Old Kingdom."

Sabriel met his gaze, and her eyes were not the uncertain, flickering beacons of adolescence.

"I am only eighteen years old on the outside," she said, touching her palm against her breast with an almost wistful motion. "But I first walked in Death when I was twelve. I encountered a Fifth Gate Rester when I was fourteen, and ban-ished it beyond the Ninth Gate. When I was sixteen I stalked and banished a Mordicant that came near the school. A weakened Mordicant, but still . . . A year ago, I turned the final page of *The Book of the Dead*. I don't feel young anymore."

"I am sorry for that," said the Colonel, then, almost as if he had surprised himself, he added, "Ah, I mean that I wish you some of the foolish joys my daughter has—some of the lightness, the lack of responsibility that goes with youth. But I don't wish it if it will weaken you in the times ahead. You have chosen a dif-ficult path."

"'Does the walker choose the path, or the path the walker?'"

Sabriel quoted, the words, redolent with echoes of Charter Magic, twining around her tongue like some lingering spice. Those words were the dedication in the front of her almanac. They were also the very last words, all alone on the last page, of *The Book of the Dead*.

"I've heard that before," remarked Horyse. "What does it mean?"

"I don't know," said Sabriel.

"It holds power when you say it," added the Colonel slowly. He swallowed, open-mouthed, as if the taste of the Charter marks was still in the air. "If I spoke those words, that's all they would be. Just words."

"I can't explain it." Sabriel shrugged, and attempted a smile. "But I do know other sayings that are more to the point at the moment, like: 'Traveler, embrace the morning light, but do not take the hand of night.' I must be on my way."

Horyse smiled at the old rhyme, so beloved of grandmothers and nannies, but it was an empty smile. His eyes slid a little away from Sabriel's and she knew that he was thinking about refusing to let her cross the Wall. Then he sighed, the short, huffy sigh of a man who is forced into a course of action through lack of alternatives.

"Your papers are in order," he said, meeting her gaze once again. "And you are the daughter of Abhorsen. I cannot do other than let you pass. But I can't help feeling that I am thrusting you out to meet some terrible danger. I can't even send a patrol out with you, since we have five full patrols already out there."

"I expected to go alone," replied Sabriel. She had expected that, but felt a tinge of regret. A protective group of soldiers would be quite a comfort. The fear of being alone in a strange and dangerous land, even if it was her homeland, was only just below the level of her excitement. It wouldn't take much for the fear to rise over it. And always, there was the picture of her father in her mind. Her father in trouble, trapped and alone in the chill waters of Death . . .

"Very well," said Horyse. "Sergeant!"

A helmeted head appeared suddenly around the doorway, and Sabriel realized two soldiers must have been standing on guard outside the dugout, on the steps up into the communication trench. She wondered if they'd heard.

"Prepare a crossing party," snapped Horyse. "A single person to cross. Miss Abhorsen, here. And Sergeant, if you or Private Rahise so much as talk in your sleep about what you may have heard here, then you'll be on gravedigging fatigues for the rest of your lives!"

"Yes, sir!" came the sharp reply, echoed by the unfortunate Private Rahise, who, Sabriel noted, did seem half-asleep.

"After you, please," continued Horyse, gesturing towards the door. "May I carry your skis again?"

The Army took no chances when it came to crossing the Wall. Sabriel stood alone under the great arch of the gate that pierced the Wall, but archers stood or knelt in a reverse arrowhead formation around the gate, and a dozen swordsmen had gone ahead with Colonel Horyse. A hundred yards behind her, past a zigzagged lane of barbed wire, two Lewyn machinegunners watched from a forward emplacement—though Sabriel noted they had drawn their sword-bayonets and thrust them, ready for use, in the sandbags, showing little faith in their air-cooled 45-rounds-per-minute tools of destruction.

There was no actual gate in the archway, though rusting hinges swung like mechanical hands on either side and sharp shards of oak thrust out of the ground, like teeth in a broken jaw, testimony to some explosion of modern chemistry or magical force.

It was snowing lightly on the Old Kingdom side, and the

wind channeled occasional snowflakes through the gate into Ancelstierre, where they melted on the warmer ground of the south. One caught in Sabriel's hair. She brushed at it lightly, till it slid down her face and was captured by her tongue.

The cold water was refreshing and, though it tasted no different from any other melted snow she'd drunk, it marked her first taste of the Old Kingdom in thirteen years. Dimly, she remembered it had been snowing then. Her father had carried her through, when he first brought her south into Ancelstierre.

A whistle alerted her, and she saw a figure appear out of the snow, flanked by twelve others, who drew up in two lines leading out from the gate. They faced outwards, their swords shining, blades reflecting the light that was itself reflected from the snow. Only Horyse looked inwards, waiting for her.

With her skis over her shoulder, Sabriel picked her way among the broken timbers of the gate. Going through the arch, from mud into snow, from bright sun into the pallid luminescence of a snowfall, from her past into her future.

The stones of the Wall on either side, and above her head, seemed to call a welcome home, and rivulets of Charter marks ran through the stones like rain through dust.

"The Old Kingdom welcomes you," said Horyse, but he was watching the Charter marks run on the stones, not looking at Sabriel.

Sabriel stepped out of the shadow of the gate and pulled her cap down, so the peak shielded her face against the snow.

"I wish your mission every success, Sabriel," continued Horyse, looking back at her. "I hope . . . hope I see both you and your father before too long."

He saluted, turned smartly to his left, and was gone, wheeling around her and marching back through the gate. His men peeled off from the line and followed. Sabriel bent down as they marched past, slid her skis back and forth in the snow, then slipped her boots into the bindings. The snow was falling steadily, but it was only a light fall and the cover was patchy. She could still easily make out the Old North Road. Fortunately, the snow had banked up in the gutters to either side of the road, and she could make good time if she kept to these narrow snow-ways. Even though it seemed to be several hours later in the Old Kingdom than it was in Ancelstierre, she expected to reach Cloven Crest before dusk.

Taking up her poles, Sabriel checked that her father's sword was easy in its scabbard, and the bells hung properly from their baldric. She considered a quick Charter-spell for warmth, but decided against it. The road had a slight uphill gradient, so the skiing would be quite hard work. In her handknitted, greasy wool shirt, leather jerkin and thick, double padded skiing knickerbockers, she would probably be too warm once she got going.

With a practiced motion, she pushed one ski ahead, the opposite arm reaching forward with her pole, and slid forward, just as the last swordsman passed her on his way back through the gate. He grinned as he passed by, but she didn't notice, concentrating on building up the rhythm of her skis and poles. Within minutes, she was practically flying up the road, a slim, dark figure against the white of the ground.

Chapter Four

SABRIEL FOUND THE first dead Ancelstierran soldier about six miles from the Wall, in the last, fading hours of the afternoon. The hill she thought was Cloven Crest was a mile or two to the north. She'd stopped to look at its dark bulk, rising rocky and treeless from the snow-covered ground, its peak temporarily hidden in one of the light, puffy clouds that occasionally let forth a shower of snow or sleet.

If she hadn't stopped, she would probably have missed the frosted-white hand that peeked out of a drift on the other side of the road. But as soon as she saw that, her attention focused and Sabriel felt the familiar pang of death.

Crossing over, her skis clacking on bare stone in the middle of the road, she bent down and gently brushed the snow away.

The hand belonged to a young man, who wore a standard-issue coat of mail over an Ancelstierran uniform of khaki serge. He was blond and grey-eyed, and Sabriel thought he had been surprised, for there was no fear in his frozen expression. She touched his forehead with one finger, closed his sightless eyes, and laid two fingers against his open mouth. He had been dead twelve days, she felt. There were no obvious signs as to what had killed him. To learn more than that, she would have to follow the young man into Death. Even after twelve days, it was unlikely he had gone farther than the Fourth Gate. Even so, Sabriel had a strong disinclination to enter the realm of the dead until she absolutely had to. Whatever had trapped—or killed—her father could easily be waiting to ambush her there. This dead soldier could even be a lure.

Quashing her natural curiosity to find out exactly what had happened, Sabriel folded the man's arms across his chest, after first unclenching the grip that his right hand still had on his sword hilt—perhaps he had not been taken totally unawares after all. Then she stood and drew the Charter marks of fire, cleansing, peace and sleep in the air above the corpse, while whispering the sounds of those same marks. It was a litany that every Charter Mage knew, and it had the usual effect. A glowing ember sparked up between the man's folded arms, multiplied into many stabbing, darting flames, then fire whooshed the full length of the body. Seconds later it was out and only ash remained, ash staining a corselet of blackened mail.

Sabriel took the soldier's sword from the pile of ashes and thrust it through the melted snow, into the dark earth beneath. It stuck fast, upright, the hilt casting a shadow like a cross upon the ashes. Something glinted in the shadow and, belatedly, Sabriel remembered that the soldier would have worn an identity disc or tag.

Shifting her skis again to rebalance she bent down and hooked the chain of the identity disc on one finger, pulling it up to read the name of the man who had met his end here, alone in the snow. But both the chain and disc were machine-made in Ancelstierre and so unable to withstand the Charter Magic fire. The disc crumbled into ash as Sabriel raised it to eye level and the chain fell into its component links, pouring between Sabriel's fingers like small steel coins.

"Perhaps they'll know you from your sword," said Sabriel. Her voice sounded strange in the quiet of the snowy wilderness and, behind each word, her breath rolled out like a small, wet fog.

"Travel without regret," she added. "Do not look back."

Sabriel took her own advice as she skied away. There was an anxiety in her now that had been mostly academic before and every sense was alert, watchful. She had always been told that the Old Kingdom was dangerous, and the Borderlands near the Wall particularly so. But that intellectual knowledge was tempered by her vague childhood memories of happiness, of being with her father and the band of Travelers. Now, the reality of the danger was slowly coming home . . .

Half a mile on she slowed and stopped to look up at Cloven Crest again, neck cricked back to watch where the sun struck between the clouds, lighting up the yellow-red granite of the bluffs. She was in cloud shadow herself, so the hill looked like an attractive destination. As she looked, it started to snow again, and two snowflakes fell upon her forehead, melting into her eyes. She blinked and the melted snow traced tear trails down her cheeks. Through misted eyes, she saw a bird of prey—a hawk or kite— launch itself from the bluffs and hover, its concentration totally centered upon some small mouse or vole creeping across the snow.

The kite dropped like a cast stone, and a few seconds later, Sabriel felt some small life snuffed out. At the same time, she also felt the tug of human death. Somewhere ahead, near where the kite dined, more people lay dead.

Sabriel shivered, and looked at the hill again. According to Horyse's map, the path to Cloven Crest lay in a narrow gully between two bluffs. She could see quite clearly where it must be, but the dead lay in that direction. Whatever had killed them might also still be there.

There was sunlight on the bluffs, but the wind was driving snow clouds across the sun and Sabriel guessed it was only an hour or so till dusk. She'd lost time freeing the soldier's spirit, and now had no choice but to hurry on if she wished to reach Cloven Crest before nightfall.

She thought about what lay ahead for a moment, then chose a compromise between speed and caution. Stabbing her poles into the snow, she released her bindings, stepped out of her skis and then quickly fastened skis and poles together to be strapped diagonally across her backpack. She tied them on carefully, remembering how they'd fallen and broken her Charter-spell on the parade ground—only that morning, but it seemed like weeks ago and a world away.

That done, she started to pick her way down the center of the road, keeping away from the gutter drifts. She'd have to leave the road fairly soon, but it looked like there was little snow on the steep, rocky slopes of Cloven Crest.

As a final precaution, she drew Abhorsen's sword, then resheathed it, so an inch of blade was free of the scabbard. It would draw fast and easily when she needed it.

Sabriel expected to find the bodies on the road, or near it, but they lay farther on. There were many footprints, and churned-up snow, leading from the road towards the path to Cloven Crest. That path ran between the bluffs, following a route gouged out by a stream falling from some deep spring higher up the hill. The path crossed the stream several times, with stepping-stones or tree trunks across the water to save walkers from wet feet. Halfway up, where the bluffs almost ground together, the stream had dug itself a short gorge, about twelve feet wide, thirty feet long and deep. Here, the pathmakers had been forced to build a bridge along the stream, rather than across it.

Sabriel found the rest of the Ancelstierran patrol here, tumbled on the dark olive-black wood of the bridge, with the water murmuring beneath and the red stone arching overhead. There were seven of them along the bridge's length. Unlike the first soldier, it was quite clear what had killed them. They had been hacked apart and, as Sabriel edged closer, she realized they had been beheaded. Worse than that, whoever . . . whatever . . . had killed them had taken their heads away—almost a guarantee that their spirits would return.

Her sword did draw easily. Gingerly, her right hand almost glued to the sword hilt, Sabriel stepped around the first of the splayed-out bodies and onto the bridge. The water beneath was partly iced over, shallow and sluggish, but it was clear the soldiers had sought refuge over it. Running water was a good protection from dead creatures or things of Free Magic, but this torpid stream would not have dismayed even one of the Lesser Dead. In Spring, fed with melted snow, the stream would burst between the bluffs, and the bridge would be knee-deep in clear, swift water. The soldiers would probably have survived at that time of year.

Sabriel sighed quietly, thinking of how easily seven people could be alive in one instant, and then, despite everything they could do, despite their last hope, they could be dead in just another. Once again, she felt the temptation of the necromancer, to take the cards nature had dealt, to reshuffle them and deal again. She had the power to make these men live again, laugh again, love again . . .

But without their heads she could only bring them back as "Hands," a derogatory term that Free Magic necromancers used for their lackluster revenants, who retained little of their original intelligence and none of their initiative. They made useful servants, though, either as reanimated corpses or the more difficult Shadow Hands, where only the spirit was brought back.

Sabriel grimaced as she thought of Shadow Hands. A skilled necromancer could easily raise Shadow Hands from the heads of the newly dead. Similarly, without the heads, she couldn't give them the final rites and free their spirits. All she could do was treat the bodies with some respect and, in the process, clear the bridge. It was near to dusk, and dark already in the shadow of the gorge, but she ignored the little voice inside her that was urging her to leave the bodies and run for the open space of the hilltop.

By the time she finished dragging the bodies back down the path a way, laying them out with their swords plunged in the earth next to their headless bodies, it was dark outside the gorge too. So dark, she had to risk a faint, Charter-conjured light, that hung like a pale star above her head, showing the path before dying out.

A slight magic, but one with unexpected consequences, for, as she left the bodies behind, an answering light burned into brilliance on the upper post of the bridge. It faded into red embers almost immediately, but left three glowing Charter marks. One was strange to Sabriel, but, from the other two, she guessed its meaning. Together, they held a message.

Three of the dead soldiers had the feel of Charter Magic about them, and Sabriel guessed that they were Charter Mages. They would have had the Charter mark on their foreheads. The very last body on the bridge had been one of these men and Sabriel remembered that he had been the only one not holding a weapon—his hands had been clasped around the bridge post. These marks would certainly hold his message.

Sabriel touched her own forehead Charter mark and then the bridge post. The marks flared again, then went dark. A voice came from nowhere, close to Sabriel's ear. A man's voice, husky with fear, backed by the sound of clashing weapons, screaming and total panic.

"One of the Greater Dead! It came behind us, almost from the Wall. We couldn't turn back. It has servants, Hands, a Mordicant! This is Sergeant Gerren. Tell Colonel . . ."

Whatever he wanted to tell Colonel Horyse was lost in the moment of his own death. Sabriel stood still, listening, as if there might be more. She felt ill, nauseous, and took several deep breaths. She had forgotten that for all her familiarity with death and the dead, she had never seen or heard anyone actually die. The aftermath she had learnt to deal with . . . but not the event.

She touched the bridge post again, just with one finger, and felt the Charter marks twisting through the grain of the wood. Sergeant Gerren's message would be there forever for any Charter Mage to hear, till time did its work, and bridge post and bridge rotted or were swept away by flood.

Sabriel took a few more breaths, stilled her stomach, and forced herself to listen once more.

One of the Greater Dead was back in Life, and that was something her father was sworn to stop. It was almost certain that this emergence and Abhorsen's disappearance were connected.

Once again, the message came, and Sabriel listened. Then, brushing back her starting tears, she walked on, up the path, away from the bridge and the dead, up towards Cloven Crest and the broken Charter Stone.

The bluffs parted and, in the sky above, stars started to twinkle, as the wind grew braver and swept the snow clouds before it into the west. The new moon unveiled itself and swelled in brightness, till it cast shadows on the snow-flecked ground.

Chapter Five

I T WAS NO more than a half-hour's steady climb to the flat top of Cloven Crest, though the path grew steeper and more difficult. The wind was strong now and had cleared the sky, the moonlight giving form to the landscape. But without the clouds, it had grown much colder.

Sabriel considered a Charter-spell for warmth, but she was tired, and the effort of the spell might cost more than the gain in warmth. She stopped instead and shrugged on a fleece-lined oil-skin that had been handed down from her father. It was a bit worn and too large, needing severe buckling-in with her sword-belt and the baldric that held the bells, but it was certainly windproof.

Feeling relatively warmer, Sabriel resumed climbing up the last, winding portion of the path, where the incline was so steep the pathmakers had resorted to cutting steps out of the granite— steps now worn and crumbling, prone to sliding away underfoot.

So prone to sliding, that Sabriel reached the top without realizing it, head down, her eyes searching in the moonlight for the solid part of the next step. Her foot was actually halfway up in the air before she realized that there wasn't a next step.

Cloven Crest lay before her. A narrow ridge where several slopes of the hill met to form a miniature plateau, with a slight depression in the middle. Snow lay in this depression, a fat, cigar-shaped drift, bright in the moonlight, stark white against the red granite. There were no trees, no vegetation at all, but in the very center of the drift, a dark grey stone cast a long moonshadow. It was twice Sabriel's girth and three times her height, and looked whole till she walked closer and saw the zigzag crack that cut it down the middle.

Sabriel had never seen a true Charter Stone before, but she knew they were supposed to be like the Wall, with Charter marks running like quicksilver through the stone, forming and dissolving, only to re-form again, in a never-ending story that told of the making of the world.

There were Charter marks on this stone, but they were still, as frozen as the snow. Dead marks, nothing more than meaning-less inscriptions, carved into a sculptured stone.

It wasn't what Sabriel had expected, though she now real-ized that she hadn't thought about it properly. She'd thought of lightning or suchlike as the splitter of the stone, but forgotten lessons remembered too late told her that wasn't so. Only some terrible power of Free Magic could split a Charter Stone.

She walked closer to the stone, fear rising in her like a toothache in its first growth, signaling worse to come. The wind was stronger and colder, too, out on the ridge, and the oilskin seemed less comforting, as its memories of her father brought back remembrance of certain pages of *The Book of the Dead* and tales of horror told by little girls in the darkness of their dormi-tory, far from the Old Kingdom. Fears came with these memo-ries, till Sabriel wrestled them to the back of her mind, and forced herself closer to the stone.

Dark patches of . . . something . . . obscured some of the marks, but it wasn't until Sabriel pushed her face almost to the stone that she could make out what they were, so dull and black in the moonlight.

When she did see, her head snapped up, and she stumbled backwards, almost overbalancing into the snow. The patches were dried blood, and when she saw them, Sabriel knew how the stone had been broken, and why the blood hadn't been cleaned away by rain or snow . . . why the stone never would be clean.

A Charter Mage had been sacrificed on the stone. Sacrificed by a necromancer to gain access to Death, or to help a Dead spirit break through into Life.

Sabriel bit her lower lip till it hurt and her hands, almost unconsciously, fidgeted, half-drawing Charter marks in nervousness and fear. The spell for that sort of sacrifice was in the last chapter of *The Book of the Dead*. She remembered it now, in sickening detail. It was one of the many things she seemed to have forgotten from that green-bound book—or had been made to forget. Only a very powerful necromancer could use that spell. Only a totally evil one would want to. And evil breeds evil, evil taints places and makes them attractive to further acts of . . .

"Stop it!" whispered Sabriel aloud, to still her mind of its imaginings. It was dark, windy and getting colder by the minute. She had to make a decision: to camp and call her guide, or to move on immediately in some random direction in the hope that she would be able to summon her guide from somewhere else.

The worst part of it all was that her guide was dead. Sabriel had to enter Death, albeit briefly, to call and converse with the guide. It would be easy to do so here, for the sacrifice had created a semi-permanent entry, as if a door had been wedged ajar. But who knew what might be lurking, watching, in the cold river beyond.

Sabriel stood for a minute, shivering, listening, every sense concentrated, like some small animal that knows a predator hunts nearby. Her mind ran through the pages of *The Book of the Dead*, and through the many hours she had spent learning Charter Magic from Magistrix Greenwood in the sunny North Tower of Wyverley College.

At the end of the minute, she knew that camping was out of the question. She was simply too frightened to sleep anywhere near the ruined Charter Stone. But it would be quicker to call her guide here—and the quicker she got to her father's house, the sooner she could do something to help him, so a compromise was called for. She would protect herself with Charter Magic as best she could, enter Death with all precaution, summon her guide, get directions and get out as quickly as possible. Quicker, even.

With decision came action. Sabriel dropped her skis and pack, stuffed some dried fruit and homemade toffee in her mouth for quick energy, and adopted the meditative pose that made Charter Magic easier.

After a bit of trouble with the toffee and her teeth, she began. Symbols formed in her mind—the four cardinal Charter marks that were the poles of a diamond that would protect her from both physical harm and Free Magic. Sabriel held them in her mind, fixed them in time, and pulled them out of the flow of the never-ending Charter. Then, drawing her sword, she traced rough outlines in the snow around her, one mark at each cardinal point of the compass. As she finished each mark, she let the one in her mind run from her head to her hand, down the sword and into the snow. There, they ran like lines of golden fire and the marks became alive, burning on the ground.

The last mark was the North mark, the one closest to the destroyed stone, and it almost failed. Sabriel had to close her eyes and use all her will to force it to leave the sword. Even then, it was only a pallid imitation of the other three, burning so weakly it hardly melted the snow.

Sabriel ignored it, quelling the nausea that had brought bile to the back of her mouth, her body reacting to the struggle with the Charter mark. She knew the North mark was weak, but golden lines had run between all four points and the diamond was complete, if shaky. In any case, it was the best she could do. She sheathed her sword, took off her gloves, and fumbled with her bell-bandolier, cold fingers counting the bells.

"Ranna," she said aloud, touching the first, the smallest bell. Ranna the sleepbringer, the sweet, low sound that brought silence in its wake.

"Mosrael." The second bell, a harsh, rowdy bell. Mosrael was the waker, the bell Sabriel should never use, the bell whose sound was a seesaw, throwing the ringer further into Death, as it brought the listener into Life.

"Kibeth." Kibeth, the walker. A bell of several sounds, a difficult and contrary bell. It could give freedom of movement to one of the Dead, or walk them through the next gate. Many a necromancer had stumbled with Kibeth and walked where they would not.

"Dyrim." A musical bell, of clear and pretty tone. Dyrim was the voice that the Dead so often lost. But Dyrim could also still a tongue that moved too freely.

"Belgaer." Another tricksome bell, that sought to ring of its own accord. Belgaer was the thinking bell, the bell most necromancers scorned to use. It could restore independent thought, memory and all the patterns of a living person. Or, slipping in a careless hand, erase them.

"Saraneth." The deepest, lowest bell. The sound of strength. Saraneth was the binder, the bell that shackled the Dead to the wielder's will.

And last, the largest bell, the one Sabriel's cold fingers found colder still, even in the leather case that kept it silent.

"Astarael, the Sorrowful," whispered Sabriel. Astarael was the banisher, the final bell. Properly rung, it cast everyone who heard it far into Death. Everyone, including the ringer.

Sabriel's hand hovered, touched on Ranna, and then settled on Saraneth. Carefully, she undid the strap and withdrew the bell. Its clapper, freed of the mask, rang slightly, like the growl of a waking bear.

Sabriel stilled it, holding the clapper with her palm inside the bell, ignoring the handle. With her right hand, she drew her sword and raised it to the guard position. Charter marks along the blade caught the moonlight and flickered into life. Sabriel watched them for a moment, as portents could sometimes be seen in such things. Strange marks raced across the blade, before transmuting into the more usual inscription, one that Sabriel knew well. She bowed her head, and prepared to enter into Death.

Unseen by Sabriel, the inscription began again, but parts of it were not the same. "I was made for Abhorsen, to slay those already Dead," was what it usually said. Now it continued, "The Clayr saw me, the Wallmaker made me, the King quenched me, Abhorsen wields me."

Sabriel, eyes closed now, felt the boundary between Life and Death appear. On her back, she felt the wind, now curiously warm, and the moonlight, bright and hot like sunshine. On her face, she felt the ultimate cold and, opening her eyes, saw the grey light of Death.

With an effort of will, her spirit stepped through, sword and bell prepared. Inside the diamond her body stiffened, and fog blew up in eddies around her feet, twining up her legs. Frost rimed her face and hands and the Charter marks flared at each apex of the diamond. Three steadied again, but the North mark blazed brighter still—and went out.

The river ran swiftly, but Sabriel set her feet against the current and ignored both it and the cold, concentrating on looking around, alert for a trap or ambush. It was quiet at this particular entry point to Death. She could hear the water tumbling

through the Second Gate, but nothing else. No splashing, or
gurgling, or strange mewlings. No dark, formless shapes or grim
silhouettes, shadowy in this grey light.

Carefully holding her position, Sabriel looked all around her
again, before sheathing her sword and reaching into one of the
thigh pockets in her woollen knickerbockers. The bell, Saraneth,
stayed ready in her left hand. With her right, she drew out a
paper boat and, still one-handed, opened it out to its proper
shape. Beautifully white, almost luminous in this light, it had one
small, perfectly round stain at its bow, where Sabriel had carefully
blotted a drop of blood from her finger.

Sabriel laid it flat on her hand, lifted it to her lips, and blew
on it as if she were launching a feather. Like a glider, it flew from
her hand into the river. Sabriel held that launching breath as the
boat was almost swamped, only to breathe in with relief as it
breasted a ripple, righted itself and surged away with the current.
In a few seconds it was out of sight, heading for the Second Gate.

It was the second time in her life that Sabriel had launched
just such a paper boat. Her father had shown her how to make
them, but had impressed on her to use them sparingly. No more
than thrice every seven years, he had said, or a price would have
to be paid, a price much greater than a drop of blood.

As events should follow as they had the first time, Sabriel
knew what to expect. Still, when the noise of the Second Gate
stilled for a moment some ten or twenty, or forty, minutes
later—time being slippery in Death—she drew her sword and
Saraneth hung down in her hand, its clapper free, waiting to be
heard. The Gate had stilled because someone . . . something . . .
was coming back from the deeper realms of Death.

Sabriel hoped it was the one she had invited with the
paper boat.

CHARTER MAGIC ON Cloven Crest. It was like a scent on the wind to the thing that lurked in the caves below the hill, some mile or more to the west of the broken Charter Stone.

It had been human once, or human-like at least, in the years it had lived under the sun. That humanity had been lost in the centuries the thing spent in the chill waters of Death, ferociously holding its own against the current, demonstrating an incredible will to live again. A will it didn't know it possessed before a badly cast hunting spear bounced from a rock and clipped its throat, just enough for a last few minutes of frantic life.

By sheer effort of will, it had held itself on the life side of the Fourth Gate for three hundred years, growing in power, learning the ways of Death. It preyed on lesser spirits, and served or avoided greater ones. Always, the thing held on to life. Its chance finally came when a mighty spirit erupted from beyond the Seventh Gate, smashing through each of the Upper Gates in turn, till it went ravening into Life. Hundreds of the Dead had followed, and this particular spirit had joined the throng. There had been terrible confusion and a mighty enemy at the very border between Life and Death, but, in the melee, it had managed to sneak around the edges and squirm triumphantly into Life.

There were plenty of recently vacated bodies where it

emerged, so the thing occupied one, animated it and ran away. Soon after, it found the caves it now inhabited. It even decided to give itself a name. Thralk. A simple name, not too difficult for a partially decomposed mouth to voice. A male name. Thralk could not remember what its original sex had been, those centuries before, but its new body was male.

It was a name to instill fear in the few small settlements that still existed in this area of The Borderlands, settlements Thralk preyed upon, capturing and consuming the human life he needed to keep himself on the living side of Death.

Charter Magic flared on Cloven Crest again, and Thralk sensed that it was strong and pure—but weakly cast. The strength of the magic scared him, but the lack of skill behind it was reassuring and strong magic meant a strong life. Thralk needed that life, needed it to shore up the body he used, needed it to replenish the leakage of his spirit back into Death. Greed won over fear. The Dead thing left the mouth of the cave and started climbing the hill, his lidless, rotting eyes fixed on the distant crest.

Sabriel saw her guide, first as a tall, pale light drifting over the swirling water towards her, and then, as it stopped several yards away, as a blurred, glowing, human shape, its arms outstretched in welcome.

"Sabriel."

The words were fuzzy and seemed to come from much farther away than where the shining figure stood, but Sabriel smiled as she felt the warmth in the greeting. Abhorsen had never explained who or what this luminous person was, but Sabriel thought she knew. She'd summoned this advisor only once before—when she'd first menstruated.

There was minimal sex education at Wyverley College— none at all till you were fifteen. The older girls' stories about menstruation were many, varied and often meant to scare. None of Sabriel's friends had reached puberty before her, so in fear and desperation she had entered Death. Her father had told her that the one the paper boat summoned would answer any question and would protect her—and so it had. The glowing spirit answered all her questions and many more besides, till Sabriel was forced to return to Life.

"Hello, Mother," said Sabriel, sheathing her sword and carefully muffling Saraneth with her fingers inside the bell.

The shining shape didn't answer, but that wasn't unexpected. Apart from her one-word greeting, she could only answer questions. Sabriel wasn't really sure if the manifestation was the very unusual dead spirit of her mother, which was unlikely, or some residual protective magic left by her.

"I don't have much time," Sabriel continued. "I'd love to ask about . . . oh, everything, I guess . . . but at the moment, I need to know how to get to Father's house from Cloven Crest . . . I mean Barhedrin Ridge."

The sending nodded, and spoke. As Sabriel listened, she also saw pictures in her head of what the woman was describing; vivid images, like memories of a journey she'd taken herself.

"Go to the northern side of the ridge. Follow the spur that begins there down till it reaches the valley floor. Look at the sky . . . there won't be any cloud. Look to the bright red star, Uallus, near the horizon, three fingers east of north. Follow that star till you come to a road that runs from south-west to north-east. Take that road for a mile to the north-east, till you reach a mile marker and the Charter Stone behind it. A path behind the stone leads to the Long Cliffs immediately north. Take the path. It ends in a door in the Cliffs. The door will answer to Mosrael. Beyond the door is a tunnel, sloping sharply upwards. Beyond the tunnel lies Abhorsen's Bridge. The house is over the bridge. Go with love—and do not tarry, do not stop, no matter what happens."

"Thank you," Sabriel began, carefully filing the words away with the accompanying thoughts. "Could you also . . ."

She stopped as the mother-sending in front of her suddenly raised both arms as if shocked, and shouted, "Go!"

At the same time, Sabriel felt the diamond of protection around her physical body twinge in warning and she became aware that the North mark had failed. Instantly, she turned on her left heel and began racing back to the border with Life, drawing her sword. The current almost seemed to strengthen against her, twining around her legs, but then fell away before her urgency. Sabriel reached the border and, with a furious thrust of will, her spirit emerged back into Life.

For a second, she was disoriented, suddenly freezing again and thick-witted. A grinning, corpse-like creature was just stepping through the failed North mark, its arms reaching to embrace her, carrion-breath misting out of a mouth unnaturally wide.

Thralk had been pleased to find the Charter Mage's spirit wandering and a broken diamond of protection. The sword had worried him a little, but it was frosted over and his shriveled eyes couldn't see the Charter marks that danced beneath the rime. Similarly, the bell in Sabriel's left hand looked like a lump of ice or snow, as if she'd caught a snowball. All in all, Thralk felt very fortunate, particularly as the life that blazed within this still victim was particularly young and strong. Thralk sidled closer still and his double-jointed arms reached to embrace Sabriel's neck.

Just as his slimy, corrupted fingers stretched forward, Sabriel opened her eyes and executed the stop-thrust that had earned her second place in Fighting Arts and, later, lost her the First. Her arm and sword straightened like one limb to their full extent and the sword-point ripped through Thralk's neck, and into eight inches of air beyond.

Thralk screamed, his reaching fingers gripping the sword to push himself free—only to scream again as Charter marks flared on the blade. White-hot sparks plumed between his knuckles and Thralk suddenly knew what he'd encountered.

"Abhorsen!" he croaked, falling backwards as Sabriel twisted the blade free with one explosive jerk.

Already, the sword was affecting the dead flesh Thralk inhabited, Charter Magic burning through reanimated nerves, freezing those all-too-fluid joints. Fire rose in Thralk's throat, but he spoke, to distract this terrible opponent while his spirit tried to shuck the body, like a snake its skin, and retreat into the night.

"Abhorsen! I will serve you, praise you, be your Hand . . . I know things, alive and dead . . . I will help lure others to you . . ."

The clear, deep sound of Saraneth cut through the whining, broken voice like a foghorn booming above the shriek of seagulls. The chime vibrated on and on, echoing into the night, and Thralk felt it bind him even as his spirit leaked out of the body and made for flight. The bell bound him to paralyzed flesh, bound him to the will of the bell-ringer. Fury seethed in him, anger and fear fueling his struggle, but the sound was everywhere, all around him, all through him. He would never be free of it.

Sabriel watched the misshapen shadow writhing, half out of the corpse, half in it, the body bleeding a pool of darkness. It was still trying to use the corpse's mouth, but without success. She considered going with it into Death, where it would have a shape and she could make it answer with Dyrim. But the broken Charter Stone loomed nearby and she felt it as an ever-present fear, like a cold jewel upon her breast. In her mind, she heard her mother-sending's words, "Do not tarry, do not stop, no matter what happens."

Sabriel thrust her sword point–first into the snow, put Saraneth away and drew Kibeth from the bandolier, using both hands. Thralk sensed it and his fury gave way to pure, unadulterated fear. After all the centuries of struggle, he knew true death had come for him at last.

Sabriel took up a careful stance, with the bell held in a curious two-handed grip. Kibeth seemed almost to twitch in her hands, but she controlled it, swinging it backwards, forwards, and then in a sort of odd figure eight. The sounds, all from the one bell, were very different to each other, but they made a little marching tune, a dancing song, a parade.

Thralk heard them and felt forces grip him. Strange, inexorable powers that made him find the border, made him return to Death. Vainly, almost pathetically, he struggled against them, knowing he couldn't break free. He knew that he would walk through every Gate, to fall at last through the Ninth. He gave up the struggle and used the last of his strength to form a semblance of a mouth in the middle of his shadow-stuff, a mouth with a writhing tongue of darkness.

"Curse you!" he gurgled. "I will tell the Servants of Kerrigor! I will be revenged . . ."

His grotesque, gulping voice was chopped off in mid-sentence, as Thralk lost free will. Saraneth had bound him, but Kibeth gripped him and Kibeth walked him, walked him so Thralk would be no more. The twisting shadow simply disappeared and there was only snow under a long-dead corpse.

Even though the revenant was gone, his last words troubled Sabriel. The name Kerrigor, while not exactly familiar, touched some basic fear in her, some memory. Perhaps Abhorsen had spoken this name, which undoubtedly belonged to one of the Greater Dead. The name scared her in the same way the broken stone did, as if they were tangible symbols of a world gone wrong, a world where her father was lost, where she herself was terribly threatened.

Sabriel coughed, feeling the cold in her lungs, and very carefully replaced Kibeth in the bandolier. Her sword seemed to have burned itself clean, but she ran a cloth over the blade before returning it to the scabbard. She felt very tired as she swung her pack back on, but there was no doubt in her mind that she must move on immediately. Her mother-spirit's words kept echoing in her mind, and her own senses told her something was happening in Death, something powerful was moving towards Life, moving towards emergence at the broken stone.

There had been too much death and too much Charter Magic on this hill, and the night was yet to reach its blackest. The wind was swinging around, the clouds regaining their superiority over sky. Soon, the stars would disappear and the young moon would be wrapped in white.

Quickly, Sabriel scanned the heavens, looking for the three bright stars that marked the Buckle of the North Giant's Belt. She found them, but then had to check the star map in her almanac, a handmade match stinking as it cast a yellow flicker on the pages, for she didn't dare use any more Charter Magic till she was away from the broken stone. The almanac showed that she had remembered correctly: the Buckle was due north in the Old Kingdom; its other name was Mariner's Cheat. In Ancelstierre, the Buckle was easily ten degrees west of north.

North located, Sabriel started to make her way to that side of the crest, looking for the spur that slanted down to the valley lost in darkness below. The clouds were thickening and she wanted to reach level ground before the moonlight disappeared. At least the spur, when found, looked like easier going than the broken steps to the south, though its gentle slope proclaimed a long descent to the valley.

In fact, it took several hours before Sabriel reached the valley floor, stumbling and shivering, a very pale Charter flame dancing a little ways in front of her. Too insubstantial to really ease her path, it had helped her avoid major disaster, and she hoped it was pallid enough to be taken for marsh-gas or chance reflection. In any case, it had proved essential when clouds closed the last remaining gap in the sky.

So much for no cloud, Sabriel thought, as she looked towards what she guessed was still north, searching for the red star, Uallus. Her teeth were chattering and would not be stilled, and a shiver that had started with her ice-cold feet was repeating itself through every limb. If she didn't keep moving, she'd simply freeze where she stood—particularly as the wind was rising once more . . .

Sabriel laughed quietly, almost hysterically, and turned her face to feel the breeze. It was an easterly, gaining strength with the minute. Colder, yes, but it also cleared the cloud, sweeping it to the west—and there, in the first cleared broom-stroke of the wind, was Uallus gleaming red. Sabriel smiled, stared at it, took stock of the little she could see around her, and started off again, following the star, a whispering voice constant in the back of her mind.

Do not tarry, do not stop, no matter what happens.

The smile lasted as Sabriel found the road and, with a good cover of snow in each gutter, she skied, making good time.

By the time Sabriel found the mile marker and the Charter Stone behind it, no trace of the smile could be seen on her pale face. It was snowing again, snowing sideways as the wind grew more frenzied, taking the snowflakes and whipping them into her eyes, now the only exposed portion of her entire body. Her boots were soaked too, despite the mutton fat she'd rubbed into them. Her feet, face and hands were freezing, and she was exhausted. She'd dutifully eaten a little every hour, but now, simply couldn't open her frozen jaws.

For a short time, at the intact Charter Stone that rose proudly behind the smaller mile-marker, Sabriel had made herself warm, invoking a Charter-spell for heat. But she'd grown too tired to maintain it without the assistance of the stone, and the spell dissipated almost as soon as she walked on. Only the mother-spirit's warning kept her going. That, and the sensation that she was being followed.

It was only a feeling, and in her tired, chilled state, Sabriel wondered if it was just imagination. But she wasn't in any state to face up to anything that might not be imagined, so she forced herself to go on.

Do not tarry, do not stop, no matter what happens.

The path from the Charter Stone was better made than the one that climbed Cloven Crest, but steeper. The pathmakers here had to cut through a dense, greyish rock, which did not erode like granite, and they had built hundreds of wide, low steps, carved with intricate patterns. Whether these meant something, Sabriel didn't know. They weren't Charter marks, or symbols of any language that she knew, and she was too tired to speculate. She concentrated on one step at a time, using her hands to push down on her aching thighs, coughing and gasping, head down to avoid the flying snow.

The path grew steeper still and Sabriel could see the cliff-face ahead, a huge, black, vertical mass, a much darker backdrop to the swirling snow than the clouded sky, palely backlit by the moon. But she didn't seem to get any closer as the path switchbacked to and fro, rising further and further up from the valley below.

Then, suddenly, Sabriel was there. The path turned again and her little will-o'-the-wisp light reflected back from a wall, a wall that stretched for miles to either side, and for hundreds of yards upwards. Clearly, these were the Long Cliffs, and the path had ended.

Almost sobbing with relief, Sabriel pushed herself forward to the very base of the cliff, and the little light rose above her head to disclose grey, lichen-veined rock. But even with that light, there was no sign of a door—nothing but jagged, impervious rock, going up and out of her tiny circle of illumination. There was no path and nowhere else to go.

Wearily, Sabriel knelt in a patch of snow and rubbed her hands together vigorously, trying to restore circulation, before drawing Mosrael from the bandolier. Mosrael, the Waker. Sabriel stilled it carefully and concentrated her senses, feeling for anything Dead that might be near and should not be woken. There was nothing close, but once again Sabriel felt something behind her, something following her, far down on the path. Something Dead, something reeking of power. She tried to judge how distant the thing was, before forcing it from her thoughts. Whatever it might be, it was too far away to hear even Mosrael's raucous voice. Sabriel stood up, and rang the bell.

It made a sound like tens of parrots screeching, a noise that burst into the air and wove itself into the wind, echoing from the cliffs, multiplying into the scream of a thousand birds.

Sabriel stilled the bell at once and put it away, but the echoes raced across the valley, and she knew the thing behind her had heard. She felt it fix its attention on where she was and she felt it quicken its pace, like watching the muscles on a racehorse going from the walk to a gallop. It was coming up the steps at least four or five at a time. She felt the rush of it in her head and the fear rising in her at equal pace, but she still went to the path and looked down, drawing her sword as she did so.

There, between gusts of snow, she saw a figure leaping from

step to step; impossible leaps, that ate up the distance between them with horrible appetite. It was manlike, more than man-high, and flames ran like burning oil on water where it trod. Sabriel cried out as she saw it, and felt the Dead spirit within. *The Book of the Dead* opened to fearful pages in her memory, and descriptions of evil poured into her head. It was a Mordicant that hunted her—a thing that could pass at will through Life and Death, its body of bog-clay and human blood molded and infused with Free Magic by a necromancer, and a Dead spirit placed inside as its guiding force.

Sabriel had banished a Mordicant once, but that had been forty miles from the Wall, in Ancelstierre, and it had been weak, already fading. This one was strong, fiery, new-born. It would kill her, she suddenly knew, and subjugate her spirit. All her plans and dreams, her hopes and courage, fell out of her to be replaced by pure, unthinking panic. She turned to one side, then the other, like a rabbit running from a dog, but the only way down was the path and the Mordicant was only a hundred yards below, closing with every blink, with every falling snowflake. Flames were spewing from its mouth, and it thrust its pointed head back and howled as it ran, a howl like the last shout of someone falling to their death, underlaid with the squeal of fingernails on glass.

Sabriel, a scream somehow stuck and choking in her throat, turned to the cliff, hammering on it with the pommel of her sword.

"Open! Open!" she screamed, as Charter marks raced through her brain—but not the right ones for forcing a door, a spell she'd learned in the Second Form. She knew it like she knew her times tables, but the Charter marks just wouldn't come, and why was twelve times twelve sticking in her head when she wanted Charter marks . . .

The echoes from Mosrael faded, and in that silence, the

pommel struck on something that thudded hollowly, rather than throwing sparks and jarring her hand. Something wooden, something that hadn't been there before. A door, tall and strangely narrow, its dark oak lined with silver Charter marks dancing through the grain. An iron ring, exactly at hand height, touched Sabriel's hip.

Sabriel dropped her sword with a gasp, grabbed the ring, and pulled. Nothing happened. Sabriel tugged again, half-turning to look over her shoulder, almost cringing at what she would see.

The Mordicant turned the last corner and its eyes met hers. Sabriel shut them, unable to bear the hatred and bloodlust glowing in its gaze like a poker left too long in the forge. It howled again and almost flowed up the remaining steps, flames dripping from its mouth, claws and feet.

Sabriel, eyes still closed, pushed on the ring. The door flew open and she fell in, crashing to the ground in a flurry of snow, eyes snapping open. Desperately, she twisted herself around on the ground, ignoring the pain in her knees and hands. Reaching back outside, she snagged the hilt of her sword and snatched it in.

As the blade cleared the doorway, the Mordicant reached it, and twisting itself sideways to pass the narrow portal, thrust an arm inside. Flames boiled from its grey-green flesh, like beads of sweat, and small plumes of black smoke spiraled from the flames, bringing with them a stench like burning hair.

Sabriel, sprawled defenseless on the floor, could only stare in terror as the thing's four-taloned hand slowly opened and reached out for her.

Chapter Seven

B UT THE HAND didn't close; the talons failed to rend
defenseless flesh.

Instead, Sabriel felt a sudden surge of Charter Magic
and Charter marks flared around the door, blazing so brightly
that they left red after-images at the back of her eyes, black dots
dancing across her vision.

Blinking, she saw a man step out from the stones of the wall,
a tall and obviously strong man, with a longsword the twin of
Sabriel's own. This sword came whistling down on the
Mordicant's arm, biting out a chunk of burning marsh-rotten
flesh. Rebounding, the sword flicked back again, and hewed
another slice, like an axeman sending chips flying from a tree.

The Mordicant howled, more in anger than in pain—but it
withdrew the arm and the stranger threw himself against the
door, slamming it shut with the full weight of his mail-clad body.
Curiously for mail, it made no sound, no jangling from the flow
of hundreds of steel links. A strange body under it too, Sabriel
saw, as the black dots and the red wash faded, revealing that her
rescuer wasn't human at all. He had seemed solid enough, but
every square inch of him was defined by tiny, constantly moving
Charter marks, and Sabriel could see nothing between them but
empty air.

He . . . it was a Charter-ghost, a sending.

Outside, the Mordicant howled again, like a steam train

venting pressure, then the whole corridor shook and hinges screeched in protest as the thing threw itself against the door. Wood splintered and clouds of thick grey dust fell from the ceiling, mocking the falling snow outside.

The sending turned to face Sabriel and offered its hand to help her up. Sabriel took it, looking up at it as her tired, frozen legs struggled to make a tenth-round comeback. Close to, the illusion of flesh was imperfect, fluid and unsettling. Its face wouldn't stay fixed, migrating between scores of possibilities. Some were women, some were men—but all bore tough, competent visages. Its body and clothing changed slightly, too, with every face, but two details always remained the same; a black surcoat with the blazon of a silver key, and a longsword redolent with Charter Magic.

"Thank you," Sabriel said nervously, flinching as the Mordicant pounded the door again. "Can . . . do you think that . . . will it get through?"

The sending nodded grimly, and let go her hand to point up the long corridor, but it did not speak. Sabriel turned her head to follow its pointing hand and saw a dark passage that rose up into darkness. Charter marks illuminated where they stood, but faded only a little way on. Despite this, the darkness seemed friendly, and she could almost taste the Charter-spells that rode on the corridor's dusty air.

"I must go on?" asked Sabriel, as it pointed again, more urgently. The sending nodded, and flapped its hand backwards and forwards, indicating haste. Behind him, another crashing blow caused another great billow of dust, and the door sounded as if it was weakening. Once again, the vile, burnt smell of the Mordicant wafted through the air.

The doorkeeper wrinkled its nose and gave Sabriel a bit of a push in the right direction, like a parent urging a reluctant child to press on. But Sabriel needed no urging. Her fear was still burning in her. Momentarily extinguished by the rescue, the smell of the Mordicant was all it needed to blaze again. She set her face upwards and started to walk quickly, into the passage.

She looked back after a few yards, to see the doorkeeper waiting near the door, its sword at the guard position. Beyond it, the door was bulging in, iron-bound planks bursting, breaking around a hole as big as a dinner plate.

The Mordicant reached in and broke off more planks, as easily as it might snap toothpicks. It was obviously furious that its prey was getting away, for it burned all over now. Yellow-red flames vomited from its mouth in a vile torrent, and black smoke rose like a second shadow around it, eddying in crazy circles as it howled.

Sabriel looked away, setting off at a fast walk, but the walk grew faster and faster, became a jog and then a run. Her feet pounded on the stone, but it wasn't until she was almost sprinting, that she realized why she could—her pack and skis were still back at the lower door. For a moment, she was struck with a nervous inclination to go back, but it passed before it even became conscious thought. Even so, her hands checked scabbard and bandolier, and gained reassurance from the cool metal of sword hilt and the hand-smoothed wood of the bell handles.

It was light too, she realized as she ran. Charter marks ran in the stone, keeping pace with her. Charter marks for light and for fleetness, and for many other things she didn't know. Strange marks and many of them—so many that Sabriel wondered how she could have ever thought that a First in magic from an Ancelstierran school would make her a great mage in the Old Kingdom. Fear and realization of ignorance were strong medicines against stupid pride.

Another howl came racing up the passage and echoed

onwards, accompanied by many crashes, and thuds or clangs of
steel striking supernatural flesh, or ricocheting off stone. Sabriel
didn't need to look back to know the Mordicant had broken
through the door and was now fighting the doorkeeper—or
pushing past him. Sabriel knew little of such sendings, but a
common failing with the sentinel variety was an inability to
leave their post. Once the creature got a few feet past the doorkeeper, the sending would be useless—and one great charge
would soon get the Mordicant past.

That thought gave her another burst of speed, but Sabriel
knew that it was the last. Her body, pushed by fear and weakened by cold and exertion, was on the edge of failure. Her legs
felt stiff, muscles ready to cramp, and her lungs seemed to bubble
with fluid rather than air.

Ahead, the corridor seemed to go on and on, sloping ever
upwards. But the light only shone where Sabriel ran, so perhaps
the exit might not be too far ahead, perhaps just past the next
little patch of darkness . . .

Even as this thought passed through her mind, Sabriel saw a
glow that sharpened into the bright tracing of a doorway. She
half gasped, half cried out, both slight human noises drowned
out by the unholy, inhuman screech of the Mordicant. It was past
the doorkeeper.

At the same time, Sabriel became aware of a new sound
ahead, a sound she had initially thought was the throb of blood
in her ears, the pounding of a racing heart. But it was outside,
beyond the upper door. A deep, roaring noise, so low it was
almost a vibration, a shudder that she felt through the floor,
rather than heard.

Heavy trucks passing on a road above, Sabriel thought,
before remembering where she was. In that same instant, she
recognized the sound. Somewhere ahead, out of these encircling

cliffs, a great waterfall was crashing down. And a waterfall that made so great a sound must be fed by an equally great river.

Running water! The prospect of it fueled Sabriel with sudden hope, and with that hope came the strength she thought beyond her. In a wild spurt of speed, she almost hit the door, hands slapping against the wood, slowing for the instant she needed to find the handle or ring.

But another hand was already on the ring when she touched it, though none had been there a second before. Again, Charter marks defined this hand, and Sabriel could see the grain of the wood and the blueing of the steel through the palm of another sending.

This one was smaller, of indeterminate sex, for it was wearing a habit like a monk's, with the hood drawn across its head. The habit was black and bore the emblem of the silver key front and back.

It bowed, and turned the ring. The door swung open, to reveal bright starlight shining down between clouds fleeing the newly risen wind. The noise of the waterfall roared through the open doorway, accompanied by flecks of flying spray. Without thinking, Sabriel stepped out.

The cowled doorkeeper came with her and shut the door behind it, before dragging a delicate, silver portcullis down across the door and locking it with an iron padlock. Both defenses apparently came out of thin air. Sabriel looked at them and felt power in them, for both were also Charter sendings. But door, portcullis and lock would only slow the Mordicant, not stop it. The only possible escape lay across the swiftest of running water, or the untimely glare of a noonday sun.

The first lay at her feet and the second was still many hours away. Sabriel stood on a narrow ledge that projected out from the bank of a river at least four hundred yards wide. A little to her right, a scant few paces away, this mighty river hurled itself over the cliff, to make a truly glorious waterfall. Sabriel leaned forward a little, to look at the waters crashing below, creating huge white wings of spray that could easily swallow her entire school, new wing and all, like a rubber duck swamped in an unruly bath.

It was a very long fall, and the height, coupled with the sheer power of the water, made her quickly look back to the river. Straight ahead, halfway across, Sabriel could just make out an island, an island perched on the very lip of the waterfall, dividing the river into two streams. It wasn't a very big island, about the size of a football field, but it rose like a ship of jagged rock from the turbulent waters.

Encircling the island were limestone-white walls the height of six men. Behind those walls was a house. It was too dark to see clearly, but there was a tower, a thrusting, pencil silhouette, with red tiles that were just beginning to catch the dawning sun. Below the tower, a dark bulk hinted at the existence of a hall, a kitchen, bedrooms, armory, buttery and cellar. The study, Sabriel suddenly remembered, occupied the second to top floor of the tower. The top floor was an observatory, both of stars and the surrounding territory.

It was Abhorsen's House. Home, although Sabriel had only visited it twice, or maybe three times, all when she was too young to remember much. That period of her life was hazy, and mostly filled with recollections of the Travelers, the interiors of their wagons, and many different campsites that all blurred together. She didn't even remember the waterfall, though the sound of it did stir some recognition—something had lodged in the mind of a four-year-old girl.

Unfortunately, she didn't remember how to get to the house. Only the words her mother-sending had given her— Abhorsen's Bridge.

She hadn't realized she'd spoken these words aloud, till the little gate warden tugged at her sleeve and pointed down. Sabriel looked and saw steps carved into the bank, steps leading right down to the river.

This time, Sabriel didn't hesitate. She nodded to the Charter sending and whispered, "Thank you," before taking the steps. The Mordicant's presence was pressing at her again, like a stranger's rank breath behind her ear. She knew it had reached the upper gate, though the sound of its battering and destruction was drowned in the greater roar of the waters.

The steps led to the river, but did not end there. Though invisible from the ledge, there were stepping-stones leading out to the island. Sabriel eyed them nervously, and looked at the water. It was clearly very deep and rushing past at an alarming speed. The stepping-stones were barely above its boisterous wavelets and, even though they were wide and cross-hatched for grip, they were also wet with spray and the slushy remnants of snow and ice.

Sabriel watched a small piece of ice from upstream hurtle by, and pictured its slingshot ride over the falls, to be smashed apart so far below. She imagined herself in its place, and then thought of the Mordicant behind her, of the Dead spirit that was at its heart, of the death it would bring, and the imprisonment she would suffer beyond death.

She jumped. Her boots skidded a little and her arms flailed for balance, but she ended up steady, bent over in a half-crouch. Hardly waiting to re-balance, she jumped to the next stone and then the one after that, and again, in a mad leapfrog through the spray and thunder of the river. When she was halfway out, with a hundred yards of pure, ferocious water behind her, she stopped and looked back.

The Mordicant was on the ledge, the silvery portcullis broken and mangled in its grip. There was no sign of the gate warden, but that was not surprising. Defeated, it would merely fade until the Charter-spell renewed itself—hours, days or even years later.

The Dead thing was curiously still, but it was clearly watching Sabriel. Even so powerful a creature couldn't cross this river and it made no attempt to do so. In fact, the longer Sabriel stared at it, the more it seemed to her that the Mordicant was content to wait. It was a sentry, guarding what might be the only exit from the island. Or perhaps it was waiting for something to happen, or for someone to arrive . . .

Sabriel suppressed a shudder and jumped on. There was more light now, heralding the advent of the sun, and she could see a sort of wooden landing stage leading up to a gate in the white wall. Treetops were also visible behind the walls, winter trees, their branches bare of green raiment. Birds flew between trees and tower, little birds launching themselves for their morning forage. It was a vision of normalcy, of a haven. But Sabriel could not forget the tall, flame-etched silhouette of the Mordicant, brooding on the ledge.

Wearily, she made the jump to the last stone and collapsed on the steps of the landing stage. Even her eyelids could barely move, and her field of vision had narrowed to a little slit directly to her front. The grain of the planks of the landing stage loomed close, as she crawled up to the gate and halfheartedly fell against it.

The gate swung open, pitching her onto a paved courtyard, the beginning of a red-brick path, the bricks ancient, their redness the color of dusty apples. The path wound up to the front door of the house, a cheerful sky-blue door, bright against whitewashed stone. A bronze doorknocker in the shape of a lion's head holding a ring in its mouth gleamed in counterpoint to the white cat that lay coiled on the rush mat before the door.

Sabriel lay on the bricks and smiled up at the cat, blinking back tears. The cat twitched and turned its head ever so slightly to look at her, revealing bright, green eyes.

"Hello, puss," croaked Sabriel, coughing as she staggered once more to her feet and walked forward, groaning and creaking with every step. She reached down to pat the cat, and froze—for, as the cat thrust its head up, she saw the collar around its neck and the tiny bell that hung there. The collar was only red leather, but the Charter-spell on it was the strongest, most enduring, binding that Sabriel had ever seen or felt—and the bell was a miniature Saraneth. The cat was no cat, but a Free Magic creature of ancient power.

"Abhorsen," mewed the cat, its little pink tongue darting. "About time you got here."

Sabriel stared at it for a moment, gave a little sort of moan and fell forward in a faint of exhaustion and dismay.

Chapter Eight

SABRIEL AWOKE TO soft candlelight, the warmth of a feather bed, and silken sheets, delightfully smooth under heavy blankets. A fire burned briskly in a red-brick fireplace and wood-paneled walls gleamed with the dark mystery of well-polished mahogany. A blue-papered ceiling with silver stars dusted across it, faced her newly opened eyes. Two windows confronted each other across the room, but they were shuttered, so Sabriel had no idea what time it was, no more than she had any remembrance of how she'd got there. It was definitely Abhorsen's House, but her last memory was of fainting on the doorstep.

Gingerly—for even her neck ached from her day and night of travel, fear and flight—Sabriel lifted her head to look around and once again met the green eyes of the cat that wasn't a cat. The creature was lying near her feet, at the end of the bed.

"Who . . . what are you?" Sabriel asked nervously, suddenly all too aware that she was naked under the soft sheets. A sensuous delight, but a defenseless one. Her eyes flickered to her sword-belt and bell-bandolier, carefully draped on a clothes-horse near the door.

"I have a variety of names," replied the cat. It had a strange voice, half-mew, half-purr, with hissing on the vowels. "You may call me Mogget. As to what I am, I was once many things, but now I am only several. Primarily, I am a servant of Abhorsen. Unless you would be kind enough to remove my collar?"

Sabriel gave an uneasy smile, and shook her head firmly. Whatever Mogget was, that collar was the only thing that kept it as a servant of Abhorsen . . . or anybody else. The Charter marks on the collar were quite explicit about that. As far as Sabriel could tell, the binding spell was over a thousand years old. It was quite possible that Mogget was some Free Magic spirit as old as the Wall, or even older. She wondered why her father hadn't mentioned it, and with a pang, wished that she had awoken to find her father here, in his house, both their troubles over.

"I thought not," said Mogget, combining a careless shrug with a limbering stretch. It . . . or he, for Sabriel felt the cat was definitely masculine, jumped to the parquet floor and sauntered over to the fire. Sabriel watched, her trained eye noting that Mogget's shadow was not always that of a cat.

A knock at the door interrupted her study of the cat, the sharp sound making Sabriel jump nervously, the hair on the back of her neck frizzing to attention.

"It's only one of the servants," Mogget said, in a patronizing tone. "Charter sendings, and pretty low-grade ones at that. They always burn the milk."

Sabriel ignored him, and said, "Come in." Her voice shook, and she realized that shaky nerves and weakness would be with her for a while.

The door swung open silently and a short, robed figure drifted in. It was similar to the upper gatewarden, being cowled and so without a visible face, but this one's habit was of light cream rather than black. It had a simple cotton underdress draped over one arm, a thick towel over the other and its Charter-woven hands held a long woollen surcoat and a pair of slippers. Without a word, it went to the end of the bed and put the garments on Sabriel's feet. Then it crossed to a porcelain basin that sat in a silver filigree stand, above a tiled area of the floor to the left of the fire. There, it twisted a bronze wheel, and steaming hot water splashed and gurgled from a pipe in the wall, bringing with it the stench of something sulphurous and unpleasant. Sabriel wrinkled her nose.

"Hot springs," commented Mogget. "You won't smell it after a while. Your father always said that having permanent hot water was worth bearing the smell. Or was it your grandfather who said that? Or great-great-aunt? Ah, memory . . ."

The servant stood immobile while the basin filled, then twisted the wheel to cut the flow as water slopped over the rim to the floor, close to Mogget—who leapt to his feet and padded away, keeping a cautious distance from the Charter sending. Just like a real cat, Sabriel thought. Perhaps the imposed shape impressed behavior too, over the years—or centuries. She liked cats. The school had a cat, a plump marmalade feline, who went by the name of Biscuits. Sabriel thought about the way it slept on the windowsill of the Prefect's Room, and then found herself thinking about the school in general, and what her friends would be doing. Her eyelids drooped as she imagined an Etiquette class, and the Mistress droning on about silver salvers . . .

A sharp clang woke her with yet another start, sending further stabs of pain through tired muscles. The Charter sending had tapped the bronze wheel with the poker from the fireplace. It was obviously impatient for Sabriel to have her wash.

"Water's getting cold," explained Mogget, leaping up to the bed again. "And they'll be serving dinner in half an hour."

"They?" asked Sabriel, sitting up and reaching forward to grab slippers and towel, preparatory to sidling out of bed and into them.

"Them," said Mogget, butting his head in the direction of the sending, who had stepped back from the basin and was now holding out a bar of soap.

Sabriel shuffled over to the basin, the towel wrapped firmly around her, and gingerly touched the water. It was delightfully hot, but before she could do anything with it, the sending stepped forward, whisked the towel off her and upended the whole basin over her head.

Sabriel shrieked, but, again before she could do anything else, the sending had put back the basin, turned the wheel for more hot water and was soaping her down, paying particular attention to her head, as if it wanted to get soap in Sabriel's eyes, or suspected an infestation of nits.

"What are you doing!" Sabriel protested, as the strangely cool hands of the sending scrubbed at her back and then, quite without interest, at her breasts and stomach. "Stop it! I'm quite old enough to wash myself, thank you!"

But Miss Prionte's techniques for dealing with domestic servants didn't seem to work on domestic sendings. It kept scrubbing, occasionally tipping hot water over Sabriel.

"How do I stop it?" she spluttered to Mogget, as still more water cascaded over her head and the sending started to scrub lower regions.

"You can't," replied Mogget, who seemed quite amused by the spectacle. "This one's particularly recalcitrant."

"What do you ... ow! ... stop that! What do you mean, this one?"

"There's lots about the place," said Mogget. "Every Abhorsen seems to have made their own. Probably because they get like this one after a few hundred years. Privileged family retainers, who always think they know best. Practically human, in the worst possible way."

The sending paused in its scrubbing just long enough to flick some water at Mogget, who jumped the wrong way and

yowled as it hit him. Just before another great basin-load of
water hit Sabriel, she saw the cat shoot under the bed, his tail
dividing the bedspread.

"That's enough, thank you!" she pronounced, as the last
drench of water drained out through a grille in the tiled area.
The sending had probably finished anyway, thought Sabriel, as it
stopped washing and started to towel her dry. She snatched the
towel back from it and tried to finish the job herself, but the
sending counterattacked by combing her hair, causing another
minor tussle. Eventually, between the two of them, Sabriel
shrugged on the underdress and surcoat, and submitted to a
manicure and vigorous hair-brushing.

She was admiring the tiny, repeated silver key motif on the
black surcoat in the mirror that backed one of the window-
shutters, when a gong sounded somewhere else in the house and
the servant-sending opened the door. A split second later,
Mogget raced through, with a cry that Sabriel thought was
"Dinner!" She followed, rather more sedately, the sending closing the door behind her.

Dinner was in the main hall of the house. A long, stately
room that took up half the ground floor, it was dominated by
the floor to ceiling stained-glass window at the western end. The
window showed a scene from the building of the Wall and, like
many other things around the house, was heavily laden with
Charter Magic. Perhaps there was no real glass in it at all, Sabriel
mused, as she watched the light of the evening sun play in and
around the toiling figures that were building the Wall. As with
the sendings, if you looked closely enough you could see tiny
Charter marks making up the patterns. It was hard to see
through the window, but judging from the sun, it was almost
dusk. Sabriel realized she must have slept for a full day, or possibly even two.

A table nearly as long as the hall stretched away from her—
a brightly polished table of some light and lustrous timber, heavily
laden with silver salt cellars, candelabra and rather fantastic-
looking decanters and covered dishes. But only two places were
fully set, with a plethora of knives, forks, spoons and other
instruments, which Sabriel only recognized from obscure draw-
ings in her Etiquette textbook. She'd never seen a real golden
straw for sucking the innards out of a pomegranate before, for
example.

One place was before a high-backed chair at the head of the
table and the other was to the left of this, in front of a cushioned
stool. Sabriel wondered which was hers, till Mogget jumped up
on the stool and said, "Come on! They won't serve till you're
seated."

"They" were more sendings. Half a dozen in all, including
the cream-dressed tyrant of the bedroom. They were all basically
the same; human in shape, but cowled or veiled. Only their
hands were visible, and these were almost transparent, as if
Charter marks had been lightly etched on prosthetic hands
carved from moonstone. The sendings stood grouped around a
door—the kitchen door, for Sabriel saw fires beyond them, and
smelled the tang of cooking—and stared at her. It was rather
unnerving, not to meet any eyes.

"Yes, that's her," Mogget said caustically. "Your new mistress.
Now let's have dinner."

None of the sendings moved, till Sabriel stepped forward.
They stepped forward, too, and all dropped to one knee, or
whatever supported them beneath the floor-length robes. Each
held out their pale right hand, Charter marks running bright
trails around their palms and fingers.

Sabriel stared for a moment, but it was clear they offered
their services, or loyalty, and expected her to do something in

return. She walked to them and gently pressed each upthrust hand in turn, feeling the Charter-spells that made them whole. Mogget had spoken truly, for some of the spells were old, far older than Sabriel could guess.

"I thank you," she said slowly. "On behalf of my father, and for the kindness you have shown me."

This seemed to be appropriate, or enough to be going on with. The sendings stood, bowed and went about their business. The one in the cream habit pulled out Sabriel's chair and placed her napkin as she sat. It was of crisp black linen, dusted with tiny silver keys, a miracle of needlework. Mogget, Sabriel noticed, had a plain white napkin, with evidence of old stains.

"I've had to eat in the kitchen for the last two weeks," Mogget said sourly, as two sendings approached from the kitchen, bearing plates that signaled their arrival with a tantalizing odor of spices and hot food.

"I expect it was good for you," Sabriel replied brightly, taking a mouthful of wine. It was a fruity, dry white wine, though Sabriel hadn't developed a palate to know whether it was good or merely indifferent. It was certainly drinkable. Her first major experiments with alcohol lay several years behind her, enshrined in memory as significant occasions shared with two of her closest friends. None of the three could ever drink brandy again, but Sabriel had started to enjoy wine with her meals.

"Anyway, how did you know I was coming?" Sabriel asked. "I didn't know myself, till . . . till Father sent his message."

The cat didn't answer at once, his attention focused on the plate of fish the sending had just put down—small, almost circular fish, with the bright eyes and shiny scales of the freshly caught. Sabriel had them too, but hers were grilled, with a tomato, garlic and basil sauce.

"I have served ten times as many of your forebears as you

have years," Mogget replied at last. "And though my powers
wane with the ebb of time, I always know when one Abhorsen
falls and another takes their place."

Sabriel swallowed her last mouthful, all taste gone, and put
down her fork. She took a mouthful of wine to clear her throat,
but it seemed to have become vinegar, making her cough.

"What do you mean by 'fall'? What do you know? What has
happened to Father?"

Mogget looked up at Sabriel, eyes half-lidded, meeting her
gaze steadily, as no normal cat could.

"He is dead, Sabriel. Even if he hasn't passed the Final Gate,
he will walk in life no more. That is—"

"No," interrupted Sabriel. "He can't be! He cannot be. He
is a necromancer . . . he can't be dead . . ."

"That is why he sent the sword and bells to you, as his
aunt sent them to him, in her time," Mogget continued, ignoring Sabriel's outburst. "And he was not a necromancer, he was
Abhorsen."

"I don't understand," Sabriel whispered. She couldn't face
Mogget's eyes anymore. "I don't know . . . I don't know enough.
About anything. The Old Kingdom, Charter Magic, even my
own father. Why do you say his name as if it were a title?"

"It is. He was the Abhorsen. Now you are."

Sabriel digested this in silence, staring at the swirls of fish
and sauce on her plate, silver scales and red tomato blurring into
a pattern of swords and fire. The table blurred too, and the room
beyond, and she felt herself reaching for the border with Death.
But try as she might, she couldn't cross it. She sensed it, but there
was no way to cross, in either direction—Abhorsen's House was
too well protected. But she did feel something at the border.
Inimical things lurked there, waiting for her to cross, but there
was also the faintest thread of something familiar, like the scent

of a woman's perfume after she has left the room, or the waft of a particular pipe tobacco around a corner. Sabriel focused on it and threw herself once more at the barrier that separated her from Death.

Only to ricochet back to Life, as sharp claws pricked her arm. Her eyes snapped open, blinking off flakes of frost, to see Mogget, fur bristling, one paw ready to strike again.

"Fool!" he hissed. "You are the only one who can break the wards of this House and they wait for you to do so!"

Sabriel stared at the angry cat, unseeing, biting back a sharp and proud retort as she realized the truth in Mogget's words. There were Dead spirits waiting, and probably the Mordicant would cross as well—and she would have faced them alone and weaponless.

"I'm sorry," she muttered, bowing her head into two frosted hands. She hadn't felt this stupidly awful since she'd burned one of the Headmistress's rose bushes with an uncontrolled Charter-spell, narrowly missing the school's ancient and much-loved gardener. She had cried then, but she was older now, and could keep the tears at bay.

"Father is not yet truly dead," she said, after a moment. "I felt his presence, though he is trapped beyond many gates. I could bring him back."

"You must not," said Mogget firmly, and his voice now seemed to carry all the weight of centuries. "You are Abhorsen, and must put the Dead to rest. Your path is chosen."

"I can walk a different path," Sabriel replied firmly, raising her head.

Mogget seemed about to protest again, then he laughed—a sardonic laugh—and jumped back to his stool.

"Do as you will," he said. "Why should I gainsay you? I am but a slave, bound to service. Why would I weep if Abhorsen falls to evil? It is your father who would curse you, and your mother too—and the Dead who will be merry."

"I don't think he's dead," Sabriel said, bright blushes of withheld emotion in her pallid cheeks, frost melting, trickling down around her face. "His spirit felt alive. He is trapped in Death, I think, but his body lives. Would I still be reviled if I brought him back then?"

"No," said Mogget, calm again. "But he has sent the sword and bells. You are only wishing that he lives."

"I feel it," Sabriel said simply. "And I must find out if my feeling is true."

"Perhaps it is so—though strange." Mogget seemed to be musing to himself, his voice a soft half-purr. "I have grown dull. This collar strangles me, chokes my wits . . ."

"Help me, Mogget," Sabriel suddenly pleaded, reaching over to touch her hand to the cat's head, scratching under the collar. "I need to know—I need to know so much!"

Mogget purred under the scratching, but as Sabriel leaned close, she could hear the faint peal of the tiny Saraneth bell cut through the purr, and she was reminded that Mogget was no cat, but a Free Magic creature. For a moment, Sabriel wondered what Mogget's true shape was, and his true nature.

"I am the servant of Abhorsen," Mogget said at last. "And you are Abhorsen, so I must help you. But you must promise me that you will not raise your father, if his body is dead. Truly, he would not wish it."

"I cannot promise. But I will not act without much thought. And I will listen to you, if you are by me."

"I guessed as much," Mogget said, twisting his head away from Sabriel's hand. "It is true that you are sadly ignorant, or you would promise with a will. Your father should never have sent you beyond the Wall."

"Why did he?" asked Sabriel, her heart suddenly leaping with the question that had been with her all her school days, a question Abhorsen had always smiled away with the one word, "Necessity."

"He was afraid," replied Mogget, turning his attention back to the fish. "You were safer in Ancelstierre."

"What was he afraid of?"

"Eat your fish," replied Mogget, as two sendings appeared from the kitchen, bearing what was obviously the next course. "We'll talk later. In the study."

Chapter Nine

L   ANTERNS LIT THE study, old brass lanterns that burned
      with Charter Magic in place of oil. Smokeless, silent and
      eternal, they provided as good a light as the electric bulbs
of Ancelstierre.

Books lined the walls, following the curves of the tower
around, save for where the stair rose from below, and the ladder
climbed to the observatory above.

A redwood table sat in the middle of the room, its legs scaled
and beady-eyed, ornamental flames licking from the mouths of
the dragon-heads that gripped each corner of the tabletop. An
inkwell, pens, papers and a pair of bronze map dividers lay
upon the table. Chairs of the same red wood surrounded it,
their upholstery black with a variation on the silver key motif.

The table was one of the few things Sabriel remembered
from her childhood visits. "Dragon desk" her father had called it,
and she'd wrapped herself around one of those dragon legs, her
head not even reaching the underside of the table.

Sabriel ran her hand over the smooth, cool wood, feeling
both her memory of it and the current sensation, then she
sighed, pulled up a chair and put down the three books she'd
tucked under her arm. Two, she put together close to her, the
other she pushed to the center of the table. This third book came
from the single glassed-in cabinet among the bookshelves and
now lay like some quiescent predator, possibly asleep, possibly

waiting to spring. Its binding was of pale green leather and Charter marks burned in the silver clasps that held it closed. *The Book of the Dead*.

The other two books were normal enough by comparison. Both were Charter Magic spell books, listing mark after mark, and how they could be used. Sabriel didn't even recognize most of the marks after chapter four in the first book. There were twenty chapters in each volume.

Doubtless there were many other books that would be useful, Sabriel thought, but she still felt too tired and shaky to get more down. She planned to talk to Mogget, then study for an hour or two, before going back to bed. Even four or five waking hours seemed too much after her ordeal, and the loss of consciousness involved in sleep suddenly seemed very appealing.

Mogget, as if he had heard Sabriel thinking of him, appeared at the top of the steps and sauntered over to sprawl on a well-upholstered footstand.

"I see you have found *that* book," he said, tail flicking backwards and forwards as he spoke. "Take care you do not read too much."

"I've already read it all, anyway," replied Sabriel, shortly.

"Perhaps," remarked the cat. "But it isn't always the same book. Like me, it is several things, not one."

Sabriel shrugged, as if to show that she knew all about the book. But that was just bravado—the inner Sabriel was afraid of *The Book of the Dead*. She had worked her way through every chapter, under her father's direction, but her normally excellent memory held only selected pages of this tome. If it changed its contents as well—she suppressed a shiver, and told herself that she knew all that was necessary.

"My first step must be to find my father's body," she said. "Which is where I need your help, Mogget."

"I have no knowledge of where he met his end," Mogget stated, with finality. He yawned, and started licking his paws.

Sabriel frowned, and found herself pulling in her lips, a characteristic she had deplored in the unpopular history teacher at school, who often went "thin-lipped" in anger or exasperation.

"Just tell me when you last saw him, and what his plans were."

"Why don't you read his diary," suggested Mogget, in a momentary break from cleaning himself.

"Where is it?" asked Sabriel, excited. A diary would be tremendously helpful.

"He probably took it with him," replied Mogget. "I haven't seen it."

"I thought you had to help me!" Sabriel said, another frown wrinkling across her forehead, reinforcing the thin lips. "Please answer my question."

"Three weeks ago," Mogget mumbled, mouth half muffled in the fur of his stomach, pink tongue alternating between words and cleansing. "A messenger came from Belisaere, begging for his help. Something Dead, something that could pass the wards, was preying on them. Abhorsen—I mean the previous Abhorsen, ma'am—suspected that there was more to it than that, Belisaere being Belisaere. But he went."

"Belisaere. The name's familiar—it's a town?"

"A city. The capital. At least it was, when there was still a kingdom."

"Was?"

Mogget stopped washing, and looked across, eyes narrowing to frowning slits. "What did they teach you in that school? There hasn't been a King or Queen for two hundred years, and not even a Regent for twenty. That's why the Kingdom sinks day by day, into a darkness from which no one will rise . . ."

"The Charter—" Sabriel began, but Mogget interrupted with a yowl of derision.

"The Charter crumbles too," he mewed. "Without a ruler, Charter Stones broken one by one with blood, one of the Great Charters twi . . . twis . . . twisted—"

"What do you mean, one of the Great Charters?" Sabriel interrupted in turn. She had never heard of such a thing. Not for the first time, she also wondered what she'd been taught in school, and why her father had kept so quiet about the state of the Old Kingdom.

But Mogget was silent, as if the things he'd already said had stopped his mouth. For a moment, he seemed to be trying to form words, but nothing came from his small red mouth. Finally, he gave up. "I cannot tell you. It's part of my binding, curse it! Suffice to say that the whole world slides into evil, and many are helping the slide."

"And others resist it," said Sabriel. "Like my father. Like me."

"It depends what you do," Mogget said, as if he doubted that someone as patently useless as Sabriel would make much difference. "Not that I care—"

The sound of the trapdoor opening above their heads stopped the cat in mid-speech. Sabriel tensed, looking up to see what was coming down the ladder, then started breathing again as she realized that it was only another Charter sending, its black habit flopping over the rungs of the ladder as it came down. This one, like the guards on the cliff corridor—but unlike the other House servants—had the silver key emblazoned on its chest and back. It bowed to Sabriel, and pointed up.

With a feeling of foreboding, Sabriel knew that it wanted her to look at something from the observatory. Reluctantly, she pushed her chair back and went over to the ladder. A cold draft was blowing in through the open trapdoor, carrying with it the chill of ice from further up the river. Sabriel shivered, as her hands touched the cold metal rungs.

Emerging into the observatory, the chill passed, for the room was still lit by the last, red light of the setting sun, giving an illusion of warmth and making Sabriel squint. She had no memory of this room, so it was with delight that she saw that it was totally walled in glass, or something like it. The bare beams of the red-tiled roof rested on transparent walls, so cleverly morticed together that the roof was like a work of art, complete with the slight draft that reduced its perfection to a more human level.

A large telescope of gleaming glass and bronze dominated the observatory, standing triumphant on a tripod of dark wood and darker iron. A tall observer's stool stood next to it, and a lectern, a star chart still spilled across it. A thick, toe wriggle-inviting carpet lay under all, a carpet that was also a map of the heavens, showing many different, colorful constellations and whirling planets, woven in thick, richly dyed wool.

The sending, who had followed Sabriel, went to the south wall and pointed out towards the southern riverbank, its pallid, Charter-drawn hand indicating the very spot where Sabriel had emerged after her underground flight from the Mordicant.

Sabriel looked there, shielding her right eye from the west-falling sun. Her gaze crossed the white tops of the river and was drawn to the ledge, despite an inner quailing about what she would see.

As she feared, the Mordicant was still there. But with what she had come to think of as her Death sight, Sabriel sensed it was quiescent, temporarily just an unpleasant statue, a foreground to other, more active shapes that bustled about in some activity behind.

Sabriel stared a little longer, then went to the telescope,

narrowly avoiding Mogget, who had somehow appeared underfoot. Sabriel wondered how he had got up the ladder, then dismissed the thought as she concentrated on what was happening
outside.

Unaided, she hadn't been certain what the shapes around
the Mordicant were, but they sprang sharply at her through the
telescope, drawn so close she felt she could somehow lean forward and snatch them away.

They were men and women— living, breathing people. Each
was shackled to a partner's leg by an iron chain and they shuffled
about in these pairs under the dominating presence of the
Mordicant. There were scores of them, coming out of the corridor, carrying heavily laden leather buckets or lengths of timber,
taking them across the ledge and down the steps to the river.
Then they filed back again, buckets empty, timber left behind.

Sabriel depressed the telescope a little, and almost growled
in exasperation and anger as she saw the scene by the river. More
living slaves were hammering long boxes together from the
timber, and these boxes were being filled with earth from
the buckets. As each box was filled, it was pushed out to bridge
the gap from shore to stepping-stone and locked in place by
slaves hammering iron spikes into the stone.

This particular part of the operation was being directed by
something that lurked well back from the river, halfway up the
steps. A man-shaped blot of blackest night, a moving silhouette.
A necromancer's Shadow Hand, or some free-willed Dead spirit
that scorned the use of a body.

As Sabriel watched, the last of four boxes was thrust out to
the first stepping-stone, spiked in place, and then chained to its
three adjacent fellows. One slave, fastening the chain, overbalanced and went headfirst into the water, his shackle-mate following a second later. Their screams, if any, were drowned by the

roar of the waterfall as its waters took their bodies. A few seconds later, Sabriel felt their lives snuffed out.

The other slaves at the river's edge stopped working for a moment, either shocked at the sudden loss, or momentarily made more afraid of the river than their masters. But the Shadow Hand on the steps moved towards them, its legs like treacle, pouring down the slope, lapping over each step in turn. It gestured for some of the nearer slaves to walk across the earth-filled boxes to the stepping-stone. They did so, to cluster unhappily amid the spray.

The Shadow Hand hesitated then, but the Mordicant on the ledge above seemed to stir and rock forward a little, so the shadowy abomination gingerly trod on the boxes—and walked across to the stepping-stone, taking no scathe from the running water.

"Grave dirt," commented Mogget, who obviously didn't need the telescope. "Carted up by the villagers from Qyrre and Roble's Town. I wonder if they've got enough to cross all the stones."

"Grave dirt," commented Sabriel bleakly, watching a fresh round of slaves arriving with buckets and more timber. "I had forgotten it could negate the running water. I thought . . . I thought I would be safe here, for a time."

"Well, you are," said Mogget. "It'll take at least until tomorrow evening before their bridge is complete, particularly allowing for a couple of hours off around noon, when the Dead will have to hide if it isn't overcast. But this shows planning, and that means a leader. Still, every Abhorsen has enemies. It may just be a petty necromancer with a better brain for strategy than most."

"I slew a Dead thing at Cloven Crest," Sabriel said slowly, thinking aloud. "It said it would have its revenge and spoke of telling the servants of Kerrigor. Do you know that name?"

"I know it," spat Mogget, tail quivering straight out behind him. "But I cannot speak of it, except to say it is one of the Greater Dead, and your father's most terrible enemy. Do not say it lives again!"

"I don't know," replied Sabriel, looking down at the cat, whose body seemed twisted, as if in turmoil between command and resistance. "Why can't you tell me more? The binding?"

"A . . . a perversion of . . . the g . . . g . . . yes," Mogget croaked out with effort. Though his green eyes seemed to grow luminous and fiery with anger at his own feeble explanation, he could say no more.

"Coils within coils," remarked Sabriel thoughtfully. There seemed little doubt that some evil power was working against her, from the moment she'd crossed the Wall—or even before that, if her father's disappearance was anything to go by.

She looked back through the telescope again and took some heart in the slowing of the work as the last light faded, though at the same time she felt a pang of sympathy for the poor people the Dead had enslaved. Many would probably freeze to death, or die of exhaustion, only to be brought back as dull-witted Hands. Only those who went over the waterfall would escape that fate. Truly, the Old Kingdom was a terrible place, when even death did not mean an end to slavery and despair.

"Is there another way out?" she asked, swivelling the telescope around 180 degrees to look at the northern bank. There were stepping-stones going there, too, and another door high on the riverbank, but there were also dark shapes clustered on the ledge by the door. Four or five Shadow Hands, too many for Sabriel to fight through alone.

"It seems not," she answered herself grimly. "What of defenses, then? Can the sendings fight?"

"The sendings don't need to fight," replied Mogget. "For

there is another defense, though it is a rather constrictive one. And there is one other way out, though you probably won't like it."

The sending next to her nodded and pantomimed something with its arm that looked like a snake wiggling through grass.

"What's that?" asked Sabriel, fighting back a sudden urge to break into hysterical laughter. "The defense or the way out?"

"The defense," replied Mogget. "The river itself. It can be invoked to rise almost to the height of the island walls—four times your height above the stepping-stones. Nothing can pass such a flood, in or out, till it subsides, in a matter of weeks."

"So how would I get out?" asked Sabriel. "I can't wait weeks!"

"One of your ancestors built a flying device. A Paperwing, she called it. You can use that, launched out over the waterfall."

"Oh," said Sabriel, in a little voice.

"If you do wish to raise the river," Mogget continued, as if he hadn't noticed Sabriel's sudden silence, "then we must begin the ritual immediately. The flood comes from meltwater and the mountains are many leagues upstream. If we call the waters now, the flood will be on us by dusk tomorrow."

Chapter Ten

THE ARRIVAL OF the floodwaters was heralded by great chunks of ice that came battering against the wooden bridge of grave dirt boxes like storm-borne icebergs ramming anchored ships. Ice shattered, wood splintered; a regular drumming that beat out a warning, announcing the great wave that followed the outriding ice.

Dead Hands and living slaves scurried back along the coffin bridge, the Dead's shadowy bodies losing shape as they ran, so they became like long, thick worms of black crepe, squirming and sliding over rocks and boxes, throwing human slaves aside without mercy, desperate to escape the destruction that came roaring down the river.

Sabriel, watching from the tower, felt the people die, convulsively swallowing as she sensed their last breaths gurgling, sucking water instead of air. Some of them, at least two pairs, had deliberately thrown themselves into the river, choosing a final death, rather than risk eternal bondage. Most had been knocked, pushed or simply scared aside by the Dead.

The wavefront of the flood came swiftly after the ice, shouting as it came, a higher, fiercer roar than the deep bellow of the waterfall. Sabriel heard it for several seconds before it rounded the last bend of the river, then suddenly, it was almost upon her. A huge, vertical wall of water, with chunks of ice on its crest like marble battlements and all the debris of four hundred miles swilling about in its muddy body. It looked enormous, far taller than the island's walls, taller even than the tower where Sabriel stared, shocked at the power she had unleashed, a power she had hardly dreamed possible when she'd summoned it the night before.

It had been a simple enough summoning. Mogget had taken her to the cellar and then down a winding, narrow stair, that grew colder and colder as they descended. Finally, they reached a strange grotto, where icicles hung and Sabriel's breath blew clouds of white, but it was no longer cold, or perhaps so cold she no longer felt it. A block of pure, blue-white ice stood upon a stone pedestal, both limned with Charter marks, marks strange and beautiful. Then, following Mogget's instruction, she'd simply placed her hand on the ice, and said, "Abhorsen pays her respects to the Clayr, and requests the gift of water." That was all. They'd gone back up the stairs, a sending locked the cellar door behind them, and another brought Sabriel a nightshirt and a cup of hot chocolate.

But that simple ceremony had summoned something that seemed totally out of control. Sabriel watched the wave racing towards them, trying to calm herself, but her breath raced in and out as quickly as her stomach flipped over. Just as the wave hit, she screamed and ducked under the telescope.

The whole tower shook, stones screeching as they moved, and for a moment, even the sound of the waterfall was lost in a crack that sounded as if the island had been leveled by the first shock of the wave.

But, after a few seconds, the floor stopped shaking, and the crash of the flood subsided to a controlled roar, like a shouting drunk made aware of company. Sabriel hauled herself up the tripod and opened her eyes.

The walls had held, and though now the wave was past, the river still raged a mere handspan below the island's defenses and was almost up to the tunnel doors on either bank. There was no sign of the stepping-stones, the coffin bridge, the Dead, or any people—just a wide, brown rushing torrent, carrying debris of all descriptions. Trees, bushes, parts of buildings, livestock, chunks of ice—the flood had claimed its tribute from every riverbank for hundreds of miles.

Sabriel looked at this evidence of destruction and inwardly counted the number of villagers who had died on the grave boxes. Who knew how many other lives had been lost, or livelihoods threatened, upstream? Part of her tried to rationalize her use of the flood, telling her that she had to do it in order to fight on against the Dead. Another part said she had simply summoned the flood to save herself.

Mogget had no time for such introspection, mourning or pangs of responsibility. He left her watching, blank-eyed, for no more than a minute, before padding forward and delicately inserting his claws in Sabriel's slippered foot.

"Ow! What did you—"

"There's no time to waste sightseeing," Mogget said. "The sendings are readying the Paperwing on the Eastern wall. And your clothing and gear have been ready for at least half an hour."

"I've got all . . ." Sabriel began, then she remembered that her pack and skis lay at the bottom end of the entrance tunnel, probably as a pile of Mordicant-burned ash.

"The sendings have got everything you'll need, and a few things you won't, knowing them. You can get dressed, pack up, and head off for Belisaere. I take it you intend to go to Belisaere?"

"Yes," replied Sabriel shortly. She could detect a tone of smugness in Mogget's voice.

"Do you know how to get there?"

Sabriel was silent. Mogget already knew the answer was "no." Hence the smugness.

"Do you have a . . . er . . . map?"

Sabriel shook her head, clenching her fists as she did so, resisting the urge to lean forward and spank Mogget, or perhaps give his tail a judicious tug. She had searched the study and asked several of the sendings, but the only map in the house seemed to be the starmap in the tower. The map Colonel Horyse had told her about must still be with Abhorsen. With Father, Sabriel thought, suddenly confused about their identities. If she was now Abhorsen, who was her father? Had he too once had a name that was lost in the responsibility of being Abhorsen? Everything that had seemed so certain and solid in her life a few days ago was crumbling. She didn't even know who she was really, and trouble seemed to beset her from all sides—even a supposed servant of Abhorsen like Mogget seemed to provide more trouble than service.

"Do you have anything positive to say—anything that might actually help?" she snapped.

Mogget yawned, showing a pink tongue that seemed to contain the very essence of scorn.

"Well, yes. Of course. I know the way, so I'd better come with you."

"Come with me?" Sabriel asked, genuinely surprised. She unclenched her fists, bent down, and scratched between the cat's ears, till he ducked away.

"Someone has to look after you," Mogget added. "At least till you've grown into a real Abhorsen."

"Thank you," said Sabriel. "I think. But I would still like a map. Since you know the country so well, would it be possible for you to—I don't know—describe it, so I can make a sketch map or something?"

Mogget coughed, as if a hairball had suddenly lodged in his throat, and thrust his head back a little. "You! Draw a sketch map? If you must have one, I think it would be better if I undertook the cartography myself. Come down to the study and put out an inkwell and paper."

"As long as I get a useable map I don't care who draws it," Sabriel remarked, as she went backwards down the ladder. She tilted her head to watch how Mogget came down, but there was only the open trapdoor. A sarcastic meow under her feet announced that Mogget had once again managed to get between rooms without visible means of support.

"Ink and paper," the cat reminded her, jumping up onto the dragon desk. "The thick paper. Smooth side up. Don't bother with a quill."

Sabriel followed Mogget's instructions, then watched with a resigned condescension that rapidly changed to surprise as the cat crouched by the square of paper, his strange shadow falling on it like a dark cloak thrown across sand, pink tongue out in concentration. Mogget seemed to think for a moment, then one bright ivory claw shot out from a white pad—he delicately inked the claw in the inkwell, and began to draw. First, a rough outline, in swift, bold strokes; the penning in of the major geo-graphical features; then the delicate process of adding important sites, each named in fine, spidery writing. Last of all, Mogget marked Abhorsen's House with a small illustration, before lean-ing back to admire his handiwork, and lick the ink from his paw. Sabriel waited a few seconds to be sure he was done, then cast drying sand over the paper, her eyes trying to absorb every detail, intent on learning the physical face of the Old Kingdom.

"You can look at it later," Mogget said after a few minutes, when his paw was clean, but Sabriel was still bent over the table, nose inches from the map. "We're still in a hurry. You'd better go and get dressed, for a start. Do try to be quick."

"I will." Sabriel smiled, still looking at the map. "Thank you, Mogget."

The sendings had laid out a great pile of clothes and equipment in Sabriel's room, and four of them were in attendance to help her get everything on and organized. She had hardly stepped inside before they'd stripped her indoor dress and slippers off, and she'd only just managed to remove her own underclothes before ghostly Charter-traced hands tickled her sides. A few seconds later, she was suffering them anyway, as they pulled a thin, cotton-like undergarment over her head, and a pair of baggy drawers up her legs. Next came a linen shirt, then a tunic of doeskin and breeches of supple leather, reinforced with some sort of hard, segmented plates at thighs, knees and shins, not to mention a heavily padded bottom, no doubt designed for riding.

A brief respite followed, lulling Sabriel into thinking that might be it, but the sendings had merely been arranging the next layer for immediate fitting. Two of them pushed her arms into a long, armored coat that buckled up at the sides, while the other two unlaced a pair of hobnailed boots and waited.

The coat wasn't like anything Sabriel had ever worn before, including the mail hauberk she'd worn in Fighting Arts lessons at school. It was as long as an hauberk, with split skirts coming down to her knees and sleeves swallow-tailed at her wrists, but it seemed to be entirely made of tiny overlapping plates, much like a fish's scales. They weren't metal, either, but some sort of ceramic, or even stone. Much lighter than steel, but clearly very strong, as one sending demonstrated, by cutting down it with a dagger, striking sparks without leaving a scratch.

Sabriel thought the boots completed the ensemble, but as the laces were done up by one pair of sendings, the other pair were back in action. One raised what appeared to be a blue and silver striped turban, but Sabriel, pulling it down to just above her eyebrows, found it to be a cloth-wrapped helmet, made from the same material as the armor.

The other sending waved out a gleaming, deep blue surcoat,

dusted with embroidered silver keys that reflected the light in all directions. It waved the coat to and fro for a moment, then whipped it over Sabriel's head and adjusted the drape with a practiced motion. Sabriel ran her hand over its silken expanse and discreetly tried to rip it in one corner, but, for all its apparent fragility, it wouldn't tear.

Last of all came sword-belt and bell-bandolier. The sendings brought them to her, but made no attempt to put them on. Sabriel adjusted them herself, carefully arranging bells and scabbard, feeling the familiar weight—bells across her breast and sword balanced on her hip. She turned to the mirror and looked at her reflection, both pleased and troubled by what she saw. She looked competent, professional, a traveler who could look after herself. At the same time, she looked less like someone called Sabriel, and more like the Abhorsen, capital letter and all.

She would have looked longer, but the sendings tugged at her sleeves and directed her attention to the bed. A leather backpack lay open on it and, as Sabriel watched, the sendings packed it with her remaining old clothes, including her father's oilskin, spare undergarments, tunic and trousers, dried beef and biscuits, a water bottle, and several small leather pouches full of useful things, each of which were painstakingly opened and shown to her: telescope, sulphur matches, clockwork firestarter, medicinal herbs, fishing hooks and line, a sewing kit and a host of other small essentials. The three books from the library and the map went into oilskin pouches, and then into an outside pocket.

Backpack on, Sabriel tried a few basic exercises, and was relieved to find that the armor didn't restrict her too much—hardly at all in fact, though the pack was not something she'd like to have on in a fight. She could even touch her toes, so she did, several times, before straightening up to thank the sendings.

They were gone. Instead, there was Mogget, stalking mysteriously towards her from the middle of the room.

"Well, I'm ready," Sabriel said.

Mogget didn't answer, but sat at her feet, and made a movement that looked very much like he was going to be sick. Sabriel recoiled, disgusted, then halted, as a small metallic object fell from Mogget's mouth and bounced on the floor.

"Almost forgot," said Mogget. "You'll need this if I'm to come with you."

"What is it?" asked Sabriel, bending down to pick up a ring; a small silver ring, with a ruby gripped between two silver claws that grew out of the band.

"Old," replied Mogget, enigmatically. "You'll know if you need to use it. Put it on."

Sabriel looked at it closely, holding it between two fingers as she slanted it towards the light. It felt, and looked, quite ordinary. There were no Charter marks on the stone or band; it seemed to have no emanations or aura. She put it on.

It felt cold as it slipped down her finger, then hot, and suddenly she was falling, falling into infinity, into a void that had no end and no beginning. Everything was gone, all light, all substance. Then Charter marks suddenly exploded all around her and she felt gripped by them, halting her headlong fall into nothing, accelerating her back up, back into her body, back to the world of life and death.

"Free Magic," Sabriel said, looking down at the ring gleaming on her finger. "Free Magic, connected to the Charter. I don't understand."

"You'll know if you need to use it," Mogget repeated, almost as if it were some lesson to be learned by rote. Then, in his normal voice: "Don't worry about it till then. Come—the Paperwing is ready."

Chapter Eleven

THE PAPERWING SAT on a jury-rigged platform of freshly sawn pine planks, teetering out over the eastern wall. Six sendings clustered around the craft, readying it for flight. Sabriel looked up at it as she climbed the stairs, an unpleasant feeling rising with her. She had been expecting something similar to the aircraft that had begun to be common in Ancelstierre, like the biplane that had performed aerobatics at the last Wyverley College Open Day. Something with two wings, rigging and a propeller—though she had assumed a magical engine rather than a mechanical one.

But the Paperwing didn't look anything like an Ancelstierran airplane. It most closely resembled a canoe with hawk-wings and a tail. On closer inspection, Sabriel saw that the central fuselage was probably based on a canoe. It was tapered at each end and had a central hole for a cockpit. Wings sprouted on each side of this canoe shape—long, swept-back wings that looked very flimsy. The wedge-shaped tail didn't look much better.

Sabriel climbed the last few steps with sinking expectations. The construction material was now clear and so was the craft's name—the whole thing was made up from many sheets of paper, bonded together with some sort of laminate. Painted powder-blue, with silver bands around the fuselage and silver stripes along the wings and tail, it looked pretty, decorative and not at all airworthy.

Only the yellow falcon eyes painted on its pointed prow hinted at its capacity for flight.

Sabriel looked at the Paperwing again, and then out at the waterfall beyond. Now, fed by floodwaters, it looked even more frightening than usual. Spray exploded for tens of yards above its lip—a roaring mist the Paperwing would have to fly through before it reached the open sky beyond. Sabriel didn't even know if it was waterproof.

"How often has this . . . thing . . . flown before?" she asked, nervously. Intellectually, she accepted that she would soon be sitting in this craft, to be launched out towards the crashing waters—but her subconscious, and her stomach, seemed very keen to stay firmly on the ground.

"Many times," replied Mogget, easily jumping from the platform to the cockpit. His voice echoed there for a moment, till he climbed back up, furry cat-face propped on the rim. "The Abhorsen who made it once flew it to the sea and back, in a single afternoon. But she was a great weather-witch and could work the winds. I don't suppose—"

"No," said Sabriel, made aware of another gap in her education. She knew that wind-magic was largely whistled Charter marks, but that was all. "No. I can't."

"Well," continued Mogget, after a thoughtful pause, "the Paperwing does have some elementary charms to ride the wind. You'll have to whistle them, though. You can whistle, I trust?"

Sabriel ignored him. All necromancers had to be musical, had to be able to whistle, to hum, to sing. If they were caught in Death without bells, or other magical instruments, their vocal skills were a weapon of last recourse.

A sending came and took her pack, helping her to wrestle it off, then stowing it at the rear of the cockpit. Another took Sabriel's arm and directed her to what appeared to be a leather half-hammock strung across the cockpit—obviously the pilot's seat. It didn't look terribly safe either, but Sabriel forced herself to climb in, after giving her scabbarded sword into the hands of yet another sending.

Surprisingly, her feet didn't go through the paper-laminated floor. The material even felt reassuringly solid and, after a minute of squirming, swaying and adjustment, the hammock-seat was very comfortable. Sword and scabbard were slid into a receptacle at her side and Mogget took up a position on top of the straps holding down her pack, just behind her shoulders, for the seat made her recline so far she was almost lying down.

From her new eye level, Sabriel saw a small, oval mirror of silvered glass, fixed just below the cockpit rim. It glittered in the late afternoon sun, and she felt it resonate with Charter Magic. Something about it prompted her to breathe upon it, her hot breath clouding the glass. It stayed misted for a moment, then a Charter mark slowly appeared, as if a ghostly finger was drawn across the clouded mirror.

Sabriel studied it carefully, absorbing its purpose and effect. It told her of the marks that would follow; marks to raise the lifting winds, marks for descending in haste, marks to call the wind from every corner of the compass rose. There were other marks for the Paperwing and, as Sabriel absorbed them, she saw that the whole craft was lined with Charter Magic, infused with spells. The Abhorsen who made it had labored long, and with love, to create something that was more like a magical bird than an aircraft.

Time passed, and the last mark faded. The mirror cleared to be only a plate of silver glass shining in the sun. Sabriel sat, silent, fixing the Charter marks in her memory, marveling at the power and the skill that had made the Paperwing and had thought of this method of instruction. Perhaps one day, she too would have the mastery to create such a thing.

"The Abhorsen who made this," Sabriel asked. "Who was she? I mean, in relation to me?"

"A cousin," purred Mogget, close to her ear. "Your great-great-great-great-grandmother's cousin. The last of that line. She had no children."

Maybe the Paperwing was her child, Sabriel thought, running her hand along the sleek surface of the fuselage, feeling the Charter marks quiescent in the fabric. She felt a lot better about their forthcoming flight.

"We'd best hurry," Mogget continued. "It will be dark all too soon. Do you have the marks remembered?"

"Yes," replied Sabriel firmly. She turned to the sendings, who were now lined up behind the wings, anchoring the Paperwing till it was time for it to be unleashed upon the sky. Sabriel wondered how many times they'd performed this task, and for how many Abhorsens.

"Thank you," she said to them. "For all your care and kindness. Goodbye."

With that last word, she settled back in the hammock-seat, gripped the rim of the cockpit with both hands, and whistled the notes of the lifting wind, visualizing the requisite string of Charter marks in her mind, letting them drip down into her throat and lips, and out into the air.

Her whistle sounded clear and true, and a wind rose behind to match it, growing stronger as Sabriel exhaled. Then, with a new breath, she changed to a merry, joyous trill. Like a bird revelling in flight, the Charter marks flowing from pursed lips out into the Paperwing itself. With this whistling, the blue and silver paint seemed to come alive, dancing down the fuselage, sweeping across the wings, a gleaming, lustrous plumage. The whole craft shook and shivered, suddenly flexible and eager to begin.

The joyous trill ended with one single long, clear note, and a Charter mark that shone like the sun. It danced to the Paperwing's prow and sank into the laminate. A second later, the yellow eyes blinked, grew fierce and proud, looking up to the sky ahead.

The sendings were struggling now, barely able to hold the Paperwing back. The lifting wind grew stronger still, plucking at the silver-blue plumage, thrusting it forward. Sabriel felt the Paperwing's tension, the contained power in its wings, the exhilaration of that last moment when freedom is assured.

"Let go!" she cried, and the sendings complied, the Paperwing leaping up into the arms of the wind, out and upward, splashing through the spray of the waterfall as if it were no more than a spring shower, flying out into the sky and the broad valley beyond.

It was quiet, and cold, a thousand feet or more above the valley. The Paperwing soared easily, the wind firm behind it, the sky clear above, save for the faintest wisps of cloud. Sabriel reclined in her hammock-seat, relaxing, running the Charter marks she'd learned over and over in her mind, making sure she had them properly pigeonholed. She felt free, and somehow clean, as if the dangers of the last few days were dirt, washed away by the following wind.

"Turn more to the north," Mogget's voice suddenly said behind her, disturbing her carefree mood. "Do you recall the map?"

"Yes," replied Sabriel. "Shall we follow the river? The Ratterlin, it's called, isn't it? It runs nor-nor-east most of the time."

Mogget didn't reply at once, though Sabriel heard his purring breath close by. He seemed to be thinking. Finally, he said, "Why not? We may as well follow it to the sea. It branches into a delta there, so we can find an island to camp on tonight."

"Why not just fly on?" asked Sabriel cheerily. "We could be in Belisaere by tomorrow night, if I summon the strongest winds."

"The Paperwing doesn't like to fly at night," Mogget said, shortly. "Not to mention that you would almost certainly lose control of the stronger winds—it is much more difficult than it seems at first. And the Paperwing is much too conspicuous, anyway. Have you no common sense, Abhorsen?"

"Call me Sabriel," Sabriel replied, equally shortly. "My father is Abhorsen."

"As you wish, mistress," said Mogget. The "mistress" sounded extremely sarcastic.

The next hour passed in belligerent silence, but Sabriel, for her part, soon lost her anger in the novelty of flight. She loved the scale of it all, to see the tiny patchworked fields and forests below, the dark strip of the river, the occasional tiny building. Everything was so small and seemed so perfect, seen from afar.

Then the sun began to sink, and though the red wash of its fading light made the aerial perspective even prettier, Sabriel felt the Paperwing's desire to descend, felt the yellow eyes focusing on green earth, rather than blue sky. As the shadows lengthened, Sabriel felt that same desire and began to look as well.

The river was already breaking up into the myriad streams and rivulets that would form the swampy Ratterlin delta, and far off, Sabriel could see the dark bulk of the sea. There were many islands in the delta, some as large as football fields covered with trees and shrubs, others no bigger than two armspans of mud. Sabriel picked out one of the medium-sized ones, a flattish diamond with low, yellow grass, a few leagues ahead, and whistled down the wind.

It faded gradually with her whistle and the Paperwing

began to descend, occasionally nudged this way or that by Sabriel's control of the wind, or its own tilt of a wing. Its yellow eyes, and Sabriel's deep-brown eyes, were fixed on the ground below. Only Mogget, being Mogget, looked behind them and above.

Even so, he didn't see their pursuers until they came wheeling out of the sun, so his yowling cry gave only a few seconds' warning, just long enough for Sabriel to turn and see the hundreds of fast-moving shapes diving down upon them. Instinctively, she conjured Charter marks in her mind, mouth pursed, whistling the wind back up, turning them to the north.

"Gore crows!" hissed Mogget, as the flapping shapes checked their dive and wheeled to pursue their suddenly enlivened prey.

"Yes," shouted Sabriel, though she wasn't sure why she answered. Her attention was all on the gore crows, trying to gauge whether they'd intercept or not. She could already feel the wind testing the edges of her control, as Mogget had prophesied, and to whip it up further might have unpleasant results. But she could also feel the presence of the gore crows, feel the admixture of Death and Free Magic that gave life to their rotten, skeletal forms.

Gore crows didn't last very long in sun and wind—these must have been made the previous night. A necromancer had trapped quite ordinary crows, killing them with ritual and ceremony, before infusing the bodies with the broken, fragmented spirit of a single dead man or woman. Now they were truly carrion birds, birds guided by a single, if stupid, intelligence. They flew by force of Free Magic, and killed by force of numbers.

Despite her quickness in calling the wind, the flock was still closing rapidly. They'd dived from high above and kept their speed, the wind stripping feathers and putrid flesh from their spell-woven bones.

For a moment, Sabriel considered turning the Paperwing back into the very center of this great murder of crows, like an avenging angel, armed with sword and bells. But there were simply too many gore crows to fight, particularly from an aircraft speeding along several hundred feet above the ground. One overeager sword thrust would mean a fatal fall—if the gore crows didn't kill her on the way down.

"I'll have to summon a greater wind!" she yelled at Mogget, who was now sitting right up on her pack, fur bristling, yowling challenges at the crows. They were very close now, flying in an eerily exact formation—two long lines, like arms outstretched to snatch the fleeing Paperwing from the sky. Very little of their once-black plumage had survived their rushing dive, white bone shining through in the last light of the sun. But their beaks were still glossily black and gleaming sharp, and Sabriel could now see the red glints of the fragmented Dead spirit in the empty sockets of their eyes.

Mogget didn't reply. Possibly, he hadn't even heard her above his yowling, and the gore crows' cawing as they closed the last few yards to attack, a strange, hollow sound, as dead as their flesh.

For a second of panic, Sabriel felt her dry lips unable to purse, then she wet them and the whistle came, slow and erratic. The Charter marks felt clumsy and difficult in her head, as if she were trying to push a heavy weight on badly made rollers—then, with a last effort, they came easily, flowing into her whistled notes.

Unlike her earlier, gradual summonings, this wind came with the speed of a slamming door, howling up behind them with frightening violence, picking up the Paperwing and shunting it forward like a giant wave lifting up a slender boat. Suddenly, they were going so fast that Sabriel could barely make out the ground below, and the individual islands of the delta merged into one continuous blur of motion.

Eyes closed to protective slits, she craned her head around, the wind striking her face like a vicious slap. The pursuing gore crows were all over the sky now, formation lost, like small black stains against the red and purple sunset. They were flapping uselessly, trying to come back together, but the Paperwing was already a league or more away. There was no chance they could catch up.

Sabriel let out a sigh of relief, but it was a sigh tempered with new anxieties. The wind was carrying them at a fearful pace, and it was starting to veer northwards, which it wasn't supposed to do. Sabriel could see the first stars twinkling now, and they were definitely turning towards the Buckle.

It was an effort to call up the Charter marks again, and whistle the spell to ease the wind, and turn it back to the east, but Sabriel managed to cast it. But the spell failed to work—the wind grew stronger, and shifted more, till they were careening straight towards the Buckle, directly north.

Sabriel, hunkered down in the cockpit, eyes and nose streaming and face frozen, tried again, using all her willpower to force the Charter marks into the wind. Even to her, her whistle sounded feeble, and the Charter marks once again vanished into what had now become a gale. Sabriel realized she had totally lost control.

In fact, it was almost as if the spell had the opposite effect, for the wind grew wilder, snatching the Paperwing up in a great spiral, like a ball thrown between a ring of giants, each one taller than the last. Sabriel grew dizzy, and even colder, and her breath came fast and shallow, trying to salvage enough air to keep her alive. She tried to calm the winds again, but couldn't gain the breath to whistle, and the Charter marks slipped from her mind, till all she could do was desperately hang on to the straps in the hammock-seat as the Paperwing tried its best to ride the storm.

Then, without warning, the wind ceased its upward dance. It just dropped, and with it went the Paperwing. Sabriel fell upwards, straps suddenly tight, and Mogget almost clawed through the pack in his efforts to stay connected with the aircraft. Jolted by this new development, Sabriel felt her exhaustion burn away. She tried to whistle the lifting wind, but it too was beyond her power. The Paperwing seemed unable to halt its headlong descent. It fell, nose tilting further and further forward till they were diving almost vertically, like a hammer rushing to the anvil of the ground below.

It was a long way down. Sabriel screamed once, then tried to put some of her fear-found strength into the Paperwing. But the marks flowed into her whistle without effect, save for a golden sparkle that briefly illuminated her white, wind-frozen face. The sun had completely set, and the dark mass of the ground below looked all too much like the grey river of Death—the river their spirits would cross into in a few short minutes, never to return to the warm light of Life.

"Loose my collar," mewed a voice at Sabriel's ear, followed by the curious sensation of Mogget digging his claws into her armor as he clambered into her lap. "Loose my collar!"

Sabriel looked at him, at the ground, at the collar. She felt stupid, starved of oxygen, unable to decide. The collar was part of an ancient binding, a terrible guardian of tremendous power. It would only be used to contain an inexpressible evil, or uncontrollable force.

"Trust me!" howled Mogget. "Loose my collar, and remember the ring!"

Sabriel swallowed, closed her eyes, fumbled with the collar and prayed that she was doing the right thing. "Father, forgive me," she thought, but it was not just to her father that she spoke, but to all the Abhorsens who had come before her—especially the one who had made the collar so long ago.

Surprisingly for such an ancient spell, she felt little more than pins and needles as the collar came free. Then it was open, and suddenly heavy, like a lead rope, or a ball and chain. Sabriel almost dropped it, but it became light again, then insubstantial. When Sabriel opened her eyes, the collar had simply ceased to exist.

Mogget sat still, on her lap, and seemed unchanged—then he seemed to glow with an internal light and expand, till he became frayed at the edges, and the light grew and grew. Within a few seconds, there was no cat-shape left, just a shining blur too bright to look at. It seemed to hesitate for a moment and Sabriel felt its attention flicker between aggression towards her and some inner struggle. It almost formed back into the cat-shape again, then suddenly split into four shafts of brilliant white. One shot forward, one aft, and two seemed to slide into the wings.

Then the whole Paperwing shone with fierce white brilliance, and it abruptly stopped its headlong dive and leveled out. Sabriel was flung violently forward, body checked by straps, but her nose almost hit the silver mirror, neck muscles cording out with an impossible effort to keep her head still.

Despite this sudden improvement, they were still falling. Sabriel, hands now clasped behind her savagely aching neck, saw the ground rushing up to fill the horizon. Treetops suddenly appeared below, the Paperwing imbued with the strange light, just clipping through the upper branches with a sound like hail on a tin roof. Then, they dropped again, skimming scant yards above what looked like a cleared field, but still too fast to land without total destruction.

Mogget, or whatever Mogget had become, braked the Paperwing again, in a series of shuddering halts that added bruises on top of bruises. For the first time, Sabriel felt the incredible relief of knowing that they would survive. One more braking effort and the Paperwing would be safely down, to skid a little in the long, soft grass of the field.

Mogget braked, and Sabriel cheered as the Paperwing gently lay its belly on the grass and slid to what should have been a perfect landing. But the cheer suddenly became a shriek of alarm, as the grass parted to reveal the lip of an enormous dark hole directly in their path.

Too low to rise, and now too slow to glide over a hole at least fifty yards across, the Paperwing reached the edge, flipped over and spiraled towards the bottom of the hole, hundreds of feet below.

Chapter Twelve

S ABRIEL REGAINED CONSCIOUSNESS slowly, her brain fumbling for connections to her senses. Hearing came first, but that only caught her own labored breathing, and the creak of her armored coat as she struggled to sit up. For the moment, sight eluded her, and she was panicked, afraid of blindness, till memory came. It was night, and she was at the bottom of a sinkhole—a great, circular shaft bored into the ground, by either nature or artifice. From her brief glimpse of it as they'd fallen, she guessed it was easily fifty yards in diameter and a hundred deep. Daylight would probably illuminate its murky depths, but starlight was insufficient.

Pain came next, hard on the heels of memory. A thousand aches and bruises, but no serious injury. Sabriel wiggled her toes and fingers, flexed muscles in arms, back and legs. They all hurt, but everything seemed to work.

She vaguely recalled the last few seconds before impact—Mogget, or the white force, slowing them just before they hit—but the actual instant of the crash might never have been, for she couldn't remember it. Shock, she thought to herself, in an abstract way, almost like she was diagnosing someone else.

Her next thought came some time later, and with it the realization that she must have passed out again. With this awakening, she felt a little sharper, her mind catching some slight breeze to carry her out of the mental doldrums. Working by touch, she unstrapped herself and felt behind her for the pack. In her current state, even a simple Charter-spell for light was out of the question, but there were candles there, and matches, or the clockwork igniter.

As the match flared, Sabriel's heart sank. In the small, flickering globe of yellow light, she saw that only the central cockpit portion of the Paperwing survived—the sad blue and silver corpse of a once marvelous creation. Its wings lay torn and crumpled underneath it, and the entire nose section lay some yards away, shorn off completely. One eye stared up at the circular patch of sky above, but it was no longer fierce and alive. Just yellow paint and laminated paper.

Sabriel stared at the wreckage, regret and sorrow coursing like influenza in her bones, till the match burnt her fingers. She lit another, and then a candle, expanding both her light and field of vision.

More small pieces of the Paperwing were strewn over a large, open, flat area. Groaning with the effort of motivating bruised muscles, Sabriel levered herself out of the cockpit to have a closer look at the ground.

This revealed the flat area to be man-made; flagstones, carefully laid. Grass had long grown between the stones, and lichen upon them, so it was clearly not recent work. Sabriel sat on the cool stones and wondered why anyone would do such work at the bottom of a sinkhole.

Thinking about that seemed to kickstart her befuddled wits and she started to wonder about a few other things. Where, for instance, was the force that had once been Mogget? And what was it? That reminded her to fetch her sword and check the bells.

Her turbanned helmet had rotated around on her head and was almost back-to-front. Slowly, she slid it around, feeling every slight movement all the way down her now very stiff neck.

Balancing her first candle on the paving in a pool of cooling wax, she dragged her pack and weapons out of the wreckage
and lit another two candles. She put one down near the first and
took the other to light her way, walking around the destroyed
Paperwing, searching for any sign of Mogget. At the dismembered prow of the craft, she gently touched the eyes, wishing she
could close them.

"I am sorry," she whispered. "Perhaps I will be able to make
a new Paperwing one day. There should be another, to carry on
your name."

"Sentiment, Abhorsen?" said a voice somewhere behind her,
a voice that managed to sound like Mogget and not at all like
him at the same time. It was louder, harsher, less human, and
every word seemed to crackle, like the electric generators she'd
used in Wyverley College Science classes.

"Where are you?" asked Sabriel, swiftly turning. The voice
had sounded close, but there was nothing visible within the
sphere of candlelight. She held her own candle higher, and transferred it to her left hand.

"Here," snickered the voice, and Sabriel saw lines of white
fire run out from under the ruined fuselage, lines that lit the paper
laminate as they ran, so that, within a second, the Paperwing was
burning fiercely, yellow-red flames dancing under thick white
smoke, totally obscuring whatever had emerged from under the
stricken craft.

No Death sense twitched, but Sabriel could almost smell the
Free Magic; tangy, unnatural, nerve-jangling, tainting the thick
odor of natural smoke. Then she saw the white fire-lines again,
streaming out, converging, roiling, coming together—and a blazing, blue-white creature stepped out from the funeral pyre of the
Paperwing.

Sabriel couldn't look at it directly, but from the corners of her arm-shielded eyes, she saw something human in shape, taller than her, and thin, almost starved. It had no legs, the torso and head balanced upon a column of twisting, whirling force.

"Free, save for the blood price," it said, advancing. All trace of Mogget's voice was lost now, submerged in zapping, crackling menace.

Sabriel had no doubt about the meaning of a blood price and who would pay it. Summoning all her remaining energies, she called three Charter marks to the forefront of her mind, and hurled them towards the thing, shouting their names.

"Anet! Calew! Ferhan!"

The marks became silver blades as they left her hand, mind and voice, flashing through the air swifter than any thrown dagger—and went straight through the shining figure, apparently without effect.

It laughed, a series of rises and falls like a dog screaming in pain, and lazily slid forward. Its languid motion seemed to declare it would have no more trouble disposing of Sabriel than it had in burning the Paperwing.

Sabriel drew her sword and backed away, determined not to panic as she had done when faced by the Mordicant. Her head flicked backwards and forwards, neck pain forgotten, checking the ground behind her and marking her opponent. Her mind raced, considering options. Perhaps one of the bells—but that would mean dropping her candle. Could she count on the crea-ture's blazing presence to light her way?

Almost as if it could read her mind, the creature suddenly started to lose its brilliance, sucking darkness into its swirling body like a sponge soaking up ink. Within a few seconds, Sabriel could barely make it out—a fearful silhouette, back-lit by the orange glow of the burning Paperwing.

Desperately, Sabriel tried to remember what she knew of Free Magic elementals and constructs. Her father had rarely mentioned them, and Magistrix Greenwood had only lightly delved into the subject. Sabriel knew the binding spells for two of the lesser kindred of Free Magic beings, but the creature before her was neither Margrue nor Stilken.

"Keep thinking, Abhorsen," laughed the creature, advancing again. "Such a pity your head doesn't work too well."

"You saved it from not working forever," Sabriel replied warily. It had braked the Paperwing, after all, so perhaps there was some good in it somewhere, some remnant of Mogget, if only it could be brought out.

"Sentiment," the thing replied, still silently sliding forward. It laughed again and a dark, tendril-like arm suddenly unleashed itself, snapping across the intervening space to strike Sabriel across the face.

"A memory, now purged," it added, as Sabriel staggered back from a second attack, sword flashing across to parry. Unlike the silver spell darts, the Charter-etched blade did connect with the unnatural flesh of the creature, but had no effect apart from jarring Sabriel's arm.

Her nose was bleeding too, a warm and salty flow, stinging her wind-chafed lips. She tried to ignore it, tried to use the pain of what was probably a broken nose to get her mind back to full operational speed.

"Memories, yes, many memories," continued the creature. It was circling around her now, pushing her back the way they'd come, back towards the fading fire of the Paperwing. That would burn out soon, and then there would only be darkness, for Sabriel's candle was now a lump of blown-out wax, falling forgotten from her hand.

"Millennia of servitude, Abhorsen. Chained by trickery,

treachery . . . captive in a repulsive, fixed-flesh shape . . . but there will be payment, slow payment—not quick, not quick at all!"

A tendril lashed out, low this time, trying to trip her. Sabriel leapt over it, blade extended, lunging for the creature's chest. But it shimmied aside, extruding extra arms as she tried to jump back, catching her in mid-leap, drawing her close.

Sword-arm pinioned at her side, it tightened its grip, till she was close against its chest, her face a finger-width from its boiling, constantly moving flesh, as if a billion tiny insects buzzed behind a membrane of utter darkness.

Another arm gripped the back of her helmet, forcing her to look up, till she saw its head, directly above her. A thing of most basic anatomy, its eyes were like the sinkhole, deep pits without apparent bottom. It had no nose, but a mouth that split the horrid face in two, a mouth slightly parted to reveal the burning blue-white glare that it had first used as flesh.

All Charter Magic had fled from Sabriel's mind. Her sword was trapped, the bells likewise, and even if they weren't, she didn't know how to use them properly against things not Dead. She ran over them mentally anyway, in a frantic, lightning inventory of anything that might help.

It was then her tired, concussed mind remembered the ring. It was on her left hand, her free hand, cool silver on the index finger.

But she didn't know what to do with it—and the creature's head was bowing down towards her own, its neck stretching impossibly long, till it was like a snake's head rearing above her, the mouth opening wider, growing brighter, fizzing with white-hot sparks that fell upon her helmet and face, burning cloth and skin, leaving tiny, tattoo-like scars. The ring felt loose on her finger. Sabriel instinctively curled her hand, and the ring felt looser still, slipping down her finger, expanding, growing, till without looking, Sabriel knew she held a silver hoop as wide or wider than the creature's slender head. And she suddenly knew what to do.

"First, the plucking of an eye," said the thing, breath as hot as the falling sparks, scorching her face with instant sunburn. It tilted its head sideways and opened its mouth still wider, lower jaw dislocating out.

Sabriel took one last, careful look, screwed her eyes tight against the terrible glare, and flipped the silver hoop up, and she hoped, over the thing's neck.

For a second, as the heat increased and she felt a terrible burning pain against her eye, Sabriel thought she'd missed. Then the hoop was wrenched from her hand and she was thrown away, hurled out like an angry fisherman's rejected minnow.

On the cool flagstones again, she opened her eyes, the left one blurry, sore and swimming with tears—but still there and still working.

She had put the silver hoop over the thing's head, and it was slowly sliding down that long, sinuous neck. The ring was shrinking again as it slid, impervious to the creature's desperate attempts to get it off. It had six or seven hands now, formed directly from its shoulders, all squirming about, trying to force fingers under the ring. But the metal seemed inimical to the creature's substance, like a hot pan to human fingers, for the fingers flinched and danced around it, but could not take hold for longer than a second.

The darkness that stained it was ebbing too, draining down through its thrashing, twisting support, leaving glowing whiteness behind. Still the creature fought with the ring, blazing hands forming and re-forming, body twisting and turning, even bucking, as if it could throw the ring like a rider from a horse.

Finally, it gave up and turned towards Sabriel, screaming and

crackling. Two long arms sprang out from it, reaching towards
Sabriel's sprawling body, talons growing from the hands, raking the
stone with deep gouges as they scrabbled towards her, like spiders
scuttling to their prey—only to fall short by a yard or more.

"No!" howled the thing, and its whole twisting, coiling body
lurched forward, killing arms outstretched. Again, the talons fell
short, as Sabriel crawled, rolled and pushed herself away.

Then the silver ring contracted once more, and a terrible
shout of anguish, rage and despair came from the very center of
the white-flaming thing. Its arms suddenly shrank back to its
torso; the head fell into the shoulders, and the whole body sank
into an amorphous blob of shimmering white, with a single,
still-large silver band around the middle, the ruby glittering like
a drop of blood.

Sabriel stared at it, unable to look aside, or do anything else,
even quell the flow from her bleeding nose, which now covered
half her face and chin, her mouth glued shut with dried and
clotting blood. It seemed to her that something was left undone,
something that she had to provide.

Nervously crawling closer, she saw that there were now
marks on the ring, Charter marks that told her what she must
do. Wearily, she got up on her knees and fumbled with the bell-
bandolier. Saraneth was heavy, almost beyond her strength, but
she managed to draw it out, and the deep, compelling voice rang
through the sinkhole, seeming to pierce the glowing, silver-
bound mass.

The ring hummed in answer to the bell and exuded a pear-
shaped drop of its own metal, which cooled to become a miniature Saraneth. At the same time, the ring changed color and
consistency. The ruby's color seemed to run, and a red wash
spread through the silver. It was now dull and ordinary, no longer
a silver band, but a red leather collar, with a miniature silver bell.

With this change, the white mass quivered, and shone bright again, till Sabriel had to shield her eyes once more. When the shadows grew together again, she looked back, and there was Mogget, collared in red leather, sitting up and looking like he was about to throw up a hairball.

It wasn't a hairball, but a silver ring, the ruby reflecting Mogget's internal light. It rolled to Sabriel, tinkling across the stone. She picked it up and slid it back on her finger.

Mogget's glow faded, and the burning Paperwing was now only faint embers, sad memories and ash. Darkness returned, cloaking Sabriel, wrapping her up with all her hurts and fears. She sat, silent, not even thinking.

A little later, she felt a soft cat nose against her folded hands, and a candle, damp from Mogget's mouth.

"Your nose is still bleeding," said a familiar, didactic voice. "Light the candle, pinch your nose, and get some blankets out for us to sleep. It's getting cold."

"Welcome back, Mogget," whispered Sabriel.

Chapter Thirteen

NEITHER SABRIEL NOR Mogget mentioned the happenings of the previous night when they awoke. Sabriel, bathing her seriously swollen nose in an inch of water from her canteen, found that she didn't particularly want to remember a waking nightmare, and Mogget was quiet, in an apologetic way. Despite what happened later, freeing Mogget's alter ego, or whatever it was, had saved them from certain destruction by the wind.

As she'd expected, dawn had brought some light to the sinkhole, and as the day progressed, this had grown to a level approximating twilight. Sabriel could read and see things close by quite clearly, but they merged into indistinct gloom twenty or thirty yards away.

Not that the sinkhole was much larger than that—perhaps a hundred yards in diameter, not the fifty she'd guessed at when she was coming down. The entire floor of it was paved, with a circular drain in the middle, and there were several tunnel entrances into the sheer rock walls—tunnels which Sabriel knew she would eventually have to take, as there was no water in the sinkhole. There seemed little chance of rain, either. It was cool, but nowhere near as cold as the plateau near Abhorsen's House. The climate was mitigated by proximity to the ocean, and an altitude that could easily be sea-level or below, for in daylight Sabriel could see that the sinkhole was at least a hundred yards deep.

Still, with a half-full canteen of water gurgling by her side, Sabriel was quite content to slouch upon her slightly scorched pack and apply herbal creams to her bruises, and a poultice of evil-smelling tanmaril leaves to her strange sunburn. Her nose was a different matter when it came to treatment. It wasn't broken—merely hideous, swollen and encrusted with dried blood, which hurt too much to clean off completely.

Mogget, after an hour or so of sheepish silence, sauntered off to explore, refusing Sabriel's offer of hard cakes and dried meat for breakfast. She expected he'd find a rat, or something equally appetizing, instead. In a way, she was quite pleased he was gone. The memory of the Free Magic beast that lay within the little white cat was still disturbing.

Even so, when the sun had risen to become a little disc surrounded by the greater circumference of the sinkhole's rim, she started to wonder why he hadn't come back. Levering herself up, she limped over to the tunnel he'd chosen, using her sword as a walking stick and complaining quietly as every bruise reminded her of its location.

Of course, just as she was lighting a candle at the tunnel entrance Mogget reappeared behind her.

"Looking for me?" he mewed, innocently.

"Who else?" replied Sabriel. "Have you found anything? Anything useful, I mean. Water, for instance."

"Useful?" mused Mogget, rubbing his chin back along his two outstretched front legs. "Perhaps. Interesting, certainly. Water? Yes."

"How far away?" asked Sabriel, all too aware of her bruise-limited mobility. "And what does interesting mean? Dangerous?"

"Not far, by this tunnel," replied Mogget. "There is a little danger getting there—a trap and a few other oddments, but nothing that will harm you. As to the interesting part, you will have to see for yourself, Abhorsen."

"Sabriel," said Sabriel automatically, as she tried to think ahead. She needed at least two days' rest, but no more than that. Every day lost before she found her father's corporeal body might mean disaster. She simply had to find him soon.

A Mordicant, Shadow Hands, gore crows—it was now all too clear that some terrible enemy was arrayed against both father and daughter. That enemy had already trapped her father, so it had to be a very powerful necromancer, or some Greater Dead creature. Perhaps this Kerrigor . . .

"I'll get my pack," she decided, trudging back, Mogget slipping backwards and forwards across her path like a kitten, almost tripping her, but always just getting out of the way. Sabriel put this down to inexplicable catness, and didn't comment.

As Mogget had promised, the tunnel wasn't long, and its well-made steps and cross-hatched floor made passage easy, save for the part where Sabriel had to follow the little cat exactly across the stones, to avoid a cleverly concealed pit. Without Mogget's guidance, Sabriel knew she would have fallen in.

There were magical wardings too. Old, inimical spells lay like moths in the corners of the tunnel, waiting to fly up at her, to surround and choke her with power—but something checked their first reaction and they settled again. A few times, Sabriel experienced a ghostly touch, like a hand reaching out to brush the Charter mark on her forehead, and almost at the end of the tunnel, she saw two guard sendings melting into the rock, the tips of their halberds glinting in her candlelight before they, too, merged into stone.

"Where are we going?" she whispered, nervously, as the door in front of them slowly creaked open—without visible means of propulsion.

"Another sinkhole," Mogget said, matter-of-factly. "It is

where the First Blood . . . ach . . ."

He choked, hissed, and then rephrased his sentence rather drably, with "It is interesting."

"What do you mean—" Sabriel began, but she fell silent as they passed the doorway, magical force suddenly tugging at her hair, her hands, her surcoat, the hilt of her sword. Mogget's fur stood on end, and his collar rotated halfway around of its own accord, till the Charter marks of binding were uppermost and clearly readable, bright against the leather.

Then they were out, standing at the bottom of another sink-hole, in a premature twilight, for the sun was already slipping over the circumscribed horizon of the sinkhole rim.

This sinkhole was much wider than the first—perhaps a mile across, and deeper, say six or seven hundred feet. Despite its size, the entire vast pit was sealed off from the upper air by a gleaming, web-thin net, which seemed to merge into the rim wall about a quarter of the way down from the surface. Sunlight had given it away, but even so, Sabriel had to use her telescope to see the delicate diamond-pattern weave clearly. It looked flimsy, but the presence of several dessicated bird-corpses indi-cated considerable strength. Sabriel guessed the unfortunate birds had dived into the net, eyes greedily intent on food below.

In the sinkhole itself, there was considerable, if uninspiring vegetation—mostly stunted trees and malformed bushes. But Sabriel had little attention to spare for the trees, for in between each of these straggling patches of greenery, there were paved areas—and on each of these paved areas rested a ship.

Fourteen open-decked, single-masted longboats, their black sails set to catch a nonexistent wind, oars out to battle an imag-inary tide. They flew many flags and standards, all limp against mast and rigging, but Sabriel didn't need to see them unfurled to know what strange cargo these ships might bear. She'd heard of this place, as had every child in the Northern parts of Ancelstierre, close to the Old Kingdom. Hundreds of tales of treasure, adventure and romance were woven around this strange harbor.

"Funerary ships," said Sabriel. "Royal ships."

She had further confirmation that this was so, for there were binding spells woven into the very dirt her feet scuffed at the tunnel entrance, spells of final death that could only have been laid by an Abhorsen. No necromancer would ever raise any of the ancient rulers of the Old Kingdom.

"The famous burial ground of the First . . . ckkk . . . the Kings and Queens of the Old Kingdom," pronounced Mogget, after some difficulty. He danced around Sabriel's feet, then stood on his hind legs and made expansive gestures, like a circus impresario in white fur. Finally, he shot off into the trees.

"Come on—there's a spring, spring, spring!" he caroled, as he leapt up and down in time with his words.

Sabriel followed at a slower pace, shaking her head and wondering what had happened to make Mogget so cheerful. She felt bruised, tired and depressed, shaken by the Free Magic monster, and sad about the Paperwing.

They passed close by two of the ships on their way to the spring. Mogget led her a merry dance around both of them, in a mad circumnavigation of twists, leaps and bounds, but the sides were too high to look in and she didn't feel like shinning up an oar. She did pause to look at the figureheads—imposing men, one in his forties, the other somewhat older. Both were bearded, had the same imperious eyes, and wore armor similar to Sabriel's, heavily festooned with medallions, chains and other decorations. Each held a sword in his right hand, and an unfurling scroll that turned back on itself in their left—the heraldic representation of the Charter.

The third ship was different. It seemed shorter and less ornate, with a bare mast devoid of black sails. No oars sprang from its sides, and as Sabriel reached the spring that lay under its stern, she saw uncaulked seams between the planking, and realized that it was incomplete.

Curious, she dropped her pack by the little pool of bubbling water and walked around to the bow. This was different too, for the figurehead was a young man—a naked young man, carved in perfect detail.

Sabriel blushed a little, for it was an exact likeness, as if a young man had been transformed from flesh to wood, and her only prior experience of naked men was in clinical cross-sections from biology textbooks. His muscles were lean and well-formed, his hair short and tightly curled against his head. His hands, well-shaped and elegant, were partly raised, as if to ward off some evil.

The detail even extended to a circumcised penis, which Sabriel glanced at in an embarrassed way, before looking back at his face. He was not exactly handsome, but not displeasing. It was a responsible visage, with the shocked expression of someone who has been betrayed and only just realized it. There was fear there, too, and something like hatred. He looked more than a little mad. His expression troubled her, for it seemed too human to be the result of a woodcarver's skill, no matter how talented.

"Too life-like," Sabriel muttered, stepping back from the figurehead, hand falling to the hilt of her sword, her magical senses reaching out, seeking some trap or deception.

There was no trap, but Sabriel did feel something in or around the figurehead. A feeling similar to that of a Dead revenant, but not the same—a niggling sensation that she couldn't place.

Sabriel tried to identify it, while she looked over the figurehead again, carefully examining him from every angle. The man's body was an intellectual problem now, so she looked without embarrassment, studying his fingers, fingernails and skin, noting how perfectly they were carved, right down to the tiny scars on his hands, the product of sword and dagger practice. There was also the faint sign of a baptismal Charter mark on his forehead, and the pale trace of veins on his eyelids.

That inspection led her to certainty about what she'd detected, but she hesitated about the action that should be taken, and went in search of Mogget. Not that she put a lot of faith in advice or answers from that quarter, given his present propensity towards behaving as a fairly silly cat—though perhaps this was a reaction to his brief experience of being a Free Magic beast again, something that might not have happened for a millennium. The cat form was probably a welcome relief.

In fact, no advice at all could be had from Mogget. Sabriel found him asleep in a field of flowers near the spring, his tail and paddy-paws twitching to a dream of dancing mice. Sabriel looked at the straw-yellow flowers, sniffed one, scratched Mogget behind the ears, then went back to the figurehead. The flowers were catbalm, explaining both Mogget's previous mood and his current somnolence. She would have to make up her own mind.

"So," she said, addressing the figurehead like a lawyer before a court. "You are the victim of some Free Magic spell and necromantic trickery. Your spirit lies neither in Life nor Death, but somewhere in between. I could cross into Death, and find you near the border, I'm sure—but I could find a lot of trouble as well. Trouble I can't deal with in my current pathetic state. So what can I do? What would Father—Abhorsen . . . or any Abhorsen—do in my place?"

She thought about it for a while, pacing backwards and forwards, bruises temporarily forgotten. That last question seemed to make her duty clear. Sabriel felt sure her father would free the man. That's what he did, that was what he lived for. The duty of an Abhorsen was to remedy unnatural necromancy and Free Magic sorcery.

She didn't think further than that, perhaps due to the injudicious sniffing of the catbalm. She didn't even consider that her father would probably have waited until he was fitter—perhaps till the next day. After all, this young man must have been incarcerated for many years, his physical body transformed into wood, and his spirit somehow trapped in Death. A few days would make no difference to him. An Abhorsen didn't have to immediately take on any duty that presented itself . . .

But for the first time since she'd crossed the Wall, Sabriel felt there was a clear-cut problem for her to solve. An injustice to be righted and one that should involve little more than a few minutes on the very border of Death.

Some slight sense of caution remained with her, so she went and picked up Mogget, placing the dozing cat near the feet of the figurehead. Hopefully, he would wake up if any physical danger threatened—not that this was likely, given the wards and guards on the sinkhole. There were even barriers that would make it difficult to cross into Death, and more than difficult for something Dead to follow her back. All in all, it seemed like the perfect place to undertake a minor rescue.

. Once more, she checked the bells, running her hands over the smooth wood of the handles, feeling their voices within, eagerly awaiting release. This time, it was Ranna she freed from its leather case. It was the least noticeable of the bells, its very nature lulling listeners, beguiling them to sleep or inattention.

Second thoughts brushed at her like doubting fingers, but

she ignored them. She felt confident, ready for what would only
be a minor stroll in Death, amply safeguarded by the protections
of this royal necropolis. Sword in one hand, bell in the other, she
crossed into Death.

Cold hit her, and the relentless current, but she stood where she
was, still feeling the warmth of Life on her back. This was the
very interface between the two realms, where she would normally plunge ahead. This time, she planted her feet against the
current, and used her continuing slight contact with Life as an
anchor to hold her own against the waters of Death.

Everything seemed quiet, save for the constant gurgling of
the water about her feet, and the far-off crash of the First Gate.
Nothing stirred, no shapes loomed up in the grey light. Cautiously,
Sabriel used her sense of the Dead to feel out anything that might
be lurking, to feel the slight spark of the trapped, but living, spirit
of the young man. Back in Life, she was physically close to him,
so she should be near his spirit here.

There was something, but it seemed further into Death than
Sabriel expected. She tried to see it, squinting into the curious
greyness that made distance impossible to judge, but nothing was
visible. Whatever was there lurked beneath the surface of the
water.

Sabriel hesitated, then walked towards it, carefully feeling
her way, making sure of every footfall, guarding against the gripping current. There was definitely something odd out there. She
could feel it quite strongly—it had to be the trapped spirit. She
ignored the little voice at the back of her mind that suggested it
was a fiercely devious Dead creature, strong enough to hold its
own against the race of the river . . .

Nevertheless, when she was a few paces back from whatever
it was, Sabriel let Ranna sound—a muffled, sleepy peal that carried

the sensation of a yawn, a sigh, a head falling forward, eyes heavy—
a call to sleep.

If there was a Dead thing there, Sabriel reasoned, it would
now be quiescent. She put her sword and bell away, edged forward to a good position, and reached down into the water.

Her hands touched something as cold and hard as ice, something totally unidentifiable. She flinched back, then reached
down again, till her hands found something that was clearly a
shoulder. She followed this up to a head, and traced the features.
Sometimes a spirit bore little relation to the physical body, and
sometimes living spirits became warped if they spent too long in
Death, but this one was clearly the counterpart of the figurehead. It lived too, somehow encased and protected from Death,
as the living body was preserved in wood.

Sabriel gripped the spirit-form under the arms and pulled.
It rose up out of the water like a killer whale, pallid white and
rigid as a statue. Sabriel staggered backwards, and the river, ever-
eager, wrapped her legs with tricksome eddies—but she steadied
herself before it could drag her down.

Changing her hold a little, Sabriel began to drag the spirit-
form back towards Life. It was hard going, much harder than
she'd expected. The current seemed far too strong for this side of
the First Gate, and the crystallized spirit—or whatever it was—
was much, much heavier than any spirit should be.

With nearly all her concentration bent on staying upright
and heading in the right direction, Sabriel almost didn't notice
the sudden cessation of noise that marked the passage of something through the First Gate. But she'd learned to be wary over
the last few days, and her conscious fears had become enshrined
in subconscious caution.

She heard, and listening carefully, caught the soft slosh-slosh
of something half-wading, half-creeping, moving as quietly as it

could against the current. Moving towards her. Something Dead was hoping to catch her unawares.

Obviously, some alarm or summons had gone out beyond the First Gate, and whatever was stalking towards her had come in answer to it. Inwardly cursing herself for stupidity, Sabriel looked down at her spirit burden. Sure enough, she could just make out a very thin black line, fine as cotton thread, running from his arm into the water—and thence to the deeper, darker regions of Death. Not a controlling thread, but one that would let some distant Adept know the spirit had been moved. Fortunately, sounding Ranna would have slowed the message, but was she close enough to Life . . .

She increased her speed a little, but not too much, pretending she hadn't noticed the hunter. Whatever it was, it seemed quite reluctant to close in on her.

Sabriel quickened her pace a little more, adrenaline and suspense feeding her strength. If it rushed her, she would have to drop the spirit—and he would be carried away, lost forever. Whatever magic had preserved his living spirit here on the boundary couldn't possibly prevail if he went past the First Gate. If that happened, Sabriel thought, she would have precipitated a murder rather than a rescue.

Four steps to Life—then three. The thing was closing now— Sabriel could see it, low in the water, still creeping, but faster now. It was obviously a denizen of the Third, or even some later Gate, for she couldn't identify what it once had been. Now it looked like a cross between a hog and a segmented worm, and it moved in a series of scuttles and sinuous wriggles.

Two steps. Sabriel shifted her grip again, wrapping her left arm completely around the spirit's chest and balancing the weight on her hip, freeing her right arm, but she still couldn't draw her sword, or clear the bells.

The hog-thing began to grunt and hiss, breaking into a diving, rushing gallop, its long, yellow-crusted tusks surfing through the water, its long body undulating along behind.

Sabriel stepped back, turned, and threw herself and her precious cargo headfirst into Life, using all her will to force them through the wards on the sinkhole. For an instant, it seemed that they would be repulsed, then, like a pin pushing through a rubber band, they were through.

Shrill squealing followed her, but nothing else. Sabriel found herself facedown on the ground, hands empty, ice crystals crunching as they fell from her frosted body. Turning her head, she met the gaze of Mogget. He stared at her, then closed his eyes and went back to sleep.

Sabriel rolled over, and got to her feet, very, very slowly. She felt all her pains come back and wondered why she'd been so hasty to perform deeds of derring-do and rescue. Still, she had managed it. The man's spirit was back where it belonged, back in Life.

Or so she thought, till she saw the figurehead. It hadn't changed at all to outward sight, though Sabriel could now feel the living spirit in it. Puzzled, she touched his immobile face, fingers tracing the grain of the wood.

"A kiss," said Mogget sleepily. "Actually, just a breath would do. But you have to start kissing someone sometime, I suppose."

Sabriel looked at the cat, wondering if this was the latest symptom of catbalm-induced lunacy. But he seemed sober enough, and serious.

"A breath?" she asked. She didn't want to kiss just any wooden man. He looked nice enough, but he might not be like his looks. A kiss seemed very forward. He might remember it, and make assumptions.

"Like this?" She took a deep breath, leaned forward, exhaled a few inches from his nose and mouth, then stepped back to see what would happen—if anything.

Nothing did.

"Catbalm!" exclaimed Sabriel, looking at Mogget. "You shouldn't—"

A small sound interrupted her. A small, wheezing sound, that didn't come from her or Mogget. The figurehead was breathing, air whistling between carved wooden lips like the issue from an aged, underworked bellows.

The breathing grew stronger, and with it, color began to flow through the carving, dull wood giving way to the luster of flesh. He coughed, and the carven chest became flexible, suddenly rising and falling as he began to pant like a recovering sprinter.

His eyes opened and met Sabriel's. Fine grey eyes, but muzzy and unfocused. He didn't seem to see her. His fingers clenched and unclenched, and his feet shuffled, as if he were running in place. Finally, his back peeled away from the ship's hull. He took one step forward, and fell into Sabriel's arms.

She lowered him hastily to the ground, all too aware that she was embracing a naked young man—in circumstances considerably different than the various scenarios she'd imagined with her friends at school, or heard about from the earthier and more privileged day-girls.

"Thank you," he said, almost drunkenly, the words terribly slurred. He seemed to focus on her—or her surcoat—for the first time, and added, "Abhorsen."

Then he went to sleep, mouth curling up at the corners, frown dissolving. He looked younger than he did as a fixed-expression figurehead.

Sabriel looked down at him, trying to ignore curiously fond feelings that had appeared from somewhere. Feelings similar to those that had made her bring back Jacinth's rabbit.

"I suppose I'd better get him a blanket," she said reluctantly, as she wondered what on earth had possessed her to add this complication to her already confusing and difficult circumstances. She supposed she would have to get him to safety and civilization, at the very least—if there was any to be found.

"I can get a blanket if you want to keep staring at him," Mogget said slyly, twining himself around her ankles in a sensuous pavane.

Sabriel realized she really was staring, and looked away.

"No. I'll get it. And my spare shirt, I suppose. The breeches might fit him with a bit of work, I guess—we'd be much the same height. Keep watch, Mogget. I'll be back in a minute."

Mogget watched her hobble off, then turned back to the sleeping man. Silently, the cat padded over and touched his pink tongue to the Charter mark on the man's forehead. The mark flared, but Mogget didn't flinch, till it grew dull again.

"So," muttered Mogget, tasting his own tongue by curling it back on itself. He seemed somewhat surprised, and more than a little angry. He tasted the mark again, and then shook his head in distaste, the miniature Saraneth on his collar ringing a little peal that was not of celebration.

Chapter Fourteen

REY MIST COILING upwards, twining around him like a clinging vine, gripping arms and legs, immobilizing, strangling, merciless. So firmly grown about his body there was no possibility of escape, so tight his muscles couldn't even flex under skin, his eyelids couldn't blink. And nothing to see but patches of darker grey, crisscrossing his vision like wind-blown scum upon a fetid pool.

Then, suddenly, fierce red light, pain exploding everywhere, rocketing from toes to brain and back again. The grey mist clearing, mobility returning. No more grey patches, but blurry colors, slowly twisting into focus. A woman, looking down at him, a young woman, armed and armored, her face . . . battered. No, not a woman. The Abhorsen, for she wore the blazon and the bells. But she was too young, not the Abhorsen he knew, or any of the family . . .

"Thank you," he said, the words coming out like a mouse creeping from a dusty larder. "Abhorsen."

Then he fainted, his body rushing gladly to welcome real sleep, true unconsciousness and sanity-restoring rest.

He awoke under a blanket, and felt a moment's panic when the thick grey wool pressed upon his mouth and eyes. He struggled with it, threw it back with a gasp, and relaxed as he felt fresh air on his face and dim sunlight filtering down from above. He looked up and saw from the reddish hue that it must be soon after dawn. The sinkhole puzzled him for a few seconds—disoriented, he felt dizzy and stupid, till he looked at the tall masts all around, the black sails, and the unfinished ship nearby.

"Holehallow," he muttered to himself, frowning. He remembered it now. But what was he doing here? Completely naked under a rough camping blanket?

He sat up, and shook his head. It was sore and his temples were throbbing, seemingly from the battering-ram effect of a severe hangover. But he felt certain he hadn't been drinking. The last thing he remembered was going down the steps. Rogir had asked him . . . no . . . the last thing was the fleeting image of a pale, concerned face, bloodied and bruised, black hair hanging out in a fringe under her helmet. A deep blue surcoat, with the blazon of silver keys. The Abhorsen.

"She's washing at the spring," said a soft voice, interrupting his faltering recollection. "She got up before the sun. Cleanliness is a wonderful thing."

The voice did not seem to belong to anything visible, till the man looked up at the nearby ship. There was a large, irregular hole in the bow, where the figurehead should have been and a white cat was curled up in the hole, watching him with an unnaturally sharp, green-eyed gaze.

"What are you?" said the man, his eyes cautiously flickering from side to side, looking for a weapon. A pile of clothes was the only thing nearby, containing a shirt, trousers and some underwear, but it was weighted down with a largish rock. His hand sidled out towards the rock.

"Don't be alarmed," said the cat. "I'm but a faithful retainer of the Abhorsen. Name of Mogget. For the moment."

The man's hand closed on the rock, but he didn't lift it. Memories were slowly sidling back to his benumbed mind, drawn like grains of iron to a magnet. There were memories of various Abhorsens among them—memories that gave him an inkling of what this cat-creature was.

"You were bigger when we last met," he hazarded, testing his guess.

"Have we met?" replied Mogget, yawning. "Dear me. I can't recall it. What was the name?"

A good question, thought the man. He couldn't remember. He knew who he was, in general terms, but his name eluded him. Other names came easily though, and some flashes of memory concerning what he thought of as his immediate past. He growled, and grimaced as they came to him, and clenched his fists in pain and anger.

"Unusual name," commented Mogget. "More of a bear's name, that growl. Do you mind if I call you Touchstone?"

"What!" the man exclaimed, affronted. "That's a fool's name! How dare—"

"Is it unfitting?" interrupted Mogget, coolly. "You do remember what you've done?"

The man was silent then, for he suddenly did remember, though he didn't know why he'd done it, or what the consequences had been. He also remembered that since this was the case, there was no point trying to remember his name. He was no longer fit to bear it.

"Yes, I remember," he whispered. "You may call me Touchstone. But I shall call you—"

He choked, looked surprised, then tried again.

"You can't say it," Mogget said. "A spell tied to the corruption of—but I can't say it, nor tell anyone the nature of it, or how to fix it. You won't be able to talk about it either and there may be other effects. Certainly, it has affected me."

"I see," replied Touchstone, somberly. He didn't try the name again. "Tell me, who rules the Kingdom?"

"No one," said Mogget.

"A regency, then. That is perhaps—"

"No. No regency. No one reigns. No one rules. There was a regency at first, but it declined . . . with help."

"What do you mean, 'at first'?" asked Touchstone. "What exactly has happened? Where have I been?"

"The regency lasted for one hundred and eighty years," Mogget announced callously. "Anarchy has held sway for the last twenty, tempered by what a few remaining loyalists could do. And you, my boy, have been adorning the front of this ship as a lump of wood for the last two hundred years."

"The family?"

"All dead and past the Final Gate, save one, who should be. You know who I mean."

For a moment, this news seemed to return Touchstone to his wooden state. He sat frozen, only the slight movement of his chest showing continued life. Then tears started in his eyes, and his head slowly fell to meet his upturned hands.

Mogget watched without sympathy, till the young man's back ceased its heaving and the harsh in-drawn gasps between sobs became calmer.

"There's no point crying over it," the cat said harshly. "Plenty of people have died trying to put the matter to rights. Four Abhorsens have fallen in this century alone, trying to deal with the Dead, the broken stones and the—the original problem. My current Abhorsen certainly isn't lying around crying her eyes out. Make yourself useful and help her."

"Can I?" asked Touchstone bleakly, wiping his face with the blanket.

"Why not?" snorted Mogget. "Get dressed, for a start. There are some things aboard here for you as well. Swords and suchlike."

"But I'm not fit to wield royal—"

"Just do as you're told," Mogget said firmly. "Think of your-self as Abhorsen's sworn sword-hand, if it makes you feel better, though in this present era, you'll find common sense is more important than honor."

"Very well," Touchstone muttered, humbly. He stood up and put on the underclothes and shirt, but couldn't get the trousers past his heavily muscled thighs.

"There's a kilt and leggings in one of the chests back here," Mogget said, after watching Touchstone hopping around on one leg, the other trapped in too-tight leather.

Touchstone nodded, divested himself of the trousers, and clambered up through the hole, taking care to keep as far away from Mogget as possible. Halfway up, he paused, arms braced on either side of the gap.

"You won't tell her?" he asked.

"Tell who? Tell what?"

"Abhorsen. Please, I'll do all I can to help. But it wasn't intentional. My part, I mean. Please, don't tell her—"

"Spare me the pleadings," said Mogget, in a disgusted tone. "I can't tell her. You can't tell her. The corruption is wide and the spell rather indiscriminatory. Hurry up—she'll be back soon. I'll tell you the rest of our current saga while you dress."

Sabriel returned from the spring feeling healthier, cleaner and happier. She'd slept well and the morning's ablutions had cleared off the blood. The bruises, swellings and sunburn had all responded well to her herbal treatments. All in all, she felt about eighty percent normal, rather than ten percent functional, and she was looking forward to having some company at breakfast other than the sardonic Mogget. Not that he didn't have his uses, such as guarding unconscious or sleeping humans. He'd also assured her that he had tested the Charter mark on the figurehead-man, finding him to be unsullied by Free Magic, or necromancy.

She'd expected the man to still be asleep, so she felt a faint frisson of surprise and suspense when she saw a figure standing by the ship's bow, facing the other way. For a second, her hand twitched to her sword, then she saw Mogget nearby, precariously draped on the ship's rail.

She approached nervously, her curiosity tempered by the need to be wary of strangers. He looked different dressed. Older and somewhat intimidating, particularly since he seemed to have scorned her plain clothing for a kilt of gold-striped red, with matching leggings of red-striped gold, disappearing into turned-down thigh boots of russet doeskin. He was wearing her shirt, though, and preparing to put on a red leather jerkin. It had detachable, lace-up sleeves, which seemed to be giving him some problems. Two swords lay in three-quarter scabbards near his feet, stabbing points shining four inches out of the leather. A wide belt with the appropriate hooks already encircled his waist.

"Curse these laces," he said, when she was about ten paces away. A nice voice, quite deep, but currently frustrated and peaking with temper.

"Good morning," said Sabriel.

He whirled around, dropping the sleeves, almost ducking to his swords, before recovering to transform the motion into a bow, culminating in a descent to one knee.

"Good morning, milady," he said huskily, head bowed, carefully not meeting her gaze. She saw that he'd found some earrings, large gold hoops clumsily pushed through pierced lobes, for they were bloodied. Apart from them, all she could see was the top of his curly-haired head.

"I'm not 'milady,'" said Sabriel, wondering which of Miss Prionte's etiquette principles applied to this situation. "My name is Sabriel."

"Sabriel? But you are the Abhorsen," the man said slowly.

He didn't sound overly bright, Sabriel thought, with sinking expectations. Perhaps there would be very little conversation at breakfast after all.

"No, my father is the Abhorsen," she said, with a stern look at Mogget, warning him not to interfere. "I'm a sort of stand-in. It's a bit complicated, so I'll explain later. What's your name?"

He hesitated, then mumbled, "I can't remember, milady. Please, call me . . . call me Touchstone."

"Touchstone?" asked Sabriel. That sounded familiar, but she couldn't place it for a moment. "Touchstone? But that's a jester's name, a fool's name. Why call you that?"

"That's what I am," he said dully, without inflection.

"Well, I have to call you something," Sabriel continued. "Touchstone. You know, there is the tradition of a wise fool, so perhaps it's not so bad. I guess you think you're a fool because you've been imprisoned as a figurehead—and in Death, of course."

"In Death!" exclaimed Touchstone. He looked up and his grey eyes met Sabriel's. Surprisingly, he had a clear, intelligent gaze. Perhaps there is some hope for him after all, she thought, as she explained: "Your spirit was somehow preserved just beyond the border of Death, and your body preserved as the wooden figurehead. Both necromantic and Free Magic would have been involved. Very powerful magic, on both counts. I am curious as to why it was used on you."

Touchstone looked away again, and Sabriel sensed a certain shiftiness, or embarrassment. She guessed that the forthcoming explanation would be a half-truth, at best.

"I don't remember very well," he said, slowly. "Though things are coming back. I am . . . I was . . . a guardsman. The Royal Guard. There was some sort of attack upon the Queen . . . an ambush in the—at the bottom of the stairs. I remember fighting, with blade and Charter Magic—we were all Charter Mages, all the guard. I thought we were safe, but there was treachery . . . then . . . I was here. I don't know how."

Sabriel listened carefully, wondering how much of what he said was true. It was likely that his memory was impaired, but he possibly was a royal guard. Perhaps he had cast a diamond of protection . . . that could have been why his enemies could only imprison him, rather than kill. But, surely they could have waited till it failed. Why the bizarre method of imprisonment? And, most importantly, how did the figurehead manage to get placed in this most protected of places?

She filed all these questions for later investigation, for another thought had struck her. If he really was a royal guard, the Queen he had guarded must have been dead and gone for at least two hundred years and, with her, everyone and everything he knew.

"You have been a prisoner for a long time," she said gently, uncertain about how to break the news. "Have you . . . I mean did you . . . well, what I mean is it's been a very long time—"

"Two hundred years," whispered Touchstone. "Your minion told me."

"Your family . . ."

"I have none," he said. His expression was set, as immobile as the carved wood of the previous day. Carefully, he reached over and drew one of his swords, offering it to Sabriel hilt-first.

"I would serve you, milady, to fight against the enemies of the Kingdom."

Sabriel didn't take the sword, though his plea made her reflexively reach out. But a moment's thought closed her open palm, and her arm fell back to her side. She looked at Mogget, who was watching the proceedings with unabashed interest.

"What have you told him, Mogget?" she asked, suspicion wreathing her words.

"The state of the Kingdom, generally speaking," replied the

cat. "Recent events. Our descent here, more or less. Your duty as Abhorsen to remedy the situation."

"The Mordicant? Shadow Hands? Gore crows? The Dead Adept, whoever it may be?"

"Not specifically," said Mogget, cheerfully. "I thought he could presume as much."

"As you see," Sabriel said, rather angrily, "my 'minion' has not been totally honest with you. I was raised across the Wall, in Ancelstierre, so I have very little idea about what is going on. I have huge gaps in my knowledge of the Old Kingdom, including everything from geography to history to Charter Magic. I face some dire enemies, probably under the overall direction of one of the Greater Dead, a necromantic adept. And I'm not out to save the Kingdom, just to find my father, the real Abhorsen. So I don't want to take your oath or service or anything like that, particularly as we've only just met. I am happy for you to accompany us to the nearest approximation of civilization, but I have no idea what I will be doing after that. And, please remember that my name is Sabriel. Not milady. Not Abhorsen. Now, I think it's time for breakfast."

With that, she stalked over to her pack, and started getting out some oatmeal and a small cooking pot.

Touchstone stared after her for a moment, then picked himself up, attached his swords, put on the sleeveless jerkin, tied the sleeves to his belt and wandered off to the nearest clump of trees.

Mogget followed him there, and watched him pick up dead branches and sticks for a fire.

"She really did grow up in Ancelstierre," said the cat. "She doesn't realize refusing your oath is an insult. And it's true enough about her ignorance. That's one of the reasons she needs your help."

"I can't remember much," said Touchstone, snapping a branch

in half with considerable ferocity. "Except my most recent past. Everything else is like a dream. I'm not sure if it's real or not, learned or imagined. And I wasn't insulted. My oath isn't worth much."

"But you'll help her," said Mogget. It wasn't a question.

"No," said Touchstone. "Help is for equals. I'll serve her. That's all I'm good for."

As Sabriel feared, there was little conversation over breakfast. Mogget went off in search of his own, and Sabriel and Touchstone were hindered by the sole cooking pot and single spoon, so they took it in turns to eat half the porridge. Even allowing for this difficulty, Touchstone was uncommunicative. Sabriel started asking a lot of questions, but as his standard response was, "I'm sorry, I can't remember," she soon gave up.

"I don't suppose you can remember how to get out of this sinkhole, either," she asked in exasperation, after a particularly long stretch of silence. Even to her, this sounded like a prefect addressing a miscreant twelve-year-old.

"No, I'm sorry . . ." Touchstone began automatically, then he paused, and the corner of his mouth quirked up with a momentary spasm of pleasure. "Wait! Yes—I do remember! There's a hidden stair, to the north of King Janeurl's ship . . . oh, I can't remember which one that is . . ."

"There's only four ships near the northern rim," Sabriel mused. "It won't be too hard to find. How's your memory for other geography? The Kingdom, for instance?"

"I'm not sure," replied Touchstone, guardedly, bowing his head again. Sabriel looked at him and took a deep breath to calm the eel-like writhings of anger that were slowly getting bigger and bigger inside her. She could excuse his faulty memory— after all, that was due to magical incarceration. But the servile manner that went with it seemed to be an affectation. He was like a bad actor playing the butler—or rather, a non-actor trying to impersonate a butler as best he could. But why?

"Mogget drew me a map," she said, talking as much to calm herself as for any real communication. "But, as he apparently has only left Abhorsen's House for a few weekends over the last thousand years, even two-hundred-year-old memories . . ."

Sabriel paused, and bit her lip, suddenly aware that her annoyance with him had made her spiteful. He looked up as she stopped speaking, but no reaction showed on his face. He might as well still be carved from wood.

"What I mean is," Sabriel continued carefully, "it would be very helpful if you could advise me on the best route to Belisaere, and the important landmarks and locations on the way."

She got the map out of the special pocket in the pack and removed the protective oilskin. Touchstone took one end as she unrolled it, and weighted his two corners with stones, while Sabriel secured hers with the telescope case.

"I think we're about here," she said, tracing her finger from Abhorsen's House, following the Paperwing's flight from there to a point a little north of the Ratterlin river delta.

"No," said Touchstone, sounding decisive for the first time, his finger stabbing the map an inch to the north of Sabriel's own. "This is Holehallow, here. It's only ten leagues from the coast and at the same latitude as Mount Anarson."

"Good!" exclaimed Sabriel, smiling, her anger slipping from her. "You do remember. Now, what's the best route to Belisaere, and how long will it take?"

"I don't know the current conditions, mi . . . Sabriel," Touchstone replied. His voice grew softer, more subdued. "From what Mogget says, the Kingdom is in a state of anarchy. Towns and villages may no longer exist. There will be bandits, the Dead, Free Magic unbound, fell creatures . . ."

"Ignoring all that," Sabriel asked, "which way did you normally go?"

"From Nestowe, the fishing village here," Touchstone said, pointing at the coast to the east of Holehallow. "We'd ride north along the Shoreway, changing horses at post houses. Four days to Callibe, a rest day there. Then the interior road up through Oncet Pass, six days all told to Aunden. A rest day in Aunden, then four days to Orchyre. From there, it would be a day's ferry passage, or two days' riding, to the Westgate of Belisaere."

"Even without the rest days, that'd be eighteen days' riding, at least six weeks' walking. That's too long. Is there any other way?"

"A ship, or boat, from Nestowe," interrupted Mogget, stalking up behind Sabriel, to place his paw firmly on the map. "If we can find one and if either of you can sail it."

Chapter Fifteen

THE STAIR WAS to the north of the middle ship of the four. Concealed by both magic and artifice, it seemed to be little more than a particularly wet patch of the damp limestone that formed the sinkhole wall, but you could walk right through it, for it was really an open door with steps winding up behind.

They decided to take these steps the next morning, after another day of rest. Sabriel was eager to move on, for she felt that her father's peril could only be increasing, but she was realistic enough to assess her own need for recovery time. Touchstone, too, probably needed a rest, she thought. She'd tried to coax more information out of him while they'd searched for the steps, but he was clearly reluctant to even open his mouth, and when he did, Sabriel found his humble apologies ever more irritating. After the door was found she gave up altogether, and sat in the grass near the spring, reading her father's books on Charter Magic. *The Book of the Dead* stayed wrapped in oilskin. Even then, she felt its presence, brooding in her pack . . .

Touchstone stayed at the opposite end of the ship, near the bow, performing a series of fencing exercises with his twin swords, and some stretches and minor acrobatics. Mogget watched him from the undergrowth, green eyes glittering, as if intent on a mouse.

Lunch was a culinary and conversational failure. Dried beef

strips, garnished with watercress from the fringes of the spring, and monosyllabic responses from Touchstone. He even went back to "milady," despite Sabriel's repeated requests to use her name. Mogget didn't help by calling her Abhorsen. After lunch, everyone went back to their respective activities. Sabriel to her book, Touchstone to his exercises and Mogget to his watching.

Dinner was not something anyone had looked forward to. Sabriel tried talking to Mogget, but he seemed to be infected with Touchstone's reticence, though not with his servility. As soon as they'd eaten, everyone left the raked-together coals of the campfire—Touchstone to the west, Mogget north and Sabriel east—and went to sleep on as comfortable a stretch of ground as could be discovered.

Sabriel woke once in the night. Without getting up, she saw that the fire had been rekindled and Touchstone sat beside it, staring into the flames, his eyes reflecting the capering, gold-red light. His face looked drawn, almost ill.

"Are you all right?" Sabriel asked quietly, propping herself up on one elbow.

Touchstone started, rocked back on his heels, and almost fell over. For once, he didn't sound like a sulky servant.

"Not really. I remember what I would not, and forget what I should not. Forgive me."

Sabriel didn't answer. He had spoken the last two words to the fire, not to her.

"Please, go back to sleep, milady," Touchstone continued, slipping back to his servile role. "I will wake you in the morning."

Sabriel opened her mouth to say something scathing about the arrogance of pretended humility, then shut it, and subsided back under her blanket. Just concentrate on rescuing Father, she told herself. That is the one important thing. Rescue Abhorsen. Don't worry about Touchstone's problems, or Mogget's curious nature. Rescue Abhorsen. Rescue Abhorsen. Rescue Abhors . . . rescue . . .

"Wake up!" Mogget said, right in her ear. She rolled over, ignoring him, but he leapt across her head and repeated it in her other ear. "Wake up!"

"I'm awake," grumbled Sabriel. She sat up with the blanket wrapped around her, feeling the pre-dawn chill on her face and hands. It was still extremely dark, save for the uneven light of the fire and the faintest brushings of dawn light above the sinkhole. Touchstone was already making the porridge. He'd also washed, and shaved—using a dagger from the look of the nicks and cuts on his chin and neck.

"Good morning," he said. "This will be ready in five minutes, milady."

Sabriel groaned at that word again. Feeling like a shambling, blanket-shrouded excuse for a human being, she picked up her shirt and trousers and staggered off to find a suitable bush en route to the spring.

The icy water of the spring completed the waking up process without kindness, Sabriel exposing herself to it and the marginally warmer air for no more than the ten seconds it took to shed undershirt, wash and get dressed again. Clean, awake and clothed, she returned to the campfire and ate her share of the porridge. Then Touchstone ate, while Sabriel buckled on armor, sword and bells. Mogget lay near the fire, warming his white-furred belly. Not for the first time, Sabriel wondered if he needed to eat at all. He obviously liked food, but he seemed to eat for amusement, rather than sustenance.

Touchstone continued being a servant after breakfast, cleaning pot and spoon, quenching the fire and putting everything away. But when he was about to swing the pack on his back, Sabriel stopped him.

"No, Touchstone. It's my pack. I'll carry it, thank you."

He hesitated, then passed it to her and would have helped her put it on, but she had her arms through the straps and the pack swung on before he could take the weight.

Half an hour later, perhaps a third of the way up the narrow, stone-carved stair, Sabriel regretted her decision to take the pack. She still wasn't totally recovered from the Paperwing crash and the stair was very steep, and so narrow that she had difficulty negotiating the spiraling turns. The pack always seemed to jam against the outside or inside wall, no matter which way she turned.

"Perhaps we should take it in turns to carry the pack," she said reluctantly, when they stopped at a sort of alcove to catch their breath. Touchstone, who had been leading, nodded and came back down a few steps to take the pack.

"I'll lead, then," Sabriel added, flexing her back and shoulders, shuddering slightly at the pack-induced layer of sweat on her back, greasy under armor, tunic, shirt and undershirt. She picked up her candle from the bench and stepped up.

"No," said Touchstone, stepping in her way. "There are guards—and guardians—on this stair. I know the words and signs to pass them. You are the Abhorsen, so they might let you past, but I am not sure."

"Your memory must be coming back," Sabriel commented, slightly peeved at being thwarted. "Tell me, is this stair the one you mentioned when you said the Queen was ambushed?"

"No," Touchstone replied flatly. He hesitated, then added, "That stair was in Belisaere."

With that, he turned, and continued up the stairs. Sabriel followed, Mogget at her heels. Now that she wasn't lumbered by her pack, she felt more alert. Watching Touchstone, she saw him pause occasionally and mutter some words under his breath. Each time, there was the faint, feather-light touch of Charter Magic. Subtle magic, much cleverer than in the tunnel below. Harder to detect and probably much more deadly, Sabriel thought. Now she knew it was there, she also picked up the faint sensation of Death. This stair had seen killings, a long, long, time ago.

Finally, they came to a large chamber, with a set of double doors to one side. Light leaked in from a large number of small, circular holes in the roof, or as Sabriel soon saw, through an overgrown lattice that had once been open to air and sky.

"That's the outside door," Touchstone said, unnecessarily. He snuffed out his candle, took Sabriel's, now little more than a stub of wax, and put both in a pocket stitched to the front of his kilt. Sabriel thought of joking about the hot wax and the potential for damage, but thought better of it. Touchstone was not the lighthearted type.

"How does it open?" asked Sabriel, indicating the door. She couldn't see any handle, lock or key. Or any hinges, for that matter.

Touchstone was silent, eyes unfocused and staring, then he laughed, a bitter little chuckle.

"I don't remember! All the way up the stair, all the words and signals . . . and now useless! Useless!"

"At least you got us up the steps," Sabriel pointed out, alarmed by the violence of his self-loathing. "I'd still be sitting by the spring, watching it bubble, if you hadn't come along."

"You would have found the way out," Touchstone muttered. "Or Mogget would. Wood! Yes, that's what I deserve to be—"

"Touchstone," Mogget interrupted, hissing. "Shut up. You're to be useful, remember?"

"Yes," replied Touchstone, visibly calming his breathing, composing his face. "I'm sorry, Mogget. Milady."

"Please, please, just Sabriel," she said tiredly. "I've only just left school—I'm only eighteen! Calling me milady seems ridiculous."

"Sabriel," Touchstone said tentatively. "I will try to remember. 'Milady' is a habit . . . it reminds me of my place in the world. It's easier for me—"

"I don't care what's easier for you!" Sabriel snapped. "Don't call me milady and stop acting like a halfwit! Just be yourself. Behave normally. I don't need a valet, I need a useful . . . friend!"

"Very well, Sabriel," Touchstone said, with careful emphasis. He was angry now, but at least that was an improvement over servile, Sabriel thought.

"Now," she said to the smirking Mogget. "Have you got any ideas about this door?"

"Just one," replied Mogget, sliding between her legs and over to the thin line that marked the division between the two leaves of the door. "Push. One on each side."

"Push?"

"Why not?" said Touchstone, shrugging. He took up a position, braced against the left side of the door, palms flat on the metal-studded wood. Sabriel hesitated, then did the same against the right.

"One, two, three, push!" announced Mogget.

Sabriel pushed on "three" and Touchstone on "push," so their combined effort took several seconds to synchronize. Then the doors creaked slowly open, sunshine spilling through in a bright bar, climbing from floor to ceiling, dust motes dancing in its progress.

"It feels strange," said Touchstone, the wood humming beneath his hands like plucked lute strings.

"I can hear voices," exclaimed Sabriel at the same time, her ears full of half-caught words, laughter, distant singing.

"I can see time," whispered Mogget, so softly that his words were lost.

Then the doors were open. They walked through, shielding their eyes against the sun, feeling the cool breeze sharp on their skin, the fresh scent of pine trees clearing their nostrils of underground dust. Mogget sneezed quickly three times, and ran about in a tight circle. The doors slid shut behind them, as silently and inexplicably as they'd opened.

They stood in a small clearing in the middle of a pine forest, or plantation, for the trees were regularly spaced. The doors behind them stood in the side of a low hillock of turf and stunted bushes. Pine needles lay thick on the ground, pinecones peeking through every few paces, like skulls ploughed up on some ancient battleground.

"The Watchwood," said Touchstone. He took several deep breaths, looked at the sky, and sighed. "It is Winter, I think—or early Spring?"

"Winter," replied Sabriel. "It was snowing quite heavily, back near the Wall. It seems much milder here."

"Most of the Wall, the Long Cliffs, and Abhorsen's House, are on, or part of, the Southern Plateau," Mogget explained. "The plateau is between one and two thousand feet above the coastal plain. In fact, the area around Nestowe, where we are headed, is mostly below sea level and has been reclaimed."

"Yes," said Touchstone. "I remember. Long Dyke, the raised canals, the wind pumps to raise the water—"

"You're both very informative for a change," remarked Sabriel. "Would one of you care to tell me something I really want to know, like what are the Great Charters?"

"I can't," Mogget and Touchstone said together. Then Touchstone continued, haltingly, "There is a spell . . . a binding on us. But someone who is not a Charter Mage, or otherwise closely bound to the Charter, might be able to speak. A child, perhaps, baptized with the Charter mark, but not grown into power."

"You're cleverer than I thought," commented Mogget. "Not that that's saying much."

"A child," said Sabriel. "Why would a child know?"

"If you'd had a proper education, you'd know too," said Mogget. "A waste of good silver, that school of yours."

"Perhaps," agreed Sabriel. "But now that I know more of the Old Kingdom, I suspect being at school in Ancelstierre saved my life. But enough of that. Which way do we go now?"

Touchstone looked at the sky, blue above the clearing, dark where the pines circled. The sun was just visible above the trees, perhaps an hour short of its noon-time zenith. Touchstone looked from it to the shadows of the trees, then pointed: "East. There should be a series of Charter Stones, leading from here to the eastern edge of the Watchwood. This place is heavily warded with magic. There are . . . there were, many stones."

The stones were still there, and after the first, some sort of animal track that meandered from one stone to the next. It was cool under the pines, but pleasant, the constant presence of the Charter Stones a reassuring sensation to Sabriel and Touchstone, who could sense them like lighthouses in a sea of trees.

There were seven stones in all, and none of them broken, though Sabriel felt a stab of nervous tension every time they left the ambience of one and moved to another, a stark picture always flashing into her head—the bloodstained, riven stone of Cloven Crest.

The last stone stood on the very edge of the pine forest, atop a granite bluff thirty or forty yards high, marking the forest's eastern edge and the end of high ground.

They stood next to the stone and looked out, out towards the huge expanse of blue-grey sea, white-crested, restless, always rolling in to shore. Below them were the flat, sunken fields of Nestowe, maintained by a network of raised canals, pumps and dykes. The village itself lay three-quarters of a mile away, high on another granite bluff, the harbor out of sight on the other side.

"The fields are flooded," said Touchstone, in a puzzled tone, as if he couldn't believe what he was seeing.

Sabriel followed his gaze, and saw that what she had taken for some crop was actually silt and water, sitting tepidly where food once grew. Windmills, power for the pumps, stood silent, trefoil-shaped vanes still atop scaffolding towers, even though a salt-laden breeze blew in from the sea.

"But the pumps were Charter-spelled," Touchstone exclaimed. "To follow the wind, to work without care . . ."

"There are no people in the fields—no one on this side of the village," Mogget added, his eyes keener than the telescope in Sabriel's pack.

"Nestowe's Charter Stone must be broken," Sabriel said, mouth tight, words cold. "And I can smell a certain stench on the breeze. There are Dead in the village."

"A boat would be the quickest way to Belisaere, and I am reasonably confident of my sailing," Touchstone remarked. "But if the Dead are there, shouldn't we . . ."

"We'll go down and get a boat," Sabriel announced firmly. "While the sun is high."

Chapter Sixteen

THERE WAS A built-up path through the flooded fields, but it was submerged to ankle-depth, with occasional thigh-high slippages. Only the raised canal drains stood well above the brackish water, and they all ran towards the east, not towards the village, so Sabriel and Touchstone were forced to wade along the path. Mogget, of course, rode, his lean form draped around Sabriel's neck like a white fox fur.

Water and mud, coupled with an uncertain path, made it slow going. It took an hour to cover less than a mile, so it was later in the afternoon than Sabriel would have wished when they finally climbed out of the water, up onto the beginnings of the village's rocky mount. At least the sky is clear, Sabriel thought, glancing up. The winter sun wasn't particularly hot and couldn't be described as glaring, but it would certainly deter most kindred of the Lesser Dead from venturing out.

Nevertheless, they walked carefully up to the village, swords loose, Sabriel with a hand to her bells. The path wound up in a series of steps carved from the rock, reinforced here and there with bricks and mortar. The village proper nestled on top of the bluff—about thirty cozy brick cottages, with wood-tile roofs, some painted bright colors, some dull, and some simply grey and weatherbeaten.

It was completely silent, save for the odd gust of wind, or the mournful cry of a gull, slipping down through the air above.

Sabriel and Touchstone drew closer together, walking almost shoulder-to-shoulder up what passed for a main street, swords out now, eyes flickering across closed doors and shuttered windows. Both felt uneasy, nervous—a nasty, tingling, creeping sensation climbing up from spine, to nape of neck, to forehead Charter mark. Sabriel also felt the presence of Dead things. Lesser Dead, hiding from sunlight, lurking somewhere nearby, in house or cellar.

At the end of the main street, on the highest point of the bluff, a Charter Stone stood on a patch of carefully tended lawn. Half of the stone had been sheared away, pieces broken and tumbled, dark stone on green turf. A body lay in front of the stone, hands and feet bound, the gaping cut across the throat a clear sign of where the blood had come from—the blood for the sacrifice that broke the stone.

Sabriel knelt by the corpse, eyes averted from the broken stone. It was only recently ruined, she felt, but already the door to Death was creaking open. She could almost feel the cold of the currents beyond, leaking out around the stone, sucking warmth and life from the air. Things lurked there too, she knew, just beyond the border. She sensed their hunger for life, their impatience for night to fall.

As she expected, the corpse was of a Charter Mage, dead but three or four days. But she hadn't expected to find the dead person was a woman. Wide shoulders and a muscular build had deceived her for a moment, but there was a middle-aged woman before her, eyes shut, throat cut, short brown hair caked with sea salt and blood.

"The village healer," said Mogget, indicating a bracelet on her wrist with his nose. Sabriel pushed the rope bindings aside for a better look. The bracelet was bronze with inlaid Charter marks of greenstone. Dead marks now, for blood dried upon the bronze, and no pulse beat in the skin under the metal.

"She was killed three or four days ago," Sabriel announced. "The stone was broken at the same time."

Touchstone looked back at her and nodded grimly, then resumed watching the houses opposite. His swords hung loosely in his hands, but Sabriel noticed that his entire body was tense, like a compressed jack-in-the-box, ready to spring.

"Whoever . . . whatever . . . killed her and broke the stone, didn't enslave her spirit," Sabriel added quietly, as if thinking to herself. "I wonder why?"

Neither Mogget nor Touchstone answered. For a moment, Sabriel considered asking the woman herself, but her impetuous desire for journeys into Death had been soundly dampened by recent experience. Instead, she cut the woman's bonds, and arranged her as best she could, ending up with a sort of curled-up sleeping position.

"I don't know your name, Healer," Sabriel whispered. "But I hope you go quickly beyond the Final Gate. Farewell."

She stood back and drew the Charter marks for the funeral pyre above the corpse, whispering the names of the marks as she did so—but her fingers fumbled and words went awry. The baleful influence of the broken stone pressed against her, like a wrestler gripping her wrists, clamping her jaw. Sweat beaded on her forehead, and pain shot through her limbs, her hands shaking with effort, tongue clumsy, seeming swollen in her suddenly dry mouth.

Then she felt assistance come, strength flowing through her, reinforcing the marks, steadying her hands, clearing her voice. She completed the litany, and a spark exploded above the woman, became a twisting flame, then grew to a fierce, white-hot blaze that spread the length of the woman's body, totally consuming it, to leave only ash, light cargo for the sea winds.

The extra strength came through Touchstone's hand, his open palm lightly resting on her shoulder. As she straightened up, the touch was lost. When Sabriel turned around, Touchstone was just drawing his right-hand sword, eyes fixed on the houses—as if he'd had nothing to do with helping her.

"Thank you," said Sabriel. Touchstone was a strong Charter Mage, perhaps as strong as she was. This surprised her, though she couldn't think why. He'd made no secret of being a Charter Mage—she'd just assumed he would only know a few of the more fighting-related marks and spells. Petty magics.

"We should move on," said Mogget, prowling backwards and forwards in agitation, carefully avoiding the fragments from the broken stone. "Find a boat, and put to sea before nightfall."

"The harbor is that way," Touchstone added quickly, pointing with his sword. Both he and the cat seemed very keen to leave the area around the broken stone, thought Sabriel. But then, so was she. Even in bright daylight, it seemed to dull the color around it. The lawn was already more yellow than green, and even the shadows looked thicker and more abundant than they should. She shivered, remembering Cloven Crest and the thing called Thralk.

The harbor lay on the northern side of the bluff, reached by another series of steps in the rocky hill, or in the case of cargo, via one of the shear-legged hoists that lined the edge of the bluff. Long wooden jetties thrust out into the clear blue-green water, sheltered under the lee of a rocky island, a smaller sibling of the village bluff. A long breakwater of huge boulders joined island and shore, completing the harbor's protection from wind and wave.

There were no boats moored in the harbor, tied up to the jetties, or at the harbor wall. Not even a dinghy, hauled up for repair. Sabriel stood on the steps, looking down, mind temporarily devoid of further plans. She just watched the swirl of the sea around the barnacled piles of the jetties; the moving shadows in the blue, marking small fish schooling about their business. Mogget sat near her feet, sniffing the air, silent. Touchstone stood higher, behind her, guarding the rear.

"What now?" asked Sabriel, generally indicating the empty harbor below, her arm moving with the same rhythm as the swell, in its perpetual tilt against wood and stone.

"There are people on the island," Mogget said, eyes slitted against the wind. "And boats tied up between the two outcrops of rock on the southwest."

Sabriel looked, but saw nothing, till she extracted the telescope from the pack on Touchstone's back. He stood completely still while she ferreted around, silent as the empty village. Playing wooden again, Sabriel thought, but she didn't really mind. He was being helpful, without metaphorically tugging his forelock every few minutes.

Through the telescope, she saw that Mogget was right. There were several boats partly hidden between two spurs of rock, and some slight signs of habitation: a glimpse of a washing line, blown around the corner of a tall rock; the momentary sight of movement between two of the six or seven ramshackle wooden buildings that nestled on the island's south-western side.

Shifting her gaze to the breakwater, Sabriel followed its length. As she'd half expected, there was a gap in the very middle of it, where the sea rushed through with considerable force. A pile of timber on the island side of the breakwater indicated that there had once been a bridge there, now removed.

"It looks like the villagers fled to the island," she said, shutting the telescope down. "There's a gap in the breakwater, to keep running water between the island and shore. An ideal defense against the Dead. I don't think even a Mordicant would risk crossing deep tidal water—"

"Let's go then," muttered Touchstone. He sounded nervous again, jumpy. Sabriel looked at him, then above his head, and saw why he was nervous. Clouds were rolling in from the south-east, behind the village—dark clouds, laden with rain. The air was calm, but now she saw the clouds, Sabriel recognized it was the calm before heavy rain. The sun would not be guarding them for very much longer and night would be an early guest.

Without further urging, she set off down the steps, down to the harborside, then along to the breakwater. Touchstone followed more slowly, turning every few steps to watch the rear. Mogget did likewise, his small cat-face continually looking back, peering up at the houses.

Behind them, shutters inched open and fleshless eyes watched from the safety of shadows, watched the trio marching out to the breakwater, still washed in harsh sunlight, flanked by swift-moving waves of terrible water. Rotten, corroded teeth ground and gnashed in skeletal mouths. Farther back from the windows, shadows darker than ones ever cast by light whirled in frustration, anger—and fear. They all knew who had passed.

One such shadow, selected by lot and compelled by its peers, gave up its existence in Life with a silent scream, vanishing into Death. Their master was many, many leagues away, and the quickest way to reach him lay in Death. Of course, message delivered, the messenger would fall through the Gates to a final demise. But the master didn't care about that.

The gap in the breakwater proved to be at least fifteen feet wide, and the water was twice Sabriel's height, the sea surging through with a rough aggression. It was also covered by archers from the island, as they discovered when an arrow struck the stones in front of them and skittered off into the sea.

Instantly, Touchstone rushed in front of Sabriel, and she felt the flow of Charter Magic from him, his swords sketching a great circle in the air in front of them both. Glowing lines followed the swords' path, till a shining circle hung in the air.

Four arrows curved through the air from the island. One, striking the circle, simply vanished. The other three missed completely, striking stones or sea.

"Arrow ward," gasped Touchstone. "Effective, but hard to keep going. Do we retreat?"

"Not yet," replied Sabriel. She could feel the Dead stirring in the village behind them and she could also see the archers now. There were four of them, two pairs, each behind one of the large, upthrust stones that marked where the breakwater joined the island. They looked young, nervous and were already proven to be of little threat.

"Hold!" shouted Sabriel. "We are friends!"

There was no reply, but the archers didn't loose their nocked arrows.

"What's the village leader's title—usually, I mean? What are they called?" Sabriel whispered hurriedly to Touchstone, once again wishing she knew more about the Old Kingdom and its customs.

"In my day . . ." Touchstone replied slowly, his swords retracing the arrow ward, attention mostly on that, "in my day—Elder—for this size of village."

"We wish to speak with your Elder!" shouted Sabriel. She pointed at the cloud-front advancing behind her, and added, "Before darkness falls!"

"Wait!" came the answer, and one of the archers scampered back from the rocks, up towards the buildings. Closer to, Sabriel realized they were probably boathouses or something like that.

The archer returned in a few minutes, an older man hobbling over the rocks behind him. The other three archers, seeing him, lowered their bows and returned shafts to quivers. Touchstone, seeing this, ceased to maintain the arrow ward. It hung in the air for a moment, then dissipated, leaving a momentary rainbow.

The Elder was named in fact, as well as title, they saw, as he limped along the breakwater. Long white hair blew like fragile cobwebs around his thin, wrinkled face, and he moved with the deliberate intention of the very old. He seemed unafraid, perhaps possessed of the disinterested courage of one already close to death.

"Who are you?" he asked, when he reached the gap, standing above the swirling waters like some prophet of legend, his deep orange cloak flapping around him from the rising breeze. "What do you want?"

Sabriel opened her mouth to answer, but Touchstone had already started to speak. Loudly.

"I am Touchstone, sworn swordsman for the Abhorsen, who stands before you. Are arrows your welcome for such folk as we?"

The old man was silent for a moment, his deep-set eyes focused on Sabriel, as if he could strip away any falsity or illusion by sight alone. Sabriel met his gaze, but out of the corner of her mouth she whispered to Touchstone.

"What makes you think you can speak for me? Wouldn't a friendly approach be better? And since when are you my sworn—"

She stopped, as the old man cleared his throat to speak and spat into the water. For a moment, she thought that this was his response, but as neither the archers nor Touchstone reacted, it was obviously of no account.

"These are bad times," the Elder said. "We have been forced to leave our firesides for the smoking sheds, warmth and comfort for seawinds and the stench of fish. Many of the people of Nestowe are dead—or worse. Strangers and travelers are rare in such times, and not always what they seem."

"I am the Abhorsen," Sabriel said, reluctantly. "Enemy of the Dead."

"I remember," replied the old man, slowly. "Abhorsen came here when I was a young man. He came to put down the haunts that the spice merchant brought, Charter curse him. Abhorsen. I remember that coat you're wearing, blue as a ten-fathom sea, with the silver keys. There was a sword, also . . ."

He paused, expectantly. Sabriel stood, silently, waiting for him to go on.

"He wants to see the sword," Touchstone said, voice flat, after the silence stretched too far.

"Oh," replied Sabriel, flushing.

It was quite obvious. Carefully, so as not to alarm the archers, she drew her sword, holding it up to the sun, so the Charter marks could clearly be seen, silver dancers on the blade.

"Yes," sighed the Elder, old shoulders sagging with relief. "That is the sword. Charter-spelled. She is the Abhorsen."

He turned and tottered back towards the archers, worn voice increasing to the ghost of a fisherman's cross-water hail. "Come on, you four. Quick with the bridge. We have visitors! Help at last!"

Sabriel glanced at Touchstone, raising her eyebrows at the implication of the old man's last three words. Surprisingly, Touchstone met her gaze, and held it.

"It is traditional for someone of high rank, such as yourself, to be announced by their sworn swordsman," he said quietly. "And the only acceptable way for me to travel with you is as your sworn swordsman. Otherwise, people will assume that we are, at best, illicit lovers. Having your name coupled to mine in such a guise would lower you in most eyes. You see?"

"Ah," replied Sabriel, gulping, feeling the flush of embarrassment come back and spread from her cheeks to her neck. It felt a lot like being on the receiving end of one of Miss Prionte's severest social put-downs. She hadn't even thought about how it would look, the two of them traveling together. Certainly, in Ancelstierre, it would be considered shameful, but this was the Old Kingdom, where things were different. But only some things, it seemed.

"Lesson two hundred and seven," muttered Mogget from somewhere near her feet. "Three out of ten. I wonder if they've got any fresh-caught whiting? I'd like a small one, still flopping—"

"Be quiet!" Sabriel interrupted. "You'd better pretend to be a normal cat for a while."

"Very well, milady. Abhorsen," Mogget replied, stalking away to sit on the other side of Touchstone.

Sabriel was about to reply scathingly when she saw the faintest curve at the corner of Touchstone's mouth. Touchstone? Grinning? Surprised, she misplaced the retort on her tongue, then forgot it altogether, as the four archers heaved a plank across the gap, the end smacking down onto stone with a startling bang.

"Please cross quickly," the Elder said, as the men steadied the plank. "There are many fell creatures in the village now, and I fear the day is almost done."

True to his words, cloud-shadow fell across them as he spoke, and the fresh scent of closing rain mingled with the wet and salty smell of the sea. Without further urging, Sabriel ran quickly across the plank, Mogget behind her, Touchstone bringing up the rear.

Chapter Seventeen

ALL THE SURVIVORS of Nestowe were gathered in the largest of the fish-smoking sheds, save for the current shift of archers who watched the breakwater. There had been one hundred and twenty-six villagers the week before—now there were thirty-one.

"There were thirty-two until this morning," the Elder said to Sabriel, as he passed her a cup of passable wine and a piece of dried fish atop a piece of very hard, very stale bread. "We thought we were safe when we got to the island, but Monjer Stowart's boy was found just after dawn today, sucked dry like a husk. When we touched him, it was like . . . burnt paper, that still holds its shape . . . we touched him, and he crumbled into flakes of . . . something like ash."

Sabriel looked around as the old man spoke, noting the many lanterns, candles and rush tapers that added both to the light and the smoky, fishy atmosphere of the shed. The survivors were a very mixed group—men, women and children, from very young to the Elder himself. Their only common characteristic was the fear pinching their faces, the fear showing in their nervous, staccato movement.

"We think one of them's here," said a woman, her voice long gone beyond fear to fatalism. She stood alone, accompanied by the clear space of tragedy. Sabriel guessed she had lost her family. Husband, children—perhaps parents and siblings too, for she wasn't over forty.

"It'll take us, one by one," the woman continued, matter-of-fact, her voice filling the shed with dire certainty. Around her, people shuffled, twitchily, not looking at her, as if to meet her gaze would be to accept her words. Most looked at Sabriel and she saw hope in their eyes. Not blind faith, or complete confidence, but a gambler's hope that a new horse might change a run of losses.

"The Abhorsen who came when I was young," the Elder continued—and Sabriel saw that at his age, this would be his memory alone, of all the villagers—"this Abhorsen told me that it was his purpose to slay the Dead. He saved us from the haunts that came in the merchant's caravan. Is it still the same, lady? Will Abhorsen save us from the Dead?"

Sabriel thought for a moment, her mind mentally flicking through the pages of *The Book of the Dead*, feeling it stir in the backpack that sat by her feet. Her thoughts strayed to her father; the forthcoming journey to Belisaere; the way in which Dead enemies seemed to be arrayed against her by some controlling mind.

"I will ensure this island is free of the Dead," she said at last, speaking clearly so all could hear her. "But I cannot free the mainland village. There is a greater evil at work in the Kingdom—that same evil that has broken your Charter Stone—and I must find and defeat it as soon as I can. When that is done, I will return—I hope with other help—and both village and Charter Stone will be restored."

"We understand," replied the Elder. He seemed saddened, but philosophic. He continued, speaking more to his people than to Sabriel. "We can survive here. There is the spring, and the fish. We have boats. If Callibe has not fallen to the Dead, we can trade, for vegetables and other stuffs."

"You will have to keep watching the breakwater," Touchstone

said. He stood behind Sabriel's chair, the very image of a stern bodyguard. "The Dead—or their living slaves—may try to fill it in with stones, or push across a bridge. They can cross running water by building bridges of boxed grave dirt."

"So, we are besieged," said a man to the front of the mass of villagers. "But what of this Dead thing already here on the island, already preying upon us? How will you find it?"

Silence fell as the questioner spoke, for this was the one answer everyone wanted to hear. Rain sounded loud on the roof in the absence of human speech, steady rain, as had been falling since late afternoon. The Dead disliked the rain, Sabriel thought inconsequentially, as she considered this question. Rain didn't destroy, but it hurt and irritated the Dead. Wherever the Dead thing was on the island, it would be out of the rain.

She stood up with that thought. Thirty-one pairs of eyes watched her, hardly blinking, despite the cloying smoke from too many lanterns, candles and tapers. Touchstone watched the villagers; Mogget watched a piece of fish; Sabriel closed her eyes, questing outward with other senses, trying to feel the presence of the Dead.

It was there—a faint, concealed emanation, like an untraceable whiff of something rotten. Sabriel concentrated on it, followed it, and found it, right there in the shed. The Dead was somehow hiding among the villagers.

She opened her eyes slowly, looking straight at the point where her senses told her the Dead creature lurked. She saw a fisherman, middle-aged, his salt-etched face red under sunbleached hair. He seemed no different than the others around him, listening intently for her reply, but there was definitely something Dead in him, or very close by. He was wearing a boat cloak, which seemed odd, since the smoking shed was hot from massed humanity and the many lights.

"Tell me," Sabriel said. "Did anyone bring a large box with them out to the island? Something, say, an arm-span square a side, or larger? It would be heavy—with grave dirt."

Murmurs and enquiries met this question, neighbors turning to each other, with little flowerings of fear and suspicion. As they talked, Sabriel walked out through them, surreptitiously loosening her sword, signaling Touchstone to stay close by her. He followed her, eyes flickering across the little groups of villagers. Mogget, glancing up from his fish, stretched and lazily stalked behind Touchstone's heels, after a warning glare at the two cats who were eyeing the half-consumed head and tail of his fishy repast.

Careful not to alarm her quarry, Sabriel took a zigzag path through the shed, listening to the villagers with studied attention, though the blond fisherman never left the corner of her eye. He was deep in discussion with another man, who seemed to be growing more suspicious by the second.

Closer now, Sabriel was sure that the fisherman was a vassal of the Dead. Technically, he was still alive, but a Dead spirit had suppressed his will, riding on his flesh like some shadowy string-puller, using his body as a puppet. Something highly unpleasant would be half-submerged in his back, under the boat cloak. Mordaut, they were called, Sabriel remembered. A whole page was devoted to these parasitical spirits in *The Book of the Dead*. They liked to keep a primary host alive, slipping off at night to sate their hunger from other living prey—like children.

"I'm sure I saw you with a box like that, Patar," the suspicious fisherman was saying. "Jall Stowart helped you get it ashore. Hey, Jall!"

He shouted that last, turning to look at someone else across the room. In that instant, the Dead-ridden Patar exploded into action, clubbing his questioner with both forearms, knocking

him aside, running to the door with the silent ferocity of a battering ram.

But Sabriel had expected that. She stood before him, sword
at the ready, her left hand drawing Ranna, the sweet sleeper, from
the bandolier. She still hoped to save the man, by quelling the
Mordaut.

Patar slid to a halt and half-turned, but Touchstone was there
behind him, twin swords glowing eerily with shifting Charter
marks and silver flames. Sabriel eyed the blades in surprise, she
hadn't known they were spelled. Past time she asked, she realized.

Then Ranna was free in her hand—but the Mordaut didn't
wait for the unavoidable lullaby. Patar suddenly screamed, and
stood rigid, the redness draining from his face, to be replaced by
grey. Then his flesh crumpled and fell apart, even his bones flaking away to soggy ash as the Mordaut sucked all the life out of
him in one voracious instant. Newly fed and strengthened, the
Dead slid out from the falling cloak, a pool of squelching darkness. It took shape as it moved, becoming a large, disgustingly
elongated sort of rat. Quicker than any natural rat, it scuttled
towards a hole in the wall and escape!

Sabriel lunged, her blade striking chips from the floor planks,
missing the shadowy form by a scant instant.

Touchstone didn't miss. His right-hand sword sheared
through the creature just behind the head, the left-wielded blade
impaling its sinuous mid-section. Pinned to the floor, the creature writhed and arched, its shadow-stuff working away from the
blades. It was remaking its body, escaping the trap.

Quickly, Sabriel stood over it, Ranna sounding in her hand,
sweet, lazy tone echoing out into the shed.

Before the echoes died, the Mordaut ceased to writhe. Form
half-lost by its shifting from the swords, it lay like a lump of
charred liver, quivering on the floor, still impaled.

Sabriel replaced Ranna, and drew the eager Saraneth. Its forceful voice snapped out, sound weaving a net of domination over the foul creature. The Mordaut made no effort to resist, even to make a mouth to whine its cause. Sabriel felt it succumb to her will, via the medium of Saraneth.

She put the bell back, but hesitated as her hand fell on Kibeth. Sleeper and Master had spoken well, but Walker sometimes had its own ideas, and it was stirring suspiciously under her hand. Best to wait a moment, to calm herself, Sabriel thought, taking her hand away from the bandolier. She sheathed her sword, and looked around the shed. To her surprise, everyone except Touchstone and Mogget was asleep. They had only caught the echoes of Ranna, which shouldn't have been enough. Of course, Ranna could be tricksome too, but its trickery was far less troublesome.

"This is a Mordaut," she said to Touchstone, who was stifling a half-born yawn. "A weak spirit, catalogued as one of the Lesser Dead. They like to ride with the Living—cohabiting the body to some extent, directing it, and slowly sipping the spirit away. It makes them hard to find."

"What do we do with it now?" asked Touchstone, eyeing the quivering lump of shadow with distaste. It clearly couldn't be cut up, consumed by fire, or anything else he could think of.

"I will banish it, send it back to die a true death," replied Sabriel. Slowly, she drew Kibeth, using both hands. She still felt uneasy, for the bell was twisting in her grasp, trying to sound of its own accord, a sound that would make her walk in Death.

She gripped it harder and rang the orthodox backwards, forwards and figure eight her father had taught her. Kibeth's voice rang out, singing a merry tune, a capering jig that almost had Sabriel's feet jumping too, till she forced herself to be absolutely still.

The Mordaut had no such free will. For a moment, Touchstone thought it was getting away, the shadow form suddenly leaping upwards, unreal flesh slipping up his blades almost to the cross-hilts. Then, it slid back down again—and vanished. Back into Death, to bob and spin in the current, howling and screaming with whatever voice it had there, all the way through to the Final Gate.

"Thanks," Sabriel said to Touchstone. She looked down at his two swords, still deeply embedded in the wooden floor. They were no longer burning with silver flames, but she could see the Charter marks moving on the blades.

"I didn't realize your swords were ensorcelled," she continued. "Though I'm glad they are."

Surprise crossed Touchstone's face, and confusion.

"I thought you knew," he said. "I took them from the Queen's ship. They were a Royal Champion's swords. I didn't want to take them, but Mogget said you—"

He stopped in mid-sentence, as Sabriel let out a heartfelt sigh.

"Well, anyway," he continued. "Legend has it that the Wallmaker made them, at the same time he—or she, I suppose—made your sword."

"Mine?" asked Sabriel, her hand lightly touching the worn bronze of the guard. She'd never thought about who'd made the sword—it just was. "I was made for Abhorsen, to slay those already Dead," the inscription said, when it said anything lucid at all. So it probably was forged long ago, back in the distant past when the Wall was made. Mogget would know, she thought. Mogget probably wouldn't, or couldn't, tell her—but he would know.

"I suppose we'd better wake everybody up," she said, dismissing speculation about swords for the immediate present.

"Are there more Dead?" asked Touchstone, grunting as he

pulled his swords free of the floor.

"I don't think so," replied Sabriel. "That Mordaut was very clever, for it had hardly sapped the spirit of poor . . . Patar . . . so its presence was masked by his life. It would have come to the island in that box of grave dirt, having impressed the poor man with instructions before they left the mainland. I doubt whether any others would have done the same. I can't sense any here, at least. I guess I should check the other buildings, and walk around the island, just to be sure."

"Now?" asked Touchstone.

"Now," confirmed Sabriel. "But let's wake everyone up first, and organize some people to carry lights for us. We'd also better talk to the Elder about a boat for the morning."

"And a good supply of fish," added Mogget, who'd slunk back to the half-eaten whiting, his voice sharp above the heavy drone of snoring fisher-folk.

There were no Dead on the island, though the archers reported seeing strange lights moving in the village, during brief lulls in the rain. They'd heard movement on the breakwater too, and shot fire arrows onto the stones, but saw nothing before the crude, oily rag-wrapped shafts guttered out.

Sabriel advanced out on the breakwater, and stood near the sea gap, her oilskin coat loosely draped over her shoulders, shedding rain to the ground and down her neck. She couldn't see anything through the rain and dark, but she could feel the Dead. There were more than she had sensed earlier, or they had grown much stronger. Then, with a sickening feeling, she realized that this strength belonged to a single creature, only now emerging from Death, using the broken stone as a portal. An instant later, she recognized its particular presence.

The Mordicant had found her.

"Touchstone," she asked, fighting to keep the shivers from

her voice. "Can you sail a boat by night?"

"Yes," replied Touchstone, his voice impersonal again, face dark in the rainy night, the lantern-light from the villagers behind him lighting only his back and feet. He hesitated, as if he shouldn't be offering an opinion, then added, "But it would be much more dangerous. I don't know this coast, and the night is very dark."

"Mogget can see in the dark," Sabriel said quietly, moving closer to Touchstone so the villagers couldn't hear her.

"We have to leave immediately," she whispered, while pretending to adjust her oilskin. "A Mordicant has come. The same one that pursued me before."

"What about the people here?" asked Touchstone, so softly the sound of the rain almost washed his words away—but there was the faint sound of reproof under his business-like tone.

"The Mordicant is after me," muttered Sabriel. She could sense it moving away from the stone, questing about, using its otherwordly senses to find her. "It can feel my presence, as I feel it. When I go, it will follow."

"If we stay till morning," Touchstone whispered back, "won't we be safe? You said even a Mordicant couldn't cross this gap."

"I said, 'I think,'" faltered Sabriel. "It has grown stronger. I can't be sure—"

"That thing back in the shed, the Mordaut, it wasn't very difficult to destroy," Touchstone whispered, the confidence of ignorance in his voice. "Is this Mordicant much worse?"

"Much," replied Sabriel shortly.

The Mordicant had stopped moving. The rain seemed to be dampening both its senses and its desire to find her and slay. Sabriel stared vainly out into the darkness, trying to peer past the sheets of rain, to gain the evidence provided by sight, as well as her necromantic senses.

"Riemer," she said, loudly now, calling to the villager who was in charge of their lantern-holders. He came forward quickly, gingery hair plastered flat on his rounded head, rainwater dripping down from a high forehead to catapult itself off the end of his pudgy nose.

"Riemer, have the archers keep very careful watch. Tell them to shoot anything that comes onto the breakwater—there is nothing living out there now. Only the Dead. We need to go back and talk to your Elder."

They walked back in silence, save for the sloshing of boots in puddles and the steady finger-applause of the rain. At least half of Sabriel's attention stayed with the Mordicant; a malign, stomachache-inducing presence across the dark water. She wondered why it was waiting. Waiting for the rain to stop, or perhaps for the now-banished Mordaut to attack from within. Whatever its reasons, it gave them a little time to get to a boat, and lead it away. And perhaps, there was always the chance that it couldn't cross the breakwater gap.

"What time is low tide?" she asked Riemer, as a new thought struck.

"Ah, just about an hour before dawn," replied the fisherman. "About six hours, if I'm any judge."

The Elder awoke crankily from his second sleep. He was loath for them to go in the night, though Sabriel felt that at least half of his reluctance was due to their need for a boat. The villagers only had five left. The others had been sunk in the harbor, drowned and broken by the stones hurled down by the Dead, eager to stop the escape of their living prey.

"I'm sorry," Sabriel said again. "But we must have a boat and we need it now. There is a terrible Dead creature in the village—it tracks like a hunting dog, and the trail it follows is mine. If I stay, it will try and come here—and, at the ebb, it may be able to cross the gap in the breakwater. If I go, it will follow."

"Very well," the Elder agreed, mulishly. "You have cleansed this island for us; a boat is a little thing. Riemer will prepare it with food and water. Riemer! The Abhorsen will have Landalin's boat—make sure it is stocked and seaworthy. Take sails from Jaled, if Landalin's is short or rotten."

"Thank you," said Sabriel. Tiredness weighed down on her, tiredness and the weight of awareness. Awareness of her enemies, like a darkness always clouding the edge of her vision. "We will go now. My good wishes stay with you, and my hopes for your safety."

"May the Charter preserve us all," added Touchstone, bowing to the old man. The Elder bowed back, a bent, solemn figure, so much smaller than his shadow, looming tall on the wall behind.

Sabriel turned to go, but a long line of villagers was forming on the way to the door. All of them wanted to bow or curtsey before her, to mutter shy thank-yous and farewells. Sabriel accepted them with embarrassment and guilt, remembering Patar. True, she had banished the dead, but another life had been lost in the doing. Her father would not have been so clumsy . . .

The second-to-last person in the line was a little girl, her black hair tied in two plaits, one on either side of her head. Seeing her made Sabriel remember something Touchstone had said. She stopped, and took the girl's hands in her own.

"What is your name, little one?" she asked, smiling. A feeling of déjà vu swept over her as the small fingers met hers—the memory of a frightened first-grader hesitantly reaching out to the older pupil who would be her guide for the first day at Wyverley College. Sabriel had experienced both sides, in her time.

"Aline," said the girl, smiling back. Her eyes were bright and lively, too young to be dimmed by the frightened despair that clouded the adults' gaze. A good choice, Sabriel thought.

"Now, tell me what you have learned in your lessons about the Great Charter," Sabriel said, adopting the familiar, motherly and generally irrelevant questioning tone of the School Inspector who'd descended on every class in Wyverley twice a year.

"I know the rhyme . . ." replied Aline, a little doubtfully, her small forehead crinkling. "Shall I sing it, like we do in class?"

Sabriel nodded.

"We dance around the stone, too," Aline added, confidingly. She stood up straighter, put one foot forward, and took her hands away to clasp them behind her back.

Five Great Charters knit the land
together linked, hand in hand
One in the people who wear the crown
Two in the folk who keep the Dead down
Three and Five became stone and mortar
Four sees all in frozen water.

"Thank you, Aline," Sabriel said. "That was very nice."

She ruffled the child's hair and hastened through the final farewells, suddenly keen to get out of the smoke and the fish-smell, out into the clean, rainy air where she could think.

"So now you know," whispered Mogget, jumping up into her arms to escape the puddles. "I still can't tell you, but you know one's in your blood."

"Two," replied Sabriel distantly. "'Two in the folk who keep the Dead down.' So what is the . . . ah . . . I can't talk about it either!"

But she thought about the questions she'd like to ask, as Touchstone helped her aboard the small fishing vessel that lay just off the tiny, shell-laden beach that served the island as a harbor.

One of the Great Charters lay in the royal blood. The second lay in Abhorsen's. What were three and five, and four that saw all in frozen water? She felt certain that many answers could be found in Belisaere. Her father could probably answer more, for many things that were bound in Life were unraveled in Death. And there was her mother-sending, for that third and final questioning in this seven years.

Touchstone pushed off, clambered aboard and took the oars. Mogget leapt out of Sabriel's arms, and assumed a figurehead position near the prow, serving as a night-sighted lookout, while mocking Touchstone at the same time.

Back on shore, the Mordicant suddenly howled, a long, piercing cry that echoed far across the water, chilling hearts on both boat and island.

"Bear a bit more to starboard," said Mogget, in the silence after the howl faded. "We need more sea-room."

Touchstone was quick to comply.

Chapter Eighteen

B Y THE MORNING of the sixth day out of Nestowe,
Sabriel was heartily tired of nautical life. They'd sailed
virtually non-stop all that time, only putting into shore
at noon for fresh water, and only then when it was sunny. Nights
were spent under sail, or, when exhaustion claimed Touchstone,
hove-to with a sea anchor, the unsleeping Mogget standing
watch. Fortunately, the weather had been kind.

It had been a relatively uneventful five days. Two days from
Nestowe to Beardy Point, an unprepossessing peninsula whose
only interesting features were a sandy-bottomed beach and a
clear stream. Devoid of life, it was also devoid of the Dead. Here,
for the first time, Sabriel could no longer sense the pursuing
Mordicant. A good, strong, south-easterly had propelled them,
reaching northwards, at too fast a pace for it to follow.

Three days from Beardy Point to the island of Ilgard, its
rocky cliffs climbing sheer from the sea, a grey and pockmarked
tenement, home to tens of thousands of seabirds. They passed it
late in the afternoon, their single sail stretched to bursting,
clinker-built hull heeling well over, bow slicing up a column of
spray that salted mouths, eyes and bodies.

It was half a day from Ilgard to the Belis Mouth, that narrow
strait that led to the Sea of Saere. But that was tricky sailing, so
they spent the night hove-to just out of sight of Ilgard, to wait
for the light of day.

"There is a boom-chain across the Belis Mouth," Touchstone explained, as he raised the sail and Sabriel hauled the sea anchor in over the bow. The sun was rising behind him, but had not yet pulled itself out of the sea, so he was no more than a dim shadow in the stern. "It was built to keep pirates and suchlike out of the Sea of Saere. You won't believe the size of it—I can't imagine how it was forged, or strung across."

"Will it still be there?" Sabriel asked, cautiously, not wanting to prevent Touchstone's strangely talkative mood.

"I'm sure of it," replied Touchstone. "We'll see the towers on the opposite shores first. Winding Post, to the south, and Boom Hook to the north."

"Not very imaginative names," commented Sabriel, unable to help herself from interrupting. It was just such a pleasure to talk! Touchstone had lapsed back into non-communication for most of the voyage, though he did have a good excuse—handling the fishing boat for eighteen hours a day, even in good weather, didn't leave much energy for conversation.

"They're named after their purpose," replied Touchstone. "Which makes sense."

"Who decides whether to let vessels past the chain?" asked Sabriel. Already, she was thinking ahead, wondering about Belisaere. Could it be like Nestowe—the city abandoned, riddled with the Dead?

"Ah," said Touchstone. "I hadn't thought about that. In my time, there was a Royal Boom Master, with a force of guards and a squadron of small, picket ships. If, as Mogget says, the city has fallen into anarchy . . ."

"There may also be people working for, or in alliance with, the Dead," Sabriel added thoughtfully. "So even if we cross the boom in daylight, there could be trouble. I think I'd better reverse my surcoat and hide my helmet wrapping."

"What about the bells?" asked Touchstone. He leaned past her, to draw the main sheet tighter, right hand slightly nudging the tiller to take advantage of a shift in the wind. "They're fairly obvious, to say the least."

"I'll just look like a necromancer," Sabriel replied. "A salty, unwashed necromancer."

"I don't know," said Touchstone, who couldn't see that Sabriel was joking. "No necromancer would be let into the city, or would stay alive, in—"

"In your day," interrupted Mogget, from his favorite post on the bow. "But this is now, and I am sure that necromancers and worse are not uncommon sights in Belisaere."

"I'll wear a cloak—" Sabriel started to say.

"If you say so," Touchstone said, at the same time. Clearly, he didn't believe the cat. Belisaere was the royal capital, a huge city, home to at least fifty thousand people. Touchstone couldn't imagine it fallen, decayed and in the hands of the Dead. Despite his own inner fears and secret knowledge, he couldn't help but be confident that the Belisaere they were sailing towards would be little different from the two-hundred-year-old images locked in his memory.

That confidence took a blow as the Belis Mouth towers became visible above the blue line of the horizon, on opposite shores of the strait. At first, the towers were no more than dark smudges, that grew taller as wind and wave carried the boat towards them. Through her telescope, Sabriel saw that they were made from a beautiful, rosy-pink stone that once must have been magnificent. Now they were largely blackened by fire; their majesty vanished. Winding Post had lost the top three storys, from seven; Boom Hook stood as tall as ever, but sunlight shone through gaping holes, showing the interior to be a gutted ruin. There was no sign of any garrison, toll collector, windlass mules, or anything alive.

The great boom-chain still stretched across the strait. Huge iron links, each as wide and long as the fishing boat, rose green and barnacle-befouled out of the water and up into each of the towers. Glimpses of it could be seen in the middle of the Mouth, when the swell dipped, and a length of chain shone slick and green in the wave trough, like some lurking monster of the deep.

"We'll have to go in close to the Winding Post tower, unstep the mast and row under the chain where it rises," Touchstone declared, after studying the chain for several minutes through the telescope, trying to gauge whether it had sunk enough to allow them passage. But even with their relatively shallow-draft boat, it would be too risky, and they daren't wait for high tide, late in the afternoon. At some time in the past, perhaps when the towers were abandoned, the chain had been winched up to its maximum tension. The engineers who'd made it would have been pleased, for there seemed to be no noticeable slippage.

"Mogget, go to the bow and keep a lookout for anything in the water. Sabriel, could you please watch the shore and the tower, to guard against attack."

Sabriel nodded, pleased that Touchstone's stint as captain of their small vessel had done a lot to remove the servant nonsense out of him and make him more like a normal person. Mogget, for his part, jumped up to the bow without protest, despite the spray that occasionally burst over his head as they cut diagonally across the swell—towards the small triangle of opportunity between shore, sea and chain.

They came in as close as they dared before unstepping the mast. The swell had diminished, for the Belis Mouth was well-sheltered by the two arms of land, but the tide had turned, and a tidal race was beginning to run from the ocean to the Saere Sea. So, even without mast and sail, they were borne rapidly towards the chain; Touchstone rowing with all his strength just to keep steerage way. After a moment, this clearly became impossible, so Sabriel took one of the oars, and they rowed together, with Mogget yowling directions.

Every few seconds, at the end of a full stroke, her back nearly level with the thwarts, Sabriel snatched a glimpse over her shoulder. They were headed for the narrow passage, between the high but crumbling seawall of Winding Post, and the enormous chain rising out of the swift-flowing sea in a swath of white froth. She could hear the melancholy groaning of the links, like a chorus of pained walruses. Even that gargantuan chain moved at the sea's whim.

"Port a little," yowled Mogget. Touchstone backed his oar for a moment, then the cat jumped down, yelling, "Ship oars and duck!"

The oars came rattling, splashing in, both Sabriel and Touchstone simply lying down on their backs, with Mogget somewhere between them. The boat rocked and plunged, and the groan of the chain sounded close and terrible. Sabriel, one moment looking up at the clear, blue sky, in the next saw nothing but green, weed-strewn iron above her. When the swell lifted the boat up, she could have reached out and touched the great boom-chain of Belis Mouth.

Then they were past, and Touchstone was already pushing out his oar, Mogget moving to the bow. Sabriel wanted to lie there, just looking up at the sky, but the collapsed seawall of Winding Post was no more than an oar-length away. She sat up and resumed her duty as a rower.

The water changed color in the Sea of Saere. Sabriel trailed her hand in it, marveling at its clear turquoise sheen. For all its color, it was incredibly transparent. The water was very deep, but she could see down the first three or four fathoms, watching small fish dance under the bubbles of their boat's wake.

She felt relaxed, momentarily carefree, all the troubles that lay ahead and behind her temporarily lost in single-minded contemplation of the clear blue-green water. There was no Dead presence here, no constant awareness of the many doors to Death. Even Charter Magic was dissipated at sea. For a few minutes, she forgot about Touchstone and Mogget. Even her father faded from her mind. There was only the sea's color, and its coolness on her hand.

"We'll be able to see the city soon," Touchstone said, interrupting her mental holiday. "If the towers are still standing."

Sabriel nodded thoughtfully, and slowly took her hand from the sea, as if she were parting from a dear friend.

"It must be difficult for you," she said, almost to herself, not really expecting him to answer. "Two hundred years gone, the Kingdom slowly falling into ruin while you slept."

"I didn't really believe it, till I saw Nestowe, and then the Belis Mouth towers," replied Touchstone. "Now I am afraid—even for a great city that I never believed could really change."

"No imagination," said Mogget, sternly. "No thinking ahead. A flaw in your character. A fatal flaw."

"Mogget," Sabriel said indignantly, angry at the cat for crushing yet another possible conversation. "Why are you so rude to Touchstone?"

Mogget hissed and the fur bristled on his back.

"I am accurate, not rude," he snapped, turning his back to them with studied scorn. "And he deserves it."

"I'm sick of this!" announced Sabriel. "Touchstone, what does Mogget know that I don't?"

Touchstone was silent, knuckles white on the tiller, eyes focused on the distant horizon, as if he could already see the towers of Belisaere.

"You'll have to tell me eventually," said Sabriel, a touch of the prefect entering her voice. "It can't be that bad, surely?"

Touchstone wet his lips, hesitated, then spoke.

"It was stupidity on my part, not evil, milady. Two hundred years ago, when the last Queen reigned . . . I think . . . I know that I am partly responsible for the failing of the Kingdom, the end of the royal line."

"What!" exclaimed Sabriel. "How could you be?"

"I am," continued Touchstone miserably, his hands shaking so much the tiller moved, giving the boat a crazy zigzag wake. "There was a . . . that is . . ."

He paused, took a deep breath, sat up a little straighter, and continued, as if reporting to a senior officer.

"I don't know how much I can tell you, because it involves the Great Charters. Where do I start? With the Queen, I guess. She had four children. Her oldest son, Rogir, was a childhood playmate of mine. He was always the leader, in all our games. He had the ideas—we followed them. Later, when we were growing up, his ideas became stranger, less nice. We grew apart. I went into the Guard; he pursued his own interests. Now I know that those interests must have included Free Magic and necromancy—I never suspected it then. I should have, I know, but he was secretive, and often away.

"Towards the end . . . I mean a few months before it happened . . . well, Rogir had been away for several years. He came back, just before the Midwinter Festival. I was glad to see him, for he seemed to be more like he was as a child. He'd lost interest in the bizarrities that had attracted him. We spent more time together again; hawking, riding, drinking, dancing.

"Then, late one afternoon—one cold, crisp afternoon, near sunset—I was on duty, guarding the Queen and her ladies. They were playing Cranaque. Rogir came to her, and asked her to come with him down to the place where the Great Stones are . . . hey, I can say it!"

"Yes," interrupted Mogget. He looked tired, like an alley cat that has suffered one kick too many. "The sea washes all things clear, for a time. We can speak of the Great Charters, at least for a little while. I had forgotten it was so."

"Go on," said Sabriel, excitedly. "Let's take advantage of it while we can. The Great Stones would be the stones and mortar of the rhyme—the Third and Fifth Great Charter?"

"Yes," replied Touchstone, remotely, as if reciting a lesson, "with the Wall. The people, or whatever they were who made the Great Charters, put three in bloodlines and two in physical constructions: the Wall and the Great Stones. All the lesser stones draw their power from one or the other.

"The Great Stones . . . Rogir came and said there was something amiss there, something the Queen must look into. He was her son, but she did not take great account of his wisdom, or believe him when he spoke of trouble with the Stones. She was a Charter Mage and felt nothing wrong. Besides, she was winning at Cranaque, so she told him to wait till morning. Rogir turned to me, asked me to intercede, and, Charter help me, I did. I believed Rogir. I trusted him and my belief convinced the Queen. Finally, she agreed. By that time, the sun had set. With Rogir, myself, three guards and two ladies-in-waiting, we went down, down into the reservoir where the Great Stones are."

Touchstone's voice faded to a whisper as he continued, and grew hoarse.

"There was terrible wrong down there, but it was Rogir's doing, not his discovery. There are six Great Stones and two were just being broken, broken with the blood of his own sisters, sacrificed by his Free Magic minions as we approached. I saw their last seconds, the faint hope in their clouding eyes, as the Queen's

barge came floating across the water. I felt the shock of the
Stones breaking and I remember Rogir, stepping up behind the
Queen, a saw-edged dagger striking so swiftly across her throat.
He had a cup, a golden cup, one of the Queen's own, to catch
the blood, but I was too slow, too slow . . ."

"So the story you told me at Holehallow wasn't true,"
Sabriel whispered, as Touchstone's voice cracked and faded, and
the tears rolled down his face. "The Queen didn't survive . . ."

"No," mumbled Touchstone. "But I didn't mean to lie. It was
all jumbled up in my head."

"What did happen?"

"The other two guards were Rogir's men," Touchstone continued, his voice wet with tears, muffled with sorrow. "They
attacked me, but Vlare—one of the ladies-in-waiting—threw
herself across them. I went mad, battle-mad, berserk. I killed
both guards. Rogir had jumped from the barge and was wading
to the Stones, holding the cup. His four sorcerers were waiting,
dark-cowled, around the third stone, the next to be broken. I
couldn't reach him in time, I knew. I threw my sword. It flew
straight and true, taking him just above the heart. He screamed,
the echo going on and on and he turned back towards me!
Transfixed by my sword, but still walking, holding that vile cup
of blood up, as if offering me a drink.

"'You may tear this body,' he said, as he walked. 'Rip it, like
some poor-made costume. But I cannot die.'

"He came within an arm's length of me, and I could only
look into his face, look at the evil that lay so close behind those
familiar features . . . then there was blinding white light, the sound
of bells—bells like yours, Sabriel—and voices, harsh voices . . .
Rogir flinching back, the cup dropped, blood floating on the
water like oil. I turned, saw guardsmen on the stairs; a burning,
twisting column of white fire; a man with sword and bells . . .

then I fainted, or was knocked unconscious. When I came to, I was in Holehallow, seeing your face. I don't know how I got there, who put me there . . . I still only remember in shreds and patches."

"You should have told me," Sabriel said, trying to put as much compassion in her voice as she could. "But perhaps it had to wait for the sea's freeing of that binding spell. Tell me, the man with the sword and bells, was it the Abhorsen?"

"I don't know," replied Touchstone. "Probably."

"Almost definitely, I would say," added Sabriel. She looked at Mogget, thinking of that column of twisting fire. "You were there too, weren't you, Mogget? Unbound, in your other form."

"Yes, I was there," said the cat. "With the Abhorsen of that time. A very powerful Charter Mage, and a master of the bells, but a little too good-hearted to deal with treachery. I had terrible trouble getting him to Belisaere, and in the end, we were not timely enough to save the Queen or her daughters."

"What happened?" whispered Touchstone. "What happened?"

"Rogir was already one of the Dead when he came back to Belisaere," Mogget said wearily, as if he were telling a cynical yarn to a crew of hard-bitten cronies. "But only an Abhorsen would have known it, and he wasn't there. Rogir's real body was hidden somewhere . . . is hidden somewhere . . . and he wore a Free Magic construct for his physical form.

"Somewhere along the path of his studies, he'd swapped real Life for power and, like all the Dead, he needed to take life all the time to stay out of Death. But the Charter made it very difficult for him to do that anywhere in the Kingdom. So he decided to break the Charter. He could have confined himself to breaking a few of the lesser stones, somewhere far away, but that would only give him a tiny area to prey on, and the Abhorsen would soon hunt him down. So he decided to break the Great

Stones, and for that he needed royal blood—his own family's blood. Or Abhorsen's, or the Clayr's, of course, but that would be much harder to get.

"Because he was the Queen's son, clever, and very powerful, he almost achieved his aims. Two of the six Great Stones were broken. The Queen and her daughters were killed. Abhorsen intervened a little too late. True, he did manage to drive him deep into Death—but since his true body has never been found, Rogir has continued to exist. Even from Death, he has overseen the dissolution of the Kingdom—a kingdom without a royal family, with one of the Great Charters crippled, corrupting and weakening all the others. He wasn't really beaten that night, in the reservoir. Just delayed, and for two hundred years he's been trying to come back, trying to re-enter Life—"

"He's succeeded, hasn't he?" interrupted Sabriel. "He's the thing called Kerrigor, the one Abhorsens have been fighting for generations, trying to keep in Death. He is the one who came back, the Greater Dead who murdered the patrol near Cloven Crest, the master of the Mordicant."

"I do not know," replied Mogget. "Your father thought so."

"It is him," Touchstone said, distantly. "Kerrigor was Rogir's childhood nickname. I made it up, on the day we had the mud fight. His full ceremonial name was Rogirek."

"He—or his servants—must have lured my father to Belisaere just before he emerged from Death," Sabriel thought aloud. "I wonder why he came out into Life so near the Wall?"

"His body must be near the Wall. He would need to be close to it," Mogget said. "You should know that. To renew the master spell that prevents him from ever passing beyond the Final Gate."

"Yes," replied Sabriel, remembering the passages from *The Book of the Dead*. She shivered, but suppressed it, before it became a racking sob. Inside, she felt like screaming, crying. She wanted to flee back to Ancelstierre, cross the Wall, leave the Dead and magic behind, go as far south as possible. But she quelled these feelings, and said, "An Abhorsen defeated him once. I can do so again. But first, we must find my father's body."

There was silence for a moment, save for the wind in the canvas and the quiet hum of the rigging. Touchstone wiped his hand across his eyes and looked at Mogget.

"There is one thing I would like to ask. Who put my spirit in Death, and made my body the figurehead?"

"I never knew what happened to you," replied Mogget. His green eyes met Touchstone's gaze, and it wasn't the cat who blinked. "But it must have been Abhorsen. You were insane when we got you out of the reservoir. Driven mad, probably by the breaking of the Great Stones. No memory, nothing. It seems two hundred years is not too long for a rest cure. He must have seen something in you—or the Clayr saw something in the ice . . . ah, that was hard to say. We must be nearing the city, and the sea's influence lessens. The binding resumes . . ."

"No, Mogget!" exclaimed Sabriel. "I want to know, I need to know, who you are. What's your connection with the Great . . ."

Her voice locked up in her throat and a startled gargle was the only thing that came out.

"Too late," said Mogget. He started cleaning his fur, pink tongue darting out, bright color against white fur.

Sabriel sighed, and looked out at the turquoise sea, then up at the sun, yellow disc on a field of white-streaked blue. A light breeze filled the sail above her, ruffling her hair in passing. Gulls rode it on ahead, to join a squawking mass of their brethren, feeding from a school of fish, sharp silver bursting near the surface.

Everything was alive, colorful, full of the joy of living. Even the salt tang on her skin, the stink of fish and her own unwashed body, was somehow rich and lively. Far, far removed from

Touchstone's grim past, the threat of Rogir/Kerrigor and the chilling greyness of Death.

"We shall have to be very careful," Sabriel said at last, "and hope that . . . what was it you said to the Elder of Nestowe, Touchstone?"

He knew immediately what she meant.

"Hope that the Charter preserves us all."

Chapter Nineteen

SABRIEL HAD EXPECTED Belisaere to be a ruined city, devoid of life, but it was not so. By the time they saw its towers, and the truly impressive walls that ringed the peninsula on which the city stood, they also saw fishing boats, of a size with their own. People were fishing from them—normal, friendly people, who waved and shouted as they passed. Only their greeting was telling of how things might be in Belisaere. "Good sun and swift water" was not the typical greeting in Touchstone's time.

The city's main harbor was reached from the west. A wide, buoyed channel ran between two hulking defensive outworks, leading into a vast pool, easily as big as twenty or thirty playing fields. Wharves lined three sides of the pool, but most were deserted. To the north and south, warehouses rotted behind the empty wharves, broken walls and holed roofs testimony to long abandonment.

Only the eastern dock looked lively. There were none of the big trading vessels of bygone days, but many small coastal craft, loading and unloading. Derricks swung in and out; longshoremen humped packages along gangplanks; small children dived and swam in between the boats. No warehouses stood behind these wharves—instead, there were hundreds of open-topped booths, little more than brightly decorated frameworks delineating a patch of space, with tables for the wares, and stools for the

vendors and favored customers. There seemed to be no shortage
of customers in general, Sabriel noted, as Touchstone steered for
a vacant berth. People were swarming everywhere, hurrying
about as if their time was sadly limited.

Touchstone let the mainsheet go slack, and brought the boat
into the wind just in time for them to lose way and glide at an
oblique angle into the fenders that lined the wharf. Sabriel threw
up a line, but before she could leap ashore and secure it to a bol-
lard, a street urchin did it for her.

"Penny for the knot," he cried, shrill voice piercing through
the hubbub from the crowd. "Penny for the knot, lady?"

Sabriel smiled, with effort, and flicked a silver penny at the
boy. He caught it, grinned and disappeared into the stream of
people moving along the dock. Sabriel's smile faded. She could
feel many, many Dead here . . . or not precisely here, but further
up in the city. Belisaere was built upon four low hills, surrounding a central valley, which lay open to the sea at this harbor. As
far as Sabriel's senses could tell, only the valley was free of the
Dead—why, she didn't know. The hills, which made up at least
two-thirds of the city's area, were infested with them.

This part of the city, on the other hand, could truly be said
to be infested with life. Sabriel had forgotten how noisy a city
could be. Even in Ancelstierre, she had rarely visited anything
larger than Bain, a town of no more than ten thousand people.
Of course, Belisaere wasn't a big city by Ancelstierran standards,
and it didn't have the noisy omnibuses and private cars that had
been significantly adding to Ancelstierran noise for the last ten
years, but Belisaere made up for it with the people. People hurrying, arguing, shouting, selling, buying, singing . . .

"Was it like this before?" she shouted at Touchstone, as they
climbed up onto the wharf, making sure they had all their possessions with them.

"Not really," answered Touchstone. "The Pool was normally full, with bigger ships—and there were warehouses here, not a market. It was quieter, too, and people were in less of a rush."

They stood on the edge of the dock, watching the stream of humanity and goods, hearing the tumult, and smelling all the new odors of the city replacing the freshness of the sea breeze. Cooking food, wood smoke, incense, oil, the occasional disgusting whiff of what could only be sewage . . .

"It was also a lot cleaner," added Touchstone. "Look, I think we'd best find an inn or hostelry. Somewhere to stay for the night."

"Yes," replied Sabriel. She was reluctant to enter the human tide. There were no Dead among them, as far as she could sense, but they must have some kind of accommodation or agreement with the Dead and that stank to her far more than sewage.

Touchstone snagged a passing boy by the shoulder as Sabriel continued to eye the crowd, nose wrinkling. They spoke together for a moment, a silver penny changed hands, then the boy slid into the rush, Touchstone following. He looked back, saw Sabriel staring absently, and grabbed her by the hand, dragging both her and the lazy, fox-fur-positioned Mogget after him.

It was the first time Sabriel had touched him since he'd been revived and she was surprised by the shock it gave her. Certainly, her mind had been wandering, and it was a sudden grab . . . his hand felt larger than it should, and interestingly calloused and textured. Quickly, she slipped her hand out of his, and concentrated on following both him and the boy, weaving across the main direction of the crowd.

They went through the middle of the open-topped market, along one street of little booths—obviously the street of fish and fowl. The harbor end was alive with boxes and boxes of fresh-caught fish, clear-eyed and wriggling. Vendors yelled their prices, or their best buy, and buyers shouted offers or amazement at the price. Baskets, bags and boxes changed hands, empty ones to be filled with fish or lobster, squid or shellfish. Coins went from palm to palm, or, occasionally, whole purses disgorged their shining contents into the belt-pouches of the stallholders.

Towards the other end it grew a little quieter. The stalls here had cages upon cages of chickens, but their trade was slower, and many of the chickens looked old and stunted. Sabriel, seeing an expert knife-man beheading row after row of chickens and dropping them to flop headless in a box, concentrated on shutting out their bewildered featherbrained experience of death.

Beyond the market there was a wide swath of empty ground. It had obviously been intentionally cleared, first with fire, then with mattock, shovel and bar. Sabriel wondered why, till she saw the aqueduct that ran beyond and parallel to this strip of wasteland. The city folk who lived in the valley didn't have an agreement with the Dead—their part of the city was bounded by aqueducts, and the Dead could no more walk under running water than over it.

The cleared ground was a precaution, allowing the aqueducts to be guarded—and sure enough, Sabriel saw a patrol of archers marching atop it, their regularly moving shapes silhouetted, shadow puppets against the sky. The boy was leading them to a central arch, which rose up through two of the aqueduct's four tiers, and there were more archers there. Smaller arches continued on each side, supporting the aqueduct's main channel, but these were heavily overgrown with thornbushes, to prevent unauthorized entry by the living, while the swift water overhead held back the Dead.

Sabriel drew her boat cloak tight as they passed under the arch, but the guards paid them no more attention than was required to extort a silver penny from Touchstone. They seemed very third-rate—even fourth-rate—soldiers, who were probably more constables and watchkeepers than anything else. None bore the Charter mark, or had any trace of Free Magic.

Beyond the aqueduct, streets wound chaotically from an unevenly paved square, complete with an eccentrically spouting fountain—the water jetted from the ears of a statue, a statue of an impressively crowned man.

"King Anstyr the Third," said Touchstone, pointing at the fountain. "He had a strange sense of humor, by all accounts. I'm glad it's still there."

"Where are we going?" asked Sabriel. She felt better now that she knew the citizenry weren't in league with the Dead.

"This boy says he knows a good inn," replied Touchstone, indicating the ragged urchin who was grinning just out of reach of the always-expected blow.

"Sign of Three Lemons," said the boy. "Best in the city, Lord, Lady."

He had just turned back from them to go on, when a loud, badly cast bell sounded from somewhere towards the harbor. It rang three times, the sound sending pigeons racketing into flight from the square.

"What's that?" asked Sabriel. The boy looked at her, open-mouthed. "The bell."

"Sunfall," replied the boy, once he knew what she was asking. He said it as if stating the blindingly obvious. "Early, I reckon. Must be cloud coming, or somefing."

"Everyone comes in when the sunfall bell sounds?" asked Sabriel.

"Course!" snorted the boy. "Otherwise the haunts or the ghlims get you."

"I see," replied Sabriel. "Lead on."

Surprisingly, the Sign of Three Lemons was quite a pleasant

inn. A whitewashed building of four storys, it fronted onto a smaller square some two hundred yards from King Anstyr's Fountain Square. There were three enormous lemon trees in the middle of the square, somehow thick with pleasant-smelling leaves and copious amounts of fruit, despite the season. Charter Magic, thought Sabriel, and sure enough, there was a Charter Stone hidden amongst the trees, and a number of ancient spells of fertility, warmth and bountitude. Sabriel sniffed the lemon-scented air gratefully, thankful that her room had a window fronting the square.

Behind her, a maid was filling a tin bath with hot water. Several large buckets had already gone in—this would be the last. Sabriel closed the window and came over to look at the still-steaming water in anticipation.

"Will that be all, miss?" asked the maid, half-curtseying.

"Yes, thank you," replied Sabriel. The maid edged out the door, and Sabriel slid the bar across, before divesting herself of her cloak, and then the stinking, sweat- and salt-encrusted armor and garments that had virtually stuck to her after almost a week at sea. Naked, she rested her sword against the bath's rim—in easy reach—then sank gratefully into the water, taking up the lump of lemon-scented soap to begin removing the caked grime and sweat.

Through the wall, she could hear a man's—Touchstone's—voice. Then water gurgling, that maid giggling. Sabriel stopped soaping and concentrated on the sound. It was hard to hear, but there was more giggling, a deep, indistinct male voice, then a loud splash. Like two bodies in a bath rather than one.

There was silence for a while, then more splashing, gasps, giggles—was that Touchstone laughing? Then a series of short, sharp, moans. Womanly ones. Sabriel flushed and gritted her teeth at the same time, then quickly lowered her head into the water so she couldn't hear, leaving only her nose and mouth exposed. Underwater, all was silent, save for the dull booming of her heart, echoing in her flooded ears.

What did it matter? She didn't think of Touchstone in that way. Sex was the last thing on her mind. Just another complication—contraception—messiness—emotions. There were enough problems. Concentrate on planning. Think ahead. It was just because Touchstone was the first young man she'd met out of school, that was all. It was none of her business. She didn't even know his real name . . .

A dull tapping noise on the side of the bath made her raise her head out of the water, just in time to hear a very self-satisfied, masculine and drawn-out moan from the other side of the wall. She was about to stick her head back under, when Mogget's pink nose appeared on the rim. So she sat up, water cascading down her face, hiding the tears she told herself weren't there. Angrily, she crossed her arms across her breasts and said, "What do you want?"

"I just thought that you might like to know that Touchstone's room is that way," said Mogget, indicating the silent room opposite the one with the noisy couple. "It hasn't got a bathtub, so he'd like to know if he can use yours when you're finished. He's waiting downstairs in the meantime, getting the local news."

"Oh," replied Sabriel. She looked across at the far, silent wall, then back to the close wall, where the human noises were now largely lost in the groaning of bedsprings. "Well, tell him I won't be long."

Twenty minutes later, a clean Sabriel, garbed in a borrowed dress made incongruous by her sword-belt (the bell-bandolier lay under her bed, with Mogget asleep on top of it), crept on slippered feet through the largely empty common room and tapped the salty, begrimed Touchstone on the back, making him spill his beer.

"Your turn for the bath," Sabriel said cheerily, "my evil-smelling swordsman. I've just had it refilled. Mogget's in the room, by the way. I hope you don't mind."

"Why would I mind?" asked Touchstone, as much puzzled by her manner as the question. "I just want to get clean, that's all."

"Good," replied Sabriel, obscurely. "I'll organize for dinner to be served in your room, so we can plan as we eat."

In the event, the planning didn't take long, nor was it slow in dampening what was otherwise a relatively festive occasion. They were safe for the moment, clean, well-fed—and able to forget past troubles and future fears for a little while.

But, as soon as the last dish—a squid stew, with garlic, barley, yellow squash and tarragon vinegar—was cleared, the present reasserted itself, complete with cares and woe.

"I think the most likely place to find my father's body will be at . . . that place, where the Queen was slain," Sabriel said slowly. "The reservoir. Where is it, by the way?"

"Under the Palace Hill," replied Touchstone. "There are several different ways to enter. All lie beyond this aqueduct-guarded valley."

"You are probably right about your father," Mogget commented from his nest of blankets in the middle of Touchstone's bed. "But that is also the most dangerous place for us to go. Charter Magic will be greatly warped, including various bindings—and there is a chance that our enemy . . ."

"Kerrigor," interrupted Sabriel. "But he may not be there. Even if he is, we may be able to sneak in—"

"We might be able to sneak around the edges," said Touchstone. "The reservoir is enormous, and there are hundreds of columns. But wading is noisy, and the water is very still—sound carries. And the six . . . you know . . . they are in the very center."

"If I can find my father and bring his spirit back to his body," Sabriel said stubbornly, "then we can deal with whatever confronts us. That is the first thing. My father. Everything else is just a complication that's followed on."

"Or preceded it," said Mogget. "So, I take it your master plan is to sneak in, as far as we can, find your father's body, which will hopefully be tucked away in some safe corner, and then see what happens?"

"We'll go in the middle of a clear, sunny day . . ." Sabriel began.

"It's underground," interrupted Mogget.

"So we have sunlight to retreat to," Sabriel continued in a quelling tone.

"And there are light shafts," added Touchstone. "At noon, it's a sort of dim twilight down there, with patches of faint sun on the water."

"So, we'll find Father's body, bring it back to safety here," said Sabriel, "and . . . and take things from there."

"It sounds like a terribly brilliant plan to me," muttered Mogget. "The genius of simplicity . . ."

"Can you think of anything else?" snapped Sabriel. "I've tried, and I can't. I wish I could go home to Ancelstierre and forget the whole thing—but then I'd never see Father again, and the Dead would just eat up everything living in this whole rotten Kingdom. Maybe it won't work, but at least I'll be trying something, like the Abhorsen I'm supposed to be and you're always telling me I'm not!"

Silence greeted this sally. Touchstone looked away, embarrassed. Mogget looked at her, yawned and shrugged.

"As it happens, I can't think of anything else. I've grown stupid over the millennia—even stupider than the Abhorsens I serve."

"I think it's as good a plan as any," Touchstone said, unexpectedly. He hesitated, then added, "Though I am afraid."

"So am I," whispered Sabriel. "But if it's a sunny day tomorrow, we will go there."

"Yes," said Touchstone. "Before we grow too afraid."

Chapter Twenty

L EAVING THE SAFE, aqueduct-bounded quarter of Belisaere
proved to be a more difficult business than entering it,
particularly through the northern archway, which led out
to a long-abandoned street of derelict houses, winding their way
up towards the northern hills of the city.

There were six guards at the archway, and they looked considerably more alert and efficient than the ones who guarded the
passage from the docks. There was also a group of other people
ahead of Sabriel and Touchstone waiting to be let through. Nine
men, all with the marks of violence written in their expressions,
in the way they spoke and moved. Every one was armed, with
weapons ranging from daggers to a broad-bladed axe. Most of
them also carried bows—short, deeply curved bows, slung on
their backs.

"Who are these people?" Sabriel asked Touchstone. "Why
are they going out into the Dead part of the city?"

"Scavengers," replied Touchstone. "Some of the people I
spoke to last night mentioned them. Parts of the city were abandoned to the Dead very quickly, so there is still plenty of loot to
be found. A risky business, I think . . ."

Sabriel nodded thoughtfully and looked back at the men,
most of whom were sitting or squatting by the aqueduct wall.
Some of them looked back at her, rather suspiciously. For a
moment, she thought they'd seen the bells under her cloak and

recognized her as a necromancer, then she realized that she and Touchstone probably looked like rival scavengers. After all, who else would want to leave the protection of swift water? She felt a bit like a hard-bitten scavenger. Even freshly cleaned and scrubbed, her clothes and armor were not the sweetest items of wear. They were also still slightly damp, and the boat cloak that covered her up was on the borderline between damp and wet, because it hadn't been hung up properly after washing. On the positive side, everything had the scent of lemon, for the Sign of Three Lemons washerfolk used lemon-scented soap.

Sabriel thought the scavengers had been waiting for the guards, but clearly they had been waiting for something else, which they'd suddenly sighted behind her. The sitting or squatting men picked themselves up, grumbling and cursing, and shuffled together into something resembling a line.

Sabriel looked over her shoulder to see what they saw—and froze. For coming towards the arch were two men, and about twenty children; children of all ages between six and sixteen. The men had the same look as the other scavengers, and carried long, four-tongued whips. The children were manacled at the ankles, the manacles fastened to a long central chain. One man held the chain, leading the children down the middle of the road. The other followed behind, plying the air above the small bodies idly with his whip, the four tongues occasionally licking against an ear or the top of a small head.

"I heard of this too," muttered Touchstone, moving up closer to Sabriel, his hands falling on his sword hilts. "But I thought it was a beer story. The scavengers use children—slaves—as decoys, or bait, for the Dead. They leave them in one area, to draw the Dead away from where they intend to search."

"This is . . . disgusting!" raged Sabriel. "Immoral! They're slavers, not scavengers! We have to stop it!"

She started forward, mind already forming a Charter-spell to blind and confuse the scavengers, but a sharp pain in her neck halted her. Mogget, riding on her shoulders, had dug his claws in just under her chin. Blood trickled down in hairline traces, as he hissed close to her ear.

"Wait! There are nine scavengers and six guards, with more close by. What will it profit these children, and all the others who may come, if you are slain? It is the Dead who are at the root of this evil, and Abhorsen's business is with the Dead!"

Sabriel stood still, shuddering, tears of rage and anger welling up in the corners of her eyes. But she didn't attack. Just stood, watching the children. They seemed resigned to their fate, silent, without hope. They didn't even fidget in their chains, standing still, heads bowed, till the scavengers whipped them up again and they broke into a dispirited shuffle towards the archway.

Soon, they were beyond the arch, heading up the ruined street, the scavenging team walking slowly behind them. The sun shone bright on the cobbled street and reflected from armor and weapons—and, briefly, from a little boy's blond head. Then they were gone, turning right, taking the way towards Coiner's Hill.

Sabriel, Touchstone and Mogget followed after ten minutes spent negotiating with the guards. At first, the leader, a large man in a gravy-stained leather cuirass, wanted to see an "official scavenger's license," but this was soon translated as a request for bribes. Then it was merely a matter of bargaining, down to the final price of three silver pennies each for Sabriel and Touchstone, and one for the cat. Strange accounting, Sabriel thought, but she was glad Mogget stayed silent, not voicing the opinion that he was being undervalued.

Past the aqueduct, and the soothing barrier of running water, Sabriel felt the immediate presence of the Dead. They were all around, in the ruined houses, in cellars and drains, lurking anywhere the light didn't reach. Dormant. Waiting for the night, while the sun shone.

In many ways, the Dead of Belisaere were direct counterparts of the scavengers. Hiding by day, they took what they could by night. There were many, many Dead in Belisaere, but they were weak, cowardly and jealous. Their combined appetite was enormous, but the supply of victims sadly limited. Every morning saw scores of them lose their hold on Life, to fall back into Death. But more always came . . .

"There are thousands of Dead here," Sabriel said, eyes darting from side to side. "They're weak, for the most part—but so many!"

"Do we go straight on to the reservoir?" Touchstone asked. There was an unspoken question there, Sabriel knew. Should they—could they—save the children first?

She looked at the sky, and the sun, before answering. They had about four hours of strong sunlight, if no clouds intervened. Little enough time, anyway. Assuming that they could defeat the scavengers, could they leave finding her father till tomorrow? Every day made it less likely his spirit and body could be brought back together. Without him, they couldn't defeat Kerrigor—and Kerrigor had to be defeated for them to have any hope of repairing the stones of the Great Charter—banishing the Dead across the Kingdom . . .

"We'll go straight to the reservoir," Sabriel said, heavily, trying to blank out a sudden fragment of visual memory; sunlight on that little boy's head, the trudging feet . . .

"Perhaps we . . . perhaps we will be able to rescue the children on the way back."

Touchstone led the way with confidence, keeping to the middle of the streets, where the sun was bright. For almost an hour, they strode up empty, deserted streets, the only sound the clacking of their boot-nails on the cobbles. There were no birds, or animals. Not even insects. Just ruin and decay.

Finally, they reached an iron-fenced park that ran around the base of Palace Hill. Atop the hill, blackened, burnt-out shells of tumbled stone and timber were all that remained of the Royal Palace.

"The last Regent burned it," said Mogget, as all three stopped to look up. "About twenty years ago. It was becoming infested with the Dead, despite all the guards and wards that various visiting Abhorsens put up. They say the Regent went mad and tried to burn them out."

"What happened to him?" asked Sabriel.

"Her, actually," replied Mogget. "She died in the fire—or the Dead took her. And that marked the end of any attempt at governing the Kingdom."

"It was a beautiful building," Touchstone reminisced. "You could see out over the Saere. It had high ceilings, and a clever system of vents and shafts to catch the light and the sea breeze. There was always music and dancing somewhere in the Palace, and Midsummer dinner on the garden roof, with a thousand scented candles burning . . ."

He sighed, and pointed at a hole in the park fence.

"We might as well go through here. There's an entrance to the reservoir in one of the ornamental caves in the park. Only fifty steps down to the water, rather than the hundred and fifty from the Palace proper."

"One hundred and fifty-six," said Mogget. "As I recall."

Touchstone shrugged, and climbed through the hole, onto the springy turf of the park. There was no one—and no thing— in sight, but he drew his swords anyway. There were large trees nearby, and accordingly, shadows.

Sabriel followed, Mogget jumping down from her shoulders to saunter forward and sniff the air. Sabriel drew her sword too, but left the bells. There were Dead about, but none close. The park was too open in daylight.

The ornamental caves were only five minutes' walk away, past a fetid pond that had once boasted seven water-spouting statues of bearded tritons. Now their mouths were clogged with rotten leaves, and the pond was almost solid with yellow-green slime.

There were three cave entrances, side by side. Touchstone led them to the largest, central entrance. Marble steps led down the first three or four feet, and marble pillars supported the entrance ceiling.

"It only goes back about forty paces into the hill," Touchstone explained, as they lit their candles by the entrance, sulphur matches adding their own noisome stench to the dank air of the cave. "They were built for picnics in high summer. There is a door at the back of this one. It may be locked, but should yield to a Charter-spell. The steps are directly behind, and pretty straight, but there are no light shafts. And it's narrow."

"I'll go first then," said Sabriel, with a firmness that belied the weakness in her legs and the fluttering in her stomach. "I can't sense any Dead, but they could be there . . ."

"Very well," said Touchstone, after a moment's hesitation.

"You don't have to come, you know," Sabriel suddenly burst out, as they stood in front of the cave, candles flickering foolishly in the sunshine. She suddenly felt awfully responsible for him. He looked scared, much whiter than he should, almost as pale as a Death-leeched necromancer. He'd seen terrible things in the reservoir, things that had once driven him mad, and despite his self-accusation, Sabriel didn't believe it was his fault. It wasn't his father down there. He wasn't an Abhorsen.

"I do have to," Touchstone replied. He bit his lower lip nervously. "I have to. I'll never be free of my memories, otherwise. I have to do something, make new memories, better ones. I need

to . . . seek redemption. Besides, I am still a member of the Royal
Guard. It is my duty."

"So be it," said Sabriel. "Anyway, I'm glad you're here."

"I am too—in a strange sort of way," said Touchstone, and
he almost, but not quite, smiled.

"I'm not," interrupted Mogget, decidedly. "Let's get on with
it. We're wasting sunlight."

The door was locked, but opened easily to Sabriel's spell, the
simple Charter symbols of unlocking and opening flowing from
her mind through to her index finger, which lay against the keyhole. But though the spell was successful, it had been difficult to
cast. Even up here, the broken stones of the Great Charter exerted
an influence that disrupted Charter Magic.

The faint candlelight showed damp, crumbly steps, leading
straight down. No curves or turns, just a straight stair leading into
darkness.

Sabriel trod gingerly, feeling the soft stone crumble under
her heavy boots, so she had to keep her heels well back on each
step. This made for slow progress, with Touchstone close behind
her, the light from his candle casting Sabriel's shadow down the
steps in front, so she saw herself elongated and distorted, sliding
into the dark beyond the light.

She smelled the reservoir before she saw it, somewhere
around the thirty-ninth step. A chill, damp smell that cut into her
nose and lungs, and filled her with the impression of a cold
expanse.

Then the steps ended in a doorway on the edge of a vast,
rectangular hall—a giant chamber where stone columns rose up
like a forest to support a roof sixty feet above her head, and the
floor before her wasn't stone, but water as cold and still as stone.
Around the walls, pallid shafts of sunlight thrust down in counterpoint to the supporting columns, leaving discs of light on the

water. These made the rim of the reservoir a complex study of light and shade, but the center remained unknown, cloaked in heavy darkness.

Sabriel felt Touchstone touch her shoulder, then she heard his whisper.

"It's about waist-deep. Try and slip in as quietly as possible. Here—I'll take your candle."

Sabriel nodded, passed the candle back, sheathed her sword, and sat down on the last step, before slowly easing herself into the water.

It was cold, but not unbearable. Despite Sabriel's care, ripples spread out from her, silver on the dark water, and there had been the tiniest splash. Her feet touched the bottom, and she only half stifled a gasp. Not from the cold, but from the sudden awareness of the two broken stones of the Great Charter. It hit her like the savage onset of gastric flu, bringing stomach cramps, sudden sweat and dizziness. Bent over, she clutched at the step, till the first pains subsided to a dull ache. It was much worse than the lesser stones, broken at Cloven Crest and Nestowe.

"What is it?" whispered Touchstone.

"Ah . . . the broken stones," Sabriel muttered. She took a deep breath, willing the pain and discomfort away. "I can stand it. Be careful when you get in."

She drew her sword, and took her candle back from Touchstone, who prepared to enter the water. Even forewarned, she saw him flinch as his feet touched the bottom, and sweat broke out in lines on his forehead, mirroring the ripples that spread from his entry.

Sabriel expected Mogget to jump up on her shoulder, given his apparent dislike for Touchstone, but he surprised her, leaping to the man. Touchstone was clearly startled too, but recovered well. Mogget draped himself around the back of Touchstone's neck, and mewed softly.

"Keep to the edges, if you can. The corruption—the break—will have even more unpleasant effects near the center."

Sabriel raised her sword in assent and led off, following the left wall, trying to break the surface tension of the water as little as possible. But the quiet slosh-slosh of their wading seemed very loud, echoing and spreading up and out through the cistern, adding to the only other noise—the regular dripping of water, plopping loudly from the roof, or more sedately sliding down the columns.

She couldn't sense any Dead, but she wasn't sure how much that was due to the broken stones. They made her head hurt, like a constant, too-loud noise; her stomach cramped; her mouth was full of the acrid taste of bile.

They had just reached the north-western corner, directly under one of the light shafts, when the light suddenly dimmed, and the reservoir grew dark in an instant, save for the tiny, soft glow of the candles.

"A cloud," whispered Touchstone. "It will pass."

They held their breath, looking up, up to the tiny outline of light above, and were rewarded when sunlight came pouring back down. Relieved, they began to wade again, following the long west-east wall. But it was short-lived relief. Another cloud crossed the sun, somewhere in that fresh air so high above them, and darkness returned. More clouds followed, till there were only brief moments of light interspersed by long stretches of total dark.

The reservoir seemed colder without the sun, even a sun diluted by passage down long shafts through the earth. Sabriel felt the cold now, accompanied by the sudden, irrational fear that they had stayed too long, and would emerge to a night full of waiting, life-hungry Dead. Touchstone felt the chill too, made more bitter by his memories of two hundred years past, when he'd waded in this same water, and seen the Queen and her two daughters sacrificed and the Great Stones broken. There had been blood on the water then, and he still saw it—a single frozen moment of time that would not get out of his head.

Despite these fears, it was the darkness that helped them. Sabriel saw a glow, a faint luminescence off to her right, somewhere towards the center. Shielding her eyes from the candle's glare, she pointed it out to Touchstone.

"There's something there," he agreed, his voice so low Sabriel barely heard it. "But it's at least forty paces towards the center."

Sabriel didn't answer. She'd felt something from that faint light, something like the slight sensation across the back of her neck that came when her father's sending visited her at school. Leaving the wall, she pushed out through the water, a V-line of ripples behind her. Touchstone looked again, then followed, fighting the nausea that rose in him, coming in waves like repeated doses of an emetic. He was dizzy too, and could no longer properly feel his feet.

They went about thirty paces out, the pain and the nausea growing steadily worse. Then Sabriel suddenly stopped, Touchstone lifting his sword and candle, eyes searching for an attack. But there was no enemy present. The luminous light came from a diamond of protection, the four cardinal marks glowing under the water, lines of force sparkling between them.

In the middle of the diamond, a man-shaped figure stood, empty hands outstretched, as if he had once held weapons. Frost rimed his clothes and face, obscuring his features, and ice girdled the water around his middle. But Sabriel had no doubt about who it was.

"Father," she whispered, the whisper echoing across the dark water, to join the faint sounds of the ever-present dripping.

Chapter Twenty-One

"THE DIAMOND IS complete," said Touchstone. "We won't be able to move him."

"Yes. I know," replied Sabriel. The relief that had soared inside her at the sight of her father was ebbing, giving way to the sickness caused by the broken stones. "I think . . . I think I'll have to go into Death from here, and fetch his spirit back."

"What!" exclaimed Touchstone. Then, quieter, as the echoes rang, "Here?"

"If we cast our own diamond of protection . . ." Sabriel continued, thinking aloud. "A large one, around both of us and Father's diamond—that will keep most danger at bay."

"Most danger," Touchstone said grimly, looking around, trying to peer past the tight confines of their candle's little globe of light. "It will also trap us here—even if we can cast it, so close to the broken stones. I know that I couldn't do it alone, at this point."

"We should be able to combine our strengths. Then, if you and Mogget keep watch while I am in Death, we should manage."

"What do you think, Mogget?" asked Touchstone, turning his head, so his cheek brushed against the little animal on his shoulder.

"I have my own troubles," grumbled Mogget. "And I think this is probably a trap. But since we're here, and the—Abhorsen Emeritus, shall we say, does seem to be alive, I suppose there's nothing else to be done."

"I don't like it," whispered Touchstone. Just standing this close to the broken stones took most of his strength. For Sabriel to enter Death seemed madness, tempting fate. Who knew what might be lurking in Death, close by the easy portal made by the broken stones? For that matter, who knew what was lurking in or around the reservoir?

Sabriel didn't answer. She moved closer to her father's diamond of protection, studying the cardinal marks under the water. Touchstone followed reluctantly, forcing his legs to move in short steps, minimizing the splash and ripple of his wake.

Sabriel snuffed out her candle, thrust it through her belt, then held out her open palm.

"Put your sword away and give me your hand," she said, in a tone that did not invite conversation or argument. Touchstone hesitated—his left hand held only a candle, and he didn't want both his swords scabbarded—then he complied. Her hand was cold, colder than the water. Instinctively, he gripped a little tighter, to give her some of his warmth.

"Mogget—keep watch," Sabriel instructed.

She closed her eyes, and began to visualize the East mark, the first of the four cardinal wards. Touchstone took a quick look around, then closed his eyes too, drawn in by the force of Sabriel's conjuration.

Pain shot through his hand and arm, as he added his will to Sabriel's. The mark seemed blurry in his head, and impossible to focus. The pins and needles that had already plagued his feet spread up above his knees, shooting them through with rheumatic pains. But he blocked off the pain, narrowing his consciousness to just one thing: the creation of a diamond of protection.

Finally, the East mark flowed down Sabriel's blade and took root in the reservoir floor. Without opening their eyes, the duo shuffled around to face the south, and the next mark.

This was harder still, and both of them were sweating and shaking when it finally began its glowing existence. Sabriel's hand was hot and feverish now, and Touchstone's flesh ricocheted violently between sweating heat and shivering cold. A terrible wave of nausea hit him, and he would have been sick, but Sabriel gripped his hand, like a falcon its prey, and lent him strength. He gagged, dry-retched once, then recovered.

The West mark was simply a trial of endurance. Sabriel lost concentration for a moment, so Touchstone had to hold the mark alone for a few seconds, the effort making him feel drunk in the most unpleasant way, the world spinning inside his head, totally out of control. Then Sabriel forced herself back and the West mark flowered under the water. Desperation gave them the North mark. They struggled with it for what seemed like hours, but was only seconds, till it almost squirmed from them uncast. But at that moment, Sabriel spent all the force of her desire to free her father, and Touchstone pushed with the weight of two hundred years of guilt and sorrow.

The North mark rolled brightly down the sword and grew to brilliance, brilliance dulled by the water. Lines of Charter-fire ran from it to the East mark, from East mark to South mark to West mark and back again. The diamond was complete.

Immediately, they felt a lessening of the terrible presence of the broken stones. The high-pitched pain in Sabriel's head dimmed; normal feeling returned to Touchstone's legs and feet. Mogget stirred and stretched, the first significant movement he'd made since taking up position around Touchstone's neck.

"A good casting," Sabriel said quietly, looking at the marks through eyes half-lidded in weariness. "Better than the last one I cast."

"I don't know how we did it," muttered Touchstone, staring down at the lines of Charter-fire. He suddenly became aware that he was still holding Sabriel's hand, and slumping like an aged wood collector under a heavy burden. He straightened up suddenly, dropping her hand as if it were the fanged end of a snake.

She looked at him, rather startled, and he found himself staring at the reflection of his candle-flame in her dark eyes. Almost for the first time, he really looked at her. He saw the weariness there, and the incipient lines of care, and the way her mouth looked a little sad around the edges. Her nose was still swollen, and there were yellowing bruises on her cheekbones. She was also beautiful and Touchstone realized that he had thought of her only in terms of her office, as Abhorsen. Not as a woman at all . . .

"I'd better be going," said Sabriel, suddenly embarrassed by Touchstone's stare. Her left hand went to the bell-bandolier, fingers feeling for the straps that held Saraneth.

"Let me help," said Touchstone. He stood close, fumbling with the stiff leather, hands weakened by the effort spent on the diamond of protection, his head bowed over the bells. Sabriel looked down on his hair, and was strangely tempted to kiss the exact center, a tiny part marking the epicenter where his tight brown curls radiated outwards. But she didn't.

The strap came undone, and Touchstone stepped back. Sabriel drew Saraneth, carefully stilling the bell.

"It probably won't be a long wait for you," she said. "Time moves strangely in Death. If . . . if I'm not back in two hours, then I probably . . . I'll probably be trapped too, so you and Mogget should leave . . ."

"I'll be waiting," replied Touchstone firmly. "Who knows what time it is down here anyway?"

"And I'll wait, it seems," added Mogget. "Unless I want to swim out of here. Which I don't. May the Charter be with you, Sabriel."

"And with you," said Sabriel. She looked around the dark

expanse of the reservoir. She still couldn't sense any of the Dead out there—and yet . . .

"We'll need it to be with us," Mogget replied sourly. "One way or another."

"I hope not," whispered Sabriel. She checked the pouch at her belt for the small things she'd prepared back at the Sign of Three Lemons, then turned to face the North mark and started to raise her sword, beginning her preparations to enter Death.

Suddenly, Touchstone sloshed forward and quickly kissed her on the cheek—a clumsy, dry-lipped peck that almost hit the rim of her helmet rather than her cheek.

"For luck," Touchstone said nervously. "Sabriel."

She smiled, and nodded twice, then looked back to the north. Her eyes focused on something not there and waves of cold air billowed from her motionless form. A second later, ice crystals began to crack out of her hair, and frost ran in lines down the sword and bell.

Touchstone watched, close by, till it grew too cold, then he retreated to the far southern vertice of the diamond. Drawing one sword, he turned outwards, holding his candle high, and started to wade around inside the lines of Charter-fire as if he were patrolling the battlements of a castle. Mogget watched too, from his shoulder, his green eyes lit with their own internal luminescence. Both of them often turned to gaze at Sabriel.

The crossing into Death was made easy—far too easy—by the presence of the broken stones. Sabriel felt them near her, like two yawning gates, proclaiming easy entry to Life for any Dead nearby. Fortunately, the other effect of the stones—the sickening illness—disappeared in Death. There was only the chill and tug of the river.

Sabriel started forward immediately, carefully scanning the

grey expanse before her. Things moved at the edge of her vision; she heard movement in the cold waters. But nothing came towards her, nothing attacked, save the constant twining and gripping of the current.

She came to the First Gate, halting just beyond the wall of mist that stretched out as far as she could see to either side. The river roared beyond that mist, turbulent rapids going through to the Second Precinct, and on to the Second Gate.

Remembering pages from *The Book of the Dead*, Sabriel spoke words of power. Free Magic, that shook her mouth as she spoke, jarring her teeth, burning her tongue with raw power.

The veil of mist parted, revealing a series of waterfalls that appeared to drop into an unending blackness. Sabriel spoke some more words, and gestured to the right and left with her sword. A path appeared, parting the waterfall like a finger drawn through butter. Sabriel stepped out onto it, and walked down, the waters crashing harmlessly on either side. Behind her, the mist closed up and, as her rearmost heel lifted to make her next step, the path disappeared.

The Second Precinct was more dangerous than the First. There were deep holes, as well as the ever-present current. The light was worse too. Not the total darkness promised at the end of the waterfalls, but there was a different quality in its greyness. A blurring effect, that made it difficult to see further than you could touch.

Sabriel continued carefully, using her sword to probe the ground ahead. There was an easy way through, she knew, a course mapped and plotted by many necromancers and not a few Abhorsens, but she didn't trust her memory to tread confidently ahead at speed.

Always, her senses quested for her father's spirit. He was somewhere in Death, she was positive of that. There was always the faintest trace of him, a lingering memory. But it was not this close to Life. She would have to go on.

The Second Gate was essentially an enormous hole, at least two hundred yards across, into which the river sank like sink-water down a drain. Unlike a normal drain, it was eerily silent, and with the difficult light, easy for the unwary to walk up to its rim. Sabriel was always particularly careful with this Gate—she had learned to sense the feel of its tug against her shins at an early age. She stopped well back when the tug came, and tried to focus on the silently raging whirlpool.

A faint squelching sound behind her made her turn, sword scything around at full arm-stretch, a great circle of Charter-spelled steel. It struck Dead spirit-flesh, sparks flying, a scream of rage and pain filling the silence. Sabriel almost jumped back, at that scream, but she held her ground. The Second Gate was too close.

The thing she'd hit stepped back, its head hanging from a mostly severed neck. It was humanoid in shape, at least to begin with, but had arms that trailed down below its knees, into the river. Its head, now flopping on one shoulder, was longer than it was wide or tall, possessed a mouth with several rows of teeth. It had flaming coals in its eyepits, a characteristic of the deep Dead, from beyond the Fifth Gate.

It snarled and brought its long, skewer-thin fingers up out of the water to try and straighten its head, attempting to rest it back atop the cleanly hewn neck.

Sabriel struck again, and the head and one hand flew off, splashing into the river. They bobbed on the surface for a moment, the head howling, eyes flaming with hate across the water. Then it was sucked down, down into the hurly-burly of the Second Gate.

The headless body stood where it was for a second, then

started to cautiously step sideways, its remaining hand groping around in front of it. Sabriel watched it cautiously, debating whether to use Saraneth to bind it to her will, and then Kibeth to send it on its way to final death. But using the bells would alert everything Dead between here and the First and Third Gates at least—and she didn't want that.

The headless thing took another step, and fell sideways into a deep hole. It scrabbled there, long arms thrashing the water, but couldn't pull itself up and out. It only succeeded in getting across into the full force of the current, which snatched it up and threw it into the whirlpool of the Gate.

Once again, Sabriel recited words of Free Magic power, words impressed into her mind long ago from *The Book of the Dead*. The words flowed out of her, blistering her lips, strange heat in this place of leeching cold.

With the words, the waters of the Second Gate slowed and stilled. The whirling vortex separated out into a long spiral path, winding downwards. Sabriel, checking for a few last holes near the edge, gingerly strode out to this path and started down. Behind and above her, the waters began to swirl again.

The spiral path looked long, but to Sabriel it seemed only a matter of minutes before she was passing through the very base of the whirlpool, and out into the Third Precinct.

This was a tricksome place. The water was shallow here, only ankle-deep, and somewhat warmer. The light was better too—still grey, but you could see farther out. Even the ubiquitous current was no more than a bit of a tickle around the feet.

But the Third Precinct had waves. For the first time, Sabriel broke into a run, sprinting as fast as she could towards the Third Gate, just visible in the distance. It was like the First Gate—a waterfall concealed in a wall of mist.

Behind her, Sabriel heard the thunderous crashing that

announced the wave, which had been held back by the same spell that gave her passage through the whirlpool. With the wave came shrill cries, shrieks and screams. There were clearly many Dead around, but Sabriel didn't spare them a thought. Nothing and no one could withstand the waves of the Third Precinct. You simply ran as fast as possible, hoping to reach the next gate—whichever way you were going.

The thunder and crashing grew louder, and one by one the various screams and shouts were submerged in the greater sound. Sabriel didn't look, but only ran faster. Looking over her shoulder would lose a fraction of a second, and that might be enough for the wave to reach her, pick her up and hurl her through the Third Gate, stunned flotsam for the current beyond . . .

Touchstone stared out past the southern vertice, listening. He had heard something, he was sure, something besides the constant dripping. Something louder, something slow, attempting to be surreptitious. He knew Mogget had heard it too, from the sudden tensing of cat paws on his shoulder.

"Can you see anything?" he whispered, peering out into the darkness. The clouds were still blocking the light from the sunshafts, though he thought the intervals of sunlight were growing longer. But, in any case, they were too far away from the edge to benefit from a sudden return of sun.

"Yes," whispered Mogget. "The Dead. Many of them, filing out of the main southern stair. They're lining up each side of the door, along the reservoir walls."

Touchstone looked at Sabriel, now covered in frost, like a wintering statue. He felt like shaking her shoulder, screaming for help . . .

"What kind of Dead are they?" he asked. He didn't know much about the Dead, except that Shadow Hands were the worst

of the normal variety, and Mordicants, like the one that had followed Sabriel, were the worst of them all. Except for what Rogir
had become. Kerrigor, the Dead Adept . . .

"Hands," muttered Mogget. "All Hands, and pretty putrescent ones too. They're falling apart just walking."

Touchstone stared again, trying by sheer force of will to
see—but there was nothing, save darkness. He could hear them,
though, wading, squelching through the still water. Too still for
his liking—suddenly he wondered if the reservoir had a drain-
hole and a plug. Then he dismissed it as a foolish notion. Any
such plug or drain cover would have long since rusted shut.

"What are they doing?" he whispered anxiously, fingering
his sword, tilting the blade this way and that. His left hand seemed
to hold the candle steady, but the little flame flickered, clear evidence of the tiny shakes that ran down his arm.

"Just lining up along the walls, in ranks," Mogget whispered
back. "Strange—almost like an honor guard . . ."

"Charter preserve us," Touchstone croaked, with a weight in
his throat of absolute dread and terrible foreboding. "Rogir . . .
Kerrigor. He must be here . . . and he's coming . . ."

Chapter Twenty-Two

S ABRIEL REACHED THE Third Gate just ahead of the wave, gabbling a Free Magic spell as she ran, feeling it fume up and out of her mouth, filling her nostrils with acrid fumes. The spell parted the mists, and Sabriel stepped within, the wave breaking harmlessly around her, dumping its cargo of Dead down into the waterfall beyond. Sabriel waited a moment more, for the path to appear, then passed on—on to the Fourth Precinct.

This was a relatively easy area to traverse. The current was strong again, but predictable. There were few Dead, because most were stunned and rushed through by the Third Precinct's wave. Sabriel walked quickly, using the strength of her will to suppress the leeching cold and the plucking hands of the current. She could feel her father's spirit now, close by, as if he were in one room of a large house, and she in another—tracking him down by the slight sounds of habitation. He was either here in the Fourth Precinct, or past the Fourth Gate, in the Fifth Precinct.

She increased her pace a little again, eager to find him, talk with him, free him. She knew everything would be all right once Father was freed . . .

But he wasn't in the Fourth Precinct. Sabriel reached the Fourth Gate without feeling any intensification of his presence. This gate was another waterfall, of sorts, but it wasn't cloaked in mist. It looked like the easy drop of water from a small weir, a matter of only two or three feet down. But Sabriel knew that if you approached the edge there was more than enough force to drag the strongest spirit down.

She halted well back, and was about to launch into the spell that would conjure her path, when a niggling sensation at the back of her head made her stop and look around.

The waterfall stretched as far as she could see to either side, and Sabriel knew that if she was foolish enough to try and walk its length, it would be an unending journey. Perhaps it eventually looped back on itself, but as there were no landmarks, stars or anything else to fix one's position, you'd never know. No one ever walked the breadth of an inner precinct or gate. What would be the point? Everyone went into Death or out of it. Not sideways, save at the border with Life, where walking along altered where you came out—but that was only useful for spirit-forms, or rare beings like the Mordicant, who took their physical shape with them.

Nevertheless, Sabriel felt an urge to walk along next to the Gate, to turn on her heel and follow the line of the waterfall. It was an unidentifiable urge, and that made her uneasy. There were other things in Death than the Dead—inexplicable beings of Free Magic, strange constructs and incomprehensible forces. This urge—this calling—might come from one of them.

She hesitated, thinking about it, then pushed out into the water, heading out parallel to the waterfall. It might be some Free Magic summoning, or it might be some connection with her father's spirit.

"They're coming down the east and west stairs too," said Mogget. "More Hands."

"What about the south—where we came in?" asked Touchstone, looking nervously from side to side, ears straining to hear every sound, listening to the Dead wading out into the reservoir to form up in their strange, regimented lines.

"Not yet," replied Mogget. "That stair ends in sunlight, remember? They'd have to go through the park."

"There can't be much sunlight," muttered Touchstone, looking at the light-shafts. Some sunshine was coming through, heavily filtered by clouds, but it wasn't enough to cause the Dead in the reservoir any distress, or lift Touchstone's spirits.

"When . . . when do you think he will come?" asked Touchstone. Mogget didn't need to ask who "he" was.

"Soon," replied the cat, in a matter-of-fact tone. "I always said it was a trap."

"So how do we get out of it?" asked Touchstone, trying to keep his voice steady. He was inwardly fighting a strong desire to leave the diamond of protection and run for the southern stair, splashing through the reservoir like a runaway horse, careless of the noise—but there was Sabriel, frosted over, immobile . . .

"I'm not sure we can," said Mogget, with a sideways glance at the two ice-rimmed statues nearby. "It depends on Sabriel and her father."

"What can we do?"

"Defend ourselves if we're attacked, I suppose," drawled Mogget, as if stating the obvious to a tiresome child. "Hope. Pray to the Charter that Kerrigor doesn't come before Sabriel returns."

"What if he does?" asked Touchstone, staring white-eyed out into the darkness. "What if he does?"

But Mogget was silent. All Touchstone heard was the shuffling, wading, splashing of the Dead, as they slowly drew closer, like starving rats creeping up to a sleeping drunk's dinner.

Sabriel had no idea of how far she'd gone before she found him. That same niggling sensation prompted her to stop, to look out into the waterfall itself, and there he was. Abhorsen. Father. Somehow imprisoned within the Gate itself, so only his head was visible above the rush of the water.

"Father!" cried Sabriel, but she resisted the urge to rush forward. At first, she thought he was unaware of her, then a slight wink of one eye showed conscious perception. He winked again, and moved his eyeballs to the right, several times.

Sabriel followed his gaze, and saw something tall and shadowy thrust up through the waterfall, arms reaching up to pull itself out of the gate. She stepped forward, sword and bell at the ready, then hesitated. It was a Dead humanoid, very similar in shape and size to the one who had brought the bells and sword to Wyverley College. She looked back at her father, and he winked again, the corner of his mouth curving up ever so slightly—almost a smile.

She stepped back, still cautious. There was always the chance that the spirit chained in the waterfall was merely the mimic of her father, or, even if it was him, that he was under the sway of some power.

The Dead creature finally hauled itself out, muscles differently arranged to a human's visibly straining along the forearms. It stood on the rim for a moment, bulky head questing from side to side, then lumbered towards Sabriel with that familiar rolling gait. Several paces away from her—out of sword's reach—it stopped, and pointed at its mouth. Its jaw worked up and down, but no sound issued from its red and fleshy mouth. A black thread ran from its back, down into the rushing waters of the Gate.

Sabriel thought for a moment, then replaced Saraneth, one-handed, and drew Dyrim. She cocked her wrist to ring the bell, hesitated—for to sound Dyrim would alert the Dead all around—then let it fall. Dyrim rang, sweet and clear, several notes sounding from that one peal, mixing together like many conversations overheard in a crowd.

Sabriel rang the bell again before the echoes died, in a series of slight wrist-twitches, moving the sound out towards the Dead creature, weaving into the echoes of the first peal. Sound seemed to envelope the monster, circling around its head and muted mouth.

The echoes faded. Sabriel replaced Dyrim quickly, before it could try and sound of its own accord, and drew Ranna. The Sleeper could quell a large number of Dead at once, and she feared many would come to the sound of the bells. They would probably expect to find a foolish, half-trained necromancer, but even so, they would be dangerous. Ranna twitched in her hand, expectantly, like a child waking at her touch.

The creature's mouth moved again, and now it had a tongue, a horrid pulpy mess of white flesh that writhed like a slug. But it worked. The thing made several gurgling, swallowing sounds, then it spoke with the voice of Abhorsen.

"Sabriel! I both hoped and feared you would come."

"Father . . ." Sabriel began, looking at his trapped spirit rather than the creature. "Father . . ."

She broke down, and started to cry. She had come all this way, through so many troubles, only to find him trapped, trapped beyond her ability to free him. She hadn't even known that it was possible to imprison someone within a Gate!

"Sabriel! Hush, daughter! We have no time for tears. Where is your physical body?"

"In the reservoir," sniffed Sabriel. "Next to yours. Inside a diamond of protection."

"And the Dead? Kerrigor?"

"There was no sign of them there, but Kerrigor is somewhere in Life. I don't know where."

"Yes, I knew he had emerged," muttered Abhorsen, via the thing's mouth. "He will be near the reservoir, I fear. We must move quickly. Sabriel, do you remember how to ring two bells simultaneously? Mosrael and Kibeth?"

"Two bells?" asked Sabriel, puzzled. Waker and Walker? At the same time? She had never even heard it was possible—or had she?

"Think," said Abhorsen's mouthpiece. "Remember. *The Book of the Dead*."

Slowly, it came back, pages floating down into conscious memory, like leaves from a shaken tree. The bells could be rung in pairs, or even greater combinations, if enough necromancers were gathered to wield the bells. But the risks were much greater . . .

"Yes," said Sabriel, slowly. "I remember. Mosrael and Kibeth. Will they free you?"

The answer was slow in coming.

"Yes. For a time. Enough, I hope, to do what must be done. Quickly, now."

Sabriel nodded, trying not to think about what he had just said. Subconsciously, she had always been aware that Abhorsen's spirit had been too long from his body, and too deep in the realm of Death. He could never truly live again. Consciously, she chose to barricade this knowledge from her mind.

She sheathed her sword, replaced Ranna, and drew Mosrael and Kibeth. Dangerous bells, both, and more so in combination than alone. She stilled her mind, emptying herself of all thought and emotion, concentrating solely on the bells. Then, she rang them.

Mosrael she swung in a three-quarter circle above her head; Kibeth she swung in a reverse figure-eight. Harsh alarm joined with dancing jig, merging into a discordant, grating, but energetic tone. Sabriel found herself walking towards the waterfall, despite all her efforts to keep still. A force like the grip of a demented giant moved her legs, bent her knees, made her step forward.

At the same time, her father was emerging from the water-fall of the Fourth Gate. His head was freed first, and he flexed his neck, then rolled his shoulders, raised his arms over his head and stretched. But still Sabriel stepped on, till she was only two paces from the rim, and could look down into the swirling waters, the sound of the bells filling her ears, forcing her onwards.

Then Abhorsen was free, and he leapt forward, thrusting his hands into the bell-mouths, gripping the clappers with his pallid hands, making them suddenly quiet. There was silence, and father and daughter embraced on the very brink of the Fourth Gate.

"Well done," said Abhorsen, his voice deep and familiar, lending comfort and warmth like a favorite childhood toy. "Once trapped, it was all I could do to send the bells and sword. Now I am afraid we must hurry, back to Life, before Kerrigor can complete his plan. Give me Saraneth, for now . . . no, you keep the sword, and Ranna, I think. Come on!"

He led the way back, walking swiftly. Sabriel followed at his heels, questions bursting up in her. She kept looking at him, looking at the familiar features, the way his hair was ragged at the back, the silver stubble just showing on his chin and side-burns. He wore the same sort of clothes as she did, complete with the surcoat of silver keys. He wasn't quite as tall as she remembered.

"Father!" she exclaimed, trying to talk, keep up with him and keep watch, all at the same time. "What is happening? What is Kerrigor's plan? I don't understand. Why wasn't I brought up here, so I would know things?"

"Here?" asked Abhorsen, without slowing. "In Death?"

"You know what I mean," protested Sabriel. "The Old Kingdom! Why did . . . I mean, I must be the only Abhorsen ever who doesn't have a clue about how everything works! Why! Why?"

"There's no simple answer," replied Abhorsen, over his shoulder. "But I sent you to Ancelstierre for two main reasons. One was to keep you safe. I had already lost your mother, and the only way to keep you safe in the Old Kingdom was to keep you either with me or always at our House—practically a prisoner. I couldn't keep you with me, because things were getting worse and worse since the death of the Regent, two years before you were born. The second reason was because the Clayr advised me to do so. They said we needed someone—or will need someone—they're not good with time—who knows Ancelstierre. I didn't know why then, but I suspect I do now."

"Why?" asked Sabriel.

"Kerrigor's body," replied Abhorsen. "Or Rogir's, to give him his original name. He could never be made truly dead because his body is preserved by Free Magic, somewhere in Life. It's like an anchor that always brings him back. Every Abhorsen since the breaking of the Great Stones has been looking for that body—but none of us ever found it, including me, because we never suspected it is in Ancelstierre. Obviously, somewhere close to the Wall. The Clayr will have located it by now, because Kerrigor must have gone to it when he emerged into Life. Right, do you want to do the spell, or shall I?"

They had reached the Third Gate. He didn't wait for her answer, but immediately spoke the words. Sabriel felt strange hearing them, rather than speaking them—curiously distant, like a far-off observer.

Steps rose before them, cutting through the waterfall and the mist. Abhorsen took them two at a time, showing surprising energy. Sabriel followed as best she could. She felt tiredness in her bones now, a weariness beyond exhausted muscles.

"Ready to run?" asked Abhorsen. He took her elbow as they left the steps and went into the parted mists, a curiously formal gesture that reminded her of when she was a little girl, demanding to be properly escorted when they took a picnic basket out on one of her father's corporeal school visitations.

They ran before the wave, with hands inside the bells, faster and faster, till Sabriel thought her legs would seize up and she'd tumble head over heels, around and around and around, finally clattering to a halt in a tangle of sword and bells.

But she made it somehow, Abhorsen chanting the spell that would open the base of the Second Gate, so they could ascend through the whirlpool.

"As I was saying," Abhorsen continued, taking these steps two at a time as well, speaking as swiftly as he climbed. "Kerrigor could never be properly dealt with till an Abhorsen found the body. All of us pushed him back at various times, as far back as the Seventh Gate, but that was merely postponing the problem. He grew stronger all the time, as lesser Charter Stones were broken, and the Kingdom deteriorated—and we grew weaker."

"Who's we?" asked Sabriel. All this information was coming too quickly, particularly when given at the run.

"The Great Charter bloodlines," replied Abhorsen. "Which to all intents and purposes means Abhorsens and the Clayr, since the royal line is all but extinct. And there is, of course, the relict of the Wallmakers, a sort of construct left over after they put their powers in the Wall and the Great Stones."

He left the rim of the whirlpool, and strode confidently out into the Second Precinct, Sabriel close at his heels. Unlike her earlier halting, probing advance, Abhorsen practically jogged along, obviously following a familiar route. How he could tell, without landmarks or any obvious signs, Sabriel had no idea. Perhaps, when she had spent thirty-odd years traversing Death, she would find it as easy.

"So," continued Abhorsen. "We finally have the chance to finish Kerrigor once and for all. The Clayr will direct you to his body, you will destroy it, and then banish Kerrigor's spirit form—which will be severely weakened. After that, you can get the surviving royal prince out of his suspended state, and with the aid of the Wallmaker relict, repair the Great Charter Stones . . ."

"The surviving royal prince," asked Sabriel, with a feeling of unlooked-for knowledge rising in her. "He wasn't . . . ah . . . suspended as a figurehead in Holehallow, was he . . . and his spirit in Death?"

"A bastard son, actually, and possibly crazy," Abhorsen said, without really listening. "But he has the blood. What? Oh, yes, yes he is . . . you said was . . . you mean—"

"Yes," said Sabriel, unhappily. "He calls himself Touchstone. And he's waiting in the reservoir. Near the Stones. With Mogget."

Abhorsen paused for the first time, clearly taken aback.

"All our plans go astray, it seems," he said somberly, sighing. "Kerrigor lured me to the reservoir to use my blood to break a Great Stone, but I managed to protect myself, so he contented himself with trapping me in Death. He thought you would be lured to my body, and he could use your blood—but I was not trapped as securely as he thought, and planned a reverse. But now, if the Prince is there, he has another source of blood to break the Great Charter—"

"He's in the diamond of protection," Sabriel said, suddenly feeling afraid for Touchstone.

"That may not suffice," replied Abhorsen grimly. "Kerrigor grows stronger every day he spends in Life, taking the strength from living folk, and feeding off the broken Stones. He will soon be able to break even the strongest Charter Magic defenses. He may be strong enough now. But tell me of the Prince's companion. Who is Mogget?"

"Mogget?" repeated Sabriel, surprised again. "But I met him at our House! He's a Free Magic—something—wearing the shape of a white cat, with a red collar that carries a miniature Saraneth."

"Mogget," said Abhorsen, as if trying to get his mouth around an unpalatable morsel. "That is the Wallmaker relict, or their last creation, or their child—no one knows, possibly not even him. I wonder why he took the shape of a cat? He was always a sort of albino dwarf-boy to me, and he practically never left the House. I suppose he may be some sort of protection for the Prince. We must hurry."

"I thought we were!" snapped Sabriel, as he started off again. She didn't mean to be bad-tempered, but this was not her idea of a heartfelt reunion between father and daughter. He hardly seemed to notice her, except as a repository for numerous revelations and as an agent to deal with Kerrigor.

Abhorsen suddenly stopped, and gathered her into a quick, one-armed embrace. His grip felt strong, but Sabriel felt another reality there, as if his arm was a shadow, temporarily born of light, but doomed to fade at nightfall.

"I have not been an ideal parent, I know," Abhorsen said quietly. "None of us ever are. When we become the Abhorsen, we lose much else. Responsibility to many people rides roughshod over personal responsibilities; difficulties and enemies crush out softness; our horizons narrow. You are my daughter, and I have always loved you. But now, I live again for only a short time—a hundred hundred heartbeats, no more—and I must win a battle against a terrible enemy. Our parts now—which perforce we must play—are not father and daughter, but one old Abhorsen, making way for the new. But behind this, there is always my love."

"A hundred hundred heartbeats . . ." whispered Sabriel, tears falling down her face. She gently pushed herself out of his embrace, and they started forward together, towards the First Gate, the First Precinct, Life—and then, the reservoir.

Chapter Twenty-Three

TOUCHSTONE COULD SEE the Dead now, and had no difficulty hearing them. They were chanting and clapping, decayed hands meeting together in a steady, slow rhythm that put all the hair on the back of his head on edge. A ghastly noise, hard sounds of bone on bone, or the liquid thumpings of decomposed, jellying flesh. The chanting was even worse, for very few of them had functioning mouths. Touchstone had never seen or heard a shipwreck—now he knew the sound of a thousand sailors drowning, all at once, in a quiet sea.

The lines of the Dead had marched out close to where Touchstone stood, forming a great mass of shifting shadow, spread like a choking fungus around the columns. Touchstone couldn't make out what they were doing, till Mogget, with his nightsight, explained.

"They're forming up into two lines, to make a corridor," the little cat whispered, though the need for silence was long gone. "A corridor of Dead Hands, reaching from the northern stair to us."

"Can you see the doorway of the stair?" Touchstone asked. He was no longer afraid, now he could see and smell the putrescent, stinking corpses lined up in mockery of a parade. I should have died in this reservoir long ago, he thought. There has just been a delay of two hundred years . . .

"Yes, I can," continued Mogget, his eyes green with sparkling fire. "A tall beast has come, its flesh boiling with dirty flames. A

Mordicant. It's crouching in the water, looking back and up like a dog to its master. Fog is rolling down the stairs behind it—a Free Magic trick, that one. I wonder why he has such an urge to impress?"

"Rogir always was flamboyant," Touchstone stated, as if he might be commenting on someone at a dinner party. "He liked everyone to be looking at him. He's no different as Kerrigor, no different Dead."

"Oh, but he is," said Mogget. "Very different. He knows you're here, and the fog's for vanity. He must have been terribly rushed making the body he wears now. A vain man—even a Dead one—would not like this body looked at."

Touchstone swallowed, trying not to think about that. He wondered if he could charge out of the diamond, flèche with his swords into that fog, a mad attack—but even if he got there, would his swords, Charter-spelled though they were, have any effect on the magical flesh Kerrigor now wore?

Something moved in the water, at the limits of his vision, and the Hands increased the tempo of their drumming, the frenzied gurgle-chanting rising in volume.

Touchstone squinted, confirming what he thought he'd seen—tendrils of fog, lazily drifting across the water between the lines of the Dead, keeping to the corridor they'd made.

"He's playing with us," gasped Touchstone, surprised by his own lack of breath for speech. He felt like he'd already sprinted a mile, his heart going thump-thump-thump-thump . . .

A terrible howl suddenly rose above the Dead drumming, and Touchstone leapt back, nearly dislodging Mogget. The howl rose and rose, becoming unbearable, and then a huge shape broke out of the fog and darkness, stampeding towards them with fearful power, great swaths of spray exploding around it as it ran.

Touchstone shouted, or screamed—he wasn't sure—threw away his candle, drew his left sword and thrust both blades out, crouching to receive the charge, knees so bent he was chest-deep in the water.

"The Mordicant!" yelled Mogget, then he was gone, leaping from Touchstone to the still-frosted Sabriel.

Touchstone barely had time to absorb this information, and a split-second image of something like an enormous, flame-shrouded bear, howling like the final scream of a sacrifice—then the Mordicant collided with the diamond of protection, and Touchstone's out-thrust swords.

Silver sparks exploded with a bang that drowned the howling, throwing both Touchstone and the Mordicant back several yards. Touchstone lost his footing, and went under, water bubbling into his nose and still-screaming mouth. He panicked, thinking the Mordicant would be on him in a second, and flipped himself back up with unnecessary force, savagely ripping his stomach muscles.

He almost flew out of the water, swords at guard again, but the diamond was intact, and the Mordicant retreating, backing away along the corridor of Hands. They'd stopped their noise, but there was something else—something Touchstone didn't recognize, till the water drained out of his ears.

It was laughter, laughter echoing out of the fog, which now billowed across the water, coming closer and closer, till the retreating Mordicant was enveloped in it, and lost to sight.

"Did my hound scare you, little brother?" said a voice from within the fog.

"Ow!" exclaimed Sabriel, feeling Mogget's claws on her physical body. Abhorsen looked at her, raising one silvery eyebrow questioningly.

"Something touched my body in Life," she explained. "Mogget, I think. I wonder what's happening?"

They stood at the very edge of Death, on the border with Life. No Dead had tried to stop them, and they'd passed easily through the First Gate. Perhaps any Dead would quail from the sight of two Abhorsens . . .

Now they waited. Sabriel didn't know why. Somehow, Abhorsen seemed to be able to see into Life, or to work out what was happening. He stood like an eavesdropper, body slightly bent, ear cocked to a non-existent door.

Sabriel, on the other hand, stood like a soldier, keeping watch for the Dead. The broken stones made this part of Death an attractive high road into Life, and she had expected to find many Dead here, trying to take advantage of the "hole." But it was not so. They seemed to be alone in the grey, featureless river, their only neighbors the swells and eddies of the water.

Abhorsen closed his eyes, concentrating even harder, then opened them to a wide-eyed stare and touched Sabriel lightly on the arm.

"It is almost time," he said gently. "When we emerge, I want you to take . . . Touchstone . . . and run for the southern stairs. Do not stop for anything, anything at all. Once outside, climb up to the top of the Palace Hill, to the West Yard. It's just an empty field now—Touchstone will know how to get there. If the Clayr are watching properly, and haven't got their whens mixed up, there'll be a Paperwing there—"

"A Paperwing!" interrupted Sabriel. "But I crashed it."

"There are several around," replied Abhorsen. "The Abhorsen who made it—the forty-sixth, I think—taught several others how to construct them. Anyway, it should be there. The Clayr will also be there, or a messenger, to tell you where to find Kerrigor's body in Ancelstierre. Fly as close to the Wall as possible, cross, find the body—and destroy it!"

"What will you be doing?" whispered Sabriel.

"Here is Saraneth," replied Abhorsen, not meeting her gaze. "Give me your sword, and . . . Astarael."

The seventh bell. Astarael the Sorrowful. Weeper.

Sabriel didn't move, made no motion to hand over bell or blade. Abhorsen pushed Saraneth into its pouch, and did up the strap. He started to undo the strap that held Astarael, but Sabriel's hand closed on his, gripping it tightly.

"There must be another way," she cried. "We can all escape together—"

"No," said Abhorsen firmly. He gently pushed her hand away. Sabriel let go, and he took Astarael carefully from the bandolier, making sure it couldn't sound. "Does the walker choose the path, or the path the walker?"

Numbly, Sabriel handed him her sword . . . his sword. Her empty hands hung open by her sides.

"I have walked in Death to the very precipice of the Ninth Gate," Abhorsen said quietly. "I know the secrets and horrors of the Nine Precincts. I do not know what lies beyond, but everything that lives must go there, in the proper time. That is the rule that governs our work as the Abhorsen, but it also governs us. You are the fifty-third Abhorsen, Sabriel. I have not taught you as well as I should—let this be my final lesson. Everyone and everything has a time to die."

He bent forward, and kissed her forehead, just under the rim of her helmet. For a moment, she stood like a stringed puppet at rest, then she flung herself against his chest, feeling the soft fabric of his surcoat. She seemed to diminish in size, till once again she was a little girl, running to his embrace at the school gates. As she could then, she heard the slow beating of his heart. Only now, she heard the beats as grains in a timepiece, counting his hard-won hundred hundreds, counting till it was time for him to die.

She hugged him tightly, her arms meeting around his back, his arms outstretched like a cross, sword in one hand, bell in the other. Then, she let go.

They turned together, and plunged out into Life.

Kerrigor laughed again, an obscene cackle that rose to a manic crescendo, before suddenly cutting to an ominous silence. The Dead resumed their drumming, softer now, and the fog drifted forward with horrible certainty. Touchstone, drenched and partly drowned, watched it with the taut nerves of a mouse captivated by a gliding snake. Somewhere in the back of his mind, he noted that it was easier to see the whiteness of the fog. Up above, the clouds had gone, and the edges of the reservoir were once again lit by filtered sunlight. But they were forty paces or more from the edge . . .

A cracking noise behind him made him start, and turn, a jolt of fear suddenly overlaid with relief. Sabriel, and her father, were returning to Life! Ice flakes fell from them in miniature flurries, and the layer of ice around Abhorsen's middle broke into several small floes and drifted away.

Touchstone blinked as the frost fell away from their hands and faces. Now Sabriel was empty-handed, and Abhorsen wielded the sword and bell.

"Thank the Charter!" exclaimed Touchstone, as they opened their eyes and moved.

But no one heard him, for in that instant a terrible scream of rage and fury burst out of the fog, so loud the columns shivered, and ripples burst out across the water.

Touchstone turned again, and the fog was flying away in shreds, revealing the Mordicant crouched low, only its eyes and long mouth, bubbling with oily flames, visible above the water.

Behind it, with one elongated hand upon its bog-clay head, stood something that might be thought of as a man.

Staring, Touchstone saw that Kerrigor had tried to make the body he currently inhabited look like the Rogir of old, but either his skills, memory or taste were sadly lacking. Kerrigor stood at least seven feet tall, his body impossibly deep-chested and narrow-waisted. His head was too thin, and too long, and his mouth spread from ear to ear. His eyes did not bear looking at, for they were thin slits burning with Free Magic fires—not eyes at all.

But somehow, even so warped, he did have a little of the look of Rogir. Take a man, make him malleable, stretch and twist . . .

The hideous mouth opened, yawning wider and wider, then Kerrigor laughed, a short laugh, punctuated by the snap of his closing jaws. Then he spoke, and his voice was as warped and twisted as his body.

"I am fortunate. Three bearers of blood—blood for the breaking! Three!"

Touchstone kept staring, hearing Kerrigor's voice, still somewhat like Rogir's, rich but rotten, wet like worm-ridden fruit. He saw both the new, twisted Kerrigor and the other, better-fashioned body he'd known as Rogir. He saw the dagger again, slashing across the Queen's throat, the blood cascading out, the golden cup . . .

A hand grabbed him, turned him around, took his left sword from his grasp. He suddenly refocused, gasping for air again, and saw Sabriel. She had his left sword in her right hand, and now took his open palm in her left, dragging him towards the south. He let her pull, following in a splashing, loose-limbed run. Everything seemed to close in then, his vision narrowing, like a half-remembered dream.

He saw Sabriel's father—the Abhorsen—for the first time

devoid of frost. He looked hard, determined, but he smiled, and bowed his head a fraction as they passed. Touchstone wondered why he was going the wrong way . . . towards Kerrigor, towards the dagger and the catching cup. Mogget was on his shoulder too, and that was unlike Mogget, going into danger . . . there was something else peculiar about Mogget too . . . yes, his collar was gone . . . maybe he should turn and go back, put Mogget's collar back on, try and fight Kerrigor . . .

"Run! Damn you! Run!" screamed Sabriel, as he half-turned. Her voice snapped him out of whatever trance he'd been in. Nausea hit, for they'd left the diamond of protection. Unwarned, he threw up immediately, turning his head as they ran. He realized he was dragging on Sabriel's hand, and forced himself to run faster, though his legs felt dead, numbed by savage pins and needles. He could hear the Dead again now, chanting, and drumming, drumming fast. There were voices too, raised loud, echoing in the vast cavern. The howl of the Mordicant, and a strange buzzing, crackling sound that he felt rather than heard.

They reached the southern stair, but Sabriel didn't slacken her pace, jumping up and off, out of the twilight of the reservoir into total darkness. Touchstone lost her hand, then found it again, and they stumbled up the steps together, swords held dangerously ahead and behind, striking sparks from the stone. Still they heard the tumult from behind, the howling, drumming, shouting, all magnified by the water and the vastness of the reservoir. Then another sound began, cutting through the noise with the clarity of perfection.

It started softly, like a tuning fork lightly struck, but grew, a pure note, blown by a trumpeter of inexhaustible breath, till there was nothing but the sound. The sound of Astarael.

Sabriel and Touchstone both stopped, almost in mid-stride. They felt a terrible urge to leave their bodies, to shuck them off as so much worn-out baggage. Their spirits—their essential selves—wanted to go, to go into Death and plunge joyfully into the strongest current, to be carried to the very end.

"Think of Life!" screamed Sabriel, her voice only just audible through the pure note. She could feel Touchstone dying, his will insufficient to hold him in Life. He seemed almost to expect this sudden summons into Death.

"Fight it!" she screamed again, dropping her sword to slap him across the face. "Live!"

Still he slipped away. Desperate, she grabbed him by the ears, and kissed him savagely, biting his lip, the salty blood filling both their mouths. His eyes cleared, and she felt him concentrate again, concentrate on Life, on living. His sword fell, and he brought his arms up around her and returned her kiss. Then he put his head on her shoulder, and she on his, and they held each other tightly till the single note of Astarael slowly died.

Silence came at last. Gingerly, they let each other go. Touchstone shakily groped around for his sword, but Sabriel lit a candle before he could cut his fingers in the dark. They looked at each other in the flickering light. Sabriel's eyes were wet, Touchstone's mouth bloody.

"What was that?" Touchstone asked huskily.

"Astarael," replied Sabriel. "The final bell. It calls everyone who hears it into Death."

"Kerrigor . . ."

"He'll come back," whispered Sabriel. "He'll always come back, till his real body's destroyed."

"Your father?" Touchstone mumbled. "Mogget?"

"Dad's dead," said Sabriel. Her face was composed, but her eyes overflowed into tears. "He'll go quickly beyond the Final Gate. Mogget—I don't know."

She fingered the silver ring on her hand, frowned, and bent

to pick up the sword she'd taken from Touchstone.

"Come on," she ordered. "We have to get up to the West Yard. Quickly."

"The West Yard?" asked Touchstone, retrieving his own sword. He was confused and sick, but he forced himself up. "Of the Palace?"

"Yes," replied Sabriel. "Let's go."

Chapter Twenty-Four

THE SUNSHINE WAS harsh to their eyes, for it was surprisingly only a little past noon. They stumbled out onto the marble steps of the cave, blinking like nocturnal animals prematurely flushed out of an underground warren.

Sabriel looked around at the quiet, sunlit trees, the placid expanse of grass, the clogged fountain. Everything seemed so normal, so far removed from the crazed and twisted chamber of horrors that was the reservoir, deep beneath their feet.

She looked at the sky too, losing focus in the blue, retreating lines of clouds just edging about the fuzzy periphery of her vision. My father is dead, she thought. Gone forever . . .

"The road winds around the south-western part of Palace Hill," a voice said, somewhere near her, beyond the blueness.

"What?"

"The road. Up to the West Yard."

It was Touchstone talking. Sabriel closed her eyes, told herself to concentrate, to get a grip on the here and now. She opened her eyes and looked at Touchstone.

He was a mess. Face blood-streaked from his bleeding lip, hair wet, plastered flat, armor and clothes darkly sodden. Water dripped down the sword he still held out, angled to the ground.

"You didn't tell me you were a Prince," Sabriel said, in a conversational tone. She might have been commenting on the weather. Her voice sounded strange in her own ears, but she didn't have the energy to do anything about it.

"I'm not," Touchstone replied, shrugging. He looked up at the sky while he spoke. "The Queen was my mother, but my father was an obscure northern noble, who 'took up with her' a few years after her consort's death. He was killed in a hunting accident before I was born . . . Look, shouldn't we be going? To the West Yard?"

"I suppose so," Sabriel said dully. "Father said there will be a Paperwing waiting for us there, and the Clayr, to tell us where to go."

"I see," said Touchstone. He came closer, and peered at Sabriel's vacant eyes, then took her unresisting and oddly floppy arm, and steered her towards the line of beech trees that marked a path to the western end of the park. Sabriel walked obediently, increasing her pace as Touchstone sped up, till they were practically jogging. Touchstone was pushing on her arm, with many backward glances; Sabriel moving with a sleepwalker's jerky animation.

A few hundred yards from the ornamental caves, the beeches gave way to more lawn, and a road started up the side of Palace Hill, switchbacking twice to the top.

The road was well-paved, but the flagstones had pushed up, or sunk down, over two decades without maintenance, and there were some quite deep ruts and holes. Sabriel caught her foot in one and she almost fell, Touchstone just catching her. But this small shock seemed to break her from the effects of the larger shock, and she found a new alertness cutting through her dumb despair.

"Why are we running?"

"Those scavengers are following us," Touchstone replied shortly, pointing back through the park. "The ones who had the children at the gate."

Sabriel looked where he pointed and, sure enough, there were figures slowly moving through the beech-lined path. All nine were there, close together, laughing and talking. They seemed confident Sabriel and Touchstone could not escape them, and their mood looked to be that of casual beaters, easily driving their stupid prey to a definite end. One of them saw Sabriel and Touchstone watching and used a gesture that distance made unclear, but was probably obscene. Laughter carried to them, borne by the breeze. The men's intentions were clear. Hostile.

"I wonder if they deal with the Dead," Sabriel said bleakly, revulsion in those words. "To do their deeds when sunlight lends its aid to the living . . ."

"They mean no good, anyway," said Touchstone, as they set off again, building up from a fast walk to a jog. "They have bows and I bet they can shoot, unlike the villagers of Nestowe."

"Yes," replied Sabriel. "I hope there is a Paperwing up there . . ."

She didn't need to expand upon what would happen if it wasn't. Neither of them were in any shape for fighting, or much Charter Magic, and nine bowmen could easily finish them off— or capture them. If the men were working for Kerrigor, it would be capture, and the knife, down in the dark of the reservoir . . .

The road grew steeper, and they jogged in silence, breath coming fast and ragged, with none to spare for words. Touchstone coughed, and Sabriel looked at him with concern, till she realized she was coughing too. The shape they were in, it might not take an arrow to finish matters. The hill would do it anyway.

"Not . . . much . . . farther," Touchstone gasped as they turned at the switchback, tired legs gaining a few seconds of relief on the flat, before starting the next incline.

Sabriel started to laugh, a bitter, coughing laugh, because it

was still a lot farther. The laugh became a shocked cry as something struck her in the ribs like a sucker punch. She fell sideways,
into Touchstone, carrying both of them down onto the hard
flagstones. A long-shot arrow had found its mark.

"Sabriel!" Touchstone shouted, voice high with fear and
anger. He shouted her name again, and then Sabriel suddenly felt
Charter Magic explode into life within him. As it grew, he leapt
up, and thrust his arms out and down towards the enemy,
towards that over-gifted marksman. Eight small suns flowered at
his fingertips, grew to the size of his clenched fists, and shot out,
leaving white trails of after-image in the air. A split second later,
a scream from below testified to their finding at least one target.

Numbly, Sabriel wondered how Touchstone could possibly
still have the strength for such a spell. Wonder became surprise
as he suddenly bent and lifted her up, pack and all, cradling her
in his arms—all in one easy motion. She screamed a little as the
arrow shifted in her side, but Touchstone didn't seem to notice.
He threw his head back, roared out an animal-like challenge, and
started to run up the road, gathering speed from an ungainly
lurch to an inhuman sprint. Froth burst from his lips, blowing
out over his chin and onto Sabriel. Every vein and muscle in his
neck and face corded out, and his eyes went wild with unseeing
energy.

He was berserk, and nothing could stop him now, save total
dismemberment. Sabriel shivered in his grasp and turned her
face into his chest, too disturbed to look on the savage, snorting
face that bore so little resemblance to the Touchstone she knew.
But at least he was running away from the enemy . . .

On he ran, leaving the road, climbing over the tumbled stones
of what had once been a gateway, hardly pausing, jumping from
one rock to another with goat-like precision. His face was as
bright red as a fire engine now, the pulse in his neck beating as

fast as a hummingbird's wings. Sabriel, forgetting her own wound in sudden fear that his heart would burst, started shouting at him, begging him to come out of the rage.

"Touchstone! We're safe! Put me down! Stop! Please, stop!"

He didn't hear her, his whole concentration bent on their path. Through the ruined gateway he ran, on along a walled path, nostrils wide, head darting from side to side like a scent-following hound.

"Touchstone! Touchstone!" Sabriel sobbed, beating on his chest with her hands. "We've got away! I'm all right! Stop! Stop!"

Still he ran, through another arch; along a raised way, the stones falling away under his feet; down a short stair, jumping gaping holes. A closed door halted him for a moment, and Sabriel breathed a sigh of relief, but he kicked at it viciously, till the rotten wood collapsed and he could back through, carefully shielding Sabriel from splinters.

Beyond the door was a large, open field, bordered by tumble-down walls. Tall weeds covered the expanse, with the occasional stunted, self-sown tree rising above them. Right at the western edge, perched where a wall had long since crumbled down the hill, there were two Paperwings, one facing south and the other north—and two people, indistinct silhouettes bordered with the flaming orange of the afternoon sun that was sinking down behind them.

Touchstone broke into a gait that could only be described as a gallop, parting the weeds like a ship ploughing a sargasso sea. He ran right up to the two standing figures, gently placed Sabriel on the ground before them—and fell over, eyes rolling back to whiteness, limbs twitching.

Sabriel tried to crawl over to him, but the pain in her side suddenly bit sharp and deadly, so it was all she could do to sit up and look at the two people, and beyond them, the Paperwings.

"Hello," they said, in unison. "We are, for the moment, the Clayr. You must be the Abhorsen and the King."

Sabriel stared, dry-mouthed. The sun was in her eyes, making it hard for her to see them clearly. Young women, both, with long blond hair and bright, piercing blue eyes. They wore white linen dresses, with long, open sleeves. Freshly pressed dresses that made Sabriel feel extremely dirty and uncivilized, in her reservoir-soaked breeches and sweaty armor. Like their voices, their faces were identical. Very pretty. Twins.

They smiled, and knelt down, one by Sabriel's side, the other by Touchstone's. Sabriel felt Charter Magic slowly welling up in them, like water rising in a spring—then it flowed into her, taking away the hurt and pain of the arrow. Next to her, Touchstone's breath became less labored, and he sank into the easy quiet of sleep.

"Thank you," croaked Sabriel. She tried to smile, but seemed to have lost the knack of it. "There are slavers . . . human allies of the Dead . . . behind us."

"We know," said the duo. "But they are ten minutes behind. Your friend—the King—ran very, very fast. We saw him run yesterday. Or tomorrow."

"Ah," said Sabriel, laboriously pushing herself up onto her feet, thinking of her father and what he had said about the Clayr confusing their whens. Best to find out what she needed to know before things got really confusing.

"Thank you," she said again, for the arrow fell on the ground as she fully straightened up. It was a hunting arrow, narrow-headed, not an armor-punching bodkin. They had only meant to slow her down. She shivered, and felt the hole between the armor plates. The wound didn't feel healed exactly—just older, as if it had struck a week ago, instead of minutes.

"Father said you would be here . . . that you have been watching for us, and watching for where Kerrigor has his body."

"Yes," replied the Clayr. "Well, not us exactly. We've only been allowed to be the Clayr today, because we're the best Paperwing pilots . . ."

"Or actually, Ryelle is . . ." one of the twins said, pointing at the other. "But since she would need a Paperwing to fly home in, two Paperwings were needed, so . . ."

"Sanar came too," Ryelle continued, pointing back at her sister.

"Both of us," they chorused. "Now, there isn't much time. You can take the red and gold Paperwing . . . we painted it in the royal colors when we knew last week. But first, there's Kerrigor's body."

"Yes," said Sabriel. Her father's—her family's—the Kingdom's enemy. For her to deal with. Her burden, no matter how heavy, and how feeble her shoulders currently felt, she had to bear it.

"His body is in Ancelstierre," said the twins. "But our vision is weak across the Wall, so we don't have a map, or know the place names. We'll have to show you—and you'll have to remember."

"Yes," agreed Sabriel, feeling like a dull student promising to deal with a question quite beyond her. "Yes."

The Clayr nodded, and smiled again. Their teeth were very white and even. One, possibly Ryelle—Sabriel had already got them confused—brought a bottle made of clear green glass out from the flowing sleeve of her robe, the telltale flash of Charter Magic showing it hadn't been there before. The other woman— Sanar—produced a long ivory wand out of her sleeve.

"Ready?" they asked each other simultaneously, and, "Yes," before their question had even penetrated Sabriel's tired brain.

Ryelle unstoppered the bottle with a resonant "pop," and in

one quick motion, poured out the contents along a horizontal line. Sanar, equally quickly, drew the wand across the falling water—and it froze in mid-air, to form a pane of transparent ice. A frozen window, suspended in front of Sabriel.

"Watch," commanded the women, and Sanar tapped the ice-window with her wand. It clouded over at that touch, briefly showed a scene of whirling snow, a glimpse of the Wall, then steadied into a moving vision—much like a film shot from a traveling car. Wyverley College had frowned on films, but Sabriel had been to see quite a few in Bain. This was much the same, but in color, and she could hear natural sounds as clearly as if she were there.

The window showed typical Ancelstierran farmland—a long field of wheat, ripe for the harvest, with a tractor stopped in the distance, its driver chatting with another man perched atop a cart, his two draft-horses standing stolidly, peering out through their blinkers.

The view raced closer towards these two men, veered around them with a snatch of caught conversation, and continued—following a road, up and over a hill, through a small wood and up to a crossroads, where the gravel intersected with a macadamized route of greater importance. There was a sign there, and the "eye," or whatever it was, zoomed up to it, till the signpost filled the whole of the ice-window. "Wyverley 2½ miles," it read, directing travelers along the major road, and they were off again, shooting down towards Wyverley village.

A few seconds later, the moving image slowed, to show the familiar houses of Wyverley village; the blacksmith-cum-mechanic's shop; the Wyvern public house; the constable's trim house with the blue lantern. All landmarks known to Sabriel. She concentrated even more carefully, for surely the vision, having shown her a fixed point of reference, would now race off to parts of Ancelstierre which were unknown to her.

But the picture still moved slowly. At a walking pace, it went through the village, and turned off the road, following a bridle-path up the forested hill known as Docky Point. A nice enough hill, to be sure, covered by a cork tree plantation, with some quite old trees. Its only point of interest was the rectangular cairn upon the hilltop . . . the cairn . . . The image changed, closing in on the huge, grey-green stones, square-cut and tightly packed together. A relatively recent folly, Sabriel remembered from their local history lessons. A little less than two hundred years old. She'd almost visited it once, but something had changed her mind . . .

The image changed again, somehow sinking through the stone, down between the lines of mortar, zigzagging around the blocks, to the dark chamber at its heart. For an instant the ice-window went completely dark, then light came. A bronze sar-cophagus lay under the cairn, metal crawling with Free Magic perversions of Charter marks. The vision dodged these shifting marks, penetrated the bronze. A body lay inside, a living body, wreathed in Free Magic.

The scene shifted, moving with jagged difficulty to the face of the body. A handsome face, that swam closer and closer into focus, a face that showed what Kerrigor once had been. The human face of Rogir, his features clearly showing that he had shared a mother with Touchstone.

Sabriel stared, sickened and fascinated by the similarities between the half-brothers—then the vision suddenly blurred, spinning into greyness, greyness accompanied by rushing water. Death. Something huge and monstrous was wading against the current, a jagged cutting of darkness, formless and featureless, save for two eyes that burned with unnatural flame. It seemed to see her beyond the ice-window, and lurched forward, two arms like blown storm clouds reaching forward.

"Abhorsen's Get!" screamed Kerrigor. "Your blood will gush upon the Stones . . ."

His arms seemed about to come through the window, but suddenly, the ice cracked, the pieces collapsing into a pile of swift-melting slush.

"You saw," the Clayr said together. It wasn't a question. Sabriel nodded, shaking, her thoughts still on the likeness between Kerrigor's original human body and Touchstone. Where was the fork in their paths? What had put Rogir's feet on the long road that led to the abomination known as Kerrigor?

"We have four minutes," announced Sanar. "Till the slavers come. We'll help you get the King to your Paperwing, shall we?"

"Yes, please," replied Sabriel. Despite the fearsome sight of Kerrigor's raw spirit form, the vision had imbued her with a new and definite sense of purpose. Kerrigor's body was in Ancelstierre. She would find it and destroy it, and then deal with his spirit. But they had to get to the body first . . .

The two women lifted Touchstone up, grunting with the effort. He was no lightweight at any time, and now was even heavier, still sodden with water from his ducking in the reservoir. But the Clayr, despite their rather ethereal appearance, seemed to manage well enough.

"We wish you luck, cousin," they said, as they walked slowly to the red and gold Paperwing, balanced so close to the edge of the broken wall, the Saere glistening white and blue below.

"Cousin?" Sabriel murmured. "I suppose we are cousins—of a sort, aren't we?"

"Blood relatives, all the children of the Great Charters," the Clayr agreed. "Though the clan dwindles . . ."

"Do you always—know what is going to happen?" Sabriel asked, as they gently lowered Touchstone into the back of the cockpit, and strapped him in with the belts normally used for securing luggage.

Both the Clayr laughed. "No, thank the Charter! Our family is the most numerous of the bloodlines, and the gift is spread among many. Our visions come in snatches and splinters, glimpses and shadows. When we must, the whole family can spend its strength to narrow our sight—as it has done through us today. Tomorrow, we will be back to dreams and confusion, not knowing where, when or what we see. Now, we have only two minutes . . ."

Suddenly, they hugged Sabriel, surprising her with the obvious warmth of the gesture. She hugged them back, gladly, grateful for their care. With her father gone, she had no family left—but perhaps she would find sisters in the Clayr, and perhaps Touchstone would be . . .

"Two minutes," repeated both the women, one in each ear. Sabriel let them go, and hurriedly took *The Book of the Dead* and the two Charter Magic books from her pack, wedging them down next to Touchstone's slightly snoring form. After a second's thought, she also stuffed in the fleece-lined oilskin and the boat cloak. Touchstone's swords went into the special holders next, but the pack and the rest of its contents had to be abandoned.

"Next stop, the Wall," Sabriel muttered as she climbed into the craft, trying not to think about what would happen if they had to land somewhere uncivilized in between.

The Clayr were already in their green and silver craft, and, as Sabriel did up her straps, she heard them begin to whistle, Charter Magic streaming out into the air. Sabriel licked her lips, summoned her breath and strength, and joined in. Wind rose behind both the craft, tossing black hair and blond, lifting the Paperwings' tails and jostling their wings.

Sabriel took a breath after the wind-whistling, and stroked

the smooth, laminated paper of the hull. A brief image of the first Paperwing came to mind, broken and burning in the depths of Holehallow.

"I hope we fare better together," she whispered, before joining with the Clayr to whistle the last note, the pure clear sound that would wake the Charter Magic in their craft.

A second later, two bright-eyed Paperwings leapt out from the ruined palace of Belisaere, glided down almost to the swell in the Sea of Saere, then rose to circle higher and higher above the hill. One craft, of green and silver, turned to the north-west. The other, of red and gold, turned south.

Touchstone, waking to the rush of cold air on his face, and the unfamiliar sensation of flying, groggily muttered, "What happened?"

"We're going to Ancelstierre," Sabriel shouted. "Across the Wall, to find Kerrigor's body—and destroy it!"

"Oh," said Touchstone, who only heard "across the Wall." "Good."

"BEG PARDON, SIR," said the soldier, saluting at the doorway to the officer's bathroom. "Duty officer's compliments and can you come straight away?"

Colonel Horyse sighed, put down his razor, and used the flannel to wipe off the remains of the shaving soap. He had been interrupted shaving that morning, and had tried several times during the day to finish the job. Perhaps it was a sign he should grow a moustache.

"What's happening?" he asked, resignedly. Whatever was happening, it was unlikely to be good.

"An aircraft, sir," replied the private, stolidly.

"From Army HQ? Dropping a message cylinder?"

"I don't know, sir. It's on the other side of the Wall."

"What!" exclaimed Horyse, dropping all his shaving gear, picking up his helmet and sword, and attempting to rush out, all at the same time. "Impossible!"

But, when he eventually sorted himself out and got down to the Forward Observation Post—an octagonal strongpoint that thrust out through the Perimeter to within fifty yards of the Wall—it quite clearly was possible. The light was fading as the afternoon waned—it was probably close to setting on the other side—but the visibility was good enough to make out the distant airborne shape that was descending in a series of long, gradual loops . . . on the other side of the Wall. In the Old Kingdom.

The Duty Officer was watching through big artillery spotter's binoculars, his elbows perched on the sandbagged parapet of the position. Horyse paused for a moment to think of the fellow's name—he was new to the Perimeter Garrison—then tapped him on the shoulder.

"Jorbert. Mind if I have a look?"

The young officer lowered the binoculars reluctantly, and handed them across like a boy deprived of a half-eaten lollipop.

"It's definitely an aircraft, sir," he said, brightening up as he spoke. "Totally silent, like a glider, but it's clearly powered somehow. Very maneuverable, and beautifully painted too. There's two . . . people in it, sir."

Horyse didn't answer, but took up the binoculars and the same elbow-propping stance. For a moment, he couldn't see the aircraft, and he hastily panned left and right, then zigzagged up and down—and there it was, lower than he expected, almost in a landing approach.

"Sound stand-to," he ordered harshly, as the realization struck him that the craft would land very close to the Crossing Point—perhaps only a hundred yards from the gate.

He heard his command being repeated by Jorbert to a sergeant, and then bellowed out, to be taken up by sentries, duty NCOs, and eventually to hand-cranked klaxons and the old bell that hung in the front of the Officer's Mess.

It was hard to see exactly who or what was in the craft, till he twiddled with the focus, and Sabriel's face leapt towards him, magnified up to a recognizable form, even at the current distance. Sabriel, the daughter of Abhorsen, accompanied by an unknown man—or something wearing the shape of a man. For a moment, Horyse considered ordering the men to stand-down, but he could already hear hobnailed boots clattering on the duckboards, sergeants and corporals shouting—and it might not really be Sabriel. The sun was weakening, and the coming night would be the first of the full moon . . .

"Jorbert!" he snapped, handing the binoculars back to the surprised and unready subaltern. "Go and give the Regimental Sergeant-Major my compliments, and ask him to personally organize a section of the Scouts—we'll go out and take a closer look at that aircraft."

"Oh, thank you, sir!" gushed Lieutenant Jorbert, obviously taking the "we" to include himself. His enthusiasm surprised Horyse, at least for a moment.

"Tell me, Mr. Jorbert," he asked. "Have you by any chance sought a transfer to the Flying Corps?"

"Well, yes, sir," replied Jorbert. "Eight times . . ."

"Just remember," Horyse said, interrupting him. "That whatever is out there may be a flying creature, not a flying machine—and its pilots may be half-rotted things that should be properly dead, or Free Magic beings that have never really lived at all. Not fellow aviators, knights of the sky, or anything like that."

Jorbert nodded, unmilitarily, saluted, and turned on his heel.

"And don't forget your sword next time you're on duty, officer," Horyse called after him. "Hasn't anyone told you your revolver might not work?"

Jorbert nodded again, flushed, almost saluted, then scuttled off down the communication trench. One of the soldiers in the Forward Observation Post, a corporal with a full sleeve of chevrons denoting twenty years' service, and a Charter mark on his forehead to show his Perimeter pedigree, shook his head at the departing back of the young officer.

"Why are you shaking your head, Corporal Anshy?" snapped Horyse, irked by his many interrupted shaves and this new and potentially dangerous appearance of an aircraft.

"Water on the brain," replied the corporal cheerfully—and

rather ambiguously. Horyse opened his mouth to issue a sharp reprimand, then closed it as the corners of his mouth involuntarily inched up into a smile. Before he could actually laugh, he left the post, heading back to the trench junction where his section and the RSM would meet him to go beyond the Wall.

Within five paces, he'd lost his smile.

The Paperwing slid to a perfect landing in a flurry of snow. Sabriel and Touchstone sat in it, shivering under oilskin and boat cloak, respectively, then slowly levered themselves out to stand knee-deep in the tightly packed snow. Touchstone smiled at Sabriel, his nose bright red and eyebrows frosted.

"We made it."

"So far," replied Sabriel, warily looking around. She could see the long grey bulk of the Wall, with the deep honey-colored sun of autumn on the Ancelstierran side. Here, the snow lay banked against the grey stone, and it was overcast, with the sun almost gone. Dark enough for the Dead to be wandering around.

Touchstone's smile faded as he caught her mood, and he took his swords from the Paperwing, giving the left sword to Sabriel. She sheathed it, but it was a bad fit—another reminder of loss.

"I'd better get the books too," she said, bending in to retrieve them from the cockpit. The two Charter Magic books were fine, untouched by snow, but *The Book of the Dead* seemed wet. When Sabriel pulled it out, she found it wasn't snow-wet. Beads of dark, thick blood were welling up out of its cover. Silently, Sabriel wiped it on the hard crust of the snow, leaving a livid mark. Then she tucked the books away in the pockets of her coat.

"Why . . . why was the book like that?" asked Touchstone, trying, and almost succeeding, to sound curious rather than afraid.

"I think it's reacting to the presence of many deaths," Sabriel replied. "There is great potential here for the Dead to rise. This is a very weak point—"

"Shhh!" Touchstone interrupted her, pointing towards the Wall. Shapes, dark against the snow, were moving in an extended line towards them, at a deliberate, steady pace. They carried bows and spears, and Sabriel, at least, recognized the rifles slung across their backs.

"It's all right," Sabriel said, though a faint stab of nervousness touched her stomach. "They're soldiers from the Ancelstierran side—still, I might send the Paperwing on its way . . ."

Quickly, she checked that they'd taken everything from the cockpit, then laid her hand on the nose of the Paperwing, just above its twinkling eye. It seemed to look up at her as she spoke.

"Go now, friend. I don't want to risk you being dragged into Ancelstierre and taken apart. Fly where you will—to the Clayr's glacier, or, if you care to, to Abhorsen's House, where the water falls."

She stepped back, and formed the Charter marks that would imbue the Paperwing with choice, and the winds to lift it there. The marks went into her whistle, and the Paperwing moved with the rising pitch, accelerating along till it leapt into the sky at the peak of the highest note.

"I say!" exclaimed a voice. "How did you do that?"

Sabriel turned to see a young, out-of-breath Ancelstierran officer, the single gold pip of a second lieutenant looking lonely on his shoulder-straps. He was easily fifty yards in front of the rest of the line, but he didn't seem frightened. He was clutching a sword and a revolver, though, and he raised both of them as Sabriel stepped forward.

"Halt! You are my prisoners!"

"Actually, we're travelers," replied Sabriel, though she did stand still. "Is that Colonel Horyse I can see behind you?"

Jorbert turned half around to have a look, realized his mistake, and turned back just in time to see Sabriel and Touchstone smiling, then chuckling, then out-and-out laughing, clutching at each other's arms.

"What's so funny?" demanded Lieutenant Jorbert, as the two of them laughed and laughed, till the tears ran down their cheeks.

"Nothing," said Horyse, gesturing to his men to encircle Sabriel and Touchstone, while he went up and carefully placed two fingers on their foreheads—testing the Charter they bore within. Satisfied, he lightly shook them, till they stopped their shuddering, gasping laughter. Then, to the surprise of some of his men, he put an arm around each of them and led them back to the Crossing Point, towards Ancelstierre and sunshine.

Jorbert, left to cover the withdrawal, indignantly asked the air, "What was so funny?"

"You heard the Colonel," replied Regimental Sergeant-Major Tawklish. "Nothing. That was an hysterical reaction, that was. They've been through a lot, those two, mark my words."

Then, in the way that only RSMs have with junior officers, he paused, crushing Jorbert completely with a judicious, and long delayed "Sir."

The warmth wrapped Sabriel like a soft blanket as they stepped out of the shadow of the Wall, into the relative heat of an Ancelstierran autumn. She felt Touchstone falter at her side, and stumble, his face staring blindly upwards to the sun.

"You both look done in," said Horyse, speaking in the kindly, slow tone he used on shell-shocked soldiers. "How about something to eat, or would you rather get some sleep first?"

"Something to eat, certainly," Sabriel replied, trying to give him a grateful smile. "But not sleep. There's no time for that. Tell me—when was the full moon? Two days ago?"

Horyse looked at her, thinking that she no longer reminded him of his own daughter. She had become Abhorsen, a person beyond his ken, in such a short time . . .

"It's tonight," he said.

"But I've been in the Old Kingdom at least sixteen days . . ."

"Time is strange between the kingdoms," Horyse said. "We've had patrols swear they were out for two weeks, coming back in after eight days. A headache for the paymaster . . ."

"That voice, coming from the box on the pole," Touchstone interrupted, as they left the zigzag path through the wire defenses and climbed down into a narrow communication trench. "There is no Charter Magic in the box, or the voice . . ."

"Ah," replied Horyse, looking ahead to where a loudspeaker was announcing stand-down. "I'm surprised it's working. Electricity runs that, Mr. Touchstone. Science, not magic."

"It won't be working tonight," Sabriel said quietly. "No technology will be."

"Yes, it is rather loud," Horyse said, in a strong voice. More softly, he added, "Please don't say anything more till we get to my dugout. The men have already picked something up about tonight and the full moon . . ."

"Of course," replied Sabriel, wearily. "I'm sorry."

They walked the rest of the way in silence, slogging along the zigzagging communication trench, passing soldiers in the fighting trenches, ready at their stand-to positions. The soldier's conversations stopped as they passed, but resumed as soon as they turned the next zig or zag and were out of sight.

At last, they descended a series of steps into Colonel Horyse's dugout. Two sergeants stood guard outside—this time, Charter Mages from the Crossing Point Scouts, not the regular garrison infantry. Another soldier doubled off to the cookhouse, to fetch some food. Horyse busied himself with a small spirit-burner, and made tea.

Sabriel drank it without feeling much relief. Ancelstierre, and the universal comforter of its society—tea—no longer seemed as solid and dependable as she had once thought.

"Now," said Horyse. "Tell me why you don't have time to sleep."

"My father died yesterday," Sabriel said, stony-faced. "The wind flutes will fail tonight. At moonrise. The Dead here will rise with the moon."

"I'm sorry to hear about your father. Very sorry," Horyse said. He hesitated, then added, "But as you are here now, can't you bind the Dead anew?"

"If that were all, yes, I could," Sabriel continued. "But there is worse to come. Have you ever heard the name Kerrigor, Colonel?"

Horyse put his tea down.

"Your father spoke of him once. One of the Greater Dead, I think, imprisoned beyond the Seventh Gate?"

"More than Greater, possibly the Great," Sabriel said bleakly. "As far as I know, he is the only Dead spirit to also be a Free Magic adept."

"And a renegade member of the royal family," added Touchstone, his voice still harsh and dry from the cold winds of their flight, unquenched by tea. "And he is no longer imprisoned. He walks in Life."

"All these things give him power," Sabriel continued. "But there is a weakness there too. Kerrigor's mastery of Free Magic, and much of his power in both Life and Death, is dependent on the continual existence of his original body. He hid it, long ago, when he first chose to become a Dead spirit—and he hid it in Ancelstierre. Near the village of Wyverley, to be exact."

"And now he's coming to fetch it . . ." said Horyse, with terrible prescience. Outwardly, he looked calm, all those long years of Army service forming a hard carapace, containing his feelings. Inwardly, he felt a trembling that he hoped wasn't being transmitted to the mug in his hand.

"When will he come?"

"With the night," replied Sabriel. "With an army of the Dead. If he can emerge out of Death close to the Wall, he may come earlier."

"The sun—" Horyse began.

"Kerrigor can work the weather, bring fog or dense cloud."

"So what can we do?" asked Horyse, turning his palms outwards, towards Sabriel, his eyes questioning. "Abhorsen."

Sabriel felt a weight placed upon her, a burden adding to the weariness that already pressed upon her, but she forced herself to answer.

"Kerrigor's body is in a spelled sarcophagus under a cairn, a cairn atop a little hill called Docky Point, less than forty miles away. We need to get there quickly—and destroy the body."

"And that will destroy Kerrigor?"

"No," said Sabriel, shaking her head wistfully. "But it will weaken him . . . so there may be a chance . . ."

"Right," said Horyse. "We've still got three or four hours of daylight, but we'll need to move quickly. I take it that Kerrigor and his . . . forces . . . will have to cross the Wall here? They can't just pop out at Docky Point?"

"No," agreed Sabriel. "They'll have to emerge in Life in the Old Kingdom, and physically cross the Wall. It would probably be best not to try and stop him."

"I'm afraid we can't do that," replied Horyse. "That's what the Perimeter Garrison is here for."

"A lot of your soldiers will die to no purpose then," said

Touchstone. "Simply because they'll be in the way. Anything, and anybody, that gets in Kerrigor's way will be destroyed."

"So you want us to just let this . . . this thing and a horde of Dead descend on Ancelstierre?"

"Not exactly," replied Sabriel. "I would like to fight him at a time and a place more of our choosing. If you lend me all the soldiers here who have the Charter mark, and a little Charter Magic, we may have enough time to destroy Kerrigor's body. Also, we will be almost thirty-five miles from the Wall. Kerrigor's power may only be slightly lessened, but many of his minions will be weaker. Perhaps so weak, that destroying or damaging their physical forms will be sufficient to send them back into Death."

"And the rest of the garrison? We'll just stand aside and let Kerrigor and his army through the Perimeter?"

"You probably won't have a choice."

"I see," muttered Horyse. He got up, and paced backwards and forwards, six steps, all the dugout would allow. "Fortunately, or unfortunately perhaps—I am currently acting as the General Officer commanding the whole Perimeter. General Ashenber has returned south, due to . . . ah . . . ill health. A temporary situation only—Army HQ is loath to give any sort of higher command to those of us who wear the Charter mark. So the decision is mine . . ."

He stopped pacing, and stared back at Sabriel and Touchstone—but his eyes seemed to see something well beyond them and the rusty corrugated iron that walled the dugout. Finally, he spoke.

"Very well. I will give you twelve Charter Mages—half of the full complement of the Scouts—but I will also add some more mundane force. A detachment to escort you to . . . what was it? Docky Point. But I can't promise we won't fight on the Perimeter."

"We need you too Colonel," Sabriel said, in the silence that followed his decision. "You're the strongest Charter Mage the Garrison has."

"Impossible!" Horyse exclaimed emphatically. "I'm in command of the Perimeter. My responsibilities lie here."

"You'll never be able to explain tonight, anyway," Sabriel said. "Not to any general down south, or to anyone who hasn't crossed the Wall."

"I'll . . . I'll think about it while you have something to eat," Horyse declared, the rattle of a tray and plates tactfully announcing the arrival of a mess orderly on the steps. "Come in!"

The orderly entered, steam rising around the edges of the silver dishes. As he put the tray down, Horyse strode out past him, bellowing.

"Messenger! I want the Adjutant, Major Tindall and the CSM from 'A' Company, Lieutenant Aire from the Scouts, the RSM and the Quartermaster. In the Operations Room in ten minutes. Oh . . . call in the Transport Officer too. And warn the Signals staff to stand by for coding."

EVERYTHING MOVED RAPIDLY after the tea was drunk. Almost too rapidly for the exhausted Sabriel and Touchstone. Judging from the noises outside, soldiers were rushing about in all directions, while they ate their belated lunch. Then, before they could even begin to digest, Horyse was back, telling them to get moving.

It was somewhat like being a bit player in the school play, Sabriel thought, as she stumbled out of the communication trench and onto the parade ground. There was an awful lot happening around her, but she didn't really feel part of it. She felt Touchstone lightly brush her arm, and smiled at him reassuringly—it had to be even worse for him.

Within minutes, they were hustled across the parade ground, towards a waiting line of trucks, an open staff car and two strange steel-plated contraptions. Lozenge-shaped, with gun turrets on either side, and caterpillar tracks. Tanks, Sabriel realized. A relatively recent invention. Like the trucks, they were roaring, engines belching blue-grey smoke. No problem now, Sabriel thought, but the engines would stop when the wind blew in from the Old Kingdom. Or when Kerrigor came . . .

Horyse led them to the staff car, opened the back door and gestured for them to get in.

"Are you coming with us?" Sabriel asked, hesitantly, as she settled back in the heavily padded leather seats, fighting a wave of tiredness that threatened immediate sleep.

"Yes," replied Horyse, slowly. He seemed surprised at his own answer, and suddenly far away. "Yes, I am."

"You have the Sight," said Touchstone, looking up from where he was adjusting his scabbard before sitting down. "What did you see?"

"The usual thing," replied Horyse. He got in the front seat, and nodded to the driver—a thin-faced veteran of the Scouts, whose Charter mark was almost invisible on his weather-beaten forehead.

"What do you mean?" asked Sabriel, but her question was lost as the driver pressed the starter switch, and the car coughed and spluttered into life, a tenor accompaniment to the bass cacophony of the trucks and tanks.

Touchstone jumped at the sudden noise and vibration, then smiled sheepishly at Sabriel, who'd lightly rested her fingers on his arm, as if calming a child.

"What did he mean 'the usual thing'?" asked Sabriel.

Touchstone looked at her, sadness and exhaustion vying for first place in his gaze. He took her hand in his own and traced a line across her palm—a definite, ending sort of line.

"Oh," muttered Sabriel. She sniffed and looked at the back of Horyse's head, eyes blurring, seeing only the line of his cropped silver hair extending just past his helmet rim.

"He has a daughter the same age as me, back at . . . somewhere south," she whispered, shivering, clutching Touchstone's hand till his fingers were as white as her own. "Why, oh why, does everything . . . everyone . . ."

The car started forward with a lurch, preceded by two motorcycle outriders and followed by each of the nine trucks in turn, carefully spaced out every hundred yards. The tanks, with tracks screeching and clanking, took a side road up to the railway siding where they would be loaded up and sent on to Wyverley Halt. It was unlikely they would arrive before night-fall. The road convoy would be at Docky Point before six in the afternoon.

Sabriel was silent for the first ten miles, her head bowed, hand still clutching tightly on Touchstone's. He sat silently too, but watching, looking out as they left the military zone, looking at the prosperous farms of Ancelstierre, the sealed roads, the brick houses, the private cars and horse-drawn vehicles that pulled off the road in front of them, cleared aside by the two red-capped military policemen on motorcycles.

"I'm all right now," Sabriel said quietly, as they slowed to pass through the town of Bain. Touchstone nodded, still watch-ing, staring at the shop windows in the High Street. The towns-people stared back, for it was rare to see soldiers in full Perimeter battle equipment, with sword-bayonets and shields—and Sabriel and Touchstone were clearly from the Old Kingdom.

"We have to stop by the Police Station, and warn the Superintendent," Horyse announced as their car pulled in next to an imposing white-walled edifice with two large, blue elec-tric lanterns hanging out the front, and a sturdy sign proclaim-ing it to be the headquarters of the Bainshire Constabulary.

Horyse stood up, waved the rest of the convoy on, then vaulted out and dashed up the steps, a curiously incongruous figure in mail and khaki. A constable descending the steps looked ready to stop him, but stopped himself instead and saluted.

"I'm all right," Sabriel repeated. "You can let go of my hand."

Touchstone smiled, and flexed his hand a little in her grip. She looked a bit puzzled, then smiled too, her fingers slowly relaxing till their hands lay flat on the seat, little fingers just touching.

In any other town, a crowd would certainly have formed

around an Army staff car with two such unusual passengers. But this was Bain, and Bain was close to the Wall. People took one look, saw Charter marks, swords and armor, and went the other way. Those with natural caution, or a touch of the Sight, went home and locked their doors and shutters, not merely with steel and iron, but also with sprigs of broom and rowan. Others, even more cautious, took to the river and its sandy islets, without even pretending to be fishing.

Horyse came out five minutes later, accompanied by a tall, serious-looking man whose large build and hawk-like visage were made slightly ridiculous by a pair of too-small pince-nez clinging to the end of his nose. He shook hands with the Colonel, Horyse returned to the car, and they were off again, the driver crashing through the gears with considerable skill.

A few minutes later, before they'd left the last buildings of the town, a bell began to ring behind them, deep and slow. Only moments later, another followed from somewhere to the left, then another, from up ahead. Soon, there were bells ringing all around.

"Quick work," Horyse shouted into the back of the car. "The Superintendent must have made them practice in the past."

"The bells are a warning?" asked Touchstone. This was something he was familiar with, and he began to feel more at home, even with this sound, warning of dire trouble. He felt no fear from it—but then, after facing the reservoir for a second time, he felt that he could cope with any fear.

"Yes," replied Horyse. "Be inside by nightfall. Lock all doors and windows. Deny entry to strangers. Shed light inside and out. Prepare candles and lanterns for when the electricity fails. Wear silver. If caught outdoors, find running water."

"We used to recite that in the junior classes," Sabriel said. "But I don't think too many people remember it, even the people around here."

"You'd be surprised, ma'am," interrupted the driver, speaking out of the corner of his mouth, eyes never leaving the road. "The bells haven't rung like this in twenty years, but plenty of folk remember. They'll tell anyone who doesn't know—don't fret about that."

"I hope so," replied Sabriel, a momentary flash of remembrance passing through her mind. The people of Nestowe, two-thirds of their number lost to the Dead, the survivors huddled in fish-drying sheds on a rocky island. "I hope so."

"How long till we reach Docky Point?" asked Touchstone. He was remembering too, but his memories were of Rogir. Soon he would look on Rogir's face again, but it would only be a husk, a tool for what Rogir had become . . .

"About an hour at the most, I should think," replied Horyse. "Around six o'clock. We can average almost thirty miles an hour in this contraption—quite remarkable. To me, anyway. I'm so used to the Perimeter, and the Old Kingdom—the small part we saw on patrol, anyway. I'd have liked to see more of it . . . gone farther north . . ."

"You will," said Sabriel, but her voice lacked conviction, even to her own ears. Touchstone didn't say anything, and Horyse didn't reply, so they drove on in silence after that, soon catching the truck convoy, overtaking each vehicle till they were in front again. But wherever they drove, the bells preceded them, every village belltower taking up the warning.

As Horyse had predicted, they arrived at Wyverley village just before six. The trucks stopped in a line all through the village, from policeman's cottage to the Wyvern pub, the men debussing almost before the vehicles stopped, quickly forming up into ranks on the road. The signals truck parked under a telephone pole and two men swarmed up to connect their wires. The military policeman went to each end of the village, to redirect traffic.

Sabriel and Touchstone got out of the car and waited.

"It's not much different from the Royal Guard," Touchstone said, watching the men hurry into their parade positions, the sergeants shouting, the officers gathering around Horyse, who was speaking on the newly connected phone. "Hurry up and wait."

"I'd have liked to see you in the Royal Guard," Sabriel said. "And the Old Kingdom, in . . . I mean before the Stones were broken."

"In my day, you mean," said Touchstone. "I would have liked that too. It was more like here, then. Here normally, I mean. Peaceful, and sort of slow. Sometimes I thought life was too slow, too predictable. I'd prefer that now . . ."

"I used to think like that at school," Sabriel answered. "Dreaming about the Old Kingdom. Proper Charter Magic. Dead to bind. Princes to be—"

"Rescued?"

"Married," replied Sabriel, absently. She seemed intent on watching Horyse. He looked like he was getting bad news over the telephone.

Touchstone didn't speak. Everything seemed to sharpen in focus for him, centering on Sabriel, her black hair gleaming like a raven's wing in the afternoon sun. I love her, he thought. But if I say the wrong thing now, I may never . . .

Horyse handed the telephone back to a signaler, and turned towards them. Touchstone watched him, suddenly conscious that he probably only had five seconds to be alone with Sabriel, to say something, to say anything. Perhaps the last five seconds they would ever have alone together . . .

I am not afraid, he said to himself.

"I love you," he whispered. "I hope you don't mind."

Sabriel looked back at him, and smiled, almost despite herself. Her sadness at her father's death was still there, and her fears for the future—but seeing Touchstone staring apprehensively at her somehow gave her hope.

"I don't mind," she whispered back, leaning towards him. She frowned. "I think . . . I think I might love you too, Charter help me, but now is—"

"The telephone line to the Perimeter Crossing Point just went out," Horyse announced grimly, shouting above the village bell even before he was close enough to talk. "A fog started rolling across the Wall over an hour ago. It reached the forward trenches at four forty-six. After that, none of the advance companies could be reached by phone or runner. I was just speaking to the Duty Officer then—that young chap who was so interested in your aircraft. He said the fog was just about to reach his position. Then the line went silent."

"So," said Sabriel. "Kerrigor didn't wait till sundown. He's working the weather."

"From the timings given by the Perimeter," Horyse said, "this fog—and whatever's in it—is moving southwards at around twenty miles an hour. As the crow flies, it'll reach us around half past seven. Dark, with the moonrise yet to come."

"Let's go then," snapped Sabriel. "The bridle-path to Docky Point starts from behind the pub. Shall I lead?"

"Best not," replied Horyse. He turned, and shouted some orders, accompanied by considerable waving and pointing. Within a few seconds, men were moving off around the pub, taking the path to Docky Point. First, the Crossing Point Scouts, archers and Charter Mages all. Then, the first platoon of infantry, bayonets fixed, rifles at the ready. Past the pub, they shook out into an arrowhead formation. Horyse, Sabriel, Touchstone and their driver followed. Behind them came the other two platoons, and the signalers, unreeling field telephone wire from a large and cumbersome drum.

It was quiet among the cork trees, the soldiers moving as silently as they could, communicating by hand signals rather than shouts, only their heavy tread and the occasional rattle of armor or equipment disturbing the quiet.

Sunshine poured down between the trees, rich and golden, but already losing its warmth, like a butter-colored wine that was all taste and no potency.

Towards the top of the hill, only the Crossing Point Scouts went on up. The lead platoon of infantry followed a lower contour around to the northern side; the other two platoons moved to the south-west and south-east, forming a defensive triangle around the hill. Horyse, Sabriel, Touchstone and the driver continued on.

The trees fell away about twenty yards from the top of the hill, thick weeds and thistles taking their place. Then, at the highest point, there was the cairn: a solid, hut-sized square of grey-green stones. The twelve Scouts were grouped loosely around it, four of them already levering one of the corner stones out with a long crowbar, obviously carried up for this purpose.

As Sabriel and Touchstone came up, the stone fell with a thud, revealing more blocks underneath. At the same time, every Charter Mage present felt a slight buzzing in their ears, and a wave of dizziness.

"Did you feel that?" asked Horyse, unnecessarily, as it was clear from everyone's expressions and the hands that had gone to ears that they all had.

"Yes," replied Sabriel. To a lesser extent, it was the same sort of feeling the Broken Stones caused in the reservoir. "It will get worse, I'm afraid, as we get closer to the sarcophagus."

"How far in is it?"

"Four blocks deep, I think," said Sabriel. "Or five. I . . . saw it . . . from an odd perspective."

Horyse nodded, and indicated to the men to keep prying

away the stones. They went to it with a will, but Sabriel noticed they kept looking at the position of the sun. All the Scouts were Charter Mages, of various power—all knew what sundown would bring.

In fifteen minutes, they'd made a hole two blocks wide and two deep in one end, and the sickness was growing worse. Two of the younger Scouts, men in their early twenties, had become violently sick and were recuperating further down the hill. The others were working more slowly, their energies directed to keeping lunches down and quelling shaking limbs.

Surprisingly, given their lack of sleep and generally run-down state, Sabriel and Touchstone found it relatively easy to resist the waves of nausea emanating from the cairn. It didn't compare with the cold, dark fear of the reservoir, there on the hill, with the sunshine and the fresh breeze, warming and cooling at the same time.

When the third blocks came out, Horyse called a brief rest break, and they all retreated down the hill to the tree line, where the cairn's sickening aura dissipated. The signalers had a telephone there, the handset sitting on the upturned drum. Horyse took it, but turned to Sabriel before the signaler wound the charging handle.

"Are there any preparations to be made before we remove the last blocks? Magical ones, I mean."

Sabriel thought for a moment, willing her tiredness away, then shook her head. "I don't think so. Once we have access to the sarcophagus, we may have to spell it open—I'll need everyone's help for that. Then, the final rites on the body—the usual cremation spell. There will be resistance then too. Have your men often cast Charter Magic in concert?"

"Unfortunately, no," replied Horyse, frowning. "Because the Army doesn't officially admit the existence of Charter Magic, everyone here is basically self-taught."

"Never mind," Sabriel said, trying to sound confident, aware that everyone around her was listening. "We'll manage."

"Good," replied Horyse, smiling. That made him look very confident, thought Sabriel. She tried to smile too, but was uncertain about the result. It felt too much like a grimace of pain.

"Well, let's see where our uninvited guest has got to," Horyse continued, still smiling. "Where does this phone connect to, Sergeant?"

"Bain Police," replied the Signals Sergeant, winding the charging handle vigorously. "And Army HQ North, sir. You'll have to ask Corporal Synge to switch you. He's on the board at the village."

"Good," replied Horyse. "Hello. Oh, Synge? Put me through to Bain. No, tell North you can't get through to me. Yes, that's right, Corporal. Thank you . . . ah . . . Bainshire Constabulary? It's Colonel Horyse. I want to speak to Chief Superintendent Dingley . . . yes. Hello, Superintendent. Have you had any reports of a strange, dense fog . . . what! Already! No, on no account investigate. Get everyone in. Shutter the windows . . . yes, the usual drill. Yes, whatever is in . . . Yes, extraordinarily dangerous . . . hello! Hello!"

He put the handset down slowly, and pointed back up the hill.

"The fog is already moving through the northern part of Bain. It must be going much faster. Is it possible that this Kerrigor could know what we're up to?"

"Yes," replied Sabriel and Touchstone, together.

"We'd better get a move on then," Horyse announced, looking at his watch. "I'd say we now have less than forty minutes."

THE LAST BLOCKS came away slowly, pulled out by sweating, white-faced men, their hands and legs shivering, breath ragged. As soon as the way was clear, they staggered back, away from the cairn, seeking patches of sunlight to combat the dreadful chill that seemed to eat at their bones. One soldier, a dapper man with a white-blond moustache, fell down the hill, and lay retching, till stretcher-bearers ran up to take him away.

Sabriel looked at the dark hole in the cairn, and saw the faint, unsettling sheen from the bronze sarcophagus within. She felt sick too, with the hair on the back of her neck frizzing up, skin crawling. The air seemed thick with the reek of Free Magic, a hard, metallic taste in her mouth.

"We will have to spell it open," she announced, with a sinking heart. "The sarcophagus is very strongly protected. I think . . . the best thing would be if I go in with Touchstone taking my hand, Horyse his, and so on, to form a line reinforcement of the Charter Magic. Does everyone know the Charter marks for the opening spell?"

The soldiers nodded, or said, "Yes, ma'am." One said, "Yes, Abhorsen."

Sabriel looked at him. A middle-aged corporal, with the chevrons of long service on his sleeve. He seemed one of the least affected by the Free Magic.

"You can call me Sabriel, if you want," she said, strangely

unsettled by what he had called her.

The corporal shook his head. "No, Miss. I knew your dad. You're just like him. The Abhorsen, now. You'll make this Dead bugger—begging your pardon—wish he'd stayed properly bloody dead."

"Thank you," Sabriel replied, uncertainly. She knew the corporal didn't have the Sight—you could always tell—but his belief in her was so concrete . . .

"He's right," said Touchstone. He gestured for her to go in front of him, making a courtly bow. "Let's finish what we came to do, Abhorsen."

Sabriel bowed back, in a motion that had almost the feel of ritual about it. The Abhorsen bowing to the King. Then she took a deep breath, her face settling into a determined mold. Beginning to form the Charter marks of opening in her mind, she took Touchstone's hand and advanced towards the open cairn, its dark, shadowy interior in stark contrast with the sunlit thistles and the tumbled stones. Behind her, Touchstone half-turned to take Horyse's calloused hand as well, the Colonel's other hand already gripping Lieutenant Aire's, Aire gripping a Sergeant's, the Sergeant the long-service Corporal's, and so on down the hillside. Fourteen Charter Mages in all, if only two of the first rank.

Sabriel felt the Charter Magic welling up the line, the marks glowing brighter and brighter in her mind, till she almost lost her normal vision in their brilliance. She shuffled forwards into the cairn, each step bringing that all-too-familiar nausea, the pins and needles, uncontrollable shaking. But the marks were strong in her mind, stronger than the sickness.

She reached the bronze sarcophagus, slapped her hand down and let the Charter Magic go. Instantly, there was an explosion of light, and a terrible scream echoed all through the cairn. The bronze grew hot, and Sabriel snatched back her hand, the palm red and blistered. A second later, steam billowed out all around the sarcophagus, great gouts of scalding steam, forcing Sabriel out, the whole line going down like dominoes, tumbling out of the cairn and down the hill.

Sabriel and Touchstone were thrown together, about five yards down from the entrance to the cairn. Somehow, Sabriel's head had landed on Touchstone's stomach. His head was on a thistle, but both of them lay still for a moment, drained by the magic and the strength of the Free Magic defenses. They looked up at the blue sky, already tinged with the red of the impending sunset. Around them there was much swearing and cursing, as the soldiers picked themselves up.

"It didn't open," Sabriel said, in a quiet, matter-of-fact voice. "We don't have the power, or the skill—"

She paused, and then added, "I wish Mogget wasn't . . . I wish he was here. He'd think of something . . ."

Touchstone was silent, then he said, "We need more Charter Mages—it would work if the marks were reinforced enough."

"More Charter Mages," Sabriel said tiredly. "We're on the wrong side of the Wall . . ."

"What about your school?" asked Touchstone, and then "Ow!" as Sabriel suddenly shot up, disrupting his balance, then "Ow!" again as she bent down and kissed him, pushing his head further into the thistle.

"Touchstone! I should have thought . . . the Senior magic classes. There must be thirty-five girls with the Charter mark and the basic skills."

"Good," muttered Touchstone, from the depths of the thistle. Sabriel put out her hands, and helped him up, smelling the sweat on him, and the fresh, pungent odor of crushed thistles. He was halfway up when she suddenly seemed to lose her enthusiasm, and he almost fell back down again.

"The girls are there," said Sabriel, slowly, as if thinking aloud. "But have I any right to involve them in something that . . ."

"They're involved anyway," interrupted Touchstone. "The only reason that Ancelstierre isn't like the Old Kingdom is the Wall, and it won't last once Kerrigor breaks the remaining Stones."

"They're only schoolchildren," Sabriel said sadly. "For all we always thought we were grown women."

"We need them," said Touchstone, again.

"Yes," said Sabriel, turning back towards the knot of men gathered as close as they dared to the cairn. Horyse, and some of the stronger Charter Mages, peering back towards the entrance and the shimmering bronze within.

"The spell failed," Sabriel said. "But Touchstone has just reminded me where we can get more Charter Mages."

Horyse looked at her, urgency in his face. "Where?"

"Wyverley College. My old school. The Fifth and Sixth Form magic classes, and their teacher, Magistrix Greenwood. It's less than a mile away."

"I don't think we've got time to get a message there, and get them over here," Horyse began, looking up at the setting sun, then at his watch—which was now going backwards. He looked puzzled for a moment, then ignored it. "But . . . do you think it would be possible to move the sarcophagus?"

Sabriel thought about the protective spell that she'd encountered, then answered. "Yes. Most of the wards were on the cairn, for concealment. There's nothing to stop us moving the sarcophagus, save the side effects of the Free Magic. If we can stand the sickness, we can shift it—"

"And Wyverly College—it's an old, solid building?"

"More like a castle than anything," replied Sabriel, seeing the way he was thinking. "Easier to defend than this hill."

"Running water . . . No? That would be too much to hope

for. Right! Private Macking, run down to Major Tindall and tell him that I want his company ready to move in two minutes. We're going back to the trucks, then on to Wyverley College— it's on the map, about a mile . . ."

"South-west," Sabriel provided.

"South-west. Repeat that back."

Private Macking repeated the message in a slow drawl, then ran off, clearly keen to get away from the cairn. Horyse turned to the long-service corporal and said, "Corporal Anshey. You look pretty fit. Do you think you could get a rope around that coffin?"

"Reckon so, sir," replied Corporal Anshey. He detached a coil of rope from his webbing as he spoke, and gestured with his hand to the other soldiers. "Come on you blokes, get yer ropes out."

Twenty minutes later, the sarcophagus was being lifted by shear-legs and rope aboard a horse-drawn wagon, appropriated from a local farmer. As Sabriel had expected, dragging it within twenty yards of the trucks stopped their engines, put out electric lights and disrupted the telephone.

Curiously, the horse, a placid old mare, didn't seem overly frightened by the gleaming sarcophagus, despite its bronze surface sluggishly crawling with stomach-churning perversions of Charter marks. She wasn't a happy horse, but not a panicked one either.

"We'll have to drive the wagon," Sabriel said to Touchstone, as the soldiers pushed the suspended coffin aboard with long poles, and collapsed the shear-legs. "I don't think the Scouts can withstand the sickness much longer."

Touchstone shuddered. Like everyone else, he was pale, eyes red-rimmed, his nose dripping and teeth chattering. "I'm not sure I can, either."

Nevertheless, when the last rope was twitched off, and the soldiers hurried away, Touchstone climbed up to the driver's seat and picked up the reins. Sabriel climbed up next to him, suppressing the feeling that her stomach was about to rise into her mouth. She didn't look back at the sarcophagus.

Touchstone said "tch-tch" to the horse, and flicked the reins. The mare's ears went up, and she took up the load, pacing forwards. It was not a quick pace.

"Is this as fast as . . ." Sabriel said anxiously. They had a mile to cover, and the sun was already bloody, a red disc balanced on the line of the horizon.

"It's a heavy load," Touchstone answered slowly, quick breaths coming between his words, as if he found it difficult to speak. "We'll be there before the light goes."

The sarcophagus seemed to buzz and chuckle behind them. Neither of them mentioned that Kerrigor might arrive, fog-wreathed, before the night did. Sabriel found herself looking behind every few seconds, back along the road. This meant catching glimpses of the vilely shifting surface of the coffin, but she couldn't help it. The shadows were lengthening, and every time she caught a glimpse of some tree's pale bark, or a white-washed mile marker, fear twitched in her gut. Was that fog curling down the road?

Wyverley College seemed much farther than a mile. The sun was only a three-quarter disc by the time they saw the trucks turn off the road, turning up the bricked drive that led to the wrought-iron gates of Wyverley College. Home, thought Sabriel for a moment. But that was no longer true. It had been home for the better part of her life, but that was past. It was the home of her childhood, when she was only Sabriel. Now, she was also Abhorsen. Now, her home lay in the Old Kingdom, as did her responsibilities. But like her, these traveled.

Electric lights burned brightly in the two antique glass lanterns on either side of the gate, but they dimmed to mere sparks as the wagon and its strange cargo drove through. One of the gates was off its hinges, and Sabriel realized the soldiers must have forced their way through. It was unusual for the gates to be locked before full dark. They must have closed them when they heard the bells, Sabriel realized, and that alerted her to something else . . .

"The bell in the village," she exclaimed, as the wagon passed several parked trucks and wheeled around to stop near the huge, gate-like doors to the main building of the school. "The bell—it's stopped."

Touchstone brought the wagon to a halt, and listened, cocking an ear towards the darkening sky. True enough, they could no longer hear the Wyverley village bell.

"It is a mile," he said, hesitantly. "Perhaps we're too far, the wind . . ."

"No," said Sabriel. She felt the air, cool with evening, still on her face. There was no wind. "You could always hear it here. Kerrigor has reached the village. We need to get the sarcophagus inside, quickly!"

She jumped down from the wagon, and ran over to Horyse, who was standing on the steps outside the partially open door, talking to an obscured figure within. As Sabriel got closer, edging through groups of waiting soldiers, she recognized the voice. It was Mrs. Umbrade, the headmistress.

"How dare you barge in here!" she was pronouncing, very pompously. "I am a very close personal friend of Lieutenant-General Farnsley, I'll have you know—Sabriel!"

The sight of Sabriel in such strange garb and circumstance seemed to momentarily stun Mrs. Umbrade. In that second of fish-mouthed silence, Horyse motioned to his men. Before Mrs. Umbrade could protest, they'd pushed the door wide open, and streams of armed men rushed in, pouring around her startled figure like a flood around an island.

"Mrs. Umbrade!" Sabriel shouted. "I need to talk to Miss Greenwood urgently, and the girls from the Senior Magic classes. You'd better get the rest of the girls and the staff up to the top floors of the North Tower."

Mrs. Umbrade stood, gulping like a goldfish, till Horyse suddenly loomed over her and snapped, "Move, woman!"

Almost before his mouth closed, she was gone. Sabriel looked back to check that Touchstone was organizing the shifting of the sarcophagus, then followed her in.

The entrance hall was already blocked by a conga line of soldiers, passing boxes in from the trucks outside, stacking them up all along the walls. Khaki-colored boxes marked ".303 Ball" or "B2E2 WP Grenade," piled up beneath pictures of prizewinning hockey teams, or gilt-lettered boards of merit and scholastic brilliance. The soldiers had also thrown open the doors to the Great Hall, and were busy in there, closing shutters and piling pews up on their ends against the shuttered windows.

Mrs. Umbrade was still in motion at the other end of the entrance hall, bustling along towards a knot of obviously nervous staff. Behind them, peering down from the main stair, was a solid rank of prefects. Behind them, higher up the stair, and just able to see, were several gaggles of non-prefectorial fifth and sixth formers. Sabriel didn't doubt that the rest of the school would be lining the corridors behind them, all agog to hear what the commotion was all about.

Just as Mrs. Umbrade reached her staff, all the lights went out. For a moment, there was total, shocked quiet, then the noise redoubled. Girls screaming, soldiers shouting, crashes and bangs as people ran into things and each other.

Sabriel stood where she was, and conjured the Charter marks for light. They came easily, flowing down to her fingertips like cool water from a shower. She let them hang there for a moment, then cast them at the ceiling, drops of light that grew to the size of dinner plates and cast a steady yellow light all down the hall. Someone else was also casting similar lights down by Mrs. Umbrade, and Sabriel recognized the work of Magistrix Greenwood. She smiled at that recognition, a slight, upturning of just one side of her mouth. She knew the lights had gone out because Kerrigor had passed the electric sub-station, and that was halfway between the school and the village.

As expected, Mrs. Umbrade wasn't telling her teachers anything useful—just going on about rudeness and some General. Sabriel saw the Magistrix behind the tall, bent figure of the Senior Science Mistress, and waved.

"And I was never more shocked to see one of our—" Mrs. Umbrade was saying, when Sabriel stepped up next to her and gently laid the marks of silence and immobility on the back of her neck.

"I'm sorry to interrupt," Sabriel said, standing next to the temporarily frozen form of the Headmistress. "But this is an emergency. As you can see, the Army is temporarily taking over. I am assisting Colonel Horyse, who is in charge. Now, we need all the girls in the two Senior Magic classes to come down to the Great Hall—with you, Magistrix Greenwood, please. Everyone else—students, staff, gardeners, everyone—must go to the top floors of the North Tower and barricade yourselves in. Till dawn tomorrow."

"Why?" demanded Mrs. Pearch, the Mathematics Mistress. "What's all this about?"

"Something has come from the Old Kingdom," Sabriel replied shortly, watching their faces change as she spoke. "We will shortly be attacked by the Dead."

"So there will be danger to my students?" Miss Greenwood

spoke, pushing her way forward, between two frightened English teachers. She looked Sabriel in the face, as if in recognition, and then added, "Abhorsen."

"There will be danger to everyone," Sabriel said bleakly. "But without the aid of the Charter Mages here, there isn't even a chance . . ."

"Well," replied Miss Greenwood, with some decision. "We'd better get organized then. I'll go and fetch Sulyn and Ellimere. I think they're the only two Charter Mages among the Prefects— they can organize the others. Mrs. Pearch, you'd better take charge of the . . . ah . . . evacuation to the North Tower, as I imagine Mrs. Umbrade will be . . . err . . . deep in thought. Mrs. Swann, you'd best round up Cook and the maids—get some fresh water, food and candles too. Mr. Arkler, if you would be so kind as to fetch the swords from the gymnasium . . ."

Seeing that all was under control, Sabriel sighed, and quickly walked back outside, past soldiers stringing oil lamps up in the corridor. Despite them, it was still lighter outside, the sky washed red and orange with the last sunlight of the day.

Touchstone and the Scouts had the sarcophagus down, and roped up. It now seemed to glow with its own, ugly inner light, the flickering Free Magic marks floating on the surface like scum, or clots in blood. Apart from the Scouts pulling the ropes, no one went close to it. Soldiers were everywhere, coiling out barbed wire, filling sandbags from the rose gardens, preparing firing positions on the second floor, tying trip flares. But in all this commotion, there was an empty circle around the glistening coffin of Rogir.

Sabriel walked towards Touchstone, feeling the reluctance in her legs, her body revolting at the thought of going any closer to the bloody luminescence of the sarcophagus. It seemed to radiate stronger waves of nausea now, now that the sun had almost fled. In the twilight, it looked larger, stronger, its magic more forceful and malign.

"Pull!" shouted Touchstone, heaving on the ropes with the soldiers. "Pull!"

Slowly, the sarcophagus slid across the old paving stones, inching towards the front steps, where other soldiers were hastily hammering a wooden ramp together, fitting it over the steps.

Sabriel decided to leave Touchstone to it, and walked a little way down the drive, to where she could see out the iron gates. She stood there, watching, her hands nervously running over the handles of the bells. Six bells, now—all probably ineffective against the awful might of Kerrigor. And an unfamilar sword, strange to her touch, even if it was forged by the Wallmaker.

The Wallmaker. That reminded her of Mogget. Who knew what he had been, that strange combination of irascible companion to the Abhorsens and blazing Free Magic construct sworn to kill them. Gone now, swept away by the mournful call of Astarael . . .

I left this place knowing almost nothing about the Old Kingdom, and I've come back with not much more, Sabriel thought. I am the most ignorant Abhorsen in centuries, and perhaps one of the most sorely tried . . .

A clatter of shots interrupted her thoughts, followed by the zing of a rocket arcing up into the sky, its yellow trail reaching down towards the road. More shots followed. A rapid volley— then sudden silence. The rocket burst into a white parachute flare, that slowly descended. In its harsh, magnesium brilliance, Sabriel saw fog rolling up the road, thick and wet, stretching back into the dark as far as she could see.

Chapter Twenty-Eight

S ABRIEL FORCED HERSELF to walk back to the main doors,
rather than break into a screaming run. Lots of soldiers
could see her—they were still placing lanterns out in lines,
radiating out from the steps, and several soldiers were holding a
coil of concertina wire, waiting to bounce it out. They looked
anxiously at her as she passed.

The sarcophagus was just slipping off the ramp into the corridor ahead of her. Sabriel could easily have pushed past it, but
she waited outside, looking out. After a moment, she became
aware that Horyse was standing next to her, his face half-lit by
the lanterns, half in shadow.

"The fog . . . the fog is almost at the gates," she said, too
quickly to be calm.

"I know," replied Horyse, steadily. "That firing was a picket.
Six men and a corporal."

Sabriel nodded. She had felt their deaths, like slight punches
in her stomach. Already she was hardening herself not to notice,
to wilfully dull her senses. There would be many more deaths
that night.

Suddenly, she felt something that wasn't a death, but things
already dead. She stood bolt upright, and exclaimed, "Colonel!
The sun is truly down—and something's coming, coming ahead
of the fog!"

She drew her sword as she spoke, the Colonel's blade

flickering out a second later. The wiring party looked around, startled, then bolted for the steps and the corridor. On either side of the door, two-man teams cocked the heavy, tripod-mounted machine-guns, and laid their swords across the newly made sandbag walls.

"Second floor, stand ready!" Horyse shouted, and above her head, Sabriel heard the bolts of fifty rifles working. Out of the corner of her eye, she saw two of the Scouts step back outside, and take up position behind her, arrows nocked, bows ready. She knew they were ready to snatch her inside, if it came to that . . .

In the expectant quiet, there were only the usual sounds of the night. Wind in the big trees out past the school wall, starting to rise as the sky darkened. Crickets beginning to chirp. Then Sabriel heard it—the massed grinding of Dead joints, no longer joined by gristle; the padding of Dead feet, bones like hobnails clicking through necrotic flesh.

"Hands," she said, nervously. "Hundreds of Hands."

Even as she spoke, a solid wall of Dead flesh hit the iron gates, throwing them over in a split second's crash. Then vaguely human forms were everywhere, rushing towards them, Dead mouths gulping and hissing in a ghastly parody of a war cry.

"Fire!"

In the instant's delay after this command, Sabriel felt the terrible fear that the guns wouldn't work. Then rifles cracked, and the machine-guns beat out a terrible, barking roar, red tracer rounds flinging out, ricocheting from the paving in a crazy embroidery of terrible violence. Bullets tore Dead flesh, splintered bone, knocked the Hands down and over—but still they came, till they were literally torn apart, broken into pieces, hung up on the wire.

The firing slowed, but before it could entirely cease, another wave of Hands came stumbling, crawling, running through the gateway, slipping, tumbling over the wall. Hundreds of them, so densely packed they crushed the wire and came on, till the last of them were mown down by the guns at the very foot of the front steps. Some, still with a slight vestige of human intelligence, retreated, only to be caught in great gouts of flame from white phosphorus grenades thrown out from the second floor.

"Sabriel—get inside!" Horyse ordered, as the last of the Hands flopped and crawled in crazy circles, till more bullets thudded into them and made them still.

"Yes," replied Sabriel, looking out at the carpet of bodies, the flickering fires from the lanterns and lumps of phosphorus burning like candles in some ghastly charnel house. The stench of cordite was in her nose, through her hair, on her clothes, the machine-gun's barrels glowing an evil red to either side of her. The Hands were already dead, but even so, this mass destruction made her sicker than any Free Magic . . .

She went inside, sheathing her sword. Only then did she remember the bells. Possibly, she could have quelled that vast mob of Hands, sent them peaceably back into Death, without— but it was too late. And what if she had been overmastered?

Shadow Hands would be next, she knew, and they could not be stopped by physical force, or her bells, unless they came in small numbers . . . and that was as likely as an early dawn . . .

There were more soldiers in the corridor, but these were mailed and helmed, with large shields and broad-headed spears streaked with silver and the simplest Charter marks, drawn in chalk and spit. They were smoking, and drinking tea from the school's second-best china. Sabriel realized they were there to fight when the guns failed. There was an air of controlled ner-vousness about them—not bravado exactly, just a strange mixture of competence and cynicism. Whatever it was, it made Sabriel walk casually among them, as if she were in no hurry at all.

"Evening, miss."

"Good to hear the guns, hey? Practically never work up north!"

"Won't need us at this rate."

"Not like the Perimeter, is it, ma'am?"

"Good luck with the bloke in the metal cigar case, miss."

"Good luck to all of you," replied Sabriel, trying to smile in answer to their grins. Then the firing started again, and she winced, losing the smile—but their attention was off her, focused back outside. They weren't nearly as casual as they pretended, Sabriel thought as she edged through the side doors leading from the corridor into the Great Hall.

Here, the mood was much more frightened. The sarcophagus was up the far end of the Hall, resting across the speaker's dais. Everyone else was as far away as possible up at the other end. The Scouts were on one side, also drinking tea. Magistrix Greenwood was talking to Touchstone in the middle, and the thirty or so girls—young women, really—were lined up on the opposite wall to the soldiers. It was all rather like a bizarre parody of a school dance.

Behind the thick stone walls and shuttered windows of the Great Hall, the gunfire could almost be mistaken for extremely heavy hail, with grenades for thunderclaps, but not if you knew what it was. Sabriel walked into the center of the Hall, and shouted.

"Charter Mages! Please come here."

They came, the young women quicker than the soldiers, who were showing the weariness of the day's work, and proximity to the sarcophagus. Sabriel looked at the students, their faces bright and open, a thin layer of fear laid over excitement at the spice of the unknown. Two of her best schoolfriends, Sulyn and Ellimere, were among the crowd, but she felt far distant from them now.

She probably looked it too, she thought, seeing respect and something like wonder in their eyes. Even the Charter marks on their foreheads looked like fragile cosmetic replicas, though she knew they were real. It was so unfair that they had to be caught up in this . . .

Sabriel opened her mouth to speak, and the noise of gunfire suddenly ceased, almost on cue. In the silence, one of the girls giggled nervously. Sabriel, however, suddenly felt many deaths come at once, and a familiar dread touched her spine with cold fingers. Kerrigor was closing in. It was his power that had stilled the guns, not a lessening of the assault. Faintly, she could hear shouts and even . . . screams . . . from outside. They would be fighting with older weapons now.

"Quickly," she said, walking towards the sarcophagus as she spoke. "We must make a handfast ring around the sarcophagus. Magistrix, if you would place everyone—Lieutenant, please put your men in among the girls . . ."

Anywhere else, at any other time, there would have been ribald jokes and giggles about that. Here, with the Dead about the building, and the sarcophagus brooding in their midst, it was simply an instruction. Men moved quickly to their places, the young women took their hands purposefully. In a few seconds, the sarcophagus was ringed by Charter Mages.

Linked by touch now, Sabriel didn't need to speak. She could feel everyone in the ring. Touchstone, to her right, a familiar and powerful warmth. Miss Greenwood, to her left, less powerful, but not without skill—and so on, right around the ring.

Slowly, Sabriel brought the Charter marks of opening to the forefront of her mind. The marks grew, power flowing round and round the ring, growing in force till it started to project inwards, like the narrowing vortex of a whirlpool. Golden light began to stream about the sarcophagus, visible streaks rotating clockwise around it, with greater and greater speed.

Still Sabriel kept the power of the Charter Magic flowing into the center, drawing on everything the Charter Mages could produce. Soldiers and schoolgirls wavered, and some fell to their knees, but the hands stayed linked, the circle complete.

Slowly, the sarcophagus itself began turning on the platform, with a hideous shrieking noise, like an enormous unoiled hinge. Steam jetted forth from under its lid, but the golden light whisked it away. Still shrieking, the sarcophagus began to spin faster and faster, till it was a blur of bronze, white steam and yolk-yellow light. Then, with a scream more piercing than any before, it suddenly stopped, the lid flying off to hurtle over the Charter Mages' heads, smashing into the floor a good thirty paces away.

The Charter Magic went too, as if earthed by its success, and the ring collapsed with fewer than half the participants still on their feet.

Wavering, her hands still tightly gripped by Touchstone and the Magistrix, Sabriel tottered over to the sarcophagus and looked in.

"Why," said Miss Greenwood, with a startled glance back up at Touchstone, "he looks just like you!"

Before Touchstone could answer, steel clashed outside in the corridor, and the shouting grew louder. Those Scouts still standing drew their swords and rushed to the doors—but before they could reach them, other soldiers were pouring in, bloodied, terrified soldiers, who ran to the corners, or threw themselves down, and sobbed, or laughed, or shook in silence.

Behind this rush came some of the heavily armored soldiery of the corridor. These men still had some semblance of control. Instead of running on, they hurled themselves back against the doors, and dropped the bar in place.

"He's inside the main doors!" one of them shouted back

towards Sabriel, his face white with terror. There was no doubt about who "he" was.

"Quick, the final rites!" Sabriel snapped. She drew her hands from the others' grasp, and held them out over the body, forming the marks for fire, cleansing and peace in her mind. She didn't look too closely at the body. Rogir did look very much like a sleeping, defenseless Touchstone.

She was tired, and there were still Free Magic protections around the body, but the first mark soon lingered in the air. Touchstone had transferred his hand to her shoulder, pouring power into her. Others of the circle had crept up and linked hands again—and suddenly Sabriel felt a stirring of relief. They were going to make it—Kerrigor's human body would be destroyed, and the greater part of his power with it . . .

Then the whole of the northern wall exploded, bricks cascading out, red dust blowing in like a solid wave, knocking everyone down in blinding, choking ruin.

Sabriel lay on the floor, coughing, hands pushing feebly on the floor, knees scrabbling as she tried to get up. There was dust and grit in her eyes, and the lanterns had all gone out. Blind, she felt around her, but there was only the still-scalding bronze of the sarcophagus.

"The blood price must be paid," said a crackling, inhuman voice. A familiar voice, though not the liquid, ruined tones of Kerrigor . . . but the terrible speech of the night in Holehallow, when the Paperwing burned.

Blinking furiously, Sabriel crawled away from the sound, around the sarcophagus. It didn't speak again immediately, but she could hear it closing in, the air crackling and buzzing at its passage.

"I must deliver my last burden," the creature said. "Then the bargain is done, and I may turn to retribution."

Sabriel blinked again, tears streaming down her face. Vision slowly came back, a picture woven with tears and the first rays of moonlight streaming through the shattered wall, a picture blurred with the red dust of pulverized bricks.

All Sabriel's senses were screaming inside her. Free Magic, the Dead, danger all around . . .

The creature that had once been Mogget blazed a little more than five yards away. It was squatter than it had appeared previously, but equally misshapen, a lumpy body slowly drifting towards her atop a column of twisting, whirling energies.

A soldier suddenly leapt up behind it, driving a sword deep into its back. It hardly noticed, but the man screamed and burst into white flames. Within a second, he was consumed, his sword a molten lump of metal, scorching the thick oak planks of the floor.

"I bring you Abhorsen's sword," the creature said, dropping a long, dimly seen object to one side. "And the bell called Astarael."

That, it laid carefully down, the silver glinting momentarily before it was lowered into the sea of dust.

"Come forward, Abhorsen. It is long since time that we begun."

The thing laughed then, a sound like a match igniting, and it started to move around the sarcophagus. Sabriel loosened the ring on her finger, and edged away, keeping the sarcophagus between them, her thoughts racing. Kerrigor was very near, but there still might be time to turn this creature back into Mogget, and complete the final rites . . .

"Stop!"

The word was like a foul lick across the face by a reptilian tongue, but there was power behind it. Sabriel stood still, against her own desire, as did the blazing thing. Sabriel tried looking past it, lidding her eyes against the light, trying to puzzle out what was happening at the other end of the Hall. Not that she really needed to see.

It was Kerrigor. The soldiers who'd barred the door lay dead around him, pale flesh islands about a sea of darkness. He had no shape now, but there were semi-human features in the great ink-splash of his presence. Eyes of white fire, and a yawning mouth that was lined with flickering coals of a red as dark as drying blood.

"Abhorsen is mine," croaked Kerrigor, his voice deep and somehow liquid, as if his words came bubbling out like lava mixed with spittle. "You will leave her to me."

The Mogget-thing crackled, and moved again, white sparks falling like tiny stars in its wake.

"I have waited too long to allow my revenge to be taken by another!" it hissed, ending on a high-pitched yowl that still had something of the cat. Then it flew at Kerrigor, a shining electric comet hurtling into the darkness of his body, smashing into his shadowy substance like a hammer tenderizing meat.

For a moment, no one moved, shocked by the suddenness of the attack. Then, Kerrigor's dark shape slowly recongealed, long tendrils of bitter night wrapping around his brilliant attacker, choking and absorbing it with the implacable voracity of an octopus strangling a bright-shelled turtle.

Desperately, Sabriel looked around for Touchstone and Magistrix Greenwood. Brick dust was still falling slowly through the moonlit air, like some deadly rust-colored gas, the bodies lying around seemingly victims of its choking poison. But they had been struck by bricks, or wooden splinters from the smash-ing of the pews.

Sabriel saw the Magistrix first, lying a little away, curled up on her side. Anyone else might have thought her merely unconscious, but Sabriel knew she was dead, struck by a long, stiletto-like splinter from a shattered pew. The iron-hard wood had driven right through her.

She knew Touchstone was alive—and there he was, propped up against a pile of broken masonry. His eyes reflected the moonlight.

Sabriel walked over to him, stepping between the bodies and the rubble, the patches of freshly spilled blood and the silent, hopeless wounded.

"My leg is broken," Touchstone said, his mouth showing the pain of it. He tilted his head towards the gaping hole in the wall. "Run, Sabriel. While he's busy. Run south. Live a normal life . . ."

"I can't," replied Sabriel softly. "I am the Abhorsen. Besides, how could you run with me, you with your broken leg?"

"Sabriel . . ."

But Sabriel had already turned away. She picked up Astarael, practiced hands keeping it still. But there was no need, for the bell was choked with brick dust, its voice silent. It would not ring true until cleaned, with patience, magic and steady nerves. Sabriel stared at it for a second, then gently placed it back down on the floor.

Her father's sword was only a few paces farther away. She picked it up, and watched the Charter marks flow along the blade. This time, they didn't run through the normal inscription, but said: "The Clayr saw me, the Wallmaker made me, the King quenched me, the Abhorsen wields me so that no Dead shall walk in Life. For this is not their path."

"This is not their path," whispered Sabriel. She took up the guard position, and looked down the Hall to the writhing hulk of darkness that was Kerrigor.

Chapter Twenty-Nine

K ERRIGOR SEEMED TO have finished with the Free Magic
         thing that had once been Mogget. His great cloud of
         darkness was complete again, with no sign of white
fire, no dazzling brilliance fighting away within.

He was remarkably still, and Sabriel had a moment's brief
hope that he was somehow wounded. Then the awful realization
came. Kerrigor was digesting, like a glutton after an overly ambitious meal.

Sabriel shuddered at the thought, bile tainting her mouth.
Not that her end was likely to be better. Both she and Touchstone
would be taken alive, and kept that way, till they pumped out
their life's blood, throats yawning, down in the dark of the
reservoir . . .

She shook her head, dispelling that image. There had to be
something . . . Kerrigor had to be weaker, so far from the Old
Kingdom . . . perhaps weakened more than her Charter Magic. She
doubted that a single bell could sway him, but two, in concert?

It was dark in the Hall, save for the moonlight falling through
the shattered wall behind her. And quiet. Even the wounded
were slipping away in silence, their cries muted, last wishes whispered. They kept their agony close, as if a scream might attract
the wrong attention. There were things worse than death in the
Hall . . .

Even in darkness, the form of Kerrigor was darker still.

Sabriel watched him carefully, undoing the straps that held Saraneth and Kibeth with her left hand. She sensed other Dead all around, but none entered the Hall. There were still men to fight, or feast upon. What went on in the Hall was their Master's business.

The straps came undone. Kerrigor didn't move, his burning eyes closed, his fiery mouth shut.

In one quick motion, Sabriel sheathed her sword, and drew the bells.

Kerrigor did move then. Swiftly, his dark bulk bounding forward, halving the gap between them. He grew taller too, stretching upwards till he almost reached the vaulted ceiling. His eyes opened to full, raging, flaming fury, and he spoke.

"Toys, Abhorsen. And too late. Much too late."

It was not just words he spoke, but power, Free Magic power that froze Sabriel's nerves, caught at her muscles. Desperately, she struggled to ring the bells, but her wrists were locked in place . . .

Tantalizingly slowly, Kerrigor glided forward, till he was a mere arm's length away, towering over her like some colossal statue of rough-hewn night, his breath rolling down on her with the stench of a thousand abattoirs.

Someone—a girl quietly coughing out her last breath on the floor—touched Sabriel's ankle with a light caress. A small spark of golden Charter Magic came from that dying touch, slowly swelling into Sabriel's veins, traveling upwards, warming joints, freeing muscles. At last it reached her wrists and hands—and the bells rang out.

It was not the clear, true sound it should be, for somehow the bulk of Kerrigor took the sound in and warped it—but it had an effect. Kerrigor slid back, and was diminished, till he was little more than twice Sabriel's height.

But he was not subject to Sabriel's will. Saraneth had not

bound him, and Kibeth had only forced him back.

Sabriel rang the bells again, concentrating on the difficult counterpoint between them, forcing all her will into their magic. Kerrigor would fall under her domination, he would walk where she willed . . .

And for a second, he did. Not into Death, for she lacked the power, but into his original body, inside the broken sarcophagus. Even as the chime of the bells faded, Kerrigor changed. Fiery eyes and mouth ran into each other like molten wax, and his shadow-stuff folded into a narrow column of smoke, roaring up into the ceiling. It hovered among the rafters for a moment, then descended with a hideous scream, straight into the Rogir-body's open mouth.

With that scream, Saraneth and Kibeth cracked, shards of silver falling like broken stars, crashing to the earth. Mahogany handles turned to dust, drifting through Sabriel's fingers like smoke.

Sabriel stared at her empty hands for a second, still feeling the harsh imprint of bell-handles . . . then, without any conscious thought, there was a sword hilt in her hand as she advanced upon the sarcophagus. But before she could see into it, Rogir stood up and looked at her—looked with the burning fire-pit eyes of Kerrigor.

"An inconvenience," he said, with a voice that was only marginally more human. "I should have remembered you were a troublesome brat."

Sabriel lunged at him, sword blowing white sparks as it struck, punching through his chest to project out the other side. But Kerrigor only laughed, and reached down till he held the blade with both hands, knuckles pallid against the silver-sparking steel. Sabriel tugged at the sword, but it would not come free.

"No sword can harm me," Kerrigor said, with a giggle like a dying man's cough. "Not even one made by the Wallmakers.

Especially not now, when I have finally assumed the last of their powers. Power that ruled before the Charter, power that made the Wall. I have it now. I have that broken puppet, my half-brother—and I have you, my Abhorsen. Power, and blood—blood for the breaking!"

He reached out, and pulled the sword farther into his chest, till the hilt was lodged against his skin. Sabriel tried to let go, but he was too quick, one chill hand clutching her forearm. Irresistibly, Kerrigor drew her towards him.

"Will you sleep, unknowing, till the Great Stones are ready for your blood?" whispered Kerrigor, his breath still reeking of carrion. "Or will you go waking, every step of the way?"

Sabriel stared back, meeting his gaze for the first time. Surely, there in the hellfire of his eyes, she could see the faintest spark of blazing white? She unclenched her left fist, and felt the silver ring slip down her finger. Was it expanding?

"What would you have, Abhorsen?" continued Kerrigor, his mouth peeling back, skin already breaking at the corners, the spirit within corroding even this magically preserved flesh. "Your lover crawls towards us—a pathetic sight—but I shall have the next kiss . . ."

The ring was hanging in Sabriel's hand, hidden behind her back. It had grown larger—but she could still feel the metal expanding . . .

Kerrigor's blistered lips moved towards hers, and still the ring moved in her hand. His breath was overpowering, reeking of blood, but she had long gone beyond throwing up. She turned her head aside at the last second, and felt, dry, corpse-like flesh slide across her cheek.

"A sisterly kiss," chuckled Kerrigor. "A kiss for an uncle who has known you since birth—or slightly before—but it is not enough . . ."

Again, his words were not just words. Sabriel felt a force grip her head, and move it back to face him, while her mouth was wedged apart, as if in passionate expectation.

But her left arm was free.

Kerrigor's head bent forward, his face looming larger and larger—then silver flashed between them, and the ring was around his neck.

Sabriel felt the compulsion snap off, and she leant back, trying to hurl herself away. But Kerrigor didn't let go of her arm. He seemed surprised, but not anxious. His right hand went up to touch the band, fingernails falling as he did so, bone already pushing through at the fingertips.

"What is this? Some relic of . . ."

The ring constricted, cutting through the pulpy flesh of his neck, revealing the solid darkness within. That too was compressed, forced inwards, pulsating as it tried to escape. Two flaming eyes looked down in disbelief.

"Impossible," croaked Kerrigor. Snarling, he pushed Sabriel away, throwing her to the floor. In the same motion he drew the sword from his chest, the blade slowly coming free with a sound like a rasp on hardwood.

Swiftly as a snake, arm and sword went out, striking through Sabriel, through armor and flesh and deep into the wooden floor beyond. Pain exploded, and Sabriel screamed, body convulsing around the blade in one awful reflexive curve.

Kerrigor left her there, impaled like a bug in a collection, and advanced upon Touchstone. Sabriel, through eyes fogged with pain, saw Kerrigor look down and rip a long, jagged splinter from one of the pews.

"Rogir," Touchstone said. "Rogir . . ."

The splinter came down with a strangled shriek of rage. Sabriel closed her eyes and looked away, slipping into a world of her own, a world of pain. She knew she should do something about the blood pouring out of her stomach, but now—with Touchstone dead—she just lay where she was, and let it bleed.

Then Sabriel realized she hadn't felt Touchstone die.

She looked again. The splinter had broken on his armored coat. Kerrigor was reaching out for another splinter—but the silver ring had slipped down to his shoulders now, shredding the flesh away as it fell, like an apple corer punching the Dead spirit out of the rotting corpse.

Kerrigor struggled and shrieked, but the ring bound his arms. Capering madly, he threw himself from side to side, seeking to cast off the silver band that held him—only causing yet more flesh to fall away, till no flesh remained, nothing but a raging column of darkness, constrained by a silver ring.

Then the column collapsed upon itself like a demolished building, to become a mound of rippling shadow, the silver ring shining like a ribbon. A gleaming red eye shone amidst the silver—but that was only the ruby, grown to match the metal.

There were Charter marks on the ring again, but Sabriel couldn't read them. Her eyes wouldn't focus, and it was too dark. The moonlight seemed to have gone. Still, she knew what must be done. Saraneth—her hand crept to the bandolier, but the sixth bell wasn't there—or the seventh, or the third. Careless of me, thought Sabriel, careless—but I must complete the binding. Her hand fell on Belgaer for a moment, and almost drew it—but no, that would be release . . . Finally, she drew Ranna, whimpering with the pain of even that small movement.

Ranna was unusually heavy, for so slight a bell. Sabriel rested it against her chest for a moment, gathering strength. Then, lying on her back, transfixed with her own sword, she rang the bell.

Ranna sounded sweet, and felt comforting, like a long-expected bed. The sound echoed through the Hall, and out, to

where a few men still battled with the Dead. All who heard it
ceased their struggles, and lay themselves down. The badly
wounded slipped easily into Death, joining the Dead who had
followed Kerrigor; those less hurt fell into a healing sleep.

The mound of darkness that had been Kerrigor split into
two distinct hemispheres, bounded by an equatorial ring of silver.
One hemisphere was as black as coal; the other a gleaming white.
Gradually, they melted into two distinct forms—two cats, joined
at the throat like Siamese twins. Then the silver ring split in two,
a ring around each neck, and the cats separated. The rings lost
their brilliance, slowly changing color and texture till they were
red leather bands, each supporting a miniature bell, a miniature
Ranna.

Two small cats sat side by side. One black, one white. Both
leaned forward, throats moving, and each spat up a silver ring.
The cats yawned as the rings rolled towards Sabriel, then curled
up and went to sleep.

Touchstone watched the rings roll through the dust, silver
flashing in the moonlight. They hit Sabriel's side, but she didn't
pick them up. Both her hands still clutched Ranna, but it was
silent, resting below her breasts. Her sword loomed above her,
blade and hilt casting the moonshadow of a cross upon her face.

Something from his childhood memory flashed through
Touchstone's mind. A voice, a messenger's voice, speaking to his
mother.

"Highness, we bring sorrowful tidings. The Abhorsen is
dead."

Epilogue

Death seemed colder than ever before, Sabriel thought, and wondered why, till she realized she was still lying down. In the water, being carried along by the current. For a moment, she started to struggle, then she relaxed.

"Everyone and everything has a time to die . . ." she whispered. The living world and its cares seemed far away. Touchstone lived, and that made her glad, inasmuch as she could feel anything. Kerrigor was defeated, imprisoned if not made truly dead. Her work was done. Soon she would pass beyond the Ninth Gate, and rest forever . . .

Something grabbed her arms and legs, picked her up out of the water and set her down on her feet.

"This is not your time," said a voice, a voice echoed by half a hundred others.

Sabriel blinked, for there were many shining human shapes around her, hovering above the water. More than she could count. Not Dead spirits, but something else, like the mother-sending called by the paper boat. Their shapes were vague, but instantly recognizable, for all wore the deep blue with the silver keys. Every one was an Abhorsen.

"Go back," they chorused. "Go back."

"I can't," sobbed Sabriel. "I'm dead! I haven't the strength . . ."

"You are the last Abhorsen," the voices whispered, the shining shapes closing in. "You cannot pass this way until there is another. You do have the strength within you. Live, Abhorsen, live . . ."

Suddenly, she did have the strength. Enough to crawl, wade and fall *back up the river, and gingerly edge back into Life, her shining escort dropping back at the very last. One of them—perhaps her father— lightly touched her hand in the instant before she left the realm of Death behind.*

A face swam into view—Touchstone's, staring down at her. Sound hit her ears, distant, raucous bells that seemed out of place, till she realized they were ambulance bells, ambulances racing in from the town. She could sense no Dead at all, nor feel any great magic, Free or Charter. But then, Kerrigor was gone, and they were nearly forty miles from the Wall . . .

"Live, Sabriel, live," Touchstone was muttering, holding her icy hands, his own eyes so clouded with tears he hadn't noticed hers opening. Sabriel smiled, then grimaced as the pain came back. She looked from side to side, wondering how long it would take Touchstone to realize.

The electric lights had come back on in parts of the Hall, and soldiers were placing lanterns out again. There were more survivors than she'd expected, tending to the wounded, propping up dangerous brickwork, even sweeping up the brick-dust and grave mold.

There were also many dead, and Sabriel sighed as she let her senses roam. Colonel Horyse, killed outside on the steps; Magistrix Greenwood; her innocent schoolfriend Ellimere; six other girls; at least half the soldiers . . .

Her eyes wandered to closer regions, to the two sleeping cats, the two silver rings next to her on the floor.

"Sabriel!"

Touchstone had finally noticed. Sabriel turned her gaze back to him, and lifted her head cautiously. He'd removed her sword, she saw, and several of her schoolfriends had cast a healing spell, good enough for the moment. Typically, Touchstone had done nothing for his own leg.

"Sabriel," he said again. "You're alive!"

"Yes," said Sabriel, with some surprise. "I am."

Lirael

To Anna, my family and friends,
and to the memory of Bytenix (1986–1999),
the original Disreputable Dog

CONTENTS

PART TWO 443

PART THREE 663

Prologue

It was a hot, steamy summer, and the mosquitoes swarmed everywhere, from their breeding grounds in the rotten, reedy shores of the Red Lake up to the foothills of Mount Abed. Small, bright-eyed birds swooped among the clouds of insects, eating their fill. Above them, birds of prey circled, to devour the smaller birds in turn.

But there was one place near the Red Lake where no mosquito or bird flew, and no grass or living thing would grow. A low hill, little more than two miles from the eastern shore. A mound of close-packed dirt and stones, stark and strange amidst the wild grassland that surrounded it, and the green forest that climbed the nearby hills.

The mound had no name. If one had ever appeared on a map of the Old Kingdom, the map was long lost. There had once been farms nearby, but never closer than a league. Even when people had lived there, they would neither look at the strange hill nor speak of it. The nearest town now was Edge, a precarious settlement that had never seen better days but had not yet given up hope of them. The townsfolk of Edge knew it was wise to avoid the eastern shore of the Red Lake. Even the animals of the forest and the meadow shunned the area around the mound, as they instinctively stayed away from anyone who seemed to be going there.

Such as the man who stood on the fringe of the forest, where the hills melted into the lakeshore plain. A thin, balding man who wore a suit of leather armor that covered him from ankle to wrist, reinforced with plates of red-enameled metal at his neck and every joint. He carried a *naked sword in his left hand, the blade balanced across his shoulder. His right hand rested against a leather bandolier worn diagonally across his chest. Seven pouches hung from the bandolier, the smallest no larger than a pillbox, the largest as big as his clenched fist. Wooden handles hung downwards out of the pouches. Black ebony handles, which his fingers crawled across like a spider along a wall.*

Anyone who had been there to see would have known that the ebony handles belonged to bells, and that in turn would identify the man by kind, if not by name. A necromancer, he carried the seven bells of his dark art.

The man looked down at the mound for some time, noting that he was not the first to come there that day. At least two people stood on the bare hill, and there was a shimmer of heat in the air that suggested that other, less visible beings stood there, too.

The man considered waiting till dusk, but he knew he didn't have that choice. This was not his first visit to the mound. Power lay far beneath it, imprisoned deep within the earth. It had called him across the Kingdom, summoning him to its presence on this Midsummer's Day. It called him now, and he could not deny it.

Still, he retained enough pride and will to resist running the last half mile to the mound. It took all his strength, but when his boots touched the bare earth at the lip of the hill, it was with deliberation and no sign of haste.

One of the people there he knew, and expected. The old man, the last of the line that had served the thing that lay under the mound, acting as a channel for the power that kept it hidden from the gaze of the witches who saw everything in their cave of ice. The fact that the old man was the last, without some sniveling apprentice at his side, was reassuring. The time was coming when it need no longer hide beneath the earth.

The other person was unknown. A woman, or something that had once been a woman. She wore a mask of dull bronze, and the heavy furs of the Northern barbarians. Unnecessary, and uncomfortable, in this

weather . . . unless her skin felt something other than the sun. She wore
several rings of bone upon her silk-gloved fingers.

"You are Hedge," the stranger declared.

The man was surprised by the crackle of power in her speech. She
was a Free Magic sorcerer, as he'd suspected, but a more powerful one
than he could have guessed. She knew his name, or one of them—the
least of his names, the one he had used most often in recent times. He,
too, was a Free Magic sorcerer, as all necromancers had to be.

"A Servant of Kerrigor," continued the woman. "I see his brand
upon your forehead, though your disguise is not without some skill."

Hedge shrugged, and touched what appeared to be a Charter mark
on his forehead. It cracked in two and fell off like a broken scab, reveal-
ing an ugly scar that crawled and wriggled on his skin. "I carry the brand
of Kerrigor," he replied evenly. "But Kerrigor is gone, bound by the
Abhorsen and imprisoned these last fourteen years."

"You will serve me now," said the woman, in tones that brooked no
argument. "Tell me how I may commune with the power that lies under
this mound. It, too, will bend itself to my will."

Hedge bowed, hiding his grin. Was this not reminiscent of how he
had come to the mound himself, in the days after Kerrigor's fall?

"There is a stone on the western side," he said, pointing with his
sword. "Swing it aside, and you will see a narrow tunnel, striking
sharply down. Follow the tunnel till the way is blocked by a slab of
stone. At the foot of the stone, you will see water seeping through. Taste
of the water, and you will perceive the power of which you speak."

He did not mention that the tunnel was his, the product of five years'
toil, nor that the seeping water was the first visible sign of a struggle for
freedom that had gone on for more than two thousand years.

The woman nodded, the thin line of pallid skin around the mask
giving no hint of expression, as if the face behind it were as frozen as the
metal. Then she turned aside and spoke a spell, white smoke gushing
from the mouthpiece of the mask with every word. When she finished,

two creatures rose up from where they'd lain at her feet, nearly invisible against the earth. Two impossibly thin, vaguely human things, with flesh of swiftly moving mist and bones of blue-white fire. Free Magic elementals, of the kind that humans called Hish.

Hedge watched them carefully and licked his lips. He could deal with one, but two might force him to reveal strengths best left veiled for the moment. The old man would be no help. Even now he just sat there, mumbling, a living conduit for some part of the power under the hill.

"If I do not return by nightfall," the woman said, "my servants will rend you asunder, flesh and spirit too, should you seek refuge in Death."

"I will wait here," Hedge replied, settling himself down on the raw earth. Now that he knew the Hish's instructions, they represented no threat. He laid down his sword and turned one ear to the mound, pressing it against the soil. He could hear the constant whisper of the power below, through all the layers of earth and stone, though his own thoughts and words could not penetrate the prison. Later, if it was necessary, he would go into the tunnel, drink of the water, and lay his mind open, sending his thoughts back along the finger-wide trickle that had broken through all seven thrice-spelled wards. Through silver, gold, and lead; rowan, ash, and oak; and the seventh ward of bone.

Hedge didn't bother to watch the woman go, or stir when he heard the sound of the great stone being rolled away, even though it was a feat beyond the strength of any normal man, or any number of normal men.

When the woman returned, Hedge was standing at the very center of the mound, looking south. The Hish stood near him, but made no move as their mistress climbed back up. The old man sat where he always had, still gibbering, though whether he spoke spells or nonsense, Hedge couldn't say. It was no magic he knew, though he felt the power of the hill in the old man's voice.

"I will serve," the woman said.

The arrogance, though not the power, was gone from her voice. Hedge saw the muscles in her neck spasm as she spoke the words. He smiled and raised his hand. "There are Charter Stones that have been raised too close to the hill. You will destroy them."

"I will," agreed the woman, lowering her head.

"You were a necromancer," continued Hedge. In years past, Kerrigor had drawn all the necromancers of the Kingdom to him, to serve as petty underlords. Most had perished, either in Kerrigor's fall or, in the years after, at the hands of the Abhorsen. Some survived still, but this woman had never been a Servant of Kerrigor.

"Long ago," said the woman.

Hedge felt the faint flicker of Life inside her, buried deep under the spell-coated furs and the bronze mask. She was old, this sorcerer, very, very old—not an advantage for a necromancer who must walk in Death. That cold river had a particular taste for those who had evaded its clutches beyond their given span of years.

"You will take up the bells again, for you will need many Dead for the work that lies ahead." Hedge unbuckled his own bandolier and handed it over cautiously, careful not to jar the bells into sound. For himself he had another set of the seven, taken from a lesser necromancer in the chaos following Kerrigor's defeat. There would be some risk retrieving them, for they lay in that main part of the Kingdom long since reclaimed by the King and his Abhorsen Queen. But he had no need of the bells for his immediate plans, and could not take them where he intended to go.

The woman took the bells but did not put on the bandolier. Instead, she stretched out her right hand, palm upwards. A tiny spark glinted there, a splinter of metal that shone with its own bright, white fire. Hedge held out his own hand, and the splinter leapt across, burying itself just under the skin, without drawing blood. Hedge held it up to his face, feeling the power in the metal. Then he slowly closed his fingers, and smiled.

It was not for him, this sliver of arcane metal. It was a seed, a seed that could be planted in many soils. Hedge had a particular purpose for it, a most fertile bed where it could grow to its full fruit. But it would likely be many years before he could plant it where it would do most harm.

"And you?" asked the woman. "What do you do?"

"I go south, Chlorr of the Mask," said Hedge, revealing that he knew her name—and much else besides. "South to Ancelstierre, across the Wall. The country of my birth, though in spirit I am no child of its powerless soil. I have much to do there, and even farther afield. But you will hear from me when I have need. Or if I hear news that is not to my liking."

He turned then, and walked off without further word. For a master need make no farewells to any of his servants.

PART ONE

THE OLD KINGDOM

Fourteenth Year of the Restoration
of King Touchstone I

Chapter One

D EEP WITHIN A dream, Liracl felt someone stroking her forehead. A gentle, soft touch, a cool hand upon her own fevered skin. She felt herself smile, enjoying the touch. Then the dream shifted, and her forehead wrinkled. The touch was no longer soft and loving, but rough and rasping. No longer cool, but hot, burning her—

She woke up. It took her a second to realize that she'd clawed the sheet away and had been lying facedown on the coarsely woven mattress cover. It was wool and very scratchy. Her pillow lay on the floor. The pillowcase had been torn off in the course of some nightmare and now hung from her chair.

Lirael looked around the small chamber, but there were no signs of any other nocturnal damage. Her simple wardrobe of dressed pine was upright, the dull steel latch still closed. The desk and chair still occupied the other corner. Her practice sword hung in its scabbard on the back of the door.

It must have been a relatively good night. Sometimes, in her nightmare-laced sleep, Lirael walked, talked, and wreaked havoc. But always only in her room. Her precious room. She couldn't bear to think what life would be like if she were forced to go back to family chambers.

She closed her eyes again and listened. All was silent, which meant that it must be long before the Waking Bell. The bell sounded at the same time every day, calling the Clayr out of their beds to join the new morning.

Lirael scrunched her eyes together more tightly and tried to go back to sleep. She wanted to regain the feel of that hand on her brow. That touch was the only thing she remembered of her mother. Not her face or her voice—just the touch of her cool hand.

She needed that touch desperately today. But Lirael's mother was long gone, taking the secret of Lirael's paternity with her. She had left when Lirael was five, without a word, without an explanation. There never was any explanation. Just the news of her death, a garbled message from the distant North that had arrived three days before Lirael's tenth birthday.

Once she had thought of that, there was no hope for sleep. As on every other morning, Lirael gave up trying to keep her eyes shut. She let them spring open and stared up at the ceiling for a few minutes. But the stone had not changed overnight. It was still grey and cold, with tiny flecks of pink.

A Charter mark for light glowed there too, warm and golden in the stone. It had shone brighter when Lirael had first awoken and grew brighter still as she swung her feet out and felt around with her toes for her half-shoes. The Clayr's halls were heated by the steam of hot springs and by magic, but the stone floor was always cold.

"Fourteen today," whispered Lirael. She had her half-shoes on, but made no move to rise. Ever since the message of her mother's death had come so close to her tenth birthday, all her birthdays had been harbingers of doom.

"Fourteen!" Lirael said again, the word laced with anguish. She was fourteen, and by the measure of the world outside the Clayr's Glacier, a woman. But here she must still wear the blue tunic of a child, for the Clayr marked the passage to adulthood not by age, but by the gift of the Sight.

Once again, Lirael closed her eyes, screwing them tight as she willed herself to See the future. Everyone else her age had the Sight. Many younger children already wore the white robe and the circlet of moonstones. It was unheard of not to have the Sight by fourteen.

Lirael opened her eyes, but she saw no vision. Just her simple room, slightly blurred by tears. She rubbed them away and got up.

"No mother, no father, no Sight," she said as she opened her wardrobe and took out a towel. It was a familiar litany. She said it often, though it always made her feel a terrible stab of sorrow in her stomach. It was like worrying a toothache with her tongue. It hurt, but she couldn't leave it alone. The wound was part of her now.

But perhaps one day soon, she would be summoned by the Voice of the Nine Day Watch. Then she would wake and say, "No mother, no father, but I have the Sight."

"I will have the Sight," Lirael muttered to herself as she eased open the door and tiptoed down the corridor to the baths. Charter marks brightened as she passed under them, bringing day from twilight. But all the other doors in the Hall of Youth remained shut. Once, Lirael would have knocked on them, laughing and calling the other orphans who lived there to an early bath.

But that was years ago. Before they had all gained the Sight.

That was also when Merell was Guardian of the Young, one who had governed her charges with a light hand. Lirael's own aunt Kirrith was Guardian now. If there was any noise, she would emerge from her room in her maroon-and-white-striped bathrobe, to order silence and respect for sleeping elders. She would make no special allowance for Lirael, either. Quite the reverse. Kirrith was the exact opposite of Lirael's mother, Arielle. She was all for rules and regulations, tradition and conformity.

Kirrith would never leave the Glacier to travel who knew where, only to return seven months gone with child. Lirael scowled at Kirrith's door. Not that Kirrith had ever told her that. Kirrith wouldn't talk about her younger sister. The little Lirael knew about her mother came from eavesdropping on her closer cousins' conversations. The ones during which they discussed what to do about a girl who so obviously didn't belong.

Lirael scowled again at that thought. The scowl didn't go away, even when she was scraping her face with pumice stone in the hot bath. Only the shock of the cold plunge in the long pool finally smoothed the lines away.

The lines came back, though, as Lirael combed her hair in the communal mirror in the changing room next to the cold pool. The mirror was a rectangle of silver steel, eight feet high and twelve feet wide, rather tarnished around the edges. Later in the morning it would be shared by up to eight of the fourteen orphans currently in the Hall of Youth.

Lirael hated sharing the mirror, because it made yet another difference more obvious. Most of the Clayr had brown skin that quickly tanned to a deep chestnut out on the glacier slopes, as well as bright blond hair and light eyes. In contrast Lirael stood out like a pallid weed among healthy flowers. Her white skin burnt instead of tanning, and she had dark eyes and even darker hair.

She knew she probably took after her father, whoever that had been. Arielle had never identified him, yet another shame for her suffering daughter to carry. The Clayr often bore children fathered by visiting men, but they didn't usually leave the Glacier to find them, and they made no secret of the fathers. And for some reason, they almost always had girls. Fair-haired, nut-brown girls with pale blue or green eyes.

Except for Lirael.

Alone in front of the mirror, Lirael could forget all that. She concentrated on combing her hair, forty-nine strokes to each side. She was feeling more hopeful. Perhaps this would be the day. A fourteenth birthday marked by the best possible present. The gift of the Sight.

Even so, Lirael had no desire to eat breakfast in the Middle Refectory. Most of the Clayr ate there, and she would have to sit at a table with girls three or even four years younger, sticking out like a thistle in a bed of well-tended flowers. A blue-clad thistle. Everyone else her age would be dressed in white, sitting at the tables of the crowned and acknowledged Clayr.

Instead, Lirael crossed two silent corridors and descended two stairways that spiraled in opposite directions, down to the Lower Refectory. This was where the traders ate, and the supplicants who came to ask the Clayr to look into their futures. The only Clayr here would be those on the kitchen or serving rosters.

Or almost the only Clayr. There was one other who Lirael hoped would come. The Voice of the Nine Day Watch. As she walked down the last steps, Lirael imagined the scene. The Voice striding down the main stairs, striking the gong, then stopping to make her announcement that the Nine Day Watch had Seen her—Seen Lirael—being crowned with the circlet of moon-stones, had Seen her gaining the Sight at last.

The Lower Refectory wasn't very busy that morning. Only three of the sixty tables were occupied. Lirael went to a fourth, as far away from the others as possible, and drew out the bench. She preferred to sit alone, even when she was not among the Clayr.

Two of the tables were occupied by merchants, probably from Belisaere, talking loudly of the peppercorns, ginger, nutmeg, and cinnamon they had imported from the far North and hoped to sell to the Clayr. Their conversation about the quality and strength of their spices was all too evidently meant to be heard by the Clayr working in the kitchens.

Lirael sniffed the air. Their claims might even be true. The scent of cloves and nutmeg from the merchants' bags was very strong, but pleasant. Lirael took it as another good omen.

The third table was taken up by the merchants' guards. Even here, inside the Clayr's Glacier, they wore armored coats of interlocking scales and kept their scabbarded swords close by, under the benches. Obviously, they thought bandits or worse could easily follow the narrow path along the river gorge and force the gate that led to the Clayr's vast complex.

Of course, they would not have been able to see most of the defenses. The river path crawled with Charter marks of hiding and blinding, and under the flat paving stones there were sendings of beasts and warriors that would rise up at the slightest threat. The path also crossed the river no less than seven times, on slender bridges of ancient construction, apparently spun from stone. Easily defended bridges—with the river Ratterlin running below, deep enough and fast enough to keep any Dead from crossing.

Even here in the Lower Refectory there was Charter Magic lying dormant in the walls, and sendings that slept in the rough-hewn stone of floor and ceiling. Lirael could see the Charter marks, faint as they were, and puzzle out the spells they made up. The sendings were harder, because only the marks to trigger them were clear. Of course, there were clearly visible marks as well, the ones that shed light here and everywhere else within the Clayr's underground domain, bored into the rock of the mountain, next to the icy mass of the Glacier.

Lirael scanned the visitors' faces. Without helmets, their close-cropped hair made it easy to see that none had the Charter mark upon their foreheads. So they almost certainly couldn't see the magic that surrounded them. Instinctively, Lirael parted her own rather too-long hair and felt her mark. It pulsed lightly under her touch, and she felt the sense of connection, the feeling of belonging to the great Charter that described the world. At least she was something of a Charter Mage, even if she didn't have the Sight.

The merchants' guards should trust more in the Clayr's defenses, Lirael thought, looking at the armored men and women again. One of them saw her glance, and met her eyes for an instant, till she looked away. In that fleeting moment, she saw a young man, his head even more closely shaven than the others, so his scalp shone when it caught the light from the Charter marks in the ceiling.

Though she tried to ignore him, Lirael saw the guard get up and walk across, his scale coat too big for someone who would not see his real growth for several years. Lirael scowled as he approached, and turned her head away even more. Just because the Clayr did occasionally take lovers from amongst the visitors, some people thought that any of the Clayr visiting the Lower Refectory would be hunting for a man. This notion seemed particularly strong among young men of sixteen or thereabouts.

"Excuse me," said the guard. "May I sit here?"

Lirael nodded reluctantly, and he sat, a cascade of scales rattling down his chest in a slow waterfall of metal.

"I'm Barra," he said cheerfully. "Is this your first time here?"

"What?" asked Lirael, puzzled and shy. "In the Refectory?"

"No," said Barra, laughing and stretching his arms out to indicate a much larger vista. "Here. In the Clayr's Glacier. This is my second visit, so if you need someone to show you around . . . though I guess your parents might trade here often?"

Lirael looked away again, feeling bright spots burn into her cheekbones. She tried to think of something to say, some snappy rejoinder, but all she could think was that even outsiders knew she wasn't really a Clayr. Even a stupid, undergrown, rattling clod like this one.

"What's your name?" asked Barra, oblivious to the blush and the terrible emptiness that had grown inside her.

Lirael swallowed and wet her lips, but no answer came. She felt as if she didn't have a name to give, or an identity at all. She couldn't even look at Barra because her eyes were full of tears, so she stared at the half-eaten pear on her plate instead.

"I just wanted to say hello," said Barra uneasily, as the silence stretched out between them.

Lirael nodded, and two tears fell on the pear. She didn't look up or try to wipe her eyes. Her arms felt as limp and useless as her voice.

"I'm sorry," Barra added as he clanked to his feet. Lirael watched him go back to his table, her eyes partly covered by a protective fall of hair. When he was a few feet away, one of the men said something, not loud enough to hear. Barra shrugged, and the men—and some of the women—burst into laughter.

"It's my birthday," Lirael whispered to her plate, her voice more full of tears than her eyes. "I must not cry on my birthday." She stood up and clumsily stepped over the bench, taking her plate and fork to the scullery hatch, being careful not to catch the eye of whichever first, second, or third cousin worked there.

She was still holding the plate when one of the Clayr came down the main stairs and struck with her metal-tipped wand the first of the seven gongs that stood on the bottom seven steps. Lirael froze, and everyone in the Refectory stopped talking as the Clayr descended, striking each gong in turn, the different notes of the gongs merging into one before they echoed away into silence.

At the bottom step, the Clayr stopped and held up her wand. Lirael's heart leapt inside her, while her stomach knotted in anxiety. It was exactly as she had imagined. So like it that she felt sure that it hadn't been imagination, but the onset of the Sight.

Sohrae, as her wand declared, was currently the Voice of the Nine Day Watch, the Voice who made the announcements when the Watch Saw something of public importance to the Clayr or the Kingdom. Most important, the Voice also announced when the Watch had Seen the girl who would be next to gain the Sight.

"Know one, know many," proclaimed Sohrae, her clear voice carrying to every corner of the Refectory and the kitchens and the scullery beyond. "The Nine Day Watch with great gladness announce that the Gift of Sight has Awoken in our sister . . ."

Sohrae took a breath to go on, and Lirael shut her eyes, knowing that Sohrae was about to say her name. It must, it must, it *must* be me, she thought. Two years later than everyone, and today my birthday. It has to—

"Annisele," intoned Sohrae. Then she turned and went up the stairs again, lightly striking the gongs, their sound a soft undercurrent to the talk that had resumed among the visitors.

Lirael opened her eyes. The world had not changed. She did not have the Sight. Everything would go on as it always had. Miserably.

"Can I have your plate, please?" asked the unseen cousin behind the scullery hatch. "Oh, Lirael! I thought you were a visitor. You'd better hurry back upstairs, dear. Annisele's Awakening will start inside the hour. This is the Voice's last stop, you know. Whyever did you eat down here?"

Lirael didn't answer. She let the plate go and crossed the Refectory like a sleepwalker, her fingers listlessly brushing the table corners as she passed. All she could think of was Sohrae's voice, running over and over in her head.

"The gift of Sight has Awoken in our sister Annisele."

Annisele. Annisele would be the one to wear the white robe, to be crowned with the silver and moonstones, while Lirael once again would have to put on her best blue tunic, the uniform of a child. The tunic that no longer had a hem because it had been let out so many times. The tunic that was still too short.

Annisele had just turned eleven ten days ago. But her birthday would be nothing compared to this day, the day of her Awakening.

Birthdays *were* nothing, Lirael thought, as she mechanically put one foot in front of the other, up the six hundred steps from the Lower Refectory to the Westway, along that path for two hundred paces, and then up the hundred and two steps to the backdoor of the Hall of Youth. She counted every step, and looked no one in the eye. All she saw was the sweep of white robes and the flash of black-slippered feet, as all the Clayr rushed to the Great Hall to honor the latest girl to join the ranks of those who Saw the future.

By the time she reached her room, Lirael found that any small joy to be had from her birthday was gone. Extinguished, snuffed out like a candle. It was Annisele's day now, Lirael thought. She had to try to be happy for Annisele. She had to ignore the terrible sorrow that was welling up in her own heart.

Chapter Two

A FUTURE LOST

L IRAEL THREW HERSELF on her bed and tried to overcome her despair. She really should get dressed for Annisele's Awakening. But every time she started to get up, she felt unable to continue, and sat back down. For the moment, getting up was impossible. All she could do was relive the awful moment in the Lower Refectory when she had not heard her name. But she managed to wrestle her mind away from that, to think about the immediate future, not the past. Lirael made a decision. She wouldn't go to Annisele's Awakening.

It was unlikely anyone would really miss her, but there was a chance somebody might come to get her. This thought gave her enough strength to finally get off the bed and investigate hiding places. Under the bed was traditional, but the underside of Lirael's simple trestle bed was both cramped and very dusty, since she hadn't followed the standard cleaning routine properly for weeks.

She considered the wardrobe for a little while. But its spare, box-like shape and pine-plank construction made her think of it as an upended coffin. This was not a new thought for Lirael. She had always had what her cousins considered a morbid imagination. As a small child she had liked to playact dramatic death scenes from famous stories. She had stopped playacting years ago, but had never stopped thinking about death. Her own, in particular.

"Death," Lirael whispered, shivering to hear the word aloud. She said it again, a little louder. A simple word, a simple way to avoid all the things that plagued her. She could avoid Annisele's Awakening, but she probably couldn't avoid all the ones that would come after that.

If she killed herself, Lirael reasoned, she wouldn't have to watch girls increasingly younger than herself gaining the Sight. She wouldn't have to stand with a bunch of children in blue tunics. Children who all peeked at her under their lashes during the Awakening ceremony. Lirael knew that look and recognized the fear in it. They were afraid that they might be like her, doomed to lack the only thing that really mattered.

And she wouldn't have to put up with the Clayr who looked at her with pity. The ones who always stopped and asked how she was. As if mere words could describe how she felt. Or as if even if she had the words, Lirael could tell them what it was like to be fourteen and without the Sight.

"Death," Lirael whispered again, tasting the word on her tongue. What else was there for her? There had always been the hope that one day she would gain the Sight. But now she was fourteen. Who had ever heard of a Clayr Sightless at fourteen? Things had never seemed quite so desperate as they were today.

"It's the best thing to do," Lirael pronounced, as if she were informing a friend of a vital decision. Her voice sounded confident, but inside she wasn't so sure. Suicide wasn't something the Clayr did. Killing herself would be the final, terrible confirmation that she just didn't belong. It probably was the best thing. How would she actually do it? Lirael's eyes strayed to where her practice sword hung in its scabbard on the back of the door. It was blunt, soft steel. She could probably fall on its point, but that would lead to a very slow and painful death. Besides, someone would almost certainly hear her screaming and get help.

There was probably a spell that would still her breath, dry up her lungs, and close her throat. But she wouldn't find that in the school texts, her workbook of Charter Magic, or the *Index of Charter Marks*, both of which lay on the desk a few paces away. She'd have to search the Great Library for such a spell, and that sort of magic would be locked away by charm and key.

That left two reasonably accessible means of ending it all: cold and height. "The glacier," whispered Lirael. That would be it, she decided. She would climb the Starmount Stair while everyone else was at Annisele's Awakening, and then throw herself onto the ice. Eventually, if anyone bothered to look, they would find her frozen, broken body—and then they would all realize how hard it was to be a Clayr without the Sight.

Tears filled her eyes as she imagined a great crowd silently watching as her body was carried through the Great Hall, the blue of her child's tunic transformed to white by the ice and snow encrusted upon it.

A knock at the door cut short her morbid daydream, and Lirael jumped up, relieved. The Nine Day Watch must have finally Seen her, for the first time ever. They'd Seen her climb out onto the glacier and go plunging down, so they'd sent someone to prevent that future, to tell her that she would gain the Sight one day, that everything would be fine.

Then the door opened, before Lirael could say "Come in." That was enough to tell her that it wasn't a Nine Day Watcher concerned for her safety. It was Aunt Kirrith, Guardian of the Young. Or more the other way round, since she never treated Lirael any differently from the others, and particularly didn't show her the affection you might expect from an aunt.

"There you are!" boomed Kirrith unnecessarily in her annoying, falsely jolly voice. "I looked for you at breakfast, but there was such a crush I just couldn't find you. Happy birthday, Lirael!"

Lirael stared at Kirrith and at the present she was holding out. A large, square package, wrapped in red and blue paper dusted with gold. Very pretty paper, too. Aunt Kirrith had never given her a present before. She explained this by saying that she never accepted presents either, but Lirael thought that this missed the point. It was all about giving, not receiving.

"Go on, open it," exclaimed Kirrith. "We haven't got much time till the Awakening. Fancy it being little Annisele!"

Lirael took the package. It was soft, but quite heavy. For a moment, all her thoughts of killing herself were gone, driven away by curiosity. What could the present be?

Then, as she felt the package again, a terrible presentiment struck her. Quickly, she tore a hole in the corner of the paper, and saw the telltale blue. "It's a tunic," said Lirael, the words seeming to come from someone else, and a long way away. "A child's tunic."

"Yes," said Kirrith, resplendent in her own white robe, the circlet of silver and moonstones secure on her white-blond head. "I noticed your old one was too short, not really seemly, with the way you've grown. . . ."

She kept on talking, but Lirael didn't hear a word. Nothing seemed real anymore. Not the new tunic in her hands. Not Aunt Kirrith talking away. Nothing.

"Come on then, get dressed!" Kirrith encouraged her, straightening the folds of her own robe. She was a large and tall woman, one of the tallest of the Clayr. Lirael felt very small in front of her, and somehow dirty compared to the great expanse of white that was Kirrith's robe. She stared at that whiteness and began to think again of ice and snow.

She was lost in her thoughts when Kirrith tapped her on the shoulder.

"What?" Lirael asked, realizing that she'd missed most of Kirrith's words.

"Get dressed!" repeated Aunt Kirrith. A slight frown folded the skin on her forehead, making her circlet move down and shadow her eyes. "It would be terribly rude to be late."

Mechanically, Lirael pulled off her old tunic and slipped on the new one. It was heavy linen, stiff with newness, so she struggled a little with it, till Aunt Kirrith pulled it down smartly. When her arms were through and the tunic settled on her shoulders, it reached just above her ankles.

"Plenty of room for growth," remarked Aunt Kirrith with satisfaction. "Now we really must get on."

Lirael looked down at the sea of blue cloth that swathed her entire body, and thought that there was more room than she could ever possibly fill. Aunt Kirrith must expect her never to wear the white of the Awakening, for this tunic would fit even if she kept on growing till she was thirty-five.

"You go on—I'll catch up in a minute," she lied, thinking of the Starmount Stair, the cliffs beyond, and the waiting ice. "I have to go to the toilet."

"Very well," said Kirrith as she hurried back out into the corridor. "But be quick, Lirael! Think of what your mother would say!"

Lirael followed her, turning left towards the nearest water closet. Kirrith turned right, clapping her hands to hasten on a trio of eight-year-olds who were dressing as they walked, their tunics half over their heads, smothering giggles.

Lirael had no idea what her mother would have said about anything. She had been teased about Arielle often enough when she was younger, before she became too much of an outsider to be teased. It was quite normal for the Clayr to seek casual lovers from visitors to the Glacier, and not even that uncommon to find one outside. But it was unheard of not to record the parentage of children.

Her mother had compounded her strangeness by leaving the Glacier—and a five-year-old Lirael—called by some vision she had not shared with the other Clayr. Years later, Aunt Kirrith had told Lirael that Arielle was dead, though no details ever came. Lirael had heard various theories, including Arielle being poisoned by jealous rivals in the court of some barbarian lordling in the frozen wastes of the North or killed by beasts. Apparently she'd been serving as a seer, something that no Clayr would think was a suitable occupation for people of their Blood.

The pain of losing her mother was locked away in Lirael's heart, but not so deep it could not be uncovered. Aunt Kirrith was an expert at bringing it back.

Once Kirrith and the three suddenly chastened girls were gone, Lirael doubled back to her room and got her outdoor gear: a coat of heavy wool, greasy with lanolin; a cap of double felt with earflaps; oilskin overshoes; fur-lined gloves; and leather goggles with lenses of smoked green glass. Part of her said it was stupid to get these things, since she was going to her death anyway, but another small voice inside her said that she might as well be properly dressed.

Because all the inhabited parts of the Clayr's domain were heated by steam piped up from the deep springs, Lirael carried her outdoor gear, the smaller items wrapped in the coat. It was going to be hot enough climbing the Starmount Stair without wearing all that wool. As a last-minute gesture of defiance, she pulled off the new tunic and threw it on the floor. Instead, she chose to put on the neutral garments worn when the Clayr were on kitchen or scullery duty in the Lower Refectory, a long grey cotton shirt that came down to the knees, over thin blue woollen leggings. There was a canvas apron that went with this ensemble, but Lirael left that behind.

It was strange slinking down the Northway with no one in sight. Normally, there would be dozens of the Clayr going about their business on this busy thoroughfare, either heading to or from the Nine Day Watch or engaged in the myriad more mundane tasks of the community. The Clayr's Glacier was really a small town, albeit a very strange one, since its primary business was to look into the future. Or, as the Clayr had to constantly explain to visitors, the numerous possible futures.

At the point where the Northway met the Zigzag, Lirael made sure she was unobserved. Then she went a few steps along the first zig of the Zigzag, looking for a small, dark hole at waist height. When she found it, she took out the key she wore on a chain around her neck. All the Clayr had such keys, and they opened most of the common doors. The Starmount Door was not often used, but Lirael didn't think it needed a special key.

There was no sign of a door around the keyhole until Lirael put in the key and turned it twice. Then a faint silvery line spread from the floor and slowly traced a doorway in the yellowish stone.

Lirael pushed the door open. Cold air rushed in, so she went through quickly. If there were any other people about, they would notice a cold breeze more quickly than anything else. The Clayr might live in a mountain that was half smothered by a glacier, but they didn't revel in the cold.

The door swung shut behind Lirael, and the silver lines that marked its outline slowly faded. Ahead of her, the steps rose up in a straight line, the Charter marks above them providing light that was dimmer than that in the main halls. The risers were higher than usual, something Lirael hadn't remembered from a class excursion many years before, when all steps had seemed high. She grimaced as she started to climb, knowing that her calf muscles would soon protest the extra six-inch rise.

There was a bronze handrail for the first hundred or so steps, where the Stair went up in a dead straight line. Lirael gripped it as she climbed, the cool of the metal soothing under her hand.

As was her habit, she started counting steps, the regular rhythm temporarily banishing the mental images of herself falling down an endless slope of ice.

She hardly noticed when the handrail stopped and the steps began to turn inwards, into the long spiral that would take her to the top of the mountain, Starmount. Its sister peak was Sunfall, and the two mountains held the glacier between them. The glacier had once had its own name, but it was long forgotten. So for thousands of years it had been called after the Clayr who lived above, beside, and sometimes beneath it. Over time that name had come to be extended to the Clayr's realm as well, so both the great mass of ice and the halls of stone were known as the Clayr's Glacier, as if they were all one.

Not that the Clayr chose rooms too close to the glacier as a rule. They had lived in the mountain for millennia, following the tunneling of the now almost extinct drill-grubs or carrying out their own magical or physical excavations. At the same time, the glacier had continued its inexorable march down the valley, and into the mountains that gripped its sides. Ice ground down and broke through stone, and the glacier was indifferent if that also meant crashing through the tunnels of the Clayr.

Of course, the Clayr could See where the glacier was going to have its unthinking way, but that hadn't stopped various ambitious builders of bygone days. Obviously they had felt their extensions would last as long as they did, and probably for at least three or four generations after them—time enough to make the work worthwhile.

Lirael thought of all those builders and wondered why the Stair had been made with such uncomfortably high steps. But after a while, even mechanically counting steps couldn't keep her imagination under rein. She started to imagine how Annisele would be looking right at that instant. Perhaps she was standing at the children's end of the Great Hall, a single figure in white amidst a field of blue. She would be staring down the other end, no doubt, barely aware of the ranks and ranks of white-clad Clayr, sitting in the pews that lined both sides of the Hall for several hundred yards, twenty-one ranks deep. Pews made from ancient dark mahogany, with silk cushions that were replaced every fifty years, with considerable ceremony.

At the far end of the Hall, there would be the Voice of the Nine Day Watch, and perhaps some of the Watchers, too, their business permitting. They would be standing around the Charter Stone that rose up from the floor of the Hall, a single menhir swarming with all the glowing, changing marks of the Charter that described everything in the world, seen or unseen. And on the Charter Stone, higher than anyone could reach, save the Voice with her metal-tipped wand, there would be the circlet of the new Clayr, the silver and moonstones reflecting the Charter marks of the Stone.

Lirael forced her tired legs up another step. Annisele's walk wouldn't be tiring at all. Just a few hundred steps, with smiling faces on all sides. Then, when the circlet was placed on her head at last, the tumult as all the Clayr rose to their feet, followed by the great cheer that would echo through the Hall and beyond. The Awakening of Annisele, a true Clayr, a mistress of the Sight. Acclaimed by one and all.

Unlike Lirael, who was, as always, alone and unregarded. She felt like crying but brushed the tears away. Only another hundred steps to go, and she would be at the Starmount Gate. Once through the gate and across the wide terrace in front of it, Lirael would stand on the edge of the glacier, looking down into icy death.

Chapter Three

A T THE TOP of the Starmount Stair, Lirael rested for a while, till the chill coming through the stone got too much to bear. Then she donned her outdoor gear, turning the world green as she slipped on her goggles. Last, she drew a silk scarf from the pocket of her coat, tied it across her nose and mouth, and folded down the earflaps of her cap.

Dressed like that, she might be one of the Clayr. No one could see her face, hair, or eyes. She looked exactly like any other Clayr. When they found her body, they wouldn't even know who it was till cap, scarf, and goggles were removed.

Lirael would look like one of the Clayr for the last time.

Even so, she hesitated before the door that led from the Stair to the Paperwing hangar and the Starmount Gate. It probably wasn't too late to go back, to say she'd eaten something that disagreed with her so she'd had to stay in her room. If she hurried, she'd almost certainly be back before everyone returned from the Awakening.

But nothing would have changed. There was nothing to look forward to down there, Lirael decided, so she might as well go and look at the cliffs. She could make her final decision there.

She took her key out again, clumsy in her gloves, and unlocked the door. A visible one, this time, but magically guarded as well. Lirael felt the Charter Magic inside it flow out through the key, through the fur of her gloves and into her hands. She tensed for a moment, then relaxed as it ebbed away again. Whatever it guarded against, the spell wasn't interested in her.

It was colder still past the door, though Lirael was still inside the mountain. This large chamber was the Paperwing hangar, where the Clayr kept their magical aircraft. Three of them slept nearby. They looked rather like slim canoes, with hawk-wings and tails. Lirael felt an urge to touch one of them, to see if it really did feel like paper, but she knew better than that. Physically, the Paperwings were made from thousands of sheets of laminated paper. But they were also made with considerable magic, and were partially sentient as a result. The painted eyes at the front of the closest green and silver craft might be dull now, but they would light up if she touched it. Lirael had no idea what it might do then. She knew the craft were controlled by whistled Charter marks, and she could whistle, but she didn't know the marks or any special technique that might be required.

So Lirael crept past the Paperwings, across to the Starmount Gate. It was huge—big enough for thirty people or two Paperwings to pass abreast—and easily four times as tall as Lirael. Fortunately, she didn't have to even try to open it, because there was a smaller sally port cut into the large Gate's left quarter. A moment's work with her key, the touch of the guarding spell, then the door was open, and Lirael stepped outside.

Cold and sunshine hit her at the same time, the former strong enough to feel even through her heavy clothes, and the latter fierce enough to make her half-close her eyes, even behind goggles.

It was a beautiful summer day. Lower down in the valley, below the glacier, it would be hot. Here it was cold, the chill mainly coming from the breeze that blew along the glacier and then up, over, and around the mountain.

Ahead of Lirael, a broad, unnaturally flat terrace was carved

into the mountainside. It was about a hundred yards long and
fifty yards wide, and snow and chunks of ice were piled up all
around it in deep drifts. But the terrace itself had only a light
dusting of snow. Lirael knew it was kept like that by Charter
sendings—magically created servants who shoveled, raked, and
repaired all the year round, oblivious to the weather. There were
none to be seen now, but the Charter Magic that would send
them into action lurked beneath the paving stones of the terrace.

On the far side of the terrace, the mountain fell away in a
sheer precipice. Lirael looked across to it but saw nothing but
blue sky and a few wisps of low cloud. She would have to cross
the terrace and look down to see the main bulk of the glacier a
thousand feet below. But she didn't cross. Instead, she pictured
what might happen if she jumped. If she threw herself out far
enough, she would fall free, down to the waiting ice and a speedy
end. If she fell short, she would hit a spur of rock maybe only
thirty or forty feet down, then slide and tumble the rest of the
way, breaking a new bone with every momentary impact.

Lirael shivered and looked away. Now that she was actually
here, only a few minutes' brisk walk from the precipice, she wasn't
sure that making her own death was such a good idea. But every
time she tried to think of a continuing future for herself, she felt
weak and blocked, as if all the ways forward were closed off by
walls too high to climb.

For now, she forced herself to move and take a few steps
across the terrace, to at least look at the drop. But her legs seemed
to have a life of their own, walking her along the length of the
terrace instead, without getting any closer to the cliff-side.

Half an hour later, she headed back to the Starmount Gate,
having walked the length of the terrace four times without once
daring to go anywhere near the cliff on the far side. The closest
she'd got was the sudden drop at the end of the terrace, where

the Paperwings actually took off. But that was a fall of only a few hundred feet, down a much less steep face of the mountain, and not onto the glacier. Even then she hadn't gone within twenty feet of the edge.

Lirael wondered how the Paperwings would launch off that far end. She had never seen one take off or land, and she spent some time trying to imagine how it would look. Obviously, they would slip along the ice and then at some point leap into the sky, but where exactly? Did they need a long run-up like the blue pelicans she'd seen on the Ratterlin, or could they shoot straight up like falcons?

All these questions made Lirael curious about how the Paperwings actually worked. She was thinking of risking a closer look at one back in the hangar when she realized that the black speck she'd noticed high above wasn't a product of her imagination, or a tiny storm cloud. It was a real Paperwing, and it was obviously coming in to land.

At the same time she heard the deep rumble of the Starmount Gate as it started to swing open. She looked back at it, then at the Paperwing again, her head moving in frantic starts. What was she going to do?

She could run across the terrace and throw herself off, but she really didn't feel like doing that. The moment of her darkest despair had passed, at least for now.

She could just stand on one side of the terrace and watch the Paperwing land, but that would almost certainly lead to a serious scolding from Aunt Kirrith, not to mention several months' worth of extra kitchen duties. Or some even worse punishment she didn't know about.

Or she could hide and watch. After all, she had wanted to see a Paperwing land.

All these options raced through her mind, and it took only

an instant for the last one to be chosen. Lirael ran to a snowdrift, sat down in it, and started to drag snow across herself. Soon she was almost completely hidden, save for the line of footprints that led across the snow to her hiding place.

Quickly, Lirael visualized the Charter, then reached into its eternal flow to pull out the three marks she needed. One by one they grew into brilliance inside her mind, filling it until she could think of nothing else. She drew them into her mouth, then puffed the marks out towards her tracks in the snow.

The spell left her as a whirling ball of frosted breath that grew until it was an arm's span wide. It drifted back across her path, sweeping her footsteps clean. Then, its work done, the ball let itself be taken by the wind, breath and Charter marks dissolving into nothing.

Lirael looked up, hoping whoever was in the Paperwing hadn't seen the strange little cloud. The aircraft was closer now, the shadow of its wings passing along the terrace as it circled once more, losing height with every pass.

Lirael squinted, her sight obscured by goggles and the snow that covered nearly all her face. She couldn't quite see who was in the Paperwing. It was a different color from the ones used by the Clayr. Red and gold, the colors of the Royal House. A messenger, perhaps? There was regular communication between the King in Belisaere and the Clayr, and Lirael had often seen messengers in the Lower Refectory. But they didn't normally arrive by Paperwing.

Some whistled notes, redolent with power, drifted down to Lirael, and for a nausea-inducing moment she felt as if she herself were flying and must turn into the wind. Then she saw the Paperwing come swooping down once more, turn into the wind, and come to a sliding, snow-spraying stop on the terrace—much too close to Lirael's hiding place for comfort.

Two people climbed wearily out of the cockpit and stretched their arms and legs. Both were so heavily wrapped in furs that Lirael couldn't see whether they were male or female. They weren't Clayr, though, she was certain, not in those clothes. One wore a coat of black and silver marten fur, the other a coat of some russet-red fur Lirael didn't recognize. And their goggles were blue lensed, not green.

The russet-furred one reached back into the cockpit and pulled out two swords. Lirael thought he—she was reasonably certain this one was a he—would hand one over, but he buckled both onto his broad leather belt, one on either side of his waist.

The other person—the one in black and silver—was a woman, Lirael decided. There was something about the way she took off her glove and rested her palm on the nose of the Paperwing, like a mother checking the temperature of a child's forehead.

Then the woman also reached into the cockpit, and she pulled out a leather bandolier. Lirael craned forward to see better, ignoring the snow that fell down inside her collar. Then she almost gasped and gave herself away, as she recognized what was in the pouches on the bandolier. Seven pouches, the smallest the size of a pillbox, the largest as long as Lirael's hand. Each pouch had a mahogany handle sticking out of it. The handles of bells, bells whose voices were stilled in the leather. Whoever this woman was, she carried the seven bells of a necromancer!

The woman put the bandolier on and reached for her own sword. Longer than the ones the Clayr used, and older, too. Lirael could feel some sort of power in it, even from where she was hidden. Charter Magic, in the sword, and in both the people.

And in the bells, Lirael realized, which finally told her who this person must be. Necromancy was Free Magic, and forbidden in the Kingdom, as were the bells that necromancers used. Except for the bells of one woman. The woman who was charged with undoing the evil that necromancers wrought. The woman who put the Dead to rest. The woman who alone combined Free Magic with the Charter.

Lirael shivered, but not from cold, as she realized that she was only about twenty yards away from the Abhorsen. Years ago, the legendary Sabriel had rescued the petrified prince Touchstone and with him defeated the Greater Dead creature called Kerrigor, who had almost destroyed the Kingdom. And she had married the Prince when he became King, and together they had—

Lirael looked at the man again, noting the two swords and the way he stood close to Sabriel. He must be the King, she realized, feeling almost sick. King Touchstone and the Abhorsen Sabriel here! Close enough to go and talk to—if she was brave enough.

She wasn't. She settled further back into the snow, ignoring the damp and the cold, and waited to see what would happen. Lirael didn't know how you were supposed to bow or curtsy or whatever it was, or what you were supposed to call the King and the Abhorsen. Most of all, she didn't know how to explain what she was doing there.

Having equipped themselves, Sabriel and Touchstone drew close together and spoke quietly, their muffled faces almost touching. Lirael strained her ears but couldn't hear anything. The wind was blowing their words the wrong way. However, it was clear that they were waiting for something—or someone.

They didn't have to wait long. Lirael slowly turned her head towards the Starmount Gate, careful not to disturb the snow packed around her. A small gathering of the Clayr was issuing out of the Gate and hurrying across the terrace. They'd obviously come straight from the Awakening, because most of them had simply thrown cloaks or coats over their white robes, and nearly all of them still wore their circlets.

Lirael recognized the two in front—the twins Sanar and Ryelle—the flawless embodiment of the perfect Clayr. Their Sight was so strong they were nearly always in the Nine Day Watch, so Lirael hardly ever crossed paths with them. They were both tall and extremely beautiful, their long blond hair shining even more brightly than their silver circlets in the sun.

Behind them came five other Clayr. Lirael knew them all vaguely and, if pressed, could recall their names and their familial relationship to her. None was closer than a third cousin, but she recognized all of them as being particularly strong in the Sight. If they weren't part of the Nine Day Watch right now, they would be tomorrow, and probably had been last week.

In short, they were seven of the most important Clayr in all the Glacier. They all held significant ordinary posts in addition to their Sighted work. Small Jasell, for example, bringing up the rear, was First Bursar, in charge of the Clayr's internal finances and its trading bank.

They were also the very last people Lirael wanted to meet somewhere she wasn't supposed to be.

Chapter Four

As SANAR AND Ryelle led the others forward, Lirael thought she would see them do whatever it was you did when you met the King and his Queen, who had the added distinction of being the Abhorsen.

But Sabriel and Touchstone didn't wait for whatever that was. They met Sanar and Ryelle with hugs and, after pushing up their goggles and removing their scarves, with kisses on both cheeks. Once again, Lirael leaned forward to hear what was being said. The wind was still blowing the wrong way, but it had lessened, so she could catch the conversation.

"Well met, cousins," said Sabriel and the King together, both smiling. Now that she could see their faces, Lirael thought they both looked very tired.

"We Saw you last night," said Sanar—or Ryelle—Lirael wasn't sure. "But we had to guess the time from the sun. I trust you haven't been waiting long?"

"A few minutes," said Touchstone. "Just long enough to stretch."

"He still doesn't like flying much," said Sabriel, with a smile at her husband. "No confidence in the pilot."

Touchstone shrugged and laughed. "You get better all the time," he said.

Lirael sensed that he wasn't just talking about flying Paperwings. There seemed to be a semi-secret line of energy and feeling that ran between Touchstone and Sabriel. They shared something unseen, something that brought laughter and the smile in Sabriel's eyes.

"We didn't See you staying," continued Sanar. "I take it we got that right?"

"You did," replied Sabriel, and the smile was gone from her eyes. "There is trouble in the West, and we cannot linger. Only long enough to take counsel. If you have any to give."

"The West again?" asked Sanar, and she shared a troubled look with Ryelle, as did the others of the Clayr behind her. "We See nothing for too great a part of the West. Some power exists there that blocks all but the briefest glimpses. Yet we know that it is from the West that trouble will come to pass. So many futures show snatches of it, but never enough to be useful."

"Plenty of present trouble, too," said the King, sighing. "I have raised six Charter Stones around Edge and the Red Lake in the last ten years. Only two remain from year to year, and I can no longer spare the time to keep repairing the others. We go there now to quell whatever the current trouble is, and to attempt to find the source, but I am not confident we will. Particularly if it is strong enough to hide from the Clayr's Sight."

"It is not always strength that can blind our Sight," said one of the Clayr, the oldest there. "Nor even evil. There are subtle powers that divert our Sight for reasons we can only guess, and there is always simply the fact that we See too many futures, too briefly. Perhaps whatever blinds us near the Red Lake is no more than this."

"If it is, then it also breaks Charter Stones with the blood of Charter Mages," said Touchstone. "And it draws the Dead and Free Magic to it more than anywhere else. Of all the Kingdom, it is the region around the Red Lake and the foothills of Mount Abed that most resists our rule. Fourteen years ago, Sabriel and

I promised that the broken Charter Stones would be made anew, the villages re-established, the people once again free to go about their lives and business, without fear of the Dead and Free Magic. We have made it so from the Wall to the Northern Desert. But we cannot defeat whatever it is that opposes us in the West. Apart from Edge itself, that part of the West is still the wilderness that Kerrigor made it over two hundred years ago."

"You grow weary of your toils," said the old Clayr suddenly, and both Touchstone and Sabriel nodded. But their shoulders were straight, and while they admitted the weariness, they gave no sign that they refused the burden.

"We get no rest," said Touchstone. "There is always some new trouble, some danger that can be dealt with only by the King or the Abhorsen. Sabriel gets the worst of it, for there are still too many Dead abroad, and too many idiots who would open further doors to Death."

"Like the one who is currently causing havoc near Edge," said Sabriel. "Or so the messages say. A necromancer or Free Magic sorcerer, one who wears a bronze mask. She—for it is reported she is a woman—has a company of both the Dead and living men, and they have been raiding farms and steadings from Edge to the east, almost as far as Roble's Town. Yet we have heard nothing from you. Surely you must have Seen some of this?"

"We rarely See anything near the Red Lake," replied Ryelle with a troubled frown. "But we usually have no problem farther afield. In this case, I regret that we have given you no warning for what has happened, and can give you no guide as to what will."

"A company of the Guard is riding from Qyrre," said Touchstone. "But they will not arrive for at least three days. We plan to be at Roble's Town ourselves by the morning."

"Hopefully a bright morning," added Sabriel. "If the reports are true, this necromancer has many Dead Hands under her control. Maybe even enough to attack a town at night, or under heavy cloud."

"I think we would definitely See an attack upon Roble's Town," said Ryelle. "And we have not."

"That's some relief," said Touchstone, but Lirael saw that he didn't entirely believe them. She was herself shocked, because she had never heard of the Sight being blocked, or of there being some place where the Clayr couldn't See. Except beyond the Wall to Ancelstierre, of course, but that was different. No magic worked in Ancelstierre, at least not once you got well south of the Wall. Or so the stories said. Lirael didn't know anyone who'd ever been to Ancelstierre, though the rumor was that Sabriel had grown up there.

The wind strengthened as Lirael mulled over what she'd heard, so she couldn't quite catch the next bit of conversation. But she saw the Clayr bow, and Sabriel and Touchstone motion for them to rise.

"Don't get formal on me!" exclaimed Touchstone. "You can't See everything, just as we can't do everything. Somehow we've managed so far, and we'll keep on managing."

"'Keeping on' being the watchword of this year and all the years behind it," said Sabriel, sighing. "Speaking of such, we'd best turn the Paperwing around and take flight again. I want to visit the House on the way to Roble's Town."

"To take counsel with—?" asked Ryelle, but the rest of her words were lost to Lirael, carried away by a gust of wind. She leaned forward a bit more, still trying not to dislodge the snow from her cap.

Sabriel said something in return, but Lirael couldn't make it out, save for the last part. ". . . still sleeps most of the year, under Ranna's . . ."

Then there was more lost talk, as they all clustered around the Paperwing and slid it around. Lirael craned forward as far as she dared, snow slipping from her face. It was infuriating to see them and hear the occasional word but not be able to understand. For a moment she even wildly thought of casting a spell to improve her hearing. She'd seen references to such a spell, but she didn't know all the marks. Besides, Sabriel and the others would almost certainly notice Charter Magic nearby.

Suddenly, the wind dropped, and Lirael could hear clearly again.

"They're still at school in Ancelstierre," Sabriel said, obviously in answer to a question asked by Sanar. "They'll be here for the holidays in three, no . . . four weeks. If all works out with this current emergency, we might just get to the Wall in time to meet them, and we had planned a few weeks together in Belisaere. But I expect some new trouble will arise that will take at least one of us away until they have to go back."

She sounded sad when she said that, Lirael thought. Touchstone must have thought so, too, because he took her hand, lending support.

"At least they're safe there," he said, and Sabriel nodded, her weariness showing through again.

"We have Seen them crossing the Wall, though it may be the next time, or the one after that," affirmed Ryelle. "Ellimere looks . . . will look . . . very like you, Sabriel."

"Fortunately," said Touchstone, laughing. "Though she takes after me in some other respects."

Lirael realized that they had been talking about their children. They had two, she knew. A Princess who was roughly her own age, and a Prince who was younger, she didn't know by how much. Sabriel and Touchstone obviously cared about them a great deal, and missed them. That made her think of her own mother and father, who must not have cared about her at all. Once again she remembered the touch of that soft, cool hand. But her mother had still left her, and who knew whether her father ever even knew of her birth?

"She will be Queen," said a strong voice, dragging Lirael's attention back to the present. "She will not be Queen. She may be Queen."

It was one of the other Clayr, an older woman, speaking in the voice of prophecy, her eyes Seeing something other than the lump of ice she was staring at. Then she gasped and stumbled forward, hands flung out to break her fall into the snow.

Touchstone lunged and caught her before she could hit the ground, setting her back on her feet. She swayed there, still unsteady, her eyes wild and dreaming.

"A far future," she said, the strange timbre of foreseeing gone from her voice. "One in which your daughter, Ellimere, was older than you are now, reigning as Queen. But I also Saw many other possible futures, side by side, where there is nothing but smoke and ashes, the whole world burnt and broken."

Lirael felt a shiver pass through her entire body as the old Clayr spoke. Her voice carried so much conviction, Lirael could almost see the desolate ruins herself. But how could the whole world be burnt and broken?

"Possible futures," interjected Sanar, trying to sound calm. "We often catch glimpses of futures that will never be. It is part of the burden of the Sight."

"Then I for one am glad I don't have it," replied Touchstone, as he let the still shaky Clayr go into the helping hands of Sanar and Ryelle. He looked up at the sun, and then across at Sabriel, who nodded. "I regret to say that we must be on our way."

He and Sabriel shared a smile at this unintentional rhyme, turning their heads so that only they and the hidden Lirael saw it. Touchstone took off his swords and stowed them in the cockpit, then took Sabriel's sword and put that away as well. Sabriel took off the bell bandolier and gently laid it down, careful to not jar the bells. Lirael wondered why they had bothered to get them out for such a short time. Then she realized that they lived so much in danger that it was second nature to keep weapons close at hand. Like the merchants' guards in the Refectory that morning. The realization that the Abhorsen and the King didn't trust the Clayr's protection made Lirael suddenly think of her own weaponless state. What would she do if she were attacked out here after everyone had gone? She wasn't sure if her key would open the sally port from the outside. She hadn't even thought about it on the way up.

Lirael stopped watching the Paperwing in order to panic, imagining a night out here and a monstrous claw dragging her out of the snow. The prospect of an unchosen death didn't appeal to her at all. Then a sudden movement caught her eye. Sabriel, now in the Paperwing, was pointing. Pointing straight at Lirael's hiding place in the snow!

"You might want to investigate that green glint," said Sabriel, her words all too clear for once. "I think whatever lies beneath it is harmless, but you never know. Farewell, cousins of the Clayr. I hope we can meet again soon, and tarry longer."

"As we hope that we can be of greater service," said Sanar, looking where Sabriel pointed. "And See more clearly, both in the West and under our own noses."

"Farewell," added Touchstone, waving from the rear of the Paperwing. Sabriel whistled, a pure sound infused with magic. The whistle rose up into the wind, turned it, and brought it down to lift the Paperwing, sending it sliding along the terrace. Sabriel and Touchstone waved; then the red and gold craft shot off the end and dropped out of sight.

Lirael held her breath, then sucked air in with relief as the Paperwing suddenly soared back into sight. It circled higher, then turned to the south and shot away, faster and faster as Sabriel called the wind behind them.

Lirael watched it go for a second, then tried to burrow deeper into the snow. Perhaps they would think she was an ice otter. But even as she disappeared into the drift, she knew it was no use. All seven of the Clayr were advancing upon her hiding place, and they did not look pleased.

Chapter Five

L IRAEL WASN'T QUITE sure how they got back into the Paperwing hangar so quickly. She knew she was grabbed by more pairs of hands than seemed possible for seven people and hustled across the snow much more uncomfortably than she could have managed on her own. For a few seconds she thought they were very, very angry with her. Then she realized they were just cold, and wanted to get back inside.

Once all were inside, it was clear that while the Clayr were not exactly furious, they weren't too happy, either. Hands snatched off her cap, goggles, and scarf without regard for the hair that was caught up in them, and seven somewhat wind-chilled faces looked down at her.

"Arielle's daughter," said Sanar, as if she were identifying a flower or a plant, dredging it up from a list. "Lirael. Not on the roster of the Watch. Therefore, not yet with the Sight. Is that correct?"

"Y-yes," stammered Lirael. No one had ever peered at her so intently before, and she generally avoided talking to other people, particularly fully fledged Clayr. Important Clayr made her nervous even when she was behaving herself. Now there were seven of them giving her their undivided attention. She wished she could somehow sink through the floor and reappear in her own room.

"Why were you hiding out there?" asked the old Clayr, who

Lirael suddenly remembered was named Mirelle. "Why aren't you at the Awakening?"

There was no warmth in her voice at all, just cold authority. Belatedly, Lirael remembered that this grey-haired, leather-faced old woman was also the commander of the Clayr's Rangers, who hunted and patrolled across Starmount and Sunfall, the glacier, and the river valley. They dealt with everything from lost travelers to foolish bandits or marauding beasts, and were not to be trifled with.

Mirelle asked her question again, but Lirael couldn't answer. Tears came into her eyes, though she managed to hold them back. Then, when it seemed Mirelle was about to shake both answer and tears out of her, she said the first thing that came into her head.

"It's my birthday. I'm fourteen."

For some reason, this seemed to be the right thing to say. All the Clayr relaxed, and Mirelle let go of her shoulders. Lirael winced. The woman had gripped her hard enough to leave bruises.

"So you're fourteen," said Sanar, much more kindly than Mirelle. "And you're worried because the Sight hasn't woken in you?"

Lirael nodded, not trusting herself to speak.

"It comes late to some of us," continued Sanar, her eyes warm and understanding. "But often the later it is, the more strongly it wakes. The Sight did not come to me and Ryelle till we were sixteen. Has no one told you that?"

Lirael looked up, fully meeting the Clayr's gaze for the first time, her eyes wide with shock. Sixteen! That was impossible!

"No," she said, the surprise and relief clear in her voice. "Not sixteen!"

"Yes," said Ryelle, smiling, taking over where Sanar left off.

"Sixteen and a half, in fact. We thought it would never come. But it did. I suppose you couldn't bear another Awakening. Is that why you came up here?"

"Yes," said Lirael, a small smile beginning to creep across her own face. Sixteen! That meant there was hope for her yet. She felt like jumping forward and hugging everybody, even Mirelle, and running down the Starmount Stair yelling for joy. All of a sudden, her plan to kill herself seemed incredibly stupid, and the hatching of it long ago and far away.

"Part of our problem back then was having too much time to think about our lack of the Sight," said Sanar, who had not missed the signs of relief in Lirael's face and posture, "since we weren't part of the Watch and didn't have the Sight training. Of course, we didn't want to do extra shifts on the roster duties, either."

"No," agreed Lirael hurriedly. Who would want to clean toilets or wash dishes any more than she had to?

"It wasn't usual for us to be assigned a post before we turned eighteen," continued Ryelle. "But we asked, and the Watch agreed that we should be given proper work. So we joined the Paperwing Flight and learned to fly. That was in the time before the return of the King, when everything was much more dangerous and unsettled, so we flew far more patrols, and farther afield, than we do now.

"After only a year of flying, the Sight woke in us. It could have been an awful year, as was the one before it, waiting and hoping for the gift, but we were too busy to even think about it much. Do you think that proper work might help you, too?"

"Yes!" replied Lirael fervently. A post would free her from the child's tunic, let her wear the clothes of a working Clayr. It would also give her somewhere to go, away from the younger children and Aunt Kirrith. She might even be able to stay away from Awakenings, depending on what the work was.

"The question is, what work would suit you best?" mused Sanar. "I do not think we have ever Seen you, so that's no help. Is there any posting you would particularly like? The Rangers? Paperwing Flight? The Merchant Office? The Bank? Building and Construction? The Infirmary? The Steamworks?"

"I don't know," said Lirael, trying to think of all the many and various jobs the Clayr did, in addition to the rostered community duties.

"What are you good at?" asked Mirelle. She looked Lirael up and down, clearly measuring her up as a potential recruit for the Rangers. The slight lift of her nose showed that she didn't seem to think much of Lirael's potential. "How's your swordcraft, and archery?"

"Not very good," replied Lirael guiltily, thinking of all the practice sessions she'd missed lately, having chosen to mope in her room instead. "I'm best at Charter Magic, I think. And music."

"Perhaps the Paperwings, then," said Sanar. Then she frowned and looked at the others. "Though fourteen is perhaps a shade too young. They can be a bad influence."

Lirael glanced at the Paperwings and couldn't hold back a small shiver. She liked the idea of flying, but the Paperwings frightened her a bit. There was something creepy about their being alive and having their own personalities. What would happen if she had to talk to one of them all the time? She hated talking to people, let alone Paperwings.

"Please," said Lirael, pursuing that thought to the logical place where she could avoid people the most. "I think I would like to work in the Library."

"The Library," repeated Sanar, looking troubled. "That can be dangerous to a girl of fourteen. Or a woman of forty, for that matter."

"Only in parts," said Ryelle. "The Old Levels."

"You can't work in the Library without going into the Old Levels," said Mirelle somberly. "At least some of the time. I wouldn't be keen on going to some parts of the Library, myself."

Lirael listened, wondering what they were talking about. The Great Library of the Clayr was enormous, but she had never heard of the Old Levels.

She knew the general layout well. The Library was shaped like a nautilus shell, a continuous tunnel that wound down into the mountain in an ever-tightening spiral. This main spiral was an enormously long, twisting ramp that took you from the high reaches of the mountain down past the level of the valley floor, several thousand feet below.

Off the main spiral, there were countless other corridors, rooms, halls, and strange chambers. Many were full of the Clayr's written records, mainly documenting the prophesies and visions of many generations of seers. But they also contained books and papers from all over the Kingdom. Books of magic and mystery, knowledge both ancient and new. Scrolls, maps, spells, recipes, inventories, stories, true tales, and Charter knew what else.

In addition to all these written works, the Great Library also housed other things. There were old armories within it, containing weapons and armor that had not been used for centuries but still stayed bright and new. There were rooms full of odd paraphernalia that no one now knew how to use. There were chambers where dressmakers' dummies stood fully clothed, displaying the fashions of bygone Clayr or the wildly different costumes of the barbaric North. There were greenhouses tended by sendings, with Charter marks for light as bright as the sun. There were rooms of total darkness, swallowing up the light and anyone foolish enough to enter unprepared.

Lirael had seen some of the Library, on carefully escorted

excursions with the rest of her year gathering. She had always hankered to enter the doors they passed, to step across the red rope barriers that marked corridors or tunnels where only authorized librarians might pass.

"Why do you want to work there?" asked Sanar.

"It—it's interesting," stammered Lirael, uncertain how she should reply. She didn't want to admit that the Library would be the best place to hide away from other Clayr. And in the back of her mind, she hadn't forgotten that in the Library she might find a spell to painlessly end her life. Not now, of course, now she knew that the Sight might come. But later, if she grew older and older without the Sight and the black despair welled up again inside her, as it had done earlier today.

"It is interesting," replied Sanar. "But there are dangerous things and dangerous knowledge in the Library, too. Does that bother you?"

"I don't know," said Lirael, honestly. "It would depend on what it was. But I really would like to work there." She paused and then said in a very low voice, "I do want to be busy, as you said, and forget about not having the Sight."

The Clayr turned away from Lirael then, and gathered together in a tight circle that excluded her, speaking in whispers. Lirael watched anxiously, aware that something momentous was going to happen to her life. The day had been horrible, but now she had hope again.

The Clayr stopped whispering. Lirael looked at them through the fall of her hair, glad that it hid her face. She didn't want them to see how badly she wanted them to let her work.

"Since it is your birthday," said Sanar, "and because we believe it will be best, we have decided that we will put you to work as you ask, in the Great Library. You should report there tomorrow morning, to Vancelle, the Chief Librarian. Unless she finds you unsuitable for some reason, you will become a Third Assistant Librarian."

"Thank you," cried Lirael. It came out as a croak, so she had to say it again. "Thank you."

"There is one more thing," said Sanar, and she came and stood so close that Lirael had to look up and meet her eyes. "You heard talk today that you should not have heard. Indeed, you have seen a visit that did not take place. The stability of a Kingdom is a fragile thing, Lirael, and easily upset. Sabriel and Touchstone would not speak so freely elsewhere, or to a different audience."

"I won't say anything to anyone," said Lirael. "I don't talk, really."

"You won't remember," said Ryelle, who had moved around behind her. She gently released the spell she'd held ready, cupped in her hand. Before Lirael could even think about countering it, a chain of bright Charter marks fell over her head, gripping her at the temples.

"At least not until you need to remember," continued Ryelle. "You will recall everything you have done today, save the visit of Sabriel and Touchstone. That memory will be gone, replaced by a walk on the terrace, and a chance meeting with us here. You seemed troubled, so we talked of work and the gaining of the Sight. That is how you gained your new post, Lirael. You will remember that, and no more."

"Yes," replied Lirael, words rolling off her lips so slowly that she seemed to be drunk or incredibly tired. "The Library. Tomorrow I report to Vancelle."

Chapter Six

THIRD ASSISTANT LIBRARIAN

THE CHIEF LIBRARIAN had a large oak-paneled office, with a very long desk that was covered in books, papers, and a large brass tray with that morning's breakfast still half-eaten upon it. There was also a long, silver-bladed sword on the desk, unsheathed, with its hilt close to the Librarian's hand.

Lirael stood in front of the desk, her head bowed, as Vancelle read the note the girl had brought from Sanar and Ryelle.

"So," said the Librarian, her deep, commanding voice making Lirael jump. "You want to be a librarian?"

"Y-yes," stammered Lirael.

"But are you suitable?" asked the Librarian. She touched the hilt of her sword, and for a moment Lirael thought Vancelle was going to pick it up and wave it around, to see if it frightened her.

Lirael was already frightened. The Librarian scared her, even without the sword. Her face gave away no feelings, and she moved with an economy of force, as if she might at any moment explode into violent action.

"Are you suitable?" asked the Librarian.

"Um, I don't . . . I don't know," whispered Lirael.

The Librarian came out from behind her desk, so swiftly that Lirael wasn't sure if she'd blinked and missed the motion.

Vancelle was only slightly taller than Lirael, but she seemed to loom over the young girl. Her eyes were bright blue, and her hair was a soft, shining grey, like the finest ash left from a cooling fire. She wore many rings on her fingers, and on her left wrist there was a silver bracelet set with seven sparkling emeralds and nine rubies. It was impossible to guess her age.

Lirael trembled as the Librarian reached out and touched the Charter mark on her forehead. She felt it flare, warm on her skin, and saw the light reflected in the Librarian's bejeweled rings and bracelet.

Whatever the Librarian felt in Lirael's Charter mark, no sign of it showed upon her face. She withdrew her hand and walked back behind her desk. Once again, she touched the hilt of her sword.

"We have never taken on a librarian whom we haven't already Seen as being a librarian," she said, tilting her head, like someone puzzling over how to hang a painting. "But no one has ever Seen you at all, have they?"

Lirael felt her mouth dry up. Unable to speak, she nodded. She felt the sudden opportunity that had been granted her slipping away. The reprieve, the chance of work, of being someone—

"So you are a mystery," continued the Librarian. "But there is no better place for mystery than the Great Library of the Clayr— and it is better to be a librarian than part of the collection."

For a moment, Lirael didn't understand. Then hope blossomed in her again, and she found her voice. "You mean . . . you mean I am suitable?"

"Yes," said Vancelle, Chief Librarian of the Great Library of the Clayr. "You are suitable, and you may begin at once. Deputy Librarian Ness will tell you what to do."

Lirael left in a daze of happiness. She had survived the ordeal. She had been accepted. She was going to be a librarian!

Deputy Librarian Ness merely sniffed at Lirael and sent her to First Assistant Librarian Roslin, who kissed her absently on the cheek and sent her to Second Assistant Librarian Imshi, who was only twenty and not long promoted from the yellow silk waist-coat of a Third Assistant to the red of a Second.

Imshi took Lirael to the Robing Room, a huge room full of all the equipment, weapons, and miscellaneous items the librarians needed, from climbing ropes to boathooks. And dozens and dozens of the special Library waistcoats, all in different sizes and colors.

"Third Assistant's yellow, Second Assistant's red, First Assistant's blue, Deputy is white, and the Chief wears black," explained Imshi, as she helped Lirael put on a brand-new yellow waistcoat over her working clothes. "Heavier than it looks, isn't it? That's because it's actually canvas, covered in silk. Much tougher that way. Now, this whistle clips on the lapel loops here, so you can bend your head and blow into it, even if something's holding your arms. But you should whistle only if you really need help. If you hear a whistle, run towards the sound and do whatever you can to help."

Lirael took the whistle, which was a simple brass pipe, and put it through the special lapel loops as instructed. As Imshi had said, she could easily blow into it just by lowering her head. But what did Imshi mean? What might be holding her arms?

"Of course, the whistle's good only when someone can hear it," continued Imshi, handing Lirael something that at first glance looked like a silver ball. She indicated that it should be placed in the front left pocket of her new waistcoat. "That's why you have the mouse. It's part clockwork, so you have to remember to wind it once a month, and the spell has to be renewed every year at Midsummer."

Lirael looked at the small silver object. It was a mouse with little mechanical legs, two bright chips of ruby for eyes, and a small key in its back. She could feel the warmth of a Charter-spell lying dormant inside it. She supposed that this would activate the clockwork mechanism at the right time and send it wherever it was supposed to go.

"What's it do?" Lirael asked, surprising Imshi a little. The younger girl hadn't spoken since they'd been introduced, and had stood there with her hair hanging over her face the whole time. Imshi had already written her off as one of the Chief's eccentric recruitment decisions, but perhaps there was still hope. She sounded interested, anyway.

"It gets help," replied Imshi. "If you're in the Old Levels or somewhere you don't think anyone will hear the whistle, put the mouse on the ground and speak or draw the activating mark, which I'll show you in a moment. Once it's activated, it'll run to the Reading Room and sound the alarm."

Lirael nodded and flicked back her hair to study the mouse more closely, running her finger over its silver back. When Imshi started to thumb through an index of Charter marks, Lirael shook her head and put the mouse in its special pocket.

"I know the mark, thanks," she said quietly. "I felt it in the spell."

"Really?" asked Imshi, surprised again. "You must be good. I can hardly manage to light a candle, or warm my toes out on the glacier."

But you have the Sight, thought Lirael. You are a real Clayr.

"Anyway, you have the whistle and the mouse," said Imshi, getting back to her task. "Here's your belt and scabbard, and I'll just see which dagger is sharpest. Ow! That'll do, I think. Now we have to put the number in the book, and you have to sign for everything."

Lirael buckled on the broad leather belt and settled the scabbard against her hip and thigh. The dagger that went into it was as long as her forearm, with a thin, sharp blade. It was steel but had been washed in silver, and there were Charter marks on the blade. Lirael touched them lightly with her finger, to see what they were supposed to do. They warmed under her touch, and she recognized them as marks of breaking and unraveling, especially useful against Free Magic creatures. They had been put there some twenty years ago, replacing older marks that had worn out. These too would last only another ten years or so, as they had not been placed with any great power or skill. Lirael thought she could possibly do better herself, though she wasn't particularly adept at working magic on inanimate objects.

Lirael looked up from the dagger and saw Imshi waiting expectantly, a quill in her hand, hovering above the huge leather-bound ledger that was chained to the desk at the front of the Robing Room.

"The number," said Imshi. "On the blade."

"Oh," said Lirael. She angled the blade till the Charter marks faded out and she could see the bare metal, and the letter and number etched there by conventional means.

"L2713," Lirael called out; then she slid the dagger home into the scabbard. Imshi wrote the number down, re-inked the quill, and passed it to Lirael to sign.

There in the ledger, in between ruled lines of red ink, was Lirael's name, the date, her position as Third Assistant Librarian, and a list of all the things she'd been given, neatly written by Imshi. Lirael scanned the list, but didn't sign.

"It says a key, here," she said cautiously, tipping up the quill so an incipient blob of ink didn't fall on the paper.

"Oh, a key!" exclaimed Imshi. "I wrote it down and then I forgot!"

She went over to one of the cupboards on the wall, opened it, and rummaged around inside. Finally, she pulled out a broad silver bracelet set with emeralds, the match of the one on her own wrist. Unlocking it, she clasped it around Lirael's right wrist.

"You'll have to go back to the Chief to have the spell inside woken up," explained Imshi, showing Lirael how two of the seven emeralds on her own bracelet swarmed with bright Charter marks. "Depending on your work and post, it will then open all the appropriate doors."

"Thanks," said Lirael briefly. She could feel the spell in the silver, Charter marks hiding deep within the metal, waiting to flow into the emeralds. There were actually seven spells, she could tell, one for each emerald. But she didn't know how they could be brought to the surface and made to work. This particular magic was beyond her.

Nor was she much wiser ten minutes later, when Vancelle took her wrist and quickly cast a spell that neither was spoken nor had any other obvious marks, signed or drawn. Whatever it was, the spell lit up only one emerald, leaving the other six dark. That, said Vancelle, was enough to open the common doors, which was more than enough for a new Third Assistant Librarian.

It took Lirael three months to work out how to wake the next four spells in her bracelet, though the secret of the sixth and seventh remained beyond her. But she didn't wake the extra spells at once, taking another month to create an illusion of the bracelet as it was supposed to be, that would sit over her own and hide the glow of the additional emeralds.

It was mainly curiosity that set her to working out the key spells. Originally she didn't plan to wake them, and intended to treat her discovery purely as an intellectual exercise. But there were so many interesting doors, hatches, gates, grilles, and locks that she couldn't help but wonder what was behind them. Once the spells in the bracelet were active, she found it very difficult not to think of using them.

Her daily work also led her into temptation. While there were Charter sendings to do much of the manual labor, ferrying materials to and from the Main Reading Room and the individual studies of scholars, all the checking, recording, and indexing was done by people. Generally, the junior librarians. There were also very special or dangerous items that had to be fetched in person, or even by large parties of armed librarians. Not that Lirael got to go on any of these exciting expeditions to the Old Levels. Nor would she, till she attained the red waistcoat of a Second Assistant, which usually took at least three years.

But in the course of her regular duties, she often passed interesting-looking corridors sealed off with red rope, or doors that beckoned to her, almost saying, "How can you walk past me every day and not want to go in?"

Without exception, any vaguely interesting portal was locked, beyond the original key spell and the sole glowing emerald of Lirael's bracelet.

Aside from the inaccessibility of the interesting parts, the Great Library met most of Lirael's hopes. She was given a small study of her own. Barely wider than her outstretched arms, it contained nothing but a narrow desk, a chair, and several shelves. But it was a refuge, somewhere she would be left alone, secure from Aunt Kirrith's intrusions. It was meant for quiet study, in Lirael's case, of the set texts of the beginning librarian: *The Librarian's Rules, Basic Bibliography*, and *The Large Yellow Book: Simple Spells for Third Assistant Librarians*. It had taken her only a month to learn everything she needed to from those volumes.

So she quietly "borrowed" any book she could get her hands on, like *The Black Book of Bibliomancy*, carelessly left off a returning list by a Deputy Librarian. And she spent a great deal of time analyzing the spells in her bracelet, slowly finding her way through the complex chains of Charter marks to find the activating symbols.

Lirael had been driven by curiosity at first, and by the sense of satisfaction she gained from working out magic that was supposed to be beyond her. But somewhere along the way, Lirael realized that she enjoyed learning Charter Magic for its own sake. And when she was learning marks and putting them together into spells, she completely forgot about her troubles and forgot about not having the Sight.

Learning to be a real Charter Mage also gave her something to do, when all the other librarians or her fellows from the Hall of Youth were engaged in more social activities.

The other librarians, particularly the dozen or so Third Assistants, had tried to be friendly at first. But they were all older than Lirael, and they all had the Sight. Lirael felt she had nothing to talk about or share with them, so she stayed silent, hiding behind her hair. After a while, they stopped inviting her to sit with them at lunch, or to play a game of tabore in the afternoon, or to gossip about their elders over sweet wine in the evening.

So Lirael was once again alone among company. She told herself that she preferred it, but she couldn't deny the pang in her heart when she saw laughing groups of young Clayr, so effortlessly talking and enjoying one another's friendship.

It was even worse when whole groups were called to join the Nine Day Watch, as happened more and more frequently during Lirael's first few months of work. Lirael would be stacking books in the Reading Room, or writing in one of the registers, when a Watch messenger would come in, bearing the ivory tokens that summoned the recipient to the Observatory. Sometimes dozens of the Clayr in the huge, domed Reading Room would each receive a token. They would smile, curse, grimace, or take it stoically; then there would be a flurry of activity as they all stopped work, drawing back their chairs, locking away books and papers in their desk drawers, or returning them to shelves or sorting tables before trooping out the doors en masse.

At first Lirael was surprised that so many were called, and she was even more surprised when some of them returned only hours or days later, instead of the usual nine days that gave the Watch its name. She initially thought it must be some peculiarity of the librarians, that so many were called at once and not for the full term. But she didn't feel like asking anyone about it, so it was some time before she got some sort of answer, when she over-heard two Second Assistant Librarians in the Binding Room.

"It's all very well to have a Ninety-Eight. But to go on to a Hundred and Ninety-Six and on up to yesterday's Seven Hundred and Eighty-Four is quite ridiculous," said one of the Second Assistants. "I mean we did all fit in the Observatory. But now there's talk of a Fifteen Sixty-Eight! That'll be nearly everybody, I should think—and making the Watch bigger doesn't seem to make it work any better than the usual Forty-Nine. I couldn't tell the difference."

"I don't mind, myself," replied the other Second Assistant as she carefully applied glue to the binding of a broken-backed book. "It makes a change from here, and at least it's over quicker with a larger Watch. But it is tedious when we have to try to focus where we can't See anything. Why don't the high-ups just admit that no one can See anything around that stupid lake and leave it at that?"

"Because it's not so simple," interrupted a stern-voiced Deputy, bearing down on them like a huge white cat on two plump mice. "All the possible futures are connected. Not being able to See where futures begin is a significant problem. You should know that, and you also should know not to talk about the business of the Watch!"

The last sentence was said with a general glare about the room. But Lirael, even half-hidden behind a huge press, felt it was particularly aimed at her. After all, everybody else in the room was a full Clayr and eligible to be a member of the Nine Day Watch.

Her cheeks burnt with embarrassment and shame as she threw all her strength into turning the great bronze handles of the screw, tightening the press. Talk slowly resumed around her, but she ignored it, concentrating only on her task.

But that was the moment when she resolved to wake the dormant magic in her bracelet, and use the spell she'd made to hide the glow of the additional emeralds.

She might not be able to join the Watch in the Observatory, but she would explore the Library.

Chapter Seven

BEYOND THE DOORS OF SUN AND MOON

E VEN AFTER SHE woke the extra spells in her bracelet, Lirael found it hard to explore the areas formerly closed to her. There was always too much work, or there were too many other librarians around. After the first two heart-thumping moments of near-discovery in front of forbidden doors, Lirael decided to put off her exploration until there were fewer people around or she could more easily escape from work.

Her first real chance came almost five months after she had donned the yellow waistcoat of a Third Assistant. She was in the Reading Room, sorting books to be returned by the sendings, who gathered close around her, their ghostly, Charter-etched hands the only visible part of their shrouded forms. They were quite simple sendings, without any higher functions, but they loved their work. Lirael liked them, too, because they didn't require her to speak or ask her questions. She simply gave the appropriate books to the right sending, and it would take them away to its area and the proper shelf or store.

Lirael was particularly good at recognizing which sending was which, a valuable skill since the embroidered signs on their cowled robes were often obscured with dust or had become unpicked and indecipherable. They didn't have official names, only descriptions of their responsibilities. But most had nicknames, like Tad, who was in charge of Traveler's Tales, A–D, or Stoney, who looked after the geology collection.

Lirael was just giving Tad a particularly large and unwieldy volume bound in leather stamped with a three-humped camel motif when the Watch messenger arrived. Lirael didn't pay much attention to her at first, because she knew no ivory token would be given to her. Then she noticed that the messenger was stopping at every desk and speaking to every person, and a hum of whispered conversation was rising behind her. Lirael surreptitiously tucked her hair behind her ears and tried to listen. At first the murmur was indistinct, but as the messenger grew closer, Lirael caught the words "Fifteen Sixty-Eight" being repeated over and over again.

For a moment she was puzzled; then she realized that this must be what the Second Assistants had been talking about. The calling of one thousand five hundred sixty-eight Clayr to the Watch—an unprecedented concentration of the Sight.

It would also take nearly every librarian out of the Library, Lirael calculated, giving her the perfect chance for a secret excursion. For the first time ever, Lirael watched the messenger's distribution of tokens with excitement rather than with her usual depression and self-pity. Now she was wishing everyone else *would* get summoned to the Watch. Trying not to look too obvious, Lirael even wandered around the other side of the desk to see if anyone had been missed.

No one had. Lirael found it strangely hard to breathe as she waited to see if anyone would remember to tell her to do something—or not to. But none of the librarians with whom she usually worked were here. Imshi was not to be seen. Lirael guessed the messenger had met her on the way and had already given her a token.

She willed them all to go and started to sort her books with a concentrated ferocity, as if she didn't care what happened around her. The sendings approved, moving faster themselves as each one took its stack of books and another moved into place.

Finally, the last bright waistcoat gleamed in the doorway and was gone. More than fifty librarians, disposed of in less than five minutes. Lirael smiled and put the last book down with a definite snap, disappointing the sending who was waiting for a full load.

Ten minutes later, to allow for stragglers, she headed down the main spiral. There was a door about a half mile down, well into the Old Levels, a particular favorite that she wanted to investigate first. It had a bright sunburst emblem upon its otherwise unremarkable wooden surface, a golden disc with rays that spread from top to bottom. Of course, there was also a red rope across it, secured at either end with wax seals bearing the book and sword symbol of the Chief Librarian.

Lirael had long since worked out how to deal with this particular annoyance. She drew a short piece of wire with two wooden handles from her waistcoat pocket and held it near her mouth. Then she spoke three Charter marks, a simple charm to heat metal. With the wire momentarily red-hot, she quickly sliced the seals away and hid them and the rope in a nearby hole in the passage wall, away from the light.

Then came the real test. Would the door open to her bracelet, or would it need the last two spells she couldn't figure out?

Holding her wrist as she'd been taught, she waved her bracelet in front of the door. Emeralds flashed, breaking through the cloaking-spell she'd put upon them—and the door swung open without a sound.

Lirael stepped through, and the door slowly shut behind her. She found herself in a short corridor and was momentarily disoriented by the bright light at the other end. Surely this passage couldn't lead outside? She was in the heart of the mountain, thousands of feet underground. Blinking against the light, she walked forward, one hand on the hilt of her dagger, the other one on the clockwork emergency mouse.

The corridor didn't lead outside, but Lirael saw how she had been misled. It opened out into a vast chamber, bigger even than the Great Hall. Charter marks as bright as the sun shone in the distant ceiling, hundreds of feet above. A huge oak tree filled the center of the room, in full summer leaf, its spreading branches shading a serpentine pool. And everywhere, throughout the cavern, there were flowers. Red flowers. Lirael bent down and picked one, uncertain if it was some sort of illusion. But it was real enough. She felt no magic, just the crisp stalk under her fingers. A red daisy, in full bloom.

Lirael sniffed it, and sneezed as the pollen went up her nose. Only then did she realize how quiet it was. This huge cavern might mimic the outside world, but the air was too still. There was no breeze, and no sound. No birds, no bees happily at work amid the pollen. No small animals drinking at the pool. There was nothing living, save the flowers and the tree. And the lights above gave no warmth, unlike the sun. This place was the same temperature as the rest of the Clayr's inhabited realm, and had the same mild humidity, from the moist heat distributed via the huge network of pipes that brought superheated water from the geysers and steam plumes far, far below.

Lovely as it was, it was a bit disappointing. Lirael wondered if this was all there was to find on her first expedition. Then she saw that there was another door—a latticed gate, rather—on the far side of the cavern.

It took her ten minutes to walk across, longer than she would have thought. But she tried not to tread on too many flowers, and she gave the tree and the pool a very wide berth. Just in case.

The gate barred the way to another corridor, one that went into darkness rather than light. The gate, a simple metal grille, had the emblem of a silver moon upon it, rather than a sun. A crescent moon, with much sharper and longer points than could be considered usual or aesthetically pleasing.

Lirael looked through the gate to the passage beyond. For some reason it made her think about the whistle on her waistcoat, and things grabbing her arms. The whistle would be useless here anyway—and the mouse, too, Lirael suddenly realized, since there was no one currently in the Reading Room to hear its squeaked alarm.

But aside from unknown dangers, there was no obvious reason not to try the gate, at least. Lirael waved her arm, and once again the emeralds flashed, but the gate didn't open. She let her hand fall, tucked her hair back out of her eyes and frowned. Clearly, this was a gate that answered only to the higher spells.

Then she heard a click, and the right-hand leaf of the gate slowly swung open—barely wide enough for Lirael to squeeze through. To make it harder, the crescent moon protruded into the open space, the sharp points level with where Lirael's neck and groin would be.

She looked at the narrow way and thought about it. What if there were something horrible beyond? But then again, what did she have to lose? Fear and curiosity fought inside her for a moment. Curiosity won.

Acting on the latter impulse, Lirael took the mouse from her pocket and put it down amongst the flowers. If something did go wrong beyond the gate, she could scream out the activating Charter mark and off it would go, taking its own devious mouseways to the Reading Room. Even if it was too late to save Lirael, it might be a useful warning to the others. According to her superiors and co-workers, it was not uncommon for librarians to lay down their lives for the benefit of the Clayr as a whole, either in dangerous research, simple overwork, or action against previously unknown dangers discovered in the Library's collection. Lirael believed this principle of self-sacrifice was particularly appropriate to herself, since the rest of the Clayr had the Sight and so needed to be alive much more than she did.

After placing the mouse, Lirael drew her dagger and slipped through the partly open gate. It was a very tight fit, and the moon's points were razor sharp, but she got through without damage to herself or her clothes. It did not occur to her that a grown man or woman would not be able to pass.

The corridor was very dark, so Lirael spoke a simple Charter-spell for light, letting it flow into her dagger. Then she held the blade up in front of her like a lantern, only not as bright. Either she'd muffed the spell a little or something was damping it.

Besides being dark, the corridor, evidently not connected to the Clayr's geothermal pipes, was also cold. Dust rose as Lirael walked, swirling around in strange patterns that Lirael thought might almost be Charter marks, ones she didn't know.

Beyond the corridor, there was a small rectangular room. Holding her dagger high, Lirael could see its shadowed corners, crawling with faint Charter marks that were so old, they'd almost lost their luminescence.

The whole room was afloat in magic—strange, ancient Charter Magic that she didn't understand and was almost afraid of. The marks were remnants of some incredibly old spell, now senile and broken. Whatever the spell had once been, now it was no more than hundreds of disconnected marks, fading into the dust.

Enough remained of the spell to make Lirael even more uneasy. There were marks of binding and imprisonment floating there, of warding and warning. Even in its broken form, the spell was trying to fulfill its purpose.

Worse than that, Lirael realized that though the marks were very old, the spell had not simply faded, as she first thought. It had been broken only recently, within weeks, or perhaps months.

In the middle of the room, there was a low table of black, glassy stone, a single slab, reminiscent of an altar. It, too, was covered in the remnants of some mighty charm or spell. Charter marks washed across its smooth surface, forever seeking connection to some master Charter mark that would draw them all together. But that mark was no longer there.

There were seven small plinths on the table, lined up in a row. They were carved of some sort of luminous white bone, and all were empty save one. The third from the left had a small model or statuette upon it.

Lirael hesitated. She couldn't quite make out what it was, but she didn't want to get any closer. Not without knowing more about the spells that had been broken here.

She stood there for some time, watching the marks and listening. But nothing changed, and the room was totally silent.

One more step forward, Lirael reasoned, wouldn't make a difference. She would see what was on the third plinth and then withdraw.

She stepped closer and raised her light.

As soon as her foot landed, she knew she'd made a mistake. The floor felt strange, unsteady under her. Then there was a terrible crack, and both feet suddenly went right through the panel of dark glass she had mistaken for more of the floor.

Lirael fell forward, only just keeping hold of her dagger. Her left hand fell on the table, instinctively grabbing the statuette. Her knees hit the lip where glass met stone, sending a jarring pain through to her head. Her feet were stinging, cut by the glass.

She looked down and saw something worse than broken glass and cut feet, something that had her moving again instantly, regardless of any further damage the shards might do.

For the glass had been the cover of a long, coffin-like trench, and there was something lying in it. Something that at first looked like a sleeping, naked woman. In the next horrified instant, Lirael saw that its forearms were as long as its legs, and bent backwards, with great claws on the ends, like those of a praying mantis. It opened its eyes, and they were silver fires, brighter and more terrible than anything Lirael had ever seen.

Even worse, there was the smell. The telltale metallic odor of Free Magic that left a sour taste in Lirael's mouth and throat and made her stomach roil and heave.

Both creature and Lirael moved at the same time. Lirael threw herself back towards the corridor as the thing struck out with its awful, elongated claws. They missed, and the monster let out a shriek of annoyance that was completely inhuman, making Lirael run faster than she had ever run before, cut feet or not.

Before the shriek had subsided, Lirael was squeezing through the gate, breathing in with such a panic that there were inches to spare. Beyond it, she turned and waved her bracelet, screaming out, "Shut! Shut!"

But the gate didn't close, and the creature was suddenly there, one leg and hideous arm thrust through. For a moment Lirael thought it wouldn't be able to pass the sharp points of the moon, but it suddenly thinned and grew taller, its body as malleable as soft clay. Its silver eyes sparkled, and it opened a mouth full of silver-spined teeth to lick its lips with a grey tongue that was striped yellow, like a leech.

Lirael didn't stay to watch it. She forgot the emergency mouse. She forgot about staying away from the pool and the tree. She just ran in an absolutely straight line, crashing through the flowers, daisy petals exploding in a cloud around her.

On and on she ran, thinking that at any moment a hooked claw would bring her down. She didn't slow at the outer corridor, and slid to a stop only just in time to avoid smashing into the door. There, she waved her bracelet and slipped through before it opened more than a crack, stripping all the buttons from her waistcoat.

On the other side, she waved her bracelet again, watching the open doorway with the wide-eyed, sick anticipation of a calf watching an approaching wolf.

The door stopped opening and slowly began to close again. Lirael sighed and fell to her knees, feeling as if she were going to vomit. She shut her eyes for a moment—and heard a snick that was not the shutting of the door.

Her eyes flashed open, and she saw a curving, insectile hook, as long as her hand, thrust through a finger-width gap. Then another followed it—and the door began to open.

Lirael's mouth went to her whistle, and its shrill cry echoed up and down the spiral. But there was no one to hear it, and when her hand went to the mouse pocket, it found a strange statuette of soft stone, not the familiar silver body of the mouse.

The door shuddered, and the gap increased, the creature clearly winning against the spell that tried to keep it shut. Lirael stared at it, unable to think of what to do next. She frantically glanced up and down the corridor, as if some unlooked-for help might come.

But none did come, and she could only think that whatever this thing was, it must not be let out into the main spiral. The words of the librarians telling her of self-sacrifice came back to her, as did her depressed climb up the Starmount Stairs only a few months before. Now that death seemed likely, she realized how much she wanted to stay alive.

Even so, Lirael knew what must be done. She drew herself up and reached into the Charter. There, in the endless flow, she drew out all the marks she knew for breaking and blasting, for fire and destruction, for blocking, barring, and locking. They came into her mind in a flood, brighter and more blinding than any light, so strong that she could barely weave them into a spell. But somehow she ordered them as she wished, and linked them together with a single master mark, one of great power, that she had never before dared to use.

With the spell ready, pent up inside her by will alone, Lirael did the bravest thing she had ever done. She touched the door with one hand, the creature's hook with the other, and spoke the master Charter mark to cast the spell.

Chapter Eight

DOWN THE FIFTH BACK STAIR

A S SHE SPOKE, heat coursed through Liracl's throat. White fire exploded through her right hand into the creature, and a titanic force was unleashed from her left, slamming the door shut. She was hurled backwards, tumbling over and over till her head struck the stone floor with a terrible crack that sent her instantly into darkness.

When she came to, Lirael had no idea where she was. Her head felt as if a hot wire had pierced her skull. It was somehow wet as well, and her throat ached as if she were in the throes of a really bad flu. For a moment she thought she was sick in bed and would soon see Aunt Kirrith or one of the other girls bending over her with a spoonful of herbal restorative. Then she realized that there was cold stone under her, not a mattress, and she was fully clothed.

Hesitantly, she touched her head, and her fingers showed her what the wetness was. She looked at the bright blood, and a wave of cold and dizziness overcame her, shooting up from her toes and through her head. She tried to call for help, but her throat was too sore. Nothing came out, only a sort of breathy buzz.

Now she remembered what she'd been trying to do, and a bolt of pure panic banished the dizziness. She tried to raise her head, but that hurt too much, so she rolled on her side instead, to see the door.

It was shut, and there was no sign of the creature. Lirael stared at the door till the grain of the wood grew blurry, uncertain that it really was closed, the creature gone. When she was absolutely sure it was shut, she turned her head away and threw up, sour bile burning her already painful throat.

She lay still after that, trying to steady her breathing and her stammering heart. A further cautious examination of her head revealed the blood to be clotting already, so it probably wasn't too serious. Her throat seemed to be worse, damaged by speaking a master Charter mark that she didn't have the strength or the experience to use correctly. She tried to say a few words, but only a hoarse whisper came out.

Next, she investigated her feet, but they turned out to be more scratched than cut, though her shoes had so many holes that they had become like sandals. Compared to her head, her feet were fine, so she decided to try standing up.

That took her several minutes, even using the wall for support. Then it took another five minutes to bend down again, pick up her dagger, and ease it into the scabbard.

After that exercise, she stood for a while, till she felt steady enough to examine the door. It was shut properly, without a gap, and she could feel her own spell, as well as the door's magical lock, holding it closed. No one could get in or out now without breaking Lirael's spell. Even the Chief Librarian would have to get her to lift it, or break it.

Thinking of the Chief made Lirael pick up as many of her torn-off buttons as she could find, and replace the red rope and the seals across the door—though calling up a spell to warm the wax was almost beyond her. When she'd finished, she walked a few steps up the main spiral, but had to sit down, too weak to go on.

Slumping down, she lapsed into a semi-conscious daze, unable to think about anything or to assess her situation. She sat for a

long time, maybe even an hour. Then some natural resilience
rose up in her, and Lirael realized where she was and the state
she was in. Bloodied, bruised, her waistcoat buttonless and torn,
her emergency mouse lost. All of which would need explanation.

The loss of the mouse reminded her of the statuette. Her
hands were much clumsier than usual, frustratingly so, but she
managed to get the small stone figure out of her pocket and set
it on her lap.

It was a dog, she saw, carved from a soft grey-blue soapstone
that was pleasant to touch. It looked like a fairly hard-bitten sort
of dog, with pointy ears and a sharp snout. But it also had a
friendly grin, and the suggestion of a tongue in the corner of its
mouth.

"Hello, dog," whispered Lirael, her voice so weak and scratchy,
she could hardly hear it herself. She liked dogs, though there were
none in the higher reaches of the Glacier. The Rangers had a
kennel for their working dogs near the Great Gate, and visitors
sometimes brought their dogs into the guest quarters and the
Lower Refectory. Lirael always said hello to the visiting dogs, even
when they were huge brindled wolfhounds with studded collars.
The dogs were always friendly to her, often more so than their
owners, who would get upset when Lirael spoke only to their
dogs and not to them.

Lirael held the dog statuette and wondered what she was
going to do. Should she tell Imshi or someone higher up about
the thing that was loose in the flower-field chamber? And admit
she had woken the extra key spells in her bracelet?

She sat there for ages, turning over ideas, scratching the stone
head of the dog as if it were a miniature real animal. Telling the
truth was probably the right thing to do, she concluded, but then
she would almost certainly lose her job—and going back to the

children's classes and the hated blue tunic would be unbearable. Once again, she toyed with the idea that death might provide an escape, but the reality of nearly being slain by the hooks of the creature made killing herself even less attractive than it had been before.

No, Lirael decided. She had got herself into trouble and she would get herself out of it. She'd find out what the creature was, learn how to defeat it, and then go and do it. It couldn't get out till then, or so she hoped. And no one else could get in, so it wouldn't be a danger to other librarians.

That left explaining her cut head, scratched feet, bruises, mislaid mouse, lost voice, and general disarray. All of which could probably be done with a single brilliant plan. Which Lirael didn't have.

"I might as well walk and think," she whispered to the dog statuette. It was oddly comforting to speak to the dog and hold it in her hand. She looked down at the way it sat, with its tail curled around its back legs, head up and forelegs straight, as if waiting for its mistress.

"I wish I had a real dog," Lirael added, groaning as she stood up and started slowly walking up the spiral corridor. Then she stopped and looked down at the statuette, a sudden wild thought blossoming in her mind. She could create a Charter sending of a dog, a complex one that could bark and everything. All she'd need was *On the Making of Sendings*, and perhaps *The Making and Mastery of Magical Beings*. Both were locked up, of course, but Lirael knew where they were. She could even make the sending look like the lovely dog statuette.

Lirael smiled at the thought of having a dog of her own. A true friend, someone she could talk to who wouldn't ask her questions or talk back. A loving and lovable companion. She tucked the statuette back in her waistcoat pocket and limped on.

A hundred yards later she abruptly stopped thinking about how to create a sending and started to worry about how she would find out what the creature in the flower room was. There were bestiaries in the Library, she knew, but finding and getting access to them could be a problem.

She kept thinking about that for another hundred yards until she realized she had a far more pressing problem. She needed to work out an explanation for her injuries and the lost mouse, with a minimum of actual lying. Lirael felt that she owed the Library a lot, and didn't want to tell an outright lie. Besides, she didn't think she could lie, if it came to heavy-duty questioning from the Chief Librarian or someone like that.

The mouse was the tricky part. She stopped moving to try to think more clearly, and she was surprised by how much her body needed the rest. Normally she ran around the Library all day, up and down the spiral, up and down ladders, in and out of rooms. Now she could barely move without a major effort of will.

A fall would explain her head injury, Lirael thought, once again feeling the cut. It had stopped bleeding, but her hair was matted with blood, and she could feel a lump coming up.

A long fall, with a terrified scream, could also explain her sore throat. Buttons could be scraped off in that sort of fall, and a mouse easily lost from a pocket.

Steps, Lirael decided. A fall down a flight of steps would best explain everything. Particularly if someone found her at the bottom of the steps, so she wouldn't have to say anything much.

It took her only a little while to work out that the Fifth Back Stair between the main spiral and the Hall of Youth would be the most likely spot for her to have an accident. She could even pick up a glass of water from the Zally Memorial Fountain on the way. You weren't allowed to take the glasses away, of course, but that was probably a bonus. It would give everybody—particularly Aunt Kirrith—something to scold her for, and they wouldn't look for more serious crimes. And a broken glass would explain her scratched feet.

Now all she had to do was get there and not meet anyone on the way. If the past extra-large Watch gatherings were any indication, the Fifteen Sixty-Eight wouldn't last much longer. There was a definite correlation between the size of a particular Watch and how long it lasted. The normal Forty-Nine lasted nine days, giving the Watch its name. But when there were more people involved, the Clayr returned much sooner. The most recent Watch had taken the participating Clayr away for less than a day.

The closer she got to the Hall of Youth, the greater the danger of meeting youngsters or others not part of the Watch. Lirael decided that if she did meet anyone, she'd just fall down and pass out, hoping that whoever it was didn't get too inquisitive.

But she didn't meet anyone before she turned off the spiral, picked up her glass of water at the Zally Fountain, went through the permanently open stone doors of the Fifth Library Landing, and reached the Fifth Back Stair. It was a narrow, circular stair, not much used since it merely connected the Library with the western side of the Hall of Youth.

Wearily, Lirael climbed the first half dozen steps, to the point where it started to turn inwards. Then she threw the glass down, wincing as it broke. After that she had to work out where to lie so it looked as if she really had fallen down the steps. This made her dizzy, so she had to sit down. And once she was sitting, it seemed quite natural to lay her head on an upper step, cushioned by an outthrust arm.

She knew she should be artistically arranging herself on the landing below, an obvious victim of a fall, but it all seemed too hard. The strength that had sustained her to this point was gone. She couldn't get up. It was so much easier to go to sleep. Beautiful sleep, where no troubles could torment her . . .

Lirael awoke to a voice urgently calling her name, and two fingers checking the pulse in her neck. This time, she came to her senses fairly quickly, grimacing as the pain returned.

"Lirael! Can you talk?"

"Yes," whispered Lirael, her voice still very weak and strangely husky. She was disoriented. Her last memory was of lying on the steps, and now she was flat on the ground. She realized that she was on the landing, looking much more like the victim of a fall than anything she could have arranged herself. She must have slipped down the steps after passing out.

A blue-waistcoated First Assistant Librarian was bending over her, peering closely at her face. Lirael blinked and wondered why this strange person was moving her hand backwards and forwards in front of Lirael's eyes. But it wasn't a strange person after all. It was Amerane, whom she had worked with for a few days last month.

"What happened?" asked Amerane, concern in her voice. "Does anything feel broken?"

"I hit my head," whispered Lirael, and she felt tears springing up in her eyes. She hadn't cried before, but now she couldn't stop, and her whole body started to shake as well, no matter how hard she tried to stay still.

"Does anything feel broken?" Amerane repeated. "Does it hurt anywhere else aside from your head?"

"N-no," sobbed Lirael. "Nothing's broken."

Amerane didn't seem to trust Lirael's opinion, because she lightly felt all the way up and down the girl's arms and legs, and gently pressed against her fingers and feet. Since Lirael didn't scream and there seemed to be no grating of bones or abnormal lumps or swellings, Amerane helped her get up.

"Come on," she said kindly. "I'll help you get to the Infirmary."

"Thanks," whispered Lirael, putting her arm around Amerane's shoulders and letting her take most of her weight. Her other hand went to her pocket, fingers wrapping around the little stone dog, its smooth surface a source of comfort, as Amerane carried her away.

Chapter Nine

CREATURES BY NAGY

A T FIRST, LIRAEL thought she would be out of the Infirmary within a day. But even three days after her "fall," she could barely speak, and she had lost all her energy, not even wanting to get up. While the pain in her head and throat lessened, fear grew everywhere else, sapping her strength. Fear of the silver-eyed, hook-handed monster that she could almost see waiting for her amidst the red daisies. Fear of her trespasses being found out, forcing the loss of her job. Fear of the fear itself, a vicious circle that exhausted her and filled what little sleep she got with nightmares.

On the morning of the fourth day, the Chief Healer clicked her teeth together and frowned at the patient's lack of progress. She called in another healer to look at Lirael, who bore this patiently. They both decided, in Lirael's hearing, that they would need to call Filris down from her dreaming room.

Lirael started nervously at this announcement. Among other things, Filris was the Infirmarian, and the oldest of the Clayr still living. For all of Lirael's life, Filris had spent most of her time in her dreaming room, and presumably working in the Infirmary as well, though Lirael had never seen her on either of the two occasions she had been hospitalized with childhood illnesses.

She had never seen any of the really old Clayr, the ones old enough to retire to dreaming rooms of their own. They needed such rooms because the Sight tended to grow progressively more difficult with age, sending more and more frequent visions, but in smaller splinters, which could not be controlled, even with the focusing powers of ice and the Nine Day Watch. It was not uncommon for some of the more ancient Clayr to perceive only these fragmented futures and not be able to interact with the present at all.

However, when Filris arrived an hour later, she came alone and clearly needed no help with the ordinary world. Lirael eyed her suspiciously, seeing a short, slight woman with hair as white as the snow atop Starmount and skin like aged parchment, the underlying veins a delicate tracery upon her face, counterpoint to the wrinkles of extreme age.

She inspected Lirael from head to foot, without speaking, her paper-dry hands gently prodding her to move in the directions she required. Finally, she looked down Lirael's throat, staring at it for some time, a small bauble of Charter-Magicked light floating an inch from Lirael's stiffening jaw. When Filris finally stopped looking, she sent the Healer from the ward and sat beside Lirael's bed. Silence crept over them, for the ward was empty now. The other seven beds were vacant.

Eventually, Lirael made a noise that was halfway between clearing her throat and a sob. She moved her hair away from her face and nervously looked at Filris—and was caught in the gaze of her pale blue eyes.

"So you are Lirael," said Filris. "And the healer tells me you fell down the stairs. But I do not think your throat was damaged by a scream. To be frank, I am surprised you are still alive. I know of no other Clayr your age—and few of any age—who could speak such a mark without being consumed by it."

"How?" croaked Lirael. "How can you tell?"

"Experience," replied Filris dryly. "I have worked in this Infirmary for over a hundred years. You are not the first Clayr I have seen suffer from the effects of attempting overambitious magic. Also, I am curious as to how you came by these other injuries at the same time, particularly since the glass dug out of your feet is pure crystal, and certainly not the same as that of the glasses from the Zally Fountain."

Lirael swallowed, but didn't speak. The silence returned. Filris waited patiently.

"I'll lose my job," whispered Lirael at last. "I'll be sent back to the Hall."

"No," said Filris, taking her hand. "What passes between us here shall go no further."

"I've been stupid," said Lirael huskily. "I've let something out. Something dangerous—dangerous to everyone. All the Clayr."

"Hmph!" snorted Filris. "It can't be that bad if it hasn't done anything in the last four days. Besides, 'all the Clayr' can look after its collective self very well. It's you I'm concerned about. You are letting your fear come between you and getting better. Now start from the beginning, and tell me everything."

"You won't tell Kirrith? Or the Chief?" asked Lirael desperately. If Filris told anybody, they'd take her away from the Library, and then she'd have nothing. Nothing at all.

"If you mean Vancelle, no I won't," replied Filris. She patted Lirael's hand and said, "I won't tell anybody. Particularly since I am coming to the conclusion that I should have looked in on you long ago, Lirael. I had no notion you were more than a child . . . but tell me. What happened?"

Slowly, her voice so soft that Filris had to lean close, Lirael told her. About her birthday, about going up to the terrace, meeting Sanar and Ryelle, getting her job and how much it had helped her. She told Filris about waking the spells in the bracelet, about the sunburst and crescent-moon doors. Her voice grew softer still as she spoke of the horror in the glass-roofed coffin. The statuette of the dog. The struggle up the spiral and the plans she had made as her mind wandered. Her faked fall.

They spoke for more than an hour, Filris questioning, bringing out all Lirael's fears, hopes, and dreams. At the end of it, Lirael felt peaceful and no longer afraid, emptied of all the knotted pain and anguish that had filled her.

When Lirael finished talking, Filris asked to see the dog statuette. Lirael took the little stone dog from under her pillow and reluctantly handed it over. She had grown very attached to it, for it was the one thing that brought her some comfort, and she was afraid that Filris would take it away or tell her it must go back to the Library.

The old woman took the statuette in both hands, cupping it so only the snout was visible, thrusting out between her withered fingers. She looked at it for a long time, then gave a deep sigh and handed it back. Lirael took it, surprised by the warmth the stone had gained from the old woman's hands. Still, Filris didn't move or speak, till Lirael sat up straighter in bed, attracting her attention.

"I'm sorry, Lirael. I thank you for telling me the truth. And for showing me the dog statuette. It has been a long time coming, so long that I had thought I would be lost in the future, too mad to see it true."

"What do you mean?" asked Lirael uneasily.

"I saw your little dog long ago," explained Filris. "When the Sight still came clearly to me. It was the last vision that came to me whole and unbroken. I Saw an old, old woman, peering closely at a small stone dog clasped in her hands. It took me many years to realize that the old woman was myself."

"Did you See me, too?" asked Lirael.

"I Saw only myself," said Filris calmly. "What it means, I'm afraid, is that we shall not meet again. I would have liked to help you defeat the creature you have released, by counsel if not by deed, for I fear that it must be dealt with as soon as you can. Things of that ilk do not wake without reason, or without help of some kind. I would also like to see your dog-sending. I regret that I will not. Most of all I regret that I have not lived enough in the present these last fifteen years. I should have met you sooner, Lirael. It is a failing of the Clayr that we tend to forget individuals sometimes, and we ignore their troubles, knowing that all such things will pass."

"What do you mean?" asked Lirael. For the first time in her life, she'd felt comfortable talking to someone about herself, about her life. Now it seemed that this was only a tantalizing taste of the intimacy other people enjoyed, as if she were fated to never have what other Clayr took for granted.

"Every Clayr is given the gift to See some portent of her death, though not the death itself, for no human could bear that weight. Almost twenty years ago I Saw myself and your little dog, and in time I realized that this was the vision that foretold my final days."

"But I need you," said Lirael, weeping, throwing her arms around the slight figure. "I need someone! I can't keep going on my own!"

"You can and you will," said Filris fiercely. "Make your dog your companion, to be the friend you need. You must learn about the creature you released and defeat it! Explore the Library. Remember that while the Clayr can See the future, others make it. I feel that you will be a maker, not a seer. You must promise me that it will be so. Promise me that you will not give in. Promise me that you will never give up hope. Make your future, Lirael!"

"I'll try," whispered Lirael, feeling the fierce energy of Filris flowing into her. "I'll try."

Filris gripped her hand, harder than Lirael would have thought possible with those thin, ancient fingers. Then she kissed Lirael on the forehead, sending a tingle of energy through her Charter mark, right through her body and out the soles of her feet.

"I was never close to Arielle, or her mother," Filris said quietly. "Too much a Clayr, I suppose, too much in the future. I am glad I was not too late to speak to you. Goodbye, my great-great-granddaughter. Remember your promise!"

With that, she walked out of the ward, straight-backed and proud, so that someone who didn't know her age would never guess that she had worked in these wards for more than a hundred years, and lived half as long again.

Lirael never saw Filris again. She wept with many others at the Farewell in the Hall, forgetting her distaste for the new blue tunic, hardly noticing that she stood a full head higher than all the other children and many of the white-clad Clayr who had newly Awoken to their gift.

She was unsure how much she cried for Filris and how much she cried for herself, left alone again. It seemed to be her fate that she would have no close friends. Only countless cousins, and one aunt.

But Lirael didn't forget Filris's words and was back at work the next day, though her voice was still weak, and she had a slight limp. Within a week, she managed to secretly obtain copies of *On the Making of Sendings* and *Superior Sendings in Seventy Days*, as *The Making and Mastery of Magical Beings* proved too difficult to spirit out of its locked case. The bestiaries proved troublesome, too, as all the ones she could find were chained to their shelves. She dipped into them when no one was around, but without immediate success. Clearly, it would take some time to find out exactly what the creature was.

Whenever she could, she passed the sunburst door and felt for her spell, checking that her magic still remained, binding door, hinges, and lock into the surrounding stone. The fear always rose in her then, and sometimes she thought she smelled the corrosive tang of Free Magic, as if the monster stood on the other side of the door, separated from her only by the thin barrier of wood and spells.

Then she would remember Filris's words, and hurry back to her study to work on her dog-sending; or to the latest bestiary she'd found, to see if it might describe a woman-like creature with eyes of silver fire and the claws of a praying mantis, a creature of Free Magic, malice, and awful hunger.

Sometimes she would wake in the night, a nightmare of the door opening fading as she struggled out of sleep. She would have checked the door more often, but following the day of the Watch of Fifteen Sixty-Eight, the Chief Librarian had ordered that all librarians must go into the Old Levels only in pairs, so it was harder to sneak there and back. The Watch had not Seen anything conclusive, Lirael heard, but the Clayr were obviously worried about something close to home. The Library was not the only department to take precautionary measures: extra Rangers patrolled the glacier and the bridges, the steampipe crews also now worked in pairs, and many internal doors and corridors were closed and locked for the first time since the Restoration.

Lirael checked the door to the flower-field room forty-two times over seventy-three days before she found a bestiary that told her what the creature was. In those ten weeks of worry, study, and preparation, she had searched through eleven bestiaries and done most of the preliminary work needed to create her dog-sending.

In fact, it was the dog-sending that was mostly on her mind when she finally did find a mention of the monster. She was thinking about when she could cast the next lot of spells even as her hands opened the small, red-bound book that was simply

titled *Creatures by Nagy*. Flicking through the pages without
expectation, her eye was caught by an engraving that showed
exactly what she was looking for. The accompanying text made
it clear that whoever Nagy was, or had been, he or she had
encountered the same sort of monster Lirael had released from
the glass-covered coffin.

> *It stands higher than a tall man, generally taking the shape
> of a comely woman, though its form is fluid. Often the
> Stilken will have great hooks or pincers in the place of
> forearms, which it uses with facility to seize its prey. Its
> mouth generally appears human till it opens, revealing double
> rows of teeth, as narrow and sharp as needles. These teeth
> may be of a bright silver, or black as night. The Stilken's eyes
> are also of silver, and burn with a strange fire.*

Lirael shivered as she read this description, making the chain
that held the book to the shelf rattle and clank. Quickly she
looked around to see if anyone had heard and would come looking between the shelves. But there was no sound save her own
breathing. This room was rarely used, housing a collection of
obscure personal memoirs. Lirael had come here merely because
Creatures by Nagy was cross-indexed in the Reading Room as
a bestiary of sorts.

Stilling her hands, she read on, the words filling only part of
her mind. The rest was struggling with the fact that, now that she
had the knowledge she sought, she must face the Stilken and
defeat it.

> *The Stilken is an elemental of Free Magic, and so it cannot
> be harmed by earthly materials, such as common steel. Nor
> can human flesh touch it, for its substance is inimical to life.*

*A Stilken cannot be destroyed, except by Free Magic, at the
hands of a sorcerer more powerful than itself.*

Lirael stopped reading, nervously swallowed and read the
last line again. "Cannot be destroyed, except by Free Magic," she
read, over and over again. But she couldn't do any Free Magic.
It wasn't allowed. Free Magic was too dangerous.

Unable to think of what she could do, Lirael read on—and
breathed a long sigh of relief as the book continued.

*However, while destruction is the province solely of Free
Magic, a Stilken may be bound by Charter Magic and
imprison'd within a vessel or structure, such as a bottle of
metal or wrought crystal (simple glass being too fragile for
surety) or down a dry well, covered by stone.*

*I have essayed this task myself, using the spells I list
below. But I warn that these bindings are of terrible force,
drawing as they do on no fewer than three of the master
Charter marks. Only a great adept—which I am not—
would dare use them without the assistance of an ensorceled
sword or a rowan wand, charged with the first circle of seven
marks for binding the elements, and in the case of fire and
air, the second circle too, and all of them linked with the
master mark—*

Lirael swallowed again, her throat suddenly sore. The nota-
tion Nagy used was for the same master mark that had burnt her.
Worse than that, she didn't know the second circle of marks for
binding fire and air, and she had no idea how they could all be
put into a sword or a rowan wand. She didn't even know where
she could find a rowan tree, for that matter.

Slowly, she shut the book and placed it back on the shelf,

careful not to rattle the chain. Part of her was frustrated. Having finally found out what the creature was, she still had to find out more. Another part of her was relieved that she would not have to confront the Stilken. Not yet.

She would have time to create her dog-sending first. At least then she would have something . . . someone to talk to about all this. Even if it couldn't talk back, or help her.

Chapter Ten

DOG DAY

THE FINAL SPELL to create the dog-sending required four hours to cast, so Lirael had to wait for another opportunity when most of the librarians would be away. If she were interrupted during the casting, all her work of the previous months would be wasted, the delicately connected network of Charter-spells broken into their component marks, rather than brought together by the final spell.

The opportunity came sooner than Lirael had expected, for whatever the Clayr were trying to See obviously still eluded them. Lirael heard other librarians muttering about the demands of the Observatory, and it was clear that the Nine Day Watch was growing in size again, starting with a ninety-eight. This time, as each new, larger Watch was called, Lirael carefully observed the time of the summons and noted when the Clayr returned. When the full Fifteen Sixty-Eight was called—amidst considerable grumbling in the Reading Room—she estimated she had at least six hours. Time enough to finish her sending.

In her study, the dog statuette sat benignly, surveying Lirael's preparations from the top of her desk. Lirael spoke to it as she locked the door, with a spell since she wasn't senior enough to rate a key or bar.

"This is it, little dog," she said cheerfully, reaching over to stroke the dog's stone snout with one finger. The sound of her own voice surprised her, not because of the huskiness that still remained from her damaged throat, but because it sounded strange and unfamiliar. She realized then that she hadn't spoken for two days. The other librarians had long accepted her silence, and she had not recently been taxed with any conversation that required more than a nod, a shake of the head, or simply instant application to an ordered task.

The beginning of the dog-sending was under her desk, hidden by a draped cloth. Lirael reached in, removed the cloth, and gently slid out the framework she had built to start the spell. She ran her hands over it, feeling the warmth of the Charter marks that swam lazily up and down the twisted silver wires that formed the shape of a dog. It was a small dog, about a foot high, the size constrained by the amount of silver wire Lirael could easily obtain. Besides, she thought a small dog-sending would be more sensible than a big one. She wanted a comfortable friend, not a dog large enough to be a guard-sending.

Aside from the framework of silver wire, the dog shape had two eyes made from jet buttons and a nose of black felt, all of them already imbued with Charter marks. It also had a tail made from braided dog hair, clipped surreptitiously from several visiting dogs down in the Lower Refectory. That tail was already prepared with Charter marks, marks that defined something of what it was to be a dog.

The final part of the spell required Lirael to reach into the Charter and pluck forth several thousand Charter marks, letting them flow through her and into the silver-wire armature. Marks that fully described a dog, and marks that would give the semblance of life, though not the actuality.

When the spell was finished, the silver wire, jet buttons, and braided dog hair would be gone, replaced by a puppy-sized dog of spell-flesh. It would look like a dog till you got close enough to see the Charter marks that made it up, but she wouldn't be able to touch it. Touching most sendings was like touching water: the skin would yield and then re-form around whatever touched it. All the toucher would feel was the buzz and warmth of the Charter marks.

Lirael sat down cross-legged next to the silver-wire model and started to empty her mind, taking slow breaths, forcing them down so far that her stomach pushed outwards as the air reached the very bottoms of her lungs.

She was just about to reach into the Charter and begin when her eye caught sight of the small stone dog, up on the desk. It somehow looked lonely up there, as if it felt left out. Impulsively, Lirael got up and set it in her lap when she sat back down. The small carving tilted slightly but stayed upright, looking at the silver-wire copy of itself.

Lirael took a few more breaths and began again. She had written out the marks she required, in the safe shorthand all Mages used to record Charter marks. But those papers stayed by her side, still in a neat pile. She found that the first marks came easily, and those after them seemed to almost choose themselves. Mark after mark leapt out of the flow of the Charter and into her mind, then as quickly out, crossing to the silver-wire dog in an arc of golden lightning.

As more and more marks rushed through her, Lirael slipped further into a trance state, barely aware of anything except the Charter and the marks that filled her. The golden lightning became a solid bridge of light from her outstretched hands to the silver wires, growing brighter by the second. Lirael closed her eyes against the glare, and she felt herself slip towards the edge of dream, her conscious mind barely awake. Images moved restlessly between the marks in her mind. Images of dogs, many dogs, of all shapes, colors, and sizes. Dogs barking. Dogs running after thrown sticks. Dogs refusing to run. Puppies waddling on uncertain paws. Old dogs shivering themselves upright. Happy dogs. Sad dogs. Hungry dogs. Fat, sleepy dogs.

More and more images flashed through, till Lirael felt she had seen glimpses of every dog that had ever lived. But still the Charter marks roared through her mind. She had long lost track of where she was up to, or which marks were next—and the golden light was too bright for her to see how much of the sending was done.

Yet the marks flowed on. Lirael realized that not only did she not know which mark she was up to—she didn't even know the marks that were passing through her head! Strange, unknown marks were pouring out of her into the sending. Powerful marks that rocked her body as they left, forcing everything else out of her mind with the urgency of their passage.

Desperately, Lirael tried to open her eyes, to see what the marks were doing—but the glow was blinding now, and hot. She tried to stand up, to direct the flow of marks into the wall or ceiling. But her body seemed disconnected from her brain. She could feel everything, but her legs and arms wouldn't move, just as if she were trying to wake herself from the end of a dream.

Still the marks came, and then Lirael's nostrils caught the terrible, unmistakable reek of Free Magic, and she knew something had gone terribly, horribly wrong.

She tried to scream, but no sound came out, only Charter marks that leapt from her mouth towards the golden radiance. Charter marks continued to fly from her fingers, too, and swam in her eyes, spilling down inside her tears, which turned to steam as they fell.

More and more marks flew through Lirael, through her tears and her silent screaming. They swarmed through like an endless flight of bright butterflies forced through a garden gate. But even as the thousands and thousands of marks flung themselves into the brightness, the smell of Free Magic rose, and a crackling white light formed in the center of the golden glow, so bright it shone through Lirael's shut eyelids, piercing her brimming eyes.

Held motionless by the torrent of Charter Magic, Lirael could do nothing as the white light grew stronger, subduing the rich golden glow of the swirling marks. It was the end, she knew. Whatever she'd done now, it was much, much worse than freeing a Stilken; so much worse that she couldn't really comprehend it. All she knew was that the marks that passed through her now were more ancient and more powerful than anything she had ever seen. Even if the Free Magic that grew in front of her spared her life, the Charter marks would burn her to a husk.

Except, she realized, they didn't hurt. Either she was in shock and already dying, or the marks weren't harming her. Any one of them would have killed her if she'd tried to use them normally. But several hundred had already stormed through, and she was still breathing. Wasn't she?

Frightened by the thought that she might not be breathing, Lirael focused all her remaining energy on inhaling—just as the tremendous flow of marks suddenly stopped. She felt her connection to the Charter sever as the last mark jumped across to the boiling mass of gold and white light that had been her silver-wire dog. Her breath came with sudden force, and she overbalanced, falling backwards. At the last moment, she caught the edge of the bookshelf, almost pulling that on top of her. But the shelf didn't quite go over, and she pulled herself back up to a sitting position, ready to use her newly filled lungs to scream.

The scream stayed unborn. Where the Free Magic and Charter marks had fought in their sparking, swirling brilliance, there was now a globe of utter darkness that occupied the space where the wire dog and the desk had been. The awful tang of Free Magic was gone, too, replaced by a sort of damp animal odor that Lirael couldn't quite identify.

A tiny pinprick star appeared on the black surface of the globe, and then another, and another, till it was no longer dark but as star-filled as a clear night sky. Lirael stared at it, mesmerized by the multitude of stars. They grew brighter and brighter, till she was forced to blink.

In the instant of that blink, the globe disappeared, leaving behind a dog. Not a cute, cuddly Charter sending of a puppy, but a waist-high black and tan mongrel that seemed to be entirely real, including its impressive teeth. It had none of the characteristics of a sending. The only hint of its magical origin was a thick collar around its neck that swam with even more Charter marks that Lirael had never seen before.

The dog looked exactly like a life-size, breathing version of the stone statuette. Lirael stared at the real thing, then down at her lap.

The statuette was gone.

She looked back up. The dog was still there, scratching its ear with a back foot, eyes half-closed with concentration. It was soaking wet, as if it had just been for a swim.

Suddenly, the dog stopped scratching, stood up, and shook itself, spraying droplets of dirty water all over Lirael and all over the study. Then it ambled across and licked the petrified girl on the face with a tongue that most definitely was all real dog and not some Charter-made imitation.

When that got no response, it grinned and announced, "I am the Disreputable Dog. Or Disreputable Bitch, if you want to get technical. When are we going for a walk?"

Chapter Eleven

SEARCH FOR A SUITABLE SWORD

T HE WALK THAT Lirael and the Disreputable Dog took that day was the first of many, though Lirael never could remember exactly where they went, or what she said, or what the Dog answered. All she could recall was being in the same sort of daze she'd had when she'd hit her head—only this time she wasn't hurt.

Not that it mattered, because the Disreputable Dog never really answered her questions. Later, Lirael would repeat the same questions and get different, still-evasive answers. The most important questions—"What are you? Where did you come from?"— had a whole range of answers, starting with "I'm the Disreputable Dog" and "from elsewhere" and occasionally becoming as eloquent as "I'm your Dog" and "You tell me—it was your spell."

The Dog also refused, or was unable, to answer questions about her nature. She seemed in most respects to be exactly like a real dog, albeit a speaking one. At least at first.

For the first two weeks they were together, the Dog slept in Lirael's study, under the replacement desk that Lirael had been forced to purloin from an empty study nearby. She had no idea what had happened to her own, as not a bit of it remained after the Dog's sudden appearance.

The Dog ate the food Lirael stole for her from the Refectory or the kitchens. She went walking with Lirael four times a day in the most disused corridors and rooms Lirael could find, a nerve-wracking exercise, though somehow the Dog always managed to hide from approaching Clayr at the last second. She was discreet in other ways as well, always choosing dark and unused corners to use as a toilet—though she did like to alert Lirael to the fact that she had done so, even if her human friend declined to sniff at the result.

In fact, apart from her collar of Charter marks and the fact that she could talk, the Disreputable Dog really did seem to be just a rather large dog of uncertain parentage and curious origin.

But of course she wasn't. Lirael sneaked back to her study one evening after dinner, to find the Dog reading on the floor. The Dog was turning the pages of a large grey book that Lirael didn't recognize, with one paw—a paw that had grown longer and separated out into three extremely flexible fingers.

The Dog looked up from the book as her supposed mistress froze in the doorway. All Lirael could think of were the words in Nagy's book, about the Stilken's form being fluid—and the way the hook-handed creature had stretched and thinned to get through the gate guarded by the crescent moon.

"You *are* a Free Magic thing," she blurted out, reaching into her waistcoat pocket for the clockwork mouse, as her lips felt for the whistle on her lapel. This time she wouldn't make a mistake. She'd call for help right away.

"No, I'm not," protested the Dog, her ears stiffening in outrage as her paw shrank back to its normal proportions. "I'm definitely not a *thing*! I'm as much a part of the Charter as you are, albeit with special properties. Look at my collar! And I am definitely not a Stilken or any other of the several hundred variations thereof."

"What do you know about Stilken?" asked Lirael. She still didn't enter the study, and the clockwork mouse was ready in her hand. "Why did you mention them in particular?"

"I read a lot," replied the Dog, yawning. Then she sniffed, and her eyes lit up with expectation. "Is that a ham bone you have there?"

Lirael didn't answer but moved the paper-wrapped object in her left hand behind her back. "How did you know I was thinking about a Stilken just then? And I still don't know you aren't one yourself, or something even worse."

"Feel my collar!" protested the Dog as she edged forward, licking her chops. Clearly the current conversation wasn't as interesting as the prospect of food.

"How did you know I was thinking about a Stilken?" repeated Lirael, giving each word a slow and considered emphasis. She held the ham bone over her head as she spoke, watching the Dog's head tilt back to follow the movement. Surely a Free Magic creature wouldn't be this interested in a ham bone.

"I guessed, because you seem to be thinking about Stilken quite a lot," replied the Dog, gesturing with a paw at the books on the desk. "You are studying everything required to bind a Stilken. Besides, you also wrote 'Stilken' fourteen times yesterday on that paper you burnt. I read it backwards on the blotter. And I've smelled your spell on the door down below, and the Stilken that waits beyond it."

"You've been out by yourself!" exclaimed Lirael. Forgetting that she had been afraid of whatever the Dog might be, she stormed in, slamming the door behind her. In the process, she dropped the clockwork mouse, but not the ham bone.

The mouse bounced twice and landed at the Dog's feet. Lirael held her breath, all too aware that the door was now shut at her back, which would greatly delay the mouse if she needed help. But the Dog didn't seem dangerous, and she was so much easier to talk to than people were . . . except for Filris, who was gone.

The Disreputable Dog sniffed at the mouse eagerly for an

instant, then pushed it aside with her nose and transferred her attention back to the ham bone.

Lirael sighed, picked up the mouse, and put it back in her pocket. She unwrapped the bone and gave it to the Dog, who immediately snatched it up and deposited it in a far corner under the desk.

"That's your dinner," said Lirael, wrinkling her nose. "You'd better eat it before it starts to smell."

"I'll take it out and bury it later, in the ice," replied the Dog. She hesitated and hung her head a little before adding, "Besides, I don't actually need to eat. I just like to."

"What!" exclaimed Lirael, cross again. "You mean I've been stealing food for nothing! If I were caught I'd—"

"Not for nothing!" interrupted the Dog, sidling over to butt her head against Lirael's hip and look up at her with wide, beseeching eyes. "For me. And much appreciated, too. Now, you really should feel my collar. It will show you that I am not a Stilken, Margrue, or Hish. You can scratch my neck at the same time."

Lirael hesitated, but the Dog felt so like the friendly dogs she scratched when they visited the Refectory that her hand almost automatically went to the Dog's back. She felt warm dog skin and the silky, short hair, and she began to scratch along the Dog's spine, up towards the neck. The Dog shivered and muttered, "Up a bit. Across to the left. No, back. Aahhh!"

Then Lirael touched the collar, just with two fingers—and was momentarily thrown out of the world altogether. All she could see, hear, and feel were Charter marks, all around, as if she had somehow fallen into the Charter. There was no leather collar under her hand, no Dog, no study. Nothing but the Charter.

Then she was suddenly back in herself again, swaying and dizzy. Both her hands were scratching the Dog under the chin, without her knowing how they had got there.

"Your collar," Lirael said, when she got her balance back. "Your collar is like a Charter Stone—a way into the Charter. Yet I saw Free Magic in your making. It has to be there somewhere . . . doesn't it?"

She fell silent, but the Dog didn't answer, till Lirael stopped scratching. Then she turned her head and jumped up, licking Lirael across her open mouth.

"You needed a friend," said the Dog, as Lirael spluttered and wiped her mouth with both sleeves, one after the other. "I came. Isn't that enough to be going on with? You know my collar is of the Charter, and whatever else I may be, it would constrain my actions, even if I did mean you any harm. And we do have a Stilken to deal with, do we not?"

"Yes," said Lirael. On an impulse, she bent down and hugged the Dog around the neck, feeling both warm dog and the soft buzz of the Charter marks in the Dog's collar through the thin material of her shirt.

The Disreputable Dog bore this patiently for a minute, then made a sort of wheezing sound and shuffled her paws. Lirael understood this from her time with the visiting dogs, and let go.

"Now," pronounced the Dog. "The Stilken must be dealt with as soon as possible, before it gets free and finds even worse things to release, or let in from outside. I presume you have obtained the necessary items to bind it?"

"No," said Lirael. "Not if you mean the stuff Nagy mentions: a rowan wand or a sword, infused with the Charter marks—"

"Yes, yes," said the Dog hastily, before Lirael could recite the whole list. "I know. Why haven't you got one?"

"They don't just lie around," replied Lirael defensively. "I thought I could get an ordinary sword and put the—"

"Take too long. Months!" interrupted the Dog, who had started pacing to and fro in a serious manner. "That Stilken will be through your door spell in a few days, I would think."

"What!" screamed Lirael. Then she said more quietly, "What? You mean it's escaping?"

"It will soon," confirmed the Dog. "I thought you knew. Free Magic can corrode Charter marks as well as flesh. I suppose you could renew the spell."

Lirael shook her head. Her throat still hadn't recovered from the master mark she'd used last time. It would be too risky to chance speaking it again before she was completely better. Not without the added strength of a Charter-spelled sword—which brought her back to the original problem.

"You'll have to borrow a sword, then," declared the Dog, fixing Lirael with a serious eye. "I don't suppose anyone will have the right sort of wand. Not really a Clayr thing, rowan."

"I don't think swords redolent with binding spells are, either," protested Lirael, slumping into her chair. "Why couldn't I just be an ordinary Clayr? If I'd got the Sight, I wouldn't be wandering around the Library getting into trouble! If I ever do get the Sight, I swear by the Charter I am never going to go exploring, ever again!"

"Mmmm," said the Dog, with an expression Lirael couldn't fathom, though it seemed to be loaded with hidden meaning. "That's as may be. On the matter of swords, you are in error. There are a number of swords of power within these halls. The Captain of the Rangers has one, the Observatory Guard have three—well, one is an axe, but it holds the same spells within its steel. Closer to home, the Chief Librarian has one, too. A very old and famous sword, in fact, most appropriately named Binder. It will do nicely."

Lirael looked at the Dog with such a blank stare that the hound stopped pacing, cleared her throat, and said, "Pay attention, Lirael. I said that you were in error about—"

"I heard what you said," snapped Lirael. "You must be absolutely mad! I can't steal the Chief's sword! She always has it with her! She probably sleeps with it!"

"She does," replied the Dog smugly. "I checked."

"Dog!" wailed Lirael, trying to keep her breathing down to less than one breath a second. "Please, please do not go looking in the Chief Librarian's rooms! Or anywhere else! What would happen if someone saw you?"

"They didn't," replied the Dog happily. "Anyway, the Chief keeps the sword in her bedroom, but not actually in bed with her. She puts it on a stand next to her bed. So you can borrow it while she's asleep."

"No," replied Lirael, shaking her head. "I'm not creeping into the Chief's bedroom. I'd rather fight the Stilken without a sword."

"Then you'll die," said the Disreputable Dog, suddenly very serious. "The Stilken will drink your blood and grow stronger from it. Then it will creep out into the lower reaches of the Library, emerging every now and then to capture librarians, to take them one by one, feasting on their flesh in some dark corner where the bones will never be found. It will find allies, creatures bound even deeper in the Library, and will open doors for the evil that lurks outside. You must bind it, but you cannot succeed without the sword."

"What if you help me?" asked Lirael. There had to be some way of avoiding the Chief, some way that didn't involve swords at all. Trying to get Mirelle's sword, or the ones from the Observatory, would not be any easier than the Chief's. She didn't even know exactly where the Observatory was.

"I'd like to," replied the Dog. "But it is your Stilken. You let it out. You must deal with the consequences."

"So you won't help," said Lirael sadly. She had hoped, just

for a moment, that the Disreputable Dog would step in and fix
everything for her. She was a magical creature, after all, possibly
of some power. But not enough to take on a Stilken, it seemed.

"I will advise," said the Dog. "As is only proper. But you will
have to borrow the sword yourself, and perform the binding.
Tonight is probably as good a time as any."

"Tonight?" asked Lirael, in a very small voice.

"Tonight," confirmed the Dog. "At the stroke of midnight,
when all such adventures should begin, you will enter the Chief
Librarian's room. The sword is on the left, past the wardrobe,
which is strangely full of black waistcoats. If all goes well, you
will be able to return it before the dawn."

"If all goes well," repeated Lirael somberly, remembering the
silver fire in the Stilken's eyes, and those terrible hooks. "Do
you . . . do you think I should leave a note, in case . . . in case all
does not go well?"

"Yes," said the Dog, removing the last small shred of Lirael's
self-confidence. "Yes. That would be a very good idea."

Chapter Twelve

INTO THE LAIR OF THE CHIEF LIBRARIAN

WHEN THE GREAT water-powered clock in the Middle Refectory showed fifteen minutes to midnight, Lirael left her hiding spot in the breakfast servery and climbed up through an air shaft to the Narrow Way, which would in turn take her to the Southscape and Chief Librarian Vancelle's rooms.

Lirael had dressed in her librarian's uniform in case she met anyone, and carried an envelope addressed to the Chief. A skeleton staff of librarians did work through the night, though they didn't usually employ Third Assistants like Lirael. If she was stopped, Lirael would claim she was taking an urgent message. In fact, the envelope contained her "just in case" note, alerting the Chief to the presence of the Stilken.

But she didn't meet anyone. No one came down the Narrow Way, which lived up to its name by being too narrow for two people to pass abreast. It was rarely used, because if you did meet someone going the other way, the more junior Clayr would have to backtrack—sometimes for its entire length, which was more than half a mile.

The Southscape was wider, and much more risky for Lirael because so many senior Clayr had rooms off its broad expanse. Fortunately, the marks that lit it so brightly during the day had faded to a glimmer at night, producing heavy shadows for her to hide in.

The door to the Chief's rooms, however, was brightly lit by a ring of Charter marks around the book-and-sword emblem that was carved into the stone next to the doorway.

Lirael looked at the lights balefully. Not for the first time, she wondered what she was doing. It probably would have been better to confess months ago when she initially got into trouble. Then someone else could deal with the Stilken—

A touch at her leg made her jump and almost scream. She stifled the scream as she recognized the Disreputable Dog.

"I thought you weren't going to help," she whispered, as the Dog jumped up and attempted to lick her face. "Get down, you idiot!"

"I'm not helping," said the Dog happily. "I've come to watch."

"Great," replied Lirael, trying to sound sarcastic. Secretly, she was pleased. Somehow, the lair of the Chief Librarian seemed less threatening with the Dog along.

"When is something going to happen?" the Dog asked a minute later, as Lirael still stood in the shadows, watching the door.

"Now," said Lirael, hoping that saying the word would give her the courage to begin. "Now!"

She crossed the corridor in ten long strides, gripped the bronze doorknob, and pushed. No Clayr needed to lock her door, so Lirael wasn't expecting any resistance. The door opened, and Lirael stepped in, the Dog whisking past her on the way.

She shut the door quietly behind her and turned to survey the room. It was mainly a living space, dominated by bookshelves on three walls, several comfortable chairs, and a tall, thin sculpture of a sort of squashed-in horse, carved out of translucent stone.

But it was the fourth wall that attracted Lirael's attention. It was a single, vast window from floor to ceiling, made of the clearest, cleanest glass Lirael had ever seen.

Through the window, Lirael could see the entire Ratterlin valley stretching southward, the river a wide streak of silver far below, shining in the moonlight. It was snowing lightly outside, and snowflakes whirled about in wild dances as they fell down the mountainside. None stuck to the window, or left any mark upon it.

Lirael flinched and stepped back as a dark shape swooped past, straight through the falling snow. Then she realized it was only an owl, heading down the valley for a midnight snack.

"There's lots to do before dawn," whispered the Dog conversationally, as Lirael kept staring out the window, transfixed by that ribbon of silver winding off to the far horizon and by the strange moonlit vista that stretched as far as she could see. Beyond the horizon lay the Kingdom proper: the great city of Belisaere, with all its marvels, open to the sky and surrounded by the sea. All the world—the world that the other Clayr Saw in the ice of the Observatory—was out there, but all she knew of it was from books or from travelers' tales overheard in the Lower Refectory.

For the first time, Lirael wondered what the Clayr were trying to See out there with the greatly expanded Watches. Where was the place that resisted the Sight? What was the future that was beginning there, perhaps even as she looked out?

Something tickled at the back of her mind, a sense of déjà vu or a fleeting memory. But nothing came, and she remained entranced, staring at the outside world.

"A lot to do!" repeated the Dog, a little louder.

Reluctantly, Lirael tore herself away and concentrated on the task at hand. The Chief's bedroom had to be beyond this room. But where was the door? There were only the window, the door leading outside, and the bookshelves. . . .

Lirael smiled as she saw that the end of one shelf was occupied by a door-handle rather than tightly packed books. Trust the Chief to have a door that doubled as a bookshelf.

"The sword is on a stand just to the left," whispered the Dog, who suddenly seemed a bit anxious. "Don't open the door too much."

"Thanks," replied Lirael as she gingerly tested the door handle, to see if it had to be pulled, pushed, or turned. "But I thought you weren't helping."

The Dog didn't answer, because as soon as Lirael touched it, the whole bookcase swung open. Lirael only just managed to get a firm enough grasp on the handle to stop it from opening completely, and had to haul it back to leave a gap wide enough for herself to slide through.

The bedroom was dark, lit only by the moonlight in the outer chamber. Lirael poked her head in very slowly and let her eyes adjust, her ears trying to catch any sound of movement or sudden waking.

After a minute or so, she could see the faint dark mass of a bed, and the regular breathing of someone asleep—though she wasn't sure if she could really hear that or was just imagining it.

As the Dog had said, there was a stand near the door. A sort of cylindrical metal cage that was open only at the top. Even in the dim light, Lirael could see that Binder was there, in its scabbard. The pommel was only a few inches below the top of the stand, in easy reach. But she would have to be right next to the stand to lift the sword high enough to clear the cage.

She ducked back out and took a deep breath. The air seemed closer in the bedroom somehow. Darker, and cloying, as if it conspired against thieves like Lirael.

The Dog looked at her and winked encouragingly. Still, Lirael's heart started to beat faster and faster as she edged back through the door, and she suddenly felt strangely cold.

A few, small, careful steps took her next to the stand. She

touched it with both hands, then gingerly moved to grab the sword by the grip, and the scabbard just below the hilt.

Lirael's fingers had barely touched the metal when the sword suddenly let out a low whistle, and Charter marks flared into brilliance across the hilt. Instantly, Lirael let go and hunched forward, trying to muffle both light and sound with her body. She didn't dare turn around. She didn't want to see the Chief awake and furious.

But there was no sudden shout of outrage, no stern voice demanding to know what she was doing. The red blur in front of her eyes faded as her night vision returned, and she cocked an ear to try and hear anything above the steady drumbeat of her own heart.

Both whistle and the light had lasted no more than a second, she realized. Even so, it was clear that Binder chose who would— or would not—wield it.

Lirael thought about this for a moment, then bent down and whispered, so low that she could hardly hear it herself.

"Binder, I would borrow you for this night, for I need your help to bind a Stilken, a creature of Free Magic. I promise that you will be returned before the dawn. I swear this by the Charter, whose mark I bear."

She touched the Charter mark on her forehead, wincing as its sudden flare of light lit up the stand. Then she touched the pommel of Binder with the same two fingers.

It didn't whistle, and the marks in its hilt merely glowed. Lirael almost sighed, but swallowed the sigh at the last moment, before it could give her away.

The sword came free of the stand without a sound, though Lirael had to lift it high over her own head for the point to clear, and it was heavy. She hadn't realized how heavy it would be, or how long. It felt as if it weighed double her little practice sword, and it was easily a third as long again. Too long to clip the scabbard to her belt, unless she wore the belt under her armpits, or let the point drag along the ground.

This sword was never made for a fourteen-year-old girl, Lirael concluded, as she edged back out and carefully shut the door. She resisted thinking any further than that.

There was no sign of the Disreputable Dog. Lirael looked around, but there was nothing big enough for the Dog to hide behind—unless she'd somehow shrunk herself and gone under one of the chairs.

"Dog! I've got it! Let's go!" hissed Lirael.

There was no answer. Lirael waited for at least a minute, though it seemed much longer. Then she went to the outer door and put her head against it, listening for footsteps in the corridor outside. Getting back to the Library with the sword would be the trickiest part of the venture. It would be impossible to explain to any Clayr she met.

She couldn't hear anything, so she slipped outside. As the door clicked shut behind her, Lirael saw a shadow suddenly stretch out of the dark edge on the other side, and a jolt of fear went through her. But once again, it was only the Disreputable Dog.

"You scared me!" whispered Lirael, as she hurried into the shadows herself, and along to the Second Back Stair that would take her directly down to the Library. "Why didn't you wait?"

"I don't like waiting," said the Dog, trotting along at her heels. "Besides, I wanted to take a look in Mirelle's rooms."

"No!" exclaimed Lirael, louder than she intended. She dropped to one knee, put the sword into the crook of one arm, and gripped the Dog's lower jaw. "I told you not to go into people's rooms! What will we do if someone decides you're a menace?"

"I *am* a menace," mumbled the Dog. "When I want to be. Besides, I knew she wasn't there. I could smell she wasn't."

"Please, please, don't go looking anywhere people might see you," begged Lirael. "Promise me you won't."

The Dog tried to look away, but Lirael held her jaw. Eventually she muttered something that possibly contained the word "promise." Lirael decided that, given the circumstances, that would have to do.

A few minutes later, slinking down the Second Back Stair, Lirael remembered her own promise to Binder. She'd sworn she'd return it to Vancelle's bedroom before dawn. But what if she couldn't?

They left the Stair and headed down the main spiral until they were almost at the door to the flower-field room. When it came in sight, Lirael suddenly stopped. The Dog, who was several yards behind, loped up and looked at her enquiringly.

"Dog," Lirael said slowly. "I know you won't help me fight the Stilken. But if I can't bind it, I want you to get Binder and take it back to Vancelle's. Before the dawn."

"You will take it back yourself, Mistress," said the Dog confidently, her voice almost a growl. Then she hesitated, and said in a softer tone, "But I will do as you ask, if it proves necessary. You have my promise."

Lirael nodded her thanks, unable to speak. She walked the final thirty feet to the door. There, she checked that the clockwork mouse was in her right waistcoat pocket and the small silver bottle in her left. Then she unsheathed Binder and, for the first time, held it as a weapon, on guard. The Charter marks on the blade burst into brilliant fire as they sensed the foe, and Lirael felt the latent strength of the sword's magic. Binder had defeated many strange creatures, she knew, and this filled her with hope— until she remembered that this was probably the first time it was being wielded by a girl who didn't really know what she was doing.

Before that thought could paralyze her, Lirael reached out and broke the locking-spell on the door. As the Dog had said, the spell had been corroded by Free Magic, a corrosion so fierce that the spell broke apart merely at her touch and a whispered command.

Then she waved her wrist. The emeralds of her bracelet flashed, and the door groaned open. Lirael braced herself for the sudden rush of the Stilken's attack—but there was nothing there.

Hesitantly, she stepped through the doorway, her nose twitching, seeking any scent of Free Magic, her eyes wide for the slightest hint of the creature's presence.

Unlike on her earlier visit, there was no bright light beyond the corridor—just an eerie glow, a Charter Magic imitation of moonlight that reduced all colors to shades of grey. Somewhere, in that half-darkness, the Stilken lurked. Lirael raised the sword higher and stepped out into the chamber, the flowers rustling under her feet.

The Disreputable Dog followed ten paces behind, every hair on her back stuck up in a ridge, a low growl rumbling in her chest. There were traces of the Stilken here, but no active scent. It was hiding somehow, waiting in ambush. For a moment the Dog almost spoke. Then she remembered: Lirael must defeat the Stilken alone. She hunkered down on her belly, watching as her mistress walked on through the flowers, towards the tree and the pool—where the Stilken's ambush must surely lie.

Chapter Thirteen

OF STILKEN AND STRANGE MAGIC

ONCE AGAIN, LIRAEL was struck by the silence in the vast chamber of flowers. Apart from the soft rustle of her passage through the daisies, there was no sound at all.

Slowly, circling every few steps to make sure nothing was creeping up on her, Lirael crossed the cavern, right up to the door with the crescent moon. It was still partly open, but she didn't venture inside, thinking that the Stilken might be able to lock her in somehow, if it was still hiding out in the field.

The tree was the most likely spot for the creature to be, Lirael thought, imagining it twined around a branch like a snake. Hidden by the thick green leaves, its silver eyes following her every movement . . .

In the strange light, the oak was only a blot of shadow. The Stilken could even be behind the trunk, slowly circling to keep the tree between it and Lirael. Lirael kept her eyes on the tree, opening them as wide as she could, as if they might capture extra light. Still nothing stirred, so she started to walk towards the tree, her steps getting shorter and shorter and her stomach tighter, twisting with dread.

She was so intent on the tree that her feet splashed into the edge of the pool before she realized it was there. Bright ripples, reflecting in the ersatz moonlight, spread for an instant, then once again the water was still and dark.

Lirael stepped back, shook her feet, and began to skirt around the pool. She could see some definition in the oak now, see separate clumps of leaves and individual branches. But there were also clots of shadow that could be anything. Every time her eyes shifted, she thought she saw movement in the darkness.

It was time for a light, she decided, even if that meant giving her own position away. She reached into the Charter, and the requisite marks began to swim into her mind—and were lost, as the Stilken erupted out of the pool beside her and attacked with its ferocious hooks.

Somehow, Binder met them in a spray of white sparks and steam, and a shock that nearly dislocated Lirael's shoulder. She stumbled back, screaming with sudden battle rage as much as panic, instinctively dropping into the guard position. Sparks flew again and water hissed as the Stilken attacked again, its hooks barely parried in time by Lirael and Binder.

Without conscious thought, Lirael gave ground, backing towards the oak. All her knowledge of the binding-spells had left her head, as had her sense of the Charter. Survival was all that mattered now, getting her sword in place to block the murderous assault of the monster.

It swung again, low, towards her legs. Lirael parried, and surprised herself as her incompletely trained muscles took over. She riposted directly at the thing's torso. Binder's point hit and skittered across its gut, sending up a blaze of sparks that peppered Lirael's waistcoat with tiny holes.

But the Stilken didn't seem hurt, only annoyed. It attacked again, every sweep of its hooks forcing Lirael back several paces. Desperately, she swung Binder, feeling the shock of every parry through to her bones. The weight of the sword was already wearing her out. She had never been much of a swordswoman and had never regretted it—till now.

She stepped back again, and her foot met slight resistance

and then went back a lot more than it should have, into an unexpected hole. Lirael lost her balance, tumbling over backwards as a sharp hook sliced the air in front of her throat.

Time seemed frozen as she fell. She saw her parry going wide as her arms windmilled in her attempt to regain her balance. She saw the hooks of the Stilken scything forward, towards her, almost certain to meet around her waist.

Lirael hit the ground hard, but she didn't notice the pain. She was already rolling aside, dimly registering that it was a hollow between two roots that had tripped her, and tree roots were pummeling her body as she rolled over them.

Earth—flowers—the distant ceiling and its Charter lights like far-off stars—earth—flowers—the artificial sky—with every roll, Lirael expected to see the Stilken's silver gaze and feel the searing pain of its hooks. But she didn't see it, and no death blow came. On the sixth roll, she stopped and threw herself forward, stomach muscles stabbing in agony as she flipped back onto her feet.

Binder was still in her hand, and the Stilken was trying to extricate its left hook from where it was stuck, deep in one of the great taproots of the oak. Instantly, Lirael realized it must have missed her as she fell—and struck the root instead.

The Stilken looked at her, silver eyes blazing, and made an awful gobbling noise, deep in its throat. Its body started to shift, weight moving from the trapped left arm to the right side of its body. It grew squatter, and muscles moved under the seemingly human skin like slugs under a leaf, gathering in the caught arm. Before the process was finished, it heaved, straining to free itself and come after Lirael.

This was her chance, Lirael knew—these scant few seconds. Charter marks flared on Binder's blade as she reached out to them, joining them to others drawn out of the Charter. Four master marks she needed, but to use them she had first to protect herself with lesser marks.

Binder helped her, and the marks slowly formed a chain in her mind, all too slowly, as the Stilken gobbled and strained, pulling its hook out inch by inch. The oak itself seemed to be trying to keep the creature trapped, Lirael realized, with that small part of her mind not totally focused on the Charter-spell. She could hear the tree rustling and creaking, as if it fought to keep the cut in its taproot closed, the hook with it.

The last mark came, flowing into Lirael with easy grace. She let the spell go, feeling its power rush through her blood and every bone, fortifying her against the four master marks she needed to call.

The first of these master marks blossomed in her mind as the Stilken finally pulled its hook free, with a great groan from the oak and a spray of white-green sap. Even with the protective spell upon her, Lirael didn't let the master mark linger in her mind. She cast it forth, sending it down Binder's blade, where it spread like shining oil, till it suddenly burst into fire, surrounding the blade with golden flames.

The Stilken, already leaping to attack, tried to twist away. But it was too late. Lirael stepped forward, and Binder leapt out in a perfect stop thrust, straight through the Stilken's neck. Golden fire raged, white sparks plumed up like a skyrocket's trail, and the creature froze a mere two paces from Lirael, its hooks almost touching her on either side.

Lirael called forth the second master mark, and it, too, ran down the blade. But when it reached the Stilken's neck, it disappeared. A moment later, the creature's skin began to crack and shrivel, blazing white light shining through when the shriveled skin sloughed off onto the ground. Within a minute, the Stilken had lost its semi-human appearance. Now it was just a featureless column of fierce white light, transfixed by a sword.

The third master mark left Binder and went into the column. Instantly, what was left of the Stilken began to shrink, dwindling away until it was a blob of light an inch in diameter, with Binder now resting point first upon it.

Lirael took the metal bottle out of her waistcoat pocket, put it on the ground, and used the sword to roll the shining remnant of the Stilken inside. Only then did she withdraw the blade, drop it, and thrust in the cork. A moment later, she sealed it with the fourth master mark, which wrapped itself around both cork and bottle in a flash of light.

For a moment the bottle jumped and wriggled in her hand, then it was still. Lirael put it back in her pocket, and sat down next to Binder, gasping. It was really over. She had bound the Stilken. All by herself.

She leaned back, wincing at the aches and pains that sprang up along her back and arms. A brief flash of light caught her eye, from somewhere over near the tree. Instantly, she was back on the alert again, her hand going to Binder, all her pains forgotten. Picking up the sword, she went to investigate. Surely there couldn't be another Stilken? Or could it have got out at the last instant? She checked the bottle, which was definitely sealed. Might there have been the briefest instant when she blinked, just as the fourth mark came?

The light flashed again, soft and golden as Lirael approached, and she sighed with relief. That had to be Charter Magic, so she was safe after all. The glow came from the hole she had tripped over.

Warily, Lirael poked at the hole with Binder, clearing the soil away. She saw that the glow came from a book, bound in what looked like fur or some sort of hairy hide. Using the sword as a lever, she flipped the book out. She'd seen the tree trying to hang on to the Stilken—she didn't want it getting a grip on her.

Once it was clear of the roots, she picked the book up. The Charter marks on its cover were familiar ones, a spell to keep the book clean and free of silverfish and moths. Lirael tucked the thick volume under her arm, suddenly conscious that she was drenched in sweat, caked in dirt and flower petals, and completely exhausted, not to mention bruised. But only her waistcoat had suffered permanent damage, drilled through by sparks in a hundred places, as if it had been attacked by incendiary moths.

The Dog rose up out of the flowers to meet her as she headed back to the exit. She had Binder's scabbard in her mouth and didn't let it go as Lirael slid the sword home.

"I did it," said Lirael. "I bound the Stilken."

"Mmmpph, mmpph, mmph," said the Dog, prancing on her back feet. Then she carefully laid the sword down and said, "Yes, Mistress. I knew you would. Reasonably certainly."

"Did you?" Lirael looked at her hands, which were starting to shake. Then her whole body was shaking, and she had to sit down till it stopped. She hardly noticed the Dog's warm bulk against her back, or the encouraging licks against her ear.

"I'll take the sword back," offered the Dog, when Lirael finally stopped shaking. "You rest here till I return. I won't be long. You will be safe."

Lirael nodded, unable to speak. She patted the Dog on the head and lay back on the flowers, letting their scent waft over her, the petals soft against her cheek. Her breathing slowed and became more regular, her eyes blinked slowly once, twice—and then they closed.

The Dog waited until she was sure Lirael was asleep. Then she let out a single short bark. A Charter mark came with it, expelled out of the Dog's mouth to hover in the air over the sleeping girl. The Dog cocked her head and looked at it with an experienced eye. Satisfied, she picked up the sword in her powerful jaws and trotted off, out into the main spiral.

When Lirael awoke, it was morning, or at least the light was bright again in the cavern. For a second she had the impression that there was a Charter mark above her head, but clearly that was only a dream, for there was nothing there when she came fully awake and sat up.

She felt very stiff and sore, but no worse than she usually did after one of the annual sword-and-bow exams. The waistcoat was beyond repair, but she had spares, and there didn't seem to be any other physical signs of her combat with the Stilken. Nothing that would require a trip to the Infirmary. The Infirmary . . . Filris. For a moment Lirael was sad she couldn't tell her great-great-grandmother that she had defeated the Stilken after all.

Filris would have liked the Disreputable Dog, too, Lirael thought, glancing over to where the hound slept nearby. She was curled into a ball, her tail wrapped completely around her back legs, almost up to her snout. She was snoring slightly and twitching every now and then, as if she dreamed of chasing rabbits.

Lirael was about to wake up the Dog when she felt the book poking into her. In the light, she realized it wasn't bound in fur or hide, but had some sort of closely knitted cover over heavy boards, which was very peculiar indeed.

She picked it up and flicked it open to the title page, but even before she read the first word, she knew it was a book of power. Every part of it was saturated with Charter Magic. There were marks in the paper, marks in the ink, marks in the stitching of the spine.

The title page said merely *In the Skin of a Lyon*. Lirael turned it over, hoping to see a list of contents, but it went straight into the first chapter. She started to read beyond the words "Chapter One," but the type suddenly blurred and shimmered. She blinked, rubbed her eyes, but when she looked again the page had the heading "Preface," though she was sure it could not have turned. She turned back, and there was the title page again.

Lirael frowned and flipped forward. It still said "Preface." Before it could change, she started to read.

"The making of Charter-skins," she read,

allows the Mage to take on more than the mere semblance or seeming of a beast or plant. A correctly woven Charter-skin, worn in the prescribed fashion, gives the Mage the actual desired shape, with all the peculiarities, perceptions, limitations, and advantages of that shape.

    This book is a theoretical examination of the art of making Charter-skins; a practical primer for the beginning shapewearer; and a compendium of complete Charter-skins, including those for the lyon, the horse, the hopping toade, the grey dove, the silver ash, and divers other useful shapes.

    The course of study contained herein, if followed with fortitude and discipline, will equip the conscientious Mage with the knowledge needed to make a first Charter-skin within three or four years.

"A useful book, that one," said the newly awake Dog, interrupting Lirael's reading by thrusting her snout across the pages, clearly demanding a morning scratch between the ears.

"Very," agreed Lirael, trying to keep reading around the Dog, without success. "Apparently if I follow the course of study in it, I'll be able to take on another shape in three or four years."

"Eighteen months," yawned the Dog sleepily. "Two years if you're lazy. Though you *wear* a Charter-skin—you don't change your own shape, as such. Make sure you start on a Charter-skin that'll be useful for exploring. You know, good at getting through small holes and so on."

"Why?" asked Lirael.

"Why?" repeated the Dog incredulously, pulling her head out from under Lirael's hand. "There's so much to see and smell here! Whole levels of the Library that no one has been into for a hundred, a thousand years! Locked rooms full of ancient secrets. Treasure! Knowledge! Fun! Do you want to be just a Third Assistant Librarian all your life?"

"Not exactly," replied Lirael stiffly. "I want to be a proper Clayr. I want to have the Sight."

"Well, maybe we'll find something that can wake it in you," declared the Dog. "I know you have to work, but there's so much other time that shouldn't go to waste. What could be better than walking where no others have walked for a thousand years?"

"I suppose I might as well," Lirael agreed, her imagination taking fire from the Dog's words. There were plenty of doors she wanted to open. There was that strange hole in the rock, for instance, down where the main spiral came to an abrupt end—

"Besides," the Dog added, interrupting her thoughts, "there are forces at work here that want you to use the book. Something freed the Stilken, and the creature's presence has woken other magics, too. That tree would not have given up the book if you weren't meant to have it."

"I suppose," said Lirael. She didn't like the idea that the Stilken had had help to break free from its prison. That implied that there was some greater force of evil down here in the Old Levels, or that some power could reach into the Clayr's Glacier from afar, despite all their wards and defenses.

If there was something like the Stilken—some Free Magic entity of great power—in the Library, Lirael felt it was her duty to find it. She felt that by defeating the Stilken, she had unconsciously taken the first step towards assuming the responsibility

for destroying anything else like the creature that might be a
threat to the Clayr.

Exploring would also fill up the time and distract her. Lirael
realized she hadn't thought much at all about Awakenings, or the
Sight, over these last few months. Creating the Dog and discov-
ering how to defeat the Stilken had filled nearly all her waking
thoughts.

"I will learn a useful Charter-skin," she declared. "And we
will explore, Dog!"

"Good!" said the Dog, and she gave a celebratory bark that
echoed around the cavern. "Now you'd better run and get washed
and changed, before Imshi wonders where you are."

"What time is it?" asked Lirael, startled. Away from the
peremptory whistle-blasts of Kirrith in the Hall of Youth, or the
chiming clock in the Reading Room, she had no idea what time
of day it was. She had thought it roughly dawn, for she felt she
hadn't had much sleep.

"One half past the . . . sixth hour of the morning," replied
the Dog, after cocking her ear, as if to some distant chime. "Give
or take . . ."

Her voice trailed off, because Lirael had already left, breaking into a somewhat limping run. The Dog sighed and launched
herself into a body-extending lope, easily catching up with Lirael
before she shut the door.

PART TWO

ANCELSTIERRE
1928 A.W.
THE OLD KINGDOM

Eighteenth Year of the Restoration of
King Touchstone I

Chapter Fourteen

PRINCE SAMETH HITS A SIX

SEVEN HUNDRED MILES south of the Clayr's Glacier, twenty-two boys were playing cricket. In the Old Kingdom, beyond the Wall that lay thirty miles to the north, it was late autumn. Here in Ancelstierre, the last days of summer were proving warm and clear, perfect for the concluding match in the fiercely contested Senior Schoolboys' Shield series, the primary focus for the sporting sixth formers of eighteen schools.

It was the last over of the match, with only one ball left to bowl, and three runs needed to win the innings, the match, and the series.

The batsman who faced that last ball was a month short of his seventeenth birthday and half an inch over six feet tall. He had tightly curling dark brown hair and distinctive black eyebrows. He was not exactly handsome, but pleasing to the eye, a striking figure in his white cricket flannels. Not that they were as crisp and starched as they had been earlier, since they were now drenched with the sweat of making seventy-four runs in partnership, sixty of them his own.

A large crowd was watching in the stands of the Bain Cricket Ground—a much larger crowd than normal for a schoolboy match, even with one of the teams coming from the nearby Dormalan School. Most of the onlookers had come to see the tall young batsman, not because he was any more talented than others on the team, but because he was a Prince. More to the point, he was a Prince of the Old Kingdom. Bain was not only the closest town to the Wall that separated Ancelstierre from that land of magic and mystery, it had also suffered nineteen years before from an incursion of Dead creatures that had been defeated only with the aid of the batsman's parents, particularly his mother.

Prince Sameth was not unaware of the curiosity the towns-folk of Bain felt towards him, but he didn't let it distract him. All his attention was on the bowler at the other end of the pitch, a fierce, redheaded boy whose ferociously quick bowling had taken three wickets already. But he seemed to be tiring, and his last over had been quite erratic, letting Sam and his batting partner, Ted Hopkiss, slog the ball all over the field in the effort to get those vital last runs. If the bowler didn't recover his strength and former precision, Sameth thought, he had a chance. Mind you, the bowler was taking his time, slowly flexing his bowling arm and looking at the clouds that were rolling in.

The weather was a bit distracting, though only to Sameth. A wind had sprung up a few minutes before. Blowing in directly from the North, it carried magic with it, picked up from the Old Kingdom and the Wall. It made the Charter mark on Sameth's forehead tingle and heightened his awareness of Death. Not that this cold presence was very strong where he was. Few people had died on the cricket pitch, at least in recent times.

At last the bowler went into his run-up, and the bright red ball came howling down the pitch, bouncing up as Sameth stepped forward to meet it. Willow met leather with a mighty crack, and the ball soared off over Sameth's left shoulder. Higher and higher, it arced over the running fielders to the stands, where it was caught by a middle-aged man, leaping out of his seat to display some long-disused cricketing form.

A six! Sameth felt the smile spread across his face as applause erupted in the stands. Ted ran down to shake his hand, babbling something, and then he was shaking hands with the opposing team and then all sorts of people as he made his way back to the changing rooms in the pavilion. In between handshakes, he looked up to where the telegraph board was clicking over. He had made sixty-six not out, a personal best, and a fitting end to his school cricket career. Probably his entire cricket career, he thought, thinking of his return to the Old Kingdom, only two months away. Cricket was not played north of the Wall.

His friend Nicholas was the first to congratulate him in the changing rooms. Nick was a superb spin bowler, but a poor batsman and an even worse fielder. He often seemed to go off in a dream, studying an insect on the ground or some strange weather pattern in the sky.

"Well done, Sam!" declared Nick, vigorously shaking his hand. "Another trophy for good old Somersby."

"It *will* be good old Somersby soon," replied Sam, easing himself onto a bench and unstrapping his pads. "Odd, isn't it? Ten years of moaning about the place, but when it's time to leave . . ."

"I know, I know," said Nick. "That's why you should come up to Corvere with me, Sam. Pretty much more of the same, university. Put off that fear of the future—"

Whatever else he was going to say was lost as the rest of the team pushed through to shake Sameth's hand. Even Mr. Cochrane, the coach and Somersby's famously irascible Games Master, deigned to clap him on the shoulder and declare, "Excellent show, Sameth."

An hour later, they were all in the school's omnibus, all damp from the sudden shower that had come with the northern wind. Patches of sun and patches of rain were alternating, sometimes only for minutes. Unfortunately, the last rainy one had come when they crossed the road to the bus.

It was a three-hour drive, almost due south to Somersby,

along the Bain High Road. So the passengers on the bus were surprised when the driver turned off the High Road just outside Bain, into a narrow, single-lane country road.

"Hold on, driver!" exclaimed Mr. Cochrane. "Where on earth are you going?"

"Detour," said the man succinctly, hardly moving his mouth. He was a replacement for Fred, the school's regular driver, who had broken his arm the day before in a fight over a disputed darts contest. "High Road's flooded at Beardsley. Heard it from a postman, back at the Cricketer's Arms."

"Very well," said Cochrane, his frown indicating the reluctance of his approval. "It is most odd. I wouldn't have thought there's been enough rain. Are you sure you know a way around, driver?"

"Yes, guv'nor," the man affirmed, something that was possibly meant to be a smile crossing his rather weasely face. "Beckton Bridge."

"Never heard of it," said Cochrane dismissively. "Still, I suppose you know best."

The boys paid little attention to this discussion, or to the road. They'd been up since four o'clock in order to get to Bain on time, and had played cricket all day. Most of them, including Nick, fell asleep. Sameth stayed awake, still buoyed up by the excitement of his winning six. He watched the rain on the windows and the countryside. They passed settled farms, the warm glow of electric light in their windows. The telegraph poles flashed by the side of the road, as did a red telephone booth as they whisked through a village.

He would be leaving all that behind soon. Modern technology like telephones and electricity simply didn't work on the other side of the Wall.

Ten minutes later, they passed another sight Sameth wouldn't see beyond the Wall. A large field full of hundreds of tents, with dripping laundry hung on every available guy rope, and a general air of disorder. The bus slowed as it passed, and Sameth saw that most of the tents had women and children clustered in their doorways, looking out mournfully into the rain. Nearly all of them had blue headscarves or hats, identifying them as Southerling refugees. More than ten thousand of them were being given temporary refuge in what the *Corvere Times* described as "the remote northern regions of the nation," which clearly meant close to the Wall.

This must be one of the refugee settlements that had sprung up in the last three years, Sameth realized, noting that the field was surrounded by a triple fence of concertina wire and that there were several policemen near the gate, the rain sluicing off their helmets and dark-blue slickers.

The Southerlings were fleeing a war among four states in the far South, across the Sunder Sea from Ancelstierre. The war had started three years previously, with a seemingly small rebellion in the Autarchy of Iskeria proving an unlikely success. That rebellion had grown to be a civil war that drew in the neighboring countries of Kalarime, Iznenia, and Korrovia, on different sides. There were at least six warring factions that Sameth knew about, ranging from the Iskerian Autarch's forces and the original Anarchist rebels to the Kalarime-backed Traditionalists and the Korrovian Imperialists.

Traditionally, Ancelstierre did not interfere with wars on the Southern Continent, trusting to its Navy and the Flying Corps to keep such trouble on the other side of the Sunder Sea. But with the war now spread across most of the continent, the only safe place for noncombatants was in Ancelstierre.

So Ancelstierre was the refugees' chosen destination. Many were turned back on the sea or at the major ports, but for every

large ship returned, a smaller vessel would make landfall somewhere on the Ancelstierran coast and disgorge the two or three
hundred refugees who had been packed aboard like sardines.

Many more drowned, or starved, but this did not discourage
the others.

Eventually, they would be rounded up and put in temporary
camps. Theoretically, they would then be eligible to become proper
immigrants to the Commonwealth of Ancelstierre, but in practice,
only those with money, connections, or useful skills ever gained
citizenship. The others stayed in the refugee camps while the
Ancelstierran government tried to work out how to send them
back to their own countries. But with the war growing worse and
getting more confused by the day, no one who had escaped it
would willingly go back. Every time mass deportment had been
attempted, it had ended in hunger strikes, riots, and every form
of possible protest.

"Uncle Edward says that Corolini chap wants to send the
Southerlings into your neck of the woods," said Nicholas sleepily,
wakened by the bus's decrease in speed. "Across the Wall. No room
for them here, he says, and lots of room in the Old Kingdom."

"Corolini is a populist rabble-rouser," replied Sameth, quoting an editorial from the *Times*. His mother—who conducted
most of the Old Kingdom's diplomacy with Ancelstierre—had an
even harsher opinion of this politician, who had risen to promi-
nence since the beginning of the Southern War. She thought he
was a dangerous egotist who would do anything to gain power.
"He doesn't know what he's talking about. They would all die in
the Borderlands. It's not safe."

"What's the problem with it?" asked Nick. He knew his
friend didn't like talking about the Old Kingdom. Sam always
said that it was not at all like Ancelstierre and that Nick
wouldn't understand. No one else knew anything much about

it, and there was little information of consequence in any library Nick had seen. The Army kept the border closed, and that was it.

"There are dangerous . . . dangerous animals and . . . um . . . things," replied Sameth. "It's like I've told you before. Guns and electricity and so on don't work. It's not like—"

"Ancelstierre," interrupted Nicholas, smiling. "You know, I've a good mind to come and visit you during the vac and see for myself."

"I wish you would," Sameth said. "I'll need to see a friendly face after six months of Ellimere's company."

"How do you know it's not your sister I want to visit?" asked Nick, with an exaggerated leer. Sam never had a good word to say about his older sister. He was about to say more, but his words were cut short as he looked out the window. Sam looked, too.

The refugee camp was long past and had given way to a fairly dense forest. The distant, rain-blurred orb of the sun hung just above the trees. Only they were both looking out the left-hand side of the bus, and the sun should have been on the right. They were going north, and must have been for some time. North, towards the Wall.

"I'd better tell Cockers," said Sameth, who was in the aisle seat. He'd just got up, and started to make his way to the front of the bus, when the engine suddenly spluttered and the bus jerked, nearly throwing Sam to the floor. The driver cursed and crashed down several gears, but the engine kept spluttering. The driver cursed again, revving the engine so hard its whine woke up anyone left asleep. Then it suddenly stopped. Both the interior light and the headlights went out, and the bus rolled to a silent stop.

"Sir!" Sam called out to Mr. Cochrane, above the sudden hubbub of waking boys. "We've been going north! I think we're near the Wall."

Cochrane, who was peering through his own window, turned back as Sam spoke and stood in the aisle, his commanding bulk enough to silence the closer boys.

"Settle down!" he said. "Thank you, Sameth. Now everyone stay in your seats, and I'll soon sort—"

Whatever he was going to say was interrupted by the sound of the driver's door, as he slammed it shut behind him. All the boys rushed to the windows, despite Cochrane's roar, and saw the driver leap the roadside wall and run off through the trees as if pursued by some mortal enemy.

"What on earth?" exclaimed Cochrane, as he turned to look out the windscreen. Whatever had scared the driver clearly didn't seem so terrible to him, since he merely opened the passenger door and stepped out into the rain, unfurling his umbrella as he did so.

As soon as he left the bus, everyone rushed to the front. Sam, from his position in the aisle, was the first to get there. Looking out, he first saw a barrier across the road, and a large red sign next to it. He couldn't quite read it, because of the rain, but he knew what it said anyway. He'd seen identical signs every holiday, when he went home to the Old Kingdom. The red signs marked the beginning of the Perimeter, the military zone that the Ancelstierran Army had established to face the Wall. Beyond that sign, the woods on either side of the road would vanish, replaced by a half-mile-wide expanse of strong points, trenches, and the coils and coils of barbed wire that stretched from the east coast to the west.

Sam remembered exactly what the sign said. Pretending he had an amazing ability to see through fogged-up windscreens, he recited the familiar warning to the others. It was important for them to know.

PERIMETER COMMAND
NORTHERN ARMY GROUP

Unauthorized egress from the Perimeter Zone
is strictly forbidden.
Anyone attempting to cross the Perimeter Zone will
be shot without warning.
Authorized travelers must report to the
Perimeter Command H.Q.
REMEMBER—NO WARNING WILL BE MADE

A moment of silence met this recitation, as the seriousness
of it sank in. Then a babble of questions broke out, but Sam didn't
answer. He had thought the driver had run away because he was
afraid of being so close to the Wall. But what if he had brought
them there on purpose? And why had he run away from the two
red-capped military policemen who were walking up from their
sentry box?

Sameth's family had many enemies in the Old Kingdom.
Some were human, and might be able to pass as harmless in
Ancelstierre. Some were not, but they might be powerful enough
to cross the Wall and get this little distance south. Especially on
a day when the wind blew from the north.

Not bothering to get his raincoat, Sam jumped down from
the bus and hurried over to where the two military policemen
had just met Mr. Cochrane. Or rather, to where the MP sergeant
had started to shout at Cochrane.

"Get everyone off that bus and get them moving back as
quick as you can," the sergeant shouted. "Run as far as you can,
then walk. Got it?"

"Why?" asked Mr. Cochrane, bristling. Like most of the
teachers and staff at Somersby, he wasn't from the North, and he
had no idea about the Wall, the Perimeter, or the Old Kingdom.
He had always treated Sameth as he treated the school's other
Prince, who was an albino from far-off Karshmel—like an

adopted child who wasn't quite a member of the family.

"Just do it!" ordered the sergeant. He seemed nervous, Sameth noted. His revolver holster was open, and he kept looking around at the trees. Like most soldiers on the Perimeter—but totally unlike any other units of the Ancelstierran Army—he also wore a long sword-bayonet on his left hip, and a mail coat over his khaki battledress, though he'd kept his MP's red cap, rather than wearing the usual neck- and nasal-barred helmet of the Perimeter garrison. Sam noted that neither of the two men had a Charter mark on his forehead.

"That's not good enough," Cochrane protested. "I insist on speaking to an officer. I can't have my boys running about in the rain!"

"We'd better do as the sergeant says," said Sam, coming up behind him. "There is something in the wood—and it's getting closer."

"Who are you?" demanded the sergeant, drawing his sword. The lance-corporal with him instantly followed suit, and started to sidle around behind. Both of them were looking at Sam's forehead, and the Charter mark that was just visible under his Cricket XI cap.

"Prince Sameth of the Old Kingdom," said Sam. "I suggest you call Major Dwyer of the Scouts, or General Tindall's head-quarters, and tell them I'm here—and that there are at least three Dead Hands in the woods over there."

"That's torn it!" swore the sergeant. "We knew something was up with this wind. How did they get—Well, it doesn't matter. Harris, double back to the post and alert HQ. Tell them we've got Prince Sameth, a bunch of schoolkids, and at least three category-A intruders. Use a pigeon and the rocket. The phone'll be out for sure. Move!"

The lance-corporal was gone before the sergeant's mouth

shut, and just as Cochrane began.

"Sameth! What are you going on about?"

"There's no time to explain," replied Sam urgently. He could sense Dead Hands—bodies infused with spirits called from Death—moving through the forest, parallel to the road. They didn't seem to have sensed the living yet, but once they did, they would be there within minutes. "We have to get everyone out of here—we have to get as far away from the Wall as we can."

"But . . . But . . ." blustered Cochrane, red-faced and astounded at the impertinence of one of his own boys ordering him around. He would have said more, if the sergeant hadn't drawn his revolver and calmly said, "Get them going now, sir, or I'll shoot you where you stand."

Chapter Fifteen

THE DEAD ARE MANY

FIVE MINUTES LATER, the entire team was out in the rain, on the road, jogging south. At Sameth's suggestion, they had armed themselves with cricket bats, metal-tipped cricket stumps, and cricket balls. The MP sergeant ran with them, his revolver continuing to silence Cochrane's protests.

The boys took it all as a bit of a joke at first, with much bravado and carrying-on. But as it got darker and the rain got heavier, they grew quieter. The jokes stopped altogether when four quick shots were heard behind them, and then a distant, anguished scream.

Sameth and the sergeant exchanged a look that combined fear and a dreadful knowledge. The shots and the scream must have come from Lance-Corporal Harris, who had gone back to the post.

"Is there a stream or other running water near here?" panted Sameth, mindful of the warning rhyme he'd known since childhood about the Dead. The sergeant shook his head but didn't answer. He kept glancing back over his shoulder, almost losing his balance as they ran. A little while after they heard the scream, he saw what he was looking for and pointed it out to Sameth: three red parachute flares drifting down from a few miles north.

"Harris must have got the pigeon off, at least," he puffed. "Or maybe the telephone worked, since his pistol did. They'll have the reserve company and a platoon of Scouts out here soon, sir."

"I hope so," replied Sameth. He could sense the Dead on the road behind them now, coming up quickly. There seemed to be no hope of safety anywhere ahead. No stout farmhouse or barn, or a stream, whose running water the Dead couldn't cross. In fact, the road went down to become a sunken lane, even darker and more closed in, a perfect site for an ambush.

As Sam thought of that, he felt his sense of Death suddenly alter. It disoriented him at first, till he realized what it was. A Dead spirit had just risen in front of them, somewhere in the darkness around the high-banked road. Worse than that, it was new, brought out of Death at that very moment. These were no self-willed Dead spirits that had infiltrated through the Perimeter. They were Dead Hands, raised by a necromancer on the Ancelstierran side of the Wall. Controlled by the necromancer's mind, they were much more dangerous than rogue spirits.

"Stop!" screamed Sam, his voice cutting through the beat of rain and footsteps on the asphalt. "They're ahead of us. We have to leave the road!"

"Who are ahead, boy?" shouted Cochrane, furious again. "This has gone quite far enough. . . ."

His voice faltered as a figure stumbled out of the shadows ahead, out into the middle of the road. It was human, or had once been human, but now its arms were hanging threads of flesh, and its head was mostly bare skull, all deep eye hollows and shining teeth. It was unquestionably dead, and the reek of decomposition rolled off it, over the soft smell of the rain. Clods of earth fell from it as it moved, showing that it had just dug itself out of the ground.

"Left!" shouted Sam, pointing. "Everyone go left!"

His shout broke the silent tableau into action, boys leaping over the stone wall that bordered the road. Cochrane was one of the first over, throwing his umbrella aside.

The Dead thing moved, too, breaking into a shambling run as it sensed the Life it craved. The sergeant propped himself against the wall and waited till it was ten feet away. Then he emptied his heavy .455 revolver into the creature's torso, five shots in quick succession, accompanied by a gasp of relief that the weapon actually worked.

The creature was knocked back and finally down, but the sergeant didn't wait. He'd been on the Perimeter long enough to know that it would get back up again. Bullets could stop Dead Hands, but only if the creatures were shredded to pieces. White phosphorus grenades worked better, burning them to ash— when they worked. Guns and grenades and all such standards of Ancelstierran military technology tended to fail the closer they got to the Wall and the Old Kingdom.

"Up the hill!" shouted Sam, pointing to a rise in the ground ahead, where the forest thinned out. If they could make it there, at least they could see what was coming and have the slight advantage of high ground.

A harsh, inhuman cry rose behind them as they ran, a sound like a broken bellows accidentally trodden on, more squeal than scream. Sam knew it came from the desiccated lungs of a Dead Hand. This one was farther to the right than the one the sergeant had shot. At the same time, he sensed others, moving around to the right and left, beginning to encircle the hill.

"There's a necromancer back there," he said as they ran. "And there must be a lot of dead bodies, not too far gone."

"A truck full of those Southerlings . . . ran off the road near here, six weeks ago," said the sergeant, speaking rapidly between breaths. "Nineteen killed. Bit of a . . . mystery where they was going . . . anyway . . . churchwarden at Archell wouldn't . . . have 'em . . . the Army crematorium neither . . . so they was buried next to the road."

"Stupid!" cried Sameth. "It's too close to the Wall! They should have been burnt!"

"Bloody paper-pushers," puffed the sergeant, nimbly ducking under a branch. "Regulations say no burying within the . . . Perimeter. But this is . . . outside, see?"

Sameth didn't answer. They were climbing the hill itself now, and he needed all his breath. He sensed there were at least twelve Dead Hands behind them now, and three or four on each side, going wide. And there was something, some presence that was probably the necromancer, back where the bodies were—or had been—buried.

The top of the hill was clear of trees, save for a few wind-blown saplings. Before they reached it, the sergeant called a halt, just short of the crest.

"Right! Get in close. Are we missing anyone? How many—"

"Sixteen, including Mr. Cochrane," said Nick, who was a lightning calculator. Cochrane glared at him but was silent, ducking his head back down as he tried to get his breath back. "Everyone's here."

"How long have we got, sir?" the sergeant asked Sam, as they both looked back down into the trees. It was hard to see anything. Visibility was reduced by both the increasingly heavy rain and the onset of night.

"The first two or three will be on us in a few minutes," said Sameth grimly. "The rain will slow them a little. We'll have to knock them down and run stumps through them, to try to keep them pinned. Nick, organize everyone into groups of three. Two batsmen and someone to hold the stumps ready. No, Hood—go with Asmer. When they come, I'll distract them with a . . . I'll distract them. Then the batsman must hit as hard as they can straight off, in the legs, and then hammer a stump through each arm and leg."

Sameth paused as he saw one of the boys eyeing the two-and-a-half-foot-long wooden stump with its metal spike on the end. From the expression on the boy's face, it was clear he couldn't imagine hammering it through anything.

"These are not people!" Sam shouted. "They're already Dead. If you don't fight them, they will kill us. Think of them as wild animals, and remember, we're fighting for our lives!"

One of the boys started crying, without making a noise, the tears falling silently down his face. At first Sam thought it was the rain, till he noticed the despairing stare that signified complete and utter terror.

He was about to try some more encouraging words when Nick pointed downhill and shouted, "Here they come!"

Three Dead Hands were coming out from the treeline, shambling like drunks, their arms and legs clearly not fully under control. The bodies had been too broken up in the crash, Sam thought, gauging their strength. That was good. It would make them slower and more uncoordinated.

"Nick, your team can take the one on the left," he commanded, speaking quickly. "Ted, yours the middle, and Jack's the right. Go for their knees and hammer the stumps home as soon as you get them down. Don't let them get a grip on you— they're much stronger than they look. Everyone else—including you, please, Sergeant, and Mr. Cochrane—hold back and help any team that gets in trouble."

"Yes, sir!" replied the sergeant. Cochrane merely nodded dumbly, staring at the approaching Dead Hands. For the first time in Sam's memory, the man's face was not flushed red. It was white, almost as white as the sickeningly pallid flesh of the approaching Dead.

"Wait for my order," shouted Sam. At the same time, he reached into the Charter. It was impossible to reach in most of

Ancelstierre, but this close to the Wall, it was merely difficult, rather like trying to swim down to the bottom of a deep river.

Sameth found the Charter and took a moment's comfort from the familiar touch of it, its permanence and its totality linking him to everything in existence. Then he summoned the marks he wanted, holding them in his mind while he formed their names in his throat. When he had everything ready, he punched out his right hand, three fingers splayed, each finger indicating one of the approaching Dead creatures.

"Anet! Calew! Ferhan!" he spat, and the marks flew from his fingers as shining silver blades, whistling through the air quicker than any eye could follow. Each one struck a Dead Hand, blowing a fist-sized hole straight through decaying flesh. All three staggered back, and one fell down, waving its arms and legs like a beetle thrown on its back.

"Bloody hell!" exclaimed one of the boys next to Sam.

"Now!" shouted Sam, and the schoolboys rushed forward with a roar, waving their makeshift weapons. Sam and the sergeant went with them, but Cochrane struck out on his own, running down the hill at a right angle to everyone else.

Then there was a blur of screaming, bats rising and falling, the dull thud of stumps being driven through Dead flesh and into the sodden ground.

Sam experienced it all in a strange frenzy, such a tangled mess of sound, images, and emotion that he was never really sure what happened. He seemed to come out of this concentrated fury to find himself helping Druitt Minor hammer a stump through the forearm of a writhing creature. Even with a stump through each limb, it still struggled, breaking one stump and almost getting free, before some of the boys in reserve cleverly rolled a boulder over the loose arm.

Everyone was cheering, Sam realized, as he stepped back and

wiped the rain off his face. Everyone except him, because he could sense more Dead, coming up from the road and on the other side of the hill. A quick survey showed that there were only three stumps left, and two of the five bats were broken.

"Get back," he ordered, quelling the cheering. "There's more on the way."

As they moved back, Nick and the sergeant came up close to Sam. Nick spoke first, quietly asking, "What do we do now, Sam? Those things are still moving! They'll get free within half an hour."

"Troops from the Perimeter will be here before then," muttered Sam, glancing at the sergeant, who nodded in affirmation. "It's the new ones coming up I'm worried about. The only thing I can think of doing . . ."

"What?" asked Nick, as Sam stopped in mid-sentence.

"These are all Dead Hands, not free-willed Dead," replied Sam. "Newly made ones. The spirits in them are just whatever the necromancer could call quickly, so they're neither powerful nor smart. If I could get to the necromancer who's controlling them, they would probably attack each other, or wander in circles. Quite a few might even snap back into Death."

"Well, let's get this necromancer chap!" declared Nick stoutly. His voice was steady, but he couldn't help a nervous look back down the hill.

"It's not as easy as that," said Sam absently. Most of his attention was on the Dead Hands he could sense around them. There were ten down near the road, and six on the other side of the hill somewhere. Both groups were getting themselves into ragged lines. Obviously, the necromancer planned to have them all attack at once, from both sides.

"It's not so easy," Sam repeated. "The necromancer is down there somewhere, physically at least. But he's almost certainly in

Death, leaving his body protected by a spell or some sort of bodyguard. To get at him, I'll have to go into Death myself—and I don't have a sword, or bells, or anything."

"Go into Death?" asked Nick, his voice rising half an octave. He was clearly about to say something else but he looked down at the staked-out Dead Hands and shut up.

"Not even time to cast a diamond of protection," Sam muttered to himself. He had never actually been into Death by himself before. He'd gone only with his mother, the Abhorsen. Now he wished desperately that she were here. But she wasn't, and he couldn't think of anything else to do. He could almost certainly get away himself, but he couldn't leave the others.

"Nick," he said, making up his mind. "I am going to go into Death. While I'm there, I won't be able to see or sense anything here. My body will seem to be frozen, so I'll need you—and you, sergeant—to guard me as best you can. I plan to be back before the Dead get here, but if I'm not, try to slow them down. Throw cricket balls, stones, and anything else you can find. If you can't stop them, grab my shoulder, but don't touch me otherwise."

"Right-oh," replied Nick. He was clearly puzzled, and afraid, but he put out his hand. Sam took it, and they shook hands, while the other boys looked at them curiously, or stared out into the rain. Only the sergeant moved, handing Sam his sword, hilt first.

"You'll need this more than I do, sir," he said. Then, echoing Sam's own thoughts, he added, "I wish your mum was here. Good luck, sir."

"Thanks," said Sam, but he handed the sword back. "I'm afraid only a spelled sword would help me. You keep it."

The sergeant nodded and took the sword. Sam dropped into a boxer's defensive stance and closed his eyes. He felt for the boundary between Life and Death and found it easily, for a moment experiencing the strange sensation of rain falling down the back of his neck while his face was hit by the terrible chill of Death, where it never rained.

Exerting all his willpower, Sam pushed towards the cold, making his spirit cross into Death. Then, without warning, he was there, and the cold was all around him, not just on his face. His eyes flashed open, and he saw the flat grey light of Death and felt the tug of the river's current at his legs. In the distance, he heard the roar of the First Gate, and shivered.

Back in Life, Nick and the sergeant saw Sam's entire body stiffen suddenly. A fog came from nowhere, twining up his legs like a vine. As they kept staring, frost formed on his face and hands—an icy coat that was not washed off by the rain.

"I'm not sure I can believe what I'm seeing," whispered Nick, as he looked away from Sam and down at the approaching Dead.

"You'd better believe it," said the sergeant grimly. "Because they'll kill you whether you believe in them or not."

Chapter Sixteen

INTO DEATH

APART FROM THE distant roar of the waterfall that marked the First Gate, it was completely silent in Death. Sam stood still, staying close to the border with Life, listening and looking. But he couldn't see very far in the peculiar grey light that seemed to flatten everything out and warp perspective. All he could see was the river around him, the water completely dark save where it rushed in white rapids around his knees.

Carefully, Sam began to walk along the very edge of Death, fighting the current that tried to suck him under and carry him off. He guessed that the necromancer would also be staying close to the border with Life, though there was no guarantee that Sam was going in the right direction to find him, or her. He wasn't skilled enough to know where he was in Death in relation to Life, except for the point where he would return to his own body.

He moved much more warily than he had when last in Death. That was a year past, with his mother, the Abhorsen, at his side. It felt very different now that he was alone and unarmed. It was true he could gain some control over the Dead by whistling or clapping his hands, but without the bells he could neither command nor banish them. And while he was a more than proficient Charter Mage, this necromancer could easily be a Free Magic adept, completely outclassing him.

His only real chance would be to creep up on the necromancer and catch him unawares, and that would be possible only if the necromancer were totally focused on finding and binding Dead spirits. Even worse, Sam realized, he was making a lot of noise by wading at right angles to the current. No matter how slowly he tried to wade, he couldn't help splashing. It was hard work, too, physically and mentally, as the river tugged at him and filled him with thoughts of weariness and defeat. It would be easier to lie down and let the river take him; he could never win. . . .

Sameth scowled and forced himself to keep wading, suppressing the morbid pressure on his mind. There was still no sign of the necromancer, and Sam began to worry that his enemy might not be in Death at all. Perhaps he was out there in Life even now, directing the Dead to attack. Nick and the sergeant would do their best to protect his body, Sam knew, but they would be defenseless against the Free Magic of the necromancer.

For a moment, Sam thought about going back—then a slight sound returned all his attention to Death. He heard a distant, pure note that seemed far away at first but was moving rapidly towards him. Then he saw the ripples that accompanied the sound, ripples that ran at a right angle to the flow of the river— straight towards him!

Sam clapped his hands to his ears, grinding his palms into his head. He knew that long, clear call. It came from Kibeth, the third of the seven bells. Kibeth, the Walker.

The single note slid between Sam's fingers and into his ears, filling his mind with its strength and purity. Then the note changed and became a whole series of sounds that were almost the same, but not. Together they formed a rhythm that shot through Sam's limbs, tweaking a muscle here and a muscle there, rocking him forward, whether he liked it or not.

Desperately, Sam tried to purse his lips, to whistle a counterspell or even just a random noise that might disrupt the bell's call. But his cheeks wouldn't move, and his legs were already stumping through the water, carrying him quickly towards the source of the sound, towards the wielder of the bell.

Too quickly, for the river found its chance in Sam's sudden clumsiness. The current surged and wove itself between Sam's feet. Caught on one leg, he teetered for a moment, then went over like a bowling pin, crashing into the river. The cold stabbed into him like a thousand thin knives, all over his body.

Kibeth's call was cut off in that moment, but it still held him, as if he were a fish on a line. Kibeth tried to walk him back, even as the current tried to keep him in its grip. Sam himself fought only to get his head clear, to get a breath of air before he was forced to take a breath of water. But the effects of the bell and the current were too much, locking him in a struggle in which he could not control his body. And while he could no longer hear Kibeth, his whole body trembled, shot through with the tremendous power of the First Gate, the waterfall that was sucking him deeper and closer with every second.

Desperately, Sam thrust his face towards the surface, and for a moment he broke free to snatch a breath. But at that instant, he heard the roar of the Gate rise to a crescendo. He was too close, he knew, and at any moment he would be swept through the Gate. Without bells, he would be easy prey for any denizen of the Second Precinct. Even if he escaped them, he was probably already too weak to resist the pull of the river. It would take him on, all the way through to the Ninth Gate and the ultimate death that lay beyond.

Then something grabbed his right wrist and he came to a sudden stop, the river raging and frothing impotently about him. Sam almost struggled against his rescuer, for fear of what it might be, but his fear of the river was greater and he needed to breathe so desperately that he could think of nothing else. So he simply fought to get a proper footing, and cough up at least some of the water that had managed to get into his throat and lungs.

Then he realized that steam was billowing from his sleeve, and his wrist was burning. He cried out. Fear of his captor rose in him again, and he was almost too afraid to look and see who—or what—it might be.

Slowly Sam raised his head. He was being held by the necromancer he'd hoped to surprise. A thin, balding man, who wore leather armor with red-enameled plates for reinforcement—and a bandolier of bells across his chest.

Here in Death, Free Magic magnified his stature, cloaking him with a great shadow of fire and darkness that moved as he moved, transforming his presence into something truly terrible and cruel. The touch of his hand blistered Sam's wrist, and flames burnt where the whites of his eyes should be.

In his left hand he held a sword level with Sam's neck, the sharp edge a few inches from his throat. Dark flames ran slowly down the blade like mercury and fell to the surface of the river, where they continued to burn as the current carried them away.

Sam coughed again, not because he needed to, but to cover an attempt to reach into the Charter. He had hardly begun when the sword swung even closer, the acrid fumes of the ensorceled blade making him cough for real.

"No," said the necromancer, his voice redolent with Free Magic, his breath carrying the reek of drying blood. Desperately, Sam tried to think of what he could do. He couldn't reach the Charter, and he couldn't fight barehanded against that sword. He couldn't even move, for that matter, as his sword-arm was held impossibly still in the necromancer's burning grasp.

"You will return to Life and seek me out," ordered the necromancer, his voice low and hard, supremely confident. It wasn't just words either, Sam realized. He felt a compulsion to do exactly what the necromancer said. It was a Free Magic spell—but one that Sam knew would not be complete till it was sealed with the power of Saraneth, the sixth bell. And there was his chance, because the necromancer would have to let go of Sam or sheathe his sword in order to wield the bell.

Let me go, Sam wished fervently, trying not to tense his muscles too much and give his intentions away. Let me go.

But the necromancer chose to sheathe his sword instead, and draw the second-largest of the bells with his right hand. Saraneth, the Binder. With it he would bind Sam to his will, though it was strange that he wanted Sam to return to Life. Necromancers did not normally care for living servants.

His grip on Sam's wrist did not slacken. The pain there was intense, so bad that it had gone beyond bearing, and his mind had decided to shut it out. If he hadn't still been able to see his fingers he would have believed that his hand had been burnt off at the wrist.

The necromancer carefully opened the pouch that held Saraneth. But before he could transfer his grip to grasp the bell by its clapper and pull it out, Sam threw himself backwards and scissored his legs around the necromancer's waist.

Both of them plunged into the icy water, the necromancer sending up a huge plume of steam as he hit. Sam was underneath, the water instantly filling his mouth and nose, beating at the last breath in his lungs. He could feel the flesh of his thighs burning, even through the cold, but he did not let go. He felt the necromancer twisting and turning to get free, and through half-closed eyes he saw that under the river, the necromancer was a shape of fire and darkness, more monstrous and much less human than he had seemed before.

With his free hand, Sam desperately clawed at the necromancer's bandolier, trying to get one of the bells. But they felt strange, the ebony handles biting to his touch, quite unlike the smooth, Charter-spelled mahogany of his mother's bells. His fingers couldn't close on any handle, his legs were slowly being unlocked by the necromancer's inhuman strength, the grip on his wrist was unrelenting—and his breath was almost gone.

Then the current quickened, picking them both up and turning them into a dizzy spin, till Sam couldn't tell which way he could stretch to find a breath. Then they were hurtling down—down through the waterfall of the First Gate.

The waterfall spun them about viciously, and then they were in the Second Precinct, and Sam couldn't hold the necromancer anymore. The man got free of Sam's scissored legs and elbowed Sam savagely in the stomach, driving the last pathetic remnant of air from his lungs in one choked-off explosion of bubbles.

Sam tried to hit back, but he was already sucking in water instead of air, and his strength was almost gone. He felt the necromancer let go and slip away from him, moving through the water like a snake, and he lost all thought save the desperate urge for survival.

A second later, he broke the surface, coughing madly, getting as much water as air. At the same time, he fought to keep his balance against the current and locate his enemy. Hope sparked in him as he caught no sign of the necromancer. And he seemed to be close to the First Gate. It was hard to tell in the Second Precinct, where some quality of the light made it impossible to see farther than you could touch.

But Sam could see the froth of the waterfall, and when he stumbled forward, he touched the rushing water of the First Gate, and all he had to remember was the spell that would let him past. It was from *The Book of the Dead*, which he had begun to study last year. As he thought of it, pages appeared in his mind, the words of the Free Magic spell shining, ready for him to say.

He opened his mouth—and two burning hands came down on his shoulders, driving him face-first into the river. This time he had no chance of holding his breath, and his scream was nothing more than bubbles and froth, barely disturbing the flow of the river.

It was pain that brought him back to consciousness. Pain in his ankles, and a strange feeling in his head. It took him a moment to realize that he was still in Death—but back at the border with Life. And the necromancer was holding him upside down by the ankles, water still pouring from his ears and nose.

The necromancer was speaking again, speaking words of power that rose up around Sam like bands of steel. He could feel them pressing against him, making him their prisoner, and he knew that he should try to resist. But he couldn't. He could barely keep his eyes open, even that small thing taking all the willpower and energy he had left.

Still the necromancer kept on speaking, the words weaving around and around him, till Sam finally understood the single most important thing: the necromancer was sending him back into Life, and this binding was to make sure that he did what he was told.

But the binding didn't matter. Nothing mattered, save that he was going back to Life. He didn't care that back in Life, he would have to follow some terrible purpose of the sorcerer. He would be back in Life. . . .

The necromancer let go of one ankle, and Sam swung like a pendulum, his head just brushing the surface of the river. The necromancer seemed to have grown much taller, for he wasn't holding his arm very high. Or perhaps, Sam thought muzzily through the pain and shock, he was the one who had shrunk.

"You will come to me in Life, near where the road sinks and

the graves lie broken," ordered the necromancer finally, when the spell had settled on Sam so tightly that he felt like a fly trussed up by a spider. But it had to be sealed by Saraneth. Sam tried to struggle as he saw the bell come out, but his body wouldn't respond. He tried to reach the Charter, but instead of the cool comfort of the endless flow of marks, he felt a great whirlpool of living fire, a maelstrom that threatened to maim his mind as much as his body had already been burnt.

Saraneth sounded, deep and low, and Sam screamed. Some instinct helped him hit the one note that would be most at discord with the bell. The scream cut through Saraneth's commanding tone, and the bell jarred in the necromancer's hand, becoming suddenly shrill and raucous. Instantly, he let go of Sam, his free hand stilling the clapper, for a bell gone awry could have disastrous consequences for its wielder.

When the bell was finally still, the necromancer turned his attention back to the boy. But there was no sign of him, and no chance the current could have taken him out of sight so soon.

Chapter Seventeen

NICHOLAS AND THE NECROMANCER

S AM RETURNED TO Life to hear the harsh tap-tap-tap of machine-gun fire and to see the landscape turned black and white by the stark brilliance of the parachute flares that were falling slowly through the rain.

Ice cracked as he moved, the frost on his clothes crazing into strange patterns. He took half a step forward and fell to his knees, sobbing with pain and shock as his fingers scrabbled at the muddy earth, seeking comfort from the feel of Life.

Slowly he became aware that there were arms around him, and people speaking. But he couldn't hear properly, because the necromancer's words kept repeating in his head, telling him what he must do. He tried to speak himself, through teeth that chattered with cold, unconsciously imitating the rhythm of the gunfire.

"Necromancer . . . sunken road . . . near graves," he said haltingly, not really knowing what he was saying or whom he was talking to. Someone touched his wrist and he screamed, the pain blinding him more than the flares that continued to blossom in the sky above. Then, after the brightness, there was sudden darkness. Sam had fainted.

"He's hurt," said Nick, staring at the blistered finger-marks on Sam's wrist. "Burnt somehow."

"What?" asked the sergeant. He was staring down the slope, watching red tracer rounds fly in low arcs from the neighboring hill down into and along the road. Every now and then one would be accompanied by the sudden bang, whoosh, and blinding sunburst of white phosphorus. Clearly the troops from the Perimeter were fighting their way towards where the sergeant and the boys were. What worried the sergeant was the way the machine-gunners were traversing their fire to the left and right of the road.

"Sam's burnt," replied Nick, unable to tear his eyes off the livid marks on his friend's wrist. "We have to do something."

"We sure do," said the sergeant, suddenly faceless again as the last flare fizzled out. "The boys down there are driving the Dead towards us—and they must think we're already done for, because they're not being real careful. We'll be taking rounds any minute now if we don't clear off."

As if to punctuate his remark, another flare arced up overhead, and a sudden flurry of tracer shot over their heads with a whip and a crack. Everybody ducked, and the sergeant shouted, "Down! Get down!"

In the light of the new flare, Nick saw dark shapes emerge from the trees and start up the hill, their telltale shambling gait showing what they were. At the same time, one of the boys farther around the hill screamed out, "They're coming up behind! Lots of—"

Whatever he was saying was drowned out by more machine-gun fire, long bursts of tracer that drew lines of red light right through the Dead, clearly hitting them many times. They twitched and staggered under the multiple impacts, but still they came on.

"Got 'em enfiladed from that hill," said the sergeant. "But they'll get here before the guns rip them apart. I've seen it before. And we'll get shot to pieces as well."

He spoke slowly, almost dumbly, and Nick realized that he wasn't able to think—that his brain had become saturated with danger and could not deal with the situation.

"Can't we signal the soldiers somehow?" he shouted above yet another burst of fire. Both the dark silhouettes of the Dead and the momentarily bright shifting lines of tracer were advancing towards them at an inexorable rate, like something slow but unstoppable, a hypnotic instrument of fate.

One line of tracer suddenly swung farther up towards them, and bullets ricocheted off stone and earth, whistling past Nick's head. He pressed himself further into the mud, and pulled Sam closer, too, shielding his unconscious friend with his own body.

"Can't we signal?" Nick repeated frantically, his voice muffled, mouth tasting dirt.

The sergeant didn't answer. Nick looked across and saw that he was lying still. His red-banded cap had come off, and his head was in a pool of blood, black in the flare light. Nick couldn't tell if he was still breathing.

Hesitantly, he reached out towards the sergeant, pushing his arm through the mud, dreadful visions of bullets smashing through the bone making him keep it as low as possible. His fingers touched metal, the hilt of the man's sword. He would have flinched and drawn back, but at that moment someone screamed behind him, a scream of such terror that his fingers convulsively gripped the weapon.

Twisting around, he saw one of the boys silhouetted, grappling with a larger figure. It had him gripped around the neck and was shaking him around like a milk shake.

Without thinking of getting shot, Nick leapt up to help. Even as he did so, other boys jumped up, too, hacking at the Dead Hand with bats, stumps, and rocks.

Within seconds they had it down and stumped through, but not quickly enough to save its victim. Harry Benlet's neck was broken, and he would never take three wickets in a single afternoon ever again, or hurdle every desk in the exam hall at Somersby just for the fun of it.

The fight with the Hand had taken them to the crest of the hill, and there Nick saw that there were Dead on both sides. Only the ones on the forward slope were being slowed by gunfire. He could see where the soldiers were firing from, and could make out groups of them. There were several machine-guns on the neighboring hill, and at least a hundred soldiers were advancing through the trees on either side of the road.

As Nick watched, he saw one line of tracer suddenly swing up towards them. It got within thirty yards and suddenly stopped. It was too far to see clearly with the rain, but Nick realized that the gun had only stopped for reloading or to shift the tripod, as soldiers moved swiftly around it. Obviously they had seen a target of opportunity: figures silhouetted on the hilltop.

"Move!" he shouted, rushing down the side of the hill in a half-crouch. The others followed in a mad, sliding dash that ended only when several boys crashed into each other and fell over.

A moment later, tracer shot overhead and the hilltop exploded in a spray of water, mud, and ricocheting bullets.

Nick instinctively ducked, though he was well down the slope. In that second, he realized three terrible facts: he had left Sam behind, halfway around the hill; they absolutely had to signal the soldiers to avoid getting shot; and even if they kept moving, the Dead would catch them before the soldiers finished off the Dead.

But with those dreadful realizations came sudden energy, and a determination Nick had never known, a clarity of thought that he'd never experienced before.

"Ted, get out your matches," he ordered, knowing Ted's affectation of smoking a pipe, though he was no good at it.

"Everyone else, get out anything you've got that's dry and will burn. Paper, whatever!"

Everyone clustered around as he spoke, their fear-filled faces revealing their eagerness to be doing something. Letters were proffered, dog-eared playing cards, and after a moment's hesitation pages torn from a notebook that had up till then contained what its owner imagined was his deathless prose. Then came the prize of the lot, a hip flask of brandy from, of all people, the very rules-conscious Cooke Minor.

The first three matches fizzled out in the rain, increasing everyone's anxiety. Then Ted used his cap to shield the fourth. It lit nicely, as did the brandy-soaked paper. A bright fire sprang up, of orange flames tinged with brandy blue, suddenly bringing color back to the monochrome landscape, lit by the seemingly endless succession of parachute flares.

"Right," snapped Nick. "Ted, will you and Mike crawl around and drag Sam back here? Stay off the crest. And do be careful of his wrists—he's burnt."

"What are you going to do?" asked Ted, hesitating as more tracer rounds flew over the hill, and white phosphorus grenades exploded in the distance. Clearly he was afraid to go but didn't want to admit it.

"I'm going to try to find the necromancer, the man who controls the things out there," said Nick, brandishing the sword. "I suggest everyone else start singing, so the Army knows there are real people here, by the fire. You'll have to keep the creatures away, too, though I'm going to try to draw the closer ones after me."

"Sing?" asked Cooke Minor. He seemed quite calm, possibly because he'd drunk half the contents of his hip flask before handing it over. "Sing what?"

"The school song," replied Nick over his shoulder as he

headed down the hill. "It's probably the only thing everybody knows."

To keep out of the way of the machine-guns, Nick ran around the hill before he headed down, towards the Dead, who were now behind their original position. As he ran, he waved the sword above his head and shouted, meaningless words that were half-drowned by the constant chatter of the guns.

He was halfway to the closest Hands when the singing started, loud enough to be heard even above the gunfire, the boys singing with a volume greater than the Somersby choirmaster would have believed possible.

Snatches of the words followed Nick as he dummied a left turn in front of the Hands and then darted right, turning back towards the trees and the road.

"Choose the path that honor takes—"

He slowed to avoid a tree trunk. It was much darker among the trees, the flare light diminished by the foliage overhead. Nick risked a glimpse behind and was both pleased and terrified to see that at least some of the Dead had turned and were following him. Terror was the stronger emotion, making him run faster between the trees than common sense called for.

"Play the game for its own sakes—"

The words of the school song were suddenly cut off as Nick left the trees, smacked into a stone wall, tumbled over it, and fell down six or seven feet into the sunken road. The sword spun out of his hand, and his palms skidded across asphalt, which took off most of the skin.

He lay on the road for a moment, gathering his wits, then started to get up. He was on his hands and knees when he became aware that someone was standing right in front of him. Leather boots, with metal plates at the knee, clanked as whoever it was stepped forward.

"So, you have come as ordered, even without Saraneth to seal the pledge," said the man, his voice somehow turning off all the other sounds that had filled Nick's ears. Gunfire, grenade explosions, the singing—all of it was gone. All he could hear was that terrible voice, a voice that filled him with indescribable fear.

Nick had started to lift his head as the man spoke, but now he was afraid to look. Instinctively he knew that this was the necromancer he'd so foolishly sought. Now all he could do was hang his head, the peak of his cricket cap shielding his face from what he knew would be a terrible gaze.

"Lift up your hand," ordered the necromancer, the words as piercing as hot wires through Nick's brain. Slowly, the boy knelt as if in prayer, his head still bowed—and he held out his right hand, bloody from the fall.

The necromancer's hand slowly came to meet it, palm outwards. For a moment, Nick thought he was going to shake hands, and he suddenly thought of the pattern in the terrible burns on Sam's wrists. A pattern of finger-marks! But he couldn't move. His body was locked in place by the power of the necromancer's words.

The necromancer's hand stopped several inches away, and something quivered under the skin of his palm, like a parasite trying to get out. Then it was free, a sliver of silver metal that slowly oriented itself towards Nick's open hand. It hung suspended for another second, then it suddenly leapt across the gap.

Nick felt it strike his hand, felt it break through his skin and enter his bloodstream. He screamed, his body arched back in convulsions, and for the first time the necromancer saw his face.

"You are not the Prince!" shouted the necromancer, and his sword flashed through the air, straight at Nick's wrist. But it stopped suddenly, less than a finger's width away, as the convulsions stopped and the boy looked up at him calmly, cradling his hand to his chest.

Inside that hand, the sliver of arcane metal swam, negotiating the complex pathway of the boy's veins. It was weak here, on the wrong side of the Wall, but not too weak to reach its ultimate destination.

It hit Nicholas Sayre's heart a minute later, and lodged there. A minute later still, puffs of thick, white smoke began to issue from his mouth.

Hedge waited, watching the smoke. But the white smoke suddenly dissipated, and Hedge felt the wind swing around to the east, and his own power diminish. He heard the sound of many hob-nailed boots farther up the road, and the whoosh of a flare being fired directly overhead.

Hedge hesitated for a moment, then leapt up the embankment with inhuman dexterity, into the trees. Lurking there, he watched as soldiers cautiously approached the unconscious boy. Some of them had rifles with bayonets fixed, and there were two with Lewin light machine-guns. These were no threat to Hedge, but there were others there, those who wielded proper swords that bore glowing Charter marks, and shields that carried the symbol of the Perimeter Scouts. These men had the Charter mark on their foreheads, and were practiced Charter Mages, even if the Army denied that any such thing existed.

There were enough of them to hold him off, Hedge knew. His Dead Hands were almost all gone, too, either immobilized in some way he still didn't understand, or driven back into Death when their newly occupied bodies were too damaged to hold them.

Hedge blinked, holding his eyes shut for a full second—his only acknowledgment that his plan had gone awry. But he had been in Ancelstierre for four years, and his other plans were in full motion. He would come back for the boy.

As Hedge fled into the darkness, stretcher bearers picked up Nick; a young officer convinced the schoolboys on the hill that they really could stop singing; and Ted and Mike tried to tell the barely conscious Sam what had happened as an Army medic looked at the burns on his wrist and legs and prepared a surette of morphine.

Chapter Eighteen

A FATHER'S HEALING HAND

THE HOSPITAL IN Bain was relatively new, built six years before, when a flurry of hospital reform came sweeping up from the South. Even in only six years, many people had died there, and it was close enough to the Wall for Sam's sense of Death to remain active. Weakened by pain and by the morphine they were giving him for it, Sam was unable to drive away his sense of Death. Always it loomed close, filling his bones with its bitter chill, making him shiver constantly and the doctors increase his medication.

He dreamed of bodiless creatures that would come from Death and finish off what the necromancer had begun, and he could not wake himself from the dreams. When he did wake, he often saw that same necromancer stalking towards him, and would scream and scream until the nurse who it really was gave him another injection and started the cycle of nightmares again.

Sam suffered four days of this, drifting in and out of consciousness, without ever really waking up, and never losing his sense of Death and the fear that accompanied it. Sometimes he was lucid enough to realize that Nick was there, too, in the next bed, his hands bandaged. Sometimes they talked briefly, but it wasn't ever a real conversation, since Sam could neither answer questions nor continue whatever talk Nick began.

On the fifth day, everything changed. Sam was once again in the grip of a nightmare, once again in Death, facing a necromancer who was many things all at once, simultaneously in, under, and above the water. Sam was running, and falling and drowning, as had actually happened, and then came the grip on his wrist . . . but this time it wasn't on his wrist, it was on his shoulder, and it was cool and comforting. A grip that somehow led him out of the nightmare, lifting him up through a sky that was all Charter marks and sunshine.

When Sam opened his eyes, he could see clearly for the first time, his vision clear of the drug haze and vertigo. He felt fingers resting lightly on his neck, on the pulse there, and knew his father's hand before he even looked up. Touchstone was right next to him, his eyes closed as he directed a healing-spell into his son's body, the marks flashing under his fingers as they left him and entered Sam.

Sam looked up at Touchstone, grateful that his father's eyes were closed and he couldn't see the pathetic relief on his son's face, or the tears that he hastened to brush away. The Charter Magic was making him warm for the first time in days. Sam could feel the marks driving the drugs out of his bloodstream, while they took over quelling the pain from his burns. But it was the mere presence of his father that had driven away the fear of Death. He could still sense Death, but it was dim and far away, and he was no longer afraid.

King Touchstone I finished the spell and opened his eyes. They were grey, like his son's, but Touchstone's were the more troubled now, and he was obviously tired. Slowly, he took his hand away from Sam's neck.

They almost hugged until Sam saw that there were two doctors, four of Touchstone's guards, and two Ancelstierran Army officers in the ward as well as a whole crowd of Ancelstierran police, soldiers, and officials gathered out in the corridor, peering in. So Sam and Touchstone gripped one another's forearms instead, Sam sitting up in the bed. Only the tightness of Sam's grip and his reluctance to let go indicated just how glad he was to see his father.

Both doctors were amazed that Sam was even conscious, and one checked the chart at the foot of the bed to affirm that the patient really had been receiving intravenous morphine for days.

"Really, this is impossible!" the doctor began, till a cold glance from one of Touchstone's guards convinced him that his conversation was currently not required. A slight further movement convinced him that his presence was not required either, and he backed away to the door. Like the King, the guards were all wearing three-piece suits of a sober charcoal grey, so as not to alarm delicate Ancelstierran sensibilities. This effect was only slightly spoiled by the fact that they also carried swords, badly disguised in rolled-up trenchcoats.

"The entourage," said Touchstone dryly, seeing Sam look out at all the people in the corridor. "I told them I was simply here as a private individual to see my son, but apparently even that requires an official escort. I hope you're feeling up to riding. If we stay here any longer, I'll be cornered by some sort of committee or politician for sure."

"Riding?" asked Sam. He had to say it twice, his throat initially too weak to get the word out. "I'm to leave school before the end of term?"

"Yes," said Touchstone, keeping his voice low. "I want you home. Ancelstierre is no longer a safe haven. The police here caught your bus driver. He was bribed, and bribed with Old Kingdom silver deniers. So one of our enemies has found a way to work on both sides of the Wall. Or has at least found out how to spend money in Ancelstierre."

"I think I'm well enough to ride," said Sam, wrinkling his

brow. "I mean, I don't know whether I'm really hurt. My wrist is sore. . . ."

He paused and looked at the bandage on his wrist. Charter marks still moved around the edge of the bandage, oozing out of his pores like golden sweat. Healing him, Sam realized, for his wrist really was only sore, where it had been excruciatingly painful before, and the pain from the lesser burns on his thighs and ankles was completely gone.

"The bandage can come off now," said Touchstone, and he began to untie it. As he unwound it, he lowered his head still closer to Sam and whispered, "You have not been badly hurt in body, Sam. But I feel that you have suffered an injury of the spirit. That will take time to heal, for it is beyond my power to repair."

"What do you mean?" asked Sam anxiously. He felt very young all of a sudden, not at all like the nearly adult Prince he was supposed to be. "Can't Mother fix it up?"

"I don't think so," said Touchstone, resting his hand on Sam's shoulder, the small white scars from years of sword practice and actual fighting bright across his knuckles in the hospital light. "But then I cannot tell the nature of it, only that it has happened. I would guess that as a result of your going into Death unprepared and unprotected, some small fragment of your spirit has been leeched away. Not much, but enough to make you feel weaker, or slower . . . basically less than yourself. But it will come back, in time."

"I shouldn't have done it, should I?" whispered Sam, looking up into his father's face, searching for some sternness or sign of disapproval. "Is Mother furious with me?"

"Not at all," said Touchstone, surprised. "You did what you thought was necessary to save the others, which was both brave and in the best traditions of both sides of the family. Your mother is more worried about you than anything else."

"Then where is she?" asked Sam, before he could stop himself. It was a petulant question, and as soon as his mouth closed, he wished he hadn't said it.

"Apparently, there is a Mordaut riding the ferryman at Oldmond," explained Touchstone patiently, as he had explained so many of Sabriel's necessary absences over the course of Sam's childhood. "We received word of it as we reached the Wall. She took the Paperwing and flew off to deal with it. She'll meet us back at Belisaere."

"If she doesn't have to go somewhere else," said Sam, knowing he was being bitter and childish. But he could have died, and apparently that still wasn't enough for his mother to come and see him.

"Unless she has to go somewhere else," agreed Touchstone, as calmly as ever. His father worked hard at staying calm, Sam knew, for there was the old berserker blood in him, and Touchstone feared its rise. The only time Sam had ever seen that fury was when a false ambassador from one of the northern clans had tried to stab Sabriel with a serving fork at a formal dinner in the Palace. Touchstone, roaring like some sort of terrible beast, had picked up the six-foot barbarian and hurled him the length of the table, onto a roast swan. This had scared everyone much more than the assassination attempt, particularly when Touchstone then tried to pick up the double throne and throw that after the man. Fortunately, he'd failed and was eventually calmed by Sabriel stroking his brow as he blindly wrenched at the marble footing of the throne.

Sam remembered this as he saw his father's eyelids close just a fraction and a line appear on his forehead.

"Sorry," Sam mumbled. "I know she has to do it. Being the Abhorsen and everything."

"Yes," said Touchstone, and Sam got a slight hint of his father's own deep feelings about the many and frequent absences required by Sabriel's battles with the Dead.

"I'd better get dressed, then," said Sam, and he swung his legs out of the bed. Only then did he notice that the opposite bed was empty and made up.

"Where's Nick?" he asked. "He was there, wasn't he? Or did I just dream that?"

"I don't know," said Touchstone, who had met his son's friend on previous visits to Ancelstierre. "He wasn't here when we arrived. Doctor! Was Nicholas Sayre in this bed?"

The doctor hurried forward. He didn't know who this strange but obviously important visitor was, or who the patient was either, since the Army had insisted on secrecy and the use of first names only. Now he wished that he hadn't heard the other patient's surname, since the name Sayre was not unknown to him. But the Chief Minister didn't have a son of that age, so the fellow could only have been a cousin or something, which was some relief.

"The patient Nicholas X," he said, emphasizing the "X," "was released to one of his parents' confidential servants yesterday. He only had minor shock and some abrasions."

"Did he leave me a message?" asked Sam, surprised that his friend wouldn't have tried to communicate in some way.

"I don't believe so—" the doctor started to say, when he was interrupted by a nurse who pushed her way through the massed ranks of blue, khaki, and grey in the corridor. She was quite young and pretty, with striking red hair not very well concealed under her starched cap.

"He left a letter, Your Highnesses," she said, with the characteristic accent of the North. Obviously a native of Bain, she knew exactly who both Sam and Touchstone were, much to the doctor's annoyance. The doctor took the letter in her out-stretched hand with a sniff and handed it to Sam, who immediately tore it open.

He didn't recognize the handwriting at first; then he realized that it was Nick's, only the individual letters were much larger and the flourishes less regular. It took a moment for him to work out that this must be a consequence of Nick's writing with heavily bandaged hands.

Dear Sam,

I hope you are soon well enough to read this. I seem to be quite recovered myself, though I admit that the events of our unusual evening are somewhat hazy. I guess you wouldn't know that I took it in my head to chase down that necromancer fellow you went after first, wherever it was you went. Unfortunately, what with the dark and the rain and perhaps a little too much zing in my step, all I managed to do was fall into the sunken road and knock myself out. I was lucky not to break any bones, the doctors say, though I have some interesting bruises. I don't expect that the debs back in Corvere will be as prepared to look at them as Nurse Moulin, though!

I understand that the Army got hold of your pater and he's coming down to take you home, so you won't be finishing the term. I daresay I won't bother either, since I already have my place at Sunbere. It won't be the same without you, or poor Harry Benlet. Or even Cochrane. They found him five miles away the next morning, apparently, gibbering and frothing, and I expect he's locked up in Smithwen Special Hospital by now. Should have been done years ago, of course.

In fact, I was thinking that I might come and visit you in your mysterious Old Kingdom before I have to go up to

college next spring. I admit that my scientific interest has
been piqued by those apparently animated corpses and your
own exhibition of whatever it was. I'm sure you think of it
as magic, but I expect it can all be explained by the proper
application of scientific method. I hope I can be the one to do
so, of course. Sayre's Theory of Surreality. Or Sayre's Law of
Magical Explication.

It's very boring in hospital, particularly if your wardmate
can't carry a conversation. So you'll have to excuse me
rambling on. Where was I? Oh yes, experiments in the Old
Kingdom. I expect the reason no one has done the proper
scientific work before is due to the Army. Would you believe
that no less than a colonel and two captains were here
yesterday, wanting me to sign the Official Secrets Act and a
declaration that I wouldn't ever speak or write of the recent
odd events near the Perimeter? They forgot sign language, so
I expect I shall inform a deaf journalist when I get back.

I won't, of course. At least not until I have something
better to tell the world—some truly great discovery.

The officers wanted you to sign as well, but since you
weren't in a signing mood, they just waited and got cross
with each other. Then I told them that you weren't even a
citizen of Ancelstierre, and they got thoughtful and had a big
discussion outside with the lieutenant in charge of the guards.
Something tells me the right hand knoweth not what the
left hand doeth, since they were from Corvere Legal Affairs
and the guards outside are from the Perimeter Scouts. I
was interested to note that the latter belong to your peculiar
religion, with the caste mark or whatever it is on their
foreheads. Not that sociology is really in my field of
interest, I hasten to add.

I must go now. The aged parents have sent some sort of

private undersecretary to the oversecretary chamberlain of the
personal privy type of fellow to collect me and take me home
to Amberne Court. Apparently Father is too busy with the
Southerling refugee problem, questions in the House and all
that sort of thing, and Uncle Edward needs his support blah
blah blah as per usual. Mother probably had a charity dinner
or something equally all-engrossing. I'll write soon so we can
arrange my visit. I expect I'll have everything prepared in a
couple of months, three at the outside.

   Chin up!

                            Nick, the mysterious patient X

Sam folded the letter, smiling. At least Nick had come out of
that awful night without any real harm, and with his sense of
humor intact. It was typical of him that the Dead had only triggered his scientific interest, rather than a much more sensible fear.

   "All well?" asked Touchstone, who had been waiting patiently.
At least half the onlookers had lost interest, Sam saw, withdraw-
ing farther down the corridor and out of sight, where they felt
they could talk.

   "Father," said Sam, "did you bring me some clothes? My
school stuff must have been ruined."

   "Damed, the bag, please," said Touchstone. "Everybody else,
outside if you don't mind."

   Like two flocks of sheep that have difficulty mixing, the
people left in the ward tried to get out while the people in the
corridor tried to help and actually made it more difficult.
Eventually, they did all get out, except for Damed—Touchstone's
principal bodyguard, a small thin man who moved alarmingly
fast. Damed handed over a compact suitcase before he left, shutting the door.

   There were Ancelstierran clothes in the bag, procured—like

Touchstone's and the guards'—from the Bain consulate of the Old Kingdom.

"Wear these for now," said Touchstone. "We'll get changed at the Perimeter. Back into sensible clothes."

"Armored coat and helmet, boots and sword," said Sameth, pulling his hospital gown off over his head.

"Yes," said Touchstone. He hesitated, then said, "Does that bother you? I suppose you could go south instead. I must return to the Kingdom. But you might be safe in Corvere—"

"No!" Sam said. He wanted to stay with his father. He wanted the heavy weight of his armored coat and the pommel of a sword under his palm. But most of all, he wanted to be with his mother in Belisaere. Because only then would he really be safe from Death . . . and the necromancer who he was sure even now waited in that cold river, waiting for Sam to return.

Chapter Nineteen

ELLIMERE'S THOUGHTS ON
THE EDUCATION OF PRINCES

AFTER TWO WEEKS of hard riding, bad weather, indifferent food, and sore muscles that were slow to re-adapt to
horseback, Sam arrived in the great city of Belisaere to
find that his mother was not there. Sabriel had already been and
gone, called away again to deal with a reported Free Magic sorcerer cum bandit chief, who was attacking travelers along the
northern extremes of the Nailway.

Within a day, Touchstone was gone, too, riding to sit at a High
Court in Estwael, where an ancient, simmering feud between two
noble families had broken out into murders and kidnappings.

In Touchstone's absence, Sam's fourteen-month-older sister
Ellimere was named co-regent, along with Jall Oren, the
Chancellor. It was a formality really, since Touchstone would
rarely be more than a few days away by message-hawk, but a formality that would greatly affect Sam. Ellimere took her responsibility seriously. And she thought that one of her duties as co-regent
was to address the shortcomings of her younger brother.

Touchstone had been gone only an hour when Ellimere
came looking for Sam. Since Touchstone had left at dawn, Sam
was still asleep. He had recovered from his physical wounds, but
he still did not feel quite himself. He grew tired more easily than
before, and wanted to be alone more. Fourteen days of rising
before dawn and riding till after dusk, accompanied by the

hearty humor of the guards, had not helped him feel less tired or more gregarious.

Consequently, he was not amused when Ellimere chose to wake him on his first morning in his own bed by ripping back the curtains, flinging his window open, and ripping the blankets off. It was already several days into winter in the Old Kingdom, and decidedly cool. The sea breeze that came roaring in could even be accurately described as cold, and all the feeble sunshine did was hurt Sam's eyes.

"Wake up! Wake up! Wake up!" caroled Ellimere, who had a surprisingly deep singing voice for a woman.

"Go away!" growled Sam, as he attempted to snatch the blankets back. A brief tug-of-war ensued, which Sam gave up when one of the blankets got ripped in half.

"Now look what you've done," Sam said bitterly. Ellimere shrugged. She was supposed to be pretty—some even considered her beautiful—but Sam couldn't see it. As far as he was concerned, Ellimere was a dangerous pest. By making her co-regent, his parents had elevated her to the status of a monster.

"I've come to discuss your schedule," said Ellimere. She sat down on the end of the bed, her back very straight and her hands clasped regally in her lap. Sam noted that she wore a fine, bell-sleeved tabard of red and spun gold over her everyday linen dress, and a sort of demi-regal circlet kept her long and immaculately brushed black hair in place. Since her normal attire was old hunting leathers with her hair carelessly tied back out of the way, her dress did not bode well for Sam's own desire for informality.

"My what?" Sam asked.

"Your schedule," continued Ellimere. "I'm sure that you were planning to spend most of your time tinkering in that smelly workshop of yours, but I'm afraid your duty to the Kingdom comes first."

"What?" asked Sam. He felt very tired, and certainly not up to this conversation. Particularly since he had indeed planned to spend most of his time in his tower workroom. For the last few days, as they'd got closer and closer to Belisaere, he'd been looking forward to the solitude and peace of sitting at his workbench, with all his tools carefully arranged on the wall, above the chest of tiny drawers, each filled with some useful material, like silver wire or moonstones. He had managed to survive the last part of the trip by dreaming up new toys and gadgets he would make in his little haven of calm and recuperation.

"The Kingdom must come first," reiterated Ellimere. "The people's morale is very important, and each member of the family must play a part in maintaining it. As the only Prince we've got, you'll have to—"

"No!" exclaimed Sam, who suddenly realized where she was heading. He jumped out of bed, his nightshirt billowing around his legs, and scowled down at his sister, until she stood up and looked down her nose at him. She not only was slightly taller than he was, but also had the advantage of wearing shoes.

"Yes," said Ellimere sternly. "The Midsummer Festival. You're needed to play the part of the Bird of Dawning. Rehearsals start tomorrow."

"But it's five months away!" protested Sam. "Besides, I don't want to be the blasted Bird of Dawning. That suit must weigh a ton, and I'd have to wear it for a week! Didn't Dad tell you I'm sick?"

"He said you needed to be busy," said Ellimere. "And since you've never danced the Bird, you'll need five months' practice. Besides, there's the appearance at the end of the Midwinter Festival, too—and that's only six weeks away."

"I haven't got the legs for it," muttered Sameth, thinking of the cross-gartered yellow stockings worn under the gold-feathered plumage of the Bird of Dawning. "Get someone with tree-trunk legs."

"Sameth! You are going to dance the Bird, like it or not," declared Ellimere. "It's about time you did something useful around here. I've also scheduled you to sit with Jall at the Petty Court every morning between ten and one, and you'll have sword practice twice a day with the Guard, of course, and you must come to dinner—no ordering meals to your grubby workshop. And for Perspective, I've assigned you to work with the scullions every second Wednesday."

Sam groaned and sank back on the bed. Perspective was Sabriel's idea. For one day every two weeks, Ellimere and Sam would work somewhere in the palace, supposedly like the ordinary people there. Of course, even when they were washing dishes or mopping floors, the servants could rarely forget that Sam and Ellimere would be Prince and Princess again tomorrow. Most of the servants dealt with the situation by pretending Sam and Ellimere weren't there, with a few notable exceptions like Mistress Finney, the falconer, who shouted at them like everyone else. So Perspective was usually a day of drudgery performed in strange silence and isolation.

"What are *you* doing for Perspective?" Sam asked, suspicious that Ellimere would skip it now she was co-regent.

"Stables."

Sam grunted. The stables were hard work, particularly since it would probably be a day of mucking out. But Ellimere loved horses and all the work around them, so she probably didn't mind.

"Mother also said you were to study this." Ellimere drew a package out of her voluminous sleeve. It wasn't immediately recognizable, being wrapped in oilskin and tied with thick, hairy twine.

Sam reached for the package, but as his fingers touched the wrapping, he felt a terrible chill and the sudden presence of Death, despite the spells and charms that were supposed to prevent any traffic with that cold realm, woven into the very stone around them.

Sam snatched his hand back and retreated to the other end of the bed, his heart suddenly thumping wildly, sweat beading his face and hands.

He knew what was inside that seemingly innocuous package. It was *The Book of the Dead.* A small volume, bound in green leather, with tarnished silver clasps. Leather and silver laden with protective magic. Marks to bind and blind, to close and imprison. Only someone with an innate talent for Free Magic and necromancy could open the book, and only an uncorrupted Charter Mage could close it. It contained all the lore of necromancy and counter-necromancy that fifty-three Abhorsens had gathered over a thousand years—and more besides, for its contents never stayed the same, seemingly altering at the book's own whim. Sam had read a little of it, at his mother's side.

"What's wrong with you?" asked Ellimere curiously, as Sam went paler and paler and his teeth began to chatter. She put the package on the end of his bed and came over, touching the back of her hand to Sam's forehead.

"You're cold," she said, surprised. "Really cold!"

"Sick," muttered Sam. He could barely speak. Fear gripped his throat. Fear of somehow being thrown into Death by the book, of being plunged once again under the surface of the cold river, to go crashing through the First Gate . . .

"Get back into bed," ordered Ellimere, suddenly solicitous. "I'll get Dr. Shemblis."

"No!" cried Sam, thinking of the court doctor and his curious, inquiring ways. "It'll pass. Just leave me alone for a while."

"All right," replied Ellimere, as she closed the window and helped re-arrange what was left of the blankets. "But don't think this is going to get you off playing the Bird of Dawning. Not unless Dr. Shemblis says you're really, really sick."

"I'm not," said Sam. "I'll be all right in a few hours."

"What happened to you, anyway?" asked Ellimere. "Dad was a bit vague, and we didn't have time to talk. Something about you going into Death and getting into trouble."

"Something like that," whispered Sam.

"Sooner you than me."

Ellimere picked up the package and hefted it curiously, then threw it down next to Sam. "I'm glad I had no aptitude for it. Imagine if you were going to be the King, and me the Abhorsen! Still, I'm glad you've already started popping into Death, because Mother certainly needs the help at the moment, and you'll be a lot more use doing that than mucking about making toys. Mind you, I was going to ask if you could make me two tennis racquets, so I suppose I shouldn't complain. I can't get anyone else to understand what I want, and I haven't played a game since I left Wyverley. You could make some, couldn't you?"

"Yes," replied Sam. But he wasn't thinking about tennis. He was thinking about the book next to him, and the fact that he was the Abhorsen-in-Waiting. Everyone expected him to succeed Sabriel. He was going to have to study *The Book of the Dead*. He would have to walk in Death again, and confront the necromancer—or even worse things, if that were possible.

"Are you sure I shouldn't get Shemblis?" Ellimere asked. "You do look very pale. I'll have someone come up with some chamomile tea, and I suppose you don't have to start your proper schedule till tomorrow. You will be better tomorrow, won't you?"

"I think so," said Sam. He was frozen immobile by the proximity of the book.

Ellimere looked at him again, with a look that contained equal parts of concern, annoyance, and irritation. Then she swung around and swept out, banging the door behind her.

Sam lay in bed, trying to take regular, slow breaths. He could feel the book next to him, almost as if it were a living thing. A coiled snake that was waiting to strike when he moved.

He lay there for a long time, listening to the sounds of the Palace that came wafting up to his tower room, even with the window closed. The regular watch-cry of the guards on the wall; the sudden conversation of people in the courtyard below, as they met on their business; the clash of sword on sword from the practice field that lay beyond the inner wall. Behind it all there was the constant crash of the sea. Belisaere was almost an island, and the Palace was built upon one of its four hills, in the north-east quarter. Sam's bedchamber was in the Sea Cliff tower, about halfway up. During the wildest winter storms, it was not unusual for sea spray to splash upon his window, despite the tower's distance from the shore.

A servant brought chamomile tea, and they spoke briefly, though Sam had no idea what he had said. The tea cooled, and the sun rose higher, till it had passed beyond his window and the air grew colder again.

Finally, Sam moved. With shaking hands, he forced himself to pick up the package. He cut the string with the knife that lay sheathed upon his bedhead and quickly unwrapped the oilskin, knowing that if he stopped, he'd be unable to go on.

Sure enough, it was *The Book of the Dead*, the green leather shining as if it were coated with sweat. The silver clasps that held it closed were clouded, their brightness dimmed. They cleared as Sam watched, and then frosted again, though he had not breathed upon them.

There was a note, too, a single sheet of rough-edged paper

that bore only a Charter mark and Sam's own name, written in Sabriel's firm, distinctive hand.

Sam picked up the note, then used the oilskin wrapper like a glove to slip the Book under his bed. He couldn't bear to look at it. Not yet.

Then he touched the Charter mark on the paper, and Sabriel's voice sounded inside his head. She spoke quickly, and from the other noises in the background, Sam guessed she had made this message immediately before flying out in her Paperwing. Flying out to combat the Dead.

Sam—

I hope you are well and can forgive me for not being there for you now. I know from your father's last message-hawk that you are fit enough to be riding home, but that your encounter in Death has left you sorely tried. I know what that can be like—and I am proud that you risked entering Death to save your friends. I don't know that I would be brave enough myself to go into Death without my bells. Be assured that any hurt to your spirit will pass in time. It is the nature of Death to take, but the nature of Life to give.

Your brave action has also shown me that you are ready to formally begin training as the Abhorsen-in-Waiting. This makes me both proud and a little sad, because it means that you have grown up. The burdens of an Abhorsen are many, and one of the worst is that we are doomed to miss so much of our children's lives—of your life, Sam.

I have delayed teaching you to some degree because I wanted you to stay the dear little boy I can so easily remember. But of course you have not been a little boy for many years, and now you are a young man and must be treated as such. Part of that is acknowledging your heritage, and the essential role you have in the future of our Kingdom.

A great part of that heritage is contained within The Book of the Dead, *which you now have. You have studied a little of it with me, but now it is time for you to master its contents, as much as this is possible for anyone to do. Certainly, in these present days, I have need of your assistance, for there is a strange resurgence of trouble from both the Dead and those who follow Free Magic, and I cannot find the source of either.*

We will speak more of this on my return, but for now I want you to know that I am proud of you, Sameth. Your father is, too. Welcome home, my son.

With all my love,
Mother

Sam let the paper fall from his grasp and fell back on the pillow. The future, so bright when that cricket ball had arced over the stands for a six, now seemed very dark indeed.

Chapter Twenty

A DOOR OF THREE SIGNS

To CELEBRATE HER nineteenth birthday, Lirael and the Dog decided to explore somewhere special, to venture through the jagged hole in the pale green rock where the main spiral of the Great Library came to a sudden end.

The hole was too small for Lirael to enter, so she had made a Charter-skin for the expedition. In the years since finding *In the Skin of a Lyon*, she had learned to make three different Charter-skins. Each had been very carefully selected for its natural advantages. The ice otter was small and lithe, and enabled Lirael to move in narrow ways and across ice and snow with ease. The russet bear was larger, and much stronger, than her natural form, and its thick fur was protection against both cold and harm. The barking owl gave her flight and made darkness no burden, though she had yet to fly outside some of the great chambers of the Library, which were never truly dark.

But the Charter-skins had their disadvantages as well. The ice otter's vision was in shades of grey, its perspective was low to the ground, and it induced a fondness for fish that lasted for days after Lirael shucked the skin. The russet bear's sight was weak, and wearing it made Lirael bad-tempered and gluttonous, also for some time after it was taken off. The barking owl was of little use in full daylight, and after wearing it Lirael would find her eyes watering under the bright lights of the Reading Room. But all in all she was pleased with the Charter-skins and the choices she had made, and proud that she had learned three Charter-skins in less time than *In the Skin of a Lyon* suggested would be possible.

Their major drawback was the time they took to prepare and put on. Typically, it would take Lirael five hours or more to prepare a Charter-skin, another hour to fold it properly so that it would last a day or two in a pouch or bag, and then at least half an hour to put on. Sometimes it took longer, particularly the ice-otter skin, because it was so much smaller than Lirael's normal form. It was like forcing a foot into a sock that was only big enough for a toe, with the sock stretching while the foot shrank. Balancing the process was quite difficult, and it always made Lirael dizzy and a bit nauseated, to feel herself both changing and shrinking.

But on her birthday, since the hole in the rock was less than two feet wide, only the ice-otter shape would do. Lirael began to put it on, as the Disreputable Dog scrabbled at the hole. Somehow the Dog made herself longer and thinner in the process, till she looked like one of the sausage dogs that the Rasseli shepherd-queens carried around their necks, as illustrated in Lirael's favorite travelogue.

After a few minutes of furious work with her back legs, the Dog disappeared. Lirael sighed, and kept forcing herself into the Charter-skin. The Dog had a well-known problem with waiting, but Lirael felt a bit aggrieved that the hound couldn't even wait on her birthday, or let her go first.

Not that she really expected it. Her birthday was Lirael's most hated time of the year, the day she was forced to remember all the bad things in her life.

This year, as on every past birthday, she had woken without the Sight. It was an old hurt now, scarred over and locked deep within her heart. Lirael had learnt not to show the pain it caused her, not even to the Disreputable Dog, who otherwise shared all her thoughts and dreams.

Nor did Lirael contemplate suicide, as she had done on her fourteenth birthday, and briefly on her seventeenth. She had managed to forge a life for herself that, if not ideal, was satisfying in many ways. She still lived in the Hall of Youth, and would till she was twenty-one and assigned her own chambers, but since she spent every waking hour in the Library, she was largely free of Kirrith's interference. Lirael had also long since stopped going to Awakenings or any other ceremonial functions that would require her to wear the blue tunic, that hated, obvious sign that she was not a proper Clayr.

She wore her Librarian's uniform instead, even at breakfast, and had taken to tying a white scarf around her head like some of the older Clayr. It hid her black hair, and in her uniform there was no doubting who she was, even amongst the visitors in the Lower Refectory.

The week before her birthday, these working clothes had been greatly enhanced by the transition from a yellow to a red waistcoat, proud symbol of Lirael's promotion to Second Assistant Librarian. The promotion was very welcome but not without trouble, as the formal letter announcing it came unexpectedly, late one afternoon. In the letter, Vancelle, the Chief Librarian, congratulated Lirael and noted that there would be a brief ceremony the next morning—at which time an additional key spell would be woken in her bracelet and certain spells taught her as was "concomitant to the responsibilities and offices of a Second Assistant Librarian in the Great Library of the Clayr."

Consequently, Lirael had stayed up all night in her study trying to put the extra key-spells she'd already awoken in her bracelet back to sleep, so as not to reveal her unauthorized wanderings. But the sleeping proved harder than the waking.

Hours and hours later, without success, her groans of despair at four in the morning had woken the Dog, who breathed on the bracelet, which returned the extra spells to their dormant state and sent Lirael into a sleep so heavy she almost missed the ceremony anyway.

The red waistcoat was an early birthday present, followed by others on the actual day. Imshi and the other young librarians who worked most closely with Lirael gave her a new pen, a slender rod of silver that was engraved with the faces of owls and had two slender claws where a variety of steel nibs could be screwed in. It came in a velvet-lined box of sweet-smelling sandalwood, with an ancient inkwell of cloudy green glass that had a golden rim etched with runes that no one could read.

Both pen and inkwell were an unspoken commentary on Lirael's now long-established habit of speaking as little as possible. She wrote notes whenever she could get away with it. In the last few years, she had rarely said more than ten words in a row, and often she would not speak to other humans for days at a time.

Of course, the other Clayr didn't know that Lirael's silence was more than made up for in her conversations with the Dog, with whom she would talk for hours. Sometimes, her superiors would ask her why she didn't like to talk, but Lirael couldn't answer. All she knew was that talking to the Clayr reminded her of all the things she couldn't talk about. The Clayr's conversations would always return to the Sight, the central focus of their lives. By not speaking, Lirael was simply protecting herself from pain, even if she wasn't conscious of the reason.

At her birthday tea in the Junior Librarians' Common Room, an informal chamber normally given to lots of talk and laughter, Lirael was able only to say "thank you," and smile, though it was a smile accompanied by teary eyes. They were very kind, her fellow librarians. But they were still Clayr first and librarians second.

Lirael's last present was from the Disreputable Dog, who gave her a big kiss. As dog kisses seemed to consist of energetic licks to the face, Lirael was happy to curtail the well-wishing by handing over the leftover cake from her birthday tea.

"That's all I get, a dog kiss," muttered Lirael. She was more than halfway into the ice-otter skin, but it would still be ten minutes before she could pursue her friend.

Lirael did not know it, but there were a number of other people who would have liked to give her a birthday kiss. Quite a few of the young men among the guards and merchants who regularly visited the Clayr had looked on her with increasing interest over the years. But she made it clear that she wanted to keep herself to herself. They also noted that she did not speak, not even to the Clayr on kitchen duty. So the young men simply watched her, and the more romantic of them dreamed of the day when she would suddenly come over and invite them upstairs. Other Clayr occasionally did so, but not Lirael. She continued to eat alone, and the dreamers continued to dream.

Lirael herself rarely thought about the fact that at nineteen she had never been kissed. She knew all about sex in theory, from the compulsory lessons in the Hall of Youth and books in the library. But she was too shy to approach any of the visitors, even the ones she saw regularly in the Lower Refectory, and there were very few male Clayr.

She often overheard the other young librarians talking freely of men, sometimes even in detail. But these liaisons were clearly not as important to the Clayr as the Sight and their work in the Observatory, and Lirael judged by their standards. The Sight was the most important, and it came first. Once she had the Sight, she might think of doing as the other Clayr did, and bring a man up to the Upper Refectory for dinner and a walk in the Perfumed Garden, and perhaps then . . . to her bed.

In fact, Lirael couldn't even imagine that any man would be interested in her, compared to a real Clayr. As in everything else, Lirael thought a real Clayr would always be more interesting and attractive than herself.

Even outside work, Lirael took a different path from the other young Clayr. When they all finished at the Library at four in the afternoon, most would go to the Hall of Youth or their own living quarters, or to one of the Refectories or the areas where Clayr gathered for recreation, like the Perfumed Garden or the Sun Steps.

Lirael always went the other way, down from the Reading Room to her study, to wake up the Disreputable Dog. She'd been given a new study with her promotion, and now had a larger room that had a tiny bathroom off it, complete with water closet, sink, and hot and cold water.

Once the Dog had been woken up and the various items that had been knocked over in their exuberant greeting had been replaced, Lirael and the Dog usually waited till the night-watch assembly, when all the librarians on duty gathered briefly in the Main Reading Room to be given their tasks. Thus safe from observation, Lirael and the Dog would creep down the main spiral, passing into the Old Levels, where the other librarians seldom came.

Over the years, Lirael had come to know the Old Levels and many of their secrets and dangers well. She had even secretly helped out other librarians, without their knowing. At least three of them would have died if Lirael and the Dog hadn't taken care of several unpleasant creatures that had somehow entered the Library.

"Come on!" said the Dog, sticking her head back out of the hole. Lirael was fully in the otter skin, but there was something strange about her stomach. It looked different, but she couldn't work out what it was. She turned around to stare at it and rolled across the floor.

"Proud of your new waistcoat, I see," said the Dog, sniffing.

"What?" asked Lirael. She sat up and bent her head down to look at her furry stomach. It was a different shade of grey than normal, but she didn't remember making any changes.

"Ice otters don't usually have red stomachs, Miss Second Assistant Librarian," said the Dog. "Come on!"

"Oh," said Lirael. She'd never changed the color of her fur before. Still, it did show at least an unconscious mastery in making a Charter-skin. She smiled, and bounded up behind the Dog. They'd always meant to find out what was down this passage, but something had always interrupted them before. Now they would discover what lay beyond the end of the main spiral.

"The tunnel has fallen in," said the Disreputable Dog, wagging her tail in a manner that diluted the apparent seriousness of the news.

"I can see that!" snapped Lirael. She was feeling irritable, mainly from having been in her ice-otter Charter-skin for the last two hours. It had started to get very uncomfortable, like extremely sweaty clothes that stick in all the wrong places. There was nothing to distract her from the discomfort, either, because the hole at the end of the main spiral had proved to be quite boring. It had widened out after a while, but otherwise simply zigzagged back and forth without coming to any interesting intersections, chambers, or doors. Now it had ended with a wall of tumbled ice that blocked their way.

"No need to get snarky, Mistress," replied the Dog. "Besides, there is a way across. The glacier has pushed through, all right, but sometime or other a drill-grub has cut through above. If we climb up we can probably use the bore to get across to the other side."

"Sorry," said Lirael, sighing, shrugging her otter shoulders in a movement that flowed right through the rest of her long white-furred body. "What are you waiting for, then?"

"It's almost dinnertime," the Dog said primly. "You'll be missed."

"You mean you'll miss whatever I can steal for you," grumbled Lirael. "No one will miss me. Besides, you don't need to eat."

"But I like to," protested the Dog, pacing backwards and forwards, nimbly avoiding the chunks of ice that had fallen from the spur of the glacier and were now blocking their further progress along the tunnel.

"Just find the way, please," instructed Lirael. "Use your famous nose."

"Aye, aye, Captain," said the Dog with resignation. She started climbing up the tumbled ice, claws leaving deep, melting cuts. "The drill-grub bore is right at the top."

Lirael bounded up after her, enjoying the almost liquid feel of being an ice otter in movement. Of course, when she stopped wearing the Charter-skin, that memory of liquid movement would make her stumble and jerk for a few minutes, till her mind realized it was connecting with different muscles.

The Disreputable Dog was already scrabbling into the drill-grub's hole—a perfectly cylindrical bore about three feet in diameter that cut straight through the ice barrier. That was only a medium-sized grub's bore. The big ones were more than ten feet across. The grubs were rare now, in all sizes. Lirael was probably one of the few inhabitants of the Clayr's Glacier who had ever seen one.

In fact, she had seen two, many years apart. Both times the Dog had smelt them first, so they had had time to get out of the way. The grubs weren't dangerous, at least intentionally, but they were slow to react, and their rotating, multiple jaws chewed up anything in their path: ice, rock, or slow-moving human.

The Dog slipped for a moment, but didn't slide back, as a real dog probably would have. Lirael noticed that her canine friend's claws had grown to twice their normal length to cope with the ice. Definitely not something a real dog could do, but Lirael had long since come to terms with the fact that she didn't really know what the Dog was. That she had been born of both Charter and Free Magic there was no doubt, but Lirael didn't care to dwell on that. Whatever the Dog was, she was Lirael's one true friend and had proved her loyalty a hundred times and more in the past four and a half years.

Despite her magical origins, the Dog's smell was all too like a real dog's, Lirael thought, particularly when she was wet. Like now, when Lirael's wrinkling otter-nose was pressed up against the Dog's hind legs and tail as she followed her through the bore. Fortunately, the tunnel wasn't long, and Lirael forgot the Dog's odor as she saw that there wasn't just more boring tunnel on the other side. She could see the glow of a Charter-Magicked ceiling, and some sort of tiled wall.

"It's old, this room," announced the Dog, as they slid out of the bore and onto the pale blue and yellow tiles of the chamber floor. Both shook off the ice with a wriggle, Lirael copying the Dog's expressive shiver from shoulder to tail.

"Yes," agreed Lirael, suppressing an urge to scratch herself vigorously around the neck. The Charter-skin was fraying already, and she would need it to go back through the bore and the tunnel. Forcing her clawed forepaws to be still, she tried to concentrate on the room, hampered by her otterish vision, with its different field of view and lack of color.

The room was lit by common Charter marks for light, glowing in the ceiling, though Lirael immediately saw that they were faded, and much older than most such marks would last. A desk of some deep red wood took up one corner, but without a chair. Empty bookcases lined one wall, glass doors shut. Charter marks for repelling dust moved endlessly across them like the sheen of oil on water.

There was a door on the far wall, of that same reddish wood, studded with tiny golden stars, golden towers, and silver keys. The golden stars were the seven-pointed variety that were the emblem of the Clayr, and the golden tower was the blazon of the Kingdom itself. The silver key Lirael did not know, though it was not an uncommon sigil. Many cities and towns used silver keys in their blazons.

She could feel considerable magic in the door. Charter marks of locking and warding ran with the grain of the wood, and there were other marks, too, describing something Lirael couldn't quite grasp.

She started towards it to see what they were, all her itchiness forgotten, but the Dog put herself in the way, as if curbing an exuberant puppy.

"Don't!" she yelped. "It has a guard-sending on it, who would only see—and slay—an ice otter. You must approach in normal form and let it sense your blood untainted."

"Oh," said Lirael, slumping down, slim head resting on her forepaws, glittering dark eyes focused on the door. "But if I change back, it'll take me at least half the night to make a new Charter-skin. We'll miss dinner—and the midnight rounds."

"Some things," the Dog said portentously, "are worth missing dinner for."

"And the rounds?" asked Lirael. "It'll be the second time this week. Even if it *is* my birthday, it will be extra kitchen duty for me—"

"I like you having extra kitchen duty," replied the Dog, licking her lips, and then licking Lirael's face for good measure.

"Eeerrggh!" exclaimed Lirael. She still hesitated, thinking not only of the extra kitchen duty but also the lecture that would accompany it from Aunt Kirrith.

But just over there, the door of stars and towers and keys beckoned. . . .

Lirael shut her eyes and began to think of the sequence of Charter marks that would unravel the otter-skin, her mind dipping into the never-ending flow of the Charter, picking out a mark here, a symbol there, weaving them into a spell. In just a few minutes she would be plain Lirael again, with her long, unruly black hair so unlike that of her blond- and brown-haired cousins; her pointy chin so much sharper than their round faces; her pale skin that would never tan, not even in the harsh sunlight reflecting off the glacial ice; and her brown eyes, when all the Clayr had blue or green. . . .

The Disreputable Dog watched her change, the ice-otter skin glowing with crawling Charter marks that spun and wove till they became a tornado of light, shining brighter and brighter and spinning faster and faster till it vanished. A slight young woman stood there, frowning, eyes tightly shut. Before her eyes opened, her hands ran over her body, checking that the red waistcoat was there, with dagger, whistle, and clockwork emergency mouse. In some of Lirael's early Charter-skins, all her clothes had fallen off in pieces when she'd shucked the skin, every seam unpicked in an instant.

"Good," said the Disreputable Dog. "Now we can try the door."

Chapter Twenty-One

BEYOND THE DOORS OF WOOD AND STONE

LIRAEL TOOK TWO steps towards the red wood door, then stopped, as Charter Magic flared and swirled before her and a fierce yellow light shone from the door-frame, forcing her to duck her head and blink.

When she looked up, a Charter-sending stood in front of the door—a creature of spell-flesh and magic-bone, conjured for a specific purpose. Not one of the passive Library helpers, but a guard of human shape, though much taller and broader than any living man, clad in silver mail, a closed steel helm hiding whatever face the spell had wrought. Its sword was in its hand, outthrust, held steady as a statue, the point a few inches from Lirael's bare throat. Unlike their spell-flesh, the weapons or tools of sendings were always made to be completely tangible. Sometimes, as Lirael suspected was the case with this sword, they were even harder, sharper, and more dangerous than they would be if wrought of steel rather than magic.

The sending held the sword extended for a few seconds without a waver. Then, so quickly she didn't see it move, the point flicked against Lirael's throat—just enough to break the skin, capturing a single bead of blood on the very tip of the blade.

Lirael gulped down a startled cry but remained frozen, fearful that it would strike again if she flinched. She knew much of the lore of sendings, having continued her studies even after "creating" the Dog. But she could not gauge the true purpose of this one. For the first time since she had gone to confront the Stilken, she felt afraid, and the chill dread of Charter Magic gone wrong welled up inside her bones.

The sending lifted its sword again, and Lirael did flinch this time, unable to control the twitch of fright. But the guard was simply making that drop of blood run down the gutter of the blade in a slow, stately roll, like a bead of oil, not leaving a trace on the Charter-woven steel. After what seemed an age, the bead reached the hilt and sank into the crossguard like butter into toast.

Behind Lirael, the Dog let out a long, half-woofed sigh, even as the sending saluted with the sword—and broke apart, the Charter symbols that had made it momentarily real spinning out into the air before fading away into nothingness. In a few seconds, no sign of the sending remained.

Lirael realized she'd been holding her breath, and let it out with a relieved whoosh. She touched her neck, expecting to feel the unpleasant wetness of blood. But there was nothing, no cut, not even a slight unevenness in the skin.

The Dog's snout nudged her behind the knee. Then the hound slipped past and grinned back at her.

"Well, you passed that test," she said. "You can open the door now."

"I'm not sure I want to," replied Lirael thoughtfully, still fingering her neck. "Maybe we should go back."

"What!" exclaimed the Dog, her ears sticking up in disbelief. "Not look? Since when have you become Miss We Shouldn't Be Here?"

"It could have cut my throat," said Lirael, her voice trembling. "It nearly did."

The Disreputable Dog rolled her eyes and collapsed onto her front paws in exasperation. "It was only testing you, to make sure you have the Blood. You're a Daughter of the Clayr—

no Charter-made creature would harm you. Though as the greater world is full of danger, you'd better start getting used to the idea that you can't give up at the first thing that scares you!"

"Am I a Daughter of the Clayr?" whispered Lirael, tears starting in her eyes. She had held her sorrow in all year, but it was always worst on her birthday. Now it could not be repressed. She crouched down and hugged the Dog, ignoring the damp reek of dog-smell. "I'm nineteen and I still haven't got the Sight. I don't look like everyone else. When that sending put out its sword, I suddenly realized that it knew. It knew I'm not a Clayr, and it was going to kill me."

"But it didn't, because you are a Clayr, idiot," said the Dog, quite gently. "You've seen the hunting dogs, how every now and then one will be born with floppy ears or have a brown back instead of gold. They're still part of the pack. You're just a floppy-ear."

"But I can't See the future!" cried Lirael. "Would the pack accept a dog that couldn't smell?"

"You can smell," said the Dog, rather illogically. She licked Lirael's cheek. "Besides, you have other gifts. None of the others are half the Charter Mage you are, are they?"

"No," whispered Lirael. "But Charter Magic doesn't count. It's the Sight that makes the Clayr. Without it, I am nothing."

"Well, perhaps there are other things you can learn," encouraged the Dog. "You might find something else—"

"What? Like an interest in embroidery?" Lirael said in a depressed monotone, cradling her head in her tear-dampened forearms. "Or perhaps you think I should take up leatherwork?"

"That," said the Dog, her voice losing all sympathy, "is self-pity, and there's only one way to deal with it."

"What?" asked Lirael sullenly.

"This," said the Dog, lunging forward and nipping her quite sharply on the leg.

"Ow!" Lirael shrieked, leaping up and stumbling against the door. "What did you do that for?"

"You were being pathetic," said the Dog, as Lirael rubbed the spot on her calf where visible tooth-marks indented her soft wool leggings. "Now you're just cross, which is an improvement."

Lirael eyed the Dog balefully but didn't answer, because she couldn't think of anything to say that wouldn't—quite accurately—be seen as sulky or bad-tempered. Besides, she remembered a particular dog bite from her seventeenth birthday and had no desire to add a nineteenth-birthday scar.

The Dog stared back, her head tilted to one side, ears cocked, waiting for some sort of reply. Lirael knew from experience that the Dog could sit like that for hours if necessary, and gave up the struggle to maintain her self-pity. Clearly, the Dog just didn't understand how important it was to have the Sight.

"So—how do I open this?" asked Lirael.

Without realizing it, she'd been leaning against the door, catching her balance there after the nip-assisted leap. She could feel the Charter Magic in it, warm and rhythmic under the palm of her hand, moving in slow counterpoint to the pulse in her wrist and neck.

"Give it a push," suggested the Dog, moving closer, sniffing at the crack where the door met the floor. "The sending probably unlocked it for you."

Lirael shrugged and placed both palms against the door. Curiously, the metal studs seemed to have moved while she wasn't looking. They had been all mixed up but were now sorted into three distinct patterns, though there was no obvious meaning to them. Lirael wasn't sure which particular symbols were under her palms, though she could feel them leaving an imprint on her skin.

Even the metal studs were impregnated with Charter symbols, Lirael felt. She didn't know precisely what they were, but it was clear the door was a major work of magic, the result of many months of superior spell-casting and equally masterful metalwork and carpentry.

She pushed once, and the door groaned. She pushed more forcefully, and it suddenly slid back like a concertina, separating into seven distinct panels. Lirael didn't notice that as this happened, one of the three symbols completely disappeared, leaving only two types of studs visible. She was overcome by a sudden surge of Charter Magic that flowed out of the door and somehow into Lirael herself. She felt it coursing through her, infusing her with a heady happiness she had not felt since the Disreputable Dog had first come to banish her loneliness. It swam in her blood, sparked in her breath—then it was gone, and she staggered against the door-frame. At the same time, the impression of the studs on her hands faded before she could see what they meant.

"Whew!" she said, shaking her head, one hand unconsciously feeling for the comforting bulk of the Dog at her side. "What was that?"

"The Door just said hello," replied the Dog. Slipping from Lirael's grasp, she was already questing ahead, paws clicking as she essayed the first steps of a flight that spun downwards into the mountain.

"What do you mean?" asked Lirael. The Dog's upthrust, wagging tail whisked down and around the curve of the spiral. "How can a door say hello? Wait! Wait for me!"

The Disreputable Dog wasn't known for listening to commands, requests, or even entreaties, but she was waiting about twenty steps lower down. There were fewer Charter marks providing light here, and the steps were covered in dark moss. Clearly no one had passed this way for a very long time.

She looked up as Lirael reached her, then immediately took off down the steps again, easily re-establishing her twenty-step lead, and was once again lost to sight, though Lirael could hear her paws steadily clicking down the steps.

Lirael sighed and followed more slowly, not trusting the moss-covered stair. There was something farther down that she didn't quite like, and she felt oppressed by some sense of unease, below the level of consciousness. A sort of vaguely unpleasant pressure that was increasing with every downwards step.

The Dog waited, at least momentarily, eight more times before they reached the bottom of the deep stairs. Lirael guessed they were now more than four hundred yards deeper under the mountain than she had ever been before. There were no ice intrusions here, either, adding to her feeling of strangeness. It wasn't like any other part of the Clayr's domain.

It kept getting darker, too, the lower they went, the old Charter marks for light fading till there were only a few flickering here and there. Whoever had built this stair had started from the bottom, Lirael realized, looking at the marks. The lower ones were much older and had not been replaced for centuries.

Normally, she didn't mind the darkness, but it was different here, deep in the mountain. Lirael called up a light herself, two bright Charter marks of illumination that she wove into her hair, to send a bobbing fall of light ahead of her as she descended.

At the bottom of the stairs, the Dog was scratching the back of her ear in front of another Charter-bound door. This one was of stone, and there were some letters carved into it, large, deep-cut letters using the Middle Alphabet, as well as the Charter symbols only a Charter Mage could see.

Lirael bent closer to read them, then recoiled, turned to the steps, and tried to run away. Somehow the Dog got between her legs, tripping her. Lirael fell and lost control of her light spell, and the bright marks went out, twisting back into the endless flow of the Charter.

For a moment of pure panic, she scrabbled in the darkness, heading for what she thought were the steps. Then her fingers met the soft, wet nose of the Dog, and she saw a faint, spectral glow outlining the shape of her canine companion.

"That was smart," said the Dog in the darkness, moving closer to woofle wetly in Lirael's ear. "I take it you didn't suddenly remember a pie in the oven?"

"The door," whispered Lirael, making no effort to get up. "It's a grave door. To a crypt."

"Is it?"

"It's got my name on it," muttered Lirael.

There was a long pause. Then the Dog said, "So you think someone went to all the trouble to make you a crypt a thousand years ago on the off chance you might turn up one day, walk in, and have a convenient heart attack?"

"No . . ."

There was another long pause, and then the Dog said, "Presuming that this actually is the door to a crypt, may I ask how rare the name Lirael is?"

"Well, I think there was a great-aunt I'm named after, and there was another one before her—"

"So if it is a crypt, it's probably that of some long-ago Lirael," the Dog suggested kindly. "But what makes you think it is a crypt door, anyway? I seem to recall there were two words on the door. And the second one didn't look like 'grave' or 'crypt.'"

"What did it say, then?" asked Lirael, wearily standing up, already mentally reaching for the Charter marks that would give her light, hands ready to sketch them in the air. She couldn't even remember reading the second word, but didn't want to admit to the Dog that she'd just had the overwhelming feeling that it was a crypt. That feeling, combined with seeing her own name, had created a moment of total panic, when her only thought was to get out, to get back to the safety of the Library.

"Something quite different," said the Dog with satisfaction, as light bloomed from Lirael's fingertips, falling cleanly on the door.

This time, Lirael looked long at the carved letters, her hands touching the deep-etched stone. Her forehead wrinkled as she read the words again and again, as if she couldn't quite put the letters together into a sensible word.

"I don't understand," she said finally. "The second word is 'path.' It says 'Lirael's Path'!"

"Guess you should go through, then," said the Dog, unperturbed by the sign. "Even if you're not the Lirael whose path it is, you are a Lirael, which in my book is a pretty good excuse—"

"Dog. Shut up," said Lirael, thinking. If this gate was the beginning of a path named for her, it had been made at least a thousand years ago. Which was not impossible, for the Clayr sometimes had visions of such far-distant futures. Or possible futures, as they called them, for the future was apparently like a many-branching stream, splitting, converging, and splitting again. Much of the Clayr's training, at least as far as Lirael knew, was in working out which possible future was the most likely—or the most desirable.

But there was a catch to the notion that the long-ago Clayr had Seen Lirael, because the Clayr of the present time couldn't See Lirael's future at all and had never been able to do so. Sanar and Ryelle had told her that even when the Nine Day Watch tried to See her, there was nothing. Lirael's future was impenetrable, as was her present. No Clayr had ever Seen her, not even in a chance-found minute showing her in the Library, or asleep in bed a month hence. Once again she was different, not able to See and also Unseen.

If even the Nine Day Watch couldn't See her, Lirael thought, how could the Clayr of a thousand years past know she would come this way? And why would they build not only this door but also the stairs? It was far more likely that this path was named for one of her ancestors, some other Lirael of long ago.

That made her feel better about opening the door. She leaned forward, pushing with both hands against the cold stone. Charter Magic flowed in this door, too, but it did not leap into her, instead just pulsing gently against her skin. It was like an old dog by the fire, content to be stroked, knowing it need not obviously show delight.

The door moved slowly inwards, resisting her push, with a long-drawn-out screech of stone on stone. Colder air flowed from the other side, ruffling Lirael's hair, making the Charter lights dance. There was a damp smell, too, and the strange, oppressive feeling Lirael had encountered on the stairs grew stronger, like the beginning buzz of a toothache that heralds future pain.

A vast chamber lay beyond the door, space stretching up and out, seemingly endless, beyond the pool of light around her. A cavern, measureless in the dark, perhaps going on forever.

Lirael stepped in and looked up, up into darkness, till her neck ached, and her eyes slowly grew accustomed to the gloom. Strange luminescence, not from Charter Magic lights, shone in patches here and there, rising up so high that the farthest glow was like a distant swathe of stars in the night. Still looking up, Lirael realized that she stood at the bottom of a deep rift that stretched up almost to the very pinnacle of Starmount itself. She looked across and saw that she stood on a broad ledge, and the rift continued past it, down into still deeper darkness, perhaps even to the root of the world itself. With that sight came recognition, for she knew only one chasm so narrow and so deep. Much higher up, it was spanned by closed bridges. Lirael had crossed it almost unknowingly many times, but had never seen its terrifying depth.

"I know this place," said Lirael, her voice small and echoing. "We're in the bottom of the Rift, aren't we?"

She hesitated, then added, "The burial place of the Clayr."

The Disreputable Dog nodded but didn't say anything.

"You knew, didn't you?" continued Lirael, still looking up. She couldn't see them, but she knew the higher reaches of the Rift were pockmarked with small caves, each one holding the mortal remains of a past Clayr. Generations of dead, carefully tucked away in this vertical cemetery. In a weird way, she could feel the presence of the graves, or the dead inside them . . . or something.

Her mother was not there, for she had died alone in some foreign land, far from the Clayr, too far for the body to be returned. But Filris rested here, as did others whom Lirael had known.

"It *is* a crypt," she said, looking sternly at the Dog. "I knew it."

"Actually it's more of an ossuary," the Dog began. "I understand that when a Clayr Sees her death, she is lowered down by rope to a suitable ledge, where she digs her own—"

"They do not!" interrupted Lirael, shocked. "They only know when, to some degree. And Pallimor and the gardeners usually prepare the caves. Aunt Kirrith says it's very ill-bred to want to dig your own cave—"

She stopped suddenly and whispered, "Dog? Am I here because they've Seen me die and I have to dig my own cave because I'm ill-bred?"

"I'm going to have to bite you properly if you keep up that

nonsense," growled the Dog. "Why this sudden preoccupation with dying, anyway?"

"Because I can feel it, feel it all around me," muttered Lirael. "Particularly here."

"That's because the doorways to Death are ajar where many people have died, or where many lie buried," said the Dog absently. "The Blood mixes a little, so there are always Clayr who are sensitive to Death. That's what you feel. You shouldn't be afraid of it."

"I'm not, really," replied Lirael, puzzled. "It's like an ache or an itch. It makes me want to do something. Scratch it. Make it go away."

"You don't know any necromancy, do you?"

"Of course not! That's Free Magic. It's forbidden."

"Not necessarily. Clayr have dabbled in Free Magic before, and some still do," said the Dog in a distracted manner. She'd caught the scent of something and was snuffling vigorously around Lirael's feet.

"Who dabbles in Free Magic?" asked Lirael. The Dog didn't answer but continued to sniff around Lirael's feet. "What can you smell?"

"Magic," said the Dog, looking up for a second before resuming her snuffle, roaming out in an ever-increasing circle. "Old, old magic. Hidden here, in the depths of the world. How very, very . . . *yow!*"

Her last words ended in a yelp as a sudden sheet of flame sprang up across the rift, heat and light exploding everywhere. Lirael, totally unprepared, staggered back, falling across the open doorway. An instant later, the Dog collided with her, smelling distinctly singed.

Inside the fiery wall, forms began to take shape, humanoid figures that flexed arms and legs within the flame. Charter marks

roared and swam in the yellow-blue-red inferno, flowing too fast
for Lirael to see what they were.

Then the figures stepped out of the flames, warriors composed entirely of fire, their swords white-hot and brilliant.

"Do something!" barked the Dog.

But Lirael just kept staring at the advancing warriors, mesmerized by the flames that flickered through their bodies. They
were all part of one great Charter-spell, she saw, one enormously
powerful sending made up of many parts. A guardian-sending,
like the one on the red wood door . . .

Lirael stood up, patted the Dog once on the head, and
walked out, straight towards the ferocious heat and the guardians
with their swords of flame.

"I am Lirael," she said, investing her speech with the Charter
marks of truth and clarity. "A Daughter of the Clayr."

Her words hung in the air for a moment, cutting through
the buzz and crackle of the fiery sendings. Then the guardians
raised their swords as if in salute—and a wave of even more intense
heat rolled forward, robbing Lirael's lungs of air. She choked,
coughed, took one step back . . . and fainted.

When she came to, the Disreputable Dog's tongue was just about
to lick her face. For about the tenth time, judging from the thick
film of dog saliva on her cheek.

"What happened?" she asked, quickly looking around. There
were no fires now, no burning guardians, but small Charter marks
for light twinkled all around her like tiny stars.

"They burnt up your air when they saluted. I think that whoever created those sendings expected people to identify themselves
from the door," said the Dog, attempting another lick, only to be
fended off. "Or else they were particularly stupid sendings. Still,
at least one of them had the good grace to throw out a handful

of these little lights. Some of your hair has been burnt off, by the way."

"Curse it!" exclaimed Lirael, examining the singed ends of her hair, where they stuck out from under her scarf. "Aunt Kirrith will notice that for sure! I'll have to tell her I leant over a candle or something. Speaking of Kirrith, we'd better start back."

"Not yet!" protested the Dog. "Not after all this effort. Besides, the lights mark a path. Look! That must be it. Lirael's Path!"

Lirael sat up and looked where the Dog was pointing—in the classic pose, one foreleg up and snout eagerly forward. Sure enough, there was a path of tiny, twinkling Charter lights, leading farther along the ledge, to where the Rift narrowed into an even more ominous darkness.

"We really should go back," she said, half-heartedly. The path of lights was there, beckoning. The sendings had let her past. There must be something at the other end worth getting to. Maybe even something that would help her gain the gift of Sight, she thought, helpless against that longing, the tiny hope that still lived inside her heart. All her years of searching in the Library had not helped her. Perhaps it would be otherwise, here in the ancient heart of the Clayr's realm.

"Come on, then," she said, pushing herself up with a groan. Burnt hair and bruises—that was all she'd found so far. "What are you waiting for?"

"You go first," retorted the Dog. "My nose still hurts from your stupid relatives' blazing doormen."

The path of lights led farther along the ledge, and the Rift narrowed, the rock walls closing in, till Lirael could reach out and run her fingers along the cold, wet stone on either side of her. She stopped doing that when she discovered that the luminescence came from a damp fungus that made her fingertips glow and smell like rotten cabbage.

As the way grew narrower, it also descended farther into the mountain, and a chill dankness banished the last remnants of heat from Lirael's scorched face. There was also a sound, a deep rumbling that vibrated up through her feet, getting louder as they walked on. At first, Lirael thought she was imagining it, that perhaps it was part of what the Dog called her sense of Death. Then she realized what it was: the full-throated roar of rushing water.

"We must be near an underground river or something," she said, nervously raising her voice to counter the rising roar of the water. Like most of the Clayr, she could barely swim, and her experience of rivers was confined to the awesome ice-melt torrents that raged from the glacier every Spring.

"We are almost upon it," replied the Dog, who could see farther in the glow of the star-lined path. "As the poet had it:

> *"Swift river born in deepest night,*
> *Rushing forth to catch the light.*
> *Deep ice and dark its swaddling cloth,*
> *The Kingdom's foes will feel its wroth.*
> *Till mighty Ratterlin spends its strength,*
> *In the Delta at full length.*

"Hmmm . . . I may have forgotten a line there. Let's see, 'Swift river—' "

"The Ratterlin's source is here?" interrupted Lirael, pointing ahead. "I thought it was just meltwater. I didn't know it had a source."

"There is a spring," replied the Dog, after a pause. "A very old spring. In the heart of the mountain, in the deepest dark. Stop!"

Lirael obeyed, one hand instinctively clutching at the loose fold of skin on the Dog's neck, just behind her collar.

At first she didn't understand why the Dog had stopped her, till the hound led her on, a few more cautious steps. With those steps, the sound of the river suddenly became a thundering roar, and cold spray slapped her in the face.

They had come to the river. The path ahead was a slender, slippery bridge of wet stone that stretched out twenty paces or more, to end in yet another door. The bridge had no rails, and was less than two feet wide. Its narrowness, and the rushing water below, were a clear indication that it was designed to be a barrier to the Dead. Nothing of that kind could cross here.

Lirael looked at the bridge, the door, then down at the dark, rushing water, feeling both fear and a terrible fascination. The constant motion of the water and the incessant roar were mesmerizing, but finally she managed to tear her gaze away. She looked at the Dog, and though her words were half-drowned by the crash of the river, exclaimed, "I am not going to cross that!"

The Dog ignored her, and Lirael started to repeat herself. But the words stayed on her tongue as Lirael saw that the Dog's paws had grown twice as large as usual, and flattened out. She also looked quite smug.

"I bet you've even grown suckers," shouted Lirael, shuddering with distaste at the thought. "Like an octopus."

"Of course I have," the Dog shouted back, lifting one paw with a squelching pop that Lirael could hear even over the river's roar. "This looks like a very treacherous bridge."

"Yes, it does," bawled Lirael, looking at the bridge again. Clearly the Dog intended to cross, and with her sucker-footed help, Lirael guessed, crossing would go from impossible to merely dangerous. Sighing, she bent down and took off her shoes, eyes blinking against the constant spray. After tying the laces of her soft leather ankle-boots through her belt, she wriggled her toes on the stone. It was very cold, but Lirael was relieved to feel faint cross-hatching that she hadn't seen in the dim light. That would give her some grip.

"I wonder what this bridge was designed to keep out," she said, carefully slipping her fingers under the Dog's collar, feeling the comforting buzz of the Charter Magic there and the even more comforting bulk of a well-balanced dog.

They had only taken the first step when Lirael voiced her second thought, her words inaudible with the river's bellow all around them.

"Or what it was designed to keep in."

Chapter Twenty-Two

POWER OF THREE

THE DOOR AT the far end of the bridge opened as soon as Lirael touched it. Once again, she felt Charter Magic flow into her, but it was not the friendly touch of the upper door, or the quiet recognition of the stone portal at the entrance to the Rift. This one was more like a wary examination, followed by immediate, but not necessarily friendly, recognition.

Under her hand, the Dog shivered as the door swung open. Lirael felt the tremor and wondered why, till she caught the distinctive, corrosive scent of Free Magic. It was coming from somewhere ahead, strangely overlaid with Charter Magic that bound and contained it.

"Free Magic," whispered Lirael, hesitating. But the Dog continued to move forward, dragging her along. Reluctantly, Lirael followed her through the doorway.

As soon as Lirael passed the threshold, the door slammed shut behind her. In an instant, the roar of the river was cut off. So was the light from the Charter-marked trail. It was dark, darker than any darkness Lirael had ever known, a true dark in which it was suddenly difficult to even imagine light. The darkness pressed upon Lirael, making her doubt her own senses. Only the Dog's warm skin under her hand told her that she was still standing, that the room had not changed, and the floor had not tilted.

"Don't move," whispered the Dog, and Lirael felt a canine

snout briefly press against her leg, as if the spoken warning weren't enough.

The smell of Free Magic grew stronger. Lirael pinched her nose with one hand, trying not to breathe anything in, while her other hand went to the clockwork emergency mouse in her waistcoat pocket. Not that it was likely that even this clever device could find its way from here to the Library.

She could feel Charter Magic building, too, strong marks floating in the air like pollen, their usual internal light dampened. She could sense Charter and Free Magic working together, winding and twisting about her, weaving some spell she couldn't even begin to identify.

Fear began to knot in Lirael's stomach, slowly spreading to paralyze her lungs. She wanted to breathe, to force air slowly in and out, to calm herself with the steadiness of her own breath. But the air was heavy with strange magic, magic she could not—would not—breathe in.

Then lights began to sparkle in the air; tiny, fragile balls of light made up of hundreds of hair-thin spines, like luminous dandelion clocks, wafting about on some breeze Lirael couldn't feel. With the lights, the taint of Free Magic abated, the Charter Magic began to strengthen, and Lirael took a slight, cautious breath.

In the strangely mottled, constantly changing light, Lirael saw that she was in an octagonal chamber. A large room, but not of cold, carved stone as she'd expected, here in the heart of the mountain. The walls were tiled in a delicate pattern of golden stars, towers, and silver keys. The ceiling was plastered and painted with a night sky, full of black, rain-fat clouds advancing upon seven bright and shining stars. And there was carpet under her bare feet, Lirael realized. A deep blue carpet, soft and warm under her toes after the cold, wet stone of the bridge.

In the middle of the room, a redwood table stood in solitary splendor, its slender legs ending in silver, three-toed feet. On its rich, polished surface there were three items, arranged in a line: a small metal case about the size of Lirael's palm; a set of what looked like metal panpipes; and a book, bound in deep blue leather with silver clasps. The table, or the items on it, were clearly the focal point for the magic, for the dandelion lights swarmed thickest there, creating an effect like luminous fog.

"Off you go, then," said the Dog, sitting back on her haunches. "That looks like what we've come for."

"What do you mean?" asked Lirael suspiciously, drawing a series of deep and calming breaths. She felt reasonably safe now, but there was a lot of magic in the room that she didn't know, and she couldn't even begin to guess what it was for or where it came from. And she could still taste Free Magic at the back of her mouth and on her tongue, a cold iron tang that just wouldn't go away.

"The doors opened for you; the path lit up for you; the guardians here didn't destroy you," said the Dog, nuzzling Lirael's open hand with her cold, damp nose. She looked up at Lirael knowingly and added, "Whatever's on that table must be meant for you. Which equally means it's not meant for me. So I'm going to sit down here. Or lie down, actually. Wake me up when it's time to go."

With that, the Dog stretched luxuriously, yawned, and lowered herself to the carpet. Comfortably settled on her side, she swished her tail a few times and then, to all appearances, fell deeply asleep.

"Oh, Dog!" exclaimed Lirael. "You can't sleep now! What'll I do if something bad happens?"

The Dog opened one eye and said, with the least possible jaw movement, "Wake me up, of course."

Lirael looked down at the sleeping Dog, then over at the table. The Stilken was the worst thing she'd encountered in the Library. But she'd found other dangerous things over the past few years—fell creatures, old Charter-spells that had unraveled or become unpredictable, mechanical traps, even poisoned book bindings. All these were the regular hazards of a librarian's life, but nothing like what she faced now. Whatever these items were, they were guarded more heavily, and with stranger and more powerful magic, than anything Lirael had ever seen.

Whatever magic was concentrated here was very old, too, Lirael realized. The walls, the floor, the ceiling, the carpet, the table—even the air in the room—were saturated with layer upon layer of Charter marks, some of them at least a thousand years old. She could feel them moving everywhere, mixing and changing. When she closed her eyes for a moment, the room felt almost like a Charter Stone, a source of Charter Magic rather than just a place upon which many spells had been cast.

But that was impossible, at least as far as she knew. . . .

Suddenly made dizzy by the thought, Lirael opened her eyes again. Charter marks flowed against her skin, into her breath, swam in her blood. Free Magic floated between the marks. The dandelion lights spread out towards her like tendrils, wrapped gently around her waist, and slowly reeled her in towards the table.

The magic and the lights made her feel light-headed and dazed, as if she'd woken from the final moments of a dream. Lirael fought the feeling for a moment, but it was a pleasant feeling, not at all threatening. She let the sleeping Dog lie and walked forward slowly, swathed in light.

Then she was suddenly at the table, with no memory of crossing the intervening space. Her hands were resting on the cool, polished surface of the table. As could be expected of a Second

Assistant Librarian, she reached for the book first, her fingers
touching the silver clasp that held it shut as she read the title
embossed in silver type upon the spine: *The Book of Remembrance
and Forgetting.*

Lirael undid the clasp, feeling Charter Magic there, too,
noting the marks that chased each other across the silver surface
and deep in the metal itself. Marks of binding and closing, burning and destruction.

But the clasp was open by the time she realized what the
marks were, and she stood unharmed. Carefully, she turned back
the cover and the title page, the crisp, leaf-thin paper turning easily.
There were Charter marks inside the pages, put there at the time
of the paper's making. And Free Magic, constrained and channeled
into place. Magic of both kinds lay in the boards and leather of the
cover, and even in the glue and stitching of the spine.

Most of all, there was magic and power in the type. In the
past, Lirael had seen similar, if less powerful, books, like *In the
Skin of a Lyon.* You could never truly finish reading such a book,
for the contents changed at need, at the original maker's whim,
or to suit the phases of the moon or the patterns of the weather.
Some of the books had contents you couldn't even remember till
certain events might come to pass. Invariably, this was an act of
kindness from the creator of the book, for such contents invariably dealt with things that would be a burden to recall with every
waking day.

The lights danced around Lirael's head as she began to read,
making shadow patterns from her hair flicker across the page. She
read the first page, then the next, then the one after. Soon Lirael
had finished the first chapter, as her hand reached out every few
minutes to turn the page. Behind her, the Dog's heavy, sleepy
breath seemed to match the slow rhythm of the turning pages.

Hours later, or even days—for Lirael had lost all knowledge

of time—she turned what seemed to be the last page and closed the book. It latched itself shut, the silver clasp snapping.

Lirael drew back at the snap but didn't leave the table. Instead, she picked up the panpipes, seven small tubes of silver, ranging in size from the length of her little finger to a little shorter than her hand. She held the pipes up to her lips, but didn't blow. They were much more than they appeared. The book had told her how the pipes were made, and how they should be used, and Lirael now knew that the Charter marks that moved in the silver were only a veneer on the Free Magic that lurked within.

She touched each of the pipes in turn, smallest to largest, and whispered their names to herself before putting the instrument back on the table. Then she picked up the last item, the small metal case. This was silver, too, etched with pleasing decorations as well as Charter marks. The latter were similar to those on the book, all threatening retribution if the box were opened by someone not of the True Blood. It didn't say which particular blood, but Lirael thought that if the book opened for her, the case would, too.

She lightly touched the catch, recoiling a little as she felt the heat of Free Magic blazing within. The case remained shut. Briefly, she thought that the book might be wrong, or she might have misread the marks, or not have the right blood. She shut her eyes and firmly pressed the catch.

Nothing terrible happened, but the case shivered in her hand. Lirael opened her eyes. The case had sprung open into two halves, hinged in the middle. Like a small mirror, to be balanced on a shelf or table.

Lirael opened it completely and placed it, vee-shaped, on the table. One side of it was silver, but the other was something she couldn't describe. Where the bright reflective surface of a mirror would be, there was a nonreflective rectangle of . . . nothing. A piece of absolute darkness, a shape of something made from the total absence of light.

The Book of Remembrance and Forgetting called it a Dark Mirror, and Lirael had read, at least in part, how it might be used. But the Dark Mirror would not work in this room, or in any part of the world of Life. It could be used only in Death, and Lirael had no intention of going there, even if the book professed to show her how to come back. Death was the province of the Abhorsen, not the Clayr, even though the peculiar use of the Dark Mirror could possibly be related to the Clayr's gift of Sight.

Lirael snapped shut the Dark Mirror and laid it on the table. But her fingers still rested upon it. She stood there like that for a full minute, thinking. Then she picked it up and slipped it into her left waistcoat pocket, to join the company of a pen nib, a length of waxed string, and a seriously foreshortened pencil. After another moment of hesitation, she picked up the panpipes and put them in her right pocket with the clockwork mouse. Finally, she picked up the *Book of Remembrance and Forgetting* and tucked it into the front of her waistcoat.

She walked back to the Disreputable Dog. It was time for the two of them to have a very serious talk about what was going on. The Book, the Dark Mirror, and the panpipes had lain here for a thousand years or more, waiting in the dark for someone the Clayr of long ago had known would come.

Waiting in the dark for a woman named Lirael.

Waiting for *her*.

Chapter Twenty-Three

A TROUBLESOME SEASON

PRINCE SAMETH STOOD shivering on the narrow sentry walk of the Palace's second tallest tower. He was wearing his heaviest fur cloak, but the wind still cut through it, and he couldn't be bothered to cast a Charter-spell for warmth. He half wanted to catch a cold, because it would mean escaping from the training schedule Ellimere had forced upon him.

He was standing on the sentry walk for two reasons. The first reason was that he wanted to look out in the hope that he would see either his father or his mother returning. The second was that he wanted to avoid Ellimere and everyone else who wanted to organize his life.

Sam missed his parents, not just because they might free him from Ellimere's tyranny. But Sabriel was constantly in demand away from Belisaere, flying her red and gold Paperwing from one trouble spot to the next. It was a bad winter, people repeatedly said in Sam's hearing, with so much activity from the Dead and from Free Magic creatures. Sam always shivered inside as they said it, knowing their eyes were on him and that he should be studying *The Book of the Dead*, preparing himself to help his mother.

He should be studying now, he thought glumly, but he continued to stare out over the frosted roofs of the city and through the rising smoke of thousands of cozy fires.

He hadn't opened the book at all since Ellimere had given

it to him. The green and silver volume remained safely locked in a cupboard in his workroom. He thought about it every day, and looked at it, but couldn't bring himself to actually read it. In fact, he spent the hours he was supposed to be studying it trying to work out how he could tell his mother that he couldn't. He couldn't read the book, and he couldn't face going into Death again.

Ellimere allowed him two hours a day for study of the book, or "Abhorsen prep" as she called it, but Sam did no reading. He wrote instead. Speech after speech in which he tried to explain his feelings and his fears. Letters to Sabriel. Letters to Touchstone. Letters to both parents. All of them ended up in the fire.

"I'll just tell her," announced Sam to the wind. He didn't speak too loudly in case the sentry on the far side of the tower heard him. The guards already thought he was a miserable excuse for a Prince. He didn't want them thinking he was a mad Prince as well.

"No, I'll tell Dad, and then he can tell her," he added after a moment's thought. But Touchstone had barely returned from Estwael when he had had to ride south to the Guard Fort at Barhedrin Hill, just north of the Wall. There had been reports that the Ancelstierrans were allowing groups of Southerling refugees to cross the Wall and settle in the Old Kingdom—or in actuality, to be killed by the creatures or wild folk who roamed the Borderlands. Touchstone had gone to investigate these reports, to see what the Ancelstierrans were up to, and to save any of the Southerlings who might have survived.

"Stupid Ancelstierrans," muttered Sam, kicking the wall. Unfortunately, his other foot slipped on the icy stone, and he skidded into the wall, smacking his funny bone.

"Ow!" he exclaimed, clutching his elbow. "Blast it!"

"You all right, sir?" asked the guard, who came at a run, his hob-nailed boots providing much better purchase than Sam's rabbit-fur slippers. "You don't want to break a leg."

Sam scowled. He knew that the prospect of his dancing the Bird of Dawning provided no end of amusement for the guards. His sense of self-worth wasn't helped by their badly disguised snickering or the ease with which Ellimere practiced her own future role, acting as co-regent with grace and authority—at least to everyone except Sam.

Sam's stumbling rehearsals for the Bird of Dawning part in the Midwinter and Midsummer Festivals was only one of the many areas in which he displayed himself as poorer royal material than his sister. He couldn't pretend enthusiasm for the dances, he often fell asleep in Petty Court, and while he knew he was a very competent swordsman, he somehow didn't feel like stretching his ability at practice with the guards.

Nor did he show up well at Perspective. Ellimere always threw herself into the task at hand, working like fury. Sam did quite the reverse, staring into space and worrying about his clouded future, often becoming so engrossed that he stopped doing whatever he was supposed to be doing.

"Sir, are you all right?" the guard repeated.

Sam blinked. There, he was doing it again. Staring into space while he thought about staring into space.

"Yes, thank you," he said, flexing his gloved fingers. "Slipped. Hit my funny bone."

"See anything interesting out there?" asked the guard. His name was Brel, Sam remembered. Quite a friendly guard, not one who stifled a smile every time Sam walked past in his Bird of Dawning costume.

"No," replied Sam, shaking his head. He looked out again, down into the interior of the city. The Midwinter Festival was to start in a few days. Construction of the Frost Fair was in full swing. A great, bustling tent town on the frozen surface of Lake Loesare, the Frost Fair had pageant wagons and players, jesters and jugglers, musicians and magicians, exhibitions and expositions, and all sorts of games, not to mention food from every corner of the Old Kingdom and beyond. Lake Loesare covered ninety acres of Belisaere's central valley, but the Frost Fair overflowed it, extending into the public gardens that lined the lakeshore.

Sam had always liked the Frost Fair, but he looked down on it now without interest. All he could feel was a cold and black depression.

"All the fun of the fair," said Brel, clapping his hands together. "It looks like it'll be a good festival this year."

"Does it?" asked Sam bleakly. He would have to dance on the final day of the Festival, as the Bird of Dawning. It was his job to carry the green sprig of Spring at the tail end of the Winter procession, behind Snow, Hail, Sleet, Fog, Storm, and Frost. They were all professional dancers on stilts, so they not only loomed threateningly over the Bird but also showed up Sam's lack of expertise.

The Winter Dance was long and complicated, weaving through two miles of the Fair's winding ways. But it was much longer than that, because there was lots of doubling back as the Six Spirits of Winter ducked around the Bird and tried to prolong their season by stealing the sprig of Spring from under Sam's golden wing, or by tripping him up with their stilts.

There had been two full rehearsals so far. The Spirits of Winter were supposed to fail at tripping the Bird, but so far even the skill of the other dancers couldn't prevent the Bird from tripping himself. By the end of the first rehearsal, the Bird had fallen three times and bent its beak twice, and certainly had extremely ruffled feathers. The second rehearsal had been even worse, when the Bird crashed into Sleet and knocked her off her stilts. The new Sleet still wouldn't talk to him.

"They say a hard practice means an easy dance," said Brel.

Sam nodded and looked away from the guard. There was no sign of a Paperwing gliding in against the wind, or a troop of horsemen bearing the royal banner on the southern road. It was a waste of time looking for his parents.

Brel coughed into his glove. Sam glanced back as the guard inclined his head and resumed his slow march around the sentry walk, his trumpet bumping gently on its strap against his back.

Sam went downstairs. He was already late for the next rehearsal.

Brel was wrong about the bad rehearsals meaning a successful dance. Sam bumbled and stumbled all his way through it, and only the professionalism and energy of the Six Spirits saved the dance from disaster.

Traditionally, all the dancers from the Festival ate with the royal family at the Palace after the dance, but Sam chose to stay away. They'd done enough to him, and he'd done enough, with the bruises to show for it. He was sure Sleet had deliberately smacked him with her stilt near the end. She was the sister of the one he'd knocked off her stilts in rehearsal.

Instead of attending the dinner, Sam retired to his workshop, trying to forget his troubles in the construction of a particularly intricate and interesting magical-mechanical toy. Ellimere sent a page to get him but could do no more without embarrassing everyone, so he was left in peace—for that night at least.

But not the next day or the days following. Ellimere couldn't—or wouldn't—see that Sam's sullenness came from genuine trouble. So she simply made up more things for him to do. Even worse, she started foisting the younger sisters of her own friends on him, clearly thinking that a good woman could sort out whatever was wrong with him. Naturally, Sam took an instant dislike to anyone Ellimere so obviously seated next to him at dinner, or who "just happened" to drop by his workroom with a broken bracelet catch to be mended. His constant worry about the book and his mother's return left him little energy to pursue friendships, let alone romantic attachments. So he earned the reputation of being stiff and distant, not only among the young women introduced to him by Ellimere, but to everyone of his own age around the Palace. Even people who had been his friends in previous years, when he was home for the holidays, found that they no longer enjoyed his company. Sam, caught up in his own troubles and busy with his official duties, hardly noticed that people of his own age avoided him.

He did talk to Brel a bit, since they both tended to be up the second tallest tower around the same time. Fortunately, the guard was not naturally talkative and also didn't seem to mind Sam's silences or his tendency to stop and just stare out over the city and the sea.

"Your birthday today," said Brel, early one clear and very cold morning. The moon was still visible, and there was a ring around it, as only happened on the coldest nights of winter.

Sam nodded. Since it occurred two weeks after the Mid-winter Festival, his birthday was always somewhat eclipsed by the greater event. This year, it was made even less spectacular by the continued absence of Sabriel and Touchstone, who could only send messages and presents that, while obviously carefully chosen, did not cheer Sam. Particularly since one was a surcoat with the silver keys of the Abhorsen on a deep blue field, quartered with the royal line's golden castle on a red field, and the other was a book entitled *Merchane on the Binding of Free Magic Elementals*.

"Get any good presents?" asked Brel.

"Surcoat," said Sam. "And a book."

"Ah," said Brel. He clapped his hands together, to regain circulation. "Not a sword, then? Or a dog?"

Sam shook his head. He didn't want a sword or a dog, but either would have been more welcome than what he had been given.

"Expect Princess Ellimere will get you something good," Brel said after a long, thoughtful pause.

"I doubt it," said Sam. "She'll probably organize some sort of *lesson*."

Brel clapped his hands together again, stood still, and slowly scanned the horizon from south to north.

"Happy birthday," he said when his head had finished its slow movement. "What is it? Eighteen?"

"Seventeen," replied Sam.

"Ah," said Brel, and he walked around to the other side of the tower to repeat his scan of the horizon.

Sam went back downstairs.

Ellimere did organize a birthday feast in the Great Hall, but it was a lackluster affair, mainly due to Sam's depressing influence. He refused to dance, because it was the one day when he could refuse, and since it was his birthday, that meant no one else could dance, either. He refused to open his presents in front of everyone because he didn't feel like it, and he merely toyed with the grilled swordfish with lime and buttered smallwheat that had once been his favorite dish. In fact, he acted like a spoiled and sulky brat of seven, rather than like a young man of seventeen. Sam knew it but felt unable to stop. It was the first time in weeks that he'd been able to refuse Ellimere's orders or, as she called them, "strong suggestions."

The feast ended early, with everyone cross and short-tempered. Sam went straight to his workroom, ignoring the whispers and sidelong looks as he left the Hall. He didn't care what everyone thought, though he was uncomfortably aware of Jall Oren's hooded eyes watching his exit. Jall would certainly report on Sam's shortcomings when his parents returned, if he didn't decide before then to deliver one of his justly feared summations of exactly what was wrong with Sam's behavior.

But even one of Jall's lectures would pale to insignificance when his mother found out the truth about her son. Beyond that revelation, Sam daren't think. He couldn't imagine what would happen, or what his own future would be. The Kingdom had to have an Abhorsen-in-Waiting and a royal heir. Ellimere was demonstrably the perfect royal heir, so Sam had to be the Abhorsen-in-Waiting. Only he couldn't do it. Not wouldn't, as everyone was bound to think. Couldn't.

That night, as he had done scores of times before, Sam unlocked the cupboard to the left of his workbench and steeled himself to look at *The Book of the Dead*. It sat on a shelf, shining with its own ominous green light that overshadowed the soft glow of the Charter lights in the ceiling.

He reached out to it, like a hunter trying to pat a wolf in the vain hope that it might be only a friendly dog. His fingers touched the silver clasp and the Charter marks laid upon it, but before he could do more, a violent shaking overtook him, and his skin turned as cold as ice. Sam tried to still the shakes and ignore the cold, but he couldn't. He snatched back his hand and retreated to the front of the fireplace, where he crouched down in misery, hugging his knees.

A week after his birthday, Sam received a letter from Nick. Or rather, the remains of a letter, because it had been written on machine-made paper. Like most products of Ancelstierran technology, the paper had begun to fail upon crossing the Wall, and it was now crumbling into its component fibers. Sam had often told Nick in the past to use hand-made paper, but he never did.

Still, there was enough of it left for Sam to deduce that Nick was asking him for an Old Kingdom visa for himself and a servant. He intended to cross the Wall at Midwinter, and he would be grateful if Sam met him at the Crossing Point.

Sam brightened. Nick could always cheer him up. He immediately consulted his almanac to see what Midwinter in Ancelstierre would correspond with in the Old Kingdom. Generally, the Old Kingdom was a full season ahead of Ancelstierre, but there were some strange fluctuations that required double-checking in an almanac, particularly around the solstices and the turn of the seasons.

Old Kingdom/Ancelstierre almanacs like Sam's had been almost impossible to obtain once, but ten years ago Sabriel had lent hers to the royal printer, who had reset it to incorporate all the handwritten comments and marginalia of Sabriel and previous Abhorsens. That had been a long and laborious process. The end result was aesthetically very pleasing, with clear, slightly indented type on crisp linen paper, but was very expensive. Sabriel and Touchstone were careful about who was allowed to have these almanacs. Sameth had been very proud when he was entrusted with one on his twelfth birthday.

Fortunately, the almanac had an exact correspondence for Midwinter, rather than just an equation for Sam to work out, requiring moon sights and other observations. On that day in Ancelstierre, it would be the Day of Ships in the Old Kingdom, in the third week of spring. It was still many weeks off, but at least Sam had something positive to look forward to.

After the letter from Nick, Sam's mood improved a little, and he got on better with everyone in the Palace except Ellimere. The rest of winter passed without either of his parents coming home, and without any particularly terrible storms or the intense, bone-numbing cold that sometimes rolled in from the northeast, accompanied by pods of lost whales who didn't otherwise enter the Sea of Saere.

Weather-wise it was a particularly mild winter, but in court and city the people still spoke of it as a bad one. There had been more trouble all over the Kingdom that season than in any of the last ten winters, trouble such as hadn't been seen since the early days of Touchstone's reign. Message-hawks flew constantly to and from the Mews Tower, and Mistress Finney grew red-eyed and even more irritable than normal, as her children, the hawks, were hard-pressed to meet the demand for communication. Many of the messages the hawks carried were reports of the Dead, and of Free Magic creatures. A large proportion turned out to be false, but all too many were real, and all required Sabriel's attention.

There was other news that troubled Sam. One letter from his father reminded him too much of the terrible day on the Perimeter, when the Dead Southerlings had attacked his cricket team and he had faced the necromancer in Death.

Sam took the letter up the second-tallest tower to read over and think, while Brel paced around him. One particular section he read three times:

> The Ancelstierran Army, presumably under instructions from the government, has allowed a group of Southerling "volunteers" to enter the Old Kingdom at one of the old Crossing Points on the Wall, in contravention of all past agreements and common sense. Obviously, Corolini has gained further support, and this is a test of his plan to send all the Southerlings into the Kingdom.
>
> I have put a stop to further crossings as best I can, and reinforced the guards at Barhedrin. But there is no guarantee that the Ancelstierrans will not send more Southerlings

*across, though General Tindall has said he will delay acting
on any such order and warn us if he can.*

*In any case, more than a thousand Southerlings have
already crossed, and they are at least four days ahead of us.
Apparently they were met by "local guides," but as no
Perimeter Scouts were allowed to escort the refugees, I do not
know whether these were even true men.*

*We will pursue, of course, but there is a smell about this
I do not like. I am certain at least one Free Magic sorcerer is
involved on our side of the Wall, and the Crossing Point the
Southerlings used is the one closest to where you were
ambushed, Sameth.*

The necromancer, thought Sam as he folded the letter. He
was glad the sun was out and that he was in the Palace, protected
by wards and guards and running water.

"Bad news?" asked Brel.

"Just news," said Sam, but he was unable to suppress a shiver.

"Nothing the King and the Abhorsen can't deal with," said
Brel, with total confidence.

"Wherever they are," whispered Sam. He put the letter inside
his coat and went back downstairs. To his workshop, to lose himself in making things, in tiny details that required all his attention
and the total dexterity of his hands.

With every step, he knew he should be going to open *The
Book of the Dead.*

Typically, Sam's parents returned on a beautiful spring evening,
long after Sam had climbed down from the tower and Brel's watch
had ended. The wind had turned to the east, the Sea of Saere was
shifting color from winter black to summery turquoise, the sun
was still warm even as it sank into the west, and the swallows that

lived in the cliffs were stealing wool from Sam's torn blanket for their nests.

Sabriel arrived first, her Paperwing skimming low over the practice yard where Sam was sweating through forty-eight patterns of attack and defense with Cynel, one of the better guards. The shadow of the Paperwing startled them both and allowed Cynel to take the final point, since she recovered while Sam was momentarily paralyzed.

His day of doom had finally come, and all his prepared speeches and letters leaked out of his brain, as if his opponent had actually pierced his head rather than triumphantly clanging her wooden sword down on his heavily padded helmet.

He was hurrying inside to change out of his practice armor when the trumpets sounded above the South Gate. At first he thought they were for his mother, till he heard other trumpets farther away, up at the West Yard, where her Paperwing would have landed. So the trumpets at the South Gate had to be announcing the King. No one else got a fanfare.

It was indeed Touchstone. Sam met him twenty minutes later in the family's private solar—a large room, three stories above the Great Hall, with a single long window that looked down upon the city rather than the sea. Touchstone was looking out at his capital as Sam came in, watching the lights come on. Bright Charter lights and soft oil lights, flickering candles and fires. It was one of the best times to be in Belisaere, at lighting-up time on a warm spring evening.

As usual, Touchstone looked tired, though he'd managed to wash and change out of armor and riding gear. He was wearing an Ancelstierran-style bathrobe, his curly hair still wet from a hasty bath. He smiled as he saw Sam, and they shook hands.

"You look better, Sam," said Touchstone, noting the flush in his son's face from the sword practice. "Though I had hoped you'd also develop as a letter writer this winter."

"Um," said Sam. He'd sent only two letters to his father all winter, and a few notes at the bottom of some of Ellimere's much more regular correspondence. Neither the letters nor the notes had contained anything very interesting and nothing at all personal. Sam had actually drafted some that did, but like the ones to his mother, they'd ended up in the fire.

"Dad, I . . ." Sam began hesitantly, and he felt a surge of relief as he finally began to broach the subject he'd stewed on all winter. "Dad, I can't—"

Before he could go on, the door swung open, and Ellimere breezed in. Sam's mouth snapped shut, and he glared at her, but she ignored him and rushed straight to Touchstone, hugging him with evident relief.

"Dad! I'm so glad you're home," she said. "And Mother, too!"

"One big happy family," muttered Sam under his breath.

"What was that?" asked Touchstone, a touch of sternness in his voice.

"Nothing," said Sam. "Where's Mother?"

"Down in the reservoir," replied Touchstone slowly. He kept one arm around Ellimere and drew Sam in with the other. "Now, I don't want you to get too worried, but she's had to go to the Great Stones, because she's been wounded—"

"Wounded!" exclaimed Ellimere and Sam together, turning in so that all three of them were in a tight circle.

"Not seriously," Touchstone said hastily. "A bite to the leg from some sort of Dead thing, but she couldn't attend to it at the time, and it went bad."

"Is she . . . is she going to . . ." Ellimere asked anxiously, staring down at her own leg in consternation. From the look on her face, it was plain that she found it hard to imagine Sabriel hurt and not completely in command of herself and everything around her.

"No, she is not going to lose her leg," Touchstone said firmly. "She's had to go down to the Great Charter Stones because both of us were simply too tired to cast the necessary healing spells. But we'll be able to down there. It is also the best place for all of us to have a private discussion. A family conference."

The reservoir where the six Great Charter Stones stood was in many ways the heart of the Old Kingdom. It was possible to access the Charter, the very wellspring of magic, anywhere in the Old Kingdom, but the presence of ordinary Charter Stones made it much easier, as if they were conduits to the Charter. However, the Great Charter Stones actually seemed to be *of* the Charter, not just connected to it. While the Charter contained and described all living things and all possibilities, and existed everywhere, it was particularly concentrated in the Great Stones, the Wall, and the bloodlines of the royal family, as well as the Abhorsens and the Clayr. Certainly, when two of the Great Stones were broken by Kerrigor, and the royal family apparently lost, the Charter itself had seemed to weaken, allowing greater free-dom to Free Magic and the Dead.

"Wouldn't it be better to have the conference up here, after Mother's cast her spell?" asked Sam.

Despite its importance to the Kingdom, the reservoir had never been his favorite place, even before he had become so afraid of Death. The Stones themselves were comforting, even keeping the water around them warm, but the rest of the reservoir was cold and horrible. Touchstone's mother and sisters had been slain there by Kerrigor, and much later, Sabriel's father had died there, too. Sam didn't want to think about what it must have been like when there were two broken Stones, and Kerrigor lurked there in the darkness with his necromantic beasts and Dead servants.

"No," replied Touchstone, who had much more reason than

his son to fear the place. But he had lost that fear years ago, in his long labor to repair the broken Stones with his own blood and fragments of barely remembered magic. "It's the only place where we will definitely not be overheard, and there are too many things you both must know, and no others should. Bring the wine, Sameth. We'll need it."

"Are you going like that?" asked Ellimere, as Touchstone strode over to the fireplace and into the left-hand side of the inglenook. He turned as she spoke, looked down on his robe and the twin swords belted across it, shrugged, and went on. Ellimere sighed and followed him, and both disappeared into the darkness behind the fire.

Sam scowled and picked up the earthenware jug of spiced wine that had been mulled and placed near the fire to keep hot. Then he followed, pressing his hand up against the rear of the inglenook, Charter marks flaring as the guard-spell let him push open the secret door. Beyond that, he could already hear his father and sister clattering down the one hundred fifty-six steps that led to the reservoir, the Great Charter Stones, and Sabriel.

Chapter Twenty-Four

COLD WATER, OLD STONE

THE RESERVOIR WAS a vast hall of silence, cold stone, and even colder water. The Great Stones stood in the darkness at its center, invisible from the landing where the Palace stairs met the water. Around the rim of the reservoir, shafts of sunlight came down from the grilled openings high above, casting cross-hatched ripples of light across the mirror-smooth surface of the water. Tall columns of white marble rose up like mute sentinels between the patches of light, supporting the ceiling sixty feet above.

The water was, as always, extremely clear. Sam dipped his hand in it as he helped his father untie the barge that was moored at the end of the Palace steps. As the water trickled between his fingers, he saw Charter marks sparkle briefly. All the water in the reservoir absorbed magic from the Great Charter Stones. Closer to the center, the water was almost more magic than anything else, and was no longer cold—or even wet.

The barge was not much more than a raft with gilded knobs on each corner. There were two of them in the reservoir, but Sabriel had obviously taken the other one. She would be on it, out there in the center, where no sunlight fell. The Great Stones glowed with all the millions of Charter marks that moved in and on them, but most of the time it was only a faint luminescence, no rival even to the filtered sunlight. They wouldn't see the glow until they were close, away from the light-dappled rim, past the third line of columns.

Touchstone undid the rope on his side, then placed his hand upon the planking and whispered a single word. Ripples moved across the still water as he spoke, and the barge began to edge away from the landing. There was no current in the reservoir, but the barge moved as if there were, or as if unseen hands pushed it through the water. Touchstone, Sam, and Ellimere stood close together in the middle, occasionally shifting balance as the barge swayed and rocked.

This was how Sam's long-dead aunts and his grandmother had traveled to their deaths, he thought. Standing on a barge—maybe even this same one, he thought, dredged up, repaired and re-gilded—all unsuspecting, till they were ambushed by Kerrigor. He had cut their throats, catching their blood in his golden cup. Royal blood. Blood for the breaking of the Great Charter Stones.

Blood for the breaking, blood for the making. The Stones had been broken by royal blood, and re-made with royal blood—his father's blood. Sam looked at Touchstone and wondered how he had done it. The weeks of laboring here alone, each morning taking a silver, Charter-spelled knife and deliberately re-opening the cuts in his palms from the day before. Cuts that had left white lines of scar tissue from his little finger to the ball of the thumb. Cutting his hands, and casting spells that he had not been sure of, spells that were terribly dangerous to the caster, even without the added risk and burden of the broken Stones.

But even more, Sam wondered about the use of blood, the same blood that ran in his veins. It felt strange to him that his pounding heart was in its way akin to the Great Stones ahead. How ignorant he was, particularly of the Charter's greater secrets.

Why was royal, Abhorsen, and Clayr blood different from normal people's—even that of other Charter Mages, whose blood was sufficient to mend or mar only the lesser Stones? The three blood-lines were known as Great Charters, like the Great Stones ahead, and the Wall. But why? Why did their blood contain Charter Magic, magic that could not be duplicated by marks drawn from the generally accessible Charter?

Sam had always been fascinated by Charter Magic, particu-larly making things with it, but the more he used it, the more he realized how little he knew. So much knowledge had been lost in the two hundred years of the Interregnum. Touchstone had passed on as much as he knew to his son, but his own specialty was in battle magic, not in making, or any deeper mysteries. He had been a Royal Guard, a bastard Prince, not a mage, at the time of the Queen's death. After that, he had been imprisoned in the shape of a ship's figurehead for two hundred years, while the Kingdom sank slowly into disorder.

Touchstone had been able to mend the Great Stones, he had said, because the broken Stones wanted to be re-made. He had made many mistakes at first, and only survived by grace of the Stones' support and strength, nothing else. Even so, it had taken many months, and as many years off his life. There had been no silver in Touchstone's hair before the mending.

The barge passed between two columns, and Sam's eyes slowly adjusted to the strange twilight. He could see the six Great Stones ahead now, tall monoliths of dark grey, their irreg-ular shapes quite different from the smooth masonry of the columns and only a third of their height. And there was the other barge, floating in the center of the ring of Stones. But where was Sabriel?

Fear suddenly gripped hard at his chest. He couldn't see his mother, and all he could think of was how the Dead Kerrigor had taken on his former human shape and lured Sam's grand-mother the Queen down to a dark and bloody death. Maybe Touchstone wasn't really Touchstone, but something else that had assumed his form. . . .

Something moved on the barge ahead. Sam, who had unconsciously held his breath, gasped and choked, thinking that all his fears were realized. Whatever it was had no human shape, rising only as high as his waist, without arms or head or dis-cernible form. A lump of writhing darkness, where his mother should be—

Then Touchstone slapped him on the back. He took a sudden breath, and the thing on the barge cast a small Charter light that sparkled in the air above like a tiny star—revealing that it was Sabriel after all. She had been lying down, wrapped in her dark blue cloak, and had just sat up. The light shone on her face now, and her familiar smile met them. But it was not the full, uncar-ing smile of complete happiness, and she looked more tired and worn than Sam had ever seen her. Always pale, her skin looked almost translucent in the Charter light, and it was sheened with the sweat of pain and suffering. For the first time, Sam saw white streaks in her hair, and he was struck with the realization that she was not ageless but would one day grow old. She was not wear-ing her bells, but the bandolier lay beside her, the mahogany handles in easy reach, as did her sword and pack.

Sam's barge drifted between two of the Stones and into the ring. All three passengers started as it crossed, feeling a sudden surge of energy and power from the Great Stones. Some weari-ness was stripped away from them, though not all. In Sam's case, the fear and guilt that he had carried all winter were lessened. He felt more confident, more like his old self. It was a feeling he hadn't had since he'd walked out onto the pitch for that final cricket match in the Schoolboys' Shield.

The two barges met. Sabriel didn't get up, but she held out her arms. A second later, she was hugging Ellimere and Sam, the barges rocking dangerously from their sudden rush and enthusiastic greetings.

"Ellimere! Sameth! I am so glad to see you, and so sorry I have been too long away," said Sabriel, after the initial very tight hug had given way to a looser one.

"That's all right, Mother," replied Ellimere, who sounded more as if she were the mother and Sabriel her daughter. "It's you we're worried about. Let's have a look at your leg."

She started to lift the cloak, but Sabriel stopped her just as Sam caught the faint, horrible smell of decaying flesh.

"It's still not pleasant," Sabriel said quickly. "A wound from the Dead rots quickly, I'm afraid. But I have cast healing-spells upon it, with the aid of the Great Stones, and fixed a poultice of feliac there, too. All will soon be well."

"This time," said Touchstone. He was standing outside the close group of Sabriel, Ellimere, and Sam, looking down at his wife.

"Your father is angry with me because he thinks I almost got myself killed," said Sabriel, with a slight grin. "I don't understand it myself, since I think he should be glad that I didn't."

Silence greeted this remark, till Sam hesitantly asked, "How badly were you hurt?"

"Badly," replied Sabriel, wincing as she moved her leg. Charter marks flared under the cloak, briefly visible even through the tightly woven wool. She hesitated, then quietly added, "If I hadn't met your father on the way back, I might not have made it here."

Sam and Ellimere exchanged horrified glances. All their lives they had heard stories of Sabriel's battles and hard-won victories. She had been wounded before, but they had never heard her admit that she might have been killed, and had never really considered the possibility themselves. She was the Abhorsen, who entered Death only of her own accord!

"But I did make it, and I am going to be absolutely fine," Sabriel said firmly. "So there is no need for anyone to fuss."

"Meaning me, I suppose," said Touchstone. He sat down with a sigh, then stood up irritably to re-arrange his swords and bathrobe before sitting again.

"The reason I am fussing," he said, "is that I am concerned that all this winter someone, or something, has been deliberately and cleverly arranging situations to put you most at risk. Look at the places you've been called to, and how there are always more Dead than were reported, and more dangerous creatures—"

"Touchstone," interrupted Sabriel, reaching out to take his hand. "Calm down. I agree. You know I agree."

"Mmph," grumbled Touchstone, but he did not say any more.

"It's true," replied Sabriel, looking squarely at Sam and Ellimere. "There is a clear pattern, and not just in the Dead that have been raised solely to ambush me. I think that the increasing number of Free Magic elementals is also connected, as is the trouble that your father has been having with the Southerling refugees."

"It almost certainly is," said Touchstone, sighing. "General Tindall believes that Corolini and his Our Country Party are being funded with Old Kingdom gold, though he cannot definitely prove it. Since Corolini and his party now hold the balance of power in the Ancelstierre Moot, they've been able to get the Southerlings moved farther and farther north. They have also made it clear that their ultimate aim is to get all the Southerling refugees moved across the Wall, into our Kingdom."

"Why?" asked Sam. "I mean, what for? It's not as if northern Ancelstierre is over-populated."

"I'm not sure," replied Touchstone. "The reasons they make public in Ancelstierre are populist rubbish, pandering to the fears of the countryfolk. But there has to be a reason why someone here is supplying them with gold—enough gold to buy the twelve seats they've picked up in the Moot. I fear that reason may have something to do with the fact that we have not been able to find more than a score of the thousand people who were sent across a month ago, and none of that score alive. The rest have simply vanished—"

"How could that many people disappear? Surely they would leave some trace," interrupted Ellimere. "Perhaps I should go—"

"No." Touchstone smiled, amused by his daughter's obvious belief that she could do a better job than he could when it came to looking for something. The smile faded as he went on. "This is not as simple as it appears, Ellimere. Sorcery is involved. Your mother thinks that we will find them when we least want to, and that they will not be living when we do."

"This is the heart of the matter," said Sabriel gravely. "Before we discuss it further, I think we should take further precautions against being overheard. Touchstone?"

Touchstone nodded and stood up. Drawing one of his swords, he concentrated for a moment. The Charter marks on his sword began to glow and move, till the whole blade was wreathed in golden light. Touchstone flicked the sword up, and the Charter marks leapt across to the nearest Great Stone, splashing on it like liquid fire.

For a moment nothing happened. Then other marks caught the light, and the golden flames spread to cover the whole Stone, roaring up like a crown-caught wildfire. More marks leapt to the next Stone till it kindled, too, and then to the next, until all six

Great Stones were ablaze, and streams of bright Charter marks flew up and across to weave a tracery of light like a dome above the two barges.

Looking over the side, Sam saw that the golden fire had spread underwater, too, forming a crazy maze of marks that covered the reservoir floor. The four were now completely enclosed by a magical barrier, one that relied upon the power of the Great Stones. He wanted to ask how it was cast, and enquire about the nature of the spell, but his mother was already speaking.

"We can talk now without fear of being overheard, by natural ears or other means," said Sabriel. She took Sam's hand, and Ellimere's, holding them tight, so they felt the calluses on her fingers and palms, the result of so many years of wielding sword and bells.

"Your father and I are certain that the Southerlings were brought across the Wall to be killed—slain by a necromancer who has used the bodies to house Dead spirits who owe him allegiance. Only Free Magic sorcery can explain how the bodies and all other traces have disappeared, unseen by our patrols or the Clayr's Sight."

"But I thought the Clayr could See everything," said Ellimere. "I mean, they often get the time wrong, but they still See. Don't they?"

"Over the past four or five years the Clayr have become aware that their Sight is clouded, and possibly has always been clouded, in the region around the eastern shores of the Red Lake and Mount Abed," said Touchstone grimly. "A large area, which not coincidentally is also where our royal writ does not hold true. There is some power there that opposes both the Clayr and our authority, blocking their Sight and breaking the Charter Stones I have set there."

"Well, shouldn't we call out the Trained Bands and take them and the Guard and go down there and sort it out once and for all?" protested Ellimere, in the same tone that Sam imagined she had used when she led the Wyverley College hockey team back in Ancelstierre.

"We don't know where—or what—it is," said Sabriel. "Every time we undertake to really search the area for the source of the trouble, something happens somewhere else. We did think we might have found the root of it five years ago, at the Battle of Roble's Town—"

"The necromancer woman," interrupted Sam, who remembered the story well. He had thought a lot about necromancers over the past months. "The one with the bronze mask."

"Yes. Chlorr of the Mask," replied Sabriel, staring out at the golden barrier, obviously recalling unpleasant memories. "She was very old, and powerful, so I had presumed she was the architect of our difficulties there. But now I am not sure. It is clear someone else is still working to befuddle the Clayr and incite trouble across the Kingdom. There is also someone behind Corolini in Ancelstierre and perhaps even the Southerling wars as well. One possibility is the man you encountered in Death, Sam."

"The . . . the necromancer?" asked Sam. His voice came out as a pathetic squeak, and he unconsciously rubbed his wrists, his sleeves briefly riding up to show the skin still scarred from the burns.

"He must have great power to raise so many Dead Hands on the other side of the Wall," replied Sabriel. "And with that power, I should have heard of him, but I have not. How has he kept himself hidden all these years? How did Chlorr hide when we scoured the Kingdom after Kerrigor's fall, and why did she reveal herself to attack Roble's Town? Now I am wondering if perhaps I underestimated Chlorr. She may even have evaded me at the last. I made her walk beyond the Sixth Gate, but I was sorely tired, and I did not follow her all the way to the Ninth. I should have. There was something strange about her, something more than the usual taint of Free Magic or necromancy. . . ."

She paused, and her eyes stared out at nothing, unfocused. Then she blinked and continued. "Chlorr was old, old enough for other Abhorsens to have encountered her in the past, and I suspect that this other necromancer is also ancient. But I have found no record of either at the House. Too much knowledge was destroyed when the Palace burnt, and more has been lost besides, simply by the march of time. And the Clayr, while they keep everything in that Great Library of theirs, rarely find any-thing useful in it. Their minds are too much bent upon the future. I should like to look there myself, but that is a task that would take months, if not years. I think Chlorr and this other necro-mancer were in league, and may be still, if Chlorr has survived. But who leads and who follows is unclear. I also fear that we will find they are not alone. But whoever or whatever moves against us, we must make sure their plans come to naught."

The light seemed to darken as Sabriel spoke, and the water rippled as if an unwanted breeze had somehow passed the pro-tection of the golden light around the Stones.

"What plans?" asked Ellimere. "What are they . . . it . . . what-ever . . . going to do?"

Sabriel looked at Touchstone, and a brief flash of uncertainty passed between them before she continued.

"We think that they plan to bring all two hundred thousand Southerling refugees into the Old Kingdom—and kill them," whispered Sabriel, as if they might be overheard after all. "Two hundred thousand deaths in a single poisoned minute, to make an avenue out of Death for every spirit that has lingered there from the First Precinct to the very precipice of the Ninth Gate. To summon a host of the Dead greater than any that has ever walked in Life. A host that we could not possibly defeat, even if all the Abhorsens who have ever lived were somehow to stand against them."

Chapter Twenty-Five

A FAMILY CONFERENCE

SILENCE GREETED SABRIEL'S words, a silence that went on and on, as they all imagined a host of the Dead two hundred thousand strong, and Sam struggled not to. A horde of the Dead, a great sea of stumbling, Life-starved corpses that stretched from horizon to horizon, inexorably marching towards him—

"That will not happen, of course," said Touchstone, breaking into Sam's terrible imaginings. "We will make sure that it doesn't, that the refugees never even cross the Wall. However, we can't stop them on our side. The Wall is too long, with too many broken gates and too many old Crossing Points on the other side. So we must ensure that the Ancelstierrans don't send them across in the first place. Consequently your mother and I have decided to go to Ancelstierre ourselves—secretly, so as not to arouse alarm or suspicion. We will go to Corvere and negotiate with their government, which will undoubtedly take several months. That means we will be relying on you two to look after the Kingdom."

More silence greeted this revelation. Ellimere looked deeply thoughtful but otherwise calm. Sam swallowed several times, then said, "What, ah, what exactly do you mean?"

"As far as both our friends and enemies need know, I will be on a diplomatic mission to the barbarian chiefs at their Southern Stop, and Sabriel will be going about her business as mysteriously as she always does," replied Touchstone. "In our absence, Ellimere will continue as co-regent with Jall Oren—everyone seems to have become accustomed to that. Sameth, you will assist her. But most important, you will continue in your studies of *The Book of the Dead*."

"Speaking of such things, I have something for you," added Sabriel, before Sam could interject. She pushed her pack across with obvious effort. "Look in the top."

Slowly, Sam undid the straps. He suddenly felt very sick, knowing that he must tell them now or he would not be able to. Ever.

There was an oilskin-wrapped package in the pack. Sameth slid it out slowly, his fingers gone cold and clumsy. His eyes seemed to be strangely blurry, too, and Sabriel sounded as if she were talking from another room.

"I found these at the House—or rather, the sendings had set them out. I don't know where they found them, or why they've got them out now. They are very, very old. So old that I have no record of who bore them first. I would have asked Mogget, but he still sleeps—"

"Except for when I caught that salmon last year," interjected Touchstone crossly. Mogget, the Abhorsen's cat-shaped familiar, was bound by Ranna, the Sleepbringer, first of the seven bells. He had woken only five or six times in nearly twenty years, on three of those occasions to steal and eat fish caught by Touchstone.

"Mogget would not wake," continued Sabriel. "But as I have my own, these are clearly meant for the Abhorsen-in-Waiting. Congratulations, Sam."

Sam nodded dumbly, the remaining package unopened in his lap. He didn't need to look to know that wrapped inside the crinkled oilskin were the seven Charter-spelled bells of an Abhorsen.

"Aren't you going to open it?" asked Ellimere.

"Later," croaked Sam. He tried to smile but only made his mouth twitch. He knew Sabriel was looking at him, but he couldn't meet her eyes.

"I'm glad the bells have come," said Sabriel. "Most Abhorsens before me worked with their successors, sometimes for many years, as I hope we will work together. According to Mogget, my father trained with his aunt for nearly a decade. I have often wished I had had the same opportunity."

She hesitated again and then said quickly, "To tell the truth, I will need your help, Sam."

Sam nodded, unable to speak, as the words of his confession dried up in his mouth. He had the birthright, he had the book, he had the bells. Obviously, he just had to try harder to read the book, he told himself, trying to overcome the panic that twisted knots in his stomach. He *would* become the proper Abhorsen-in-Waiting everyone expected and needed. He had to.

"I'll do my best," he said, finally looking Sabriel in the eyes. She smiled, with a smile that made her whole face bright, and hugged him.

"I have to go to Ancelstierre, for I still know their ways much better than your father does," she said. "And quite a few of my old school friends have become influential, or have married so. But I didn't want to leave without knowing there was an Abhorsen here to protect the people from the Dead. Thank you, Sam."

"But I'm not . . ." Sam cried out before he could stop himself. "I'm not ready. I haven't finished the book, I mean, and—"

"I'm sure you know more than you think," Sabriel said. "In any case, there should be little trouble now that spring is in full bloom. Every stream and river is flowing with snow-melt and spring rain. The days are getting longer. There never are any major threats from the Dead this late in spring, or through the summer.

The most you'll have to deal with is a rogue Hand or perhaps a Mordaut. I have every confidence you can manage that."

"What about the missing Southerlings?" asked Ellimere, with a look that spoke volumes about her confidence in Sam. "Nine hundred Dead are a major threat."

"They must have disappeared into the area around the Red Lake, or the Clayr would have Seen them," said Sabriel. "So they should be confined there by the spring floods. I would go and deal with them first, but the greater danger lies with the many more Southerlings in Ancelstierre. We will have to trust in the flooded rivers, and in you, Sam."

"But—" Sam began.

"Mind you, the necromancer or necromancers who oppose us are not to be trifled with," continued Sabriel. "If they dare to confront you, you must fight them in Life. Do not fight one of them in Death again, Sam. You were brave to do so before, but also lucky. You must also be very careful with the bells. As you know, they can force you into Death, or trick you into it. Use them only when you are confident you have learned the lessons in the book. Do you promise?"

"Yes," said Sam. Somehow or other he barely had breath for that single word. But there was relief in it, for he'd been given a reprieve of sorts. He could probably sort out most of the Lesser Dead with Charter Magic alone. His resolution to be a proper Abhorsen had not banished the fear that still lurked in his heart, and his fingers were cold where they touched the wrapped-up bells.

"Now," said Touchstone, "I wonder if you have any insights into dealing with the Ancelstierrans, you two, from your schooling there. This Corolini, for instance, the leader of the Our Country Party. Could he be from the Old Kingdom himself, do you think?"

"After my time," said Ellimere, who had been a whole year out of school and seemed to consider her Ancelstierran days as ancient history.

"I don't know," replied Sam. "He was in the newspapers a lot before I left, but they never mentioned where he came from. My friend Nicholas might know, and he would be able to help, I think. His uncle is the Chief Minister, Edward Sayre, you know. Nick is coming to visit me next month, but you should be able to catch him before he leaves."

"He's coming here?" asked Touchstone. "I'm surprised they'll let him. I don't think the Army has issued a permit in years, apart from that lot of refugees—and that was a political show. The Army didn't have a choice."

"Nick can be very persuasive," said Sam, thinking of various scrapes Nick had talked him into at school—and less often, out of the blame afterwards. "I asked Ellimere to seal a visa for him, for our side."

"I sent it ages ago," said Ellimere, with a snide glance at Sam. "Some of us are efficient, you know."

"Good," said Touchstone. "It will be a useful connection, and important for one of Ancelstierre's ruling families to see that we do not invent the stories they hear about the Kingdom. I'll also make sure the Barhedrin Guard Post provides an escort from the Wall. It wouldn't help negotiations if we lose the Chief Minister's nephew."

"What are we negotiating with?" asked Ellimere. "I mean, down in Corvere they like to pretend we don't even exist. I was always having to convince stuck-up city girls that I wasn't making the Kingdom up."

"Two things," replied Sabriel. "Gold and fear. We have only a modest amount of gold, but it might be enough to tip the balance if it goes into the right pockets. And there are many

Northerners who remember when Kerrigor crossed the Wall. We shall try to convince them that this will happen again if they send the Southerling refugees north."

"It couldn't be Kerrigor, could it?" asked Sam. "I mean, whoever is behind all the trouble."

"No," said Sabriel and Touchstone together. They exchanged a look, obviously remembering the terrible past and what Kerrigor had tried to do, both here in the Old Kingdom and in Ancelstierre.

"No," repeated Sabriel. "I looked in on Kerrigor when I visited the House. He sleeps still and forever under Ranna's spell, locked in the deepest cellar, bound with every Mark of ward and guard your father and I have ever known. It is not Kerrigor."

"Whoever, or whatever, it is, they shall be dealt with," said Touchstone, his voice powerful and regal. "We four shall see to that. But for now, I suggest we all drink some mulled wine and talk of better things. How was the Midwinter Festival? Did I tell you that I danced the Bird of Dawning when I was your age, Sam? How did you do?"

"I forgot the cups," said Sam, handing over the still-warm jug.

"We can drink from the jug," said Sabriel, after a moment when no one chose to answer Touchstone's question. She took the jug and expertly poured a stream of wine into her mouth. "Ah, that's good. Now tell me, how was your birthday, Sam? A good day?"

Sam answered mechanically, hardly noticing Ellimere's rather more pointed interjections. Clearly, his parents hadn't spoken to Jall yet, or they would be asking different questions. He was relieved when they started questioning Ellimere, gently teasing her about her tennis and all the young men who were trying to learn this new sport. Obviously, gossip about his sister had traveled

faster than news of Sam's shortcomings. He was brought briefly
back into the conversation when Ellimere accused him of refusing to make any more racquets, which was a shame because no
one else could make them quite so well, but a quick promise to
produce a dozen dropped him out again.

The others continued to talk for a while, but the dark future
weighed heavily on them all. Sameth, for his part, couldn't stop
thinking about the book and the bells. What would he do if he
were actually called upon to repel an incursion by the Dead?
What would he do if it turned out to be the necromancer who'd
tortured him in Death? Or even worse, what if there were some
still more powerful enemy, as Sabriel feared?

Suddenly he blurted out, "What if it . . . this Enemy . . . isn't
behind Corolini? What if he's going to do something else while
you're both gone?"

The others, who were in the middle of a conversation about
Heria, who'd tripped over her own dress and catapulted into Jall
Oren at an afternoon party in honor of the Mayor of Sindle,
looked up, startled.

"If that is so, we will be just a week away, ten days at the
most," said Sabriel. "A message-hawk to Barhedrin, a rider to the
Perimeter, a telegraph from there or Bain to Corvere, train back
to Bain—maybe even less than a week. But we think that whatever this Enemy—as you have dubbed it so well—plans, it must
involve a great number of the Dead. The Clayr have Seen many
possible futures in which our entire Kingdom is nothing more
than a desert, inhabited only by the Dead. What else could bring
this about but the sort of massing of the Dead that we suspect?
And that could be brought about only by killing all those poor,
unprotected refugees. Our people are too well guarded. In any
case, apart from Belisaere, there are not two hundred thousand
people in one place in all the Kingdom. And certainly not two

hundred thousand without a single Charter mark amongst them."

"I don't know what else it could be," said Sam heavily. "I just wish you weren't going."

"Being the Abhorsen is a weighty responsibility," Sabriel said quietly. "One that I understand you are wary of shouldering, even when it is shared with me. But it is your destiny, Sam. Does the walker choose the path, or the path the walker? I am sure you will do very well, and we will soon all be together again, speaking of happier things."

"When do you go?" asked Sam, unable to hide the hope of delay from his voice. Maybe he would be able to talk to Sabriel tomorrow, to get her help with *The Book of the Dead*, to overcome his paralyzing fear.

"Tomorrow, at dawn," replied Sabriel reluctantly. "Provided my leg is healed enough. Your father will ride with the real embassy to the Northern Barbarians, and I will fly west. But I will double back to pick him up tomorrow night, and we will then fly south to the House, to try to consult again with Mogget, then on to Barhedrin and the Wall. Hopefully this will confuse any spies who may be watching."

"We would stay longer," said Touchstone sadly, looking at his small family, so rarely all together in one place. "But as always, duty calls—and we must answer."

Chapter Twenty-Six

A LETTER FROM NICHOLAS

SAM LEFT THE reservoir that night with an empty wine jug, a bandolier of bells, a heavy heart, and much to think upon. Ellimere went with him, but Sabriel stayed behind, needing to spend the night within the circle of Great Charter Stones to speed her healing. Touchstone stayed with her, and it was obvious to the two children that their parents wished to be alone. Probably to discuss the shortcomings of their son, Sam thought as he wearily climbed the stairs, the package of bells in his hand.

Ellimere wished him an almost friendly good night at the door to her chambers, but Sam didn't go to bed. Instead he climbed another twisting stair to his tower workroom and spoke the word that brought the Charter lights to life. Then he put the bells in a different cupboard from the book, locking them out of sight if not out of mind. After that, he half-heartedly tried to resume work on a clockwork and Charter Magic cricketer, a batsman six inches high. He had some ideas of making two teams and setting them to play, but neither the clockwork nor the magic yet worked to his satisfaction.

Someone knocked on the door. Sam ignored it. If it was a servant, he'd call or go away. If it was Ellimere, she'd just barge in.

The knock was repeated, there was some sort of muffled call, and Sam heard something slide under the door, followed by footsteps going back down the stairs. A silver tray was on the floor,

with a very ragged-looking letter upon it. Judging from the state
it was in, it had to be from Ancelstierre, and that meant it was
from Nicholas.

Sam sighed, put on his white cotton gloves, and picked up a
pair of tweezers. Receiving one of Nick's letters was always
more of a forensic exercise than a matter of reading. He picked
up the tray and carried it over to his bench, where the Charter
marks were brightest, and began to peel the paper apart and
piece the rotten bits together.

Half an hour later, as the clock in the Grey Tower clanged
out a dozen strokes for midnight, the letter was laid out clearly
enough to read. Sam bent over it, his frown deepening the further he read.

> Dear Sam,
>
> Thanks for organizing the Old Kingdom visa for me.
> I don't know why your Consul at Bain was so reluctant to
> give me one. Lucky you're a Prince, I guess, and can get
> things done. I didn't have any trouble at this end. Father
> called Uncle Edward, who pulled the appropriate strings.
> Practically no one in Corvere even knew you could get a
> permit to cross the Perimeter. Anyway, I suppose it shows
> that Ancelstierre and the Old Kingdom aren't that different.
> It all comes down to who you know.
>
> In any case, I intend to leave Awengate tomorrow, and if
> all the train connections go smoothly, I will be in Bain by
> Saturday and across the Wall by the 15th. I know this is
> earlier than we agreed, so you won't be able to meet me, but
> I'm not just rushing in on my own. I've hired a guide—a
> former Crossing Point Scout I ran into in Bain. Quite
> literally, in fact. He was crossing the road to avoid a
> demonstration by these One Country fellows, stumbled and

nearly knocked me over. But it was a fortuitous meeting, as he knows the Old Kingdom well. He also confirmed something I've read about a curious phenomenon called the Lightning Trap. He has seen it, and it certainly sounds worth studying.

So I think we will go and take a look at this Lightning Trap en route to your undoubtedly charming capital of Belisaere. My guide didn't seem at all surprised that I knew you, by the way. Perhaps he is as unimpressed by royalty as some of our former schoolfellows!

In any case, the Lightning Trap is apparently near a town called Edge, which I understand is not too far out of the direct route north to you. If only you people believed in normal maps and not quasi-mystical memorization aided by blank pieces of paper!

I look forward to seeing you in your native habitat— almost as much as I look forward to investigating the curious anomalies of your Old Kingdom. There is surprisingly little written about it. The College library has only a few old and highly superstitious texts and the Radford little more. It never gets mentioned in the papers, either, except obliquely when Corolini is raving on in the Moot about sending "undesirables and Southerlings" to what he calls "the extreme North." I expect that I will be an advance guard of one "undesirable" in his terms!

Everything about the Old Kingdom seems to fall under a conspiracy of silence, so I am sure there will be many things for an ambitious young scientist to discover and reveal to the world.

I hope you are quite recovered, by the way. I have been ill myself, on and off, with chest pains that seem to be some sort of bronchitis. Strangely enough, they get worse the farther

south I go, and were terrible in Corvere, probably because the
air is absolutely filthy. I've spent the last month in Bain, and
have barely been troubled. I expect I will be even better in
your Old Kingdom, where the air should be positively
pristine.

  In any case, I look forward to seeing you soon, and
remain your loyal friend,

                                        Nicholas Sayre

P.S. I don't believe Ellimere is really six foot six and weighs
twenty stone. You would have mentioned it before.

Sameth put the letter down, careful not to break what was
left of it.

After he'd finished, he read the letter again, hoping that the
words had somehow changed. Surely Nick wouldn't cross into the
Old Kingdom with only a single—and possibly untrustworthy—
guide? Didn't he realize how dangerous the Borderlands near the
Wall were? Particularly to an Ancelstierran, lacking a Charter
mark and any sense of magic. Nick wouldn't even be able to test
whether his guide was a real man, a tainted Charter bearer, or even
a Free Magic construct, powerful enough to cross the Perimeter
without detection.

Sam bit his lip at the thought, teeth tapping at the skin in
unconscious concern, and consulted his almanac. According to
that, the fifteenth was three days ago, so Nick must have already
crossed the Wall. So it was too late to get there, even by Paperwing,
or to find one of the Palace message-hawks and send it with
orders to the guards. Nick had a visa for himself and a servant,
so the Barhedrin Post wouldn't detain him. He would be in the
Borderlands now, heading towards Edge.

Edge! Sam bit his lip harder. That was far too close to the

Red Lake, and the region where the necromancer Chlorr had destroyed the Stones and even now the Enemy hid and hatched its plans against the Kingdom. It was the worst possible place for Nick to go!

A knock at the door interrupted his thoughts and made him bite his lip even harder, so he tasted blood. Irritated, he called out, "Yes! Who is it!"

"Me!" said Ellimere, breezing in. "I hope I'm not disturbing the act of creation or anything?"

"No," Sameth replied warily. He indicated his workbench with a half wave and a shrug, implying that his work wasn't going well.

Ellimere looked around with interest, since Sam usually pushed her out whenever she tried to come in. The small tower room had been given to Sameth on his sixteenth birthday and had had much use since then. Currently, the two workbenches were covered in the paraphernalia of a jeweler and many tools and devices that were obscure to her. There were also some small figurines of cricketers, thin bars of gold and silver, reels of bronze wire, a scattering of sapphires, and a small but still-smoking forge built into the room's former fireplace.

And there was Charter Magic everywhere. The faded after-images of Charter marks shone in the air, crawled lazily across the walls and ceiling, and clustered by the chimney. Clearly Sameth was not just creating costume jewelry or the promised extra tennis racquets.

"What are you making?" Ellimere asked curiously. Some of the Charter symbols, or rather the fading reflections of them, were extremely powerful. They were marks she would be reluctant to use herself.

"Things," said Sameth. "Nothing you'd be interested in."

"How do you know?" asked Ellimere. The familiar tide of

resentment was rising between them.

"Toys," snapped Sam, holding up his little batsman, which suddenly swung its tiny bat before freezing back into immobility. "I'm making toys. I know it's not a fit occupation for a Prince, and I should be asleep getting ready for a fun new day of dance classes and Petty Court, but I . . . can't sleep," he concluded wearily.

"Neither can I," said Ellimere in a conciliatory tone. She sat down in the one other chair, and added, "I'm worried. About Mother."

"She said she'd be fine. The Great Stones will heal her."

"This time. She needs help with her work, Sam, and you're the only person who can do it."

"I know," said Sam. He looked away, down at Nick's letter. "I know."

"Well," Ellimere continued uncomfortably, "I just wanted to say that studying to be the Abhorsen is the most important thing, Sam. If you need more time, you just have to say, and I'll reorganize your schedule."

Sam looked at her, surprised. "You mean take time away from the Bird of Dawning, or those afternoon parties with your friends' stupid sisters?"

"They're not—" Ellimere started to say; then she took a deep breath and said, "Yes. Things are different now. Now we know what's going on. I shall be spending more time with the Guard myself. Getting ready."

"Ready?" asked Sam nervously. "So soon?"

"Yes," said Ellimere. "Even if Mother and Dad are successful in Ancelstierre, there's going to be trouble. Whatever is behind it all isn't going to lie still while we stop its plans. Something will happen, and we need to be ready. *You* need to be ready, Sam. That's all I wanted to say."

She got up and left. Sam stared into space. There was nowhere to turn. He had to become a proper Abhorsen-in-Waiting. He had to help fight whatever the Enemy was. The people expected it. Everyone depended on him.

And so, he suddenly realized, did Nicholas. He had to go and find Nicholas, to save his friend before he got in trouble, because no one else would.

Suddenly Sam was filled with purpose, a feeling of decision that he didn't examine too closely. His friend was in danger, and he must go to save him. He would be away from *The Book of the Dead* and his Princely chores for only a few weeks. He would probably be able to find Nick quite quickly and bring him to safety, particularly if he could take half a dozen of the Royal Guard. As Sabriel had said, there was little chance of the Dead doing anything, what with the spring floods.

Somewhere deep down a small voice was telling him that what he was really doing was running away. But he smothered the voice with other more important thoughts, and didn't even look at the cupboards that held the book and the bells.

Once the decision was made, Sam thought about how it could be done. Ellimere would never let him go, he knew. So he must ask his father, and that meant rising before dawn in order to catch Touchstone in his wardrobe.

Chapter Twenty-Seven

DESPITE HIS GOOD intentions, Sam overslept and missed Touchstone's departure from the Palace. Thinking that he might catch him at the South Gate, he ran down Palace Hill and then along the broad, tree-lined Avenue of Stars, named after the tiny metal suns embedded in its paving stones. Two guards ran with him, easily keeping pace despite the weight of their mail hauberks, helmets, and boots.

Sam had just sighted the rear ranks of his father's escort when he heard the cheers of the crowd and the sudden blare of trumpets. He jumped up on a cart that was stopped in the traffic and looked over the heads of the crowd. He was just in time to see his father ride out through the high gate of Belisaere, red and gold cloak streaming behind him over the horse's hindquarters, the early sun just catching his crown-circled helmet before he passed into the shadow of the gate.

Royal guards rode in front of and behind the King, twoscore tall men and women, bright mail flashing from the vertical cuts in their red and gold surcoats. The guards would continue north tomorrow, Sam knew, with someone dressed as Touchstone. The King would actually be flying south to Ancelstierre with Sabriel, to try to forestall the death of two hundred thousand innocents.

Sameth kept watching even after the last guard passed the gate and the normal traffic resumed; people, horses, wagons, donkeys, pushcarts, pullcarts, beggars . . . all flowed past him, but he didn't notice.

He had missed Touchstone, and now he would have to make up his mind all on his own.

Even when he crossed to the center of the road and turned against the tide flowing out of the city, his gaze was absent. Only the vacuum created around him by two burly guards prevented several pedestrian accidents.

Since Sam had started to think about going to find Nicholas, he found that he couldn't stop. He was sure that the letter was real. Sam was the only one who knew Nick well enough to track him down, the only one with a friendship bond that finding magic could flow through.

The only one who could save him from whatever trouble was brewing for everyone around the Red Lake.

But that meant Sam would have to leave Belisaere, abandoning his duties. He knew that Ellimere would never give him permission.

These thoughts, and multiple variations of them, swirled through his mind as he and his guards passed under one of the huge aqueducts that fed the city with pure, snow-melt water. The aqueducts had proved their worth in other ways, too. Their fast-flowing waters were a defense against the Dead, particularly during the two centuries of the Interregnum.

Sameth thought of that, too, as he heard the deep bellow of the aqueduct above his head. For a moment his conscience twinged. He was supposed to be a defense against the Dead himself.

He left the cool shadow of the aqueduct and began heading along the Avenue of Stars before the wearying climb up the switchbacked King's Road that led to Palace Hill. Ellimere was probably already waiting for him back at the Palace, since both of them were to sit in Petty Court this morning. She would be cool and composed in her judicial robes of black and white, holding the wand of ivory and the wand of jet that were used in the truth-testing spell. She would be cross that he was sweaty, dirty, inappropriately dressed, and unequipped—his wands had disappeared, though he had the vague notion that they might have rolled under his bed.

Petty Court. Belisaere Festival duties. Tennis racquets. *The Book of the Dead*. All of it surged up like a great dark wave that threatened to engulf him.

"No," he whispered, stopping so suddenly that both his guards nearly ran into him. "I'll go. I'll go tonight."

"What was that, sir?" asked Tonin, the younger of the two guards. She was the same age as Ellimere, and they had been friends since they had played together as children. She was nearly always one of his guards on his rare excursions into the city, and Sameth felt sure she reported his every movement to the Princess.

"Um, nothing, Tonin," replied Sameth, shaking his head. "I was just thinking aloud. Guess I'm not used to getting up before dawn."

Tonin and the other guard exchanged semi-tolerant glances behind his back as they moved on. They got up every day before dawn.

Sameth didn't know what his guards were thinking, as they finished the climb up the hill and entered the cool, fountain-centered court that led to the west wing of the Palace. But he'd seen the looks they'd exchanged, and he had a general idea that they did not consider him the perfect pattern of a Prince. He suspected most of the city folk shared their opinion. It was galling to someone who had been one of the leading lights of his school in Ancelstierre. There he had excelled at everything that was important. Cricket in the summer and Rugby in the winter. And he'd been first in chemistry class and in the top classes for everything else. Here, he couldn't seem to do anything right.

The guards left him outside his room, but Sam didn't immediately change into his judge's robes or make any motion to use the basin and ewer of water that stood in the tiled alcove that served him as a bathroom. The Palace, rebuilt with economy following its destruction by fire, did not have the steampipes and hot-water systems of Abhorsen's House or the Clayr's Glacier. Sam had plans for such a system, and indeed some of the original works remained deep below Palace Hill, but he had not had time to investigate the magic and engineering required to make it happen.

"I will go," he declared again, to the painting on the wall that showed a pleasant harvest scene. The reapers did not react, nor did the pitchfork crew, as he added, "The only question is—how?"

He paced around the room. It was not large, so he had made twenty circuits before he made a decision, at the same time he arrived in front of the silver mirror that hung on the wall to the right of his simple iron-framed bed.

"I'll be someone else," he said. "Prince Sameth can stay behind. I'll be Sam, a Traveler going to rejoin his band after seeking treatment for a sickness in Belisaere."

He smiled at that, looking at himself in the mirror. Prince Sameth looked back at him, resplendent in red and gold jerkin, somewhat sweaty white linen shirt, tan doeskin breeches, and gilt-heeled knee boots. And above the court finery a pleasant face, with the potential to be striking one day, although Sam didn't see that. Too youthful and open, he decided. His face lacked the definition of experience. He needed a scar or a broken nose or something like that.

As he looked, he was also reaching into the endless swim of the Charter, picking out a mark here, a symbol there, linking them into a chain in his mind. Holding them there, he drew the final Charter mark in front of his eyes with his forefinger, and all the marks rushed out, to hang in the air, a glowing constellation of magic symbols.

Sameth looked at them carefully, checking the spell before he stepped right into the glowing pattern. The marks brightened as they touched his skin, sparking against the Charter mark on his forehead, flowing in streaks of golden fire across his face.

He shut his eyes as the fire reached them, ignoring the tingle under his eyelids and a sudden urge to sneeze. He stood that way for several minutes, till the tingle vanished. He sneezed explosively, inhaled with equal force—and opened his eyes.

In the mirror, there were still the same clothes, with the same build of man inside them. But the face had changed. Sam the Traveler stared back, a man reminiscent of Prince Sameth but clearly several years older, with a carefully shaven mustache and goatee. His hair was a different color, too, lighter and straighter, and much longer at the back.

Better. Much better. Sameth—no, Sam—winked at the reflection and started to undress. His old hunting leathers would be best, and some plain shirts and underdrawers. He could buy a cloak in the city. And a horse. And a sword, since he couldn't take the Charter-Magicked blade his mother had given him on his sixteenth birthday. It wouldn't take a glamour and was too recognizable.

But he could take some of the things he'd made himself, he realized as he kicked off his boots and dug out some well-worn but durable thigh boots of black calfskin.

Thinking of his tower workshop inevitably led him to *The Book of the Dead*. Well, he certainly wouldn't take *that*. Just a quick run up the stairs, pick up a few things, including his little store of gold nobles and silver deniers, and then he'd be off!

Except that he couldn't go up to his workshop looking as he did now. And he also had to do something that would allay Ellimere's suspicions—otherwise he'd be chased down and brought back. Forcibly, he imagined, since the guards would have no problem taking Ellimere's orders over his own.

He sighed and sat down on the bed, boots in hand. Obviously this escape—or rather rescue expedition—was going to take more preparation than he thought. He'd have to make a temporary Charter sending that was a reasonable duplicate of himself and set up some situation so Ellimere couldn't get too close a look.

He could probably say that he had to do something from *The Book of the Dead* that required staying in his workroom for three days or so, to give himself a head start on any search. It wasn't as if he were completely giving up studying to be the Abhorsen. He just needed a break, he told himself, and three weeks of rescuing Nicholas had to be more important than three weeks of study that he could easily make up on his return.

Even if Ellimere asked the Clayr to find out where he was, a three-day start should be enough. Presuming she worked out what had happened after the third day and sent a message-hawk to the Clayr, it would be at least two days before they replied. Five days, in all.

He'd be halfway to Edge by then. Or a quarter of the way, he thought, trying to remember exactly how far away the little town on the Red Lake actually was. He'd have to get a map and look up the latest *Very Useful Guide* to see where to stop on the way.

Really, there were more than a dozen things to do before he could escape, Sam thought, dropping the boots to stand in front of the mirror again. The glamour would have to go for a start, if he didn't want to be arrested by his own guards.

Who would have thought that starting an adventure was so difficult?

Glumly, he began the process of dissolving the Charter-spell that disguised him, letting the component marks twist away and fall back into the Charter. As soon as that was done, he would go up to the tower room and begin to get organized. Provided, of course, that Ellimere didn't intercept him and take him off to Petty Court.

Chapter Twenty-Eight

SAM THE TRAVELER

ELLIMERE DID INTERCEPT Sam, so the rest of his day was lost to Petty Court: the sentencing of a thief who tried to lie despite the truth-spell turning his face bright yellow with every falsehood; the arbitration of a property dispute that defied any hard and fast truths as all the original parties were dead; the rapid processing of a series of petty criminals who confessed immediately, hoping that not having to bespell them would improve the court's outlook; and a long and boring speech from an advocate, which turned out to be irrelevant, as it relied on a point of law overturned by Touchstone's reforms more than a decade ago.

The night, however, was not taken up by official duties, though Ellimere once again produced a younger sister of one of her thousands of friends to sit next to Sam at dinner. To her surprise, Sam was quite talkative and friendly, and for days afterwards she defended him when other girls told tales of his distance.

After dinner, Sam told Ellimere that he would be studying for the next three days, and had to immerse himself in a spell that required total concentration. He would get food and water from the kitchens and then would be in his bedchamber and must not be disturbed. Ellimere took the news surprisingly well, which made Sam feel bad. But even that could not curb his growing excitement, and the long hours creating a very basic sending of himself did not diminish his sense of expectation. When he finished it at a little past midnight, the sending looked quite like him from the door, though it had no depth from other angles. And if it was spoken to, it could shout "Go away!" and "I'm very busy" in a fair imitation of his voice.

With the sending done, Sam went to his workroom and picked up his ready money and some of the things he had made, which might prove useful for the journey. He did not look at the cupboards, which stood like disapproving guardians in the corners of the room.

But he dreamed of them when he finally got to bed. He dreamed that he climbed the stairs again, and opened the cupboards, and put on the bandolier of bells and opened the book, and read words that burst into fire, and the words picked him up and swept him into Death, plunging him into the cold river, and he couldn't breathe—

He woke, thrashing in his bed, the sheets tangled around his neck, cutting off his air. He fought them in a panic, till he realized where he was and his heart began to slow from its frenzied pumping. Off in the distance, a clock struck the hour, followed by the shouts of the Watch, announcing all was well. It was four o'clock. He'd had only three hours' sleep, but he knew he could sleep no more. It was time to cast the glamour upon himself. Time for Sam the Traveler to take his leave.

It was still dark when Sam slipped out of the Palace, in the cool morning just before the dawn. Cloaked in Charter-spells of quiet and unseeing, he slipped down the stairs, past the guard post in the Southwest Courtyard, and along the steeply sloping corridor down to the gardens. He avoided the guards who tramped between the roses in the lowest terrace, and went out through a sally port that was locked by steel and spell. Fortunately, he had stolen the key for the lock, and the door knew him by his Charter mark.

Out in the lane that ran into the King's Road, he slung his surprisingly heavy saddlebags over his shoulder and wondered whether he should have gone through them again and taken things out, because they were bursting at the seams. But he couldn't think of anything to leave behind, and he was taking just the bare essentials: a cloak; spare shirts, trousers, and under-clothes; a sewing kit; a bag of soaps and toiletries with a razor he hardly needed to use; a copy of *The Very Useful Guide*; some friction matches; slippers; two gold bars; an oilskin square that could be used as a makeshift tent; a bottle of brandy, a piece of salted beef, a loaf of bread, three ginger cakes; and a few devices of his own making. Besides what was in the saddlebags, he had only a broad-brimmed hat, a belt purse, and a fairly nondescript dagger. His first stop would be the central market to buy a sword, and then he would go to the Horse Fair at Anstyr's Field for a mount.

As he left the lane and stepped out into the King's Road to join the already rapidly building bustle of men, women, children, dogs, horses, mules, carts, beggars, and who-knew-what on the street, Sam felt a tremendous lift to his spirits, a feeling he hadn't had for years. It was the same sense of joy and expectation he'd felt as a child being given an unexpected holiday. Freed of responsibility, suddenly given license to have fun, to run, to scream, to laugh.

Sam did laugh, trying a deeper chuckle to fit his new per-sonality. It came out rather strained, almost a gurgle, but he didn't mind. Twirling his new, Charter-Magicked mustache, he quick-ened his pace. Off to adventure—and, of course, to rescue Nicholas.

Three hours later, most of his pre-dawn exuberance was gone. His guise as a Traveler was very good for not being recognized, but it didn't help him get attention from merchants and horse-traders. Travelers were not known as great customers, for they rarely had any coins, preferring to barter services or goods.

It was also unseasonably warm, even for so late in spring, making the sword buying in the crowded market sweaty and unpleasant, with every second seeming to last an hour.

The horse-trading was even worse, with great swarms of flies settling on the eyes and mouths of man and beast alike. It was no wonder, Sameth thought, King Anstyr had ordered the Horse Fair set up three miles from the city all those centuries ago. The Fair had ceased during the years of the Interregnum, but had begun to grow again in Touchstone's reign. Now the permanent stables, corrals, and bidding rings covered a good square mile, and there were always more strings of horses in the pastures that surrounded the Horse Fair proper. Of course, finding a horse that you wanted to buy among the multitude took considerable time, and there was always competition for the better horses. People from all over the Kingdom, and even barbarians from the North, came to buy at the Fair, particularly at this time of year.

Despite the crowds, the flies, and the competition, Sameth came out of his two purchasing ordeals quite happily. A plain but serviceable longsword hung at his hip, its sharkskin hilt rough under his tapping finger. A somewhat nervous bay mare followed behind, constrained by a leading rein from giving in to her neuroses. Still, she seemed sound enough and was neither too noticeable nor expensive. Sam was toying with calling her Tonin after his least favorite guard, but he decided that this was both childish and vindictive. Her previous owner had—somewhat enigmatically—called her Sprout, and that would do.

Once out of the stink and crowding of the Horse Fair, Sam mounted up, weaving Sprout through the steady stream of traffic,

finding his way past carts and peddlers, donkeys with empty pan-
niers going away from the city and those with full ones going in,
gangs of workmen relaying the stone pavers of the road, and all
the nondescript journeyers in between. Not far out of the city
he was overtaken by a King's Messenger on a black thorough-
bred that would have set the buyers bidding furiously at the Fair,
and then later by a quartet of guards, setting a pace that could be
maintained only in the knowledge that fresh horses awaited
them at every posting house on the road. Both times Sam
slouched in the saddle and pulled his hat down to shadow his
face, even though the glamour still held.

With the help of *The Very Useful Guide*, Sam had already
decided on his first stop. He would take the Narrow Way along
the isthmus that joined Belisaere to the mainland because there
was no other way to go. Then he would take the high road south
to Orchyre. He had considered going west to Sindle and then to
the Ratterlin, where he could take a boat as far as Qyrre. But *The
Very Useful Guide* mentioned a particularly good inn at Orchyre
that served a famous jellied eel. Sam was partial to jellied eel and
saw no reason why he shouldn't take the most comfortable way
to Edge.

Not that he was entirely sure what the most comfortable
way would be after Orchyre. The Great South Road followed
the east coast most of the way down, but Edge was all the way
across on the west coast. So he would have to cut west sooner or
later. Perhaps he could even leave the royal roads, as they were
called, and cut cross-country from Orchyre, trusting that he
would be able to find country roads that would take him in
the right direction. The danger in that lay in the spring floods.
The royal roads mostly had decent bridges, but the country roads
did not, and their usual fords might be impassable now.

In any case, that was all in the future and not to be worried about till after Orchyre. The town was two days' steady riding away, and he could think about his next stage en route, or that evening when he planned to put up at some inn.

But planning the next stage of his journey was the last thing on Sameth's mind when he finally reached a village and a staging inn that could be considered far enough away from Belisaere to stop. He'd ridden only seven leagues, but the sun was already setting, and he was exhausted. He'd had too little sleep the night before, and his backside and thighs were reminding him that he'd hardly ridden all winter.

By the time he saw the swinging sign that declared the inn's name to be The Laughing Dog, he could do little more than tip the ostler to look after Sprout and collapse on a bed in the best room in the house.

He woke several times in the night, the first to kick off his boots and the second to relieve himself in the bedpan (with a broken lid) thoughtfully provided by the inn. The third time he woke, it was to insistent knocking on the door and the first rays of sunlight slipping through the shuttered windows.

"Who is it?" groaned Sameth, sliding out of the bed and into his boots. His joints were stiff, and he felt awful, particularly in his slept-in clothes, which smelled dreadfully of horse. "Is it breakfast?"

There was no answer save more knocking. Grumbling, Sameth went to the door, expecting some zany or village fool to grin up at him from behind a breakfast tray. Instead, he was greeted by two wide-shouldered men wearing the red and gold sashes of the Rural Constabulary over their leather cuirasses.

One, clearly the senior, carried some authority in his stern face and silver, short-buzzed hair. He also had a Charter mark on his forehead, which his younger assistant did not.

"Sergeant Kuke and Constable Tep," announced the silver-haired man, thrusting past Sameth quite roughly. His companion also pushed in, quickly closing the door after him and letting the bar fall back in place.

"What do you want?" asked Sam, yawning. He didn't intend to be rude, but he had no idea that they had an interest in him and had knocked on his door by choice rather than chance. His only previous experience with the Rural Constabulary was seeing them on parade, or inspecting some post of theirs with his father.

"We want a word," said Sergeant Kuke, standing close enough that Sam could smell the garlic on his breath and see the marks where he'd scraped the stubble off his chin not long before. "Let's be beginning with your name and station."

"I am called Sam. I'm a Traveler," replied Sameth, his eye following the constable, who had moved to the corner of the room and was examining his sword, propped against the saddlebags. For the first time, he felt a twinge of apprehension. These constables might not be the clodpolls he thought. They might even discover who he was.

"Unusual for a Traveler to stay at a posting inn, let alone the best room in the house," said the constable, turning back from Sam's sword and saddlebags. "Unusual to tip the ostler a silver denier, too."

"Unusual for a Traveler's horse not to have a brand, or clan tokens in its mane," replied the sergeant, talking as if Sam wasn't there. "It'd be pretty strange to see a Traveler without a clan tattoo. I wonder if we'd see one on this laddie, if we looked. But maybe we should start looking in those bags, Tep. See if we can find something to tell us who we've got here."

"You can't do that!" exclaimed Sam, outraged. He took a step towards the constable, but stopped abruptly as sharp steel pricked through his linen shirt, just above his belly. Looking down, he saw a poniard held steadily in Sergeant Kuke's hand.

"You could tell us who you really are and what you're up to," said the sergeant.

"It's none of your business!" exclaimed Sam, throwing his head back in disdain. As he did so, his tousled hair flew back, revealing the Charter mark on his forehead.

Instantly Kuke called out a warning, and the poniard was at Sam's neck, and his right arm pinioned behind him. Of all things the constables might fear, the bearer of a false or corrupted Charter mark was one of the worst, for he could only be a Free Magic sorcerer, a necromancer, or some thing that had taken human shape.

Almost at the same time, Tep opened a saddlebag and lifted out a dark leather bandolier, a bandolier of seven tubular pouches that ranged in size from a pillbox to a large jar. Wooden handles of dark mahogany thrust out of the pouches, making it quite clear what the bandolier held. The bells that Sabriel had sent to Sameth. The bells that he had locked away in his workroom and definitely hadn't packed.

"Bells!" exclaimed Tep, dropping them in fright and leaping back, almost as if he'd drawn out a nest of writhing serpents. He didn't notice the Charter marks that thronged upon both bandolier and handles.

"A necromancer," whispered Kuke, and Sam heard the sudden fear in his voice and felt the hold on him slackening, the poniard drifting away from his throat, the hand that held it beset by sudden shivering.

In that instant, Sameth pictured two Charter marks in his mind, drawing them from the endless flow like a skilled fisherman selecting his catch from a glittering shoal. He let the marks infuse into his held breath—then he blew them out, at the same time throwing himself to the ground.

One mark flew true, striking Tep with sudden blindness. But Kuke must have been some small Charter Mage himself, for he countered the spell with a general warding, the air sparking and flashing as the two Charter marks met.

Then, before Sam could even get up, Kuke's poniard stabbed out, sinking deep into his leg, just above the knee.

Sam screamed, the noise adding to Tep's shouts of blind despair as he groped around the room and Kuke's even louder shouts of "Necromancer!" and "A rescue!" That would bring every constable for miles and any guards who might be on the road. Even concerned citizens might come, but it would be brave ones since the word "necromancer" had been heard.

After the first split-second shock of pain, when his whole mind seemed to crack open, Sam instinctively did what he'd been taught to save his life in the event of an assassination attempt. Drawing several Charter marks in his mind, he let them grow in his throat and roared out a Death-spell to strike everyone unprotected in the room.

The marks left him like an incandescent spark, leaping to the two constables with terrible force. In a second, it was quiet, as Kuke and Tep tumbled to the floor like broken-stringed puppets.

Sam pushed himself to his feet, the realization of what he'd done rising through the pain. He'd killed two of his father's men . . . his own men. They'd simply been doing their job. The job that he was afraid to do. Protecting people from necromancers and Free Magic and whatever else . . .

He didn't stop to think any further. The pain was coming back, and he knew he had to get away. In a panic, he picked up his bags, thrust the cursed bells back in, buckled the sword around his waist, and left.

He didn't know how he managed the stairs, but a moment later he was in the common room, with people staring at him as they backed against the walls. He stared back, wide-eyed and wild, and limped through, leaving bloody footprints on the floor.

Then he was in the stables, saddling Sprout, the horse blowing wide-nostriled, eyes white with fear at the scent of human blood. Mechanically, he soothed her, hands moving without conscious thought.

A year later, or in no time at all, or somewhere in between, Sam was in the saddle, kicking Sprout into a trot and then a canter, all the while feeling his blood washing down his leg like warm water, filling up his boot till it overflowed the rolled-back top. Some part of his mind screamed at him to stop and tend to the wound, but the greater part shouted it down, wanting only to flee, flee the scene of his crime.

Instinctively, he headed west, putting the rising sun at his back. He zigzagged for a while, to lay a false trail, then took a straight track through the fields, towards a dark expanse of forest, not too far ahead. He had only to reach it and he could hide, hide and tend his hurt.

Finally, Sam reached the comforting shadow of the trees. He went in as far as he could and fell off his horse. Pain climbed up his leg, spiking all the way. The green world of the forest spun and lurched sickeningly, refusing to hold still. The morning light had gone from yellow to grey, like an overcooked egg. He couldn't focus on the healing spell. The Charter marks eluded him, slipping from his mind. They simply wouldn't line up as they should.

It was all too hard. Easier to let go. To fall asleep, to drift into Death.

Except that he knew Death, knew its chill. He was already falling into the cold current of the river. If he could have been sure of being taken under by that current, rushed through the cascade of the First Gate and then onwards, he might have given in. But he knew the necromancer who'd burnt him was waiting for him in Death, waiting for an Abhorsen-in-Waiting too incompetent to manage the manner of his own passing. The necromancer would catch him, take his spirit, and bind it to his will, use him against his family, his Kingdom. . . .

Fear grew in Sam, sharper than the pain. He reached for the Charter marks of healing once more—and found them. Golden warmth grew in his weakly gesturing hands and flowed into his leg, through the black and sodden trouser. He felt its heat rushing through, all the way to the bone, felt the skin and blood vessels knit together, the magic bringing everything back to the way it was supposed to be.

But he'd lost too much blood too quickly for the spell to render him completely whole. He tried to get up but couldn't. His head fell back, the leaf litter making him a pillow. He tried to force his eyes wide open but couldn't. The forest spun again, faster and faster, and then everything went black.

Chapter Twenty-Nine

THE DISREPUTABLE DOG woke with great reluctance, spending a number of minutes in stiff-legged stretching, yawning, and eye rolling. Finally, she shook herself and headed for the door. Lirael stood where she was, her arms crossed sternly across her chest.

"Dog! I need to talk to you!"

The Dog acted surprised, putting her ears back with a sudden jerk. "Shouldn't we be hurrying home? It's after midnight, you know. Third hour of the morning, in fact."

"No!" exclaimed Lirael, all thoughts of talks forgotten. "It can't be! We'd better hurry!"

"Still, if you want to have a talk," said the Dog, sitting back on her haunches and cocking her head in a prime listening attitude, "there's no time like the present, I always say."

Lirael didn't answer. She rushed to the door, pulling on the Dog's collar as she passed, yanking her upright.

"Ow!" yelped the Dog. "I was only joking! I'll hurry!"

"Come on, come on!" snapped Lirael, pushing her hands against the door and then trying to pull at it, which was difficult because it didn't have a handle or a knob. "Oh, how does this open?"

"Ask it," replied the Dog, calmly. "There's no point pushing."

Lirael let out a huff of frustration, took a deep breath, and then forced herself to say, "Please open, door."

The door seemed to think about it for a moment, then slowly swung inwards, giving Lirael enough time to back away. The roar of the river rose through the doorway, and a cool breeze came with it, lifting Lirael's sadly singed hair. The wind also brought something else, something that attracted the Dog's attention, though Lirael couldn't tell what it was.

"Hmmm," said the Dog, turning one ear towards the door and the Charter-lit bridge beyond it. "People. Clayr. Possibly even an aunt."

"Aunt Kirrith!" exclaimed Lirael, jumping nervously. She looked around wildly, seeking another way out. But there was nowhere to go except back across the slippery, river-washed bridge. And now she could see bright Charter lights out in the Rift, lights made fuzzy by the mist and spray from the river.

"What'll we do?" she asked, but her question echoed in the room, taking up the space where there should have been an answer. Quickly, Lirael looked back, but there was no sign of the Disreputable Dog. She had simply disappeared.

"Dog?" whispered Lirael, eyes scanning the room as tears started to blur her vision. "Dog? Don't leave me now."

The Dog had left before when people might have seen her, and every time she did, Lirael harbored the secret fear that her one and only friend would never come back. She felt that familiar fear uncoil in her stomach, adding to the fear she felt from what she'd learned. Fear of the secret knowledge she felt seething and broiling in the book she held under her arm. It was knowledge that she didn't want to have, for it was not of the Clayr.

A single tear ran down her cheek, but she quickly wiped it away. Aunt Kirrith wouldn't have the satisfaction of seeing her cry, she decided, tilting her head back to keep further tears at bay. Aunt Kirrith always seemed to expect the worst of Lirael, seemed to think that she would commit terrible crimes and never amount to anything. Lirael felt that it was all because she wasn't a proper Clayr, though some part of her mind had to acknowledge that this was the way Aunt Kirrith treated anybody who departed from her stupid standards.

Lirael kept her head proudly tilted back until she took her first step on the bridge, when she had to look down, down into the roiling mist and the fast-rushing water. Without the Dog's solid, sucker-footed body at her side, she found the bridge much, much scarier. Lirael took one step, faltered, then started to sway. For a moment, she felt she would fall, and in a panic she crouched down on all fours. *The Book of Remembrance and Forgetting* shifted as she moved, and it almost fell out of her shirt as well. But Lirael shoved it back in and started to crawl across the narrow bridge.

Even crawling took all her concentration, so she didn't look up until she was almost across. She was now also acutely aware that her hair was burnt and her clothes totally soaked by the spray that kept washing over the bridge. And she was barefoot.

When she finally did look up, she let out a stifled scream and made a reflexive hop like a frightened rabbit. Only the quick hands of the two closest Clayr saved her from a potentially fatal fall into the swift, cold waters of the Ratterlin.

They were also the people who had given her the shock, the last two people Lirael would expect to see looking for her: Sanar and Ryelle. As always, they looked calm, beautiful, and sophisticated. They were in the uniform of the Nine Day Watch, their long blond hair elegantly contained in jeweled nets and their long white dresses sprinkled with tiny golden stars. They also held wands of steel and ivory, proclaiming that they were the joint Voice of the Watch. Neither of them looked a day older than when Lirael had first met them properly, out on the Terrace on her fourteenth birthday. They were still everything Lirael thought the Clayr should be.

Everything she wasn't.

There were a whole lot of the Clayr behind them, as well. More of the highest, including Vancelle, the Chief Librarian, and what looked like more of the Nine Day Watch. Quickly counting, Lirael realized that it probably was *all* of the current Nine Day Watch. Forty-seven of them, lined up behind Sanar and Ryelle, white shapes in the darkness of the Rift.

But the total absence of Aunt Kirrith was the worst sign. That meant that whatever she'd done was punishable by something far worse than extra kitchen duties. Lirael couldn't even imagine what sort of punishment required the presence of the entire Watch. She'd never even heard of them leaving the Observatory, not all together.

"Stand up, Lirael," said one of the twins. Lirael realized that she was crouching, still supported by the two Clayr. Gingerly, she stood up, trying to avoid meeting their gaze, not to mention all the other blue and green eyes that she was sure were noting just how brown and muddy her own eyes were.

Words rose up in her mind, but her throat closed when they tried to pass. She coughed, and stuttered, then finally managed to whisper, "I . . . I didn't mean to come here. It just . . . happened. And I know I missed dinner . . . and the midnight rounds. I'll make it up somehow. . . ."

She stopped as Sanar and Ryelle glanced at each other and laughed. But it was kind, surprised laughter, not the scorn she feared.

"We seem to have established a tradition of meeting you in strange places on your birthday," said Ryelle—or perhaps it was Sanar—looking down at the book poking out of Lirael's shirt and the silver panpipes glinting from her waistcoat pocket. "You need not worry about the rounds or a missed dinner. You seem to have claimed a birthright of sorts tonight, one that has waited long for your coming. Everything else is of little consequence."

"What do you mean by a birthright?" asked Lirael. The Sight was the Clayr's birthright, not a trio of strange magical devices.

"You know that alone amongst the Clayr you have never been Seen in the visions," the other twin began. "Never a glimpse, at least till now. But an hour ago, we—that is, the Nine Day Watch—Saw that you would be here, and in another place also. None of us even suspected that this bridge existed, nor the room beyond. But it is clear that while the Clayr of today have not Seen you in their visions, the Clayr of long ago Saw enough to prepare this place and the things you hold. To prepare you, in fact."

"Prepare me for what?" asked Lirael, panicked by the sudden attention. "I don't want anything! All I want is to be . . . to be normal. To have the Sight."

Sanar—for it was Sanar who had spoken last—looked down at the young woman, seeing the pain in her. Since their first meeting five years before, she and her sister had kept a cautious eye on Lirael, and they knew more about her life than their young cousin suspected.

She chose her words carefully.

"Lirael, the Sight may yet come to you in time, and be the stronger for the waiting. But for now you have been given other gifts, gifts that I am sure will be sorely needed by the Kingdom. And as all of us of the Blood are given gifts, we are also laden with the responsibility to use them wisely and well. You have the potential for great power, Lirael, but I fear that you will also face great tests."

She paused, staring into the billowing cloud of mist behind Lirael, and her eyes seemed to cloud, too, as her voice grew deeper and became less friendly, more impersonal and strange.

"You will meet many trials on a path that lies unseen, but you will never forget that you are a Daughter of the Clayr. You may not See, but you will Remember. And in the Remembering, you will see the hidden past that holds the secrets of the future."

Lirael shivered at the words, for Sanar had spoken with the truth of prophecy, and her eyes were sparkling with a strange, icy light.

"What do you mean by great tests?" Lirael asked, when the last faint echo of Sanar's words were lost, drowned in the roar of the river.

Sanar shook her head and smiled, the moment of the vision lost. Unable to speak, she looked at her sister, who continued.

"When we Saw you here this evening, we also Saw you somewhere else, somewhere we have labored for many years to See, without success," said Ryelle. "On the Red Lake, in a boat of woven reeds. The sun was high and bright, so we know it will be in summer. You looked much as you do now, so we know it is in the summer coming that you will be there."

"There will be a young man with you," continued Sanar. "A sick or wounded man, one we were asked to seek for the King. We do not know exactly where he is now, or how or when he will come to the Red Lake. He is surrounded by powers that cloak our vision, and his future is dark. But we do know that he lies at the center of some great and terrible danger. A danger not just to him but to all of us, to the Kingdom. And he will be there with you, in the reed boat, at the height of summer."

"I don't understand," whispered Lirael. "What's that to do with me? I mean, the Red Lake, this man, and everything? I'm just a Second Assistant Librarian! What have I got to do with it?"

"We don't know," answered Sanar. "The visions are fragmented, and a dark cloud spreads like spilt ink across the pages of possible futures. All we know is that this man is important, for both good and ill, and we have Seen you with him. We think that you must leave the Glacier. You must go south and find the reed boat on the Red Lake, and find him."

Lirael looked at Sanar's lips, still moving, but she could hear no sound save the cry of the river. The sound of the water rushing to be free of the mountain, flowing away, away to some distant and unknown land.

I'm being thrown out, she thought. I don't have the Sight, I've grown too old, and they're throwing me out—

"We have also had another vision of the man," Sanar was saying as Lirael's hearing came back. "Come, we will show you, so you will know him at the proper time, and know something of the danger he is in. But not here—we must go up to the Observatory."

"The Observatory!" exclaimed Lirael. "But I'm not . . . I haven't Awoken—"

"I know," said Ryelle, taking her hand to lead her. "It is difficult for you to gaze upon your heart's desire when you may not possess it. If the danger were any less, or someone else could shoulder the burden, we would not press you so. If the vision were not of this place that resists us, we could probably show you elsewhere, too. But now we need the power of the Observatory, and the full strength of the Watch."

They walked back along the Rift, with Sanar and Ryelle on either side of an unprotesting Lirael. Lirael briefly felt what the Dog had called her sense of the Dead, a sort of pressure from all the dead Clayr buried throughout the Rift, but she paid it no heed. It was like someone far away calling someone else's name. All she could think of was that they were making her leave. She would be alone again, because the Disreputable Dog might not come. The Dog might not even be able to exist outside the

Clayr's Glacier, like a sending that couldn't leave its bounds.

Halfway back along the Rift towards the door where she'd come in, Lirael was surprised to see that a long bridge of ice had spanned the depths. The Clayr were walking back across it and then into a deep cave-mouth on the other side of the Rift. Ryelle saw her look and explained, "There are many ways to and from the Observatory, when we have need. This bridge will melt when we have all crossed."

Lirael nodded dumbly. She'd always wondered where the Observatory actually was, and had tried to find it on more than one occasion. She'd had many daydreams of finding her way there, and finding her Sight within. But all those daydreams were destroyed now.

Across the bridge, the cave-mouth led into a rudely dug tunnel that sloped up quite steeply. It was hard going, and Lirael was hot and out of breath when the tunnel finally flattened out. Ryelle and Sanar stopped then, and Lirael wiped the sweat from her eyes before she looked around. They had left stone behind. Now there was nothing but ice all around, blue ice that reflected the Charter lights the Clayr carried. They had come to the heart of the Glacier.

A gate was carved in the ice, flanked by two guards in full mail, holding shields that bore the golden star of the Clayr. Their faces were stern under their open helms. One carried an axe that gleamed with Charter marks, the other a sword that shone brighter than the lights, casting a thousand tiny reflections in the ice. Lirael stared at the guards, for they were clearly Clayr, but no one she knew, which she had thought impossible. There were less than three thousand Clayr in the Glacier, and she had lived here all her life.

"I See you, Voice of the Nine Day Watch," said the woman with the axe, speaking in a strange, formal tone. "You may pass."

But the other with you has not Awoken. By the ancient laws, she must not be allowed to See the secret ways."

"Don't be silly, Erimael," said Sanar. "What ancient laws? It's Lirael, Arielle's daughter."

"Erimael?" whispered Lirael, peering at the severe face, sharply defined by the edges of her helm. Erimael had joined the Rangers six years ago and hadn't been seen since. Lirael had thought Erimael must have been killed in an accident and that she'd missed her Farewell, as she had missed so many other events that required her to don the blue tunic.

"The laws are clear," said Erimael, still in the same stern voice, though Lirael saw her gulp nervously. "I am the Axe-Guard. She must be blindfolded if you wish her to pass."

Sanar snorted and turned to the other woman. "And what says the Sword-Guard? Don't tell me you agree?"

"Yes, unfortunately," said the other woman, who Lirael realized was much older. "The letter of the law is strict. Guests must be blindfolded. Anyone who is not an Awoken Clayr is a guest."

Sanar sighed and turned to Lirael. But Lirael had already hung her head, to hide her humiliation. Slowly, she undid her head scarf, folded it into a narrow band, and bound it around her head, covering her eyes. Behind the soft darkness of the cloth, she wept silently, the blindfold soaking up her tears.

Sanar and Ryelle took her hands again, and Lirael felt the sympathy in their touch. But it did not matter. This was even worse than when she was fourteen, standing alone in her blue tunic, suffering the public shame of not being a Clayr. Now she was irrevocably marked as an outsider. Not a Clayr at all, of any kind. Only a guest.

She asked only two questions as Ryelle and Sanar led her through what felt like a complicated, maze-like passage.

"When will I have to go?"

"Today," replied Ryelle, as she stopped Lirael and prepared her for another sharp turn by gently pushing her elbow till she was facing the right way. "That is to say, as soon as possible. A boat is being prepared for you. It will be spelled to take you down the Ratterlin to Qyrre. From there you should be able to get some constables or even some of the Guard to escort you to Edge, on the Red Lake itself. It should be a fast and uneventful journey, though we wish we could See some of it beforehand."

"Am I to go alone?"

Lirael couldn't see, but she sensed Sanar and Ryelle exchanging glances, silently working out who would speak. At last Sanar said, "That is how you have been Seen, so I'm afraid that is how you will have to go. I wish it were otherwise. We would fly you down by Paperwing, but all the Paperwings have been Seen elsewhere, so the river it must be."

Alone. Without even her one friend, the Disreputable Dog. It didn't really matter what happened to her now.

"There are some steps down here," said Ryelle, stopping Lirael again. "About thirty, I think. Then we will be in the Observatory, and you can take the blindfold off."

Lirael mechanically went with the twins down the steps. It was unsettling, not being able to see where her feet were going, and some of the steps seemed lower than the others. To make it worse, there was a weird rustling noise all around, and occasionally the hint of whispers or smothered conversations.

Finally, they arrived on level ground and took a half dozen steps forward. Sanar helped untie her blindfold.

Light was the first thing Lirael noticed, and space, and then the massed ranks of the Clayr, silently standing in their white, rustling robes. She stood in the center of a huge chamber carved entirely out of ice, a vast cave easily as large as the Great Hall she knew and hated so much. Charter Magic lights shone everywhere, reflecting from the many facets of the ice, so that there was not a hint of darkness anywhere.

Lirael instinctively looked down when she saw all the other Clayr, so she couldn't meet anyone's eyes. But as she cautiously peered out from behind her protective fall of singed hair, she saw that they were not looking at her. They were all looking up. She followed their gaze and saw that the angled ceiling was perfectly smooth and flat, one single enormous sheet of clear ice, almost like an enormous, opaque window.

"Yes," said Sanar, noting Lirael's stare. "That is where we focus our Sight, so all the fragments of the vision can become one, and everyone can See."

"I think we may begin," announced Ryelle, looking around at the massed, silent ranks of the Clayr. Nearly every Awoken Clayr was there, to join a Watch of Fifteen Sixty-Eight. They stood in a series of ever-wider circles around the small central area where Lirael, Sanar, and Ryelle stood, like some strange concentric orchard of white trees that bore silver and moonstone fruit.

"Let us begin!" cried Sanar and Ryelle, and they lifted their wands and clashed them together like swords. Lirael jumped as all the gathered Clayr shouted back, a great bellow that she felt through her bones.

"Let us begin!"

As one, the Clayr in the closest circle joined hands, snapping together as in a military drill. Then the next circle joined hands, and the next, a wave of movement rippling from the center to the farthest circle in the Observatory, till all was still again.

"Let us See!" cried Sanar and Ryelle, clashing their wands again. This time, Lirael was prepared for the shout that came back, but not for the magic that followed. Charter marks seemed to well up out of the icy floor, flowing up through the Clayr of the first circle, till there were so many, they brimmed over and flowed into the next circle, and then the one after that. Charter marks that flowed like thick golden fog up the Clayr's bodies and along their arms.

Lirael watched the magic grow as it passed each circle, saw it wrap itself around the bodies of her cousins. She could see the Charter marks, feel the magic in her pounding heart, hunger for it. But it remained alien, somehow beyond her, as no other Charter Magic had ever been.

Then the outermost circle of the Clayr broke their hand-clasps and held their arms up towards the distant, icy ceiling. Marks flowed from them into the air, falling upwards like golden dust caught in shafts of sunlight. When it hit the ice, it splashed there, as if it were glorious paint and the ice a blank canvas waiting to come alive.

Each circle followed in turn, till all the magic they'd summoned had risen to fill the whole huge ice ceiling with swirling Charter marks. They stared at it, entranced, and Lirael saw their eyes move as if they all watched something there. But she saw nothing, nothing save the swirl of magic that she couldn't understand.

"Look," said Ryelle softly, and the wand she held suddenly became a bottle of bright green glass.

"Learn," said Sanar, and she waved her wand in a pattern directly above Lirael's head.

Then Ryelle threw the contents of the bottle, seemingly at Lirael. But as the liquid flew over her head, Sanar's wand transformed it into ice. A pane of pure, translucent ice that hung horizontally in the air directly above Lirael's head.

Sanar tapped this pane with her wand, and it began to glow a deep, comfortable blue. She tapped it again, and the blue fled to the edges. Lirael stared at it, and then through it, and as she stared, she realized that this strange, suspended pane was helping her See what the Clayr Saw. The meaningless patterns on the ice ceiling above were starting to become clear. Hundreds, maybe even thousands of tiny pictures were joining together to make up a larger picture, like the puzzle pictures she'd played with as a child.

It was a picture of a man standing with his foot on a rock, Lirael saw now. He was looking at something below him.

Curious, Lirael craned her head back for a better view. That made her dizzy for an instant, and then it seemed as if she were falling upwards, through the blue pane and all the way up into the ceiling, falling into the vision. There was a flash of blue and a touch of something that made her shiver—and she was there!

She was standing next to the man. She could hear his rasping, unhealthy-sounding breath, smell the faintest hint of sweat, feel the heat and humidity of a summer day.

And she could taste the awful taint of Free Magic, stronger and more vile than she could ever have imagined, stronger even than her memory of the Stilken. So strong that the bile rose in her throat and she had to force it back, and dots danced before her eyes.

Chapter Thirty

NICHOLAS AND THE PIT

H E WAS YOUNG, Lirael saw, about her own age. Nineteen or twenty. And obviously ill. He was tall, but stooped over, as if a nagging pain bit his middle. His blond, unkempt hair was clean, but hung together like damp string. His skin was too pink in the cheeks and grey around his lips and eyes. Those eyes were blue, but dulled. He held a pair of dark spectacles loosely in one hand, the arms repaired with twine and one green lens cracked and starred.

He was standing on some sort of artificial hill of rough, loose earth, peering shortsightedly down towards a deep pit, a gaping hole in the ground. The pit—or whatever was in it—was the source of the Free Magic that was making Lirael nauseated, even through the vision. She could feel waves of it pulsating out of the scarred earth, cold and terrible, eating into her bones, biting away deep inside her teeth.

The pit had obviously been freshly dug. It was at least as wide across as the Lower Refectory, which could hold four hundred people. A spiral path wound around its edges, disappearing down into the dark depths. Lirael couldn't see how deep it was, but there were people carrying baskets of dirt and rock up and empty baskets back down. Slow, tired people, who seemed quite strange to Lirael. Their clothes were dirty and torn, but even so, Lirael could see that their cut and color were quite unlike anything she'd ever seen. And nearly all of them wore blue hats or the knotted remnants of blue headscarves.

Lirael wondered how on earth they could work with the corrosive taint of Free Magic all around, and looked at them more closely. Then she gasped and tried to move back, but the vision held her.

They weren't people. They were Dead. She could feel them now, feel the chill of Death close by. These workers were Dead Hands, enslaved by some necromancer's will. The blue hats shaded sightless eye sockets, the blue scarves held together rotting heads.

Lirael suppressed her instinctive desire to vomit and quickly looked at the young man next to her, fearful that he might be the necromancer and could somehow see her. But he had no Charter mark on his brow, either whole or perverted to Free Magic. His forehead was clear, save for dirty beads of sweat that had caught the dust from the air, and there was no sign of any bells.

He was looking up now, looking at the sky, and shaking some metal object on his wrist. Perhaps in ritual, Lirael thought. She suddenly felt sorry for him, and had a strange urge to touch the curve of his neck where it joined his ear, just with the very tip of her fingers. She even started to reach out, and was only reminded of where—and what—she was when he spoke.

"Damn it!" he muttered. "Why does nothing work?"

He lowered his arm but kept looking up. Lirael looked, too, seeing the dark thunderclouds that roiled there, low and close. Lightning flickered, but there was no cool breeze, no scent of rain. Just the heat and the lightning.

Then, without warning, a blinding bolt of lightning struck down into the pit, lighting the black depths in a bright flash of incandescence. In that moment, Lirael saw hundreds of Dead Hands digging, digging with tools if they had them and with their own rotting hands if not. They paid no attention to the lightning, which burnt and blackened several of their number, nor the deafening crash of thunder that came at almost the same time.

Within a few seconds, another bolt followed the first, seemingly hitting exactly the same place. Then another and another, thunder booming on and on, shaking the ground at Lirael's feet.

"Four in approximately fifty seconds," remarked the man to himself. "It's getting more frequent. Hedge!"

Lirael didn't understand this last call till a man strode out of the pit below and waved. A thin, balding man, clad in leather armor with gold-etched red enamel steel plates at his throat, elbows, and knees. He had a sword at his side—and a bandolier of bells across his chest, black ebony handles poking out of red leather pouches. Perversions of Charter marks moved across both wood and leather, leaving after-images of fire.

Even from so far away, he smelt of blood and hot metal. He must be the necromancer the Dead Hands served—or one of the necromancers, for there were many Dead. But this one was not the source of the Free Magic that burnt at Lirael's lips and tongue. Something far worse than he lay hidden in the depths of the pit.

"Yes, Master Nicholas?" called the man. Lirael noted that he waved the two Dead Hands that followed him back down into the shadows, as if he didn't want them too clearly seen.

"The lightning comes more quickly," said the young man, so identifying himself to Lirael as Nicholas. But what manner of man—a man without a Charter mark—would a necromancer call Master?

"We must be close," he added, his voice going hoarse. "Ask the men if they will work an extra shift tonight."

"Oh, they'll work!" shouted the necromancer, laughing at some private jest. "Do you want to come down?"

Nicholas shook his head. He had to clear his throat several

times before he could shout back, "I feel . . . I feel unwell again, Hedge. I'm going to lie down in my tent. I will look later. But you must call me if you find anything. It will be metal, I think. Yes, shining metal," he continued, eyes staring as if he saw it in front of him. "Two shining metal hemispheres, each taller than a man. We must find them quickly. Quickly!"

Hedge half bowed, but he didn't answer. He climbed out of the pit, leaving it to walk up to the hill of tailings where Nicholas stood.

"Who is that with you?" shouted Hedge, pointing.

Nicholas looked to where he pointed but saw nothing save the afterglow of the lightning and the image of the shining hemispheres—the image he saw in all his waking moments, as if it were imprinted on his brain.

"Nothing," he muttered, looking straight at Lirael. "No one. I am so tired. But it will be a great discovery—"

"Spy! You'll burn at the feet of my Master!"

Flames leapt from the necromancer's hands and spilled on the ground, red flames cloaked in black, choking smoke. They raced up the hill like wildfire, straight towards Lirael.

At the same time, she saw Nicholas's eyes suddenly focus on her. He reached out one hand in greeting, saying, "Hello! But I expect you're only another hallucination."

Then hands gripped her shoulders and she was pulled back into the Observatory as the red fire struck where she'd been and boiled up into a narrow column of fiery destruction and blackest smoke.

Ice shattered, and Lirael blinked. When she opened her eyes, she was standing between Ryelle and Sanar again, in a pool of broken shards, with pieces of blue ice sprinkled across her head and shoulders.

"You Saw," said Ryelle. It wasn't a question.

"Yes," replied Lirael, sorely troubled, as much by the experience of the vision as by what she'd Seen. "Is that what it is like to have the Sight?"

"Not exactly," replied Sanar. "We mostly See in short flashes, brief fragments from many different parts of the future, all mixed up. Only together, in the Watch, here in the Observatory, can we unify the vision. Even then, only the person who stands where you have stood will See it all."

Lirael thought about that and craned her head back again, ice dribbling down her neck under her shirt. The distant ceiling was only a patch of ice again. She looked back down and saw that all the Clayr were leaving without a word or a backwards glance. The outer ring had gone before she even noticed, and now the next was uncurling into a single file, leaving by a different door. There seemed to be many exits from the Observatory, Lirael thought. Soon she would take one herself, never to return again.

"What," Lirael began, forcing herself to think about the vision, "what am I supposed to do?"

"We don't know," said Ryelle. "We have been trying to See around the Red Lake for several years, without success. Then all of a sudden we Saw you in the room below, the vision we have shown you, and then a glimpse of you and the man in a boat upon the lake. All are obviously linked in some way, but we have not been able to See more."

"The man Nicholas is the key," said Sanar. "Once you find him, we think, you will know what to do."

"But he's with a necromancer!" exclaimed Lirael. "They're digging up something terrible! Shouldn't we tell the Abhorsen?"

"We have sent messages, but the Abhorsen and the King are in Ancelstierre, where they hope to avert a trouble that is also probably connected with whatever is in the pit that you Saw. We have also alerted Ellimere and her co-regent, and it is possible they will also act, perhaps with Prince Sameth, the Abhorsen-in-Waiting. But whatever they do, we know that it is you who must find Nicholas. It seems a little thing, I know, a meeting between two people on a lake. But it is the only future we can See now, with all else hidden from us, and it offers our only hope to avert disaster."

Lirael nodded, white-faced. Too many things were happening, and she was too tired and emotionally exhausted to cope. But it did seem that she was not just being thrown out. She really did have something important to do, not just for the Clayr, but for the whole Kingdom.

"Now, we must prepare you for the journey," added Sanar, obviously noting Lirael's weariness. "Is there anything personal you wish to take, or something special we can provide?"

Lirael shook her head. She wanted the Disreputable Dog, but that didn't seem possible, if the Clayr hadn't Seen her. Perhaps her friend was gone forever now, the spell that had brought her meeting some condition that triggered its end.

"My outdoor things, I suppose," she whispered finally. "And a few books. I suppose I should take the things I found, too."

"You should," said Sanar, obviously curious as to what exactly they were. But she didn't ask, and Lirael didn't feel like talking about them. They were just more complications. Why had they been left for her? What use would they be out in the wide world?

"We must also outfit you with a bow and sword," said Ryelle. "As befits a Daughter of the Clayr gone a-voyaging."

"I'm not very good with a sword," Lirael said in a small voice, choking a little at being called a Daughter of the Clayr. Those words, so long sought, sounded empty to her now. "I'm all right with a bow."

She didn't explain that she was competent with the laminated short bow used by the Clayr only because she shot rats in the Library, using blunted arrows so as not to puncture books. The Dog liked to retrieve the arrows but wasn't interested in eating the rats, unless Lirael cooked them with herbs and sauce, which she naturally refused to do.

"I hope you will need neither weapon," said Sanar. Her words seemed loud, echoing out into the huge cavern of ice. Lirael shivered. That hope seemed likely to be false. Suddenly it was cold. Nearly all the Clayr had gone, all fifteen hundred of them, in a matter of minutes, as if they had never been there. Only two armored guards remained, watching from the end of the Observatory. One had a spear and the other a bow. Lirael didn't need to get closer to know that these were also weapons of power, imbued with Charter Magic.

They had stayed, she knew, to make sure she was blind-folded. She looked away and took her scarf off, folding it with slow, deliberate movements. Then she tied it across her eyes and stood stiffly, waiting for Sanar and Ryelle to take her arms.

"I am sorry," said Sanar and Ryelle, at the same time, their voices blending into one. They sounded to her as if they were apologizing not just for the blindfold, but for Lirael's whole life.

By the time they reached her small chamber off the Hall of Youth, Lirael had not slept or eaten for more than eighteen hours. She was staggering with fatigue, so Sanar and Ryelle continued to support her. She was so tired that she didn't even realize Aunt Kirrith was present until she was taken into a sudden, unwel-come, extremely tight embrace.

"Lirael! What have you done now!" Aunt Kirrith exclaimed, her voice booming from somewhere above Lirael's head, which was kept firmly pressed into her aunt's neck. "You're too young to go off into the world!"

"Aunt!" protested Lirael, trying to free herself, embarrassed to be treated like a little girl in front of Ryelle and Sanar. It was typical of Aunt Kirrith to try to hug her when she didn't want her to, and to not hug her when she did want to be hugged.

"It'll be just like your mother all over again," Kirrith was saying, seemingly as much to the twins as to Lirael. "Going off who knows where and getting involved in who knows what with who knows whom. Why, you might even come back—"

"Kirrith! Enough!" snapped Sanar, surprising Lirael. She had never heard anyone speak to Kirrith like that. It was clearly a shock to Kirrith, too, because she let go of Lirael and took a deep, dignified breath.

"You can't talk to me like that, San . . . Ry . . . whichever one you are," Aunt Kirrith finally said after several deep breaths. "I'm Guardian of the Young, and I am in authority here!"

"And we, for the moment, are the Voice of the Clayr," replied Sanar and Ryelle in unison, lifting the wands they still held. "We have been invested with the powers of the Nine Day Watch. Do you challenge our right, Kirrith?"

Kirrith looked at them, tried to take an even deeper breath, and failed, her breath wheezing out of her like that of a toad that has been stepped on. It was clearly a recognition of their authority, if not a very dignified one.

"Fetch the things you want to take, Lirael," said Sanar, touching her on the shoulder. "We must soon go down to the boat. Kirrith, perhaps if we could speak outside?"

Lirael nodded wearily and went to the chest that held her clothes, while the others went out and shut the door. Without looking, she reached in. Her hand hit something hard, and her fingers were around it before she looked and gave a little gasp of recognition. It was the old soapstone carving of the hard-bitten dog, the one she'd found in the Stilken's chamber, the one that had vanished when the Disreputable Dog had appeared.

Lirael hugged it close to her chest for a moment, a faint hope breaking through her weariness. It was not the Dog, but it was a hint that the Dog could be summoned again. Smiling, she put the statuette in the pocket of a clean waistcoat, making sure its soapstone snout could not be seen poking out. She put the Dark Mirror in the same pocket and the panpipes in the other one, and transferred *The Book of Remembrance and Forgetting* to a small shoulder bag that seemed exactly made for it. The clockwork emergency mouse she put in a corner of the chest, followed by the whistle. Neither of them could help her where she was going now.

As she undressed and quickly washed, thankful for the larger room and simple bathroom she'd moved to on her eighteenth birthday, Lirael considered changing her clothes completely, to wear something that did not identify her as a Clayr. But when it came time to dress, she once again donned the working clothes of a Second Assistant Librarian. That was what she was, she told herself. She had earned the right to the red waistcoat. No one could take that away, even if she wasn't a proper Clayr.

She had just rolled some spare clothes into her cloak, and was thinking about her heavy wool coat and its likely usefulness in late spring and summer, when there was a knock on the door, followed immediately by Kirrith.

"I didn't mean any nastiness about your mother," Kirrith said from the doorway, sounding subdued. "Arielle was my little sister, and I loved her well. But she was outlandish, if you know what I mean, and prone to trouble. Always getting into scrapes and . . . well . . . it's not been easy, what with being Guardian and having to keep everyone in line. Perhaps I haven't shown you . . . well, it's hard when you can't See how others feel or will feel about you. What I mean to say is that I loved your mother—and I love you, too."

"I know, Auntie," replied Lirael, not looking back as she threw her coat back in the chest. Even a year ago she would have given anything to hear those words, to feel that she belonged. Now it was too late. She was leaving the Glacier, leaving it as her mother had done years before, when she had abandoned her daughter seemingly without a care.

But that was all history, Lirael thought. I can leave it behind, start my story afresh. I don't need to know why my mother left, or who my father was. I don't need to know, she repeated to herself.

I don't need to know.

But while she mumbled those words under her breath, her mind kept turning to *The Book of Remembrance and Forgetting* in the bag at her side, and the pipes and Dark Mirror in her waistcoat pockets.

She didn't need to know what had happened in the past. But while she had always been alone among the Clayr for her blindness to the future, now she was alone in another way as well. In a perverse reversal of all her hopes and dreams, she had been granted the exact opposite of her heart's desire.

For with the Dark Mirror, and her new-found knowledge, she could See into the past.

Chapter Thirty-One

A VOICE IN THE TREES

HIDDEN A MERE hundred yards into the fringe of the forest, Prince Sameth lay like a dead man, sprawled where he'd fallen from his horse. One leg was caked with drying blood, and black-red blotches marked the green leaves of the bushes that shivered around him in the breeze. Only a close inspection would have shown that he was still breathing.

Sprout, proving less neurotic than expected, grazed quietly nearby. Occasionally her ears twitched and her head went up, but all through the long day nothing disturbed her contented munching.

In the late afternoon, when the shadows began their slow crawl out from the trees to stretch and join together, the breeze picked up and relieved the heat of the late-spring day. It blew over Sam, partly covering him with leaves, twigs, wind-caught spider-webs, beetle carcasses, and feathery grasses.

One thin blade of grass caught up against his nose and was trapped there, tickling his nostril. It rustled this way, then that, but didn't shift. Sameth's nose twitched in response, twitched again, then finally burst out in a sneeze.

Sam woke up. At first he thought he was drunk, hungover, and suffering. His mouth was dry, and he could taste the stench of his own breath. His head ached with a fierce pain, and his legs hurt even more. He must have passed out in someone's garden, which was incredibly embarrassing. He had been this drunk only once before, and hadn't wished to repeat the experience.

He started to call out, but even as the dry, pathetic croak left his lips, he remembered what had happened.

He'd killed two constables. Men who were trying to do their duty. Men who had wives, family. Parents, brothers, sisters, children. They would have left their homes in the morning with no expectation of sudden death. Perhaps their wives were even now waiting for them to come home for the evening meal.

No, thought Sameth, levering himself up to look bleakly at the red light of the setting sun filtering through the trees. They had fought early in the morning. The wives would know by now that their husbands were never coming home.

Slowly, he pushed himself further upright, brushing the forest debris from his clothes. He had to push the guilt down, too, at least for the moment. Survival required it.

First of all, he had best cut away his trouser leg and look at the wound. He dimly remembered casting the spell that had undoubtedly saved his life, but the wound would still be fragile, liable to reopen. He had to bind it up, for he was far too weak to cast another healing spell.

After that, he would somehow stand up. Stand up, catch the faithful Sprout, and ride deeper into the forest. He was somewhat surprised that he hadn't already been discovered by the local constabulary. Unless he had laid a more confusing trail than he'd thought, or they were waiting for reinforcements to arrive before they started looking for what they assumed to be a murderous necromancer.

If the constables—or even worse, the Guard—found him now, he'd have to tell them who he was, Sam decided. And that would mean a shameful return to Belisaere, there to be tried by Ellimere and Jall Oren. Public disgrace and infamy would be sure to follow. The only other alternative would be a dishonorable covering up of his awful deed.

Either situation would be intolerable. The disappointment he could already imagine on his parents' faces would be too much to bear. No doubt his inability to be the Abhorsen-in-Waiting would also come out, and they would despair of him completely.

Better that he disappear. Go into the forest and hide out while he recovered, then continue to Edge with a newly conjured visage, for he was sure Nick still needed help. At least he would be able to do that. Not even Nick could get into more trouble than Sam had managed to get into himself.

Making the decisions proved easier than putting them into practice. Sprout backed away from him, her nostrils flaring, as he tried to grab her reins. She didn't like the smell of blood, or the occasional grunts of pain Sam let out as he accidentally put weight on his wounded leg.

Finally, he managed to push her into a sort of natural cul-de-sac, where three trees prevented any further retreat. Mounting proved to be another challenge. Pain flared as he swung his leg over, gasping at the hurt.

Now Sam was faced with another problem. It was rapidly getting dark, and he had no idea where to go. Civilization and all it offered lay east, north, and south, but he dared not go until he was strong enough to cast another spell to change his and Sprout's looks. Westward, there were many forest paths of doubtful use and direction. There might be some settlements or lone houses somewhere within the forest, but he couldn't visit them with any safety, either.

Worse, he had only a single canteen of yesterday's water, a hunk of very stale bread, and a lump of salted beef, his emergency provision in case he needed a snack between inns. The ginger cakes were long gone, eaten on the road.

It began to rain, the wind having brought clouds over from

the sea—only a light spring shower, but it was enough to make Sam curse and wrestle with his saddlebags, trying to pull out his cloak. If he caught a cold on top of his existing hurts, there was no knowing how he'd end up. In a forest grave, most likely, he thought bitterly, not dug by human hands. Just a mound of wind-borne bits and pieces, linked by the grass growing up around his pathetic remains.

He was just thinking about this dismal future when his fingers, pulling at the cloak, felt leather and cold metal instead of wool. Instantly, he snatched his hand away, the tips of his fingers cold and already turning blue. The knowledge of what he'd just touched made him bend over his saddle horn and let out a great sob of despair and fright.

The Book of the Dead. He'd left it behind in his workroom, but it had refused to be left. Just like the bells. He would never be rid of them, even wounded and alone in this dark forest. They would follow him forever, even into Death itself.

He was just about to let himself break down when a voice came from the darkness between the trees.

"A little lost princeling, weeping in the forest? I would have thought you had more steel in your spine, Prince Sameth. Still, I am often wrong."

The voice had an electric effect on Sameth and Sprout. The Prince shot bolt upright in the saddle, gasped at the pain, and tried to draw his sword. Sprout, equally surprised, leapt forward into an instant canter, weaving amid the trees without a thought for her rider and low-slung branches.

Horse and rider raced along in a cacophony of breaking branches, shouts, and whinnies. They continued in this fashion for at least fifty yards before Sameth got Sprout under control and managed to turn her back in the direction the voice had come from.

He also managed to draw his sword. It was half-dark now, the tree-trunks pale ashen streaks in the gathering gloom, supporting branches where leaves hung like heavy clots of darkness. Whoever . . . whatever . . . had spoken could easily creep up on him now, but it was better to face it than be knocked off by a branch in panicked flight.

The voice had been unnatural. He'd tasted Free Magic in it, and something else. It wasn't a Dead creature—no, not that. But it could be a Stilken or Margrue, Free Magic elementals that occasionally hungered for the taste of Life. He wished now that he had read the book that he'd been given for his birthday, the one on binding, by Merchane.

Something rustled in the leaves of the closest tree, and Sam started again, lifting his sword to the guard position. Sprout fidgeted, kept in check only by the pressure of Sam's knees. The effort sent bolts of pain up Sam's side, but he did not ease off.

There was something moving all right, moving up the trunk—there—no, there. It was jumping from branch to branch, moving behind him. Maybe more than one. . . .

Desperately, Sam tried to reach the Charter to draw out the marks needed for a magical attack. But he was too weak, the pain in his leg too strong, too fresh. He couldn't keep the marks in his mind. He couldn't remember the spell he wanted to form.

Perhaps the bells, he thought in desperation, as whatever it was moved again. But he didn't know how to use the bells against the Dead, let alone Free Magic beings. His hand shook at the thought of using the bells, and he was reminded of Death. At the same time a fierce determination rose in him. Whatever ill luck had dogged him, he would not just lie down and die. He might be afraid, but he was a royal Prince, the son of Touchstone and Sabriel, and he would sell his life as dear as his strength could make it.

"Who calls Prince Sameth?" he shouted, words harsh in the darkling forest. "Show yourself, before I wreak a spell on you of great destruction!"

"Save the theatrics for those who respond to them," replied the voice, this time accompanied by the flash of two piercing green eyes, reflecting the last of the sun on a branch high above Sam's head. "And count yourself lucky that it's only me. You've left blood enough around to call a brace of hormagants."

With that speech, a small white cat leapt from the tree, catapulted off a lower branch, and landed a cautious distance from Sprout's forefeet.

"Mogget!" exclaimed Sam, peering down at him with dizzy incredulity. "What are you doing here?"

"Looking for you," said the cat. "As should be startlingly obvious to even the most dull-witted Prince. Loyal servant of the Abhorsen, that's me. Ready to baby-sit at a moment's notice. Anywhere. No trouble at all. Now get off that horse and make a fire, just in case there actually are some hormagants about. I don't suppose you've been sensible enough to bring anything to eat?"

Sameth shook his head, feeling something not exactly as positive as relief pass through him. Mogget *was* a servant of the Abhorsen, but he was also a Free Magic being of ancient power. The red collar he wore, engrained with Charter marks, and the miniature bell that hung from it, were the visible signs of the power that bound him. Once it had been Saraneth, the Binder, that rang on that collar. Since the defeat of Kerrigor, the bell that bound Mogget was a tiny Ranna. Ranna the Sleepbringer, the first of the seven bells.

Sameth had hardly ever spoken to Mogget, for the strange cat-being had been awake only once when Sam was at Abhorsen's House, and that had been ten years before. As on the more recent occasion, he'd woken just long enough to steal Touchstone's fresh-caught salmon, and had addressed few words to the boy of seven who had stared incredulously as the "always sleeping" cat removed a fish as large as itself from a silver platter.

"I really don't understand," mumbled Sameth as he gingerly lowered himself off Sprout's back. "Did Mother send you to look for me? How did she wake you up?"

"The Abhorsen," replied Mogget, between bouts of licking his paw in a rather stately fashion, "had nothing directly to do with it. Having been associated with the family for so long, I am simply aware of when my services are required. For example, when a new set of bells appears, suggesting that an Abhorsen-in-Waiting is ready to come into his inheritance. Having woken, I simply followed the bells.

"But the return of Cassiel's bells did not waken me," continued Mogget, switching to his other paw. "I was already awake. Something is happening in the Kingdom. Things long dormant are stirring, or being woken, and the ripples of their waking have spread to Abhorsen's House, for whatever wakes threatens the Abhorsen—"

"Do you know what it is exactly?" Sam interrupted anxiously. "Mother said she feared some ancient evil was planning terrible things. I had thought it might be Kerrigor."

"Your uncle Rogir?" replied Mogget, as if answering a question about some slightly eccentric relative rather than the fearful Greater Dead Adept that Kerrigor had ultimately become. "Ranna holds him tighter than she does me. He sleeps in the deepest cellar of Abhorsen's House. And there he will sleep till the end of time."

"Ah," sighed Sam, relieved.

"Unless whatever is stirring wakes him up as well," Mogget added thoughtfully. "Now tell me why my leisurely journey to Belisaere and its justly famous fish markets has been suddenly interrupted by a side trip to a forest. Where do you think you're going, and why are you going there?"

"I'm going to find my friend Nicholas," explained Sam, though he felt Mogget's green eyes boring into him, seeking out the deeper reasons that he continued to hide from himself. Avoiding that gaze, he pushed together a small pyramid of twigs and dried leaves, and lit it with a friction match struck against his boot.

"And who is Nicholas?" asked Mogget.

"He's an Ancelstierran, a friend of mine from school. I'm worried because he has no idea what it's really like over here. He doesn't even believe in Charter Magic—or any other magic, for that matter," said Sam, as he added some larger sticks to the fire. "He thinks everything can be explained scientifically, the same way Ancelstierran things work. Even after the Dead attacked us near the Perimeter, he still wouldn't accept that there isn't some explanation other than magic. He's *very* stubborn. Once he decides something is just so, he won't change his mind unless you can prove it with mathematics or something he accepts. And he's important in Ancelstierre, because he's the Chief Minister's nephew. I mean, you probably know that Mother and Dad are going to negotiate—"

"Where is this Nicholas?" interrupted Mogget, hooding his eyes. Sameth could see the flames reflected in them for a moment before the lids closed, and he shivered. In the eyes of some Dead creatures, those flames would not be a reflection.

"He was supposed to wait for me to meet him at the Wall, but he's already crossed. At least that's what he said in his letter. He hired a guide, and he's going to look for some old legend called the Lightning Trap on the way to Belisaere," continued Sameth, feeding a larger branch into the fire. "I don't know what that is, or how he heard about it, but apparently it's somewhere near Edge.

And of course that's where Mother and Dad think the Enemy is."

His voice trailed off as he realized that Mogget didn't seem to be listening.

"The Lightning Trap, near the Red Lake," muttered Mogget, his eyes closing to narrow slits of darkness. "The King and the Abhorsen in Ancelstierre, trying to stop a great multitude going to their deaths. A friend of the Abhorsen-in-Waiting, a Prince of sorts himself on the other side of the Wall. The Clayr Sightless, save for visions of total ruin . . . This does not bode well, and the connections cannot be purely coincidence. The Lightning Trap. I have not heard that name precisely, but something stirs. . . . Sleep grips and dulls my memory. . . ."

Mogget's voice had grown softer as he spoke, drifting into something like a growl. Sam waited for the cat to say something more, then realized that the growl had become a snore. Mogget was asleep.

Shivering—but not with cold—Sam put another branch in the fire and was comforted by the flare of friendly light. It had stopped raining, or never got properly started. Just a bit of spitting and a slight drop in temperature. But this was not good news to Sam, who would have preferred to be enduring heavy rain. The last few days had been unseasonably warm for the time of year, with summer heat in late spring, and teasing rain that had never quite developed into a real storm. That meant the spring floods would be sinking early. And the Dead would roam further afield, not confined by running water.

He looked at Mogget again and was startled to see one bright eye watching him, sparkling in the firelight, while the other eye was firmly closed.

"How were you wounded?" purred the cat, voice low, words matching the crackle of the fire. He sounded as if he already knew the answer, but wanted to confirm something.

Sam blushed and hung his head, hands unconsciously linking in an attitude of prayer.

"I got in a fight with two constables. They thought I was a
necromancer. The bells . . ." His voice trailed off, and he gulped.
Mogget kept staring at him with that one sardonic eye, obviously
waiting to hear more.

"I killed them," whispered Sam. "A Death-spell."

There was a long silence. Mogget opened his other eye and
yawned, pink mouth revealing sharp, ever-so-white teeth.

"Idiot. Worse than your father. Guilt, guilt, guilt," he said,
mid yawn. "You didn't kill them."

"What!" exclaimed Sam.

"You can't have killed them," replied Mogget, turning around
several times to knead the leaves into a more comfortable bed.
"They're royal servants, sworn to the King. They carry his protection, even from one of his wayward children. Mind you, any
other innocents about would have been slain. Very clumsy of
you, to use that spell."

"I didn't think," replied Sam woodenly. He was enormously
relieved that he wasn't a murderer. Now he could feel angry at
Mogget for making him feel like a foolish schoolboy.

"Obviously," agreed Mogget. "And you haven't started thinking, either. If they'd died, you would have felt it. You're the
Abhorsen-in-Waiting, Charter help us."

Sam bit back an angry reply as he realized that the cat was correct. He *hadn't* felt the constables die. Mogget kept watching him,
his eyes still slitted, apparently viewing Sam with deep suspicion.

"Coils within coils," murmured the cat. "Fleas upon fleas,
idiots begetting idiots—"

"What?"

"Mmm, just thinking," whispered Mogget. "You should try
it sometimes. Wake me in the morning. It may be quite difficult."

"Yes, Sire," said Sam, mustering as much sarcasm as possible. It had no effect upon Mogget, who now seemed to be really asleep.

"I always wondered why Dad said you were too big for your boots," Sam added, straightening his leg out in front of him and checking the bandage. He didn't add that when he had been seven years old and newly at school in Ancelstierre, he had pointed to an illustration from "Puss in Boots" and loudly repeated something his father had once said to Sabriel: "That bloody cat of yours is too big for his boots."

It had also been the first time he'd worn the dunce cap and stood in the corner. "Bloody" was not in the accepted vocabulary for the young gentlemen of Thorne Preparatory School.

Mogget didn't reply. Sam poked his tongue out at him, then dragged a half-rotted stump onto the fire, hopping on his good leg. The stump would burn till dawn, but just in case, he broke up some deadfall branches and laid them close by.

Then he lay down himself, with his sword under his hand and Sprout's saddle under his head. It was a warm night, so he didn't need his cloak or Sprout's odorous saddle blanket. Sprout herself dozed nearby, hobbled to prevent her starting off on her own nervous adventures. Mogget slept at Sam's side, more like a hunting dog than a cat.

For a few moments Sam thought about staying awake to keep watch, but he didn't have the strength to keep his eyes open. Besides, they were in the heartland of the Kingdom, close to Belisaere. It had been safe here for the last decade at least. What could possibly trouble them?

Many things, Sam thought, as sleep battled with his awareness of all the subtle sounds of the night forest. He was deeply troubled by Mogget's enigmatic words, and was still cataloguing potential horrors and matching them to sounds when exhaustion overcame him and he fell asleep.

He awoke to the touch of sunlight on his face, filtered through the canopy of trees. The fire continued to smolder, smoke meandering about till he sat up, when it changed direction and blew across his face.

Mogget was still sleeping, now curled up into a tight white ball, almost buried in the leaves.

Sam yawned and tried to stand up. He'd forgotten about his leg, which had stiffened so much that he promptly fell over, letting out a shriek of pain. That startled Sprout, who jumped as far as her hobbles allowed her and rolled her eyes. Sam muttered soothing words at her while he used a hefty sapling to haul himself upright.

Mogget didn't wake then or later, sleeping on while Sam finished re-dressing his wound and cast a small Charter-spell to dull the pain and keep infection at bay. The cat stayed asleep even when Sam got out some bread and beef for a not very satisfactory breakfast.

After he'd eaten, Sam brushed Sprout and then saddled up. With nothing left to do but cover the remnants of the fire, he decided it was time to endure more of Mogget's insults.

"Mogget! Wake up!"

The cat didn't stir. Sam leaned down closer and shouted, "Wake up!" again, but Mogget didn't even twitch an ear.

Finally, he reached out and shook the little cat gently behind the collar. Aside from his feeling the buzz and interplay of Free and Charter Magic, nothing happened. Mogget slept on.

"What am I supposed to do with you?" asked Sam, looking down at him. This whole adventure/rescue business was getting out of hand. It was only his third day out of Belisaere, and he was already off the high road, wounded, and in the company of a strange and potentially extremely dangerous Free Magic construct. His question dredged up another one he'd been trying to avoid: What was he going to do now himself?

He didn't expect an answer to either question, but after a moment, a muffled reply came from the apparently still sleeping cat.

"Put me in a saddlebag. Wake me up when you find some decent food. Preferably fish."

"All right," replied Sam with a shrug. Picking up the cat without moving his wounded leg proved difficult, but eventually he managed it. Cradling Mogget in one forearm, he delicately transferred him to the left saddlebag, after checking that it wasn't the one with the bells and *The Book of the Dead*. He didn't like the idea of all three being put together, though he knew no reason why they shouldn't be.

Eventually Mogget was safely installed, with just his head poking out of the bag.

"I'm going to ride west through this small forest, then across the open country to the Sindlewood," explained Sam as he turned the stirrup and put his boot through, ready to mount. "We'll go through the Sindlewood to the Ratterlin, then follow it south till we can get a boat to take us to Qyrre. From there it shouldn't take long to get to Edge, and hopefully we'll find Nick straightaway. Does that sound like a good plan?"

Mogget didn't answer.

"So a day or so in this forest," continued Sam as he mustered his strength to swing up and over. He liked talking about his plans out loud—it made them seem more real and sensible. Particularly when Mogget was asleep and couldn't criticize them. "When we come out, we're bound to find a village, or a charcoal burner's camp or something. They'll sell us whatever we need before we cross the Sindlewood. There're probably woodcutters or people like that there, too."

He stopped talking as he mounted up, suppressing a cry of

pain. His injured leg was feeling better than the day before, but not by much. And he felt a bit dizzy now, almost lightheaded. He'd have to be careful.

"By the way," he said, clicking Sprout into a walk, "last night you seemed to know something about this Lightning Trap Nick has gone to look for. You didn't like the sound of it, but you fell asleep before saying anything else. I was wondering if it had anything to do with the necromancer—"

"Necromancer?" came the immediate, yowled reply. Mogget erupted out of the saddlebag and crouched in front of Sam, looking in every direction, his fur standing on end.

"Um, not here. I was just saying that you started to talk about the Lightning Trap, and I wondered if it had to do with Chlorr of the Mask, or the other necromancer, the one . . . the one I fought."

"Humph," snorted Mogget darkly, subsiding back into the saddlebag.

"Well, tell me something!" demanded Sam. "You can't just sleep all day!"

"Can't I?" asked Mogget. "I could sleep all year. Particularly since I have no fish, which I note you have failed to procure."

"So what is the Lightning Trap?" prompted Sam, pulling lightly on the reins to direct Sprout towards a more westerly and well-traveled path.

"I don't know," Mogget said softly. "But I mislike the sound of it. A Lightning Trap. A gatherer of lightning? Surely it cannot be—"

"What?" asked Sam.

"It is probably only a coincidence," replied Mogget heavily, his eyes closing once more. "Perhaps your friend does only go to see a place where lightning strikes more commonly than it should. But there are powers working here, powers that hate everything of the Charter, Blood, and Stone. I smell plots and long-laid plans, Sameth. I do not like it at all."

"So what should we do?" Sam asked anxiously.

"We must find your friend Nick," whispered Mogget as he drifted back into sleep. "Before he finds . . . whatever it is that he seeks."

Chapter Thirty-Two

"WHEN THE DEAD DO WALK, SEEK WATER'S RUN"

GOADED ON BY Mogget's alarming presentiment, Sam pressed himself and Sprout hard—so they left the small, unnamed forest earlier than expected, on the evening of the first day, and began to cross the rolling green hills of the farmland beyond. This was part of the Middle Lands of the Old Kingdom, a wide belt of small villages, farm steadings, and sheep, stretching west across the country almost as far as Estwael and Olmond. Apart from Sindle to the north, there were no towns until Yanyl, twenty leagues past the western shore of the Ratterlin. Largely depopulated during the Interregnum, the area had recovered quickly during Touchstone's reign, but there were still far fewer people than in the heyday of the Kingdom.

Since his former disguise was now a liability, Sam removed the Charter-spell that disguised him as a Traveler and resumed his normal appearance. Sprout was already disguised by the mud on her legs and her very ordinary looks. In his sweaty, dirt-stained clothes, it was hard to tell what Sam looked like, anyway. He had a story ready, should he be asked. He would say he was the younger son of a Belisaere merchant's guard captain, traveling from the north to a cousin near Chasel, who would employ him as a retainer.

He also re-bound his wound and managed to slip on his spare trousers, so as not to show an obviously wounded, blood-stained leg. His limp he could not disguise, unlike his hat, which suffered the indignity of having its brim cut in half, rendering it both less shady and less distinctive.

Soon after leaving the forest, they entered a village, or a hamlet, really, since it boasted only seven houses. There was a Charter Stone nearby, though. Sam could feel it, somewhere behind the houses. He was tempted to find it and use it to help him cast another, stronger healing spell, but the villagers would surely notice him then.

The place lacked an inn. Though a comfortable bed was beyond hope, he did manage to buy some almost-fresh bread, a freshly cooked rabbit, and several small, sweet apples from a woman who was taking a cartload of fair-day purchases home to her farm.

Mogget slept through this transaction, hidden under the loosely tied flap of the saddlebag, which was just as well. Sam didn't know how he would even begin to explain why a white cat rode with him. It was better not to tempt interest.

Sam kept on riding till it was too dark to see and Sprout wandered into the mud on either side of what was supposed to be a road. He conjured a small Charter light, and they found an open-sided hayrick in which to take shelter. Mogget slept on, oblivious to the removal of the saddlebags and the scraping of at least some of the mud from man and horse.

Sam tried to wake him, to learn more about the Lightning Trap. But the bell that bound Mogget worked too well, its sleepy chime sounding whenever the cat moved as if to wake up. The miniature Ranna made even Sam weary when he leaned too close, so he fell asleep next to the cat in a most uncomfortable position.

The next day was much the same as the first. Not surprisingly, considering his thin bed of leftover straw, Sam found it easy to rise before dawn, and once again he pushed Sprout to a pace beyond her liking.

He met few people on the road—which was not much more than a track—and spoke little but pleasantries to them, for fear of discovery. Just enough to seem normal, when he bought some food, or asked about the best way through Sindlewood to the Ratterlin.

He had a fright in one village, when he stopped to buy some grain for Sprout and a bag of onions and parsnips for himself. Two constables rode straight towards him, but they didn't slow, merely nodding as they passed, riding back eastwards. Apparently, the word had not spread either about a dangerous necromancer-at-large or a missing Prince, or else he didn't look as if he could be either one. Whatever the cause, Sam was grateful.

In the main, it was an uneventful if tiring journey. Sam spent much of the time thinking about Nick, his parents, and his own shortcomings. These thoughts always led back to the Enemy. The more he thought about it, the more Sam was convinced that the necromancer who had burnt him must be the architect of all the current troubles. That necromancer had the power, and he had shown his hand by trying to capture and dominate Sam.

Mostly Sam agonized over what he should do and what might happen. He constructed many quite horrifying scenarios in his head, and he generally failed to work out what the best course of action would be if they turned out to be true. Each passing day made him envision more horrible possibilities. Every day Sam was more acutely aware that Nicholas might have already found something inimical in the Lightning Trap. Perhaps his doom.

Four days after his encounter with the constables, Sam found himself looking down from a pastured hill into the shadowy green borders of the ancient forest known as Sindlewood. It looked much larger, darker, and more overgrown than the small wood where he'd met Mogget. The trees were taller, too, at least the ones he could see on the fringe, and there was no obvious path.

Even as Sam looked at the forest, his thoughts were far away. Nick's situation weighed heavily on him, as did the presence of *The Book of the Dead* and the bells. All these things were closely entwined now, for it seemed that Sam's best hope of rescuing Nick—if he was in trouble—lay in mastering the skills of an Abhorsen. If Nick was held by the Enemy, he would probably be used to blackmail the Chief Minister in Ancelstierre and stop Sabriel and Touchstone's plan to prevent the Southerlings' being massacred, which in turn would mean an invasion by the Dead and the end of the Old Kingdom, and . . .

Sam sighed and looked back at the saddlebags. His imagination was getting out of control. But whatever was really happening, he would have to make a supreme effort to read the book, in order to become a rescuer and not just an idiot riding into disaster, getting himself killed or enslaved for nothing.

Of course, there was always the possibility that Mogget was lying. Sam was somewhat suspicious of Mogget, having the dim recollection that the cat never left Abhorsen's House without the Abhorsen. True, Sabriel couldn't have taken him into Ancelstierre on a diplomatic mission, and it was possible that she had granted him freedom to leave the House. But Sabriel also had the ring that could control the Free Magic being that would result if Mogget were unbound. If the creature within Mogget should be freed, it would kill any Abhorsen it could. Which, in this case, meant Sam. Surely Sabriel wouldn't have let the cat out without making sure it also brought Sam the ring.

Maybe it was her very absence in Ancelstierre, on the other side of the Wall, that had allowed Mogget to do what he liked.

Or perhaps Mogget had even been suborned by the Enemy and was actually guiding Sameth to his doom. . . .

Busy thinking unpleasant thoughts and trying to direct Sprout the best way down the hill, Sam was totally unprepared for the cold shiver that suddenly touched his spine. In that same instant, he realized he was being watched. Watched by something Dead.

The old rhyme, drilled into him since childhood, leapt into his head:

When the Dead do walk, seek water's run,
For this the Dead will always shun.
Swift river's best or broadest lake
To ward the Dead and haven make.
If water fails thee, fire's thy friend;
If neither guards, it will be thy end.

Even as the words were running through his head, Sam looked at the sun. There was little more than an hour of daylight left. Simultaneously he looked for running water—a stream or river—and saw a reflection, silver in the shadows, near the edge of the forest. Farther away than he would have liked.

He directed Sprout towards it, feeling the fear rise in him, coursing through his muscles. He couldn't see the Dead creature, but it was close. He felt its spirit like a clammy touch upon his skin. It must be strong, too, or it would not risk even the waning sun.

Sam's knees twitched, the reflex of an overwhelming urge to kick Sprout into a gallop. But they were still going down the hill, on broken ground. If Sprout fell on him, he would be trapped, easy prey for the Dead. . . .

No. Best not to think of that. He looked around again, squinting against the yellow-red sun, low in the sky. The creature was somewhere behind him . . . and no . . . to the right.

His fear grew as Sam realized there were two creatures, per-haps more. They must be Shadow Hands, slinking from the shade of rock to rock, almost impossible to see till they reared up to attack.

Fumbling, he reached back and opened the saddlebag. If he couldn't reach running water in time, the bells would be his only defense against Shadow Hands. A fairly pathetic defense, since he didn't know how to use them properly and they might easily work against him.

He felt one of the Dead move again, and his heart stammered at the awful swiftness of the thing. It was right next to him and he still couldn't see it, even in bright sunlight!

Then he looked up. A black speck hovered above him, just beyond arrow-shot. And another, behind the first and farther up.

Not Shadow Hands at all. Gore Crows. And where there were two, there would be many more. Gore Crows were always cre-ated in flocks, made from ordinary crows killed with ritual and ceremony, then infused with the splintered fragments of just one Dead spirit. Guided by this shattered but single intelligence, these decaying lumps of rotten flesh and feathers flew by force of Free Magic—and killed by force of numbers.

But as Sam scanned the horizon, he could see no more than two. Surely no necromancer would waste his power on just a pair of Gore Crows. They were too easy to kill in anything less than a flock. A sword-stroke could smash a single crow, but even a mighty warrior could be defeated by a hundred Gore Crows attacking at once, sharp beaks striking at the eyes and neck.

It was also unusual for them to be out under the sun. The spell that drove them was quickly eroded by heat and light, even as their physical forms were shredded by the wind.

Unless, Sam suddenly thought, there really were only two Gore Crows, sharing the Dead vitality that would normally be spent on hundreds of crow bodies. If this was the case, they would last much longer and would be stronger under the sun. They could also be used in other ways than to merely attack.

Like watching, he thought grimly, as neither Dead bird sought to come any closer. They were keeping station above him, circling slowly, probably marking him for the assault of other Dead come nightfall.

As if to confirm his thoughts, one of the Gore Crows—the one farther away—let out a mocking, scratchy caw and turned away to the south, dropping rotten feathers as it flew, propelled more by magic than by the occasional beats of its wings.

It looked all too much like a messenger, with its partner the shadower, staying high to follow wherever Sam might go.

For a moment he contemplated casting a spell of destruction upon it, but it was too far away and obviously well instructed in caution. Besides, he was still weak from his wounded leg. He knew he must save his powers for the night.

Keeping a wary eye on the black speck above him, Sam urged Sprout on. The stream didn't look like much from here, but it would offer some protection. After a moment's hesitation, he also drew out the bell-bandolier and put it on. The weight of the bells and their power lay heavily upon his chest, and shortened and shallowed his breath. But if worst came to worst, he would try to use the lesser bells, drawing on the lessons he'd had from his mother. They were supposed to be merely a prelude for the study he'd abandoned. Ranna, at least, he could probably wield without fear of being forced unwillingly into Death.

A nagging voice at the back of his mind said that even now it was not too late to pick up *The Book of the Dead*, to learn more of the birthright that could save him. But even his fear of an attack by the Dead was not enough to conquer Sam's fear of the book. Reading it, he might find himself taken into Death. Better to fight the Dead in Life, with what little knowledge he had, than to confront them in Death itself.

Behind him, Sam thought he heard a chuckle, a muffled laugh that didn't sound like Mogget. He turned, hand instinctively going to his sword, but there was nothing and no one there. Just the sleeping cat in one saddlebag, and *The Book of the Dead* in the other. Sam let go of the hilt, already sweaty from his trembling fingers, and looked down at the stream again. If the bed was smooth, he would ride along it as far as he could. If he was lucky, it might even take him as far west as the Ratterlin, a mighty river even one of the Greater Dead couldn't cross.

And from there, a secret and cowardly voice said in his mind, he could take a boat to Abhorsen's House. He would be safe there. Safe from the Dead, safe from everything. But what, another voice asked, would happen to Nick, to his parents, to the Kingdom? Then both voices were lost as Sam concentrated on guiding Sprout down the hillside, towards the promised safety of the stream.

Sam lost sight of the Gore Crow when the last of the daylight was eaten up by the shadows of the trees and the falling darkness. But he could still feel the Dead spirit above him. It was lower now, braver with the cloaking night about it.

But not brave enough to descend too close to the running water that burbled on either side of Sam's temporary camp. The stream had proved to be a bit of a disappointment, and a clear indication that the spring floods were already receding. It was only thirty feet wide, and shallow enough to wade in. But it would help, and Sam had found an islet, no more than a narrow strip of sand, where the water ran swiftly on either side.

He had a fire going already, since there was no point trying to hide with the Gore Crow circling above. All he had to do to make his camp as secure as possible was to cast a diamond of protection large enough for himself, the horse, and the fire.

If he had the strength to do it, Sam thought, as he made Sprout stand still. As an afterthought, he also took off the bandolier of bells, which had grown no easier to bear. Then he limped to take up a spell-casting stance in front of Sprout, unsheathed his sword, and held it outstretched. Keeping this pose, he took four slow, deliberate breaths, drawing as much oxygen into his tired body as he could.

He reached out for the four cardinal Charter marks that would create the points of the diamond of protection. Symbols formed in his mind, plucked out of the flow of the never-ending Charter.

He held them in his mind, breath ragged at the effort, and drew the outline of the first mark—the Eastmark—in the sand in front of him. As he finished, the Eastmark in his head ran down into the blade like golden fire. It filled the outline he'd made in the sand with light.

Sam limped behind Sprout, past the fire, and drew the Southmark. As this one flared into life, a line of yellow fire ran to it from the Eastmark, forming a barrier impenetrable to both the Dead and physical danger. Intent on moving on, Sam didn't look. If he faltered now, the diamond would be incomplete.

Sam had cast many diamonds of protection before, but never when he was wounded and so weary. When the last mark, the Northmark, finally flared up, he dropped his sword and collapsed, wheezing onto the damp sand.

Sprout, curious, turned her head back to look at him, but she didn't move. Sam had thought he would have to spell her into immobility to keep her from accidentally moving out of the diamond, but she didn't stir. Perhaps she could smell the Gore Crow.

"I take it we're in danger," said a yawning voice close to Sam's ear. He sat up and saw Mogget extricating himself from the saddlebag, which lay next to the fire and a probably insufficient pile of rather damp wood.

Sam nodded, temporarily unable to speak. He pointed up at the sky, which was now beginning to show single stars and the great white swathe of the Mare's Tail. There were black clouds too, high to the south, crackling with distant lightning, but no sign of rain.

The Gore Crow was invisible, but Mogget seemed to know what Sam was pointing at. The cat rose up on his hind legs and sniffed, one paw absently batting down an oversized mosquito that had probably just dined on Sam.

"A Gore Crow," he said. "Only one. Strange."

"It's been following us," said Sam, slapping several mosquitoes that were coming in to land on his forehead. "There were two, but the other one flew away. South. Probably to get orders. Curse these bugs!"

"There is a necromancer at work here," agreed Mogget, sniffing the air again. "I wonder if he . . . or she . . . has been searching for you specifically. Or is it just bad luck for a wayward traveler?"

"It could be the one who caught me before, couldn't it?" asked Sam. "I mean, he knew where I was with the cricket team. . . ."

"Perhaps," replied Mogget, still staring up at the night sky. "It is unlikely that there would be Gore Crows here, or that any lesser necromancer would dare to move against you, unless there is a guiding force behind them. Certainly these Crows are more daring than they have any right to be. Have you caught me a fish?"

"No," replied Sam, surprised by the sudden change of subject.

"How inconsiderate of you," said Mogget, sniffing. "I suppose I'll have to catch one myself."

"No!" exclaimed Sam, levering himself up. "You'll break the diamond! I haven't got the strength to cast it again. Ow! Charter curse these mosquitoes!"

"I won't break it," said Mogget, walking over to the Westmark and carefully poking out his tongue. The mark flashed white, dazzling Sam. When his vision cleared, Mogget was standing upright on the other side, intent on the water, one paw raised, like a fishing bear.

"Show-off," muttered Sam. He wondered how the cat had done it. The diamond was unbroken, the lines of magical fire streaming without pause between the brightness of the cardinal marks.

If only the diamond kept the mosquitoes out as well, he thought, slapping several more into bloody oblivion against his neck. Clearly their bites did not come into the spell's definition of physical harm. Suddenly he smiled, remembering something he'd packed.

He was getting this object out of the saddlebag when the Westmark flashed again, reacting to Mogget's return. The cat had two small trout in his mouth, their scales reflecting rainbows in the mix of firelight and Charter glow.

"You can have this one to cook," said Mogget, dropping the smaller one next to the fire. "What is that?"

"It's a present for my mother," replied Sam proudly, setting down a bejeweled clockwork frog that had the interesting anatomical addition of wings made of feathery bronze. "A flying frog."

Mogget watched with interest as Sam lightly touched the frog's back and it began to glow with Charter Magic as the sending inside the mechanical body waked from sleep. It opened one turquoise eye, then the other, lids of paper-thin gold sliding back. Then it flapped its wings, brazen feathers clashing.

"Very pretty," said Mogget. "Does it *do* anything?"

The flying frog answered the question itself, suddenly leaping into the air, a long and vibrantly red tongue flashing out to grab several startled mosquitoes. Wings beating furiously, it spiraled after several more, ate them, and then dived back down to land contentedly near Sam's feet.

"It catches bugs," stated Sam with considerable satisfaction. "I thought it would be handy for Mother, since she spends so much time in swamps hunting the Dead."

"You made it," said Mogget, watching the flying frog leap again to twirl and twist after its quarry. "Completely your invention?"

"Yes," replied Sam shortly, expecting some criticism of his handiwork. But Mogget was silent, just watching the frog's aerobatics, his green eyes following its every move. Then the cat shifted his gaze to Sam, making him nervous. He tried to meet that green stare, but he had to look away—and he suddenly realized that there were Dead nearby. Lots of Dead, drawing closer with every second.

Mogget obviously felt them, too, for he leapt up and hissed, the hair on his back rising to a ridge. Sprout smelt them, and shivered. The Flying Frog flew to the saddlebags and climbed in.

Sam looked out into the darkness, shielding his eyes from the firelight. The moon was occluded by cloud, but starlight reflected from the water. He could feel the Dead, out there in the forest, but the darkness lay too heavy under the branches of the old tangled trees. He couldn't see anything.

But he could hear twigs cracking, and branches snapping back, and even the occasional heavy footfall, all against the constant burble of the stream. Whatever was coming, some of them at least had physical forms. There could be Shadow Hands out there as well. Or Ghlims or Mordaut or any of the many kinds of Lesser

Dead. He could feel nothing more powerful, at least for now.

Whatever they were, there were at least a dozen of them, on both sides of the stream. Forgetting his tiredness and his limp, Sam moved around the diamond, checking the marks. The running water was neither deep nor fast enough to do more than discourage the Dead. The diamond would be their true protection.

"You may have to renew the marks before dawn," said Mogget, watching Sam's inspection. "It hasn't been cast very well. You should get some sleep before you try again."

"How can I sleep?" whispered Sam, instinctively keeping his voice down, as if it mattered whether the Dead could hear him. They already knew where he was. He could even smell them now—the disgusting odor of decaying flesh and gravemold.

"They're only Hands," said Mogget, looking out. "They probably won't attack as long as the diamond lasts."

"How do you know that?" asked Sam, wiping the sweat from his forehead, along with several crushed mosquitoes. He thought he could see the Dead now—tall shapes between the darker trunks of the trees. Horrible, broken corpses forced back into Life to do a necromancer's bidding. Their intelligence and humanity ripped from them, leaving only inhuman strength and an insatiable desire for the life they could no longer have.

His life.

"You could walk out there and send them all back to Death," suggested Mogget. He was starting to eat the second fish, beginning with the tail. Sam hadn't seen him eat the first one.

"Your mother would," Mogget added slyly, when Sam didn't speak.

"I'm not my mother," replied Sam, dry-mouthed. He made no move to pick up the bells, though he could feel them there on the sand, calling out to him. They wanted to be used against the Dead. But they could be dangerous to the wielder, most of them, or tricksome at least. He would have to use Kibeth to make the Dead walk back into Death, and Kibeth could easily send him walking instead.

"Does the walker choose the path, or the path the walker?" Mogget asked suddenly, his eyes once again intent on Sam's sweating face.

"What?" asked the Prince, distracted. He'd heard his mother say that before, but it didn't mean anything to him then or now. "What does that mean?"

"It means that you've never finished *The Book of the Dead*," said Mogget in a strange tone.

"Well, no, not yet," said Sam wretchedly. "I'm going to, it's just that I—"

"It also means that we really are in trouble," interrupted Mogget, switching his gaze to the outer darkness. "I thought you would at least know enough to protect yourself by now!"

"What do you see?" asked Sam. He could hear movement upstream, the sudden splintering of trees and the crash of rocks into the water.

"Shadow Hands have come," replied Mogget bleakly. "Two of them, well back in the trees. They are directing the Hands to dam the stream. I expect they will attack when the water no longer flows."

"I wish . . . I wish I were a proper Abhorsen," whispered Sam.

"Well you should be, at your age!" said Mogget. "But I suppose we will have to make do with whatever you do know. By the way, where is your own sword? An unspelled blade will not cut the stuff of Shadow Hands."

"I left it in Belisaere," Sam said, after a moment. "I didn't think . . . I didn't understand what I was doing. I thought Nick was probably in trouble, but not this much."

"That's the problem with growing up as a Prince," growled Mogget. "You always think that everything will get worked out for you. Or you turn out like your sister and think nothing gets done unless you do it. It's a wonder any of you are ever any use at all."

"What can I do now?" asked Sam humbly.

"We will have a little time before the water slows," replied Mogget. "You should try to place some magic in your blade. If you can make that Frog, I'm sure that will not be beyond you."

"Yes," said Sam dully. "I do know how to do that."

Concentrating on the blade, he delved once more into the Charter, reaching for marks of sharpness and unraveling, magic that would wreak havoc upon Dead flesh or spirit-stuff.

With an effort, he forced the marks into the blade, watching them slowly move like oil upon the metal, soaking into the steel.

"You are skilled," remarked the cat. "Surprisingly so. Almost you remind me of—"

Whatever he was about to say was lost as a terrible scream split the night, accompanied by frenzied splashing.

"What was that?" exclaimed Sam, going to the Northmark, his newly spelled sword held at guard.

"A Hand," replied Mogget, chuckling. "It fell in. Whoever controls these Dead is far away, my Prince. Even the Shadow Hands are weak and stupid."

"So we may have a chance," whispered Sam. The stream seemed little affected by the dam building upstream, and the diamond still shone brightly. Perhaps nothing would happen before the dawn.

"We have a good chance," said Mogget. "For tonight. But there will be another night tomorrow, and perhaps another after that, before we can reach the Ratterlin. What of them?"

Sam was still trying to think of an answer when the first of the Dead Hands came screaming across the water—and ran full tilt into the diamond, silver sparks exploding everywhere into the night.

Chapter Thirty-Three

FLIGHT TO THE RIVER

DAWN CAME SLOWLY to the outer fringes of the Sindlewood, light trickling over the treetops long before it penetrated the darker depths. When it did finally reach the lower regions, it was no longer a burning heat, but a greenish, diluted light that simply pushed the shadows back rather than extinguished them.

The sunlight reached Sameth's magic-girded islet much later than he would have liked. The fire had long since burnt itself out, and as Mogget had predicted, Sam had had to renew the diamond of protection long before the first hint of dawn, drawing on reserves of energy he hadn't known he possessed.

With the light came the full evidence of the night's work. The streambed was almost dry, the Dead-made dam upstream still holding. Six Charter-blasted corpses lay piled all around the islet: husks vacated by the Dead when the protective magic of the diamond burnt through too many nerves and sinews, rendering the bodies useless.

Sam looked at them warily, through red-rimmed puffy eyes, watching the sunlight crawl across the stinking remnants. He'd felt the Dead spirits shucking the bodies as snakes shed their skins, but in the confusion of their suicidal attacks, he wasn't sure whether all of them had gone. One might be lurking still, husbanding its strength, enduring the sun, hoping Sam would be overconfident and step out of the diamond.

He could still feel Dead nearby, but that was probably the Shadow Hands, taking up daytime refuges in rabbit holes or otter holts, slipping down into the dark earth under the rocks, where they belonged.

At last full sunshine lit the whole streambed, and Sam's sense of the Dead faded, save for the ever-present Gore Crow, circling high overhead. He sighed with relief, and stretched, trying to relieve the cramp in his sword-arm and the pain in his wounded leg. He was exhausted, but he was alive. For another day, at least.

"We'd better start moving," said Mogget, who had slept most of the night, ignoring the slam and sizzle of the Dead Hands' attempts to break through the diamond. He looked ready to slip back into that sleep at a moment's notice.

"If the Gore Crow's stupid enough to get close, kill it," he added, yawning. "That will give us a chance to escape."

"What will I kill it with?" asked Sam wearily. Even if the Gore Crow came closer, he was too tired to cast a Charter-spell, and he didn't have a bow.

There was no answer from Mogget. He was already asleep again, curled up in the saddlebag, ready to be put on Sprout. Sam sighed and forced himself to get on with the job of saddling up. But his mind, tired as it was, still grappled with the problem of the Gore Crow. As Mogget said, as long as it tracked them, other Dead would be able to find them easily. Perhaps it would be one of the Greater Dead next, or a Mordicant, or even just larger numbers of Lesser Dead. Sam would have to spend at least the next two nights in the forest, and he would be weaker and more tired with every passing hour. He might not even be able to cast a diamond of protection. . . .

But, he thought, looking down at the dry streambed and the hundreds of beautifully round pebbles there, I do have the strength to put a mark of accuracy on a stone, and make a sling from my spare shirt. He even knew how to use one. Jall Oren had been keen on tutoring the royal children in all manner of weapons.

For the first time in days, a smile crept upon Sam's face, banishing the weariness. He looked up. Sure enough, the Gore Crow was circling lower than yesterday, overconfident from Sam's lack of a bow and obvious inability to do anything. It would be a long shot, but a Charter-spelled stone should go the distance.

Still grinning, Sam knelt down, surreptitiously picked up several likely stones, and ripped the sleeves from his spare shirt. He'd let the Gore Crow follow them for a while, he decided, and grow even more confident. Then it would pay the price for spying on a scion of the Old Kingdom.

Sam led Sprout westwards along the streambed, till it joined another, larger watercourse, and he had a choice of directions. Upstream to the northeast or downstream to the southwest.

At the junction, he hesitated, using Sprout's bulk to shield himself from view as he cast a mark upon the stone and settled it into the makeshift sling. The Gore Crow, seeing his hesitation, circled lower to make sure it could see which way he chose. It was obviously put off by the running water of the larger stream and perhaps hoped he'd turn back.

Sam waited till its spiral turned it closest to him. Then he stepped away from Sprout, the sling whirring above his head. At just the right moment, he yelled "Hah!" and let the stone fly.

The Gore Crow had only an instant to react, and being stupid, sunstruck, and Dead, it simply flew straight into the rocketing stone, meeting it in an explosion of feathers, dry bones, and putrid gobbets of meat.

With great satisfaction and then outright joy, Sam watched the disgusting creature fall. The crushed ball of feathers landed with a splash in the stream, and the fragment of Dead spirit inside it was instantly banished back to whence it came. Better still, it would drag all the other fragments of that same spirit back into Death. So any Gore Crows that shared it would be dropping inexplicably, wherever they might be.

With the fall of the Gore Crow, he could sense no Dead nearby. The Shadow Hands would be long hidden now, as would any Dead Hands that remained. The intelligence that commanded them from afar might guess that Sam would take the southwest stream towards the Ratterlin, but whoever or whatever it was would not know for sure, and might split its forces, increasing his chance of evasion and escape.

"We have a chance, faithful horse," announced Sam cheerfully, leading Sprout towards an animal track that ran parallel to the stream. "We have a definite chance."

But hope seemed to slip from Sam's grasp as the day progressed and the going became slower and more difficult, so he couldn't ride Sprout. The stream had grown considerably deeper and faster, but also much narrower, barely three or four strides across, so it was impossible to stand in it or make a camp that would be protected on both sides.

The track had grown narrower, too, and overgrown. Sam had to hack through low branches, high shrubs, and barbed coils of blackberries. His hands became heavily scratched, attracting hordes of flies to the lines of drying blood. That would attract the Dead later, too. They could smell blood a long way away, though fresh would bring them faster.

By late afternoon, Sam had begun to despair. He was really exhausted now. There would be no question of casting a diamond of protection this coming night. He would pass out just trying to visualize the marks—and the Dead would find his defenseless body stretched out upon the ground.

His weariness was closing down his senses, too, narrowing

his sight to a blinkered view and his hearing to little more than a muffled awareness of Sprout's hooves, dull upon the soft, forgiving forest floor.

In that state, it took him several seconds to realize that Sprout's hooves were suddenly making a sharper sound, and the cool green light of the forest had given way to something much sharper and more bright. He looked up, blinking, and saw that they had come to a wide clearing. The clearing was easily a hundred paces wide, cutting through the forest from the southeast to the northwest, continuing in both directions as far as he could see. Saplings had grown up on its borders, but the middle was stark and bare—and there was a paved road in the middle of it.

Sam stared at the road and then at the sun, which he'd barely been able to see under the forest's shady roof.

"About two, maybe three hours to dusk," he mumbled to Sprout, as he fiddled with the stirrup and mounted up. "You've had a good meal of grain today, haven't you, Sprout? Not to mention an easy walk, without carrying me. Now you can pay me back, because we are going to ride."

He chuckled then, thinking of an expression from the moving pictures he'd often seen in the Somersby Orpheum in Ancelstierre.

"We're going to ride, Sprout!" he repeated. "Ride like the wind!"

An hour and a half later, Sprout was no longer running like the wind, but back at a walk, legs trembling, sweat drenching her flanks, and froth forming at her mouth. Sam wasn't in much better shape, walking again himself, to give Sprout a chance to recover. He wasn't sure now what hurt more—his leg or his backside.

Even so, they had covered six or seven leagues, thanks to the road. It was no royal road now, but it had been built and drained properly long ago, and so was more than serviceable.

They were currently climbing up a slight ridge, the road attacking it directly rather than winding around. Sam lifted his head as they approached the top, hoping for a glimpse of the Ratterlin before the day came to an end. By his reckoning, the ride—and the road—had saved more than a day of foot travel through the forest, so they should be close to the river. They *must* be close to the river. . . .

He stood on his toes for a moment but still couldn't see. It was an annoying ridge, this one, full of false heights and annoying dips along the way. But surely in a moment he would see the Ratterlin!

Clip! Clop! Sprout's hooves sounded loud on the road, as loud as Sam's own beating heart, but much, much slower. His heart was racing, racing with a combination of hope and fear.

There was the real crest ahead. Sam pushed forward, trying to see, but the sun was setting directly in front of him, a huge red disc sinking into the west, blinding him.

He screwed his eyes almost shut and shielded them with a hand, looking again—and there, under the sun, was a thick ribbon of blue, reflecting orange-red streaks back into the sky.

"The Ratterlin! Ow!" exclaimed Sam, stubbing his toe as he stumbled over the rise. But he ignored the momentary pain. There was the swift river whose waters would bar any Dead. The river that would save him!

Except, he thought, with sudden dread, it was still half a league away, and the night had almost come. And with it, he realized, so had the Dead. There were Dead creatures not too far away—perhaps even ahead of him. This road—and the point where it joined the Ratterlin towpath—would be an obvious point to be watched.

Worse than that, he thought, looking down at the river, he

hadn't actually planned what he'd do once he reached it. What if there was no boat or raft to be found?

"Hurry," said Mogget from the saddlebag behind him, making Sam jump in surprise and start leading Sprout on again. "We must head for the mill and take shelter there."

"I can't see a mill," said Sam doubtfully, shielding his eyes once more. He couldn't see any detail near the river at all. His eyes were blurry from lack of sleep, and he felt as stupid as a Dead Hand.

"Of course there's a mill," snapped Mogget, leaping down from the saddlebag onto Sam's shoulder, making him start again. "The wheel does not turn—so we can hope it is abandoned."

"Why?" asked Sam blearily. "Wouldn't it be better if there's people? We can get food, drink—"

"Would you bring the Dead upon a miller and his family?" interrupted Mogget. "It will not be long before they find us—if they haven't already."

Sam didn't reply, merely encouraging Sprout with a gentle slap to the neck. Perhaps he wouldn't weary her too much if he hung on the stirrup, he thought. He hoped she'd make the distance, because he didn't think he could walk that far unaided.

As usual, Mogget was right. Sam could feel the Dead closer now and, looking up, saw two black specks spiraling down out of the night that swept in from the east. Clearly the particular necromancer who drove them had no shortage of Gore Crows. And where the Crows flew, there would soon be others, brought out of Death to seek their prey.

Mogget saw the Gore Crows, too, and whispered in Sam's ear.

"There can be little doubt, now. This is the work of a necromancer who bears you particular ill will, Prince Sameth. His servants will seek you wherever you flee, and he will use all the creatures of Death to drive you to your doom."

Sam swallowed. The dire pronouncement echoed in his ears, imbued with the faint hint of the Free Magic power that was contained within the cat form on his shoulder. He slapped Sprout on the rump to get her going; then he said the first thing that came into his head.

"Mogget. Shut up."

Sprout fell a hundred yards from the mill, worn out by her earlier gallop and the dead weight of Sam hanging on a stirrup. He let go just in time to avoid being trapped under her. Mogget leapt off his shoulder to get even farther out of the way.

"Foundered," said Mogget briskly, without looking at her, his green eyes peering sharply back into the night. "They're getting closer."

"I know!" said Sam, urgently pulling the saddlebags free and slinging them over his shoulder. He bent down to stroke Sprout's head, but she didn't respond. Her eyes showed white and rolled almost completely back. He took the reins and tried to pull her up, but she made no move to help, and he was too weak to force her.

"Hurry!" urged Mogget, pacing around him. "You know what to do."

Sam nodded and glanced back at the Dead. There were a score or more of them, dim, lumbering shapes in the gathering darkness. Their masters had clearly driven them hard from some distant cemetery or boneyard, walking them even under the sun. Consequently, they were slow, but implacable. If he lingered even for a minute longer, they would fall upon him like rats on a worn-out dog.

He drew his dagger and felt Sprout's neck. The pulse of her main artery was weak and erratic under his fingers. He rested the dagger there but didn't push it in.

"I can't," he whispered. "She might recover."

"The Dead will drink her blood and feast upon her flesh!" exclaimed Mogget. "You owe her better than that. Strike!"

"I can't take a life. Even that of a horse, in mercy," said Sam, standing up unsteadily. "I realized that after . . . after the constables. We'll wait together."

Mogget hissed, then jumped across Sprout's neck, one paw tracing a line of white fire across the horse's neck. For an instant, nothing happened. Then blood burst out in a terrible fountain, splashing Sam's boots and throwing hot drops across his face. Sprout gave a single, convulsive shudder—and died.

Sam felt her die and turned his head away, unable to look at the dark pool that stained the ground beneath her.

Something nudged at his shins. Mogget, urging him into motion. Blindly, he turned away and began to trudge towards the mill. Sprout was dead, and he knew Mogget had done the only possible thing. But it just didn't seem right.

"Quickly!" urged the cat again, dancing around his feet, a white blur in the darkness. Sam could hear the Dead behind him now, hear the clicking of their bones, the screech of dry knees bent at angles impossible in Life. Fear fought the tiredness in him, made him move, but the mill seemed so far away.

He stumbled and almost fell, but somehow recovered. The pain in his leg jabbed at his head again, clearing it a little. His horse might be dead, but there was no reason why he should join her in Death. Only his weariness had made that seem attractive—for a moment.

There was the mill ahead, built out into the mighty Ratterlin, with the mill race, sluice gate, and wheel cut into the shore. He need only reach the race and open the sluice gate, and the mill would be defended by swift water, diverted from the river.

He risked a look over his shoulder and stumbled again, surprised by the dark and the nearness and number of the Dead. There were far more than a score of them now, moving in lines from all directions, the closest little more than forty yards away. Their corpse-white faces looked like flocks of bobbing moths, stark in the starlight.

Many of the Dead wore the remnants of blue scarves and blue hats. Sam stared at them. They were dead Southerlings! Probably some of the ones his father had tried to find.

"Run, you idiot!" shouted Mogget, streaking ahead himself, as the Dead behind seemed to finally realize that their quarry might escape them. Dead muscles squealed, suddenly forced into speed, and Dead throats cried strange, desiccated battle cries.

Sam didn't look again. He could hear their heavy footfalls, the squelch of rotten meat pushed beyond even its magically supported limits. He pushed himself, breaking into a run, his breath burning in his throat and lungs, muscles sending streaks of pain through the length of his body.

He made the mill race—a deep, narrow channel—barely ahead of the Dead. Four steps and he was over the planks of the simple bridge, kicking it down into the race. But the channel was dry, so the first Dead Hands simply hurled themselves down and began to claw up the other side. Behind them came more Hands, line after line of them, a tide of Dead that could not be turned back.

Desperately, Sam rushed to the sluice gate and the wheel that would lift it, to send the roaring waters of the Ratterlin into the race and across the climbing Dead.

But the wheel was rusted tight, the sluice gate stuck in place. Sam put all his weight on the iron wheel, but it simply broke, leaving him clutching a piece of the rusted rim.

Then the first Dead Hand pulled itself out of the mill race and turned towards him. It was dark, true dark now, but Sam could just make it out. It had been human once, but the magic that had brought it back to Life had twisted the body as if following a mad artist's whim. Its arms trailed below its knees, its head no longer sat upon a neck but sank into its shoulders, and the mouth had split upwards, usurping the place that had once held a nose. There were more behind it, other twisted shapes, using the blades of the water-wheel like steps to climb out of the mill race.

"Through here!" commanded Mogget, his tail flicking as he leapt through a doorway into the mill itself. Sam tried to follow, but the Dead Hand barred his way, skeletal mouth grinning with too many teeth, its long hands outstretched with grasping, bare-boned fingers.

Sam drew his sword and hacked at it, all in one swift motion. The Charter marks on the blade blazed, silver sparks spewing into the night as spelled metal ate into Dead flesh.

The Hand reeled back, broken but not beaten, one arm hanging from a single strip of sinew. Sam punched it farther away with the pommel of his sword, back into two more that sought to close in. Then he swung around to strike at one leaping up behind him, and backed into the mill.

"The door!" spat Mogget from somewhere at his feet, and Sam reached out and felt wood. Desperately he gripped the door's edge and slammed it in the grinning faces of the Dead. Mogget jumped up, fur brushing Sam's hand, and a heavy thump told him the cat had just pushed down the bar. The door, at least for the moment, was closed.

He couldn't see a thing. It was completely, suffocatingly dark. He couldn't even see the bright white coat of Mogget.

"Mogget!" he yelped, panic in his voice. The single word was suddenly drowned in a violent crash as the Dead Hands threw themselves against the door. They were too stupid to find some timber to use as a ram.

"Here," said the cat, calm as ever. "Reach down."

Sam reached, more urgently than he would have liked to admit, fingers grasping Mogget by his Charter-spelled collar. For an awful moment, he thought he'd inadvertently pulled the collar off. Then the cat moved, the miniature Ranna tinkled, and he knew the collar had stayed on. Ranna's sound sent a wave of drowsiness against him, but that was nothing compared to the relief of feeling the collar still tight against that feline neck. With the Dead so close and the door already splintering under their attack, it would take more than a miniature Ranna to send him into sleep.

"This way," said Mogget, a disembodied voice in the darkness. Sam felt him move again and quickly hurried after, every sense alert to the door behind.

Then Mogget suddenly turned, but Sam kept going for a step, his sword hitting something solid and rebounding, almost hitting him in the face. Sam sheathed his sword, nearly stabbing himself, and reached out to touch whatever it was.

His hand traced another door—a door that must lead to the river itself. He could hear the water rushing by, just audible under the crash of the Dead Hands hurling themselves against the other door. The noise reverberated up into the higher reaches of the mill. Despite the noise, they hadn't got in, and Sam offered up silent thanks to the miller who had built so well.

His trembling hands found the bar and lifted it, then the ring that turned the lock. He twisted it, met resistance, then twisted again, fear shooting through him. Surely this door couldn't be locked from the outside?

Behind him, he heard screaming hinges finally give way, and the other door exploded inwards. Dead Hands came bounding through, croaking cries that were inhuman echoes of the triumphant yells of the Living.

Sam turned the ring the other way, and the door suddenly swung open. He went with it, sprawling outside and down some steps that led to a narrow landing stage. He landed there with a thud that sent a blinding pain through his wounded leg, but he didn't care. At last he had reached the Ratterlin!

He could see again, at least somewhat, by the stars above and their reflections in the water. There was the river, rushing past, little more than an arm's length away. There was a tin bathtub, too, a big one, of the kind used to bathe several children at once, big enough for a grown person to lounge in. Sam saw it and, in the same instant, picked it up and pushed it into the river, holding it against the current with one hand while he dropped his sword and the saddlebags in.

"I take it back," said Mogget, jumping in. "You're not as stupid as you look."

Sam tried to answer, but his face and mouth seemed unable to move. He climbed into the bathtub, clutching at the last step of the landing stage. The tub sank alarmingly, but even when he was fully in, it still had several inches of freeboard.

He pushed off as the Dead poured out of the door. The first one recoiled at the proximity of so much running water. But the others pushed behind it, and the Hand fell—straight at Sam's makeshift boat.

The Dead creature screamed as it bounced on the steps, sounding almost alive for a brief second. Its hands scrabbled as it fell, trying to hold on to something, but it succeeded only in changing the direction of its fall. A second later, it entered the Ratterlin, and its scream was lost in a fountain of silver sparks and golden fire.

It had missed the boat by only a few feet. The wave from its impact almost swamped the bathtub. Sam watched the creature's last moments, as did the Dead halted in the doorway above, and felt enormous relief well up inside him.

"Amazing," said Mogget. "We actually got away. What are you doing?"

Sam stopped squirming and silently held out the cake of dried, sun-shriveled soap he'd just sat on. Then he put his head back and draped his hands over the sides to rest in the sweet river that had rescued them.

"In fact," said Mogget, "I think I can even say 'Well done.'"

Sam didn't answer, because he'd just passed out.

PART THREE

THE OLD KINGDOM

Eighteenth Year of the Restoration of
King Touchstone I

Chapter Thirty-Four

FINDER

THE BOAT WAS tied up at a subterranean dock that Lirael knew about but had visited only once, years before. It was built all along one end of a vast cavern, with sunlight pouring in at the other end where it opened out onto the world, the Ratterlin welling up with frothing vigor below the dock. A line of icicles across the cavern-mouth testified to the presence of the glacier above, as did the occasional fall of ice and snow.

There were several boats tied up, but Lirael instinctively knew that the slim, curving vessel with the single mast was hers. She had a carved fantail at her stern and an arching figurehead at the bow—a woman with wide-awake eyes. Those eyes seemed to be looking straight at Lirael, as if the boat knew who her next passenger would be. For a moment Lirael thought the figurehead might even have winked at her.

Sanar pointed and said, "That is *Finder*. She will take you safely down to Qyrre. It is a journey she has made a thousand times or more, there and back, with or against the current. She knows the river well."

"I don't know how to sail," said Lirael nervously, noting the Charter marks that moved quietly over the hull, mast, and rigging of the boat. She felt very small and stupid. The sight of the outside world beyond the cavern-mouth combined with her weariness and made her want to hide somewhere and go to sleep. "What will I have to do?"

"There is little you need attend to," replied Sanar. "*Finder* will do most of it herself. But you will have to raise and lower the sail, and steer a little. I will show you how."

"Thank you," said Lirael. She followed Sanar into the boat, grabbing at the gunwale as *Finder* rocked beneath her. Ryelle passed Lirael's pack, bow, and sword across, and Sanar showed her where to stow the pack in the oilskin-lined box at the vessel's forepeak. The sword and bow went into special waterproof cases on either side of the mast, to be more accessible.

Then Sanar showed Lirael how to raise and lower *Finder*'s single triangular mainsail, and how the boom would move. *Finder* would trim the sail herself, Sanar explained, and would guide Lirael's hand on the tiller. Lirael could even let the boat steer herself in an emergency, but the vessel preferred to feel a human touch.

"We hope that there will be no danger on the way," said Ryelle, when they had finished showing Lirael over the boat. "Normally the river-road is quite safe to Qyrre. But we cannot now be sure of anything. We do not know the nature of whatever lies in the pit you Saw, or its powers. Just in case, it would be best to anchor in the river at night, rather than going ashore— or to tie up at an island. There are many of those downstream. At Qyrre and onwards, you should seek whatever help you can get from the Royal Constables. Here is a letter from us as the Voice of the Watch, for that purpose. If we are lucky, there will also be guards present, and the Abhorsen may have returned from Ancelstierre. Whatever you do, you must make sure that you travel with a large and well-armed party from Qyrre to Edge. From there, I fear, we cannot advise you. The future is clouded, and we can See you only on the Red Lake, with nothing before or beyond that."

"All summed up, that means 'Be very careful,'" said Sanar.

She smiled, but there was the hint of a frown in her forehead and at the corners of her eyes. "Remember that this is only one possible future we See."

"I will be careful," promised Lirael. Now that she was actually in the boat and about to depart, she felt very nervous. For the first time, she would be going out into a world that was not bounded by stone or ice, and she would have to see and speak to many strangers. More than that, she was going into danger, against a foe she knew nothing about and was ill prepared to face. Even her mission was vague. To find a young man, somewhere on a lake, sometime this summer. What if she did find this Nicholas and somehow survived all the looming dangers? Would the Clayr let her back into the Glacier? What if she was never allowed to return?

But at the same time Lirael also felt a blooming sense of excitement, even of escape, from a life that she couldn't admit was stifling her. There was *Finder*, and the sunshine beyond, and the Ratterlin streaming away to lands she knew only from the pages of books. She had the dog statuette, and the hope her canine companion would return. And she was going on official business, doing something important. Almost like a real Daughter of the Clayr.

"You may need this, too," said Ryelle, handing over a leather purse, bulging with coins. "The Bursar would have you get receipts, but I think you will have enough to worry about without that."

"Now, let us see you raise the sail yourself, and we will bid you farewell," continued Sanar. Her blue eyes seemed to see into Lirael, perceiving the fears that she had not voiced. "The Sight does not tell me so, but I am sure we will meet again. And you must remember that, Sighted or not, you *are* a Daughter of the Clayr. Remember! May fortune favor you, Lirael."

Lirael nodded, unable to speak, and hauled on the halyard to raise the sail. It hung slackly, the cavern dock being too sheltered for any wind.

Ryelle and Sanar bowed to her, then cast off the ropes that held *Finder* fast. The Ratterlin's swift current gripped the boat, and the tiller moved under Lirael's hand, nudging her to direct the eager vessel out towards the sunlit world of the open river.

Lirael looked back once as they passed from the shade of the cavern to the sun, with the icicles tinkling far above her head. Sanar and Ryelle were still standing on the dock. They waved as the wind came to fill *Finder*'s sail and ruffle Lirael's hair.

I have left, thought Lirael. There could be no turning back now, not against the current. The current of the river held the boat, and the current of her destiny held her. Both were taking her to places that she did not know.

The river was already wide where the underground source came to join it, fed by the lakes of snow-melt higher up, and the hundred small streams that wound their way like capillaries through and around the Clayr's Glacier. But here, only the central channel—perhaps fifty yards across—was deep enough to be navigable. To either side of the channel, the Ratterlin shallowed, content to sheet thinly across millions of clean-washed pebbles.

Lirael breathed in the warm, river-scented air and smiled at the heat of the sun on her skin. As promised, *Finder* was moving herself into the swiftest race of the river, while the mainsheet imperceptibly slackened till they were running before the wind from the north. Lirael's nervousness about sailing lessened as she realized that *Finder* really did look after herself. It was even fun, speeding along with the breeze behind them, the bow sending up a fine spray as it sliced through the small waves caused by wind and current. All Lirael needed to make the moment perfect was the presence of her best friend, the Disreputable Dog.

She reached into her waistcoat pocket for the soapstone statuette. It would be a comfort just to hold it, even if it would not be practicable to try the summoning spell until she got to Qyrre and could get the silver wire and other materials.

But instead of cool, smooth stone, she felt warm dog skin—and what she pulled out was a very recognizable pointy ear, followed by an arc of round skull and then another ear. That was immediately followed by the Disreputable Dog's entire head, which was much too big by itself to fit in the pocket—let alone the rest of her.

"Ouch! Tight fit!" growled the Dog, pushing out a foreleg and wiggling madly. Another foreleg impossibly followed, and then the whole dog leapt out, shook hair all over Lirael's leggings, and turned to give her an enthusiastic lick.

"So we're off at last!" she barked happily, mouth open to catch the breeze, tongue lolling. "About time, too. Where are we going?"

Lirael didn't answer at first. She just hugged the Dog very tightly and took several quick, jarring breaths to stop herself crying. The Dog waited patiently, not even licking Lirael's ear, which was a handy target. When Lirael's breathing seemed to get back to normal, the Dog repeated her question.

"More like *why* are we going," said Lirael, checking her waistcoat pocket to make sure the Dog's exit hadn't taken the Dark Mirror with it. Strangely enough, the pocket wasn't even stretched.

"Does it matter?" asked the Dog. "New smells, new sounds, new places to piss on . . . begging your pardon, Captain."

"Dog! Stop being so excited," ordered Lirael. The Dog partly obeyed, sitting down at her feet, but her tail kept wagging, and every few seconds she snapped at the air.

"We're not just going on one of our normal expeditions, like in the Glacier," Lirael explained. "I have to find a man—"

"Good!" interrupted the Dog, leaping up to lick her exuberantly. "Time you were bred."

"Dog!" Lirael, protested, forcing her back down. "It's not about that! This man is from Ancelstierre and he's trying to . . . dig up, I think . . . some ancient thing. Near the Red Lake. A Free Magic thing, so powerful it made me sick even when Ryelle and Sanar only showed it to me through a vision. And there was a necromancer who saw me, and lightning kept hitting the hole in the ground—"

"I don't like the sound of that," said the Dog, suddenly serious. Her tail stopped waving, and she looked straight at Lirael, no longer snuffling the air. "You'd better tell me more. Start at the beginning, from when the Clayr came to find you down below."

Lirael nodded and went over everything that the twins had said, and described the vision that they'd shared with her.

By the time she'd finished, the Ratterlin had widened into the mighty river that most of the Kingdom knew. It was over half a mile wide, and very deep. Here in the middle, the water was dark and clear and blue, and many fish could be seen, silver in the depths.

The Dog lay with her head upon her forelegs and thought deeply. Lirael watched her, looking at the brown eyes that seemed to focus on far distant things.

"I don't like it," the Dog said finally. "You're being sent into danger, and no one really knows what's going on. The Clayr unable to See clearly, the King and the Abhorsen not even in the

Kingdom. This hole in the ground that eats up lightning reminds me of something very bad indeed . . . and then there's this necromancer, as well."

"Well, I suppose we could go somewhere else," Lirael said doubtfully, upset by the strength of the Dog's reaction.

The Dog looked at her in surprise. "No, we can't! You have a duty. I don't like it, but we've got it. I never said anything about giving up."

"No," agreed Lirael. She was about to say that she hadn't suggested it, either. She was just stating a possibility. But it would clearly be better to let the point lie.

The Dog was silent for a while. Then she said, "Those things that were left for you in the room. Do you know how to use them?"

"They might not even be meant for me," Lirael said. "I just happened to find them. I don't want them, anyway."

"Choosers will be beggars if the begging's not their choosing," said the Dog.

"What does that mean?"

"I have no idea," said the Dog. "Now, do you know how to use the things that were left for you?"

"Well, I have read *The Book of Remembrance and Forgetting*," Lirael replied half-heartedly. "So I guess I know the theory—"

"You should practice," declared the Dog. "You may need actual expertise later on."

"But I'll have to go into Death," Lirael protested. "I've never done that before. I'm not even sure I should. I'm a Clayr. I should be Seeing the future, not the past."

"You should use the gifts you have been given," said the Dog. "Imagine how you'd feel if you gave me a bone and I didn't eat it."

"Surprised," replied Lirael. "But you do bury bones some-times. In the ice."

"I always eat them eventually," said the Dog. "At the right time."

"How do you know this is the right time for me?" asked Lirael suspiciously. "I mean, how do you even know what my gifts are for? I haven't told you, have I?"

"I read a lot. It comes from living in a library," said the Dog, answering the second question first. "And there's lots of islands ahead. An island would be a perfect place to stop. You can use the Dark Mirror on one of them. If anything follows you back from Death, we can get on the boat and just sail away."

"You mean if something Dead attacks me," said Lirael. That was the real danger. She actually did want to look into the past. But she didn't want to go into Death to do it. *The Book of Remembrance and Forgetting* told her how, and assured her she could come back. But what if it was wrong?

And the panpipes were all very well, in their way, as a weapon and protection against the Dead. Seven pipes, named after the seven bells used by a necromancer. Only they weren't as powerful as the bells, and one part of the book said that "though generally the instrument of a Remembrancer, the pipes are not infrequently used by Abhorsens-in-Waiting, till they succeed to their bells." Which didn't make the pipes sound all that fantastic.

But even if the pipes were not as strong as the bells, the book seemed to think they were powerful enough to assure her safety. Provided she could use them properly, of course, having only book-learning to go on. Still, there was something she particularly wanted to see. . . . "We do need to get to Edge as soon as possible," she said with deliberation. "But I suppose we could take a few hours off. Only I need to nap for a while first. When I wake up, we'll stop at an island, if there's one near. Then . . . then I will go into Death, and look into the past."

"Good," said the Dog. "I could do with a walk."

Chapter Thirty-Five

REMEMBRANCER

LIRAEL STOOD WITH the Dog in the center of a small island, surrounded by stunted trees and bushes that couldn't grow higher in the rocky ground. *Finder's* mast towered behind them, no more than thirty paces away, showing where safety lay if they had to flee from something coming out of Death.

In preparation for entering that cold realm, Lirael buckled on the sword the Clayr had given her. The weight felt strange on her hip. The broad leather belt was tight against her lower stomach, and the sword, while longer and heavier than her practice sword, somehow felt familiar, though she had never seen it before. She would have remembered its distinctive silver-wired hilt and pommel with a single green stone set in bronze.

Lirael held the panpipes in her left hand, watching the Charter marks move across the silver tubes, weaving in with the Free Magic that lurked there. She looked at each pipe, remembering what the book had said about them. Her life could well depend on knowing which pipe to use. She said the names aloud, under her breath, to secure them in her mind and to delay actually going into Death.

"First, and least, is Ranna," recited Lirael, the relevant page from *The Book of Remembrance and Forgetting* clear in her head. "Ranna, the Sleepbringer, will take all those who hear it into slumber.

"Second is Mosrael, the Waker. One of the most dangerous bells, and still so in any form. Its sound is a seesaw that will throw the piper further into Death, even as it brings the listener into Life.

"Third is Kibeth, the Walker. Kibeth gives freedom of movement to the Dead, or forces the Dead to walk at the piper's will. But Kibeth is contrary and can make the piper walk where she would not choose to go.

"Fourth is Dyrim, the Speaker, of melodious tone. Dyrim may grant speech to the dumb, tongue-lost Dead, or give forgotten words their meaning. Dyrim may also still a tongue that moves too freely.

"Fifth is Belgaer, the Thinker, which can restore independent thought, and memory, and all the patterns of what was once in Life. Or, in a careless hand, erase them. Belgaer is troublesome, too, always seeking to sound of its own accord.

"Sixth comes Saraneth, also known as the Binder. Saraneth speaks with the deep voice of power, shackling the Dead to the wielder's will."

Lirael paused before she recited the name of the seventh and last pipe, the longest, its silver surface forever cold and frightening under her touch.

"Astarael, the Sorrowful," whispered Lirael. "Properly sounded, Astarael will cast all who hear it deep into Death. Including the piper. Do not call upon Astarael unless all else is lost."

"Sleeper, Waker, Walker, Speaker, Thinker, Binder, and Weeper," said the Dog, taking a break from a heavy-duty scratching of her ear. "Bells would be better, though. Those pipes are really only for children to practice with."

"Ssshhh," said Lirael. "I'm concentrating."

She knew better than to ask the Dog how she knew the names

of the pipes. The impossible hound had probably read *The Book of Remembrance and Forgetting* herself, while Lirael slept.

Having mentally prepared herself to use the panpipes—or to use only some of them—Lirael drew her sword, noting the play of Charter marks along its silvered blade. There was an inscription, too, she saw. She held the blade to the light and read it aloud.

"The Clayr Saw me, the Wallmakers made me, my enemies Remember me."

"A sister sword to Binder," remarked the Dog, nosing it with interest. "I didn't know they had that one. What's it called?"

Lirael twisted the blade to see if there was something written on the other side, but as she did so, the first inscription changed, the letters shimmering into a new arrangement.

" 'Nehima,' " read Lirael. "What does that mean?"

"It's a name," said the Dog blandly. Seeing Lirael's expression, she cocked her head to one side and continued, "I suppose you could say it means 'forget-me-not.' Though the irony is that Nehima herself is long forgotten. Still, better a sword than a block of stone, I suppose. It's certainly an heirloom of the house, if ever I saw one," the Dog added. "I'm surprised they gave it to you."

Lirael nodded, unable to speak, her thoughts once again turning back to the Glacier and the Clayr. Ryelle and Sanar had just casually handed the sword to her. Made by the Wallmakers themselves, it must be one of the greatest treasures the Clayr possessed.

A nudge at her leg reminded her of the business at hand, so she blinked away an incipient tear and focused all her thought, as *The Book of Remembrance and Forgetting* had told her to. Apparently she should feel Death and then sort of reach out to it. It was easier in places where lots of people had died, or were buried, but theoretically it was possible anywhere.

Lirael closed her eyes to concentrate harder, furrows forming across her forehead. She could feel Death now, like a cold pressure against her face. She pushed against it, feeling its chill sink into her cheekbones and lips, soaking into her outstretched hands. It was strange with the sun still hot against her bare neck.

It grew colder still, and colder, as the chill moved up her feet and legs. She felt a tug against her knees, a tug that wasn't one of the Dog's gentle reminders. It was like being gripped by a current, a strong current that wanted to take her away and force her under.

She opened her eyes. A river flowed against her legs, but it was not the Ratterlin. It was black and opaque, and there was no sign of the island, the blue sky, or the sun. The light was grey, grey and dull as far as she could see, out to a totally flat horizon.

Lirael shuddered, not just from the cold, for she had successfully entered Death. She could hear a waterfall somewhere in the distance. The First Gate, she supposed, from the description in the book.

The river tugged at her again, and without thinking, she went with it for a few steps. It tugged again, even harder, the cold spreading into her very bones. It would be easy to let that chill spread through her entire body, to lie down and let the current take her where it willed—

"No!" she snapped, forcing herself back a step. This was what the book had warned her about. The river's strength wasn't just in the current. She had also to resist its compulsion to walk farther into Death, or to lie down and let it carry her away.

Fortunately, the book was also right about something more favorable. She could feel the way back to Life, and instinctively knew exactly where to go and how to get back there, which was a relief.

Apart from the distant roar of the First Gate, Lirael could hear nothing else moving in the river. Lirael listened carefully, nerves drawn tight, muscles ready for immediate flight. Still there was nothing, not even a ripple.

Then her Death sense twitched, and she quickly scanned the river to either side of her again. For a moment, she thought she saw something move on the surface, a thin line of darkness under the water, moving farther back into Death. But then it was gone, and she could neither see nor sense anything. After a minute, she wasn't even sure if there had been anything there in the first place.

Sighing, she carefully sheathed her sword, put the panpipes back in her waistcoat pocket, and drew out the Dark Mirror. Here, in the First Precinct of Death, she could look just a little way into the past. To look further back, she would have to travel deeper in, past the First Gate or even far beyond it. But today she only planned to look back a matter of twenty years or so.

The click that accompanied the opening of the Mirror seemed far too loud, echoing across the dark waters. Lirael flinched at the sound—then screamed as it was followed by a loud splash directly behind her!

Reflexively, she jumped—farther into Death— swapped the Mirror into her left hand, and drew her sword, all before she even knew what was happening.

"It's only me," said the Dog, her tail slapping the water as it wagged. "I got bored waiting."

"How did you get here?" whispered Lirael, sheathing her sword with a shaking hand. "You scared me to death!"

"I followed you," said the Dog. "It's just a different sort of walk."

Not for the first time, Lirael wondered what the Dog really was, and the extent of her powers. But there was no time for speculation now. *The Book of Remembrance and Forgetting* had warned her not to stay too long in any one place in Death, because things would come looking. Things she didn't want to meet.

"Who's going to guard my body if you're here?" she asked reproachfully. If anything happened to her body back in Life, she would have no choice but to follow the river onwards, or to become some sort of Dead spirit herself, eternally trying to get back into Life, by stealing someone else's body. Or to become a shadow, drinking blood and Life to keep itself out of Death.

"I'll know if anyone comes close," said the Dog, sniffing the river. "Can we go farther in?"

"No!" snapped Lirael. "I'm going to use the Dark Mirror here. But you're going back straight away! This is Death, Dog, not the Glacier!"

"True," mumbled the Dog. She looked up pleadingly at Lirael and added, "But it's only the very edge of Death—"

"Back! Now!" commanded Lirael, pointing. The Dog stopped her pleading look, showed the whites of her eyes in disapproval, and slunk away with her tail down. A second later, she vanished—back into Life.

Lirael ignored her and opened the Mirror, holding it close to her right eye. "Focus on the Mirror with one eye," the book had said, "and look into Death with the other, lest harm befall you there."

Good advice, but hardly practical, Lirael thought, as she struggled to focus on two different things at once. But after a minute, the Mirror's opaque surface began to clear, its darkness lifting. Instead of looking at her reflection, Lirael found that she was somehow looking through the mirror, and it was not the cold river of Death she saw beyond. She saw swirling lights, lights that she soon realized were actually the passage of the sun across the sky, so fast it was a blur. The sun was going backwards.

Excitement grew in her as she realized this was the beginning of the magic. Now she had to think of what she wanted to see. She began to form an image of her mother in her mind, borrowing more from the charcoal drawing Aunt Kirrith had given her years ago than from her own recollection, which was the mixed-up memory of a child, all feelings and soft-edged images.

Holding the picture of her mother in her head, she spoke aloud, infusing her voice with the Charter marks she'd learned from the book, symbols of power and command that would make the Dark Mirror show her what she wanted to see.

"My mother I knew, a little," Lirael said, her words loud against the murmur of the river. "My father I knew not, and would see through the veil of time. So let it be."

The swift passage of backwards suns began to slow as she spoke, and Lirael felt herself drawn closer to the image in the Mirror, till a single sun filled all her vision, blinding her with its light. Then it was gone, and there was darkness.

Slowly, the darkness ebbed, and Lirael saw a room, strangely superimposed upon the river of Death she saw through her other eye. Both images were blurry, as if her eyes were full of tears, but they were not. Lirael blinked several times, but the vision grew no clearer.

She saw a large room—a hall, in fact—dominated at one end by a large window, which was a blur of different colors rather than clear glass. Lirael sensed there was some sort of magic in the window, for the colors and patterns changed, though she couldn't see it clearly enough to make it out.

A long, brilliantly polished table of some light and lustrous wood stretched the full length of the hall. It was loaded with silver of many kinds: candelabra with beeswax candles burning clean yellow flames, salt cellars and pepper grinders, sauce boats and tureens, and many ornaments Lirael had never seen. A roast goose, half-carved, sat on a platter, encircled by plates of lesser foods.

There were only two people at the table, sitting at the other end, so Lirael had to squint to try to see them more clearly. One, a man, sat at the head of the table in a high-backed chair, almost a throne. Despite his simple white shirt and lack of jewelry, he had the bearing of a man of rank and power. Lirael frowned and shifted the Dark Mirror a little, to see if she could make the vision sharper. Rainbows briefly rippled through the room, but nothing else seemed to change.

There were spells to use to refine the vision, but Lirael didn't want to try them just yet, in case they made the vision go away completely. Instead she concentrated on the other person. She could see her more clearly than the man.

It was her mother. Arielle, Kirrith's little sister. She looked beautiful in the soft candlelight, her long blond hair hanging in a brilliant waterfall down the back of her dress, an elegant creation of ice-blue adorned with golden stars. It was cut low across the neck and back, and she wore a necklace of sapphires and diamonds.

As Lirael concentrated, the vision of the past grew sharper around the two people, but even muddier everywhere else, as if all the color and light were gathering around the point of her focus. At the same time, her view of the river of Death clouded. Sounds began to come to her, as if she were listening to two people conversing as they walked towards her. They were speaking in the courtly fashion, which was rarely used in the Glacier. Obviously they didn't know each other very well.

"I have heard many strange things under this roof, Mistress," the man was saying as he poured himself more wine, waving back a sending servant that had begun to attend to him. "But none so strange as this."

"It is not something I sought," replied the woman, her voice strangely familiar to Lirael's ears. Surely she didn't remember it? She had been only five when Arielle had abandoned her. Then she realized that it was Kirrith's voice it reminded her of. Though it was sweeter than Kirrith's had ever been.

"And none of your Vision-Sisters have Seen what you wish of me?" asked the man. "None of the Nine Day Watch?"

"None," said Arielle, bending her head, a blush spreading across her neck. Lirael watched in amazement. Her own mother embarrassed! But then the Arielle she saw here wasn't much older than herself. She seemed very young.

The man seemed to be thinking along similar lines, because he said, "My wife has been dead these eighteen years, but I have a daughter grown who would be near your age. I am not unfamiliar with the . . . the . . ."

"Imaginings of young women? Or the infatuations of youth?" interrupted Arielle, looking back up at him, her face angry now. "I am five and twenty, sir, and no girlish virgin dreaming of her mate. I am a Daughter of the Clayr, and nothing but my Sight would have brought me here to lie with a man I have never met who is old enough to be my father!"

The man put his cup down and smiled ruefully, but his eyes were tired and untouched by the smile.

"I beg your pardon, Mistress. In truth, I heard the sound of prophecy when you first spoke to me today, but I put it from my mind. I must leave here tomorrow, to face many perils. I have no time for thoughts of love, and I have been proven a less than perfect parent. Even if I were not away tomorrow, and could linger here with you, any child you bear would likely see little of its father."

"This is not a matter of love," said Arielle quietly, meeting his gaze. "And a single night may beget a child as well as a year of striving. As it will, for I have Seen her. As to the lack of a father, I fear she will have neither parent for very long."

"You speak of a certainty," said the man. "Yet the Clayr often See many threads, which the future may weave this way or that."

"I See only a single thread in this, sir," said Arielle, reaching across to take the man's pale hand in her own brown fingers. "I am here, called by the visions granted by my Blood, as you are governed by yours. It is meant to be, cousin. But perhaps we can at least enjoy our single night, forgetting higher reasons. Let us to bed."

The man hesitated, his fingers open. Then he laughed, and raised Arielle's hand to his lips for a gentle kiss.

"We shall have our night," he said, rising from the chair. "I know not what it means, or what future we will here secure. But for once I am tired of responsibility and care! As you say, my dear cousin, let us to bed!"

The two embraced, and Lirael shut her right eye, stricken with embarrassment and a slight, uneasy feeling of shame. If she kept watching, she might even see the moment of her own conception, and that was too embarrassing to even contemplate. But even with her eye shut, the vision lingered, till Lirael blinked it away, this time with an actual tear.

She had secretly expected more from the vision, some indication of her parents' having a forbidden love or some great bond that would be revealed to their daughter. But it seemed she was the result of a single evening's coupling, which was either predestined or the result of her mother's mad imagination. Lirael didn't know which would be worse. And she still had no clear idea who her father was, though some of the things she had seen and heard were certainly suggestive and would require further thought.

Snapping the mirror shut, she put it back into her belt pouch. Only then did she realize that the sound of the First Gate had stopped. Something was coming through the waterfall—something from the deeper reaches of Death.

Chapter Thirty-Six

A DENIZEN OF DEATH

A FEW SECONDS after Lirael noticed the silence of the First Gate, the sound of the crashing water resumed. Whatever had stilled it had passed through, and was now in the First Precinct of Death. With Lirael.

Lirael peered into the distance, unable to see anything moving. The grey light and flatness of the river made it hard to work out distances, and she had no idea whether the First Gate was as close as it sounded. She knew it was marked by a veil of mist, and she couldn't see it.

To be on the safe side, Lirael drew both sword and pipes and took several steps towards Life, till she was close enough to feel its warmth at her back. She should cross now, she knew, but a daredevil curiosity gripped her and kept her there—the urge to see, albeit briefly, a denizen of Death.

When she did see the first signs of it, all her curiosity was gone in an instant, replaced by fear. For something was approaching under the river, not upon it, a vee of ripples heading straight for her, moving swiftly against the current. Something large and hidden, able to cloak itself against her senses. She hadn't felt its presence at all, and saw the ripples purely by chance, as a result of her own caution.

Instantly, she felt for Life again, but at the same time, the vee exploded into a leaping figure, a shape of fire and darkness. It held a bell, a bell that rang with power, fixing her on the very border of Life and Death.

The bell was Saraneth, Lirael somehow knew, recognizing it deep in her bones as the bell's fierce power fought against her straining muscles. But a raw Saraneth, one that was not partnered with Charter Magic, as in her pipes or an Abhorsen's bells. There was more power here, and less art. It had to be the bell of a Free Magic sorcerer. A necromancer!

She could feel the wielder's will behind the bell, seeking domination of her spirit, an implacable force of hatred beating down her own pathetic resistance. Now Lirael saw the wielder clearly, despite the steam that eddied around his body as if he were a hot iron plunged into the river.

It was Hedge, the necromancer from the vision the twins had shown her. She could feel the fires of Free Magic that burnt in him, defeating even the chill of Death.

"Kneel before your master!" commanded Hedge, striding towards her, the bell in one hand, a sword burning with dark, liquid flames in the other. His voice was harsh and cruel, the words infused with fire and smoke.

The necromancer's command struck at Lirael like a blow, and she felt her knees unlock, her legs beginning to crumple. Hedge already had her in his power, the deep commanding tone of Saraneth still ringing in her ears, echoing inside her head, a sound she couldn't dislodge from her mind.

He came still closer, the sword raised above his head, and she knew that it would soon fall upon her unprotected neck. Her own sword was in her hand, the Charter marks burning like golden suns as Nehima reacted angrily to the Free Magic menace that approached. But her sword arm was locked at the elbow by her enemy's will, held in place by the terrible power of the bell.

Desperately she tried to pour strength into her arm, to no avail. Then she tried to reach into the Charter, to draw forth a spell to blast the necromancer with silver darts or red-gold fire.

"Kneel!" the necromancer commanded again, and she knelt, the cold river clutching at her stomach and breasts, welcoming her in its soon-to-be-permanent embrace. The muscles in her neck twitched and stood out in cords as she fought the compulsion to bend her head.

Then she realized that by giving in, just a little, she could bend her head down, enough so her lips could touch the panpipes held in her frozen left hand. So she submitted, too quickly, lips meeting silver with bloody force, not even knowing which pipe would sound. At the worst, it would be Astarael, and then she would take the necromancer with her into the deeper realms of Death.

She blew as hard as she could, forcing all that remained of her will into directing the clear note that cut through the echoing remnants of the necromancer's bell.

The pipe was Kibeth. The sound struck Hedge as he swung for a beheading blow. It caught his feet with joyful trickery, spinning him around completely. His sword-stroke swung wide, high above Lirael, and then Kibeth was walking and dancing him like a drunken fool, sending him cavorting towards the First Gate.

But even surprised by Kibeth, his will and Saraneth fought to hold Lirael as she tried to throw herself back into Life. Her arms and legs felt like clumsy sacks of earth, the river like quicksand, trying to suck her under. Desperately, she pushed to free herself, reaching towards Life, reaching for the day, for the Dog, for everything she loved.

Finally, as if a rope that held her snapped, Lirael pitched forward into sunlight and cool breezes, but not before the necromancer had shouted out his farewell, in words as cold and threatening as the river of Death itself.

"I know you! You cannot hide! I will—"

His last words were cut off as Lirael completely re-occupied her body, senses re-arranging themselves for the living world. As the Book had warned, there was ice and frost all over her, lining every fold of her clothing. There was even an icicle hanging from her nose. She broke it off, which hurt, and sneezed.

"What! What was that!" barked the Dog, who was practically under her feet. Clearly, she had sensed that Lirael had been attacked.

"A n-necromancer," said Lirael, shivering. "The one . . . the vision . . . that the Clayr showed me. Hedge. He . . . he . . . almost killed me!"

The Dog growled, low in her throat, and Lirael suddenly noticed that she had grown as tall as her own shoulder and now sported much larger and sharper teeth. "I knew I should have stayed with you, Mistress!"

"Yes, yes," mumbled Lirael. She still could hardly speak, her breath coming in little panicked pants. She knew the necromancer couldn't follow her back here—he would have to return to his own body in Life. Unfortunately, her little Kibeth pipe wouldn't have walked him far. He was easily powerful enough to come back and send Dead spirits through to pursue her. The bodiless ones.

"He'll send something after me. We've got to get out of here!"

The Dog growled again but didn't object as Lirael stumbled back across the stony island, intent on getting aboard *Finder* as quickly as possible. She circled behind Lirael, so every time the girl looked back nervously, there was the Dog, standing between her and danger.

A few minutes later, safe in the swift waters of the Ratterlin, Lirael collapsed from the shock, lying down in the boat with just one hand lightly touching the rudder. *Finder* could be trusted to steer her own course.

"I would have bitten that necromancer's throat out," said the

Dog, after letting Lirael gasp and shake for several minutes. "He'd have had cause to remember my teeth!"

"I don't think he would notice if you *did* rip his throat out," said Lirael, shivering. "He felt more Dead than alive. He said, 'I know you,'" she continued slowly, looking up at the sky, angling her face back to catch more of the sun, delighting in its blessed heat upon her still frosted lips and nose. "How could he know me?"

"Free Magic eats up necromancers," said the Dog, shrinking herself down to a less belligerent and more conversational size. "The power they seek to wield—the Free Magic they profess to master—ultimately devours them. That power recognizes your Blood. That's probably what he meant by 'I know you.'"

"I don't like the thought of anyone outside the Glacier knowing me," said Lirael, shuddering. "Knowing who I am. And that necromancer's probably with Nicholas now, in Life. So when I find Nicholas, I'll find the necromancer. Like a bug going to a spider to find a fly."

"Tomorrow's trouble," said the Dog, soothing her, not very convincingly. "At least we're done with today's. We're safe on the river."

Lirael nodded, thinking. Then she sat up and scratched the Dog under the chin and all around her ears.

"Dog," she said hesitantly, "there's Free Magic in you, maybe even more than the Charter Magic in your collar. Why don't you . . . why aren't you . . . why aren't you like the necromancer?"

The Dog sighed, with a meaty "oof" that made Lirael wrinkle her nose. The hound tilted her head to one side, thinking before she answered.

"In the Beginning, all magic was Free Magic—unconstrained, raw, unchanneled. Then the Charter was created, which took most of the Free Magic and made it ordered, subject to structure, constrained by symbols. The Free Magic that remained separate from the Charter is the Free Magic of necromancy, of Stilken, Margrue, and Hish, of Analem and Gorger, and all the other fell creatures, constructs, and familiars. It is the random magic that persists outside the Charter.

"There is also the Free Magic that helped make the Charter but was not consumed by it," continued the Dog. "That is quite different from the Free Magic that would not join in the creation of the Charter."

"You speak of the Beginning," said Lirael, who wasn't at all sure she understood. "But could that be before the Charter? It doesn't have a Beginning—or an End."

"Everything has a Beginning," replied the Dog. "Including the Charter. I should know, since I was there at the birth of it, when the Seven chose to make the Charter and the Five gave themselves to the making. In a sense, you were there, too, Mistress. You are descended from the Five."

"The Five Great Charters?" asked Lirael, fascinated by this information. "I remember the rhyme about that. It must have been one of the first things we memorized as children."

She sat up even straighter, and clasped her hands behind her back, unconsciously assuming the recital position she'd learned as a child.

> *"Five Great Charters knit the land,*
> *Together linked, hand in hand.*
> *One in the people who wear the crown,*
> *Two in the folk who keep the Dead down,*
> *Three and Five became stone and mortar,*
> *Four sees all in frozen water."*

"Yes," said the Dog. "A good rhyme for pups to learn. The Great Charters are the keystones of the Charter. The bloodlines,

the Wall, and the Charter Stones all come from the original sacrifice of the Five, who poured their power into the men and
women who were your ancestors. Some of those, in turn, passed
that power into stone and mortar, when blood alone was judged
to be too easily diluted or led astray."

"So if the Five were sort of . . . dissolved into the Charter, what
happened to the other two?" asked Lirael, digesting this information with a frown. Everything she had read said the Charter
had always existed and always would. "You said there were Seven
who chose to make the Charter."

"It began with the Nine," replied the Dog quietly. "Nine
who were most powerful, who possessed the conscious
thought and foresight that raised them above all the tens of
thousands of Free Magic beings that clamored and strove to
exist upon the earth. Yet of the Nine, only Seven agreed to
make the Charter. One chose to ignore the Seven's work but
was finally bound to serve the Charter. The Ninth fought and
was barely defeated."

"That's number eight and nine," said Lirael, counting on her
fingers. "This would be much easier to understand if they had
names instead of numbers. Anyway, you still haven't explained
what happened to . . . um . . . six and seven. Why didn't they
become part of the Great Charters?"

"They put a great deal of their power into the bloodlines,
but not all their being," replied the Dog. "But I suspect they were
perhaps less tired of conscious, individual existence. They wished
to go on, in some form or another. I think they wanted to see what
happened. And the Seven did have names. They are remembered
in the bells and in the pipes you have in your belt. Each of those
bells has something of the original power of the Seven, the
power that existed before the Charter."

"You're not . . . you're not one of the Seven, are you?" asked

Lirael, after a moment of anxiety-laden silence. She couldn't imagine that one of the creators of the Charter, no matter how much power it had given away, would condescend to be her friend. Or would continue to do so once its true loftiness had been established.

"I'm the Disreputable Dog," replied the Dog, licking Lirael's face. "Just a leftover from the Beginning, freely given to the Charter. And I'll always be your friend, Lirael. You know that."

"I guess I do," replied Lirael doubtfully. She hugged the Dog tight, her face pressed into the hound's warm neck. "I'll always be your friend, too."

The Dog let Lirael keep on hugging, but her ears were pricked, listening to the world around them. Her nose kept sniffing the air, trying to get more of the scent that had come back from Death with Lirael. A disturbing scent, one the Dog hoped was purely from her own imagination and long memory, because it was not the smell of just one human necromancer, no matter how powerful. It was much, much older, and much more frightening.

Lirael stopped hugging when the Dog's wet smell began to overcome her, and she moved back to take the tiller. *Finder* kept steering herself, but Lirael felt a surge of welcome recognition as Charter marks blossomed under her hand, warm and comforting after the chill of Death.

"We'll probably see the Sindle Ferry later today," remarked Lirael, her brow furrowing as she recalled the maps she had rolled, unrolled, catalogued, and repaired in the Library. "We're making good time—we must have come twenty leagues already!"

"Towards danger," said the Dog, moving aft to flop down at Lirael's feet. "We mustn't forget that, Mistress."

Lirael nodded, thinking back to the necromancer and Death. It seemed unreal now, out in the sunshine, with the boat sailing so cheerfully down the river. But it had been all too real then.

And if the necromancer's words were true, not only did he know her, he might know where she was going. Once she left the Ratterlin, she would be relatively easy prey for the necromancer's Dead servants.

"Perhaps I should make a Charter-skin soon," she said. "The barking owl. Just in case."

"Good idea," said the Dog, slurring. Her chin was propped on Lirael's foot, and she was drooling profusely. "By the way, did you see anything in the Dark Mirror?"

Lirael hesitated. She'd momentarily forgotten. The vision of the past had been put out of her mind by the necromancer's attack.

"Yes." The Dog waited for her to go on, but Lirael was silent. Finally, the hound raised her head and said, "So you are a Remembrancer now. The first in these last five hundred years, unless I am mistaken."

"I suppose I am," said Lirael, not meeting the Dog's eyes. She didn't want to be a Remembrancer, as the book called someone who Saw into the past. She wanted to See into the future.

"And what did you See?" prompted the Dog.

"My parents." Lirael blushed as she thought again of how close she had come to seeing her parents making love. "My father."

"Who was he?"

"I don't know," replied Lirael, frowning. "I would recognize a portrait, I think. Or the room that I saw. It doesn't really matter, anyway."

The Dog snorted, indicating that Lirael hadn't fooled her one bit. Obviously, it mattered a lot, but Lirael didn't want to talk about it.

"*You're* my family," said Lirael quickly, giving the Dog a quick hug. Then she stared deliberately ahead at the shining waters of the Ratterlin. The Dog really was her only family, even more than the Clayr she had lived with all her life.

They had shown she would never be truly one of them, she thought as she tightened her headscarf, remembering how the silk had felt against her eyes. Families did not blindfold their own children.

Chapter Thirty-Seven

A BATH IN THE RIVER

FOLLOWING SANAR AND Ryelle's advice, Lirael spent her first night away from the Clayr's Glacier anchored in the lee of a long, thin island in the very middle of the Ratterlin, with more than four hundred yards of swift, deep water on either side.

Soon after dawn, following a breakfast of oatmeal, an apple, a rather tough cinnamon cake, and several mouthfuls of clear river water, Lirael drew in the anchor, stowed it, and whistled for the Dog. She came swimming across from the island, where she'd performed her canine duty for the other dogs who might one day visit it.

They had just raised the sail and were beginning to reach before the wind when the Dog suddenly went stiff-legged and pointed across the bow, letting out a warning yip.

Lirael ducked her head down so she could see under the boom, her gaze following the line pointed by the Dog's forelimb at some object two or three hundred yards downstream. At first, she couldn't make out what it was—something metal on the surface of the river, reflecting the morning sun. When she did recognize it, she had to peer more carefully to re-affirm her initial judgment.

"That looks like a metal bathtub," she said slowly. "With a man in it."

"It *is* a bathtub," said the Dog. "And a man. There's something else, too . . . you'd best nock an arrow, Mistress."

"He looks unconscious. Or dead," replied Lirael. "Shouldn't we just sail around?"

But she left the tiller to *Finder*, took out the bow, and quickly strung it. Then she loosened Nehima in its sheath and took an arrow from the quiver.

Finder seemed to share the Dog's desire for caution, for she turned away from a direct intercept. The bathtub was traveling much more slowly than they were, propelled only by the current. With the wind on her beam, *Finder* was considerably faster and could curve around in an arc to pass the bathtub and keep going.

Keeping going was what Lirael wanted to do. She didn't want to have anything to do with strangers before she absolutely had to. But then, she would have to deal with people sooner or later, and he did look as if he was in trouble. Surely he wouldn't have chosen to be out in the Ratterlin in a craft as unreliable as a metal bathtub?

Lirael frowned and tugged her scarf down lower over her forehead, so it shaded her face. When they were only fifty yards away, and about to pass the tub, she also nocked an arrow, but did not draw. The man was definitely unaware of *Finder*'s approach, since he hadn't so much as twitched. He was on his back in the bath, with his arms hanging over the sides and his knees drawn up. Lirael could see the hilt of a sword at his side, and there was something across his chest—

"Bells! A necromancer!" exclaimed Lirael, drawing her bow. He didn't look like Hedge, but any necromancer was dangerous. Putting an arrow in him would simply be insurance. Unlike their Dead servants, necromancers had no trouble with running water. This one was probably pretending to be hurt, to lure her into an ambush.

She was just about to loose the arrow when the Dog suddenly barked, "Wait! he doesn't smell like a necromancer!"

Surprised, Lirael jerked, let go—and the arrow sped through the air, passing less than a foot above the man's head. If he'd sat up, it would have pierced his throat or eye, killing him instantly.

As the arrow arced downward to plop into the water well past the tub, a small white cat emerged from under the man's legs, climbed onto his chest, and yawned.

This provoked an immediate response from the Dog, who barked furiously and lunged at the water. Lirael only just managed to drop her bow and grab the hound's tail before the Dog went over the side.

The Dog's tail was waving happily, at such a speed Lirael had difficulty hanging on to it. Whether this was actual friendliness or excitement at the prospect of chasing a cat, Lirael didn't know.

All the noise finally woke the man in the tub. He sat up slowly, obviously dazed, the cat moving up to perch precariously on his shoulder. At first, he looked the wrong way for the source of the barking; then he turned, saw the boat—and instantly went for his sword.

Swiftly, Lirael picked up her bow and nocked another arrow. *Finder* turned into the wind so they slowed, giving Lirael a reasonably stable platform from which to shoot.

The cat spoke, words coming out amidst another yawn.

"What are you doing here?"

Lirael jumped in surprise but managed not to drop her arrow.

She was about to answer when she realized the cat was speaking to the Dog.

"Humph," replied the Dog. "I thought someone as slippery as *you* would know the answer to that. What are you called now?

And who is that sorry ragamuffin with you?"

"I am called Mogget," said the cat. "Most of the time. What name do you—"

"This sorry ragamuffin can speak for himself," interrupted the man angrily. "Who or what are you? And you, too, mistress! That's one of the Clayr's boats, isn't it? Did you steal it?"

Finder yawed at this insult, and Lirael tightened her grip on the bow, right hand creeping to the string. He was obviously a very arrogant ragamuffin, and younger than she was, to boot. And he was wearing a necromancer's bells! Apart from that, he was quite handsome, which was another black mark as far as she was concerned. The good-looking men were always the ones who came up to her in the Refectory, certain that she would never refuse their attentions.

"I am the Disreputable Dog," said the Dog, quite calmly. "Companion to Lirael, Daughter of the Clayr."

"So you got stolen as well," said Sam grumpily, hardly thinking about what he was saying. He hurt all over, and Mogget's presence on his shoulder was both extremely uncomfortable and annoying.

"I am Lirael, Daughter of the Clayr," pronounced Lirael, her anger overriding her familiar feeling of being an imposter. "Who or what are you? Besides insufferably rude?"

The man—boy, really—stared back at her, till the blush spread further across her face and Lirael bent her head, hiding under her hair and scarf. She knew well what he was thinking.

She couldn't possibly be a Daughter of the Clayr. The Clayr were all tall and blond and elegant. This girl . . . woman . . . was dark-haired and wore odd clothes. Her bright-red waistcoat was not at all like the star-dusted white robes of the Clayr he'd seen in Belisaere. And she lacked the aloof confidence of the seeresses, who had always made him nervous when he had met them by chance in the corridors of the Palace.

"You don't look like a Daughter of the Clayr," he said, paddling the bathtub a bit closer. The current was already taking him past *Finder*, and he had to battle just to keep in place. "But I guess I can take your word for it."

"Stop!" commanded Lirael, half drawing her bow. "Who are you? And why are you wearing the bells of a necromancer?"

Sam looked down at his chest. He'd forgotten he was wearing the bandolier. Now he was aware of how cold it was, how it pressed against his chest and made breathing difficult.

He unbuckled the bandolier as he tried to work out something inconclusive to say, but Mogget beat him to it.

"Well met, Mistress Lirael. This ragamuffin, as your servant so aptly described him, is His Highness Prince Sameth, the Abhorsen-in-Waiting. Hence the bells. But on to more serious matters. Could you please rescue us? Prince Sameth's personal vessel is not quite what I am used to, and he is eager to catch me a fish before my morning nap."

Lirael looked at the Dog questioningly. She knew who Prince Sameth was. But why on earth would the second child of King Touchstone and the Abhorsen Sabriel be floating in a bathtub in the middle of the Ratterlin, leagues from anywhere?

"He's a royal Prince, all right," said the Dog, quietly sniffing. "I can smell his Blood. He's wounded, too—it is making him irritable. Not much more than a pup, really. You'd best be careful of the other. The Mogget. I know him of old. He's the Abhorsen's servant all right, but he's Free Magic, of the bound variety. He doesn't serve of his own free will, and you must never loose his collar."

"I suppose we have to pick them up," said Lirael slowly, hoping the Dog would contradict her. But the Dog simply stared back, looking amused. *Finder* finally settled the matter by moving her tiller a little, and the boat started to head slowly towards the bathtub.

Lirael sighed and put away the bow, but took care to draw her sword instead, in case the Dog was mistaken. What if this Prince Sameth was actually a necromancer, and not the Abhorsen-in-Waiting at all?

"Leave your sword by your side," Lirael called. "And you, Mogget, sit under the Prince's legs. When you're alongside, don't move until I tell you."

Sam didn't answer immediately. Lirael saw him whisper to the cat and realized that he was having a conversation similar to the one she'd had with the Dog.

"All right!" Sam shouted after listening to the cat, and he pushed his sword cautiously down to the bottom of the tub, with the bells. He looked feverish, Lirael thought as they drew closer; he was very flushed on the cheeks and around the eyes.

Mogget climbed down gracefully, disappearing below the rim of the bathtub. The makeshift vessel continued on its way, spinning in the current. *Finder* moved, too, tacking across the wind to come broadside.

Boat and bathtub met with a loud clang. Lirael was surprised by how low in the water the tub was—it hadn't seemed so submerged from a distance. The Prince scowled up at her, but true to his word, he didn't move.

Quickly, Lirael reached across with her left hand and touched the Charter mark on his forehead, her sword held ready to strike if the mark was false or corrupted. But her finger felt the familiar warmth of the true Charter, bright and strong. Despite what the Dog had told her, the Charter certainly seemed to go on forever, without Beginning or End.

Hesitantly, Sam stretched out his hand, too, obviously waiting for permission, with the sharp point of her sword so near.

She nodded, and he touched her forehead with two fingers, the Charter mark there flashing brilliantly, brighter even than the sun on the river.

"Well, I guess you can get out of the bathtub," said Lirael, breaking the silence. She felt suddenly nervous again, having to share the boat with a stranger. What would she do if he wanted to talk all the time, or tried to kiss her or something? Not that he seemed to be in any shape to do much of anything. She put her sword down and reached out to help him up, wrinkling her nose. He smelt of blood and dirt and fear, and obviously hadn't washed for days.

"Thank you," muttered Sam, slithering over the gunwale, his legs cramped and useless. Lirael saw him bite his lip against the pain, but he didn't cry out. When his legs were swung over, he took a breath and said shakily, "Could . . . could you get my sword, and the bells and the saddlebags? I'm afraid I can hardly move."

Lirael quickly complied. She lifted the saddlebags out last. As they came free, the balance of the bathtub shifted, and one end went briefly underwater. For a second it righted itself, riding still lower in the river. Then a slight wave filled one end beyond recovery, and it flipped over, sinking like a strange silver fish into the clear water below.

"Farewell, brave vessel," whispered Sam, watching as it sank below the upper band of light into the darkness of the deep. He sat back and let out a sigh that was half pain and half relief.

Mogget had jumped as the tub filled and was now facing the Dog, so close their noses almost touched. Both just sat there, staring, but Lirael suspected they were communicating in some way unknown to their human "masters." It didn't look entirely friendly. Both of them had their backs up, and the Dog was growling, low and soft, the sound rolling out from deep in her chest.

Lirael busied herself turning *Finder* back downriver, ducking under the boom as it swung across. The boat hardly needed her help, but it was easier than talking. Once that was done, the silence grew oppressive. The two animals still stood nose-to-nose. Eventually, Lirael felt she had to say something. She wished she were back in the Library and could just write a note.

"What . . . um . . . happened to you?" she asked Sam, who had settled himself at full length in the bottom of the boat. "Why were you in a bathtub?"

"It's a long story," said Sam weakly. He tried to sit up to see her better, but his head dropped back and bumped on a thwart. "Ow! In the simple version, I guess you could say I was escaping from the attentions of the Dead, and the tub happened to be the best boat available."

"The Dead? Near here?" asked Lirael, shivering as she thought of her own encounter with Death. With the necromancer Hedge. She'd presumed that in Life he would be near the Red Lake, as he was in the vision. But that might not have actually happened yet. Perhaps Hedge was somewhere close, right now—

"Several leagues upstream, last night," said Sam, prodding the flesh around his wound with a finger. It was tender and felt tight against the trouser leg, a sure sign that the spell to contain infection had failed in the face of his weariness and over-exertion.

"That looks bad," said Lirael, who could see the dark stain of old blood showing through the cloth. "Did the necromancer do it?"

"Mmm?" asked Sam, who felt like he might pass out again. Pressing on the wound had been a big mistake. "There was no necromancer there, fortunately. The Dead were following set orders, and not being too smart about it. I got stabbed earlier."

Lirael thought for a moment, unsure what to tell him. But he was a royal Prince and the Abhorsen-in-Waiting.

"It's just that I fought a necromancer yesterday," she said.

"What!" exclaimed Sam, sitting up, despite a sudden wave of nausea. "A necromancer? Here?"

"Not exactly," said Lirael. "We were in Death. I don't know where he was physically."

Sam groaned and fell backwards again. This time Lirael saw it coming and just managed to catch his head.

"Thanks," muttered Sam. "Was . . . was he sort of thin and bald, with red armor plates at his elbows?"

"Yes," whispered Lirael. "His name is Hedge. He tried to cut my head off."

Sam made a sort of coughing noise and turned towards the gunwale, the muscles in his neck straining. Lirael just managed to get her hands free before he threw up over the side. He hung there for a few minutes after that, then feebly splashed his face with cold river water.

"Sorry," he said. "Nervous reaction, I suppose. Did you say you fought this necromancer in Death? But you're a Clayr. Clayr don't go into Death. I mean, nobody does, except necromancers and my mother."

"I do," mumbled Lirael back. She blushed again. "I'm . . . I'm a Remembrancer. I had to find out something there, something in the past."

"What's a Remembrancer? What's the past got to do with Death?" asked Sam. He felt delirious. Either Lirael was raving or he was somehow not able to understand what she was saying.

"I think," said the Dog, turning from her nose-to-nose communication with the cat, "that my mistress should tend to your wound, young Prince. Then we might all start at the beginning."

"That could take a while," said Mogget gloomily, searching for fish over the side. Whatever he'd been communicating with the Dog, their body language indicated that he'd come out second best.

"The necromancer," whispered Sam. "Did he burn you, too?"

"No," replied Lirael, puzzled. "Who did he burn?"

Now she was confused. But Sam didn't answer. His eyelids fluttered once, then closed.

"You'd best tend to his wound, Mistress," said the Dog.

Lirael sighed in exasperation, got out her knife, and began to cut Sam's trouser leg away. At the same time, she reached out to the Charter, pulling out the marks for a spell that would cleanse the wound and knit the tissue back together.

Explanations would obviously have to wait.

THE EXPLANATIONS HAD to wait almost the whole day, because Sam didn't wake up until *Finder* gently beached herself on a sandy spit, and Lirael began to set up camp on the adjoining island. Over a dinner of grilled fish, dried tomatoes, and biscuit, they told each other their stories. Lirael was surprised by how easy it was to talk to him. It was almost like talking to the Dog. Perhaps it was because he wasn't a Clayr, she thought.

"So you've Seen Nicholas," said Sam heavily. "And he's definitely with this necromancer, Hedge. Digging up some terrible Free Magic thing. I guess that must be the Lightning Trap he wrote to me about. I was hoping—stupidly, I suppose—that it was all a coincidence. That Nick wouldn't have anything to do with the Enemy, that he was really going to the Red Lake because he'd heard about something interesting."

"I didn't See it myself," Lirael said reluctantly, to forestall any requests that she use her supposed Sight to find out more. "I mean they showed it to me. It took a Watch of more than fifteen hundred Clayr to See near the pit. But they didn't know when it was . . . or will be. It might not have happened yet."

"I guess he hasn't been in the Kingdom for that long," said Sam doubtingly. "But I would think he would have made it to the Red Lake by now. And the digging you Saw might have started without him. The Dead in the blue caps and scarves must

be Southerling refugees, the ones who came across the Wall
more than a month ago."

"Well, according to the Clayr's other vision, I will find
Nicholas at the Red Lake sometime soon," said Lirael. "But I
don't want to go there unprepared. Not if Hedge is with him."

"This is getting worse by the day," said Sam, groaning and
cradling his head in his hands. "We'll have to send a message to
Ellimere. And, I don't know . . . get my parents back from
Ancelstierre. Only then there're the Southerlings to worry about.
Maybe Mother could come back and Dad could stay there—"

"I think the Clayr have already sent messages," said Lirael.
"But they don't know as much as we do, so we should send some,
too. Only we'll have to do something ourselves, won't we? It'll
take too long for the King and the Abhorsen to even hear about
this, let alone come back."

"I suppose so," said Sam, without enthusiasm. "I just wish
Nick had waited for me at the Wall."

"He probably didn't have a choice," said the Dog, who was
curled up at Lirael's feet, listening. Mogget lay nearby, his paws
extended towards the dying remnants of the cooking fire, clean
fishbones near his face. As soon as he'd eaten dinner, he'd fallen
asleep, ignoring Sam and Lirael's conversation.

"I suppose so," agreed Sam as he absently looked at the scars
on his wrists. "That necromancer, Hedge, must have . . . must
have got hold of him when we were at the Perimeter. I never
actually saw Nick after that. We just exchanged letters. I guess I'll
just have to keep trying to find the dumb bastard."

"He looked sick," said Lirael, surprised by the feeling of
concern that rose in her from the memory. He'd reached out his
hand to her and said hello. . . . "Sick and confused. I think the
Free Magic was affecting him, but he didn't realize what it was."

"Nick never really understood what it was like here, or

accepted the idea that magic works," said Sam, staring into the embers. Nick had only got worse as he got older, always asking why. He'd never accepted anything that seemed to contradict his understanding of the forces of nature and the mechanics of how the world worked.

"I don't understand Ancelstierre," said Lirael. "I mean I've heard about it, but it might as well be another world."

"It is," said the Dog. "Or it's best to think of it that way."

"It always seemed somehow less real than here," said Sam, still staring at the fire, not really listening. He was watching the sparks fly up now, trying to count the number of them in each little flurry. "A really detailed dream, but sort of washed out, like a thin watercolor. Softer, somehow, even with their electric light and engines and everything. I guess it was because there was hardly any magic at school, because we were too far from the Wall. I could weave shadows and do tricks with light sometimes, but only when the wind blew from the north. Sometimes I felt like part of me was asleep, not being able to reach the Charter."

He fell silent, still staring at the embers. After a few minutes, Lirael spoke again. "Getting back to what we're going to do," she said hesitantly. "I was going to Qyrre, to get the constables or the Royal Guard there to escort me to Edge. But it seems that Hedge already knows about me—about us—so that can't be a very sensible thing to do. I mean I still have to get to the Red Lake, but not so openly. It would be stupid to just tie up at the Qyrre jetty and get out, wouldn't it?"

"Yes," agreed the Dog, looking up at her, proud that she had worked this out for herself. "There was a smell about Hedge, a smell of power strong enough for me to catch when Lirael escaped him. I think he is more than a necromancer. But whatever he is, he is clever, and has long prepared to move against the Kingdom. He will have servants among the living as well as the Dead."

Sameth didn't answer for a moment. He tore his gaze away from the fire, frowning as he saw Mogget's sleeping form. Now that Nicholas was definitely known to be in the clutches of the Enemy, Sam didn't know what to do. Rescuing Nicholas had seemed like a good idea back in the safety of his tower room—simpler, uncomplicated.

"We can't go to Qyrre," he said. "I was thinking we should go to the House—Abhorsen's House, I mean. I can send message-hawks from there, and we can . . . uh . . . get stuff for the journey. Mail hauberks. A better sword for me."

"And it would be safe," said the Dog, with a penetrating look at Sam.

Sam looked away, unable to meet the Dog's eyes. Somehow she knew his secret thoughts. Half of him said he would have to go on. Half of him said that he couldn't. He felt sick with the tension of it. Wherever he went, he could not escape being the Abhorsen-in-Waiting, and all too soon he would be shown to be an imposter.

"I think that's a good idea," said Lirael. "It's on the Long Cliffs, isn't it? We can strike west from there, staying off the roads. Are there any horses at the House? I can't ride, but I could wear a Charter-skin while you—"

"My horse is dead," interrupted Sam, suddenly white-faced. "I don't want another one!"

He got up abruptly and limped out into the darkness, staring at the Ratterlin, watching the silver ripples in its dark expanse. He could hear Lirael and that Dog creature—which was too much like Mogget for comfort—talking behind him, too low to make out the words. But he knew they were talking about him, and he felt ashamed.

"He's a spoilt brat!" whispered Lirael crossly. She wasn't used to this sort of behavior. On her explorations she had done what she wanted, and in the Library there was strict discipline and a chain of command. Sam had provided useful information, but otherwise he seemed to be a nuisance. "I was just trying to make some sort of plan. Maybe we should leave him behind."

"He is troubled," acknowledged the Dog. "But he has also been through much that tested him beyond all expectation—and he is hurt and afraid. He will be better tomorrow, and in the days to come."

"I hope so," said Lirael. Now that she knew more about Nicholas, the Lightning Trap, and the attacks of the Dead upon Sam, she realized she would probably need all the help she could get. The entire Kingdom would need all the help it could get.

"It is his job, after all," she added. "Being the Abhorsen-in-Waiting. I should be safely back at the Glacier while he deals with Hedge and whatever else is out there!"

"If the Abhorsen and the King are correct about Hedge's plans, nowhere will be safe," said the Dog. "And all who bear the Blood must defend the Charter."

"Oh, Dog!" Lirael said plaintively, giving the hound a hug. "Why is everything so difficult?"

"It just is," said the Dog, woofling in her ear. "But sleep will make it seem easier. A new day will bring new sights and smells."

"How will that help?" grumbled Lirael. But she lay down on the ground, dragging her pack over to use as a pillow. It was too hot for a blanket, even with the slight breeze off the river. Hot and awfully humid, with mosquitoes and sand-flies into the bargain. Summer had not yet begun as far as the Kingdom's calendar was concerned, but the weather had paid no attention to human reckoning. And there was no sign of a cooling rainstorm.

Lirael swatted a mosquito, then turned her head as Sam came back and rummaged in his saddlebag. He was getting something out—a bright, sparkling object. Lirael sat up as she saw it was a jeweled frog. A frog with wings.

"I'm sorry I behaved badly before," Sam mumbled, setting down the flying frog. "This will help with the mosquitoes."

Lirael didn't need to ask how. It became clear immediately as the frog executed a backwards somersault and used its tongue to collect two particularly large and blood-laden mosquitoes.

"Ingenious," said the Dog sleepily, lifting her head for a moment from the comfortable hole she'd scratched out to sleep in.

"I made it for my mother," said Sam, self-pity evident in his voice. "That's about the only thing I'm really good at. Making things."

Lirael nodded, watching the frog wreak havoc on the local insect population. It moved effortlessly, bronze wings beating as fast as a hummingbird's, making a soft sound like tightly closed shutters moving slightly in the wind.

"Mogget had to kill her," Sam said suddenly, looking back into the fire. "My horse, Sprout. I pushed her too hard. She foundered. I couldn't do the mercy stroke. Mogget had to cut her throat, to make sure the Dead didn't kill her and grow stronger."

"It doesn't sound like there was much choice," said Lirael uncomfortably. "I mean, there was nothing else you could have done."

Sam was silent, staring at the few red coals that remained, seeing the shapes and patterns of orange, black, and red. He could hear the Ratterlin's subdued roar all around, the wheezing breath of the sleeping Dog. He could practically feel Lirael sitting there, three or four steps away, waiting for him to say something.

"I should have done it," he whispered. "But I was afraid. Afraid of Death. I always have been."

Lirael didn't say anything, feeling even more uncomfortable now. No one had ever shared something so personal with her

before, least of all something like this! He was the Abhorsen's
son, the Abhorsen-in-Waiting. It simply wasn't possible that he
could be afraid of Death. That would be like a Clayr who was
afraid of the Sight. That was beyond imagining.

"You're tired and wounded," she said finally. "You should
rest. You'll feel better in the morning."

Sam turned to look at her but kept his head down, not
meeting her gaze.

"You went into Death," muttered Sam. "Were you afraid?"

"Yes," acknowledged Lirael. "But I followed what it said in
the book."

"The book?" asked Sam, shivering despite the heat. "*The
Book of the Dead*?"

"No," replied Lirael. She'd never even heard of *The Book of
the Dead*. "*The Book of Remembrance and Forgetting*. It deals with
Death only because that's where a Remembrancer has to go to
look into the past."

"Never heard of it," muttered Sam. He looked at his saddlebags as if they were bulging poison sacs. "I'm supposed to be
studying *The Book of the Dead*, but I can't stand looking at it. I
tried to leave it behind, but it followed me, with the bells. I . . .
I can't get away from it, but I can't look at it, either. And now I'll
probably need them both to save Nick. It's so bloody unfair. I
never asked to be the Abhorsen-in-Waiting!"

I never asked for my mother to walk away from me when I
was five, or to be a Clayr without the Sight, thought Lirael. He
was young for his age, this Prince Sameth, and, as the Dog said,
he was tired and wounded. Let him have his bout of self-pity. If
he didn't snap out of it tomorrow, the Dog could bite him. That
had always worked on her.

So instead of saying what she thought, Lirael reached out to
touch the bandolier lying at Sam's side.

"Do you mind if I look at the bells?" she asked. She could feel their power, even as they lay there quiescent. "How do you use them?"

"*The Book of the Dead* explains their use," he said reluctantly. "But you can't really practice with them. They can only be used in earnest. No! Don't . . . please don't take them out."

"I'll be careful," said Lirael, surprised at his reaction. He had gone pale, quite white in the darkness, and was shivering. "I do know a bit about them already, because they're like my pipes."

Sam shuffled back a few steps, the panic rising in him. If she dropped a bell or accidentally rang one, they might both be hurled into Death. He was afraid of that, desperately afraid. At the same time, he felt a sudden urge to let her take the bells, as if that might somehow break their connection with him.

"I suppose you can look at them," he said hesitantly. "If you really want to."

Lirael nodded thoughtfully, running her fingers over the smooth mahogany handles and the rich, beeswax-treated leather. She had a sudden urge to put on the bandolier and walk into Death to try the bells. Her little panpipes were a toy in comparison.

Sam watched her touch the bells and shivered, remembering how cold and heavy they had felt upon his chest. Lirael's scarf had fallen back, letting her long black hair tumble out. There was something about her face in the firelight, something about the way her eyes reflected the light, that made Sam feel odd. He had the sense that he'd seen her before. But that was impossible, as he'd never been to the Glacier, and she'd never left it until now.

"Could I also have a look at *The Book of the Dead*?" asked Lirael, unable to disguise the eagerness in her voice.

Sam stared at her, his mind paralyzed for a moment. "*The Book of the Dead* could d-d-destroy you," he said, his voice betraying him with a stutter. "It's not to be trifled with."

"I know," said Lirael. "I can't explain, but I feel that I must read it."

Sam considered. The Clayr were cousins of the royal line and the Abhorsen, so he supposed Lirael had the Bloodright. Enough not to get destroyed straightaway. She had also studied *The Book of Remembrance and Forgetting*, whatever that was, which seemed to have made her something of a necromancer, at least as far as traveling in Death was concerned. And her Charter mark was true and clear.

"It's there," he said roughly, pointing at the appropriate saddlebag. He hesitated, then backed away, till he was a good ten paces from the fire, closer to the river, with both the Dog and Mogget between him and Lirael—and the book. He lay down, purposefully looking away from Lirael. He didn't want to even see the book. His flying frog jumped after him and rapidly cleared the mosquitoes away from his makeshift bed.

Sam heard the straps of the saddlebags being opened behind his back. Then came the soft brilliance of a Charter light, the snap of silver clasps—and the ruffling of pages. There was no explosion, no sudden fire of destruction.

Sam let out his breath, closed his eyes, and willed himself to sleep. He would be at Abhorsen's House within a few days. Safe. He could stay there. Lirael could go on alone.

Except, his conscience said as he drifted off, Nicholas is *your* friend. It's *your* job to deal with necromancers. And it's *your* parents who would expect you to face the Enemy.

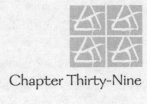

Chapter Thirty-Nine

HIGH BRIDGE

S AM FELT MUCH better the next morning, physically, at least. His leg was greatly improved by Lirael's healing magic. But mentally he felt very nervous about the responsibilities that once again weighed upon him.

Lirael, on the other hand, was physically exhausted but mentally very invigorated. She'd stayed up all night reading *The Book of the Dead*, finishing the last page just as the sun rose, its heat quickly banishing the last few cool hours of the night.

Much of the book was already lost to her. Lirael knew she'd read the whole thing, or had at least read every page she'd turned. But she had no sense of the totality of the text. *The Book of the Dead* would require many re-readings, she realized, as it could offer something new each time. In many ways, she felt it recognized her lack of knowledge, and had given her the bare minimum she was capable of understanding. The book had also raised more questions for her about Death, and the Dead, than it had answered. Or perhaps it had answered, but she would not remember until she needed to know.

Only the last page stayed fixed in her mind, the last page with its single line.

Does the walker choose the path, or the path choose the walker?

She thought about that question as she stuck her head in the river to try to wake herself up, and was still thinking about it as she retied her scarf and straightened her waistcoat. She was reluctant to part with the bells and *The Book of the Dead*, but she finally returned them to Sam's saddlebags as he finished his own morning ablutions farther downstream, behind some of the island's sparse foliage.

They didn't talk as they loaded the boat, not so much as a word about the book or the bells, or Sam's confession of the previous night. As Lirael raised *Finder*'s sail and they set off downriver again, the only sound was the flapping of the canvas as she slowly hauled in the mainsheet, accompanied by the rush of water under the keel. Everyone seemed to agree that it was too early for conversation. Especially Mogget. He hadn't even bothered to wake up and had had to be carried aboard by Sam.

It wasn't until they were well under way that Lirael passed around some of her plate-sized cinnamon cakes, breaking them into manageable hunks. The Dog ate hers in one and a half gulps, but Sam looked at his askance.

"Do I risk my teeth on it or just suck it to death?" he asked, with an attempt at a smile. Clearly he felt better, Lirael thought. It was better than the dismal self-pity of the night before.

"You could give it to me," suggested the Dog, without moving her gaze from the hand that held the cake.

"I don't think so," said Sam, taking a bite and making an effort to chew. Then he held out the uneaten half and said, with his mouth full, "But I'll trade you this half for a close look at your collar."

Before he finished speaking, the Dog lunged forward, gulped the cake, and put her chin on Sam's thigh, her neck in easy reach.

"Why do you want to look at the Dog's collar?" asked Lirael.

"It has Charter marks I've never seen," replied Sam, reaching down to touch it. It looked like leather with Charter marks set upon it. But as his fingers met the surface, Sam realized it wasn't leather at all. It was nothing but Charter marks, a great sea of marks, stretching into forever. He felt as if he could push his whole hand into the collar, or dive in himself. And within that great pool of magic, there were very few Charter marks that he actually knew.

Reluctantly, he pulled his hand away, and then, on a whim, scratched the Dog's head between the ears. She felt exactly as a normal dog should, just as Mogget felt like a cat. But both were intensely magical beings. Only Mogget's collar was a binding-spell of great force, and the Dog's collar was something very different, almost like a part of the Charter itself. It had something of the same feel as a Charter Stone.

"Excellent," sighed the Dog, responding to the scratching. "But do my back as well, please."

Sam complied, and the Dog stretched out under his fingers, luxuriating in the treatment. Lirael watched, suddenly struck by the realization that she'd never before seen the Dog with another person. The hound had always disappeared when any other people were around.

"Some of the Charter marks in your collar are familiar," said Sam idly, as he scratched and watched the morning sun play across the water. It was going to be another very hot day, and he'd lost his hat. It must have come off when he fell down the steps of the mill's landing stage.

The Dog didn't answer, merely wriggling to direct Sam's scratching hand farther down her back.

"Only I can't think where I've seen them," continued Sam, pausing to concentrate. He didn't know what the Charter marks were for, but he had seen them somewhere else. Not in a grimoire or a Charter Stone, but on some object or something solid. "Not in Mogget's collar—those are quite different."

"You think too much," growled the Dog, though not angrily. "Just keep scratching. You can do under my chin as well."

"You're a very demanding Dog for a supposed servant of the Clayr," said Sam. He looked at Lirael and added, "Is she always like this?"

"Pardon?" asked Lirael, who had started thinking about *The Book of the Dead* again. It took an effort for her to pay attention to Sam, and for a moment she wished she were back in the Great Library, where no one spoke to her unless they had to.

Sam repeated his question, and Lirael looked at the Dog. "She's usually worse," she replied. "If it's not food she's after, it's scratching. She's incorrigible."

"That's why I'm the *Disreputable* Dog," said the Dog smugly, wagging her tail. "Not just the Dog. But you'd better stop scratching now, Prince Sameth."

"Why?"

"Because I can smell people," replied the Dog, forcing herself up. "Beyond the next bend."

Sam and Lirael looked, but couldn't see any sign of habitation or another vessel on the river. The Ratterlin had turned into a wide bend, and the riverbanks were rising into high bluffs of pinkish stone, obscuring the view ahead.

"I can hear roaring, too," added the Dog, who was now perched on the bow, her ears erect and quivering.

"Like rapids?" asked Lirael nervously. She trusted *Finder*, but didn't fancy shooting any waterfalls in her—or in any boat, for that matter.

Sam stood up next to her, keeping one hand on the boom for balance, and tried to see ahead. But whatever was there lay beyond the bend. He took another look at the riverbanks, noting that they'd risen up to become real cliffs, and that the river was getting narrower, and was perhaps only a few hundred yards wide ahead.

"It's okay," he said, and then, seeing her puzzlement at the Ancelstierran expression, he added, "I mean it's all right. We're coming to the High Bridge Gorge. The river gets a lot narrower, and faster, but not so bad that boats can't get through. And the river is lower than it should be at this time of year, so I bet it won't be too fast."

"Oh, High Bridge," said Lirael, with considerable relief. She'd read about High Bridge, and had even seen a hand-colored etching of it. "We actually sail under the town, don't we?"

Sam nodded, thinking. He'd been to the town of High Bridge only once, over a decade ago, with his parents. They'd reached it overland, not on the Ratterlin, but he did remember Touchstone pointing out the guardboats that patrolled upstream of the town, and in the pool beyond High Bridge, where the river widened again. They not only kept at least that part of the Ratterlin free of river pirates but also exacted tolls from traders. Ellimere had probably already given the river-guards orders to "escort" him ashore and return him to Belisaere.

Which would be one way of reaching safety, he thought, and it would make Ellimere responsible for whatever happened next. But he would have to face up to his fight with the constables, and it would mean a delay in any attempt to rescue Nick. And he had no doubt Lirael would choose to go on without him.

"We do, don't we?" repeated Lirael. "Sail under it?"

"What?" asked Sam, who was still wondering what would be the best thing for him to do. "Yes . . . yes, we do. Um, I'd better lie down under a blanket or something before we're in sight of the town."

"Why?" asked Lirael and the Dog at the same time.

"Because he's a truant Prince," yawned Mogget, walking up and stretching on his back paws to look ahead. "He ran away, and his sister wants him back for the Belisaere Festival, to play the Summer Fool or some such."

"The Bird of Dawning," corrected Sam with embarrassment as he got down into the scuppers, ready to hide.

"When you said you'd left Belisaere to look for Nicholas, I thought you meant you'd been sent by your parents!" exclaimed Lirael, unconsciously taking on the tone she used to scold the Dog. "The way I've been sent by the Clayr. You mean they don't even know what you're doing?"

"Er . . . no," replied Sam sheepishly. "Though Dad might have guessed that I've gone to meet Nick. If they know I've gone, that is. It depends where they are in Ancelstierre. But I'll explain when we send messages. The only problem is that Ellimere has probably ordered all the Guard and the Constabulary to send me back to Belisaere if they can."

"Great," said Lirael. "I was counting on your being useful if we did need to get help along the way. A royal Prince, I thought—"

"Well, I could still be useful—" Sam began to say, but at that moment they rounded the bend, and the Dog let out a warning bark. Sure enough, a guardboat was moored to a large buoy mid river—a long, slim galley of thirty-two oars in addition to its square-rigged sail. As *Finder* appeared round the bend, a sailor cast off from the buoy, and others raised the red sail, the golden tower of the royal service gleaming upon it.

Sam hunkered down still lower, pulling the blanket across his face. Something touched his cheek as he settled down, and he started, thinking it was a rat. Then he realized Mogget was slinking under the blanket, too.

"No sense in their wondering why an aristocratic cat would share deck space with a mangy dog," whispered Mogget, close to

Sam's ear under the stifling blanket. "I wonder if they'll do that old trick city guards do with hay wagons, when they suspect smuggling."

"What's that?" Sam whispered back, though he had the feeling he didn't want to know.

"They stick everything with spears to make sure there's nothing—or no one—hidden there," said Mogget absently. "Mind if I move under your arm?"

"They won't do that," said Sam, firmly. "They'll see this is one of the Clayr's boats."

"Will they? They might—but Lirael doesn't look like a Clayr, does she? You yourself suspected her of stealing this boat."

"Quiet down there," woofed the Dog, close by Sam's other ear. Then he felt her bulk settle in at his side—on top of the blanket. It moved again after that, as Lirael tugged on it so it looked like covered baggage rather than a body.

Nothing happened for at least ten minutes. Mogget seemed to go back to sleep, and the Dog rested more of her weight against Sam's side. Sam found that while all he could see was the underside of the blanket, he could hear all sorts of sounds he hadn't noticed before: the creak of the clinker-built hull, the splash of the bow wave, the faint hum of the rigging, and the clatter of the boom as they turned into the wind and stopped.

Then he heard another sound—the heavy splash of many oars moving in unison, and a voice calling the time. "With a will, and a way, that's a stroke and a lay, with a will, and way . . . oars up and in!"

There came a shout, so loud and close it almost made Sam flinch.

"What vessel, and where are you bound?"

"The Clayr's boat *Finder*," Lirael said, but her voice was lost in the rush of the river. She forced herself to shout, surprised by the strength of her own voice. "The Clayr's boat *Finder*. Bound for Qyrre."

"Oh, aye, I know *Finder*," replied the voice, less formal now. "And she obviously knows your hand, Mistress—so you may pass. Will you be stopping to climb up to town?"

"No," said Lirael. "I travel on urgent business for the Clayr."

"No doubt, no doubt," replied the guardboat commander, nodding at Lirael across the forty feet of water that separated the two vessels. "There's trouble brewing, for sure. You'd best beware of the riverbanks, for there have been reports of Dead creatures. Just like the old days, before the return of the King."

"I'll be careful," shouted Lirael. "Thank you for the warning, Captain. May I go on now?"

"Pass, friend," shouted the guard, waving his hand. At that motion, the oars dropped in again, the men straining at their benches. The steers-woman put the rudder over, and the guardboat drove hard away, bow slicing through the current. Lirael saw something metallic glisten under the water as the galley rose up, and she realized it was a long steel ram. The guardboat clearly had the means to sink any craft that didn't stop at its hail.

As they passed, one of the guards looked at Lirael strangely, and she saw his hand creeping to the string of his bow. But none of the others so much as looked at her, and after a moment, the strange guard turned away, leaving Lirael with a feeling of unease. For a moment, she felt she had smelled the metallic tang of Free Magic. She looked at the Dog, and saw that she was staring back at the same guard, all the hair on her back on end.

Sam listened to the steady swish of the oars as the galley drew away, and the receding voice of the cantor. "Are they gone?"

"Yes," said Lirael slowly. "But you'd better stay hidden. They're still in sight, and we're coming up to High Bridge now. And there was something not quite right about one of them. I caught the hint of Free Magic, as if it might not have been a man at all."

"It can't have been Free Magic," said Sam. "The river is flowing too strongly."

"Unlike the Dead, not all things of Free Magic turn back from running water," said Mogget. "Only those with common sense."

"The cat speaks truly," added the Disreputable Dog. "Running water is no bar to those of the Third Kindred, or anything infused with the essence of the Nine. I would not expect such things here, but I did smell something of that ilk aboard the guardboat, Prince Sameth. Something that had only the semblance of a man. Fortunately, it did not dare reveal its presence among so many. But we must be on our guard."

Sam sighed and fought back the temptation to peel the blanket aside just a little bit. It was very hard to lie in darkness going into possible danger. And he'd never seen High Bridge from the water, and it was supposed to be one of the most spectacular sights in the Kingdom.

Lirael certainly thought so. Despite the increasing current, she was content to let *Finder* steer, choosing to gape, instead.

High Bridge had originally been an enormous natural bridge of stone, resting upon the cliffs of the gorge, with the Ratterlin rushing under it four hundred forty feet below. Over the centuries, the natural grandeur of the bridge had been augmented by the human buildings upon it. The first of the buildings constructed there was a castle, built to take advantage of the protection offered by so much deep running water beneath it. No Dead creatures could come against its walls, for they must also pass above the river's swift waters.

This had proved to be an enormous attraction during the years of the Interregnum, when the great majority of Charter Stones in the Kingdom were broken and the villages that depended upon them for safety destroyed, leaving the Dead and those in league with them free to do as they chose. Within a few years, the original castle had been surrounded by houses, inns, warehouses, windmills, forges, manufactories, stables, taverns, and all manner of other buildings. Many were actually dug down into the bridge itself, for the stone was several hundred feet thick. The bridge was more than a mile broad, too, though not very long, the distance between the eastern and western cliffs once being famously covered in a single bowshot by the archer Aylward Blackhair.

Lirael was staring up at this strange metropolis when she heard a woman's shout, seemingly from the figurehead at the front of the boat. At the same time *Finder*'s tiller shot out of her hand, pushing hard over to the left. Instantly, the boom swung violently across and the boat heeled over to the right, her starboard quarter almost in the river, spray and water foaming in across the side.

Sam found himself piled up against the starboard rail. Somehow both Mogget and the Dog had ended up on top of him, along with what felt like everything else. And water was pouring in on him in bucketloads.

Sam thrust his hands out of the blanket and clawed along the side of the boat, reaching out for the rail. But his hands went straight into rushing water, and Sam realized that *Finder* was heeled over so far she must be about to capsize. Desperately he struggled to free himself of Mogget, Dog, baggage, and blanket, at the same time as he shouted, "Lirael! Lirael! What's happening?"

Chapter Forty

L IRAEL WAS TOO busy pulling herself back into the boat to answer. The boom had caught her on the shoulder, knocking her overboard before she even knew what was happening. Fortunately, she'd managed to grab the rail and hang on, looking up fearfully as *Finder*'s hull towered above her, so far over it seemed certain the boat would capsize—with Lirael underneath.

Then, as quickly as she'd heeled over, *Finder* righted herself, the sudden lurch helping Lirael fling herself back in, to end up in a terrible tangle of blanket, Sam, Dog, Mogget, lots of odds and ends, and sloshing water.

At the same time, *Finder* passed under High Bridge, moving out of sunlight into the strange, cool twilight, as the Ratterlin streamed into the vast tunnel made by the bridge of stone high overhead.

"What happened?" spluttered Sam when he finally got free of the wet blanket. Lirael was already by the tiller, completely drenched, her hand gripped around something projecting from the stern.

"I thought *Finder* had gone mad," said Lirael. "Till I saw this."

Sam shuffled back, cursing the blanket that was still tangled around his legs. It wasn't exactly dark under High Bridge, because light did come in from either end, but it was a strange light, like sun slowly breaking through fog, soft and diffused by the water. The Dog rushed over to look, too, but Mogget sniffed and padded to the bow, to begin the long process of licking himself dry.

The Dog saw what Lirael held before Sam did, and growled. There was a splintered hole through the port side of the stern, under the gunwale, where Lirael had been sitting before *Finder* had knocked her over with the boom. In her hand Lirael held the crossbow bolt that had made the hole. Its shaft was painted white, and it was fletched with raven feathers.

"It must have just missed you!" exclaimed Sam, as he put three of his fingers through the hole.

"Only thanks to *Finder*," said Lirael, stroking the tiller gently. "Look at what it did to my poor boat."

"It would have gone straight through you, even if you'd had armor on," said Sam grimly. "That's a war bolt—not a hunting quarrel. And a very good shot. Too good to be natural."

"They'll probably try again on the other side—or before," said Lirael, looking up with alarm at the stone high above them. "Are there any openings above us, do you know?"

"No idea," said Sam. He followed her gaze and could see only unbroken yellow stone. But the bridge was several hundred feet above them, and the light bad. There could be any number of dark openings he just couldn't see.

"I can't see any, Mistress," growled the Dog as she craned her head back, too. "But we'll be through in a few minutes, with this current."

"Do you know how to cast an arrow ward?" Sam asked Lirael. The current was indeed taking them along at a rapid rate, and the bright, sunlit arch that marked the other side of the bridge was getting closer all too quickly.

"No," said Lirael nervously. "I was probably supposed to. I skipped fighting arts quite a lot."

"All right," Sam said. "Why don't we swap places? I'll sit here and steer, but with an arrow ward at my back. You get ready with your bow, prepared to shoot back. Mogget—you've got the best eyes—you spot for Lirael."

"The Horrible Hound, or whatever she calls herself, can do that," declared Mogget, from the bow. "I'm going back to sleep."

"But what if the ward doesn't work?" protested Lirael. "You're already wounded—"

"It'll work," said Sam, moving up, so Lirael had little choice but to get out of the way. "I used to practice with the Guard every day. Only a spelled arrow or bolt can get through."

"But it might be spelled," said Lirael, quickly re-stringing her bow with a dry string from a waxed packet. The black and white bolt had not carried any scent of magic, but that did not mean the next would be unspelled.

"It still has to be stronger than the ward," said Sam confi-dently—much more confidently than he actually felt. He had cast arrow wards many times, but never in an actual fight. Touchstone had taught him the spell when Sam was only six years old, and the arrows fired to test it were mere toys with cushioned heads made from the rags of old pajamas. Later, he had graduated to blunted arrows. He had never been tested against a war bolt that could punch through an inch of plate steel.

Sam sat by the tiller and turned to face the stern. Then he began to reach for the Charter marks he needed. He usually used his sword to trace the ward in the air, but he had been taught to use only his hands if need be, and that worked just as well.

Lirael saw his hands and fingers move swiftly and surely, Charter marks beginning to glow in the air. They hung there, shining, just beyond the arc his fingertips were describing. Whatever else he might be, she thought, Sam was a very powerful Charter Mage. And he might be afraid of Death and the Dead, but he wasn't a coward. She wouldn't want to be sitting there with only a spell between her and the razored edges of a crossbow bolt traveling with killing speed. She shivered. If it were not for *Finder*, she would probably already be dead, or bleeding to death in the scuppers.

Lirael's stomach muscles tightened at that thought, and she paid careful attention to nocking her arrow. Whoever the hidden killer was, Lirael would try her best to make sure he didn't get more than one shot.

Sam finished describing the full circle of the arrow ward but remained crouched at the stern. His hands continued to move, drawing Charter marks that fled his fingers to join the glowing circle above and behind him.

"Have to keep it going," he said, panting. "Bit of a drawback. Get ready! We'll be out in a sec—"

They suddenly burst out into sunshine, and Sam instinctively shrank to present a smaller target.

Lirael, kneeling by the mast and looking up, was momentarily blinded. In that second, the assassin fired. The bolt flew true. Lirael screamed a warning, but the sound was still in her throat when the black-feathered quarrel hit the arrow ward—and vanished.

"Quick!" gasped Sam, the strain of maintaining the spell showing in his face and straining chest.

Lirael was already searching for the crossbowman. But there were many windows and openings up there, either in the stone of the Bridge itself or in the buildings that were built upon it. And there were people all over the place, too, in windows, on balconies, leaning over railings, swinging on platforms roped to plaster walls. . . . She couldn't even begin to find the shooter.

Then the Dog moved up next to Lirael, raised her head—and howled. It was an eerie, high tone that seemed to echo across the water, up the sides of the river gorge, and everywhere across the town itself. It sounded as if scores of wolves had suddenly appeared on the river, in the town, and all around.

Everywhere, people stopped moving and stared. Except in one window, about halfway up. Lirael saw someone there suddenly fling the shutters wide open, one hand still clutching a crossbow.

She drew and shot as he stood there, but her arrow was caught by an errant breeze and went wide, striking the wall above his head. As Lirael nocked another arrow, the assassin stood up in the window frame, precariously balanced on the sill.

The Dog drew breath and howled again. The assassin dropped his crossbow so he could jam his fingers in his ears. But even then he couldn't block out the terrible sound, and his legs moved of their own accord, stepping out into space. Desperately, he tried to hurl his upper body backwards into the room, but he seemed to have no control at all below the waist. A moment later, he fell, following the crossbow down four hundred feet into the water. He kept his fingers in his ears all the way down, and his legs kept moving even though there was nothing to tread but air.

The Dog stopped howling as the assassin's body hit the water, and both Sam and Lirael flinched as they felt him die. They watched the ripples spread till they met *Finder*'s wash and disappeared.

"What did you do?" asked Lirael, carefully replacing her bow. She'd never seen or felt anyone actually die before. She had only attended Farewells, with the death made distant, all wrapped up with ceremony and tradition.

"I made him walk," growled the Dog, sitting back on her haunches, a ridge of hair along her back stiff and angry. "He would have killed you if he could, Mistress."

Lirael nodded and gave the Dog a quick hug. Sam watched

them warily. That howl was pure Free Magic, with no Charter Magic in it at all. The Dog seemed friendly and appeared to be devoted to Lirael, but he could not forget how dangerous she was. There was also something about the howl that reminded him of something, some magic he had experienced that he couldn't quite place.

At least Mogget's case was straightforward. He was a Free Magic creature, bound and safe while he wore the collar. The Dog appeared to be a free-willed blend of the two magics, which was completely beyond anything Sam had ever heard about. Not for the first time, he wished that his mother were here. Sabriel would know what the Dog was, he felt sure.

"We'd better swap places again," said Lirael urgently. "There's another guardboat ahead."

Sam quickly scrunched down, on the opposite side from the Dog, who looked at him and grinned, showing a very sharp, very white, and very large set of teeth. Sam forced himself to smile back, remembering the advice he'd been given about dogs when he was a boy. Never let them know you're afraid. . . .

"Ugh! There's a lot of water here," he complained as he lay down, squelching, and drew the sodden blanket towards him. "I should have bailed it out in the tunnel."

He was just about to draw the blanket over his face when he saw Mogget, still sunning and grooming himself on the bow.

"Mogget!" he commanded. "You should hide, too."

Mogget looked pointedly at the water swishing around Sam's legs and stuck out his small pink tongue.

"Too wet for me," he said. "Besides, the guardboat will stop us for sure. They will have been signaled from the town after this canine show-off's demonstration of vocal talents—though hopefully no one will recognize what that actually was. So you might as well sit up."

Sam groaned and sloshed upright. "You might have told me before I lay down," he said bitterly, picking up a tin cup and beginning to bail.

"It would be best if we can get past without being stopped," the Dog commented, sniffing the air. "There may be more enemies concealed aboard this guardboat, too."

"There's more room to maneuver up ahead," said Lirael. "But I don't know if it's enough to evade the guardboat."

The eastern side of the river was the main river-port for High Bridge. Twelve jetties of various lengths thrust out into the river, most of them cluttered with trading boats, whose masts made a forest of bare poles. Behind the jetties, there was a quay carved into the stone of the gorge, a long terrace cluttered with cargoes being readied to go aboard the boats or up to the town. Beyond the quay, there were several steep stairways that ran up the cliff-face to the town, in between the derrick cables that lifted up the multitude of boxes and chests, barrels and bales.

But the western side of the river was open, save for a few trading boats ahead of them downstream, and the one guardboat, which was already slipping its mooring. If they could get past the guardboat and keep ahead, there was nothing to stop them.

"They've got at least twenty archers on that boat," said Sam doubtfully. "Do you think we can just sail past?"

"I suppose it depends how many—if any—of them are agents of the Enemy," said Lirael as she hauled the mainsheet tighter, trimming the sail for more speed. "If they're real guards, they won't shoot at a royal Prince and a Daughter of the Clayr. Will they?"

"I suppose it's worth a try," muttered Sam, who couldn't think of an alternative plan. If the guards were real guards, the worst that would happen was that he would be returned to Belisaere. If they weren't, it would be best to stay as far away as possible. "What if the wind drops?"

"We'll whistle one up," said Lirael. "Are you much of a weather-worker?"

"Not by my mother's standards," replied Sam. Weather magic was mostly performed with whistled Charter marks, and he was no great whistler. "But I can probably raise a wind."

"This is not a brilliant plan, even by your mother's standards," commented Mogget, who was watching the guardboat raise its sail, obviously intent on an intercept. "Lirael doesn't look like a Daughter of the Clayr. Sameth looks like a scarecrow, not a royal Prince. And the commander of this guardboat may not recognize *Finder*. So even if they *are* all real guards, they probably will just feather us with arrows if we try to sail past. Personally, I don't want to be made into a pincushion."

"I don't think we have a choice," said Sam slowly. "If even two or three of them belong to the Enemy, they will attack. If we can conjure up enough of a wind, we might be able to stay out of bowshot anyway."

"Fine!" muttered Mogget. "Wet, cold, and full of holes. Another fun day on the river."

Lirael and Sam looked at each other. Lirael took a deep breath. Charter marks flowered in her mind, and she let them flow into her lungs and throat, circling there. Then she whistled, and the pure notes leapt up into the sky.

Answering the whistle, the river behind them darkened. Ripples and white peaks sprang up across the water and streaked across towards *Finder* and her waiting sail.

A few seconds later, the wind hit. The boat heeled over and picked up speed, the rigging adding its own whistle at the sudden pressure. Mogget hissed his lack of appreciation and hastily sprang back from the bow as spray flew over where he'd been a moment before.

Still Lirael whistled, and Sam joined in, their combined weather spell weaving the wind behind *Finder*'s quarter, at the same time stripping it away from the guardboat, whose sail lay limp and airless.

But the guardboat had oars, and expert rowers. The cantor sped his call, and the oars dipped in faster rhythm as the galley rushed forward to intercept *Finder*, water suddenly foaming around its bow, the bright metal of the ram gleaming in the sun.

Chapter Forty-One

FREE MAGIC AND THE FLESH OF SWINE

"THEY'LL BE WITHIN bowshot in a few minutes," warned Mogget gloomily, gauging with a jaundiced eye the distance to the galley, and then the proximity of the western shore. "I suppose we'll end up having to swim for our miserable lives."

Lirael and Sam exchanged glances of concern, reluctant to agree aloud with the cat. Despite their spell-woven wind and their current scudding run across the water, the galley was still too fast. They were as close as they dared to the shore, and were rapidly running out of river to maneuver in.

"I guess we'd better heave to and risk the presence of enemies among the guards," said Sam, who was acutely aware that he had already injured two constables. "I don't want any of us to get shot because they think we're smugglers or something, and I definitely don't want to hurt any guards. Once they find out I am who I am, I'll order them to let you go. And who knows? I might be lucky. Maybe Ellimere hasn't ordered my arrest after all."

"I don't know—" Lirael started to say, her voice anxious. There was still a slight chance they might get past. But she'd hardly said a word when the Dog barked in interruption.

"No! There are at least three or four Free Magic creatures aboard that boat! We mustn't stop!"

"Smells all right to me," said Mogget, shuddering as more spray spumed in over the bow. "But then I don't have your famous nose. However, as I can see a half dozen archers getting ready to shoot, perhaps you actually can smell something."

Sam saw that Mogget was quite correct. The guardboat was angling to cross their path, but six archers were already formed up on the forward deck, arrows nocked. Obviously they intended to shoot first and make polite enquiries later.

"Are the archers human?" asked Sam quickly.

The Dog sniffed the air again before replying. "I cannot tell. I think most of them are. But the captain—the one with the plumed hat—has only the semblance of a man. It is a construct, made from Free Magic and the flesh of swine. That odor I cannot mistake."

"We have to show the human archers who they're shooting at!" Sam exclaimed. "I should have brought a shield with the royal blazon or something. They'd never dare shoot at us then, even if they're ordered to."

"Of course!" said Lirael, suddenly slapping herself on the forehead. "Here, take this!"

"What!" shouted Sam, throwing himself back to clutch at the tiller as Lirael let go. "What do I do? I don't know how to sail!"

"Don't worry, she steers herself," Lirael shouted back as she crawled forward to the storage box in the forepeak. It was a matter of only twelve feet, but Lirael found it hard going, since *Finder* was heeled over at a sharp angle and the boat kept leaping up and then coming down with a bone-jarring smack every few yards.

"Are you sure?" Sam shouted again. He could feel the pressure on the tiller, and he felt that only his white-knuckled grip was keeping them from veering sharply into the riverbank. Experimentally, he opened his fingers for a second, ready to grab hold again immediately. But nothing happened. *Finder* kept her course, the tiller barely moving. Sam sighed in relief, but his sigh became a choking cough as he saw a flight of arrows snap away from the guardboat—straight at him.

"Too far yet," said the Dog, casting a professional eye on the arrows' flight, and sure enough, the arrows plunged into the water a good fifty yards away.

"Not for long," grumbled Mogget. He jumped yet again to try to find a drier spot. He seemed to have found it near the mast when a slight twitch of the tiller—without Sam's cooperation—caught a small wave and neatly sloshed it in and over his back.

"I hate you!" hissed Mogget in the general direction of the boat's figurehead as the water drained away from his feet. "At least that rowboat looks dry. Why don't we just let ourselves be captured? We've got only the Dog's nose to say the captain is a construct."

"They're shooting at us, Mogget!" said Sam, who wasn't entirely sure whether Mogget was joking.

"There are two other constructs on board besides the captain," growled the Dog, whose nose was still vigorously sampling the air. She was getting bigger, Sam noticed, and fiercer-looking. Clearly she expected a fight, discounting whatever Lirael thought she was doing up at the bow.

"Got it!" exclaimed Lirael, as another flight of arrows sped towards them. This time, they splashed into the river no more than two arms' lengths away. Sam could probably have touched the closest one.

"What?" shouted Sam. He simultaneously reached into the Charter to begin making an arrow ward. Not that it would be much use against six archers at once. Not when he wasn't up to his full strength.

Lirael held up a large square of black cloth and let it flap into the breeze, revealing a brilliant silver star shining in the middle of it. The wind almost tore it from her grasp, but she clutched it to her chest and began to crawl back to the mast.

"*Finder*'s flag," she shouted as she pulled out a halyard and started to unscrew the pin in a shackle so it could be put through an eyelet in the banner. "I'll have it up in a minute."

"We don't have a minute!" screamed Sam, who could see the archers about to loose again. "Just hold it out!"

Lirael ignored him. Quickly she fitted the shackles at each end, screwing in the pins with what looked like deliberate slowness to Sam. He was about to lunge forward and grab the damned flag when Lirael suddenly let it go and pulled on the halyard—as five more arrows leapt towards them from the guardboat.

Finder reacted first, nudging the tiller over to turn the bow into the wind. Instantly, she lost speed, the sail flapping and clapping like maniacal applause. Sam ducked as she did it, and the tiller smacked him in the jaw, hard enough to make him think he'd been shot—at least for a moment. Then it swung back again, just missing him, as the boat returned to her original course.

But those few seconds of lost speed had been vital, Sam realized, as the arrows that should have struck them plunged into the water only a few feet ahead.

Then the great silver star of the Clayr billowed out from the mast, shining in the sun. Now there could be no doubt about whose boat this was, for the flag was not just a thing of cloth but, like *Finder* herself, was imbued with Charter Magic. Even in the darkest night, the starry banner of the Clayr would shine. In the bright day, it was almost blinding in its brilliance.

"They've stopped rowing," announced the Dog cheerily, as the guardboat suddenly lost way in a confusing pick-up-sticks jumble of oars. Sam relaxed and let the beginnings of the arrow ward fade away, so he could start checking whether he'd lost any teeth.

"But two archers are still going to shoot," the Dog continued, making Sam groan and hurriedly try to reach for the Charter marks he'd just let go.

"Yes . . . no . . . the other four are overpowering them. The captain is shouting . . . it has revealed itself!"

Sam and Lirael looked back at the guardboat. It was a mess of struggling figures, accompanied by shouting, screaming, and the clash of weapons. In the middle of it, a column of white fire suddenly appeared, with a whoosh loud enough to make the Dog's ears crinkle back and to make the others flinch. The column roared up twelve feet or more, then slid sideways and arced over the side.

For a moment, Sam and Lirael thought it would sink and disappear, but it actually bounced off the river as if the water were springy grass. Then the column started to move towards them, and it began to transform itself into something else. Soon it was no longer a tall streak of white fire but a gigantic burning boar, complete with tusks. It ran after *Finder* in great splashing leaps, squealing as it ran, a sound that sent a wave of nausea through everyone who heard it.

Sam was the first to react. He picked up Lirael's bow and sent four arrows in quick succession into the thing that was fast catching up to them. All struck it head on, but they had no effect save for a sudden flurry of sparks. The arrows turned instantly into molten metal and ash.

Sam was reaching for another arrow when Lirael thrust her hand past him, and she screamed a spell over the wind. A golden net flew from her fingers, spreading wider and wider as it crossed the intervening water. It met the boar-thing as it jumped, wrapping it in ropes of yellow red fire that dampened the thing's white-hot brilliance. Boar and net came plunging down, and both disappeared under the surface of the river, cutting off the terrible squealing. As the waters of the Ratterlin closed over the boar, an enormous plume of steam shot up for at least a hundred feet. When it subsided, there was no sign of either net or Free Magic creature, save for many small pieces of what looked like long-decayed meat, morsels that even the ravenous seagulls overhead chose to avoid.

"Thank you," said Sam, after it became clear that nothing more was going to come from the guardboat or out of the depths. He knew the net-spell Lirael had used but hadn't thought it would work against something that looked so powerful.

"Mogget suggested it," said Lirael, who was clearly surprised both by that and by the fact that the spell had worked so well.

"While that kind of construct can move across running water, it is destroyed by total immersion," explained Mogget. "Slowing it for even a moment was enough."

He looked slyly at the Dog, and added, "So you see that this hound is not the only one who knows of such things. Now I really must have a little nap. I trust that some fish will be forthcoming when I wake?"

Sam nodded wearily, though he had no idea how he was going to catch any. He almost patted Mogget, as Lirael so often did the Dog. But something in the cat's green eyes made him pull his hand back before the motion was really begun.

"Sorry I didn't think of the flag earlier," said Lirael as they sped on. The spell-wind had lessened, but it still blew quite strongly at their backs. "There's a whole pile of stuff there I looked at for only a second when we first left the Glacier."

"I'm glad you remembered it when you did," said Sam, his words slightly muffled as he tested the operation of his jaw. It seemed to be only bruised, and he still had all his teeth. "And this wind will come in handy. We should get to the House by tomorrow morning."

"Abhorsen's House," Lirael said thoughtfully. "It's built on an island, isn't it? Just before the waterfall where the Ratterlin goes over the Long Cliffs?"

"Yes," replied Sam, thinking of that raging cascade and how grateful he was going to be to have its protection. Then it occurred to him that far from thinking of the waterfall as safety, Lirael was probably wondering how they would reach the House without going over the mighty falls and down to certain destruction.

"Don't worry about the waterfall," he explained. "There's a sort of channel behind the island, where the current isn't as strong. It goes back almost a league, so as long as you enter it at the right point and stay in it, there's no problem. The Wallmakers made it. They built the House, too. It's brilliant work—the channel, I mean. I tried to make a model of it once, using the waterfall and pools on the second terrace at home. The Palace. But I couldn't spell the current to split. . . ."

He stopped talking as he realized Lirael wasn't listening. She had an abstract expression on her face, and her eyes were focused over his shoulder, into the distance.

"I didn't realize I was that boring," he said with an annoyed smile. Sam wasn't used to pretty girls ignoring him. And Lirael was pretty, he suddenly realized, potentially even beautiful. He hadn't noticed before.

Lirael started, blinked, and said, "Sorry. I'm not used to . . . People don't talk to me much back home."

"You know, you'd look a lot better without that scarf," said Sam. She really was attractive, though something about her face unsettled him. Where had he seen her? Perhaps she looked like one of the girls Ellimere had forced on him back in Belisaere.

"You know, you remind me of someone. I don't suppose I could have met one of your sisters or something, could I? I don't remember ever seeing any dark-haired Clayr, though."

"I don't have any sisters," replied Lirael absently. "Only cousins. Lots and lots of cousins. And an aunt."

"You could change into one of my sister's dresses at the House. It'd give you a chance to get out of that waistcoat," said Sam. "Do you mind if I ask how old you are, Lirael?"

Lirael looked at him, puzzled at the question, till she saw the glint in his eye. She knew that look from the Lower Refectory. She looked away and pulled up her scarf, trying to think of something to say. If only Sam could have just stayed like the Dog, she thought. A comforting friend, without the complication of romantic interest. There had to be something she could do to completely discourage him, short of throwing up or otherwise making herself totally unattractive.

"I'm thirty-five," she said at last.

"Thirty-five!" exclaimed Sam, "I mean, I beg your pardon. You don't look . . . you seem much younger—"

"Ointments," said the Dog, sporting a wicked, one-sided grin that only Lirael could see. "Unguents. Oils from the North. Spells of seeming. My mistress works hard to keep her youth, Prince."

"Oh," said Sam, leaning back against the stern rail. Surreptitiously he looked at Lirael again, trying to see some lines he'd missed or something. But she really didn't look a day older than Ellimere. And she certainly didn't act like a much older woman. She wasn't all that confident or outgoing, for a start. Perhaps it was because she was a librarian, Sam thought, as he tried to make out what he thought was probably a very shapely form under the baggy waistcoat.

"Enough of that talk, Dog!" commanded Lirael, turning her

head to hide her own smile from Sam. "Make yourself useful and keep an eye out for danger. I'm going to make myself useful by weaving a Charter-skin."

"Aye, aye, Mistress," growled the Dog. "I will keep watch."

The hound stretched and yawned, then jumped to the bow, sitting down right in the path of the spray, her mouth wide open and tongue lolling. How she stayed upright and steady was a mystery, Lirael thought, though she had the unpleasant notion that the Dog might have grown suckers on her bottom.

"Mad. Absolutely mad," said Mogget, as he watched the Dog get drenched. The cat had resumed his post near the mast and was once again licking himself dry. "But then, she always was."

"I heard that!" barked the Dog, without looking back.

"Of course you did," said Mogget, sighing, and he licked away at his collar. He looked up at Lirael, his green eyes twinkling with wickedness, and added, "I don't suppose I could trouble you to take off my collar so I can get properly dry?"

Lirael shook her head.

"Well, I suppose if the village idiot here wouldn't do it, there was no chance you would," grumbled Mogget, inclining his head at Sameth. "It's enough to make me wish I'd volunteered in the first place. Then I wouldn't be forced out all the time on these barbaric boat trips."

"What didn't you volunteer for?" asked Lirael curiously. But the little cat only smiled. A smile that had rather too much of the carnivorous hunter in it, Lirael thought. Then he twitched his head, Ranna tinkled, and he was asleep, sprawled out in the noonday sun.

"Be careful with Mogget," Sam warned, as Lirael succumbed to the temptation to scratch the cat's furry white belly. "He's nearly killed my mother in his unbound form. Three times, in fact, during the time she's been the Abhorsen."

Lirael pulled her hand back just as Mogget opened one eye and made an—apparently playful—swipe with one claw-extended paw.

"Go back to sleep," said the Dog from the bow, without looking around. She certainly seemed confident that Mogget would obey.

Mogget winked at Lirael, holding her gaze for a moment. Then that one sharp green eye closed, and he really did seem to fall asleep, Ranna tinkling at his neck.

"Well," Lirael said. "Time to make a Charter-skin."

"Do you mind if I watch?" asked Sam eagerly. "I've read about Charter-skins, but I thought the art was lost. Even Mother doesn't know how to make one. What shapes do you know?"

"I can make an ice otter, a russet bear, or a barking owl," replied Lirael, relieved to see that the spasm of romantic interest that had gripped Sam had passed. "You can watch if you like, but I don't know what you'll see. They're basically just very long and complex chains of Charter marks and joining-spells—and you have to hold them in your head all at the same time. So I won't be able to talk or explain or anything. And it will probably take me until sunset. Then I have to fold it exactly right so it can be used later."

"Fascinating," said Sam. "Have you tried putting the completed spell into an object? So that the whole chain of marks is there, ready to be pulled out when you need it, but it hasn't actually been cast?"

"No," replied Lirael. "I didn't know that it was possible."

"Well, it's difficult," explained Sam eagerly. "It's sort of like repairing a Charter Stone. I mean, you have to use some of your own blood to prepare whatever is going to hold the spell. Royal blood, that is, though Clayr or Abhorsen blood should work equally well. You need to be very careful, of course, because if you get it wrong . . . Anyway, let's see your Charter-skin first. What is it going to be?"

"A barking owl," replied Lirael, with a sense of foreboding. She didn't need the Sight to know that Sameth would like to ask an awful lot of questions. "And it'll take about four hours. Without," she added firmly, "any interruptions."

Chapter Forty-Two

SOUTHERLINGS AND A NECROMANCER

THE SUN WAS setting, sending a red light across the broad river. Despite Sam and Lirael's earlier weather spell, the wind had turned and was blowing strongly from the south. Even against the wind, *Finder* continued to make good time, tacking in long diagonals between the eastern and western shores.

As Lirael had expected, Sam hadn't been able to stop himself asking questions. But even with the interruptions she had managed to create the Charter-skin of a barking owl and fold it up properly for later use.

"That was fascinating," said Sam. "I'd like to learn how to make one myself."

"I've left *In the Skin of a Lyon* back at the Glacier," replied Lirael. "But you can have it if you ever go there. It belongs to the Library, but I expect you'd be allowed to borrow it."

Sam nodded. The prospect of him visiting the Clayr's Glacier seemed exceedingly remote. It was just another piece of a future that he couldn't imagine. All he could think of was reaching the safe haven of the House.

"Can we sail through the night?" he asked.

"Yes," replied Lirael. "If the Dog is prepared to stay up as lookout, to help *Finder*."

"I will," barked the Disreputable Dog. She had not shifted from her position at the bow. "The sooner we're there, the better.

There is a foul scent on this wind, and the river is too deserted to be normal."

Sam and Lirael both looked around. They had been so intent on the Charter-skin that they hadn't noticed the complete absence of any other boats, though there were a number anchored close to the eastern shore.

"No one's followed us down from High Bridge, and we have passed only four craft coming from the south," said the Dog. "This cannot be normal for the Ratterlin."

"No," Sam agreed. "Whenever I've been on the river, there've always been lots of boats. Even in winter. We should have seen some of the wood barges at least, heading north."

"I haven't seen a single craft all day," said the Dog. "Which means that they have stopped somewhere, to take shelter. And the boats I've seen tied up have all been out on the jetties or moored to buoys. As far as they can get from the land."

"There must be more of the Dead, or those Free Magic constructs, all along the river," said Lirael.

"I knew Mother and Dad shouldn't have gone," said Sam. "If they'd known—"

"They would still have gone," interrupted Mogget with a yawn. He stretched, and tasted the air with his delicate pink tongue. "As per usual, trouble comes in several directions at once. I think some is coming our way, for I am afraid to say that the hound is correct. There *is* a reek on this breeze. Wake me if something unpleasant seems likely to occur."

With that, he settled back down again, curling into a tight white ball.

"I wonder what Mogget would call 'something unpleasant,'" muttered Sam nervously. He picked up his sword and drew it partially out of the scabbard, checking that the Charter marks he'd put there still flourished.

The Dog sniffed the air again as the boat came about, onto a port tack. Her nose quivered, and she raised her snout higher as the scent grew stronger.

"Free Magic," she said finally. "On the western shore."

"Where, exactly?" asked Lirael, shading her eyes with her hand. It was hard to see anything to the west, against the setting sun. All she could make out was tangled groves of willows between empty fields, a few makeshift jetties, and the semi-submerged stone walls of a large fish trap.

"I can't see," replied the Dog. "I can only smell. Somewhere downstream."

"I can't see anything, either," added Sam. "But if the Free Magic isn't on the river, we can just sail past."

"I can smell people, too," reported the Dog. "Frightened people."

Sam didn't say anything. Lirael glanced at him and saw that he was biting his lip.

"Could it be the necromancer?" Lirael asked. "Hedge?"

The Dog shrugged. "I cannot tell from here. The scent of Free Magic is strong, so it could be a necromancer. Or perhaps a Stilken or Hish."

Lirael swallowed nervously. She could bind a Stilken, since she had Nehima to help. And Sam, the Dog, and Mogget. But she didn't want to have to.

"I knew I should have read that book," muttered Sam. He didn't say which book.

They sat in silence for a minute, as *Finder* continued on her way towards the western shore. The sun was sinking fast now, more than half of its ruddy disc below the horizon. The stars were starting to become brighter as darkness fell.

"I suppose we'd better . . . we'd better take a look," Sam said at last, with obvious effort. He buckled on his sword, but made no move to pick up the bandolier of bells. Lirael looked at them and wished she could take them up, but they were not hers. It was up to Sam to decide what to do with them.

"If we tie up at that next jetty, will we be close?" Lirael asked the Dog. The hound nodded her head. Without needing orders, *Finder* turned towards the jetty.

"Wake up, Mogget!" said Sam, but he spoke softly. It had grown quiet on the river with the fall of night. He did not want his voice to carry over the soft burble of the current.

Mogget did not stir. Sam spoke again and scratched the cat's head, but Mogget continued to sleep.

"He'll wake when he needs to," said the Dog. She also spoke softly. "Prepare yourselves!"

Finder expertly slid up to the jetty as Lirael lowered the sail. Sam jumped ashore, his sword drawn, closely followed by the Dog.

Lirael joined them a moment later, Nehima bare, the Charter marks on the blade glowing in the twilight.

The Dog sniffed the air again and cocked one ear. All three stood still. Listening. Waiting.

Even the hungry gulls had stopped calling. There was no sound, save their own breathing and the rush of the river under the jetty.

Off in the distance, the silence was suddenly broken by a long-drawn-out scream. Then, as if that were a signal for noise to begin, it was followed by muffled shouts and more screams.

At the same time, Lirael and Sam both felt several people die. Though it was far away, they flinched at the shock of the deaths and then again as it was quickly repeated. There was something else there, too, that they could sense. Some power over Death.

"A necromancer!" blurted Sam. He took a step back.

"The bells," said Lirael, and she looked down at the boat. Mogget was awake now, his green eyes gleaming in the dark. He was perched upon the bell-bandolier.

"They're coming this way," announced the Dog calmly.

The shouts and screams grew closer. But Lirael and Sam still couldn't see anything beyond the line of willows. Then, fifty yards downstream, a man burst out of the trees and fell into the water. He went under at once but bobbed to the surface some distance out. He swam for a few strokes, then turned on his back to float, too weary or too hurt to keep swimming.

Behind him, a burnt and blackened corpse shambled to the water's edge and let out a horrible, gobbling cry as it saw its prey escape. Repelled by the swift flow of the river, the Dead Hand staggered back into the trees.

"Come on," said Lirael, though she could barely get out the words. She drew her panpipes and marched off. The Dog followed her. Sam hesitated, staring out into the darkness.

More people screamed and shouted beyond the trees. No words were clear, but Sam knew they were desperately afraid, and the shouts were for help.

He looked back at the bells. Mogget met his gaze, unblinking. "What are you waiting for?" asked the cat. "My permission?"

Sam shook his head. He felt paralyzed, unable to reach for the bells or to follow Lirael. She and the Dog were almost at the end of the jetty. He could sense the Dead nearby, less than a hundred yards away, and the necromancer with them.

He had to do something. He had to act. He had to prove to himself he wasn't a coward.

"I don't need the bells!" he shouted, and he ran down the jetty, his boots echoing on the wooden planks. He burst past the surprised Lirael and the Dog, and sprinted through the gap where the willows had been pruned back.

He was past the trees in an instant and out in a twilit paddock. A Dead Hand rushed at him. He cut its legs away and kicked it over, all in one fluid motion. Before it could rise, he jumped over it and ran on.

The necromancer. He had to kill the necromancer, before he could drag him into Death. He had to kill him as quickly as he could.

A hot rage rose in him, banishing the fear. Sam growled and ran on.

Lirael and the Dog emerged from the willows to see Sam charge. The Dead Hand he'd cut down scrabbled towards them, but Lirael had the panpipes ready at her lips. She chose Saraneth and blew a strong, pure note, its commanding tones stopping the Hand in its tracks. Without a pause, Lirael changed to Kibeth, and a trill of dancing notes sent the corpse somersaulting backwards even as the Spirit inhabiting it was forced to walk back into Death.

"It's gone," said the Dog, loping forward. Lirael ran, too, but not with Sam's reckless abandon.

It was still light enough to see that thirty or forty Dead Hands had surrounded a group of men, women, and children. Obviously, they'd tried to reach the safety of the river, only to fail at the very last. Now they had formed a ring with the children at the center, a last desperate defense.

Lirael could sense the Dead Hands . . . and something else, something strange and much more powerful. It was only when she saw Sam charge past the Hands and scream a challenge that she realized that it had to be the necromancer.

The people were screaming, too, and shouting, and crying. The Dead roared and screeched back, as they pulled their victims down and ripped their throats out or rent them limb from limb. Makeshift clubs and sharpened branches struck at the Dead, but their wielders did not know how to use them to best effect, and they were heavily outnumbered.

Lirael looked across and saw the necromancer turn to face Sam. He raised his hands, and the hot metal smell of Free Magic suddenly filled the air. A moment later, a blinding, blue white spark exploded out, leaping across to strike the charging boy.

At the same time, the Dead Hands howled in triumph as they burst through the ranks of struggling men and women and into the inner circle of children.

Lirael turned her easy run into an all-out sprint. Whoever she tried to help, it looked like she would be too late.

Sam saw the necromancer raise his hands and saw the bronze of his face. Even as he threw himself to the side, his mind raced. A bronze face! Then this wasn't Hedge, but Chlorr of the Mask, the creature his mother had fought years ago!

The bolt sizzled past him, missing him by a few inches. Heat from its passage struck him, and the grass behind him burst into flame.

Sam slowed down as he reached into the Charter and pulled out four marks. He drew them with his free hand, fingers flashing too quickly to follow. A triangular silver blade suddenly materialized in his grip. Before it was even fully formed, Sam threw it.

The blade spun as it shot through the air. Chlorr easily ducked it, but the spinning blade turned a few paces beyond her and came shooting back.

Sam rushed forward as the blade struck the necromancer in the arm. He expected it to almost sever that limb, but there were only a burst of golden flame, a gout of white sparks, and a smoldering sleeve.

"Fool," said Chlorr, raising her sword. Her voice crawled across his skin like a thousand tiny insects. Her breath stank of death and Free Magic. "You have no bells."

In that instant, Sam realized that Chlorr didn't have any bells, either. Nor were there any human eyes behind the mask. Pools of fire burnt there, and white smoke puffed from the mouth-hole.

Chlorr was no longer a necromancer. She was one of the Greater Dead. Sabriel *had* finished her as a living being.

But someone had brought her back.

"Run!" shouted Lirael. "Run!"

She stood between the last four survivors and those Dead Hands who had resisted the panpipes. Lirael had blown on Saraneth till her face was blue, but there had just been too many of them for her to deal with, the power of the pipes too slight. The Dead who were left didn't seem affected at all.

Worse still, the children wouldn't run. They were too shocked, incapable of doing anything, let alone understand what Lirael was shouting at them.

A Dead Hand lunged, and Lirael thrust at it. The Dog leapt at another, knocking it down. But a third, a low, loping thing with elongated jaws, got past them. It rushed at a small boy who could not stop screaming. The jaws closed, and the scream was instantly cut off.

Sobbing with fury and revulsion, Lirael spun around and hewed off the thing's head, Nehima showering silver sparks as it cut through. But even then the Dead Hand functioned, the spirit inside indifferent to any physical harm. She cut at it again and again, but Dead fingers still clutched its victim, and the head still gnashed its teeth.

Sam parried another blow from the thing that had once been Chlorr. Her strength was incredible, and once again he nearly lost his sword. His hand and wrist were numb, and the Charter marks he'd spelled so laboriously into the blade were slowly being destroyed by Chlorr's power. When they were gone, the blade would shatter—

He staggered back and glanced quickly around the field. He could just make out Lirael and the Dog, fighting with at least a half dozen Dead Hands. He'd heard the pipes before, the voices of Saraneth and Kibeth, though strangely different from the bells he knew. They had sent most of the spirits animating the Hands back into Death, but had had no effect upon Chlorr.

Chlorr struck again, hissing. Sam dodged. Desperately, he tried to think of what he could do. There had to be some spell, something that would at least hold her back long enough for him to get away. . . .

Lirael and the Dog struck together, smashing the last Dead Hand to the ground. Before it could get up, the Dog barked in its face. Instantly, it went limp, no more than a ghastly, misshapen corpse, the spirit banished.

"Thanks," gasped Lirael. She looked around her, at the grotesque forms of Dead Hands and the pathetic bodies of their victims. Desperately, she hoped to see even just one of the children. But there was no one standing except her and the Dog. There were bodies everywhere, sprawled on the blood-soaked ground. The cast-off remnants of the Dead Hands piled up with the slaughtered people.

Lirael closed her eyes, her sense of Death almost overpowering her. That sense confirmed what her eyes had already told her.

No one had survived.

She felt sick, the gorge rising in her throat. But as she bent forward to throw up, she suddenly heard Sam shouting. She straightened up, opened her eyes, and looked around. She couldn't see Sam, but off in the distance there was a blaze of golden fire, interspersed with huge showers of white sparks. It might have been a fireworks display, but Lirael knew better.

Even so, it took her a few seconds to work out what Sam was shouting.

When it finally percolated into her stunned, shocked mind, all thought of throwing up disappeared. She jumped over the bodies of the Dead Hands and their victims and started to run.

Sam was shouting, "Help! Lirael! Dog! Mogget! Anyone! Help!"

Sam's sword had broken on the last exchange of blows. It had snapped off near the hilt, leaving him with a useless dead weight, devoid of magic.

Chlorr laughed. A laugh strange and distant behind her mask, as if it echoed from inside some far-off hall.

She had grown taller as she had stalked after Sam, visibly a thing of darkness under the rotting, splitting furs. Now she stood head and shoulders above him, white smoke drifting from her mouth as she raised her sword again. Red fire flowed along the blade, and flaming drops fell to the grass.

Sam threw the hilt at her face and jumped back, shouting, "Help! Lirael! Dog!"

The sword came down. Chlorr leapt forward as well, faster and farther than Sam had expected. The blade whisked past his nose. Shocked, he shouted again, "Mogget! Anyone! Help!"

Lirael saw the necromancer's sword of red fire come blazing down. Sam fell under the blow, and the red fire obscured Lirael's vision.

"Sam!" she screamed.

As she screamed, the Disreputable Dog sprang ahead, leaping in great bounds towards Sam and the necromancer.

For a panicked second, Lirael thought Sam had been killed. Then she saw him roll aside, untouched. The necromancer raised her sword again, and Lirael burst her lungs trying to get there in time to do something. But she could not. She was still forty or fifty yards away, and her mind was empty of all the spells that might have crossed the distance and distracted the enemy.

"Die!" whispered Chlorr, raising her sword two-handed above her head, the blade pointing straight down. Sam looked up at it and knew he could not get out of the way in time. She was too fast, too strong. He half raised his hand and tried to speak a Charter mark, but the only one that came to mind was something useless, some mark used in making his toys.

The blade came down.

Sam screamed.

The Disreputable Dog barked.

There was Charter Magic in the bark. It hit Chlorr as she struck. Her arms flashed gold and sizzled, white smoke gouting out of a thousand tiny holes. The blow that should have impaled Sam went awry, the sword sinking deep into the earth, so close that his hip was burnt by the flame.

All Chlorr's unnatural strength had gone into the blow. Now she struggled to free the weapon as the Dog advanced upon her, growling. The hound had grown and was now the size of a desert lion, with teeth and claws to match. Her collar shone with golden fire, the Charter marks shifting and joining in a wild dance.

The Dead creature let the sword go and backed away. Sam struggled to his feet as Chlorr drew back. He clenched his fists as he tried to calm himself, in preparation for casting a spell.

Lirael arrived a second later, completely out of breath. Gasping, she slowed to a walk and moved up behind the Dog.

Chlorr raised one shadowy fist, her fingernails elongating into thin blades of darkness. White smoke still eddied around her, but the holes in her arm had already closed.

She took one step forward, and the Dog barked again.

There was Free Magic power in this bark, reinforced with Charter-spells. Her collar shone even brighter, and Sam and Lirael had to half-close their eyes.

Chlorr flinched and raised her hands to shield her face. More white smoke poured out from behind her mask, and her body changed shape under the furs. She began to collapse in on herself, her clothes crumpling as the shadowflesh within leaked away.

"Curse you!" she shrieked.

The furs fell to the ground, and the bronze mask bounced on top of them. A shadow as dark and thick as ink flowed away from the Dog and Lirael, moving faster than any liquid ever spilled.

Lirael started to follow, but the Dog blocked her way.

"No," said the Dog. "Let it go. I have only forced it out of its shape. It is too powerful for me to send back into Death alone, or destroy."

"It was Chlorr," said Sam, white-faced and shivering. "Chlorr of the Mask. A necromancer my mother fought years ago."

"It is one of the Greater Dead now," said Mogget. "Back from beyond the Seventh or Eighth Gate."

Sam jumped several feet into the air. When he looked down, Mogget was sitting quite calmly near Chlorr's sword, as if he'd been there all the time.

"Where were you?" Sam asked.

"I've been looking around while you took care of things here," explained Mogget. "Chlorr has fled but will return. There are more Dead Hands less than two leagues to the west. A hundred of them at least, with Shadow Hands to lead them."

"A hundred!" exclaimed Sam as Lirael said, "Shadow Hands!"

"We'd better get back to the boat," said Sam. He looked at Chlorr's sword, quivering in the earth. No flames ran down it now, but the steel was as dark as ebony and etched with strange runes that wriggled and convulsed and made him feel nauseated.

"We should destroy this," he said. His head felt strangely fuzzy, and he found it difficult to think. "But . . . but I don't know how to do it quickly."

"What about all these people?" asked Lirael. She couldn't call them bodies. She still couldn't believe they were all dead. It had happened so quickly, in just a few frenzied minutes.

Sam looked across the field. There were more stars out now, and a slim crescent of a moon had risen. In the cool light he saw that many of the slain people wore blue hats or scarves. A scrap of blue material was caught in the claws of one of the Dead that Lirael had banished with her pipes.

"They're Southerlings," he said, surprised.

He walked over for a closer look at the nearest body, a fair-haired boy who couldn't have been more than sixteen. Sam's eyes showed more puzzlement than fear, as if he couldn't believe what was happening. "Southerling refugees. I guess they were trying to escape."

"Escape from what?" asked Lirael.

Before anyone could answer, a Dead creature howled in the distance. A moment later the howl was taken up by many desiccated, decaying throats.

"Chlorr has reached the Hands," said Mogget urgently. "We must leave now!"

The cat hurried away. Sam started to follow, but Lirael grabbed him by the arm.

"We can't just leave!" protested Lirael. "If we leave them, their bodies will get used—"

"We can't stay!" protested Sam. "You heard Mogget. There are too many to fight, and Chlorr will come back, too!"

"We have to do something!" Lirael said. She looked at the Dog. Surely the Dog would help her! They had to perform the cleansing rite on the bodies or bind them so they couldn't be used to house spirits brought from Death.

But the Dog shook her head. "There's no time," she said sadly.

"Sam can get the bells!" protested Lirael. "We have to—"

The hound nudged Lirael behind the knee, pushing her on. The girl stumbled forward, tears welling up in her eyes. Sam and Mogget were already well ahead, hurrying towards the willows.

"Hurry!" said the Dog anxiously, after a glance over her shoulder. She could hear the clicking of many bones and smell decaying flesh. The Dead were closing fast.

Lirael wept as she broke into a shambling jog. If only she could run faster, or knew how to use the panpipes better. She might have been able to save even one of the refugees.

One of the refugees. One *had* got away from the Dead.

"The man!" she exclaimed, breaking into a run. "The man in the river! We have to rescue him!"

Chapter Forty-Three

FAREWELL TO *FINDER*

EVEN WITH THE Dog's highly developed sense of smell and Mogget's unrivaled night vision, it took almost an hour to find the Southerling who'd managed to reach the river.

He was still floating on his back, but his face was barely above the surface, and he didn't seem to be breathing. But as Sam and Lirael pulled him in closer to the boat, he opened his eyes and groaned with pain.

"No, no," he whispered. "No."

"Hold him," whispered Lirael to Sam. She quickly reached into the Charter, drawing out several marks of healing. She spoke their names and cupped them in her hand. They glowed there, warm and comforting, as she sought any obvious wounds to place them for best effect. Once the spell was active, they could pull him out of the water.

There was a huge dark stain of dried blood on the man's neck. But when she moved her hand to it, he cried out and tried to escape from Sam's grasp.

"No! The evil!"

Lirael pulled her hand back, puzzled. It was obviously Charter Magic she was about to cast. The golden light was clear and bright, and there was no stench of Free Magic.

"He's a Southerling," whispered Sam. "They don't believe in magic, even the superstitions the Ancelstierrans believe in, let alone our magic. It must have been terrible for them when they crossed the Wall."

"Land across the Wall," sobbed the man. "He promised us land again. Farms to build, a place of our own . . ."

Lirael tried again to place the spell, but the man shrieked and fought against Sam's hold. The waves he made ducked his head under several times, till Lirael had to take her hand away and let the spell go, away into the night.

"He's dying," said Sam. He could feel the man's life ebbing away, feel the cold touch of Death reaching out to him.

"What can we do?" asked Lirael. "What—"

"All dead," said the man, coughing. Blood came out with the river-water, bright in the moonlight. "At the pit. They were dead, but still they did his bidding. Then the poison . . . I told Hral and Mortin not to drink . . . four families—"

"It's all right," said Sam soothingly, though his voice was nearly breaking. "They . . . they got away."

"We ran, and the Dead followed," whispered the Southerling. His eyes were bright, but they saw something other than Sam and Lirael. "Night and day we ran. They dislike the sun. Torbel hurt his ankle, and I couldn't . . . couldn't carry him."

Lirael reached across and stroked the man's head. He flinched at first, but relaxed as he saw no strange light in her hands.

"The farmer said the river," continued the dying man. "The river."

"You made it," said Sam. "This is the river. The Dead cannot cross running water."

"Ahh," sighed the man, and then he was gone, slipping away to that other river, the one that would carry him to the Ninth Gate and beyond.

Sam slowly let go. Lirael raised her hand. The water closed

over the man's face, and *Finder* steered away.

"We couldn't save even one," whispered Lirael. "Not even *one*."

Sam didn't answer. He sat staring past her, out at the moon-lit river.

"Come here, Lirael," said the Dog gently, from her post at the bow. "Help me keep watch."

Lirael nodded, her lower lip trembling as she tried to keep herself from sobbing. She clambered over the thwarts and threw herself down next to the Dog, and hugged her as hard as she could. The Dog bore this without a word, and said nothing about the tears that spilled off onto her coat.

Eventually, Lirael's grip loosened, and she slid down. Sleep had claimed her, the kind of sleep that comes only after all strength is exhausted and battles won or lost.

The Dog shifted a little to make Lirael more comfortable and twisted her head to look behind her in a way no normal dog could twist. Sam was asleep, too, curled up in the stern, the tiller moving slightly above his head.

Mogget seemed to be asleep, at his customary post near the mast. But he opened one bright green eye as the Dog looked back.

"I saw it, too," said Mogget. "On the Greater Dead, that Chlorr."

"Yes," said the Dog, her voice troubled. "I trust you will have no trouble remembering where your loyalties lie?"

Mogget didn't answer. He slowly closed his eye, and a small and secret smile spread across his mouth.

All through the night, the Disreputable Dog sat at the bow, while Lirael tossed and turned beside her. They passed Qyrre in the early, silent hours of the morning, merely a white sail in the distance. Though it had been her original destination, *Finder* did not try to put in to the dock.

Lirael experienced a mild attack of panic when she awoke to the sound of a waterfall ahead. At this distance, it sounded like the buzz of many insects, and it took her a moment to figure out what it was. Once she did, she had a few anxious moments till she realized that *Finder* was traveling quite slowly compared to the tree branches, leaves, and other flotsam racing past on either side of them.

"We're in the channel, approaching Abhorsen's House," explained the Dog, as Lirael rubbed the sleep out of her eyes and stretched, in a futile effort to relieve her aches and kinks.

All the deaths of the night before seemed long ago. But not at all like a dream. Lirael knew that the face of the last Southerling, his look of relief as he finally knew he had escaped the Dead, would stay with her forever.

As she stretched, she looked at the huge mass of spray thrown up by the Ratterlin's fall over the Long Cliffs ahead. The river seemed to disappear into a great cloud that smothered the cliffs and the land beyond in a giant, undulating quilt of white. Then, just for a moment, the mist parted, and she saw a bright tower, its red-tiled, conical roof catching the sun. It looked like a mirage, shimmering in the cloud, but Lirael knew that she had come to Abhorsen's House at last.

As they drew closer, Lirael saw more red-tiled roofs emerge from the cloud, hinting at other buildings grouped around the tower. But she couldn't see more, because the whole island the House was built on was surrounded by a whitewashed stone wall that was at least forty feet high. Only the red tiles and some tree-tops were visible.

She heard Sam come forward from the stern, and he was soon next to her, looking ahead. By unspoken consent, they didn't talk about what had happened, though the silence was heavy between them.

Finally, desperate to say something, Sam took on the role of a tour guide.

"It doesn't look it, but the island is larger than a football field. Um, that's a game I used to play at school, in Ancelstierre. Anyway, the island is about three hundred yards long and a hundred yards wide. There's a garden and an orchard as well as the House itself—you can just see the blossoms on the peach trees, over on the right. Too early for fruit, though, unfortunately. The peaches here are fantastic, Charter knows why. The House isn't much compared to the Palace in size, but it is bigger than it looks, and there's a lot packed into it. Quite a bit different from your Glacier, I guess."

"I like it already," said Lirael, smiling, still looking ahead. There was the faint hint of a rainbow in the cloud, arching over the white walls, framing the House with a border of many colors.

"Just as well," muttered Mogget, as he appeared suddenly at Lirael's elbow. "Though you should be warned about the cooking."

"Cooking?" asked the Dog, licking her lips. "What's wrong with it?"

"Nothing," said Sam sternly. "The sendings are very good cooks."

"Do you have sendings for servants?" asked Lirael, who was curious about the difference between the Abhorsen's life and the Clayr's. "We do most of the work ourselves at the Glacier. Everyone has to take turns, especially with the cooking, though there are some people who specialize."

"No one apart from the family ever comes here," replied Sam. "I mean the extended family—those of the Blood, like the Clayr. And no one has to do anything, really, because there are so many sendings, all eager to help. I think they get bored when the place is empty. Every Abhorsen makes a few sendings, so they kind of multiply. Some are hundreds of years old."

"Thousands," said Mogget. "And senile, most of them."

"Where do we land?" asked Lirael, ignoring Mogget's mutterings. She couldn't see any gate or landing spot in the northern wall.

"On the western side," said Sam, raising his voice to counter the increasing roar of the falls. "We skirt around the island, almost to the waterfall. There's a landing stage there for the House, and the stepping-stones across to the western tunnel. Look, you can see where the tunnel entrance is, up on the bank."

He pointed at a narrow ledge halfway up the western riverbank, a grey stone outcrop almost as high as the House. If there was a tunnel entrance there, Lirael couldn't see it through the mist, and it seemed perilously close to the waterfall.

"You mean there are stepping-stones across that?" exclaimed Lirael, pointing to the edges where the waters rushed over in a torrent that was at least two hundred yards wide, extremely deep and going at a speed Lirael couldn't even guess at. Worse than that, Sam had told her that the waterfall was more than a thousand feet high. If they were somehow drawn out of the channel, *Finder* would go over in seconds, and it was a very long way to fall.

"On both sides," shouted Sam. "They go to the riverbanks, and then there are tunnels that lead down to the bottom of the cliffs. Or you can keep going over the banks and stay on the plateau, if you want."

Lirael nodded and gulped, looking at the point where the stepping-stones must cross from the House to the western shore. She couldn't even see them under all the spray and the churning of the water. She hoped she wouldn't need to, and remembered the Charter-skin that was now safely rolled up in the bag that held *The Book of Remembrance and Forgetting*, ready to be put on. She could just fly across in the shape of a barking owl, screeching all the way.

A few minutes later, *Finder* was next to the whitewashed walls. Lirael looked up at them, drawing an imaginary line from the boat's mast to the top of the walls. Somehow, the walls looked even higher close up, and they had curious marks that even fresh whitewash couldn't conceal. The sort of stains left by a flood that had reached almost to the top.

Then they were at the wooden landing stage. *Finder* gently bumped against the heavy canvas fenders that hung there, but any sound from the bump was totally lost in the stomach-vibrating crash of the waterfall. Sam and Lirael quickly unloaded everything, gesturing to make themselves understood. The waterfall was too loud for them to hear even a shout, unless—as Sam demonstrated to Lirael—he was right against her ear, and then it hurt.

When everything was piled up on the landing stage, with Mogget perched on Lirael's pack and the Dog happily catching spray in her mouth, Lirael kissed *Finder*'s figurehead on the cheek and pushed the boat off the jetty. She thought she saw the carved face of the woman wink, and her lips curve up in a smile.

"Thank you," she mouthed, while Sam bowed at her side, showing his respect. *Finder* flapped her sail in answer, then swung about and began to move upstream. Sam, watching carefully, noted that the current in the channel had reversed and was moving north, against the flow of the river. Once again, he wondered how it was done and tried to think of how he could get to look at the Charter Stones that were sunk deep in the riverbed below. Perhaps Lirael would teach him how to make an ice-otter Charter-skin—

A touch at his arm broke his reverie, and he turned to pick up his saddlebags and sword. Then he led the way to the gate and pushed it open. As soon as they passed through, the noise of the waterfall practically ceased, so Lirael had to listen carefully to hear even a distant roar. She could hear birds in the trees instead, and many bees buzzing past on their way to the peach blossoms. The mist also parted above and around Abhorsen's House, for Lirael stood in sunshine, which quickly dried the spray that had fallen on her face and clothes.

There was a red-brick path ahead, bordered by a lawn and a line of shrubs with clumps of odd, stick-shaped yellow flowers. The path led to the front door of the House, which was painted a cheerful sky blue, bright against the whitewashed stone on either side of it. The House itself seemed normal enough. It was mainly one large building of three or four stories, in addition to the tower. It also had some sort of inner courtyard, too, because Lirael could see birds flying in and out. There were many windows, all quite large, and it exuded comfort and welcome. Clearly Abhorsen's House was not a fortification, relying on means other than architecture for its defense.

Lirael raised her arms to the sun and drank in the clear air, and the faint perfume from the gardens, of flowers and fertile soil and green growing things. She suddenly felt peaceful, and strangely at home, though it was so different from the enclosed tunnels and chambers of the Glacier. Even the gardens in the vast chambers there, with their painted ceilings and Charter-mark suns, could not begin to duplicate the vastness of the blue sky and the true sun.

She exhaled slowly and was about to drop her arms when she saw a small speck high above her. A moment later it was joined by a dark cloud of many somewhat larger things. It took Lirael a few seconds to realize that the smaller speck was a bird that seemed to be diving straight at her, and the larger specks were also birds—or things that flew like birds. At the same time her Death sense twinged, and Sam cried out next to her.

"Gore Crows! They're after a message-hawk!"

"They're actually below it," said the Dog, her head craned back. "It's trying to dive through!"

They watched anxiously as the message-hawk fell, zigzagging slightly to try to avoid the Gore Crows. But there were hundreds of them, and they spread across a wide area, so the hawk had no choice but to try to smash through where they were fewest. It selected its point and closed its wings, dropping even faster, as if it were a stone thrown straight down.

"If it makes it through, they won't dare pursue," said Sam. "Too close to the river, and the House."

"Go!" whispered Lirael, staring up at the hawk, willing it to go even faster. It seemed to fall for ages, and she realized it must have been very high indeed. Then all of a sudden it hit the black cloud, and there was an explosion of feathers and Gore Crows hurtling in all directions, while still more flew in. Lirael held her breath. The hawk didn't re-appear. Still the Gore Crows flew in, till there were so many in a small area that they began to collide, and black, broken bodies began to fall.

"They got it," said Sam slowly. Then he shouted. A small brown bird suddenly dropped out of the swirling mass of Gore Crows. This time it fell seemingly out of control, lacking the fierce direction and purpose they'd seen before. A few Gore Crows broke off to pursue it, but they had gone only a little way before they pulled up and sheered off, repelled by the force of the river and the protective magics of the House.

The hawk fell further, as if it were dead or stunned. But only forty or fifty feet above the garden, it suddenly spread its wings, breaking its fall just enough to swoop in and land at Lirael's feet. It lay there, feathered breast panting, and the marks of the Gore Crows' attacks obvious in its tattered plumage and bleeding head. But its yellow eyes were still lively, and it hopped easily enough onto Sam's wrist when he bent down and offered it a place on the cuff of his shirt.

"Message for Prince Sameth," it said, in a voice that was not any bird's. "Message."

"Yes, yes," said Sam soothingly, gently stroking its feathers back into place. "I am Prince Sameth. Tell me."

The bird cocked its head to one side and opened its beak. Lirael saw the hint of Charter marks there, and she suddenly understood that the bird carried a spell inside it, a spell that was probably cast upon it while it was still in its egg, to grow as it grew.

"Sameth, you idiot, I hope this finds you at the House," said the message-hawk, its voice changing again. Now it seemed to be a woman. From the tone of voice and the expression on Sam's face, Lirael guessed that it was his sister, Ellimere.

"Father and Mother are still in Ancelstierre. There is greater trouble there than they feared. Corolini is definitely under the influence of someone from the Old Kingdom, and his Our Country Party grows more influential in the Moot. More and more refugees are being moved nearer the Wall. There are also reports of Dead creatures all along the Ratterlin's western shores. I am calling up the Trained Bands and will be marching south to Barhedrin with them and the Guard within two weeks, to try to prevent any crossings. I don't know where you are, but Father says it is essential that you find Nicholas Sayre and return him to Ancelstierre at once, as Corolini claims we have kidnapped him to use as a hostage to influence the Chief Minister. Mother sends her love. I hope you can do something really useful for a change—"

The voice suddenly stopped, having reached the limit of the message-hawk's rather tiny mind. The bird made a peeping sound and started to preen itself.

"Well, let's go in and get cleaned up," said Sam slowly, though he kept staring at the hawk as if it might speak again. "The send-ings will look after you, Lirael. I guess we should talk about every-thing at dinner tonight?"

"Dinner!" exclaimed Lirael. "We'd better talk about it before then. It sounds like we should be off again straightaway."

"But we only just got here—"

"Yes," agreed Lirael. "But there're the Southerlings, and your friend Nicholas is in danger. It may be that every hour counts."

"Particularly since whoever controls Chlorr and the other Dead knows we're here," growled the Dog. "We must move quickly before we are besieged."

Sam didn't answer for a moment. "Okay," he said quickly. "I'll meet you for lunch in an hour, and we can . . . uh . . . work out what to do next."

He stalked off ahead, his limp suddenly becoming notice-ably worse, and pushed the front door open. Lirael followed more slowly, her hand loosely draped over the Dog's back. Mogget walked next to them for a few paces, then used the Dog's back to springboard himself onto Lirael's shoulder. She jumped as he landed, but relaxed as she realized he had sheathed his claws. The little cat carefully draped himself around her neck and then seemed to go to sleep.

"I'm so tired," Lirael said as they stepped over the threshold. "But we really can't wait, can we?"

"No," growled the Dog as she looked around the entrance hall, sniffing. There was no sign of Sam, but a sending was retreat-ing with the message-hawk on its gloved hand, and two other sendings were waiting at the foot of the main staircase. They wore long habits of light cream, with deep cowls covering their heads, hiding their lack of faces. Only their hands were visible, pale ghostly hands made of Charter marks, which occasionally sparkled as they moved.

One came forward and bowed deeply to Lirael, then beckoned to her to follow. The other went straight to the Disreputable
Dog and took her by the collar. No words were spoken, but both
the Dog and Mogget seemed to guess the sending's intentions.
Mogget, despite appearing to be asleep, was the first to react. He
leapt from Lirael's neck and ran through a cat door under the
stairs, displaying a speed and liveliness Lirael hadn't seen before.
The Dog was either less quick on the uptake or was less practiced in evading the attentions of the sendings of Abhorsen's
House.

"A bath!" she yelped in indignation. "I'm not having a bath!
I swam in the river only yesterday. I don't need a bath!"

"Yes you do," said Lirael, wrinkling her nose. She looked at
the sending and added, "Please make sure she has one. With soap.
And scrubbing."

"Can I at least have a bone afterwards?" asked the downcast
Dog, looking back with pleading eyes as the sending led her away.
Anyone would think she was going to prison, or worse, Lirael
thought. But she couldn't help herself running over to kiss the
hound on the nose.

"Of course you can have a bone, and a big lunch as well. I'm
going to have a bath, too."

"It's different for dogs," said the Dog mournfully, as the sending opened a door to the inside courtyard. "We just don't like
baths!"

"I do, though," whispered Lirael, looking down at her sweat-
stained clothing and running her fingers through her dirty hair.
For the first time she noticed that there was blood on her as well.
The blood of innocents. "A bath and clean clothes. That's what
I need."

The sending bowed again and led her to the stairs. Lirael
followed obediently, enjoying the different creaks in each step as

they climbed. For the next hour, she thought, I will forget about everything.

But even as she followed the sending, she was thinking of the Southerlings who had tried so hard to escape. Escape the pit where their fellows had been killed and forced into servitude. The pit she had seen, with Nicholas standing alone on a hill of spoil, while a necromancer and his lightning-blackened corpses labored to dig up something that Lirael was sure should never again see the light of day.

WHEN LIRAEL CAME back downstairs, she was very clean indeed. The sending had proved to be a true believer in scrubbing and plenty of hot water—the latter supplied by hot springs, Lirael guessed, for the first few basins had been accompanied by a nasty sulphurous whiff, exactly as sometimes happened back in the Glacier.

The sending had put out rather fancy clothes for her, but Lirael had refused them. She put on her spare Librarian's outfit instead. She had worn the uniform for so long that she felt strange without it. At least in her red waistcoat she could feel something like a proper Clayr.

The sending was still trailing after her with a surcoat folded over its arm. It had been quite insistent that she try it on, and Lirael had been hard pressed to explain that waistcoats and surcoats simply didn't go together.

Another sending opened the double doors to the right of the stairs as she came down. The bronze knobs were turned by pale spell-hands, hands that stood out in stark relief against the dark oak as the sending pushed the door open. Then the sending moved aside and bowed its cowled head—and Lirael caught her first glimpse of the main hall. It took up at least half the ground floor, but it was not the size that immediately struck Lirael. She was seized with an intense feeling of déjà vu as she looked down the length of the hall to the great stained-glass window that showed the building of the Wall. And there was the long, brilliantly polished table laden with silver, and the high-backed chair.

Lirael had seen all of this before, in the Dark Mirror. Only then the chair had been occupied by the man who was her father.

"There you are," said Sam from behind her. "I'm sorry I'm late. I couldn't get the sendings to give me the right surcoat—they've dug up something odd. Must be getting senile, like Mogget said."

Lirael turned around and looked at his surcoat. It had the golden towers of the royal line, but they were quartered with a strange device she had never seen—some sort of trowel or spade, in silver.

"It's the Wallmakers' trowel," explained Sam. "But they've all been gone for centuries. A thousand years at least. . . . I say, I like your hair," he added as Lirael continued to stare at him. She wasn't wearing her headscarf. Her black hair was brushed and shining, and the waistcoat didn't really hide her slender form. She really was very attractive, but something about her now struck him as rather forbidding. Whom did she remind him of?

Sam pushed past the sending that was holding the door open, and was halfway to the table when he realized that Lirael hadn't moved. She was still standing in the doorway, staring at the table.

"What?" he asked.

Lirael couldn't speak. She beckoned to the sending that carried her surcoat. Lirael took it and unfolded it so she could see the blazon.

Then she folded the surcoat again, shut her eyes for a silent count of ten, unfolded it, and stared at it again.

"What is it?" asked Sam. "Are you all right?"

"I . . . I don't know how to say this," Lirael began, as she undid her waistcoat and handed it to the sending that appeared at her elbow. Sam started at her sudden undressing, but he was even more shocked when she put on her surcoat and slowly smoothed it out.

On the coat were the golden stars of the Clayr quartered with the silver keys of the Abhorsen.

"I must be half Abhorsen," said Lirael, in a tone that indicated she hardly believed it herself. "In fact, I think I'm your mother's half-sister. Your grandfather was my father. I mean, I'm your aunt. Half-aunt. Sorry."

Sam shut his eyes for several seconds. Then he opened them, trod like a sleepwalker over to a chair, and sat down. After a moment, Lirael sat down opposite him. Finally he spoke.

"My aunt? My mother's half-sister?" He paused. "Does she know?"

"I don't think so," muttered Lirael, suddenly anxious again. She hadn't really thought about the full ramifications of her birth. How would the famous Sabriel feel about the sudden appearance of a sister? "Surely not—or she would have found me long ago. I only worked it out myself by using the Dark Mirror. I wanted to see who my father was. I looked back and saw my parents in this very room. My father was sitting in that chair. They had only one night together, before he had to go away. I suppose that was the year he died."

"Can't have been," said Sam, shaking his head. "That was twenty years ago."

"Oh," said Lirael, blushing. "I lied. I'm only nineteen."

Sam looked at her as if any more revelations would turn his brain. "How did the sendings know to give you that surcoat?" he asked.

"I told them," said Mogget, his head popping up from a chair nearby. It was obvious that he'd been snoozing, because his fur was sticking up all on one side.

"How did you know?" asked Sam.

"I have served the Abhorsens for many centuries," said Mogget, preening. "So I tend to know what's what. Once I realized that Sam was not the Abhorsen-in-Waiting, I kept my eyes open for the real one to turn up, because the bells wouldn't have appeared unless her arrival was imminent. And I was here when Lirael's mother came to see Terciel—that is, the former Abhorsen. So it was rather elementary. Lirael was clearly both the former Abhorsen's daughter and the Abhorsen-in-Waiting the bells were meant for."

"You mean I'm not the Abhorsen-in-Waiting? She is?" asked Sam.

"But I can't be!" exclaimed Lirael. "I mean, I don't want to be. I'm a Clayr. I suppose I am a Remembrancer as well, but I am . . . I am a Daughter of the Clayr!"

She had shouted the last words, and they echoed through the hall.

"Complain all you like, but the Blood will out," said Mogget when the echoes faded. "You are the Abhorsen-in-Waiting, and you must take up the bells."

"Thank the Charter!" sighed Sam, and Lirael saw that there were tears in his eyes. "I mean, I was never going to be any good with them, anyway. You'll be a much better Abhorsen-in-Waiting, Lirael. Look at the way you went into Death with only those little pipes. And you fought Hedge and got away. All I managed to do was get burnt, and let him get to Nicholas."

"I am a Daughter of the Clayr," insisted Lirael, but her voice sounded weak even to her. She had wanted to know who her father was. But being the Abhorsen-in-Waiting, and one day— hopefully long distant—the Abhorsen, was a much more difficult thing to accept. Her life would be dedicated to hunting down and destroying or banishing the Dead. She would travel all over the Kingdom, instead of living the life of a Clayr within the confines of the Glacier.

"'Does the walker choose the path, or the path the walker?'" she whispered, as the final page from *The Book of the Dead* came shining into her mind. Then another thought struck her, and she went white.

"I'll never have the Sight, will I?" she said slowly. She was half Clayr, but it was the Abhorsen's blood that ran strongest in her veins. The gift she had longed for her entire life was finally and absolutely to be denied to her.

"No, you won't, Mistress," said the Dog calmly, as she came in behind Lirael and put her snout on Lirael's lap. "But it is your Clayr heritage that gives you the gift of Remembrance, for only a child of Abhorsen and Clayr can look into the past. You must grow in your own powers—for yourself, for the Kingdom, and for the Charter."

"I will never have the Sight," Lirael whispered again, very slowly. "I will never have the Sight. . . ." She clasped her arms around the neck of the strangely clean Dog, not even noticing that the hound smelled sweetly of soap, for the first and probably last time. But she did not cry. Her eyes were dry. She just felt very cold, unable to warm herself with the Dog's comforting heat.

Sam watched her shiver but did not shift from his chair. He felt as if he should go over and comfort her somehow, but didn't quite know how. It wasn't as if she were a young woman or a girl. She was an aunt, and he didn't know how to behave. Would she be offended if he tried to hug her?

"Is it . . . is the Sight really that important to you?" he asked hesitantly. "You see," he continued, twisting his linen napkin, "I feel . . . I feel amazingly relieved that I don't have to be the

Abhorsen-in-Waiting. I never wanted the sense of Death, or to go into Death or any of it. And when I did, that time, when the necromancer . . . when he caught me . . . I wanted to die, because then it would be over. But I somehow got out, and I knew that I couldn't ever go into Death again. It was just everyone else expecting me to follow in Mother's footsteps, because Ellimere was so obviously going to be the Queen. I thought maybe it was the same for you. You know, all the other Clayr have the Sight, so that's the only thing that matters, even if you don't want it. It would be the only way to meet their expectations, like me being the Abhorsen-in-Waiting. Only I didn't want to be what they wanted, and you did. . . . I'm babbling, aren't I? Sorry."

"More than a hundred words in a row," remarked Mogget. "And most of them made sense. There is hope for you yet, Prince Sameth. Particularly since you are quite right. Lirael is so obviously an Abhorsen that wanting the Sight must be solely a peculiarity of her upbringing in that ridiculously cold mountain of theirs."

"I wanted to belong," said Lirael quietly, sitting up. It was only the shock of losing a childhood dream, she told herself. In a way, she'd known ever since she had been blindfolded before being allowed into the Observatory, or perhaps since Sanar and Ryelle had waved her farewell. She had known that her life would change, that she would never have the Sight, never be truly one of the Clayr. At least she had something else now, she told herself, trying to still the terrible sense of loss. Much better to be the Abhorsen-in-Waiting than a Sightless Clayr, a freak. If only her head could make her heart believe that was true.

"You belong here," said Mogget simply, waving one white and pink paw around the Hall. "I am the oldest servant of the Abhorsens, and I feel it in my very marrow. The sendings likewise. Look at the way they cluster there, just to see you. Look at the

Charter lights that burn brighter above you than anywhere else. This whole House—and its servants—welcome you, Lirael. So will the Abhorsen, and the King, and even your niece, Ellimere."

Lirael looked around, and sure enough, there was a great throng of sendings clustered around the door to the kitchen, filling the room beyond. At least a hundred of them, some so old and faded that their hands were barely visible—just suggestions of light and shadow. As she looked, they all bowed. Lirael bowed in return, feeling the tears she had held back flow freely down her cheeks.

"Mogget is correct," woofled the Dog, her chin securely resting on Lirael's thigh. "Your Blood has made you what you are, but you should remember that it is not just the high office of Abhorsen-in-Waiting you have gained. It is a family you have found, and all will welcome you."

"Absolutely!" exclaimed Sam, jumping up with sudden excitement. "I can't wait to see Ellimere's face when she hears I've found our aunt! Mother will love it, too. I think she's always been a bit disappointed with me as Abhorsen-in-Waiting. And Dad doesn't have any living relatives, because he was imprisoned for so long as a figurehead down in Hole Hallow. It'll be great! We can have a welcoming party for you—"

"Aren't you forgetting something?" interrupted Mogget, with a very sarcastic meow. He continued, "There is the little matter of your friend Nicholas, and the Southerling refugees, and the necromancer Hedge, and whatever they're digging up near the Red Lake."

Sam stopped speaking as if he had been physically gagged, and sat back down, all his enthusiasm erased by a few short words.

"Yes," said Lirael heavily. "That is what we should be concerning ourselves with. We have to work out what to do. That's more important than anything else."

"Except lunch, because no one can plan on an empty stomach," interrupted Mogget, loudly seconded by a hungry bark from the Dog.

"I suppose we do have to eat," agreed Sam, signaling to the sendings to begin serving the luncheon.

"Shouldn't we send the messages first, to your parents and Ellimere?" asked Lirael, though now that she could smell the tasty aromas coming from the kitchen, food did seem to be of prime importance.

"Yes, we should," agreed Sam. "Only I'm not sure exactly what to say."

"Everything we have to, I suppose," said Lirael. It was an effort to get her thoughts together. She kept looking down at the silver keys on her surcoat and feeling dizzy and sort of sick. "We need to make sure that Princess Ellimere and your parents know what we know, particularly that Hedge is digging up something best left buried, something of Free Magic, and that Nick is his captive, and Chlorr has been brought back as a Greater Dead spirit. And we should tell them that we're going to find and rescue Nick and stop whatever the Enemy plans to do."

"I suppose so," agreed Sam half-heartedly. He looked down at the plate the sending had just put in front of him, but his attention was clearly not on the poached salmon. "It's only . . . if I'm not the Abhorsen-in-Waiting, I'm not really going to be able to do much. I was thinking of staying here."

Silence greeted his words. Lirael stared at him, but he wouldn't meet her gaze. Mogget kept eating calmly, while the Dog let out a soft growl that vibrated through Lirael's leg. Lirael looked at Sam, wondering what she could say. Even now she wished she could write a note, push it across the table, and go away to her room. But she was no longer a Second Assistant Librarian of the Great Library of the Clayr. Those days were gone, vanished with everything else that had defined her previous existence and identity. Even her librarian's waistcoat had been spirited away by the sendings.

She was the Abhorsen-in-Waiting. That was her job now, Lirael thought, and she must do it properly. She would not fail in the future, as she had failed the Southerlings on the banks of the Ratterlin.

"You can't, Sameth. It isn't just rescuing your friend Nicholas. Think about what Hedge is trying to do. He's planning to kill two hundred thousand people and unleash every spirit in Death upon the Kingdom! Whatever he's digging up must be part of that. I can't even begin to face it all alone, Sam. I need your help. The Kingdom needs your help. You may not be the Abhorsen-in-Waiting anymore, but you are still a Prince of the Kingdom. You cannot just sit here and do nothing."

"I'm . . . I'm afraid of Death," sobbed Sam, holding up his burnt wrists so Lirael could see the scars there, scarlet burns against the lighter skin. "I'm afraid of Hedge. I . . . I can't face him again."

"I'm afraid, too," Lirael said quietly. "Of Death and Hedge and probably a thousand other things. But I'd rather be afraid and do something than just sit and wait for terrible things to happen."

"Hear, hear," said the Dog, raising her head. "It's always better to be doing, Prince. Besides, you don't smell like a coward—so you can't be one."

"You didn't hide from the crossbowman at High Bridge," added Lirael. "Or the construct when it came across the water. That was brave. And I'm sure that whatever we face won't be as bad as you think."

"It will probably be worse," said Mogget cheerfully. He

seemed to be enjoying Sam's humiliation. "But think of how much worse it would be to sit here, not knowing. Until the Dead choke the Ratterlin and Hedge walks across the dry bed of the river to batter down the door."

Sam shook his head and muttered something about his parents. Obviously he didn't want to believe Mogget's predictions of doom and was still clutching at straws.

"The Enemy has set many pieces in motion," Mogget said. "The King and the Abhorsen seek to counter whatever brews in Ancelstierre. They must succeed in stopping the Southerlings from crossing the Wall, but surely that is only part of the Enemy's plans—and because it is the most obvious, perhaps the least of them."

Sam stared down at the table. All his hunger was gone. Finally he looked up. "Lirael," he said, "do you think I'm a coward?"

"No."

"Then I guess I'm not," said Sam, his voice growing stronger. "Though I am still afraid."

"So you'll come with me? To find Nicholas, and Hedge?"

Sam nodded. He didn't trust himself to speak.

Silence fell in the hall, as they all thought of what lay ahead. Everything had changed, transformed by history and fate and truth. Neither Sam nor Lirael were who they had been, only a little while before. Now they both wondered what all this meant, and where their new lives would lead them.

And where—and how soon—those new lives might end.

Epilogue

Dear Sam,

I am writing to you local-style, with a quill pen and some wretchedly thick paper that soaks up the ink like a sponge. My fountain pen has clogged irreparably, and the paper I brought with me has succumbed to some sort of rot. A fungus, I think.

Your Old Kingdom is certainly inimicable to the products of Ancelstierre. Clearly the level of moisture in the air and the proliferation of local fungi is as abrasive as conditions in the tropics, though I would not have expected it from the latitude.

I have had to cancel most of my planned experiments, due to problems with equipment and some quite alarming experimental errors on my part, invalidating the results. I put this down to the illness I have suffered from ever since I crossed the Wall. Some sort of fever that greatly weakens me and has encouraged hallucinatory episodes.

Hedge, the man I hired in Bain, has proved to be a great asset. Not only did he help me pinpoint the location of the Lightning Trap from all the local rumors and superstitious ramblings, but he has overseen the excavation with commendable zeal.

We had quite a lot of trouble hiring local workers

at first, till Hedge hit upon the idea of recruiting from
what I understand to be a lazaret or leper colony of
sorts. The workers from there are quite able-bodied
but shockingly disfigured, and they smell atrocious. In
daylight, they go about completely muffled in cloaks
and swaddling rags, and they seem much more
comfortable after dark. Hedge calls them the Night
Crew, and I must agree this is an appropriate name.
He assures me the disease is not readily contagious,
but I avoid all physical contact, to be on the safe side.
It is interesting that they share the same preference for
blue hats and scarves as the Southerlings.

The Lightning Trap is as fascinating as I expected.
When we first found it, I observed lightning striking a
small hillock or mound more than twice every hour
for several hours, with thunderstorms overhead on an
almost daily basis. Now, as we get closer to the true
object that is buried underneath, the lightning comes
even more frequently, and there is a constant storm
overhead.

From what I have read and—you will laugh at me
for this, because it is most uncharacteristic—from
what I have dreamt, I believe that the Lightning Trap
itself is composed of two hemispheres of a previously
unknown metal, buried some twenty or thirty fathoms
below the mound, which we found to be completely
artificial and very difficult to break into, with all sorts
of odd building materials. Including bone, if you can
believe it. Now the excavation goes much faster, and I
expect we shall make our discovery within a few days.

I had planned to go on to Belisaere at that point,
to meet you, leaving the experiment in abeyance for a

few weeks. But the state of my health is such that a return to Ancelstierre seems prudent, away from this inclement air.

I will take the hemispheres with me, having procured suitable import licenses from Uncle Edward. I believe they are unusually dense and heavy, but I expect to be able to ship them from the Red Lake downriver to the sea, and from there to a little place north of Nolhaven on the west coast. There is a deserted timber mill there, which I have procured for use as an experimental station. Timothy Wallach—one of my fellow students at Sunbere, though he is in Fourth Year—should already be there, setting up the Lightning Farm I have designed to feed power into the hemispheres.

It is indeed pleasant to have private means and powerful relatives, isn't it? It would be very hard to get things done without them. Mind you, I expect my father will be quite cross when he discovers I have spent a whole quarter's allowance on hundreds of lightning rods and miles of extra-heavy copper wire!

But it will all be worth it when I get the Lightning Trap to my experimental station. I am sure that I will be quickly able to prove that the hemispheres can store incalculable amounts of electrical energy, all drawn from storms. Once I have solved the riddle of extracting that power again, I shall need only to replicate them on a smaller scale, and we shall have a new source of limitless, inexpensive power! Sayre's Super Batteries will power the cities and industries of the future!

As you can see, my dreams are as large as my

seriously enlarged head. I need you to come and
shrink it, Sam, with some criticism of my person or
abilities!

In fact, I hope you will be able to come and see
my Lightning Farm in all its glory. Do try, if it is at all
possible, though I know you dislike crossing the Wall. I
understand from my last conversation with Uncle
Edward that your parents are already in Ancelstierre,
discussing Corolini's plans to settle the Southerling
refugees in your deserted lands near the Wall. Perhaps
you could tie in a visit to them with a side trip to see
my work?

In any case, I look forward to seeing you before
too long, and I remain your loyal friend,

Nicholas Sayre

*Nick put the pen down and blew on the paper. Not that it needed
it, he thought, looking at the blurred lines where the ink had spread,
making a mockery of his penmanship.*

*"Hedge!" he called, sitting back to quell a wave of dizziness and
nausea. These fits often came over him now, especially after concentrating
on something. His hair was falling out, too, and his gums were sore. But
it couldn't be scurvy, for his diet was varied and he drank a glass of fresh
lime juice every day.*

*He was about to call for Hedge again when the man appeared at the
tent door. Barbarously clad, as usual, but the man was very efficient. As
you would expect from a former sergeant in the Crossing Point Scouts.*

*"I have a letter to go to my friend Prince Sameth," said Nick,
folding the paper several times and sealing it with a blob of wax
straight from the candle and a thumbprint. "Can you see it gets sent
by messenger or whatever they have here? Send someone to Edge, if
necessary."*

"Don't worry, Master," replied Hedge, smiling his enigmatic smile. "I'll see it's taken care of."

"Good," mumbled Nick. It was too hot again, and the lotion he'd brought to repel insects was not working. He'd have to ask Hedge again to do whatever it was he did to keep them at bay . . . but first there was the ever-present question—the status of the pit.

"How goes the digging?" Nick asked. "How deep?"

"Twenty-two fathoms by my measure," replied Hedge, with great enthusiasm. "We will soon be there."

"And the barge is ready?" asked Nick, forcing himself to keep upright. He really wanted to lie down, as the room started to spin and the light began to gain a strange redness that he knew was only in his own eyes.

"I need to recruit some sailors," said Hedge. "The Night Crew fear water, because of their . . . affliction. But I expect my new recruits to arrive any day. Everything is taken care of, Master," he added, as Nick didn't reply. But he was looking at the young man's chest, not at his eyes. Nick stared back at him, unseeing, his breath coming in ragged gasps. Somewhere deep inside, he knew that he was fainting, as he so often did in front of Hedge. A damnable weakness he could not control.

Hedge waited, licking his lips nervously. Nick's head swayed forward and back. He groaned, his eyelids flickering. Then he sat up, bolt straight in his chair.

Nick had indeed fainted, and there was something else behind his eyes, some other intelligence that had lain dormant. It suddenly sang now, accompanied by fumes of acrid white smoke that coiled out of Nick's nose and throat.

"I'll sing you a song of the long ago—
  Seven shine the shiners, oh!
  What did the Seven do way back when?
  Why, they wove the Charter then!

Five for the warp, from beginning to end.
Two for the woof, to make and mend.
That's the Seven, but what of the Nine—
What of the two who chose not to shine?
The Eighth did hide, hide all away,
But the Seven caught him and made him pay.
The Ninth was strong and fought with might,
But lone Orannis was put out of the light,
Broken in two and buried under hill,
Forever to lie there, wishing us ill."

There was silence for a moment after the song, then the voice whispered the last two lines again.

"'Broken in two and buried under hill, Forever to lie there, wishing us ill'. . . . But it is not my song, Hedge. The world spins on without my song. Life that knows not my lash crawls unbidden wherever it will go. Creation runs amok, without the balance of destruction—and my dreams of fire are only dreams. But soon the world will fall asleep, and it will be my dream that all will dream, my song that will fill every ear. Is it not so, my faithful Hedge?"

Whatever spoke did not wait for Hedge to answer. It went on immediately, in a different, harsher tone, no longer singing. "Destroy the letter. Send more Dead to Chlorr and make sure that they slay the Prince, for he must not come here. Walk in Death yourself, and keep watch for the spying Daughter of the Clayr, and kill her if she is seen again. Dig faster, for I . . . must . . . be . . . whole . . . again!"

The last words were shouted with a force that threw Hedge against the rotting canvas of the tent, to burst out into the night. He looked back through the rent, fearful of worse, but whatever had spoken through Nick was gone. Only an unconscious, sick young man remained, blood slowly trickling from both nostrils.

"I hear you, Lord," whispered Hedge. "And as always, I obey."

Abhorsen

To Anna and Thomas Henry Nix

CONTENTS

PART THREE 999

Prologue

Fog rose from the river, great billows of white weaving into the soot and smoke of the city of Corvere, to become the hybrid thing that the more popular newspapers called smog and the Times *"miasmic fog." Cold, dank, and foul-smelling, it was dangerous by any name. At its thickest, it could smother, and it could transform the faintest hint of a cough into pneumonia.*

But the unhealthiness of the fog was not its chief danger. That came from its other primary feature. The Corvere fog was a concealer, a veil that shrouded the city's vaunted gaslights and confused both eyes and ears. When the fog lay on the city, all streets were dark, all echoes strange, and everywhere set for murder and mayhem.

"The fog shows no signs of lifting," reported Damed, principal body-guard to King Touchstone. His voice showed his dislike of the fog even though he knew it was only a natural phenomenon, a blend of industrial pollution and river-mist. Back in their home, the Old Kingdom, such fogs were often created by Free Magic sorcerers. "Also, the . . . telephone . . . is not working, and the escort is both understrength and new. There is not one of the officers we usually have among them. I don't think you should go, sire."

Touchstone was standing by the window, peering out through the shutters. They'd had to shutter all the windows some days ago, when some of the crowd outside had adopted slingshots. Before that, the demonstrators hadn't been able to throw half bricks far enough, as the mansion that housed the Old Kingdom Embassy was set in a walled park, and a good fifty yards back from the street.

Not for the first time, Touchstone wished that he could reach the Charter and draw upon it for strength and magical assistance. But they were five hundred miles south of the Wall, and the air was still and cold. Only when the wind blew very strongly from the north could he feel even the slightest touch of his magical heritage.

Sabriel felt the lack of the Charter even more, Touchstone knew. He glanced at his wife. She was at her desk, as usual, writing one last letter to an old school friend, a prominent businessman, or a member of the Ancelstierre Moot. Promising gold, or support, or introductions, or perhaps making thinly veiled threats of what would happen if they were stupid enough to support Corolini's attempts to settle hundreds of thousands of Southerling refugees over the Wall, in the Old Kingdom.

Touchstone still found it odd to see Sabriel dressed in Ancelstierran clothes, particularly their court clothes, as she was wearing today. She should be in her blue and silver tabard, with the bells of the Abhorsen across her chest, her sword at her side. Not in a silver dress with a hussar's pelisse worn on one shoulder, and a strange little pillbox hat pinned to her deep-black hair. And the small automatic pistol in her silver mesh purse was no substitute for a sword.

Not that Touchstone felt at ease in his clothes either. An Ancelstierran shirt with its stiff collar and tie was too constricting, and his suit offered no protection at all. A sharp blade would slide through the double-breasted coat of superfine wool as easily as it would through butter, and as for a bullet . . .

"Shall I convey your regrets, sire?" asked Damed.

Touchstone frowned and looked at Sabriel. She had been to school in Ancelstierre, she understood the people and their ruling classes far better than he did. She led their diplomatic efforts south of the Wall, as she had always done.

"No," said Sabriel. She stood up and sealed the last letter with a sharp tap. "The Moot sits tonight, and it is possible Corolini will

present his Forced Emigration Bill. Dawforth's bloc may just give us the votes to defeat the motion. We must attend his garden party."

"In this fog?" asked Touchstone. "How can he have a garden party?"

"They will ignore the weather," said Sabriel. "We will all stand around, drinking green absinthe and eating carrots cut into elegant shapes, and pretend we're having a marvelous time."

"Carrots?"

"A fad of Dawforth's, introduced by his swami," replied Sabriel. "According to Sulyn."

"She would know," said Touchstone, making a face—but at the prospect of raw carrots and green absinthe, not Sulyn. She was one of the old school friends who had been so much help to them. Sulyn, like the others at Wyverley College twenty years ago, had seen what happened when Free Magic was stirred up and grew strong enough to cross the Wall and run amok in Ancelstierre.

"We will go, Damed," said Sabriel. "But it would be sensible to put in place the plan we discussed."

"I do beg your pardon, Milady Abhorsen," replied Damed. "But I'm not sure that it will increase your safety. In fact, it may make matters worse."

"But it will be more fun," pronounced Sabriel. "Are the cars ready? I shall just put on my coat and some boots."

Damed nodded reluctantly and left the room. Touchstone picked out a dark overcoat from a number that were draped across the back of a chaise longue and shrugged it on. Sabriel put on another—a man's coat—and sat down to exchange her shoes for boots.

"Damed isn't concerned without reason," Touchstone said as he offered his hand to Sabriel. "And the fog is very thick. If we were at home, I wouldn't doubt it was made with malice aforethought."

"The fog is natural enough," replied Sabriel. They stood close together and knotted each others' scarves, finishing with a soft, brushing kiss. "But I agree it may well be used against us. Yet I am so close to forming an alliance against Corolini. If Dawforth comes in, and the Sayres stay out of the matter—"

"Little chance of that unless we can show them we haven't made off with their precious son and nephew," growled Touchstone, but his attention was on his pistols. He checked both were loaded and there was a round in the chamber, hammer down and safety on. "I wish we knew more about this guide Nicholas hired. I am sure I have heard the name Hedge before, and not in any positive light. If only we'd met them on the Great South Road."

"I am sure we will hear from Ellimere soon," said Sabriel as she checked her own pistol. "Or perhaps even from Sam. We must leave that matter, at least, to the good sense of our children and deal with what is before us."

Touchstone grimaced at the notion of his children's good sense, handed Sabriel a grey felt hat with a black band, twin to his own, and helped her remove the pillbox and pin her hair up underneath the replacement.

"Ready?" he asked as she belted her coat. With their hats on, collars up, and scarves wound high, they looked indistinguishable from Damed and their other guards. Which was precisely the idea.

There were ten bodyguards waiting outside, not including the drivers of the two heavily armored Hedden-Hare automobiles. Sabriel and Touchstone joined them, and the twelve huddled together for a moment. If any enemies were watching beyond the walls, they would be hard put to make out who was who through the fog.

Two people went into the back of each car, with the remaining eight standing on the running boards. The drivers had kept the engines idling for some time, the exhausts sending a steady stream of warm, lighter emissions into the fog.

At a signal from Damed, the cars started down the drive, sounding their Klaxons. This was the signal for the guards at the gate to throw it open, and for the Ancelstierran police outside to push the crowd apart. There was always a crowd these days, mostly made up of Corolini's supporters: paid thugs and agitators wearing the red armbands of Corolini's Our Country party.

Despite Damed's worries, the police did their job well, separating the throng so that the two cars could speed through. A few bricks and stones were hurled after them, but they missed the riding guards or bounced off the hardened glass and armor plate. Within a minute, the crowd was left behind, just a dark, shouting mass in the fog.

"The escort is not following," said Damed, who was riding the running board next to the front car's driver. A detachment of mounted police had been assigned to accompany King Touchstone and his Abhorsen Queen wherever they went in the city, and up to now they had performed their duty to the expected standards of the Corvere Police Corps. This time the troopers were still standing by their horses.

"Maybe they got their orders mixed up," said the driver through her open quarter window. But there was no conviction in her voice.

"We'd better change the route," ordered Damed. "Take Harald Street. Left up ahead."

The cars sped past two slower automobiles, a heavily laden truck, and a horse and wagon, braked sharply, and curved left into the broad stretch of Harald Street. This was one of the more modern promenades, and better lit, with gas lamps on both sides of the street at regular intervals. Even so, the fog made it unsafe to drive faster than fifteen miles per hour.

"Something up ahead!" reported the driver. Damed looked up and swore. As their headlights pierced the fog, he saw a great mass of people blocking the street. He couldn't make out what was on the banners they held, but it was easy enough to recognize it as an Our Country demonstration. To make it worse, there were no police to keep them in check. Not one blue-helmeted officer in sight.

"Stop! Back up!" said Damed. He waved at the car behind, a

double signal that meant "Trouble!" and "Retreat!"

Both cars started to back up. As they did, the crowd ahead surged forward. They'd been silent till then. Now they started shouting, "Foreigners out!" and "Our Country!" The shouts were accompanied by bricks and stones, which for the moment fell short.

"Back up!" shouted Damed again. He drew his pistol, holding it down by his leg. "Faster!"

The rear car was almost back at the corner when the truck and the wagon they'd passed pulled across, blocking the way. Masked men dropped out of the backs of both vehicles, sending the fog shivering as they ran. Men with guns.

Damed knew even before he saw the guns that this was what he had feared all along.

An ambush.

"Out! Out!" he shouted, pointing at the armed men. "Shoot!"

Around him the other guards were opening car doors for cover. A second later they opened fire, the deeper boom of their pistols accompanied by the sharp tap-tap-tap of the new, compact machine rifles that were so much handier than the Army's old Lewins. None of the guards liked guns, but they had practiced with them constantly since coming south of the Wall.

"Not the crowd!" roared Touchstone. "Only armed targets!"

Their attackers were not so careful. They had gone under their vehicles, behind a post box, and down on the footpath beside a low wall of flower boxes, and were firing wildly.

Bullets ricocheted off the street and the armored cars in mad, zinging screeches. There was noise everywhere, harsh, confused sound, a mixture of screaming and shouting combined with the constant crack and chatter of gunfire. The crowd, so eager to rush forward only seconds before, had become a terrible, tumbling crush of people trying to flee.

Damed rushed to a knot of guards crouched behind the engine of the rear car.

"The river," he shouted. "Go through the square and down the Warden Steps. We have two boats there. You'll lose any pursuit in the fog."

"We can fight our way back to the Embassy!" retorted Touchstone.

"This is too well planned! The police have turned, or enough of them! You must get out of Corvere. Out of Ancelstierre!"

"No!" shouted Sabriel. "We haven't finished—"

She was cut off as Damed violently pushed her and Touchstone over and leapt above them. With his legendary quickness, he intercepted a large black cylinder that was tumbling through the air, trailing smoke behind it.

A bomb.

Damed caught and threw it in one swift motion, but even he was not fast enough.

The bomb exploded while it was still in the air. Packed with high explosive and pieces of metal, it killed Damed instantly. The blast broke every window for half a mile and momentarily deafened and blinded everyone within a hundred yards. But it was the thousands of metal fragments that did the real damage, ripping and screaming through the air, to bounce off stone or metal, or all too often to cut through flesh.

Silence followed the explosion, save for the roar of the burning gas from the shattered lamps. Even the fog had been thrown back by the force of the blast, which had cleared a great circle open to the sky. Rays of weak sunshine filtered through, to illuminate a scene of terrible destruction.

There were bodies strewn all around and under the cars, not one overcoated guard still on his or her feet. Even the car's armored windows were broken, and the occupants were slumped in death.

The surviving assassins waited for a few minutes before they crawled out from behind the low wall and moved forward, laughing and congratulating one another, their weapons cradled casually under their arms or across their shoulders with what they imagined was debonair style.

The talk and laughter were too loud, but they didn't notice. Their *senses were battered, their minds in shock. Not only from the explosion or the terrible sights that drew closer and more real with every step, or even with relief at being alive in the midst of so much death and destruction.*

The real shock came from the realization that it was three hundred years since a King and a Queen had been slain on the streets of Corvere. Now it had happened again—and they had done the deed.

PART ONE

Chapter One

A HOUSE BESIEGED

THERE WAS ANOTHER fog, far away from the smog of Corvere. Six hundred miles to the north, across the Wall that separated Ancelstierre from the Old Kingdom. The Wall where the Old Kingdom's magic really began and Ancelstierre's modern technology failed.

This fog was different from its far-southern cousin. It was not white but the dark grey of a storm cloud, and it was completely unnatural. This fog had been spun from air and Free Magic and was born on a hilltop far from any water. It survived and spread despite the heat of a late-spring afternoon, which should have burned it into nothing.

Ignoring sun and light breezes, the fog spread from the hill and rolled south and east, thin tendrils creeping out in advance of the main body. Half a league on from the hill, one of these tendrils separated into a cloud that rose high in the air and crossed the mighty river Ratterlin. Once across, it sank to sit like a toad on the eastern bank, and new fog began to puff out of it.

Soon the two arms of fog shrouded both western and eastern shores of the Ratterlin, though the sun still shone on the river in between.

Both river and fog sped at their very different paces towards the Long Cliffs. The river dashed along, getting faster and faster as it headed to the great waterfall, where it would plunge down more than a thousand feet. The fog was slow and threatening. It thickened and rose higher as it rolled on.

A few yards before it reached the Long Cliffs, the fog stopped, though it still grew thicker and rose higher, threatening the island that sat in the middle of the river and on the edge of the waterfall. An island with high white walls that enclosed a house and gardens.

The fog did not spread across the river, nor lean in too far as it rose. There were unseen defenses that held it back, that kept the sun shining on the white walls, the gardens, and the red-tiled house. The fog was a weapon, but it was only the first move in a battle, only the beginning of a siege. The battle lines were drawn and the House invested.

For the whole river-circled isle was Abhorsen's House. Home to the Abhorsen, whose birthright and charge was to maintain the borders of Life and Death. The Abhorsen, who used necromantic bells and Free Magic, but who was neither necromancer nor Free Magic sorcerer. The Abhorsen, who sent any Dead who trespassed in Life back to whence they came.

The creator of the fog knew that the Abhorsen was not actually in the House. The Abhorsen and her husband, the King, had been lured across the Wall and would presumably be dealt with there. That was part of her Master's plan, long since laid but only recently begun in earnest.

The plan had many parts, in many countries, though the very heart and reason for it lay in the Old Kingdom. War, assassination, and refugees were elements of the plan, all manipulated by a scheming, subtle mind that had waited generations for everything to come to fruition.

But as with any plan, there had already been complications and problems. Two of them were in the House. One was a young woman, who had been sent south by the witches who lived in the glacier-clad mountain at the Ratterlin's source. The Clayr, who Saw many futures in the ice, and who would certainly try to twist the present to their own ends. The woman was one of their elite mages, easily identified by the colored waistcoat she wore. A red waistcoat, marking her as a Second Assistant Librarian.

The maker of the fog had seen her, black haired and pale skinned, surely no older than twenty, a mere fingernail sliver of an age. She had heard the young woman's name, called out in desperate battle.

Lirael.

The other complication was better known, and possibly more trouble, though the evidence was conflicting. A young man, hardly more than a boy, curly haired from his father, black eyebrowed from his mother, and tall from both. His name was Sameth, the royal son of King Touchstone and the Abhorsen Sabriel.

Prince Sameth was meant to be the Abhorsen-in-Waiting, heir to the powers of *The Book of the Dead* and the seven bells. But the maker of the fog doubted that now. She was very old, and once she had known a great deal about the strange family and their House in the river. She had fought Sameth barely a night past, and he had not fought like an Abhorsen; even the way he cast his Charter Magic was strange, reminiscent of neither the royal line nor the Abhorsens.

Sameth and Lirael were not alone. They were supported by two creatures who appeared to be no more than a small bad-tempered white cat and a large black and tan dog of friendly disposition. Yet both were much more than they seemed, though exactly what they were was another slippery piece of information. Most likely they were Free Magic spirits of some kind, bound in service to the Abhorsen and the Clayr. The cat was known to some degree. His name was Mogget, and there was speculation about him in certain books of lore. The Dog was a different matter. She was new, or so old that any book that told of her was long since dust. The creature in the fog thought the latter. Both the young woman and her hound had come from the Great Library of the Clayr. It was likely both of them, like the Library, had hidden depths and contained unknown powers.

Together, these four could be formidable opponents, and they represented a serious threat. But the maker of the fog did not have to fight them directly, nor could she, for the House was too well guarded by both spell and swift water. Her orders were to make sure that they were trapped in the House. The House was to be besieged while matters progressed elsewhere—until it was too late for Lirael, Sam, and their companions to do anything at all.

Chlorr of the Mask hissed as she thought of those orders, and fog billowed around what passed for her head. She had once been a living necromancer, and she took orders from no one. She had made a mistake, a mistake that had led to her servitude and death. But her Master had not let her go to the Ninth Gate and beyond. She had been returned to Life, though not in any living form. She was a Dead creature now, caught by the power of bells, bound by her secret name. She did not like her orders yet had no choice but to obey.

Chlorr lowered her arms. A few feathery tendrils of fog issued from her fingers. There were Dead Hands all around her, hundreds and hundreds of swaying, suppurating corpses. Chlorr had not brought the spirits that inhabited these rotten, half-skeletal bodies out of Death, but she had been given command of them by the one who had. She raised one thin, long arm of shadow and pointed. With sighs and groans and gurgles and the clicking of frozen joints and broken bones, the Dead Hands marched forward, sending the fog swirling all around them.

☥✦◇

"There are at least two hundred Dead Hands on the western bank, and fourscore or more to the east," reported Sameth. He straightened up from behind the bronze telescope and swung it down out of the way. "I couldn't see Chlorr, but she must be there somewhere, I guess."

He shivered as he thought of the last time he'd seen Chlorr, a thing of malignant darkness looming above him, her flaming sword about to fall. That had been only the night before, though it already felt much longer ago.

"It's possible some other Free Magic sorcerer could have raised this mist," said Lirael. But she didn't believe it. She could sense the same brooding power out there that she'd felt last night.

"Fog," said the Disreputable Dog, who was delicately balanced on the observer's stool. Apart from the fact that she could talk, and the bright collar made of Charter marks around her neck, she looked just like any other large black and tan mongrel dog. The kind that smiled and wagged their tails more than they barked and growled. "I think it has thickened sufficiently to be called fog."

The Dog; her mistress, Lirael; Prince Sameth; and the Abhorsen's cat-shaped servant, Mogget, were all in the observatory that occupied the topmost floor of the tower on the northern side of Abhorsen's House.

The observatory's walls were entirely transparent, and Lirael found herself taking nervous glances at the ceiling, because it was hard to see if anything was holding it up. The walls were not glass either, or any material she knew, which somehow made it even worse.

But she didn't want her nervousness to show, so Lirael turned her most recent twitch into a nod of agreement as the Dog spoke. Only her hand betrayed her feelings, as she kept it resting on the Dog's neck, for the comfort of warm dog skin and the Charter Magic in the Dog's collar.

Though it was only early afternoon, and the sun still shone directly down on the House, the island, and the river, there was a solid mass of fog on either bank, billowing up in sheer walls that kept on climbing and climbing, though they were already several hundred feet high.

The fog was clearly sorcerous in origin. It had not risen from the river as a normal fog would, or come with lowering cloud. This fog had flowed in from the east and west at the same time, moving swiftly regardless of the wind. Thin at first, it had grown thicker with every passing minute.

A further indication of the fog's strangeness lay directly to the south, where it stopped sharply just before it might mix with the natural mist thrown up by the great waterfall where the river flung itself over the Long Cliffs.

The Dead had come soon after the fog. Lumbering corpses who climbed clumsily along the riverbanks, though they feared the swift-flowing water. Something was driving them on, something hidden farther back in the fog. Almost certainly that something was Chlorr of the Mask, once a necromancer, now herself one of the Greater Dead. A very dangerous combination, Lirael knew, for Chlorr had probably retained much of her old sorcerous knowledge of Free Magic, combined with whatever powers she had gained in Death. Powers that were likely to be dark and strange. Lirael and the Dog had briefly driven Chlorr away in the last night's battle on the riverbank, but it had not been a victory.

Lirael could feel the presence of the Dead and the sorcerous nature of the fog. Though Abhorsen's House was defended by deep running water and many magical wards and guards, she still shivered, as if a cold hand had trailed fingers across her skin.

No one commented on the shiver, though Lirael felt embarrassed at how obvious it had been. No one said anything, but they were all looking at her. Sam, the Dog, and Mogget, all waiting as if she were going to pronounce some great wisdom or insight. For a moment Lirael felt a surge of panic. She wasn't used to taking the lead in conversation, or in anything else. But she was the Abhorsen-in-Waiting now. While Sabriel was across the Wall in Ancelstierre, she was the only Abhorsen. The Dead, the fog, and Chlorr were her problems. And they were only minor problems, compared to the real threat—whatever Hedge and Nicholas were digging up near the Red Lake.

I'll have to pretend, thought Lirael. I'll have to act like an Abhorsen. Maybe if I act well enough, I'll come to believe it myself.

"Apart from the stepping-stones, is there any other way out?" she asked suddenly, turning south to look at the stones that were just visible under the water, leading out to both eastern and western banks. Stepping-stones was not quite the right name, Lirael thought. Jumping-stones would be more appropriate, as they were set at least six feet apart and were very close to the edge of the waterfall. If you missed a jump, the river would snatch you up and the waterfall would throw you down. Down a very long way, under a great weight of crushing water.

"Sam?"

Sam shook his head.

"Mogget?"

The little white cat was curled up on the blue and gold cushion that had briefly been on the observer's stool, before it was knocked off by a paw and put to better use on the floor. Mogget was not actually a cat, though he had the shape of one. The collar of Charter marks with its miniature bell—Ranna, the Sleepbringer—showed that he was much more than any simple talking cat.

Mogget opened one bright-green eye and yawned widely.

Ranna tinkled on his collar, and Lirael and Sam found them-selves yawning as well.

"Sabriel took the Paperwing, so we cannot fly out," he said. "Even if we could fly, we'd have to get past the Gore Crows. I suppose we could call a boat, but the Dead would follow us along the banks."

Lirael looked out at the walls of fog. She had been the Abhorsen-in-Waiting for only two hours, and already she didn't know what to do. Except that she had an absolute conviction that they must leave the House and hurry to the Red Lake. They had to find Sam's friend Nicholas and stop him from digging up whatever it was that was imprisoned deep beneath the earth.

"There might be another way," said the Dog. She jumped down from the stool and began to tread a circle near Mogget as she spoke, high-stepping as if she were pressing down grass beneath her paws rather than cool stone. On "way" she suddenly collapsed onto the floor near the cat and slapped a heavy paw near the cat's head. "Though Mogget won't like it."

"What way?" Mogget hissed, arching his back. "I know of no way out but the stepping-stones, or the air above, or the river—and I have been here since the House was built."

"But not when the river was split and the island made," said the Dog calmly. "Before the Wallmakers raised the walls, when the first Abhorsen's tent was pitched where the great fig grows now."

"True," conceded Mogget. "But neither were you."

There was the hint of a question, or doubt, in Mogget's last words, thought Lirael. She watched the Disreputable Dog care-fully, but all the hound did was scratch her nose with both forepaws before continuing.

"In any case, there was once another way. If it still exists, it is deep, and it could be dangerous in more ways than one. Some might say it would be safer to cross the stones and fight our way through the Dead."

"But not you?" asked Lirael. "You think there is an alternative?"

Lirael was afraid of the Dead, but not so much that she could not face them if she had to. She was just not entirely confident in her newfound identity. Perhaps an Abhorsen like Sabriel, in the full flower of her years and power, could simply leap across the stepping-stones and put Chlorr, the Shadow Hands, and all the other Dead to rout. Lirael thought if she tried that herself, she would end up retreating back across the stones and quite likely fall into the river and be smashed to pieces in the waterfall.

"I think we should investigate it," pronounced the Dog. She stretched out, almost hitting Mogget again with her paws, then slowly stood up and yawned, revealing many extremely large, very white teeth. All of this, Lirael was sure, was to annoy Mogget.

Mogget looked at the Dog through narrowed eyes.

"Deep?" mewed the cat. "Does that mean what I think it does? We cannot go there!"

"She is long gone," replied the Dog. "Though I suppose something might linger. . . ."

"She?" asked Lirael and Sameth together.

"You know the well in the rose garden?" asked the Dog. Sameth nodded, while Lirael tried to remember if she'd seen a well as they'd crossed the island to the House. She did vaguely recall catching a glimpse of roses, many roses sprawled across trellises that rose up past the eastern side of the lawn closest to the House.

"It is possible to climb down the well," continued the Dog. "Though it is a long climb, and narrow. It will bring us to even deeper caves. There is a way through them to the base of the waterfall. Then we will have to climb back up the cliffs again, but I expect we will be able to do that farther west, bypassing Chlorr and her minions."

"The well is full of water," said Sam. "We'll drown!"

"Are you sure?" asked the Dog. "Have you ever looked in it?"

"Well, no," said Sam. "It's covered, I think. . . ."

"Who is the 'she' you mentioned?" asked Lirael firmly. She knew very well from past experience when the Dog was avoiding an issue.

"Someone once lived down there," replied the Dog. "Someone who had considerable and dangerous powers. There might be some remnant of her there."

"What do you mean, 'someone'?" asked Lirael sternly. "How could someone have lived deep underneath Abhorsen's House?"

"I refuse to go anywhere near that well," interjected Mogget. "I suppose it was Kalliel who thought to dig into forbidden ground. What use to add our bones to his in some dark corner of the depths?"

Lirael's gaze flicked across to Sam for an instant, then back to Mogget. She regretted it instantly, for it showed her own doubts and fears. Now that she was the Abhorsen-in-Waiting, she had to set an example. Sam had been open about his fear of Death and the Dead, and his desire to hide out here in the heavily protected House. But he had overcome his fear, at least for now. How could Sam continue to be brave if she didn't set an example?

Lirael was also his aunt. She didn't feel like an aunt, but she supposed that it carried certain responsibilities towards a nephew, even one who was only a few years younger than herself.

"Dog!" ordered Lirael. "Answer me plainly for once. Who . . . or what . . . is down there?"

"Well, it's difficult to put into words," said the Dog. She shuffled her front paws again. "Particularly since there's probably no one down there at all. If there is, I suppose that you would call her a leftover from the creation of the Charter, as am I, and so many others of varying stature. But if she is there, or some part of her, then it's possible she is as she was, which is dangerous in a very . . . *elemental* . . . way, though it's all so long ago and really I'm only telling you what other people have said or written or thought. . . ."

"Why would she be down there?" asked Sameth. "Why under Abhorsen's House?"

"She's not exactly anywhere," replied the Dog, who was now scratching at her nose with one paw and totally failing to meet anybody's eyes. "Part of her power is invested here, so if she were to be anywhere, it's likely to be here, and that's where if she were anywhere she'd be."

"Mogget?" asked Lirael. "Can you translate anything the Dog has said?"

Mogget didn't answer. His eyes were shut. Somewhere in the space of the Dog's answer he had curled up and gone to sleep.

"Mogget!" repeated Lirael.

"He sleeps," said the Dog. "Ranna has called him into slumber."

"I think he only listens to Ranna when he feels like it," said Sam. "I hope Kerrigor sleeps more soundly."

"We can look, if you like," said the Dog. "But I am sure we would know if he had woken. Ranna has a lighter hand than Saraneth, but she holds tightly when she must. Besides, Kerrigor's power lay in his followers. His art was to draw upon them, and his downfall was to depend upon it."

"What do you mean?" asked Lirael. "I thought he was a Free Magic sorcerer who became one of the Greater Dead?"

"He was more than that," said the Dog. "For he had the

royal blood. Mastery of others ran deep in him. Somewhere in Death, Kerrigor found the means to use the strength of those who swore allegiance to him, through the brand he burned upon their flesh. If Sabriel had not accidentally used a most ancient charm that severed him from this power, I think Kerrigor would have triumphed. For a time, at least."

"Why only for a time?" asked Sam. He wished he had never mentioned Kerrigor in the first place.

"I think he would eventually have done what your friend Nicholas is doing now," said the Dog. "And dug up something best left alone."

No one said anything to that.

"We're wasting time," Lirael said finally.

She looked out at the fog on the western bank again. She could feel many Dead Hands there, more than could be seen, though there were plenty enough of those. Rotting sentries, wreathed in fog. Waiting for their enemy to come out.

Lirael took a deep breath and made her decision.

"If you think we should climb down the well, Dog, then that is the way we will go. Hopefully we will not encounter whatever remnant of power lurks below. Or perhaps she will be friendly, and we can talk—"

"No!" barked the Dog, surprising everyone. Even Mogget opened an eye but, seeing Sam looking at him, hastily shut it again.

"What?" asked Lirael.

"If she is there, which is very unlikely, you musn't speak to her," said the Dog. "You must not listen to her or touch her in any way."

"Has anyone ever heard or touched her?" asked Sam.

"No mortal," said Mogget, raising his head. "Nor passed through her halls, I would guess. It is madness to try. I always wondered what happened to Kalliel."

"I thought you were asleep," said Lirael. "Besides, she might ignore us as we ignore her."

"It is not her ill will I am afraid of," said Mogget. "I fear her paying us any attention at all."

"Perhaps we should—" said Sam.

"What?" asked Mogget nastily. "Stay here all nice and safe?"

"No," replied Sam quietly. "If this woman's voice is so dangerous, then perhaps we should make earplugs before we go. Out of wax, or something."

"It wouldn't help," said Mogget. "If she speaks, you will hear her through your very bones. If she sings . . . We had best hope she will not sing."

"We will avoid her," said the Dog. "Trust to my nose. We will find our path."

"Can you tell us who Kalliel was?" asked Sam.

"Kalliel was the twelfth Abhorsen," replied Mogget. "A most untrusting individual. He kept me locked up for years. The well must have been dug then. His grandson released me when Kalliel disappeared, and he inherited his grandsire's bells and title. I do not wish to share Kalliel's doom. Particularly down a well."

Lirael twitched as she suddenly felt some shift out in the fog. The brooding presence that had been lurking farther back was moving. She could sense it, a being far more powerful than the Shadow Hands who were beginning to flicker in and out of the edge of the fog.

Chlorr was coming closer, almost down to the riverbank. Or if not Chlorr, someone of equal or greater power. Perhaps it was even the necromancer she had encountered in Death.

Hedge. The same necromancer who had burned Sam. Lirael could still see the scars on Sam's wrists, through the slits in the sleeves of his surcoat.

That surcoat was another mystery—for another day, Lirael thought wearily. A surcoat that quartered the royal towers with a device that had not been seen for millennia. The trowel of the Wallmakers.

Sam caught her glance and picked at the heavy golden thread where the Wallmakers' symbol was woven through the linen. It was only slowly entering his head that the sendings hadn't made a mistake with the surcoat. For a start, it was new made, not some old thing they'd dragged out of a musty cupboard or centuries-old laundry basket. So he probably was entitled to wear it for some reason. He was a Wallmaker as well as a royal Prince. But what did that mean? The Wallmakers had disappeared millennia ago, putting themselves into the creation of the Wall and the Great Charter Stones. Quite literally, as far as Sam knew.

For a moment, he wondered if that would be his destiny, too. Would he have to make something that would end his life, at least as a living, breathing man? For the Wallmakers weren't exactly dead, Sam thought, remembering the Great Charter Stones and the Wall. They were more transformed or transfigured.

Not that he fancied that, either. In any case, he was far more likely to simply get killed, he thought, as he looked out to the fog and felt the cold presence of the Dead within it.

Sam touched the gold thread on his chest again and took comfort from it, his fear of the Dead receding. He had never wanted to be an Abhorsen. A Wallmaker was much more interesting, even if he didn't know what it meant to be one. It would have the added benefit of driving his sister, Ellimere, crazy, since she would never believe he didn't know and couldn't, rather than wouldn't, explain what it was to be a Wallmaker.

Presuming he ever saw Ellimere again . . .

"We'd best be moving," said the Dog, startling both Lirael and Sam. Lirael had been staring out into the fog again, too, lost in her own thoughts.

"Yes," said Lirael, tearing her gaze away. Not for the first time, she wished she were back in the Great Library of the Clayr. But that, like her lifelong wish to wear the white robes and the silver-and-moonstone crown of a fully fledged Daughter of the Clayr, had to be pushed away and buried deep. She was an Abhorsen now, and there was a great and momentous task ahead of her.

"Yes," she repeated. "We'd best be moving. We will go by way of the well."

Chapter Two

INTO THE DEEP

I T TOOK LITTLE more than an hour to prepare for their departure, once the decision had been made. Lirael found herself wearing armor for the first time since her Fighting Arts lessons many years before—but the coat the sendings brought her was much lighter than the mail hauberks the Clayr kept in their schoolroom armory. It was made of tiny overlapping scales or plates of some material Lirael didn't recognize, and despite its length to her knees and its long, swallow-tailed sleeves, it was quite light and comfortable. It also didn't have the characteristic odor of well-oiled steel, for which Lirael was grateful.

The Disreputable Dog told her the scales were a ceramic called "gethre," made with Charter Magic but not magic in itself, though it was stronger and lighter than any metal. The secret of its making was long lost, and no new coat had been made in a thousand years. Lirael felt one of the scales and was surprised to find herself thinking, "Sam could make this," though she had no real reason to suppose that he could.

Over the armored coat, Lirael wore the surcoat of golden stars and silver keys. The bell-bandolier would lie across that, but Lirael had yet to put it on. Sam had reluctantly taken the panpipes, but Lirael kept the Dark Mirror in her pouch. She knew it was very likely that she would need to look into the past again.

Her sword, Nehima, her bow and quiver from the Clayr, and

a light pack cleverly filled by the sendings with all manner of things that she hadn't had a chance to look at completed her equipment.

Before she went to join Sam and Mogget downstairs, Lirael paused for a moment to look at herself in the tall silver mirror that hung on the wall of her room. The image that faced her bore little resemblance to the Second Assistant Librarian of the Clayr. She saw a warlike and grim young woman, dark hair bound back with a silver cord rather than hanging free to disguise her face. She no longer wore her librarian's waistcoat, and instead of a library-issue dagger, she had long Nehima at her side. But she couldn't completely let go her former identity. Taking the end of a loose thread from her waistcoat, she drew out a single strand of red silk, wound it around her little finger several times to make a ring, tied it off, and tucked it into the small pouch at her belt with the Dark Mirror. She might not wear the waistcoat any longer, but part of it would always travel with her.

She had become an Abhorsen, Lirael thought. At least on the outside.

The most visible sign of both her new identity and her power as the Abhorsen-in-Waiting was the bell-bandolier. The one Sabriel had given to Sam after it had mysteriously appeared in the House the previous winter. Lirael loosened the leather pouches one by one, slipping her fingers in to feel the cool silver and the mahogany, and the delicate balance between Free Magic and Charter marks in both metal and wood. Lirael was careful not to let the bells sound, but even the touch of her finger on a bell rim was enough to summon something of the voice and nature of each bell.

The smallest bell was Ranna. Sleeper, some called it, its voice a sweet lullaby calling those who heard it into slumber.

The second bell was Mosrael, the Waker. Lirael touched it ever so lightly, for Mosrael balanced Life with Death. Wielded properly, it would bring the Dead back into Life and send the wielder from Life into Death.

Kibeth was the third bell, the Walker. It granted freedom of movement to the Dead, or it could be used to make them walk where the wielder chose. Yet it could also turn on a bell-ringer and make her march, usually somewhere she would not wish to go.

The fourth bell was called Dyrim, the Speaker. This was the most musical bell, according to *The Book of the Dead*, and one of the most difficult to use as well. Dyrim could return the power of speech to long-silent Dead. It could also reveal secrets, or even allow the reading of minds. It had darker powers, too, favored by necromancers, for Dyrim could still a speaking tongue forever.

Belgaer was the name of the fifth bell. The Thinker. Belgaer could mend the erosion of mind that often occurred in Death, restoring the thoughts and memory of the Dead. It could also erase those thoughts, in Life as well as in Death, and in necromancers' hands had been used to splinter the minds of enemies. Sometimes it splintered the mind of the necromancer, for Belgaer liked the sound of its own voice and would try to steal the chance to sing of its own accord.

The sixth bell was Saraneth, also known as Binder. Saraneth was the favorite bell of all Abhorsens. Large and trustworthy, it was powerful and true. Saraneth was used to dominate and bind the Dead, to make them obey the wishes and directions of the wielder.

Lirael was reluctant to touch the seventh bell, but she felt it would not be diplomatic to ignore the most powerful of all the bells, though it was cold and frightening to her touch.

Astarael, the Sorrowful. The bell that sent all who heard it into Death.

Lirael withdrew her finger and methodically checked every pouch, making sure the leather tongues were in place and the straps tight but also able to be undone with one hand. Then she put the bandolier on. The bells were hers, and she had accepted the armament of the Abhorsens.

Sam was waiting for her outside the front door, sitting on the steps. He was similarly armored and equipped, though he did not have a bow or a bell-bandolier.

"I found this in the armory," he said, holding up a sword and tilting the blade so that Lirael could see the Charter marks etched into the steel. "It isn't one of the named swords, but it is spelled for the destruction of the Dead."

"Better late than never," remarked Mogget, who was sitting on the front step looking sour.

Sam ignored the cat, pulled out a sheet of paper from inside his sleeve, and handed it to Lirael.

"This is the message I've sent by message-hawk to Barhedrin. The Guard post there will send it on to the Wall, and it will be passed through to the Ancelstierrans, who will . . . um . . . send it by a device called a telegraph to my parents in Corvere. That's why it's written in telegraphese, which is pretty strange if you're not used to it. There were four hawks in the mews—not counting the one from Ellimere, which won't fly again for a week or two—so I've sent two to Belisaere for Ellimere and two to Barhedrin."

Lirael looked down at the paper and the words printed in Sam's neat hand.

TO   KING TOUCHSTONE AND ABHORSEN
            SABRIEL
            OLD KINGDOM EMBASSY CORVERE
            ANCELSTIERRE
COPY   ELLIMERE VIA MESSAGEHAWK

HOUSE SURROUNDED DEAD PLUS CHLORR
NOW GREATER DEAD STOP HEDGE IS
NECROMANCER STOP NICK WITH HEDGE STOP
THEY EVIL UPDUG NEAR EDGE STOP GOING
EDGE SELF PLUS AUNT LIRAEL FORMER CLAYR
NOW ABHORSENINWAITING STOP PLUS
MOGGET PLUS LIRAEL APOSTROPHE ESS
CHARTER DOG STOP WILL DO WHAT CAN STOP
SEND HELP COME SELVES EXPRESS URGENT
STOP SENT TWO WEEKS PRIOR MIDSUMMER
DAY SAMETH END

The message was indeed written strangely, but it made sense, thought Lirael. Given the limitations of the message-hawks' small minds, "telegraphese" was probably a good form of communication even when a telegraph was not involved.

"I hope the hawks make it," she said as Sam took the paper back. Somewhere out in the fog lurked Gore Crows, a swarm of corpse birds animated by a single Dead spirit. The message-hawks would have to get past them, and perhaps other dangers as well, before they could speed on to Barhedrin and Belisaere.

"We cannot count on it," said the Dog. "Are you ready to go down the well?"

Lirael walked down the steps and took a few paces along the redbrick path. She shrugged her pack higher up her back and tightened the straps. Then she looked up at the sunny sky, now only a very small patch of blue, the walls of fog hemming it in on three sides and the mist from the waterfall on the fourth.

"I guess I'm ready," she said.

Sam picked up his pack, but before he could put it on, Mogget leapt onto it and slid under the top flap. All that could be seen of him were his green eyes and one white-furred ear.

"Remember I advised against this way," he instructed. "Wake me when whatever terrible thing is about to happen happens, or if it appears I might get wet."

Before anyone could answer, Mogget wriggled deeper into the pack, and even his eyes and that one ear disappeared.

"How come I get to carry him?" asked Sam aggrievedly. "He's supposed to be the Abhorsen's servant."

A paw came back out of the pack, and a claw pricked into the back of Sam's neck, though it didn't break the skin. Sam flinched and swore.

The Dog jumped up at the pack and braced her forepaws on it. Sam staggered forward and swore again as the Dog said, "No one will carry you if you don't behave, Mogget."

"And you won't get any fish, either," muttered Sam as he rubbed his neck.

Either one or both of these threats worked, or else Mogget had subsided into sleep. In any case, there was no reappearance of the claw or the cat's sarcastic voice. The Dog dropped down, Sam finished adjusting the straps on his pack, and they set off along the brick path.

As the front door shut behind them, Lirael turned back and saw that every window was crowded with sendings. Hundreds of them, pressed close together against the glass, so their hooded robes looked like the skin of some giant creature, their faintly glowing hands like many eyes. They did not wave or move at all, but Lirael had the uncomfortable feeling that they were saying goodbye. As if they did not expect to see this particular Abhorsen-in-Waiting return.

The well was only thirty yards from the front door, hidden beneath a tangled network of wild roses that Lirael and Sam had to tear away, pausing every few minutes to suck their thorn-pierced fingers. The thorns were unusually long and sharp, Lirael thought, but she had limited experience with flowers. The Clayr had underground gardens and vast greenhouses lit by Charter marks, but most were dedicated to vegetables and fruit, and there was only one rose garden.

Once the rose vines were cleared away, Lirael saw a circular wooden cover of thick oak planks, about eight feet in diameter, set securely inside a low ring of pale white stones. The cover was chained in four places with bronze chains, the links set directly into the stones and bolted to the wood, so there was no need for padlocks.

Charter marks of locking and closing drifted across both wood and bronze, gleaming marks only just visible in the sunlight, till Sam touched the cover and they flared into sudden brightness.

Sam laid his hand on one of the bronze chains, feeling the marks within it and studying the spell. Lirael looked over his shoulder. She didn't know even half of the marks, but she could hear Sam muttering names to himself as if they were familiar to him.

"Can you open it?" asked Lirael. She knew scores of spells for opening doors and gates, and had practical experience of opening ways into many places she wasn't supposed to have entered in the Great Library of the Clayr. But she instinctively knew none of them would work here.

"I think so," Sam replied hesitantly. "It's an unusual spell, and there are a lot of marks I don't know. As far as I can work out, there are two ways it can be opened. One I don't understand at all. But the other . . ."

His voice trailed off as he touched the chain again and Charter Marks left the bronze to drift across his skin and then flow into the wood.

"I think we're supposed to breathe on the chains . . . or kiss

them . . . only it has to be the right person. The spell says 'my
children's breath.' But I can't work out whose children or what
that means. Any Abhorsen's children, I guess."

"Try it," suggested Lirael. "A breath first, just in case."

Sam looked doubtful but bent his head, took a deep breath,
and blew on the chain.

The bronze fogged from the breath and lost its shine.
Charter marks glittered and moved. Lirael held her breath. Sam
stood up and edged away, while the Disreputable Dog came
closer and sniffed.

Suddenly the chain groaned aloud, and everyone jumped
back. Then a new link came out of the seemingly solid stone, followed by another and another, the chain rattling as it coiled to
the ground. In a few seconds there was an extra six or seven feet
of chain piled up, enough to allow that corner of the well cover
to be lifted free.

"Good," said the Disreputable Dog. "You do the next one,
Mistress."

Lirael bent over the next chain and breathed lightly upon it.
Nothing happened for a moment, and she felt a stab of uncertainty. Her identity as an Abhorsen was so new, and so precarious, that it could be easily doubted.

Then the chain frosted, the marks shone, and the links came
pouring out of the stone with the sharp rattle of metal. The
sound was echoed almost immediately from the other side, as
Sam breathed on the third chain.

Lirael breathed on the last chain, touching it for a moment
as she took in a breath. She felt the marks shiver under her fingers, the lively reaction of a Charter-spell that knew its time had
come. Like a person tensing muscles in that frozen instant before
the beginning of a race.

With the loosening of the chains, Lirael and Sam were able

to lift one end of the cover and slide it away. It was very heavy, so they didn't drag it completely off, just making an opening large enough for them to climb down with their packs on.

Lirael had expected a wet, dank smell to come up from the open well, even though the Dog had said it wasn't full of water. There was a smell, strong enough to overcome the scent of the roses, but it wasn't of old standing water. It was a pleasant herbal odor that Lirael couldn't identify.

"What can I smell?" she asked the Dog, whose nose had often picked up scents and odors that Lirael could neither smell, spell, or imagine.

"Very little," replied the Dog. "Unless you've improved recently."

"No," said Lirael patiently. "There's a particular smell coming out of the well. A plant, or an herb. But I can't place it."

Sam sniffed the air and his forehead furrowed in thought.

"It's something used in cooking," he said. "Not that I'm much of a cook. But I've smelled this in the Palace kitchens, when they were roasting lamb, I think."

"It's rosemary," said the Dog shortly. "And there is amaranth, too, though you probably cannot smell it."

"Fidelity in love," said a small voice from Sam's backpack. "With the flower that never fades. And you still say she is not there?"

The Dog didn't answer Mogget but stuck her snout down the well. She sniffed around for at least a minute, pushing her snout farther and farther down the well. When she pulled back, she sneezed twice and shook her head.

"Old smells, old spells," she said. "The scent is already fading."

Lirael sniffed experimentally, but the Dog was right. She could smell only the roses now.

"There is a ladder," said Sam, who was also looking into the well, a Charter-conjured light bobbing above his head. "Bronze, like the chains. I wonder why. I can't see the bottom, though—or any water."

"I'll go first," said Lirael. Sam seemed about to protest but stepped away. Lirael didn't know whether this was because he was afraid or because he was acquiescing—to the familial authority of Lirael as his newfound aunt or because she was now the Abhorsen-in-Waiting.

She looked into the well. The bronze ladder gleamed near the top, disappearing down into darkness. Lirael had climbed up, down, and through many dark and dangerous tunnels and passages in the Great Library of the Clayr. But that had been in more innocent times, even though she had experienced her share of danger. Now she felt a sense of great and evil powers at work in the world, of a terrible fate already in motion. The Dead surrounding the House were only a small and visible part of that. She remembered the vision the Clayr had shown her, of the pit near the Red Lake, and the terrible stench of Free Magic from whatever was being unearthed there.

Climbing down this dark hole was only the beginning, Lirael thought. Her first step onto the bronze ladder would be the first real step of her new identity, the first step of an Abhorsen.

She took one last look at the sun, ignoring the climbing walls of fog to either side. Then she knelt down and gingerly lowered herself into the well, her feet finding secure footholds on the ladder.

After her came the Disreputable Dog, her paws elongating to form stubby fingers that gripped the ladder better than any human fingers could. Her tail brushed in Lirael's face every few rungs, sweeping across with greater enthusiasm than Lirael could have mustered if she'd had a tail of her own.

Sam came last, his Charter light still hovering above his head, Mogget securely fastened in his backpack.

As Sam's hobnailed boots clanged on the rungs, there was an answering clatter above as the chains suddenly contracted. He barely had time to bring in his hands before the cover was dragged across and slammed into place with a rattle and a deafening crash.

"Well, we won't be going back that way," said Sam, with forced cheerfulness.

"If at all," whispered Mogget, his voice so low that it was possible no one heard him. But Sam hesitated for a moment, and the Dog let out a low growl, while Lirael continued to climb down, cherishing that last memory of the sun as they descended farther into the dark recesses of the earth.

Chapter Three

AMARANTH, ROSEMARY, AND TEARS

THE LADDER WENT down and down and down. At first Lirael counted the rungs, but when she got to 996, she gave up. Still they climbed down. Lirael had conjured a Charter light herself. It hovered about her feet, to complement the one Sam had dancing above his head. In the light of these two glowing balls, with the shadows of the rungs flickering on the wall of the well, Lirael found it easy to imagine that they were somehow stuck on the ladder, repeating the same section time after time.

A treadmill that they could never leave. This fancy grew on her, and she started to think it real, when suddenly her foot met stone instead of bronze, and her Charter light rebounded as high as her knee.

They had reached the bottom of the well. Lirael pronounced a Charter mark, and her light flew up to join the spoken word, circling her head. In its light she saw that they had come to a rectangular chamber, roughly hewn from the rich red rock. A passage led off from the chamber into darkness. There was an iron bucket next to the passage, filled with what looked like torches, simple lengths of wood topped with oil-soaked rags.

Lirael walked forward as the Disreputable Dog jumped down behind her, closely followed by Sam.

"I suppose this is the way," Lirael whispered, indicating the passage. Somehow she felt that it was safer not to raise her voice.

The Dog sniffed at the air and nodded.

"I wonder if I should take—" Lirael said, reaching out for one of the torches. But even before her hand could close on it, the torch puffed into dust. Lirael flinched, almost falling over the Dog, who stepped back into Sam.

"Watch it!" Sam called out. His voice echoed in the well shaft and reverberated past Lirael down the corridor.

Lirael reached out again, more gingerly, but the other torches also simply fell into dust. When she touched the bucket, it collapsed in on itself, becoming a pile of rusted shards.

"Time never truly falters," said the Dog enigmatically.

"I guess we have to go on," said Lirael, but she was really only speaking to herself. They didn't need the torches, but she would have felt better with one.

"The faster the better," said the Dog. She was sniffing the air again. "We do not want to tarry anywhere under here."

Lirael nodded. She took one step forward, then hesitated and drew her sword. Charter marks burned brightly on the blade as it came free of the scabbard, and the name of the sword rippled down the steel, briefly changing into the inscription Lirael had seen before. Or was it different? She couldn't remember, and the words rippled away too quickly for her to be sure.

"The Clayr Saw a sword and so I was. Remember the Wallmakers. Remember Me."

Whatever it said, the extra light reassured Lirael, or perhaps it was just the feel of Nehima in her hand.

She heard Sam draw his sword behind her. He waited for a few seconds as she started on again. Obviously he did not want to trip and impale the Dog or Lirael from behind, a precaution Lirael thoroughly approved.

For the first hundred paces or so, the passageway was of worked stone. Then that suddenly ended and they came to a

tunnel that was not the work of any tool. The red rock gave way
to a pallid greenish-white stone that reflected the Charter lights,
making Lirael hood her eyes. The tunnel seemed to have been
eroded rather than worked, and there were the patterns of many
swirls and eddies upon the ceiling, floor, and walls. Yet even these
seemed strange, contrary to what they ought to be, though Lirael
didn't know why. She just felt their strangeness.

"No water ever cut this way," said Sam. He was whispering,
too, now. "Unless it flowed back and forth at the same time on
different levels. And I have never seen this kind of stone."

"We must hurry," said the Dog. There was something in her
voice that made Lirael move more quickly. An anxiety she had
not heard before. Perhaps it was even fear.

They began to walk more swiftly, as fast as they could without risk of tripping over or falling into some unsuspected hole.
The strange, glowing tunnel continued on for what felt like several miles, then opened into a cavern, again carved by unknown
means out of the same reflective stone. There were three tunnels
off this, and Lirael and Sam stopped while the Dog sniffed carefully at each entrance.

There was a pile of what Lirael thought was stone in one
corner of the cavern, but when she looked at it more closely, she
realized it was actually a mound of old, powdery bones mixed
with pieces of metal. Touching the mound with the corner of
her boot, she separated out several shards of tarnished silver and
the fragment of a human jaw, still showing one unbroken tooth.

"Don't touch it," Sam warned in a hasty whisper, as Lirael
bent to inspect the metal fragments.

Lirael stopped, her hand still outstretched.

"Why not?"

"I don't know," replied Sam, an unconscious shiver rippling
across his neck. "But that's bell metal, I think. Best to leave it alone."

"Yes," agreed Lirael. She stood up and couldn't help shivering herself. Human bones and bell metal. They had found Kalliel. What was this place? And why was the Dog taking so long to decide which way to go?

When she voiced the question, the Disreputable Dog stopped her sniffing and pointed her right paw to the center tunnel.

"This one," she said, but Lirael noted a certain lack of enthusiasm in the Dog. The hound had not spoken with total confidence, and even her pointing had wavered. If she had been in a pointing competition, she would have lost points.

The tunnel was significantly wider than the previous one, and the ceiling higher. It also felt different to Lirael, and not because there was more room to move. At first she couldn't place what it was; then she realized the air around her was growing colder. And she had a strange sensation around her feet and ankles, almost as if there were something rushing around her heels. A current that swished one way and then the other, but there was no water there.

Or was there? When she looked directly in front or down, Lirael saw stone. But when she looked out of the corners of her eyes, she could see dark water flowing. Coming from behind them, pushing past, and then curling back, like a wave falling upon the shore. A wave that was trying to knock them down and sweep them back the way they'd come.

In a very unsettling way, it reminded her of the river of Death. But she did not feel they were in Death, and apart from the growing cold and the peripheral view of the river, all her senses told her that she was firmly in Life, though in a very strange tunnel, far underground.

Then she smelled rosemary again, with something sweeter, and at that moment the bells in the bandolier across her chest began to vibrate in their pouches. Their clappers stilled by leather tongues, they could not sound, but she could feel them moving and shaking, as if they were trying to break free.

"The bells!" she gasped. "They're shaking. . . . I don't know what . . ."

"The pipes!" cried Sam, and Lirael heard a brief cacophany as the panpipes sounded with the voices of all seven bells, before they were suddenly cut off.

"No!" shouted a voice that was not instantly recognizable as Mogget's. "No!"

"Run!" roared the Dog.

Amidst the shouts and yells and roaring, the Charter light above Lirael's head suddenly dimmed to little more than a faint glow.

Then it went out.

Lirael stopped. There was some light from the marks on Nehima's blade, but these were fading, too, and the sword was twisting strangely in her hand. Undulating in a way that no thing of steel could ever move, it had become alive, not so much a sword anymore as an eel-like creature, writhing and growing in her grasp. The green stone on the pommel had become a bright, lidless eye, and the silver wire on the hilt had become a row of shining teeth.

Lirael shut her eyes and sheathed the sword, ramming it hard into the scabbard before she let go with relief. Then she opened her eyes and looked around. Or tried to. All the golden Charter light was gone, and it was dark. The total darkness of the deep earth.

In the black void Lirael heard cloth tear and rip, and Sam cried out.

"Sam!" she cried. "Over here! Dog!"

There was no answer, but she heard the Dog growl, and then

there was a soft, low laugh. A horrible, gloating chuckle that set
the hair on the back of her neck on edge. It was made worse
because there was something familiar in it. Mogget's laugh,
twisted and made more sinister.

Desperately Lirael tried to reach for the Charter, to summon
a new light spell. But there was nothing there. Instead of the
Charter she felt a terrible, cold presence that she knew at once.
Death. That was all she could feel.

The Charter was gone, or she could not reach it.

Panic began to flower in her as the gloating chuckle deepened and the darkness pressed upon her. Then Lirael's eyes registered a faint change. She became aware of subtle greys in the
darkness, and she felt a momentary hope that there would be
light. Then she saw the barest fingernail scraping of illumination
spark and fizz and steadily grow till it became a pool of fierce,
bright, white light. With the light came the hot metal stench of
Free Magic, a smell that rolled across in waves, each one causing
a reflex gag as the bile rose in Lirael's throat.

Sam moved with the light, appearing at Lirael's side as if he'd
flown there. His backpack was open at the top, ragged edges
showing where something had cut free. His sword was sheathed,
and he was holding the panpipes with both hands, fingers
jammed on the holes. The pipes were vibrating, sending out a
low hum that Sam was desperately trying to stifle. Lirael had her
own arm pressed along the bell-bandolier, to try to still the bells.

The Dog stood between the pool of white fire and Lirael,
but it was not the Dog as Lirael knew her. She still had a dog
shape, but the collar of Charter marks was gone, and she was
once more a creature of intense darkness outlined with silver
fire. The Dog looked back and opened her mouth.

"She is here!" boomed a voice that was the Dog's and yet
not the Dog's, for it penetrated Lirael's ears and sent sharp pains

coursing through her jaw. "The Mogget is free! Run!"

Lirael and Sam stood frozen as the echoes of the Dog's voice rolled past them. The pool of white fire was sparking and crackling, spinning counterclockwise as it rose up to form the shape of a spindly, too-thin humanoid.

But beyond the thing that was Mogget unbound, an even brighter light shone. Something so bright that Lirael realized she had shut her eyes and was seeing it through her eyelids, eyelids seared through with the image of a woman. An impossibly tall woman, her head bowed even in this high tunnel, reaching out her arms to sweep up the Mogget creature, the Dog, Lirael, and Sam.

A river flowed around and in front of the shining woman. A cold river that Lirael knew at once. This was the river of Death, and this creature was bringing it to them. They would not cross into it but be swamped and taken away. Thrown down and taken up, carried in a rush to the First Gate and beyond. They would never be able to make their way back.

Lirael had time to think only a few final, awful thoughts.

They had failed so soon.

So many depended on them.

All was lost.

Then the Disreputable Dog shouted, "Flee!" and barked.

The bark was infused with Free Magic. Without opening her eyes, without conscious thought, Lirael swung around and suddenly found herself running, running headlong, running as she had never run before. She ran without care, into the unknown, away from the well and the House, her feet finding the twists and turns of the tunnel even though they left the white light behind and in the darkness Lirael couldn't tell whether her eyes were open or not.

Through caverns and chambers and narrow ways she ran, not knowing whether Sam ran with her or whether she was pursued. It was not fear that drove her, for she didn't feel afraid. She was somewhere else, locked away inside her own body, a machine that drove on and on without feeling, acting on directions that had not come from her.

Then, as suddenly as it began, the compulsion to run stopped. Lirael fell to the floor, shuddering, trying to draw breath into her starved lungs. Pain shot through every muscle, and she curled into a ball of cramps, frantically massaging her calf muscles as she bit back cries of pain.

Someone was near her doing the same thing, and as reason returned, Lirael saw that it was Sam. There was a dim light falling from somewhere ahead, enough to make him out. A natural light, though much diffused.

Hesitantly Lirael touched the bell-bandolier. It was still, the bells quiescent. Her hand fell to Nehima's hilt, and she was relieved to feel the solidity of the green stone in the pommel, and the silver wire no more than silver wire.

Sam groaned and stood up. He leaned against the wall with his left hand and stowed the panpipes away with his right. Lirael watched that hand flicker in a careful movement, and a Charter light blossomed in his palm.

"It was gone, you know," he said, sliding back down the wall to sit facing Lirael. He seemed calm but was obviously in shock. Lirael realized she was, too, when she tried to stand up and simply couldn't.

"Yes," she replied. "The Charter."

"Wherever that was," continued Sam, "the Charter wasn't. And who was *she*?"

Lirael shook her head, as much to clear it as to indicate her inability to answer. She shook it again immediately, trying to force her thoughts back into action.

"We'd better . . . better go back," she said, thinking of the

Dog facing both Mogget and that shining woman alone in the darkness. "I can't leave the Dog."

"What about *her*?" asked Sam, and Lirael knew who he meant. "And Mogget?"

"You need not go back," said a voice from the dark reaches of the passage. Lirael and Sam instantly leapt up, finding new strength and purpose. Their swords were out and Lirael found she had one hand on Saraneth, though she had no idea what she was going to do with the bell. No wisdom from *The Book of the Dead* or *The Book of Remembrance and Forgetting* came unbidden into her head.

"It's me," said the voice in an aggrieved tone, and the Disreputable Dog slowly walked into the light, her tail between her legs and her head bowed. Apart from this uncharacteristic pose, she seemed back to normal—or what was normal for her—with the deep, rich glow of many Charter Marks once more around her neck, and her short hair dusty and golden save for her back, where it was black.

Lirael didn't hesitate. She put Nehima down and flung herself on the Dog, burying her face in her friend's neck. The Dog licked Lirael's ear without her usual enthusiasm, and she didn't try even one affectionate nip.

Sam hung back, his sword still in his hand.

"Where is Mogget?" he asked.

"She wished to speak to him," replied the Dog, throwing herself sorrowfully across Lirael's feet. "I was wrong. I put you in terrible danger, Mistress."

"I don't understand," Lirael replied. She felt incredibly tired all of a sudden. "What happened? The Charter . . . the Charter seemed to suddenly . . . not be."

"It was her coming," said the Dog. "It is her fate, that her knowing self will be forever outside what she chose to make, the

Charter that her unknowing self is part of. Yet she stayed her hand when she could so easily have taken you to her embrace. I do not know why, or what it may mean. I believed her to be past any interest in the things of this world, and so I thought to pass here unscathed. Yet when ancient forces stir, many things are woken. I should have guessed it would be so. Forgive me."

Lirael had never seen the Dog so humbled, and it scared her more than anything that had happened. She scratched her around the ears and along the jaw, seeking to give as much comfort as she took. But her hands shook, and she felt that at any moment she would shudder into tears. To try to stop them, she took slow breaths, counting them in, and counting them out.

"But . . . what will happen to Mogget?" asked Sam, his voice unsteady. "He was unbound! He'll try to kill the Abhorsen . . . Mother . . . or Lirael! We haven't got the ring to bind him again!"

"Mogget has long avoided her," mumbled the Dog. She hesitated, then quietly said, "I don't think we need to worry about Mogget anymore."

Lirael let out her breath and didn't take another. How could Mogget not be coming back?

"What?" asked Sam. "But he's . . . well, I don't know, but powerful . . . a Free Magic spirit. . . ."

"Who is she?" asked Lirael. She spoke very sternly as she took the Disreputable Dog by the jaw and stared into her deep, dark eyes. The Dog tried to turn away, but Lirael held her fast. The hound shut her eyes hopefully, only to be foiled as Lirael blew on her nose and they snapped open again.

"It won't help you to know, because you can't understand," said the Dog, her voice filled with great weariness. "She doesn't really exist anymore, except every now and then and here and there, in small ways and small things. If we had not come this way, she would not have been, and now that we have passed, she will not be."

"Tell me!"

"You know who she is, at least in some degree," said the
Dog. She tapped her nose against Lirael's bell-bandolier, leaving
a wet mark on the leather of the seventh bell, and a single slow
tear rolled down her snout to dampen Lirael's hand.

"Astarael?" whispered Sam in disbelief. The most frightening bell of them all, the one he had never even touched in his
brief time as custodian of that set of bells. "The Weeper?"

Lirael let the Dog go, and the hound promptly pushed her
head farther into Lirael's lap and let out a long sigh.

Lirael scratched the Dog's ears again, but even with the feel
of warm dog skin under her hand, she could not help asking a
question she had asked before.

"What are you, then? Why did Astarael let you go?"

The Dog looked up at her and said simply, "I am the
Disreputable Dog. A true servant of the Charter, and your friend.
Always your friend."

Lirael did weep then, but she wiped the tears away as she
lifted the Dog by her collar and moved her away so she could
stand up. Sam picked up Nehima and silently handed the sword
to her. The Charter marks on the blade rippled as Lirael touched
the hilt, but no inscription became visible.

"If you are sure Mogget will not be coming, bound or
unbound, then we must go on," said Lirael.

"I suppose so," said Sam doubtfully. "Though I feel . . . feel
sort of strange. I got kind of used to Mogget, and now he's
just . . . just gone? I mean, has she . . . has she killed him?"

"No!" answered the Dog. She seemed surprised at the suggestion. "No."

"What then?" asked Sam.

"It is not for us to know," said the Disreputable Dog. "Our

task lies ahead, and Mogget lies behind us now."

"You're absolutely sure he won't come after Mother or Lirael?" asked Sam. He knew Mogget's recent history well and had been warned since he was a toddler of the danger of removing Mogget's collar.

"I am sure that your mother is safe from Mogget across the Wall," replied the Dog, only half-answering Sam's question.

Sam did not look entirely convinced, but he slowly nodded in reluctant acceptance of the Dog's assurance.

"We haven't got off to a good start," muttered Sam. "I hope it gets better."

"There is sunlight ahead, and a way out," said the Dog. "You will be happier under the sun."

"It should be dark by now," said Sam. "How long have we been underground?"

"Four or five hours, at least," replied Lirael with a frown. "Maybe more, so that can't be sunshine."

She led the way across the cavern, but as they drew closer to the entrance, it was clear that it *was* sunshine. Soon they could see a narrow cleft ahead, and through it a clear blue sky, misted with spray from the great waterfall.

Once through the cleft, they found themselves several hundred yards to the west of the waterfall, at the base of the Long Cliffs. The sun was halfway up the sky to the west, the sunshine making rainbows in the huge cloud of spray that hung above the falls.

"It's afternoon," said Sam, shielding his eyes to look near the sun. He looked along the line of the cliffs, then held up his hand to gauge how many fingers the sun was above the horizon. "Not past four o'clock."

"We've lost practically a whole day!" exclaimed Lirael. Every delay meant a greater chance of failure, and her heart sank at this further setback. How could they have spent almost twenty-four hours underground?

"No," said the Disreputable Dog, who was watching the sun and sniffing the air. "We have not lost a day."

"Not more?" whispered Lirael. Surely not. If they had somehow spent weeks or more underground, it would be too late to do anything. . . .

"No," continued the Dog. "It is the same day we left the House. Perhaps an hour since we climbed down the well. Maybe less."

"But—" Sam started to say something, then stopped. He shook his head and looked back at the cleft in the cliff.

"Time and Death sleep side by side," said the Dog. "Both are in Astarael's domain. She has helped us, in her own way."

Lirael nodded, though she didn't feel as if she'd been helped. She felt shocked and tired, and her legs hurt. She wanted to curl up in the sun and wake up in the Great Library of the Clayr with a sore neck from sleeping at her desk and a vague memory of disturbing nightmares.

"I can't sense any Dead down here," she said, after dismissing her daydream. "Since we've been given the gift of an afternoon, I guess we'd better use it. How do we get back up the cliffs?"

"There is a path about a league and a half to the west," said Sam. "It's narrow and mostly steps, so it's not often used. The top of that should be well clear of the fog and Chlorr's minions. Beyond that, the Western Cut is at least twelve or so leagues farther on. That's where the road goes through."

"What is the stepped path called?" asked the Dog.

"I don't know. Mother just called it the Steps, I think. It's quite strange really. The path is only wide enough for one, and the steps are low and deep."

"I know it," said the Dog. "Three thousand steps, and all for the sweet water at the foot."

Sam nodded. "There is a spring there, and the water is good. You mean someone built the whole path just to get a drink of good water?"

"Water, yes, but not to drink," said the Dog. "I am glad the path is still there. Let us go to it."

With that, the hound sprang forward, jumping over the sprawl of boulders that helped conceal the cleft and the caves beyond.

Lirael and Sam followed more sedately, clambering between the stones. Both were still sore, and they had many things to think about. Lirael in particular was thinking of the Dog's words: "When ancient forces stir, many things are woken." She knew that whatever Nicholas was digging up was both powerful and evil, and it was clear that its emergence had set many things in motion, including a rising of the Dead across the whole Kingdom. But she had not considered that other powers might also be woken, and how that might affect their plans.

Not that they really had a plan, Lirael thought. They were simply rushing headlong to try to stop Hedge and save Nicholas and keep whatever it was safely buried in the ground.

"We should have a proper plan," she whispered to herself. But no brilliant thoughts or strategies came to mind, and she had to concentrate on climbing between and over stones as she followed the Disreputable Dog along the base of the Long Cliffs, with Sam close behind.

Chapter Four

BREAKFAST OF RAVENS

THE SUN HAD almost set by the time Lirael, Sam, and the Dog arrived at the foot of the Steps, and the shadow of the Long Cliffs stretched far across the Ratterlin plain. Lirael easily found the spring—a clear, bubbling pool ten yards wide—but it took longer to find the beginning of the steps, as the path was narrow, cut deeply into the face of the cliff, and disguised by many overhangs and jutting buttresses of jagged stone.

"Can we climb it by night?" asked Lirael uncertainly, looking up at the shadowed cliff above them and the last faint touch of sun a thousand feet above. The cliff stretched up even farther than that, and she couldn't see the top. Lirael had climbed many stairs and narrow ways in the Clayr's Glacier, but she had little experience of traveling in the open under sun and moon.

"We shouldn't risk a light," replied the Dog, who had been uncharacteristically silent. Her tail still hung limply, without its usual wag or spring. "I could lead you, though it will be dangerous in the dark if any steps have fallen away."

"The moon will be bright," said Sam. "It was in its third quarter last night, and the sky is reasonably clear. But it will not rise till the early morning. An hour after midnight at least. We should wait till then, if not overnight."

"I don't want to wait," Lirael muttered. "I have this feeling . . . an anxiety I can't describe. The vision the Clayr told me about, me with Nicholas, on the Red Lake . . . I feel it slipping away, as

if I'll somehow miss the moment. That it will become the past
rather than a possible future."

"Falling off the Long Cliffs in the dark won't get us there
any faster," said Sam. "And I could do with a bite to eat and a
few hours' rest before we get climbing."

Lirael nodded. She was tired, too. Her calves ached, and her
shoulders were sore from the weight of the pack. But there was
another weariness, too, one that she was sure Sam shared. It was
a weariness of the spirit. It came from the shock of losing
Mogget, and she really just wanted to lie down by the cool
spring and go to sleep in the vain hope that the new day would
be brighter. It was a feeling she recognized from her younger
days. Then it had been the vain hope that she would sleep and
in the morning awake with the Sight. Now she knew that the
new day could bring nothing good. They needed to rest, but not
for too long. Hedge and Nicholas would not rest, nor would
Chlorr and her Dead Hands.

"We'll wait for the moon to rise," she said, slipping the pack
off her shoulders and sitting down next to it on a convenient
boulder.

The next instant she was back on her feet, sword in hand
even before she realized she'd drawn it, as the Dog catapulted
past her with a sudden bark. It took Lirael a moment to hear that
the bark had no magical resonance, then another to spot the
target of the Dog's attack.

A rabbit zigzagged between the fallen stones, desperately
trying to evade the pursuing Dog. The chase ended some distance away, but it was not clear with what result. Then a great
plume of dirt, dust, and stones flew up, and Lirael knew the
rabbit had gone to ground and the Dog had begun to dig.

Sam was still sitting next to his pack. He had half-risen several seconds after Lirael, had caught on what was happening, and

had sat back down. Now he was looking at the torn hole in the top flap of his pack.

"At least we're alive," said Lirael, mistaking his silent scrutiny of the tear for remorse at the loss of Mogget.

Sam looked up, surprised. He had a sewing kit in his hand and was about to open it.

"Oh, I wasn't thinking about Mogget. At least not right then. I was wondering how best to sew up this hole. I'll have to patch it, I think."

Lirael laughed, a peculiar half-hearted sort of laugh that just escaped her.

"I'm glad you can think of patches," she said. "I . . . I can't help thinking of what happened. The bells trying to sound, the white lady . . . Astarael . . . the presence of Death."

Sam selected a large needle and bit off a length of black thread from a bobbin. He frowned as he threaded the needle, then spoke off to the setting sun, not directly to Lirael.

"It's strange, you know. Since I learned that you were the Abhorsen-in-Waiting, not me, I haven't felt afraid. I mean I've been scared, but it wasn't the same. I'm not responsible now. I mean, I am responsible because I'm a Prince of the Kingdom, but it's normal things I'm responsible for now. Not necromancers and Death and Free Magic creatures."

He paused to knot the end of the thread, and this time he did look at Lirael.

"And the sendings gave me this surcoat. With the trowel. The Wallmakers' trowel. They gave it to me, and I've been thinking that it's as if my ancestors are saying it's all right to make things. That's what I'm meant to do. Make things, and help the Abhorsen and the King. So I'll do that, and I'll do my best, and if my best isn't good enough, at least I will have done everything I could, everything that is in me. I don't have to try to be someone else, someone I could never be."

Lirael didn't answer. Instead, she looked away, back to where the Dog was returning, a limp rabbit in her jaws.

"Dimsher," pronounced the Dog, repeating herself more clearly after she dropped the rabbit at Lirael's feet. Her tail had started to wag again, just at the tip. "Dinner. I'll get another one."

Lirael picked up the rabbit. The Dog had broken its neck, killing it instantly. Lirael could feel its spirit close by in Death, but she walled it out. It hung heavy in her hand, and she wished that they could simply have eaten the bread and cheese the sendings had packed for them. But dogs will be dogs, she thought, and if rabbits beckon . . .

"I'll skin it," offered Sam.

"How will we cook it?" asked Lirael, gladly handing over the rabbit. She had eaten rabbits before, but only either raw, in her Charter-skin of a barking owl, or cooked and served in the refectories of the Clayr.

"A small fire under one of these boulders should be all right," replied Sam. "In a little while, anyway. The smoke won't be visible, and we can shield the flame well."

"I'll leave it to you," said Lirael. "The Dog will eat hers raw, I'm sure."

"You should sleep," said Sam as he tested the blade of a short knife with his thumb. "You can get an hour while I prepare the rabbit."

"Looking after your old aunt," said Lirael with a smile. She was only two years older than Sameth, but she had once told him she was much older, and he had believed her.

"Helping the Abhorsen-in-Waiting," said Sameth, and he bowed, not entirely in jest. Then he bent down and, with a practiced move, made a cut and pulled the skin off the rabbit in one piece, like taking the cover off a pillow.

Lirael watched him for a moment, then turned away and lay down on the stony ground with her head on her pack. It wasn't at all comfortable, particularly since she was still in armor and kept her boots on. But it didn't matter. She lay on her back and looked up at the sky, watching the last blue fade away, the black creep in, and the stars begin to twinkle. She could not feel any Dead creatures close, or sense any hint of Free Magic, and the weariness that had been in her came back a hundredfold. She blinked twice, three times; then her eyes would stay open no more, and she sank into a deep and instant sleep.

When she awoke, it was dark, save for the starlight and the dim red glow of a well-hidden fire. She saw the silhouette of the Dog sitting nearby, but there was no sign of Sam at first, till she saw a man-sized lump of darkness stretched along the ground.

"What time is it?" she whispered, and the Dog stirred and padded over to her.

"Close to midnight," replied the Dog quietly. "We thought it best to let you sleep, and then I convinced Sam it would be safe for him to sleep, too, leaving me on guard."

"I bet that wasn't easy," said Lirael, levering herself up and groaning at her stiffened muscles. "Has anything happened?"

"No. It is quiet, save for the usual things of the night. I expect Chlorr and the Dead still watch the House, and will do so for many days yet."

Lirael nodded as she groped between the boulders and trod gingerly over to the spring. It was the only patch of brightness in the calm, dark night, its silver surface picking up the starlight. Lirael washed her face and hands, the cold shock of the water bringing her fully awake.

"Did you eat my share of the rabbit?" Lirael whispered as she made her way back to her pack.

"No, I did not!" exclaimed the Dog. "As if I would! Besides,

Sameth kept it in the pot. With the lid on."

Not that this would have stopped the Dog, thought Lirael as she found the small cast-iron traveling pot by the side of the dying fire. The pieces of rabbit inside had been simmered over-long, but the stew was still warm and tasted very good. Either Sam had found herbs or the sendings had packed them, though Lirael was glad that there was no hint of rosemary. She did not want to smell that herb.

By the time she'd finished the rabbit and washed her hands and scrubbed the pot clean with a handful of grit at the spring, the moon had begun to rise. As Sam had said, it was somewhat past three quarters, well on its way to the full, and the sky was clear. Under its light Lirael could clearly make out details on the ground. It would be enough to climb the Steps.

Sam woke quickly when she shook him, his hand going to his sword. They didn't speak—something about the quiet of the night forestalled any conversation. Lirael covered the fire as Sam splashed water on his face, and they helped each other shoulder their packs. The Dog loped backwards and forwards as they got ready, her tail wagging, all eagerness to be off again.

The Steps began in a deep cut that went straight into the cliff for twenty yards, so at first it seemed it would become a tunnel. But it was open to the sky, and it soon turned to run along and up the cliff, striking westward. Each step was exactly the same size, in height and breadth and depth, so the climb was regular and relatively easy, though still exhausting.

As they climbed, Lirael came to understand that the cliff was not, as she had thought, a single almost vertical face of rough stone. It was actually composed of hundreds of faces of slipped rock, as if a sheaf of paper had been propped up and many indi-vidual pages had slipped down. The stepped path was mainly built between and on top of the faces, running along till it had to turn and be cut back deeper into the cliff in order to reach the next higher face.

The moon rose higher as they climbed, and the sky became much lighter. There was moon shadow now, and whenever they stopped for a rest, Lirael looked out to the lands beyond, to the distant hills to the south and the silver-brushed trail of the Ratterlin to the east. She had often flown in owl shape above the Clayr's Glacier and the twin mountains of Starmount and Sunfall, but that was different. Owl senses were not the same, and back there she had always known that come the dawn, she would be safely tucked in bed, secure in the fastness of the Clayr. Those flights had been pure adventure. This was something much more serious, and she could not simply enjoy the cool of the night and the bright moon.

Sam looked out, too. He couldn't see the Wall to the south— it was over the horizon—but he recognized the hills. Barhedrin was one, Cloven Crest of old, where there was a Charter Stone and, since the Restoration, a tower that was the Guard's southernmost headquarters. Beyond the Wall was the country of Ancelstierre. A strange country, even to Sameth, who had gone to school there. A country without the Charter, or Free Magic, save for its northern regions, close to the Old Kingdom. Sameth thought of his mother and father there, far off to the south. They were trying to find a diplomatic solution to stop the Ancelstierrans from sending Southerling refugees across the Wall, to their certain deaths and, after that, to serve at the command of the necromancer Hedge. It could be no coincidence, Sam thought grimly, that this Southerling refugee problem had arisen at the same time that Hedge was masterminding the digging up of the ancient evil that was imprisoned near the Red Lake. It all smacked of a long-term, well-laid plan, on both sides of the Wall.

Which was extremely unusual and did not bode well. What could a necromancer of the Old Kingdom really hope to gain from the world beyond the Wall? Sabriel and Touchstone thought their Enemy's plan was to bring hundreds of thousands of the Southerlings across the Wall, kill them by poison or spell, and make them into an army of the Dead. But the more Sam thought about it, the more he wondered. If that was the Enemy's sole intention, what was being dug up? And what part did his friend Nicholas have to play in it all?

The rests became more frequent as the moon slowly drifted down the sky. Though the steps were regular and well made, it was a steep climb, and they were tired to begin with. The Dog kept loping ahead, occasionally doubling back to make sure her mistress was keeping up, but Lirael and Sam were faltering. They trod with mechanical regularity, and their heads were bowed. Even the sight of a nest full of cliff owl chicks near the path attracted only a brief look from Lirael and not even a glance from Sameth.

They were still climbing when a red glow started to the east, coloring the moon's cold light. Soon it became bright enough to make the moon fade, and birds began to sing. Tiny swifts issued from cracks all along the cliff, flying out to chase insects rising with the morning wind.

"We must be close to the top," said Sam as they paused to rest, the three of them strung out along the narrow way: the Dog at the top, as high as Lirael's head, and Sameth below her, his head at about her knee level.

Sam leaned against the cliff face as he spoke, only to recoil with a cry as an unnoticed thorn tree pricked him in the legs.

For a moment Lirael thought he would fall, but he recovered his balance and twisted himself around to pick out the thorns.

The Steps were considerably scarier in daylight, Lirael thought, as she looked down. All it would take was a step to the left and she would fall, if not the whole way down, at least to the next rock slip. That was twenty yards below them here, enough to break bones if it didn't kill immediately.

"I never realized!" said Sam, who had stopped pulling out thorns and was kneeling down to brush away the dust and fragments of stone on the steps in front of him. "The steps are made of brick! But they would have had to cut into the stone anyway, so why face the stone with brick?"

"I don't know," replied Lirael, before she caught on that Sam had actually been asking himself. "Does it matter?"

Sam stood up and brushed his knees.

"No, I suppose not. It's just odd. It must have been an enormous job, particularly as I can't see any sign of magical assistance. I suppose sendings could have been used, though they do tend to shed the odd mark here and there. . . ."

"Come on," said Lirael. "Let's get to the top. Perhaps there will be some clue to the Steps' making there."

But well before they came to the top of the Steps, Lirael had lost all interest in plaques or builder's monuments. A terrible foreboding that had been lurking in the back of her mind grew stronger as they climbed the last few hundred feet, and slowly it became more and more concrete. She could feel a coldness in her gut, and she knew that what awaited them at the top would be a place of death. Not recent death, not within the day, but death nonetheless.

She knew Sam felt it, too. They exchanged bleak looks as the Steps widened at last near the top. Without needing to talk about it, they moved from single file to a line abreast. The Dog grew slightly larger and stayed close to Lirael's side.

Lirael's sense of death was confirmed by the breeze that hit them on the last few steps. A breeze that carried with it a terrible smell, giving a few moments' warning before they reached the top of the Steps, to look out on a barren field strewn with the bodies of many men and mules. A great gathering of ravens clustered around and on the corpses, tearing at flesh with their sharp beaks and squabbling amongst themselves.

Fortunately, it was immediately clear the ravens were normal birds. They flew away as soon as the Disreputable Dog ran forward, croaking their displeasure at the interruption to their breakfast. Lirael could not sense any Dead among them, or nearby, but she still drew Saraneth and her sword, Nehima. Even from a distance, her necromantic senses told her the bodies had been there for days, though the smell could have told her just as much.

The Dog ran back to Lirael and tilted her head in question. Lirael nodded, and the hound loped off, sniffing the ground around the bodies in wider and wider circles till she disappeared out of sight behind a particularly large clump of thorn trees. There was a body hanging from the tallest tree, tossed there by some great wind or a creature far stronger than any man.

Sam came up next to Lirael, his sword in hand, the Charter marks on the blade glowing palely in the sun. It was full dawn now, the light rich and strong. It seemed wrong for this field of death, Lirael thought. How could good sunshine play across such a place? There should be fog and darkness.

"A merchant party by the look of them," said Sam as they advanced closer. "I wonder what . . ."

It was clear from the way the bodies lay that they had been fleeing something. All the merchants' bodies, distinguishable by their richer clothes and lack of weapons, lay closer to the Steps. The guards had fallen defending their employers, in a line some twenty yards farther back. A last stand, turning to face an enemy they could not outrun.

"A week or more ago," said Lirael as she walked towards the bodies. "Their spirits will be long gone. Into Death, I hope, though I am not sure they have not been . . . harvested for use in Life."

"But why leave the bodies?" asked Sam. "And what could have made these wounds?"

He pointed at a dead guardsman, whose mail hauberk had been pierced in two places. The holes were about the size of Sam's fists and were scorched around the edges, the steel rings and the leather underneath blackened as if by fire.

Lirael carefully returned Saraneth to its pouch and walked over to take a closer look at the body and the strange wounds. She tried not to breathe as she got closer, but a few paces away she suddenly stopped and gasped. With that gasp the awful stench entered her nose and lungs. It was too much, and she began to gag and had to turn away and throw up. As soon as she did, Sam immediately followed suit, and they both emptied their stomachs of rabbit and bread.

"Sorry," said Sam. "Can't stand other people being sick. Are you all right?"

"I knew him," said Lirael, glancing back at the guardsman. Her voice trembled until she took a deep breath.

"I knew him. He came to the Glacier years ago, and he talked to me in the Lower Refectory. His hauberk didn't fit him then."

She took the bottle Sam offered her, poured some water into her hands, and rinsed out her mouth.

"His name was . . . I can't quite remember. Larrow, or Harrow. Something like that. He asked me my name, and I never answered—"

She hesitated, about to say more, but stopped as Sam suddenly whipped around.

"What was that?"

"What?"

"A noise, somewhere over there," replied Sam, pointing to a dead mule that was lying on the lip of a shallow erosion gully that led down to the cliffs. Its head hung over the gully and was out of sight.

As they watched, the mule shifted slightly; then with a jerk, it slid over the edge and into the gully. They could still see its hindquarters, but most of it was hidden. Then the mule's rump and back legs began to shake and shiver.

"Something's eating it!" exclaimed Lirael in disgust. She could see drag marks on the ground now, all leading to the gully. There had been more bodies of mules and men. Someone . . . or something had dragged them to the narrow ditch.

"I can't sense anything Dead," said Sam anxiously. "Can you?"

Lirael shook her head. She slipped off her pack and took up her bow, strung it, and nocked an arrow. Sam drew his sword again.

They advanced slowly on the gully while more and more of the mule disappeared from sight. Closer, they could hear a dry gulping noise, rather like the sound of someone shoveling sand. Every now and then it would be accompanied by a more liquid gurgle.

But they still couldn't see anything. The gully was deep and only three or four feet wide, and whatever was in it lay directly under the mule. Lirael still couldn't sense anything Dead, but there was a faint tang of something in the air.

Both of them recognized what it was at the same time. The acrid, metallic odor characteristic of Free Magic. But it was very faint, and it was impossible to tell where it was coming from. Perhaps the gully, or possibly blowing in on the faint breeze.

When they were only a few paces from the edge of the gully, the rear legs of the mule disappeared with a final shake, its hooves flying in a grim parody of life. The same liquid gurgle accompanied the disappearance.

Lirael stopped at the edge and looked down, her bow drawn, a Charter-spelled arrow ready to fly. But there was nothing to shoot. Just a long streak of dark mud at the bottom of the gully, with a single hoof sinking under the surface. The smell of Free Magic was stronger, but it was not the corrosive stench she had encountered from the Stilken or other lesser Free Magic elementals.

"What is it?" whispered Sam. His left hand was crooked in a spell-casting gesture, and a slim golden flame burned at the end of each finger, ready to be thrown.

"I don't know," said Lirael. "A Free Magic thing of some kind. Not anything I've ever read about. I wonder how—"

As she spoke, the mud bubbled and peeled back, to reveal a deep maw that was neither earth nor flesh but pure darkness, lit by a long, forked tongue of silver fire. With the open maw came a rolling stench of Free Magic and rotten meat, an almost physical assault that sent Lirael and Sam staggering back even as the tongue of silver fire rose into the air and struck down where Lirael had stood a moment before. Then a great snake head of mud followed the tongue, rearing out of the gully, looming high above them.

Lirael loosed her arrow as she stumbled back, and Sam thrust out his hand, shouting the activating marks that sent a roaring, crackling fountain of fire towards the thing of mud and blood and darkness that was rising up. Fire met silver tongue, and sparks exploded in all directions, setting the grass alight. Neither arrow nor Charter fire seemed to affect the creature, but it did recoil, and Lirael and Sam had no hesitation in running farther back.

"Who dares disturb my feasting!" roared a voice that was many voices and one, mixed with the braying of mules and the cries of dying men. "My feast so long since due!"

In answer Lirael dropped her bow and and drew Nehima. Sam muttered marks and drew them into the air with his sword and hand, knitting together many complex symbols. Lirael took a half step forward to guard Sam while he completed the spell.

Sam finished with a master mark that wreathed his hand in golden flames as he drew it in the air. It was a mark that Lirael knew could easily immolate an unready caster, and she flinched slightly as it appeared. But it left Sam's hand easily, and the spell hung in the air, a glowing tracery of linked marks, rather like a belt of shining stars. He took one end gingerly, swung the whole thing round his head, and let it fly at the creature, simultaneously shouting out, "Look away!"

There was a blinding flash, a sound like a choir screaming, and silence. When they looked back, there was no sign of the creature. Just small fires burning in the grass, coils of smoke twining together to cast a pall across the field.

"What was that?" asked Lirael.

"A spell for binding something," replied Sam. "I was never quite sure what, though. Do you think it worked?"

"No," said the Dog, her sudden appearance making Lirael and Sam jump. "Though it was quite bright enough to let every Dead thing between here and the Red Lake know where we are."

"If it didn't work, then where is that thing?" asked Sam. He looked around nervously as he spoke. Lirael looked, too. She could still smell the Free Magic, though once more only faintly, and it was impossible to tell where it was coming from amidst the eddying smoke.

"It's probably under our feet," said the Dog. She suddenly thrust her nose into a small hole and snorted. The snort sent a gout of dirt flying into the air. Lirael and Sam jumped away, hesitated on the brink of flight, then slowly stood back-to-back, their weapons ready.

Chapter Five

BLOW WIND, COME RAIN!

"EXACTLY WHERE UNDER our feet!?" exclaimed Sam. He looked down anxiously, his sword and spell-casting hand ready.

"What can we do?" asked Lirael quickly. "Do you know what that was? How do we fight it?"

The Dog sniffed scornfully at the ground.

"We will not need to fight. That was a Ferenk, a scavenger. Ferenks are all show and bluster. This one lies under several ells of earth and stone now. It will not come out till dark, perhaps not even till dark tomorrow."

Sam scanned the ground, not trusting the Dog's opinion, while Lirael bent down to talk to the hound.

"I've never read anything about Free Magic creatures called Ferenks," said Lirael. "Not in any of the books I went through to find out about the Stilken."

"There should be no Ferenk here," said the Dog. "They are elemental creatures, spirits of stone and mud. They became nothing more than stone and mud when the Charter was made. A few would have been missed, but not here . . . not in a place so traveled. . . ."

"If it was just a scavenger, what killed these poor people?" asked Lirael. She'd been wondering about the wounds she'd seen and not liking the direction her thoughts were going in. Most of the corpses had, like the guardsman, two holes bored right through them, holes where clothing and skin were scorched around the edges.

"Certainly a Free Magic creature, or creatures," said the Dog. "But not a Ferenk. Something akin to a Stilken, I think. Perhaps a Jerreq or a Hish. There were many thousands of Free Magic creatures who evaded the making of the Charter, though most were later imprisoned or made to serve after a fashion. There were entire breeds, and others of a singular nature, so I cannot speak with absolute certainty. It is complicated by the fact that there was a forge here long ago, inside the ring of thorns. There was a creature bound inside the stone anvil of that forge, yet I can find neither anvil nor any other remnants. Possibly whatever was bound here killed these people, but I think not. . . ."

The Dog paused to sniff the ground again, wandered in a circle, absently snapped at her own tail, and then sat down to offer her conclusion.

"It might have been a twinned Jerreq, but I am inclined to think the killing here was done by two Hish. Whatever did the deed, it was done in the service of a necromancer."

"How do you know that?" asked Sam. He'd stopped circling when the Dog started, though he still kept on looking at the ground. Now he was looking for signs of a stone anvil as well as an erupting Ferenk. Not that he'd ever seen an anvil here.

"Tracks and signs," replied the Dog. "The wounds, the smells that remain, a three-toed impression in soft soil, the body hung in the tree, the thorns stripped from seven branches in celebration . . . all this tells me what walked here, up to a point. As to the necromancer, no Jerreq or Hish or any of the other truly dangerous creatures of Free Magic has woken in a thousand years save to the sound of Mosrael and Saraneth, or by a direct summons using their secret names."

"Hedge was here," whispered Lirael. Sam flinched at the name, and the burn scars on his wrists darkened. But he did not look at the scars or turn away.

"Perhaps," said the Dog. "Not Chlorr, anyway. One of the Greater Dead would leave different signs."

"They died eight days ago," continued Lirael. She did not question how she knew this. Now that she had seen the corpses more closely, she just knew. It was part of her being an Abhorsen. "Their spirits were not taken. According to *The Book of the Dead*, they should not be past the Fourth Gate. I could go into Death and find one. . . ."

She stopped as both the Dog and Sam shook their heads.

"I don't think that's a good idea," said Sam. "What could you learn? We know that there are bands of the Dead and necromancers and who knows what else roaming around."

"Sam is right," said the Dog. "There is nothing useful to learn from their deaths. And since Sam has already announced our presence with Charter Magic, let us give these poor people the cleansing fire, so that their bodies may not be used. But we should be quick."

Lirael looked across the field, blinking as the sun cut across her eyes, over to where the young man who had once been Barra lay. The name came to her as she looked. She had thought of finding Barra in Death, and telling his spirit that the girl he had probably forgotten years ago had always wished she had talked to him, kissed him even, done anything other than hide behind her hair and weep. But even if she could find Barra in Death, she knew he would be long past any concerns of the living world. It would not be for him that she sought his spirit, but for herself, and she could not afford the luxury.

All three of them stood together over the closest body. Sam drew the Charter mark for fire, the Disreputable Dog barked one for cleansing, and Lirael drew those for peace and sleep and pulled all the marks together. The marks met and sparked on the man's chest, became leaping golden flames, and a second later exploded to immolate the entire body. Then the fire died as quickly as it had come, leaving only ash and lumps of melted metal that had once been belt buckle and knife blade.

"Farewell," said Sam.

"Go safely," said Lirael.

"Do not come back," said the Dog.

After that, they did the ritual individually, moving as quickly as they could among the bodies. Lirael noticed that Sam was at first surprised, then obviously relieved, that the Disreputable Dog could cast the Charter marks and perform a rite that no necromancer or pure Free Magic creature could do, because of the rite's inherent opposition to the forces they wielded.

Even with the three of them performing the rite, the sun was high and the morning almost gone by the time they finished. Not counting the unknown number of people taken by the Ferenk to its muddy lair, thirty-eight men and women had died in the field of thorn trees. Now they were only piles of ash in a field of rotting mules and ravens, who had come back, croaking their dissatisfaction at the diminution of their feast.

It was Lirael who first noticed that one of the ravens was not actually alive. It sat on the head of a mule, pretending to pick at it, but its black eyes were firmly fixed on Lirael. She had sensed its presence before seeing it, but hadn't been sure whether it was the deaths of eight days ago she felt, or the presence of the Dead. As soon as she met its gaze, she knew. The bird's spirit was long gone, and something festering and evil lived inside the feathered body. Something once human, transformed by ages spent in Death, years misspent in an endless struggle to return to Life.

It was not a Gore Crow. Though it wore a raven's body, this was a much stronger spirit than was ever used to animate a flock of just-killed crows. It was out in the glare of the full sun, and so must be a Fourth or Fifth Gate Rester at least. The raven body it used had to be fresh, for such a spirit would corrode the flesh of whatever it inhabited within a day.

Lirael's hand flew to Saraneth, but even as she drew the bell, the Dead creature shot into the air and flew swiftly west, hugging the ground and twisting among the thorn trees. Feathers and bits of dead flesh dropped as it flew. It would be a skeleton before it went much farther, Lirael realized, but then it did not need feathers to fly. Free Magic propelled it, not living sinew.

"You should have got it," criticized the Dog. "It could still hear the bell, even past those thorn trees. Let's hope it was an independent spirit; otherwise we'll have Gore Crows—at the least—all over us."

Lirael returned Saraneth to its pouch, carefully holding the clapper till the leather tongue slipped into place to keep the bell still.

"I was surprised," she said quietly. "I'll be quicker next time."

"We'd better move on," said Sam. He looked at the sky and sighed. "Though I had hoped to have a bit of a rest. It's too hot to walk."

"Where are we going?" asked Lirael. "Is there a wood or anything nearby that will hide us from the Gore Crows?"

"I'm not sure," said Sam. He pointed north, where the ground rose up to a low hill, the thorn trees giving way to a field that once must have been cultivated, though it was now home to weeds and saplings. "We can take a look from that rise. We have to head roughly northwest anyway."

They did not look back as they left what had become a

funerary ground. Lirael tried to look everywhere else, her sight and sense of Death alert for any slight indication of the Dead. The Dog loped along next to her, and Sam walked to her left, a few steps behind.

They followed the remnants of a low stone wall up the hill. Once it would have separated two fields, and there might have been sheep on the higher pasture and crops below. But that was long ago, and the wall had not been mended for decades. Somewhere, less than a league or so away, there would be a ruined farmhouse, ruined yards, a choked well. The telltale signs that people had once lived there and had not fared well.

From their high point they could see the Long Cliffs stretching out to the east and west, and the undulating hills of the plateau. They could see the Ratterlin stretching from north to south, and the plume of the waterfall. Abhorsen's House was hidden by the hills, but the tops of the fog banks that still surrounded it were eerily visible.

Several hundred years ago, before Kerrigor's rise, they would also have seen farms and villages and cultivated fields. Now, even twenty years after King Touchstone's Restoration, this part of the Kingdom was still largely deserted. Small forests had joined to become larger ones, single trees had become small forests, and drained marshes had returned happily to swamps. There were villages out there somewhere, Lirael knew, but none she could see. They were few and far between, because just a handful of Charter Stones had been replaced or restored. Only Charter Mages of the royal line could make or mend a Charter Stone—though the blood of any Charter Mage could break a normal stone. Too many Charter Stones had been broken in the two hundred years of the Interregnum for even twenty years of hard work to fix.

"It's at least two, maybe three days' solid march to Edge," said

Sam, pointing nor-norwest. "The Red Lake is behind those mountains. Which we pass to the south, I'm glad to say."

Lirael shielded her eyes against the sun with her hand and squinted. She could just make out the peaks of a distant mountain range.

"We may as well get started then," she said. Still shading her eyes, she gradually turned a full circle, looking up into the sky. It was a beautiful, clear blue, but Lirael knew that all too soon she would see telltale black blots—distant flocks of Gore Crows.

"We could head for Roble's Town first," suggested Sam, who was also looking up at the sky. "I mean, Hedge is going to know where we are anyway soon, and we might be able to get some help in Roble's Town. There'll be a Guard post there."

"No," said Lirael thoughtfully. She could see a line of puffy, black-streaked clouds far to the north, and it had given her an idea. "We'd just be getting other people into trouble. Besides, I think I know how to get rid of the Gore Crows, or hide from them at least—though it won't be pleasant. We'll try it a bit later on. Closer to nightfall."

"What do you plan, Mistress?" asked the Dog. She had collapsed near Lirael's feet, her tongue lolling out as she panted to cool down after the climb. This was a difficult task, since the sky was clear and the day was getting hotter and hotter as the sun climbed.

"We'll whistle down those rain clouds," replied Lirael, pointing at the distant cushion of dark cloud. "Good heavy rain and wind will blow away the Gore Crows, make us hard to find, and cover our tracks as well. What do you think?"

"An excellent plan!" exclaimed the Dog with approval.

"Do you think we can bring that rain down here?" asked Sam dubiously. "I reckon that cloud is about as far away as High Bridge."

"We can try," said Lirael. "Though there is more cloud to the west. . . ."

Her voice trailed off as she really focused on the blacker cloud beyond the hills, close to the western mountains. Even from this far away she could sense a wrongness in it, and as she stared, she saw the sheen of lightning within the cloud.

"I guess not that cloud."

"No," growled the Dog, her voice very deep, rumbling in her chest. "That is where Hedge and Nicholas are digging. I fear that they may have already uncovered what they seek."

"I'm sure Nick doesn't know he's doing anything bad," said Sam quickly. "He's a good man. He wouldn't do anything that would hurt anyone intentionally."

"I hope so," said Lirael. She was wondering once again what they would do when they got there. Why did Hedge need Nicholas? What was being dug up? What was their Enemy's ultimate plan?

"We'd better keep moving, anyway," she said, tearing her gaze away from the distant dark cloud and its flickering lightnings to look at the rolling land to the west. "What if we follow that valley? It goes in the right direction, and there's quite a lot of tree cover and a stream."

"That should be practically a small river," said Sam. "I don't know what's happened to the spring rains down here."

"Weather can be worked two ways," said the Dog absently. She was still looking towards the mountains. "It may be no accident that the rain clouds hug the north. It would be good to bring them south for several reasons. I would like it even more if we could stop that lightning storm."

"I guess we could try," said Sam doubtfully, but the Dog shook her head.

"That storm would not answer to any weather magic," she

said. "There is too much lightning, and that confirms a fear I had hoped to lay to rest. I had not thought they would find it so quickly, or that it could be so easily untombed. I should have known. Astarael does not lightly tread the earth, and a Ferenk released already . . ."

"What is *it*?" asked Lirael nervously.

"The thing that Hedge is digging up," said the Dog. "I will tell you more when needs must. I do not wish to fill your bones with fear, or tell ancient tales for no purpose. There are still several possible explanations and ancient safeguards that might yet hold even if the worst is true. But we must hurry!"

With that, the Dog leapt up and shot off down the hill, grinning as she zigzagged around white-barked saplings with silver-green leaves and shot over yet another ruined stone wall.

Lirael and Sam looked at each other and then at the lightning storm.

"I wish she wouldn't do that," complained Lirael, who had opened her mouth to ask another question. Then she went down after the Dog, at a considerably slower pace. Magical dogs might not tire, but Lirael was already very weary. It would be a long and exhausting afternoon, if no worse, for there was always the chance the Gore Crows would find them.

"What have you done, Nick?" whispered Sam. Then he followed Lirael, already pursing his lips and thinking about the Charter marks that would be needed to shunt a rain cloud two hundred miles across the sky.

They walked steadily all afternoon, with only short breaks, following a stream that flowed through a shallow valley between two roughly parallel lines of hills. The valley was lightly wooded, the shade saving them from the sun, which Lirael was finding particularly troubling. She was already sunburnt a little on the nose and cheekbones, and had neither the time nor the energy to soothe her skin with a spell. This was also a niggling reminder of the differences that had plagued her all her life. Proper Clayr were brown skinned, and they never burnt—exposure to sun simply made them darker.

By the time the sun had begun its slow fall behind the western mountains, only the Dog was still moving with any grace. Lirael and Sam had been awake for nearly eighteen hours, most of it climbing up the Long Cliffs or walking. They were stumbling, and falling asleep on their feet, no matter how they tried to stay alert. Finally Lirael decided that they had to rest, and they would stop as soon as they saw somewhere defensible, preferably with running water on at least one side.

Half an hour later, as they kept stumbling on and the valley began to narrow and the ground to rise, Lirael was prepared to settle for anywhere they could simply fall down, with or without running water to help defend against the Dead. The trees were also thinning out, giving way to low shrubs and weedy grass as they climbed. Another field that was returning to the wild, and totally indefensible.

Just when Lirael and Sam could hardly take another step, they found the perfect place. The soft gurgle of a waterfall announced it, and there was a shepherd's hut, built on stilts across the swift water at the foot of a long but not very high waterfall. The hut was both shelter and bridge, so solidly built of ironwood that it showed little sign of decay, save for some of the shingles missing from the roof.

The Dog sniffed around outside the river hut, pronounced it dirty but habitable, and got in the way as Lirael and Sam tried to climb the steps and enter.

It was filthy inside, having at some time been subject to a flood that had deposited a great deal of dirt on the floor. But

Lirael and Sam were past caring about that. Whether they slept on dirt outdoors or in, it was all one.

"Dog, can you take the first watch?" asked Lirael, as she gratefully shrugged off her pack and settled it in one corner.

"I can watch," protested Sam, belying his words with a mighty yawn.

"I will watch," said the Disreputable Dog. "Though there may be rabbits. . . ."

"Don't chase them out of sight," warned Lirael. She drew Nehima and laid the sword across her pack, ready for quick use, then did the same with the bell-bandolier. She kept her boots on, choosing not to speculate on the state of her feet after two days' hard traveling.

"Wake us in four hours, please," Lirael added as she slumped down and leant back against the wall. "We have to call the rain clouds down."

"Yes, Mistress," replied the Dog. She had not come in but sat near the rushing water, her ears pricked to catch some distant sound. Rabbits, perhaps. "Do you want me to bring you a boiled egg and toast as well?"

There was no answer. When the Dog looked in a moment later, both Lirael and Sam were sound asleep, slumped against their packs. The Dog let out a long sigh and slumped down herself, but her ears stayed upright and her eyes were keen, gazing out long after the summer twilight faded into the night.

Near midnight, the Dog shook herself and woke Lirael with a lick on her face and Sam with paw pressed heavily on his chest. Each woke with a start, and both reached for their swords before their eyes adjusted to the dim light from the glow of the Charter marks in the Dog's collar.

Cold water from the stream woke them a little more, followed by necessary ablutions slightly farther afield. When they came back, a quick meal of dried meat, compressed dry biscuits, and dried fruit was eaten heartily by all three, though the Dog regretted the absence of rabbit or even a nice bit of lizard.

They couldn't see the rain clouds in the night, even with a star-filled sky and the moon beginning its rise. But they knew the clouds were there, far to the north.

"We will have to go as soon as the spell is done," warned the Dog, as Lirael and Sam stood under the stars quietly discussing how they would call the clouds and rain. "Such Charter Magic will call anything Dead within miles, or any Free Magic creatures."

"We should press on anyway," said Lirael. The sleep had revived her to some degree, but she still wished for the comfort of the sleeping chair in her little room in the Great Library of the Clayr. "Are you ready, Sam?"

Sam stopped humming and said, "Yes. Um, I was wondering whether you might consider a slight variation on the usual spell? I think that we will need a stronger casting to bring the clouds so far."

"Sure," said Lirael. "What do you want to do?"

Sam explained quickly, then went through it again slowly as Lirael made certain she knew what he planned to do. Usually both of them would whistle the same marks at the same time. What Sam wanted to do was whistle different but complementary marks, in effect weaving together two different weatherworking spells. They would end and activate the spell by speaking two master marks at the same time, when one was normally all that would be used.

"Will this work?" asked Lirael anxiously. She had no experience of working with another Charter Mage on such a complex spell.

"It will be much stronger," said Sam confidently.

Lirael looked at the Dog for confirmation, but the hound wasn't paying attention. She was staring back towards the south, intent on something Lirael and Sam couldn't see or sense.

"What is it?"

"I don't know," replied the Dog, turning her head to the side, her pricked ears quivering as she listened to the night. "I think something is following us, but it is still distant. . . ."

She looked back at Lirael and Sam.

"Do your weather magic and let us be gone!"

A league or more downstream of the shepherd's hut, a very short man—almost a dwarf—was paddling in the shallows. His skin was as white as bone, and the hair on his head and beard was whiter still, so white it shone in the darkness, even under the shadow of the trees where they overhung the water.

"I'll show her," muttered the albino, though no one was there to hear his angry speech. "Two thousand years of servitude already, and then to—"

He stopped mid word and swooped into the stream, one knobby-fingered hand plunging into the water. It emerged a moment later holding a struggling fish, which he immediately bit behind its eyes, severing the spinal cord. His teeth, bright in the starlight, were sharper by far than any human's.

The dwarf tore at the fish again, blood dribbling down his beard. In a few minutes he'd eaten the whole thing, spitting out the bones with curses and grumbling between bites over the fact that he'd wanted a trout and had got a redjack.

When he finished, he carefully cleaned his face and beard and dried his feet, though he left the bloodstains on the simple robe he wore. But as he walked along the bank of the stream, the stains faded and the cloth was once again clean and white and new.

The robe was fastened around the little man's waist with a

red leather belt, and where the buckle should have been there was a tiny bell. All this time the albino had held it, using only one hand to catch the fish and clean himself. But his caution failed when he stumbled on a slippery patch of grass. The bell sang out as he fell to one knee, a bright sound that paradoxically made the man yawn. For a moment it seemed he might lie down there and then, but with an obvious effort he shook his head and stood up.

"No, no, sister," he muttered, clutching the bell even more fiercely. "I have work to do, you see. I cannot sleep, not now. There are miles to go, and I must make the most of two legs and two hands while I still have them."

A night bird called nearby and the man's head flashed around, instantly spotting it. Still holding the bell, he licked his lips and, taking one slow step after the other, began to stalk it. But the bird was wary, and before the albino could pounce, it flew away, calling plaintively into the night.

"I never get dessert," complained the man. He turned back to the stream and began to follow it westwards once again, still holding the bell and muttering complaints.

Chapter Six

THE SILVER HEMISPHERES

ONE HUNDRED AND twenty miles to the northwest of Abhorsen's House, the eastern shores of the Red Lake lay in darkness, even though a new day had dawned. For it was not the dark of night but of storm, the sky heavy with black clouds, that stretched for several leagues in all directions. The darkness had already lasted for more than a week. What little sunlight came through the cloud was weak and pale, and the days were lit by a strange twilight that did no favor to any living thing. Only at the epicenter of this immovable cluster of storm clouds was there any other light, and that was sudden, harsh and white, from the constant assault of lightning.

Nicholas Sayre had grown used to the twilight, as he had grown used to many other things, and he no longer thought it strange. But his body still rebelled, even when his mind did not. He coughed and held his handkerchief against his nose and mouth. Hedge's Night Crew were sterling workers, but they did smell awful, as if the flesh were rotting on their bones. Generally he didn't like to get too close—in case whatever they had was contagious—but he'd had to this time, to check out what was happening.

"You see, Master," Hedge explained, "we cannot move the two hemispheres any closer together. There is a force that keeps them apart, no matter what methods we employ. Almost as if they are identical poles of a magnet."

Nick nodded, absorbing this information. As he'd dreamt, there had been two silver hemispheres hidden deep underground, and his excavation had found them. But his sense of triumph at their discovery was soon dispelled by the logistical problems of getting them out. Each hemisphere was seven feet in diameter, and the strange metal it was made of was much heavier than it should be, weighing even more than gold.

The hemispheres had been buried some twenty feet apart, separated by a strange barrier made of seven different materials, including bone. Now that they were being raised, it was clear that this barrier had helped negate the repulsive force, for the hemispheres simply could not be brought within fifty feet of each other.

Using rollers, ropes, and over two hundred of the Night Crew, one of the hemispheres had been dragged up the spiral ramp and over the lip of the pit. The other lay abandoned a good distance down the ramp. The last time they had tried to drag and push up the lower hemisphere, the repulsive force had been so great it was hurled back down, crushing many of the workers beneath it.

In addition to this strange repulsive force, Nick noted, there were other effects around the hemispheres. They seemed to generate an acrid, hot-metal smell that cut through even the fetid, rotting odor of the Night Crew. The smell made him sick, though it did not seem to affect either Hedge or his peculiar laborers.

Then there was the lightning. Nick flinched as yet another bolt struck down, momentarily blinding him, deafening thunder coming an instant later. The lightning was striking even more frequently than before, and now both hemispheres were exposed, Nick could see a pattern. Each hemisphere was struck eight times in a row, but the ninth bolt would invariably miss, often striking one of the workers.

Not that this seemed to affect them, part of Nick's mind observed. If they didn't catch alight or get completely dismembered, they kept on working. But this information didn't stay in his head, as Nick's thoughts always came back to his primary goal with an intense focus that banished all extraneous thoughts.

"We will have to move the first hemisphere on," he said, fighting the shortness of breath that came with the nausea he suffered whenever he went too close to the silver metal. "And we will need an additional barge. The two hemispheres won't fit on the one we've got, not with a fifty-foot separation. I hope the import license I have will allow two shipments. . . . In any case, we have no choice. There must be no delay."

"As you say, Master," replied Hedge, but he kept staring at Nick as if he expected something else.

"I meant to ask if you'd found a crew," Nick said at last, when the silence became uncomfortable. "For the barges."

"Yes," replied Hedge. "They gather at the lakeside. Men like me, Master. Those who served in the Army of Ancelstierre, down in the trenches of the Perimeter. At least till the night drew them from their pickets and listening posts and made them cross the Wall."

"You mean deserters? Are they trustworthy?" Nick asked sharply. The last thing he wanted was to lose a hemisphere through human stupidity, or to introduce some additional complication for when they crossed back into Ancelstierre. That simply could not be allowed to happen.

"Not deserters, sir, oh, no," replied Hedge, smiling. "Simply missing in action, and too far from home. They are quite trustworthy. I have made certain of that."

"And the second barge?" Nick asked.

Hedge suddenly looked up, nostrils flaring to sniff the air, and he didn't answer. Nick looked up, too, and a heavy drop of rain splashed upon his mouth. He licked his lips, then quickly spat as a strange, numbing sensation spread down his throat.

"This should not be," Hedge whispered to himself, as the rain came heavier and a wind sprang up around them. "Summoned rain, coming from the northeast. I had best investigate, Master."

Nick shrugged, uncertain what Hedge was talking about. The rain made him feel peculiar, recalling him to some other sense of himself. Everything around him had assumed a dream-like quality, and for the first time he wondered what on earth he was doing.

Then a strange pain struck him in the chest and he doubled over. Hedge caught him and laid him down onto earth that was rapidly turning into mud.

"What is it, Master?" asked Hedge, but his tone was inquisitive rather than sympathetic.

Nick groaned and clutched at his chest, his legs writhing. He tried to speak, but only spittle came from his lips. His eyes flickered wildly from side to side, then rolled back.

Hedge knelt by him, waiting. Rain continued to fall on Nick's face, but now it sizzled as it hit, steam wafting off his skin. A few moments later, thick white smoke began to coil out of the young man's nose and mouth, hissing as it met the rain.

"What is it, Master?" repeated Hedge, his voice suddenly nervous.

Nick's mouth opened, and more smoke puffed out. Then his hand moved, quicker than Hedge could see, fingers clutching at the necromancer's leg with terrible force. Hedge clenched his teeth, fighting back the pain, and asked again, "Master?"

"Fool!" said the thing that used Nick as its voice. "Now is not the time to seek our enemies. They will find this pit soon enough, but by then we will be gone. You must procure an additional barge at once, and load the hemispheres. And get this body out of the rain, for it is already too fragile, and much remains to be done. Too much for my servants to laze and chatter!"

The last words were said with venom, and Hedge screamed as the fingers on his leg dug in like a steel-toothed mantrap. Then he was released, to fall back into the mud.

"Hurry," whispered the voice. "Be swift, Hedge. Be swift."

Hedge bowed where he was, not trusting himself to speak. He wanted to edge out of reach of the grasping, inhuman power of those hands, but he feared to move.

The rain grew heavier, and the white smoke began to sink back into Nick's nose and mouth. After a few seconds it disappeared completely, and he went totally limp.

Hedge caught his head just before it splashed back into a puddle. Then he lifted him up and carefully arranged him over his shoulders in a fireman's lift. A normal man's leg would have been broken by the force exerted through Nick's hand, but Hedge was no normal man. He lifted Nick easily, merely grimacing at the pain in his leg.

He'd carried Nick halfway back to his tent before the inert body on his shoulders twitched and the young man began to cough.

"Easy, Master," said Hedge, increasing his pace. "I'll soon have you out of the rain."

"What happened?" asked Nick, his voice rasping. His throat felt as if he'd just smoked half a dozen cigars and drunk a bottle of brandy.

"You fainted," replied Hedge, pushing through the flaps of the tent door. "Are you able to dry yourself and get to bed?"

"Yes, yes, of course," snapped Nick, but his legs trembled as Hedge put him down, and he had to balance himself against a traveling chest. Overhead, the rain beat out a steady rhythm on the canvas, accentuated every few minutes by the dull bass boom of thunder.

"Good," replied Hedge, handing him a towel. "I must go and give the Night Crew their instructions; then I have to go and . . . acquire another barge. It would probably be best if you rested here, sir. I will make sure someone—not one of the afflicted—brings your meals and empties the necessaries and so forth."

"I'm quite able to look after myself," replied Nick, though he couldn't stop shivering as he stripped off his shirt and began to weakly towel his chest and arms. "Including overseeing the Night Crew."

"That will not be required," said Hedge. He leaned over Nick, and his eyes appeared to grow larger and fill with a flickering red light, as if they were windows to a great furnace somehow burning inside his skull.

"It would be best if you rested here," he repeated, his breath hot and metallic on Nick's face. "You do not need to supervise the work."

"Yes," agreed Nick dully, the towel frozen in mid motion. "It would be best for me to rest . . . here."

"You will await my return," commanded Hedge. His usual subordinate tone was completely gone, and he loomed over Nick like a headmaster about to cane a pupil.

"I will await your return," Nick repeated.

"Good," said Hedge. He smiled and turned on his heel, striding back out into the rain. It evaporated instantly into steam as it touched his bare head, wreathing him with a strange white halo. A few steps later, the steam wafted away, and the rain simply plastered down his hair.

Back in his tent, Nick suddenly started drying himself again.

That done, he put on a pair of badly repaired pajamas and went to his bed of piled furs. His camp bed from Ancelstierre had broken days before, the springs collapsing into rust and the canvas crumbling with mildew.

Sleep came quickly, but not rest. He dreamed of the two silver hemispheres, and his Lightning Farm that was being set up across the Wall. He saw the hemispheres absorbing power from a thousand lightning strikes and, as they drew power, overcoming the force that kept them apart. He saw them finally hurtle together, charged with the strength of ten thousand storms . . . but then the dream began again from the beginning, so he couldn't see what happened when the hemispheres met.

Outside, the rain came down in sheets and the lightning struck again and again into and around the pit. Thunder rumbled and shook as the Dead Hands of the Night Crew strained at the ropes, slowly dragging the first silver hemisphere towards the Red Lake and the second hemisphere up and out of the pit.

Chapter Seven

A LAST REQUEST

I T WAS STILL raining two days after Lirael and Sam's all-too-successful weather working. Despite the oilskin coats thoughtfully packed by the sendings back at the House, they were completely, and seemingly permanently, sodden. Fortunately the spell was finally weakening, particularly the wind-summoning aspect, so the rain had lessened and was no longer driving horizontally into their faces, and they weren't being assaulted by sticks, leaves, and other wind-borne debris.

On the positive side, as Lirael had to remind herself every few hours, the rain had made it absolutely impossible for any Gore Crows to find them. Though that was somehow not as cheering as it should have been.

It also wasn't cold, which was another positive. They would have frozen to death otherwise, or exhausted themselves into immobility by using Charter Magic to stay alive. Both the wind and the rain were warm, and if there had been even an hour or two without them, Lirael would have thought their weather working a great success. As it was, misery rather tainted any pride in the spell.

They were getting close to the Red Lake now, climbing up through the lush forested foothills of Mount Abed and her sisters. The trees grew close here, forming a canopy overhead, interspersed with many ferns and plants Lirael knew only from books. The leaf litter from all of them was thick on the ground, making a carpet over the mud. Because of the rain, there were thousands of tiny rivulets of water everywhere, cascading among tree roots, down stone, and around Lirael's ankles. When she could see her ankles, because most of the time her legs were buried up to the shins in a mixture of wet leaves and mud.

It was very hard going, and Lirael was more tired than she had thought possible. The rests, when they had them, consisted of finding the largest tree with the thickest foliage to keep out the rain, and the highest roots to sit on, to keep out of the mud. Lirael had found that she could sleep even in these conditions, though more than once she awoke, after the scant two hours they allowed themselves, to find herself lying in the mud rather than sitting above it.

Of course, once they got back out in the rain, the mud soon washed off. Lirael wasn't sure which was worse. Mud or rain. Or the middle course: the first ten minutes after moving out of shelter, when the mud was getting washed off and running down her face, hands, and legs.

It was at exactly that time after a rest, with her total attention on getting the mud out of her eyes as they climbed up yet another gully, that they found a dying Royal Guard, propped up against the trunk of a sheltering tree. Or rather, the Disreputable Dog found her, sniffing her out as she scrabbled ahead of Lirael and Sam.

The Guardswoman was unconscious, her red and gold surcoat stained black with blood, her mail hauberk ripped and torn in several places. She still held a notched and blunted sword firmly in her right hand, while her left was frozen in a spell-casting gesture she would never complete.

Both Lirael and Sam knew that she was almost gone, her spirit already stepping across the border into Death. Quickly Sam bent down, calling up the most powerful healing spell he knew. But even as the first Charter mark flowered brightly in his mind, she was dead. The faint sheen of life in her eyes disappeared, replaced by a dull, unseeing gaze. Sam let the healing mark go and brushed her eyelids gently shut.

"One of Father's Guards," he said heavily. "I don't know her, though. She was probably from the Guard tower at Roble's Town or Uppside. I wonder what she was doing . . ."

Lirael nodded, but she couldn't tear her gaze away from the corpse. She felt so useless. She kept on being too late, too slow. The Southerling in the river, after the battle with Chlorr. Barra and the merchants. Now this woman. It was so unfair that she should die alone, with only a few minutes between death and rescue. If only they'd been quicker climbing the hill, or if they hadn't stopped for that last rest . . .

"She was a few days dying," said the Disreputable Dog, sniffing around the body. "But she can't have come far, Mistress. Not with those wounds."

"We must be close to Hedge and Nick then," said Sam, straightening up to cast a wary eye around. "It's so hard to tell under all these trees. We could be near the top of the ridge or still have miles to go."

"I guess I'd better find out," said Lirael slowly. She was still looking down at the dead body of the Guard. "What killed her, and where the enemy are."

"We must hurry then," said the Dog, jumping up on her hind legs with sudden excitement. "The river will have taken her some distance."

"You're going into Death?" asked Sam. "Is that wise? I mean, Hedge could be nearby—or even waiting in Death!"

"I know," said Lirael. She had been thinking exactly the same thing. "But I think it's worth the risk. We need to find out exactly where Nick's diggings are, and what happened to this

Guard. We can't just keep blindly marching on."

"I suppose so," said Sam, biting his lip with unconscious anxiety. "What will I do?"

"Watch over my body while I'm gone, please," said Lirael.

"But don't use any Charter Magic unless you have to," added the Dog. "Someone like Hedge can smell it from miles away. Even with this rain."

"I know that," replied Sam. He betrayed his nervousness by drawing his sword, as his eyes kept moving, checking out every tree and shrub. He even looked up, just in time to receive a trickle of rain that had made it through the thick branches overhead. It ran down his neck and under the oilskin, to make him even less comfortable. But nothing lurked in the branches of the tree, and from what little he could see of the sky, it seemed empty of anything but rain and clouds.

Lirael drew her sword, too. She hesitated over which bell to choose for a moment, her hand flat against the bandolier. She had entered Death only once before, when she had been so nearly defeated and enslaved by Hedge. This time, she told herself, she would be stronger and better prepared. Part of that meant choosing the right bell. Her fingers lightly touched each pouch till the sixth one, which she carefully opened. She took out the bell, holding it inside its mouth so the clapper couldn't sound. She had chosen Saraneth, the Binder. Strongest of all the bells save Astarael.

"I am coming, too, aren't I?" asked the Dog eagerly, jumping around Lirael's feet, her tail wagging at high speed.

Lirael nodded her acquiescence and began to reach out for Death. It was easy here, for the Guard's passing had created a door that would link Life and Death at this spot for many days. A door that could work both ways.

The cold came quickly, banishing the humidity of the warm

rain. Lirael shivered but kept forcing herself forward into Death, till
the rain and the wind and the scent of wet leaves and Sam's watching face were all gone, replaced by the chill, grey light of Death.

The river tugged at Lirael's knees, willing her onwards. For
a moment she resisted, reluctant to give up the feel of Life at her
back. All she had to do was take one step backwards, reach out
to Life, and be back in the forest. But she would have learned
nothing. . . .

"I am the Abhorsen-in-Waiting," she whispered, and she felt
the river's tug lessen. Or perhaps she just imagined it. Either way,
she felt better. She had a right to be here.

She took her first slow step forward, and then another and
another, until she was walking steadily forward, the Disreputable
Dog plunging along at her side.

If she was lucky, Lirael thought, the Guard would still be on
this side of the First Gate. But nothing was moving anywhere
she could see, not even drifting on the surface, caught by the
current. In the far distance was the roar of the Gate.

She listened carefully to that—for the roar would stop if the
woman went through—and kept walking, careful to feel for pot-
holes or sudden dips. It was much easier going with the current,
and she relaxed a little, but not so much that she lowered sword
or bell.

"She is just ahead, Mistress," whispered the Dog, her nose
twitching only an inch above the surface of the river. "To the
left."

Lirael followed the Dog's pointing paw and saw that there
was a dim shape under the water, drifting with the current
towards the First Gate. Instinctively, she stepped forward, thinking to physically grab the Guard. Then she realized her mistake
and stopped.

Even the newly Dead could be dangerous, and a friend in

Life would not necessarily be so here. It was safer not to touch. Instead she sheathed her sword and, keeping Saraneth stilled with her left hand, transferred her right to grasp the bell's mahogany handle. Lirael knew she should have flipped it one-handed and begun to ring it at the same time, and she knew she could if she had to, but it seemed sensible to be more cautious. After all, she had never used the bells before. Only the panpipes, and they were a lesser instrument of power.

"Saraneth will be heard by many, and afar," whispered the Dog. "Why don't I run up and grab her by the ankle?"

"No." Lirael frowned. "She's a Royal Guard, Dead or not, and we have to treat her with respect. I'll just get her attention. We won't be waiting around anyway."

She rang the bell with a simple arcing motion, one of the easiest peals described in *The Book of the Dead* for Saraneth. At the same time, she exerted her will into the sound of the bell, directing it at the submerged body floating away ahead.

The bell was very loud, eclipsing the faint roar of the First Gate. It echoed everywhere, seeming to grow louder rather than fainter, the deep tone creating ripples on the water in a great ring around Lirael and the Dog, ripples that moved even against the current.

Then the sound wrapped around the spirit of the Guard, and Lirael felt her twist and wriggle against her will like a fresh-hooked fish. Through the echo of the bell, she heard a name, and she knew that Saraneth had found it out and was giving it to her. Sometimes it was necessary to use a Charter-spell to discover a name, but this Guard had no defenses against any of the bells.

"Mareyn," said the echo of Saraneth, an echo that sounded only inside Lirael's head. The Guard's name was Mareyn.

"Stay, Mareyn," she said in a commanding tone. "Stand, for I would speak with you."

Lirael felt resistance from the Guard then, but it was weak. A moment later the cold river frothed and bubbled, and the spirit of Mareyn stood up and turned to face the bell wielder who had bound her.

The Guard was too newly dead for Death to have changed her, so her spirit looked the same as her body out in Life. A tall, strongly built woman, the rents in her armor and the wounds in her body as clear here in the strange light of Death as they had been under the sun.

"Speak, if you are able," ordered Lirael. Again, being newly Dead, Mareyn could probably talk if she chose. Many who dwelled long in Death lost the power of speech, which could only then be restored by Dyrim, the speaking bell.

"I . . . am . . . able," croaked Mareyn. "What do you want of me, Mistress?"

"I am the Abhorsen-in-Waiting," declared Lirael, and those words seemed to echo out into Death, drowning the small still voice inside her that wanted to say, "I am a Daughter of the Clayr."

"I would ask the manner of your death and what you know of a man called Nicholas and the pit he has dug," she continued.

"You have bound me with your bell and I must answer," said Mareyn, her voice devoid of all emotion. "But I would ask a boon, if I may."

"Ask," said Lirael, flicking her glance to the Disreputable Dog, who was circling behind Mareyn like a wolf after a sheep. The Dog saw her looking, wagged her tail, and started to circle back. She was obviously just playing, though Lirael didn't understand how she could be so lighthearted here in Death.

"The necromancer of the pit, whose name I dare not speak," said Mareyn. "He killed my companions, but he laughed and let me crawl away, wounded as I was, with the promise that his servants would find me in Death and bind me to his service. I feel that this is so, and my body also lies unburnt behind me. I do not wish to return, Mistress, or to serve such a one as he. I ask you to send me on, where no power can turn me back."

"Of course I will," said Lirael, but Mareyn's words sent a stab of fear through her. If Hedge had let Mareyn go, he had probably had her followed and knew where her body was. It might be under observation at this moment, and it would be easy enough to set a watch in Death for Mareyn's spirit when it came. Hedge—or his servants—might be approaching in both Life and Death, right now.

Even as she thought that, the Dog's ears pricked up and she growled. A second later Lirael heard the roar of the First Gate falter and become still.

"Something comes," warned the Dog, nose snuffling at the river. "Something bad."

"Quickly then," Lirael said. She replaced Saraneth and drew Kibeth, transferring the bell to her left hand so she could also unsheath Nehima. "Mareyn, tell me where the pit is, in relation to your body."

"The pit lies in the next valley, over the ridge," replied Mareyn calmly. "There are many Dead there, under constant cloud and lightning. They have made a road, too, along the valley floor to the lake. The young man Nicholas lives in a patchwork tent to the east of the pit. . . . Something comes for me, Mistress. Please, I beg you to send me on."

Lirael felt the fear within Mareyn's spirit, even though her voice had the steady, uninflected tone of the Dead. She heard it and responded instantly, ringing Kibeth above her head in a figure-eight pattern.

"Go, Mareyn," she said sternly, her words weaving into the toll of the bell. "Walk deep into Death and do not tarry, or let any bar your path. I command thee to walk to the Ninth Gate and go beyond, for you have earned your final rest. Go!"

Mareyn jerked completely around at that last word and began to march, her head high and arms swinging, as she must once have marched in Life on the parade ground at the barracks at Belisaere. Straight as an arrow she marched, off towards the First Gate. Lirael saw her falter for a moment in the distance, as if something had tried to waylay her, but then she marched on, till the roar of the First Gate stilled to mark her passage.

"She's gone," remarked the Dog. "But whatever came through is here somewhere. I can smell it."

"I can feel it, too," whispered Lirael. She swapped bells again, taking up Saraneth. She liked the security of the big bell, and the deep authority of its voice.

"We should go back," said the Dog, her head slowly moving from side to side as she tried to locate the creature. "I don't like it when they're clever."

"Do you know what it is?" whispered Lirael as they began to trudge back to Life, zigzagging so her back was never truly turned. As on her first trip, it was much harder going against the current, and it seemed colder than ever, too, leaching away at her spirit.

"Some sneaker from beyond the Fifth Gate, I think," said the Dog. "Small, and long since whittled down from its original—There!"

She barked and dashed through the water. Lirael saw something like a long, spindle-thin rat—with burning coals for eyes—leap aside as the Dog struck. Then it was coming straight at her, and she felt its cold and powerful spirit rise against her, out of all proportion to its rat-like form.

She screamed and struck at it with her sword, blue-white sparks streaming everywhere. But it was too quick. The blow glanced off, and it snapped at her left wrist, at the hand that held the bell. Its jaws met her armored sleeve, and black-red flames burst out between its needle-like teeth.

Then the Dog fastened her own jaws on the creature's middle and twisted it off Lirael's arm, the hound's bloodcurdling growl adding to the sound of the thing squealing and Lirael's scream. A moment later all were drowned in the deep sound of Saraneth as Lirael stepped back, flipped the bell, caught the handle, and rang it, all in one smooth motion.

Chapter Eight

THE TESTING OF SAMETH

S AM WALKED AROUND his small perimeter again, checking to make sure nothing was approaching. Not that he could see much through the rain and the foliage. Or hear anything, for that matter, till it would be too close for him to do anything but fight.

He checked Lirael again for any sign of change, but she remained in Death, her body still as a statue, rimed with ice, cold billowing out to freeze the puddles at her feet. Sam thought about breaking off a piece of ice to cool himself down but decided against it. There were several large Dog footprints in the middle of the frozen puddle, for the Disreputable Dog—unlike her mistress—was able to bodily cross into Death, confirming Sam's guess that her physical form was entirely magical.

The Guard's body was still propped up against the tree as well. Sam had considered laying her out properly, but that seemed stupid when it meant putting her body down into the mud. He wanted to give her body a proper ending, too, but didn't dare use the Charter Magic required. Not until Lirael came back, at least.

Sam sighed at that thought and wished he could shelter out of the rain against the tree until Lirael did return. But he was acutely aware that he was responsible for Lirael's safety. He was alone again, in effect, now without even the dubious companionship of Mogget. It made him nervous, but the fear that had been with him all through his flight from Belisaere was gone. This time he simply didn't want to let Aunt Lirael down. So he hefted his sword and began once again to walk around the tight ring of trees he'd selected as his patrol route.

He was halfway around when he heard something above the steady sound of the rain. The soggy snap of wet twigs breaking underfoot, or something like it. A sound out of keeping for the forest.

Immediately, Sam knelt down behind the checkered trunk of a large fern and froze, so he could hear better.

At first, all he heard was the rain and his own beating heart. Then he caught the sound again. A soft footfall, leaves crushed underfoot. Someone—or something—was trying to sneak up on him. The sounds were about twenty feet away, lower down the slope, hidden by all the green undergrowth. Coming closer very slowly, just a single pace every minute or so.

Sam glanced back at Lirael. There was no sign of her returning from Death. For a moment, he thought he should run and tap her on the shoulder, to alert her to come back. It was very tempting, because then she could take charge.

He dismissed the thought. Lirael had a task to do, and so did he. There would be time enough to call her back if he had to. Perhaps it was only a big lizard crawling up between the ferns, or a wild dog, or one of those large black flightless birds that he knew lived in these mountains. He couldn't remember what they were called.

It wasn't anything Dead. He would have sensed it for sure, he thought. A Free Magic creature would be sizzling from the rain, and he'd smell it. Probably . . .

It moved again, but not uphill. It was circling around, Sam realized. Perhaps trying to work its way past them to attack down the slope. That would be a human trick.

It could be a necromancer, said a fearful part of Sam's mind.

Not Dead, so you couldn't sense it. Wielding Free Magic, but not of it, so you couldn't smell anything. It could even be *him*. It could be Hedge.

Sam's sword hand began to tremble. He gripped the hilt tighter, made the trembling stop. The burn scars on his wrists grew livid, bright with the effort.

This is it, he told himself. This was the test. If he didn't face whatever was out there now, he would know he was a coward forever. Lirael didn't think he was, nor the Dog. He had run from Astarael, but not out of fear. He had been made to by magic, and Lirael had run, too. There was no shame in that.

It moved again, slinking closer. Sam still couldn't see it, but he was sure he knew where it was.

He reached into the Charter and felt his heart slow from a frantic pace as he was embraced by the familiar calm of the magic that linked all living things. Drawing in the air with his free hand, Sam called forth four bright Charter marks. The fifth he spoke under his breath, into his cupped hand. When the marks joined, Sam held a dagger that was like a sunbeam caught in his hand. Too bright to look at directly, but golden at a glance.

"For the Charter!"

Sun dagger in one hand, sword in the other, Sam roared a battle cry and leapt forward, crashing through the ferns, slipping in the mud, half-falling down the slope. He saw a flash of movement behind a tree and changed direction, still roaring, his father's berserker blood beating in his temples. There was the enemy, a strange pallid little man—

Who disappeared.

Sam tried to stop. He dug his heels in, but his feet skidded in the mud and he ran straight into a tree trunk, rebounded into a fern, and fell flat on his back. Down in the mud, he remembered his arms master telling him, "Most who go down in a battle never get up again. So don't bloody well fall down!"

Sam dropped the sun dagger, which was extinguished immediately, the individual marks melting into the ground, and pushed himself up. He had been down for only a second or two, he thought, as he stared wildly around. But there was no sign of the . . . whatever it was. . . .

Lirael.

The thought struck him like a blow, and instantly he was running up the slope he'd just careered down, grabbing at ferns and branches and anything that could make him go faster. He had to get back! What if Lirael was attacked while she was still in Death? Struck from behind with a dagger, or a knife? She wouldn't have a chance.

He made it back to the small clearing. Lirael still stood there. Icicles made from raindrops hung from her outstretched arms. The frozen pool around her feet had spread, so strange in this warm forest. She was unharmed.

"Lucky I was here," said a voice behind Sam. A familiar voice. Mogget's voice.

Sam whirled around.

"Mogget? Is that you? Where are you?"

"Here, and regretting it as per usual," replied Mogget, and a small white cat sauntered out from behind a fern tree.

Sam did not relax his guard. He could see that Mogget still wore his collar, and there was a bell on it. But it could be a trick. And where . . . or who . . . was that strange pale man?

"I saw a man," said Sam. "His hair and skin were white, white as snow. White as your fur . . ."

"Yes," yawned Mogget. "That was me. But that shape was forbidden to me by Jerizael, who was . . . let me see . . . she was the forty-eighth Abhorsen. I cannot use it in the presence of an

Abhorsen, even an apprentice, without prior permission. Your mother does not generally give me permission, though her father was more flexible. Lirael cannot currently say yea or nay, so once again you see me as I am."

"The Dog said that she . . . Astarael . . . wasn't going to let you go," said Sam. He had not lowered his sword.

Mogget yawned again, and the bell rang on his neck. It *was* Ranna—Sam recognized both the voice and his own reaction: he couldn't help yawning himself.

"Is that what that hound said?" remarked the cat as he padded over to Sam's pack and delicately sliced open half the stitches on the patch with one sharp claw so he could climb in. "Astarael? Is that who it was? It's been so long, I can't really remember who was who. In any case, she said what she wanted to say, and then I left. Wake me up when we're somewhere dry and comfortable, Prince Sameth. With civilized food."

Sam slowly lowered his sword and sighed in exasperation. It clearly was Mogget. Sam just wasn't sure if he was pleased or not that the cat had returned. He kept remembering that gloating chuckle in the tunnel below the House, and the stench and dazzle of Free Magic. . . .

Ice cracked. Sam whirled about again, his heart hammering. With the cracking of the ice, he heard the echo of a distant bell. So distant it might have been a memory, or an imagined sound.

More ice cracked, and Lirael fell to one knee, ice flaking off her like a miniature snowstorm. Then there was a bright flash, and the Dog appeared, jumping around anxiously and growling deep in her chest.

"What happened?" asked Sam. "Are you hurt?"

"Not really," said Lirael, with a grimace that showed there was something wrong, and she held up her left wrist. "Some horrible little Fifth Gate Rester tried to bite my arm. But it didn't get through the coat—it's only bruised."

"What did you do to it?" asked Sam. The Dog was still running around as if the Dead creature might suddenly appear.

"The Dog bit it in half," said Lirael, forcing herself to take several long, slow breaths. "Though that didn't stop it. But I made it obey me in the end. It's on its way to the Ninth Gate—and it won't be coming back."

"You really are the Abhorsen-in-Waiting now," said Sam, admiration showing in his voice.

"I guess I am," replied Lirael slowly. She felt as if she'd claimed something when she'd announced herself as such in Death. And lost something, too. It was one thing to take up the bells at the House. It was another to actually use the bells in Death. Her old life seemed so far away now. Gone forever, and she did not yet know what her new life would be, or even what she was. She felt uncomfortable in her own skin, and it had nothing to do with the melting ice, or the rain and mud.

"I can smell something," announced the Dog.

Lirael looked up and for the first time noticed that Sam was much muddier than he had been, and was bleeding from a scratch across the back of his hand, though he didn't appear to have noticed it.

"What happened to you?" she asked sharply.

"Mogget came back," replied Sam. "At least I think it's Mogget. He's in my pack. Only at first he was a sort of really short albino man and I thought he was an enemy—"

He stopped talking as the Dog prowled over to his pack and sniffed at it. A white paw flashed out, and the Dog jerked back just in time to avoid a clawed nose. She settled back on her haunches, and her forehead furrowed in puzzlement.

"It is the Mogget," she confirmed. "But I don't understand—"

"She gave me what she chooses to call another chance," said a voice from inside the pack. "More than you've ever done."

"Another chance at what?" growled the Dog. "This is no time for your games! Do you know what is being dug up four leagues from here?"

Mogget thrust his head out of the pack. Ranna jangled, sending a wave of weariness across all who heard the bell.

"I know!" spat the little cat. "I didn't care then and I don't care now. It is the Destroyer! The Unmaker! The Unraveler—"

Mogget paused for breath. Just as he was about to speak again, the Dog suddenly barked, a short, sharp bark infused with power. Mogget yowled as if his tail had been trodden on and sank hissing back into the pack.

"Do not speak Its name," ordered the Dog. "Not in anger, not when we are so close."

Mogget was silent. Lirael, Sam, and the Dog looked at the pack.

"We have to get away from here." Lirael sighed, wiping the most recent raindrops off her forehead before they could get into her eyes. "But first I want to get something straight."

She approached Sam's pack and leaned over it, careful to stay out of striking distance of a paw.

"Mogget. You are still bound to be a servant of the Abhorsens, aren't you?"

"Yes," came the grudging reply. "Worse luck."

"So you will help me, help us, won't you?"

There was no answer.

"I'll find you some fish," interjected Sam. "I mean, when we're somewhere where there are fish."

"And a couple of mice," added Lirael. "If you like mice, that is."

Mice chewed books. All librarians disliked mice, and Lirael

was no exception. She was quite pleased to discover that becoming an Abhorsen had not removed that essential part of the librarian in her. She still hated silverfish as well.

"There is no point bargaining with the creature," said the Dog. "He will do as he is told."

"Fish when available, and mice, and a songbird," said Mogget, emerging from the pack, his little pink tongue tasting the air as if the fish were even now in front of him.

"No songbird," said Lirael firmly.

"Very well," agreed Mogget. He cast a disdainful glance at the Dog. "A civilized agreement, and in keeping with my current form. Food and lodging in return for what help I care to offer. Better than being a slave."

"You are a—" the Dog began hotly, but Lirael grabbed her collar and she subsided, growling.

"There's no time for bickering," said Lirael. "Hedge let Mareyn—the Guard—go, intending to enslave her spirit later—a slow death makes for a more powerful spirit. He knows roughly where she died, and he may have had other servants in Death who will report my presence. So we need to get going."

"We should . . ." Sam began as Lirael started to walk off. "We have to give her a proper ending."

Lirael shook her head, a diagonal motion that was neither agreement nor refusal, but simply weariness.

"I must be tired," she said, wiping her brow again. "I promised her I would."

Like the bodies of the merchant party, Mareyn's body, if left here, could become inhabited by another Dead spirit, or Hedge might be able to use it for even worse things.

"Can you do it, Sam?" Lirael asked, rubbing her wrist. "I'm a bit worn out, to be honest."

"Hedge may smell the magic," warned the Dog. "As may any

Dead creatures that are close enough. Though the rain will help."

"I've already cast a spell," said Sam apologetically. "I thought we were being attacked—"

"Don't worry," interrupted Lirael. "But hurry."

Sam went over to the body and drew the Charter marks in the air. A few seconds later, a white-hot shroud of fire enveloped the body, and soon there was nothing left for any necromancer save the blackened rings of mail.

Sam turned to go then, but Lirael stepped forward, and three simple Charter marks fell from her open hand into the bark of the tree above the ashes. She spoke to the marks, placing her words there for any Charter Mage to hear in the years ahead, for as long as the tree might stand.

"Mareyn died here, far from home and friends. She was a Royal Guard. A brave woman, who fought against a foe too strong for her. But even in Death she did her duty and more. She will be remembered. Farewell, Mareyn."

"A fitting gesture," said the Dog. "And a—"

"Fairly stupid one," interrupted Mogget, from behind Sam's head. "We'll have the Dead down on us in minutes if you keep doing all this magic."

"Thank you, Mogget," said Lirael. "I'm glad you're helping us already. We are leaving now, so you can go back to sleep. Dog—please scout ahead. Sam—follow me."

Without waiting for an answer, she struck off up towards the ridgeline, heading for a point where the trees clustered more thickly together. The Dog ran up behind her, then slipped around to get ahead, her tail wagging.

"Bossy, isn't she?" remarked Mogget to Sam, who was following more slowly. "Reminds me of your mother."

"Shut up," said Sam, pushing aside a branch that threatened to slap him in the face.

"You do know that we should be running as fast as we can in the other direction," said Mogget. "Don't you?"

"You told me before, back at the House, that's there's no point running away or trying to hide," snapped Sam. "Didn't you?"

Mogget didn't answer, but Sam knew he hadn't fallen asleep. He could feel the cat moving around in his pack. Sam didn't repeat his question, because the slope was becoming steeper and he needed all his breath. Any thoughts of conversation quickly slipped away as they climbed farther, weaving between the trees and over fallen logs, torn out of the hillside by the wind and their inability to set deep roots.

At last they reached the ridge, sodden despite their oilskins, and wretchedly tired from the climb. The sun, lost somewhere in cloud, was not far off setting, and it was clear they couldn't go much farther before nightfall.

Lirael thought of calling a rest, but when she gestured at the Dog, the hound ignored her, pretending she couldn't see the frantic hand signals. Lirael sighed and followed, thankful that the Dog had turned to the west and was following the ridge now, instead of climbing down. They kept on for another thirty minutes or so, though it felt like hours, till at last they came to a point where a landslide had carved out a great swathe of open ground down the northern face of the ridge.

The Dog stopped there, choosing a stand of ferns that would shelter them. Lirael sat down next to her, and Sam staggered in a minute later and collapsed like a broken concertina. As he sat, Mogget climbed out of his pack and stood on his hind legs, using Sam's head as a rest for his two front paws.

The four of them looked down through the clearing, out and along the valley, all the way to the Red Lake, a dull expanse of water in the distance, lit by flashes of lightning and what little of the setting sun made it through the cloud.

Nick's pit was clearly visible, too, an ugly wound of red dirt and yellow clay in the green of the valley. The land around it was constantly struck by lightning, the boom of the thunder rolling back to the four watchers, a constant background noise. Hundreds of figures, made tiny by the distance, toiled around the pit. Even from a few miles away, Lirael and Sam could feel that they were the Dead.

"What are the Hands doing?" whispered Lirael. Though they were hidden high on the ridge amongst the trees and ferns, she still felt that they were on the verge of detection by Hedge and his servants.

"I can't tell," replied Sam. "Moving something—that glittering thing—I think. Towards the lake."

"Yes," said the Dog, who was standing absolutely stiff next to Lirael. "They are dragging two silver hemispheres, three hundred paces apart."

Behind Sam's ear, Mogget hissed, and Sam felt a shudder run down his spine.

"Each hemisphere imprisons one half of an ancient spirit," said the Dog. Her voice was very low. "A spirit from the Beginning, from before the Charter was made."

"The one you said to Mogget not to name," whispered Lirael. "The Destroyer."

"Yes," said the Dog. "It was imprisoned long ago, and trapped within the silver hemispheres; and the hemispheres were buried deep beneath wards of silver, gold, and lead; rowan, ash, and oak; and the seventh ward was bone."

"So it's still bound?" whispered Sam urgently. "I mean, they might have dug up the hemispheres, but it's still bound inside them, isn't it?"

"For now," said the Dog. "But where the prison fails, little hope can be placed in the bonds. Someone must have found a way to join the hemispheres, though I cannot guess how, and where they are taking them. . . .

"I am sorry to have failed you, Mistress," she added, sinking down on her belly, her chin digging into the ground with misery.

"What?" asked Lirael, looking down at the dejected Dog. For a moment she couldn't think of anything to say. Then she felt a little voice inside her ask, "What would an Abhorsen do?" and she knew that she must be what she was supposed to be. Undaunted, even though she felt exactly the opposite.

"What are you talking about? It's not your fault."

Her voice trembled for a second, but she disguised it with a cough before continuing.

"Besides, the . . . the Destroyer is still bound. We'll just have to stop those hemispheres joining or whatever it is Hedge plans to do with them."

"We should rescue Nick," said Sam. He swallowed audibly, then added, "Though there's an awful lot of Dead down there."

"That's it!" exclaimed Lirael. "That's what we can do to start with, anyway. Nick will know exactly where they plan to take the hemispheres."

"She plans like your mother, too," said Mogget. "What are we supposed to do? Walk down there and ask Hedge to hand over the boy?"

"Mogget—" Sam started to say, and the Dog growled, but Lirael spoke over them. A plan of sorts had come to mind, and she wanted to get it out before it started to sound hopeless even to her.

"Don't be silly, Mogget. We'll rest for a while; then I'll put on the Charter-skin I made on the boat and fly down as an owl. The Dog can fly down, too, and between both of us, we'll find Nick and sneak him away. You and Sam can follow us down, and we'll rendezvous near running water—that stream over there. By then we'll have daylight and running water, and we can find out what's happening from Nick. What do you think?"

"That is only the fourth-most stupid plan I have ever heard from an Abhorsen," replied Mogget. "I like the part about sleeping for a while, though you neglected to mention dinner."

"I'm not sure you should be the one to fly down," said Sam uncomfortably. "I'm sure I could get the hang of the owl shape, and I might be better able to convince Nick to come with us. And how can the Dog fly?"

"There won't be any convincing required," growled the Dog. "Your friend Nick must be largely a creature of the Destroyer. He will have to be compelled—and we must be wary of him and any powers he may have been granted. As to flying, I just make myself smaller and grow some wings."

"Oh," said Sam. "Of course. Grow some wings."

"We'll have to watch out for Hedge, too," added Lirael, who was belatedly wondering if perhaps there wasn't a better plan after all. "But it will have to be me who uses the Charter-skin. I made it to my size—it wouldn't fit you. I hope it isn't too crumpled in my pack."

"It'll take me at least two hours to get down to that creek—since I can't fly," said Sam, looking down the ridge. "Perhaps we should all go on later tonight; then you can fly from there. That way I'll be closer and ready immediately if there's any trouble. And you could lend me your bow, so I can spell some arrows while I'm waiting."

"Good idea," said Lirael. "We should go on. But the bow won't be much use if it keeps raining—and I don't think we can risk any more weather magic to stop it. That will give us away for sure."

"It'll stop before dawn," said the Dog with great authority.

"Humph," replied Mogget. "Anyone could have told them that. It's stopping now, for that matter."

Sam and Lirael looked up through the canopy of the trees, and sure enough, though the storm to the northwest was constant, the clouds above and to the east were parting to show the fading red wash of the sun and the first star of the night. It was Uallus, the red star that showed the way north. Lirael was heartened to see it, though she knew it was only a shepherd's tale that said Uallus granted luck if it was the first star in the sky.

"Good," said Lirael. "I hate flying in the rain. Wet feathers are a pain."

Sam didn't answer. It was getting dark, but the lightning around the pit made it possible to make out some things down in the valley in a sort of stop-start way. There was a square-shaped blob that could easily be a tent. Presumably Nick's tent, for there were no others visible.

"Hang on, Nick," whispered Sam. "We'll save you."

FIRST INTERLUDE

TOUCHSTONE'S HAND CLASPED Sabriel's shoulder as they lay under the car. Neither of them could hear after the explosion, and they were dazed from the shock. Many of their guards were dead around them, and their eyes could not process the dreadful human wreckage that surrounded them. In any case, they were intent on their would-be assassins. They could see their feet approaching, and their laughter sounded muffled and distant, like noisy neighbors on the other side of a wall.

Touchstone and Sabriel crawled forward, their pistols in their hands. The two guards who had also made it under the car crawled forward, too. One was Veran, Sabriel saw, still clutching her pistol despite the blood that ran down her hands. The other survivor was the oldest of all the guards, Barlest, his grizzled hair stained and no longer white. He had a machine rifle and was readying it to fire.

The assassins saw the movement, but it was too late. The four survivors fired almost at the same time, and the laughter was drowned in an assault of sudden gunfire. Empty brass cartridges rattled on the underside of the car, and acrid smoke billowed out between the wheels.

"To the boat!" shouted Barlest to Sabriel, gesturing behind him. She couldn't hear him properly at first, till he had shouted it three times: "Boat! Boat! Boat!"

Touchstone heard it, too. He looked at Sabriel, and she saw the fear in his eyes. But it was fear for her, she knew, not for himself. She gestured back towards the lane that ran between the houses behind them. That would take them to Larnery Square and the Warden Steps. They had boats there, and more guards disguised as river traders. Damed had carefully prepared several escape routes, but this was the closest. As in everything, he had thought only of the safety of his King and Queen.

"Go!" shouted Barlest. He had changed the drum on his automatic rifle, and he began firing short bursts to the right and left, forcing any of their attackers who had made it back to cover to keep their heads down.

Touchstone gripped Barlest's shoulder for a brief, final moment, then wriggled around and moved across to the other side of the car. Sabriel crawled next to him, and they briefly touched hands. Veran, next to her, took a deep breath and hurled herself out, leaping to her feet and running the second she was clear of the car. She got to the lane, crouched behind a fire hydrant, and covered Sabriel and Touchstone as they followed. But for the moment there were no shots apart from the disciplined bursts from Barlest, still under the car.

"Come on!" roared Touchstone, turning at the entrance to the lane. But Barlest did not come, and Veran grabbed Touchstone and Sabriel and pushed them down the lane, shouting, "Go! Go!"

They heard Barlest shout a battle cry behind them, heard his footsteps as he charged out from under the car on the opposite side. There was one long shuddering burst of automatic fire and several louder, single shots. Then there was silence, save for the clattering of their own boots on the cobbles, the pant of their labored breaths, and the beating of their hearts.

Larnery Square was empty. The central garden, usually the

habitat of nannies and babies, was completely devoid of life. The explosion had probably happened only a few minutes ago, but that was enough. There had been plenty of trouble in Corvere since the rise of Corolini and his Our Country thugs, and the ordinary citizens had learned when to retreat quickly from the streets.

Touchstone, Sabriel, and Veran ran grimly through the square and clattered down the Warden Steps on the far side. A drunken bargeman saw them, three gun-wielding figures splattered in blood and worse, and was not so drunk that he got in the way. He cowered to one side, hunching himself into as small a ball as possible.

The Sethem River flowed dirtily past the short quay at the end of the steps. A man dressed in the oilskin thigh boots and assorted rags of a tide dredger stood there, his hands inside a barrel that he'd presumably just salvaged from the muddy river flats. As he heard the clatter on the stairs, his hands came out holding a sawed-off shotgun, the hammers cocked.

"Querel! A rescue!" shouted Veran.

The man carefully decocked the shotgun, pulled a whistle out from under his many-patched shirt and blew it several times. There was an answering whistle, and several more Royal Guards leapt up from a boat that was out of sight beneath the quay, the river being at low tide. All the guards were armed and expecting trouble, but from their expressions none expected what they saw.

"An ambush," exclaimed Touchstone quickly as they approached. "We must be away at once."

Before he could say any more, many hands grabbed him and Sabriel and practically threw them onto the deck of the waiting boat, Veran jumping on after them. The craft, a converted river tramp, was six or seven feet below the quay, but there were more hands to catch them. Even as they were hustled into the heavily sandbagged cabin, the engine was going from a slow idle to a heavy throb and the boat was shuddering into motion.

Sabriel and Touchstone looked at each other, reassuring themselves that they were still alive and relatively unhurt, though they were both bleeding from small shrapnel cuts.

"That is it," said Touchstone quietly, setting his pistol down on the deck. "I am done with Ancelstierre."

"Yes," said Sabriel. "Or it is done with us. We will not find any help here now."

Touchstone sighed and, taking up a cloth, wiped the blood from Sabriel's face. She did the same for him; then they stood and briefly embraced. Both were shaking, and they did not try to disguise it.

"We had best see to Veran's wounds," said Sabriel as they let go of each other. "And plot a course to take us home."

"Home!" confirmed Touchstone, but even that word wasn't said without both of them feeling an unspoken fear. Close as they had come to death today, they feared their children would face even greater dangers, and as both of them knew so well, there were far worse fates than simple death.

PART TWO

Chapter Nine

A DREAM OF OWLS AND FLYING DOGS

NICK WAS DREAMING the dream again, of the Lightning Farm, and the hemispheres coming together. Then the dream suddenly changed, and he seemed to be lying on a bed of furs in a tent. There was the slow beat of rain on the canvas above his head, and the sound of thunder, and the whole tent was lit by the constant flicker of lightning.

Nick sat up and saw an owl perched on his traveling chest, looking at him with huge, golden eyes. And there was a dog sitting next to his bed. A black and tan dog not much bigger than a terrier, with huge feathery wings growing out of its shoulders.

At least it's a different dream, part of him thought. He had to be almost awake, and this was one of those dream fragments that precede total wakefulness, where reality and fantasy mix. It was his tent, he knew, but an owl and a winged dog!

I wonder what that means, Nick thought, blinking his dream eyes.

Lirael and the Disreputable Dog watched him look at them, his eyes sleepy but still full of a fevered brightness. His hand clutched at his chest, fingers curled as if to scratch at his heart. He blinked twice, then shut his eyes and lay back on the furs.

"He really is sick," whispered Lirael. "He looks terrible. And there's something else about him . . . I can't tell properly in this shape. A wrongness."

"There is something of the Destroyer in him," growled the

Dog softly. "A sliver of one of the silver hemispheres, most like, infused with a fragment of its power. It is eating away at him, body and spirit. He is being used as the Destroyer's avatar. A mouthpiece. We must not awaken this force inside him."

"How do we get him out without doing that?" asked Lirael. "He doesn't even look strong enough to leave his bed, let alone walk."

"I can walk," protested Nick, opening his eyes and sitting up again. Since this was his dream, surely he could participate in the conversation between the winged dog and the talking owl. "Who is the Destroyer, and what's this about eating away at me? I just have a bad influenza or something.

"Makes me hallucinate," he added. "And have vivid dreams. A winged dog! Hah!"

"He thinks he's dreaming," said the Dog. "That's good. The Destroyer will not rise in him unless it feels threatened or there is Charter Magic close. Be careful not to touch him with your Charter-skin, Mistress!"

"Can't have an owl sit on my head," giggled Nick dreamily. "Or a dog, neither."

"I bet he can't get up and get dressed," Lirael said archly.

"I can so," replied Nick, immediately swiveling his legs across and sliding out of bed. "I can do anything in a dream. Anything at all."

Staggering a little, he took off his pajamas, unconscious of any need for modesty in front of his dream creatures, and stood there, stark naked. He looked very thin, Lirael thought, and was surprised to feel a pang of concern. You could see his ribs—and everything else for that matter. "See?" he said. "Up and dressed."

"You need some more clothes," suggested Lirael. "It might rain again."

"I've got an umbrella," declared Nick. Then his face

clouded. "No—it broke. I'll get my coat."

Humming to himself, he crossed to the chest and reached for the lid. Lirael, surprised, flew away just in time and went to perch on the vacated bed.

"The Owl and the Pussycat went . . ." sang Nick as he pulled out underwear, trousers, and a long coat and put them on, bypassing a shirt. "Except I've got it wrong in my dream . . . because you're not a pussycat. You're . . . a . . .

"A winged dog," he finished, reaching out to touch the Disreputable Dog on the nose. The solidity of that touch seemed to surprise him, and the fever flush deepened on his face.

"Am I dreaming?" he said suddenly, slapping himself in the face. "I'm not, am I? I'm . . . only . . . going . . . mad."

"You're not mad," soothed Lirael. "But you are sick. You have a fever."

"Yes, yes, I do," agreed Nick fretfully, feeling his sweaty forehead with the back of his hand. "Must go back to bed. Hedge said, before he went to get the other barge."

"No," Lirael commanded, her voice strangely loud from the owl's small beak. Hearing that Hedge was absent made her certain they must seize this opportunity. "You need fresh air. Dog— can you make him walk? Like you did the crossbowman?"

"Perhaps," growled the Dog. "I feel several forces at work within him, and even a fragment of the bound Destroyer is a power to be reckoned with. It will also alert the Dead."

"They're still dragging the hemispheres to the lake," said Lirael. "They'll take a while to get here. So I think you'd better do it."

"I'm going back to bed," declared Nick, holding his head in his hands. "And the sooner I get home to Ancelstierre, the better."

"You're not going back to bed," growled the Dog, advancing

upon him. "You're coming for a walk!"

With that word, she barked, a bark so deep and loud that the tent shook, poles quivering in resonance. Lirael felt the force of it strike her, ruffling her feathers. It sent sparks flying off her, too, as the Free Magic fought the Charter marks of her altered shape.

"Follow me!" ordered the Dog as she turned and left the tent. Nick took three steps after her but paused at the entrance, clutching at a canvas flap.

"No, no, I can't," he muttered, his muscles moving in weird spasms under the skin of his neck and hands. "Hedge told me to stay. It's best I stay."

The Dog barked again, louder, the noise carrying even above the constant thunder. A corona of sparks flared about Lirael, and the discarded pajamas under her claws suddenly caught fire, forcing her to fly out of the tent.

Nick shuddered and twisted as the force of the bark hit him. He fell to his knees and began to crawl out of the tent, groaning and calling out to Hedge. Lirael circled above him, looking to the west.

"Stand," commanded the Dog. "Walk. Follow me."

Nick stood, took several steps, then froze in place. His eyes rolled back, and tendrils of white smoke began to drift out of his open mouth.

"Mistress!" shouted the Dog. "The fragment wakes within him! You must resume your form and quell it with the bells!"

Lirael dropped like a stone, instantly calling up the Charter marks to unravel the owl skin she wore. But not before her huge golden owl eyes had cut through the lightning-laced night to where the Dead toiled to move the silver hemispheres. Hundreds of Dead Hands were already throwing down their ropes and turning towards the tent. A moment later they began to run, the massed sound of hundreds of dried-out joints clicking in a ghastly undercurrent to the thunder. The Hands at the front fought one another to get past, as they were drawn by the lure of magic and the promise of a rich life for the taking. Life to assuage their eternal hunger.

The Dog barked again as the smoke rose from Nick's nose, but it seemed to have little effect. Lirael could only watch the white smoke coil, as she was momentarily caught within a shining tornado of light, while the Charter-skin spun back into its component marks.

Then she was there in her own form, hands reaching for Saraneth and Nehima. But something else was there, too, some presence that burned inside Nick, filling him with an internal glow that set the raindrops sizzling as they touched his skin. The hot-metal stench of Free Magic rolled off him in a wave as a voice that was not Nicholas's came out of his mouth, accompanied by puffs of white smoke.

"How dare— Ah . . . I should have expected you, meddler, and one of your sister's get—"

"Quick, Lirael," shouted the Dog. "Ranna and Saraneth together, with my bark!"

"To me, my servants!" shouted the voice from Nick, a voice far louder and more horrible than could come from any human throat. It carried even over the thunder, rolling out across the valley. All the Dead heard, even those who still labored stupidly on the ropes, and they all hurried, a tide of rotten flesh that flowed around both sides of the pit, rushing towards the beacon of the burning tent, where their ultimate Master called.

Others heard it, too, though they were farther away than any sound could carry. Hedge cursed and turned aside to slay an unlucky horse, so that he could make a mount that would not shy to carry him. Many leagues to the east, Chlorr turned away from the riverbank near Abhorsen's House and began to run, a great shape of fire and darkness that moved faster than any human legs could take her.

Lirael dropped her sword and drew Ranna, so hastily the bell tinkled briefly and a wave of tiredness washed across her. Her wrist still hurt from her encounter in Death, but neither pain nor Ranna's protest were enough to stop her. The relevant pages from *The Book of the Dead* shone in her mind, showing her what to do. So she did it, joining Ranna's gentle sound with Saraneth's deep strength, and with them the imperative sharp bark of the Dog.

The sound wrapped around Nick, and the voice that spoke from him was dampened. But a raging will fought against the spell, a will that Lirael could feel pushing against her, fighting against the combined powers of bell and bark. Then suddenly that resistance snapped, and Nick fell to the ground, the white smoke retreating rapidly back into his nose and throat.

"Hurry! Hurry! Get him up!" urged the Dog. "Cut south and head for the rendezvous. I'll hold them off here!"

"But—Ranna and Saraneth—he'll be asleep," protested Lirael as she put the bells away and hauled Nick upright. He was much lighter than she expected, even lighter than he looked. Obviously he was worn to the bone.

"No, only the shard within him sleeps," said the Dog rapidly. She had absorbed her wings and was growing to her combat size. "Slap him—and run!"

Lirael obeyed, though she felt cruel. The slap stung her palm, but it certainly woke Nick up. He yelped, looked around wildly, and struggled against Lirael's grip on his arm.

"Run!" she commanded, dragging him along, with a momentary pause to pick up Nehima. "Run—or I'll stick you with this."

Nick looked at her, the burning tent, the Dog, and the

onrushing horde of what he thought of as diseased workers, his face blank with shock and amazement. Then he started running, obeying Lirael's push on his arm to make him head south.

Behind them, the Dog stood in the light of the fire, a grim shadow now easily five feet tall at the shoulder. The Charter marks that ran in her collar glowed eerily with their own colors, stronger than the red and yellow blaze of the burning tent. Free Magic pulsed under the collar, and red flames dripped like saliva from her mouth.

The first mass of Dead Hands saw her and slowed, uncertain of what she was and how dangerous she might be.

Then the Disreputable Dog barked, and the Dead Hands shrieked and howled as a power they knew and feared gripped them, a Free Magic assault that made them shuck their putrescent bodies . . . and forced them to walk back into Death.

But for every one that fell, there were another dozen charging forward, their grasping, skeletal hands ready to grip and tear, their broken, grave-bleached teeth anxious to bite into any flesh, magical or not.

Chapter Ten

PRINCE SAMETH AND HEDGE

LIRAEL WAS HALFWAY back to the rendezvous with Sam
when Nick fell and could not get up. His face was
blotched with fever and exertion, and he could not get
his breath. He lay on the ground looking up at her dumbly, as if
waiting for execution.

Which was probably what it looked like, she realized, since
she was standing above him with a naked sword held high.
Lirael sheathed Nehima and stopped frowning, but she saw
that he was too ill and tired to understand that she was trying to
reassure him.

"Looks like I'm going to have to carry you," she said, her
voice mixed with equal parts of exhaustion and desperation. He
wasn't at all heavy, but it was at least half a mile to the stream.
And she didn't know how long the shard of the Destroyer or
whatever it was in him would stay subdued.

"Why . . . why are you doing this?" croaked Nick as she levered him across her shoulders. "The experiment will go on
without me, you know."

Lirael had been taught how to do a fireman's carry back in
the Great Library of the Clayr, though she hadn't practiced it in
several years. Not since Kemmeru's illicit still had caught fire
when Lirael was doing her turn on the librarians' fire brigade.
She was pleased she hadn't forgotten the technique, and that
Nick was a lot lighter than Kemmeru. Not that it was a fair

comparison, as Kemmeru had insisted on being carried out with her favorite books.

"Your friend Sam can explain," puffed Lirael. She could still hear the Dog barking somewhere behind her, which was good, but it was hard to see where she was going, since there was only the soft predawn light, not even strong enough to cast a shadow. It had been much easier crossing this stretch of valley as an owl.

"Sam?" asked Nick. "What's Sam got to do with this?"

"He'll explain," Lirael said shortly, saving her breath. She looked up, trying to fix her position by Uallus again. But they were still too close to the pit, and all she could see was thunderclouds and lightning. At least it had stopped raining, and the more natural clouds were slowly blowing away.

Lirael kept on going, but with a growing suspicion that she'd somehow veered off the track and was no longer heading in the right direction. She should have paid more attention when she was flying, Lirael thought, when everything had been laid out below her in a beautiful patchwork.

"Hedge will rescue me," Nick whispered weakly, his voice hoarse and strange, particularly since it was coming from somewhere near her belt buckle, as he was draped over her back.

Lirael ignored him. She couldn't hear the Dog anymore, and the ground was getting boggy under her feet, which couldn't be right. But there was a dim mass of something ahead. Bushes perhaps. Maybe the ones that lined the stream where Sam was waiting.

Lirael pressed forward, Nick's extra weight pushing her feet deep into the soggy ground. She could see what lay ahead, now she was close enough and more light trickled in from the rising sun. It was reeds, not bushes. Tall rushes with red flowering heads, the rushes that gave the Red Lake its name, from their pollen that colored the lakeshores with a brilliant scarlet wash.

She'd gone completely the wrong way, Lirael realized. Somehow she must have turned west. Now she was on the shore of the lake, and the Gore Crows would soon find her. Unless, she thought, they couldn't see her. She shifted Nick higher and bent over a little more to balance the load. He groaned in pain, but Lirael ignored him and pressed on into the reeds.

Soon the mud gave way to water, up to her shins. The reeds grew closer together, their flowery heads towering over her. But there was a narrow path where the reeds were beaten down, allowing passage through them. She took the path, winding deeper and deeper into the reedy marsh.

Sam drew another mark out of the endless flow of the Charter and forced it into the arrow he was holding across his knees, watching it spread like oil over the sharp steel of the head. It was the final mark for this arrow. He had already put marks of accuracy and strength into the shaft, marks for flight and luck into the fletching, and marks for unraveling and banishment into the head.

It was the last arrow of twenty, all now spelled to be weapons of great use against the Lesser Dead, at the least. It had taken Sam two hours to do all twenty, and he was a little weary. He was unaware that it would have taken most Charter Mages the better part of a day. Working magic on inanimate objects had always come easily to Sam.

He was doing his work while sitting on the dry end of a half-submerged log that stuck out of the stream. It was a good stream from Sam's point of view, because it was at least fifteen yards wide, very deep, and fast. It could be crossed via the log and jumping across a couple of big stones, but Sam didn't think the Dead would do that.

Sam put the finished arrow back into the quiver built into

Lirael's pack and slung that on his back. His own pack was pushed up against the stream bank, with Mogget asleep in the top of it. Though not anymore, Sam noticed, as he bent down to see it more clearly in the predawn light. The patch on the flap had gone completely, and there was no sign of the cat in the top pocket.

Sam looked around carefully, but he couldn't see anything moving, and the light wasn't good enough to see anything stand-ing still or hiding. He couldn't hear anything suspicious either— just the burble of the stream and the distant thunder from the lightning storm around the pit.

Mogget had never slipped off like this before, and Sam trusted the little white cat thing even less than he had before their experience in the strange tunnels under the House. Slowly he took Lirael's bow from its cover and nocked an arrow. His sword was at his side, but with the dawn, it was just light enough to shoot a little way with accuracy. At least across the stream, which Sam had no intention of crossing.

Something moved on the other side. A small, white shape, slinking near the water. It was probably Mogget, Sam thought, peering into the gloom. Probably.

It came closer, and his fingers twitched on the string.

"Mogget?" he whispered, nerves strung as taut as the bow.

"Of course it is, stupid!" said the white shape, leaping nimbly from rock to rock and then to the log. "Save your arrows—you'll need them. There's about two hundred Dead Hands headed this way!"

"What!" exclaimed Sam. "What about Lirael and Nick? Are they all right?"

"No idea," said Mogget calmly. "I went to see what was hap-pening when our canine companion started to bark. She's head-ing this way—hotly pursued—but I couldn't see Lirael or your troublesome friend. Ah—I think that's the Disgusting Dog now."

Mogget's words were followed by an enormous splash as the Dog suddenly appeared on the opposite bank and dived into the stream, sending a cascade of water in all directions, but mostly over Mogget.

Then the Dog was next to them, shaking herself so vigorously that Sam had to hold his bow out of the way.

"Quick," she panted. "We need to get out of here! Stay on this side and head downstream!"

As soon as she'd spoken, the Dog was off again, loping easily along beside the stream. Sam leapt off the log, swooped upon his pack, picked it up, and stumbled after the Dog, questions falling out of his mouth as he ran. With Lirael's pack on his back, the bow and an arrow in one hand, and his own pack in the other hand, it took most of his concentration not to fall over and into the stream.

"Lirael . . . and Nick? What . . . can't we stop . . . got to rearrange all this . . ."

"Lirael went into the reeds, but the necromancer suddenly showed up so I couldn't follow without leading him to her," said the Dog, turning her head back as she ran. "*That's* why we can't wait!"

Sam looked back, too, and immediately fell over his pack and dropped both bow and arrow. As he stumbled to his feet, he saw a wall of Dead Hands lurch to a stop on the other side of the stream, back up near the sunken log. There were hundreds of them, a great dark mass of writhing figures that immediately started to parallel the dog's course on the opposite bank.

In the midst of the Dead Hands, one figure stood out. A man cloaked in red flame, riding a horse that was mostly skeleton, though some flesh still hung on its neck and withers.

Hedge. Sam felt his presence like a shock of cold water, and a sharp pain in his wrists. Hedge was shouting something—per-

haps a spell—but Sam didn't hear it because he was scrabbling to
pick up the bow and get another arrow. It was still quite dark,
and a fair distance, he thought, but not too far for a lucky shot,
in the stillness before the dawn.

As quick as that thought, he nocked an arrow and drew. For
an instant, his whole concentration was on a line between himself and that shape of fire and darkness.

Then he loosed, and the spelled arrow flew like a blue spark
from him. Sam watched it, filled with hope as it sped as true as
he could wish, and arrow met necromancer with a blaze of
white fire against the red. Hedge fell from his skeleton horse,
which reared and then dived forward, smashing through several
ranks of Dead Hands to plunge into the water in an explosion
of white sparks and high-pitched screaming. Instinctively, it had
known how to free itself and die the final death.

"That'll annoy him," said Mogget from somewhere near
Sam's feet.

Sam's sudden hope died as he saw Hedge stand up, pluck the
arrow from his throat, and throw it on the ground.

"Don't waste another on him," said the Dog. "He cannot be
slain by any arrow, no matter the spells laid upon it."

Sam nodded grimly, threw the bow aside, and drew his
sword. Though the stream might hold the Dead Hands back, he
knew that it would not stop Hedge.

Hedge drew his own sword and walked forward, his Dead
Hands parting to make a corridor. At the edge of the stream the
necromancer smiled an open smile, and red fire licked about his
teeth. He put one boot in the stream—and smiled again as the
water burst into steam.

"Go and help Lirael," Sam ordered the Dog. "I'll hold off
Hedge as long as I can. Mogget—will you help me?"

Mogget didn't answer, and he was nowhere to be seen.

"Good luck," said the Dog. Then she was gone, racing along the bank to the west.

Sam took a deep breath and crouched into a defensive stance. This was his worst fear, come into terrible reality. Alone again, and facing Hedge.

Sam reached into the Charter, as much for comfort as to be ready to cast a spell. His breathing steadied as he felt its familiar flow all around him, and almost without thinking he began to draw out Charter marks, whispering their names quietly as they fell into his open hand.

Hedge took another step. He was wreathed in steam now and almost completely obscured, the stream bubbling and roiling both upstream and down. With a shrinking feeling, Sam saw that the necromancer was actually boiling the stream dry. There was already significantly less water below him, the streambed was becoming visible, and the Dead Hands were starting to move.

Hedge wouldn't even have to fight him, Sam thought. All he had to do was stand in the stream, and his Dead Hands would cross and finish Sam off. Though he had the panpipes, Sam didn't know how to use them properly, and there were simply too many Hands.

There was only one thing he could do. Sam would have to attack Hedge in the stream and kill him before the Hands could cross. If he could kill Hedge, a little nagging voice said from deep inside his mind. Wouldn't it be better to run away? Run away before you are burnt again, and your spirit ripped out of your flesh and taken by the necromancer. . . .

Sam buried that thought away, sending the nagging voice so far into the recesses of his mind that it was just a meaningless squeak. Then he let the Charter marks he already held in his hand fall into nothingness, reached into the Charter again, and drew out a whole new string of marks. As he summoned them,

Sam hurriedly traced the marks on his legs with a finger. Marks of protection, of reflection, of diversion. They joined and shimmered there, wrapping his legs in Charter Magic armor that would resist the steam and boiling water.

He looked down for only ten, or perhaps fifteen seconds. But when he looked back up, Hedge was gone. The steam was dissipating, and the water was flowing again. The Dead Hands were turning their backs to him and lumbering away, leaving the ground churned up and littered with pieces of rotting flesh and splintered bone.

"Either you were born to a different death, Prince," remarked Mogget, who had appeared at Sam's feet like a newly sprung plant, "or Hedge just found something more important to do."

"Where were you?" asked Sam. He felt strangely deflated. He'd been all ready to plunge into the stream, to fight it out, and now all of a sudden it was just a quiet morning again. The sun was even up, and the birds had resumed their singing. Though only on his side of the stream, Sam noticed.

"Hiding, like any sensible person would when confronted by a necromancer as powerful as Hedge," replied Mogget.

"Is he that powerful?" asked Sam. "You must have encountered many necromancers, serving my mother and the other Abhorsens."

"They didn't have help from the Destroyer," said Mogget. "I must say I'm impressed with what it can do, even bound as it is. A lesson for us all, that even trapped inside a lump of silver metal—"

"Where do you think Hedge went?" interrupted Sam, who wasn't really listening.

"Back to those lumps of metal, of course," yawned Mogget. "Or after Lirael. Time for me to have a nap, I think."

Mogget yawned again, then yelped in surprise as Sam grabbed him and shook him, setting Ranna jangling on his collar.

"You have to track the Dog! We have to go and help Lirael!"

"That's no way to ask me." Mogget yawned again, as waves of sleep from Ranna washed over both of them. Sam suddenly found that he was sitting down, and the ground felt so comfortable. All he had to do was lie back and put his hands behind his head. . . .

"No! No!" he protested. Staggering to his feet, he plunged into the stream and pushed his face into the water.

When he climbed out, Mogget was back in his pack. Fast asleep, a wicked grin on his little face.

Sam stared down at him and ran his hands through his dripping hair. The Dog had run off downstream. What had she said? "Lirael went into the reeds."

So if Sam followed the stream to the Red Lake, there was a good chance he'd find Lirael. Or some sign of her, or the Dog. Or Mogget might wake up.

Or Hedge might come back. . . .

Sam didn't want to just sit where he was. Lirael might need his help. Nicholas might need his help. He had to find them. Together, they might survive long enough to do something about this Destroyer trapped in the silver hemispheres. Alone, they could only fail and fall.

Sam packed away Lirael's bow and the dropped arrow. Then he balanced the two packs using a single strap on each shoulder, made sure Mogget would not fall out even though the cat deserved to, and started west, the stream burbling along beside him.

Chapter Eleven

HIDDEN IN THE REEDS

LIRAEL MORE THAN half-expected to find a boat made of woven reeds, since the Clayr had Seen her and Nicholas in it on the Red Lake. Even so, she was very much relieved when she did stumble across the strange craft, because the water was now well above her thighs. If it had got any deeper, she would have had to turn back or risk Nick's drowning, since she couldn't carry him any other way than the fireman's lift, which put his head about two feet lower than hers.

Carefully, she unloaded him into the center of the canoe-like boat, quickly grabbing the sides as it tipped. The boat was about twice as long as she was tall, but very narrow apart from its midsection—so there would be only just enough room for both of them.

Nick was semiconscious, but he rallied as they sat quietly in the boat, and Lirael considered her options. The reeds leaned over them, creating a secret bower, and small waterbirds called plaintively nearby, with the occasional splash as one dived after some fishy treat.

Lirael sat with her sword across her lap and a hand on the bell-bandolier, listening. The marsh birds would be happily piping and fishing, then they would suddenly go silent and hide deeper in the reeds. Lirael knew it was because Gore Crows were flying low overhead. She could feel the cold spirit that inhabited them, single-mindedly following the orders of its necromancer master. Searching for her.

The boat was exactly as the Clayr had said it would be, but Lirael felt a strange new fear as she sat rocking in it. This was the limit of the Clayr's vision. They had Seen her here with Nicholas, but no further, and they had not Seen what Nicholas was. Was their Sight limited because this was the end? Was Hedge about to appear through the reeds? Or would the Destroyer emerge from within the slight young man opposite her?

"What are you waiting for?" Nick asked suddenly, showing himself to be more recovered than she'd thought. Lirael jumped as he spoke, setting the boat rocking more violently. Nick's voice was loud, strange in the quiet world of the reeds.

"Silence!" ordered Lirael in a stern whisper.

"Or what?" asked Nick with some bravado. But he spoke more softly, and his eyes were on her sword.

A few seconds passed, then Lirael said, "We're waiting for noon, when the sun is brightest and the Dead are weak. Then we'll head along the lakeshore and, hopefully, make it to a meeting place where your friend Sameth will be."

"The Dead," said Nick with a superior smile. "Some local spirits to appease, I take it? And you mentioned Sam before. What's he got to do with this? Did you kidnap him, too?"

"The Dead . . . are the Dead," replied Lirael, frowning. Sam had mentioned that Nick didn't understand, or even try to comprehend, the Old Kingdom, but this blindness to reality could not be natural. "You have them working in your pit. Hedge's Dead Hands. And no, Sam is working with me to rescue you. You obviously don't understand the danger."

"Don't tell me Sam has fallen back into all this superstition," said Nick. "The Dead, as you call them, are simply poor unfortunates who suffer from something like leprosy. And far from rescuing me, you have taken me away from an important scientific experiment."

"You saw me as an owl," said Lirael, curious to find exactly how blinkered he was. "With the winged dog."

"Hypnosis . . . or hallucinations," replied Nick. "As you can see, I'm not well. Which is another reason I shouldn't be in this . . . this compost heap of a craft."

"Curious," said Lirael thoughtfully. "It must be the thing inside you that has closed your mind. I wonder what purpose that serves."

Nick didn't reply, but he rolled his eyes eloquently enough, obviously dismissing whatever Lirael had to say.

"Hedge will rescue me, you know," he said. "He's a very resourceful chap, and he's just as keen to stay on schedule as I am. So whatever mad belief has seized you, you should give it up and go home. In fact, I'm sure there would be some sort of reward if you returned me."

"A reward?" Lirael laughed, but with bitterness. "A horrible death and eternal servitude? That's the 'reward' for anyone living who goes near Hedge. But tell me—what is your 'experiment' all about?"

"Will you let me go if I tell you?" asked Nick. "Not that it's terribly secret. After all, you won't be publishing in Ancelstierran scientific journals, will you?"

Lirael didn't answer either question. She just looked at him, waiting for him to talk. He met her gaze at first, then faltered and looked away. There was something unnerving about her eyes. A toughness he had never seen in the young women he knew from the debutante parties in Corvere. It was partly this that made him talk, and partly a desire to impress her with his knowledge and intelligence.

"The hemispheres are a previously unknown metal that I postulate has an almost infinite capacity to absorb electrical energy for later discharge," he said, arching his fingers together. "They also create some sort of ionized field that attracts the thunderstorms, which in turn create lightning that is drawn down by the metal. Unfortunately, that ionized field also prevents working of the metal, as steel or iron tools cannot be brought close.

"It is my intention to connect the hemispheres to a Lightning Farm, which a trusted associate of mine is building in Ancelstierre even as we speak. The Lightning Farm will be composed of a thousand connected lightning rods that will draw down the full electrical force of an entire storm—rather than just a number of strikes—and feed it into the hemispheres. This power will . . . ah . . . repolarize . . . or demagnetize . . . the two hemispheres so they can be brought together as one. This is the ultimate goal. They must be brought together, you see. It is absolutely essential!"

He collapsed back with the last word, his breath coming in ragged gasps.

"How do you know?" asked Lirael. To her it sounded like the sort of waffle used by false seers and charlatan mages, as much to convince themselves as anything.

"I just know," whispered Nick. "I am a scientist. When the hemispheres are in Ancelstierre, I will be able to prove my theories, with proper instruments and proper help."

"Why do the hemispheres have to be brought together?" asked Lirael. That seemed to be the weakest point of his belief, and the most dangerous, for bringing the hemispheres together would make whatever was trapped inside them whole. It was only as she asked it that she realized there was a more important question.

"They have to be," replied Nick, puzzlement showing clearly on his face. Obviously he couldn't think clearly about it at all. "That should be obvious."

"Yes, of course," said Lirael, soothingly. "But I'm curious about how you will get the hemispheres to Ancelstierre. And where exactly is your Lightning Farm? It must be hard to set something like that up. I mean, it would take an awful lot of space."

"Oh, it's not as difficult as you might think," said Nick. He seemed relieved to be moving away from the subject of bringing the hemispheres together. "We'll take the metal down to the sea in barges, and then follow the coast south. Apparently the waters are too disturbed and the weather too foggy as a rule to go all the way by sea. We'll take them ashore just north of the Wall, drag them over that, and then it's only a matter of ten or twelve miles to Forwin Mill, where my Lightning Farm is being built. It should be just about completed by the time we arrive, all being well."

"But . . ." Lirael said, "how will you get them over the Wall? It is a barrier to the Dead and all such things. You won't be able to get the hemispheres across the Wall."

"Rubbish!" exclaimed Nick. "You're as bad as Hedge. Except that he at least is prepared to try, provided I let him do some mumbo jumbo first."

"Oh," said Lirael. Obviously Hedge—or more likely his ultimate Master—had found a way to get the hemispheres across the Wall. It had been a vain hope anyway, because Lirael knew Hedge had crossed more than once, and Kerrigor and his army had crossed years ago. She'd just hoped the hemispheres would be prevented.

"Won't . . . ah . . . won't you have difficulties with the authorities in Ancelstierre?" Lirael asked hopefully. Sam had told her about the Perimeter the Ancelstierrans had built to stop anything from entering their country from the north. She had no idea what she could do if the hemispheres were taken out of the Old Kingdom.

"No," said Nick. "Hedge says there won't be any trouble he can't handle, but I think he was a bit of a smuggler in the past, and he does have rather unconventional ways. I prefer to work within the law, so I got all the usual customs permits and approvals and so on. Though I admit that they're not for things from the Old Kingdom, because officially there is no Old Kingdom, so there are no forms. I also have a letter from my uncle, granting approval for me to bring across whatever I need for my experiment."

"Your uncle?"

"He's the Chief Minister," Nick replied proudly. "Seventeen years as CM this year—with a three-year break in the middle when the Moderate Reform lot got it. The most successful CM the country has ever had, though of course he's having trouble now, with the continental wars and all the Southerling refugees pouring in. Still, I don't think Corolini and his ragtag bunch will get the numbers to unseat him. He's my mother's oldest brother, and a damn good chap. Always happy to help a deserving nephew."

"Those papers would have burned in your tent," suggested Lirael, clutching at another hope.

"No," said Nick. "Thanks to Hedge again. He suggested I leave them with the fellow who's meeting us over the Wall. Said they'd rot, which in hindsight is absolutely true. Now—are you going to let me go?"

"No," said Lirael. "You're being rescued, whether you like it or not."

"In that case I shan't tell you any more," Nick proclaimed petulantly. He laid himself back down again, rustling against the rushes.

Lirael watched him, thoughts churning in her head. She

hoped Ellimere had received Sam's message, and at this moment there might be a strong force of Guards riding to the rescue. Sabriel and Touchstone might also be rushing north from Corvere. They could even be about to cross the Wall.

But all of them would be heading for Edge, while the hemispheres that held the bound thing slipped away—into Ancelstierre, where the ancient spirit of destruction could gain its freedom, free from interference by the only people who understood the danger.

Nick was watching her, too, she realized, as those thoughts clamored in her mind. But not with puzzlement or enmity. He was just looking, tilting his head on the side, with one eye partly closed.

"Pardon me," he said. "I was wondering how you knew Sam. Are you a . . . um . . . a princess? Only, if you're his fiancée or something, I thought I should know. To . . . ah . . . offer my congratulations, as it were. And I don't even know your name."

"Lirael," Lirael replied shortly. "I'm Sam's aunt. I'm the Ab— Well, let's say I sort of work with Sam's mother, and I also . . . was . . . a Second Assistant Librarian and a Daughter of the Clayr, though I don't expect you know what those titles mean. I'm not at all sure myself at the moment."

"His aunt!" exclaimed Nick, a flush of embarrassment rather than fever coloring his face. "How can you be—I mean, I had no idea. I apologize, ma'am."

"And I'm . . . I'm much older than I look," Lirael added. "In case you were going to ask."

She was a little embarrassed herself, though she couldn't think why. She still didn't know how to talk about her mother. In some ways it was more painful thinking about her now that she knew about her father and how she had come to be conceived. One day, she thought, she would find out exactly what had happened to

Arielle, and why she had chosen to go away.

"Wouldn't dream of it," replied Nick. "You know, this sounds stupid, but I feel much better here than I have for weeks. Never would have thought a swamp could be a tonic. I haven't even fainted today."

"You did once," said Lirael. "When we first took you from the tent."

"Did I?" asked Nick. "How embarrassing. I seem to be fainting a lot. Fortunately it tends to be when Hedge is there to catch me."

"Can you tell when you're about to faint?" asked Lirael. She hadn't forgotten the Dog's warning about how long the fragment would be subdued, and she was fairly certain she could not quell it again by herself.

"Usually," said Nick. "I get nauseous first and my eyesight goes peculiar—everything goes red. And something happens to my sense of smell, so I get the sensation of something burning, like an electric motor fusing. But I do feel much better now. Perhaps the fever's broken."

"It isn't a fever," Lirael said wearily. "Though I hope it is better, for both our sakes. Sit still now—I'm going to paddle us out a bit farther. We'll stay in the reeds, but I want to see what's happening on the lake. And please keep quiet."

"Sure," said Nick. "I don't really have a choice, do I?"

Lirael almost apologized, but she held it back. She did feel sorry for Nick. It wasn't his fault he had been chosen by an ancient spirit of evil to be its avatar. She even felt sort of maternal to him. He needed to be tucked in bed and fed willow-bark tea. That thought led to the idle speculation of what he might look like if he were well. He could be quite handsome, Lirael thought, and then instantly banished the notion. He might be an unwitting enemy, but he was still an enemy.

The reed boat was light, but even so it was hard work paddling with just her hands. Particularly since she also had to keep an eye on Nicholas in case of trouble. But he seemed content to lie back on the high prow of the reed boat. Lirael did catch him looking at her surreptitiously, but he didn't try to escape or call out.

After about twenty minutes of difficult paddling, the reeds began to thin out, the red water paled into pink, and Lirael could see the muddy lake bottom. The sun was well and truly up, so Lirael chanced pushing the boat to the very fringe of the reed marsh so she could look out on the lake but keep hidden.

They were still covered overhead because of the way the reeds leaned into one another. Even so, Lirael was relieved to discover that she couldn't sense any Gore Crows about. Probably because there was a strong current beyond the reedy shores, combined with the bright sun of morning.

Though there were no Gore Crows in sight, there was something moving out on the surface of the lake. For a second Lirael's heart lifted as she thought it might be Sam, or a force of Guards. Then she realized what it was, just as Nick spoke.

"Look—my barges!" he called, sitting up and waving. "Hedge must have got the other one—and loaded already!"

"Quiet!" hissed Lirael, reaching out to drag him down.

He offered no resistance but suddenly frowned and clutched his chest. "I think . . . I think I was counting my chickens before—"

"Fight it!" interrupted Lirael urgently. "Nick—you have to fight it!"

"I'll try—" Nick began, but he didn't finish his sentence, his head falling back with a dull, reedy thud. His eyes showed white, and Lirael saw a thin tendril of smoke begin to trickle from his nose and mouth.

She slapped him hard across the face.

"Fight it! You're Nicholas Sayre! Tell me who you are!"

Nick's eyes rolled back, though smoke still trickled from his nose.

"I'm . . . I'm Nicholas John Andrew Sayre," he whispered. "I'm Nicholas . . . Nicholas . . ."

"Yes!" urged Lirael. She put her sword down by her side and took his hands, shuddering as she felt the Free Magic coursing in the blood under his cold skin. "Tell me more about yourself, Nicholas John Andrew Sayre! Where were you born?"

"I was born at Amberne, my family home," whispered Nick. His voice grew stronger and the smoke receded. "In the billiard room. No, that's a joke. Mother would kill me for that. I was born all proper for a Sayre, doctor and midwives in attendance. Two midwives, no less, and the society doctor . . ."

Nick closed his eyes, and Lirael gripped his hands tighter.

"Tell me . . . anything!" she demanded.

"The specific gravity of orbilite suspended in quicksilver is . . . I don't know what it is. . . . The snow in Korrovia is confined to the southern Alps, and the major passes are Kriskadt, Jorstschi, and Korbuk. . . . The average blue-tailed plover lays twenty-six eggs in the course of its fifty-four-year lifespan. . . . More than a hundred thousand Southerlings landed illegally in the last year. . . . The chocolate tree is an invention of—"

He stopped suddenly, took a deep breath, and opened his eyes. Lirael kept holding his hands for a moment, but when she saw no sign of smoke or strangeness in his gaze, she dropped them and took up her sword again, resting the blade across her thighs.

"I'm in trouble, aren't I?" said Nick. His voice was unsteady. He looked down at the bottom of the boat, hiding his face, taking very controlled breaths.

"Yes," said Lirael. "But Sameth and I, and the . . . our friends . . . will do the best we can to save you."

"But you don't think you can," said Nicholas softly. "This . . . thing . . . inside me. What is it?"

"I don't know," replied Lirael. "But it is part of some great and ancient evil, and you are helping it to be free. To wreak destruction."

Nick nodded slowly. Then he looked up and met Lirael's gaze.

"It's been like a dream," he said simply. "Most of the time I don't really know whether I'm awake or not. I can't remember things from one minute to the next. I can't think of anything except the hemi—"

He stopped talking. Fear flashed in his eyes and he reached out for Lirael. She took his left hand but kept hold of her sword. If the thing inside him took over and wouldn't let her go, she knew she would have to cut her way free.

"It's okay, it's okay, it's okay," Nick repeated to himself, rocking backwards and forwards as he spoke. "I've got it under control. Tell me what I have to do."

"Keep fighting," Lirael instructed, but she didn't know what else to tell him. "If we can't keep you, then when the time comes, you must do whatever you can to stop . . . to stop it. Promise me you will!"

"I promise," groaned Nick through clenched teeth. "Word of a Sayre. I'll stop it! I will! Talk to me, please, Lirael. I have to think about something else. Tell me . . . tell me . . . where were you born?"

"In the Clayr's Glacier," said Lirael nervously. Nick's grip was tightening, and she didn't like it. "In the Birthing Rooms of the Infirmary. Though some Clayr have their babies in their own rooms, most of us . . . them . . . have their children in the Birthing Rooms because everyone's there and it's more communal and fun."

"Your parents," gasped Nick. He shuddered and started to

speak very quickly. "Tell me about them. Nothing to tell about mine. Father's a bad politician, though enthusiastic with it. His older brother is the success. Mother goes to parties and drinks too much. How is it you are Sameth's aunt? I don't understand how you could be Touchstone's or Sabriel's sister. I've met them. Much older than you. Ancient. Must be forty, if a day. . . . Speak to me, please, speak to me—"

"I'm Sabriel's sister," said Lirael, though the words felt strange on her tongue. "Sabriel's sister. But not by the same mother. Her . . . my father was . . . . um . . . with my mother only for a little while, before he died. I didn't even know who he was till quite recently. My mother . . . my mother went away when I was five. So I didn't know my father was the Abhorsen— Oh no!"

"Abhorsen!" cried Nick. His body convulsed, and Lirael felt his skin suddenly grow even colder. She hurriedly wrenched her hand free and backed as far away as she could, cursing herself for saying "Abhorsen" aloud when Nicholas was already on the edge of losing control. Of course it would set off the Free Magic inside him.

White smoke began to pour out of Nick's nose and mouth. White sparks flickered behind his tongue as he desperately tried to speak. He mouthed it, but only smoke came out, and it took a moment for Lirael to work out what it was he was trying to say.

"No!" Or perhaps "Go!"

Chapter Twelve

THE DESTROYER IN NICHOLAS

OR A MOMENT, Lirael was caught in indecision, unable to decide whether to simply jump overboard and flee, or to reach for her bells. Then she acted, drawing Ranna and Saraneth, a difficult operation while sitting with a sword across her thighs.

Nick still hadn't moved, but the white smoke was billowing out in slow, deliberate tendrils that reached this way and that, as if they had a life of their own. The nauseating stench of Free Magic came with them, biting at Lirael's nose, bile rising in her throat in response.

She didn't wait to see more but rang the bells together, focusing her will into a sharp command directed at the figure in front of her and the drifting smoke.

Sleep, Lirael thought, her whole body tense with the effort of concentrating the power of the two bells. She could feel Ranna's lullaby and Saraneth's compulsion, loud as they echoed across the water. Together they wreathed Nicholas with magic and sound, sending the Free Magic spirit inside him back into its parasitic sleep.

Or not, Lirael saw, as the white smoke only recoiled, and the bells began to glow with a strange red heat, their voices losing pitch and clarity. Then Nick sat up, his eyes still rolled back and unseeing, and the Destroyer spoke through his mouth.

Its words struck at Lirael with physical force, the marrow in her bones suddenly burning and her ears pierced with a sudden, sharp ache.

"Fool! Your powers are thin hand-me-downs to pit against me! I almost sorrow that Saraneth and Ranna live on only in you and your trinkets. Be still!"

The last two words were spoken with such force that Lirael screamed with sudden pain. But the scream became a choking gurgle as she ran out of air. The thing inside Nick—the fragment—had bound her so fast that even her lungs were frozen. Desperately she tried to breathe, but it was no use. Her entire body was paralyzed, inside and out, held by a force she could not even begin to combat.

"Farewell," said the Destroyer. Then it stood Nick's body up, carefully balancing as the reed boat swayed, and waved at the barges. At the same time, it shouted a name that echoed through the whole lake valley.

"Hedge!"

Panicking, Lirael tried to breathe again and again. But her chest remained frozen, and the bells lay lifeless in her still hands. Wildly, she ran through Charter marks in her head, trying to think of something that might free her before she died of asphyxiation.

Nothing came to her, nothing at all, till she suddenly noticed she did have some sensation. In her thighs, where Nehima lay across her legs. She could only just see it there—being unable to move her eyes—but Charter marks were burning on the blade and flowing from there into her, fighting the Free Magic spell that held her in its deathly grip.

But the marks were only slowly defeating the spell. She would have do something herself, because at this rate, she would asphyxiate before her lungs were freed.

Desperate to do anything, she found she could twist her

calves from side to side, trying to rock the boat. It wasn't very stable, so perhaps if it went over and distracted the Free Magic spirit . . . it might break the spell.

She rocked again, and water slopped into the craft, soaking into the tightly corded reeds. Still Nick's body didn't turn, his legs unconsciously adapting to the swaying motion. The thing inside him was clearly intent on the approaching barges and the hemispheres that held its greater self.

Then Lirael blacked out, her body starving for air. She came to in an instant, more panicked adrenaline flooding through her veins, and rocked again as hard as she could.

The reed boat rolled—but it didn't go over. Lirael screamed inside and rocked for what she knew would be the last time, using every muscle that had been freed by her sword.

Water sloshed in like a tide, and for a brief moment, the boat seemed about to capsize. But the lakefolk had woven it too well, and it righted. Nick's body, surprised by the violence of the roll, didn't. He swayed one way, made a grab at the prow, swung back the other—and fell into the lake.

Instantly, Lirael took a breath. Her lungs stayed frozen for a moment, then inflated with a shudder she felt through her entire body. The spell had broken with Nick's fall. Sobbing and panting, she thrust the bells back into their pouches and grabbed her sword, the Charter marks in the hilt pulsing with warmth and encouragement.

All the time, she was looking for the Nick creature. At first there was no sign of anything moving in the water. Then she saw a great steaming and bubbling a few yards away, as if the lake were boiling. A hand—Nick's hand—reached up and gripped the side of the boat, tearing away a whole section of the woven reeds with impossible strength; his mouth cleared the water, and a high-pitched scream of anger sent every marsh bird within a mile into panicked flight.

It sent Lirael, too. Instinctively, she jumped straight off the other side of the boat as far as she could, smashing into the reeds and water and starting off at a wading run. The terrible scream came again, followed by a violent splashing. For a moment Lirael thought that Nick was right behind her; but instead there was a violent explosion of water and broken reeds: Nick had picked up the entire boat and thrown it at her. If she had been a little slower, it would have been the boat that struck her back, rather than spray and some harmless bits of reed.

Before he could do anything else, Lirael redoubled her efforts to get away. The water wasn't as deep as she expected—only up to her chest—but it slowed her down, so every second she thought the creature would catch her, or strike her with a spell. Desperately, she headed back towards shallower water, hacking at the reeds with Nehima to speed the way.

She didn't look back, because she couldn't face what she might see, and she didn't stop, not even when she was lost in the rushes with no idea where she was going, and her lungs and muscles ached and burned with the effort of moving.

Finally, she was forced to a halt when the cramp in her side became impossible to ignore, and her legs were unable to hold her up out of the water. Fortunately, it was only knee-deep now, so Lirael sat down, crushing reeds into a wet and muddy seat.

All her senses were attuned to pursuit, but there didn't seem to be anything behind her—at least nothing she could hear over the pounding of her heart echoing through every blood vessel in her entire body.

She rested there, in the muddy water, for what seemed like a long time. Finally, when she felt as if she could move without bursting into tears or vomiting, she got up and sloshed forward again.

As she waded, she thought about what she'd done—or

hadn't done. Over and over the scene played through her head. She should have been quicker with the bells, she thought, remembering her hesitation and clumsiness. Maybe she should have stabbed Nick—though that didn't seem right, since he had no idea what lurked within him, awaiting the chance to manifest itself. It probably wouldn't even have helped, since the fragment could probably inhabit a Dead Nick as easily as it did while he lived. Perhaps it could even have got inside her. . . .

The Clayr's vision of a world destroyed was also prominent in her mind. Had she missed her chance to stop the Destroyer? Were those few minutes with Nick in the reed boat some great cusp of destiny? A vital chance that she could have grasped but failed to?

She was still thinking about that when the water she was racing through turned to actual mostly solid mud, instead of muddy water. The reed clumps started to thin out, too, so clearly she was coming to the edge of the marsh. But as this particular marsh stretched in patches for a good twenty miles along the eastern shore of the Red Lake, Lirael still didn't really know where she was.

She took a guess at south from the position of the sun and the length of a tall reed's shadow, and started to head that way, keeping to the fringe of the marsh. It was harder going than dry ground, but safer if there were Dead about, forced out into the sun by Hedge.

Two hours later Lirael was wetter and more miserable than ever, thanks to an unexpectedly deep hole along the way. She was almost completely covered in a sticky and revolting mixture of red reed pollen and black mud. It stank, and she stank, and there seemed no end to the marsh, and no sign of her friends, either.

Doubts began to assail her even more strongly, and Lirael

began to fear for her companions, particularly the Disreputable
Dog. Perhaps she had been overcome by the sheer numbers of
the Dead, or had been overmastered by Hedge, in the same way
even the fragment in Nick had swatted her magic aside as if it
didn't exist.

Or perhaps they were wounded, or still fighting, she
thought, forcing herself to greater speed. Without her and the
bells, they would be much weaker against the Dead. Sam hadn't
even finished reading *The Book of the Dead*. He wasn't an
Abhorsen. What if there was a Mordicant pursuing them, or
some other creature that was strong enough to endure the sun
at noon?

Thinking about that made her leave the rushes and start
alternately running and walking along firmer ground. Run a
hundred paces, walk a hundred paces—all the while keeping an
eye out for Gore Crows, other Dead, or the human servants of
Hedge.

Once she saw—and felt—Dead nearby, but they were Dead
Hands fleeing in the distance, seeking some refuge from the
harsh sun that was eating into them, flesh and spirit, the sun that
would send them back into Death if they could not find a cave
or unoccupied grave.

Soon she felt like an animal that is both hunter and
hunted—like a fox or a wolf. All she could concentrate on was
getting to the stream as quickly as possible, to search along its
length to find either her friends or—as she feared—some evidence of what had happened to them. At the same time, she had
the unpleasant sensation that some enemy was about to appear
from behind every slight rise or shrunken tree, or dive down
from the sky.

At least it was much easier to see where she was going, Lirael
thought, as she noted the line of trees and bushes that marked the

stream. It was less than a half mile away, so she redoubled her running, doing two hundred paces at a stretch instead of one.

She was up to 173 running paces when something burst out of the line of trees, straight towards her.

Instinctively Lirael reached for her bow—which wasn't there. She changed that movement to a swing across her body to draw her sword and kept on running.

She was just about to scream and turn the run into a charge when she recognized the Disreputable Dog and let out a glad cry instead, a cry that was met by the Dog's happy yelp.

A few minutes later they met in a tangle of jumping, licking, and dancing around (on the Dog's part) and hugging, kissing, and keeping her sword out of the way (on Lirael's part).

"It's you, it's you, it's you!" woofed the Dog, wiggling her hindquarters and squeaking.

Lirael didn't say anything. She knelt and put her head against the Dog's warm neck and sighed, a sigh that held all her troubles in it.

"You smell worse than I usually do," observed the Dog, after the initial excitement had worn off and she had had a chance to sniff Lirael's mud-covered body. "You'd better get up. We have to get back to the stream. There are still plenty of Dead about—Hedge seems to have abandoned them to do what they will. At least so we suppose, since the lightning storm—presumably following the hemispheres—has moved out over the lake."

"Yes," said Lirael, after they'd started walking back. "Hedge is there. Nick . . . the thing inside . . . called out to him from the reeds. They have two barges, and they're taking the hemispheres to Ancelstierre."

"It rose again in Nick," mused the Dog. "That didn't take long. Even the fragment must be stronger than I would have thought."

"It was a lot stronger than I ever imagined," replied Lirael, shivering. They were almost at the stream, and there was Sam waiting in the shadow of the trees, with an arrow nocked ready to fire. How was she going to explain to him that she'd rescued Nicholas—and lost him again?

Suddenly, Sam moved, and Lirael stopped in surprise. It looked as if he was going to shoot her—or the Dog. She just had time to duck as his bow twanged, and an arrow leapt out—straight at her head.

Chapter Thirteen

DETAILS FROM THE DISREPUTABLE DOG

AS SHE DUCKED, Lirael suddenly sensed a Gore Crow's cold presence directly above her. An instant later its dive was arrested, and it smacked into the ground, transfixed by Sam's arrow, the Charter Magic he'd set in the sharp point sparking as it ate into the splinter of Dead Spirit that was trying to crawl away.

Lirael found herself instinctively with a bell in hand, looking up for more Gore Crows. There was another, diving down, but an arrow lofted up and met it, too. This missile punched straight through the ball of feathers and dried bone and kept on going—but the Gore Crow didn't, and another fragment of Dead Spirit writhed on the ground near the first, suffering in the sunshine.

Lirael looked at the bell in her hand, and the spirit fragments, pools of inky darkness that were already creeping together, seeking to join for greater strength. The bell was Kibeth, which was appropriate, so she rang it in a quick S shape, producing a clear and joyful tune that made her left foot break out into a little jig.

It had a more inimicable effect upon the remnant spirit fragments of the Gore Crows. The two blots reared up like salted leeches and almost somersaulted as they sought to evade the sound. But there was nowhere for them to go, nowhere they could escape Kibeth's peremptory call. Except the one place the spirit never wished to see again. But it had no choice. Shrieking inside, the spirit obeyed the bell, and the two blots vanished into Death.

Lirael cast her eye around the sky again and smiled in satisfaction as three more distant black dots fell earthwards: Gore Crows destroyed when the first two banished fragments sucked the rest of the shared spirit back into Death. Then she put the bell away and walked forward to greet Sam, the Disreputable Dog taking a quick side trip to sniff at the crow feathers, to make absolutely sure the spirit was gone and there was nothing worth eating.

Sam, like the Dog, also seemed extremely happy to see Lirael, and was even about to give her a welcoming hug—till he smelled the mud. That made him change his open arms into an expansive welcoming gesture. Even so, Lirael noticed that he was looking behind her for someone else.

"Thanks for shooting the crows," she said. Then she added, "I lost Nick, Sam."

"Lost him!"

"There's a fragment of the Destroyer inside him, and it took him over. I couldn't stop it. It almost killed me when I tried."

"What do you mean a fragment of the Destroyer? Inside him how?"

"I don't know!" snapped Lirael. She took a deep breath before continuing. "Sorry. The Dog says that there's a sliver of the metal from one of the hemispheres inside Nicholas. I don't know any more than that, though it does explain why he's working with Hedge."

"So where is he?" asked Sam. "And what . . . what are we going to do now?"

"He's almost certainly on the barges Hedge is using to transport the hemispheres," replied Lirael. "To Ancelstierre."

"Ancelstierre!" exclaimed Sam, his surprise echoed by Mogget, who emerged from Sam's pack. The little cat took several steps towards Lirael; then his nose wrinkled and he backed away.

"Yes," said Lirael heavily, ignoring Mogget's reaction. "Apparently Hedge—or the Destroyer itself, I suppose—knows some way to get across the Wall. They're taking the hemispheres by barge as close as they can. Then they'll cross the Wall and go to a place called Forwin Mill, where Nick will use a thousand lightning rods to funnel the entire power of a storm into the hemispheres. This will somehow help them come together, and then, I imagine, whatever it is will be whole again, and unbound. Charter knows what will happen then."

"Total destruction," said the Dog bleakly. "The end of all Life."

Silence greeted her words. The Dog looked up to see Sam and Lirael staring at her. Only Mogget was unmoved, choosing that moment to clean his paws.

"I suppose it is time to tell you exactly what we face," said the Dog. "But we should find somewhere defensible first. All the Dead that Hedge used to dig the pit are still about, and those strong enough to face the day will be hungry for life."

"There's an island at the mouth of the stream," said Sam slowly. "It's not much, but it would be better than nothing."

"Lead on," said Lirael wearily. She wanted to collapse on the spot and block her ears from whatever the Dog was going to tell them. But this wouldn't help. They had to know.

The island was a tumbled patch of rocks and stunted trees. It had once been a low hillock on the edge of the lake, with the stream on one side, but centuries ago the lake had risen or the streambed split. Now the island stood in the broad mouth of the stream, surrounded by swift water to the north, south, and east, and the deep waters of the lake to the west.

They waded across, Mogget clinging to Sam's shoulder and the Dog swimming in the middle. Unlike most dogs, Lirael noticed, her friend actually stuck her whole head underwater, ears and all. And whatever power fast-moving water had over the Dead and some Free Magic creatures clearly didn't apply to the Disreputable Dog.

"How come you like to swim but hate baths?" asked Lirael curiously as they reached dry ground and found a sandy patch between the rocks to set up a makeshift camp.

"Swimming is swimming, and the smells stay the same," said the Dog. "Baths involve soap."

"Soap! I would love some soap!" exclaimed Lirael. Some of the mud and reed pollen had come off in the stream, but not enough. She felt so filthy that she couldn't think straight. But she knew from long experience that any delay would only encourage the Dog to avoid telling them anything. She sat down on her pack and looked expectantly at the Dog. Sam sat down, too, and Mogget leapt down and stretched for a moment before settling comfortably into the warm sand.

"Tell us," ordered Lirael. "What is the thing bound in the hemispheres?"

"I suppose the sun is high enough," said the Dog. "We will not be bothered for a few hours yet. Though it might perhaps—"

"Tell us!"

"I am telling you," protested the Dog with great dignity. "It's just finding the best words. The Destroyer was known by many names, but the most common is one that I will write here. Do not speak it unless you must, for even the name has power, now that the silver hemispheres have been brought out under the sky."

The Dog flexed her paw, and a single sharp claw popped out. She scratched seven letters in the sand, using the modern

version of the alphabet favored by Charter Mages for nonmagi-
cal communication about magical topics.

The letters she wrote spelled out a single word.

ORANNIS.

"Who . . . or what . . . is this thing?" asked Lirael when she'd
silently read the name. She already had a feeling that it would be
worse than she expected. There was a great but subtle tension in
the way Mogget was crouched, his green eyes fixed on the letters, and the Dog wouldn't meet her eyes.

The Dog didn't answer at first but shuffled her paws and
coughed.

"Please," said Lirael gently. "We have to know."

"It is the Ninth Bright Shiner, the most powerful Free
Magic being of them all, the one who fought the Seven in the
Beginning, when the Charter was made," said the Dog. "It is the
Destroyer of worlds, whose nature is to oppose creation with
annihilation. Long ago, beyond counting in years, It was
defeated. Broken in two, each half bound within a silver hemisphere, and those hemispheres secured with seven bonds and
buried deep beneath the earth. Never to be released, or so it was
thought."

Lirael nervously tugged at her hair, wishing she could disappear behind it forever. She felt a nervous desire to laugh or
scream or fall to the ground weeping. She looked at Sam, who
was biting his lip, unconscious of the fact that he had really
bitten it and blood was trickling down his chin.

The Dog did not say anything more, and Mogget just kept
staring at the letters.

ORANNIS.

"How can we defeat something like that?" burst out Lirael.
"I'm not even a proper Abhorsen yet!"

Sam shook his head as she spoke, but whether it was in

negation or agreement, Lirael couldn't tell. He kept on shaking it, and she realized it was simply that he couldn't fully grasp what the Dog had told them.

"It is still bound," said the Dog gently, giving Lirael an encouraging lick to her hand. "While the hemispheres are separate, the Destroyer can use only a small portion of Its power, and none of Its most destructive attributes."

"Why didn't you tell me this before!"

"Because you were not strong enough in yourself," explained the Dog. "You did not know who you are. Now you do, and you are ready to know fully what we face. Besides, I was not sure myself until I saw the lightning storm."

"I knew," said Mogget. He stood up and stretched out to a surprising length before sitting back and inspecting his right paw. "Ages ago."

The Dog wrinkled her nose in obvious disbelief and kept talking.

"The most disturbing aspect of this is that Hedge is taking the hemispheres to Ancelstierre. Once they are across the Wall, I do not know what is possible. Perhaps these massed lightning rods of Nick's will enable the Destroyer to join the hemispheres and become whole. If It does, then everyone . . . and everything is doomed, on both sides of the Wall."

"It was always the most powerful and cunning of the Nine," mused Mogget. "It must have worked out that the only place It could come back together was somewhere It had never existed. And then somehow It must have learned that we infringed upon a world beyond our own, for the Destroyer was bound long before the Wall was made. Clever, clever!"

"You sound like you admire It," said Sam somewhat bitterly. "Which is not the right attitude for a servant of the Abhorsens, Mogget."

"Oh, I do admire the Destroyer," replied Mogget dreamily, his pink tongue licking the corners of his white-toothed mouth. "But only from a distance. It would have no qualms about annihilating me, you know—since I refused to ally with It against the Seven when It gathered Its host all those long-lost dreams ago."

"Only sensible thing you ever did," growled the Dog. "Though not as sensible as you could have been."

"Neither for nor against," said Mogget. "I would have lost myself either way. Not that it helped me any in the end, choosing the middle road, for I've lost most of myself anyway. Well, lackaday. Life goes on, there are fish in the river, and the Destroyer heads for Ancelstierre and freedom. I am curious to hear your next plan, Mistress Abhorsen-in-Waiting."

"I'm not sure I have one," replied Lirael. Her brain was saturated with danger. She couldn't even begin to comprehend the threat the Destroyer posed. That left room for tiredness, hunger, and a fierce loathing for her muddy, stinking body to become uppermost in her thoughts. "I think I have to get clean and eat something. Only I do have one question first. Or two questions, I guess.

"First of all, if the Destroyer does join Itself back together in Ancelstierre, can It do anything? I mean, both Charter and Free Magic don't work on the other side of the Wall, do they?"

"Magic fades," answered Sam. "I could do Charter Magic at school, thirty miles south of the Wall, but none at all in Corvere. It also depends on whether the wind blows from the north or not."

"In any case, the Destroyer is a source of Free Magic in Itself," said the Dog, her brow wrinkled in thought. "Should It become whole and free, It could range wherever It wills, though I do not know how It would manifest Itself beyond the Kingdom. The Wall alone could not stop It, for the stones carry the power of only two of the Seven, and it took all of them to bind the Destroyer in the long ago."

"That leads to my next question," said Lirael wearily. "Do either of you know—or remember—exactly *how* It was split in two by the Seven and bound into the hemispheres?"

"I was already bound, like so many others," sniffed Mogget. "Besides, I am not really who I was even one millennium ago, let alone what I was in the Beginning."

"In a way I was present," said the Dog after a long pause. "But I, too, am only a shadow of what I once was, and my clear memories all stem from a later time. I do not know the answer to your question."

Lirael thought of a particular passage in *The Book of Remembrance and Forgetting* and sighed. She had heard the term "the Beginning" before but only now could place it as coming from that book.

"I think I know how to find out, though I don't know whether I'll be able to do it. But first of all I have to wash before this mud eats through my clothes!"

"And think of a plan?" Sam asked hopefully. "I guess we'll have to try to stop the hemispheres crossing the Wall, won't we?"

"Yes," said Lirael. "Keep watch, will you?"

She walked carefully down to the stream proper, thankful that it was another unseasonably hot day. She had considered stripping off for a complete wash but decided against it. Whatever the scales of her armored coat were called or made of, they weren't metal, so there was no danger of rust. And she didn't like the idea of being surprised by the Dead while seminaked. Besides, it was hot, the rain had long gone, and she would dry off quickly.

She put her sword on the bank, close at hand, and the bell-bandolier next to it. Both would need serious cleaning, too, and the bandolier rewaxing. Her surcoat almost had to be scraped off, there was so much mud in and under it. She rolled it up and carried it into a convenient pool, out of the main current.

A sound made her look around, but it was only the Disreputable Dog, carefully sliding down the bank with something bright and yellow in her mouth. She spat it out as she reached Lirael, followed by a mixture of dog spit and bubbles.

"Yeerch," said the Dog. "Soap. See how much I love you?"

Lirael smiled and caught the soap, let the stream take the coating of dog saliva off, and started to lather herself and her clothes. Soon she was entirely covered in soapy foam but wasn't much cleaner, since the mud and the red pollen were very resistant, even to soap and water. Her surcoat looked as if it would be permanently stained until she had the time and energy to do some laundry magic.

Washing it without the help of magic gave her something to do while she thought about their next step. The more she considered it, the more it became clear that they couldn't stop Hedge from transporting the hemispheres through the Old Kingdom. Their only real chance was to stop him and the hemispheres at the Wall. That meant going into Ancelstierre, to enlist whatever help they could get there.

If despite their efforts Hedge did get the hemispheres over the Wall, then there would still be one last chance: to stop Nick's Lightning Farm from being used to make the Destroyer whole.

And if that failed . . . Lirael didn't want to think about any last resorts beyond that.

When she judged herself to be about as clean as possible without entirely new clothes, Lirael waded back out to take care of her equipment. She carefully wiped the bandolier and waxed it with a lump of lovely-smelling beeswax, and went over Nehima with goose grease and a cloth. Then she put surcoat, bell–bandolier, and sword baldric back on, over her armor.

Sam and the Disreputable Dog stood on the largest of the rocks, watching both the lakeshore and the sky above. There was no sign of Mogget, though he could easily be back in Sam's pack. Lirael climbed up to the rock to join Sam and the Dog. She chose a small patch of sunshine between the two, sat down, and ate a cinnamon biscuit to satisfy her immediate pangs of hunger.

Sam watched her eat, but it was obvious he couldn't wait for her to finish and start talking.

Lirael ignored him at first, till he pulled a gold coin out of his sleeve and tossed it in the air. It spun up and up, but just when Lirael thought it would come down, it hovered, still spinning. Sam watched it for a while, sighed, and clicked his fingers. Instantly, the coin dropped into his waiting hand.

He repeated this process several times till Lirael snapped.

"What is that?"

"Oh, you're finished," said Sam innocently. "This? It's a feather-coin. I made it."

"What is it for?"

"It isn't for anything. It's a toy."

"It's for annoying people," said Mogget from Sam's pack. "If you don't put it away, I shall eat it."

Sam's hand closed on the coin, and it went back up his sleeve.

"I suppose it does annoy people," he said. "This is the fourth one I've made. Mother broke two, and Ellimere caught the last one and hammered it flat, so it could only wobble about close to the ground. Anyway, now that you've finished eating—"

"What!" asked Lirael.

"Oh, nothing," Sam replied brightly. "Only I was hoping we could discuss what . . . what we're going to do."

"What do you think we should do?" asked Lirael, suppressing the irritation that the feather-coin had created. Despite everything, Sam appeared to be less tense and nervous than she'd expected. Perhaps he had become fatalistic, she thought, and wondered if she had as well. Faced by an Enemy that was so clearly beyond them, they were just resigned to doing whatever they could before they got killed or enslaved. But she didn't feel fatalistic. Now that she was clean, Lirael felt curiously hopeful, as if they actually could do something.

"It seems to me," Sam said, pausing to chew his lip thoughtfully again. "It seems to me that we should try to get to this Torwin Mill—"

"Forwin Mill," interrupted Lirael.

"Forwin, then," continued Sam. "We should try to get there first, with whatever help we can muster from the Ancelstierrans. I mean, they don't like anyone bringing anything in from the Old Kingdom, let alone something magical they don't understand. So if we can get there first and get help, we could have Nick's Lightning Farm dismantled or destroyed before Hedge and Nick arrive with the hemispheres. Without the Lightning Farm, Nick won't be able to feed power into the hemispheres, so It will stay bound."

"That's a good plan," said Lirael. "Though I think we should work on stopping the hemispheres before they can cross the Wall."

"There is another problem that makes both plans a bit iffy," said Sam hesitantly. "I think those Edge sailing barges do the journey from Edge to the Redmouth in under two days. Faster with a spelled wind. It's not far from there to the Wall, maybe half a day depending on how fast they can drag the hemispheres. It'll take us at least four or five days to walk there. Even if we manage to find some horses today, we'll be at least a day behind."

"Or more," said Lirael. "I can't ride a horse."

"Oh," said Sam. "I keep forgetting you're a Clayr. Never seen one of them on a horse. . . . I guess we'll have to hope that the Ancelstierrans won't let them cross. Though I'm not sure they could stop even Hedge by himself, unless there were a lot of Crossing Point Scouts—"

Lirael shook her head. "Your friend Nick has a letter from his uncle. I don't know what a Chief Minister is, but Nick seemed to think that it would force the Ancelstierrans to allow him to bring the hemispheres across the Wall."

"How come he's always 'your friend Nick' when he makes things difficult?" protested Sam. "He *is* my friend, but it's the Destroyer and Hedge making him do all this stuff. It's not his fault."

"Sorry," sighed Lirael. "I know it's not his fault, and I won't call him 'your friend Nick' anymore. But he does have that letter. Or actually, someone on the other side of the Wall has it, who will be meeting them."

Sam scratched his head and frowned in exasperation.

"It depends on where they cross and who is in charge," he said despondently. "I guess they'll be intercepted at the Perimeter by a patrol, who will probably be all regular Army and not Scouts, and only the Scouts are Charter Mages. So they might let Nick and Hedge and everyone go through the Perimeter. I don't think any of the normal patrols could stop Hedge anyway, even if they wanted to. If only we could get there first! I know General Tindall well—he commands the Perimeter. And we would be able to wire my parents at the embassy in Corvere. If they're still there."

"Can we sail ourselves?" asked Lirael. "Where could we get a boat that's faster than the barges?"

"Edge would be the closest," replied Sam. "At least a day

north, so we'd lose as much time as we gained. If Edge is still there. I don't want to think about how Hedge got his barges."

"Well, what about downstream?" asked Lirael. "Is there a fishing village or something?"

Sam shook his head absently. There was an answer, he knew. He could feel an idea just lurking out of reach. How could they reach the Wall faster than Hedge and Nick?

Land, sea . . . and air.

"Fly!" he exclaimed, jumping up and throwing his arms in the air. "We can fly! Your owl Charter-skin!"

It was Lirael's turn to shake her head.

"It would take me at least twelve hours to make two Charter-skins. Maybe more, since I need some sort of rest first. And it takes weeks to learn how to fly properly."

"But I won't need to," said Sam excitedly. "Look—I watched you making the barking owl skin before and I noticed that there's only a few key Charter marks that set how big it is, right?"

"Maybe," said Lirael dubiously.

"Well, my idea is that you make a really big owl, big enough to carry me and Mogget in your claws," continued Sam, gesturing wildly. "It wouldn't take any longer than it usually does. Then we fly to the Wall . . . um, cross it . . . and take it from there."

"An excellent idea," said the Dog, her expression a mixture of surprise and approval.

"I don't know," said Lirael. "I'm not sure a giant Charter-skin would work."

"It will," said Sam confidently.

"I don't suppose there's much else we can do," Lirael said quietly. "So I guess I'd better give it a go. Where's Mogget? I'm curious to see what he thinks of your plan."

"It stinks," said Mogget's muffled voice from the shade

below the boulder. "But there's no reason why it won't work."

"There's one other thing I guess I might have to do later," Lirael said hesitantly. "Is it possible to enter Death on the other side of the Wall?"

"Sure, depending how far into Ancelstierre you go, just like with magic," Sam replied, his voice suddenly very serious. "What . . . what is it you might have to do?"

"Use the Dark Mirror and look back into the past," Lirael said, her voice unconsciously taking on some of the timbre of a Clayr's prophecy. "Back to the Beginning, to see how the Seven defeated the Destroyer."

Chapter Fourteen

FLIGHT TO THE WALL

"IT WAS HUGE," sobbed the man, panic in his eyes and voice. "Bigger than a horse, with wings . . . wings that blocked the sky. And it had a man in its claws, dangling . . . horrible . . . horrible! The screeching . . . you must have heard the screeching?"

The other members of the small band of Travelers nodded, many of them looking up into the fading light of the evening sky.

"And something else was flying with it," whispered the man. "A dog. A dog with wings!"

His listeners exchanged glances of disbelief. A giant owl they could accept, after the screeching they'd heard. This was the Borderlands, after all, and in troubled times. Many things they had thought never to see had walked the earth in the last few days. But a winged dog?

"We'd best move along," said the leader, a tough-looking woman who bore the Charter mark on her forehead. She sniffed the air and added, "There's something odd about, all right. We'll go on to the Hogrest, unless anyone has a better idea. Somebody help Elluf, too. Give him some wine."

Quickly, the Travelers broke their camp and unhobbled their horses. Soon, they were headed north, with the unfortunate Elluf swigging from a wineskin as if it were water.

South of the Travelers, Lirael flew with gradually slowing wing beats. It was much, much harder to fly as a twenty-times-sized barking owl than as a normal one, particularly carrying Sam, Mogget, and both packs. Sam had helped along the way by casting Charter marks of strength and endurance into her, but a large part of the sustaining magic had been absorbed by the Charter-skin itself.

"I have to set down," she called to the Disreputable Dog, who was flying behind her, as pain coursed through her wings again. She picked a clear glade amongst the mass of trees and started to glide in for a landing.

Then she suddenly saw their destination. There, beyond the forest—a long grey line snaking along the crest of a low hill, going from east to west as far as she could see. The Wall that separated the Old Kingdom from Ancelstierre.

And on the far side of the Wall, darkness. The full dark, near midnight of an Ancelstierran early spring, spreading up to the Wall, where it suddenly met the warmth of an Old Kingdom summer evening. It gave Lirael an instant headache, her owl eyes unable to adjust to the contradiction—sunset here and night over there.

But there was the Wall, and buoyed up by this sighting, she forgot her pain and the intended landing site. With a push of her wings she lofted up again, heading straight for the Wall, a triumphant screech splitting the night.

"Don't try to cross!" Sam called urgently from below, as he swung in the makeshift harness of sword baldrics and pack straps that was held tight by her claws. "We have to land on this side, remember!"

Lirael heard him, recalled his warnings about the Perimeter on the Ancelstierran side, and dropped one wing. Immediately this became a diving turn, followed by frenzied flapping as Lirael realized she'd misjudged their airspeed and was about to plow Sam, Mogget, and herself into the ground at a painful velocity.

The flapping worked, after a fashion. Sam picked himself off the ground, checked that his bruised knees still functioned, and went over to the enormous owl who lay next to him, apparently stunned.

"Are you all right?" he asked anxiously, uncertain how he could check. How did you feel an owl's pulse, particularly an owl that was twenty feet long?

Lirael didn't answer, but faint lines of golden light began to run in hairline cracks through the giant owl shape. The lines ran together till Sam could see individual Charter marks; then the whole thing began to blaze so brightly that Sam had to back off, shielding his eyes against the brilliance.

Then there was only soft twilight in his eyes, as the sun slowly set on the Old Kingdom side. And there was Lirael, lying spread-eagled on her stomach, groaning.

"Ow! Every muscle in my entire body hurts," she muttered, slowly pushing herself up with her hands. "And I feel absolutely disgusting! Worse than the mud, that Charter-skin. Where's the Dog?"

"Here, Mistress," answered the Disreputable Dog, rushing over to surprise Lirael with a lick to her open mouth. "That was fun. Particularly flying over that man."

"That wasn't intentional," said Lirael, using the Dog as a crutch to help herself up. "I was just as surprised as he was. Let's just hope that we've saved enough time to make it worthwhile."

"If we can get across the Wall—and the Perimeter—tonight, we have to be ahead of Hedge," said Sam. "How fast can a barge go, after all?"

It was a rhetorical question, but it was answered.

"With a spelled wind, they could sail more than sixty

leagues in a day and night," said Mogget, a hidden voice of authority from inside Sam's pack. "I would presume they reached the Redmouth around noon today. From there, who knows? It depends how quickly they can move the hemispheres. They may even have crossed, and time is disjointed between the Old Kingdom and Ancelstierre. Hedge—aided by the Destroyer—may even be able to manipulate that difference to gain a day . . . or more."

"Ever cheerful, aren't you, Mogget?" said Lirael. She actually felt surprisingly cheerful herself, and not as tired as she'd thought she was. She felt quietly proud that the giant owl Charter-skin had worked, and she was sure that they had got ahead of Hedge and his barges.

"I suppose we should push on," she said. Better not to count her apples before the tree grew. "Sam, I hadn't actually thought of this, but how will we get into Ancelstierre? How do we get across the Wall?"

"The Wall is the easy part," replied Sam. "There are lots of old gates. They'll be locked and warded, except for the one at the current Crossing Point, but I think I can open them."

"I'm sure you can," said Lirael encouragingly.

"The Perimeter is more difficult in some ways. They shoot on sight over there, though most of the troops are around the Crossing Point, so there will only be a chance of a patrol this far west. To be on the safe side, I was thinking we might take on the semblance of an officer and a sergeant from the Crossing Point Scouts. You can be the sergeant, with a head wound—so you can't talk and get us into trouble. They might believe that— enough not to shoot us straightaway."

"What about the Dog and Mogget?" asked Lirael.

"Mogget can stay in my pack," said Sam. With a backwards glance towards the cat, he added, "But you have to promise to be quiet, Mogget. A talking pack will get us killed for sure."

Mogget didn't answer. Sam and Lirael took this to be a surly agreement, since he didn't protest.

"We can disguise the Dog with a glamour as well," continued Sam. "To make her look like she's got a collar and breastplate like the Army sniffer dogs."

"What do they sniff?" asked the Disreputable Dog with interest.

"Oh, bombs and other . . . um . . . exploding devices—like the blasting marks we use, only made from chemicals, not magic," explained Sam. "Down south, that is. But they have special dogs on the Perimeter that sniff out the Dead or Free Magic. The dogs are much better than ordinary Ancelstierrans at detecting such things."

"Naturally," said the Disreputable Dog. "I take it I'm not allowed to talk, either?"

"No," confirmed Sam. "We'll have to give you a name and number, like a real sniffer dog. How about Woppet? I knew a dog called that. And you can have my old service number from the cadet corps at school. Two Eight Two Nine Seven Three. Or Nine Seven Three Woppet for short."

"Nine Seven Three Woppet," mused the Dog, rolling the words around in her mouth as if they were something potentially edible. "A curious name."

"We'd better cast the illusions here for us to take on," said Sam. "Before we try to cross the Wall."

He looked at the full dark of the Ancelstierran night beyond the Wall and said, "We need to cross before dawn, which can't be too far away. We're less likely to run into a patrol at night."

"I've never cast a glamour before," said Lirael doubtfully.

"I have to do them anyway," replied Sam. "Since you don't know what we want to look like. They're not that hard—a lot easier than your Charter-skins. I can do three easily enough."

"Thank you," said Lirael. She sat down next to the Dog, easing her aching muscles, and scratched the hound under the collar. Sam walked a few paces away and began to reach into the Charter, gathering the marks that he needed for casting the spells of disguise.

"Funny to think he's my nephew," whispered Lirael to the Dog. "It feels very strange. An actual family, not just a great clan of cousins, like the Clayr. To be an aunt, as well as having one. To have a sister, too . . ."

"Is it good as well as strange?" asked the Dog.

"I haven't had a chance to think about it," replied Lirael, after a moment of thoughtful silence. "It's sort of good and sort of sad. Good, because I am . . . I am an Abhorsen, blood and bone, so I have found where I belong. Sad, because all my life before was about not belonging, not being properly one of the Clayr. I spent so many years wanting to be something I wasn't. Now I think if I could have become a Clayr, would it have been enough for me? Or would I simply be unable to imagine being anything else?"

She hesitated, then quietly added, "I wonder if my mother knew what my childhood would be. But then Arielle was a Clayr, too, and probably couldn't comprehend what it would be like growing up at the Glacier without the Sight."

"That reminds me," Mogget said, unexpectedly emerging from the pack, his left ear crumpled by his rapid exit. "Arielle. Your mother. She left a message with me when she was at the House."

"What!" exclaimed Lirael, jumping over to grab Mogget by the scruff of the neck, ignoring Ranna's call to sleep and the unpleasant interchange of Free Magic under cat skin and the Charter-spelled collar. "What message? Why didn't you give it to me before?"

"Hmmm," replied Mogget. He pulled himself free, catching his collar against Lirael's hand. She let go just before he could slip out of the leather band, and Ranna's warning chime made the cat stop wriggling. "If you listen, I'll tell you—"

"Mogget!" growled the Dog, stalking over to breathe in the cat's face.

"Arielle Saw me with you, near the Wall," said Mogget quickly. "She was sitting in her Paperwing, and I was handing her a package—I had a different form in those days, you understand. In fact, I probably wouldn't have remembered this if I hadn't taken that shape again after my forced conversation under the House. It's funny how in man shape I remember things differently. I suppose I had to forget in order to not remember until I was where she Saw me—"

"Mogget! The message!" pleaded Lirael.

Mogget nodded and licked his mouth. Clearly he would proceed only in his own time.

"I handed her the package," he continued. "She was looking into the mist above the waterfall. There was a rainbow there that day, but she did not see it. I saw her eyes cloud with the Sight, and she said, 'You will stand by my daughter near the Wall. You will see her grown, as I will not. Tell Lirael that . . . that my going will be . . . will have been . . . no choice of mine. I have linked her life and mine to the Abhorsen, and put the feet of both mother and daughter on a path that will limit our own choosing. Tell her also that I love her, and will always love her, and that leaving her will be the death of my heart.'"

Lirael listened intently, but it was not Mogget's voice she heard. It was her mother's. When the cat finished, she looked up at the red-washed sky above and the glittering stars beyond the Wall, and a single tear ran down her cheek, leaving a trail of silver, caught by the last moments of evening light.

"I've made your glamour," said Sam, who had been so intent

on his spells that he had totally missed what Mogget said. "You just need to step into it. Make sure you keep your eyes closed."

Lirael turned to see the glowing outline hanging in the air and stumbled towards it. She had her eyes closed well before she walked into the spell. The golden fire spread across her face like warm, welcoming hands and brushed away her tears.

Chapter Fifteen

THE PERIMETER

"Sarge—there's definitely something moving out there," whispered Lance Corporal Horrocks, as he looked out over the sights of his Lewin machine-gun. "Should I let 'em have a few rounds?"

"No bloody fear!" Sergeant Evans whispered back. "Don't you know anything? If it's a haunt or a Ghlim or something, it'll just come over here and suck your guts out! Scazlo—get back and tell the Lieutenant something's up. The rest of you, pass the word to fix bayonets, quiet like. And don't nobody do nothing unless I say so."

Evans looked again himself as Scazlo hurried back down the communications trench behind them. All along the main fighting trench there was the click of bayonets being fixed as quietly as possible. Evans himself strung his bow and loaded a flare pistol with a red cartridge. Red was the sign for an incursion from across the Wall. At least it would be the sign if it worked, he thought. There was a warm, northerly wind blowing in from the Old Kingdom. It was good for taking the chill out of the icy mud of the trenches, for spring had yet to fully banish the past winter, but it also meant that guns, planes, trip flares, mines, and everything else technological might not work.

"There's two of them—and something, looks like a dog," whispered Horrocks again, his trigger finger slowly curling back from its orthodox position held straight against the trigger guard.

Evans peered into the darkness, trying to make something out himself. Horrocks wasn't too bright, but he did have extraordinary night vision. A lot better than Evans. He couldn't see anything, but there were tin cans tinkling together on the wire. Someone . . . or something . . . was slowly coming through.

Horrocks's finger was inside the trigger guard now, the safety off, a full drum of ammunition on top, a round in the chamber. All he needed was the word, and maybe the wind to change.

Then he suddenly sighed, his trigger finger came out again, and he leaned back from the stock.

"Looks like some of our mob," he said, no longer whispering. "Scouts. An officer and some poor bastard with a bandaged head. And one of them . . . you know . . . smeller dogs."

"Sniffer dogs," corrected Evans automatically. "Shut up."

Evans was thinking about what to do. He'd never heard of Old Kingdom creatures taking the shape of an Ancelstierran officer or an Army dog. Practically invisible shadows, yes. Ordinary-looking Old Kingdom folk, yes. Flying horrors, yes. But there was always a first time—

"What's up, Evans?" asked a voice behind him, and he felt an internal relief he would never show. Lieutenant Tindall might be a General's son, but he wasn't a good-for-nothing staff officer. He knew what was what on the Perimeter—and he had the Charter mark on his forehead to prove it.

"Movement in front, about fifty yards out," he reported. "Horrocks thinks he can see a couple of Scouts, one wounded."

"And a smell . . . sniffer dog," added Horrocks.

Tindall ignored him, stepping up to peer over the parapet himself. Two dim shapes were definitely closing, whoever they were. But he could sense no inimicable force or dangerous magic. There was something . . . but if they were Crossing Point

Scouts, they would both be Charter Mages as well.

"Have you tried a flare?" he asked. "White?"

"No, sir," said Evans. "Wind's northerly. Didn't think it would work."

"Very well," said the Lieutenant. "Warn the men that I'm going to cast a light out in front. Everyone to stand ready for my orders."

"Yes, sir!" confirmed Evans. He turned to the man at his side and said quietly, "Stand to the step! Light in front! Pass it on."

As the word rippled down the line, the men stood up on the firing step, tension evident in their postures. Evans couldn't see all the platoon—it was too dark—but he knew his corporals at each end would sort them out.

"Casting now," said Lieutenant Tindall. A faint Charter mark for light appeared in his cupped hand. As it began to brighten, he threw it overarm like a cricket ball, directly out in front.

The white spark became brighter as it flew through the air, till it became a miniature sun, hovering unnaturally over No Man's Land. In its harsh light all shadows were banished, and two figures could clearly be seen following the narrow zigzagged trail through the wire entanglements. As Horrocks had said, they had a sniffer dog with them, and both wore the khaki uniforms of the Ancelstierran Army under the mail coats that were peculiar to the Perimeter Forces. Some indefinable unorthodoxy about their webbing gear and weapons also proclaimed them to be members of the Northern Perimeter Reconnaissance Unit, or as they were better known, the Crossing Point Scouts.

As the light fell on them, one of the two men put up his hands. The other, who was bandaged around the head, followed suit more slowly.

"Friendly forces! Don't shoot!" shouted Sameth as the Charter light slowly faded above him. "Lieutenant Stone and

Sergeant Clare coming in. With a sniffer dog!"

"Keep your hands up and come in single file!" shouted Tindall. Aside to his sergeant, he said, "Lieutenant Stone? Sergeant Clare?"

Evans shook his head. "Never heard of 'em, sir. But you know the Scouts. Keep themselves to themselves. The Lieutenant does look sort of familiar."

"Yes," murmured Tindall, frowning. The approaching officer did look vaguely familiar. The wounded sergeant was moving with the shuffling gait of someone forcing himself into action despite constant pain. And the sniffer dog had the correct khaki breastplate with its number stenciled on in white, and a broad, spiked leather collar. All together, they looked authentic.

"Stop there!" Tindall called as Sameth trod down a piece of unsupported concertina wire, only ten yards from the trench. "I'm coming out to test your Charter marks."

"Cover me," he whispered aside to Evans. "You know the drill if they're not what they seem."

Evans nodded, stuck four silver-tipped arrows in the mud between the duckboards for quick use, and nocked another. The Army didn't issue or even recognize the use of bows and silver arrows, but like a lot of such things on the Perimeter, every unit had them. Many of the men were practiced archers, and Evans was one of the best.

Lieutenant Tindall looked at the two figures, dim shapes again now that his spell was fading. He'd kept one eye closed against the light, as taught, to preserve his night vision. Now he opened it, noting once again that it didn't seem to make that much of a difference.

He drew his sword, the silver streaks on it shining even with the dim starlight, and climbed out of the trench, his heart thumping so loud, it seemed to be echoing inside his stomach.

Lieutenant Stone stood waiting, his hands held high. Tindall approached him carefully, all his senses open to any sensation, any hint or scent of Free Magic or the Dead. But all he could feel was Charter Magic, some fuzzy, blurring magic that wrapped both men and the dog. Some protective charm, he presumed.

At arm's length, he gently placed his sword point against the stranger Lieutenant's throat, an inch above where the mail coat laced. Then he reached forward and touched the Charter mark on the man's forehead with the index finger of his left hand.

Golden fire burst from the mark as he touched it, and Tindall felt himself fall into the familiar, never-ending swirl of the Charter. It was an unsullied mark, and Tindall felt relief as strongly as he felt the Charter.

"Francis Tindall, isn't it?" asked Sam, thankful that he'd made a luxurious mustache part of the glamour that disguised him with the uniform and accoutrements of a Scout officer. He'd met the young officer several times the year before at the regular official functions he always attended in term time. The Lieutenant was only a few years older than Sam. Francis's father, General Tindall, commanded the entire Perimeter Garrison.

"Yes," replied Francis, surprised. "Though I don't recall?"

"Sam Stone," said Sameth. But he kept his hands up and jerked his head back. "You'd better check Sergeant Clare. But be careful of his head. Arrow wound on the left side. He's pretty groggy."

Tindall nodded, stepped past, and repeated the procedure with sword and hand on the wounded sergeant. Most of the man's head was roughly bandaged, but the Charter mark was clear, so he touched it. Once again he found it uncorrupted. This time he also realized that the power within the Sergeant was very, very strong—as had been Lieutenant Stone's. Both these soldiers were enormously powerful Charter Mages, the strongest he'd ever encountered.

"They're clear!" he shouted back to Sergeant Evans. "Stand the men down and get the listening posts back out!"

"Ah," said Sam. "I wondered how you picked us up. I didn't expect the trenches here to be manned."

"There's some sort of emergency farther west," explained Tindall, as he led the way back to the trench. "We were ordered out only an hour ago. It's lucky we were still here, in fact, since the rest of the battalion is halfway to Bain. Called out in support of the civil authorities. Probably trouble with the Southerling camps again, or Our Country demonstrations. Our company was the rear party."

"An emergency west of here?" asked Sam anxiously. "What kind of emergency?"

"I haven't had word," replied Tindall. "Do you know something?"

"I hope not," replied Sam. "But I need to get in touch with HQ as quickly as possible. Do you have a field telephone with you?"

"Yes," replied Tindall. "But it's not working. The wind from across the Wall, I expect. The one at the Company CP might just work, I suppose, but otherwise you'll have to go all the way back to the road."

"Damn!" exclaimed Sam as they climbed down into the trench. An emergency to the west. That had to have something to do with Hedge and Nicholas. Absently, he returned Evans's salute and noted all the white faces staring at him out of the darkness of the trench, faces that showed their relief that he was not a creature of the Old Kingdom.

The Dog jumped down beside him, and the closest soldiers flinched. Lirael climbed down slowly after the hound, her muscles still sore from flying. It was strange, this Perimeter, and frightening, too. She could feel the vast weight of many deaths here, everywhere about her. There were many Dead pressing against the border with Life, prevented from crossing only by the wind flutes that sang their silent song out in No Man's Land. Sabriel had made them, she knew, for wind flutes would stand only as long as the current Abhorsen lived. When she passed on, the wind flutes would fail with the next full moon, and the Dead would rise, till they were bound again by the new Abhorsen. Which, Lirael realized, would be herself.

Lieutenant Tindall noticed her shiver and looked at her with concern.

"Shouldn't we get your Sergeant to the regimental aid post?" he asked. There was something peculiar about the Sergeant, something that made him difficult to look at directly. If he looked out of the corners of his eyes, Tindall could see a fuzzy aura that didn't quite match the outline he was expecting. That bandolier was odd, too. Since when did the Scouts carry bandoliers of rifle ammunition? Particularly when neither of them was carrying a rifle?

"No," said Sam quickly. "He'll be all right. We have to get to a phone as fast as possible and contact Colonel Dwyer."

Tindall nodded but didn't say anything. The nod hid a flash of concern across his face, and the thoughts that were racing through his head. Lieutenant Colonel Dwyer, who commanded the Crossing Point Scouts, had been on leave for the last two months. Tindall had even seen him off, following a memorable dinner at his father's headquarters.

"You'd better come with me to the Company CP," he said finally. "Major Greene will want to have a word."

"I must telephone," Sam insisted. "There's no time for talking!"

"Major Greene's telephone may be operational," said

Tindall, trying to keep his voice as even as possible. "Sergeant Evans—take charge of the platoon. Byatt and Emerson . . . follow on. Keep those bayonets fixed. Oh, Evans—send a runner for Lieutenant Gotley to join me at the CP. I think we might need his signals expertise."

He led the way off down the communications trench, Sam, Lirael, and the Dog following. Evans, who had caught his Lieutenant's eye and call for the only other Charter Mage in the company besides Major Greene, held Byatt and Emerson back for a few moments, whispering, "Something funny's up, lads. If the boss gives the word, or there's any sign of trouble, stick those two in the back!"

Chapter Sixteen

A MAJOR'S DECISION

SAMETH'S HEART FELL as Lieutenant Tindall led them into a deep dugout about a hundred yards behind the fighting trench. Even in the dim light of an oil lamp, he could see it looked too much like the abode of a lazy and comfort-loving officer—who probably wouldn't even listen, let alone understand what they needed to do.

There was a woodstove burning fiercely in one corner, an open bottle of whisky on the map table, and a comfortable armchair wedged in one corner. Major Greene, in turn, was wedged in the chair, looking red faced and cantankerous. But he did have his boots on, Sam noted, a sword next to his chair, and a holstered revolver that hung by its lanyard from a nearby peg.

"What's this?" bellowed the Major, creakily rising up as they ducked under the lintel and spread out around the map table. He was old for a major, Sam thought. Pushing fifty at least, and imminent retirement.

Before he could speak, Lieutenant Tindall—who'd moved around behind them—said, "Imposters, sir. Only I'm not sure what kind. They do bear uncorrupted Charter marks."

Sam stiffened at the word "imposters," and he saw Lirael grab the Dog's collar as she growled, deep and angrily.

"Imposters, hey?" said Major Greene. He looked at Sam, and for the first time Sam realized the old officer had a Charter mark on his forehead. "What do you have to say for yourselves?"

"I'm Lieutenant Stone of the NPRU," said Sam stiffly. "That is Sergeant Clare and the Sniffer Dog Woppet. I need to phone Perimeter HQ urgently—"

"Rubbish!" roared the Major, without any anger. "I know all the officers of the Scouts, the NCOs, too. I was one for long enough! And I'm pretty familiar with the sniffer dogs, and that one ain't of the breed. I'd be surprised if it could smell a cow pat in a kitchen."

"I could so," said the Dog indignantly. Her words were met by a hushed silence; then the Major had his sword out and leveled at them, and Lieutenant Tindall and his men had moved forward, sword and bayonet points only inches behind Sam's and Lirael's unprotected necks.

"Oops," said the Dog, sitting down and resting her head on her paws. "Sorry, Mistress."

"Mistress?" exclaimed Greene, his face going even redder. "Who are you two? And what is that?"

Sam sighed and said, "I am Prince Sameth of the Old Kingdom, and my companion is Lirael, the Abhorsen-in-Waiting. The Dog is a friend. We are all under a glamour. Do I have your permission to remove it? We'll glow a bit, but it isn't dangerous."

The Major looked redder-faced than ever, but he nodded.

A few minutes later Sam and Lirael stood in front of Major Greene wearing their own clothes and faces. Both were obviously very tired, and clearly had suffered much in recent times. The Major looked at them carefully, then down at the Dog. Her breastplate had disappeared and her collar changed, and she looked larger than before. She met his gaze with a sorrowful eye, then spoiled it by winking.

"It is Prince Sameth," declared Lieutenant Tindall, who'd edged around to see their faces. There was a strange expression on his face. A sympathetic look, and he nodded twice at Sameth, who looked surprised. "And she looks . . . I beg your pardon, ma'am. I mean to say you look very like Sabriel, I mean the Abhorsen."

"Yes, I am Prince Sameth," said Sam slowly, with little expectation that this overweight, soon-to-be-retired Major would be much help. "I urgently need to contact Colonel Dwyer."

"The phone doesn't work," replied the Major. "Besides, Colonel Dwyer is on leave. What's this urgent need to communicate?"

Lirael answered him, her voice cracked and croaking from the onset of a cold, caused by the sudden transition from a warm Old Kingdom summer to the Ancelstierran spring. The oil lamp flared as she spoke, sending her shadow flickering and dancing across the table.

"An ancient and terrible evil is being brought into Ancelstierre. We need help to find It and stop It—before It destroys your country and then our own."

The Major looked at her, his red face set in a frown. But it wasn't a frown of disbelief, as Sam had feared.

"If I didn't know what your title signified, and recognize the bells you wear," the Major said slowly, "I would suspect you of overstatement. I don't think I have ever heard of an evil so powerful it could destroy my entire country. I wish I weren't hearing about it now."

"It is called the Destroyer," said Lirael, her voice soft, but charged with the fear that had been growing since they had left the Red Lake. "It is one of the Nine Bright Shiners, the Free Spirits of the Beginning. It was bound and broken by the Seven and buried deep beneath the ground. Only now the two metal hemispheres that hold It prisoner have been dug up by a necromancer called Hedge, and even as we talk here, he could be bringing them across the Wall."

"So that's what it is," said the Major, but there was no satisfaction in his voice. "I had a carrier pigeon from Brigade about
trouble to the west and a defense alert, but there's been nothing
since. Hedge, you say? I knew a sergeant of that name, in the
Scouts when I first joined. Couldn't be him, though—that was
thirty-five years ago and he was fifty if he was a day—"

"Major, I have to get to a telephone!" interrupted Sameth.

"At once!" declared the Major. He seemed to be recalled to
a more vigorous and perhaps younger version of himself. "Mister
Tindall, pull your platoon in and tell Edward and CSM Porrit to
organize a move. I'm going to take these two—"

"Three," said the Dog.

"Four," interrupted Mogget, poking his head out of Sam's
pack. "I'm tired of keeping quiet."

"He's a friend, too," Lirael assured the soldiers hastily, as
hands once more went for swords and bayonets swung back.
"Mogget is the cat and the Disreputable Dog is the . . . um . . .
dog. They are . . . er . . . servants of the Clayr and the Abhorsen."

"Just like the Perimeter! It never rains but it pours," declared
the Major. "Now, I'm going to take you four back to the reserve
line road, and we'll try the phone there. Francis, follow to the
transport rendezvous as fast as you can."

He paused and added, "I don't suppose you know where this
Hedge is going, if they've got across the Perimeter?"

"Forwin Mill, where there is something called a Lightning
Farm that they will use to free the Destroyer," said Lirael. "They
may have no difficulty getting across the Perimeter. Hedge has
the Chief Minister's nephew with him, Nicholas Sayre, and
they're being met by someone who has a letter from the Chief
Minister allowing them to bring the hemispheres in."

"That wouldn't be sufficient," declared the Major. "I suppose it might work at the Crossing Point, but there'd be hours of to and fro with Garrison at Bain and even Corvere. No one in their right mind would fall for it on the real Perimeter. They'll have to fight their way through, though if an alert was sounded an hour ago, they probably already have. Orderly!"

A corporal, a burning cigarette disguised in one cupped hand, poked his head into the dugout entrance.

"Get me a map that covers Forwin Mill, somewhere west of here! I've never heard of the bloody place."

"It's about thirty miles down the coast from here, sir," volunteered Tindall, stopping in mid rush for the exit. "I've been fishing there—there's a loch with quite good salmon. It is a few miles outside the Perimeter Zone, sir."

"Is it? Humph!" remarked Greene, his face once again turning a deeper shade of red. "What else is there?"

"There was an abandoned sawmill, a broken-down dock, and what's left of the railway they once used to bring the trees down from the hills," said Tindall. "I don't know what this Lightning Farm might be, but there is—"

"Nicholas had the Lightning Farm built there," interrupted Lirael. "Quite recently, I think."

"Any people about the place?" asked the Major.

"There are now," replied Lieutenant Tindall. "Two Southerling refugee camps were built there late last year. Norris and Erimton they're called, in the hills immediately above the loch valley. There might be fifty thousand refugees there, I suppose, under police guard."

"If the Destroyer is made whole, they will be among the first to die," said the Dog. "And Hedge will reap their spirits as they cross into Death, and they will serve him."

"We'll have to get them out of there, then," said the Major. "Though being outside the Perimeter makes it difficult for us to do anything. General Tindall will understand. I only hope General Kingswold has gone home. He's an Our Country supporter through and through—"

"We must hurry!" Lirael suddenly interrupted. There was no time for more talk. A terrible sense of foreboding gripped her, as if every second they spent here was a grain of sand lost from a nearly empty hourglass. "We have to get to Forwin Mill before Hedge and the hemispheres!"

"Right!" shouted Major Greene, suddenly energized again. He seemed to need spurring along every now and then. He snatched up his helmet, threw it on his head, and snagged his revolver by the lanyard with the return motion. "Carry on, Mister Tindall. Quickly now!"

Everything did happen very quickly then. Lieutenant Tindall disappeared into the night, and the Major led them at a trot down another communications trench. Eventually it rose out of the ground and became a simple track, identified every few yards with a white-painted rock that shone faintly in the starlight. There was no moon, though one had risen on the Old Kingdom side, and it was much colder here.

Twenty minutes later, the wheezing—but surprisingly fit—Major slowed to a walk, and the track joined a wide asphalt road that stretched as far as they could see by starlight, due east and west. Telephone poles lined the road, part of the network that connected the full length of the Perimeter.

A low, concrete blockhouse brooded on the other side of the road, fed from the telegraph poles with a spaghetti-like pile of telephone wires.

Major Greene led the way inside like some corpulent missile, shouting to wake the unfortunate soldier who was slumped over a switchboard desk, his head nestled in a web of lines and plugs.

"Get me Perimeter HQ!" ordered the Major. The semiconscious soldier obeyed him, plugging in lines with the dumb expertise of the highly trained. "General Tindall in person! Wake him up if necessary!"

"Yes sir, yes, sir, yes," mumbled the telephone orderly, wishing that he had chosen a different night to drink his secret hoard of rum. He kept one hand over his mouth to try to keep the smell from the ferocious Major and his strange companions.

When the call went through, Greene grabbed the handset and spoke quickly. Obviously he was talking to various unhelpful in-between people, because his face kept getting redder and redder, till Lirael thought his skin would set his mustache on fire. Finally he reached someone who he listened to for a minute, without interruption. Then he slowly put the handset back in its cradle.

"There is an incursion happening at the western end of the Perimeter right now," he said. "There were reports of red distress rockets, but we've lost communication from Mile One to Mile Nine, so it's a broad attack. No one knows what's going on. General Tindall has already ordered out a flying column, but apparently he's gone to some other trouble at the Crossing Point. The shiny-bum staff colonel on the other end has ordered me to stay here."

"Stay here! Can't we go west and try and stop Hedge at the Wall?" asked Lirael.

"We lost communication an hour ago," said Major Greene. "It hasn't been re-established. No more rockets have been seen. That means there is no one left alive to fire any. Or else they've run away. In either case, your Hedge and his hemispheres will already be over the Wall and past the Perimeter."

"I don't understand how they could have caught up with us," said Lirael.

"Time plays tricks between here and home," said Mogget

sepulchrally, frightening the life out of the telephone operator. The little cat jumped out of Sam's pack, ignored the soldier, and added, "Though I expect it will be slow going, dragging the hemispheres to this Forwin Mill. We may have time to get *there* first."

"I'd better get in touch with my parents," said Sam. "Can you patch into the civilian telephone system?"

"Ah," said the Major. He rubbed his nose and seemed unsure of what he was going to say. "I thought you would have known. It happened almost a week ago. . . ."

"What?"

"I'm sorry, son," said the Major. He braced himself to attention and said, "Your parents are dead. They were murdered in Corvere by Corolini's radicals. A bomb. Their car was totally destroyed."

Sam listened blank faced to the Major's words. Then he slid down the wall and put his head in his hands.

Lirael touched Sam's left shoulder, and the Dog rested her nose on his right. Only Mogget seemed unaffected by the news. He sat next to the switchboard operator, his green eyes sparkling.

Lirael spent the next few seconds walling off the news, pushing it down to where she had always pushed her distress, somewhere that allowed her to keep on going. If she lived, she would weep for the sister she had never known, as she would weep for Touchstone, and her mother, and so many other things that had gone wrong in the world. But now there was no time for weeping, since many other sisters, brothers, mothers, fathers, and others depended on them doing what must be done.

"Don't think about it," said Lirael, squeezing Sam's shoulder. "It's up to us now. We have to get to Forwin Mill before Hedge does!"

"We can't," said Sam. "We might as well give up—"

He stopped himself in mid sentence, let his hands fall from his face, and stood up, but hunched over as if there were a pain in his gut. He stood there silently for almost a minute. Then he took the feather-coin out of his sleeve and flipped it. It spun up to the ceiling of the blockhouse and hung there. Sam leaned against the wall to watch it, his body still crooked but his head craned back.

Eventually he stopped looking at the spinning coin and straightened up, until he was standing at attention opposite Lirael. He didn't snap his fingers to recall the coin.

"I'm sorry," he whispered. There were tears in his eyes, but he blinked them back. "I'm . . . I'm all right now."

He bent his head to Lirael and added, "Abhorsen."

Lirael shut her eyes for a moment. That single word brought it all home. She was the Abhorsen. No longer in waiting.

"Yes," she said, accepting the title and everything that went with it. "I am the Abhorsen, and as such, I need all the help I can get."

"I'll come with you," said Major Greene. "But I can't legally order the company to follow. Though most of 'em would probably volunteer."

"I don't understand!" protested Lirael. "Who cares what's legal? Your whole country could be destroyed! Everybody killed everywhere! Don't you understand?"

"I understand. It's just not that simple . . ." the Major began. Then he paused, and his red face went blotchy and pale at the temples. Lirael watched his brow furrow up as if a strange thought were trying to break free. Then it cleared. Carefully he put his hand into his pocket, then suddenly withdrew it and punched his newly brass-knuckled fist into the Bakelite exchange board, its delicate internal mechanisms exploding with a rush of sparks and smoke.

"Damn it! It is that simple! I'll order the company to go. After all, the politicos can only shoot me for it later if we win. As for you, Private, if you mention a word of this to anyone, I'll feed you to the cat thing here. Understand?"

"Yum," said Mogget.

"Yes, sir!" mumbled the telephone operator, his hands shaking as he tried to smother the burning wreckage of his switchboard with a fire blanket.

But the Major hadn't paused for his answer. He was already out the door, shouting at some poor subordinate outside to "Hurry up and get the trucks going!"

"Trucks?" asked Lirael as they rushed out after him.

"Um . . . horseless wagons," said Sam mechanically. The words came out of his mouth slowly, as if he had to remember what they were. "They'll . . . they'll get us to Forwin Mill much faster. If they work."

"They might well do so," said the Dog, lifting her nose and sniffing. "The wind is veering to the southwest and it's getting colder. But look to the west!"

They looked. The western horizon was lit by bright flashes of lightning, and there was the dull rumble of distant thunder.

Mogget watched, too, from his post back on top of Sam's pack. His green eyes were calculating, and Lirael noticed he was counting quietly aloud. Then he sniffed with a disgruntled tone.

"How far did that boy say Forwin Mill was?" he asked, noting Lirael's look.

"About thirty miles," said Sam.

"About five leagues," said Lirael at the same time.

"That lightning is due west, and six or seven leagues away. Hedge and his cargo must still be crossing the Wall!"

SECOND INTERLUDE

THE BLUE POSTAL Service van crunched its gears as it slowed to take the turnoff from the road into the bricked drive. Then it had to slow even more and judder to a stop, because the gates that were normally open were closed. There were also people with guns and swords on the other side. Armed schoolgirls in white tennis dresses or hockey tunics, who looked as if they should be holding racquets or hockey sticks rather than weapons. Two of them kept their rifles trained on the driver while another two came through the little postern gate in the wall, the naked blades they held at the ready catching the light of the late-afternoon sun.

The driver of the van looked up at the gilt, mock-Gothic letters above the gate that read "Wyverley College" and the smaller inscription below, which said, "Established in 1652 for Young Ladies of Quality."

"Peculiar bloody quality," he muttered. He didn't like to feel afraid of schoolgirls. He looked back into the interior of the van and said more loudly, "We're here. Wyverley College."

There was a faint rustle from the back, which grew into a series of thumps and muffled exclamations. The driver watched for a second, as the mailbags stood up and hands reached out from the inside to open the drawstrings at the top. Then he turned his attention back to the front. Two of the schoolgirls were coming to his window, which he immediately wound down.

"Special delivery," he said, with a wink. "I'm supposed to say Ellie's dad and mum and that'll mean something to you, so you don't go sticking me with a sword or shooting me neither."

The closer girl, who could be no more than seventeen, turned to the other—who was even younger—and said, "Go and get Magistrix Coelle.

"You stay where you are and keep your hands on the wheel," she added to the driver. "Tell your passengers to keep still, too."

"We can hear you," said a voice from the back. A woman's voice, strong and vibrant. "Is that Felicity?"

The girl started back. Then, keeping her sword on guard in front of her, she peered through the window, past the driver.

"Yes, it's me, ma'am," said the girl cautiously. She stepped back and made a signal to the rifle girls, who relaxed slightly but did not lower their weapons, much to the driver's discomfort. "Do you mind waiting till Magistrix Coelle comes down? We can't be too careful today. There is a wind from the north, and reports of other trouble. How many of you are there?"

"We'll wait," said the voice. "Two. There's myself, and . . . Ellimere's father."

"Um, hello," said Felicity. "We had news . . . that you . . . though Magistrix Coelle did not believe it. . . ."

"Do not speak of that for now," said Sabriel. She had climbed out of the mailbag and was now crouched behind the driver. Felicity peered in again, reassuring herself that the woman she saw was in fact Ellimere's mother. Even though Sabriel was wearing blue Postal Service overalls and a watch cap pulled low over her night-black hair, she was recognizable. But Felicity was still wary. The true test would come when Magistrix Coelle tested these people's Charter marks.

"Here is your payment, as agreed," said Sabriel, passing a

thick envelope to the driver. He took it and immediately looked inside, a slight smile touching his mouth and eyes.

"Much obliged," he said. "And I'll keep my mouth shut, too, as I promised."

"You'd better," muttered Touchstone.

The driver was clearly offended by this remark. He sniffed and said, "I live near Bain and always have, and I know what's what. I didn't help you for the money. That's just a sweetener."

"We appreciate your help," said Sabriel, with a quelling glance at Touchstone. Being cooped up in a mailbag for several hours had not done anything for his temper, nor did waiting, now that they were so close to the Wall and home. Wyverley College was only forty miles south of the border.

"Here, I'll bloody well give it back," said the driver. He dragged out the envelope and thrust it towards Touchstone.

"No, no, consider it a just reward," Sabriel said calmly, and pushed the envelope back. The driver resisted for a moment, then shrugged and replaced the money somewhere inside his jacket and settled sulkily down in his seat.

"Here is the magistrix," said Felicity with relief, as she looked back at an older woman and several students who were coming down the drive. They appeared to have emerged out of nowhere, for the main school building was out of sight around the bend, cloaked by a line of closely hugging poplars.

Once Magistrix Coelle arrived, it was only a matter of minutes before Sabriel and Touchstone had the Charter marks on their foreheads assessed for purity and they were all on their way to the school, and the postal van on its way back to Bain.

"I knew the news was false," said Magistrix Coelle as they walked quickly—almost at a trot—up to the huge, gate-like doors of the main building. "The *Corvere Times* ran a photo of two burnt-out cars and some bodies but had little else to say. It seemed very much a put-up job."

"It was real enough," said Sabriel grimly. "Damed and eleven others were killed in that attack, and two more of our people outside Hennen. Perhaps more have been killed. We split up after Hennen, to lay false trails. None of our people have beaten us here?"

Coelle shook her head.

"Damed won't be forgotten," said Touchstone. "Or Barlest, or any of them. We will not forget our enemies, either."

"These are terrible times," sighed Coelle. She shook her head several times again as they went inside, past more armed schoolgirls, who looked on in awe at the legendary Sabriel and her consort, even if he was only the King of the Old Kingdom and nowhere near as interesting. Sabriel had once been one of them. They kept looking long after Coelle had ushered the distinguished visitors through a door to the Visiting Parents' parlor, possibly the most luxuriously appointed room in the whole school.

"I trust the things we left have not been disturbed?" asked Sabriel. "What is the situation? What news?"

"Everything is as you left it," replied Coelle. "We have no real trouble yet. Felicity! Please have the Abhorsen's trunk brought up from the cellar. Pippa and Zettie . . . and whoever is hall monitor today . . . can help you. As to news, I have messages and—"

"Messages! From Ellimere or Sameth?" asked Touchstone urgently.

Coelle took two folded pieces of paper from her sleeve and passed them across. Touchstone grabbed them eagerly and stood close to Sabriel to read them, as Felicity and her cohorts surged past and disappeared through one of the heavy, highly polished doors.

The first message was written in blue pencil on a torn piece of letterhead that had the same bugle-and-scroll symbol that had adorned the side of the postal van. Touchstone and Sabriel read it through carefully, deep frowns appearing on both their foreheads. Then they read it again and looked at each other, deep surprise clear on their faces.

"One of our old girls sent that," contributed Coelle nervously, as no one said anything. "Lornella Acren-Janes, who is assistant to the Postmaster General. A copy of a telegram, obviously. I don't know if it ever went to your embassy."

"Can it be trusted?" asked Touchstone. "Aunt Lirael? Abhorsen-in-Waiting? Is this some other ploy to cloud our minds?"

Sabriel shook her head.

"It sounds like Sam," she said. "Even though I don't understand it. Clearly much has been going on in the Old Kingdom. I do not think we will quickly come to the root of it all."

She unfolded the second piece of paper. Unlike the first, this was thick, handmade paper, and there were only three symbols upon it. Quiescent Charter marks, dark on the white page. Sabriel ran her palm across them, and they sprang into bright, vivid life, almost leaping into her hand. With them came Ellimere's voice, clear and strong as if she stood next to them.

"Mother! Father! I hope you get this very quickly. The Clayr have Seen much more, too much to tell in this message. There is great danger, beyond our imagining. I am at Barhedrin with the Guard, the Trained Bands, and a Seven Hundred and Eighty-Four of the Clayr. The Clayr are trying to See what we must do. They say Sam is alive and fighting, and that whatever we do, you must get to Barhedrin by Anstyr's Day or it will be too late. We have to take the Paperwings somewhere. Oh—I have an aunt, apparently your half-sister . . . What? Don't interrupt—"

Ellimere's voice stopped mid word. The Charter marks

faded back into the paper.

"An interruption mid spell," said Touchstone with a frown. "It's unlike Ellimere not to redo it. Whose half-sister? She cannot be mine—"

"The important fact is that the Clayr have finally Seen something," said Sabriel. "Anstyr's Day . . . we need to consult an almanac. That must be soon . . . very soon . . . we will have to go on immediately."

"I'm not sure you'll be able to," said Coelle nervously. "That message got here only this morning. A Crossing Point Scout brought it. He was in a hurry to get back. Apparently there has been some sort of attack from across the Wall, and—"

"An attack from across the Wall!" interrupted Sabriel and Touchstone together. "What kind of attack?"

"He didn't know," stammered Coelle, taken aback at the ferocity of the question, Sabriel and Touchstone both leaning in close to her. "It was in the far west. But there is also trouble at the Crossing Point. Apparently General Kingswold, the visiting Inspector General, has declared for the Our Country government, but General Tindall refuses to recognize it or Kingswold. Various units have taken sides, some with Tindall, some with Kingswold—"

"So Corolini has openly tried to seize power?" asked Sabriel. "When did this happen?"

"It was in this morning's paper," replied Coelle. "We haven't had the afternoon edition. There is fighting in Corvere. . . . You didn't know?"

"We've got this far by hidden ways, avoiding contact with Ancelstierrans as much as possible," said Touchstone. "There hasn't been a lot of time to read the papers."

"The *Times* said the Chief Minister still controls the Arsenal, Decision Palace, and Corvere Moot," said Coelle.

"If he holds the Palace, then he still controls the Hereditary Arbiter," said Touchstone. He looked at Sabriel for confirmation. "Corolini cannot form a government without the Arbiter's blessing, can he?"

"Not unless everything has crumbled," said Sabriel decisively. "But it doesn't matter. Corolini, the attempted coup—it is all a sideshow. Everything that has happened here is the work of some power from the Old Kingdom—our kingdom. The continental wars, the influx of Southerling refugees, the rise of Corolini, everything has been orchestrated, planned for some purpose we do not know. But what can a power from our Kingdom want in Ancelstierre? I can understand sowing confusion in Ancelstierre to facilitate an attack across the Wall. But for what? And who?"

"Sam's telegram mentions Chlorr," said Touchstone.

"Chlorr is only a necromancer, though a powerful one," said Sabriel. "It must be something else. 'Evil updug . . . I mean dug up . . . near Edge—' "

Sabriel stopped in mid sentence as Felicity and her three cohorts staggered in, carrying a long, brassbound trunk. They put it down in the middle of the floor. Charter marks drifted in lazy lines along the lid and across the keyhole. They flared into brilliant life as Sabriel touched the lock and whispered some words under her breath. There was a snick, the lid lifted a finger's breadth, then Sabriel flung it open to reveal clothes, armor, swords, and her bell-bandolier. Sabriel ignored these, digging down one side to pull out a large, leather-bound book. Embossed gold type on the cover declared the book to be *An Alamanac of the Two Countries and the Region of the Wall*. She flicked quickly through its thick pages till she came to a series of tables.

"What is today?" she asked. "The date?"

"The twentieth," said Coelle.

Sabriel ran her finger down one table and then across. She stared at the result, and her finger ran again through the numbers as she quickly rechecked it.

"When is it?" asked Touchstone. "Anstyr's Day?"

"Now," said Sabriel. "Today."

Silence greeted her words. Touchstone rallied a moment later.

"It should still be morning in the Kingdom," he said. "We can make it."

"Not by road, not with the Crossing Point uncertain," said Sabriel. "We are too far south to call a Paperwing—"

Her eyes flashed at a sudden idea. "Magistrix, does Hugh Jorbert still lease the school's west paddock for his flying school?"

"Yes," replied Coelle. "But the Jorberts are on holiday. They won't be back for a month."

"We can't fly in an Ancelstierran machine," protested Touchstone. "The wind is from the north. The engine will die within ten miles of here."

"If we get high enough, we should be able to glide over," said Sabriel. "Though not without a pilot. How many of the girls are taking flying lessons?"

"A dozen perhaps," said Coelle reluctantly. "I don't know if any of them can fly alone—"

"I have my solo rating," interrupted Felicity eagerly. "My father used to fly with Colonel Jorbert in the Corps. I have two hundred hours in our Humbert trainer at home and fifty in the Beskwith here. I've done emergency landings, night flying, and everything. I can fly you over the Wall."

"No, you cannot," said Magistrix Coelle. "I forbid it!"

"These are not ordinary times," said Sabriel, quelling Coelle with a glance. "We all must do whatever we can. Thank you,

Felicity. We accept. Please go and get everything ready, while we get changed into more suitable clothes."

Felicity let out an excited yell and raced out, her followers close behind. Coelle made a motion as if to restrain her but did not follow through. Instead, she sat down on the closest arm-chair, took a handkerchief out of her sleeve, and wiped her fore-head. The Charter mark there glowed faintly as the cloth passed over it.

"She's a student," protested Coelle. "What will I tell her parents if . . . if she doesn't . . ."

"I don't know," said Sabriel. "I have never known what to tell anybody. Except that it is better to do something than noth-ing, even if the cost is great."

She did not look at Coelle as she spoke, but out through the window. In the middle of the lawn there was an obelisk of white marble, twenty feet high. Its sides were carved with many names. They were too small to be read from the window, but Sabriel knew most of the names anyway, even when she had not known the people. The obelisk was a memorial to all those who had fallen on a terrible night nearly twenty years before, when Kerrigor had come across the Wall with a horde of Dead. There were the names of Colonel Horyse, many other soldiers, school-girls, teachers, policemen, two cooks, a gardener . . .

A flash of color beyond the obelisk caught Sabriel's eye. A white rabbit ran across the lawn, hotly pursued by a young girl, her pigtails flying as she vainly tried to capture her pet. For a moment Sabriel was lost in time, taken back to another fleeing rabbit, another pigtailed schoolgirl.

Jacinth and Bunny.

Jacinth was one of the names on the obelisk, but the rabbit outside might well be some distant descendant of Bunny. Life did go on, though it was never without struggle.

Sabriel turned away from the window and from the past. The future was what concerned her now. They had to reach Barhedrin within twelve hours. She startled Coelle by ripping off her blue coveralls, revealing that she was naked underneath. When Touchstone began to unbutton his coveralls, Coelle squealed and fled the room.

Sabriel and Touchstone looked at each other and laughed. Just for an instant, before they began to dress rapidly in the clothes from the trunk. Soon they looked and felt like themselves again, in good linen underwear, woolen shirt and leggings, and armored coats and surcoats. Touchstone had his twin swords, Sabriel her Abhorsen's blade, and most important of all, she once again wore her bandolier of bells.

"Ready?" asked Sabriel as she settled the bandolier across her chest and adjusted the strap.

"Ready," confirmed Touchstone. "Or as ready as I'm going to get. I hate flying at the best of times, let alone in one of those unreliable Ancelstierran machines."

"I expect it's going to be worse than usual," said Sabriel. "But I don't think we have any choice."

"Of course," sighed Touchstone. "I hesitate to ask—in what particular way will it be worse than usual?"

"Because, unless I miss my guess," said Sabriel, "Jorbert will have flown his wife out in the two-seater Beskwith. That will leave his single-seater Humbert Twelve. We are going to have to lie on the wings."

"I am always amazed at what you know," said Touchstone. "I am at a loss with these machines. All of Jorbert's flying conveyances looked the same to me."

"Unfortunately they are not," said Sabriel. "But there is no other way home that I can think of. Not if we are to make Barhedrin before the end of Anstyr's Day. Come on!"

She strode out of the room and did not pause to look back to see if Touchstone was following. Of course, he was.

Jorbert's flying school was a very small affair, not much more than a hobby for the retired Flying Corps colonel. There was a single hangar a hundred yards from his comfortable extended farmhouse. The hangar sat on the corner of Wyverley College's West Field, which, suitably lined with yellow-painted oil drums, served as the runway.

Sabriel was correct about the aeroplane. There was only one, a boxy green single-seater biplane that to Touchstone looked as if it depended far too much on its many supporting struts and wires all holding together.

Felicity, almost unrecognizable in helmet, goggles, and fur flying suit, was already in the cockpit. Another girl stood by the propeller, and there were two more crouched by the wheels under the fuselage.

"You'll have to lie on the wings," shouted Felicity cheerfully. "I forgot that the Colonel took the Beskwith. Don't worry, it's not that difficult. There are handholds. I've done it heaps of times . . . well, twice . . . and I've wing walked, too."

"Handholds," muttered Touchstone. "Wing walking."

"Quiet," ordered Sabriel. "Don't upset our pilot."

She climbed nimbly up the left side and laid herself across the wing, taking a secure hold on the two handgrips. Her bells were a nuisance, but she was used to that.

Touchstone climbed less nimbly up the right side—and almost put his foot through the wing. Disturbed to find it was only fabric stretched over a wooden frame, he lay down with extreme care and tugged hard on the handholds. They didn't come off, as he had half-expected they might.

"Ready?" asked Felicity.

"Ready!" shouted Sabriel.

"I suppose so," muttered Touchstone. Then, much louder, he called out a hearty "Yes!"

"Contact!" ordered Felicity. The girl at the front spun the propeller expertly and stepped back. The prop swung around as the engine coughed, faltered for a moment, then sped up into a blur as the engine caught.

"Chocks away!"

The other girls pulled at their ropes, dragging out to either side the chocks that held the wheels. The plane rocked forward, then slowly bumped around in a slow arc till it was lined up on the runway and facing the wind. The sound of the engine rose higher, and the plane started forward, bumping even more, as if it were an ungainly bird that needed to jump and flap a long way to get airborne.

Touchstone watched the ground ahead, his eyes watering as their speed increased. He had expected the plane to take off like a Paperwing—fairly quickly and with ease and elan. But as they sped down the field, and the low stone wall at the northern end grew closer and closer, he realized that he knew nothing about Ancelstierran aircraft. Obviously they would leap into the sky sharply at the very end of the field.

Or not, he thought a few seconds later. They were still on the ground and the wall was only twenty or thirty paces in front of them. He started to think it would be better to let go and try and jump away from the imminent wreck. But he couldn't see Sabriel on the other wing, and he wasn't going to jump without her.

The plane lurched sideways and bounced up into the air. Touchstone sighed with relief as they cleared the wall with inches to spare, then yelled as they went back down again. The ground came up hard, and he was too winded to do anything else as they bounced again and then were finally climbing into the sky.

"Sorry!" shouted Felicity, her voice barely audible over the engine and the rush of air. "Heavier than usual. I forgot."

He could hear Sabriel shouting something on the other side but could not hear the words. Whatever it was, Felicity was nodding her head. Almost immediately the plane began to spiral back to the south, gaining height. Touchstone nodded to himself. They would need to get as high as they could in order to have the greatest gliding range. With a north wind, it was likely the engine would fail within ten miles of the Wall. So they would have to be able to glide at least that far, and preferably a bit farther. It would not do to land in the Perimeter.

Not that landing in the Old Kingdom would be easy. Touchstone looked at the fabric wing shivering above him and hoped that most of the plane was man-made. For if parts of it were not, they would fall apart too soon, the common fate of Ancelstierran devices and machinery once they were across the Wall.

"I am never flying again," muttered Touchstone. Then he remembered Ellimere's message. If they did manage to land on the other side of the Wall, and get to Barhedrin, then they would have to fly somewhere in a Paperwing, to engage in a battle with an unknown Enemy of unknown powers.

Touchstone's face set in grim lines at that thought. He would welcome that battle. He and Sabriel had struggled too long against opponents manipulated from afar. Now whatever it was had come out in the open, and it would face the combined forces of the King, the Abhorsen, and the Clayr.

Provided, of course, that the King and the Abhorsen managed to survive this flight.

PART THREE

Chapter Seventeen

COMING HOME TO ANCELSTIERRE

"W IND'S VEERING NOR-NOREAST, sir," reported Yeoman Prindel as he watched the arrow on the wind gauge, which was mechanically linked to the weathervane several floors above them. As the arrow swung, the electric lights overhead flickered and went out, leaving the room lit by only two rather smoky hurricane lamps. Prindel looked at his watch, which had stopped, and then at the striped time candle between the hurricane lamps. "Electric failure at approximately 1649."

"Very good, Prindel," replied Lieutenant Drewe. "Order the switch to oil and sound general quarters. I'm going up to the light."

"Aye, aye, sir," replied Prindel. He uncovered a speaking tube and bawled down it, "Switch to oil! General quarters! I say again, general quarters!"

"Aye, aye!" came echoing out the speaking tube, followed by the scream of a hand-cranked siren and the clang of a cracked handbell, both of which could be heard throughout the light-house.

Drewe shrugged on his blue duffel coat and strapped on a broad leather belt that supported both a revolver and a cutlass. His blue steel helmet, adorned with the crossed golden keys emblem that proclaimed his current post as the Keeper of the Western Light, completed his equipment. The helmet had belonged to his predecessor and was slightly too large, so Drewe always felt a bit like a fool when he put it on, but regulations were regulations.

The control room was five floors below the light. As Drewe climbed steadily up the steps, he met Able Seaman Kerrick rushing down.

"Sir! You'd better hurry!"

"I am hurrying, Kerrick," Drewe replied calmly, hoping his voice was steadier than his suddenly accelerating heart. "What is it?"

"Fog—"

"There's always fog. That's why we're here. To warn any ship not to sail into it."

"No, no, sir! Not on the sea! On the land. A creeping fog that's coming down from the north. There's lightning behind it, and it's heading for the Wall. And there's people coming up from the south, too!"

Drewe abandoned his calm, drilled into him with so much care at the Naval College he'd left only eighteen months before. He pushed past Kerrick and took the rest of the steps three at a time. He was panting as he pushed open the heavy steel trapdoor and climbed into the light chamber, but he took a deep breath and managed to present some semblance of the cool, collected naval officer he was supposed to be.

The light was off and wouldn't be lit for another hour or so. There was a dual system, one oil and clockwork, the other fully electric, to cater to the strange way that electricity and technology failed when the wind blew from the north. From the Old Kingdom.

Drewe was relieved to see his most experienced petty officer was already there. Coxswain Berl was outside on the walkway, big observer's binoculars pressed to his eyes. Drewe went

out to join him, bracing himself for the cold breeze. But when
he went out, the wind was warm, another sign that it came from
the north. Berl had told him the seasons were different across the
Wall, and Drewe had been at the Western Light long enough to
believe him now, though he had dismissed the notion at first.

"What's going on?" Drewe demanded. The regular sea fog
was sitting off the coast, as it always did, night and day. But there
was another, darker fog rolling down from the north, towards the
Wall. It was strangely lit by flashes of lightning and stretched to
the east as far as Drewe could see.

"Where are these people?"

Berl handed him the binoculars and pointed.

"Hundreds of them, Mister Drewe, maybe thousands. Southerlings, I reckon, from the new camp at Lington Hill. Heading
north, trying to get across the Wall. But they aren't the problem."

Drewe twiddled with the focus knob, clanged the binoculars against the rim of his helmet, and wished he could be more
impressive in front of Berl.

He couldn't see anything at all at first, but as he got the focus
right, all the fuzzy blobs sharpened and became running figures.
There were thousands of them, men in blue hats and women in
blue scarves, and many children dressed completely in blue. They
were throwing planks onto the concertina wire, forcing their
way through and cutting where they had to. Some had already
made it through the No Man's Land of wire and were almost at
the Wall. Drewe shook his head at the sight. Why on earth were
they trying to get into the Old Kingdom? To make matters even
more confusing, some of the Southerlings who had made it to
the Wall were starting to run back. . . .

"Has Perimeter HQ been informed about these people?" he
asked. There was an Army post down there, at least a company
in the rear trenches with pickets and listening posts spread out

forward and back. What were the pongoes doing?

"The phones will be out," said Berl grimly. "Besides, those people aren't the problem. Take a look at the leading edge of that fog, sir."

Drewe swung the binoculars around. The fog was moving faster than he'd thought, and it was surprisingly regular. Almost like a wall itself, moving down to meet the one of stone. Strange fog, with lightning illuminating it from the inside . . .

Drewe swallowed, blinked, and fiddled with the focus knob on the binoculars again, unable to believe what he was seeing. There were things in the forefront of the fog. Things that might have once been people but now were not. He'd heard stories of such creatures when he was first posted to shore duty in the north, but hadn't really believed them. Walking corpses, inexplicable monsters, magic both cruel and kind. . . .

"Those Southerlings won't stand a chance," whispered Berl. "I grew up in the north. I seen what happened twenty years ago at Bain—"

"Quiet, Berl," ordered Drewe. "Kerrick!"

Kerrick poked his head out the door.

"Kerrick, get a dozen red rockets and start firing them. One every three minutes."

"R-red rockets, sir?" quavered Kerrick. Red rockets were the ultimate distress signal for the lighthouse.

"Red rockets! Move!" roared Drewe. "Berl! I want every man but Kerrick assembled outside in five minutes, number-three rig and rifles!"

"Rifles won't work, sir," said Berl sadly. "And those Southerlings wouldn't have got across the Perimeter unless the garrison was already dead. There was a whole Army company down there—"

"I've given you an order! Now get to it!"

"Sir, we can't help them," Berl pleaded. "You don't know what those things can do! Our standing orders are to defend the lighthouse, not to—"

"Coxswain Berl," Drewe said stiffly. "Whatever the Army's failings, the Royal Ancelstierran Navy has never stood by while innocents die. It will not start doing so under my command!"

"Aye, aye, sir," said Berl slowly. He raised one brawny hand in salute, then suddenly brought it crashing down on Drewe's neck, under the rim of the officer's helmet. The Lieutenant crumpled into Berl's arms, and the coxswain laid him gently down on the floor and took his revolver and cutlass.

"What are you looking at, Kerrick! Get those bloody rockets firing!"

"But—but—what about—"

"If he comes to, give him a cup of water and tell him I've taken command," ordered Berl. "I'm going down to prepare the defenses."

"Defenses?"

"Those Southerlings came from the south, straight through the Army lines. So there's something already on this side, something that fixed the soldiers good and proper. Something Dead, unless I miss my guess. We'll be next, if they aren't here already. So get going with the bloody rockets!"

The big petty officer shouted the last words as he climbed through the hatch and slammed it behind him.

The clang of the hatch was still echoing as Kerrick heard the first shouts, somewhere down in the courtyard. Then there was more shouting, and a terrible scream and a confusing hubbub of noise: yelling and screaming and the clash of steel.

Trembling, Kerrick opened the rocket store and wrestled one out. The launcher was set up on the balcony rail, but though he'd done it a hundred times in training, he couldn't get the rocket to sit in it. When it was finally home, he pulled too quickly on the cord to ignite it, and his hands were burned as the rocket blasted into the sky.

Sobbing from pain and fear, Kerrick went back to get another rocket. Above his head, red blossoms fell from the sky, bright against the cloud.

Kerrick didn't wait three minutes to fire the next one, or the next.

He was still firing rockets when the Dead Hands came up through the hatch. The fog was all around the lighthouse by then, only Kerrick, his rockets, and the light room above the wet, flowing mass of mist. The fog looked almost like solid ground, so convincing that Kerrick hardly thought twice when the Dead creature came smashing through the glass door and reached out to rend him with hands that had too many fingers and ended in curved and bloody bone.

Kerrick jumped, and for a few steps the fog did seem to support him, and he laughed hysterically as he ran. But he was falling, falling, all the same. The Dead Hands watched him go, a tiny spark of Life that all too soon went out.

But Kerrick had not died in vain. The red rockets had been observed to the south and east. And in the light room, Lieutenant Drewe came to and staggered to his feet as Kerrick fell. He saw the Dead and, in a flash of inspiration, pulled the lever that released the striker and the pressurized oil.

Light flared atop the lighthouse, light magnified a thousand-fold by the best lenses ever ground by the glass masters of Corvere. The beam shone out on two sides, bracketing the Dead on the balcony. They screeched and shielded their decaying eyes. Desperately, the young naval officer slammed the clockwork gear into neutral and leaned on the capstan, to turn the light around. It had been designed for this, in case of total mechanical failure, but not to be pushed by one man.

Desperation and fear provided the necessary strength. The light turned to catch the Dead full in its hot white beam. It didn't hurt them, but they hated it, so they retreated, taking Kerrick's way, out into the fog. Unlike Kerrick, the Dead Hands survived the fall, though their bodies were smashed. Slowly they pulled themselves upright and, on jellied, broken limbs, began the long climb back up the stairs. There was Life there, and they wanted the taste of it, the annoyance of the light already forgotten.

Nick woke to thunder and lightning. As always in recent times, he was disoriented and dizzy. He could feel the ground moving unsteadily beneath him, and it took him a moment to realize that he was being carried on a stretcher. There were two men at each end, marching along with their burden. Normal men, or normal enough. Not the leprous pit workers Hedge called the Night Crew.

"Where are we?" he asked. His voice was hoarse, and he tasted blood. Hesitantly he touched his lips, and he felt the dried blood caked there. "I'd like a drink of water."

"Master!" shouted one of the men. "He's awake!"

Nick tried to sit up, but he didn't have the strength. All he could see above was thunderclouds and lightning, which was striking down somewhere ahead. The hemispheres! It all came back to him now. He had to make sure the hemispheres were safe!

"The hemispheres!" he shouted, pain spiking in his throat.

"They're safe," said a familiar voice. Hedge suddenly towered above him. He's got taller, Nick thought irrationally. Thinner, too. Sort of stretched out, like a toffee being fought over by two children. And he had seemed to be balding before, and now he had hair. Or was it shadow, curling across his forehead?

Nick shut his eyes. He couldn't think where he was or how he had got here. Obviously he was still sick, more seriously ill than before, or they wouldn't have to carry him.

"Where are we?" Nick asked weakly. He opened his eyes again, but he couldn't see Hedge, though the man answered from somewhere close by.

"We are about to cross the Wall," replied Hedge, and he laughed. It was an unpleasant laugh. But Nick couldn't help laughing, too. He didn't know why, and he couldn't make himself stop till he choked and had to.

Beyond Hedge's laugh and the constant boom of thunder, there was another noise. Nick couldn't identify it at first. He kept listening as his stretcher bearers stolidly carried him forward, till at last he thought he knew what it was. The audience at a football game or a cricket match. Shouting and yelling at a win. Though the Wall would be an odd place to have a game. Perhaps the soldiers at the Perimeter played, he thought.

Five minutes later Nick could hear screaming in the crowd noise, and he knew it was no football game. He tried to sit up again, only to be pressed back down by a hand that he knew was Hedge's, though it was black and burnt-looking, and there were red flames where the fingernails should be.

Hallucinations, Nick thought desperately. Hallucinations.

"We must cross quickly," said Hedge, instructing the stretcher bearers. "The Dead can keep the passage for only a few more minutes. As soon as the hemispheres are through, we will run."

"Yes, sir," chorused the stretcher bearers.

Nick wondered what Hedge was talking about. They were passing between two lines of his strange, afflicted laborers now. Nick tried not to look at them, at the decaying flesh held together by torn blue rags. Fortunately, he couldn't see their ravaged faces. They were all facing away, like some sort of back-to-front honor guard, and they had linked their arms.

"The hemispheres are across the Wall!"

Nick didn't know who spoke. The voice was strange and echoing, and it made him feel unclean. But the words had an immediate effect. The stretcher bearers began to run, bouncing Nick up and down. He gripped the sides and, on the peak of one of the bounces, used its extra momentum to sit up and look around.

They were running into a tunnel through the Wall that separated the Old Kingdom and Ancelstierre. A low, arched tunnel cut through the stone. It was packed with the Night Crew from beginning to end, great lines of them with their arms linked and only a very narrow passage in between the lines. Every man and woman was glowing with golden light, but as Nick got closer, he saw that the glow was from thousands of tiny golden flames, which were spreading and joining, and the people farther inside the wall were actually on fire.

Nick cried out in horror as they entered the tunnel. There was fire everywhere, strange golden fire that burnt without smoke. Though the Night Crew were being consumed by it, they did not attempt to flee, or cry out, or do anything to stop it. Even worse than that, Nick realized that as individuals were consumed by the fire, others would step into their places. Hundreds and hundreds of blue-clad men and women were pouring in from the far side, to maintain the lines.

Hedge was struggling ahead, Nick saw. But it was not exactly Hedge. It was more a Hedge-shaped thing of darkness, limned with red fire that fought against the gold. Every step he took was clearly an effort, and the gold flames seemed almost a physical force that was trying to prevent his crossing through the tunnel in the Wall.

Suddenly a whole group of the Night Crew ahead blazed, like candles collapsing into a final pool of wax, and disappeared completely. Before the people on either side could relink arms or new Night Crew rush in, the golden fire took advantage of the gap and roared out all the way across the tunnel. The stretcher bearers saw it, and they swore and screamed, but they kept on running. They hit the fire like swimmers running from the shore into surf, diving through it. But though the stretcher and its bearers made it through, Nick was plucked off the stretcher by the fire, wrapped in flame, and tumbled down onto the stone floor of the tunnel.

With the golden fire came a piercing cold pain in his heart, as if an icicle had been thrust through his chest. But it also brought a sudden clarity to his mind, and sharper senses. He could see individual symbols in the flames and the stones, symbols that moved and changed and formed in new combinations. These were the Charter marks he'd heard about, Nick realized. The magic of Sameth . . . and Lirael.

Everything that had happened recently rushed back into his head. He remembered Lirael and the winged dog. The flight from his tent. Hiding in the reeds. His conversation with Lirael. He had promised her that he would do whatever he could to stop Hedge.

The flames beat at Nick's chest but did not burn his skin. They tried to attack what was in him, to force the shard from his body. But it was a power beyond the magic of the Wall, and that power chose to re-assert itself even as Nick tried to embrace the Charter fire, grabbing at flames and even attempting to swallow flickers of golden light.

White sparks spewed out of Nick's mouth, nose, and ears, and his body suddenly uncurled, went ramrod straight, and flipped upright, elbows and knees vertically locked. Like some inflexible doll, Nick tottered forward, the golden flames raging at every step. Deep within his own mind he knew what was happening, but he was only an observer. He had no power over his own muscles. The shard had control, though it didn't know how to make him walk properly.

Joints locked, Nick lumbered on, past countless ranks of burning Night Crew, as more and more of them poured into the tunnel from the far end. Many of them hardly looked like Night Crew at all but could almost be normal men and women, their skin and hair fresh and alive. Only their eyes proclaimed their difference, and somewhere deep inside, Nick knew that they were dead, not just sick. Like their more putrescent brethren, these new arrivals also wore blue caps or scarves.

Ahead of him Hedge burst out of the tunnel and turned back to gesture at Nick. He felt the gesture like a physical grasp, dragging him forward even faster. The golden fire reached out to him everywhere it could, but there were too many Night Crew, too many burning bodies. The fire could not reach Nicholas, and finally he staggered out of the tunnel, away from the golden flames.

He had crossed the Wall and was in Ancelstierre. Or rather in the No Man's Land between the Wall and the Perimeter. Normally this would be a quiet, empty place of raw earth and barbed wire, made somehow peaceful by the soft whisper of the wind flutes that Nick had always presumed to be some sort of weird decoration or memorial. Now it was wreathed in fog, fog eerily underlit by the low, red glow of the setting sun and flashes of lightning. The fog thinned in places as it rolled inexorably south, revealing scenes of awful carnage. The white mass was like the curtain of a horror show, briefly drawing back to show piles of corpses, bodies everywhere, bodies hanging on the wire and piled on the ground. They were all blue capped and blue scarved, and Nick finally recognized that they were slain Southerling refugees, and that in some horrible way, that was who Hedge's Night Crew had also been.

Lightning crackled above him, and thunder rumbled. Fog billowed apart, and Nick caught a glimpse of the hemispheres a little way ahead, roped onto the huge sleds that Nick knew had been waiting for them when they off-loaded the barges at the Redmouth. But he couldn't remember that happening, or anything between talking to Lirael in the reed boat and his awakening just before crossing the Wall. The hemispheres had been dragged here, obviously by the men who were dragging them now. Normal men, or at least not the Night Crew. Men dressed in strange, ragged combinations of Ancelstierran Army uniforms and Old Kingdom clothes, khaki tunics contrasting with hunting leathers, bright colored breeches, and rusty mail.

The force that had propelled him through the tunnel suddenly retreated, and Nick fell at Hedge's feet. The necromancer was at least seven feet tall now, and the red flames burning around his flesh and in his eye sockets were brighter and more intense. For the first time, Nick was frightened of him, and he wondered why he hadn't been all along. But he was too weak to do anything but crouch at Hedge's feet and clutch at his chest, where the pain still throbbed.

"Soon," said Hedge, his voice rumbling like the thunder. "Soon our master will be free."

Nick found himself nodding enthusiastically and was as frightened by this as he was by Hedge. He was already drifting back into that dreamy state where all he could think about was the hemispheres and his Lightning Farm, and what had to be done—

"No," whispered Nick. What must *not* be done. He didn't know what was happening, and until he did know, he wasn't going to do anything. "No!"

Hedge recognized that Nick spoke with an independent voice. He grinned, and fire flickered in his throat. He lifted Nick up like a baby and cradled him to his chest, against the bandolier of bells.

"Your part is nearly done, Nicholas Sayre," he said, and his breath was hot like steam and smelled of decay. "You were never more than an imperfect host, though your uncle and father have proved to be more helpful than even I could have hoped, albeit unwittingly."

Nick could only stare up at the burning eyes. Already he had forgotten everything that had come back to him in the tunnel. In Hedge's eyes he saw the silver hemispheres, the lightning, the joining that he knew once again was the single high purpose of his own short life.

"The hemispheres," he whispered, almost ritually. "The hemispheres must be joined."

"Soon, Master, soon," crooned Hedge. He stalked over to the waiting bearers and laid Nicholas down on the stretcher, stroking his chest just above his heart with a blackened, still-burning hand. What little was left of Nick's Ancelstierran shirt dissolved at Hedge's touch, showing bare skin that was blue with deep bruising. "Soon!"

Nick watched dully as Hedge walked away. No independent thought was left to him. Only the burning vision of the hemispheres and their ultimate joining. He tried to sit up to look at them but didn't have the strength, and in any case the fog was thickening once again. Wearied by the effort, Nick's hands fell to the ground on either side of the stretcher, and one finger touched a piece of debris that sent a strange feeling through his arm. A sharp pain and a gentle, healing warmth.

He tried to close his hand on the object, but his fingers

refused. With considerable effort Nick rolled over to see exactly what it was. He peered down from the stretcher and saw it was a piece of broken wood, a fragment of one of the smashed wind flutes, like the one whose stump he could see a few feet away. The fragment was still infused with Charter marks, which flowed over and through the wood. As Nick watched them, something stirred in the recesses of his mind. For a moment he remembered who he really was once more, and recalled the promise he had given to Lirael.

His right hand would not obey him, so Nicholas leaned over even more and tried to pick up the wooden fragment with his left hand. He succeeded for a few seconds, but even his left hand was no longer his to command. His fingers opened, and the piece of the wind flute fell on the stretcher, between Nick's left arm and his body, not quite touching on either side.

Hedge did not walk far from Nicholas. He strode through the fog, which parted before him, straight to the largest pile of Southerling corpses. They had been killed by the Dead that Hedge had raised earlier that day from the temporary cemeteries around the camps. He was amused by the notion of using Southerling Dead to kill Southerlings. They had also killed the soldiers in the quaintly named Western Strongpoint, and the sailors in the lighthouse.

Hedge had crossed the Wall three times that day. Once to set the initial attacks in motion in Ancelstierre, which was no great task; second to go back to prepare the crossing of the hemispheres, which was much more difficult; and the third time with the hemispheres and Nicholas. He would never need to cross again, he knew, for the Wall would be one of the first things his master would destroy, along with all other works of the despised Charter.

All that remained to be done here was to go into Death and compel as many spirits as he could find to return and inhabit these bodies. Though Forwin Mill was less than twenty miles away and they should be able to reach it by morning, Hedge knew the Ancelstierran Army would attempt to prevent their breaking out of the Perimeter. He needed Dead Hands to fight the Army, and most of the ones he'd brought from the north and those created earlier that day in the Southerling camp cemeteries had been consumed in the crossing of the Wall, used up in order to get the hemispheres across.

Hedge drew two bells from his bandolier. Saraneth, for compulsion. Mosrael, to wake the spirits who slumbered here in No Man's Land, now freed from the chains of the hated Abhorsen's wind toys. He would use Mosrael to rouse as many as possible, though use of that bell would send him far into Death himself. Then he would come back through the gates and precincts, using Saraneth to drive any other spirits he could find into Life.

There would be plenty of bodies for all.

But before he could begin, he sensed something coming through the darkness. Ever careful, Hedge put Mosrael away, lest it sound of its own accord, and drew his sword instead, whispering the words that set the dark flames running down the blade.

He knew who it was, but he did not trust even the bounds and charms he had laid upon her. Chlorr was one of the Greater Dead now. In Life she had come under the sway of the Destroyer, but in Death she was somewhat beyond that control. Hedge had forced her obedience by other means, and as always with a necromancer's control over such a spirit, this obedience could be tenuous.

Chlorr appeared as a shape of darkness that was only vaguely human, with misshapen appendages upon a bulky torso that suggested two arms, two legs, and a head. Deep fires burned where eyes should be, though the fires were too large and too widely set apart. Chlorr had crossed the Wall with Hedge the first time and had led the surprise attack on the Ancelstierran Army garrison, in their Western Strongpoint. They had not expected an assault from the south. Chlorr had reaped many lives and was all the more powerful for it. Hedge watched her warily and kept a firm grip on Saraneth. The bells did not like to serve necromancers, and even a bell that an Abhorsen would find steady had to be shown who was master at all times.

Chlorr bowed, somewhat ironically in Hedge's estimation. Then she spoke, a misshapen mouth forming in the cloud of darkness. The words were a gibberish, slurred and broken. Hedge frowned and raised his sword. The mouth firmed up, and a tongue of blood-red fire flickered from side to side in the hideous maw.

"Your pardon, Master," said Chlorr. "Many soldiers are coming on a road from the south, riding horses. Some are Charter mages, though they are not adept. I slew those who came first, but there are many more behind, so I returned to warn my master."

"Good," said Hedge. "I am about to prepare a new host of Dead, which I will send to you when they are ready. For now, gather here all the Hands that you can and attack these soldiers. The Charter Mages in particular must be slain. Nothing must delay our lord!"

Chlorr bent her great, shapeless head. Then she reached back behind her and dragged forward a man who had been hidden by the fog and her dark bulk. He was a thin, little man, his coat ripped off his back to show a classic clerk's white shirt, complete with sleeve protectors. She held him by the neck just with two huge fingers, and he was almost dead from terror and lack of air. He fell to his knees in front of Hedge, gasping for breath and sobbing.

"This is yours, or so he says," said Chlorr. Then she strode off, her hands reaching out to touch any Dead Hands that were close by. As she touched them, they shuddered and jerked, then slowly began to follow her. But there were surprisingly few Hands left, and none at all in the tunnel through the Wall. Chlorr was careful not to go near the brooding mass of stone that still shimmered every now and then with golden light. Even she did not take crossing the Wall lightly, and possibly could not have done it without Hedge's help and the sacrifice of many lesser Dead.

"Who?" demanded Hedge.

"I'm . . . I'm Deputy Leader Geanner," sobbed the man. He proffered an envelope. "Mister Corolini's assistant. I've brought you the treaty letter . . . the permission to cross . . . to cross the Wall—"

Hedge took the envelope, which burst into flame as he touched it and was consumed, grey flakes of ash falling from his blackened hand.

"I do not need permission," whispered Hedge. "From anyone."

"I've also come for the . . . the fourth payment, as agreed," continued Geanner, staring up at Hedge. "We have done all you asked."

"All?" asked Hedge. "The King and the Abhorsen?"

"D . . . d . . . dead," gasped Geanner. "Bombed and burnt in Corvere. There was nothing left."

"The camps near Forwin Mill?"

"Our people will open the gates at dawn, as instructed. The handbills have been printed, with translations in Azhdik and Chellanian. They will believe the promises, I'm sure."

"The coup?"

"We are still fighting in Corvere and elsewhere, but . . . but I'm sure Our Country will prevail."

"Then everything I need has been done," said Hedge. "All save one thing."

"What's that?" asked Geanner. He looked up at Hedge but barely had begun to scream before the burning blade came down and took his head from his shoulders.

"A waste," croaked Chlorr, who was returning with a string of Hands shambling behind her. "The body is useless now."

"Go!" roared Hedge, suddenly angry. He sheathed his sword all bloody and drew Mosrael again. "Lest I send you into Death and summon a more useful servant!"

Chlorr chuckled, a sound like dry stones rattling in an iron bucket, and disappeared off into the night, a line of perhaps a hundred Dead Hands shambling after her. As the last one crossed into the forward trenches, Hedge rang Mosrael. A single note issued from the bell, starting low and gradually increasing in both volume and pitch. As the sound spread, the bodies of the Southerlings began to twitch and wriggle, and the mounds of corpses became alive with movement. At the same time, ice formed on Hedge. Still Mosrael sounded, though its wielder was already stalking through the cold river of Death.

Chapter Eighteen

CHLORR OF THE MASK

LIRAEL AWOKE WITH a start, her heart pounding and her hands scrabbling for bells and sword. It was dark, and she was trapped in some chamber . . . no, she realized, coming fully awake. She was sleeping in the back of one of the noisy conveyances—a truck, Sam called it. Only it wasn't noisy now.

"We've stopped," said the Dog. She thrust her head out the canvas flap to look around, and her voice became rather muffled. "I think rather unexpectedly."

Lirael sat up and tried to banish the sensation of being recently clubbed on the head and made to drink vinegar. She still had her cold. At least it was no worse, though the Ancelstierran spring had yet to fully flower and winter had not given up its grip on nighttime temperatures.

The stop certainly seemed unexpected, judging from the amount of swearing coming from the driver up front. Then Sam drew back the flap completely from the outside, narrowly escaping a welcoming full-face lick from the Disreputable Dog. He looked tired, and Lirael wondered if he'd been able to sleep after hearing the terrible news about his parents. She'd fallen asleep almost as soon as they'd got in the . . . truck . . . though she had no idea how long she'd been asleep. It didn't feel long, and it was still very dark, the only light coming from the Dog's collar.

"The trucks have stalled," reported Sam. "Though the wind's practically a westerly. I think we're getting too close to the hemispheres. We'll have to walk from here."

"Where are we?" Lirael asked. She stood up too quickly, and her head hit the canvas canopy, just missing one of the steel struts. There was a lot of noise outside now—shouting and the crash of hobnailed boots on the road—but behind all that there was also a constant dull booming. In her half-asleep state, it took a moment for her to understand it wasn't thunder, which she half-expected, but something else.

The Dog jumped out over the tailgate, and Lirael followed, somewhat more sedately. They were still on the Perimeter road, she saw, and it looked like early morning. The moon was up, a slim crescent rather than the nearly full moon of the Old Kingdom. It was subtly different in shape and color, too, Lirael noted. Less silver, and more a pale buttercup yellow.

The booming noise was coming from farther south, and there was a faint whistling with it. Lirael could see bright flashes on the horizon there, but it was not lightning. There was thunder as well, to the west, and the flashes from that direction were definitely lightning. As she looked, Lirael thought she caught the faintest whiff of Free Magic, though the wind was indeed a southerly. And she could sense Dead somewhere up ahead. Not more than a mile away.

"What is that noise, and the lights?" she asked Sam, pointing south. He turned to look but had to step back before he could answer, as soldiers started to trot past the trucks.

"Artillery," he said after a moment. "Big guns. They must be far enough back, so they aren't affected by the Old Kingdom or the hemispheres and can still fire. Um, they're sort of like catapults that throw an exploding device several miles, which hits the ground or blows up in the air and kills people."

"A total waste of time," interrupted Major Greene, who had come puffing up. "You can't hear any shells exploding, can you?

So all they're doing is lobbing what might as well be big rocks over, and even a direct hit with an unexploded shell won't do anything to the Dead. It'll just be a big mess for the ordnance people to clear up. Thousands of UXBs, and most of them white phosphorus. Nasty stuff! Come on!"

The Major puffed on past, with Lirael, the Dog, and Sam following. They left their packs in the trucks, and for a moment Lirael thought Mogget was still asleep in Sam's. Then she saw the little white cat up ahead behind the first double-timing platoon, dashing along the roadside as if he were chasing a mouse. As he pounced, she recognized that was exactly what he was doing. Hunting something to eat.

"Where are we?" asked Lirael as she easily caught up to Major Greene. He looked at her, took a coughing breath, and nodded his head at Lieutenant Tindall, who was up ahead. Lirael got the hint. She ran forward to the younger officer and repeated her question.

"About three miles from the Perimeter's Western Strongpoint," replied Tindall. "Forwin Mill is about sixteen miles south of there, but hopefully we'll be able to stop this Hedge at the Wall—First Platoon, halt!"

The sudden order surprised Lirael, and she ran on a few steps before she saw the soldiers in front had stopped. Lieutenant Tindall barked out some more orders, repeated by a sergeant at the front, and the soldiers ran off to either side of the road, readying their rifles.

"Cavalry, ma'am!" snapped Tindall, taking her arm and urging her to the side of the road. "We don't know whose."

Lirael rejoined Sam and drew her sword. They stared down the road, listening to the beat of hooves on the metaled road. The Dog stared, too, but Mogget played with the mouse he'd caught. It was still alive, and he kept letting it go, only to snap it up after it had run a few feet, holding it frantic and terrified in his partly open mouth.

"Not Dead," pronounced Lirael.

"Or Free Magic," said the Disreputable Dog with a loud sniff. "But very afraid."

They saw the horse and rider a moment later. He was an Ancelstierran soldier, a mounted infantryman, though he had lost his carbine and saber. He shouted as he saw the soldiers.

"Get out of the way! Get out of here!"

He tried to ride on, but the horse shied as soldiers spilled out on the road. Someone grabbed the bridle and brought the horse to a halt. Others dragged the man roughly from the saddle as he tried to slap the horse on with his hands.

"What's going on, man?" asked Major Greene roughly. "What's your name and unit?"

"Trooper 732769 Maculler, sir," replied the man automatically, but his teeth chattered as he spoke, and sweat was pouring down his face. "Fourteenth Light Horse, with the Perimeter Flying Detachment."

"Good. Now tell me what's going on," said the Major.

"Dead, all dead," whispered the man. "We rode in from due south, through the fog. Strange, twisty fog . . . We caught them with these big silver . . . like half oranges, but huge . . . They were putting them on carts, but the draft horses were dead. Only they weren't dead, they moved. The horses were pulling the carts even though they were dead. Everyone dead . . ."

Major Greene shook him, very hard. Lirael put her hand forward as if to stop him, but Sam held her back.

"Report, Trooper Maculler! The situation!"

"They're all dead but me, sir," said Maculler simply. "Me and Dusty fell in the charge. By the time we got up, it was all over. Something made us sick. Maybe there was gas in the fog.

Everyone in the reconaissance troop went down, the horses, too, or running free. Then there were these things lying all around the carts. Bodies, we thought, dead Southerlings, but they got up as we fell. I saw them, swarming over my mates . . . thousands of monsters, horrible monsters. They're coming this way, sir."

"The silver hemispheres," interrupted Lirael urgently. "Which way did the carts go?"

"I don't know," mumbled the man. "They were headed south, straight at us, when we ran into them. I don't know after that."

"Hedge is across and the hemispheres are already on their way to the Lightning Farm," said Lirael to the others. "We have to get there before they do! It's our last chance!"

"How?" asked Sam, his face white. "If they're already across the Wall . . ."

Lieutenant Tindall had the map out and was trying the switch on a small electric flashlight, which failed to work. Suppressing a curse with an apologetic glance at Lirael, he held the map to the moonlight.

As he did, Lirael felt her Death sense twitch, and she looked up. She couldn't see anything down the road ahead, but she knew what was coming. Dead Hands. A very large number of Dead Hands. And there was something else, too. A familiar cold presence. One of the Greater Dead, not a necromancer. It had to be Chlorr.

"They're coming," she said urgently. "Two groups of Hands. About a hundred in front, and a lot more farther back."

The Major barked out orders and soldiers ran in all directions, mostly forward, carrying tripods, machine-guns, and other gear. A medical orderly led Trooper Maculler away, his horse following obediently behind. Lieutenant Tindall shook the map and squinted at it.

"Always on the bloody folds, or where a map joins!" he

cursed. "It looks like we could head southeast from the cross-roads back there, then cut southwest and loop up to Forwin Mill from the south. The trucks might work if we do it that way. We'll have to push them back to start with."

"Get to it then!" roared Major Greene. "Take your platoon to push. We'll hold out here as long as we can."

"Chlorr leads them," said Lirael to Sam and the Dog. "What should we do?"

"We cannot reach the Lightning Farm before Hedge on foot," said Sam quickly. "We could take that man's horse, but only the two of us could ride, and it is sixteen miles in the dark—"

"The horse is done in," interrupted Mogget. He was chewing, and the words weren't very clear. "Couldn't carry two if it wanted to. Which it doesn't."

"So we'll have to go with the soldiers," said Lirael. "Which means holding off Chlorr and the first wave of the Dead long enough to get the trucks pushed back to where they'll work."

She looked down the road past the soldiers, who were kneeling behind a tripod-mounted machine-gun. There was just enough moon- and starlight to make out the road and the stunted bushes on either side, though they were stark and color-less. As she watched, darker shapes blotted out the lighter parts of the landscape. The Dead, shambling close together in an unplanned and unorganized mob. A larger, darker shape was at the fore, and even from several hundred yards away, Lirael could see the fire that burned inside the shadow.

It was Chlorr.

Major Greene saw the Dead, too, and suddenly shouted right near Lirael's ear.

"Company! Two hundred yards at twelve o'clock, Dead things en masse in the road, fire! Fire! Fire!"

His shouts were followed by the mass clicking of triggers, loud even after the shouts. But nothing else happened. There was no sudden assault of sound, no crack of gunfire. Just clicks and muttered exclamations.

"I don't understand," said Greene. "The wind's westerly, and the guns usually work long after the engines stop!"

"The hemispheres," said Sam, with a glance at the Dog, who nodded. "They are a source of Free Magic on their own, and we are close to them. Hedge has probably also worked the wind. We might as well still be in the Old Kingdom, as far as your technology goes."

"Damn! First and Second Platoon, form up on the road, two ranks on the double!" ordered Greene. "Archers at the rear! Gunners, take your bolts and draw your swords!"

There was a sudden bustle as the machine-gunners took the bolts out of their weapons and drew their swords. Lirael drew her sword, too, and after a moment's hesitation Saraneth. She wanted to use Kibeth for some reason—it felt more familiar to her touch—but to deal with Chlorr she would need the authority of the bigger bell.

"I thought it was later than twelve o'clock," she said to Sam as they moved up to take a position in the forward line of soldiers. There were about sixty of them in two lines across the road and out into the fields on either side. The front line all wore mail, and their rifles were fixed with long sword bayonets that shone with silver. The second rank were archers, though Lirael could tell by looking at the way they held their bows that only half of them really knew what they were doing. Their arrows were silvered, too, she noticed with approval. That would help a little against the Dead.

"Um, Major Greene's 'twelve o'clock' meant 'straight ahead'; the time is about two in the morning," replied Sam, after a glance at the night sky. Obviously he knew the Ancelstierran stars as well as the Old Kingdom ones, for the heavens here meant nothing to Lirael.

"Front rank kneel!" ordered Major Greene. He stood at the front with Lirael and Sam and cast a sideways glance at the Disreputable Dog, who was growing to her full fighting size. The soldiers next to the hound shifted nervously, even as they knelt and set their bayoneted rifles out at a forty-five degree angle, so the front rank was a thicket of spears.

"Archers stand ready!"

The archers nocked arrows but did not draw. The Dead were approaching at a steady pace, but they were not close enough for Lirael and Sam to make out individuals in the dark other than Chlorr. The clicking of their bones could be heard, and the shuffle of many misshapen feet upon the road.

Lirael felt the tension and fear in the soldiers around her. The drawn-in breaths that were not released. The nervous shifting of feet and the fussing with equipment. The silence after the Major's shouted orders. It would not take much to set them fleeing for their lives.

"They've stopped," said the Dog, her keen eyes cutting through the night.

Lirael peered ahead. Sure enough, the dark mass did seem to have stopped, and the red glint from Chlorr was moving sideways rather than ahead.

"Trying to outflank us?" asked the Major. "I wonder why."

"No," said Sam. He could sense the much larger group of Dead farther back. "She's waiting for the second lot of Dead. Close to a thousand, I'd say."

He spoke softly, but there was a ripple among the nearer soldiers at his last words, a ripple that went slowly through both lines as his words were repeated.

"Quiet!" ordered Greene. "Sergeant! Take that man's name!"

"Sir!" confirmed several sergeants. Most of them had just been whispering themselves, and none made even a show of writing something in their field notebooks.

"We can't wait," said Lirael anxiously. "We have to get to the Lightning Farm!"

"We can't turn our backs on this lot either," said Greene. He bent close, the Charter Mark on his forehead glowing softly as it responded to the Charter Magic in the Dog, and whispered, "The men are close to breaking. They're not Scouts, not used to this sort of thing."

Lirael nodded. She gritted her teeth, marking a moment of indecision, then stepped out from the front rank.

"I'll take the fight to Chlorr," she declared. "If I can defeat her, the Hands may wander off or go back to Hedge. They'll fight badly, anyway."

"You're not going without me," said the Dog. She stepped forward, too, with an excited bark, a bark that echoed out across the night. There was something strange about that bark. It made everyone's hair stand on end, and the bell in Lirael's hand chimed quietly before she could still it. Both sounds made the soldiers even jumpier.

"Or me," said Sam stoutly. He stepped forward as well, his sword bright with Charter marks, his cupped left hand glowing with a prepared spell.

"I'll come and watch," said Mogget. "Maybe you'll scare a couple of mice out of their holes."

"If you'll let an old man fight with you—" Greene began, but Lirael shook her head.

"You stay here, Major," she said, and her voice was not that of a young woman but of an Abhorsen about to deal with the Dead. "Protect our rear."

"Yes, ma'am," said Major Greene. He saluted and stepped back into the line.

Lirael walked ahead, the gravel of the road crunching under her feet. The Disreputable Dog was at her right hand and Sam on her left. Mogget, a swift white shape, ran along the roadside, darting backwards and forwards, presumably in search of more mice to torment.

The Dead did not move towards Lirael as she marched on, but as she got closer, she saw they were spreading out, moving into the fields to present a broader front. Chlorr waited on the road, a tall shape, darker than the night save for her burning eyes. Lirael could feel the Greater Dead's presence like a chill hand upon the back of her neck.

When they were about fifty yards away, Lirael stopped, the Dog and Sam a half step behind her. She held Saraneth high, so the bell shone silver in the moonlight, the Charter marks glowing and moving upon the metal.

"Chlorr of the Mask," shouted Lirael, "return to Death!"

She flipped the bell, catching it by the handle and ringing it at the same time. Saraneth boomed out across the night, the Dead Hands flinching as the sound hit them. But it was for Chlorr the bell sounded, and all Lirael's power and attention were focused on that spirit.

Chlorr raised her shadow-bladed sword above her head and screamed back in defiance. Yet the scream was drowned in the continued tolling of the bell, and Chlorr took a step back even as she brandished her sword.

"Return to Death!" ordered Lirael, walking forward, swinging Saraneth in slow loops that were straight out of a page of *The Book of the Dead* that now shone so brightly in her mind. "Your time is over!"

Chlorr hissed and took another step backwards. Then a new

sound joined the bell. A peremptory bark, impossibly sustained, stretching on and on, sharper and higher pitched than Saraneth's deep voice. Chlorr raised her sword as if to parry the sounds but took two more steps back. Confused Dead Hands staggered out of her way, gobbling their distress from their decayed throats.

Sam's arm circled in an overarm bowling motion, and golden fire suddenly exploded on and around Chlorr and splashed onto the Hands, who screamed and writhed as it ate into their Dead flesh.

Then a small white shape suddenly appeared almost at Chlorr's feet. A cat, capering on its hind feet, batting at the air in front of the Greater Dead spirit.

"Run! Run away, Chlorr No-Face!" laughed Mogget. "The Abhorsen comes to send you beyond the Ninth Gate!"

Chlorr swung at the cat, who nimbly leapt aside as the blade swept past. Then the Greater Dead thing turned the swing into a leap, a great leap across thirty feet over the heads of the Dead Hands behind her. Transforming as she leapt, she became a great raven-shaped cloud of darkness that sped across the fields to the north, to the Wall and safety, pursued by the sound of Saraneth and the bark of the Dog.

Chapter Nineteen

A TIN OF SARDINES

As Chlorr fled, the mass of Dead Hands erupted like an anthill splashed with hot water. They ran in all directions, the most stupid of them towards Lirael, Sam, and the Dog. Mogget ran between their legs, laughing, as Charter Magic fire burnt through their sinews and sent them crashing to the ground, the Dog's barking sent their spirits back into Death, and Saraneth commanded them to relinquish their bodies.

In a few mad minutes, it was all over. The echoes of bell and bark died away, leaving Lirael and her companions standing on an empty road under the moon and stars, surrounded by a hundred bodies that were no more than empty husks.

The silence was broken by cheering and yelling from the soldiers behind them. Lirael ignored it and called out to Mogget.

"Why did you tell Chlorr to run? We were winning! And what was that No-Face thing about?"

"It was quicker, which I thought was the point," said Mogget. He went up to Sam's feet and sat there, yawning. "Chlorr was always overcautious, even when she was an A— alive. I'm tired now. Can you carry me?"

Sam sighed. He sheathed his sword and picked the cat up, letting the little beast rest in the crook of his arm.

"It *was* quicker," he said to Lirael apologetically. "And I hate to mention it, but there are a lot more Dead Hands coming . . . and Shadow Hands, unless I'm mistaken. . . ."

"You're not mistaken," growled the Dog. She was looking suspiciously at Mogget. "Though like my Mistress, I am not satisfied with the Mogget's motivation or explanation, I suggest we leave immediately. We have little time."

As if in answer to her words, the sound of truck engines came from down the road. Obviously Lieutenant Tindall and his men had pushed them back far enough, and they could start again.

"I hope we can loop around," said Sam anxiously as they ran to the trucks. "If the wind changes again, we'll be stranded even farther away."

"We could try and work it . . ." Lirael began. Then she shook her head. "No, of course not. That would only make it worse for the Ancelstierran . . . what do you call it? Technologia?"

"Close enough," puffed Sam. "Come on!"

They had caught up with Major Greene and the rear platoon, who were double-timing back to the trucks. The Major beamed at them as they matched his pace, and several soldiers slapped their rifles in salute. The atmosphere was very different from what it had been only a few minutes before.

Lieutenant Tindall was waiting by the lead truck, studying the map once again, this time with the aid of a working electric flashlight. He looked up and saluted as Lirael, Sam, and Major Greene approached.

"I've found a road that will work," he said quickly. "I think we might even be able to beat Hedge there!"

"How?" asked Lirael urgently.

"Well, the only road south from the Western Strongpoint winds up through these hills here," he said, pointing. "It's a single lane and not even metaled. Heavily laden wagons—as Maculler described them to me—will take a day at least to get up through there. They can't possibly be at the Mill before late afternoon!"

We can be there soon after dawn."

"Good work, Tindall," exclaimed the Major, clapping him on the back.

"Is there any other way the hemispheres could be taken to the Mill?" asked Sam. "This has all been planned so carefully by Hedge. In both the Kingdom and here . . . everything was prepared. Using the Southerlings to make more Dead, the wagons ready . . ."

Tindall looked at the map again. The flashlight beam darted in several directions over it as he thought about possible alternatives.

"Well," he said finally, "I suppose they could take the hemispheres by wagon to the sea, load them on boats, and take them south and then up the loch to the old dock at the Mill. But there's nowhere to load them near the Western Strongpoint—"

"Yes there is," said the Major, suddenly grim again. He pointed at a single symbol on the map, a vertical stroke surrounded by four angled strokes. "There's a Navy dock at the Western Light."

"That's what Hedge will be doing," said Lirael, suddenly chill with certainty. "How quickly can they go by sea?"

"Loading the hemispheres would take a while," said Sam, joining the cluster of heads bent over the map. "And they'll have to sail, not steam. But Hedge will work the wind. I'd say less than eight hours."

There was a moment of silence after his words; then by unspoken consent, the huddle exploded into action. Greene snatched the map and hauled himself up into the cab of the first truck, Lirael and her companions ran to the back to jump in, and Lieutenant Tindall ran along the road waving his hand and shouting, "Go! Go!" as the trucks revved higher and slowly began to move out, their headlights flickering as the engines took the strain.

In the back of the truck, Sam put Mogget on top of his many-times-mended pack and sat down next to it. As he did, he pulled a small metal container out of his belt pouch and set it next to the cat's nose. For a few seconds, the cat appeared to be sound asleep. Then one green eye opened a fraction.

"What's that?" asked Mogget.

"Sardines," said Sam. "I knew they were standard rations, so I got a few tins for you."

"What are sardines?" asked Mogget suspiciously. "And why is there a key? Is this some sort of Abhorsen joke?"

In answer Sam tore the key off and slowly unwound the top of the tin. The rich smell of sardines spilled out. Mogget watched the procedure avidly, his eyes never leaving the tin. When Sam put it down, narrowly avoiding cutting himself as the truck went over a series of bumps, Mogget sniffed the sardines cautiously.

"Why are you giving me this?"

"You like fish," said Sam. "Besides, I said I would."

Mogget tore his gaze away from the sardines and looked at Sam. His eyes narrowed, but he saw no sign of guile in Sam's face. The little cat shook his head and then ate the sardines in a flash, leaving the tin spotless and empty.

Lirael and the Dog glanced at this exhibition of gluttony, but both were more interested in what was going on outside and behind them. Lirael pushed aside the canvas flap, and they looked past the three following trucks. Lirael could sense the second, much larger group of Dead and Shadow Hands that was advancing along the road. The Shadow Hands, which were both more powerful than the Dead Hands and unconstrained by flesh, were moving very swiftly, some of them leaping and gliding like enormous bats ahead of the main body of their shambling, corpse-dwelling brethren. They would undoubtedly wreak great trouble somewhere, but she could not spare them any further thought.

The greater danger lay to the west, and already a little south, where lightning played on the horizon. Lirael noticed that the other, artificial thunder from the Ancelstierran artillery had ceased some time before, but she had been too busy to hear it stop.

"Dog," whispered Lirael. She drew the Dog closer and hugged her about the neck. "Dog. What if we're too late to destroy the Lightning Farm? What if the hemispheres join?"

The Dog didn't say anything. She snuffled at Lirael's ear instead and thumped her tail on the truck floor.

"I have to go into Death, don't I?" whispered Lirael. "To use the Dark Mirror and find out how It was bound in the Beginning."

Still the Dog didn't speak.

"Will you come with me?" asked Lirael, her whisper so low no human could have heard it.

"Yes," said the Dog. "Wherever you walk, I will be there."

"When should we go?" asked Lirael.

"Not yet," muttered the Dog. "Not until there is no other choice. Perhaps we will still reach the Lightning Farm before Hedge."

"I hope so," said Lirael. She hugged the Dog again, then let her go and settled back onto her own pack. Sam was already asleep on the opposite side of the truck, with Mogget curled up against him, the empty sardine tin sliding about on the wooden floor of the truck. Lirael picked it up, wrinkled her nose, and wedged it into a corner where it wouldn't rattle.

"I will keep watch," said the Disreputable Dog. "You should sleep, Mistress. There are still several hours before the dawn, and you will need all your strength."

"I don't think I can sleep," said Lirael quietly. But she leaned back on her pack and closed her eyes. Her whole body felt edgy, and if she had been able to, she would have got up and practiced with her sword, or done something to try to drain the feeling off with exercise. But there was nothing she could do in the back of a moving vehicle. Except lie there and worry about what lay ahead. So she did that, and surprisingly soon crossed the line between wakeful worrying and troubled sleep.

The Dog lay with her head on her paws and watched Lirael toss and turn, and mumble in her sleep. Beneath them, the truck rattled and vibrated, the roar of the engine going up and down as the vehicle negotiated bends and rises and falls in the road.

After an hour or so, Mogget opened one eye. He saw the Dog watching and quickly shut it again. The Dog quietly got up and stalked over, pushing her snout down right against Mogget's little pink nose.

"Tell me why I shouldn't take you by the scruff of your neck and throw you off right now," whispered the Dog.

Mogget opened one untroubled eye again.

"I'd only run behind," he whispered back. "Besides, She gave me the benefit of the doubt. Can you do anything less?"

"I am not so charitable," said the Dog, showing her teeth. "Let me remind you that should you turn, I will make it my business to see that you are ended for it."

"Will you?" purred Mogget, opening his other eye. "What if you can't?"

The Dog growled, low and menacing. It was enough to wake Sam, who blinked and reached for his sword.

"What is it?" he asked sleepily.

"Nothing," said the Dog. She turned back to Lirael and plonked herself down with a frustrated sigh. "Nothing to worry about. Go back to sleep."

Mogget smiled and shook his head, the miniature Ranna tinkling. Sam yawned mightily at the sound and slipped back against his pack, asleep again in an instant.

⊕♣⊕

Nicholas Sayre swam into wakefulness like a fish rising to a fly. A slow ascent that left him gasping and confused, flopping about like that same fish fresh caught on the shores of a loch—which was where he was. He sat up and looked around. Some part of his mind was comforted by the fact that he was in a twilight world made by the storm clouds above him and that lightning was crackling down less than fifty yards away. He was less interested in the pallid half sun in the east, just rising above the ridge.

Nicholas was lying on a pile of straw next to a hut, off to one side of what had once been an active wharf. Twenty yards away Hedge's men swore and cursed as they wrestled with sheer-legs, ropes, and pulleys to swing one of the silver hemispheres ashore from a small coastal trader. Another coaster stood off the wharf, several hundred yards into the loch, carefully positioned not to get close enough for the hemispheres to work their violent repulsion on each other.

Nicholas smiled. They were at Forwin Mill. He couldn't remember how they had done it, but they had got the hemispheres across the Wall. The Lightning Farm was ready, and all they had to do was join the hemispheres and everything would fall into place.

Thunder cracked, and someone screamed. A man fell away from the boat, his skin blackened and hair on fire. He lay on the dock, writhing and groaning till one of the other men stepped down and quickly cut his throat. Nick watched it all happen quite calmly. It was just the price of dealing with the hemispheres, and they were all that mattered.

Slowly, Nick got up, first to all fours, and then fully upright. It was hard work, and he had to clutch at the broken drainpipe of the hut for a while, till the dizziness passed. But slowly he grew steadier. Another man died as he stood there, but Nick didn't even notice. He had eyes only for the sheen of the hemispheres and the progression of the work. Soon the first hemisphere would be ready to be shifted into the ruined shell of the timber mill. It would be loaded into a special cradle mounted on a waiting railway wagon, one of two on the same short stretch of track.

At least that was what Nicholas had ordered. It occurred to him that he hadn't actually inspected the Lightning Farm. He had drawn the plans and paid for its construction before leaving for the Old Kingdom. That seemed like a very long time ago. He had never seen the Lightning Farm in actuality. Only in paper plans, and in his troubled dreams.

He was still weak from the illness he'd picked up across the Wall, too weak to easily walk around. He needed a stick or a crutch. There was a stretcher nearby, a simple thing of canvas and wood. Perhaps he could pull out one of the poles and use that as a staff, Nick thought. Very slowly and with infinite care, he walked over to the stretcher, cursing his weakness as he nearly fell. He knelt down and removed the pole, dragging it out of the canvas loops. It was easily eight feet long, and a bit heavy, but it would be better than nothing.

He was about to use it to stand up when he saw something glowing on the stretcher. A piece of splintered wood, painted with strange luminous symbols. Puzzled, he reached out to pick it up.

As he touched it, his body convulsed and he was violently sick. But even as he vomited, he kept one finger on what he now knew was a fragment of a wind flute. He couldn't pick it up, for his hand refused to obey him and close, but he could touch it. As long as he touched it, memory came rushing back. As long as he touched it, he was really Nicholas Sayre and not some puppet of the shining hemispheres so close by.

"Word of a Sayre," he whispered, remembering Lirael again. "I must stop this."

He stayed crouched over the pole, over his own vomit, just touching the fragment, while his mind worked fiercely at his predicament. As soon as he let the charm go, he would regress, go back to being a mindless servant. He could not pick it up or carry it in his hands. Yet there had to be some way he could keep it close enough to work its magic, to remind him who he was.

Nick inspected himself. He was both shocked and scared by how thin he had become, and by the blue and purple bruising that extended all down the left side of his chest. His shirt was merely threads and tatters, and his trousers were not much better, secured at his skinny waist not by a belt but by a piece of tarred rope. The pockets were gone, as were his underclothes.

But the cuffs on his trousers were still turned up. Nick felt in them with his right hand, making sure they would hold. The fine woolen cloth was thinner than it had been only weeks before, but it would not easily tear.

Panting with the effort, he maneuvered his ankle as close to the wind flute fragment as he could, pulled the cuff open, and used his other hand to sweep the chunk of wood toward it. It took a couple of attempts, but finally he got it in. As he did, he forgot what he was doing, till a few seconds later the trouser cuff hit against his skin. Pain shot through his ankle, but it was bearable.

He didn't want to look at the hemispheres, but he found himself doing so anyway. The first one was on the wharf. Many people were swarming about it, tying new ropes for dragging and untying the ones used to swing it ashore. Nick saw that many of the workers grabbing the landward ropes were Night Crew again. Somewhat better-looking ones, though still rotting under their blue hats and scarves.

No, Nick thought, as the wooden charm slapped against his

ankle. They were not diseased humans but Dead creatures, corpses brought into a semblance of life by Hedge. Unlike the normal men, they did not seem troubled by close proximity to the hemispheres, or by the constant lightning.

As if even thinking his name summoned Hedge, in the after-flash of the most recent lightning strike, the necromancer suddenly appeared at the side of the hemisphere. Once again Nick was surprised by how monstrous Hedge had become. Shadows crawled across his skull, twining into the fire deep in his eyes, and his fingers dripped with red, viscous flames.

The necromancer walked to the bow of the coaster and shouted something. Men moved quickly to obey, though it was clear they were nearly all wounded in some way, or sick. They cast off and raised sail, and the boat slid away from the wharf. The other, loaded coaster immediately began to make its approach.

Hedge watched it come in and raised his hands above his head. Then he spoke, harsh words that made the air ripple around him and the ground shiver. He stretched out one hand towards the waters of the loch and called again, making gestures that left after-trails of red fire in the air.

Fog began to rise out of the loch. Thin white tendrils spiraled up and up, dragging thicker trails of mist behind them. Hedge gestured to the right and left, and the tendrils spread sideways, dragging more fog up out of the water to form a wall that slowly extended down the full length of the loch. As it spread sideways, it also rolled forward, towards the wharf, the timber mill, the loch valley, and the hills beyond.

Hedge clapped his hands and turned back. His eyes fell on Nick, who instantly looked down and clutched at his chest. He heard the necromancer approach, his heels loud on the wooden planks.

"Hemispheres," mumbled Nick quickly as the footsteps

stopped in front of him. "The hemispheres must . . . we must . . ."

"All progresses well," said Hedge. "I have raised a sea fog that will resist any attempts to move it, should there be any amongst our enemies skilled enough to try. Do you wish to instruct me further, Master?"

Nick felt something move in his chest. Like a panicked heartbeat, only stronger and much more frightening and repulsive. He gasped at the pain of it and fell forward, his hands scrabbling at the planks, fingernails breaking as he tore at the wood.

Hedge waited till the spasm subsided. Nick lay there panting, unable to speak, waiting for unconsciousness and the thing within him to take over. But it did not rise, and after several minutes Hedge walked away.

Nick rolled onto his back and watched the fog roll across the sky, blanketing out the storm clouds, though not the lightning. Fog lit by lightning was not a sight he had ever expected to see, he thought, some part of him making notes at the strange effects.

But the greater part of his mind was given over to something much more important. He had to stop Hedge from using the Lightning Farm.

Chapter Twenty

THE BEGINNING OF THE END

D AWN WAS BREAKING as the truck engines began to cough and splutter once again, then ground to a halt. Lieutenant Tindall swore as his red Chinagraph pencil slipped, and the dot he was making on the map became a line, which he turned into a cross. The cross was marked on the thickly clustered contour lines that marked the descent into Forvale, a broad valley that was separated from Forwin Loch and the mill by a long, low ridge.

Lirael had fallen asleep again as the trucks had driven through the night. So she had missed the small dramas that filled the hours as the trucks sped on, not stopping for anything, the drivers pushing much faster than common sense allowed. But they had good luck, or made their own, and there had been no major accidents. Plenty of minor collisions, scrapes, and scares, but no major accidents.

Lirael was also unaware of the desertions during the night. Every time the trucks had slowed to negotiate a sharp bend, or had been forced to stop before crawling across a washed-out section of what was a very secondary road, soldiers who could not face the prospect of further encounters with the Dead leapt from the trucks and disappeared into the darkness. The company had more than a hundred men when it left the Perimeter. By the time they came to Forvale, there were only seventy-three left.

"Debus! On the double!"

The Company Sergeant-Major's shouts woke Lirael. She jerked up, one hand already scrabbling at a bell, the other on Nehima. Sam reacted in a very similar way. Disoriented and scared, he stumbled towards the tailgate, right behind the Disreputable Dog, who jumped out a moment later.

"Five-minute rest! Five minutes! Do your business and be quick about it! No brew-ups!"

Lirael climbed out of the truck, yawned, and rubbed her eyes. It was still half dark, the eastern sky light beyond the ridge but without any sign of the actual sun. Most of the sky was beginning to turn blue, save for a patch not far away that was dark and threatening. Lirael saw it out of the corner of her eye, turned swiftly, and had her worst fears realized. Lightning flashed in the cloud. Lots of lightning, more than ever before, and it was striking down across a wider area. All beyond the ridge.

"Forwin Loch, and the mill," said Major Greene. "They lie beyond that ridge. What the—"

They had all been looking across to the ridge. Now Greene pointed down into the valley that lay between them. It was lush green farmland, divided into regular five-acre fields by wire fences. Sheep occupied some of the fields. But on the southern end of the valley there was a moving mass of blue. Thousands of people, a great crowd of blue-scarved and blue-hatted Southerlings, a huge migration all across the valley.

Greene and Tindall had their binoculars to their eyes in a flash. But Lirael did not need binoculars to see which way the great crowd was heading. The leading groups were already turning to the west, to the ridge and Forwin Mill beyond. To the Lightning Farm, where from the look of the storm the hemispheres were already in place.

"We have to stop them!" said Sam. He was pointing at the Southerlings.

"It is more important to stop the hemispheres from being joined," said Lirael. She hesitated for a second, unsure of what to do or say. Only one course seemed obvious. They had to get up on the western ridge to see what was happening beyond it, and that meant crossing the valley as quickly as possible. "We need to get up on that ridge! Come on!"

She started off down the road into the valley, jogging slowly at first but slowly increasing her speed. The Dog ran at her side, her tongue lolling out. Sam followed a half minute later, Mogget riding on his shoulders. Major Greene and Lieutenant Tindall were slower, but they were both soon bellowing orders, and the soldiers were running back from the ditch on the side of the road and forming up.

The road was more of a track, but once down the hill it cut straight through the fields, crossed the stream in the center of the valley at a concrete ford or sunken bridge, and then ran along the side of the ridge.

Lirael ran as she had never run before. A lone figure, she splashed across the ford and cut in front of the Southerlings. Closer to, she saw that they were in family groups, often of many generations. Hundreds of families. Grandparents, parents, children, babies. They all had the same scared look on their faces, and nearly everyone, no matter how old or small, was weighed down with suitcases, bags, and small bundles. Some had strange possessions, small machines and metal objects that Lirael did not know but Sam recognized as sewing machines, phonographs, and typewriters. Strangely, nearly all the adults also clutched small pieces of paper.

"They must not be allowed to cross the ridge," said the Dog as Lirael slowed to look at them. "But we must not stop. I fear the lightning is increasing."

Lirael halted for a second and turned back. Sam was about

fifty yards behind, running with grim determination.

"Sam!" Lirael shouted. She indicated the Southerlings, who were starting to turn towards the ridge. Some younger men were already climbing the slope. "Stop them! I'm going on!"

Lirael began to run again, ignoring the pain from an incipient stitch in her side. With every forward step it seemed to her that the lightning beyond the ridge was spreading, and the thunder was growing louder and more frequent. Lirael left the road and began to zigzag up a long spur that ran up to the ridge. To help her along, she grabbed at stones and the branches of the white-barked trees that were dotted along the slope.

She could feel the Dead beyond the ridge as she climbed. No more than a score at first, but at least a dozen more appeared as she climbed. Obviously Hedge was bringing spirits in from Death. He must have found a source of corpses somewhere. Lirael did not think they would be Shadow Hands, for it took longer to prepare a spirit for Life if there was no flesh to house it in. At least it was supposed to take longer. Lirael was afraid that she had no idea what Hedge was capable of.

Then, without warning, she was on top of the ridge and there were no more white-barked trees, no great boulders. She could see clearly down the bare western slope to the blue waters of the loch. The hillside had been totally cleared, swept clean as if by fire and a giant broom, leaving only furrowed brown dirt. But the dirt had sprouted a strange crop. Slender metal poles, twice Lirael's height. Hundreds of them, spaced six feet apart, and joined at the roots by fat black cables that snaked down the slope and into a ramshackle stone building that had lost its roof. Parallel metal lines laid on top of many short wooden beams formed a track of some sort. They ran on the ground through the building, ending abruptly twenty yards on either side of it. There were two flatbed metal-wheeled wagons on the line, one at each end. Lirael instinctively knew that these were for the hemispheres. They would be mounted on the wagons and somehow be brought together by using the power of the lightning storm.

Lightning flashed as if to punctuate her thoughts. It came forking down all around the quay, so bright that Lirael had to shield her eyes with her hand. She knew what she would see there, because she could smell the hot-metal scent, the corrosive smell of Free Magic. It turned her stomach, and she was thankful that she hadn't eaten for hours.

One of the silver hemispheres was already on the quay. It flashed blue as the lightning struck it. The other hemisphere was on a boat out on the loch. Though most of the lightning was hitting the hemispheres, Lirael saw that it was also spreading out and up the slope, and most of the strikes hit the tall poles. They were lightning rods, the thousand lightning rods that together made up Nicholas's Lightning Farm.

As if the dark clouds above were not enough, fog was beginning to swirl off the loch. Lirael could sense this was a magical fog, built with real water, so it would be much harder to force back or dispel. She felt the Free Magic working in it, and the source of it. Hedge was somewhere down on the quay. There were Dead down there with him, moving the first hemisphere, and there were more Dead around the various small buildings that lined the quay. Lirael could sense them moving about, with Hedge at the center of everything. She felt like a fly on the edge of a cobweb, feeling the movement of the great mother spider at the center and its many offspring farther around the web.

Lirael drew Nehima, and then after a moment's hesitation her hand fell on Astarael. The Weeper. All who heard her would be thrown into Death, including Lirael. If she could get close enough, she could send Hedge and all the Dead a long, long way.

Hedge, at least, would probably be able to return to Life, but there was a slim chance Lirael could return as well, and it would gain her precious time.

But as she started to draw the bell out of the bandolier, the Dog jumped up against her and pushed Lirael's hand away with her nose.

"No, Mistress," she said. "Astarael alone cannot prevail here. We are too late to prevent the hemispheres from being joined."

"Sam, the soldiers . . ." said Lirael. "If we attack at once—"

"I do not think we would easily pass through this Lightning Farm," said the Dog, shaking her head. "The Destroyer's power is less constrained here, and the Destroyer is directing the lightning. Besides, the Dead here are led by Hedge, not Chlorr."

"But if the hemispheres join . . ." Lirael whispered to herself. Then she swallowed and said, "It's time, isn't it?"

"Yes," said the Dog. "But not here. Hedge will have noticed us, as we have noticed him. His mind is on the hemispheres for the moment, but I do not think it will be long before he orders an attack."

Lirael turned to retreat back down the eastern side of the ridge, then stopped and looked back.

"Nicholas? What about him?"

"He is beyond our help now," replied the Dog sadly. "When the hemispheres join, the shard within him will burst from his heart to become part of the whole. But he will know nothing of it. It will be a swift end, though I fear Hedge will enslave his spirit."

"Poor Nick," said Lirael. "I should never have let him go."

"You had no choice," said the Dog. She nudged Lirael behind the knee, anxious to make her move. "We must hurry!"

Lirael nodded and turned back to retrace her path down the slope. As she hurried down, sliding and almost falling in the steeper parts, she thought of Nicholas and then of everyone else, including herself. Perhaps Nick would have the easiest path. After all, it was likely he would be only the first to die, unknowing. Everyone else would be only too aware of their fate, and they would probably all end up serving Hedge.

Lirael was halfway down when an enormously loud, booming voice filled the valley. It shocked her for a second, till she recognized it was Sam, his speech greatly magnified by Charter Magic. He was standing on a large boulder only a hundred yards or so farther down the spur, his hands cupped around his mouth, his fingers glowing from the spell.

"Southerlings! Friends! Do not go beyond the western ridge! Only death awaits you there! Do not believe the papers you hold—they offer only lies! I am Prince Sameth of the Old Kingdom, and I promise to give land and farms to everyone who stays in the valley! If you stay in the valley, you will be given farms and land beyond the Wall!"

Sam repeated his message as Lirael panted to a stop next to his boulder. Below it, Major Greene's men were strung out in a long line along the bottom of the ridge. The Southerlings were gathered beyond that line, overlapping it by several hundred yards at the southern end. Most of them had stopped to listen to Sam, but a few were still climbing up the ridge.

Sam stopped talking and jumped down.

"Best I can do," he said anxiously. "It might stop some of them. If they even understood what I was saying."

"Nothing else we can do," said Major Greene. "We can't shoot the beggars, and they'd overwhelm us if we tried to stop them with just the bayonet. I'd like a word with the police who were supposed to be—"

"One of the hemispheres is already ashore, and the other is close behind," interrupted Lirael, her news provoking instant attention. "Hedge is there, and he is raising a fog and creating many more Dead. The Lightning Farm is also beginning to work, and the Destroyer is calling down and directing the lightning."

"We'd best attack at once," said Major Greene. He started to take a breath to shout, but Lirael interrupted him again.

"No," she said. "We can't get through the Lightning Farm, and there are too many Dead. We cannot stop the hemispheres from joining now."

"But that's . . . that means we've lost," said Sam. "Everything. The Destroyer—"

"No," snapped Lirael. "I'm going into Death, to use the Dark Mirror. The Destroyer was bound and broken in the Beginning. Once I find out how it was done, we can do it again. But you will have to protect my body until I can come back, and Hedge is sure to attack."

As she spoke, Lirael looked firmly into Sam's eyes, then Major Greene's and the two Lieutenants', Tindall and Gotley. She hoped some sort of confidence was being transferred. She had to believe that there was an answer in Death, in the past. Some secret that would let them defeat Orannis.

"The Dog is coming with me," she said. "Where's Mogget?"

"Here!" said a voice near her feet. Lirael looked down and saw Mogget in the shadow of the boulder, licking the second of two empty sardine tins.

"I thought he might as well have them," said Sam quietly, with a shrug.

"Mogget! Help in any way you can," ordered Lirael.

"Any way I can," confirmed Mogget with a sly smile. His confirmation sounded almost like a question.

Lirael looked around, then strode to the middle of a ring of lichen-covered stones, where the spur rose slightly again after coming down the ridge. She checked that the Dark Mirror was in her belt pouch. Then she drew Nehima and Saraneth. This time she held the bell by the handle, straight down. It could sound more easily by accident but also could be more quickly used.

"I'll go into Death here," she said. "I'm depending on you to protect me. I'll be back as soon as I can."

"Do you want me to come with you?" asked Sam. He took out the panpipes and gripped the hilt of his sword. Lirael could tell he meant what he said.

"No," said Lirael. "I think you'll have enough to do here. Hedge is not going to leave us alone on his doorstep. Can't you feel the Dead on the move? We will be attacked here soon, and someone has to protect my living self while I am in Death. I charge you with that, Prince Sameth. If you have time, cast a diamond of protection."

Sam nodded gravely and said, "Yes, Aunt Lirael."

"Aunt?" asked Lieutenant Tindall, but Lirael hardly heard him. She carefully squatted down and hugged the Disreputable Dog, fighting back the terrible feeling that it might be the last time she would feel soft dog hair against her living cheek.

"Even if I do find out how the Seven bound the Destroyer, how can *we* do it?" she whispered in the Dog's ear, so softly no one else could hear. "How can we?"

The Disreputable Dog looked at her with sad brown eyes but didn't answer. Lirael matched her gaze and then smiled, a rueful, bittersweet smile.

"We've come a long way from the Glacier, haven't we?" she said. "Now we're going farther still."

She stood up and reached out to Death. As the chill sank into her bones, she heard Sam say something, and a distant shout. But the sounds faded, as did the light of day. Lifting her sword, Lirael strode into Death, her faithful hound at her heels.

Sam's death sense twitched. Lirael's breath steamed out, and frost formed on her mouth and nose. The Disreputable Dog stepped forward at her side and disappeared, leaving a momentary outline of golden light that slowly faded into nothing.

"Nick! What about Nick!" Sam suddenly called. He hit himself in the head and swore. "I should have asked!"

"Movement on the ridge!" someone called out, and there was a general flurry of activity. Tindall and Gotley ran to their platoons, and Major Greene shouted orders. The Southerlings, who had sat down to listen to Sam, stood up. Individual Southerlings began to climb up the ridge; then there was a general surge forward by the whole huge crowd of people.

At the same time, there was a sudden increase of lightning beyond the ridge, and the thunder rolled in, louder and more constant.

"I'm going to close the company in," shouted Greene. "We'll form an all-around defense here."

Sam nodded. He could sense Dead moving beyond the ridge. Fifty or sixty Dead Hands, headed their way.

"There are Dead coming," he said. He looked up at the ridge, then back at Lirael and at the Southerlings beyond. They were all starting to trudge forward, towards the ridge, not farther back into the valley. The soldiers were already running back towards the spur, the line contracting. There was nothing between the Southerlings and their doom.

"Damn!" swore Greene. "I thought you'd stopped them!"

"I'm going to talk to them!" declared Sam, making an instant decision. The Dead were at least five minutes away, and Lirael had charged him earlier to stop the Southerlings. She would not be in danger if he was quick. "I'll be back in a few minutes. Major Greene, do not leave Lirael! Mogget, protect her!"

With that, he ran down towards a particular group of Southerlings he'd seen before but hadn't really registered as important till a moment before, when he was struck by a sudden thought. The group was led by an ancient matriarch, white haired and much better dressed than everyone around her. She was also supported by several younger men and women. It was the only group that was not obviously a family, without children and without baggage. The matriarch was the leader, Sam thought. He knew that much about the Southerlings. Someone who might be able to turn back the human tide.

If only he could convince her in the next few minutes. When the Dead attacked, anything could happen. The Southerlings might panic, and many would run the wrong way and be trampled. Or they might refuse the evidence of their own eyes and continue blindly on over the ridge, driven by optimism and hope that finally they would find somewhere to call home.

Chapter Twenty-One

DEEPER INTO DEATH

LIRAEL DIDN'T PAUSE to look around as she entered Death and the current gripped her, trying to drag her under in that first shocking instant of total cold. She pushed forward at once as the Disreputable Dog bounded ahead, sniffing the river for any hint of lurking Dead.

As Lirael waded, she anxiously ran through the key lessons she had learned from *The Book of the Dead* and *The Book of Remembrance and Forgetting*. Their pages shone in her mind, telling her about each of the Nine Precincts and the secrets of the Nine Gates. But knowing these secrets—even from a magical book—was not the same as having experienced them. And Lirael had never been past the First Precinct, never even crossed the First Gate.

Nevertheless, she strode forward confidently, forcing her doubts as far back in her mind as they would go. Death was no place for doubts. The river would be quick to attack any weakness, for it was only strength of will that kept the current from sucking away Lirael's spirit. If she faltered, the waters would take her under, and all would be lost.

She came to the First Gate surprisingly quickly. One minute it had been a distant roar and a far-off wall of mist that stretched as far as she could see to the left and right. Now, what seemed only a moment later, Lirael was standing close enough to touch the mist, and the roar of the rapids on the other side was very loud.

Words came to her then, words of power impressed on her mind by both books. She spoke them, feeling the Free Magic writhe and sizzle on her tongue and lips as the words flew out of her mouth.

The veil of mist parted as she spoke, slowly rolling aside to reveal a series of waterfalls that seemed to drop down forever into a dark and endless chasm. Lirael spoke again and gestured to right and left with her sword. A path appeared, cut deep into the waterfall, like a narrow pass between two liquid mountains. Lirael stepped onto the path, the Dog so close that she was almost tangled up in Lirael's legs. As they walked, the mist closed up, and the path faded behind them.

After they'd gone on, a very small, sneaking spirit rose from the water near the First Gate and began to walk towards Life, following an almost invisible black thread connected to its navel. It twitched and gibbered as it walked, anticipating the reward its master would give for news of these travelers. Perhaps it would even be allowed to stay in Life and be given a body, that greatest and most treasured delight.

The passage through the First Gate was deceptive. Lirael couldn't tell how long it took, but soon the river had once again become a flat and endless expanse as it resumed its flow through the Second Precinct. Lirael began to probe the water ahead with her sword as soon as she left the path, checking the footing. This precinct was similar to the First, but it had deep, dangerous holes as well as the ever-present current. It was made even more difficult by a blurring effect that made the grey light fuzzy and indistinct, so Lirael couldn't see much farther than she could touch with her sword held out at full stretch.

There was an easy way through, a path charted by previous Abhorsens and recorded in *The Book of the Dead*. Lirael took it, though she didn't trust her book learning enough to give up probing with her sword. But she did count out her steps as the Book instructed, and she took the memorized turns at each point.

She was so intent on doing that, lost in the cadence of her steps, that she almost fell into the Second Gate. The Dog's quick grab for her belt pulled her to safety as she took one step too many, counting "Eleven" even as her brain said "Stop at Ten."

As quick as that thought she tried to draw back, but the Second Gate's grip was much stronger than the normal current of the river. Only her valiant Dog anchor saved her, though it took all the strength of both of them to drag Lirael back from the precipice of the gate.

For the Second Gate was an enormous hole, into which the river sank like sinkwater down a drain, creating a whirlpool of terrible strength.

"Thanks," said Lirael, shaking as she looked into the whirlpool and contemplated what might have happened. The Dog didn't reply at once, as she was untangling her jaws from a sadly battered piece of leather that had previously been a serviceable belt.

"Take it steady, Mistress," the Dog advised quietly. "We will need haste elsewhere, but not here."

"Yes," agreed Lirael, as she forced deep, slow breaths into her lungs. When she felt calmer, she stood up straight and recited further words of Free Magic, words that filled her mouth with a sudden heat, a strange glow against her deeply chilled cheeks.

The words echoed out, and the spiraling waters of the Second Gate slowed and then stopped completely, as if the whole whirlpool had been snap frozen. Now each swirl of current had become a terrace, making up one long spiral path down to the vortex of the Gate. Lirael stepped down to the start of the path and began to walk. Behind her, and above, the whirlpool began to swirl again.

It seemed she would have to circle around a hundred times or more to reach the bottom, but once again Lirael knew it was deceptive. It took only a few minutes to traverse the Second Gate, and she spent the time thinking about the Third Precinct and the trap it held for the unwary.

For the river there was only ankle deep, and a little warmer. The light was better, too. Brighter and less fuzzy, though still a pallid grey. Even the current wasn't much more than a tickle around the ankles. All in all, it was a much more attractive place than the First or Second Precincts. Somewhere ill-trained or foolish necromancers might be tempted to tarry or rest.

If they did, it wouldn't be for long—because the Third Precinct had waves.

Lirael knew it, and she left the Second Gate at a run. This was one of the places in Death where haste was necessary, she thought as she pushed her legs into an all-out sprint. She could hear the thunder of the wave behind her, a wave that had been held in check by the same spell that calmed the whirlpool. But she didn't look and concentrated totally on speed. If the wave caught her, it would crash her through the Third Gate, and she would drift on, stunned and unable to save herself.

"Faster!" shouted the Dog, and Lirael ran even harder, the sound of the wave so close now, it seemed certain to catch them both.

Lirael reached the mists of the Third Gate only a step or two in front of the rushing waters, frantically calling out the necessary Free Magic spell as she ran. This time the Dog was in front, the spell only just parting the mists ahead of her snout.

As they halted, panting, in the mist door created by the spell, the wave broke around them, hurtling its cargo of Dead into the waterfall beyond. Lirael waited to catch her breath and a few seconds more for the path to appear. Then she walked on, into the Fourth Precinct.

They crossed this precinct rapidly. It was relatively straight-forward, without holes or other traps for the unwary, though the current was strong again, stronger even than in the First Precinct. But Lirael had grown used to its cold and cunning grip.

She remained wary. Besides the known and charted dangers of each precinct, there was always the possibility of something new, or something so old and infrequent, it was not recorded in *The Book of the Dead*. Besides such anomalies, the Book hinted at powers that could travel in Death, besides the Dead them-selves, or necromancers. Some of these entities created odd local conditions, or warped the usual natures of the precincts. Lirael supposed that she herself was one of the powers that altered the nature of the river and its gates.

The Fourth Gate was another waterfall, but it was not cloaked in mist. At first sight it looked like an easy drop of only two or three feet, and the river appeared to keep on flowing after it.

Lirael knew better, from *The Book of the Dead*. She stopped a good ten feet back, and spoke the spell that would let her pass. Slowly, a dark ribbon began to roll out from the edge of the waterfall, floating in the air above the water below. Only three feet wide, it seemed to be made of night—a night without stars. It stretched out horizontally from the top of the waterfall into a distance Lirael couldn't make out.

She stepped onto the path, moved her feet a little to get a better balance, and began to walk. This narrow way was not only the path through the Fourth Gate, it was also the sole means of crossing the Fifth Precinct. The river was deep here, too deep to wade, and the water had a strong metamorphic effect. A necromancer who spent any time in its waters would find both spirit and body altered, and not for the better. Any Dead spirit who managed to wade back this way would not resemble its once-living form.

Even crossing the precinct by means of the dark path was dangerous. Besides being narrow, it was also the favored means for the Greater Dead or Free Magic beings to cross the Fifth Precinct themselves—going the other way, towards Life. They would wait for a necromancer to create the path, then rush down it, hoping to overcome the pathmaker with a sudden, vicious attack.

Lirael knew that, but even so, it was only the Dog's quick bark that warned her as something came ravening down the path ahead, seemingly out of nowhere. Once human, its long sojourn in Death had transformed it into something hideous and frightening. It scuttled forward on its arms as well as legs, moving all too like a spider. Its body was fat and bulbous, and its neck jointed so it could look straight ahead even when on all fours.

Lirael only had an instant to thrust her sword forward as it attacked, the point piercing one blobby cheek, bursting out the back of its neck. But it still pushed on, despite the blaze of white sparks that fountained everywhere as Charter Magic ate into its spirit-flesh. It thrust itself almost up to the hilt, red-fire eyes focused on Lirael, its too-wide mouth drooling spit and hissing.

Lirael kicked at it to try to get it off her sword, and rang Saraneth at the same time. But she was unbalanced, and the bell didn't ring true. A discordant note echoed out into Death, and instead of feeling her will concentrated on the Dead thing, and the beginnings of domination, Lirael felt distracted. Her mind wandered, and for an instant she forgot what she was doing.

A second or a minute later she realized it, and a shock ran through her, fear electrifying every nerve in her body. She looked, and the Dead creature was almost off her sword, ready to attack again.

"Still the bell!" barked the Dog, as she made herself smaller and tried to get between Lirael's legs to attack the creature. "Still the bell!"

"What?" exclaimed Lirael; then the shock and the fear ran through her again as she felt her hand still ringing Saraneth, without her being aware of it. Panicked, she forced it to be still. The bell sounded once more and then was silent as she fumbled it back into its pouch.

But once again she was distracted—and in that moment the creature attacked. This time it leapt at her, planning to crush her completely beneath its ghastly, pallid bulk. But the Dog saw the monster tense, and she guessed its intention. Instead of slipping between Lirael's legs, she threw herself forward and planted two heavy forepaws on Lirael's back.

The next thing Lirael knew, she was on her knees, and the creature was flying over her. One barbed finger grasped a lock of her hair as it passed, tearing it out by the roots. Lirael hardly noticed, as she frantically turned herself around on the narrow path and stood up. All her confidence was gone, and she didn't trust her balance, so it wasn't a fast maneuver.

But when she turned, the creature was gone. Only the Dog remained. A huge Dog, the hair on her back up like a boar-bristle hairbrush, red fire dripping from teeth the size of Lirael's fingers. There was a madness in her eyes as she looked back at her mistress.

"Dog?" whispered Lirael. She'd never feared her friend before, but then she'd never walked this far into Death, either. Anything could happen here, she felt. Anyone and . . . anything could change.

The Dog shook herself and grew smaller, and the madness in her eyes subsided. Her tail began to wag, and she worried the base of it for a second before walking up to lick Lirael's open hand.

"Sorry," she said. "I got angry."

"Where did it go?" asked Lirael, looking around. There was nothing on the path as far as she could see, and nothing in the river below them. She didn't think she'd heard a splash. Had she? Her mind was addled, still resonating with the discord of Saraneth.

"Down," replied the Dog, gesturing with her head. "We'd best hurry. You should draw a bell, too. Perhaps Ranna. She is more forgiving here."

Lirael knelt and touched noses with the Dog.

"I couldn't do this without you," she said, kissing her on the snout.

"I know, I know," replied the Dog distractedly, her ears twitching around in a semicircular motion. "Can you hear something?"

"No," replied Lirael. She stood up to listen, and her hand automatically freed Ranna from the bandolier. "Can you?"

"I thought someone . . . something was following before," said the Dog. "Now I'm certain. Something is coming up behind us. Something powerful, moving fast."

"Hedge!" exclaimed Lirael, forgetting about the crisis of confidence in her balance as she turned and hurried along the path. "Or could it be Mogget again?"

"I do not think it is Mogget," said the Dog with a frown. She stopped to look back for a moment, her ears pricked forward. Then she shook her head. "Whoever it is . . . or whatever . . . we should try to leave it behind."

Lirael nodded as she walked and took a firmer grip on both bell and sword. Whatever they met next, from in front or behind, she was determined not to be surprised.

Chapter Twenty-Two

JUNCTION BOXES AND SOUTHERLINGS

THE FOG HAD hidden the quay and was drifting inexorably up the slope. Nick watched it roll and watched the lightning that shot through it. Unpleasantly, it made him think of luminous veins in partly transparent flesh. Not that there was anything living that had flesh like that. . . .

There was something he had to do, but he couldn't remember what it was. He knew the hemispheres were not far away, through the fog. Part of him wanted to go over to them and oversee the final joining. But there was another, rebellious self that wanted exactly the opposite, to stop the hemispheres from joining by whatever means possible. They were like two whispering voices inside his head, both so strident that they mixed and became unintelligible.

"Nick! What have they done to you?"

For a moment Nick thought this was a third voice, also inside his head. But as it repeated the same words, he realized it wasn't.

Laboriously, Nick staggered around. At first he couldn't see anything through the fog. Then he spotted a face peering out from behind the corner of the nearest shed. It took a few seconds for him to work out who it was. His friend from the University of Corvere. Timothy Wallach, the slightly older student who he'd hired to oversee the construction of the Lightning Farm. Usually Tim was a debonair and somewhat languid individual, who was always impeccably dressed.

Tim didn't look like that now. His face was pale and dirty, his shirt had lost its collar, and there was mud all over his shoes and trousers. Crouched down behind the hut, he constantly shook, as if he had a fever or was scared out of his mind.

Nick waved and forced himself to take a few shambling steps to Tim, though he had to clutch at the wall in the last second to stop himself from falling.

"You have to stop him, Nick!" Tim exclaimed. He didn't look at Nick but everywhere else, his eyes flickering fearfully from side to side. "Whatever he's doing . . . you're both doing . . . it's wrong!"

"What?" asked Nick wearily. The walk had tired him, and one of the internal voices had become stronger. "What are we doing? It's a scientific experiment, that's all. And who is the him I have to stop? I'm in charge here."

"Him! Hedge!" blurted Tim, pointing back towards the hemispheres, where the fog was thickest. "He killed my work-men, Nick! He killed them! He pointed at them and they fell down. Just like that!"

He mimicked a spellcasting movement with his hand and started to sob, without tears, his words tumbling out in a mix-ture of gasps and cries.

"I saw him do it. It was only—only . . ."

He looked at his watch. The hands were stuck in place, stopped forever at six minutes to seven.

"It was only six to seven," whispered Tim. "Robert saw the coasters coming in, and woke us all up, so we could celebrate the completion of the work. I went back to the hut for a bottle I've been saving. . . . I saw it all through the window—"

"Saw what?" asked Nick. He was trying to understand what had upset Tim so much, but there was an awful pain in his chest, and he simply couldn't think. He couldn't put the concept of Hedge together with Tim's murdered workers.

"There's something wrong with you, Nick," Tim whispered, crawling back away from him. "Don't you understand? Those hemispheres are pure poison, and Hedge killed my workmen! All of them, even the two apprentices. I saw it!"

Without warning, Tim suddenly retched violently, coughing and gasping, though nothing came out. He had already thrown everything up.

Nick watched dumbly, as something inside him reveled at this news of death and misery and an opposing force writhed against it with feelings of fear, revulsion, and terrible doubt. The pain in his chest redoubled, and he fell down, clawing at his heart and his ankle.

"We have to get away," said Tim, wiping his mouth with the back of one shaking hand. "We have to warn somebody."

"Yes," whispered Nick. He had managed to sit up but was still hunched over, one pale hand over his heart, the other clutching the fragment of wind flute through his trouser cuff. He fought against the pain in both places and the pressure in his head. "Yes—you go, Tim. Tell her . . . tell them I'll try and stop it. Tell her—"

"What? Who?" asked Tim. "You have to come with me!"

"I can't," whispered Nick. He was remembering again. Talking to Lirael in the reed boat, trying to keep the shard of the Destroyer within him at bay. He remembered the nausea, and the metallic bite on his tongue. He could feel it again now, rising up.

"Go!" he said urgently, pushing at Tim to make him go away. "Run, before I— Aah!"

He stifled a scream, fell down, and curled into a ball. Tim crawled around to him and saw Nick's eyes roll back. For a moment he contemplated picking him up. Then he saw the white smoke trickling out of Nick's slack-jawed mouth.

Fear overcame everything then, and he started to run, between the lightning rods, up the hill. If only he could get over the ridge, get out of sight. Away from the Lightning Farm and the steadily rising fog. . . .

Behind him, Nick's hand gripped his trouser cuff even more tightly. He was whispering to himself, jumbled words spilling out in a frenzy.

"Corvere capital of two million principal products manufactured banking the attraction between two objects is directly proportional to the product of the day breaks not it is my heart four thousand eight hundred and the wind shifts generally in direction white wild Father help me Mother Sam help me Lirael—"

Nick stopped, coughed, and drew breath. The white smoke drifted off into the fog, and no new smoke emerged. Nick drew in two more shaky breaths, then experimentally let go of his trouser cuff and the piece of wind flute inside it. He felt a chill run through his body as he let go, but he still knew who he was and what he must do. Using the corner of the building, he hauled himself upright and staggered off into the fog. As always, the silver hemispheres glowed in his mind, but he had forced them into the background. Now he was thinking of the blueprints of the Lightning Farm. If Tim had made it according to Nick's design instructions, then one of the nine electrical junction boxes would be just around the corner of the main mill building.

Nick almost ran into the western wall of the mill, the fog was so thick. He skirted around it to the north as quickly as he could, staying away from the southern end, where the Dead labored to lift the first hemisphere onto a flatbed railway wagon.

The hemispheres. They glowed in Nick's mind brighter than the lightning flashes. He was suddenly struck with a compulsion to make sure that they were properly lifted into the cradles, that the cables were correctly joined, the track sanded for traction in this wet fog. He had to see to it. The hemispheres had to be joined!

Nick fell to his knees on the railway, and then forward, to lie curled up across the cold steel and the worn wooden sleepers. He clutched at his trouser cuff, fighting against that overwhelming urge to turn right and go over to the hemisphere on its railway wagon. Desperately he thought of Lirael lifting him into the reed boat, of his promise to her. His friend Sam, picking him up after he'd been knocked out by a fast ball playing cricket. Tim Wallach, bow tied and dapper, pouring him a gin and tonic.

"Word of a Sayre, word of a Sayre, word of a Sayre," he repeated over and over again.

Still mumbling, he forced himself into a crawl. Across the track, ignoring the splinters from the old railway sleepers. He crawled to the far side of the mill, and used the wall to half crawl, half stumble down to the junction box, which was actually a small concrete hut. Here, hundreds of cables from the lightning rods fed into one of the nine master cables, each as thick as Nick's body.

"I'll stop it," he whispered to himself as he reached the junction box. Deafened by thunder, half blind from the lightning, and crippled by pain and nausea, he reached up and tried to open the metal door that was marked with a vivid yellow lightning bolt and the word "DANGER."

The door was locked. Nick shook the handle, but that small act of defiance did nothing but use up his last store of energy. Exhausted, Nick slid back down and sprawled across the doorway.

He had failed. Lightning continued to spread up the slope, accompanied by fog and booming thunder. The Dead continued to struggle with the hemispheres. One was on its railway wagon, which was being moved along the rails to the far end of the line, even as the Dead who pushed it were struck again and again by lightning. The other hemisphere was swinging off the coaster— till lightning burned the rope and it came crashing down, crushing several Dead Hands. But when the hemisphere was raised, the crushed Hands came slithering out. No longer recognizable as anything remotely human, and no use in the work, they squirmed their way east. Up the ridge, to join the Dead that Hedge had already sent to make sure that the final triumph of the Destroyer was not delayed.

"You have to believe me!" exclaimed Sam in exasperation. "Tell her again that I promise on the word of a Prince of the Old Kingdom that every single one of you will be given a farm!"

A young Southerling was translating for him, though Sam was sure that like most Southerlings, the matriarch understood at least spoken Ancelstierran. This time she interrupted the interpreter halfway through and thrust the paper she held out to Sam. He took it and quickly scanned it, acutely aware that he had only a minute or two left before he had to go back to Lirael.

The paper was printed on both sides, in several languages. It was headed "Land for the Southerling People" and then went on to promise ten acres of prime farmland for every piece of paper that was presented to the "land office" at Forwin Mill. There was an official-looking crest, and the paper supposedly came from the "Government of Ancelstierre Resettlement Office."

"This is a fake," Sam protested. "There is no Ancelstierre Resettlement Office, and even if there were, why would they want you to go to somewhere like Forwin Mill?"

"That is where the land is," replied the young translator smoothly. "And there must be a Resettlement Office. Why else would the police let us leave the camps?"

"Look at what's happening over there!" screamed Sam,

pointing at the thunderclouds and the constant forks of lightning, all of which were now easily visible, even from the valley floor. "If you go there, you will be killed! That is why they let you out! It solves a problem for them if you all get killed and they can say it wasn't their fault!"

The matriarch straightened her head and looked at the lightning playing along the ridge. Then she looked at the blue sky to the north, south, and east. She touched the interpreter's arm and said three words.

"You promise us on your blood?" asked the interpreter. He pulled out a knife made from the ground-down end of a spoon. "You will give us land in your country?"

"Yes, I promise on my blood," said Sam quickly. "I will give you land and all the help we can so you can live there."

The matriarch held out her palm, which was marked with hundreds of tiny dotted scars that formed a complex whorl. The interpreter pricked her skin with the knife and twisted it around a few times, to form a new dot.

Sam held out his hand. He didn't feel the knife. All his concentration was behind him, his ears straining to hear any sound of an attack.

The matriarch spoke quickly and held her palm out. The interpreter gestured for Sam to hold his palm against hers. He did so, and she gripped his hand with surprising strength from her bony old fingers.

"Good, excellent," babbled Sam. "Have your people go back to the other side of the stream and wait there. As soon as I can, we will . . . I will arrange for you to be given your land."

"Why do we not wait here?" asked the interpreter.

"Because there's going to be a battle," said Sam anxiously. "Oh, Charter help me! Please go back beyond the stream! Running water will be the only protection you have!"

He turned and ran away before any more questions could be asked. The interpreter called after him, but Sam did not answer. He could feel the Dead coming down this side of the ridge, and he was terribly afraid he had been away from Lirael too long. She was up there on the spur, and he was her main protector. There was only so much Ancelstierrans could do, even those who had some slight mastery of Charter Magic.

Sam did not see, because he was sprinting for all he was worth, but behind him the interpreter and the matriarch spoke heatedly. Then the interpreter gestured back towards the center of the valley and the stream. The matriarch looked once more towards the lightning, then tore up the paper she held, threw it to the ground, and spat on it. Her action was mimicked by those around her, and then by others, and a great paper tearing and spitting slowly spread throughout the vast crowd. Then the matriarch turned and began to walk east, to the middle of the valley and the stream. Like a flock following its bellwether, all the other Southerlings turned as well.

Sam was panting up the spur, three quarters of the way back, when he heard shouts ahead.

"Halt! Halt!"

Sam couldn't sense the Dead so close, but he found extra speed from somewhere, and his sword leapt into his hand. Startled soldiers stepped aside as he ran past them and up to Lirael. She was still standing frozen in the ring of stones. Greene and two soldiers were in front of her. About ten feet in front of them, two more soldiers were standing over a young man with their bayonets to his throat. The youth was lying still on the ground and was shrieking. His clothes and skin were blackened, and he had lost most of his hair. But he was not a Dead Hand. In fact, Sam saw that this scorched fugitive was not much older than he was.

"It's not me, it's not me, I'm not them, they're behind me," he shrieked. "You have to help me!"

"Who are you?" asked Major Greene. "What is happening over there?"

"I'm Timothy Wallach," gasped the young man. "I don't know what's happening! It's a nightmare! That . . . I don't know what he is . . . Hedge. He killed my workmen! All of them. He pointed at them and they died."

"Who's behind you?" asked Sam.

"I don't know," sobbed Tim. "They were my men. I don't know what they are now. I saw Krontas struck directly by lightning. His head was on fire, but he didn't stop. They are—"

"The Dead," said Sam. "What were you doing at Forwin Mill?"

"I'm from the University of Corvere," whispered Tim. He made a visible effort to get himself under control. "I built the Lightning Farm for Nicholas Sayre. I didn't . . . I don't know what it's for, but it's nothing good. We have to stop it being used! Nick said he'll try, but—"

"Nicholas is there?" snapped Sam.

Tim nodded. "But he's in bad shape. He hardly knew who I was. I don't think there's much chance of him doing anything. And there was white smoke coming out of his nose—"

Sam listened with a sinking heart. He knew from Lirael that the white smoke was the sign of the Destroyer taking control. Any faint hope he'd had that Nick might escape was dashed. His friend was lost.

"What can be done?" asked Sam. "Is there any way to disable the Lightning Farm?"

"There are circuit breakers in each of the nine junction boxes," whispered Tim. "If they were opened . . . But I don't know how many circuits are actually needed. Or . . . or you could cut the cables from the lightning rods. There are a thousand and one lightning rods, and since they're already being struck by lightning . . . you'd need very special gear."

Sam didn't hear Tim's last few words. All thoughts of Nick's plight and the Lightning Farm were swept away as a cold sensation froze the hair on the back of his neck. His head snapped up, and he pushed past Tim. The first wave of Dead were almost upon them, and any question of doing something to any junction boxes was academic.

"Here they come!" he shouted, and jumped up on a rock, already reaching into the Charter to prepare destructive spells. He was surprised by how easy it was. The wind was still blowing from the west, and it should have been harder this far from the Wall. But he could feel the Charter strongly, almost as clear and present as it was in the Old Kingdom, though it was somehow inside him as much as it was outside.

"Stand ready!" shouted Greene, his warning repeated by sergeants and corporals in the ring of soldiers around Lirael's frozen form. "Remember, nothing must get through to the Abhorsen! Nothing!"

"The Abhorsen." Sam closed his eyes for a second, willing that pain away. There was no time to grieve or think about the world without his parents. He could see the Dead Hands lumbering down the slope, gathering speed as they sensed the Life ahead.

Sam readied a spell and quickly looked around. All the bowmen had arrows nocked, and they were teamed with pairs of bayonet men. Greene and Tindall were next to Sam, both ready with Charter spells. Lirael was several paces behind them, secure with soldiers all around her.

But where was Mogget? The little white cat was nowhere to be seen.

Chapter Twenty-Three

THE FIFTH GATE was a reverse waterfall: a waterclimb. The river hit an unseen wall and kept on flowing up it. The dark ribbon path that crossed the Fifth Precinct ended short of this waterclimb, leaving a gap. Lirael and the Dog stared up from the end of the path, their stomachs crowding their throats. It was very disorienting to see water rising where it should fall, though fortunately it blurred into grey fuzziness before it went too far up. Even so, Lirael had the unpleasant feeling that she was no longer subject to normal gravity and might fall upwards, too.

That feeling was fueled by the knowledge that this was actually what was going to happen when she spoke the Free Magic spell to cross the Fifth Gate. There was no path or stair here— the spell simply made sure the waterclimb didn't take you too far.

"You'd better hold my collar, Mistress," said the Dog, eyeing the rising water. "The spell won't include me otherwise."

Lirael sheathed her sword and grabbed the Dog's collar, her fingers feeling the warmth and comfortable familiarity of the Charter marks that made it up. She had a strange sense of déjà vu as she pushed her fingers through, as if she knew the Charter marks from somewhere else—somewhere relatively new, not just from the thousand times she had held the collar. But she had no time to follow that feeling to some conclusion.

Holding the Dog tight, Lirael spoke the words that would carry them up the waterclimb, once again feeling the heat of Free Magic through her nose and mouth. She would likely lose her voice from it eventually, she thought, but it also seemed to have cured her Ancelstierran cold. Though she might still have a cold in her real body, out in Life. She didn't know enough about how things like that in Death would affect her in Life. Of course, if she were slain in Death, her body would die in Life as well.

The spell was slow to start, and for a moment Lirael contemplated saying it again. Then she saw a sheet of water reach out of the surface of the waterclimb, moving like a strange, very thin, very wide tentacle. It crossed the gap to the ribbon path in a series of shuddering extensions and wrapped around Lirael and the Dog like a large blanket, without actually touching them. Then it began to rise up the waterclimb, moving at the same rate as the vertical current—taking Lirael and her closely gripped hound with it.

They rose steadily for several minutes, till the precinct below was lost in the fuzzy grey light. The waterclimb continued upwards—perhaps forever—but the extension that held Lirael stopped. Then it suddenly snapped back into the face of the waterclimb—throwing its passengers out the other side.

Lirael blinked as she hurtled into what her common sense told her should be a cliff, but the back of the waterclimb no more followed common sense than the waterclimb acknowledged gravity. Somehow, it had pushed them through to the next precinct. The Sixth, a place where the river became a shallow pool and there was no current at all. But there were lots and lots of Dead.

Lirael felt them so strongly, they might have been standing next to her—and some probably were, under the water. Instantly, she let go of the collar and drew Nehima, the sword humming as it sprang from its scabbard.

The sword, and the bell she held, were warning enough for most of the Dead. In any case, the great majority were simply waiting here till something happened and they were forced to go on, since they lacked the will and the knowledge to go back the other way. Very few were actively struggling back towards Life.

Those that were saw the great spark of Life in Lirael, and they hungered for it. Other necromancers had assuaged their hunger in the past and helped them back from the brink of the Ninth Gate—willingly or not. This one was young, and should thus be easy prey for any of the Greater Dead who chanced to be close.

There were three who were.

Lirael looked out and saw that huge shadows stalked between the apathetic lesser spirits, fires burning where once their living forms had eyes. There were three close enough to intercept her intended path—and that was three too many.

But once again *The Book of the Dead* had advice upon such a confrontation in the Sixth Precinct. And, as always, she had the Disreputable Dog.

As the three monstrous Greater Dead thrust their way towards her, Lirael replaced Ranna and drew Saraneth. Carefully composing herself this time, she rang it, joining her indomitable will with its deep call.

The Dead creatures hesitated as Saraneth's strong voice echoed out across the Precinct, and they prepared to fight, to struggle against this presumptuous necromancer who thought to bend them to her will.

Then they laughed, awful laughter that sounded like a great crowd of people caught between absurdity and sorrow. For this necromancer was so incompetent that she had focused her will not upon them, but on the Lesser Dead who lay all around.

Still laughing, the Greater Dead plunged forward, greedy now, each warily eyeing the others to gauge if they were weak enough to push out of the way. For whoever reached this necromancer first would gain the delight of consuming the greater part of her life. Life and power, the only things that were of any use for the long journey out of Death.

They didn't even notice the first few spirits who clutched at their shadowy legs or bit at their ankles, shrugging them off as a living person might ignore a few mosquito bites.

Then more and more spirits began to rise out of the water and hurl themselves at the three Greater Dead. They were forced to stop and swat these annoying Lesser Dead away, to rip them apart and rend them with their fiery jaws. Angrily, they stomped and threshed, roaring with anger now, the laughter gone.

Distracted, the Greater Dead closest to Lirael hardly noticed the Charter Spell that revealed its name to her, and it didn't see her as she walked almost right up to where it fought against a churning mass of its lesser brethren.

But Lirael gained the creature's full attention when a new bell rang, replacing Saraneth's strident commands with an excitable march. This bell was Kibeth, close by the thing's head, sounded with a dreadful tone specifically for its hearing. A tune that it couldn't ignore, even after the bell had stopped.

"Lathal the Abomination!" commanded Lirael. "Your time has come. The Ninth Gate calls, and you must go beyond it!"

Lathal screamed as Lirael spoke, a scream that carried the anguish of a thousand years. It knew that voice, for Lathal had made the long trek into Life twice in the last millennium, only to be forced back into Death by others with that same cold tone. Always, it had managed to stop itself being carried through to the ultimate gate. Now Lathal would never walk under the sun again, never drink the sweet life of the unsuspecting living. It was too close to the Ninth Gate, and the compulsion was strong.

Drubas and Sonnir heard the bell, the scream, and the voice, and knew that this was no foolish necromancer—it was the Abhorsen. A new one, for they knew the old and would have run from her. The sword was different, too, but they would remember it in future.

Still screaming, Lathal turned and stumbled away, the Lesser Dead tearing at its legs as it staggered and tumbled through the water and constantly tried to turn back without success.

Lirael didn't follow, because she didn't want to be too close when it passed the Sixth Gate, in case the sudden current took her, too. The other Greater Dead were moving hastily away, she noted with grim satisfaction, clubbing a path through the clinging spirits who still harassed them.

"Can I round them up, Mistress?" asked the Dog eagerly, staring after the retreating shapes of darkness with tense anticipation. "Can I?"

"No," said Lirael firmly. "I surprised Lathal. Those two will be on their guard and would be much more dangerous together. Besides, we haven't got time."

As she spoke, Lathal's scream was suddenly cut off, and Lirael felt the river current suddenly spring up around her legs. She set her feet apart and stood against it, leaning back on the rock-steady Dog. The current was very strong for a few minutes, threatening to drag her under; then it subsided into nothing— and once again the waters of the Sixth Precinct were still.

Immediately, Lirael began to wade through to the point where she could summon the Sixth Gate. Unlike the other precincts, the Gate out of the Sixth Precinct wasn't in any particular place. It would open randomly from time to time— which was a danger—or it could be opened anywhere a certain distance away from the Fifth Gate.

Just in case it was like the previous gate, Lirael clutched the Disreputable Dog's collar again, though it meant sheathing Nehima. Then she recited the spell, wetting her lips between the phrases to try to ease the blistering heat of the Free Magic.

As the spell built, the water drained away in a circle about ten feet wide around and under Lirael and the Dog. When it was dry, the circle began to sink, the water rising around it on all sides. Faster and faster it sank, till they seemed to be at the base of a narrow cylinder of dry air bored into three hundred feet of water.

Then, with a great roar, the watery sides of the cylinder collapsed, pouring out in every direction. It took a few minutes for the waters to pass and the froth and spray to subside; then the river slowly ebbed back and wrapped around Lirael's legs. The air cleared, and she saw that they were standing in the river, the current once again trying to pull them under and away.

They had reached the Seventh Precinct, and already Lirael could see the first of the Three Gates that marked the deep reaches of Death. The Seventh Gate—an endless line of red fire that burned eerily upon the water, the light bright and disturbing after the uniform greyness of the earlier precincts.

"We're getting closer," said Lirael, in a voice that revealed a mixture of relief that they'd made it so far and apprehension at where they still had to go.

But the Dog wasn't listening—she was looking back, her ears pricked and twitching. When she did look at Lirael, she simply said, "Our pursuer is gaining on us, Mistress. I think it is Hedge! We must go faster!"

Chapter Twenty-Four

MOGGET'S INSCRUTABLE INITIATIVE

NICK DRAGGED HIMSELF up and leaned against the door. He'd found a bent nail on the ground, and armed with that and a dim memory of how locks worked, he tried once more to get into the concrete blockhouse that housed one of the nine junction boxes that were vital to the operation of the Lightning Farm.

He could hear nothing but thunder now, and he couldn't look up, because the lightning was too close, too bright. The thing inside him wanted him to look, to make sure the hemispheres were being properly loaded into the bronze cradles. But even if he gave in to that compulsion, his body was too weak to obey.

Instead he slipped back down to the ground and dropped the nail. He started to search for it, even though he knew it was useless. He had to do something. However futile.

Then he felt something touch his cheek, and he flinched. It touched it again—something wetter than the fog, and rasping. Gingerly, he opened his eyes to narrow slits, bracing himself for the white flash of lightning.

He got that, but there was another, softer whiteness as well. The fur of a small white cat, who was delicately licking his face.

"Go away, cat!" mumbled Nick. His voice sounded small and pathetic under the thunder. He made a flapping motion with his hand and added, "You'll get struck by lightning."

"I doubt it," replied Mogget, close to his ear. "Besides, I've decided to take you with me. Unfortunately. Can you walk?"

Nick shook his head and found, to his surprise, that he did have tears left after all. He wasn't surprised by a talking cat. The world was crumbling around him, and anything could happen.

"No," he whispered. "There is something inside me, cat. It won't let me leave."

"The Destroyer is distracted," said Mogget. He could see the second hemisphere being fitted into its cradle on the railway wagon, the burnt and broken Dead Hands laboring on with mindless devotion. Mogget's green eyes reflected a tapestry of lightnings, but the cat didn't blink.

"As is Hedge," he added. Mogget had already done a careful reconnaissance, and had seen the necromancer standing in the cemetery that had once served a thriving timber town. Hedge was covered in ice, obviously engaged in gathering reinforcements in Death and sending them back. With great success, Mogget knew, from the many rotten corpses and skeletons that were already digging themselves out of their graves.

Nick somehow knew that this was his last chance, that this talking animal was like the Dog of his dream, connected with Lirael and his friend Sam. Summoning his last reserves of strength, he pushed himself up to a sitting position—but that was all. He was too weak and too close to the hemispheres.

Mogget looked at him, his tail waving to and fro in annoyance.

"If that's the best you can do, I suppose I'll have to carry you," said the cat.

"H . . . how?" mumbled Nick. He couldn't even begin to wonder how the little cat intended to carry a grown man. Even one as reduced as he was.

Mogget didn't answer. He just stood up on his back paws— and began to change.

Nick stared at the spot where the little white cat had been. His eyes watered from the glare of the constant lightning. He had seen the animal change, but even so he had trouble believing what he saw.

For instead of a small cat, there was now a very short, thin-waisted, broad-shouldered man. He wasn't much taller than a ten-year-old child, and he had the white-blond hair and translucently pale skin of an albino, though his eyes weren't red. They were bright green, and almond shaped—exactly like the cat's had been. And he had a bright red leather belt around his waist, from which hung a tiny silver bell. Then Nick noticed that the white robe this apparition wore had two wide bands around the cuffs, dusted with tiny silver keys—the same silver keys he'd seen on Lirael's coat.

"Now," said Mogget cautiously. He could sense the fragment of the Destroyer inside Nick, and even with the greater part intent on its joining, he knew he had to be careful. But trickery might serve where strength would not. "I'm going to pick you up, and we're going to go and find a really good place where we can watch the hemispheres join."

At the mention of the hemispheres, Nick felt a burning, white-hot pain through his chest. Yes, they were close, he could feel them. . . .

"I must oversee the work," he croaked. He shut his eyes again, and the vision of the hemispheres burned in his mind brighter than any lightning.

"The work is done," soothed Mogget. He picked Nick up and held him in his unnaturally strong arms, though he was careful not to touch Nick's chest. The albino looked somewhat like an ant, carrying a load larger than himself slightly away from his own body. "We're only going somewhere to have a better view. A view of the hemispheres when they join."

"A better view," mumbled Nick. Somehow that quietened the ache in his breast, but it also let him think again with his own mind.

He opened his eyes and met the green ones of his bearer. He was unable to decipher the emotions there. Was it fear—or excited anticipation?

"We have to stop it!" he wheezed, and the pain came back with such force that he screamed, a scream drowned in thunder. Mogget bent his head down closer, as Nick continued in a whisper. "I can show you . . . ah . . . unscrew the junction boxes . . . disconnect the master cables . . ."

"It's too late for that," said Mogget. He began to head up between the lightning rods, ducking and weaving with a foresight that indicated he could predict where and when the lightning would strike.

Behind and below Mogget and his burden, one of the last of Hedge's living workers connected the master cables into the cradles that held the hemispheres atop the railway trucks. The trucks were positioned fifty yards apart on the short stretch of railway line, and the hemispheres had been set up so their flat bottoms faced each other and projected out from the cradles. The cables fed into the bronze framework that held each hemisphere. There was no sign of anything that would drive the railway trucks—and the hemispheres—together, but clearly that was the intention.

Many of the lightning rods were being hit and already were feeding power into the hemispheres. Long blue sparks were crackling around the railway cars, and Mogget could feel the greedy sucking of the Destroyer, and the stir of the ancient entity within the silver metal.

The albino began to move faster, though not as fast as he could, in order not to alarm the shard inside Nick. But the young man lay quiet in his arms, one part of his mind content that it was too late to stop the joining, the other part grieving that he had failed.

Soon there was visible evidence that Orannis flexed against its bonds. The lightning ceased around the hemispheres themselves and began to move outwards, as if pushed back by some unseen hand. Instead of a concentrated series of strikes in and around the railway cars, the lightning began to hit more and more of the lightning rods that dotted the hillside. There was also more lightning coming down from the storm. Where there had been nine bolts every minute in a small area around the hemispheres, now there were ninety across the hillside, then several hundred, as the storm above roiled and thundered, spreading across the entire Lightning Farm.

Within a few minutes, there was no lightning at all in the center of the storm. But down below, the hemispheres glowed with newfound power, and every time Mogget glanced back, he could see dark shadows writhing deep inside the silver metal. In each hemisphere, the shadows moved to darken the side closest to the other, raging against the repulsion that still kept them apart.

More lightning struck, the crash of the thunder shaking the ground. The hemispheres glowed brighter still, and the shadows grew darker. With a shriek of protesting metal from long-disused wheels, the railway cars began to roll together.

"The hemispheres join!" shouted Mogget, and he ran faster up the hillside, zigzagging between the lightning rods, his body hunched over to protect his burden from the violent energies that struck down all around them.

Inside Nick's heart, a small sliver of metal quivered, feeling the attraction of its greater whole. For an instant, it moved against the heart wall, as if to burst forth in bloody glory. But the attractive force was not yet strong enough and was too far away. Instead of erupting out through flesh and bone, the shard of the Destroyer caught the flow out through a bright artery, and began to retrace the passage it had made almost a year before.

✥✥✥

Sam lowered his hand as a Dead Hand fell shrieking, golden Charter fire eating away at every sinew. Flopping and writhing, it crawled behind two burning trees. Smoke from the fires rose up in spirals, looking like outriders for the huge bank of fog that was rolling over the top of the ridge above.

"Wish my arrows did that," remarked Sergeant Evans. He'd put several silver arrows into that same Dead Hand, but they had only slowed it down.

"The spirit is still there," said Sam grimly. "Only the body is useless to it now."

He could feel many more Dead, climbing up the other side of the ridge, advancing with the fog. So far, Sam and the soldiers had managed to repel the first attack. But that had been only a half dozen Dead Hands.

"They're making us keep our distance while they prepare for the main attack, I reckon," said Major Greene, tipping back his helmet to wipe a sheen of sweat from his forehead.

"Yes," agreed Sam. He hesitated, then quietly said, "There are about a hundred Dead Hands out there, and more appearing every minute."

He looked behind him to where Lirael's ice-encrusted body stood between the rocks, and then around the ring of soldiers. Their ranks were thinner than before. None had been slain by the Dead, but at least a dozen or more of them had simply run away, too scared to stand and fight. The Major had reluctantly let them go, muttering something about not being able to shoot them when the whole company shouldn't be there anyway.

"I wish I knew what was happening!" Sam burst out. "With Lirael—and those Charter-cursed hemispheres!"

"The waiting's always the worst," said Major Greene. "But I don't think we'll be waiting long, one way or another. That fog is coming down. We'll be under it in a few minutes."

Sam looked ahead again. Sure enough, the fog was moving faster, long tendrils pushing down the slope, with the bulk of the fog behind. At the same time, he felt a great surge of the Dead rise all along the ridge.

"Here they come!" shouted the Major. "Stand fast, lads!"

There were too many to blast with Charter spells, Sam realized. He hesitated for a moment, then got out the panpipes Lirael had given him and lifted them to his mouth. He might not be the Abhorsen-in-Waiting anymore, but he would have to act the part now in the face of the onrushing Dead.

Then Sam lost sight of the Major, his whole attention on the advancing Dead and the panpipes. He put his lips to the Saraneth pipe, drew a great breath in through his nose—and blew, the pure, strong sound cutting through the thunder and the damping fog.

With that sound, Sam exerted his will, feeling it stretch across the battleground, encompassing more than fifty Dead Hands. He felt their downward rush slow, felt them fight against him, their spirits raging as dead flesh struggled to keep moving forward.

For an instant, Sam held them all in his grip, and the Dead Hands slowed to a halt, till they stood like grim statues, wreathed in wisps of fog. Arrows plunged at them, and some of the closer soldiers dashed forward to hack at legs or pierce their knees with bayonets.

Still the spirits inside the dead flesh fought, and Sam knew he could not gain total domination. He left Saraneth echoing on the hillside and switched his mouth to the Ranna pipe. But he had to draw breath again, and in that brief moment, the sound of Saraneth faded and Sam's will was broken. He lost control, and all along the line, the Dead shivered into movement and once more charged down the spur, hungry for Life.

Chapter Twenty-Five

THE NINTH GATE

LIRAEL AND THE Dog crossed the Seventh Precinct at a run, not even pausing as Lirael sang out the spell to open the Seventh Gate. Ahead of them, the line of fire shivered at her words, and directly in front, it leapt up to form a narrow arch, just wide enough for them to pass.

As she ducked through, Lirael glanced back—and saw a man-shaped figure rushing after them, himself a thing of fire and darkness, holding a sword that dripped red flames the match of those in the Seventh Gate.

Then they were through to the Eighth Precinct, and Lirael had to quickly gasp out another spell to ward off a patch of flame that reared up out of the water towards them. These flames were the main threat in the precinct, for the river was lit with many floating patches of fire that moved according to strange currents of their own or flared up out of nowhere.

Lirael narrowly averted another, and hurried past. She felt a tiny muscle above her eye start to twitch uncontrollably, a symptom of nervous fear, as individual fires roared everywhere in sight, some moving fast, some slow. At the same time, she expected Hedge to suddenly come up from behind and attack.

The Dog barked next to her, and a huge thicket of fire swerved aside. She hadn't even seen it beginning to flare, her mind so much occupied by the ones she could see and the threat of what might be coming from behind.

"Steady, Mistress," said the Dog calmly. "We'll be through this lot soon."

"Hedge!" gulped Lirael, then immediately shouted two words to send a long snake of fire twirling into another, the two joining in a combustionary dance. They seemed almost alive, she thought, watching them twirl. More like creatures than burning patches of oily scum, which is what they looked like when they didn't move. They also differed from normal fires in another way, Lirael realized, because there was no smoke.

"I saw Hedge," she repeated once the immediate threat of immolation had passed. "Behind us."

"I know," said the Dog. "When we get to the Eighth Gate, I'll stay here and stop him while you go on."

"No!" exclaimed Lirael. "You have to come with me! I'm not afraid of him . . . it's . . . it's just so inconvenient!"

"Look out!" barked the Dog, and they both jumped aside as a great globe of fire swung past, close enough to choke Lirael with its sudden heat. Coughing, she bent over—and the river chose that moment to try to pull her legs out from under her.

It almost worked. The current's sudden surge made Lirael slip, but she went down only as far as her waist, then used her sword like a crutch to lever herself up again with a single springing leap.

The Dog had already plunged under to haul her mistress out, and the hound looked very embarrassed when she emerged, soaking, to find Lirael not only still vertical but mostly dry.

"Thought you went in," she mumbled, then barked at a fire, as much to move the conversation on as to divert the intruder.

"Come on!" said Lirael.

"I'm going to wait and ambush—" the Dog started to say, but Lirael turned on her and grabbed her by the collar. The mulish Dog set her haunches down at once, and Lirael tried to drag her.

"You're coming with me!" ordered Lirael, her tone of command watered down by the quaver in her voice. "We'll fight Hedge together—when we have to. For now, let's hurry!"

"Oh, all right," grumbled the Dog. She got up and shook herself, splashing copious amounts of the river onto Lirael.

"Whatever happens," Lirael added quietly, "I want us to be together, Dog."

The Disreputable Dog looked up at her with a troubled eye but didn't speak. Lirael almost said something else, but it got choked up in her throat, and then she had to ward off another incursion by floating fires.

When that was done, they strode off side by side and, a few minutes later, stepped confidently into the wall of darkness that was the Eighth Gate. All light vanished, and Lirael could see nothing, hear nothing, and feel nothing, including her own body. She felt as if she had suddenly become a disembodied intelligence that was totally alone, cut off from all external stimuli.

But she had expected it, and though she couldn't feel her own mouth and lips, and her ears could hear no sound, she spoke the spell that would take them through this ultimate darkness. Through to the Ninth and final Precinct of Death.

The Ninth Precinct was utterly different from all other parts of Death. Lirael blinked as she emerged from the darkness of the Eighth Gate, struck by sudden light. The familiar tug of the river at her knees disappeared as the current faded away. The river now only splashed gently round her ankles, and the water was warm, the terrible chill that prevailed in all other precincts of Death left behind.

Everywhere else in Death always had a closed-in feeling, due to the strange grey light that limited vision. Here it was the opposite. There was a sensation of immensity, and Lirael could see for miles and miles, across a great flat stretch of sparkling water.

For the first time, she could also look up and see more than a grey, depressing blur. Much more. There was a sky above her, a night sky so thick with stars that they overlapped and merged to form one unimaginably vast and luminous cloud. There were no distinguishable constellations, no patterns to pick out. Just a multitude of stars, casting a light as bright as but softer than the living world's sun.

Lirael felt the stars call to her, and a yearning rose in her heart to answer. She sheathed bell and sword and stretched her arms out, up to the brilliant sky. She felt herself lifted up, and her feet came out of the river with a soft ripple and a sigh from the waters.

Dead rose, too, she saw. Dead of all shapes and sizes, all rising up to the sea of stars. Some went slowly, and some so fast they were just a blur.

Some small part of Lirael's mind warned that she was answering the Ninth Gate's call. The veil of stars was the final border, the final death from which there could be no return. That same small conscience shrieked about responsibility, and Orannis, and the Disreputable Dog, and Sam, and Nick, and the whole world of Life. It angrily kicked and screamed against the overwhelming feeling of peace and rest offered by the stars.

Not yet, it cried. Not yet.

That cry was answered, though not by any voice. The stars suddenly retreated, became immeasurably far away. Lirael blinked, shook her head, and fell several feet to splash down next to the Dog, who still gazed up at the luminous sky.

"Why didn't you stop me?" Lirael asked, made cross by the scare she'd had. Another few seconds and she would have been unable to return, she knew. She would have gone beyond the Ninth Gate forever.

"It is something that all who walk here must face themselves," whispered the Dog. She still stared up and did not look at Lirael. "For everyone, and everything, there is a time to die.

Some do not know it, or would delay it, but its truth cannot be denied. Not when you look into the stars of the Ninth Gate. I'm glad you came back, Mistress."

"So am I," said Lirael nervously. She could see Dead emerging all along the dark mass of the Eighth Gate. Every time one came out, she tensed, thinking it must be Hedge. She could feel more Dead than she could see, but they were all simply coming through and immediately falling skywards, to disappear amongst the stars. But Hedge, who must have been only a few minutes behind Lirael and the Dog, did not come through the Eighth Gate.

Still the Dog looked up. Lirael finally noticed, and her heart nearly stopped. Surely the Dog wouldn't answer the summons of the Ninth Gate?

Finally, the Dog looked down and made a slight woofing sound.

"Not yet my time, either," she said, and Lirael let out her breath. "Shouldn't you be doing what we came here for, Mistress?"

"I know," said Lirael wretchedly, all too conscious of the time wasted. She touched the Dark Mirror in her pouch. "But what if Hedge comes while I'm looking?"

"If he hasn't come through now, he probably won't," replied the Dog, sniffing the river. "Few necromancers risk seeing the Ninth Gate, for their very nature is to deny its call."

"Oh," said Lirael, much relieved by this advice.

"He will certainly be waiting for us somewhere on the way back, though," continued the Dog, bursting that small bubble of relief. "But for now, I will guard you."

Lirael smiled, a troubled smile that conveyed her love and gratitude. She was twice vulnerable, she thought, with her body out in Life guarded by Sam, and now her spirit here in Death, guarded by the Dog.

But she had to do what must be done, regardless of the risk.

First of all she pricked the point of her finger with Nehima before sheathing the sword again. Then she took out the Dark Mirror and opened it with a decisive snap.

Blood dripped down her finger, and a drop fell. But it flew up towards the sky instead of down to the river. Lirael didn't notice. She was remembering pages from *The Book of Remembrance and Forgetting*, concentrating as she held her finger close to the Mirror and touched a single bright drop to its opaque surface. As the drop touched, it spread, to form a thin sheen across the dark surface of the glass.

Lirael lifted the Mirror and held it to her right eye, while still looking out on Death through her left eye. The blood gave the Mirror a faint red tinge, but that quickly faded as she focused, and the darkness began to clear. Once again, Lirael saw through the Mirror into some other place, but she could still also see the sparkling waters of the Ninth Precinct. The two visions merged, and Lirael saw the swirling lights and the sun fleeing backwards somehow through the waters of Death, and she felt herself falling faster and faster into some incredibly distant past.

Now Lirael began to think of what she wanted to see, and her left hand fell to unconsciously touch each of the bells in her bandolier in turn.

"By Right of Blood," she said, her voice growing stronger and more confident with each word, "by Right of Heritage, by Right of the Charter, and by Right of the Seven who wove it, I would see through the veil of time, to the Beginning. I would witness the Binding and Breaking of Orannis and learn what was and what must become. So let it be!"

Long after she spoke, the suns still ran backwards, and Lirael fell farther and farther into them, till all the suns were one, blinding her with light. Then the light faded, and she gazed out to a dark void. There was a single point of light within the void, and she fell towards that, and soon it was not a light but a moon and then a huge planet that filled the horizon, and she was falling through its sky and gliding in the air above a desert that stretched from horizon to horizon, a desert that Lirael somehow knew encompassed this whole world. Nothing stirred upon the baked, parched earth. Nothing grew or lived.

The world spun beneath her, faster and faster, and Lirael saw it in earlier times, saw how all life had been extinguished. Then she fell through the suns again and saw another void, another single, struggling world that would become a desert.

Six times, Lirael saw a world destroyed. The seventh time, it was her own world she saw. She knew it, though there was no landmark or feature that told her so. She saw the Destroyer choose it, but this time others chose it, too. This would be the battleground where they would confront the Destroyer; this was where sides must be chosen and loyalties decided for all time.

The vision Lirael saw then seemed to last for many days, and many horrors. But at the same time, through her other eye she saw the Dog pacing backwards and forwards, and Lirael knew that little time had passed in Death.

Finally, she saw enough, and could bear to see no more. She shut both eyes, snapped the mirror shut, and slowly sank to her knees, holding the small silver case between her clasped hands. Warm water lapped around her, but it offered no comfort.

When she opened her eyes a moment later, the Dog licked her on the mouth and looked at her with great concern.

"We have to hurry," said Lirael, pushing herself upright. "I didn't really understand before. . . . We have to hurry!"

She started back towards the Eighth Gate and drew both sword and bell with new decisiveness. She had seen what Orannis could do now, and it was far worse than she had ever imagined. Truly, It was aptly named the Destroyer. Orannis existed solely to destroy, and the Charter was the enemy that had stopped It doing so. It hated all living things and not only wanted to destroy them—It had the power to do so.

Only Lirael knew how Orannis could be bound anew. It would be difficult—perhaps even impossible. But it was their one chance, and she was full of single-minded determination to get back to Life. She had to make it happen. For herself, for the Dog, Sam, Nick, Major Greene and his men, for the people of Ancelstierre who would die without even knowing their danger, and for all those in the Old Kingdom. Her cousins of the Clayr. Even Aunt Kirrith . . .

Thoughts of them all, and her responsibility, filled her head as she approached the Eighth Gate, the words of the opening spell on her lips. But even as she opened her mouth to speak the words, there was a gout of flame from the darkness of the Gate, directly opposite Lirael and the Dog.

Wreathed in that flame, Hedge lunged through. His sword cut at Lirael's left arm, and he struck so hard that she dropped Saraneth, its brief jangle quickly swallowed by the river. The clang of ensorcelled steel on gethre plates echoed across the water. The armor held, but even so Lirael's arm beneath was badly bruised—for the second time in only a few days.

Lirael barely managed to parry the next cut for her head. She leapt back and got in the way of the Dog, who was about to leap forward. Pain coursed through Lirael's left arm, shooting up through her shoulder and neck. Nevertheless, she reached for a bell.

Hedge was quicker. He had a bell in his hand already, and he rang it. Saraneth, Lirael recognized, and she steeled herself to resist its power. But nothing came with the peal of the bell. No compulsion, no test of wills.

"Sit!" commanded Hedge, and Lirael suddenly realized that

Hedge had focused Saraneth's power upon the Disreputable Dog.

Growling, the Dog froze, halfway back on her haunches, ready to spring. But Saraneth had her in its grip, and she was unable to move.

Lirael circled around the Dog, moving to try to cut at Hedge's bell arm, as he had cut hers. But he moved, too, circling back the other way. There was something odd about his fighting stance, Lirael noted. She couldn't think what it was for a moment. Then she realized that he kept his head angled down, and he never looked up. Clearly, Hedge was afraid to see the stars of the Ninth Gate.

He started to move towards her, but she circled back again, keeping the motionless Dog between them. As she passed in front, Lirael saw the hound wink.

"You have led me a long chase," said Hedge. His voice was flavored with Free Magic, and he sounded much more like something Dead than a living man. He looked like it, too. He towered over Lirael, and there were fires everywhere within him, glowing red in his eyes and mouth, dripping from his fingers and shining through his skin. Lirael wasn't even sure he was a living man. He was more like a Free Magic spirit himself, only clad in human flesh. "But it is finished now, here and in Life. My master is whole again, and the destruction has begun. Only the Dead walk in the living world, to praise Orannis for Its work. Only the Dead—and I, the faithful vizier."

His voice had a hypnotic quality about it. Lirael realized he was trying to distract her while he went for a killing blow. He hadn't tried the bell upon her, which was curious—but then, she'd broken free of Hedge and Saraneth before.

"Look up, Hedge," she answered, as they circled again. "The Ninth Gate calls. Can't you feel the summons of the stars?"

She lunged at him on "stars," but Hedge was ready, and

more practiced with a sword. He parried, and his swift riposte cut the fabric of her surcoat directly above her heart.

Quickly, she backed off again, this time circling away from the Dog. Hedge followed, his head still bent, watching her through hooded eyes.

Behind him, the Dog stirred. Slowly, she raised one paw from the shallow river, careful not to make a splash. Then she began to sneak after the necromancer as he stalked towards Lirael.

"I don't believe you about the Destroyer, either," said Lirael as she backed away, hoping her voice would cover the sound of the Dog's advance. "I would know if anything had happened to my body in Life. Besides, you wouldn't bother with me if It were already free."

"You are an annoyance, nothing more," said Hedge. He was smiling now, and the flames on his sword grew brighter, feeding off his expectation of a kill. "It pleases me to finish you. There is no more to it than that. As my Master destroys that which displeases, so do I!"

He slashed viciously down at her. Lirael barely managed to parry and push his sword aside. Then they were locked together, body to body, his head bent over hers and his metallic, flame-ridden breath hot upon her cheek as she turned away.

"But perhaps I will play a little with you first." Hedge smiled, disengaged, and stepped back.

Lirael struck at him with all her strength and anger. Hedge laughed, parried, stepped back once more—and tumbled over the Disreputable Dog.

He dropped his sword and bell at once, and clapped his hands to his eyes as he struck the water with the hiss and roar of steam. But he was an instant too late. He saw the stars as he fell, and they called to him, overcoming the weight of spells and power that had kept him in the living world for more than a hundred years.

Always postponing Death, always searching for something that could let him stay forever under the sun. He thought he had found it, serving Orannis, for he cared nothing about anyone else or any other living thing. The Destroyer had promised him the reward of eternal life and even greater dominion over the Dead. Hedge had done everything he could to earn it.

Now, with a single glimpse of those beckoning stars, it was all stripped away. Hedge's hands fell back. Starlight filled his eyes with glowing tears, tears that slowly quenched his internal fires. The coils of steam wafted away, and the river grew quiet. Hedge raised his arms and began his own fall towards the sky, the stars, and the Ninth Gate.

The Disreputable Dog picked up Lirael's bell from the river and took it to her, careful not to let it sound. Lirael accepted it in silence and put it away. There was no time to savor their triumph over the necromancer. Lirael knew that he was only ever a lesser enemy.

Together they crossed the Eighth Gate, both filled with a terrible fear. The fear that though Hedge's words were lies, they would become the truth before they could get back to Life.

Lirael was further burdened by the weight of knowledge. Now she knew how to bind the Destroyer anew, but she also knew it couldn't be done just by her. Sam would need to be the heir of the Wallmakers in truth and not just be entitled to wear their silver trowel on his surcoat.

Others of the Blood would be needed, too, and they just weren't there.

Even worse, the binding was only half of what must be done. Even if Lirael and Sam could somehow manage that, there was the breaking, and that would require more courage than Lirael thought she had.

Chapter Twenty-Six

SAM AND THE SHADOW HANDS

As THE DEAD broke free of Saraneth's hold, Sam blew on the Ranna pipe. But the soft lullaby was too late, and Sam's breath too hasty. Only a half dozen of the Dead lay down to sleep under Ranna's spell, and the bell caught several soldiers, too. The other ninety or more Dead Hands charged down out of the fog, to be met by swords, bayonets, silver blades, and the white lightning of the Charter Mages.

For a furious, frenzied minute of hacking and dodging, Sam couldn't see what was happening. Then the Hand in front of him collapsed, its legs cut away. Sam was surprised to see that he'd done that himself, the Charter marks on his sword blazing with blue-white fury.

"Try the pipes again!" shouted the Major. He stepped in front of Sam to engage the next broken-jawed apparition. "We'll cover you!"

Sam nodded and brought the pipes to his lips again with new determination. The Dead had driven the defenders back with their charge, and now Lirael was only a few feet behind him, a frozen statue who would be totally vulnerable to attack.

Most of the Dead Hands were fresh corpses, still clad in their workers' overalls. But many were inhabited by spirits that had lain long in Death, who quickly transformed the dead flesh they now occupied, making it less human and more like the dreadful shapes they'd assumed in Death. One came at Sam now, wriggling like a snake between Major Greene and Lieutenant Tindall, its lower jaw unhinged for a larger bite. Reflexively, Sam stabbed it through the throat. Sparks flew as the Charter marks on the blade destroyed dead flesh. It wriggled and threshed but couldn't free itself from the sword, so the thing's spirit began to crawl out of its fleshy husk, like a worm of darkness leaving a totally rotten apple.

Sam looked down at it and felt his fear replaced by a hot anger. How dare these Dead intrude upon the world of Life? His nostrils flared, and his face reddened, as he drew breath to blow upon the pipe. This was not the Dead's path, and he would make them choose another.

Lungs expanded to the full, he chose the Kibeth pipe and blew. A single note sounded, high and clear—but then it somehow became a lively, infectious jig. It cheered the soldiers and even made them smile, their weapons moving with the rhythm of Kibeth's song.

But the Dead heard a different tune, and those with working mouths and lungs and throats let out terrible howls of fear and anguish. But howl as they would, they couldn't drown out Kibeth's call, and the Dead Spirits began to move against their will, thrust out of the decaying flesh they occupied and back into Death.

"That's shown them!" shouted Lieutenant Tindall, as the Dead Hands fell all along the line, leaving empty corpses, the guiding spirits driven back into Death by Kibeth.

"Don't get too excited," growled the Major. He looked swiftly around and saw several men on the ground, clearly dead or dying. There were many wounded heading back to the aid post set up at the base of the spur, some of them supported by far too many able-bodied companions. Considerably more men were simply fleeing down the hill, back towards the Southerlings and the relative protection of the stream.

Most of the company had fled, in fact, and Greene felt a pang of disappointment in what he knew would be his last command. But the great majority of the men were conscripts, and even those who'd served on the Perimeter for a while would never have seen so many Dead.

"Damn them! Just when we're winning, the fools!"

Lieutenant Tindall had noticed the fleeing men at last, with all the indignation of his youth. He made as if to start after them, but Major Greene held him back.

"Let them go, Francis. They're not the Scouts, and this is too much for them. And we need you here—that was probably only the first wave. There will be more."

"Yes, and soon," confirmed Sam hurriedly. "Major—we need to bring everyone in closer to Lirael. I'm afraid if even one Dead creature gets past—"

"Yes!" agreed the Major fervently. "Francis, Edward—close up, everyone, quick as you can. See what you can do for the wounded, too, but I don't want to lose any more effectives. Go!"

"Yes, sir!" the two Lieutenants snapped in unison. Then they were shouting orders, and the sergeants were relaying them with extra flavor. There were only thirty or so soldiers left, and within a minute they were almost shoulder to shoulder in a tight ring around Lirael's iced-over form.

"How many more of the Dead are coming?" asked the Major, as Sam stared up into the fog. It was still spreading, and growing thicker, wisps winding around them as it rolled downhill. There was more lightning beyond the ridge, too, and the storm clouds had spread across the sky like a great inky stain, in parallel with the white fog below.

"I'm not sure." Sam frowned. "More and more of them keep emerging into Life. Hedge must be in Death himself, and is sending them out. He has to have found an old graveyard or some other supply of bodies, because they're all Dead Hands so far. Timothy said he only had sixty workers, and they were all in the first attack."

Both glanced over at Tim Wallach as Sam spoke. He had taken a dead soldier's rifle, sword bayonet, and helmet and now stood in the ring—much to everyone's surprise, perhaps including his own.

"It's always better to be doing," said Sam, quoting the Disreputable Dog. As he said it, he realized that he actually believed it now. He was still scared, still felt the knot of apprehension in his guts. But he knew it wouldn't stop him from doing what had to be done. It was what his parents would expect, Sam thought, but he did not dwell on that. He could not think of Sabriel and Touchstone, or he would fall apart—and he could not, must not, do that.

"My philosophy exactly—" the Major began to say; then he saw Sam shiver and reach for his panpipes.

"Shadow Hands!" Sam exclaimed, pointing with his sword as he put the pipes to his lips.

"Stand ready!" roared the Major, reaching into the Charter for marks of fire and destruction, though he knew they would be of little use against Shadow Hands. They had no bodies to burn or flesh to break. The Charter Magic the soldiers knew might slow them, but that was all.

Up on the ridge, four vaguely human shapes of utter darkness came down through the fog, rippling across rock and thorn. Silent as the grave, they ignored the arrows that passed straight through them and glided inexorably forward—directly towards Lirael and the gap between the boulders where Sam, Major Greene, and Lieutenant Tindall stood to bar their way.

When they were only twenty yards away, one Shadow Hand

paused—and pounced upon a wounded soldier who'd been overlooked, lying under the overhang of a large rock. Frantically, he tried to stand and get away, but the Shadow Hand wrapped all around him like a shroud and sucked his life away.

As the soldier's dying scream gurgled into nothing, Sam took a breath and blew desperately on the Saraneth pipe. He had to dominate the Shadow Hands, bend them to his will, for he and his allies had no other weapons that would work. His sword, and the marks it bore, would hurt them, but no more.

So he blew, and prayed to the Charter that he would have the strength to overcome the Shadow Hands.

Saraneth's strong voice cut through even the thunder. Immediately, Sam felt the Shadow Hands resist his dominion. They raged against his will, and sweat broke out all over his body from the effort. It was all he could do just to stop them in place. These spirits were old, and much stronger than the Dead Hands Sam had sent walking into Death with Kibeth. It took all his strength to stop them moving forward, as they constantly pushed against the bonds Saraneth had—oh so lightly—woven around them.

Slowly, the world narrowed for Sam, till all he could sense was the four spirits and their struggle against him. Everything else was gone—the dampness of the fog, the soldiers around him, the thunder and lightning. There was only him and his opponents.

"Bow down to me!" he shouted, but it was with his mind and will, not a shout any human ears could hear. Sam heard the voiceless spirits answer back the same way, a chorus of mental howls and hissing that clearly defied him.

They were clever, these Shadow Hands. One would pretend to falter, but as Sam concentrated his will against that one, the others would counterattack, almost breaking his hold.

Gradually, Sam became aware that they were not only resisting him, they were actually eroding the binding. Every time he shifted his concentration, they would shuffle forward a little. Just a few steps, but gradually the gap was closing. Soon they would be able to leap past him, drain the life from the soldiers at his side—and attack the defenseless body of Lirael.

He also became aware that only a few seconds had actually passed since he had started blowing through the Saraneth pipe—and he had yet to take another breath. Though the sound of the pipe continued, it was weakening. If only he could pause, refill his lungs, and sound Saraneth again, he could greatly strengthen the binding. Sam knew he was close to total command of these spirits, yet not close enough. He also knew that if he shifted his full concentration away from the four Shadow Hands to take a breath, they would be upon him.

Given that, all he could do was continue the battle of wills and try to slow them down even more. Lirael could return at any moment and banish them with the bells. Sam just had to hold them for long enough.

He stopped even trying to take a breath, shunting his body's urgent demands for air into a corner of his mind. Nothing was as important as stopping the Shadow Hands. He would concentrate every last particle of his mind and power upon them and every last wisp of air into the pipe. They would not reach Lirael. They must not. She was the last hope for the entire world against the Destroyer.

Besides, she was his blood kin, and he had promised.

The Shadow Hands took another step closer, and Sam's entire body shuddered with effort as he tried to force them back, his muscles reflecting the struggle of his mind. But he was growing weaker, he knew, and the Dead stronger. He was also close to passing out from lack of breath, and an almost overpowering urge to step back was rising inside him. Get out of the way! Take a breath! Let these monsters past!

But as he fought the Dead, he fought his own fears, pushing them away into the same distant corner of his mind that so badly wanted to draw air into his lungs. They would stay there, and he was determined to fight well beyond his last breath. At the same time, he tried desperately to think of some stratagem or cunning ploy.

Nothing came to him, and though he hadn't seen or felt them move, the Shadow Hands had stolen some ground. They were now only just out of sword's reach, tall columns of inky blackness, spreading a chill colder than the coldest of winter days.

The two on the outside were moving around him, Sam realized, though not by much. Clearly they intended to surround and smother him with their shadow stuff, to wrap him in a cocoon of four hungry spirits. Then they would move on to Lirael.

Fire suddenly burst out around the head of the closest Shadow Hand, a fist-sized globe of pure blue flame. But the Dead creature didn't so much as flinch, and the fire spluttered out into the individual marks that had made it, and these vanished into the fog.

Another Charter-spell struck, to no effect, save to set one of the stunted trees alight as the fire rebounded off the shadowy form of the Dead. Sam realized that Major Greene and Lieutenant Tindall were trying to help him with these spells, but he could spare neither thought nor breath to warn them of the uselessness of fire against such an enemy.

All Sam's attention was on the Dead. In turn, all their attention was focused back on him, and on the struggle between them.

So neither noticed the fog suddenly swirl around them, as if disturbed by some mighty gust of air, nor the shouts and cries of the soldiers behind them.

That is, till they heard the bell. A strong, ferocious chime that fell from the air above them. It gripped the four Shadow

Hands like a puppet master picking up marionettes to put back in the box. Unable to resist, they bent down, their shadowy heads raised to beg wordlessly for mercy.

No mercy was forthcoming. Another bell rang, building an angry, violent dance over the broad shout of the first. The Shadow Hands jerked upright at its sharp song, their shadow stuff stretching into thin lines, as if they were being sucked through a narrow hole.

Then they were gone, summarily executed, this time for good.

Sam fell to his knees as the Dead disappeared and drew a long, shuddering breath into his desperate lungs. Above him, a bright blue and silver Paperwing hovered for a moment, like a giant hawk over its prey. Then it fell quickly and circled down to the valley floor, where the ground was level and clear enough to land. Sam stared at it and at the two other Paperwings that were gliding down in front of the Southerlings.

Three Paperwings. The craft that had passed overhead was blue and silver, and that was the Abhorsen's color. The second was of green and silver, for the Clayr. The third was the red and gold of the royal line. Two of the three paperwings had a passenger as well as a pilot.

"I don't understand," whispered Sam. "Who wields the bells?"

Mogget was just short of the top of the ridge, zigzagging between Dead Hands and lightning rods, when he heard the bells. He smiled and paused to shout at the single Dead Hand who stood in his way.

"Hear the full voice of Saraneth! Flee while you still can!"

As a ploy, it didn't work. The Dead Hand was too newly returned to Life, too stupid to understand Mogget's words, and it didn't have Mogget's unnaturally keen hearing. It hadn't heard the bells through the thunder, and it had no sense of the power unleashed beyond the ridge. As far as it was concerned, living prey had just stopped in front of it. Close enough to grab.

Rotting fingers leapt out, clutching the little albino's leg. Mogget yowled and kicked back, the dry bones of his captor snapping with the force of the blow. But still it hung on, and other Dead were lumbering towards Mogget now, drawn by the prospect of Life to feast on.

Mogget yowled again and put Nick down. Then he whipped around, his long-nailed fingers scratching and his sharp-toothed mouth fastening on the Dead Hand's wrist.

If it still had human intelligence, the Hand would have been surprised, because no man ever fought like this one, with an arched back and a wild combination of hissing, biting, and scratching.

Mogget bit through the Dead creature's wrist, severing it completely. Instantly, he sprang back, picked up Nick, dodged around the Hand, and sprinted off with a triumphant yowl.

The creature ignored its missing hand and tried to follow them. Only then did it discover that its strange opponent had clawed through its hamstrings as well. It took two uncertain steps and fell, the Dead spirit that inhabited it already looking desperately around for some other body to inhabit.

By then, Mogget was on the other side of the ridge. He held Nick's arm out to one side as he ran, keeping it well away from his own body. That arm shook and shivered, muscles twitched under the skin, and dark bruises blossomed all around the elbow and forearm.

Behind Mogget, the lightning storm began to abate and the thunder to lessen. The fog was still lit with electric blue around the edges—but at the center, both the fog and the storm clouds above it had become a bright, bright red.

Chapter Twenty-Seven

WHEN THE LIGHTNING STOPS

S AM PICKED HIMSELF up. He felt very weak, washed out, and confused. Slowly he turned to look down at the three Paperwings in the valley, several hundred yards away. They looked very small in front of the crowd of Southerlings. Magical flying craft made from laminated paper and Charter Magic, they were rather like large, brilliantly feathered birds.

The pilots and passengers from the three Paperwings were already climbing out of their craft. Sam stared at them, unable to believe who he was seeing.

"That's the King and the Abhorsen, isn't it, Prince Sameth?" asked Lieutenant Tindall. "I thought they were dead!"

Sam nodded and smiled and shook his head at the same time. He felt an irresistible spring of relief flow up through every part of his body. He didn't know whether to laugh or cry or sing, and was unsurprised to find that tears were running down his cheeks and laughter had come unbidden and was leaping out of his mouth. Because the people climbing out of the blue and silver Paperwing were indisputably Touchstone and Sabriel. Alive and well, all tales of their demise proven false in that single joyous sight.

But the surprises did not end there. Sam wiped the tears away, calmed his laughter before it became hysterical, and caught his breath as he saw a young, raven-haired woman vault out of the red and gold craft and run to catch up with his parents, her sword already out and flashing. Behind her, two very blond, brown-skinned, and willowy women were leaving the green and silver Paperwing, a little more sedately but also in a hurry.

"Who's that girl?" asked Lieutenant Tindall, with more than professional interest in their saviors. "I mean, who are those ladies?"

"That's my sister, Ellimere!" exclaimed Sam. "And two of the Clayr, by the look of them!"

He started to run down to them but stopped after only two paces. They were all hurrying up, and his place was here, by Lirael. She was still frozen in place, still somewhere in Death, facing who knew what dangers. That realization brought Sam back to the current situation. The Dead had fled from Saraneth as wielded by the Abhorsen. But they were only lesser minions of the real Enemy.

"The lightning has stopped," said Tim Wallach. "Listen—there's no thunder now."

Everyone turned back to the ridge. Sam's feelings of relief vanished in an instant. The thunder and lightning had faded away to nothing, sure enough, but the fog was as thick as ever. It was no longer lit with blue flashes but by a steady, pulsing red that grew brighter as they watched—as if an enormous heart of fire grew in the valley beyond.

Something was coming down from the ridge, a shape that seemed to have too many arms, an awful silhouette backlit by the blood-red glow from behind the ridge.

Sam raised his sword and felt for the panpipes. Whatever this was didn't seem to be Dead—or at least he couldn't sense it. But it carried the hot stench of Free Magic with it—and it was coming straight towards him.

Then the thing shouted, with the voice of Mogget.

"It's me—Mogget! I've got Nicholas!"

The fog eddied, and Sam saw that the voice came from the strange little man with the pale hair and skin who he had last seen on the hill above the Red Lake. He was carrying an emaciated body that just might be Nick. Whoever it was, Mogget held the man's right arm out to the side, where it writhed and twitched with a life of its own, all too like a tentacle.

"What is that?" asked Major Greene quietly as he signaled his men to close up again around Lirael.

"It's Mogget," replied Sam with a frown. "He had that shape in my grandfather's time. And that . . . . that is my friend Nick."

"Of course it is!" shouted Mogget, who hadn't stopped walking down. "Where is the Abhorsen? And Lirael? We must hurry—the hemispheres have almost joined. If we can get Nicholas farther away, the fragment will not be able to join and the hemispheres will be incomplete—"

He was interrupted by a terrible scream. Nick's eyes flashed open and his whole body jerked into rigidity, one arm pointed back towards the loch valley like a gun. Something brighter than the sun flared at his fingertip for a moment, then it flashed over the ridge, too fast to follow.

"No!" Nick screamed. His mouth frothed with bloody foam, and his fingers clutched uselessly at empty air. But his scream was lost in another sound, a sound that welled up from the red heart of the fog beyond the ridge. An indescribable shout of triumph, greed, and fury. With that shout, a column of fire boiled up to the sky. It climbed up and up till it loomed high above the ridge. The fog swirled around it like a cloak and began to burn away.

"Free!" boomed the Destroyer. The word howled across the watchers like a hot wind, stripping the moisture from their eyes and mouths. On and on the sound carried, echoing from distant hills, screaming through far-off towns, striking fear into all who heard it, long after the word itself was lost.

"Too late," said Mogget. He laid Nick carefully down on the rocky ground and crouched himself. His pale hair began to spread down his neck and face, and his bones contracted and tightened under the skin. Inside a minute, he was once again a little white cat, with Ranna tinkling on his collar.

Sam hardly noticed the transformation. He hurried up to Nick and bent over him, already reaching for the strongest Charter marks he knew for healing, assembling them in his mind. There was no question that his friend was dying. Sam could feel his spirit slipping through to Death, see the terrible pallor of Nick's face, the blood on his mouth, and the deep bruises on his chest and arm.

Golden fire grew in Sam's gesturing hands as he pulled marks from the Charter with ferocious haste. Then he gently laid his palms on Nick's chest and sent the healing magic into his damaged body.

Only the spell wouldn't take hold. The marks slid away and were lost, and blue sparks crackled under Sam's palms. He cursed and tried again, but it was no use. There was still too strong a residue of Free Magic in Nick, and it repulsed all Sam's efforts.

All it did do was bring Nick back into consciousness—of a sort. He smiled as he saw Sam, thinking himself back at school again, struck down by a fastball. But Sam was in some weird armor, not in cricket whites. And there was thick fog behind him, not bright sunshine, and stones and stunted trees, not new-mown grass.

Nick remembered, and his smile disappeared. With memory came pain, everywhere in his body, but there was a welcome lightness as well. He felt clear and unrestricted, as if he were a prisoner freed from a lifetime locked in a single room.

"I'm sorry," he gasped, the blood in his mouth choking him

as he spoke. "I didn't know, Sam. I didn't know . . ."

"It's all right," said Sam. He wiped the bloody froth away from Nick's mouth with the sleeve of his surcoat. "It's not your fault. I should have realized something had happened to you. . . ."

"The sunken road," whispered Nick. He closed his eyes again, his breath coming in choking gasps. "After you went into Death on the hill. I can remember it now. I ran down to see what I could do and fell into the road. Hedge was waiting. He thought I was you, Sam. . . ."

His voice trailed off. Sam bent over him again, trying to force the healing marks into him by strength of will. For the third time, they slid off.

Nick's lips moved and he said something too faint to hear. Sam bent still closer, his ear to Nick's mouth, and he took his hand and held it as if he might physically drag his friend back from Death.

"Lirael," whispered Nick. "Tell Lirael I remembered her. I tried . . ."

"You can tell her yourself," Sam said urgently. "She'll be here! Any moment. Nick—you have to fight it!"

"That's what she said," coughed Nick. Specks of blood stained Sam's cheek, but he didn't move. He didn't hear the soft bark of the Dog as she returned to Life, or the cracking of ice, or Lirael's exclamation of surprise. For Sam, there was only the space he and Nicholas occupied. Everything else had ceased to exist.

Then he felt a cold hand on his shoulder, and he looked around. Lirael was standing there. She was still covered in frost. Ice flaked from her as she moved. She looked at Nick, and Sam saw a fleeting expression that he could not place. Then it was gone, visibly repressed by a hardness that reminded Sam of his mother.

"Nick's dying," said Sam, his eyes bright with tears. "The

healing spells won't— The shard flew out of him— I can't do anything!"

"I know how to bind and break the Destroyer," said Lirael urgently. She turned her gaze away from Nick and looked directly at Sam. "You have to make a weapon for me, Sam. Now!"

"But Nick!" protested Sam. He didn't let go of his friend's hand.

Lirael glanced at the column of fire. She could feel its heat now, could gauge the state of the Destroyer's power by its color and the height of the flames. There were still minutes left—but very few of them. Even twice as many would not be enough for Nick.

"There's . . . there's nothing you can do for Nick," she said, though the words came out with a sob. "There's no time, and I need . . . I need to tell you what must be done. We have a chance, Sam! I didn't think we would, but the Clayr did See who was needed and they're here. But we have to act now!"

Sam looked down at his best friend. Nick's eyes were open again, but he was looking past Sam, at Lirael.

"Do what she says, Sam," Nick whispered, attempting a smile. "Try and make it right."

Then his eyes lost their focus, and his ragged breath bubbled away to nothing. Both Sam and Lirael felt his spirit slip away, and they knew that Nicholas Sayre was dead.

Sam opened his hand and stood up. He felt old and tired, his joints stiff. He was bewildered, too, unable to accept that the body at his feet was Nick's. He had set out to save him, and he had failed. Everything else seemed doomed to failure, too.

Lirael grabbed him as he swayed in front of her, his eyes unfocused. The shock broke through the distance he felt around him, and he reluctantly met her gaze. She swung him around and pointed to Sabriel, Touchstone, Ellimere, and the two Clayr, who were moving rapidly up the spur.

"You need to get a drop of blood from me, your parents, Ellimere, and Sanar and Ryelle, and bind it with yours into Nehima with the metal from the panpipes. Can you do that? Now!"

"I haven't got a forge," Sam replied dumbly, but he accepted Nehima from Lirael's hand. He was still looking down at Nick.

"Use magic!" shrieked Lirael, and she shook him, hard. "You're a Wallmaker, Sam! Hurry!"

The shaking brought Sam all the way back to the present. He suddenly felt the heat of the fiery column, and the full dread of the Destroyer filled his bones. Turning away from Nick, he used the sword to cut his palm, wiping the blood along the blade.

Lirael cut herself next, letting the blood flow down the blade.

"I'll remember," she whispered, touching the sword. Then in the next breath, conscious of how little time they had, she shouted at the soldiers.

"Major Greene! Get all your people back to the Southerlings! Warn them! You must all stay on the other side of the stream and lie down as low as you can. Do not look towards the fire, and when it suddenly brightens, close your eyes! Go! Go!"

Before anyone could respond, Lirael was shouting again, this time at the group led by Sabriel, which was almost upon them.

"Hurry! Please hurry! We have to make at least three diamonds of protection here within the next ten minutes! Hurry!"

Sam rushed down to meet his parents, his sister, and the two Clayr, holding the bloody sword flat, ready to take more contributions. As he walked, he built a spell of forging and binding in his mind, knitting the marks together into one long and complex net. When the blade was fully blooded, he would lay the pipes upon it and the spell over it all entire. If it worked, blood and metal would join in the making of a new and unique sword. If it worked . . .

Behind him, the Dog slunk over to the sprawled, silent body of Nicholas. She looked around to make sure no one was paying any attention, then barked softly in his ear.

Nothing happened. The Dog looked puzzled, as if she expected an immediate effect, and licked his forehead. Her tongue left a glowing mark. Still nothing happened. After a moment, the Dog left the corpse and bounded across to join Lirael, who was casting the Eastmark of a very large diamond of protection. It was to be the outermost of three, if there was time to cast them. If there was not, they would not survive.

Beyond the ridge, the huge column of fire burned with increasing heat, though it stayed a terrible, disturbing red. The red of bright blood, fresh from a wound.

Chapter Twenty-Eight

THE SEVEN

"SAMETH, WHAT HAVE you done now!" were the first words out of Ellimere's mouth. But she belied her speech with an attempt to hug him, which Sam had to shrug away.

"No time to explain!" he exclaimed as he held out the bloodied Nehima. "I need some of your blood on the blade; then you have to go and help Aunt Lirael."

Ellimere immediately complied. In earlier times, Sam would have been surprised by his sister's instant cooperation. But Ellimere was no fool, and the towering column of fire beyond the ridge was clearly only the beginning of something terrible and strange.

"Mother! Father! I'm . . . I'm so glad you're not dead!" Sam cried as Ellimere ran past, her cut palm still dripping blood, and Sabriel and Touchstone clambered up.

"Likewise," said Touchstone, but he wasted no time either, holding out his hand so Sam could make the cut. Sabriel put hers out at the same time, but she ruffled Sam's head with her other hand.

"I have a sister, or so the Clayr tell me, and a new Abhorsen-in-Waiting," said Sabriel as they wiped their palms on the steel, the marks glowing as they felt the kinship of Blood to Charter. "And you have found a different path but one no less important. I trust you have been helpful to your aunt?"

"Yes, I suppose," replied Sam. He was trying to keep all the spell for the forging in his head, and he didn't have time to talk. "She needs help now. Three diamonds of protection!"

Sabriel and Touchstone were gone before Sam finished speaking. The two Clayr stood in front of him, holding out their hands. Wordlessly, Sam cut gently into their palms, and they also marked the blade with blood. Sam hardly saw them do it, so many Charter marks were whirling around in his head. He didn't feel them take his elbows, either, and lead him back up the hill. He couldn't think of such mundanities as walking. He was lost in the Charter, dredging up marks he hardly knew. Thousands and thousands of Charter marks that filled his head with light, spreading inwards and outwards, ordering themselves into a spell that would join with Nehima and the seven pipes to replicate a weapon that was as deadly to its wielder as to its target.

There was no time for greetings farther up the ridge, either. Lirael simply snapped out orders as Ellimere, Sabriel, and Touchstone arrived. She sent them to help make the first three marks of each diamond of protection, saving the last mark till everyone was inside and the diamonds could be completed. For a moment, Lirael had stumbled over her instructions, fearing that they might protest, for who was she to give orders to the King and the Abhorsen? But they didn't, quickly going to their tasks, building the diamonds jointly to save time, each taking a cardinal mark.

Major Greene hadn't questioned her orders either, Lirael noticed with relief. What was left of his company was running pell-mell across the valley, the able-bodied carrying the wounded, with the Major's shouts speeding them on the way. They were shouting at the Southerlings, too, telling them to lie down and look away. Lirael hoped the Southerlings would listen, though the sight of the whirling column of fire had the power to entrance as well as terrify.

Sam staggered up between Sanar and Ryelle, who smiled at Lirael as they brought him to the center of the incipient diamond. Lirael smiled back, a brief smile that took her back for a moment to the twins' words the day she had left the Glacier. "You must remember that, Sighted or not, you *are* a Daughter of the Clayr."

Lirael closed the outer diamond with a cardinal mark and stepped inside the next incomplete diamond. As she passed him, Touchstone let the Northmark flow down his sword to close the second diamond behind her. He smiled at Lirael as they stepped back inside the third and final diamond, and she saw the strong resemblance between him and his son.

Sabriel herself closed the inner diamond. In only a few minutes they had raised magical defenses of triple strength. Lirael hoped it would be enough and they would survive to do what must be done. She had a momentary panic then, and had to quickly count on her fingers to make sure they had the necessary seven. Herself, Sameth, Ellimere, Sabriel, Touchstone, Sanar, Ryelle. That was seven, though she was not sure it was really the right seven.

The lines of the diamond shone golden but were pallid in comparison with the fierce light of the column of fire. Vast as that roaring column was, Lirael knew it was only the first and least of the nine manifestations of the Destroyer's power. Worse was to come, and soon.

Sam knelt over sword and panpipes, weaving his spell. Lirael checked that the Dog and Mogget were safely inside the diamond, and noticed that Nick's body was inside, too, which somehow seemed right. There was also a large thistle bush, which was annoying and showed her haste. She hadn't had time to think about where the diamonds should be.

Everyone within the diamonds, save Sam, was stiff and

awkward for a moment, in that strange calm before impending disaster. Then Sabriel took Lirael into a loose embrace and kissed her lightly on the cheek.

"So you are the sister I never knew I had," said Sabriel. "I would wish that we had met earlier, and on a more auspicious occasion. We have had many revelations thrust upon us, more than my tired mind can take in, I fear. We have gone by boat and van and aeroplane and Paperwing to come here, almost without rest, and the Clayr have Seen a great deal very suddenly. They tell me that we face a great spirit of the Beginning, and that you are not only heir to my office but a Remembrancer, too, and you have Seen the past as other Clayr See the future. So please tell us—what must we do?"

"I'm so glad you're all here now," replied Lirael. It was terribly tempting to just fall apart during this brief lull, but she could not. Everything depended upon her. Everything.

She took a deep breath and continued, "The Destroyer is building up to Its second manifestation, which I hope . . . I hope the diamonds will save us from. Afterwards, It will diminish for a little time, and it is then we must go down to It, warding ourselves against the fires that the second manifestation will leave behind. The binding spell we will use ourselves is simple, and I will teach it to you now. But first, everyone must take a bell from me . . . or from the Abhorsen."

"Call me Sabriel," said Sabriel firmly. "Does it matter which bell?"

"There will be one that feels right, one that will speak to your blood. Each of us will be standing for one of the original Seven, as they live on in our bloodline and in the bells," stammered Lirael, nervous about instructing her elders. Sabriel was quite frightening up close, and it was hard to remember that she was her own sister, not just the near-legendary binder of the

Dead. But Lirael did know what she was doing. She had seen in the Dark Mirror how the binding had been done and how it must be done again, and she could feel the affinities between the bells and the people.

Though there was something strange about Sanar and Ryelle. Lirael looked at them, and her heart almost stopped as she realized that as twins, their spirits were intertwined. They could wield only one bell between them. There would only be six of the needed seven.

She stood frozen and horrified as the others stepped forward and took their bells from Sabriel.

"Saraneth for me, I think," said Sabriel, but she left the bell in the bandolier. "Touchstone?"

"Ranna for me," replied Touchstone. "The Sleeper seems very appropriate, given my past."

"I will take a bell from my aunt, if I may," said Ellimere. "Dyrim, I think."

Lirael mechanically handed the bell to her niece. Ellimere looked very like Sabriel, with the same sort of contained force inside her. But she had her father's smile, Lirael saw, even through her panic.

"We will hold Mosrael together," said Sanar and Ryelle in unison.

Lirael shut her eyes. Maybe she hadn't counted right, she thought. But she could feel who should have which bell. She opened her eyes again and with shaking hands started to undo a strap on her bandolier.

"Sam will have Belgaer, and . . . and I will wield both Astarael and . . . and Kibeth, to make the seven."

She spoke as confidently as she could, but there was a quaver in her voice. She could not wield two bells. Not for this binding. There had to be seven wielders, not just seven bells.

"Hmmph," woofed the Dog, standing up and wriggling her hindquarters in a somewhat embarrassed fashion. "Not Kibeth. I shall stand for myself."

Lirael's hand fumbled on the strap that held Astarael silent, and she only just managed to prevent the bell's mournful call, which would send all who heard it into Death.

"But you said you weren't one of the Seven!" Lirael protested, though she had long suspected the truth about the Dog. She just hadn't wanted to admit it, even to herself, for the Dog was her best and oldest friend, long her only friend. Lirael could not imagine *Kibeth* as her friend.

"I lied," said the Dog cheerily. "That's one of the reasons I'm the Disreputable Dog. Besides, I'm only what's left of Kibeth, in a roundabout, hand-me-down sort of way. Not quite the same. But I'll stand against the Destroyer. Against Orannis, as one of your Seven."

As the Dog spoke the Destroyer's name, the column of fire roared higher still and punched through the remnants of the storm clouds. It was more than a mile high now, and dominated all the western sky, its red light defeating the yellow of the sun.

Lirael wanted to say something, but the words were choked by incipient tears. She did not know whether they were of relief or sadness. Whatever was to come, she knew nothing would ever be the same with her and the Disreputable Dog.

Instead of speaking, she scratched the Dog's head. Just twice, running her fingers through the soft dog hair. Then she quickly recited the binding spell, showing everyone the marks and words they would have to use.

"Sam is making the sword that I will use to break the Destroyer once It is bound," Lirael finished. At least she hoped he was. As if to reinforce her hope, she added, "He is a true inheritor of the Wallmaker's powers."

She gestured to where Sam was bent over Nehima, his hands moving in complex gestures, the names of Charter marks tumbling from his mouth as his hands wove the glowing symbols into a complex thread that tumbled out of the air and spilled down upon the naked blade.

"How long will it take?" asked Ellimere.

"I don't know," whispered Lirael. Then she repeated herself more loudly. "I don't know."

They stood and waited, anxious seconds stretching out awfully into minutes as Sam called forth his Charter marks and Orannis rumbled beyond the ridge, both of them building very different spells. Lirael found herself looking down into the valley every few seconds, where it looked like Major Greene might be having some success at making the Southerlings lie down; then she would look at Sam; then at the Destroyer's fire; and then start all over again, full of different anxieties and fears everywhere she looked.

The Southerlings were still too close, Lirael knew, though they were considerably lower in the valley than they had been. Sam did not seem to be getting any nearer to finishing. The Destroyer was growing taller and stronger, and any minute Lirael knew it would assume its second manifestation, the one for which it was named.

The Destroyer.

Everyone jumped as Sam suddenly stood. They jumped again as he spoke seven master marks, one after the other. A river of molten gold and silver flame fell from his outstretched hands down upon Lirael's bloody sword and the panpipes, which he'd separated into individual tubes and laid along the length of the silvered blade.

Moments later, the Destroyer flashed brighter and the ground rumbled beneath their feet.

"Look away and close your eyes!" screamed Lirael. She threw one arm across her face and crouched, facing down towards the valley. Behind her a shining silver globe—the joined hemispheres—ascended to the sky atop the column of fire. As it rose, the sphere grew brighter and brighter till it was more brilliant than the sun had ever been. It hovered high in the air for a few seconds, as if surveying the ground, then sank back out of sight.

For nine very long seconds, Lirael waited, her eyes screwed shut, her face pushed into her very dirty sleeve. She knew what was to come, but it did not help her.

The explosion came as she counted nine, a blast of white-hot fury that annihilated everything in the loch valley. The mill and the railway were vaporized in the first flash. The loch boiled dry an instant later, sending a vast cloud of superheated steam roaring to the sky. Rocks melted, trees became ash, the birds and fishes simply disappeared. The lightning rods flashed into molten metal that was hurled high into the air, to fall back as deadly rain.

The blast sheared the top of the ridge completely off, destroying earth, rocks, lightning rods, trees, and everything else. Anything left that could burn did, till it was extinguished seconds later by the wind and the steam.

The outermost diamond of protection took what was left of the blast after it destroyed the protective earth of the hill. The magical defense flared for an instant, then was gone.

The second diamond had the hot wind and the steam that could strip flesh from bone. It lasted only seconds till it too gave way.

The third and final diamond held for more than a minute, repelling a hail of stones, molten metal, and debris. Then it also failed, but not until the worst had passed. A hot—but bearable—wind rushed in as the diamond fell and washed around the

Seven as they crouched on the ground, their eyes still shut, shaken in body and mind.

Above them, a huge cloud of dust, ash, steam, and destruction rose, climbing thousands of feet till it spread out like a toadstool top, to cover all in shadow.

Lirael was the first to recover. She opened her eyes to see ash falling all around like blackened snow, and their little diamond-shaped patch of unharmed dirt an island in a wasteland where all color had drained away under a sky that was like a cloudy night, with no hint of sun. But it was not the shock it could have been. She had seen it already in the past, and her mind was fully occupied, racing ahead to what they must do. To what she would have to do.

"Protect yourselves against the heat!" she shouted, as the others slowly stood and looked around, shock and horror in their eyes. Quickly, she called the marks of protection into being, letting them flow out of her mind and across her skin and clothing. Then she looked for the weapon she hoped Sam had made.

Sam held it by the blade and looked puzzled, as if uncertain what he'd wrought. He offered it to Lirael, and she took the hilt, not without a stab of fear. It was not Nehima anymore, and it was not the same sword. It was longer than it had been, with a much broader blade, and the green stone was gone from the pommel. Charter marks ran everywhere through the metal, which had a silvery-red sheen, as if it had been washed in some strange oil. An executioner's sword, Lirael thought. The inscription on the blade seemed the same. Or was it? She couldn't recall exactly. Now it simply said, "Remember Nehima."

"Is that it?" asked Sam. He was white-faced with shock. He looked past her to the valley, but he could not see anything of the Southerlings or Major Greene and his men. There was too much dust and there was little light. But he couldn't hear anything either. No screams or shouts for help, and he feared the worst. "I did what you said."

"Yes," croaked Lirael, her throat dry. The sword was heavy in her hand, and even heavier on her heart. When . . . if . . . they bound Orannis, this was what she would use to break It in two, for no binding could long contain the Destroyer if It was left entire. This weapon could break Orannis, but only at the cost of the wielder's life.

Her life.

"Does everyone have a bell?" she asked quickly, to distract herself. "Sabriel, please give Belgaer to Sam, and tell him the binding spell."

She didn't wait for an answer but led the way across the blasted ridge, down through the fires and the broken hillside, the pools of ash and the cooling metal. Down to the shores of the dry loch, where the Destroyer momentarily rested before its third manifestation, which would unleash even greater powers of destruction.

A grim party followed her, each holding a bell, the binding spell Lirael had taught them repeated over and over in every head.

As they got closer, the stench of Free Magic overcame the smoke, till its acid reek cut at their lungs and waves of nausea struck. It seemed to eat at their very bones, but Lirael would not slow her pace for pain or sickness, and the others followed her lead, fighting against the bile in their throats and the cramps that bit inside.

The steam had fallen back as fog, and the cloud above brought a darkness close to night, so Lirael had little to guide her but instinct. She chose the way by what felt worst, sure that this would lead them to the sphere that was the core of the Destroyer. She knew that if they slowed to try to pick a path by more conventional means, they would soon see a new column of flame, a beacon that would only signal failure.

Then, quite suddenly, Lirael saw the sphere of liquid fire that was the current manifestation of the Destroyer. It hung in the air ahead of her, dark currents alternating with tongues of fire upon its smooth and lustrous surface.

"Form a ring around It," commanded Lirael, her voice weak and small in this abyss of destruction, amidst the darkness and the fog. She drew Astarael in her left hand, wincing at the pain. In all the rush, she'd forgotten about Hedge's blow. There was still no time to do anything for it, but then the thought flashed through her mind that soon it wouldn't matter. The sword she rested on her right shoulder, ready to strike.

Silently, her companions—her family, old and new, Lirael realized with a pang—spread out to form a ring around the sphere of fire and darkness. Only then did Lirael realize that she had not seen Mogget since the destruction, though he had been inside the diamonds of protection. She could not see him now, and another little fear flowered in her heart.

The ring was complete. Everyone looked to Lirael. She took a deep breath and coughed, the corrosive Free Magic eating at her throat. Before she could recover and begin the spell, the sphere began to expand, and red flames leapt out from it, towards the ring of Seven, like a thousand long tongues that sought to taste their flesh.

As the flames writhed, Orannis spoke.

Chapter Twenty-Nine

THE CHOICE OF YRÆL

"So Hedge has failed me, as such servants do," said Orannis, its voice low like a whisper but harsh and penetrating. "As all living things must fail, till silence rings me in eternal calm, across a sea of dust.

"And now another Seven comes, all a-clamor to lock Orannis once more in metal, deep under earth. But can a Seven of such watered blood and thinner power prevail against the Destroyer, last and mightiest of the Nine?"

Orannis paused for a moment of terrible, absolute silence. Then it spoke three words that shook everyone around it, striking them like a harsh slap across the face.

"I think not."

The words were said with such power that no one could move or speak. Lirael had to start the binding spell, but her throat was suddenly too dry for speech, her limbs too heavy to move. Desperately, she fought against the force that held her, drawing on the pain in her arm, the shock of seeing Nick's dying face, and the awful and total destruction all around.

Her tongue moved then, and she found a hint of moisture in her mouth, even as Orannis swelled towards the ring of Seven, its tongues of flame reaching out to wrap around the fools who sought to fight it.

"I stand for Astarael against you," croaked Lirael, sketching a Charter mark with the tip of her sword. The mark hung there, glowing, and the fiery tongues recoiled from it—a little.

It was enough to free the others and begin the spell of binding. Sabriel drew a mark with her sword, and said, "I stand for Saraneth against you." Her voice was strong and confident, lending hope to all the others.

"I stand for Belgaer against you," said Sam, his voice growing in strength and anger as he thought of Nick, his bloodless face looking up as he told him to "make it right." Quickly, he drew his Charter mark, fingers almost flinging it in front of him.

"I stand for Dyrim against you," Ellimere pronounced proudly, as if it were a challenge to a duel. Her mark was drawn deliberately, like a line in the sand.

"As I did then, so do I now," said the Disreputable Dog. "I am Kibeth, and I stand against you."

Unlike the others, she didn't draw a Charter mark, but her body rippled, brown dog skin giving way to a rainbow of marks that moved across her in strange patterns and conjunctions of shape and color. One of these marks drifted in front of her snout, and she blew on it, sending it out in front to hang in the air.

"We stand as one, for Mosrael, against you," intoned Sanar and Ryelle in unison. They drew their mark together, in bold strokes with their clasped hands.

"I am Torrigan, called Touchstone, and I stand for Ranna against you," declared Touchstone, and his voice was that of a king. He drew his mark, and as it flared, he was first to sound his bell. Then the Clayr added Mosrael's voice, the Dog began a rhythmic bark, Ellimere swung Dyrim, Sam rang Belgaer, and Sabriel let Saraneth call deep and low over them all.

Finally, Lirael swung Astarael, and her mournful tone joined the ring of sound and magic that surrounded Orannis. Normally, Weeper would throw all who heard her into Death. Here, combined with the other six voices, her sound evoked a sorrow that

could not be answered. Together, the bells and Dog sang a song
that was more than sound and power. It was the song of the
earth, the moon, the stars, the sea, and the sky, of Life and Death
and all that was and would be. It was the song of the Charter,
the song that had bound Orannis in the long ago, the song that
sought to bind the Destroyer once again.

On and on the bells went, till they seemed to echo everywhere inside Lirael. She was saturated with their power, like a
sponge that can take no more. She could feel it inside her and in
the others, a welling up that filled them all and then had to go
rushing out.

It did, flowing into the mark she'd drawn, which grew
bright and spread sideways to become a strand of light that
joined the next mark, and then the next, to form a glowing ring
that closed around the globe of Orannis, a shining band in orbit
around the dark and threatening sphere.

Lirael spoke the rest of the binding spell, the words flying
out of her on a flood tide of power. With the spell, the ring grew
brighter still and began to tighten, forcing back the tongues of
flame. It sent them writhing in retreat, back into the sphere of
darkness that was Orannis.

Lirael took a step forward, and all the seven did the same,
closing the human ring behind the magic one of light. Then
they took another step, and another, as the spell-ring tightened
further, constricting the sphere itself. All around, the bells rang
on in glory, the Dog's bark a rhythm the bellringers followed
without conscious thought. A great feeling of triumph and relief
began to swell in Lirael, tempered with the dread of the sword
on her shoulder. Soon she would wield it and, all too soon,
would walk once more to the Ninth Gate, never to return.

Then the spell-ring stopped. The bells faltered as the ringers
halted behind it in mid step. Lirael flinched, feeling a backlash of

power, as if she'd suddenly walked into an unexpected wall.

"No," Orannis said, its voice calm, devoid of all emotion.

The spell-ring shivered as Orannis spoke, and began to expand again, forced outwards by the growing sphere. The tongues of fire re-appeared, more numerous than before.

The bells still rang, but the ringers were forced to step back, their faces showing emotions that ranged from grim despair to doomed determination. The spell-ring faded as it opened out, stretched too thin by the growing power of Orannis.

"Too long did I linger in my metal tomb," spoke Orannis. "Too long have I borne the affront of living, crawling life. I am the Destroyer—and all will be destroyed!"

With the last word, the flames lashed out and gripped the spell-ring with a thousand tiny fingers of dark fire. They twisted and wrenched at it every way, hastening its destruction.

Lirael saw it happen as if she were far away. All was lost now. There was nothing else to do or try. She had seen the Beginning, and seen Orannis bound. Then, the Seven had prevailed. Here, they had failed. Lirael had known and accepted the certainty of her own death in this venture, and thought it a fair price for the defeat of Orannis and the saving of all she loved and knew.

Now, they would all merely be the first of a multitude to die, till Orannis brooded on a world of ash and cinders, kept company only by the Dead.

Then, in the midst of despair, Lirael heard Sam speak and saw a flash of brilliant light flow up next to him, to form a tall shape of white fire that was only vaguely human.

"Be free, Mogget!" shouted Sam, as he held a red collar high. "Choose well!"

The shape of fire grew taller. It turned away from Sam towards Sabriel, and its head descended as if it might suddenly bite. Sabriel looked up at it stoically, and it hesitated. Then it flowed over to Lirael, and she felt the heat of it, and the shock of its own Free Magic that mixed with the lung-destroying impact of Orannis.

"Please, Mogget," whispered Lirael, too soft to be heard by anyone at all.

But the white shape did hear. It stopped and turned inwards, to face Orannis, changing from a pillar of fire to a more human shape, but one with skin as bright as a burning star.

"I am Yrael," it said, casting a hand out to throw a line of silver fire into the breaking spell-ring, its voice crackling with force. "I also stand against you."

The spell-ring tightened again, and everyone automatically stepped forward. This time, it didn't stop but contracted again. As the ring tightened, the tongues of flame blew out, and the sphere grew darker. Then it began to glow with a silver sheen, the silver of the hemispheres that had bound Orannis for so long.

Lirael stepped forward again, her eyes fixed on the shrinking sphere. Dimly she was aware that Astarael still rang in her hand, as she was even more faintly aware that Yrael was singing now, singing over the bells and the barking, his voice weaving into the song.

The sphere contracted still further, the silver spreading through it like mercury spilt in water, traveling in slow coils. When it became fully silver, Lirael knew she must strike, in the few moments when Orannis was completely bound. Bound not by the Seven, but by the Eight, she realized, for Mogget—Yrael—could be nothing else but the Eighth Bright Shiner, who was himself bound by the Seven in the long ago.

Bells rang, Yrael sang, Kibeth barked, Astarael mourned. The silver spread, and Lirael moved in closer and raised the weapon Sam had made for her from blood and sword and the spirit of the Seven in the panpipes.

Orannis spoke then, in bitter, cutting tones.

"Why, Yrael?" it said, as the last of the dark gave way to silver, and the shining sphere of metal sank slowly to the ground. "Why?"

Yrael's answer seemed to travel across a great space, words trickling into Lirael's consciousness as she raised her sword still higher, body arching back, preparing for the mighty blow that must cut through the entire sphere.

"Life," said Yrael, who was more Mogget than it ever knew. "Fish and fowl, warm sun and shady trees, the field mice in the wheat, under the cool light of the moon. All the—"

Lirael didn't hear any more. She gathered up all her courage and struck.

Sword met silver metal with a shriek that silenced everything, the blade cutting through in a blaze of blue-white sparks that fountained up into the ashen sky.

Even as it cut, the sword melted and red fire streaked up into Lirael's hand. She screamed as it hit, but hung on, putting all her weight and strength and fury into the blow. She could feel Orannis in the fire, feel it in the heat. It was seeking its last revenge on her, filling her with its destructive power, a power that would burn her into ash.

Lirael screamed again as the flames engulfed the hilt, her hand now no more than a lump of pain. But still she held on, to complete the breaking.

The sword broke through, the sphere split asunder. Even knowing she would fail, Lirael tried to let go. But Orannis had her, its spirit kept momentarily whole by the thin bridge of her sword, the last remnants of the blade between the hemispheres. A bridge to her destruction.

"Dog!" screamed Lirael instinctively, not knowing what she said, pain and fear overwhelming her intention to simply die.

Again she tried to open her hand, but her fingers were welded to the metal, and Orannis was in her blood, spreading through to consume her in its final fire.

Then the Dog's teeth suddenly closed on Lirael's wrist. There was a new pain, but a clean one, sharp and sudden. Orannis was gone from her, as was the fire that threatened to destroy her. A moment later, Lirael realized that the Dog had bitten off her hand.

All that remained free of Orannis's vengeful power was directed at the Disreputable Dog. Red fire flowered about her as she spat out the hand, throwing it between the hemispheres, where it writhed and wriggled like a dreadful spider made from burned and blackened flesh.

A great gout of flame erupted and engulfed the Dog, sending Lirael stumbling back, her eyebrows frizzled into nothing. Then, with a long, final scream of thwarted hope, the hemispheres hurtled apart. One narrowly missed Lirael, tumbling past her into the loch and the returning sea. The other flew up past Sabriel, to land behind her in a flurry of dust and ash.

"Bound and broken," whispered Lirael, staring at her wrist in disbelief. She could still feel her hand, but there was nothing there save a cauterized stump and the burnt ends of her sleeve.

She started to shake then, and the tears came, till she couldn't see for crying. There was only one thing she knew to do, so she did it, stumbling forward blindly, calling to the Dog.

"Here," called the Dog softly, in answer to the call. She was lying on her side where the sphere had been, upon a bed of ash. Her tail wagged as she heard Lirael, but only the very tip of it, and she didn't get up.

Lirael knelt by her side. The hound didn't seem hurt, but Lirael saw that her muzzle was now frosted white, and the skin was loose around her neck, as if she had suddenly become old.

The Dog raised her head very slowly as Lirael bent over her, and gave her a little lick on the face.

"Well, that's done, Mistress," she whispered, her head dropping back. "I have to leave you now."

"No," sobbed Lirael. She hugged her with her handless arm and buried her cheek against the Dog's snout. "It was supposed to be me! I won't let you go! I love you, Dog!"

"There'll be other dogs, and friends, and loves," whispered the Dog. "You have found your family, your heritage; and you have earned a high place in the world. I love you, too, but my time with you has passed. Goodbye, Lirael."

Then she was gone, and Lirael was left bowed over a small soapstone statue of a dog.

Behind her, she heard Yrael speak, and Sabriel, and the brief chime of Belgaer, so strange after the massed song of all the bells, its single voice freeing Mogget from his millennia of servitude. But the sound was far away, in another place, another time.

Sam found Lirael a moment later, curled up in the ash, the carving of the Dog nestled in the crook of her handless arm. She held Astarael—the Weeper—with her remaining hand, her fingers clenched tight around the clapper so it could not sound.

Nick stood in the river and watched with interest as the current tugged at his knees. He wanted to go with that current, to lie down and be swept away, taking his guilt and sorrow with him to wherever the river might go. But he couldn't move, because he was somehow fixed in place by a force that emanated from the patch of heat on his forehead, which was very strange when everything else was cold.

After a time that could have been minutes or hours or even days—for there was no way to tell whether time meant anything at all in this place of constant grey light—Nick noticed there was a dog sitting next to him. A large brown and black dog, with a serious expression. It looked kind of familiar.

"You're the dog from my dream," said Nick. He bent down to scratch it on the head. "Only it wasn't a dream, was it? You had wings."

"Yes," agreed the dog. "I'm the Disreputable Dog, Nicholas."

"Pleased to meet you," said Nick formally. The Dog offered a paw, and Nicholas shook it. "Do you happen to know where we are? I thought I—"

"Died," replied the Dog cheerily. "You did. This is Death."

"Ah," replied Nick. Once he might have wanted to argue about that. Now he had a different perspective, and other things to think about. "Do you . . . did they . . . the hemispheres?"

"Orannis has been bound anew," announced the Dog. "It is once again imprisoned in the hemispheres. In due course, they will be transported back to the Old Kingdom and buried deep beneath stone and spell."

Relief crossed Nick's face and smoothed out the lines of worry around his eyes and mouth. He knelt down beside the Dog to hug her, feeling the warmth of her skin in sharp contrast to the chill of the river. The bright collar around her neck was nice, too. It gave him a warm feeling in his chest.

"Sam and . . . and Lirael?" asked Nick hopefully, his head still bowed, close to the Dog's ear.

"They live," replied the Dog. "Though not without scathe. My mistress lost her hand. Prince Sameth will make her one, of course, of shining gold and clever magic. Lirael Goldenhand, she'll be forever after. Remembrancer and Abhorsen, and much else besides. But there are other hurts, which require different remedies. She is very young. Stand up, Nicholas."

Nicholas stood. He wavered a little as the current tried to trip him and take him under.

"I gave you a late baptism to preserve your spirit," said the Dog. "You bear the Charter mark on your forehead now, to balance the Free Magic that lingers in your blood and bone. You will find Charter mark and Free Magic both boon and burden, for they will take you far from Ancelstierre, and the path you will walk will not be the one you have long thought to see ahead."

"What do you mean?" asked Nick in bewilderment. He touched the mark on his forehead and blinked as it flared with sudden light. The Dog's collar shone, too, with many other bright marks that surrounded her head with a corona of golden light. "What do you mean, far from Ancelstierre? How can I go anywhere? I'm dead, aren't—"

"I'm sending you back," said the Dog gently, nudging Nick's leg with her snout, so he turned to face towards Life. Then she barked, a single sharp sound that was both a welcome and a farewell.

"Is this allowed?" asked Nick as he felt the current reluctantly release him, and he took the first step back.

"No," said the Dog. "But then I am the Disreputable Dog."

Nick took another step, and he smiled as he felt the warmth of Life, and the smile became a laugh, a laugh that welcomed everything, even the pain that waited in his body.

In Life, his waking eyes looked up, and he saw the sun breaking through a low, dark cloud, and its warmth and light fell on a diamond-shaped patch of earth where he lay, safe amidst ruin and destruction. Nick sat up and saw soldiers approaching, picking their way across an ashen desert. Southerlings followed the soldiers, their just-scrubbed hats and scarves bright blue, the only color in the wasteland.

A white cat suddenly appeared next to Nicholas's feet. He sniffed in disgust and said, "I might have known"; then he looked past Nick at something that wasn't there and winked, before trotting off in a northerly direction.

The cat was followed a little later by the weary footsteps of six people, who were supporting the seventh. Nick managed to stand and wave, and in the space of that tiny movement and its startled response, he had time to wonder what all the future held, and think that it would be much brighter than the past.

The Disreputable Dog sat with her head cocked to one side for several minutes, her wise old eyes seeing much more than the river, her sharp ears hearing more than just the gurgle of the current. After a while a small, enormously satisfied rumble sounded from deep in her chest. She got up, grew her legs longer to get her body out of the water, and shook herself dry. Then she wandered off, following a zigzag path along the border between Life and Death, her tail wagging so hard, the tip of it beat the river into a froth behind her.

NICHOLAS SAYRE
AND THE
CREATURE IN THE CASE

"I AM GOING back to the Old Kingdom, Uncle," said Nicholas Sayre. "Whatever Father may have told you. So there is no point in your trying to fix me up with a suitable Sayre job or a suitable Sayre marriage. I am coming with you to what will undoubtedly be a horrendous house party only because it will get me a few hundred miles closer to the Wall."

Nicholas's uncle Edward, more generally known as The Most Honorable Edward Sayre, Chief Minister of Ancelstierre, shut the red-bound letter book he was reading with more emphasis than he intended, as their heavily armored car lurched over a hump in the road. The sudden clap of the book made the bodyguard in front look around, but the driver kept his eyes on the narrow country lane.

"Have I said anything about a job or a marriage?" Edward enquired, gazing down his long, patrician nose at his nineteen-year-old nephew. "Besides, you won't even get within a mile of the Perimeter without a pass signed by me, let alone across the Wall."

"I could get a pass from Lewis," said Nicholas moodily, referring to the newly anointed Hereditary Arbiter. The previous Arbiter, Lewis's grandfather, had died of a heart attack during Corolini's attempted coup d'état half a year before.

"No, you couldn't, and you know it," said Edward. "Lewis has more sense than to involve himself in any aspect of government other than the ceremonial."

"Then I'll have to cross over without a pass," declared Nicholas angrily, not even trying to hide the frustration that had built up in him over the past six months, during which he'd been forced to stay in Ancelstierre. Most of that time spent wishing he'd left with Lirael and Sam in the immediate aftermath of the Destroyer's defeat, instead of deciding to recuperate in Ancelstierre. It had been weakness and fear that had driven his decision, combined with a desire to put the terrible past behind him. But he now knew that was impossible. He could not ignore the legacy of his involvement with Hedge and the Destroyer, nor his return to Life at the hands—or paws—of the Disreputable Dog. He had become someone else, and he could only find out who that was in the Old Kingdom.

"You would almost certainly be shot if you try to cross illegally," said Edward. "A fate you would richly deserve. Particularly since you are not giving me the opportunity to help you. I do not know why you or anyone else would want to go to the Old Kingdom—my year on the Perimeter as General Hort's ADC certainly taught me the place is best avoided. Nor do I wish to annoy your father and hurt your mother, but there *are* certain circumstances in which I might grant you permission to cross the Perimeter."

"What! Really?"

"Yes, really. Have I ever taken you or any other of my nephews or nieces to a house party before?"

"Not that I know—"

"Do I usually make a habit of attending parties given by someone like Alastor Dorrance in the middle of nowhere?"

"I suppose not. . . ."

"Then you might exercise your intelligence to wonder why you are here with me now."

"Gatehouse ahead, sir," interrupted the bodyguard as the car rounded a sweeping corner and slowed down. "Recognition signal is correct."

Edward and Nicholas leaned forward to look through the open partition and the windscreen beyond. A few hundred yards in front, a squat stone gatehouse lurked just off the road, with its two wooden gates swung back. Two slate-gray Heddon-Hare roadsters were parked, one on either side of the gate, with several mackintosh-clad, weapon-toting men standing around them. One of the men waved a yellow flag in a series of complicated movements that Edward clearly understood and Nicholas presumed meant all was well.

"Proceed!" snapped the Chief Minister. Their car slowed more, the driver shifting down through the gears with practiced double-clutching. The mackintosh-clad men saluted as the car swung off the road and through the gate, dropping their salute as the rest of the motorcade followed. Six motorcycle policemen were immediately behind, then another two cars identical to the one that carried Nicholas and his uncle, then another half dozen police motorcyclists, and finally four trucks that were carrying a company of fully armed soldiery. Corolini's attempted putsch had failed, and there had surprisingly been no further trouble from the Our Country Party since, but the government continued to be nervous about the safety of the nation's Chief Minister.

"So, what is going on?" asked Nicholas. "Why are you here?

And why am I here? Is there something you want me to do?"

"At last, a glimmer of thought. Have you ever wondered what Alastor Dorrance actually does, other than come to Corvere three or four times a year and exercise his eccentricities in public?"

"Isn't that enough?" asked Nick with a shudder. He remembered the newspaper stories from the last time Dorrance had been in the city, only a few weeks before. He'd hosted a picnic on Holyoak Hill for every apprentice in Corvere and supplied them with fatty roast beef, copious amounts of beer, and a particularly cheap and nasty red wine, with predictable results.

"Dorrance's eccentricities are all show," said Edward. "Misdirection. He is in fact the head of Department Thirteen. Dorrance Hall is the Department's main research facility."

"But Department Thirteen is just a made-up thing, for the moving pictures. It doesn't really exist . . . um . . . does it?"

"Officially, no. In actuality, yes. Every state has need of spies. Department Thirteen trains and manages ours, and carries out various tasks ill suited to the more regular branches of government. It is watched over quite carefully, I assure you."

"But what has that got to do with me?"

"Department Thirteen observes all our neighbors very successfully, and has detailed files on everyone and everything important within those countries. With one notable exception. The Old Kingdom."

"I'm not going to spy on my friends!"

Edward sighed and looked out the window. The drive beyond the gatehouse curved through freshly mown fields, the hay already gathered into hillocks ready to be pitch-forked into carts and taken to the stacks. Past the fields, the chimneys of a large country house peered above the fringe of old oaks that lined the drive.

"I'm not going to be a spy, Uncle," repeated Nicholas.

"I haven't asked you to be one," said Edward as he looked back at his nephew. Nicholas's face had paled, and he was clutching his chest. Whatever had happened to him in the Old Kingdom had left him in a very run-down state, and he was still recovering. Though the Ancelstierran doctors had found no external signs of significant injury, his X-rays had come out strangely fogged and all the medical reports said Nick was in the same sort of shape as a man who had suffered serious wounds in battle.

"All I want you to do is to spend the weekend here with some of the Department's technical people," continued Edward. "Answer their questions about your experiences in the Old Kingdom, that sort of thing. I doubt anything will come of it, and as you know, I strictly adhere to the wisdom of my predecessors, which is to leave the place alone. But that said, they haven't exactly left us alone over the past twenty years. Dorrance has always had a bit of a bee in his bonnet about the Old Kingdom, greatly exacerbated by the . . . mmm . . . event at Forwin Mill. It is possible that he might discover something useful from talking to you. So if you answer his questions, you shall have your Perimeter pass on Monday morning. If you're still set on going, that is."

"I'll cross the Wall," said Nick forcefully. "One way or another."

"Then I suggest it be my way. You know, your father wanted to be a painter when he was your age. He had talent too, according to old Menree. But our parents wouldn't hear of it. A grave error, I think. Not that he hasn't been a useful politician, and a great help to me. But his heart is elsewhere, and it is not possible to achieve greatness without a whole heart."

"So all I have to do is answer questions?"

Edward sighed the sigh of an older and wiser man talking to a younger, inattentive, and impatient relative.

"Well, you will have to appear a little bit at the party. Dinner and so forth. Croquet perhaps, or a row on the lake. Misdirection, as I said."

Nicholas took Edward's hand and shook it firmly.

"You are a splendid uncle, Uncle."

"Good. I'm glad that's settled," said Edward. He glanced out the window. They were past the oak trees now, gravel crunching beneath the wheels as the car rolled up the drive to the front steps of the six-columned entrance. "We'll drop you off, then, and I'll see you Monday."

"Aren't you staying here? For the house party?"

"Don't be silly! I can't abide house parties of any kind. I'm staying at the Golden Sheaf. Excellent hotel, not too far away. I often go there to get through some serious confidential reading. Place has got its own golf course, too. Thought I might go round tomorrow. Enjoy yourself!"

Nicholas hardly caught the last two words as his door was flung open and he was assisted out by Edward's personal bodyguard. He blinked in the afternoon sunlight, no longer filtered through the smoked glass of the car's windows. A few seconds later, his bags were deposited at his feet; then the Chief Minister's cavalcade started up again and rolled out the drive as quickly as it had arrived, the Army trucks leaving considerable ruts in the gravel.

"Mr. Sayre?"

Nicholas looked around. A top hatted footman was picking up his bags, but it was another man who had spoken. A balding, burly individual in a dark-blue suit, his hair cut so short it was practically a monkish tonsure. Everything about him said policeman, either active or recently retired.

"Yes, I'm Nicholas Sayre."

"Welcome to Dorrance Hall, sir. My name is Hedge—"

Nicholas recoiled from the offered hand and nearly fell over the footman. Even as he regained his balance, he realized that the man had said *Hodge* and then followed it up with a second syllable.

Hodgeman. Not *Hedge.*

Hedge the necromancer was finally, completely, and utterly dead. Lirael and the Disreputable Dog had defeated him, and Hedge had gone beyond the Ninth Gate. He couldn't come back. Nick knew he was safe from him, but that knowledge was purely intellectual. Deep inside him, the name of Hedge was linked irrevocably with an almost primal fear.

"Sorry," gasped Nick. He straightened up and shook the man's hand. "Ankle gave way on me. You were saying?"

"Hodgeman is my name. I am an assistant to Mr. Dorrance. The other guests do not arrive till later, so Mr. Dorrance thought you might like a tour of the grounds."

"Um, certainly," replied Nick. He fought back a sudden urge to look around to see who might be listening and, as he started up the steps, resisted the temptation to slink from shadow to shadow just like a spy in a moving picture.

"The house was originally built in the time of the last Trouin-Durville Pretender, about four hundred years ago, but little of the original structure remains. Most of the current house was built by Mr. Dorrance's grandfather. The best feature is the library, which was the great hall of the old house. Shall we start there?"

"Thank you," replied Nicholas. Mr. Hodgeman's turn as a tour guide was quite convincing. Nicholas wondered if the man had to do it often for casual visitors, as part of what Uncle Edward would call "misdirection."

The library was very impressive. Hodgeman closed the double doors behind them as Nick stared up at the high dome of the ceiling, which was painted to create the illusion of a storm at sea. It was quite disconcerting to look up at the waves and the tossing ships and the low scudding clouds. Below the dome, every wall was covered by tiers of shelves stretching up twenty or even twenty-five feet from the floor. Ladders ran on rails around the library, but no one was using them. The library was silent; two crescent-shaped couches in the center were empty. The windows were heavily curtained with velvet drapes, but the gas lanterns above the shelves burned very brightly. The place looked like there should be people reading in it, or sorting books, or something. It did not have the dark, dusty air of a disused library.

"This way, sir," said Hodgeman. He crossed to one of the shelves and reached up above his head to pull out an unobtrusive, dun-colored tome, adorned only with the Dorrance coat of arms, a chain argent issuant from a chevron argent upon a field azure.

The book slid out halfway, then came no farther.

Hodgeman looked up at it. Nick looked too.

"Is something supposed to happen?"

"It gets a bit stuck sometimes," replied Hodgeman. He tugged on the book again. This time it came completely out.

Hodgeman opened it, took a key from its hollowed-out pages, pushed two books apart on the shelf below to reveal a keyhole, inserted the key, and turned it. There was a soft click, but nothing more dramatic. Hodgeman put the key back in the book and returned the volume to the shelf.

"Now, if you wouldn't mind stepping this way," Hodgeman said, leading Nick back to the center of the library. The couches had moved aside on silent gears, and two steel-encased segments of the floor had slid open, revealing a circular stone staircase leading down. Unlike the library's brilliant white gaslights, it was lit by dull electric bulbs.

"This is all rather cloak-and-dagger," remarked Nick as he headed down the steps with Hodgeman close behind him.

Hodgeman didn't answer, but Nick was sure a disapproving glance had fallen on his back. The steps went down quite a long way, equivalent to at least three or four floors. They ended in front of a steel door with a covered spy hole. Hodgeman pressed a tarnished bronze bell button next to the door, and a few seconds later, the spy hole slid open.

"Sergeant Hodgeman with Mr. Nicholas Sayre," said Hodgeman.

The door swung open. There was no sign of a person behind it. Just a long, dismal, white-painted concrete corridor stretching off some thirty or forty yards to another steel door. Nick stepped through the doorway, and some slight movement to his right made him look. There was an alcove there, with a desk, a red telephone on it, a chair, and a guard—another plainclothes policeman type like Hodgeman, this time in shirtsleeves, with a revolver worn openly in a shoulder holster. He nodded at Nick but didn't smile or speak.

"On to the next door, please," said Hodgeman.

Nick nodded back at the guard and continued down the concrete corridor, his footsteps echoing just out of time with Hodgeman's. He heard behind him the faint ting of a telephone being taken off its cradle and then the low voice of the guard, his words indistinguishable.

The procedure with the spy hole was repeated at the next door. There were two policemen behind this one, in a larger and better-appointed alcove. They had upholstered chairs and a leather-topped desk, though it had clearly seen better days.

Hodgeman nodded at the guards, who nodded back with slow deliberation. Nick smiled but got no smile in return.

"Through the left door, please," said Hodgeman, pointing. There were two doors to choose from, both of unappealing, unmarked steel bordered with lines of knuckle-size rivets.

Hodgeman departed through the right-hand door as Nick pushed the left, but it swung open before he exerted any pressure. There was a much more cheerful room beyond, very much like Nick's tutor's study at Sunbere, with four big leather club chairs facing a desk, and off to one side a liquor cabinet with a large, black-enameled radio sitting on top of it. There were three men standing around the cabinet.

The closest was a tall, expensively dressed, vacant-looking man with ridiculous sideburns whom Nick recognized as Dorrance. The second-closest was a fiftyish man in a hearty tweed coat with leather elbow patches. The skin of his thick neck hung over his collar, and his fat face was much too big for the half-moon glasses that perched on his nose. Lurking behind these two was a nondescript, vaguely unhealthy-looking shorter man who wore exactly the same kind of suit as Hodgeman but in a much more untidy way, so he looked nothing like a policeman, serving or otherwise.

"Ah, here is Mr. Nicholas Sayre," said Dorrance. He stepped forward, shook Nick's hand, and ushered him to the center of the room. "I'm Dorrance. Good of you to help us out. This is Professor Lackridge, who looks after all our scientific research."

The fat-faced man extended his hand and shook Nick's with little enthusiasm but a crushing grip. Somewhere in the very distant past, Nick surmised, Professor Lackridge must have been a rugby enthusiast. Or perhaps a boxer. Now, sadly, run to fat, but the muscle was still there underneath.

"And this is Mr. Malthan, who is . . . an independent adviser on Old Kingdom matters."

Malthan inclined his head and made a faint, repressed gesture with his hands, turning them toward his forehead as if to brush his almost nonexistent hair away. There was something about the action that triggered recognition in Nick.

"You're from the Old Kingdom, aren't you?" he asked. It was unusual for anyone from the Old Kingdom to be encountered this far south. Very few travelers could get authorization from both King Touchstone and the Ancelstierran government to cross the Wall and the Perimeter. Even fewer would come any farther south than Bain, which was at least a hundred and eighty miles north. They didn't like it, as a rule. It didn't feel right, Sam had always said.

But then, this little man didn't have the Charter Mark on his forehead, which might make it more bearable for him to be on this side of the Wall. Nick instinctively brushed his dark forelock aside to show his Charter Mark, his fingers running across it. The Mark was quiescent under his touch, showing no sign of its connection to the magical powers of the Old Kingdom.

Malthan clearly saw the Mark, even if the others didn't. He

stepped a little closer to Nick and spoke in a breathy half whine.

"I'm a trader, out of Belisaere," he said. "I've always done a bit of business with some folks in Bain, as my father did before me, and his father before him. We've a Permission from the King, and a Permit from your government. I only come down here every now and then, when I've got something special-like that I know Mr. Dorrance's lot will be interested in, same as my old dad did for Mr. Dorrance's granddad—"

"And we pay very well for what we're interested in, Mr. Malthan," Dorrance interrupted him. "Don't we?"

"Yes, sir, you do. Only I don't—"

"Malthan has been very useful," interjected Professor Lackridge. "Though we must discount many of his, ahem, traveler's tales. Fortunately he tends to bring us interesting artifacts in addition to his more colorful observations."

"I've always spoken true," said Malthan. "As this young man can tell you. He has the Mark and all. He knows."

"Yes, the forehead brand of that cult," remarked Lackridge, with an uninterested glance at Nick's forehead, the Mark mostly concealed once more under his floppy forelock. "Sociologically interesting, of course. Particularly its regret-table prevalence among our Northern Perimeter Reconnais-sance Unit. I trust it is only an affectation in your case, young man? You haven't gone native on us?"

"It isn't just a religious thing," Nick said carefully. "The Mark is more of a . . . a connection with . . . how can I ex-plain . . . unseen powers. Magic—"

"Yes, yes. I am sure it seems like magic to you," said Lackridge. "But the great majority of it is easily explained as mass hallucination, the influence of drugs, hysteria, and so forth. It is the minority of events that defy explanation but leave clear physical effects that we are interested in—such as the explosion at Forwin Mill." He looked over his half-moon glasses at Nicholas.

Dorrance looked at him as well, his stare suddenly intense.

"Our studies there indicate that the blast was roughly equivalent to the detonation of twenty thousand tons of nitro-cellulose," continued Lackridge. He rapped his knuckles on the desk as he exclaimed, "Twenty thousand tons! We know of nothing capable of delivering such explosive force, particularly as the bomb itself was reported to be two metallic hemispheres, each no more than ten feet in diameter. Is that right, Mr. Sayre?"

Nick swallowed, his throat moving in a dry gulp. He could feel sweat forming on his forehead and a familiar jangling pain in his right arm and chest.

"I . . . I don't really know," he said after several long seconds. "I was very ill. Feverish. But it wasn't a bomb. It was the Destroyer. Not something our science can explain. That was my mistake. I thought I could explain everything under our natural laws, our science. I was wrong."

"You're tired, and clearly still somewhat unwell," said Dorrance. His tone was kindly, but the warmth did not reach his eyes. "We have many more questions, of course, but they can wait until the morning. Professor, why don't you show Nicholas around the establishment. Let him get his bearings. Then go back upstairs, and we can all resume life as normal, what? Which reminds me, Nicholas—everything discussed down here is absolutely confidential. Even the existence of this facility must not be mentioned once you return to the main house. Naturally you will see me, Professor Lackridge, and the others at dinner, but in our public roles. Most of the guests have no idea that Department Thirteen lurks beneath their feet, and we want it to remain that way. I trust you won't have a problem keeping our existence all to yourself?"

"No, not at all," muttered Nick. Inside he was wondering how he could avoid answering questions but still get his pass to cross the Perimeter. Lackridge obviously didn't believe in Old Kingdom magic, which was no great surprise. After all, Nick had been like that himself. But Dorrance had voiced no such skepticism, nor had he shown it by his body language. Nick definitely did not want to discuss the Destroyer and its nature with anyone who might seriously look into what it was or what had happened at Forwin Mill.

He didn't want to dabble in anything to do with Old Kingdom magic, especially without proper instruction, even two hundred miles south of the Wall.

"Follow me, Nicholas," said Lackridge. "You, too, Malthan. I want to show you something related to those photographic plates you found for us."

"I need to catch my train," muttered Malthan. "My horses . . . stabled near Bain . . . the expense . . . I'm eager to return home."

"We'll pay you a little extra," said Dorrance, the tone of his voice making it clear Malthan had no choice. "I want Lackridge to see your reaction to one of the artifacts we've picked up. I'll see you at dinner, Nicholas."

Dorrance shook Nick's hand in parting, gave a dismissive wave to Lackridge, and ignored Malthan completely. As Dorrance turned back to his desk, Nick noticed a paperweight sitting on top of the wooden in-box. A lump of broken stone, etched with intricate symbols. They did not shine or move about, not so far from the Old Kingdom; but Nick recognized their nature, though he did not know their dormant power or meaning. They were Charter Marks. The stone itself looked as if it had been broken from a greater whole.

Nick looked at Dorrance again and decided that even if it meant having to work out some other way to get across the Perimeter, he was not going to answer any of Dorrance's questions. Or rather, he would answer them vaguely and badly, and generally behave like a well-meaning fool.

Hedge had been an Ancelstierran originally, Nick remembered as he followed Malthan and the professor out. Dorrance struck him as someone who might be tempted to walk a path similar to Hedge's.

They left through the door Nick had come in by, out through the opposite door, and then rapidly through a confusing maze of short corridors and identical riveted metal doors.

"Bit confusing down here, what?" remarked Lackridge. "Takes a while to get your bearings. Dorrance's father built the original tunnels for his underground electric railway. Modeled on the Corvere Metro. But the tunnels have been extended even farther since then. We're just going to take a look in our holding area for objects brought in from north of the Wall or found on our side, near it."

"You mentioned photographic plates," said Nick. "Surely no photographic equipment works over the Wall?"

"That has yet to be properly tested," said Lackridge dismissively. "In any case, these are prints from negative glass plates taken in Bain of a book that was brought across the Wall."

"What kind of book?" Nick asked Malthan.

Malthan looked at Nick, but his eyes failed to meet the younger man's gaze. "The photographs were taken by a former associate of mine. I didn't know she had this book. It burned of its own accord only minutes after the photographs were captured. Half the plates also melted before I could get them far enough south."

"What was the title of the book?" asked Nick. "And why 'former' associate?"

"She burned with the b-b-book," whispered Malthan with a shiver. "I do not know its name. I do not know where Raliese might have got it."

"You see the problems we have to deal with," said Lackridge with a sneer at Malthan. "He probably bought the plates at a school fete in Bain. But they are interesting. The book was some kind of bestiary. We can't read the text as yet, but there are very fine etchings—illustrations of the beasts."

The professor stopped to unlock the next door with a large brass key, but he opened it only a fraction. He turned to Malthan and Nick and said, "The photographs are important, as we already had independent evidence that at least one of the beasts depicted in that book really does exist—or existed at one time—in the Old Kingdom."

"Independent evidence of one of those things?" squeaked Malthan. "What kind of—"

"This," declared Lackridge, opening the door wide. "A mummified specimen!"

The storeroom beyond was cluttered with boxes, chests, and paraphernalia. For a second, Nick's eye was drawn to two very large blowups of photographs of Forwin Loch, which were leaning on the wall near the door. One showed a scene of industry from the last century, and the other showed the destruction wrought by Orannis—the Destroyer.

But the big photographs held his attention for no more than a moment. There could be no question what Lackridge was referring to. In the middle of the room there was a glass cylinder about nine feet high and five feet in diameter. Inside the case, propped up against a steel frame, was a nightmare.

It looked vaguely human, in the sense that it had a head, a torso, two arms, and two legs. But its skin or hide was of a strange violet hue, crosshatched with lines like a crocodile's, and looked very rough. Its legs were jointed backward and ended in hooked hooves. The arms stretched down almost to the floor of the case, and ended not in hands but in clublike appendages that were covered in inch-long barbs. Its torso was thin and cylindrical, rather like that of a wasp. Its head was the most human part, save that it sat on a neck that was twice as long; it had narrow slits instead of ears, and its black, violet-pupiled eyes—presumably glass made by a skillful taxidermist—were pear-shaped and took up half its face. Its mouth, twice the width of any human's, was almost closed, but Nick could see teeth gleaming there.

Black teeth that shone like polished jet.

"No!" screamed Malthan. He ran back down the corridor as far as the previous door, which was locked. He beat on the metal with his fists, the drumming echoing down the corridor.

Nick pushed Lackridge gently aside with a quiet "Excuse me." He could feel his heart pounding in his chest, but it was not from fear. It was excitement. The excitement of discovery, of learning something new. A feeling he had always enjoyed, but it had been lost to him ever since he'd dug up the metal spheres of the Destroyer.

He leaned forward to touch the case and felt a strange, electric thrill run through his fingers and out along his thumbs.

At the same time, there was a stabbing pain in his forehead, strong enough to make him step back and press two fingers hard between his eyes.

"Not a bad specimen," said Lackridge. He spoke conversationally, but he had come very close to Nick and was watching him intently. "Its history is a little murky, but it's been in the country for at least three hundred years and in the Corvere Bibliomanse for the past thirty-five. One of the things my staff has been doing here at Department Thirteen is cross-indexing all the various institutional records, looking for artifacts and information about our northern neighbors. When we got Malthan's photographs, Dorrance happened to remember he'd seen an actual specimen of one of the creatures somewhere before, as a child. I cross-checked the records at the Bibliomanse and found the thing, and we had it brought up here."

Nick nodded absently. The pain in his head was receding. It appeared to emanate from his Charter Mark, though that should be totally quiescent this far from the Wall. Unless there was a roaring gale blowing down from the north, which he supposed might have happened since he came down into Department Thirteen's subterranean lair. It was impossible to tell what was going on in the world above them.

"Apparently the thing was found about ten miles in on our side of the Wall, wrapped in three chains," continued Lackridge. "One of silver, one of lead, and one made from braided daisies. That's what the notes say, though of course we don't have the chains to prove it. If there was a silver one, it must have been worth a pretty penny. Long before the Perimeter, of course, so it was some time before the authorities got hold of it. According to the records, the local folk wanted to drag it back to the Wall, but fortunately there was a visiting Captain-Inquirer who had it shipped south. Should never have gotten rid of the Captain-Inquirers. Wouldn't have minded being one myself. Don't suppose anyone would bring them back now. Lily-livered lot, the present government . . . excepting your uncle, of course. . . ."

"My father also sits in the Moot," said Nick. "On the government benches."

"Well, of course, everyone says my politics are to the right of old Arbiter Werris Blue-Nose, so don't mind me," said Lackridge. He stepped back into the corridor and shouted, "Come back here, Mr. Malthan. It won't bite you!"

As Lackridge spoke, Nick thought he saw the creature's eyes move. Just a fraction, but there was a definite sense of movement. With it, all his sense of excitement was banished in a second, to be replaced by a growing fear.

It's alive, thought Nick.

He stepped back to the door, almost knocking over Lackridge, his mind working furiously.

The thing is alive. Quiescent. Conserving its energies, so far from the Old Kingdom. It must be some Free Magic creature, and it's just waiting for a chance—

"Thank you, Professor Lackridge, but I find myself suddenly rather keen on a cup of tea," blurted Nick. "Do you think we might come back and look at this specimen tomorrow?"

"I'm supposed to make Malthan touch the case," said Lackridge. "Dorrance was most insistent upon it. Wants to see his reaction."

Nick edged back and looked down the corridor. Malthan was crouched by the door.

"I think you've seen his reaction," he said. "Anything more would simply be cruel, and hardly scientific."

"He's only an Old Kingdom trader," said Lackridge. "He's not even strictly legal. Conditional visa. We can do whatever we like with him."

"What!" exclaimed Nick.

"Within reason," Lackridge added hastily. "I mean, nothing too drastic. Do him good."

"I think he needs to get on a train north and go back to the Old Kingdom," said Nick firmly. He liked Lackridge less and less with every passing minute, and the whole Department Thirteen setup seemed very dubious. It was all very well for his uncle Edward to talk about having extralegal entities to do things the government could not, but the line had to be drawn somewhere, and Nick didn't think Dorrance or Lackridge knew where to draw it—or if they did, when not to step over it.

"I'll just see how he is," added Nick. An idea started to rise from the recesses of his mind as he walked down the corridor toward the crouched and shivering man pressed against the door. "Perhaps we can walk out together."

"Mr. Dorrance was most insistent—"

"I'm sure he won't mind if you tell him that I insisted on escorting Malthan on his way."

"But—"

"I am insisting, you know," Nick cut in forcefully. "As it is, I shall have a few words to say about this place to my uncle."

"If you're going to be like that, I don't think I have any choice," said Lackridge petulantly. "We were assured that you would cooperate fully with our research."

"*I* will cooperate, but I don't think Malthan needs to do

any more for Department Thirteen," said Nick. He bent down and helped the Old Kingdom trader up. He was surprised by how much the smaller man was shaking. He seemed totally in the grip of panic, though he calmed a little when Nick took his arm above the elbow. "Now, please show us out. And you can organize someone to take Malthan to the railway station."

"You don't understand the importance of our work," said Lackridge. "Or our methods. Observing the superstitious re-actions of northerners and our own people delivers legitimate and potentially useful information."

This was clearly only a pro forma protest, because as Lackridge spoke, he unlocked the door and led them quickly through the corridors. After a few minutes, Nick found that he didn't need to half carry Malthan anymore, but could just point him in the right direction.

Eventually, after numerous turns and more doors that required laborious unlocking, they came to a double-width steel door with two spy holes. Lackridge knocked, and after a brief inspection, they were admitted to a guardroom inhabited by five policeman types. Four were sitting around a linoleum-topped table under a single suspended lightbulb, drinking tea and eating doorstop-size sandwiches. Hodgeman was the fifth, and clearly still on duty, as unlike the others he had not removed his coat.

"Sergeant Hodgeman," Lackridge called out rather too loudly. "Please escort Mr. Sayre upstairs and have one of your other officers take Malthan to Dorrance Halt and see he gets on the next northbound train."

"Very good, sir," replied Hodgeman. He hesitated for a moment, then with a curiously unpleasant emphasis, which Nick would have missed if he hadn't been paying careful attention, he said, "Constable Ripton, you see to Malthan."

"Just a moment," said Nick. "I've had a thought. Malthan can take a message from me over to my uncle, the Chief Minister, at the Golden Sheaf. Then someone from his staff can take Malthan to the nearest station."

"One of my men would happily take a message for you, sir," said Sergeant Hodgeman. "And Dorrance Halt is much closer than the Golden Sheaf. That's all of twenty miles away."

"Thank you," said Nick. "But I want the Chief Minister to hear Malthan directly about some matters relating to the Old Kingdom. That won't be a problem, will it? Malthan, I'll just write something out for you to take to Garran, my uncle's principal secretary."

Nick took out his notebook and gold propelling pencil and casually leaned against the wall. They all watched him, the five policeman with studied disinterest masking hostility, Lackridge with more open aggression, and Malthan with the sad eyes of the doomed.

Nick began to whistle tunelessly through his teeth, pretending to be oblivious to the pent-up institutional aggression focused upon him. He wrote quickly, sighed and pretended to cross out what he'd written, then ripped out the page, palmed it, and started to write again.

"Very hard to concentrate the mind in these underground chambers of yours," Nick said to Lackridge. "I don't know how you get anything done. Expect you've got cockroaches too . . . maybe rats . . . I mean, what's that?"

He pointed with the pencil. Only Malthan and Lackridge turned to look. The policemen kept up their steady stare. Nick stared back, but he felt a slight fear begin to swim about his stomach. Surely they wouldn't risk doing anything to *Edward Sayre*'s nephew? And yet . . . they were clearly planning to imprison Malthan at the least, or perhaps something worse. Nick wasn't going to let that happen.

"Only a shadow, but I bet you do have rats. Stands to reason. Underground. Tea and biscuits about," Nick said as he ripped out the second page. He folded it, wrote "Mr. Edmund Garran" on the outside, and handed it to Malthan, at the same time stepping across to shield his next action from everyone except Lackridge, whom he stumbled against.

"Oh, sorry!" he exclaimed, and in that moment of apparently lost balance, he slid the palmed first note into Malthan's still open hand.

"I . . . ah . . . still not quite recovered from the events at Forwin Mill," Nick mumbled, as Lackridge suppressed an oath and jumped back.

The policemen had stepped forward, apparently only to catch him if he fell. Sergeant Hodgeman had seen him stumble before. They were clearly suspicious but didn't know what he had done. He hoped.

"Bit unsteady on my pins," continued Nick. "Nothing to do with drink, unfortunately. That might make it seem worthwhile. Now I must get on upstairs and dress for dinner. Who's taking Malthan over to the Golden Sheaf?"

"I am, sir. Constable Ripton."

"Very good, Constable. I trust you'll have a pleasant evening drive. I'll telephone ahead to make sure that my uncle's staff are expecting you and have dinner laid on."

"Thank you, sir," said Ripton woodenly. Again, if Nick hadn't been paying careful attention, he might have missed the young constable flicking his eyes up and down and then twice toward Sergeant Hodgeman—a twitch Nick interpreted as a call for help from the junior police officer, looking for Hodgeman to tell him how to satisfy his immediate masters as well as insure himself against the interference of any greater authority.

"Get on with it then, Constable," said Hodgeman, his words as ambiguous as his expression.

"Let's all get upstairs," Nick said with false cheer he dredged up from somewhere. "After you, Sergeant. Malthan, if you wouldn't mind walking with me, I'll see you to your car. Got a couple of questions about the Old Kingdom I'm sure you can answer."

"Anything, anything," babbled Malthan. He came so close, Nick thought the little trader was going to hug him. "Let us get out from under the earth. With that—"

"Yes, I agree," interrupted Nick. He gestured toward the door and met Sergeant Hodgeman's stare. All the policemen moved closer. Casual steps. A foot slid forward here, a diagonal pace toward Nick.

Lackridge coughed something that might have been "Dorrance," scuttled to the door leading back to the tunnels, opened it just wide enough to admit his bulk, and squeezed through. Nick thought about calling him back but instantly dismissed the idea. He didn't want to show any weakness.

But with Lackridge gone, there was no longer a witness. Nick knew Malthan didn't count, not to anyone in Department Thirteen.

Sergeant Hodgeman pushed one heavy-booted foot forward and advanced on Nick and Malthan till his face was inches away from Nick's. It was an intimidating posture, long beloved of sergeants, and Nick knew it well from his days in the school cadets.

Hodgeman didn't say anything. He just stared, a fierce stare that Nick realized hid a mind calculating how far he could go to keep Malthan captive, and what he might be able to do to Nicholas Sayre without causing trouble.

"My uncle is the Chief Minister," Nick whispered very softly. "My father a member of the Moot. Marshal Harngorm is my mother's uncle. My second cousin is the Hereditary Arbiter himself."

"As you say, sir," said Hodgeman loudly. He stepped back, the sound of his heel on the concrete snapping through the tension that had risen in the room. "I'm sure you know what you're doing."

That was a warning of consequences to come, Nick knew. But he didn't care. He wanted to save Malthan, but most of all at that moment he wanted to get out under the sun again. He wanted to stand aboveground and put as much earth and concrete and as many locked doors as possible between himself and the creature in the case.

Yet even when the afternoon sunlight was softly warming his face, Nick wasn't much comforted. He watched Constable Ripton and Malthan leave in a small green van that looked exactly like the sort of vehicle that would be used to dispose of a body in a moving picture about the fictional Department Thirteen. Then, while lurking near the footmen's side door, he saw several gleaming, expensive cars drive up to disgorge their gleaming, expensive passengers. He recognized most of the guests. None were friends. They were all people he would formerly have described as frivolous and now just didn't care about at all. Even the beautiful young women failed to make more than a momentary impact. His mind was elsewhere.

Nick was thinking about Malthan and the two messages he carried. One, the obvious one, was addressed to Thomas Garran, Uncle Edward's principal private secretary. It said:

Garran

Uncle will want to talk to the bearer (Malthan, an Old Kingdom trader) for five minutes or so. Please ensure he is then escorted to the Perimeter by Foxe's people or Captain Sverenson's, not D13. Ask Uncle to call me urgently. Word of a Sayre.

Nicholas.

The other, more hastily scrawled, said:

Send telegram TO MAGISTRIX WYVERLEY COLLEGE NICK FOUND BAD KINGDOM CREATURE DORRANCE HALL TELL ABHORSEN HELP.

There was every possibility neither message would get through, Nick thought. It would all depend on what Dorrance and his minions thought they could get away with. And that depended on what they thought they could do to one Nicholas Sayre before he caused them too much trouble.

Nick shivered and went back inside. As he expected, when he asked to use a telephone, the footman referred him to the butler, who was very apologetic and bowed several times while regretting that the line was down and probably would not be fixed for several days, the telegraph company being notoriously slow in the country.

With that avenue cut off, Nick retreated to his room, ostensibly to dress for dinner. In practice he spent most of the time writing a report to his uncle and another telegram to the Magistrix at Wyverley College. He hid the report in the lining of his suitcase and went in search of a particular valet who he knew would be accompanying one of the guests he had seen arrive, the aging dandy Hericourt Danjers. The permanent staff of Dorrance Hall would all really be Department Thirteen agents, or informants at the least, but it was much less likely the guests' servants would be.

Danjers's valet was famous among servants for his ability with shoe polish, champagne, and a secret oil. So neither he nor anyone else in the belowstairs parlor was much surprised when the Chief Minister's nephew sought him out with a pair of shoes in hand. The valet was a little more surprised to find a note inside the shoes asking him to go out to the village and secretly send a telegram, but as the note was wrapped around four double-guinea pieces, he was happy to do so. When he'd finished his duties, of course.

Back in his room, Nick dressed hastily. As he tied his bow tie, his hands moved automatically while he wondered what else he should be doing. All kinds of plans raced through his head, only to be abandoned as impractical, or foolish, or likely to make matters worse.

With his tie finally done, Nick went to his case and took

out a large leather wallet. There were three things inside. Two
were letters, both written neatly on thick, linen-rich handmade
paper, but in markedly different hands.

The first letter was from Nick's old friend Prince Sameth.
It was concerned primarily with Sam's current projects and
was illustrated in the margins with small diagrams. Judging
from the letter, Sam's time was being spent almost entirely on
the fabrication and enchantment of a replacement hand for
Lirael, and the planning and design of a fishing hut on an
island in the Ratterlin Delta. Sam did not explain why he
wanted to build a fishing hut, and Nick had not had a reply to
his most recent letter seeking enlightenment. This was not
unusual. Sam was an infrequent correspondent, and there was
no regular mail service of any kind between Ancelstierre and
the Old Kingdom.

Nick didn't bother to read Sam's letter again. He put it
aside, carefully unfolded the second letter, and read it for the
hundredth or two hundredth time, hoping that this time he
would uncover some hidden meaning in the innocuous words.

This letter was from Lirael, and it was quite short. The
writing was so regular, so perfectly spaced, and so free of ink
splotches that Nick wondered if it had been copied from a
rough version. If it had, what did that mean? Did Lirael
always make fine copies of her letters? Or had she done it
just for him?

Dear Nick,

I trust you are recovering well. I am much better,
and Sam says my new hand will be ready soon.
Ellimere has been teaching me to play tennis, a game
from your country, but I really do need two hands. I

have also started to work with the Abhorsen. Sabriel, I mean, though I still find it hard to call her that. I still laugh when I remember you calling her "Mrs. Abhorsen, Ma'am Sir." I was surprised by that laugh, amidst such sorrow and pain. It was a strange day, wasn't it? Waiting for everything to be discussed and sorted and explained just enough so we could all go home, with the two of us lying side by side on our stretchers with so much going on all around. You made it better for me, telling me about my friend the Disreputable Dog. I am very grateful for that. That is why I'm writing, really, and Sam said he was send-ing something so this could go in with it.

    Be well.

    Lirael, Abhorsen-in-Waiting and Remembrancer

Nick stared at the letter for several minutes after he fin-ished reading it, then gently folded it and returned it to the wallet. He drew out the third thing, which had come in a pack-age with the letters three weeks ago, though it had apparently left the Old Kingdom at least a month before that. It was a small, very plain dagger, the blade and hilt blued steel, with brass wire wound around the grip, the pommel just a big teardrop of metal.

Nick held it up to the light. He could see faint etched sym-bols upon the blade, but that was all they were. Faint etched symbols. Not living, moving Charter Marks, bright and flow-ing, all gold and sunshine. That's what Charter-spelled swords normally looked like, Nick knew, the marks leaping and splashing across the metal.

Nick knew he ought to be comforted. If the Charter Marks

on his dagger were still and dead, then the thing beneath the house should be as well. But he knew it wasn't. He'd seen its eyes flicker.

There was a knock on the door. Nick hastily put the dagger back in its sheath.

"Yes!" he called. The sheathed dagger was still in his hand. For a moment he considered exchanging it for the slim .32 automatic pistol in his suitcase's outer pocket. But he decided against it when the person at the door called out to him.

"Nicholas Sayre?"

It was a woman's voice. A young woman's voice, with the hint of a laugh in it. Not a servant. Perhaps one of the beautiful young women he'd seen arrive. Probably a not very successful actor or singer, the usual adornments of typical country house parties.

"Yes. Who is it?"

"Tesrya. Don't say you don't remember me. Perhaps a glimpse will remind you. Let me in. I've got a bottle of champagne. I thought we might have a drink before dinner."

Nick didn't remember her, but that didn't mean anything. He knew she would have singled him out from the seating plan for dinner, homing in on the surname Sayre. He supposed he should at least tell her to go away to her face. Courtesy to women, even fortune hunters, had been drummed into him all his life.

"Just one drink?"

Nick hesitated, then tucked the sheathed dagger down the inside of his trousers, at the hip. He held his foot against the door in case he needed to shut it in a hurry; then he turned the key and opened it a fraction.

He had the promised glimpse. Pale, melancholy eyes in a very white face, a forced smile from too-red lips. But there were also two hooded men there. One threw his shoulder against the door to keep it open. The other grabbed Nick by the hair and pushed a pad the size of a small pillow against his face.

Nick tried not to breathe as he threw himself backward, losing some hair in the process, but the sickly-sweet smell of chloroform was already in his mouth and nose. The two men gave him no time to recover his balance. One pushed him back to the foot of the bed, while the other got his right arm in a wrestling hold. Nick struck out with his left, but his fist wouldn't go where he wanted it to. His arm felt like a rubbery length of pipe, the elbow gone soft.

Nick kept flailing, but the pad was back on his mouth and nose, and all his senses started to shatter into little pieces like a broken mosaic. He couldn't make sense of what he saw and heard and felt, and all he could smell was a sickly scent like a cheap perfume badly imitating the scent of flowers.

In another few seconds, he was unconscious.

Nicholas Sayre returned to his senses very slowly. It was like waking up drunk after a party, his mind still clouded and a hangover building in his head and stomach. It was dark, and he was disoriented. He tried to move and for a frightened instant thought he was paralyzed. Then he felt restraints at his wrists and thighs and ankles and a hard surface under his head and back. He was tied to a table, or perhaps a hard bench.

"Ah, the mind wakes," said a voice in the darkness. Nick thought for a second, his clouded mind slowly processing the sound. He knew that voice. Dorrance.

"Would you like to see what is happening?" asked Dorrance. Nick heard him take a few steps, heard the click of a rotary electric switch. Harsh light came with the click, so bright that Nick had to screw his eyes shut, tears instantly welling up in the corners.

"Look, Mr. Sayre. Look at your most useful work."

Nick slowly opened his eyes. At first all he could see was a naked, very bright electric globe swinging directly above his head. Blinking to clear the tears, he looked to one side. Dorrance was there, leaning against a concrete wall. He smiled and pointed to the other side, his hand held close against his chest, fist clenched, index finger extended.

Nick rolled his head and then recoiled, straining against the ropes that bound his ankles, thighs, and wrists to a steel operating table with raised rails.

The creature from the case was right next to him. No longer in the case, but stretched out on an adjacent table ten inches lower than Nick's. It was not tied up. There was a red rubber tube running from one of Nick's wrists to a metal stand next to the creature's head. The tube ended an inch above the monster's slightly open mouth. Blood was dripping from the tube, small dark blobs falling in between its jet black teeth.

Nick's blood.

Nick struggled furiously for another second, panic building in every muscle. The ropes did not give at all, and the tube was not dislodged. Then, his strength exhausted, he stopped.

"You need not be concerned, Mr. Nicholas Sayre," said Dorrance. He moved around to look at the creature, gently tapping Nick's slippered feet as he passed. "I am taking only a pint. This will all just be a nightmare in the morning, half remembered, with a dozen men swearing to your conspicuous consumption of brandy."

As he spoke, the light above him suddenly flared into white-hot brilliance. Then, with a bang, the bulb exploded into powder and the room went dark. Nick blinked, the afterimage of the filament burning a white line across the room. But even with that, he could see another light. Two violet sparks that were faint at first but became brighter and more intense.

Nick recognized them instantly as the creature's eyes. At the same time, he smelled a sudden, acrid odor, which got stronger and stronger, coating the back of his mouth and making his nostrils burn. A metallic stench that he knew only too well.

The smell of Free Magic.

The violet eyes moved suddenly, jerking up. Nick felt the rubber hose suddenly pulled from his wrist and the wet sensation of blood dripping down his hand.

He still couldn't see anything save the creature's eyes. They moved again, very quickly, as the thing stood up and crossed the room. It ignored Nick, though he struggled violently against his bonds as it went past. He couldn't see what happened next, but something . . . or someone . . . was hurled against his table, the impact rocking it almost to the point of toppling over.

"No!" shouted Dorrance. "Don't go out! I'll bring you blood! Whatever kind you need—"

There was a tearing sound, and flickering light suddenly filled the room. Nick saw the creature silhouetted in the doorway, holding the heavy door it had just ripped from its steel hinges. It threw this aside and strode out into the corridor, lifting its head back to emit a hissing shriek that was so high-pitched, it made Nick's ears ring.

Dorrance staggered after it for a moment, then returned and flung open a cabinet on the wall. As he picked up the telephone handset inside, the lights in the corridor fizzed and went out.

Nick heard the dial spin three times. Then Dorrance swore and tapped the receiver before dialing again. This time the phone worked, and he spoke very quickly.

"Hello? Lackridge? Can you hear me? Yes . . . ignore the crackle. Is Hodgeman there? Tell him 'Situation Dora.' All the fire doors must be barred and the exit grilles activated. No, tell him now. . . . 'Dora' . . .Yes, yes. It worked, all too well. She's completely active, and I heard Her clearly for the first time, speaking directly into my head, not as a dreaming voice. Sayre's blood was too rich, and there's something wrong with it. She needs to dilute it with normal blood. . . . What? Active! Running around! Of course you're in danger! She doesn't care whose blood. . . . We need to keep Her in the tunnels; then I'll find someone . . . one of the servants. Just get on with it!"

Nick kept silent, but he remembered the dagger at his hip. If he could bend his hand back and reach it, he might be able to unsheath it enough to work the rope against the blade. If he didn't bleed to death first.

"So, Mr. Sayre," said Dorrance in the darkness. "Why would your blood be different from that of any other bearer of the Charter Mark? It causes me some distress to think I have given Her the wrong sort. Not to mention the difficulty that now arises from Her desire to wash Her drink down."

"I don't know," Nick whispered after a moment's hesitation. He'd thought of pretending to be unconscious, but Dorrance would certainly test that.

In the distance, electric bells began a harsh, insistent clangor. At first none sounded in the corridor outside, then one stuttered into life. At the same time, the light beyond the door flickered on, off, and on again, before giving up in a shower of sparks that plunged the room back into total darkness.

Something touched Nick's feet. He flinched, taking off some skin against the ropes. A few seconds later there was a click near his head, a whiff of kerosene; and a four-inch flame suddenly shed some light on the scene. Dorrance lifted his cigarette lighter and set it on a head-high shelf, still burning.

He took a bandage from the same shelf and started to wind it around Nick's wrist.

"Waste not, want not," said Dorrance. "Even if your blood is tainted, it has succeeded beyond my dearest hopes. I have long dreamed of waking Her."

"It, you mean," croaked Nick.

Dorrance tied off the bandage, then suddenly slapped Nick's face hard with the back of his hand.

"You are not worthy to speak of Her! She is a goddess! A goddess! She should never have been sent away! My father was a fool! Fortunately I am not!"

Nick chose silence once more, and waited for another blow. But it didn't come. Dorrance took a deep breath, then bent under the table. Nick craned his head to see what he was doing but could hear only the rattle of metal on metal.

The man emerged holding two sets of old-style handcuffs, the kind whose cuffs were screwed in rather than key locked. He quickly handcuffed Nick's left wrist to the metal rail of the bed, then did the same with the second set to his right wrist.

"It has been politic to play the disbeliever about your Charter Magic," he said as he screwed the handcuffs tight. "But She has told me different in my dreams, and if She can rise so far from the Wall, perhaps your magic will also serve you . . . and ropes do burn or fray so easily. Rest here, young Nicholas. My mistress may soon need a second drink, whether the taste disagrees with Her or not."

After shaking the handcuffs to make sure they were secure, Dorrance picked up his still-burning cigarette lighter and left, muttering something to himself that Nick couldn't quite hear. It didn't sound entirely sane, but Nick didn't need to hear bizarre mumblings to know that Dorrance was neither the harmless eccentric of his public image or the cunning spymaster of his secret identity. He was a madman in league with a Free Magic creature.

As soon as Dorrance had gone, Nick tested the handcuffs, straining against them. But he couldn't move his hands more than a few inches off the table, certainly not far enough to reach the screws. However, he could reach the pommel of his dagger with the tips of three fingers. After a few failed attempts, he managed to get the blade out, and by rolling his body, he sliced through the rope on his left wrist, cutting himself slightly in the process.

He was trying to move his left ankle up toward his hand when he heard the first distant gunshots and screams. There were more, but they got fainter and fainter, lending hope that the creature was moving farther away.

Not that it made much difference, Nick thought as he rattled his handcuffs in frustration. He couldn't get free by himself. He would have to work out a plan to get Dorrance to at least uncuff him when he returned. Then Nick might be able to surprise him. If he did return. Until then, Nick decided, he should try to rest and gather his strength. As much as the adrenaline coursing through his bloodstream would let him rest, immobilized on a steel operating table in a secret underground facility run by a lunatic, with a totally inimical creature on the loose.

He lay in silence for what he estimated was somewhere between fifteen minutes and an hour, though he was totally unable to judge the passage of time when he was in the dark and so wound up with tension. In that time, every noise seemed loud and significant, and made him twist and tilt his head, as if by moving his ears he could better capture and identify each sound.

There was silence for a while, or near enough to it. Then he heard more gunshots but without the screams. The shots were repeated a few seconds later, louder and closer, and were followed by the slam and echo of metal doors and then hurrying footsteps. Of more than one person.

"Help!" cried Nick. "Help! I'm tied up in here!"

He figured it was worth calling out. Even fanatical Department Thirteen employees must have realized by now that Dorrance was crazy and he'd unleashed something awful upon them.

"Help!"

The footsteps came closer, and a flashlight beam swung into the room, blinding Nick. Behind its yellow nimbus, he saw two partial silhouettes. One man standing in front of another.

"Get those shackles off and untie him," ordered the second man. Nick recognized the voice. It was Constable Ripton. The man who shuffled ahead, allowing the light to fall on his face and side, was Professor Lackridge. A pale and trembling Lackridge, who fumbled with the screws of the handcuffs. Ripton was holding a revolver on him, but Nick doubted that was why the scientist was so scared.

"Sorry to take so long, sir," said Ripton calmly. "Bit of a panic going on."

Nick suddenly understood what Ripton had actually been trying to convey with his quick glances back in the guardroom. His uncle's words ran through his head.

It is watched over quite carefully, I assure you.

"You're not really D13, are you? You're one of my uncle's men?"

"Yes, sir. Indirectly. I report to Mr. Foxe."

Nick sat up as the handcuffs came off, and quickly sliced through the remaining ropes. He was not entirely surprised to see the faint glimmer of Charter Marks on the blade, though they were nowhere near as bright and potent as they'd be near the Wall.

"Can you walk, sir? We need to get moving."

Nick nodded. He felt a bit light-headed but otherwise fine, so he guessed he hadn't lost too much blood to the creature.

"Sorry," Lackridge blurted out as Nick slid off the table and stood up. "I never . . . never thought that this would happen. I never believed Dorrance, thought only to humor him. . . . He said that she spoke to him in dreams, and if it was more awake, then . . . We hoped to be able to discover the secret of waking mental communication. . . . It was—"

"Mind control is what Dorrance thought he could get from it," Ripton said, interrupting him. He tapped his coat pocket. "I've got your diary here. Mind control through people's dreams. And you just went along with whatever Dorrance wanted, you stupid sod."

"What's actually happening?" asked Nick. "Has it killed anyone?"

Lackridge choked out something unintelligible.

"Anyone! It's killed almost everyone down here, and by now it's probably upstairs killing everyone there," said Ripton. "Guns don't work up close to it, bullets fired farther back don't do a thing, and the electric barrier grilles just went *phhht* when it walked up! As soon as I figured it was trying to get out, I doubled around behind it. Now I reckon we follow its path outside and then run like the clappers while it's busy—"

"We can't do that," said Nick. "What about the guests? And the servants—even if they do work for D13, they can't be abandoned."

"There's nothing we can do," said Ripton. He no longer appeared so calm. "I don't know what that thing is, but I do know that it has already killed a dozen highly trained and fully armed D13 operatives. Killed them and . . . and drunk their blood. Not . . . not something I ever want to see again. . . ."

"I know what it is," said Nick. "Somewhat. It is a Free Magic creature from the Old Kingdom. A source of Free Magic itself, which is why guns and electricity don't work near it. I would have thought that bullets coming in from farther away would at least hurt it, though. . . ."

"They bounced off. I saw the lead splashes on its hide. . . . Here's a flashlight. You go in front, Professor. Get your key ready."

"We have to try to save the people upstairs," Nick said firmly as they nervously entered the corridor, flashlight beams probing the darkness in both directions. "Has it definitely already got out of here?"

"I don't know! It was through the second guardroom. The library exit might slow it more. It's basically a revolving re-inforced concrete-and-steel slab, like a vault door. Supposed to be bombproof—"

"Is there another way up?"

"No," said Ripton.

"Yes," said Lackridge. He stopped and turned, the bronze key gleaming in his hand. Ripton stepped back, and his finger whipped from resting outside the trigger guard to curl directly around the trigger.

"The dumbwaiter!" Lackridge blurted out. "Dorrance has a dumbwaiter from the wine cellar below us here, which goes up through his office to the pantry above."

"What time is it?" asked Nick.

"Half eight," said Ripton. "Or near enough."

"The guests will be at dinner," said Nick. "They won't have heard what's going on down here. If we can take the dumb-waiter to the pantry, we might be able to get everyone out of the house before the creature breaks through to the library."

"And then what?" asked Ripton. "Talk as we go. Head for the office, Prof."

"It's not a Dead thing, so running water won't do much," said Nick as they broke into a jog. "Fire might, though. . . . If we made a barrier of hay and set it alight, that could work. It would attract attention at least. Bring help."

"I don't think the sort of help we need exists around here," said Ripton. "I've never been up north, but I know people in the NPRU, and this is right up their alley. Things like this just don't happen down here."

"No, they don't," said Nick. "They wouldn't have happened

this time, either, only Dorrance fed his creature the wrong blood."

"I don't understand," Lackridge said, puffing after them. Now that they were heading for a possible exit, he had gotten more of a grip on himself. "I didn't believe him . . . but . . . Dorrance thought the blood of one of you people with the Charter brand would rouse the creature a little, without danger. Then when we got you to come in for the Forwin Mill investigation, he saw you had a Charter Mark. The opportunity was too good to resist—"

"Shut up!" ordered Ripton. As Lackridge calmed down, the policeman got more tense.

"Dorrance worships the creature, but I don't think even he wanted it this active," snapped Nick. "I can't explain the whole thing to you, but my blood is infused with Free Magic as well as the Charter. I guess the combination is what got the creature going so strongly . . . but it was too rich or something; that's why it's trying to dilute it with normal blood. . . . I wonder if that means that the power it got from my blood will run out. Maybe it'll just drop at some point. . . ."

Lackridge shook his head, as if he still couldn't believe what he was hearing, despite the evidence.

"It might come back for a refill from you as well," said Ripton. "Here's the office. You first, Professor."

"But what if the creature's in there?"

"That's why you're going first," said Ripton. He gestured with his revolver, and when Lackridge still didn't move, he pushed him hard with his left hand. The bulky ex-boxer rebounded from the door and stood there, his eyes glazed and jowls shivering.

"Oh, I'll go first!" said Nick. He pushed Lackridge aside a

little more gently, turned the door handle, and went into Dorrance's office. It was the room he'd been in before, with the big leather club chairs, the desk, and the liquor cabinet.

"It's empty—come on!"

Ripton locked the door after them as they entered the room, and then he slid the top and bottom bolts home.

"Thought I heard something," he whispered. "Maybe it's coming back. Keep your voices down."

"Where's the dumbwaiter?" asked Nick.

Lackridge crossed to a bookshelf and pressed a corner. The whole shelf swung out an inch, allowing Lackridge to get a grip and open it out completely. The beam of Nick's flashlight revealed a square space behind it about three feet high and just as wide: a small goods elevator or dumbwaiter.

"We'll have to go one at a time," said Ripton. He slipped his revolver into his shoulder holster, laid his flashlight on the desk, and dragged one of the heavy studded leather chairs against the door. "You first, Mr. Sayre. I think it must have heard us, or smelled us, or something; there's definitely movement outside—"

"Let me go!" Lackridge burst out, darting toward the elevator. He was brought up short as Ripton whirled around and kicked him behind the knee, bringing him crashing down, his fall rattling the bottles in the liquor cabinet.

Nick hesitated, then climbed into the dumbwaiter. There were two buttons on the outside frame of the elevator, one marked with an up arrow and one with a down; but as he expected, neither did anything. However, there was a hatch in the ceiling, which when pushed open revealed a vertical shaft and some heavily greased cables. The shaft was walled with old yellow bricks, and some had been removed every few feet to make irregular, but usable, hand and footholds.

Nick ducked his head out and said, "It's electric, not working. We'll have to climb the—"

His voice was drowned out as the metal office door suddenly rang like a bell and the middle of it bowed in, struck with tremendous force from the other side.

"Fire!" Nick shouted as he jumped out of the elevator. "Start a fire against the door!"

He rushed to the liquor cabinet and ripped it open as the creature struck the door again. This second blow sheared the top bolt and bent the top half of the door over, and a dark shape with glowing violet eyes could be seen beyond the doorway. At the same time, Ripton's flashlight shone intensely bright for a second, then went out forever.

The remaining flashlight, left in the elevator, continued to shine erratically. Nick frantically threw whisky and gin bottles at the base of the door, and Ripton struck a match on the chair leg, swearing as it burst into splinters instead of flame. Then his second match flared and he flicked it across to the alcohol-soaked chair, and there was a blue flash and a ball of flame exploded around the door, searing off both Ripton's and Nick's eyebrows.

The creature made a horrid gargling, drowning sound and backed away. Nick and Ripton retreated to the wall and hunched down to try to get below the smoke, which was already filling the room. Lackridge was still slumped on the floor, not moving, the smoke twirling and curling over his back.

"Go!" Ripton coughed, gesturing with his thumb at the dumbwaiter.

"What about . . . ridge?"

"Leave him!"

"You go!"

Ripton shook his head, but when Nick crawled across to Lackridge, Ripton climbed into the dumbwaiter. The professor was a dead weight, too heavy for Nick to move without standing up. As he tried again, an unopened bottle exploded behind him, showering the back of his neck with hot glass. The smoke was getting thicker with every second, and the heat more intense.

"Get up!" Nick coughed. "You'll die here!"

Lackridge didn't move.

Flames licked at Nick's back and he smelled burning hair. He could do nothing more for the professor. He had only reduced his own chances of survival. Cradling his arms around his head, Nick dived into the dumbwaiter.

He had hoped for clean air there, but it was no better. The elevator shaft was acting as a chimney, sucking up the smoke. Nick felt his throat and lungs closing up and his arms and legs growing weaker. He thrust himself through the hatch, climbed onto the roof of the dumbwaiter, and felt about for the hatch cover, slapping it down in the hope that this might stop some of the smoke. Then, coughing and spitting, he found the first missing bricks and began to climb.

He could hear Ripton somewhere up above him, coughing and swearing. But Nick wasn't listening for Ripton. All his senses were attuned to what might be happening lower down. Would the creature come through the fire and swarm up the shaft?

The smoke did begin to thin a little as Nick climbed, but it was still thick enough for him to smash his head into Ripton's boots after he had climbed up about forty feet. The sudden shout it provoked confirmed that Ripton had been thinking about where the creature was as well.

"Sorry!" Nick gasped. "I don't think it's following us."

"There's a door here. I'm standing on the edge of it, but I can't slide the bloody thing— Got it!"

Light spilled into the shaft as smoke wafted out of it. Hard white gaslight. Ripton stepped through, then turned to help Nick pull himself up and over.

They were in a long whitewashed room lined from floor to ceiling with shelves and shelves of packaged food of all varieties. Tins and boxes and packets and sacks and bottles and puncheons and jars.

There was a door at the other end. It was open, and a white-clad cook's assistant was staring at them openmouthed.

"Fire!" shouted Nick, waving his arms to clear the smoke that was billowing out fast from behind him. He started to walk forward, continuing to half shout, his voice raspy and dulled by smoke. "Fire in the cellars! Everyone needs to get out, to the . . . Which field is closest, with hay?"

"The home meadow," croaked Ripton. He cleared his throat and tried again. "The home meadow."

"Tell the staff to evacuate the house and assemble on the home meadow," Nick ordered in his most commanding manner. "I will tell the guests."

"Yes, sir!" stammered the cook's assistant. There was still a lot of smoke coming out, even though Ripton had managed to close the door to the dumbwaiter. "Cook will be angry!"

"Hurry up!" said Nick. He strode past the assistant and along a short corridor, to find himself in the main kitchen, where half a dozen immaculately white-clad men were engaged in an orderly but complex dance around a number of counters and stove tops, directed by the rapid snap of commands from a small, thin man with the tallest and whitest hat.

"Fire!" roared Nick. "Get out to the home meadow! Fire!"

He repeated this as he strode through the kitchen and out the swinging doors immediately after a waiter who showed the excellence of his training by hardly looking behind him for more than a second.

As Nick had thought, the dinner guests were making so much noise of their own that they would never have heard any kind of commotion deep in the earth under their feet. Even when he burst out of the servants' corridor and jumped onto an empty chair near the head of the table that was probably his, only five or six of the forty guests looked around.

Then Ripton fired two rapid shots into the ceiling.

"Ladies and gentlemen, I do beg your pardon!" shouted Nick. "There is a fire in the house! Please get up at once and follow Mr. Ripton here to the home meadow!"

Silence met this announcement for perhaps half a second; then Nick was assaulted with questions, comments, and laughter. It was such a babble that he could hardly make out any one coherent stream of words; but clearly half the guests thought this was some game of Dorrance's; a quarter of them wanted to go and get their jewels, favorite coats, or lapdogs; and the last quarter intended to keep eating and drinking whether the house burned down around them or not.

"This isn't a joke!" Nick screamed, his voice barely penetrating the hubbub. "If you don't go now, you'll be dead in fifteen minutes! Men have already died!"

Perhaps ten of the guests heard him. Six of them pushed their chairs back and stood. Their movement caused a momentary lull, and Nick tried again.

"I'm Nicholas Sayre," he said, pointing at his burnt hair

and blackened dress shirt, and his bloodied cuffs. "The Chief Minister's nephew. I am not playing games for Dorrance. Look at me, will you! Get out now or you will die here!"

He jumped down as merry pandemonium turned into panic, and almost knocked down the butler, who had been standing by to either assist or restrain him; Nick couldn't be sure which.

"You're D13, right?" he asked the imposing figure. "There's been an accident downstairs. There is a fire, but there's an . . . animal . . . loose. Like a tiger, but much stronger, fiercer. No door can hold it. We need to get everyone out on the home meadow, and get them building a ring of hay. Make it about fifty yards in diameter, and we'll gather in the middle and set it alight to keep the animal out. You understand?"

"I believe I do, sir," said the butler, with a low bow and a slight glance at Ripton, who nodded. The butler then turned to look at the footmen, who stood impassively against the wall as guests ran past them, some of them screaming, some giggling, but most fearful and silent. He tuned his voice to a penetrating pitch and said, "James, Erik, Lancel, Benjamin! You will lead the guests to the home meadow. Lukas, Ned, Luther, Zekall! You will alert Mrs. Krane, Mr. Rowntree, Mr. Gowing, and Miss Grayne, to have all their staff immediately go to the home meadow. You will accompany them. Patrick, go and ring the dinner gong for the next three minutes without stopping, then run to the home meadow."

"Good!" snapped Nick. "Don't let anyone stay behind, and if you can take any bottles of paraffin or white spirits out to the meadow, do so! Ripton, lead the way to the library."

"No, sir," said Ripton. "My job's to get you out of here. Come on!"

"We can bar the doors! What the—"

Nick felt himself suddenly restrained by a bear hug around his arms and chest. He tried to throw himself forward but couldn't move whoever had picked him up. He kicked back but was held off the ground, his feet uselessly pounding the air.

"Sorry, sir," said Ripton, edging well back so he couldn't be kicked. "Orders. Take him out to the meadow, Llew."

Nick snapped his head back, hoping to strike his captor's nose, but whoever held him was not only extremely big and strong but also a practiced wrestler. Nick craned around and saw he was in the grip of a very tall and broad footman, one he had noticed when he had first arrived, polishing a suit of armor in the entrance hall that, though man-size, came up only to his shoulder.

"Nay, you shan't escape my clutch, Master," said Llew, striding out of the dining room like a determined child with a doll. "Won the belt at Applethwick Fair seven times for the wrestling, I have. You get comfortable and rest. It baint far to the home meadow."

Nick pretended to relax as they joined the column of people going through the main doors and out across the graveled drive and lawn. It was still quite light, and a harvest moon was rising, big and kind and golden. Many of the people slowed down as the sudden hysteria of Nick's warning ebbed. It was a beautiful night, and the home meadow looked rustic and inviting, with the haycocks still standing, the work of spreading the hay into a defensive ring not yet begun, though the butler was already directing servants to the task.

Halfway across the lawn, Nick suddenly arched his back and tried to twist sideways and out of Llew's grip, but to no avail. The big man just laughed.

The lawn and the meadow were separated by a fence in a ditch, or ha-ha, so as not to spoil the view. Most of the guests and staff were crossing this on a narrow mathematical bridge that supposedly featured no nails or screws, but Llew simply climbed down. They were halfway up the other side when there was a sudden, awful screech behind them, a shrill howl that came from no human throat or any animal the Ancels-tierrans had ever heard.

"Let me go!" Nick ordered. He couldn't see what was happening, save that the people in front had suddenly started running, many of them off in random directions, not to what he hoped would be safety. If they could get the hay spread quickly enough and get it alight . . .

"Too late to go back now, sir," said Ripton. "Let him go, Llew! Run!"

Nick looked over his shoulder for a second as they ran the last hundred yards to the center of the meadow. Smoke was pouring out of one wing of the house, forming a thick, puffy worm that reached up to the sky, black and horrid, with red light flickering at its base. But that was not what held his attention.

The creature was standing on the steps of the house, its head bent over a human victim it held carelessly under one arm. Even from a distance, Nick knew it was drinking blood.

There were people running behind Nick, but not many; and while they might have been dawdling seconds before, they were sprinting now. For a moment Nick hoped that everyone had gotten out of the house. Then he saw movement behind the creature. A man casually walked outside to stand next to it. The creature turned to him, and Nick felt the grip of horror as he expected to see it snatch the person up. But it didn't. The creature returned to its current victim, and the man stood by its side.

"Dorrance," said Ripton. He drew his revolver, rested the barrel on his left forearm, and aimed for a moment, before holstering the weapon again. "Too far. I'll wait till the bastard's closer."

"Don't worry about Dorrance for the moment," said Nick. He looked around. The guests were all clustered together in the center of the notional fifty-yard-diameter circle, and only the servants were spreading hay, under the direction of the butler. Nick shook his head and walked over to the guests. They surged toward him in turn, once again all speaking at the same time.

"I demand to know—"

"What is going on?"

"Is that . . . that animal really—"

"Clearly this is not properly—"

"This is an outrage! Who is respons—"

"Shut up!" roared Nick. "Shut up! That animal is from the Old Kingdom! It will kill all of us if we don't keep it out with fire, which is why everybody needs to start spreading hay in a ring! Hurry!"

Without waiting to see their response, Nick ran to the nearest haycock and tore off a huge armful of hay and ran to add it to the circle. When he looked up, some of the guests were helping the servants, but most were still bickering and complaining.

He looked across at the house. The creature was no longer on the steps. There was a body sprawled there, but Dorrance had vanished as well.

"Start pouring the paraffin!" shouted Nick. "Get more hay on the ring! It's coming!"

The butler and some of the footmen began to run around the circle, spraying white petroleum spirit out of four-gallon tins.

"Anyone with matches or a cigarette lighter, stand by the ring!" yelled Nick. He couldn't see the creature, but his forehead was beginning to throb, and when he pulled his dagger out an inch, the Charter Marks were starting to glow.

Two people suddenly jumped the hay and ran across the meadow, heading for the drive and the front gate. A young man and woman, the woman throwing aside her shoes as she ran. She was the one who had come to his door, Nick saw. Tesrya, as she had called herself.

"Come back!" shouted Nick. "Come back—"

His voice fell away as a tall, strange shape emerged from the sunken ditch of the ha-ha, its shadow slinking ahead. Its arms looked impossibly long in the twilight, and its legs had three joints, not two. It began to lope slowly after the running couple, and for a brief instant Nick thought perhaps they might have a chance.

Then the creature lowered its head. Its legs stretched; the lope became a run and then a blurring sprint that caught it up with the man and woman in a matter of seconds. It knocked them down with its clubbed hands as it overshot them, turning to come back slowly as they flopped about on the ground like fresh-caught fish.

Tesrya was screaming, but the screams stopped abruptly as the creature bent over her.

Nick looked away and saw a patch of tall yellow flowers near his feet. Corn daisies, fooled into opening by the bright moonlight.

. . . wrapped in three chains. One of silver, one of lead, and one made from braided daisies . . .

"Ripton!"

"Yes, sir!"

Nick jumped as Ripton answered from slightly behind him and to his left.

"Get anyone who can make flower chains braiding these daisies, and those poppies over there too. The maids might know how."

"What?"

"I know what it sounds like, but there's a chance that thing can be restrained with chains made from flowers."

"But . . ."

"The Old Kingdom. Magic. Just make the chains!"

"I knows the braiding of flowers," Llew said, bending down to gently pick a daisy in his huge hand. "As does my kin here, my nieces Ellyn and Alys, who are chambermaids and will have needle and thread in their apron pockets."

"Get to it then, please," said Nick. He looked across at where the young couple had fallen. The creature had been there only seconds ago, but now it was gone. "Damn! Anyone see where it went?"

"No," snapped Ripton. He spun around on the spot as he tried to scan the whole area outside the defensive circle.

"Light the hay! Light the hay! Quickly!"

Ripton struggled with his matches, striking them on his heel, but others were quicker. Guests with platinum and gold cigarette lighters flicked them open and on and held them to the hay; kitchen staff struck long, heavy-headed matches and threw them; and one old buffer wound and released a clockwork cigar fire starter, an affectation that had finally come into its own.

Accelerated by paraffin, brandy, and table polish, the ring of hay burst into flames. But not everywhere. While the fire leapt high and smoke coiled toward the moon over most of the ring, one segment about ten feet long remained stubbornly dark, dank, and unlit. The meadow was sunken there, and wet, and the paraffin had not been spread evenly, pooling in a hole.

"There it is!"

The creature came out of the shadow of the oaks near the drive. Its strangely jointed legs propelled it across the meadow in a sprint that would have let it run down a leopard. It moved impossibly, horribly fast, coming around the outside of the ring. Nick and Ripton started to run too, even though they knew they had no chance of beating the creature.

It would be at the gap in seconds. Only one person was close enough to do anything—a kitchen maid running with a lit taper clutched in her right hand, her left holding up her apron.

The creature was far faster, but it had farther to go. It accelerated again, becoming a blur of movement.

Everyone within the ring watched the race, all of them desperately hoping that the fire would simply spread of its own accord, all of them wishing that this fatal hole in their shield of fire would not depend upon a young woman, an easily extinguished taper, and an apron that was too long for its wearer.

Six feet from the edge of the hay, the apron slipped just enough for the girl to trip over the hem. She staggered, tried to recover her balance, and fell, the taper dropping from her hand.

Though she must have been shocked and bruised by the

fall, the maid did not lie there. Even as the creature bunched its muscles for the last dash to the gap, the young woman picked up the still-burning taper and threw it the last few feet into the center of the dark section.

It caught instantly, fed by a pool of paraffin that had collected in the dip in the ground. Blue fire flashed over the hay, and flames licked up toward the yellow moon.

The creature shrieked in frustration, its hooked heels throwing up great clods of grass and soil as it checked its headlong rush. For a moment it looked as if it might try to jump the fire, but instead it turned and loped back to the ha-ha, disappearing out of sight.

Nick and Ripton stopped and bent over double, resting their hands on their knees, panting as they tried to recover from their desperate sprint.

"It doesn't like fire," Ripton coughed out after a minute. "But we haven't got enough hay to keep this circle going for more than an hour or so. What happens then?"

"I don't know," said Nick. He was acutely aware of his ignorance. None of this would be happening if the creature hadn't drunk his blood. *His* blood, pumping furiously around his body that very second but a mystery to him. He knew nothing about its peculiar properties. He didn't even know what it could do, or why it had been so strong that the creature needed to dilute it with the blood of others.

"Can you do any of that Old Kingdom magic the Scouts talk about?"

"No," said Nick. "I . . . I'm rather useless, I'm afraid. I've been planning to go to the Old Kingdom . . . to learn about, well, a lot of things. But I haven't managed to get there yet."

"So we're pretty well stuffed," said Ripton. "When the fire

burns down, that thing will just waltz in here and kill us all."

"We might get help," said Nick.

Ripton snorted. "Not the help we need. I told you. Bullets don't hurt it. I doubt even an artillery shell would do anything, if a gunner could hit something moving that fast."

"Keep your voice down," Nick muttered. Most of the people inside the ring were huddled right in the center, as much to get away from the drifting smoke of the fires as for the psychological ease of being farther away from the creature. But a knot of half a dozen guests and servants was only a dozen yards away, the servants helping the kitchen maid up and the guests getting in the way. "I meant Old Kingdom help. I sent a message with Malthan. A telegram for him to send to some people who can get a message to the Old Kingdom quickly."

Ripton bent his head and mumbled something.

"What? What did you say?"

"Malthan never made it past the village," Ripton muttered. "I handed him over to two of Hodgeman's particular pals at the crossroads. Orders. I had to do it, to maintain my cover."

Nick was silent, his thoughts on the sad, frightened, greedy little man who was now probably dead in a ditch not too many miles away.

"Hodgeman said you'd never follow up what happened to Malthan," said Ripton. "He said your sort never did. You were just throwing your weight around, he said."

"I would have checked," said Nick. "I would have left no stone unturned. Believe me."

He looked around at the ring of fire. Sections of it were already dying down, generating lots of smoke but little flame. If Malthan had managed to send the telegram six or more hours ago, there might have been a slim chance that the Abhorsen . . . or Lirael . . . or somebody competent to deal with the creature would have been able to get there before they ran out of things to burn.

"Hodgeman's dead now, anyway. He was one of the first that thing got."

"I sent another message," said Nick. "I bribed Danjers's valet to go down to the village and send a telegram."

"Nowhere to send one from there," said Ripton. "Planned that way, of course. D13 keeping control of communications. The closest telephone would be at Colonel Wrale's house, and that's ten miles away."

"I don't suppose he would have managed it anyway—"

Nick broke off and peered at the closer group of people and then at the central muddle, wiping his eyes as a tendril of smoke wafted across.

"Where is Danjers? I don't remember seeing him at the dinner table, and he's pretty hard to miss. What's the butler's name again?"

"Whitecrake," said Ripton, but Nick was already striding over to the butler, who was issuing orders to his footmen, who in turn were busy feeding the fires with more straw.

"Whitecrake!" Nick called before he had closed the distance between them. "Where is Mr. Danjers?"

Whitecrake rotated with great dignity, rather like a dreadnought's gun turret, and bowed, allowing Nick to close the distance before he replied.

"Mr. Danjers removed himself from the party and left at five o'clock," he said. "I understand that the curtains in the dining room clashed with his waistcoat."

"His man went with him?"

"Naturally," said Whitecrake. "I believe Mr. Danjers intended to motor over to Applethwick."

Nick felt every muscle in his shoulders and neck suddenly relax, as a ripple of relief passed through on its way to his toes.

"We'll be all right! Danjers's valet is bound to have sent that telegram! Let's see, if they got to Applethwick by seven thirty . . . the telegram would be at Wyverley by eight at the latest. . . . They'd get the message on to the Abhorsen's House however they do it. . . . Then if someone flew by Paperwing to Wyverley, they've got those aeroplanes at the flying school there to fly south . . . though I suppose not at night, even with this moon. . . ."

The tension started to come back as Nick came to the realization that even if the Abhorsen or King Touchstone's Guard had already received his message, there was no way anyone could be at Dorrance Hall before the morning, at the very earliest.

Nick looked up from the fingers he'd been counting on and saw that Ripton, Whitecrake, several footmen, a couple of maids, and a number of the guests were all hanging on his every word.

"Help will be coming," Nick announced firmly. "But we have to make the fires last as long as we can. Everything that can burn must be gathered within this ring. Every tiny piece of straw, any spare clothes, papers you may have on you, even banknotes . . . need to be gathered up. Mr. Whitecrake, can you take charge of that? Ripton, a word if you don't mind."

No one objected to Nick's taking command, and he hardly noticed himself that he had. He had often taken the lead among his school friends and at college, his mind usually grasping any situation faster than his fellows did and his aristocratic heritage providing more than enough self-confidence. As he turned away and walked closer to the fire, Ripton followed at his heels like an obedient shadow.

"There won't be any useful help till morning at the earliest," Nick whispered, his voice hardly audible over the crackle of the fire. "I mean Old Kingdom help. Provided Danjers's man did send the telegram."

Ripton eyed the burning straw.

"I suppose there's a chance the fire'll last till dawn, if we rake it narrower and just try to maintain a bit of flame and coals. Do you . . . Is there a possibility that . . . that thing doesn't like the sun, as well as fire?"

"I don't know. But I wouldn't count on it. From the little I heard my friend Sam talk about it at school, Free Magic creatures roam the day as freely as they do the night."

"Maybe it'll run out of puff," said Ripton. "Like you said. Dorrance didn't even expect it to wake up, and here it is running around—"

"What's that noise?" interrupted Nick. He could hear a distant jangling, carried on the light breeze toward him. "Is that a bell?"

"Oh no . . ." groaned Ripton. "It's the volunteer fire brigade from the village. They know they're not to come here, no matter what. . . ."

Nick looked around at the ring of red fire, and beyond that at the vast column of spark-lit smoke that was winding up from Dorrance Hall. No firefighter would be able to resist that clarion call.

"They're probably only the first," he said quietly. "With this moon, the smoke will be visible for miles. We'll probably have town brigades here in an hour or so, as well as all the local volunteers for a dozen miles or more. I'll have to stop them."

"What! If you leave the circle, that monster will be on you in a second!"

Nick shook his head.

"I've been thinking about that. It ran away from me after it drank just a little of my blood. Dorrance was yelling something about getting it other blood to dilute mine. It could easily have killed me then, but it didn't."

"You can't go out," said Ripton. "Think about it! It's drunk enough in the last hour to dilute your blood a hundred times over! It could easily be ready for more. And it's *your* blood that revved it up in the first place. It'll kill you and get more powerful, and then it'll kill us!"

"We can't just let it kill the firemen," Nick said stubbornly. He started to walk to the other side of the circle, closer to the drive. Ripton hurried along beside him. "I might be able to hurt . . . even kill . . . the creature with this."

He pulled out Sam's dagger and held it up. Fire and moonlight reflected from the blade, but there was green and blue and gold there, too, as Charter Marks swam slowly across the metal. Not fully active, but still strange and wonderful under the Ancelstierran moon.

Ripton did not seem overly impressed.

"You'd never get close enough to use that little pigsticker. Llew! Llew!"

"You're not catching me like that again," said Nick, without slowing down. He stowed the dagger away and picked up a rake, ready to make a gap in the burning barrier. A glance over his shoulder showed him the huge-shouldered Llew getting up from where he was braiding flowers. "If I want to go, you're going to let me this time."

"Too late," said Ripton. "There's the fire engine."

He pointed through the smoke. An ancient horse-drawn tanker, of a kind obsolete everywhere save the most rural counties, was coming up the drive, with at least fourteen volunteer firemen crammed on or hanging off it. They were in various states of uniform, but all wore gleaming brass helmets. Several firemen on horseback came behind the engine, followed by a farm truck loaded with more irregular volunteers, who were armed with fire beaters and buckets. Two small cars brought up the rear, transporting another four brass-helmeted volunteers.

"How did they—"

"There's another entrance to the estate from the village by the gamekeeper's cottage. Cuts half a mile off the front drive."

Nick plunged at the fire with the rake, and dragged some of the burning hay aside before he had to fall back from the smoke and heat. After a few seconds to recover, he pushed forward again, widening the gap. But it was going to take a few minutes to get through, and the firemen would be at the meadow before he could get out.

After his third attempt he reeled back into the grasp of Llew, who held Nick as he tried to swipe his legs with the rake, till Ripton grabbed it and twisted it out of his hands.

"Hold hard, Master!" said Llew.

"It's not attacking them!" cried Ripton. "Just keep still and take a look."

Nick stopped struggling. The fire engine had come to a halt as close as the men and horses could stand the heat, some fifty yards from the house. Firemen leapt off onto the lawn and began to bustle about with hoses as the truck and cars screeched to a halt behind them, throwing up gravel. The two mounted firemen continued on toward the meadow, their horses' hooves clattering on the narrow bridge over the ha-ha.

"It'll take the horsemen," said Nick. "It *must* be hiding in the ditch."

But the riders passed unmolested over the bridge and across the meadow, finally wheeling about close enough to the ring of fire for one of them to shout, "What on earth is happening here?"

Nick didn't bother to answer. He was still looking for the creature. Why hadn't it attacked?

Then he saw it through the swirling smoke. Not attacking anyone, but slinking up from the ha-ha and across the meadow toward the drive. Dorrance was riding on its back, like a child on a bizarre mobile toy, his arms clasped around the creature's long neck. He pointed toward the gatehouse, and the creature began to run.

"It's running away!" exclaimed Ripton.

"It's running," echoed Nick. "I wonder where?"

"Who cares!" Ripton exclaimed happily.

"I do," said Nick. He slipped free of Llew's suddenly relaxed grasp, took a deep, relatively smoke-free breath, sprinted forward, and jumped the ring of fire where he'd already made a partial gap.

He landed clear, fell forward, and quickly rolled in the grass to extinguish any flames that might have hitched a ride. He felt hot but not burned, and he had not breathed in any great concentration of smoke.

Looking back, he saw Ripton and Llew frantically raking the fire apart, but they had not dared to jump after him. He got up and ran toward the lawn, the parked cars, the fire engine, and the burning house.

There was only one reason the creature would flee now. It had nothing to fear from any weapons the Ancelstierrans could bring to bear. It could have stayed and killed everybody and drunk their blood. It must have decided to cut and run because the power it had gained from Nick's blood was waning and it didn't dare drink any more from him. That meant it would be heading north, toward the Old Kingdom, to find fresh victims to replenish its strength. Victims who bore the Charter Mark on their foreheads.

Nick couldn't let it do that.

He reached the rearmost car and vaulted into the driver's seat, deaf to the roar of the fire, the thud of the pumps, and the contained shriek of the high-pressure hoses. Even when Nick pressed the starter button, none of the firemen looked around, the sound of the little two-seater's engine lost amid all the noise and action.

The car was a Branston Four convertible, very similar to the Branston roadster Nick used to rent occasionally when he was at Sunbere. He slapped the gear lever into reverse with the necessary double tap and gently pulled the hand throttle. The little car rolled back onto the lawn. Nick tapped the lever into the first of the two forward gears and nudged forward.

The firemen still hadn't noticed, but as Nick opened up the hand throttle, the car backfired, hopped forward, and stalled. Someone, presumably the owner of the car, shouted. Nick saw a bronze-helmeted head approaching in the side-view mirror. To his left, Ripton and Llew charged up out of the ha-ha.

He depressed the clutch, hit the starter again, and hoped

he had the throttle position right. The car backfired once more and leapt six feet forward, and then the engine suddenly hit a sweet, drumming note. The speedometer stopped hiccuping up and down and started to slowly climb toward the top speed of thirty-five miles per hour. A breeze ruffled Nick's hair, undiminished by the tiny windscreen.

The bronze helmet disappeared from the mirror as the car accelerated along the drive. Ripton and Llew got almost close enough to lay a hand on the rear bumper before they, too, were left behind. Ripton shouted something, and a second later, Nick felt something rebound off his shoulder and land on the seat next to him. He glanced down and saw a chain of yellow daisies, punctuated every ten blooms or so with a red poppy.

Nick didn't bother switching on the car's headlights. The moon was so bright that he could even read the dashboard dials and see the drive clearly. What he couldn't see was the creature and Dorrance, but he had to presume they were heading for the front gate. The wall around the estate was probably no great barrier for the creature, but if it didn't need to climb it, he hoped, it wouldn't.

His guess was rewarded as he turned out of the gate and stopped to look in both directions, up and down the lane. It was darker here, the road shadowed by the trees on either side. But on a slight rise, several hundred yards distant, Nick caught sight of the odd silhouette of the creature, with Dorrance still riding on its back. It disappeared over the crest, running very fast and keeping to the road.

Nick sped after it, the little car vibrating as he wrenched the hand throttle out as far as it would go. The speedometer went past the curlicued *35* that indicated the car's top speed and got stuck against the raised letter *n* that completed the word *Branston* on the dial. But even at that speed, by the time he got to the top of the rise, the creature and Dorrance were gone. The lane kept on, with a very gentle curve to the left, so if Nick's quarry was anywhere within a mile, he should have been able to see them in the clear, cool light of the vast moon overhead.

Various possibilities whisked through Nick's mind. The most disturbing was the thought that they had seen him and were hiding off the road, the creature ready to spring on him as he passed. But the most likely possibility quickly replaced that fear. He hadn't seen it at first, because of the trees, but another road joined the lane just before it started to curve away. The creature must have gone that way.

Nick took the corner a little too fast, and the car slid off the paved road and onto the shoulder, sending up a spray of clods and loose asphalt. For a moment he felt the back end start to slide out, and the steering wheel was loose in his hands, as if it were no longer connected to anything. Then the tires bit again, and he overcorrected and fishtailed furiously for thirty yards before getting fully under control.

When he could properly look ahead, Nick couldn't see the creature and Dorrance. But this road only continued for another two hundred yards, ending at a small railway station. It was not much more than a signal box, a rudimentary waiting room, a platform, and the stationmaster's house set some distance away. A single line of track looped in from the southwest, ran along the platform, then looped back out again, to join the main line that ran straight and true a few minutes' walk away.

It had to be Dorrance Halt, the private railway station for Dorrance Hall. There was a train waiting at the platform, gray-white smoke busily puffing out of the locomotive and steam wafting around its wheels. It was a strangely configured train, in that there were six empty flatcars behind the engine, then a private car. Dorrance's private car, with his crest upon the doors.

Nick suddenly realized the significance of the blazon of the silver chain. Dorrance's several-times-great-grandfather must have been the Captain-Inquirer who found the creature, and the money gained from the sale of a silver chain was part of the current Dorrance's inheritance.

The significance of the empty flatcars was also apparent to Nick. They were there to separate the locomotive from any Free Magic interference caused by the creature. Dorrance had thought out this mode of transport very carefully. Perhaps he had always planned to take the creature away by train. The thing's long-term goal must always have been to return to the Old Kingdom.

Even as Nick pushed the little Branston to its utmost, the locomotive whistled and began to pull out of the station. As the rearmost carriage passed the waiting room, the electric lights outside fizzed and exploded. The train slowly picked up speed, the gouts of smoke from its funnel coming faster as it rolled away.

Nick wrenched the throttle completely out of its housing, drove off the road, raced through the station garden in a cloud of broken stakes and tomato plants, and drove onto the platform in a desperate effort to crash into the train and stop the creature's escape.

But he was too late. All he could do was lock his knee and try to push his foot and the brake pedal through the floor, as the Branston squealed and slid down the platform, prevented from sliding off the end only by a slow-speed impact with a long and very sturdy line of flowerpots.

Nick stood up and watched the train rattle onto the main line. For a moment, he thought he saw the glow of the creature's violet eyes looking back at him through the rear window of the carriage. But, he told himself as he put the flower chain around his neck and then jumped out of the badly dented Branston, it was probably just a reflection from the moon.

A sound from the waiting room made Nick jump and draw his dagger, but he sheathed it again straightaway. A man wearing a railway-uniform coat over blue-striped pajamas was standing in the doorway, staring, as Nick had just done, at the departing train.

"Where's that train going?" Nick demanded. "When's the next train coming here?"

"I . . . I . . . saw a real monster!" said the man. His eyes were wide with what Nick at first thought was shock but slowly realized was actually delight. "I saw a monster!"

"You're lucky it left you alive to remember it," said Nick. "Now answer my questions! You're the stationmaster, aren't you? Get a grip on yourself!"

The man nodded but didn't look at Nick. He kept staring after the train, even as it disappeared from sight.

"Where's that train going?"

"I . . . I don't know. It's Mr. Dorrance's private train. It's been waiting for days, the crew sleeping over at the house . . . then the call to be ready came only an hour ago. It got a slot going north, that's all I know, direct from Central at Corvere. I guess it'd be going to Bain. You know, I never thought I'd see something like that, with those huge eyes, and those spiked hands. Not here, not—"

"When's the next train north?"

"The Bain Flyer," the man replied automatically. "But she's an express. She doesn't stop anywhere, least of all here."

"When is it due to go past?"

"Ten-oh-five."

Nick looked at the clock above the waiting room, but it was electric and so had ceased to function. There was a watch chain hanging from the stationmaster's pocket, so he snagged that and drew out a regulation railway watch. Mechanical clockwork did not suffer so much from Free Magic, and its second hand was cheerfully moving round. According to the watch, it was three minutes to ten.

"What's the signal for an obstruction on the line?" snapped Nick.

"Three flares: two outside, one on the track," the man said. He suddenly looked at Nick, his attention returned to the here and now. "But you're not—"

"Where are the flares?"

The stationmaster shook his head, but he couldn't hide an instinctive glance toward a large red box on the wall to the left of the ticket window.

"Don't try to stop me," said Nick very forcefully. "Go back to your house and, if your phone's working, call the police. Tell them . . . Oh, there's no time! Tell them whatever you like."

The flares were ancient, foot-long things like batons, which came in two parts that had to be screwed together to mix the chemicals that in turn ignited the magnesium core. Nick grabbed a handful and rushed over the branch line to the main track. Or what he hoped was the main track. There were four railway lines next to each other, and he couldn't be absolutely sure which one Dorrance's train had taken heading north.

Even if he got it wrong, he told himself, any engineer seeing three red flares together would almost certainly stop. He screwed the first flare together and dropped it on the track, then the other two followed quickly, one to either side.

With the flares gushing bright-blue magnesium and red iron flames, Nick decided he couldn't afford explanations, so he crossed the tracks and crouched down behind a tree to wait.

He didn't have to wait long. He had barely looked over his shoulder at the expanding pall of smoke from Dorrance Hall, which now covered a good quarter of the sky, before he heard the distant sound of a big, fast-moving train. Then, only seconds after the noise, he saw the triple headlights of the engine as it raced down the track toward him. A moment later there was the shriek of the whistle, and then the awful screech of metal on metal as the driver applied the brakes, a screech that intensified every few seconds as the emergency brakes in each of the following carriages came on hard as well.

Nick, on hearing the horrid scream of emergency braking and seeing the sheer speed of the approaching lights, suddenly remembered the boast of the North by Northwest Railway, that its trains averaged 110 miles per hour, and for a fearful moment he wondered if he'd made a terrible mistake. It was one thing to risk his life pursuing the creature, but quite another if he was responsible for derailing the Bain Flyer and killing all the passengers on board.

But despite the noise and speed, the train was slowing under total control, on a long straight path. It came to a shrieking, sparking halt just short of the flares.

Even before it completely stopped, the engineer jumped

down from the engine and conductors leapt from almost every one of the fifteen carriages. No one got out on the far side, so it was relatively easy for Nick to run from his tree, climb the steps of a second-class carriage, and go inside without being observed—or so he hoped.

The carriage was split into compartments, with a passageway running down the side. Nick quickly glanced into the first compartment. It had six passengers in it, almost the full complement of eight. Most of them were squashed together trying to look out the window, though one was asleep and another reading the paper with studied detachment. For a brief second, Nick thought of going in, but he dismissed the notion immediately. The passengers would have been together for hours, and the appearance of a bloodied, blackened young man with burnt eyebrows could not go unnoticed or unremarked. Somehow, Nick doubted that any explanation he could provide would satisfy the passengers, let alone the conductor.

Instead, Nick looked up at the luggage rack that ran the length of the carriage. It was pretty full, but he saw a less-populated section. Even as he hoisted himself up and discovered that his chosen resting place was on top of a set of golf clubs and an umbrella, the engine whistled twice, followed by the sound of doors slamming and then the appearance of a conductor and two large, annoyed male passengers, who had just come back aboard.

"I don't know what the railway's coming to."

"Wrack and ruin, that's what."

"Now, now, gentlemen, no harm's done. We'll make up our time, you'll see. We're expected in at twenty-five minutes after midnight, and the Bain Flyer is never late. The railway will buy you a drink or two at the station hotel, and all will be right with the world."

If only, thought Nicholas Sayre. He waited for the men to move along, then wriggled into a slightly less uncomfortable position and rearranged the flower chain across his chest so it would not get crumpled. He lay there, thinking about what had happened and what could happen, and built up plan after plan the way he used to build matchstick towers as a boy, only to have them suffer the same fate. At some point, they always fell over.

Finally, it hit him. Dorrance and the creature had gotten away. At least, they'd gotten away from him. His part in the whole sorry disaster was over. Even if Dorrance's special train was going to Bain, they would arrive at least fifteen minutes ahead of Nick. And there was a good chance that Ripton would have made it to a phone, so the authorities would be alerted. The police in Bain had some experience with things crossing the Wall from the Old Kingdom. They'd get help—Charter Mages from the Crossing Point Scouts. There would be lots of people much more qualified than Nick to deal with the creature.

At least I tried, Nick thought. When I see Lirael . . . and Sam . . . and the Abhorsen—though I hope I don't have to explain it to her—then I can honestly say I really did my best. I mean, even if I had managed to catch up with them, I don't know if I'd have been able to do anything. Maybe my Charter-spelled dagger would have worked . . . maybe I could have tried something else. . . .

Nick suddenly felt very tired, and sore, the weariness more urgent than the pain. Even his feet hurt, and for the first time he realized he was still wearing carpet slippers. He was sure his shoes had been wonderfully shined, but by now they would be ash in the ruins of Dorrance Hall.

Nick shook his head at the thought, pushed back on the golf bag, and, without meaning to, fell instantly asleep.

He woke to find something gripping his elbow. Instantly he lashed out with his fist, connecting with something fleshy rather than the scaly, hard surface his dreaming mind had suggested might be the case.

"Ow!"

A young man dressed in ludicrously bright golfing tweeds looked up at Nick, his hand covering his nose. Other passengers were already in the corridor, most of them with their bags in hand. The train had arrived in Bain.

"You've broken my nose!"

"Sorry!" Nick said as he vaulted down. "I'm very sorry! Mistaken identity. Thought you were a monster."

"I say!" called out the man. "Wait a moment. You can't just hit a man and run away!"

"Urgent business!" Nick replied as he ran to the door, weaving past several other passengers, who quickly stood aside. "Nicholas Sayre's the name. Many apologies!"

He jumped out onto the platform, half expecting to see it swarming with police, soldiers, and ambulance attendants. He would be able to report to someone in authority and then check into the hotel for a proper rest.

But there was only the usual bustle of a big country station in the middle of the night, with the last important train finally in. Passengers were disembarking. Porters were gathering cases. A newspaper vendor was hawking a late edition of the *Times*, shouting, "Flood kills five men, three horses. Getcher paper! Flood kills three—"

There'd be a different headline in the next edition, Nick

thought, though it almost certainly wouldn't be the real story. "Fire at Country House' would be most likely, with the survivors paid or pressured to shut up. He would probably get to read it over breakfast, which reminded him that he was extremely hungry and needed to have a very late, much-delayed dinner. Of course, in order to eat, he'd need to get some money, and that meant . . .

"Excuse me, sir, could I see your ticket, please?"

Nick's train of thought derailed spectacularly. A railway inspector was standing too close to him, looking sternly at the disheveled, blackened, eyebrowless young man in ruined evening wear with a chain of braided daisies around his neck and carpet slippers on his feet.

"Ah, good evening," replied Nick. He patted his sides and tried to look somewhat tipsy and confused, which was not hard. "I'm afraid I seem to have lost my ticket. And my coat. And for that matter my tie. But if I could make a telephone call, I'm sure everything can be put right."

"Undergraduate, are you, sir?" asked the inspector. "Put on the train by your friends?"

"Something like that," admitted Nick.

"I'll have your name and college to start with," said the inspector stolidly. "Then we can see about a telephone call."

"Nicholas Sayre," replied Nick. "Sunbere. Though technically I'm not up this term."

"Sayre?" asked the inspector. "Would you be . . ."

"My uncle, I'm afraid," said Nick. "That's whom I need to call. At the Golden Sheaf Hotel, near Applethwick. I'm sure that if there is a fine to pay, I'll be able to sort something out."

"You'll just have to purchase a ticket before you leave the

station," said the inspector. "As for the phone call, follow me and you can—"

He stopped talking as Nick suddenly turned away from him and stared up at the pedestrian bridge that crossed the railway tracks. To the right, in the direction of the station hotel and most of the town, everything was normal, the bridge crowded with passengers off the Flyer eager to get to the hotel or home. But to the lonely left, the electric lights on the wrought-iron lampposts were flickering and going out. One after the other, each one died just as two porters passed by, wheeling a very long, tall box.

"It must be the . . . but Dorrance was at least fifteen minutes ahead of the Flyer!"

"You're involved in one of Mr. Dorrance's japes, are you?" The inspector smiled. "His train just came in on the old track. Private trains aren't allowed on the express line. Hey! Sir! Come back!"

Nick ran, vaulting the ticket inspection barrier, the inspector's shouts ignored behind him. All his resignation burned away in an instant. The creature was here, and he was still the only one who knew about it.

Two policemen belatedly moved to intercept him before the stairs, but they were too slow. Nick jumped up the steps three at a time. He almost fell at the top step, but turned the movement into a flèche, launching himself into a sprint across the bridge.

At the top of the stairs at the other end, he slowed and drew his dagger. Down below, at the side of the road, the tall box was lying on its side, open. One of the two porters was sprawled next to it, his throat ripped out.

There was a row of shops on the other side of the street,

all shuttered and dark. The single lamppost was also dark. The moon was lower now, and the shadows deeper. Nick walked down the steps, dagger ready, the Charter Marks swimming on the blade bright enough to shed light. He could hear police whistles behind him and knew that they would be there in moments, but he spared no attention from the street.

Nothing moved there until Nick left the last step. As he trod on the road, the creature suddenly emerged from an alcove between two shops and dropped the second porter at its hoofed feet. Its violet eyes shone with a deep, internal fire now, and its black teeth were rimmed with red flames. It made a sound that was half hiss and half growl and raised its spiked club hands. Nick tensed for its attack and tried to fumble the flower chain off his neck with his left hand.

Then Dorrance peered over the creature's shoulder and whispered something in its ear slit. The thing blinked, single eyelids sliding across to dim rather than close its burning violet eyes. Then it suddenly jumped more than twenty feet—but away from Nick. Dorrance, clinging to it for dear life, shouted as it sped away.

"Stay back, Sayre! It just wants to go home."

Nick started to run, but stopped after only a dozen strides, as the creature disappeared into the dark. It had evidently not exhausted all the power it had gained from Nick's blood, or perhaps simply being closer to the Old Kingdom lent it strength.

Panting, his chest heaving from his exertion, Nick looked back. The two policemen were coming down the stairs, their truncheons in hand. The fact that they were still approaching indicated they had not seen the creature.

Nick sheathed his dagger and held up his hands. The policemen slowed to a walk and approached warily. Then

Nick saw a single headlight approaching rapidly toward him. A motorcycle. He stepped out into the street and waved his hands furiously to flag the rider down.

The motorcyclist stopped next to Nick. He was young and sported a small, highly-trimmed mustache that did him no favors.

"What occurs, old man?"

"No . . . time . . . to explain," gasped Nick. "I need your bike. Name's Sayre. Nicholas."

"The fast bowler!" exclaimed the rider as he casually stepped off the idling bike, holding it upright for Nick to get on. He was unperturbed by the sight of Nick's strange attire or the shouts of the policemen, who had started to run again. "I saw you play here last year. Wonderful match! There you are. Bring the old girl back to Wooten, if you don't mind. St. John Wooten, in Bain."

"Pleasure!" Nick said as he pushed off and kicked the motorcycle into gear. It rattled away barely ahead of the running policemen, one of whom threw his truncheon, striking Nick a glancing blow on the shoulder.

"Good shot!" cried St. John Wooten, but the policemen were soon left behind as easily as the creature had left Nick.

For a few minutes Nick thought he might catch up with his quarry fairly soon. The motorcycle was new and powerful, a far cry from the school gardener's old Vernal Victrix he'd learned on back at Somersby. But after almost sliding out on several corners and getting the wobbles at speed, Nick had to acknowledge that his lack of experience was the limiting factor, not the machine's capacity. He slowed down to a point just slightly beyond his competence, a speed insufficient to do more than afford an occasional glimpse of the creature and Dorrance ahead.

As Nick had expected, they soon left even the outskirts of Bain behind, turning right onto the Bain High Road, heading north. There was very little traffic on the road, and what there was of it was heading the other way. At least until the creature ran past. Those cars or trucks that didn't run off the road as the driver saw the monster stalled to a stop, their electrical components destroyed by the creature's passage. Nick, coming up only a minute or so later, never even saw the drivers. As might be expected this far north, they had instantly fled the scene, looking for running water or, at the very least, some friendly walls.

The question of what the creature would do at the first Perimeter checkpoint was easily answered. When Nick saw the warning sign he slowed, not wanting to be shot. But when he idled up to the red-striped barrier, there were four dead soldiers lying in a row, their heads caved in. The creature had killed them without slowing down. None of them had even managed to get a shot off, though the officer had his revolver in his hand. They hadn't been wearing mail this far south, or the characteristic neck- and nasal-barred helmets of the Perimeter garrison. After all, trouble came from the north. This most southern checkpoint was the relatively friendly face of the Army, there to turn back unauthorized travelers or tourists.

Nick was about to go straight on, but he knew there were more stringent checkpoints ahead, before the Perimeter proper, and the chance of being shot would greatly increase. So he put the motorcycle in neutral, sat it on its stand, and, looking away as much as he could, took the cleanest tunic, which happened to be the officer's. It had a second lieutenant's single pip on each cuff. The previous wearer had probably been much the same age as Nick, and moments before must have been proud of his small command, before he lost it, with his life.

Nick figured wearing the khaki coat would at least give him time to explain who he was before he was shot at. He shrugged it on, left it unbuttoned with the flower chain underneath, got back on the motorcycle, and set off once more.

He heard several shots before he arrived at the next checkpoint, and a brief staccato burst of machine-gun fire, followed a few seconds later by a rocket arcing up into the night. It burst into three red parachute flares that slowly drifted north by northwest, propelled by a southerly wind that would usually give comfort to the soldiers of the Perimeter. They would not have been expecting any trouble.

The second checkpoint was a much more serious affair than the first, blocking the road with two heavy chain-link-and-timber gates, built between concrete pillboxes that punctuated the first of the Perimeter's many defensive lines, a triple depth of concertina wire five coils high that stretched to the east and west as far as the eye could see.

One of the gates had been knocked off its hinges, and there were more bodies on the ground just beyond it. These soldiers had been wearing mail coats and helmets, which hadn't saved them. More soldiers were running out of the pillboxes, and there were several in firing positions to the side of the road, though they'd stopped shooting because of the risk of hitting their own people farther north.

Nick throttled back and weaved the motorcycle through the slalom course of bodies, debris from the gate, and the live but shaken soldiers who were staring north. He was just about to accelerate away when someone shouted behind him.

"You on the motorcycle! Stop!"

Nick felt an urge to open the throttle and let the motor-cycle roar away, but his intelligence overruled his instinct. He stopped and looked back, wincing as the thin sole of his left carpet slipper tore on a piece of broken barbed wire.

The man who had shouted ran up and, greatly surprising Nick, jumped on the pillion seat behind him.

"Get after it!"

Nick only had a moment to gain a snapshot of his un-expected passenger. He was an officer, not visibly armed, wearing formal dress blues with more miniatures of gallantry medals than he should have, since he looked no more than twenty-one. He had the three pips of a captain on his sleeves and, more important, on his shoulders the metal epaulette tags NPRU, for the Northern Perimeter Reconnaissance Unit, or as it was better known, the Crossing Point Scouts.

"I know you, don't I?" shouted the captain over the noise of the engine and rush of the wind. "You tried out for the Scouts last week?"

"Uh, no," Nick shouted back. He had just realized that he knew his passenger too. It was Francis Tindall, who had been at Forwin Mill as a lieutenant six months ago. "I'm afraid I'm . . . well, I'm Nicholas Sayre."

"Nick Sayre! I bloody hope this isn't going to be like last time we met!"

"No! But that creature is a Free Magic thing!"

"Got a hostage, too, from the look of it. Skinny old duffer. Pointless carrying him along. We'll still shoot."

"He's an accomplice. It's already killed a lot of people down south."

"Don't worry, we'll settle its hash," Tindall shouted confidently. "You don't happen to know exactly what kind of Free Magic creature it is? Can't say I've ever seen anything like it, but I only got a glimpse. Didn't expect anything like that to run past the window at a dining-in night at Checkpoint Two."

"No, but it's bulletproof and it gets power by drinking the blood of Charter Mages."

Whatever Tindall said in response was lost in the sound of gunfire up ahead, this time long, repeated bursts of machine-gun fire, and Nick saw red tracer bouncing up into the air.

"Slow down!" ordered Tindall. "Those are the enfilading guns at Lizzy and Pearl. They'll stop firing when the thing hits the gate at Checkpoint One."

Nick obediently slowed. The road was straight ahead of them, but dark, the moon having sunk farther. The red tracer was the only thing visible, crisscrossing the road four or five hundred yards ahead of them.

Then big guns boomed in unison.

"Star shell," said Tindall. "Thanks to a southerly wind."

A second after he spoke, four small suns burst high above, and everything became stark black and white, either harshly lit or in blackest shadow.

In the light, Nick saw another deep defensive line of high concertina wire, and another set of gates. He also saw the creature slow not at all, but simply jump up and over thirty feet of wire, smashing its way past the two or three fast but foolish soldiers who tried to stick a bayonet in it as it hit the ground running.

Dorrance was no longer on its back.

Nick saw him a moment later, lying in the middle of the road. Braking hard, he lost control of the bike at the last moment, and it flipped up and out, throwing both him and Tindall onto the road, but fortunately not at any speed.

Nick lay there for a moment, the breath knocked out of him by the impact. After a minute, he slowly got to his feet. Captain Tindall was already standing, but only on one foot.

"Busted ankle," he said as he hopped over to Dorrance. "Why, it's that idiot jester Dorrance! What on earth would someone like him be doing with that creature?"

"Serving Her," whispered Dorrance, his voice startling both Tindall and Nick. The older man had been shot several times and looked dead, his chest black and sodden with blood. But he opened his eyes and looked directly at Nick, though he clearly saw something or someone else. "I knew Her as a child, in my dreams, never knowing She was real. Then Malthan came, and I saw Her picture, and I remembered Father sending Her away. He was mad, you know. Lackridge found Her for me again. It was as I remembered, Her voice in my head. . . . She only wanted to go home. I had to help Her. I had to . . ."

His voice trailed away and his eyes lost their focus. Dorrance would play the fool no more in Corvere.

"If it wants to go north, I suppose we could do worse than just let it go across the Wall," said Tindall. He waved at someone at the checkpoint and made a signal, crossing his arms twice. "If it can, of course. We can send a pigeon to the Guards at Barhedrin, leave it to them to sort out."

"No, I can't do that," said Nick. "I . . . I'm already responsible for loosing the Destroyer upon them, and I did nothing to help fight it. Now I've done it again. That creature would not be free if it weren't for me. I can't just leave it to Lirael, I mean the Abhorsen . . . or whoever."

"Some things are best left to those who can deal with

them," said Tindall. "I've never seen a Free Magic creature move like that. Let it go."

"No," said Nick. He started walking up the road. Tindall swore and started hopping after him.

"What are you going to do? You have the Mark, I know, but are you a Mage?"

Nick shook his head and started to run. A sergeant and two stretcher bearers were coming through the gate, while many more soldiers ran purposefully behind them. With star shell continuing to be fired overhead, Nick could clearly see beyond the gates to a parade ground, with a viewing tower or inspection platform next to it, and beyond that a collection of low huts and bunkers and the communications trenches that zigzagged north.

"The word for the day is *Collection* and the countersign is *Treble*," shouted Tindall. "Good luck!"

Nick waved his thanks and concentrated on ignoring the pain in his feet. Both his slippers were ripped to pieces, barely more than shreds of cloth holding on at the heels and toes.

The sergeant saluted as he went past, and the stretcher bearers ignored him, but the two soldiers at the gate aimed their rifles at him and demanded the password. Nick gave it, silently thanking Tindall, and they let him through.

"Lieutenant! Report!" shouted a major Nick almost ran into as he entered the communications trench on the northern side of the parade ground. But he ignored the instruction, dodging past the officer. A few steps farther on, he felt something warm strike his back, and his arms and hands suddenly shone with golden Charter Magic fire. It didn't harm him at all, but actually made him feel better and helped him recover his breath. He ran on, oblivious to the shocked Charter Mage behind him, who had struck him with his strongest spell of binding and immobility.

Soldiers stood aside as he ran past, the Charter Magic glow alerting them to his coming. Some cheered in his wake, for they had seen the creature leap over them, and they feared that it might return before a Scout came to deal with it, as they dealt with so many of the strange things that came from the north.

At the forward trench, Nick found himself suddenly among a whole company of garrison infantry. All one hundred and twenty of them clustered close together in less than sixty yards of straight trench, all standing to on the firing step, looking to the front. The wind was still from the south, so their guns would almost certainly work, but none was firing.

A harried-looking captain turned to see what had caused the sudden ripple of movement among the men near the communications trench, and he saw a strange, very irregularly dressed lieutenant outlined in tiny golden flames. He breathed a sigh of relief, hopped down from the step, and stood in front of Nick.

"About time one of you lot got here. It's plowing through the wire toward the Wall. D Company shot at it for a while, but that didn't work, so we've held back. It's not going to turn around, is it?"

"Probably not," said Nick, not offering the certainty the captain had hoped for. He saw a ladder and quickly climbed up it to stand on the parapet.

The Wall lay less than a hundred yards away, across barren earth crisscrossed with wire. There were tall poles of carved wood here and there, quietly whistling in the breeze among the metal pickets and the concertina wire. Wind flutes of the Abhorsen, there to bar the way from Death. A great many people had died along the Wall and the Perimeter, and the border between Life and Death was very easily crossed in such places.

Nick had seen the Wall before, farewelling his friend Sam on vacation. But apart from a dreamlike memory of it wreathed in fierce golden fire, he had never seen it as more than an antiquity, just an old wall like any other medieval remnant in a good state of preservation. Now he could see the glow of millions of Charter Marks moving across, through, and under the stones.

He could see the creature, too. It was surrounded by a nimbus of intense white sparks as it used its club hands to smash down the concertina wire and wade directly toward a tunnel that went through the Wall.

"I'm going to follow it," said Nick. "Pass the word not to shoot. If any other Scouts come up, tell them to stay back. This particular creature needs the blood of Charter Mages."

"Who should I say—"

Nick ignored him, heading west along the trench to the point where the creature had begun to force its path. There were no soldiers there, only the signs of a very rapid exodus, with equipment and weapons strewn across the trench floor.

Nick climbed out and started toward the Wall. It was night in the Old Kingdom, a darker night without the moon, but the star-shell light spread over the Wall, so he could see that it was snowing there, not a single snowflake coming south.

He lifted the daisy-chain wreath over his head and held it ready in his left hand, and he drew the dagger with his right. The flowers were crushed, and many had lost petals, but the chain was unbroken, thanks to the linen thread sewn into the stems. Llew and his nieces really had known their business.

Nick was halfway across the No Man's Land when the creature reached the Wall. But it did not enter the tunnel, instead hunkering down on its haunches for half a minute before easing itself up and turning back. It was still surrounded by white sparks, and even thirty yards away Nick could smell the acrid stench of hot metal. He stopped, too, and braced himself for a sudden, swift attack.

The creature slowly paced toward him. Nick lifted the wreath and made ready to throw or swing it over the creature's head. But it didn't attack or increase its pace. It walked up close and bent its long neck down.

Nick didn't take his eyes off it for even a microsecond. As soon as he was sure of his aim, he tossed the wreath over the creature's head. The chain settled on its shoulders, the yellow and red flowers taking on a bluish cast from the crackling sparks that jetted out from the creature's hide.

"Let us talk and make truce, as the day's eye bids me do," a chill, sharp voice said directly into Nick's mind, or so it felt. His ears heard nothing but the wind flutes and the jangle of cans tied to the wire. "We have no quarrel, you and I."

"We do," said Nick. "You have slain many of my people. You would slay more."

The creature did not move, but Nick felt the mental equivalent of a snort of disbelief.

"These pale, insipid things? The blood of a great one moves in you, more than in any of the inheritors that I have drunk from before. Come, shed your transient flesh and travel with me back to our own land, beyond this prison wall."

Nick didn't answer, for he was suddenly confused. Part of

him felt that he could leave his body and go with this creature, which had somehow suddenly become beautiful and alluring in his eyes. He felt he had the power to shuck his skin and become something else, something fierce and powerful and strange. He could fly over the Wall and go wherever he wanted, do whatever he wanted.

Against that yearning to be untrammeled and free was another set of sensations and desires. He did want to change, that was true, but he also wanted to continue to be himself. To be a man, to find out where he fitted in among people, specifically the people of the Old Kingdom, for he knew he no longer could be content in Ancelstierre. He wanted to see his friend Sam again, and he wanted to talk to Lirael. . . .

"Come," said the creature again. "We must be away before any of Astarael's get come upon us. Share with me a little of your blood, so that I may cross this cursed Wall without scathe."

"Astarael's get?" asked Nick. "The Abhorsens?"

"Call them what you will," said the creature. "One comes, but not soon. I feel it, through the bones of the earth beneath my feet. Let me drink, just a little."

"Just a little . . ." mused Nick. "Do you fear to drink more?"

"I fear," said the creature, bowing its head still lower. "Who would not fear the power of the Nine Bright Shiners, highest of the high?"

"What if I do not let you drink, and I do not choose to leave this flesh?"

"Your will is yours alone," said the creature. "I shall go back and reap a harvest among those who bear the Charter, weak and prisoned remnant of my kin of long ago."

"Drink then," said Nick. He cut the bandage at his wrist and, wincing at the pain, sliced open the wound Dorrance had made. Blood welled up immediately.

The creature leaned forward, and Nick turned his wrist so the blood fell into its open mouth, each drop sizzling as it met the thing's internal fires. A dozen drops fell; then Nick took his dagger again and cut more deeply. Blood flowed more freely, splashing over the creature's mouth.

"Enough!" said the voice in his mind. But Nick did not withdraw his hand, and the creature did not move. "Enough!"

Nick held his hand closer to the creature's mouth, sparks enveloping his fingers, to be met by golden flames, blue and gold twirling and wrestling, as if Charter Magic visibly sought dominance over Free Magic.

"Enough!" screamed the silent voice in Nick's head, driving out all other thoughts and senses, so that he became blind and dumb and couldn't feel anything, not even the rapid stammer of his own heartbeat. "Enough! Enough! Enough!"

It was too much for Nick's weakened body to bear. He faltered, his hand wavering. As the blood missed the creature's mouth, it staggered, too, and fell to one side. Nick fell also, away from it, and the voice inside his head gave way to blessed silence.

His vision returned a few seconds later, and his hearing. He lay on his back, looking up at the sky. The moon was just about to set in the west, but it was like no moonset he had ever seen, for the right corner of it was diagonally cut off by the Wall.

Nick stared at the bisected moon and thought that he should get up and see if the creature was moving, if it was going to go and attack the soldiers in order to dilute his blood once again. He should bandage his wrist, too, he knew, for he could feel the blood still dripping down his fingers.

But he couldn't get up. Whether it was blood loss or simply exhaustion from everything he'd been through, or the effects of the icy voice on his brain, he was as limp and helpless as a rag doll.

I'll gather my strength, he thought, closing his eyes. I'll get up in a minute. Just a minute . . .

Something warm landed on his chest. Nick forced his eyes to open just enough to look out. The moon was much lower, now looking like a badly cut slice of pumpkin pie.

His chest got even warmer, and with the warmth, Nick felt just a tiny fraction stronger. He opened his eyes properly and managed to raise his head an inch off the ground.

A coiled spiral made up of hundreds of Charter Marks was slowly boring its way into his chest, like some kind of celestial, star-wrought drill, all shining silver and gold. As each Mark went in, Nick felt strength return to more far-flung parts of his body. His arms twitched, and he raised them too, and saw a nice, clean, Army-issue bandage around his wrist. Then he regained sensation in his legs and lifted them up, to see his carpet slippers had been replaced with more bandages.

"Can you hear me?" asked a soft voice, just out of sight. A woman's voice, familiar to Nick, though he couldn't place it for a second.

He turned his head. He was still lying near the Wall, where he'd fallen. The creature was still lying there, too, a few steps away. Between them, a young woman knelt over Nick. A young woman wearing an armored coat of laminated plates, and over it a surcoat with the golden stars of the Clayr quartered with the silver keys of the Abhorsen.

"Yes," whispered Nick. He smiled and said, "Lirael."

Lirael didn't smile back. She brushed her black hair back from her face with a golden-gloved hand, and said, "The spells are working strangely on you, but they are working. I'd best deal with the Hrule."

"The creature?"

Lirael nodded.

"Didn't I kill it? I thought my blood might poison it. . . ."

"It has sated it," said Lirael. "And made it much more powerful, when it can digest it."

"You'd better kill it first, then."

"It can't be killed," said Lirael. But she picked up a very odd-looking spear, a simple shaft of wood that was topped with a fresh-picked thistle head, and stepped over to the creature. "Nothing of stone or metal can pierce its flesh. But a thistle will return it to the earth, for a time."

She lifted the spear high above her head and drove it down with all her strength into the creature's chest. Surprisingly, the thistle didn't break on the hide that had turned back bullets; it cut through as easily as a hand through water. The spear quivered there for a moment; then it burst, shaft and point together, like a mushroom spore. The dust fell on the creature, and where it fell, the flesh melted away, soaking into the ground. Within seconds there was nothing left, not even the glow of the violet eyes.

"How did you know to bring a thistle?" Nick asked, and then cursed himself for sounding so stupid. And for looking so pathetic. He raised his head again and tried to roll over, but Lirael quickly knelt and gently pushed him back down.

"I didn't. I arrived an hour ago, in answer to a rather confused message from the Magistrix at Wyverley. I expected merely to cross here, not to find one of the rarest of Free Magic creatures. And . . . and you. I bound your wounds and put some healing charms upon you, and then I went to find a thistle."

"I'm glad it was you."

"It's lucky I read a lot of bestiaries when I was younger," said Lirael, who wouldn't look him in the eye. "I'm not sure even Sabriel would know about the peculiar nature of the Hrule. Well, I'd best be on my way. There are stretcher bearers waiting to come over to take you in. I think you'll be all right now. There's no lasting damage. Nothing from the Hrule, I mean. No new lasting effects, that is. . . . I really do have to get going. Apparently there's some Dead thing or other farther south—the message wasn't clear. . . ."

"That was the creature," said Nick. "I sent a message to the Magistrix. I followed the creature all the way here from Dorrance Hall."

"Then I can go back to the Guards who escorted me here," Lirael said, but she made no move to go, just nervously parted her hair again with her golden-gloved hand. "They won't have started back for Barhedrin yet. That's where I left my Paperwing. I can fly by myself now. I mean, I'm still—"

"I don't want to go back to Ancelstierre," Nick burst out. He tried to sit up and this time succeeded, Lirael reaching out to help him and then letting go as if he were red-hot. "I want to come to the Old Kingdom."

"But you didn't come before," said Lirael. "When we left and Sabriel said you should because of what . . . because of what had happened to you. I wondered . . . that is, Sam thought later, perhaps you didn't want to . . . that is, you needed to stay in Ancelstierre for some person, I mean reason—"

"No," said Nick. "There is nothing for me in Ancelstierre. I was afraid, that's all."

"Afraid?" asked Lirael. "Afraid of what?"

"I don't know," said Nick. He smiled again. "Can you give me a hand to get up? Oh, your hand! Sam really did make a new one for you!"

Lirael flexed her golden, Charter-spelled hand, opening and closing the fingers to show Nick that it was just as good as one of flesh and bone, before she gingerly offered both her hands to him.

"I've had it for only a week," she said shyly, looking down as Nick stood not very steadily beside her. "And I don't think it will work very far south of here. Sam really is a most useful nephew. Do you think you can walk?"

"If you help me," said Nick.